Jih's Journey

By Xavier Giovanni McClean
Edited by M. B. O.

The Jih's Journey Series: Book One

Contents

5

Character Portraits

Jih (Gee)

Hyu (Hue)

Kag (Kah-g)

Bani (Bahn-ee)

Dran (Dr-ahn)

Hizo (Hi-so)

Tur (Tour)

Narro (Naur-oh)

Trekkal (Trek-uhl)

Fahlrit (Fall-rit)

Jarzill (Jar-zill)

Osa (Oh-sa)

Eshe (Esh-uh)

Ozul (O-zull)

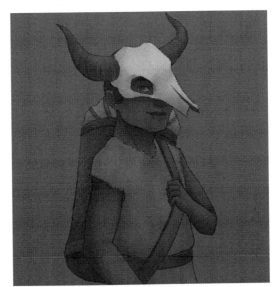

Dronall (Druh-nall)

Nezzall (Nuh-zall)

Sadal (Sa-dahl)

Deeso (D-so)

Cikya (Seek-ah)

Zulag (Zoo-lag)

Ronkalk (Ron-kalk)

The Story

The following events depicted within Jih's Journey are a microcosm of events within the Paleolithic era that occurred thousands of years ago. This period of the past was an utterly brutal time, and this is a content advisory. This book features depictions of gore, cannibalism, depression, suicide, abuse, child death and animal death. Reader discretion is advised.

In The Beginning: I

A young and tired boy rushed through the undergrowth of trees and bushes as his heart raced. The clink of stone in a bag strapped to his side increased in volume as he sped up. The land was unkempt and wild, as vines and brambles obscured the way home. He regretted his decision of taking a different path than the road most traveled, but it was not in vain. The bounty he held was a prized source of flint needed to make anything he desired. He was filled with exhaustion as he gripped a carved and shaped stone, desperate to cut a path for himself. With every breath, beads of sweat hit the very plants he manipulated before touching the ground. The ground was wet from the rains of the early morning that pierced through the rainforest canopy. His feet were bare and bled slightly from his rushing, as thorns scraped the bottom half of his body. The sound of ambient thunder in the sky accompanied each strike that he made. Each shade of green in the trees was more deceiving than the last as the boy's brown eyes looked forward and carved away at a seemingly infinite layer of foliage. All the while, the sound of clicking insects and birds filled his eardrums. His senses were overwhelmed by the number of stimuli going on around him. His feet and ankles hurt, but he worked through the pain. His biggest concern was the snarls of enraged hyenas that took refuge close to him. His ears were primed to pick these up out of the cacophony of jungle life around him. Hyenas were a scourge on the land past areas his people deemed safe, their handiwork could be seen everywhere with broken bones and claw marks along the ground. An inexperienced hunter could easily fall prey to them, and he lacked a weapon of his own.

One pack of hyenas were resting, but the boy's presence reminded them of their intense hunger. Out of everything that inhabited the jungle, the scent of man was one to be feared and drove predators with rage. The four hyenas reared up and started their pursuit from a haphazardly constructed den planted between foliage. Their brown spotted coats, tight bodies, and sharp claws were all advantages to help them on the hunt. Compared to the extravagant colors of the rainforest, these drab animals were able to disguise themselves long enough for the kill. One of their ears turned, tuned to the sound of chopping in the distance. Another dug its claws into the soil while waiting for the order from the largest who stood as the matriarch. Their panicked yelps that sounded through the forest urged the boy to keep going but his smell already reached the group. The footsteps of the animals became ever louder as they broke through the layers of forest. Their bodies braved the dense foliage as broken branches fell to the floor in their lust for blood. Other creatures dispersed, not wanting to get involved with the pursuit. Not without a plan, the boy picked up a few rocks, and expertly launched them through the brush with a heavy thud diverting their direction. The cantankerous hyenas were just as willing to fight among themselves as anything else, and a heavy sound to the forest floor mocked that of more satisfying prey. The boy used this knowledge to his advantage. The pack of four split off from another, three hyenas were successfully off the trail, but the matriarch remained.

The boy noticed the unusual calm that came by as the sounds of the hyenas vanished, but his pace didn't slow. The matriarch laid low, her claws embedded in the soil as she inched closer and waited patiently to make her strike. The last layer of foliage was carved down where the presence of tents, open fire pits, and others of his kind going about their day came into his vision. Unlike the northern part of the jungle filled with danger, this village was cleared and heavily maintained. The boy's face was filled with relief as the productivity of home was seen in the distance. Men were gathered hauling wood to various locations, while their women counterparts bound vines together into essential fibers. They wore an assortment of clothing, with those of higher status wearing furs compared to leaves and grass. Some chose to go without clothes at all, and left their backs bare in the wind that blew, with only a simple covering of the bottom. They worked in tandem as they were dispersed through the village. He could see that new additions to their band were coming as the skeletons of homes could be seen in the distance. Their discussions were held over open fire as he emerged with a small grin. He was never happier to have the scent of smoke and burning wood fill his nose. He made his presence known to the group in the distance. He waved a hand, dropping his carved stone and held up the bag with the gathered flint. While the boy continued his walk into the village, the snarls he desperately avoided sounded once again, just barely picking it up through his ears. He looked behind him to see a rumble in the brush and the matriarch emerged.

A cold sweat of terror came over him as he froze entirely. He thought he'd been so careful, and now he endangered everyone, including himself. His arm tensed as he recalled dropping the only thing he could use for defense. He slowly turned himself around to look the hyena in the eyes. For some reason, it had yet to attack him. He noticed that the hyena studied its surroundings, animals rarely breached the security they made, and this was a new experience. Luckily, strength came in numbers. A foolhardy creature, the hyena sought to use its size to intimidate, and made the decision to rush wildly into the campsite. Immersed in discussion, the voice of an older woman called back as her face filled with horror at the scene before her. She quickly got up and observed the two figures. Her look of panic turned the heads of many as she frantically gripped a spear that leaned on the side of a home. Her entire body vibrated with adrenaline and disgust at the animal that would threaten her livelihood, and most importantly, her son. Quickly, she pointed and directed people into positions before calling out in the distance.

"Jih! Come to Hizo! Denmey is dangerous, mind your surroundings!" Hizo commanded as Jih ran as fast he could.

Behind her, Hizo saw the others run to grab their weapons or hide in their homes. Some of her comrades held torches and clubs, they were eager to rout the horrid beast. With her son in grasp, Hizo took a defensive stance. Hizo's long parted hair draped down her shoulders and swayed as she stepped forward. A cool breeze came through the open camp and her grass coverall flowed with it. Hizo held a long spear composed of hardy jungle wood with a fashioned flint tip on the end. Freshly cleaned, the process would begin anew with blood on it. Hizo quickly ran forward and held the spear out perpendicular to her body. The matriarch accepted the challenge and charged towards Hizo. She swung with precision as the creature ducked and bared its teeth. The hyena reared up and hit the soil once more before lashing out with its teeth. Hizo stepped to the side, using the wood first to disorient the creature. A loud strike hit it, as the hyena noticed the growing mob that came before it.

The hyena was pelted with rocks that were thrown by others a considerable distance away while her eyes remained poised on Hizo. Hizo egged on the challenge, as she kicked up dirt with her feet and agitated the creature. It lunged for her leg but was too slow to contend with the fast footwork of Hizo. The matriarch used the rest of its power to charge and jumped, while Hizo slashed the creature upwards. She sliced its stomach as it cried in helplessness. It landed on the ground with a flat thud that disoriented its senses. The hyena leaked blood at an exuberant rate as the grass was painted red. Droplets from the animal's innards poured out in increasing volume. The animal lost all control of its body, as it flailed helplessly, exacerbating the process. The hyena's intestines were exposed as its entrails poured out in agony. Hizo looked over the hyena with disgust as she reared the spear once more and jammed it through the creature's head. She turned the spear with a loud crunch that pierced the animal's brain. Hizo chopped the creatures' head off and tossed it to the side as she examined her weapon that was muddled with blood and gray matter.

Once the kill was done, the mob took what they could salvage and threw the bloodied corpse into the jungle. The concern of scavengers was minimal as hyenas were a foul creature both in life and death. Hizo grabbed her son's face and took a long look into his eyes. As the only thing she had left, Hizo was a fanatical protector. Jih's father died early in his life to a leopard attack, but his mother Hizo was a pillar of their community. As she whittled spears and other weapons out of wood for training, she taught the children proper hunting and self-defense techniques. While Jih expected a scowl for such foolishness, his mother was filled with pride as she analyzed Jih from head to toe. She ran her hand through his muddled brown hair that parted at the top and draped down his face. It was caked with mud and sweat that she removed with her hands and wiped on her legs. His forehead was rough with a protruding brow ridge, as she tapped it with the back of her hand and let out a small grin. She tapped her own which was less pronounced as Jih smiled along with her. They both shared a dark brown hue on their skin that glistened in the sunlight that peaked. Hizo investigated her son's dress which was tattered, but repairs could be made later. Jih wore an outfit of grass and fibers that the two sewed together, popular dress with the material present in their lands.

After examining her son, Hizo let Jih go and gave him an affirming nod. Jih looked to the ground in embarrassment still as he observed onlookers with distaste evident on their faces. Jih's attempts to conform to the group only furthered their negative opinions. While Hizo was beloved by many for her competence, this extension was not given to Jih who remained unproven. Jih and Hizo belonged to an immensely hierarchical society where children and those of lower status were to comply without question. Perceived troublemakers didn't last long, and social isolation could be as hazardous to survival than anything else. Hizo hoped to strengthen Jih to one day be a leader of their people.

"You did well. Head to arena for training." Hizo said as she pointed some distance away to see the other children leaving their parents. Jih nodded in return, knowing he would see his mother shortly.

Without much to say, Jih didn't bother looking at any adults who looked him over. Hizo was highly respected, and no words would be openly exchanged about her son. On his walk, Jih could see the various teams of adults working on their respective tasks. Anything close to a break was rare, save for the occasional festival or the arrival of another band which took all interest. The ground before him was bare as dense grasses were cut down by sharpened multipurpose hand-axes[1]. Jih hoped that his bounty of flint could prove useful to make more for the group's needs. Any successful member of his group would never leave home without one. Jih's thoughts of home came to mind as he passed by it, a structure that Jih was especially proud of. Jih had low confidence in himself, as he didn't have many talents and was considered by the band to be passing at best, but he had an eye for stone and its various applications. He remembered placing medium sized stones arranged in an oval of varying lengths. He and Hizo labored for days making cuts of wood into set pieces and placing them into the ground that built the skeleton of their home. Jih built a fireplace in the center of the house so that light and heat for cooking could be used. The roof was also covered in thatch from palm leaves or animal furs and had a small opening for smoke to disperse.

Jih made his way to the training area at the opposite end of camp, marked with an arrangement of smooth stones put into an oval shape much like their home. The arena was a fair distance from any residences that occupied the background. Past the west end of the arena was brush where Hizo would teach them essential techniques to surviving in the jungle. Associated with the arena were piles of wood shaped into various states and a pile of processed animal skins placed on leaves that served as temporary bandages for injuries in combat. The arena itself had deep rings cut into the soil dug by hand-axe that represented specific ranges for respective weaponry. The first rings were for close quarters combat with clubs and knives, while others represented spear combat. Hizo's specialization was the spear above all else and ensured that her son would learn this method as well. Jih huddled himself quietly into the growing arrivals as he waited. Much like the adults, Jih could see that there were noticeable differences between the children as well. Those from families that had the good grace of their ruling body of The Council wore varying animal furs, while he and others wore grass. The most extravagant furs came from tiger and leopard, while those of humbler origin wore deer fur. The mass of students

---

[1] Hand-axes and axes are two different stone tools. Hand-axes are carved and sharpened stones that serve as multipurpose tools that can be held with one hand. These are used for various actions such as butchery and are carried around. Axes hold a wooden handle and are more specialized for chopping wood or used as a weapon.

that came to hear Hizo's words resounded as news of a momentous event was to occur today. At eighty members strong, Jih's band had eighteen that were children old enough to learn her techniques and begin the process of adulthood.

Jih noticed a crowd formed as he overheard the words of one boy known as Chak. At fifteen, Chak was the oldest of them and was an overachiever in every sense of the word. He could lift a boulder with ease or so he claimed. Every inch of him was deemed perfect by those that saw him and he made sure to boast about his victories to many. He exaggerated even the most minor of accomplishments as epic displays of power, encouraged by the others. Jih found Chak irritating but knew that his skill still far exceeded many of their own. Chak was naturally gifted and had gotten the eye of The Council for quite some time. An inflated ego was expected. Chak stood proudly, with his head raised as he basked in his own glory. On his skin were the marks of orange dye that resembled tiger stripes, which was naturally feared for its strength. His neck bore a bone necklace that clinked when he moved around and captivated those that saw him. To many of Jih's friends, he was beyond strength, having gone on solo hunts and making quick work for the group.

Jih had a scowl apparent on his face but tried his best to hide his disdain as he moved forward to greet Chak. In the crowd, Jih met the eyes of the other children who gave him varying looks. Word traveled quickly through the village and his performance from earlier was already a topic of discussion in their minds, for one witnessed what happened. With all eyes on him, Jih needed to honor tradition that lasted for thousands of years. Although the feeling of anger filled him to the point of seeing red, Jih composed himself and lowered his head to Chak when interacting with him. Chak's orange markings made him untouchable and Jih was bound to obey no matter how harsh the treatment he endured. The group opened and dispersed to give the two room.

"Coward known as Jih. Chak witnessed your lack of bravery. One Denmey too mighty for you! Mother will not save Jih this time." Chak spat as Jih folded his arms.

"Jih sees mark of The Council on Chak. It is...well earned." Jih replied, ignoring Chak's blatant disrespect. Chak's inflated ego took even the slightest bit of tone past utter fealty as a sign of protest. He shook his head and clinked his bone necklace, grabbing the attention of others. He tugged at his cape that draped behind him, a tiger fur that was expensive.

"You mock Chak, there is no grace in your voice." Chak mentioned as he balled his hand up into a fist and pushed Jih.

Jih spat at his feet, a mistake that few in the crowd noticed with their eyes poised on him. Jih's eyes met with the scowl of a girl his age as he dared speak against Chak. Jih was met with the overwhelming physicality of Chak, as he was pushed to the ground. Jih fell backwards, saving himself further embarrassment as he got up quickly.

"You will learn Jih, like all outsiders have. Face Chak in arena. Chak has seen you practice, there is skill, but none that compares." Chak threatened, while his speech was cut short by the presence of Hizo's figure walking in the distance.

No matter how many years Jih and Hizo spent among them, he was always painted as an outsider for their arrival here as a young boy. At fourteen, Jih was in this village for a decade growing up with them, but the memory of adults kept their origins well known and with it came suspicion. It wasn't an entire loss, as Jih had friends of his own to rely on. With Hizo arriving in the arena, the few discussions that were had wrapped up swiftly as they took their places in line. Jih saw a boy's head stick out, one by the name of Kag. Kag was a head taller than Jih, carrying the same rough forehead as himself. His eyes were bright and full of life that inspired others and were accompanied with a large grin. Kag was Jih's best friend from the first days of him joining The Elders. They were the same age and inseparable. An early riser, Kag would often wait outside of Jih's home and greet him with a warm smile. While Jih retained a much more serious outlook on life, Kag was sociable and humorous, taking his time to pull pranks and be silly in times that surely needed it. Kag radiated an energy that was able to make even the darkest days a bit brighter.

His sister, the youngest of all of them, at age twelve was Hyu. Hyu's expression was noted in her eyebrows that could tell a story all their own. She was shorter than the others but made up for it in her physical and mental flexibility. Hyu and Kag wore outfits of deer fur and held more prestige than Jih. Originally, they were orphaned but were mentored by a member of The Council from an early age and were exceptional. Just short of a genius, Hizo plucked Hyu a year early for training as she was observant and learned quickly. Hyu could be seen from anywhere from her long hair that draped behind her, barely touching the forest floor. She tied it together with a band made from animal sinew during training. Despite initial concerns from Hizo, her hair being grabbed in combat specifically, it didn't impede her ability to defend herself. Hyu was as sociable as Kag, if not more so, as she bounced around talking to others, but took her education seriously. Jih wasn't sure how to feel about Hyu, but he felt better when she was around. She held a bored look on her face as she stuck her tongue out to Kag while Jih averted his eyes to the ground.

Hizo stayed quiet as she gestured towards a pile of wood with sharpened spears. Hizo held her arms behind her as she spoke, nodding to allow them to break rank and grab their weapons for today's lesson. The undisciplined among them were already clamoring to claim their favorite weapon while Jih stood still.

"Collect your weapons and we will begin." Hizo commanded.

Hizo stepped forward to the pile of wood and lifted a large wooden spear slowly for the group to see. Education was important in their society, so even the most mischievous would pay attention to what the adults were demonstrating. She then opened her hand for the group to grab ones that fit best and to follow as she did. There was a brief exchange of sharpened sticks as some were unwieldy for those who got to pick last. Jih normally waited to pick last for practice as he knew some had a preference, while the ever-impatient Kag grabbed two, one for himself and Jih. Before grabbing her spear, Hyu looked at the pile of animal skins. Hizo raised an eyebrow at this notion but made no comment. The observant Hyu noticed that Jih's feet were still bleeding from his previous injury. She ripped off a small portion of animal skin she worked on earlier. Hyu walked over to Jih and tapped his shoulder. Jih stumbled on his wording but was relieved as Hyu pointed downwards.

"Blood leaks, it must be closed." Hyu mentioned as Jih slowly lifted his injured feet. He felt the tight strain of Hyu's hands as he felt himself bound. Jih watched as the brown skins were placed around his body and tied together in a tight knot. Jih was eternally grateful as he gave it a quick rotation of the foot and the bandage held. Before Jih could say another word, Hyu vanished into the crowd and grabbed her spear.

Hizo instructed them to take form now that all their spears were given. Hizo demonstrated a form that was matched as well as they could. She walked forward among the ranks, with her gentle but firm hand guiding them as she spoke.

"Never forget, we are The Elders. Holders of knowledge, we work hard so that ancestors are happy. Work makes us happy." Hizo echoed, the same speech she was given when she and Jih first arrived in this village.

"We walked many miles to come here, and the world was empty. Life was given and we made The Old Way. Our knowledge of stone to build community." Hizo said as she withdrew a carved stone from inside her grass covering.

As Hizo continued, Jih closed his eyes and recounted his heritage. He recalled the oral history lessons passed down by The Council which were some of the oldest in the world[2]. Many of these involved how to master the use of fire, traverse the coasts, and make powerful tools to aid them in their daily struggles. Jih felt a strong legacy weigh on top of him and such things were stressful to the other children that stood with him. Jih had yet to find his true purpose but took every day in stride.

"It is here on Sunda-" Hizo continued, her voice stopping short as she anticipated a wave of excitement to fall over her students. She leaned back on her weapon and saw the movement of their feet while they attempted to keep rank.

"Sunda! Sunda! Sunda!" The crowd of children said in unison as they started to get excited. Their desire to dance with enjoyment and shaking was led by Kag who let out a low chant that carried over the crowd. He gave Jih a look with his eyebrows as he prompted him to join in and the others followed suit. Chak huffed at the display, but not one to be upstaged, spoke the loudest and clearest of the bunch. After some brief movement among them, Hizo regained control over her flock and moved her hands to get them to separate. Hizo lifted her spear and watched as the others moved their spears around their arms. Hizo reminded them of a well-crafted spear's heft as they needed two hands to properly anchor themselves.

"Arms straight. Twist tightly." Hizo demonstrated, gritting her teeth as she stomped her foot down and thrust the spear forward. Jih watched a few children back away instinctively as Hizo's speed left an afterimage of the spear in the air. She emulated

---

[2] Jih's people are the group known today as Homo erectus. Homo erectus is an archaic human species from the Pleistocene era, appearing about 2 million years ago in Africa. The last known population lived in what is now modern-day Java about 110,000 years ago.

the sound of pierced flesh with her voice as she did so. She kept a generally neutral appearance but couldn't help but smile as she saw Jih and the others attempting the same pose in unison. This carried on for some time until she ordered them to practice and apply their previous lessons. Sparring was an essential part of development and Hizo sought to give Jih as much experience as possible. Jih's sparring partner was usually Kag, but Chak volunteered first and was given the approval to pick anyone he wanted. Chak left his place in line and Jih kept a still expression as he saw Chak weigh his decision carefully for show. Jih understood he and Chak had already agreed to a duel.

As Jih was called forth, the other children clamored among themselves while Hizo stood quietly. Jih looked behind him and gave a glare as he looked up to Chak. Kag raised an eyebrow at the matchup but seemed confident in his friend's skill. Chak was a brutal opponent, but Jih could match in technical skill. As Hizo's son, he was expected to perform well and set an example for others. Jih and Chak were directed by Hizo to opposing ends of the arena and given one minute to compose themselves before the fight began. Hyu watched with curiosity as the two moved closer to one another. Jih was mostly Kag's friend rather than her own, but she had a few good conversations from time to time. Chak, however, was reprehensible with his behavior. Hyu was trying to avoid him as he made his interest known to her by leaving strange offerings at her and Kag's tent. Chak left the severed heads of his kills with an accompanying crown of flowers wrapped together to show his prowess and creativity at the same time. One or the other could be a decent gift, but the delivery of both was terrifying. This was considered an unorthodox form of courtship as this mixed two forms of energy as one and disrupted balance.

The rules of Hizo's matches were simple. While a formalized rule set was used for adults, Hizo ended a match when a weapon was broken, or another yielded in defeat. Hizo officiated the match once Jih and Chak took their respective ends of the arena and clinked their spears once. Kag and the other children clapped and placed their hands on the soil to generate music. Chak operated on a principle of pure power as Jih could hear the wave of the spear's strike long after he moved to position. He shook his body as he attempted to jostle Jih's concentration. Jih took a deep breath as he sidestepped and dodged. As he turned, he could see Kag staring while clapping with the others. Jih could dodge all he wished, but he needed to bring the power to Chak. Jih used the wood of his own spear to channel Chak's power to the neutral ground as he hit the edge of Chak's spear. Chak gritted his teeth in annoyance, it would take some effort for him to get the win he felt he deserved.

Jih felt invigorated by the music produced by the other students. As he evaluated Chak's strikes, he was able to block them effectively and slammed hard with the stick to the back of Chak's leg. With the weapons made of wood, Hizo effectively cut down their lethality, only an occasional bruise showed if one wasn't careful. Jih lunged forward and brought the fight to Chak much to Kag's enjoyment. Hizo lifted her head in observation and noted how much attention the two paid to her forms. The sound of the wood cracking at once filled the village as some turned their heads to witness the display. Sparring duels were few far and between for Hizo, but ones that lasted this long came as a pleasant surprise.

Hizo's observation was interrupted by Tur, the local woodworker of the band, and a good friend of hers. They often collaborated on projects together, and he filled the void for Jih and many others as a surrogate father figure, but he could be harsh in his delivery. Although not a member of The Council, he chased trends with vigor and had a taste for high quality, being rarely ever seen with anything past leopard fur, as he had friends in high places. He wore this over his body, standing proudly as he noticed a few onlookers. Tur gave a smug grin to a few children who could only dream of having such prestige. He huffed as his focus turned towards the battle. Hizo turned in confusion as she wasn't expecting any visitors for their lesson. Kag shot Hyu a look that had her turn her head slightly to get a better look as they remained in position. The fight still raged on between Jih and Chak as the two traded blows. Tur leaned close and observed as he crouched next to Hizo.

"Tur sees fight is going well." He spoke to Hizo as she remained silent. Hizo couldn't spare to avert her gaze for even a moment but nodded at her friend's words.

"Tur has news to give Hizo. Is she ready for it?" Tur questioned as the pair kept their eyes on Jih.

While Tur shared a close friendship with Hizo, this love wasn't transferable to Jih. Tur found Chak's ambition far more useful for his needs and mentored him personally when his duties were taken care of for the day. For Tur, he had personal investment in Jih's suffering and found it difficult at times to mask his distaste for the boy. Tur instilled in Chak early that any advantage should be exploited for personal gain, the world of politics for an adult was brutal, and for children it remained such the same. He watched with interest as Chak fought dirty, seeing no viable option to match Jih's stalwart defense. He kicked up the soil in annoyance, and without a proper outlet for his growing rage, headed straight to Jih. Chak lifted his foot and used the weight of the spear to balance himself as he kicked Jih harshly.

"That is not fair! No kicking in spear fight!" Jih complained as he coughed with a kick to the stomach. He spat in the soil and grimaced at Chak, who ran towards him and used his bodyweight to push him to the soil. Hizo didn't interfere as she wondered how her son would react.

"This news? What of it to Hizo and her flock?" Hizo asked, letting out a breath of relief as she saw Jih jump and slam the spear down, letting out a satisfying yell in defiance.

"The Council has seen vision. Woodyaan of old age and many battles. Recognition Hunt is tomorrow. We will feast later today." Tur explained to Hizo.

"Tur, they are..." Hizo said with worry evident on her face as she eyed the rest of her students. She looked behind her and tried to suppress the doubt she had about their abilities.

"Not ready? Hizo can tell The Council. They will not be pleased. Their vision has seen it and tomorrow will be the day. It has been willed." Tur stretched and placed his arm on Hizo's shoulder in support.

Hizo gave a small gulp in her throat as failure was something she hoped to avoid at all costs. She'd heard the rumors of social failures and wished to avoid this fate for herself or Jih. As the conversation between Hizo and Tur continued, Jih and Chak stood with sweat over their bodies. Jih was surprised at his resilience while Chak was further angered at Jih's defiance. The durability of their weapons waned steadily, and Chak exploited this by ending the fight with a hard slam that broke Jih's weapon in two. Jih placed the splattered wooden spears to the ground and lowered his head to yield as he lost the battle. Chak found this unsatisfactory and sought blood as he raised his fist and attacked Jih. Jih was blindsided by such a punch as he raised his hands to defend himself and grab Chak. Chak pinned him to the ground and punched him in the face, giving him a swollen cheek. The music stopped abruptly as the children panicked among themselves. Kag ran over to Jih and attempted to dislodge Chak from Jih. Hyu glared at Tur who laughed at the display while Hizo ran to end the fighting.

"Enough!" Hizo screamed loudly, the likes of which hadn't been heard with such vigor in a long time.

"Jih yielded and yet you continued. Chak, this is unacceptable." Hizo said as she grabbed Chak's arm and twisted in irritation. Chak met Tur's gaze as he was quiet. Chak knew he was being watched and took his punishment in stride; he considered it a fair blow for putting Jih in his place. As tensions ran high, Hizo called for Tur to announce the news to everyone else.

"Recognition Hunt is tomorrow morning. The Council has willed it. A feast will be tonight. When lesson ends, head home to prepare." Tur stated as he saw the looks of excitement on the students' faces. With all the excitement of the match and now this news, Hizo found it far too difficult to maintain control. She gave a sigh and dismissed them for now while she needed to help prepare for the festivities. While Hizo felt that there should be more retribution for Chak's misconduct, she knew the Recognition Hunt would be enough punishment as it was.

As the crowd dispersed at Hizo's instruction, they bowed their heads thanking her. Their footsteps accumulated dust behind them as they ran home, happy to tell their parents the exciting news. A few remained behind, including Kag and Hyu. Jih massaged his wound as he looked up to see the supportive hand of Kag open and inviting. Jih grabbed his friend's hand and felt its firm grip as he was hoisted upwards while Hyu offered a small smile.

"Brother! Kag has been waiting! Jih stood for himself today." Kag said as he embraced Jih and Jih returned it in kind. Kag extended his hand out and held it to a fist while he turned his gaze to Hizo. Jih was happy to retrieve his friends for the time being. Hyu gave a satisfied look at her handiwork as Jih's bandages stayed in place the entire time. Hyu prompted Kag to bow her head in respect to Hizo before making their leave. Hyu looked at the tired Jih with a tilt of her head before bringing it back to normal.

"Chak and his foolishness will hurt us all. Remind him of that more often." Hyu said with a laugh as she gave Jih a pat on the arm. With that, Jih and his friends went their separate ways.

Hizo held Jih's hand as they walked home and crawled through the entrance of their home. While doing so, the village started to get things together for the festivities. Hizo looked at Jih as he gave a yawn. She couldn't help but give a proud smile to Jih for standing up for himself. Her son was going to be respected one way or another. Jih quickly went to sleep to recover from his injuries while Hizo left to labor for the rest of the morning and afternoon. Hizo joined the other adults who moved into formation to get everything ready as she trained for ages ago. While Jih was left to himself, Hizo waved to the others who returned from the forest and carried various treasures. Most of these were of little interest to Hizo except for collected flowers. It was considered a sign of good fortune among their people to carry flowers that were the favorite colors of those going to hunt. Hizo was unable to go into the forest to claim her son's favorite flower. She'd forgotten to do so with all her responsibilities, but a trusted friend delivered on her behalf. Hizo was integral to organizing the cleanup for the village where she and countless others organized their piles of materials and got rid of any refuse that would contaminate their space. She used her son's tools to cut the high grass that grew around the edges of their village. Hizo looked up from her duties to see a wonderful yellow flower in a man's hands and pointed to the direction of her and Jih's home. It was placed tenderly on the side of the home so that all could see it. She hoped that Jih's performance during the Recognition Hunt would get her son the acceptance they worked so hard to achieve.

The Council stepped forward from their communal tent that was sequestered some distance from the main camp. Built like that of homes belonging to the village, it was rare that they all exited at the same time. The Council was the most important body that The Elders possessed, they carried the highest amount of knowledge in any given field and had the utmost admiration and respect of almost everyone. It was late afternoon as the sun waned in the sky and those that participated were adorned with body paint and ornaments of assorted sizes that glistened in the sunlight. Hizo and the other adults worked to the bone to decorate the village for their entrance and just barely made it in time. These favorite flowers plucked from the far reaches of the jungle were planted at the edge of the participants' homes to outline a path they would go towards and give their speech. During a celebration, all work ceased, and left in the wake were half-processed animal skins and stone tools that would be started the next morning. Tur and Hizo surveyed their handiwork and nodded in satisfaction. A woman nearby cupped her hands together and let out a yell announcing the presence of The Council that would come forward.

The men wore red pigment along their skin, while their women counterparts donned blue as their attire. Speaking on their behalf was a short woman who went by the name of Ilol. She wore no covering as she guided the other members of The Council through the route. People exited their homes in anticipation of their arrival with glee and graciousness in their hearts, holding and offering whatever possessions they stored in their homes. Smoothed stones and bird feathers were among the most popular gifts. Jih woke up to the sound of rustling outside his home and remembered that the feast started soon. He found that many other children were poised waiting to hear the words of The Council. Jih stepped outside of his home and walked over to join the growing crowd that developed. Jih's eyes widened as he recognized his stoneworking teacher from the sound of her voice. She looked indistinguishable from other adults most of the time, but here Jih could only be impressed even further.

"We have seen vision." Ilol stated with much pride, as she looked back to see approving nods from the other members of The Council. The Council pointed eastwards as the crowd dispersed to reveal Chak at the end who incited celebration.

"Now is the time! Chak will lead you!" Ilol shouted, as Chak came forward to fanfare. He absorbed every bit of glory with tears of euphoria in his eyes. Tur shook his head in satisfaction as he was proud of his mentee. Hizo's mind drew to Jih, but she decided to stick with Tur as she had questions.

"What happens now?" Hizo asked in a whisper to Tur.

"They make the kill tomorrow. Today, we will celebrate. Jih will do fine." Tur replied to Hizo, hoping to ease her concerns. To keep things possible for the young initiates, predators were not considered valid targets for the Recognition Hunt and with some relief, the adults could rest somewhat easier as they looked towards the fate of their offspring.

To Jih's surprise, The Council summoned all children to come forward. He moved his way through the crowd and saw the wave of Hyu invite him over to join while the rest dispersed. Jih gave a small grin at Hyu's invitation and pressed forward while he met the eye of other children who embraced The Council as they stood triumphantly. Jih looked at the crowd that gathered as they offered small gifts of meat and fruit to their young hunting group. They wore an assortment of clothing, as many wore grass skirts and outfits strewn from leaves, while some adults wore furs with ornaments made from bone. Some went without, leaving their chests bare to the sun. Jih noticed Kag pick up a mango from a bed of leaves and chewed happily while receiving a nod from him. While many of the adolescents were happy to get the attention of the band and that of The Council, Jih felt a grave sense of unease. He knew that most of them wouldn't return. Everyone thinks of themselves as the exception until they face a rhino running at breakneck speed.

Before a Recognition Hunt began, a customary feast was held as adults brought an exuberant amount of food for the band to eat. Tur and the other adults that worked to throw the feast looked very tired but fulfilled as they saw the approval of The Council, and more importantly the young that ate happily. It was a celebration of life, but there was an undertone attached. The adults that Jih knew were simply the survivors of such a ritual, the hunt was brutal, violent, and a concise test of every facet of learning given to them.

Jih could hardly enjoy the gifts left out as he thought about this reality. He rubbed his stomach as he eyed the food but was too worried. Kag and Hyu prompted Jih to eat as they wouldn't have access to food unless they gathered it on their quest the next day. Games were played and memories of previous hunts were shared by the adults to encourage the young to be excited. For many, this would be the first time their talent as individuals would come to fruition.

Chak absorbed every amount of praise given to him as he gave an excited smile that contrasted from Jih's own concern. The children received a performance with dance synchronized to chants as food was exchanged. Smoked tapir skewers were a popular pick that was tasty and nutritious. Demand was high as Jih secured a piece for himself. Good food was hard to come by as he saw Hizo busy attempting to strike up conversation with other adults, trapped in her interactions with Tur.

Following the festivities that raged through the night, the adults hung around and talked through the night at campfires, while it was expected for the young to go to their huts and sleep early to prepare. Jih gave his goodbye to Kag and Hyu as they went separate ways for the night. Jih crawled into his hut and remained awake, unable to sleep. Jih fiddled through the night and made as many hand-axes out of leftover stone as he could for his group. By the time Jih collapsed out of exhaustion, he had a sizable pile next to him. As he lay still, Hizo entered as he slept and looked at her son resting before retiring on a bed of leaves all her own.

In The Beginning: II

Jih was shaken awake by Kag who came to collect him for the hunt. Jih wiped away the drool pool from his face and gathered his hand-axes for the group before following his best friend. Amid the darkness, Kag's white smile stuck out to him as he extended his hand that Jih grabbed. The low fire that was lit in their firepit extinguished itself overnight. Everyone else was in the center of town already. The sun had yet to rise, dawn stretching across the darkened sky as the sun still slumbered below the horizon as the two boys hurried to meet the others carrying their weapons. The hunting party was divided into ten boys and eight girls. This was no simple deer hunt, but something far more interesting. While the adults and Chak, as the hunting leader, knew of the animal they were after, Jih was left in the dark as to what they could be hunting. With little said, the group figured out their roles quickly as they were prepared for this reality for some time. Jih gave his hand-axes to those that wanted them, with the extras left behind.

Jih entered the center of camp with Kag shortly behind him as he looked to see the faces of the adults he'd seen yesterday wearing a white pigment on their face. The small glimpses of light from carried torches filled the early dawn. The flickering of the flames distorted their faces as they bunched together to give them good tidings for the journey. Hizo stood among them and gave Jih and Kag a nod before shuttling them towards the rest of the children. Hyu held her ground for the two to slip in and wait as she observed the array of torches and campfires spread throughout which lit the surrounding area. Chak stood, well-rested and energized as ever as he gave Hyu a glare before returning his attention to a more important manner. In the low light provided by the campfires, Chak's orange pigment struck out easily as he stood surrounded by his allies. Although only Chak donned the official stripes, those he appointed were treated as second-in-command for the hunt, and quickly settled into a role of authority. Chak's followers gathered around him but only at a distance as they were held back by two others.

The boy next to Chak was known as Vut, and the girl close by went by Dran. Vut aspired to be like Chak in a lot of ways, emulating his movements and reinforcing his ego, but he had a personality of his own if you gained his friendship. He had a knack for pointing out good sources of flint, so Jih appreciated his insight on the matter. The two didn't converse much outside of that. Vut had a build that echoed that of Kag, he was somewhat lanky and wore a grass covering over his body with two straps made of fibers that held it together. Vut had a nearly bald head that was cut down to the lowest bits of hair and had a slight overbite that was evident as he closed his mouth.

Dran had a sound mind for strategy, and she was often seen talking with Chak to plan out the hunts. She wore a covering of grass that was split in half that exposed her stomach and a sash of fibers over her right shoulder. Her hair rarely touched her shoulders as it was tied back with string. Dran chewed on a piece of wood while waiting for instructions. Much like Jih, Dran was far more serious than most and took every challenge with the utmost severity. Dran observed the trio as they walked closer to her, and she narrowed her eyes in annoyance. Respect for Dran was earned and not given, and so she remained skeptical regarding the rest of her cohort. She respected authority and was drawn to Chak's command of the crowd. Her goals were unknown to the others, but she remained a steady confidant for Chak. Jih looked back at Kag who was easily smitten by her face. Jih could hardly understand it, Dran didn't get an ounce of sleep as her eyes looked sunken from bags underneath, something she and Jih both shared. She lifted an eyebrow at Jih before rolling her eyes. Hyu stewed in anger as she looked at Dran, Jih didn't want to ask about their history. Jih knew he needed to follow orders and would play along to survive. After this, they would be free to go their separate ways and move on with their lives.

The Council walked forward and formed a circle around the new hunting party. They reiterated the severity of the mission and that to pass, they needed to find the creature that Chak was assigned.

"Today, you must work as one. You know what must be done." The voice of Illol boomed through the stillness of the night as the adults of The Elders knelt to the ground at their words. Chak took this action as praise for himself and looked in satisfaction at the legion of brown eyes now under his command. He met the eyes of Tur whose face painted white stuck out in the crowd. He gave Chak a nod of support as he looked at the boy's chest and his symbol of power.

Chak pounded his chest as his bone ornament clinked to get the group moving while they still had the morning ahead of them. He paused as he noticed Hizo come forward. She opened her arms to Jih, while Kag and Hyu waited. She noticed and waved for them to join her as the other two hugged her from behind. The rest of her students gathered around her with much pride in their teacher. Chak waited last and gave Hizo a hug. Jih and the other children steadied their pace through the village, for some, this would be the first time leaving the familiar hunting grounds and comforts of home. Jih was not one of these people, but the feeling of emptiness took hold all the same. The outline of their village became more faded as the group entered the northern jungles. Hizo silently walked behind them, stopping just short of the village boundary where she was joined by Tur and other adults who watched for some time, until their figures vanished from view within the forest.

The hunting party made their way through the ever-familiar rivers and forest to uncharted territory further north than they were used to. The trees were filled with eyes that stared back at them while the canopy obscured any light that came through. The obnoxious humming of insects flying around bothered them as many swatted the air in irritation. The early morning sun had barely come out, as two of the group carried torches to light the path. One in the front and one in the back. The forest was anything but silent, as the yelping sound of hyenas and other creatures were audible from miles away. Jih shook his head trying to ignore his encounter with the matriarch and focused on the task at hand. Chak had kept his silence on what they were looking for, as they seemed destined to travel in one specific direction.

"How long?" Kag whispered to Jih. Kag's impatience was apparent as they trudged through the leagues of foliage in their way. The two hung towards the back, while Hyu bounced around, telling stories to keep morale high. While Jih had painted her as a quiet type, she did well with others, and it came in handy as petty disputes were handled quickly when she came. Although she avoided talking with Chak and his associates, she did her best to make sure they weren't going to endanger the safety of anyone else.

"Maybe two days." Jih lamented, as most of his hunts with Hizo took a few hours. While Jih wasn't aware exactly of what they searched for, two days was the average time it took for previous Recognition Hunts to be completed and was a reasonable estimate.

Finding and killing the animal was half the battle, but the real struggle was bringing it back home before it got picked clean by scavengers waiting in the wings. Jih looked ahead of him as he could see bushes being cut by Vut and Dran who were commanded by Chak to dispose of them while he stood. Jih scoffed at such a measure, but he noted that even in the dark, they had to be using his high-quality hand-axes for this terrain. Jih gave a small laugh to himself knowing that through his tools, he could get through any situation. With the day finally giving light, the undergrowth continued to stay thick as the chopping hands for foliage changed. While one or two could fit through the dense brush without issue, an entire contingent of people needed to work together. Jih and Kag were at the front now, moving branches out of the way as they carved a haphazard path forward.

Jih looked behind him as he stretched his hand out, helping others move through the brush. Jih watched as they carefully lowered their heads, hoping to avoid getting caught in brambles. The hunting party was in high spirits, but the sobering concern of Vut soon filled the air around them. They approached a clearing made by a band in years past as Jih noted the mark of a hand-axe on a few trees. Vut looked over towards a decaying tree and picked up a heavy branch that was present on the ground. He examined the wood and slammed the ground with it twice, the sound reverberated through the environment. Vut waited for the rest of the line to meet as they bunched together. Dran cupped her hands with her mouth to announce their presence in case any stragglers needed to go before they were left behind. The group stopped as they waited to see what Vut had to say.

"Weypeu prints. Fresh." Vut mentioned with his hand held up, as he knelt to get a better look at the ground. Dran snatched the free torch at the front and knelt to meet Vut as she held it over to the soil to get a better look. Her face showed fear as she nodded to confirm Vut's words. Dran voiced these concerns down the line that made their way so that all could hear. While Vut spoke, Hyu passed along a torch from higher in the line to Jih.

"For Muucu. Do not drop...or set yourself on fire. Hyu can not heal this." Hyu warned Jih as she passed him the torch. While deer fur was also prone to burning, it was far easier for his grass outfit to be set ablaze.

The group bathed themselves in the smoke that emitted from the torch as it was a good way to mask their scent, but also made it less likely for mosquitoes to come in their direction. They were an irritating insect responsible for much annoyance and in extreme cases, death.

Jih's attention to Hyu was quickly diverted as Vut's words entered his mind. Tiger territory was incredibly dangerous, they didn't go for man often, but an encounter never turned out well. Dran urged them to huddle together at their backs. They walked slowly, each of them at a different point so that they could lock eyes with the beast and let the others know if running was possible. The tiger liked to attack from behind, so it came to reason that if no behind existed, the tiger would let them pass. As they walked, Dran noted the soil changed and was flooded with water. The environment of the swamps that tested the might of the party was indeed a harsh one. Every missed log under the shade of the mangroves could have easily been a crocodile waiting for an easy lunch. The group hoisted their legs up in annoyance at the uncomfortable feeling of water along their ankles. Hyu's eyes scanned the muddy water for stingrays that made their home there. She was fascinated with the creatures themselves but also was fearful of their venom. In the event she or anyone else accidentally triggered one, it was best to let them die peacefully.

Kag ran ahead of Jih as water dripped down his legs to check on his sister. As he stomped around, the sound of mud sloshed beneath his and the others' feet. Kag barged through without a care in the world to the rest of the line, pushing others as he did so. Hyu felt herself grabbed by Kag as he placed his head on her shoulder. Hyu gave a sigh but patted her brother on the cheek to soothe him. Jih and the others hadn't anticipated a stark change in terrain so quickly, but these lands weren't well known. The decay of the mangroves was evident as they approached a sizable clearing that shaped itself to be open grassland. Jih advised them to look to find dry land and evaluate supplies before going further. His words fell a bit short outside of the immediate people who heard him, but his concern was sent up the chain. Chak was the first to hit dry land and situated himself on a nearby stump. He held up his fist and stopped the party, while he motioned for Vut to approach him.

"What does Vut see, hmm?" Chak questioned Vut for his input. Vut was taken aback as he wasn't anticipating such a request to come from Chak. He took a deep breath and nodded as his eyes scanned the open grasses beyond him. His eyes looked towards a pile of rocks as he turned behind him searching for Jih. Vut waved him forward while waiting for Jih to advance. While Dran and Chak thought little of Jih, Vut cared to remember Jih's proficiency with stone. He was a scholar of The Old Way much like Jih was[3].

"There is hotspark[4] here." Vut noted, his finger pointing out the assorted piles of rocks that seemed ripe for use.

---

[3] "The Old Way" or the actual name of Acheulean technology is a stone tool tradition that first developed about 1.76 million years ago and is the form of tools that Jih's people retain to this very day.
[4] Emic word for flint.

"Spears will be made." Jih locked eyes with Vut. One of the girls accompanied them as the lookout for predators. Tool making was a long process that needed the utmost concentration and was hardly mobile. Jih and Vut would have to start over if they were disturbed, which made her job incredibly important.

The rest of the party took a moment to rest and dry off as the sun's rays went down on them. They wiped the sweat off their faces and observed some of the animals that came by. A small herd of water buffalo made themselves known as their calls could be heard in the distance. They stared in the distance at the group of kids while chewing grass. Chak rubbed his stomach in hunger as he imagined the largest of them roasting over a fire while he took the animal's skull as a trophy for his own. Chak stopped for a second as their ears turned to a snarl and accompanying scream in the distance. As Chak looked to count the group, he noticed that one boy wandered off to the source of the sound. Chak heard a shout from the boy as he turned his head, but instead decided to use his role and delegate instead. Chak picked Hyu, Kag, and Dran to investigate while he sat back and waited.

The three ran towards the boy to find him looking in shock at a man who had been disemboweled from the waist; the marks were clear that he crossed paths with the tiger. The blur of orange was just out of their range of vision, out of sight but not out of mind. His face was filled with anguish and grief as he vainly reached out to get the aid of those in front of him. Dran gritted her teeth as she found the situation uncomfortable. It was evident he was beyond any reasonable help, but Hyu attempted her best to soothe him as she grasped his hand. Hyu noticed his entrails were poured out onto the dirt and looked away as he attempted to stuff his intestines back into his body. He wore a whittled down conch shell on his neck, and an axe by his side, also made from the same material. He writhed in pain, looking at Kag, who scrambled to stop the bleeding as best as they could before succumbing to his wounds.

Dran looted the body and took the axe with her while Kag and Hyu looked over the man's corpse. Their training led them to look at injuries with curiosity rather than the disgust that their previous friend had. Hyu knew that the wound was deep, and he had lost much blood. Kag suggested in the event any of them get injured, they make a needle from bone to sew the wound together, much as how The Council did for their furs. Dran saw an opportunity to impress Chak with not only her ability in the field, but her desire to appeal to his other qualities. Dran had personal investment in Chak's success, she genuinely believed in his leadership much like Tur did. She also knew that Chak was a collector of the new and fascinating. As Dran approached, she gave a warm touch on Chak's shoulder. She locked eyes with Chak and got his attention briefly. Dran presented the axe as a gift to Chak who looked at it with questions in his mind. Chak said nothing as he snatched it from her to manipulate in his hands. He stood up some distance from the others and gave it a mighty swing as he listened to the sound it made. He hadn't seen the utility of such technology before, as The Elders sourced their technology from lithics, rather than shell of this new group. He decided to keep it as his personal weapon, while he waited for Jih and Vut to return with the flint as promised.

Jih and Vut worked to process the flint into spear points, while the girls harvested wood from the mangrove and bound plants to make fibers. Jih and Vut sat on the grass as they tossed each other a spare rock to use for their purposes. Jih folded his legs and held the flint in his left hand, while using the other rock in his right. He carefully held his breath as he stayed perfectly still. He hit the right side of the flint with the rock and saw a few flakes jettison off to the ground. Jih hoped to make a triangle out of a circle as he and Vut compared designs. Jih nodded and continued as he slammed the rock hard on the ground, accidently missing the flint piece entirely. Vut chuckled as he saw Jih do this, but out of understanding rather than mockery. Jih followed through with patience and a few hours later, there were several sizeable points made. Jih held up one by the smoothed end as he used another rock to scrap the edges of the top, making them sharpened for combat. Vut ran his finger down the edge and retracted it in surprise while Jih gave a smug grin. Far from being a professional stoneworker yet, these would get the job done as they made one of each. The girls met their end as well, poised over an array of chiseled wood and fibers bound to hold the points in place. Vut whistled to the group, and called the rest of them over as he watched them go to their assorted weapons. Jih assisted with those that were struggling as he went over the wrapping process with his own weapon. Together, they made some functional spears that could at the very least kill some small game, and with ingenuity, get to the target unharmed.

The hunting party clutched their new weapons and continued traveling the open plain and stopped as they watched a giant pangolin feed on ants. The animal walked around aimlessly while it used its claws to dig into the dirt. Its brown scales looked sharp as the animal breathed and curled its tail around.

"Kavagol!" Hyu pointed out as she tapped Jih's arm and pointed at the scales of the creature. Jih knew Hizo always coveted having a pangolin skin at home, it was a sign of protection and good fortune among their people.

A few of the other members of the hunting party stopped as well, enjoying the sight before them. The pangolin stuck out its tongue and kicked up soil with its claws. The group kept their distance watching as Kag looked up to see the clouds overhead shaped to reveal rain on the horizon. Some of their group was further along down the field as Chak stopped and yelled across the plains for them to catch up or be left behind. The sky opened, releasing a torrent of rain that soaked the ground beneath them. The hunting party ran quickly as they could, hoping to find another patch of forest to hide in as they lacked any protection. As they ran, Jih could see the outline of Chak vanish into brush once more. They were met with more undergrowth, but this time less developed. The damage from a forest fire destroyed much of the debris they worked through previously. Kag went to work grabbing large leaves to use as a reprieve from the rain while he was joined by a few others. Jih and Hyu reunited with Kag as they carefully grasped the leaves from the tree.

"When it rains, it pours! Brother, your grass will grow strong from rains! Haha!" Kag joked as he laughed while Jih shook his head trying to dry himself. The first thing on their minds was to make a new fire and dry off while Chak thought of another plan.

Chak found a dry patch of land under some dense forest canopy and ordered the group to make temporary shelters from large leaves and wood. Dran organized a sleeping shift schedule while a small fire was constructed to keep the place alight. The clouds above them showed an ominous signal with rain staying for some time. Although more time could have been spent on the road, Chak decided that resting would be better suited for the group. Jih had no complaints about this, instead choosing to sit on a log while he avoided the torrential downpour above. Kag was surprisingly full of energy and volunteered to do the first watch of the night with two others. Jih attempted to catch a moment's rest. He was once again shrouded by darkness as his vision came to. The sound of the thunder and subsequent rainstorm caused those who were able to sleep to wake up as the ground pooled around them. Hyu climbed a tree and looked above hoping to find some sort of path for them to take through the moonlight. It was far too dark for her to make out anything of real significance, but she saw that there was a gradual disappearance of trees further out.

"Forest thins further north. It is dark, do we think the risk is worth it?" Hyu commented from above, as Jih looked upwards to see Hyu suspended on two thick branches. She descended from the tree after her observation was made and walked to join the others.

The group moved to find new ground and found a better location. This was less forested, but the rain was far less. There wasn't much else to do, so the others talked among themselves as they waited for a command from Chak. Chak walked around, evaluating the strength of his hunting party as he tossed a stick into the fire. The embers cracked as his shadow distorted among the trees and bushes, stretching out to inhuman proportions. Some of his admirers noted this as another sign of strength to come. While Chak was tight-lipped about the hunt they were undergoing, some speculated about the beast.

"What will die?" One of the girls asked as she was moving kindling to increase another fire's size. She moved aside for Dran who nodded in respect as she crouched down and felt the warmth of the fire fill the air.

"Yaan. It is obvious, look how many of us there are." Dran commented as she put her hands over the fire. Vut returned with some berries he sniffed out and ate them, much to the look of disdain he got from the others who hadn't eaten for some time.

"There are many. A certain Yaan or Zaan?[5]" Hyu said, as she walked closer to the flames. The fire had increased in intensity so she could make out the vision of others through their temporary encampment.

"This one?" A boy asked, as he stuck his left arm straight out under his nose. Mimicry of creatures was a popular pastime among Jih and his people as they crafted stories regarding their place in the world.

---

[5] Both Elephant - 'Yaan' and Mammoth - 'Zaan' are words derived from the Mongolian word for elephant. It is likely their word is onomatopoeia for the mammoths that used to roam their steppe homes in years long past.

Hyu laughed as the boy flopped his arm around from side to side, emulating an elephant's long trunk. Dran bent a stick near her nose, and held it angled to the ground. Hyu nodded, understanding the animal they were after with a slight smile. Kag kept his eyes fixed on Dran some distance away but talked to Jih as he did so.

"Yaan is very big." Jih said with some worry in his voice. Jih had thought for a party this large, there would have been perhaps a rhino or a giant tapir as a choice, but an elephant? Did The Council really have that much trust in them? Adults felt hesitant about taking on elephants without help from another band, and they had basic weaponry.

"Much meat to bring back." Kag stated. His mouth salivated at the thought of some freshly cooked meat. His stomach rumbled as did the others. Elephant meat was a delicacy, as finding one isolated from the herd and the difficulty of the kill was astronomically high. Jih reasoned that there must be a calf they were pursuing if this was the case.

"How will we do it?" Jih inquired as he wiped mud off his legs.

"Many will carry meat." Kag suggested as he thought of ways the elephant hide could be used.

The discussion of the night vanished as the camp was still. Chak pushed the group to wake up as Jih and the rest of the party gathered their things with dirt and leaves caked onto their faces. With their total travel time being about two days as Jih anticipated, the fruits of their labor had finally come to pass. The vision of the tree line cleared to reveal an open spring with a small tract of grassland. The spring, on further examination, was more of a sizeable lake that served as a boundary for what lay beyond. For many of the adults in the band, this was the furthest of their hunting range. No one in living memory would venture out further on their own. Jih noted they came across many other creatures of notable size and strength but ignored them all for the chosen target. A breath of relief came upon the others as the hell of the trees was behind them now, at least for this point of the hunt.

"Chak. We are here." One of the girls singled out the elephant sipping water.

It was exactly as described to him, an old elephant sighted by The Council, known for its shy and elusive nature. Hyu wondered how The Council was able to determine its pattern, elephants weren't creatures of habit in her observations. The elephant seemed withered as it stood attempting to scoop mud and toss it around. From a distance it looked humorous, as its tusks were so massive, the trunk was instead carried over on the side drooping over. The creature had a clipped ear and claw markings on the side of its hide, it had seen battle already and seemed to have been nursing its wounds. It poured water over itself as it did so. If the creature were to fight back, it would still be a strong adversary for the group despite its condition. Jih and the others hoped sheer numbers would win the day for them, but Chak came forward with a plan. Dran ordered the others to grab their weapons as she and Vut were to delegate instructions. Chak knocked his fist on the side of a tree to get the group's attention and then spoke.

"We attack Woodyaan." Chak said as he pointed triumphantly out in the direction where the animal lay. The elephant's eye turned slightly as it surveyed its environment before drinking more water.

"Attack...how?" Hyu asked, her voice low but audible enough to rouse a perturbed expression from Chak.

Chak expected the rest of the band to follow his lead without the need to communicate. His selfishness was as vast as his talent and the two collided often. Chak huffed in annoyance at Hyu's question. While most felt this was a legitimate thing to ask, Chak was offended as he outranked her. Hyu, who had said very little on their journey to him personally, was now willing to question him so openly? Chak wouldn't entertain a response on his own. He let his subordinates do the talking for him as he turned his head away from Hyu. Chak detailed the plan with them in the early morning while the others only speculated on what was to be done.

"Surround on all sides." Vut explained, as he gestured to Chak who stood waiting. Chak scowled at the rest of the group, hoping to make sure that everyone else didn't challenge his authority.

"Water hole sinks deep. Woodyaan drowns, there we will kill." Dran confirmed, making a splashing noise with her mouth.

"It will not escape." Chak added on, as he hoped to shut down any more discussion.

The group nodded at the plan. It certainly was plausible, trapping the elephant and moving it back towards the sinkhole so it could collapse under its own weight was a crafty decision. There was some concern however on a few faces. Jih's face was among them. Kag noticed this and wondered if he and his friend came to the same conclusion. This plan was hardly sound, but few were willing to challenge Chak's authority on the matter. He had the favor of the adults with orange stripes on his person, and so it was told. Jih, however, had other plans.

"Jih does not agree." Jih stated, prompting looks of shock and anger among the others. Jih froze as he struggled with the onlookers glaring towards him. The balance of power was significantly uneven, but Jih did not see himself as a manipulator. He was concerned about his wellbeing, and that of the others. Jih knew fully well the consequences of never being told the word no in his life, and he didn't want to fall victim to Chak's arrogance. The ever-observant Kag backed up his friend's statement without question.

"Too dangerous." Kag agreed, while exaggerating his support for Jih with a strong pat on the back.

"Why Jih?" Chak asked, shaking his axe in visible anger. Dran gave a look of genuine concern as Chak started to unravel slightly. The last thing anyone wanted was something rash to happen that would endanger their success.

"Do not question Chak." Dran said defensively, her expression soured towards Jih. The others could feel the tension that filled the void with their group, everyone hadn't eaten for some time and people were getting angry. Anger was a mistake that could get them killed.

"Quiet Dran." Hyu said in annoyance to her. Jih gave a raise of his eyebrows as thanks to Hyu while Hyu gave a slight glance back before returning her attention to Chak's words.

"Not all can swim, some will drown." Jih looked at their hunting party, a few who had looks of embarrassment on their faces at the fact.

"Sacrifice Chak can make." Chak said, closing his fist, and gesturing towards his orange coating.

Jih closed his mouth and put his foot in the dirt. He didn't agree with the plan but couldn't argue against The Council's wishes anymore. Chak was the leader and so his word took precedence. Jih felt that was a mistake, but he needed to follow through for the sake of the group. Jih looked at the rest of his comrades who were shaking with anxiety. Jih empathized greatly with the others as an elephant was the stuff of nightmares and to be treated so callously by Chak was hardly motivating. Jih looked up to the above canopy and took a deep breath to ground himself for battle. The wistful nature of the leaves and wind could calm anything including his fast-beating heart that pulsed with every second they remained waiting. With that in mind, he prepared with the others to get into position and follow orders. After the drama settled, Chak removed his bone necklace and placed it on a nearby log. He wanted to be sure that he left no tell for the elephant to pick up his noise as he moved. Chak was the first to go, with Jih and Kag shortly behind him, while the others slowly advanced. They started in a single file line but dispersed gradually to anticipate the elephant's movements and escape attempts.

The elephant lifted its head up, sensing their approach. The animal continued bleeding and in its hysteria, let out a mighty sound from its mouth, warning the others to leave. Unfettered, the hunting party let out a yell of their own hoping to scare the beast. Hyu, as graceful as she was, grabbed a few rocks, and cast the first stone to distract the creature while maneuvering through the muddy shoreline. Bits of mud spattered around her as she attempted to keep balance. Hyu minded her range and moved her head to summon the rest. Most of the hunting party grabbed rocks and followed her advance, launching whatever they had on them. Chak gave a mighty yell as he commanded those with spears to join him on the assault. To the animal's exposed wounds, the pelting of stones was bothersome, and it shifted position for a charge. Kag carried a spear and jammed it tight into the already open wound of the animal. He held out a hand to Jih, warning him that the elephant's rage was directed towards him. The elephant's trunk swept at the feet of Jih who maneuvered just in time out of the way. Jih's heart raced as he tried to make sense of what he needed to do. He observed the creature as he held out his spear and swiped the air, hoping to disorient the elephant's vision.

The tusks were unwieldy for the creature but in a rush of uncharacteristic speed, the elephant was able to skewer one of the boys straight in the stomach clean through. Blood soon pooled in the mud. His upper half was torn apart from the impact and landed in the dirt as it moved its head in a rage. The boy's body was crushed by the elephant's foot and a splattering of blood and skin riddled the shore. The dirt sunk lower into the ground as the elephant advanced forward. It let out a loud bellow from its mouth once more as it boasted victory. The chaos was too frantic for the hunting party to grieve, or even perceive that one of their own had fallen. The elephant reared up on the sandy banks, and one of the girls held a spear to stab the exposed underbelly. She misjudged the power in which the elephant returned to the ground and was crushed under its massive weight. Chak's hope in his plan wavered, but he always had a plan. Not one to give up so easily, Chak ordered the others to attack as one instead as separate. He let out a whistle and called forth the rock throwers who ran with intensity down the shoreline. They each spread themselves apart a few feet from one another as they carried more rocks. His gambit paid off, with the elephant rearing again, but was unable to advance more as the weight had sunken it into the mud that was now forming at an alarming rate within the area.

Jih took to the water a short distance away to anticipate where the elephant would land so he could jam his spear into its skull. He felt his grass clothing become damp once again as bits and pieces fell apart, while the rest hung on his skin. As the elephant descended further into the spring, Jih could feel the slight vortex that was forming from the change in pressure. As Jih was far too light, he was unaffected but watching the elephant collapse in on itself was a sight to behold. It remained quite chaotic however, as the others were working to pelt it to death with stones, and the more daring went to attack in the muddy water. The elephant's howl filled the forest, its pained cries reaching out to any that would listen. Jih swam closer and met with a few others by the other edge of the bank. Jih could hardly breathe as he saw the direction of Chak pointing to the animal's back. Jih took to the water with a few others. He climbed on the half-submerged elephant and dug into the animal's skull with his spear, wincing in pain as he was damaging his own hand with so much force.

"Arms tight and twist." Jih repeated to himself as he managed to pierce the thick portions of the skull, hearing a satisfying crunch. Blood loss had eventually spelled doom for the animal, and the party was able to finally rest for just a moment. The elephant hit the ground with a resounding thud that was cut short by the impact of the mud. Now that the animal was dead, butchering it was going to be no easy task. The meat was also very wet, and Jih hoped that it would be at least somewhat edible after being drenched in freshwater.

While the others were triumphant to claim victory, Kag looked in the distance to the rest of the tree line. A large cracking sound of wood snapping followed by a low rumbling sound could be heard. Kag strained his eyes to notice that the trees caved in slightly.

"Trees are moving...?" Kag mumbled to himself as he tried to make sense of what was happening. He breathed heavily, finally getting a moment to rest. While most didn't catch Kag's question as they were recovering, Hyu remained ever tuned in and she shot her brother a look of shock. Hyu quickly stepped forward as she moved to follow Dran. Dran made her way over to address Chak. Hyu placed her hand on Dran's shoulder, yanking her back. Dran was too exhausted to comment on Hyu's presence as she held her arm out attempting to wave to Chak.

"More of the herd?" Chak questioned aloud, as he could only hear a lone noise, and not that of the other elephant's herd who would have been close by.

"We must go." Hyu said with much worry in her voice to Dran who was keeled over, out of breath.

She struggled to rally the others to come ashore and meet with her. A bull straight tusked elephant, fresh from having fought another, thundered its way through without a care in the world. Its thirst was immense, and for what they knew, this was the only spring for a large distance. It was obvious that anything could come here, and now the full ramifications of that have come to fruition. A look of fear filled the group immediately as they were surely horrified. Standing at about eighteen feet tall and weighing twenty tons it was a sight to behold. Its skin was a light gray that contrasted from the sea of green around them, and its eyes were yellow with streaks of red. The elephant's trunk dripped water as it let out a triumphant shout with its mouth. Hyu and the others could see themselves in the creature's gaze and were horrified. What kind of luck could have befallen them to meet such a mighty creature? Hyu, who had much knowledge on fauna, lost all color in her face.

"K-Kwiekyaan!" Hyu stuttered as the others of their party were in conversation. She pointed, trembling as she felt the very earth itself shake under its might. The rest of the hunting party grabbed their spears and were shaken with fear as their teeth chattered. Many could not bear to look the beast in the eye as the creature inhabited the darkest of legends. As they stomped the earth and carved out paths in the world, they left a wake of utter ruin and destruction behind them.

They weren't prepared, as an injured animal not nearly this size had already been difficult to handle, and they had lost two already. Its face was adorned with a thick tar-like secretion that could only mean the animal was in its musth stage, and the group was on a collision course for its rage. Bull elephants in this cycle of life were to be avoided at all costs, for they were filled with much destructive power as trees fell to their whim. Nothing would be spared as the animal ran its tusks into the ground, in a hope of relieving itself in some way. Those loyal to Chak and his plans grabbed what remained of their weapons to attempt to scare it off, but many already turned tail. Chak for all his strength and glory, was no match for the straight-tusked elephant. Chak ordered those who would listen to stay, and two boys retreated from the rest of the hunting party and joined him. They flanked Chak with their spears as Chak gave them an approving nod at their bravery. Dran jostled herself out of Hyu's grip for the moment as she soon made her way over to Chak. Hyu watched as Dran went off, not willing to sacrifice her life for someone that wasn't her brother. Dran arrived at the scene and heard Chak's loud yell. He was hoping to pull off the same stunt as their retired foe, but this was no mere beast. The elephant looked at the display of bravado from the boys and focused on Chak.

"Leave!" Chak shouted, his voice irritating the animal as it picked up his speech.

The elephant cleared its nostrils and moved its trunk to Chak. Spared a goring by its tusks, Chak was instead grabbed by the arm with the elephant's trunk, and before he could react, he was catapulted into the air. Chak's fleeting moments of consciousness were too slow to comprehend what happened to him. His arm was severed from his body by the sheer force of strength, where he was thrown aside to a tree with a resounding thud as his skull cracked before his own blood hit the ground. He didn't make a sound. He was already dead by the time he touched the tree. His bloody arm with exposed tendon and bone hung in the trunk and was dropped by the elephant. The rest of Chak's body practically fell apart with the amount of force as a branch fell to the floor after making contact. Now, they had no leader and no plan.

Enraged now, the elephant let out another shout from its trunk and stomped around, frantically overturning rocks and crushing logs beneath its weight. Jih witnessed this and retreated for a moment as he saw the rest of the hunting party vanish to the familiar woodland they emerged from for the hunt. Jih's mind quickly remembered camp which wasn't too far from the absolute carnage occurring from him and went to work. He arrived with weapon in hand. He held his spear to the ground and twisted it, detaching his spear point from the long stick he made. He then hastily wrapped some fibers around the top of the stick. A few eager members of his group had already lit a fire which was just what he needed. Jih waited as the fibers and wood caught flame. He crafted a torch and ran as fast as he could while trying not to blow it out. Jih hoped that the burning torch would be enough to scare it away, as fire made all animals submit, or so he thought. Jih gasped for breath as his friends scattered hoping to get away from the beast. The afterimage of Chak's downfall played through Dran's mind. Dran's thought process was immobilized by both absolute fear and grief over the quick loss of Chak. Her knees touched the ground as her vision clouded with tears. Her body single mindedly crawled to grab the boy's arm in vain. Jih saw this and moved quickly to retrieve her, there would be no more death today if he could help it.

"Dran! Come with Jih!" He shouted, as the elephant began wailing on another tree.

The unresponsive Dran was egged on by Kag and the others to get away as quickly as possible. The monster before them was distracted but could easily plow down the entire forest to get to them. Jih hoisted Dran over his shoulder and dragged steadily by Jih. Jih let out a grunt as she was far heavier than he seemed to have anticipated. The animal turned its gaze onto him, Jih waved the torch around in his free hand, hoping to scare it away. It would be difficult, as the elephant's response was to grab a log and toss it in his direction with incredible force. Jih felt his heart jump out of his body as he saw the large log just barely miss the two of them. Kag ran to support Jih as Dran was nonresponsive and the two dragged her to safety.

"We must move or die!" Kag yelled past the thundering footsteps of the elephant.

Jih winced at a scenario that came to mind, but really had no other options; he quickly tossed the torch and set alight a portion of the forest near him, hoping that would be enough to scare it away while they struggled to get back. The elephant continued to rage onwards, but the rise of the flames compelled it to reconsider. Hyu and the others waited at their hidden camp, and quickly embraced the three as they returned unharmed. Jih looked behind them, watching the fire he created slowly consume much of the treeline. They had failed to the highest degree, and now behind them was a fire that could close them in if they weren't careful.

"We have failed." Hyu said with a serious tone to her voice as she looked at the ground. Hyu lifted her head to see that others began crying as they noticed that Chak was not among them that returned.

"Chak..." Dran uttered as she was given water from another member of the party. Dran's eyes peered over to the bone necklace left on the log by Chak. Her tired arms reached over and barely clung to it with the edge of her finger. It was to be her most prized possession.

Once the atmosphere settled, the group paused to rest and heal their injured. Hyu was quick at work to look at the cuts of the wounded, as she urged Kag to look among the trees for any aid.

"Kag. Please find Marubaat for wound. This one is deep and needs help." Hyu said as she lifted a girl's hand that was cut from slipping in the mud. Jih looked to find a few of the leftover fibers and passed them to Hyu for assistance. Jih noticed that while many were concerned about their wellbeing, the topic of the hour was Chak who was being mourned. Jih felt it to be distasteful to say how he truly felt. Hyu could see that Kag had much to say on the matter, and while she offered only a glare to her brother, he spoke anyway.

"Kag is confused. We mourn for Chak, what of others, hmm? Did they not die as well?" Kag asked in indignation. While Jih and Hyu were more attuned to the social climate, Kag was always outspoken and more driven by emotion. His goofy demeanor often kept him deflected from the gossip that emerged among them.

One boy who was uninjured rose and gripped a branch in anger at Kag's words. He cracked his neck as he looked at Kag in disgust. Chak's death was fresh, and already he spoke such falsehoods. A few others made their distaste known at Kag's comments by glares and scowls on their faces.

"Kag, you are foolish. It is best you stay quiet. We are hurt and must endure-" The boy said as he threatened Kag with shaking the branch. Kag exhaled air out of his nose in annoyance.

"No! Kag will not be silent. Chak knew you could not swim and yet told you to do so. That is not leadership. Kag knows leadership. It is from Jih." Kag stated, as he called Jih forward. Jih hadn't bothered to make much of a case for himself, but he stood as Kag recalled Jih's deeds over the past two days.

"Kag hears your words behind back. Jih made tools for us to use. These were before we left for hunt, one of which you hold. Jih cuts plants with hand-axe. Jih carried injured and dealt with Kwiekyaan while you cowered." Kag spat out in anger as the boy offered no retort.

"Chak was our leader! No speech will make Jih worthy. He is an outsider!" The boy grimaced, while Jih spat in anger at his comment. Both Jih and Hizo worked relentlessly to do their best for the group and their status as refugees followed them wherever they went. Kag looked at Jih as he placed his hand on his friend's shoulder. Kag knew that Jih was primed for more, but today would not be that day.

Jih decided to take Kag's pep talk to heart as he tried to diffuse the tension between the other boy and Kag. He turned his head to see the despondent Dran and frowned at her state of being. No matter how awful Chak or Dran were, the fate of being ripped apart by an elephant was a fate none deserved.

"We must make our way home before the rain comes. Let us go." Jih said to the others as they slowly picked themselves up and continued. Kag and the boy stared down at one another but lowered their stances at the behest of Jih. Despite Jih's anger at his treatment at the hands of Chak, he knew that their senses were bewildered for the two days they were hunting. As the party continued to make their way through the brush one by one, Jih stayed behind as Dran refused to move. Kag followed the current of people and looked back at the nearly empty camp. He nodded his head for Jih to join him at the front. Jih returned his nod in understanding, but before he left, he took a knee and offered his hand to Dran. He waited for some time as Hyu lingered with her hands grasping the trunk of a tree while the sounds of rustling became further distant. Hyu waited before turning to see Kag already left. Not wanting to be left behind, she sped off. Jih could hear Hyu's words through the brush as he suppressed a smile.

"Hyu will wait for Jih, but not forever!"

After some time, Dran lifted her head up and looked at Jih's open hand. She grabbed it to support herself and the two walked together in silence distant from the others.

"Sacrifice to make..." Kag joked darkly to himself as he looked behind him one last time and recalled the site of destruction that the elephant left in its wake.

The journey home was a silent and empty-handed one as they saw the impact of what the hunt truly meant. The two other boys that deserted the group were never found, and the rest of the party assumed the worst to come. In time, the familiar sights of home came, and Tur was the first one to notice them returning. The mass of children returned as they stepped into the boundaries of their village. Tur cupped his hands and yelled for the attention of applicable adults.

"Our warriors have returned to us! Victory at hand!" Tur said, while many dropped their tools to hear his words.

The adults shed their white paint and since returned to their duties. If nothing was heard for three days, a team of scouts were sent out to recover the children. Tur gathered everyone around who looked with a big smile on their face. Hizo and other parents watched with glee as one by one, their respective child came forward. Hizo held her breath as she watched other parents retrieve their child. The promise of cooked food and a warm bed awaited them as they returned and embraced their loved ones. Tur's face frowned as he frantically searched, with no sign of Chak. He kept his composure as he knew his champion led his forces to victory.

Exhausted and drained of energy, the last batch that stepped into view was Jih and a few others, including Hyu and Kag. Hizo ran to Jih and her students, happy that they returned home safely, but noted the casualties. Hizo knew every single member of her flock intimately and felt her heart race. Hizo's eyes scanned the surroundings and saw there were some missing. She looked for Dran among them and breathed a sigh of relief as she was met by her father. A sullen feeling came over her that dampened her immense pride in her son. Hizo looked upwards and saw that The Council sat on a small slope in plain dress and observed the scene. It was clear to them that the true lesson of the Recognition Hunt was not achieved.

The truth behind this hunt was that the tasks were meant to be monumentally difficult and impossible to complete. It was to test their strengths and cooperation as a group, but also to test their insight. An elephant was a difficult task for adults, let alone children. Chak was supposed to be overruled, listening to the demands of the majority, and making the mature decision to return when conditions were better. Instead of perceived wisdom and cooperation, he used his rank to silence dissent and paid for it with his life. Although Chak's hunting party succeeded in killing their elephant, it was his hubris that endangered the group and killed many. The knowledge of when to cut your losses is invaluable, when there is only one life to live. The survivors of this experience understood this better than any but empathized with the new adults who were unsure how to process this information.

Hizo held up a finger to Jih and promised his favorite food would be waiting. Before they could go home, Hizo needed to trade for one special ingredient, a sprinkle of citrus for flavor. She ran quickly and hoped to catch another one of her friends before they went back to their duties. In the time where Jih remained, he saw that Tur still waited for the bushes to rustle and Chak to return. Jih gave a small gulp as it clearly hadn't set in that Chak wouldn't come back. While Jih despised Chak, he didn't think he needed to die for it and decided to reach out. Jih took a deep breath and attempted to console him as Tur stood with his arms folded. Tur's stare was defiant as he saw Jih looking at his leopard print covering. He withdrew away in irritation. His cheery face was dark and cold, for the possibility of failure from Chak gave him physical illness. It wasn't natural; his destiny was to be far greater than anyone realized. Tur planned every aspect of Chak's life, from the food he would eat to be strong for battle, to his choice of a partner to further the line. It was he who saw that Hyu was destined to be with Chak and inserted this seed into his mind.

"Tur." Jih said as he immediately regretted his decision.

Jih was hardly one to like Tur, but his pain was known, and he attempted to reach out where Hizo could not. Jih met the shaken composure of Tur who gave him an enraged glare. While Jih attempted to open his mouth, Tur pointed at him in disgust. Tur lost his child early in life and it was evident that Chak filled the void. It was accepted by the other adults, and nobody spoke on this matter as his own birth parents were put to death for a crime against their people. The son of murderers, Chak was left without guidance and Tur bravely took this challenge. Tur had no outlet for his rage at Chak's death and pointed his anger onto Jih who stood in his path.

"Tur will never forgive this. You killed my son!" Tur shouted as onlookers turned away in embarrassment.

The silent Dran observed quietly as she briefly gravitated from her father. She positioned herself next to the wall of a nearby hut. Unlike Tur, Dran didn't blame Jih for Chak's death. She couldn't find any reason as he saved her life. Dran's eyes shifted from Jih and Tur in debate to the slope where the members of The Council sat. Dran's emptiness was filled with disdain for The Council as she radiated in anger. Dran held little personal rapport with others but felt a grave injustice was brought on her and Chak respectively. Jih anticipated the worst to come and yet it never felt as raw hearing those words. He was filled with anger as it was Chak's stupidity that led to his death, but he was powerless to say otherwise. Tur controlled the narrative and Jih knew he had to acquiesce. Jih lowered his head and said nothing more as he saw the wave of Hizo in the distance. He followed the path of the village back to his home and thought nothing more than to get some chicken soup in his stomach.

A Sight From Above

In the years that followed Jih and his friends' return to The Elders from their Recognition Hunt, resounding changes were made. The crafty Tur accomplished his dream of securing power as a member of The Council. As the oldest surviving member of the band, he held the highest rank among them and ruled his community with a desire to craft it as he saw fit. While The Council was still highly respected for their tradition, Tur cultivated an environment of fear and deceit that overlayed the central camp. Friendships were fickle and people were quick to point fingers at inefficiency, lest they fear retribution from The Council. For many, this was life as it was, but there were those who remembered when times were better. Jih stood outside his home with his arms folded as he observed the robotic nature of people moving through the village. Trail lines in the grass from moved rocks were visible in the distance. Some members of the band sat with their legs folded on the ground and built various projects. Work was constant and there was always something to do. Most bands in the area were a quarter of their size, but through careful planning and alliance building, they were able to stand tall above the rest with few challenging them. Almost thirty years have flown by in the blink of an eye for the members of The Elders. Jih was now 42 years old; the smooth face that his mother once cherished was now withered with the passage of time. His face was covered with a dark brown beard with the occasional patch of gray. His eyes retained their dark brown hue but were marred with exhaustion on his face. His hair was also still black, with some grays he attempted to bury in vain by rubbing dirt in.

Once quite small, he now stood at around 5'7. His stamina wasn't what it used to be, but he prided himself and his strength on a powerful command in combat, aided by a trusted spear. Jih wasn't as physically imposing as others of his kind but was crafty and could find solutions to problems that others neglected. It was for this, people flocked to his style of leadership. Jih couldn't afford to be seen being viewed as lazy while he watched others around him haul meat on animal skins or hunch over a firepit sharpening tools; he searched for a way to be useful. Jih's eyes scanned the village, and he noticed a man with a limp that came towards their boundary. Jih observed his dress and noted he was not one of their own, but a member from another band known as The Jagged Bark. Visitors were common as The Elders occupied ideal hunting grounds. The man wore a covering of straw and the pelt of a deer that draped over his shoulders. The straw left small fragments behind him that frayed off, leaving a small path as he continued to make his way. His arms swayed through the holes of his outfit as he slowly made his way over. Jih gave a wave over to signal he would address him.

Jih moved past the ceaseless productivity around him as his face lightened up to see the man. He was a well-traveled emissary of The Jagged Bark, keeping up the long-held tradition between the two bands. As Jih walked towards him, he held out his hand that Jih grasped in kind. Jih saw that the man was unarmed which was unusual for travel between these lands. The Elders prioritized safety above all else, but only within their areas of influence.

"Welcome brother. What brings you to camp?" Jih questioned as he evaluated the man's condition. Jih lifted an eyebrow as he noticed a peculiar wound on the man's head. His breathing was staggered, and he knew something was amiss, but considered it bad form to point this out without just cause.

"We request...hunting...in your lands. Perkaku[6] tracks have been found here." The man commented as he gestured to the ground.

The Jagged Bark band were steadfast in their friendship, offering bounties of fruit for an assortment of goods scavenged from the wilderness. Jih knew that his asking was only a formality and permission would always be given. Jih looked at the man's wound again with more concern as he noticed the emissary before him support his head with his hand as blood continued to seep out of his wound. The droplets slid down his brow to pepper the soil below.

"Of course, The Jagged Bark are allies. Tell Jih what happened to you. What animal did this?" Jih inquired about the man's wounds. His face held a frown as his people made a great effort to keep the jungles safe.

"Animal...? Only animal that did this was Neck-Shells. They come for our shores." The man coughed as Jih walked over to support him. Jih's face frowned as he listened to the man's words. The Neck Shells were a nuisance to others but weren't known to venture in their lands.

Jih hoisted him over his shoulders but stopped as the frame of Tur increased in his vision. Jih exhaled in frustration as Tur was a constant meddler in the affairs of everyone else. While the rest of The Council was content to perform just for ceremonies, Tur saw The Elders as his personal labor force. Jih's patience wore thin as he saw the old man up close. Tur kept his remarkable leopard print clothing and wore a necklace bearing multiple crocodile teeth. On his left shoulder was a mass of white feathers tied and sewn together. His face held a scowl now with white and gray that accompanied the hair on his body. Tur could walk on his own on occasion, but mostly carried a giant staff to use as a walking stick. Tur surveyed his kingdom with the utmost contempt for those out of line as his eyes shifted through the camp. Jih and Tur met each other's gaze and stood opposed to one another. Tur shifted his head and noticed The Jagged Bark member that was in Jih's care. Tur stepped forward and moved close to Jih and opened discussion. He mashed his staff into the soil as a tuft of dirt spat out beneath it.

"Jih. What did you tell this man? Did you tell him The Jagged Bark may come? All of them?" Tur inquired with a raised eyebrow. Tur sniffed and indulged his self-importance by prompting Jih to lower his head with his hand.

---

[6] Emic word for giant tapir.

"This one is injured. We can not spare the supplies. He should make his leave." Tur added on before Jih could say another word. Jih felt an inconceivable anger at Tur as he heard his words. Jih hung his head low as he listened before making his opinion known.

"Tur, they are our allies. The Jagged Bark has always hunted here. This was will of Illol." Jih stated in irritation as he stood with his foot tapping. Jih was astonished at Tur's callousness towards those deemed to be their allies. Oaths were important things to uphold, but Tur felt such commitments to be shortsighted.

"Strange things happen in our forest Jih. Do they not?" Tur said as he looked over the emissary from The Jagged Bark.

Jih shot a glare at Tur as he was dismissive of the man's condition. Tur was more aggressive in enforcing The Elders' sense of borders than other leaders in the area. While stating that the world was more dangerous and they needed to be prepared, Jih looked at his clothing and saw Tur wanted to protect his supply of fur. Furs were important to any band's livelihood, but exceptions had to be made to keep balance in the land. Jih feared Tur's callousness would have its consequences but lacked the rank to argue further. Jih chose to comply maliciously when possible.

"Have him gone by my return. There is much to be done here." Tur ordered as he cracked his neck.

The sound of his bones creaking was uncomfortable to both Jih and the emissary. Jih watched as Tur made his way, finally giving reprieve of his vitriol. Jih's eyes were set on a new target, he made his way to the eastern end of the village. The visage of huts diminished behind them as they continued their path. Out in the distance was a lone tent that handled injuries. Hyu and Kag worked in this area as the doctors of the camp, taking in and dealing with any sort of injuries that came their way. Jih was comfortable in their expertise and knew immediately that this emissary could be saved with their care.

As Jih walked, he attempted to usher the man quickly from onlookers. He felt slight sorrow at the state of his home. Tur's presence suffocated any enjoyment that sprouted up past his watch. Jih and the other man continued to pass an array of homes spaced out before the two locked eyes with a sentry guarding the exit. Sentries were important at night to keep out predators, but in the day, they only served as enforcers for Tur to interrogate people as they stated their purpose of entry out of the village. Jih couldn't help but shake his head as the sentries started young. She was a teenager with short hair and wore a covering of palm leaves and grass as sweat poured over her. She held a spear whittled from wood while standing, with her eyes poised on Jih and the man. She struggled slightly to hold the spear up as she kept her position, not having moved for quite some time.

"Jih is taking this one to healer. We will return soon." Jih mentioned to the sentry as she nodded and allowed the two outside. Now some distance away, Jih shook his head in irritation while the other man spoke.

"Neck-Shells are dangerous Jih. Doubt may come in your mind; we have seen them."

Jih hadn't traveled much outside of their hunting grounds when it came to the spread of news. Despite working in politics as needed, the news of the outside world didn't appeal to him compared to his love for stone working. The Hunting and Scouting Teams were far more informed regarding the outer workings of the jungle, but he gave a nod to signal he was still listening. Jih fought with a Neck-Shell man over a claimed kill by the ocean but hadn't considered them to be nearly as a threat as he's heard. Jih decided to put this thought to the side for now as their destination was reached. Jih raised an eyebrow as he saw a collection of calabashes hanging from the side of their tent. Hyu emerged from inside and stood up, ducking her head underneath the entrance. Jih watched as she cupped the bottoms of the fruit with her hands, moving them slightly as she peered inside the opening. Jih let out a yell to announce his presence as Hyu turned around to give a grin before releasing the fruit. Her cheery demeanor hardened as she saw the injured person before her.

"Kag! Come quickly, we have an injury. Head wound, there is much blood." Hyu said as Jih heard rumbling from the tent.

While Kag fiddled inside, Jih moved slightly to accommodate Hyu as she ran to help Jih support the injured man. She subtly arched her back and prompted Jih to do the same as they fixed the man's position so he would be able to walk easier. The two stepped in unison, taking the injured man through the entrance of the tent where Kag labored in the back. From the outside, the tent was rather drab but, in its isolation, it was able to flourish as a functional station for healing. Their operation was away from much of the main village where the smell of burned flesh and disease did not offend the sensibilities of others and additionally isolated predators from camp.

Jih's eyes studied the inside of the tent, he was fortunate enough to not end up here injured as he was a careful hunter. Although Hyu and Kag were excellent doctors, many members of The Elders had long standing fears of treatment for it could be as painful as the sickness. The centerpiece of the tent was warm with a lit campfire as smoke billowed through an opening of the roof. The smell of burning jungle wood and soot drowned out dried blood. Jih noticed right away Hyu's hand guiding him to move aside for the moment as she held the injured man up on the tent's wall. Jih did as he was advised and took a moment to observe his partner in such awe. Hyu's black hair remained large and poufy as it flowed down her shoulders, just barely scraping the soil while she stood on her knees. Hyu's face was sculpted with a strong jaw that accentuated her smile. Her brown eyes were full of life, despite seeing it fade away from those who perished in this place. A small piece of the ongoing fire reflected from her pupils and her stare could put any at ease. She wore two deer pelts that were tied together over her body with a leather band at the center from top to bottom. Hyu spoke with a low voice to her patients that often masked the severity of their illness.

"He was attacked by Neck-Shells. Not animal bite." Jih said to Hyu as he watched her raise an eyebrow in thought at his injury. Jih and the others were aware of the potential dangers involved with animal bites and their capacity to cause infections in the body if left untreated.

"Jih, hand Hyu nearby Tenkay. Any will do. The man must drink much, for he lost blood." Hyu said as Jih nodded. Hyu had seen far worse than this man's injury, but the nature of it brought concern to her. The Council declared peace was among the bands, but this seemed to be a vain hope rather than a definitive statement.

Jih maneuvered himself around Hyu and the injured man as he noticed Kag was still busy working on something in the corner. Hollowed out coconuts filled with warm rainwater were set aside on a small bed of leaves a short distance away. Jih carefully grasped the coconut and moved it over, taking great care not to spill a drop. Hyu grabbed the man's jaw and forced it open, while extending her hand out to Jih. He passed her the coconut water, and the man drank as she nodded. While the man drank, Kag finally finished with his task. Kag's hands were wrapped with fiber bandages as he gently held a salve made from Indian Copperleaf. He wrapped the bandages carefully around the man's head as Kag held him down. The man's arms flailed in pain as the salve irritated the wound. Kag held a stern look on his face as the man continued to move his arms until at last, he rested.

"Excellent job sister! Marubaat did the work, but Hyu did her part." Kag teased as Hyu stood up with crossed arms.

Kag reasoned he would check on the man from time to time as he slept. Kag was about to speak once more but was met with Hyu's back as she turned to address Jih. Now that work was done for now, she inched over to Jih and gave an affectionate rub in his hair. Jih gave a smile with clean teeth as Hyu leaned forward and tensed her nose. Jih matched this in kind and the two rubbed noses in pure bliss. Jih felt a wave of euphoria come over him as he caressed Hyu's hands and stared into her eyes. While not much time with them was spent together, Jih savored the few times he was able to visit the pair in their element. Kag slapped the ground, prompting Jih and Hyu to pay attention to their boisterous companion.

"Brother! Kag has not seen you on this side for some time. Tur works us hard and works you to death!" Kag joked as Jih instinctively looked behind him. Kag's laugh stifled slightly as he noticed Jih's fear was genuine.

"Sister, Kag has gathered many plants. Kag will entertain Jih as you sort. An oath was made!" Kag said with a hearty laugh.

Hyu stuck out her tongue and curled it as an insult to her brother. Her eyes looked towards a large bag filled with red leaves. Jih watched as she walked over and sorted. Hyu's hand waved off Jih as she was working. Kag decided to get some fresh air as he grabbed Jih by the arm and led him to the outside of the tent. The two sat down and folded their legs as the shade of a large tree bearing citrus loomed over them.

"Jih, Kag has been waiting for this day. Let us play a game, it will lift your pain." Kag said with a smirk. Jih hadn't noticed, but from behind Kag was a small leather bag with seashells scavenged from the ocean. Jih watched as Kag poured them out and carefully took a small pebble that fit just between his fingers.

"Jih will play your game. Jih likes to win Kag, so make this good." Jih said with a grin as he moved his head past Kag. Hyu was always on his mind as he confided in her often, and his concerns of the injured man hardly vanished.

No matter how old Kag was, Jih could see his best friend's face with such clarity. The old Kag now had a full beard of brown hair. His cheekbones were sharp, and a smile rarely left his face as he entertained himself with many jokes. Like Hyu, he wore two deer pelts that were tied together by fibers. His brow was as rough as Jih's and defined the rest of his face. His eyes were a dark brown much like Hyu's, but they were far more tired despite his demeanor. Kag moved the pebble around in his hand to show Jih that his actions were genuine. He then used sleight of hand to hide the pebble's location as Kag gestured to the three shells. Kag continued to move them around on the grass as he sorted. Kag knew that Jih was an experienced player, so he needed to get creative to pull one on his friend.

"Jih, Kag has question." Kag asked, while he continued to sort the shells. Jih noted that Kag had a strange sorting pattern that was hard to discern. He did not favor going clockwise or counterclockwise but was sporadic in how he decided to move the three. The disarray bothered Jih immensely, but he kept it to himself before his face could betray him. Jih raised an eyebrow at his friend as he was aware that he was trying to distract his concentration.

"Jih knows what you are doing Kag." Jih teased as he was met with an indignant nod from Kag.

"Not at all! Kag has burning question. Kag has seen Vauval again, is it bird or not? [7]" Kag said with a chuckle as he heard the collective sighs of Jih and Hyu from opposing ends.

"Jih has told Kag already. Vauval does not lay egg, bird does. Hyu collects bird eggs." Jih huffed as he averted his gaze from the shells to look at Kag. The sounds of nature encroached on their dwelling as the sound of their fellow band members grew quiet. Work further on in the distance stopped as the Hunting Team made their return with fresh kills, lunch was to be served soon.

"Oh-Has Jih seen it? It flies! All birds do." Kag commented as he raised his finger at Jih.

"Muccu also flies, is this bird as well?" Jih retorted in dismay to Kag's comments.

"From a certain point of view, yes." Kag snickered as he sat back. He opened his arms out to Jih to pick a shell of his choosing now that they were properly sorted. Jih stared at Kag for some time as Kag's grin grew with every passing moment. He raised his finger, looking for the shell that gave interest to the most, but Kag's laughter was almost too much to contain.

---

[7] Emic word for bat. Vauval in this case refers to the Sunda Flying Fox.

Jih shook his head at Kag as he prompted him to stand. Jih wiped his forehead as sweat accumulated. His eyes searched for movement in the trees in the vain hope a breeze would relieve them both.

"Jih knows you are cheating Kag. Secrets are something you rarely hold and you were never good at it. Rise, confirm the truth of Jih." Jih mentioned as Kag's laughter subsided. Kag wiped a tear from his eye as he shrugged his shoulders.

"You know Kag too well." Kag said as he shook his clothing for the pebble to fall to the bottom. Kag scratched his back as he adjusted the fur covering him.

Hyu called for Kag and Jih to enter the tent as her sorting was finished, stifling their discussion for now. As Jih and Kag entered inside, Kag looked over the sleeping man and let out a sigh of relief as his chest moved up and down. Jih walked over to Hyu and placed his hand on her shoulder with a grin.

"Hyu is finished. You have gathered many red plants, is this for celebration?" Hyu commented as Kag turned his around to address her. Kag walked forward and raised an eyebrow as he was confused about her comment. Hyu emphasized her point by gesturing to the pile of gathered roots and plants sorted in the corner where Kag processed them. Hyu leaned her head on Jih as she rolled her eyes. Kag crouched down and examined the leaves before turning to address Jih.

"Brother! Kag has another question." Kag stated as he got Jih's attention. Jih scratched his head regarding Hyu's comment but chose to ignore it. Kag lifted a finger as he grabbed two leaves, one plant with a light green tone while the other was deep green. He placed the first in Jih's hand and gave an exaggerated grin.

"What does this look like?" Kag questioned, as he gave his sister a sarcastic grin. Jih's eyes darted from Kag to the leaf in slight disbelief of what he was answering.

"This one is green." Jih said, watching Kag place a leaf back in the pile. Kag nodded approvingly, and then showed him another leaf to which Jih affirmed Kag's statement.

"Both are red." Hyu said, where she mimicked Kag's stance as she folded her arms.

Hyu's face was annoyed as Jih and Kag gave each other a glance, suppressing their laughter. She sighed, happy deep down nonetheless that much hadn't changed from their years in childhood. Hyu had sorted Kag's plants before, mostly determining the difference by texture or smell over anything else. It was evident that Hyu saw things differently than Jih and Kag, but they were unsure of what to do with this news. Has she seen this way the entire time and made no statement about it? Hyu thought nothing different of her situation but found it amusing the topic never came up. Hyu didn't gather plants in the same way as the others, so her perception of color didn't impede her daily life.

Hyu decided to step outside to get some air as she urged Jih and Kag to join her. The three sat in a circle with their legs folded and absorbed their surroundings, until Jih heard a rustling of bushes a short distance away. Jih reflexively stood up and scanned the horizon as this was not the usual path taken to this area of the village. Kag and Hyu were laxer as they knew it was likely a deer, or some other animal that stumbled their way inside. Hyu turned around to hear the noise of two people, one was a sobbing child and the other was a stern figure lecturing them. Hyu's intuition was correct, she saw first a young boy with a gracious wound on his hand and his older caretaker. Dran interrupted the three's relaxation by calling their attention to an injured boy that she herded along. She grabbed the boy's bare shoulder and pushed him forward in the direction of the others.

"Hyu! Kag! Be useful and help Dran. There is problem." Dran said as she moved to see the three sitting down. Her already irritated face turned to a scowl at their wasted time.

Dran was the same age as Jih and Kag, but the stress of her work was far more strenuous. Dran's short hair was gray with gleams of black that radiated in the sunlight. Her eyes were a light brown and held a stare that could pierce even the toughest of wills. While the others wore fur, Dran wore a humble outfit weaved from grass. A sash around it with a green fiber tied the material and was draped over her shoulder. In her travels, she used it to hold materials as needed. Dran was strong both in morals and physicality as she was responsible for teaching essential survival skills. Dran took up the mantle of trainer after Hizo died; she taught her students early that using the hand to defend themselves against something like a snake was a terrible idea, as you could potentially lose your entire arm in the process. This one was lucky, and she hoped that the mistake would not be repeated. Kag and Hyu immediately went to her, and asked what was wrong with the child. The boy was clearly inexperienced as a hunter and looked away in embarrassment as Hyu stared at him. Tears were in the boy's eyes as the pain from his bite upset him immensely. She knelt to him as some of her large hair touched his shoulders. The injury was obvious, but Hyu found it better to hear her patient's view on what happened.

"What has happened?" She asked the small boy. He still refused to answer, which prompted her to look at Dran. Dran shot him a glare as she nudged the boy who showed Hyu his hand. Hyu pursed her lips and looked at Dran. The boy's hand was bleeding, so she knew the wound was fresh at least. It was also quite deep. She slowly moved the boy's hand looking at his expression as he winced in pain.

"Sarmpa bite[8]. He did not think and attacked too early." Dran explained, with her tone upsetting the boy further. Jih observed the scene, remembering his inexperience and could only give a look of sympathy. Although Jih's own patience with children wore thin at times, he was aware of how much of an ask they were required to know at such a young age. Dran was competent but she was not his mother.

"Which one? What is the color? Hyu needs to know more." Hyu asked Dran, her tone increasing in worry as she wondered if she needed to start digging a grave. While some in the community attempted to suck snake bite venom out, Hyu knew this was a pointless endeavor. The effect of the cobra's venom was far too powerful for any home

---

[8] Emic word for snake. Sarmpa refers to all sorts of snakes, but poisonous ones like cobras are called Nagpu!

remedy to cure. Hyu recalled the amount of material they had in reserve as she looked to Kag for a second opinion.

"Not Nagpu, the boy lives." Kag interjected as he analyzed the boy's injury. If the wound became too infected, he figured numbing the pain would be best as Hyu would likely have to remove the entire hand. Jih was out of his element when it came to matters of healing, but he absorbed a lot of information from watching Hyu and Kag. There was no tool he could construct to fix a tapeworm, but basic first aid was essential to know, and he worked with that. Kag vanished for a time to retrieve a resin he produced sometime earlier.

"Jih. Come with Hyu." Hyu prompted him towards the screaming boy. Jih held his distaste as he complied, placing his hands on him. Hyu directed Jih to hold down the boy while she waited for Kag's return. The boy's face contorted in pain as he kicked Jih in the stomach. Jih let out a slight cough and scowled at the boy as he used his arm to press him down to the ground. Kag returned with a calabash filled to the brim in his hand. It contained a frothy solution that he poured over the wound. His arms shook slightly as he tried to get the precise dose needed to clean the wound. Dran watched with suspicion as she held her tongue on the matter. Healing was a complicated manner and Dran chose to speak only about things she knew with absolute certainty. Hyu ripped a portion of her clothing to use as a bandage over the boy's hand as Kag continued to pour.

"Is it fixed? Dran must go soon with young one." Dran asked, as she stepped backwards.

Her eyes met Jih's as they shared a mutual awkward moment. She recoiled at the scene with the child kicking and screaming while Hyu did her best to calm the loud child down. After some time, Dran gritted her teeth in annoyance. She was at her wit's end with no sign of the child's hysterics ending. Hyu gave the two a sly grin; as far as she was concerned, her job was complete, and the rest was up to Dran. Hyu gave a gentle wave as Dran scooped the child off his feet and carried them over her shoulder. Dran made her leave without another word as she was in a rush to rid herself of everyone else.

Kag cracked his knuckles as he did his good deed for the day and prompted the others to return to their discussion. While many in their group worked extensively, Hyu and Kag were able to take longer breaks due to the nature of their work. As the doctors of the camp, Hyu and Kag only really needed to work when someone was injured, and they had a large surplus of material to work with. Kag decided to pique the other two's interest on a matter he heard about a few days prior.

"Kag has heard something big." He said to Jih and Hyu who returned his look. Hyu moved her arm, prompting Kag to explain further. Kag looked above him and pointed for Jih and Hyu to follow his finger. Jih leaned in with curiosity on his face. Kag was not one to participate in gossip often, so the news was especially interesting to their ears.

"Old Man Tur saw sky. Big rock is coming, he will speak of it today." Kag mentioned as he stretched his arms out as wide as possible. Kag's grin softened slightly as he saw Jih's stern expression. Jih held out his hand to stop Kag for the moment as he scoffed at the mention of Tur. There was bad blood between the two for years. Hyu frowned as she placed her hand on Jih's shoulder in solidarity. Tur soured his relationship with many people in his drive for power and it showed in full. Hyu gestured to other homes in various stages of construction in the distance. Jih and the others found Tur's will to be fickle as rain when he couldn't decide.

"Homes for our allies are still not built. Hyu has spoken to Tur of this. We must host with kindness." Hyu mentioned as Jih let out an exasperated sigh.

"Tur always hated Jih. One week ago, Jih made great kill for The Council-" Jih complained as he grabbed a branch and packed loose dirt with it.

"Hyu remembers this. It was a great kill, Hyu cornered it in tree. Jih brought Onpeu[9] pelt to The Council. Many are impressed. Tur? Tur says, Chak would have gotten Weypeu pelt. There is no pleasing Tur, so worry not." Hyu commented. Jih decided to stop himself short before he went on another rant again and diverted the conversation back to the meteor.

"Big rock? Where will it come from?" Jih asked in confusion. The sky was a vague term, as many things called it home. Was it something as important as the moon? Jih knew the moon watched over them when the sun needed to rest, and they would never fall to darkness. Jih could recall many of The Elder's oral histories, but he'd never seen a meteor before. From what he could understand, there was one such event on the eve of he and Hizo's arrival at their new home.

"Hyu knows of sky rock. Rock flies to send message." Hyu said, running her finger in the air. She darted her head, happily sending a good deal of her hair into Kag's face. She gave a small laugh as Kag wiped his face in response.

"Rocks do not fly Hyu." Kag argued, moving closer to her to emphasize his point. Hyu turned up her nose at him.

"Birds do, they have wings. Rocks fall." Kag added on.

"Rock must be bird then. You said Vauval was bird! Rock is from sky. Birds are in sky. Can Kag fly?" Hyu said as she waved her hands around. Kag rolled his eyes at Hyu's comment, he wasn't aware that she overheard he and Jih's earlier discussion.

"We should go to beach, for we can see power rock there." Jih recommended, as he tried to bring down the brewing argument between the two of them. The coastline of the beach was a perfect vantage point for those who wanted to see something as promising as a potential meteor shower. Other than the vast emptiness of the blue ocean, there was nothing to impede their view. Jih longed to smell the coastline and feel the sand beneath his feet once more.

"Beach is Neck-Shell territory...Kag has heard things." Kag noted, as his eyes darted to the tent where their patient still healed. Kag wasn't opposed to the idea, but there was some hesitation in his voice. If the Neck-Shells were truly as fierce as they were stated to be, they would need to be careful. Jih shared the same sentiment as Kag, he was

---

[9] Emic name for leopard.

the one who heard the man's warning but had faith in himself and the others as warriors. Hyu gave a sly grin to the two as she leaned in to offer her perspective.

"We will sneak then." Hyu mentioned, as she referenced the many times as children they left their tents to explore the outer regions of camp in the dead of night. Irresponsible surely, but always a good time, especially when others joined their adventures.

"It is settled. Hyu and Jih will meet Kag. Bring Bani also if her health is fair." Jih declared as he got up, with Hyu following behind him. Out of Kag's range of hearing, the two spoke to one another. Jih nodded to Kag as he ventured back in the tent and attended to his duties. Hyu carried a concerned look on her face that carried to Jih's. As partners, the two confided in one another on anything, even their loved ones. Hyu cupped her hand to obscure her words as she spoke low to Jih.

"Hyu is worried for Bani. There are suspicions, but Hyu must check later. Do not return home just yet Jih. Talk to those under you as well, you are missed by Stoneworking Team." Hyu stated to Jih as he nodded. Jih left Hyu after rubbing noses once more.

As Hyu watched Jih head towards the opposing end of the village, she couldn't help but be proud of her partner. Hyu encouraged Jih to include himself in discussions more often and the fruits of this finally sprouted. Jih was hardly the shy outsider she'd gotten to know all those years ago. Despite Tur's harsh governance, word spread for some time that Jih was to finally be inducted into The Council, but these were still just rumors. Jih was a bit secluded, and kept a small friend group, so Hyu pushed him to talk to the rest of the band when he could. Jih made his way closer to the village center and found himself involved in a conversation with a member of the Stoneworking Team. Jih wasn't used to delegating responsibilities but as one of the most experienced, he was often sought out by aspiring stone makers to learn all the secrets of The Old Way. The man before him was a recent survivor of the Recognition Hunt and still working on the trade. Jih could tell as he still wore his initiation colors on his skin that poked out from his grass clothing.

"Jih! Mant has question. Where can bloodstone[10] be found?" Mant asked, scratching his chin. Jih was confused at such a question. A stone of that caliber was hardly given to anyone, especially a newcomer to the team. Jih looked at his own hands, noting the number of times he needed to be healed by Hyu or Kag.

"Bloodstone is purple or black. It is near volcano and very sharp. Do not touch this without help. Only Jih can touch it without getting hurt." Jih commented as he lectured Mant on the various intricacies of working this rock.

Dran stood near a tent and witnessed this conversation, while she chewed on a torn stalk of sugarcane. She was trying to keep her anger under control as she was being berated for the treatment of the young boy that had been injured earlier. The screams of the parents wearing leopard fur dulled her senses as she balled up a fist. Dran locked eyes with Jih some distance from him and looked away upon him noticing. He raised an

---

[10] Emic word for obsidian.

eyebrow at this and left the other stoneworker once he found an opportunity to leave the conversation. In addition to training in the arena and the children, Dran was responsible for maintaining the camp's defenses. As Jih expected, Dran was busy getting an earful from the parents of the young boy that was injured previously. Jih did his best to ignore the conversation but felt somewhat bad for her. Children were dumb and making mistakes was expected. Dran was tired, already having the ire of The Council for some time due to her statements against them that reached their ear. One problem seemed to stack up to another. As the parents left, Dran turned to face Jih.

"Dran, why do you call Jih? Jih was busy with more important tasks." Jih questioned, turning his head to address the bothered woman before him.

"Dran is more important. Jih came on his own, Dran said nothing." Dran said as she withdrew the chewed stalk from her teeth and threw it to the ground beside her. Jih stood some distance from her as he folded his arms. He stayed silent, allowing her to deliver the important news she had to offer.

"There is news. Hunting Team has gathered more food for festival. We need to secure it. All adults will be on watch for food guard. No exceptions." Dran stated as she sized him up with her eyes.

Jih scratched his head, curious about what prompted this sudden change. Most adults were able to defend their immediate family but not much else, while some warriors that excelled in the field were to be the warriors that The Elders called for combat. The thought of the inexperienced teenagers that Dran trained to be fighters also worried him quite a bit.

"All? Hyu and Kag are-" Jih asked, his thoughts immediately shifting to those two. Dran blew air out of her nose in protest, which prompted Jih to speak again, more directly this time.

"Why? Kag and Hyu are healers. Warriors will defend the food." Jih added. Unlike Dran, Jih felt secure in his statement. The Jagged Bark would always come forward for festivals and take guard when needed. This was one of many agreements long held between the two bands and this kept peace in the region.

"Dran says all. Jih may think otherwise but it will not work. Big pile of meat means more to guard it. This is simple. Neck-Shells are waiting to strike. Dran can feel it coming and is ready. Will Jih be?" Dran stated to him.

Jih wasn't sure what to make of this new change, a large raid hadn't occurred in years by those far worse than the Neck-Shells, so why all the extra security now? One injured man was a concern, but hardly a problem for a group their size. He could reason that The Council's demands were starting to wear Dran down as she thought of ways to keep everyone safe. Despite Tur's meddling, Jih made a resounding effort to keep relations good and cemented this by taking care of their injured today. Jih connected the dots and realized there was a large accumulation of meat and other resources that was indicative of some sort of festival starting. The Council often obscured their plans, but the various hunting parties were bringing massive kills home. Dran feared this amount of meat in such a short time would paint a target on them.

"Tur does not listen to Dran. Jih rubbed his nose on foot of Tur, maybe he will for you?" Dran taunted as Jih shook his head in righteous anger.

Unlike many who saw The Council's leadership as something to emulate, Dran remained a skeptic of the mysterious and all-knowing tent dwellers even from a young age. Her slander of them gave her unwanted attention and hostility. The Council had a historical rivalry with her, and this carried over far into adulthood. Dran's opinion of The Council was incredibly low, and her opinion of Jih matched it. Those that went about the song and dance of trying to appeal to their whims were viewed as weak in her eyes.

"Jih does not think-" Jih said, being interrupted by Dran.

"Jih knows much of rock, this is true, but not tactics. Dran learned from Hizo. Talk to Tur." Dran said, walking over and poking her finger into Jih's chest.

Jih glared at Dran with a rising anger in his stomach. Jih found Tur easily to be insufferable but dealing with Dran could be its own problem to begin with. He calmed himself down by recalling all the evidence. The likelihood of a raid was low, The Council told all that the game was plentiful and there was little to be concerned about. While Tur could only spout lies, the rest of The Council was held in high regard by Jih. He stormed off to find Hyu once more before he made an outburst.

Kag left Hyu to greet his partner Bani. Upon arriving at their home located on the southern end of the village, Kag lifted a leather flap and crawled inside. Bani was bedridden for the time being, so Kag did his best to make sure she was getting everything she needed. Arranged around the back walls of the tent were a small collection of hollow calabashes now empty of water. Kag recalled he grasped a bundle of yellow flowers from his work tent and placed them at the edge of her feet. Kag moved along the floor of their home and admired Bani's beauty and resolve. Bani rested on a bed of leaves that grew slightly cold as the campfire inside was not lit. In the low light of their tent, Kag could still recall every detail of Bani. Her eyes were a light brown that reflected light. Bani's black hair was parted at the top and a large singular braid accompanied the back to reach her shoulder. At the end of this braid was an extravagant red flower tied into her hair that never left her side. She wore a humble outfit of grass that made a small shifting sound as she helped herself up. Her eyes darted to the flowers on the floor and looked back at Kag. She embraced him with love in her heart and manipulated a flower in her fingertips.

She and Jih both shared yellow as their favorite color and became fast friends due to this. Kag was fortunate for their friendship, as it was due to Jih that Kag had found Bani to begin with. She was thirty-five, a few years younger than the rest of their generation. Like Jih and Hizo, Bani was an outsider to The Elders. Jih was foraging on his own and found her naked and abandoned. Seeing as she had no other options, he extended a hand to her to come with him and live with their band. She arrived three years prior and found it hard to integrate, which is what Jih expected. Hyu brought her to meet Kag and before she knew it, the two never left each other's side. The Council had forbidden the pairing, for it was found that Bani was of a band that had been hostile in years past. Only through Jih's sly negotiations was he able to convince the highest to allow her to be among them.

"Kag will see sky rocks with Hyu and Jih. Will Bani come?" He asked Bani who nodded slowly. She turned her head, getting a good look at Kag once more as she moved the back of her hand across his face.

"Be careful, Kag. Neck-Shells are ruthless. Some may think otherwise, but Bani has heard things." She warned him, as she pointed to her axe. Along the wall of their hut were replicated attempts of Neck-Shell technology. Much like Jih, she enjoyed tinkering as she was too ill to move around for the moment. She asked children who left the vicinity of the camp to drop off shells for her to grab. She tried to understand how such slow-moving creatures, conch shells, could be such a powerful tool for all sorts of things. Perhaps there was something to learn from such barbarians such as the Neck-Shells.

Kag rested with Bani for some time until the rumbling of others across their dwelling woke them both once more. From the words they could hear outside their home, Tur was getting ready to gather everyone together. Synchronized yells through the camp increased in volume. The echo of the village center called for all. Kag looked up at Bani who nodded, signaling to Kag that she was ready to leave and hear Tur's words. Although Bani hardly felt well, the punishment from not attending Tur's speech was a far greater fear than any. Kag gently guided Bani out of the entrance of their home and supported her as they slowly made their way over. His head turned in the search for Jih and Hyu.

As work stopped, those around the village center placed down their tools and turned their attention to The Council who stood ready to give an answer. The Council pointed upwards with their eyes fixated towards the sky. Little by little, other adults stopped their tasks and align themselves in the direction of them as the sky's clouds opened to reveal calm. The only one to avert their gaze was Tur as he scanned the crowd looking for all that came forth. Tur pounded his walking stick and any discussion ceased.

"Tur has witnessed great vision. The sky will turn red, and the moon holds message for us. Tur is unsure when this will be, but it will come. Look to the night, for rocks will come from sky. This has happened four times in our stories. This will be the fifth." Tur narrated, his voice carrying over the village. Tur gestured behind him towards the outskirts of their home. Jih and Hyu were together some distance away from the main speech. While not directly close by, Tur's words traveled far and rang in the ears of Jih who carried a scowl on his face.

"There are those who wish to take what we possess. We will not give it to them. The Elders have worked hard for what they earned. Tur has heard rumors from you all. Neck-Shells are small and weak like Muucu. They are mud beneath your foot. Focus on work and what is important." Tur warned as he held out his walking stick in the direction of the crowd.

Dran listened to the speech conducted by Tur and could only shake her head at what she was hearing. It was only moments ago that The Council confided in Dran their collective concerns about the strength of their defenses, but what mattered most was the crowd. She could only stand in pure awe at the stupidity of her people and how they accepted Tur's words without question. Dran watched as some people patted the soil below with their hands praising Tur for his strong hand. The rest of The Council nodded in acknowledgment to Tur's words as they ended the workday early to prepare for viewing the meteor shower. As the group dispersed, Kag and Bani did not look pleased from the speech. Kag and Bani shared a low opinion of Tur due to their connection to Jih, but the cracks of his leadership were apparent to both. They decided to table their thoughts and wait until reuniting with Jih and Hyu to discuss further.

After another nap in their home, the time for night came, and Kag wished to see if Tur's prediction had really come true. Jih and Hyu started a small fire at the edge of the beach, where they had a full view of the stars above. Jih enjoyed the sound of the waves that hit the shores while Hyu hummed alongside him. Hyu's humming reminded him of much simpler times. Jih hoped that Kag remembered their instructions and watched Hyu place more wood to strengthen the fire. The water glistened with the light of the moon, as the waves calmly hit the shore. The silhouettes of Kag and Bani appeared in the distance. Jih stood up and waved them over, watching with glee as their shadowy forms moved closer and through the light, he could see his friends. Hyu embraced both Kag and Bani welcoming them to sit and wait for the sky to reveal itself. Kag knew that Tur's words were untested and so he waited with skepticism.

To pass the time, the four made pictographs in the sand, laughing at their strange proportions. Jih drew an outline of Hyu with long tendrils for hair and a small face with a line for her mouth and two large eyes. Jih was proud of his handiwork as he inspected the others. Kag depicted a coconut while Hyu made a fish. Bani still concentrated on her design but made a hand-axe in the sand. Jih raised his eyebrows at Bani in surprise at how extensive it matched his own creations. Out of the four of them, Bani had the most detailed drawing by far, much to Kag's pride. It was Hyu first, who lifted her head up to see the first of many strange streaks to come in the sky. In a sea of black and blue, the meteorites of legend raced across with no end in sight. The light from the meteor shower reflected off the waves of the ocean. Jih and Kag looked up and stared at the sky, while their fingers tracked their direction. Jih figured that the rocks directions were north of where they sat, but just how far was north?

"Sky rock is...powerful." Jih said as the sky was alight.

Kag and Hyu said nothing, as their eyes were filled with tears. Bani shared Jih's stoic outlook as she pondered their significance and what this meant for the rest of the band. The display of such beauty moved them, and they were sure others in their band felt the same way. The sky gave them a message to figure out on their own. It was as if the Earth itself stopped moving as they looked above. Kag nodded his head, noting that Tur's vision was indeed true. This was a sign that his leadership would guide them somewhere far as he hoped. The lines left by the meteors as they zoomed past the skies of Sundaland were distinct, and those who looked up that night had many revelations about what they witnessed. Jih's eyes fixated on one trail that was the largest among them and yet moved the quickest. He knew he needed to know more. Jih's eyes met Hyu's, and she shared the excitement of adventure. They willed to one another that they would go as one at some point to see the power rock up close.

There was more to the vision that Tur had also predicted. The moon was a highly important entity for The Elders, it was how the children that were born received their names. Expectant parents did not name their child, this was the job of The Council who referred to the phase of the moon the child was born under the previous night. Both Hyu and Kag were born under a New Moon, and their names were given as such. Jih was named by Hizo, and did not understand this custom, but respected it, nonetheless. The moon would be covered in a lunar eclipse soon, but it was unknown when this would be. The implications of such an event are rare, and it was up to The Council to delegate what to do under such immense power. Jih and the others left the fire going, knowing that the sea's brisk air would douse the flames shortly.

As the four headed home, there was much discussion on what the meteors meant and their overall message. Adults sat by open pit fires and offered their theories while children picked up small rocks to simulate what they witnessed. Tur sought to nip conspiracies in the bud and forbade discussion of the recent events much to the disappointment of many. A topic like this could hardly be suppressed and would make good conversation for tomorrow's workday. Tur reasoned it would be better if the experts figured out what to do before things spiraled out of control.

Those Who Wander

Leisure time was something enjoyed even by the adults when they could, and Hyu had her own hobbies. One thing she cherished the most as a child was collecting bird eggs. Whenever The Elders moved to a new camp, she always looked for them, both as a mental note to what wildlife was present, but she appreciated the aesthetic value attached to them. Hyu and Jih slept on a bed of deer fur with a smaller one serving as a cover for night. Jih, who had trouble sleeping for many nights, was at long last able to rest soundly. While he usually joined her on these outings, she was perfectly fine going solo. His usual tossing and turning was still, it seemed that seeing the meteors the previous night put him at ease. There was more to come. Hyu gave a quiet exit from her home as she set out early. Hyu gave a respectful nod to a spear that was propped along the outside wall of their home. The pair held their own weapons, Jih's flint spear was unwieldly for the tent, so he placed it outside. Hyu carried with her a whip made from the tail of a stingray that she rolled up and tied to her with fibers. More traditional weapons, like that of a spear or club, were boring to her.

The stillness of the day was met with a low hanging fog that filled the village. Hyu's mind drifted to her work once more as she looked to the eastern end of the village. She wouldn't be able to go about her day guilt free until she checked on the emissary left behind from The Jagged Bark. Hyu remembered that he stayed overnight in their medical tent as he recovered from his injury. Hyu appreciated the quiet of the early morning before others went about their duties. Hyu walked with purpose as she headed to the tent. She walked in front of the entrance and lifted the fur flap to enter inside. Hyu's hair emerged first with her face following next.

"Man from The Jagged Bark. Hyu has come to-" Hyu commented as she saw that the man's presence was missing. She looked around in slight confusion, it looked like Kag hadn't come by the tent either. Her eyes looked towards a small net she decided to borrow from Kag for her bird eggs.

Hyu grabbed it and left without a second thought. She hoped to find any type of egg, but a black eagle was at the top of the list. Anything from black eagles, down to the feathers, were a prized find for trade, and the shell of the egg was soft to the touch. She sniffed the still air of camp as the campfires placed around town fizzled out, where the smoke settled along the ground before vanishing entirely. Hyu's travel took her near the communal tent of The Council. The outskirts of the camp were still visible from her location as she decided to start the climb close and move inward. She had a theory that the activity of the camp moved the bird's nesting places, but she needed to test it out. Her walk took her to the extent of the outer forest where a line of trees appeared in her vision. The last stretch of the village stood behind her. Hyu envisioned herself as completely alone and closed her eyes. She tried to listen to the flight of the birds as they settled from tree to tree. Much like her brother with plants, Hyu could tell the various species of birds just by listening to their flight pattern. She looked behind her however as there was an irritating sound. Hyu gritted her teeth in annoyance as Tur's inconsiderate yelling broke the peace.

Hyu could make out the conversation between him and another figure in the distance. Hyu's eyes widened as she realized this was the emissary now fully healed. The man wore a much more esteemed dress than straw. He wore a tailored coat of serow fur that was suited for his rank. He carried some other processed furs in addition to prepare for his leave. Tur was displeased as he and the emissary remained in intense discussion. The old man was filled with anger as his face contorted. Hyu watched as Tur approached him and used a free hand to knock the carried pelts to the ground. He flailed his arms around and used his height to intimidate the emissary further.

"What is the meaning of this? You wear Sahroh pelt? This is from land of Tur and The Elders. You have no right to it. This is for leaders only, not messengers." Tur spat with anger as he used his foot to kick dirt over the donated pieces. Prior to their arrival, Jih arranged with the Hunting Team for emissaries from The Jagged Bark to be given a gift of pelts from their supply. This was a worthy sacrifice in their eyes to keep their support as always. The demands of the world were changing, and The Elders were built to accommodate just as they always have.

"This was gift to us. Jih and your Hunting Team willed it so. Your people are generous, but you are rotten. Leader of The Jagged Bark will hear about this!" The emissary shouted, his voice carrying over to a few curious adults who were observing the conversation. Tur crumpled his hands together as he hated being challenged openly. Tur knew he couldn't show weakness and decided to double down on his attitude.

"Who do you speak to? You come to land of Tur, ambushed by an enemy, use our resources, and all you do is take. You have put us at risk. This is all you and other outsiders do. They take from hardworking people like us. Jih did not have authority to do this." Tur said as he raised his fist to the man. Tur's demeanor was unbecoming as he spat with each word. Hyu could see the emissary's face change as his eyes hit the soil. He felt genuinely upset about compromising Jih but was unaware that Tur did not sanction the gift. Though tradition guided their interactions, the right was reserved by living leaders to amend the agreed terms.

"Our patience has run thin. Keep your pelts, your greed will keep you well stocked. Give thanks to the healers who respect The Old Ways." The emissary said in dismay before turning to no longer acknowledge Tur. As he faded into obscurity, Tur could still be seen waving his staff in the air while onlookers witnessed this event. For Tur, his outbursts and perceived slight disrespect incited him further, but also embarrassed him in front of the village as his authority was often unquestioned.

Hyu did her best to forget the scene before her and focus on her hobby. She barely got the time to do what she wanted, and Tur wasn't getting in the way of that. Hyu smelled the air, it rained the previous night as she looked at the dirt. Her feet were marred with mud, and a slip could be dangerous. As Hyu found her first tree to check for eggs, she wiped her feet at the base of it, hoping to retain as much traction as she could. She placed her whip down to use both her hands for the climb. The black eagle nested high, so Hyu would need to go quite some distance off the ground. Unlike many who stood by the ground, Hyu lacked a fear of heights. She saw each branch as another steppingstone to reach what she yearned for. Hyu gripped herself steadily towards the tree and held her breath. Unknown to Hyu was an orangutan's stare that watched her climb up. Her eyes met the animal who was secure with fresh fruit nearby.

"Arancu-Onru...Where is the bird Hyu seeks?" Hyu asked jokingly to the orangutan that chewed leaves as it dropped a half-eaten fig on the ground.

Hyu predicted the few second long drop it took for the fig to hit the ground before it landed with a soft thud. She raised her eyebrows at the orangutan a few times, entertaining herself as it stopped to stare again before moving away. She let out a small sigh and began her descent down below. Hyu looked behind her as she emerged deeper into the jungle. Hyu was concerned about the drama and its consequences that would be distributed to the rest of them later. For now, she was at peace looking for an ideal tree. Hyu rested her head against the trunk and used her fist to tap the wood. Hollow trees were too flimsy for her needs when animals dug inside them. She located another tree of interest with a thicker frame. Her eyes looked below and saw some discarded branches and leaves to see the above branches were inhabited. Hyu started to climb some distance from her orangutan friend, this time finding some helmeted hornbill nests that were heavily guarded. She saw that the orangutan from before was near once again. Her face scrunched in thought as she wondered if the animal was following her for some reason. Hyu held on tightly with one hand, as she waved her free hand and made a small screech, hoping to scare off the birds. The hornbills simply did nothing, ignoring her. Why was it that these birds had no fear of humans?

She knew that reaching directly into the nests was asking for trouble, so she thought of something else. She grabbed her whip, carefully placing the handle in her mouth as she ascended further and decided to use the cracking sound to instead rout the birds. This did the trick as a few hornbills panicked and caused a ruckus. Hyu couldn't help but have a sly look on her face as she carefully scooped the eggs into her hand to place in the net below. One of the hornbills attempted to dive towards Hyu to knock her off the tree. She quickly pressed herself against the tree, barely dodging the bird's pecks. The flap of feathers and rapid pecking increased in volume as it hacked away pieces of wood. Hyu watched as small chips of wood hit the ground while she stood still.

The orangutan that seemed to watch Hyu intently ended up being her savior, as it bellowed out loudly, diverting the bird's attention to the new arrival. She breathed a sigh of relief as she was looking at a 5-foot fall if she missed. She quickly made her descent with the new bounty of eggs and shook her head at making such a rookie mistake. She collected about six in all, and while this wasn't the bounty she was looking for, it was getting harder to find the good stuff. The animals became more daring in their attempts to secure safety for themselves, and this was no different for the humans of Sundaland. Hyu decided to see if she could find herself a snack, this time safely on the ground as she looked over again at her collection of eggs. She looked to the treeline to see if the orangutan would make another appearance, but it seemed her luck had run out for now. She let out a small sigh and pressed forward where she reached a point of a long flowing river. She placed her bounty down and scooped some water and splashed her face with the rest to cool down. Hyu dipped her hair in the river giving it some much needed moisture against the humidity of the early morning. As she headed back, she felt her stomach rumble and looked for a nearby clump of bushes to relieve herself. While she handled business, she overheard the conversation of two people talking. Hyu noted the tone of their voices were riddled with inexperience. They spoke plainly about their intentions to one another and hardly imagined anyone would take note of their words.

"Bhet will be new leader." The first voice, male in its nature, spoke.

"How? Bhet has one hand." The accompanying voice spoke, her tone dismissive of the man's statement.

"Bhet has plan. Targets have been made and we will attack soon."

"We agreed to peace." She said, her voice annoyed at the prospect.

"Things have changed for Neck-Shells." The man said, with a point to his stomach. He hadn't eaten in some time, and it was evident that the Neck-Shells were targeting the less able to find food suitable for them. At first, Hyu cared little for their conversation, but the mention of the Neck-Shells piqued her interest. She listened further, as her eyes widened hearing more of what the two were discussing.

"One camp was raided, and they went north. North to the jungles thick with Muucu. We will find them in time." The male voice stated.

It was here that Hyu realized just what she was hearing. She remembered that the emissary Jih recovered mentioned his attack from the Neck-Shells and his ominous warning that they were next. Who was Bhet and what did he want from The Elders? Hyu quietly cleaned herself and crawled away from the bush as she tried to figure out where the voices were coming from. While she slowly moved along the ground towards her belongings, her mind wandered with questions. What were the Neck-Shells doing so far from their territory? From what she knew from the Scouting Team, they rarely hunted for food on land, preferring to take what they wanted from smaller groups. As they ruled the coast, their implements were based on shells and other gifts only the ocean could provide. The Neck-Shells were pitiful at tracking deer, and it was out of the question to take on something as powerful as a tiger. Hyu felt as if she had come across something far more sinister than a simple inland hunt.

She stood up and quietly dragged her belongings on the ground. Hyu knelt to obscure her presence as she looked for any wildlife that may expose her position. Hyu held her breath as she focused on tracking their movements through the brush. Hyu's hand caressed a tree trunk and scaled it to get a better vantage point and saw the two conversing some distance from her. Her eyes noted they were shorter than her by about a head. Their skin was a dark brown much like her own that glistened in the beams of sunlight that pierced the jungle clearing. Their open mouths showed intentionally filed teeth that vaguely resembled fangs. Hyu noted there was little difference in dress, as they only wore grass skirts to cover themselves. Their bare chests were lathered in some sort of solution. Hyu couldn't make out exactly what it was, but it reminded her of the numerous concoctions Kag made to reduce swelling from poisonous plants. Their identity as Neck-Shells was definite, as she saw carved conch shells that made a necklace. She remembered she saw someone with such an ornament as a young girl. It seemed this was the standard and not the exception. She pulled her head back as she eavesdropped on the conversation between the two Neck-Shells. Hearing enough, Hyu knew she needed to leave before things got dangerous. She recalled her conversation with Jih some time ago. Hyu hated to admit it, but Dran was perfectly correct in her assessment of the situation. Something was coming and they needed to be prepared for it. She looked at their weapons and realized the two were not hunters at all but scouts. Their weapons were not suitable for any serious engagements with animal or man but could pose a problem if left unchecked.

"Rama wants to eat?" The man asked again, this time pointing at her.

She nodded in agreement, for what needed to be done would require the utmost faith in Bhet for this to work. His leadership was untested, but for the Neck-Shells they anticipated the ultimate reward of peace and security. Hyu began her descent down the tree, moving very slowly to hide her activity from the two onlookers. Hyu had done her best to conceal herself, but dust from the forest floor entered her nose, and she let out a loud sneeze. The two Neck-Shells ceased their conversation, as they looked around to find the source of the noise. They were aware it was human and swiped at the bushes. Hyu sweat profusely as she wanted to avoid conflict. She was some distance away and kept herself low along the ground. There was no need for death today, as she was concerned about making sure her eggs weren't broken on the trip back. She had already spent so long looking for them.

"Reveal yourself!" The one known as Rama shouted. Hyu saw that the two had their backs turned and took the opportunity to make her escape.

Unfortunately for Hyu, the route she had in mind ran directly in the path of the two Neck-Shells. They located her and uttered a primal scream as they ran towards her. Outpacing her now, the young couple withdrew their weapons. Hyu got a closer look as she saw the knives they wielded, which were small boards of wood embedded with shark teeth. If they were to touch her, she would bleed no differently than a slain buffalo. She needed to be careful and decided to see if they would be willing to look the other way, at least long enough for her to plan an escape.

"Hyu wishes to leave." She addressed the pair. The two were confused as they were not used to someone holding their ground. Hyu was nervous about the overall situation, but she kept a calm face. Hyu knew that these Neck-Shells were out of their element and could hardly contend with her experience. She lowered her head graciously, opting to give the two Neck-Shells an out and to forget they saw each other.

"We have other plans." The man said to her as he pointed his knife. Rama followed his lead; she was confident that two-on-one against a woman at Hyu's age would be a quick fight. Hyu didn't have bloodlust in her heart to provoke them as they wanted, but she would oblige them with a quick death as they so decided.

"To die young saddens Hyu." Hyu commented, as she moved her hand towards her whip.

The moment Hyu grabbed her whip, it wouldn't be put away until blood was spilled. Hizo instilled in all her students that a weapon was made to kill and if used, it must do so. The Neck-Shells remained ever bloodthirsty, charging Hyu with incredible speed. Rama circled Hyu, while the man rushed in, checking her with his shoulder. Hyu raised her arm, and cracked the whip at Rama's feet, causing her to jump backwards to dodge. Hyu's attention turned to the man who attacked her. Being this close, Hyu curled up her free hand into a fist and punched him in the jaw, his mouth pooling with blood as he bit his tongue. He swung his knife, nailing Hyu in the hand, where part of her skin peeled off and bled. The tears on Hyu's skin were irritated as the blow of the wind agitated her wound. Hyu bit her lip in pain, but it was a mere flesh wound compared to what she was prepared to unfold. The man became overconfident, as he urged Rama to support him from behind and to finish the kill.

"Rama! The knife, move it to her heart!" He shouted at her to move.

Hyu's hit from the knife was a worthy sacrifice as he was in range for her to grab his wrist. She twisted his arm hard as he reflexively fell to his knees to wrestle her grip. Her knowledge of the body was unmatched, as she contorted her adversary with ease. He attempted to switch hands with his knife but was met with a swift kick in the ribs by Hyu. He was knocked some distance away from her and was caught by Rama. On the receiving end was Hyu's whip, which cracked twice on his flesh. His skin split open immediately, her whip effortlessly cracking the shell pendant on his chest. Blood pooled to the ground as the assault was relentless.

His chest practically caved open from the force, and yet he remained alive. Hyu's whip had a particular quality about it that made it a feared weapon. As it was forged from the tail of a stingray, her whip emitted venom from the barbed ends. The man buckled under the weight of his injuries. The Neck-Shell man clawed at the air unable to reach Hyu. His breathing slowed, his swings stopped, all the while Hyu stood motionless, glaring at him. He felt his brain was melting before him, as he let out a deranged scream. His mouth foamed with saliva and blood. The open cavity around his chest was discolored and slowly turned into a red mass. He no longer felt his entire body and his vision faded. He vomited the very little contents of his stomach out to the ground. Rama was utterly terrified at this but rushed to attack Hyu, hoping to get an advantage. Hyu stood still and raised her arm with one singular motion. It happened too quickly for her to process but she too was struck down, in the face, as her cheek and jawline were torn asunder.

The impact from the whip completely knocked her to the floor, with the barb leaving a parallel exit wound as it dragged the flesh from her face. The spare bits of flesh dangled from side to side as Rama slowly crawled to her compatriot's body while she writhed in pain. Hyu packed her things, wrapping her whip back up carefully and adjusting her net. Rama coughed, as her vision doubled, and she felt necrosis setting in. She looked at the knife that fell to the forest floor and grabbed it. Her hands were shaking so much, and the pain was so unbearable, she used the remaining bits of her strength to jam the knife into her throat. Rama's body had expelled a rapid amount of blood, even more so with the self-inflicted wound on her throat to end the pain. The man blindly tried to muster all he had left to attack Hyu who looked off into the distance. He was already dead.

Hyu observed her handiwork as the blood of the two decaying Neck-Shells littered the soil. She shook her head in disappointment as she sullied the home of the orangutans she held dear. Her thoughts on the people in question, however, were far more removed. Hyu whistled on her way back as she gave no mind to the corpses left behind. She felt no ill will as she warned them of the path they chose to follow. The news she had to offer was the most important. She looked up to the trees one last time to look for the orangutan, and out of the corner of her eyes, she saw a small streak of orange move through the trees. Hyu promised she would return with a mango, just like he wanted. Hyu ran as fast as she could as she nursed her wound. As Hyu ran, she looked back one last time to ensure she wasn't being pursued by anyone else. The last thing she wanted to do was bring extra heat to their camp while unprepared. Without thinking twice, Hyu arrived back home. She quickly dropped her stuff off in front of her and Jih's home while she received odd looks from those around her.

Hyu was always seen as rational and calm, but the severity of her movements caused some concern within the ranks. With some time passing from her earlier excursion, the camp was active as ever. People were still focused on the meteor and the trails left in the sky at night but the intrigue from Tur and the emissary now dominated village discussion. Hyu ignored everyone and made her way directly to The Council's tent. The flap of their home opened without warning, as Hyu's large hair came through first, and then herself as she crawled in and stood up. The Council looked bewildered as they saw Hyu arrive with a trail of blood leaking behind her from her hand. The interior of The Council's tent was much larger than that of normal dwellings as it was a communal living space for eight people. Hyu could see the spaced-out beds of leaves and furs where the group slept and discussed various events. A hearth with high quality jungle logs occupied the center and burned brightly while The Council placed themselves on one side and Hyu on the other. The space between them and Hyu was a barrier both physical and artificial as she knew she was out of place here. A billow of low smoke filled the room as the last bits of firewood burnt.

"What is this display?!" One of the younger members of The Council shouted in indignation.

His thick black and gray beard obscured his mouth as he rose to walk over to Hyu. His pace was stopped by the long staff held by Tur. The man lowered his head in acknowledgement to Tur's authority as he receded back from Hyu. Tur remained on the ground with his legs folded as he studied Hyu carefully. Tur rarely respected anyone else, but he saw the audience of Hyu and Kag often. The pair occasionally visited The Council to assess the health of the leadership. In his mid-60s, Tur was among the oldest of The Council and was consulted on many matters regarding his health. Tur called Hyu over with his hand and waited for her approach. Hyu knelt and lifted Tur up along with his staff. Although Tur was far from a completely frail man, Hyu could tell that age withered him down like all things.

"Tell The Council your news." Tur demanded as he leaned against the wall of the hut. Hyu looked into the enraged eyes of the other members of The Council with disdain as she spoke. She took a deep breath as she knew she'd only be able to deliver this once before her concerns were swept aside.

"Neck-Shells will break our peace. Hyu bears the mark. Hyu heard it while foraging." She mentioned and showed her hand out to them. She winced slightly as the wind moved above her wound. Tur looked at the others, who were still visibly offended from Hyu's untimely entrance. Hyu described her encounter with remarkable detail as The Council shook their heads in thought. One of the men of The Council huffed at the end of Hyu's tale with a smug attitude in his voice.

"You were foraging and not healing? We have teams for this reason." One member of The Council chided to which Hyu gritted her teeth in response.

"Supplies must be gathered somehow. Hyu has legs that work and must contribute. What is it you do?" Hyu spoke back. Her response was met with the grimace of another member of The Council. A woman wearing an assortment of shell beads and tiger fur spoke out, pointing her finger at Hyu.

"You have heard wrong. Neck-Shells have taken much meat recently. They will honor the deal." She stated while Tur nodded in agreement. Hyu moved her arms in dismay as the outcome she expected made itself possible. Hyu wouldn't believe the words that came out of her mouth. Their leadership was truly gutless when the time came to it. Hyu was far from hopeless however, and where she could not appeal to their judgement out of duty, she decided to attack their vanity instead.

"Many have come to The Council with news. You ignore their call, for what? Why hold fear in your hearts? Are we not the best band of our land?" Hyu demanded of them. She met the staring eyes of The Council who were more concerned with Hyu's presentation than the news itself. The Council's silence after her words bothered Hyu to the point where her foot sunk into the soil.

"Hyu knows more is wanted! We have it and it will be taken." Hyu countered in anger.

She had no time to deal with the demands of decorum as she felt their lives were at risk. She couldn't believe that after all she had done for the leadership, they tossed her suggestion aside. Tur decided to weigh his opinion on the matter to settle things. The Council clinked their ornaments together as they bickered among themselves regarding the news. Despite promoting the message that the Neck-Shells were hardly anything to be concerned about, they were a divided party on the issue of the Neck-Shell band for some time. The Scouting Team's reports were censored and not given out to the other adults in a desire to keep stability within the village. Tur saw news like this as a distraction to the workflow that adults did daily and problems that could be handled in the shadows should stay that way. As The Elders were isolated, this was easy enough to do but the words of The Jagged Bark carried much weight. Anecdotal evidence rose and it was harder to suppress that the Neck-Shells coveted their lands. The desire to fight was something that many considered, but for veterans such as Tur, he knew that to face the Neck-Shells with their warriors only spelled destruction. It was better in his mind to placate their demands for now.

"Reason has come with meat. Hunger is for meat, not blood of The Elders." Tur said, with a stomp of his staff into the ground.

"Neck-Shells have yet to attack. It has been for many moons now and yet nothing." Another man noted, generating some nods from the rest of the members. The Council lamented at how many of the younger adults cried wolf at the impending doom of the Neck-Shells that seemed to never come. The Council asserted that their negotiation skills would win them the day. In the past, they fought brutal campaigns against hostiles but came out on top each time when violence came. Why would this be any different?

"Tur does not believe this. You ate with Hizo, her story is known to all." Hyu spat in anger. Hyu involved Tur's ties to Hizo when she wanted to make her point across. In life, the two were incredibly close friends, and to this day, Tur felt a lasting connection to her long after her passing.

"Do not invoke her. Hizo lives on with the leadership. You will leave now and have nothing more to say." Tur said with a light cough as the other members of The Council clinked their ornaments in solidarity with Tur's statement.

Tur waved his finger at Hyu and pointed to the exit of their tent. His face scrunched up in irritation at Hyu's attempts to undermine his authority. It was clearly time for Hyu to make her leave as The Council now entirely stonewalled her. She exited the tent flap and made her way home to her and Jih's tent where he waited inside to tell her news of his own. She looked at her hand and winced in pain as she pressed down on it to try to stem the bleeding. Jih got up to embrace Hyu but saw something else was amiss. Jih felt a rush of anxiety flow over him as he noted Hyu's emotional state. Hyu hardly got angry, but her energy filled the room as Jih met her eyes.

"Hyu has returned. What happened to you?" Jih asked as he placed his hand on her shoulder. It was evident that Hyu had gone through much as he slept. Jih felt a tinge of guilt course through him. His eyes darted to her hand that had the open wound, and he quickly tore off a portion of his clothing, where he wrapped it as a bandage with much care. His eyes searched for a prepared rub around to treat her injury.

"Neck-Shells attacked Hyu. Do not fear, for they are dead." Hyu explained as she cracked her knuckles in defiance.

Jih nodded, with a look of concern as she decided to lie down on her bed. Hyu looked around as she recalled leaving her items at the front of their tent earlier. Jih reassured Hyu that her bounty was safe as he woke up earlier and retrieved them. He opened the net she brought in and noted the new eggs that she brought. Her treasured black eagle eggs were not present, but Jih knew he would look for these later. He placed them carefully at an isolated corner of their hut, where a few other multicolored eggs joined the batch. Hyu revealed to Jih that she went to The Council with news of her encounter and that it fell on deaf ears. It was clear that through the smokescreen of The Council's tent, the opinions of those they considered below them were not to be considered, at a risk to everyone. Although Jih hadn't thought the Neck-Shells to be raid capable with their level of organization, he was aware of their combat prowess, having had to ward them off when hunting on his own. Hyu turned her head to look at Jih and patted the ground next to her. Jih yawned and sat down next to her. He stretched his body and rolled over, stopping before locking eyes with Hyu once more. Jih and Hyu always communicated their issues to one another; with a union of over twenty years, it was practically a form of telepathy between the pair.

"Hyu ran to trouble with Tur, hmm?" Jih said with a slight laugh as the answer was incredibly obvious.

"Those Neck-Shells. This happened to Jih before, that one kill a few weeks ago. That one was weak but there are others. This happened to Dran as well. Are these connected?" Jih noted, as he was aware of the Neck-Shells' brutality. For now, they had been spared the brunt of the fighting, with other bands revolting against them only to be crushed.

"Hyu grows tired of little change. They keep her in tent away from things." Hyu replied to Jih. She exhaled in thought to Jih's question.

"Dran is right about Neck-Shells. What will we do? What can be done?" Hyu questioned aloud. Jih blinked in shock at hearing Hyu's admission of the fact as he recalled their decades long animosity towards one another. As he heard this, he tapped Hyu's shoulder to reveal the important news he received in her absence.

"Things will change Hyu. Jih will join The Council soon." Jih declared with pride.

Hyu's expression had a confused look on her face. Jih had his own busy day while Hyu was out. Jih mentioned to Hyu how he was confronted at his workstation by a representative of The Council and called to their tent. In the smoky haze of the fire, Tur pointed his finger to Jih while the other members of The Council outlined their instructions of succession. His stoneworking teacher Illol died in the past year, and it was decided on her deathbed that out of her promised students, Jih would be the one to carry her mantle as Stone Breaker on the anniversary of her passing. Stone Breaker was the highest honor that could be given and had detailed proficiency with every type of stone among their peoples, including the notoriously difficult obsidian.

"Does Jih think this will fix things? It is much deserved to be the rank of Stone Breaker." Hyu asked. She gave a small grin as she attempted to show support for Jih.

"Jih must try. We have wanted this for some time, this is our dream. Jih is now going to achieve it. Tur and The Elders told Jih. It was willed by Illol, the great woman. Ceremony is on quarter moon." Jih said happily.

Hyu gave Jih a tight hug as she was thrilled with the news. Her head rested on his shoulders as she draped her arms around Jih and wrapped them tightly. Despite her recent grievances with The Council, she knew that Jih could make a difference and that was one of their goals finally met. Jih wanted to be a part of The Council for some time, as he felt he could change things internally for the better. He was surely qualified, with the blessing of the late Ilol, and the void that was left was to now be filled by a new toolmaker. Jih did not keep many personal possessions, but he always kept his late master's hand-axe that he used as the gold standard for all his productions. It was weathered and hardy but remained an ever-valuable tool. The quarter moon was only one week away. There was much preparation to be done on both Jih and Hyu's part, in addition to that of the other adults in the camp. As Hyu and Jih went to sleep, the words from Tur once again hung in her mind.

"Reason has come with meat. Hunger is for meat, not blood of The Elders."

Blood In The Sand

Despite their warnings the previous week, The Council decided to proceed with Jih's induction as a new member replacing the late Ilol. Preparations were made ahead of time to ensure that everything would line up correctly. The village was bustling with activity on a scale not seen in years. The induction of a new member of The Council was a rare event, many adults lived and died without seeing a change in leadership as Tur remained among the ranks for years. Jih watched with increasing excitement as his head peeked out to see decorations of bone hanging on the sides of people's homes. On the ground in front of various tents were bundles of feathers and other materials. As much as this was a celebration for Jih, this was also a time of mourning for Illol as she was now considered officially passed to the next life. Jih and his people lacked a dedicated pantheon but were aware of otherworldly forces outside their control to some degree. These measures were to ensure balance in the village and to give a proper send off to Illol after her death the previous year. While most adults were focused on the spectacle of the event, Dran's responsibility lay with making sure everything would occur without issue. It was with her patience and tactical mind that the other adults didn't need to worry about other things and focus on the event in question. Dran was certain of her plan to keep the area secure for the ceremony as she explained it at length to The Council the day before. She arranged her best warriors at different corners of their camp to rotate as sentries. The Jagged Bark were to come by with some warriors on loan for the week both as honored guests for the occasion and to act as extra security. Dran found herself at the foot of The Council's tent where they stood outside applying pigments to one another in preparation for the event. Tur let out an audible groan as he saw Dran's presence. Dran was thorough to the point of the annoyance of the others.

Tur shook his head at Dran as she failed to wear her customary dress and instead retained her grass covering. For special occasions such as this one or a union between two loved ones, adults would often construct their own clothing that differed from what they worked in. Feathers from the forest were a popular addition to augment one's look with a reasonable amount of effort put into it. Dran's lack of participation was considered an insult to not only everyone else who prepared but to the late Illol. Tur's patience was already dwindling short. Tur slept terribly the night before and his disdain for stopping work to organize an event in honor of Jih of all people angered him to no end.

"Dran must go over defenses with The Council one more time." Dran said as she clasped her hands together.

Dran detested The Council as much as they did to her, but she required their cooperation to make this event run as smoothly as possible. She hadn't received word yet on the arrival time of The Jagged Bark. The Scouting Team reported that the usual route was around a day and a half which should lead them to arrive later this afternoon if all done well. Dran's palms sweated slightly as she became incredibly anxious when a plan deviated past her expectations.

"Dran has told The Council five separate times. Will six change anything?" Tur mentioned, with him waving his hand at her in dismissal.

"The Jagged Bark will arrive like desperate Denmey for meat. Stay the course and calm yourself. We are aware of what needs to be done. You do your job." Tur ordered coldly to Dran.

Dran recognized one of her students in the distance carrying a small basket filled with berries to be crushed. He moved quickly and only lowered his head in respect to Dran before going to work. Tur made no comment as he continued to have his face meticulously painted red in their tradition. Dran shook her head and walked off as she'd seen enough. Out of the distance, she made her aggression known by beating a branch against a tree for some time until it broke. For now, it would be branches, but she imagined that one day, it would be Tur's neck instead. She took it upon herself to arm the guards with the best axes and spears that the Stoneworking Team could produce. As she continued to organize, Jih and Hyu were preparing for the most important part of the ceremony.

The inside of their home was driven with excitement of today's events. Hyu gathered a pile of animal skins to drape over Jih while he attempted to meditate and ground himself. He took a deep breath that was interrupted by the presence of Hyu staring directly at him. He veered his head back and opened his eyes. Jih lost his concentration to see a pile of fur that far outclassed his normal deer pelt that he wore. He raised his eyebrow in confusion at Hyu. Some of these furs were of exquisite quality and he wondered how they managed to slip pass Tur's ironclad greed.

"Gift from Stoneworking Team. They are proud of you. Hyu is proud of you." Hyu said as she leaned in to rub noses with Jih.

Jih returned the gesture in kind and held the various furs with two hands. Jih was briefly immobilized with the sheer amount of kindness given to him by his team. Furs such as these were incredibly expensive trade items and now, he could have his pick of any. He couldn't believe how soft and how well put together they were. Jih had always seen the amount of tiger and leopard fur that graced The Council and now he could be among them. He stripped down from his usual dress into ceremonial wear and stood nude as he looked to find what suited him best. Jih imagined himself in the tiger skin, but this was far too bold. He was a skilled fighter and technician with the spear, but he was a craftsman primarily. He skipped the leopard fur entirely due to its association with Tur. Out of all the skins around, he settled on a buffalo hide that fit snugly over his body and an associated loincloth made from the same material. Jih hardly found himself to be a materialistic person and did not care about being associated with fierce animals. The buffalo was an herbivore but an animal that defended its herd with strength. Unlike the other animals chosen, the buffalo also had qualities about it that benefited others besides its pelt. The meat was delicious, and the horns made good tools for sharpening stones and for trade. Jih saw himself as useful as the buffalo and decided to pick this. Jih flexed his arms as he felt powerful while Hyu delighted him with a clap.

In their hearth at the back of their home, she had a small fire prepared with the smell of cooking meat and some vegetables Kag picked from the ground. The heat finally picked up and the food started to simmer. She spent much of the previous day hunting for a chicken to prepare Jih's favorite meal. Jih walked over to see Hyu's handiwork and gave a nod of approval. While not his mother's, Hyu spent a good deal of time perfecting the formula and testing it against Jih's own broth. The amount was small as finding a chicken suitable for meat was hard to come by, but he felt whole with it. Hyu was not a skilled cook, Jih prepared practically all their meals, but she felt this was a special occasion and made something worth the immense effort. Kag contributed as well, picking various plants to use as seasoning to soothe Jih's palette.

"Poulji soup for Jih[11]." Hyu said happily, as she cupped a small wooden bowl for him to drink. Jih took a deep sniff and savored every bit with a small amount falling down his mouth.

"Is Jih ready?" Hyu asked, as she peeked her head outside the tent to see people winding down on their tasks.

"Blood tastes terrible." Jih exclaimed as he reeled at the thought of drinking blood. It was an acquired taste and one that he did not find nourishing. Before Jih could venture outside to face his new destiny, Hyu held out her hand once more to stop him. She took a deep breath and pointed to him.

"Hyu agrees. Now, close your eyes Jih." She said with a laugh.

Hyu crafted him a necklace as a surprise to wear when the opportunity struck. It was now she felt it was appropriate. Hyu walked behind him and tied the tight strings together. The necklace was simple in its design but had the claw of a tiger that took center attention. Jih felt the supportive tap of Hyu and opened his eyes. He held the tiger claw and examined it closely as he noted its sharpness. He had full faith in his partner's abilities, but he couldn't hide the questions on his face.

"Hyu searched far for Jih." Hyu offered her explanation as she was unwilling to reveal how she came across such a material. Some things just needed to have mystery to them.

Outside of their moment, the village continued onward with the proceedings. A yell from a loud man signaled to the others to begin the call. Men of all ages hit the ground in synchronization as they drummed up a beat for Jih to emerge. The soil lifted as the clapping grew louder in volume. Hyu nodded for Jih to emerge first as she was right behind him. The two held hands as they were greeted by the excitement of the outside world and waved to those that they knew closest. Kag and Bani took a point towards the middle so they could anticipate their arrival. The pair wore an arrangement of binturong fur with yellow flowers tied into their hair. For Kag, this was one of the nicest things he

---

[11] Emic word for chicken.

owned and only wore it on special occasions. Jih smiled as he was nearly knocked over by Kag who broke formation to give Jih a hug. Bani playfully pulled him back while nodding respectively to both Jih and Hyu. As the pair walked from their home to the central point of the village, it was time for The Council to do their part as well.

Tur motioned for the other members of The Council to follow as they began. It was his responsibility as leader to start the long walk. This was Tur's favorite part of the festivities as it was pure showmanship, and he could show off his success to the peons that strived for his approval. Their arrival was noted with a hollowed calabash that reverberated in the form of music. Jih observed their home in all its glory with awe. The youngest children spent their time picking flowers to place down throughout the camp, to purify the space for the day. They gathered as many yellow flowers as they could to welcome Jih. The adults of the band also gathered yellow pigments and lathered a crushed solution on Jih's body. For official proceedings, Jih would be coated in red like the other men of The Council, but his inaugural pigment could be whatever color he chose. The crowd dispersed as Tur made his arrival in his signature leopard pelt but wore an accompanying tiger cape to go with it. Some members of the band immediately bowed their heads in respect as Tur continued onward. The rest of The Council enjoyed their time in the sun as well, noting who praised them adequately in the back of their minds. Tur and Jih stood opposed from one another and stared.

"Tur wishes Hizo was here." Tur mentioned, as he extended his hand to Jih. Jih grabbed it and was whisked closer to Tur where the two could talk as one without onlookers. Hyu glared at Tur before finding herself distracted with those waving to her.

"This changes nothing. Illol was good to us, and she will be honored. This is her will, not the will of Tur." He said in a whisper to Jih.

Jih nodded in agreement, giving the old man a strong hug that pressed on his bones. Jih heard a satisfying crack as he let himself free of Tur before turning to face Hyu. Jih was aware of the social game they had to play to keep up appearances, he'd been doing it his entire life. Despite the hostility between the two, Jih was able to suppress his negative emotions for the sake of the ceremony. Jih wiped away a small tear in his eye as he looked to see Kag and Bani waving to him, along with the faces of many others. He was not used to this much attention on him at any given point. This moment was much like how he felt as a child preparing for the Recognition Hunt. He remembered the prying eyes of the band looking to see what promise would come from him, but now he had a different set of circumstances. The weather was clear as the sun waited high above, with beams of light piercing through the leaves.

While being inducted into The Council was an insular event, friends of the band would often make their welcome, offering pieces of meat or smooth stones found from the shoreline. It was a show of support for longtime allies. Tur looked around the boundaries of the village while the rest of the band celebrated. The Jagged Bark was running later than expected. Tur was already irritated at their actions towards his fur supply and felt further disrespected. Tur considered his options as he noticed Dran looking uneasy. He locked eyes with her from a distance to ensure everything was going as they hoped. In the distant past, raids were a simple affair. A few youths looking to prove themselves would arrive and make some loud noise only to be scared off by clubs and stone throws.

Tur looked to see the rest of The Council gathered around Jih. Tur walked over and recalled his duties that came with inducting a new member. Tasks of all kinds stopped for the day, and a wild hog was slain after the bowl of blood had been consumed. Vut was responsible for wrangling the bearded pig and held it hostage until they were ready. The Council passed around turtle-shell bowls of pigments, and dipped their hands in, each holding a varying color that would be applied onto his skin. They were to represent their mastered knowledge and Jih picked a color of his own. Jih felt his face and body marked with a rainbow of pigments and was given a small wooden bowl filled with the blood of various animals. A sharpened stick was used to siphon a small drop from each of The Council's fingers, as it slipped into the bowl. This would ensure that they were now merged as one collective over the individual. Jih held his nose as he took a knee and drank. He was surrounded by enthusiastic cheering and clapping as the liquid fell down his mouth. Jih stuck out his dark red tongue proving that he had consumed the blood and rose with distinction.

Each of them spoke with much passion in their voices. Their knowledge seemed ever infinite, as they recalled the conditions of the day Jih was born with such accuracy and conviction, it had to be true. Tur recalled the story of Hizo, and he echoed the account of her arrival and Jih in tow to the other members of The Council. Once the speech concluded, Vut dragged out the pig that was to be slain. It squealed loudly as Vut attempted to hold it down with another man. Jih was given a knife by Tur to finish the kill as he folded his arms. Jih gave a single slice to the throat and ensured the pig's death was swift. Tur made no comment as the rest of the band butchered the pig and prepared the meal. While this occurred, members of the band swayed back and forth. The band was in a trance, with the sound of pounding trees and rhythmic chanting filling the space. In pure nirvana, they entrusted themselves to fate. While the pig roasted, hours seemed to have passed by as they danced with no sign of stopping. Hyu and Jih shared a dance as they hopped together in a small circle. Bani moved sticks on the ground for her and Kag to jump, with others following suit.

Dran observed the scene with a surprising amount of hope as she rubbed her stomach. She felt it was fine to keep her same clothing as she was only security and felt out of place to begin with. The smell of cooked pig was appealing as she hadn't eaten all day, but another smell entered her nose. As Dran was on the outskirts of the village, she had a more direct view of what was going on. In the far distance, Dran could barely see two figures through the brush. She was unsure of what to make of this until she saw a small streak of orange and red. The new smell that Dran realized was the smell of burning wood. Her eyes expanded as she saw the treeline quickly engulfed with fire. She ran as fast as she could to the village center where her voice was drowned out by the sounds of the festivities. Jih noticed Dran's panicked expression and tapped Hyu to inquire if she knew what was going on. As the two looked at one another, Jih heard the voice of Tur call to him.

"Jih-" Tur opened his mouth to address him.

Tur's question was interrupted as he saw the head of a young child turn her ears to a sound in the distance. Though his hearing was not as good as it used to be, Tur felt something was amiss as children were often stuck in ignorance. His words were interrupted by a much louder call to action. The obnoxious piercing boom of a conch shell horn filled the air as it cut through the music and dancing. Four men and three women adorned with shell garb came towards the scene with weaponry, which at first did not raise much alarm. The Elders looked to The Council for strength as they remembered Tur's words of their weakness. The adults stood firm and gathered next to The Council. Raids were to steal food, food that would be reallocated that very night. The Elders had a small supply of meat stored some distance from the camp, with most used for the ceremony, and it was assumed that they would rummage it before being sent away.

What changed their minds however was the intended direction of the raid. The raiders ignored their food storage but instead kept their pursuit towards their buildings. The calm and confident feeling eroded into a sense of utter dread and panic. The various adults looked at each other and ran in the direction of their respective homes, with some choosing to hide while others fought. Hyu and Jih knew what needed to be done. The pair headed towards their home to acquire their weapons for battle. Hyu equipped her whip and Jih extended his hand out and caught his spear thrown by Hyu. Jih held his weapon close as he quickly evaluated its fighting condition. The wood was strong, and the stone head was polished and ready for battle. Jih used these to hunt traditionally, but now they would take a human life. Dran prioritized the children's safety above all else and guided them in the direction of the shore while she ran to grab her spear from the arena. The children instinctively ran towards the direction of the southern shoreline, a maneuver implemented in case they needed to move to the mangroves. They would hide there and wait out any pursuers as nature did the rest. Jih was quickly joined by the other defenders of his band, carrying clubs and hand-axes.

Kag moved to secure Bani and evacuate some of The Council who had dispersed at the sign of danger. In his older years, Kag was not as focused on offense as his sister. His directive was to take the wounded to safety as well as he could. The enemy moved with a fierceness not known to Jih or Hyu before, the Neck-Shells could never muster up energy like this. Kag noted their style was unseen and almost foreign in its nature. With Bhet in the shadows, the first part of his plan was in fruition. One of the Neck-Shell women continued the spread of the fire and carried a torch to initiate a controlled burn. It hadn't been known to The Elders, but the Neck-Shell scouts Dran spotted placed special fish oil to increase the intensity of heat. The smell of burnt fish filled their noses as the treeline smoldered in the distance. The wall of flames that engulfed the undergrowth below made it impossible to go through to safety. A few members of The Elders attempted to brave the wall but were met with searing burns on their bodies. Bloodcurdling screams filled the air as people were engulfed in the flames before falling silent and roasting with the rest. The warriors were engaged in combat as they were ignoring the fire spreading throughout. Three Neck-Shell men rushed to the interior of the treeline where they dodged stones that were being thrown at them. Two of these men chose to prioritize Jih, seeing his new markings and grabbed another one of the torches. The disarray of the village was palpable as houses collapsed in on themselves and the Neck-Shells were wrath incarnate. Some decided to set the homes aflame and engulfed those that hid inside. Jih could only watch with hatred and sorrow as good people burned to death in front of him.

The first of the men swung wildly at Jih, keeping him distracted while the second attacked with the torch. He was given a scalding mark on his back, but it was not here that Jih would die. He quickly turned in the mud and kicked a large amount of it in their faces. Jih let out a small grin, as he lowered his body to crouch. He felt the presence of Hyu close by as her whip pressed forward behind him to see his first assailant disarmed. The man's arm was properly fileted with the whip's impact and blood pooled to the ground. Jih heard the man's scream as the venom took hold of his body, there was nothing left for him to do. Jih then sidestepped to skewer his second attacker in the ribs, where blood seeped out and the attacker's breathing lapsed as he keeled over. Jih kept a wide berth of room for him to operate as he used his spear to separate himself from the growing group of Neck-Shells. Hyu broke from Jih as she saw Dran in the distance and decided to come over to assist her.

The Neck-Shell women ran to torch as many structures that were in the vicinity, adding fuel to the fire that steadily grew around them. Dran waited patiently behind a still built hut, skewering one directly in the neck as she motioned to usher her remaining students that flocked towards her to safety. What she came to realize but couldn't communicate with the others in the fighting was that the Neck-Shells didn't operate alone. Dran saw two figures come towards her and she took a battle stance. She saw the frame of Hyu in the chaos come closer to her as the crack of the whip fell one for her. Dran ducked from the swing of a man with a conch-shell gauntlet and kicked him to the ground below. Dran gritted her teeth as the man hopelessly used his gauntlet to defend himself. Dran jabbed with her spear and shattered the implement in two. She repeated her stroke and lodged her weapon in the man's throat. Her eyes were filled with bloodlust as she scanned the horizon for her next target. Dran couldn't hide her shock as she saw the leaf-based clothing worn by members of The Jagged Bark.

"Deception!" Hyu said, her anger given to three who ran to engage in combat with Dran.

It wasn't enough that The Jagged Bark failed to answer the call for help, the outcome was far worse than they imagined. After Tur's physical outburst against their emissary, The Jagged Bark decided that their relationship with The Elders needed to change. Bhet gave them a better offer. Instead of annihilation, he decided to make them vassals to his growing influence. Dran was overrun by two of The Jagged Bark but was surprised by Hyu's arrival. Hyu collided with one of them using her shoulder to push them to the ground. She grabbed the long hair of the man and used her bodyweight to press them down on the soil until they suffocated. Dran killed the other without a second thought and gave a grunt of acknowledgement as Hyu shook her head to return to support Jih in the front.

Four more of the regular Neck-Shells came pooling into the ruins that were developing, as Hyu kept her back to Jih. While Jih's eyes were focused on trying to find the enemy, Hyu sought to assist Kag and searched for the wounded. Jih ran to get a head start on the raiders who pounded the ground with a heavy conch shell axe. Hyu turned around to see one man wearing a conch shell covering his hand as a spiked knuckle gauntlet. With her quick thinking, she shattered the piece, leaving Jih only to receive a minor punch in the arm. She was tackled to the ground from behind, as a woman with a shark tooth knife rushed to attack her. Jih ran to her and pushed her to the ground, allowing Hyu to escape while he placed his hands on her throat, choking her to death. Once the job was done, Jih got up to grab his spear and saw that Hyu had turned around, herself geared to go in a different direction. Jih started to panic as the billows of smoke rose to consume the camp in its hazardous warmth. He watched as some of the remaining fighters of their group coughed profusely.

"Hyu! Come with Jih!" Jih shouted at her over the rising screams around them. Jih ran to grab Hyu for just a quick moment before he felt Hyu's touch point to the other direction.

"No! Hyu must protect our knowledge!" She exclaimed, her finger pointing in the direction of The Council where a few other warriors ran to ensure that they were safe.

While Hyu's grievances with The Council were numerous, it would be pointless to let them die for it. Jih nodded in understanding and wished her well with a quick nose rub. He had the utmost faith in Hyu. Jih's next concern was Kag, as his eyes scanned the chaos that ensued. He was missing and feared for the worse, but his attention was brought to two young boys who seemed to have been missed by the evacuation efforts. While Kag had done the best he could, there were still two members of The Council unaccounted for. He frantically cut down vines with his hand-axe to make enough space for Bani and a few of the others to fit within the bushes before going back to the battle at hand.

"Kag will return." He said, with his voice shaking as he attempted to convince himself of his words. Kag surveyed the ongoing devastation with sorrow in his heart. A raid of this scale was nothing he would have anticipated and the reasoning for the Neck-Shells attacks was unknown. His faith shattered entirely in the cause as he worked to find survivors in the growing confusion.

The young boys that accompanied Jih were powerless to help their new leader, as a man from the Jagged Bark cut them down with his axe. Jih could only watch in sheer horror as their heads were busted open and bits of brain and broken bone leaked from them. The children were not yet trained in how to defend themselves effectively and thought that their presence could aid their warriors in battle. In a rush of blind rage, Jih ran over and tackled the man to the ground. He ripped off the gifted shells from his necklace and punched through their teeth. His bloody hand attempted to stuff the shells down their throat until the body lay still. The children were the future and with each deceased person, there was another that could no longer hold the legacy of the previous generation.

Hyu and Kag by chance were running in the same direction and met with one another as they located the two remaining members of The Council, too frail to defend themselves against the onslaught of stones and flurry of fists thrown at them. Kag was happy to see his sister as she made quick work of the Neck-Shells guarding them prior. It was a depressing sight to behold, as a few of their own adults were cut down. Kag picked up a flint knife from the battlefield, and immediately stabbed a Neck-Shell in the stomach, ripping their entrails to the ground below. Seeing an opportunity, Kag grabbed the two bloody Council members and ushered them to walk towards the hiding place he picked out. Removal of the remaining ones was now their objective. Jih ran to the tent next to Kag's and found a Neck-Shell with intent of burning it to the ground. Jih was able to use surprise to his advantage and stabbed the man with intense ferocity as the torch sat just a mere distance away from the structure. Sweat accumulated on Jih's face as he ran out of energy. The effectiveness of newfound alliance for The Jagged Bark and Neck-Shells turned the wheels in Jih's mind. Jih noted that their skill was variable, some were hardened killers, while others were immensely easy to fell.

Kag saw one last child attempting to hide from the fighting as she curled into a ball. Kag locked eyes with the young girl but she was too traumatized to move. He placed his spear down to remind her that he wasn't hostile and waved her over gently. Kag was vulnerable as he knelt to defend the child with his life. As Kag was distracted, the girl cried and pointed, showing a Neck-Shell woman with a spear who rushed towards him, angled to be in for a clean kill. By the time Kag sighted her, he was already too far to grab his own spear. Kag's eyes widened as he instinctively covered the girl with his body and accepted the end that had come. While he hugged her tightly to take the hit, Kag opened his eyes to see Hyu had instead run to her, taking the spear head on, as it entered through her ribs. The amount of force generated by Hyu's speed colliding ended up knocking the woman to the ground, and she hit her head, rendering her unconscious. Hyu fell to the ground and clutched the side of her stomach in immense pain as she attempted to crawl.

Hyu spat out blood as she looked at her brother, who for the first time in her life, was filled with genuine rage. She knew this was a stupid decision to make, but her whip lacked the range to keep Kag safe at that distance. He and the girl would have died without her interfering. Kag was not a skilled fighter, and it would have ended in more misery. The light of the flames illuminated the camp, but a sullen red mist filled the air. Hyu mustered up a smile as she knew that the time was upon them. The Elders were so distracted in their fighting that they didn't notice dusk turned to night. The moon was blood red as the lunar eclipse Tur predicted came true. The Neck-Shells that saw this premonition in the sky organized a mighty stampede. The universe was ready to smite them for their actions, and they sounded the conch horn to retreat into the night. Screams from the combined Neck-Shell and Jagged Bark party continued until they vanished into the night. Only the sounds of death and the ambient flames filled the silent village. The observant Bhet waited behind for details of the attack.

Kag was too overwhelmed to speak, but Hyu's gaze met with her brother. She figured it would now be best to reveal the thought process behind her actions. In most circumstances, Hyu was more than happy to have Kag do things on her behalf, but Kag's life now was too important. Although Hyu and Jih didn't want a family further than their own, she knew the root cause of Bani's illness. Hyu reasoned with herself that a new life to come into the world needed two parents just as they did long ago. Hyu would be doing a disservice otherwise as she wouldn't want to imagine a world without her brother to raise her niece or nephew.

"Bani has...child. Let Hyu go." She said, as Kag desperately ripped off portions of his animal skins to try and patch her wound. Kag said nothing as tears filled his eyes, he saw the outline of Jih far in the distance searching around for any other non-combatants. He selflessly moved the injured to spots in the bushes to attend to later. Kag attempted to yell out to Jih, frantically begging Hyu to survive but his call fell upon deaf ears. Kag coughed as the last bits of soot from the burning wood settled throughout the camp. The fire from the forest continued to rage in smaller quantities while The Elders held out hope for rain to come.

"Jih...will understand. Kag. Turn Hyu to him. Hyu must see his face." She said, as Kag held his sister while she bled out. Per Hyu's last request, he turned her to see Jih helping people just as she knew his personality best. It was the last memory she wished to have before she died. Never had Kag felt so useless in his life. Kag reflected on the death of their parents at a young age, and how he was entrusted to keep Hyu safe for as long as he could. With the death of his younger sibling, he considered himself a failure to the one task that mattered the most. Kag turned his gaze at the small girl who remained helpless and unmoved as she shook in fear. Kag exhaled and shook his head. He wanted to comfort the child and tell her everything would be fine, but he could not.

The Council were bewildered by such treachery, as the ones Kag hid talked among themselves. What could have caused this deception? The land was plentiful, and the ocean could provide. Fruit was practically falling from the trees, this was what they had told themselves, but the reality on the ground was much more different. The Council were in disarray on what could have been the result of The Jagged Bark choosing to make alliance with the raiders over their longstanding tradition. Tur stood in silence as he gave no opinion on the matter. In the back of his mind, Tur had reason to believe that his own actions were a significant factor in relations falling flat. This only lasted a short time as their outburst only justified his claims and thoughts of their behavior. The chaos of the fighting ended with the withdrawal of most of the Neck-Shells. The remaining ones that were injured and unable to retreat, were either held as captives for some time, or decapitated with their severed heads placed on the ground as a warning to anyone else. Jih returned to what was left of his home, calling out for Hyu and Kag now that the dust settled. It took some time for him to compose himself, but only Kag answered Jih's call. He prompted him to come over and before him was Hyu's corpse. It was not in Jih to attempt to shake her awake, the blood below her ensured she had no way to be alive. Jih knelt with his spear, and hugged her closely, while Kag went to grab Bani before he returned. Jih felt the need to cry but his eyes were empty. Jih immediately regretted his decision to not go with Hyu to secure The Council as she wanted. Jih reasoned that if he were there, perhaps it could have been him instead. Hyu was more valuable to the band, she was one of only two healers and Jih was well aware of this and the impact it would cause in the aftermath to come.

Once the fighting ceased, Dran and a few other adults did a count of the slain. The chaos had brought everything into disarray as she tried to maintain order as well as she could. While some were calling on her to find The Council, Dran's priorities lay elsewhere as she searched the remains of partially burned huts for survivors. Eventually, her travels took her to where a familiar pair stood. She saw Jih and Kag, with Bani in tow. Their faces were embedded into her memory. Jih stood with Hyu's body as Dran approached, her bloodlust vanishing from slaughtering Neck-Shells as she saw the results of what happened. Kag's face was filled with tears as he tried to put on a good face for the others, while Bani held her head to the ground. The only one that could look her in the face was Jih. Dran knew that it was her responsibility above all else for the safety of the camp and her inability to keep everyone safe weighed heavily on her. Dran and the others knew that death was expected, and it was something that came for all. It hurt all the same, especially when it came to someone with experience. Fighting for The Elders was, to this point, a rare but gruesome endeavor. She was not prepared for a raid this intricate, but no excuse could rectify the damage caused. Dran expected rage and anger, the things she reacted with the most and knew how to handle, but Jih's eyes were empty. Dran wasn't sure what hurt her more, the guilt that befell her as she saw the wounded attempt to collect themselves, or the utter silence that emanated from Jih as he held Hyu in his arms. She walked away without a second thought.

Jih had such confidence in Hyu, it never entered his mind that she could have died in battle, but that fate was not to be. The three mourned silently while the remaining adults attempted to try and rebuild quickly for the fear of predators soon took their mind. The smell of shed blood was an invitation for tigers to make their way. One adult went past the camp to retrieve the children who managed to run to the mangrove, while The Council checked among their ranks as well. One passed from their wounds, but in all, remained firm and steady to lead once again. The remaining members that hadn't scattered about spent the night taking watch, for there was much to do in the morning.

The Council were the first to wake and were in deep talks about where to go from here. Jih attempted to sleep under the stars, in the remains of what was left of his partially burnt hut. He did not sleep at all; in fact he laid motionless as he looked at the moon still in its eclipse. What did this mean? The little possessions Jih had were now just objects of the past. Hyu's eggshells were crushed, and his master's hand-axe was looted from his home. Jih lay on his back and drifted his fingers over the tiger claw that made his necklace. A small boy arrived by Jih's home and innocently moved his head inside what remained. Jih looked back at his surprised visitor. Jih had no doubt that one of his parents were slain in the aftermath of the raid. Though Jih was filled with grief, it was considered improper to do so in front of children. Jih returned his look with bloodshot eyes and heard the commotion of surviving adults at the village center. Jih mustered the strength to get up and join the others as he listened to the discussion.

Many of the adults pondered what to do with the bodies, with Dran having the idea to make a large bonfire not too far from their camp to burn the remains of the Neck-Shells. She hoped to keep the other adults busy while she thought of an explanation to give to The Council. For Dran, this was the worst nightmare she could have come up with, and the price of being right was immense. Dran initiated the cleanup process as adults dispersed to gather their tools and chop wood. Jih gestured to what remained of their processed stone piles to sharpen them while he stood and watched. Although Dran gave a look to Jih, she was not able to muster any words. The last thing she would do at a time like this was ask for his assistance after the death of a loved one. Dran could only watch as the village cooperated in complete silence with only the sound of their tools filling the village center. Devoid of emotion, the band was exhausted and saw nothing more than monotony as a brief escape from their woes. The land smelled of burning flesh for much time as they tended to their own. Jih left wanting to rid himself of the process and to find comfort through Kag and Bani. While Jih slept, Kag and Bani held Hyu's body overnight. The two took care of Hyu's remains by covering her with ash to ward off scavengers and to keep her prepared for burial.

Kag and Bani shared a glance as they saw the sobering figure of Jih approach them. His hair was unwell, and his skin was bruised. His clothing was tattered as it was torn in combat or burnt off by the flames. The weight of Hyu's death was so massive he felt lifting his arms to greet them was impossible. The time to bury her would be as soon as Jih approached them. Jih took a deep breath, and his first steps without Hyu, were directly to Kag and Bani who also shared little sleep that night. Kag and Jih looked at one another and nodded knowing what needed to be done. Jih picked up a spare hand-axe off the ground and passed it to Bani while he and Kag approached Hyu gently. Kag propped up Hyu as best as he could while Jih assisted. Their walk was silent as they moved past the boundary line of their northern end of camp. Their destination was the beach that they treasured and viewed the meteors that were filled with immense power and mystique. As they approached the beach the smell of saltwater filled their noses. Jih found it difficult to compose himself as he stopped moving to absorb the smell. His eyes met the sandbanks where he and Hyu went multiple times in his life. Bani looked to Jih and Kag as she was unsure of where exactly Hyu could be buried. Her eyes met the sea, but she was horrified at the idea of her bones washing up back to shore. Jih reassured Bani with a small grin that took immense energy to muster.

Jih knew the spot where Hyu wanted to be buried, it was a special place by the beach. In their youth, the two visited there countless times as an escape from many things. It was an incredibly small patch of forest that one had to crawl into, much like their own huts. It was a continuous wall of green that between the brambles, one could see the ocean. The sounds of the waves could lull anyone to sleep. Jih could hear Hyu's humming still as he gestured with his head to proceed. A wall of poisonous plants gated the spot and no animals bothered to nest there. Kag prompted Bani to duck her head carefully to not touch the vines with her skin exposed as it caused a terrible rash. Inside the green space, there was a sizeable amount of room to rest. Jih looked above as bits of sunlight pierced through the growth and the smell of salt carried through.

Jih and Kag used the hand-axe to move a quantity of soil while Bani watched quietly. There was some risk involving Hyu's burial in what was now Neck-Shell territory, but Jih figured this was the perfect place to encapsulate their shared love for each other and the ocean. Jih and Kag dug the grave as low as they could. Each layer of unearthed soil was a struggle as the two paused from memories of Hyu entering their minds. After some time, Jih and Kag placed the soil back by hand, as her body was covered. The last thing the trio saw was Hyu's face, as a clump of dirt buried it below. Bani patted the earth's layers steadily as she let out a small sigh. Kag took a moment to rest his head on top of the grave, while Jih and Bani exited to briefly looked for stones. They collected an assortment of them, placing them on top in rows of eight and looked at their handiwork. As a stone worker, Jih prioritized finding rocks that left a particular luster on them when in the presence of sunlight. He wanted Hyu's resting place to be as bright as the day was when she lived.

Without much said, the three then left Hyu to rest and returned to camp. Jih saw there wasn't much that changed from their absence but there was a disturbance. Out of the brush, one of the errand boys for The Council emerged. He motioned for Jih to come over, as he made his way with Kag and Bani. The two noted that Jih now had official business to attend to and let him on his way. Jih followed the boy's pace and faced six of The Council who sat outside in a circle with crossed legs. Tur prioritized repairs of The Council tent as the Woodworking Team labored in the distance under his strict guidance. Jih looked at all of them in silence and was prompted to sit down by Tur. Tur held out his staff and pointed it at Jih. His scowl didn't leave his face as Jih soon saw why. As he sat down, Jih watched Dran storm off in the distance, it was clear by her walk she received a verbal lashing from The Council for how everything went the night before. Jih felt there was some blame, but he doubted Dran's warning at first about the raid, as did many other adults to begin with. Jih understood it was a horrid feeling to have been proven right at such a cost. Jih couldn't understand why he felt the gaze of his new cohort filled with vitriol. Jih anticipated a well-done job, as aside from Hyu and other casualties, they weren't wiped off the face of the planet with such a large size of enemy attackers. This opinion, however, changed as he saw what happened to Dran.

"Jih made big mistake. The Council teaches, not fights. You were to come with us." One of the women stated in anger to him.

Jih was visibly confused as he was never told this information. Jih weighed the words of his superior's statement before speaking. Was he not supposed to defend the weak? He thought of his mother's teachings and how it conflicted with the narrative placed before him. Power only wished to protect power when times were tough. Jih knew he had a case to make and sought to defend his actions.

"Jih saved lives. Twenty are dead, there could be much more." Jih said to himself as he stomped his foot on the ground in defiance at her words. Jih watched as a few eyes watched his movement and straightened their posture in response.

"Fighting is dangerous. Jih could have died. Knowledge of stone would be lost, you know how to work bloodstone. Many do not have this gift." One man voiced support for the other member. Jih gritted his teeth in frustration. If Jih did nothing, they would have been cut down to pieces, and this discussion would be nonexistent. How ungrateful could one group of people be? Jih empathized with Dran immediately as doing what was right only ended in unwarranted discipline.

One woman spoke out in defense of Jih, the quiet Aab, who mastered all there was to know of furs. Aab was a frail woman with little hair on her head. Compared to the more extravagant outfits worn by The Council, she wore an assortment of leather that was covered with black eagle feathers. White whisps and wrinkles accompanied her face as she concentrated on his words.

"Jih defended the future." She noted, and observed the many kids who were put to work with their parents in gathering materials to rebuild. Jih offered a supportive nod with some relief that people could see reason. He continued his defense by assuring The Council he held no ill will towards them as a group but only with Tur.

"Jih not upset with The Council. This is fault of Tur alone." Jih said calmly, as he looked towards him. Aab raised her head at his comment, while the other remaining members glared at Jih for such harsh words. Aab and Tur were partnered but she often let the bombastic Tur handle himself in discussion. Tur, usually needing help to get up, now stood on his own. He remained enraged at such foolish words brought before him.

"Tur? Tur leads The Council. Tur has kept us alive. Our furs are gone, and we must start anew. We are poor and no trade will be met with us." His voice spat out in rage. His old voice carried through the camp where the occasional onlooker turned their heads at the display.

"Alive? Hyu is dead. Neck-Shells brought much death. Our allies have betrayed us. Tur has saved nothing." Jih countered, pointing to the mass burning pile of bodies some distance from their camp. Jih's frustration with Tur was brewing steadily from the minute he was initiated. He was aware of the words spoken to him, that being among them would not end their decades-long feud.

"The Council-" Tur said, getting interrupted by Jih once more.

"The Council was warned by many. Tur ignored them all." He said, curling his hand into a fist.

Jih respected each member of The Council immensely in years past and the institution itself. His tolerance of Tur only lasted if Hizo lived, and she was long gone. Now, he couldn't as much as utter the man's name without contempt on his face. Death claimed the lives of twenty who have yet to reach their peak and Tur was concerned on keeping profit with his furs. Jih's hut was burned and Hyu now was but a living memory. Jih attempted to sway the conversation back to the people at hand who were responsible for keeping their power.

"Many died saving The Council. What do we say of them? We must give them something." Jih said, with regret heavy in his voice. Jih was reminded of the conversation had after Chak's death. It was detestable that Chak was given a week's worth of required mourning but for the other fallen members of their hunt, nothing was given to the parents involved.

"That is their job. Jih will understand later." Tur stated flatly, getting a surprised response from Jih and even from one of the younger members. While some may have found this bout of wits entertaining, some of The Council wished to lead. Aab spoke, prompting the two men to quiet down as they stewed in anger. Aab turned her head gently and extended her arm out of respect. Jih grabbed it kindly for a short amount of time before letting go. He kept quiet as he focused on hearing the old woman's low voice.

"Jih. Aab admits mistake was made. The Jagged Bark were a prized ally. It will take a generation to win their trust once more." She said, retaining an ounce of humility as the stubborn Tur and other members crossed their arms. She looked at the soil before addressing him.

"The Council has decided on new plan." Aab exclaimed as she made it known to him. Jih nodded in acceptance, knowing that his responsibility as the newest member was to do the will of The Council for the time being. Jih anticipated the act of preparing for conflict and was more than ready to do what it took to seek vengeance for Hyu and the rest of the fallen. Aab shot a look at Tur, seeing that he had calmed down and now was willing to speak again.

"Jih. Go to Neck-Shell territory." Tur ordered Jih with confidence in his voice.

"For? Jih does not understand." Jih commented, as his eyes met that at The Council's. Some distance away, the ever-curious Kag watched for a few moments as he saw The Council meeting outside. He knew that they had a plan of some sort, but he needed to get all the details from Jih.

"We have decided peace is best." Aab mentioned, as she waved her hand among the other members who nodded in support of their decision made without his knowledge.

"Neck-Shells are raiders, they are unreasonable." Jih countered with anger in his voice. Jih was remarkably upset, with such a decision like this made without his knowledge, he felt as if his role was purely ceremonial and not one of substance as he anticipated. Those outside The Council now saw Jih in a position of power and authority, but he remained confined by the rules before him. How could they agree to try peace again? Their last deal fell in smoke.

"Neck-Shells broke last terms. The agreement means nothing." Jih added on, his confusion prompting looks of disdain from the rest of the group. Jih was truly unsure of why his fellow band members would consider seeing peace with the enemy. The Neck-Shells as he, Kag, and Bani knew were only barbarians who didn't respect things such as diplomacy or peace. They only took what they wanted, when they wanted, and that their kindness was a resource to be exploited.

"Neck-Shells have new leader." One of the men next to Tur reasoned with him, sensing Jih's rising anger. Emotions were running high and for good reason, as the second deal with the Neck-Shells was a controversial vote, but one that needed making according to The Council.

"You will deal with Neck-Shells, and you will return with news. Make peace or do not return." Tur mentioned to Jih as he motioned for him to stand up.

Aab watched as Tur extended his hand to Jih and the two shook hands signifying his agreement to the terms. Seeing no viable solutions left other than to comply, Jih walked out calmly without another word to the other members, while his rage ran through his body. Jih approached the cluster of tents where he lived and punched a wall in frustration. He made a proper hole in the thatch as a disappointed child went back to work repairing it. Tur mumbled some words to himself as he watched Jih storm off.

"Hizo would be ashamed."

The Stone and Shell: I

Jih continued his pace from the meeting with The Council. His disgust at Tur and the other's conduct was small in comparison to stomaching the task given to him. The idea of working with the Neck-Shells in any capacity was considered cowardice at best and heinous at worst. Jih was fresh from burying Hyu and now he was given the burden of responsibility to grovel for peace with no end in sight. He compared the problem to his childhood in attempting to deal with Chak. Reasoning with him was impossible as he simply recognized it as a sign of weakness. Only violence could possibly rectify the atrocities given to his people.

Jih recalled the number of duties he still had to address despite his new rank. Although he hadn't been given an exact time to do his task with heading to Neck-Shell territory, he naturally treated it with urgency. He headed home quickly to grab his spear and brave the travels of the beach but was waved at by Kag. Jih was in a rush, but he slowed his pace to accommodate Kag who asked for his presence. Jih hadn't realized that Kag was watching the meeting's proceedings from a distance. Kag was concerned about the state of Jih's health but chose not to address this yet. Jih motioned for him to follow and Kag sped up to catch up to Jih's increasingly fast pace. The pair found themselves cutting through a small circle of women wearing various deer furs on the ground that were processing freshly captured material. The smell of fresh berries filled their noses as they did so. Kag turned his head around to catch one last sniff but received a glare and graciously gave a grin for them both as an apology. The two of them made their way to Jih's home and talked in the comfort of their isolation. Jih's face couldn't hide his stress as Kag looked over at him. Jih looked over his shoulder as he felt Kag was going to ask him a question.

"Jih is upset again. What happened now?" Kag asked as he noticed Jih's expression.

Although Kag lacked the details of how The Council operated, he could surely see that there was a lot to address. Aside from Tur's meddling, members of The Council held an isolationist view when it came to interacting with the other appendages that made up The Elders. They wanted little to do outside of rituals when leadership was surely needed. Kag was happy to be left alone to do the job he spent decades learning, but a lack of communication was a horrible outcome. His focus was on Jih, but he could already see that people were starting to run themselves thin in attempting to recover from the raid's damage.

"Jih must go to Neck-Shells. The Council wants peace, deal should be made by today." Jih said with complete disdain in his voice. Kag moved closer and placed his hand on Jih's shoulder in support.

"Peace? Ha-Ha! Many say Kag is amusing." Kag said with a hearty laugh as he slapped Jih on the back. Jih's still expression caused Kag's laughter to subside quickly noting the severity of the situation.

"Jih will go now. The sun is still high, and progress must be made." Jih said as he placed his right hand to his forehead. Jih's eyes squinted as he tried to track the movement of the sun. He lowered his head down slightly as the sun was incredibly bright in their village clearing. Jih didn't anticipate relations with the Neck-Shells being a lengthy process, they were simple people with simple desires. Jih noticed that Kag held a look of determination on his face that could only mean one thing.

"Kag will come and protect leader." Kag mentioned, with a twist of his arms as he felt a rush of energy.

Jih looked Kag over with respect for his friend. Jih noted that Kag wasn't the best fighter and thought his talents could be best at home, but an extra hand could make all the difference. Nobody else was willing to back him up. Jih was happy to have Kag accompany him on official business but saw that Kag was unarmed. Kag lifted a finger for Jih to stay where he was as he wandered off. After some time, Kag returned with a borrowed spear of his own. Kag held his hand out for Jih to give his blessing on the tool for the trek. Kag held the spear with two hands and pointed the lethal end towards the ground as he passed it to Jih. Jih examined the spear for anything that would be a risk to their mission.

"Hmm. The stone is good. The wood is aged but will work." Jih mentioned as he instinctively traced the outline of the spearhead with his finger.

He held it with a single hand as he used his knuckle to knock on the wood and look for signs of hollowing. On occasion, insects could eat at the integrity of the wood for spears. The most trained of their warriors would douse their spear handles in smoke from nearby to deter them. Jih shrugged his shoulders as he evaluated the weapon was less heavy than previous spears he designed. Hizo taught Jih early that the right type of wood was essential as it was used to take much of the impact from striking over the user themselves. Kag was delighted to see Jih in his element as a newly minted Stone Breaker, one of the few silver linings of the previous week's events.

"Protection." Kag commented as he gave him reassurance with a goofy smile from end to end.

The two made their leave as they noticed one of Tur's sentries monitoring the exit towards the beach. At first, Jih was stopped but on further examination, the man humbly lowered his head and allowed the pair to pass. Jih and Kag continued their path as they gradually reached the outskirts of their village which was marked by dense foliage. The last of the small huts made om their camp were but specks outside the dense undergrowth. Although the road to Neck-Shell territory was well-traveled, enemies and predators could be anywhere so they chose to speak little that would reveal their location. The familiar forest was now burned as the aftermath of the jungle fire gave its toll. Past the array of green that survived the damages, there were entire sections filled with soot, ash, and deceased wood. Once the pair assessed they were alone now, Kag had long waited to get Jih's reaction on an important issue. Jih pressed on ahead as he remembered an alternative route to the shore and could continue further to reach the Neck-Shell heartland. The two came across a log that blocked the usual path forward which was wedged deep between two trees. Jih and Kag diverted course to cut around the plants before going back to their normal route.

"Kag has news for Jih." Kag stated with much joy as he withdrew a knife to start cutting through thicker foliage. Jih could feel his friend's happiness and he nodded in anticipation. Jih urged Kag to speak by moving his hand along while Kag attempted to piece together what he wanted to say. Kag took a deep breath to ground himself and gave Jih the most neutral face he could muster.

"Bani will have child." Kag said as he yanked apart a few loose vines that he tossed behind them.

Jih couldn't hide his confusion but as he remembered Hyu's long visits with Bani, the pieces started to fall together. Jih gave a small laugh as he appreciated how discrete she could be. Kag was her own brother and had no idea. Jih wiped his eyes briefly in shock as reality hit him. He knew Kag always wanted to be a father and now his time would come. Jih and Hyu made the decision a long time ago that children were not something they needed to be complete. They were fine with their own company and The Council additionally had rules to keep numbers under control, forbidding them to turn a group that couldn't afford to feed their members. Some considered their decision selfish, but Jih felt the opposite. Forcing someone to be a parent that wasn't equipped for the job would make a terrible leader. He had the utmost confidence in Kag and would do whatever he could to keep him safe. Jih's eyes scanned the brush, and he ducked low to find the way through. He stuck out his hand for Kag to grab. Jih heaved Kag forward and held his ground as Kag's momentum met with his. Jih hoped that the way back would be easier after their business was dealt with. The two stood at a clearing in the forest that was visibly maintained by human hands and was the extent of the Neck-Shell's current territory.

Jih moved backwards to give Kag room as Jih lowered his head and stared at Kag. Jih tapped his forehead and Kag immediately smiled as he walked over to Jih. The two slammed their foreheads together and gave a hearty laugh of pride. The two rubbed their heads in unison with a small grin as Jih noted he was not as hard-headed, in the literal sense, as he used to be. The two continued onwards as they conversed about what day they predicted the child would be born.

"This is good to hear. Bani is often quiet, when did Kag know?" Jih asked as he continued his pace. He pointed upwards advising Kag to watch the thick branches of a nearby citrus tree as they continued to the trail.

"Hyu told Kag before..." Kag said, cutting himself off. He decided to change the topic and center it on the new life that would begin. Kag coughed and thought about the circumstances regarding birth. Aside from Bani's health, Kag now had to consider the time of day, the season, and the phase of the moon in which they would be born.

"Did The Council name Jih?" Kag inquired as he lowered his head to avoid some branches that were closing in his field of view. Jih nodded no, and reminded Kag that he joined the band when he was very young with his parents. He didn't know why they left but remembered small bits and pieces that drove them to wander until settling where they were now.

"Jih was given by Hizo, not picked by The Council." Jih commented. Kag responded with a short grunt as he thought over Jih's response. While Kag certainly liked his own name, he wondered what other names he could have gone with, and that of Hyu as well. He shrugged his shoulders in resignation as he was perfectly fine with his name.

The thick brush that they had walked through gradually thinned as the sound of ocean water and the smell of salt filled their noses. Jih never felt more relieved to meet the beach after the claustrophobia of the tight brush. The thick brush that wrapped itself around his arms and legs irritated Jih as he felt no different than a cornered animal. The Neck-Shells were a band that stuck to the coastlines often, only retreating into the deeper forest to get material for building their homes. The sea provided everything else, including the dreaded conch shells, they implemented to great effect in the forms of weaponry. In days past, Jih and the other children would swim along these coastlines diving to capture clams and fish to bring back home and to play in the water. Now, this was undisputed territory of the Neck-Shells and they needed to remain vigilant. Jih and Kag walked forward from the forest and felt the sand on their toes. Kag looked behind him as they emerged about forty minutes away from Hyu's burial mound. He nodded and remembered the importance of this mission. Hyu's death would not go unpunished or left in vain. Kag's concentration was broken by Jih who pointed to a figure in the distance.

An ear-shattering noise shouted some distance from the two of them; it was a scout that looked ahead for any travelers on the beaches they claimed as their territory. Jih placed his spear down and waved his hand in the air as a sign of non-hostility. Kag did the same as the two were probed to go further. The two gathered their weapons once more and followed the envoy before them. Some curious Neck-Shells arrived on the scene to greet their new visitor. An older mother with clothing woven from fibers held a shark tooth knife in her hand as she eyed the pair. Jih noticed a few children gathered around her work themselves up after their arrival as they fidgeted. Her hands were held out to block her children from getting closer. Jih and Kag could feel grimaces as the young threw small rocks in their direction. Jih felt comfortable in his guess that the Neck-Shells had as much to say about them than anyone else. Kag noticed their stomachs were empty and food was getting harder to come by. The land was not a forgiving place, and the sea was harsher. The raids would only continue in volume now they feared.

"Hatred is taught early." Kag noted as he returned an angry face at the children who backed off slowly.

Jih kept his laughter to himself as he tried to keep up appearances for the leader that was sure to arrive. Instead, Jih and Kag were treated to a group of four Neck-Shell men. The quartet boasted large beards and uncut hair. Jih noticed they only wore a loincloth as clothing while the brisk sea air hit their backs. They held axes with handles made from wood, but a worked conch shell served as the blade. Jih noted their ignorance of stone tools but could not deny the lethality involved. He sized up the potential combat of the men, he could take two comfortably but defending Kag was his priority.

"Why are you here?" The tallest among the four stated as he held his hand out to Jih. Jih chose his words carefully while Kag kept his eyes peeled on the other men who had their axes at the ready. While the group was tense in their wording, the Neck-Shells felt fundamentally secure. The Elders were a weak band despite their size, and they hoped to exploit it by any means. A smug look of satisfaction came as Jih's exhausted tone shone through his voice.

"The Elders want peace. The Council demands it. We will meet with leader, Jih knows this is not you." Jih addressed, with his finger pointed to the smoke rising from a settlement behind them. He looked at the man once more and noted how similar he looked to the others around him. Jih still wore his buffalo hides from the previous night while Kag backed him by sticking his spear into the sand and holding a menacing pose. Two of the surrounding men huffed their chests to match Kag's adopted bravado while they waited for their leader to speak.

"You are not leader either. He wears Onpeu fur, you wear that of Ker-Mah. This interests us, two people who meet on behalf of others. We will take you to Bhet. Your offer should amuse us." The man retorted as he blew air from his nostrils. The men looked at one another and decided to adhere to Jih's request, while keeping their weapons pointed at them. Kag looked at Jih but waited for his response before trying anything rash. The group of men retreated towards an enclave from the beach where small fires were lit out in the open. Jih and Kag were stopped as they saw they needed to surrender their arms before entering the camp.

"Drop your spears." One of the Neck-Shell men ordered Jih and Kag.

The pair did as they were told and one of them laughed as they complied without question. Jih's eyes followed their dropped spears as they touched the sand with a hearty thud. The man who ordered them to disarm collected their weapons and would return them on their leave. Jih highly doubted their claims but an audience with Bhet is what he needed the most. The tallest among the Neck-Shells saw it fit to narrate his people's achievements to the lesser members of The Elders. To combat the breeze from the sea, the Neck-Shells built small occupying mounds of dirt that kept the heat in. Jih and Kag observed the Neck-Shell camp and its inhabitants. It was far smaller than their own but saw that it seemed to be split into two separate locations. The first of these was a penetrative settlement that destroyed some of the forest but opened out towards the sea. Kag tried to understand the origin of where they gathered their wood, the coast's trees were better for boats, but building material was best extracted from the jungle. Jih reasoned that a worker's camp comprised the second settlement of the Neck-Shells deeper in the forest to supply wood as needed. Jih and Kag listened to the man explain their customs as was appropriate for any guest, even those that were raided. There were digging sticks scattered throughout as the Neck-Shell men labored to dig new constructions while the women stripped fish and prepared clothing. Piles of sand and dirt riddled the landscape as new building foundations were made. There were no guided paths like that of his home and people placed themselves without order.

The Neck-Shells lived in a combination of packed dirt and wood that made the structure of their homes. They lacked flaps for doors and were open, so Jih and Kag could look inside of any if they chose. One man who sat outside his home on a stump was certainly the leader Jih had imagined. His neck was adorned with a red shell with spines fixed to it with string. His chest was littered with wounds. His left hand was chopped down to a nub and he was missing a few teeth. His face was marred with scars but none of that mattered as the control he exerted over the Neck-Shells was absolute. He needed no council, for he was his own man and his people valued him above all else. Jih held his breath as near where he sat was the corpse of a fallen Neck-Shell. The Neck-Shells were as brutal to their own as those they encountered. The Elders buried their dead, but here the man placed his feet on a body as if it were no different from the ground. It was difficult for Jih and Kag to keep their disgust and fear hidden inside.

"What band are you?" Bhet asked, his expression one of curiosity.

Diplomatic visits were not his strong suit, but those that appealed to his interests were worth at least some conversation. His eyes scanned Jih's clothing and could tell he was a man of means. Bhet had an eye for more for his people and felt they needed to get it. Bhet was unsure of how old Jih was, but he assumed they were reasonably of the same generation. Bhet had stood out among the Neck-Shell leadership where his age and experience were an asset over the young warrior champions held by other bands. Bhet suppressed and incorporated The Jagged Bark from shared interest and wondered how far his sway could truly go.

"Jih and Kag. From The Elders, Jih stands for The Council." Jih explained.

"This one is Bhet. Neck-Shell leader, now speak." Bhet said introducing himself as he heard the concerns of his new guests.

As was customary, Jih and Kag extended their weapon hands as a sign of peace. Jih went first due to his status and gripped the man's right hand with a solid shake. Kag lifted an eyebrow as he returned the same gesture. Jih nodded to sit down and folded his legs while Kag copied his movements. Presentation meant everything when it came to negotiations. If Jih spoke while standing, Bhet would feel insecure as he remained seated and that would only cause more problems. He sat down to be on an equal footing and wanted nothing to be misconstrued. Bhet remained slightly elevated on the stump as he looked to face both Jih and Kag. Jih was aware that he was a guest in their home and Bhet's ego needed to be placated. Jih held little interest in small talk and decided the best move was to come honest with the issue at hand. His mind raced to get the words out of his mouth of how ludicrous a request he was forced to make.

"The Council wants peace Bhet. What will we do for it?" Jih stated with feigned confidence in his statement. Bhet straightened his posture as he gave Jih a look of visible confusion that made Kag stew in anger. Kag wanted nothing more than to swing wildly at Bhet, but he noted Jih's calm demeanor that hid his true thoughts.

"Peace? You live to talk." Bhet commented as he moved a rock through his fingers. Bhet's head turned to look at Kag who was inching to say anything while Jih remained quiet. Kag's volatile personality interested Bhet as it was less trained than Jih's. Jih operated on how he spoke with The Jagged Bark, but the Neck-Shells were a far different entity entirely.

"That is not peace. We-" Kag interjected and bit his tongue as he tried not to speak out of term. Keeping his emotions in check was difficult for Kag who always spoke what was on his mind, but for now he would remember his role as support.

"We must hunt undisturbed. There has been much death." Jih explained, as he held his hand up to Kag. Kag silenced himself as he saw Jih pointing into the woods that were marked with blood and the slashes of clubs and spears in skirmishes from other groups.

"The woods are ours. Your people are weak to find no new lands." Bhet spat on the ground with vitriol in his speech. Jih frowned as he immediately came up with a response. While weak in combat strategy, The Elders hardly dealt with resource insecurity due to their efficiency. Jih found it pathetic that the Neck-Shells could send their children to bed hungry while the adults subsisted on chewing bark for sustenance.

"Your people starve. Jih can see through their stomach, as clear as the saltwater you drink." Jih retorted with annoyance in his voice. It was evident that these words had gotten Bhet as he remained silent before speaking. Although Bhet was bloodthirsty, his bottom line to secure resources for his people was a relatable goal of any person. Bhet's incursions into the woods for food were not successful as the ocean yielded little this season.

"You use words. Words that do not feed Neck-Shells." Bhet stated, his tone dismissive of the points Jih had made. He would rather die than admit his leadership had flaws, something that certainly other Neck-Shells tried to oblige. While Kag remained quiet, Jih saw his chance to speak. Jih nudged Kag to comment so that he could also show some legitimacy as the other Neck-Shell men came behind their leader and listened.

"Neck-Shells need food. The dry season will come for our lands. What will you tell them when empty-handed?" Kag commented, looking at some of Bhet's men who massaged their stomachs. Starvation was a great motivator in ousting people from power and Bhet's eyes widened as he hadn't accounted for the changes in weather. His mind lay on the lunar eclipse the night before, a blood red moon meant a crisis of great renown to come. Bhet was still untested as a leader when it came to administration, and he secretly feared for his life.

"Neck-Shells do need it. Will The Elders give to us? Or should we take again?" Bhet asked as his eyes met Kag's. Jih saw an opportunity, the only one he could really muster any real chance of getting a solution. He decided that he would agree to the terms in full but would fight to get what he wanted. Jih was aiming for enough time to stall and think of a better plan.

"The Elders will give in full for peace. Give Jih an amount." Jih mentioned slamming his hand on the soil as a sign of his severity. Kag was shocked at Jih's admission of this as he figured the negotiation power was now solely in Bhet's hands. He crunched his face in thought as he debated what rationale Jih could have. Bhet decided to meet Jih as he offered and gave a number as high as he could without endangering the legitimacy of the demand.

"Bhet finds this amusing. The Jagged Bark offered men for peace. The Elders give food for it. Which is more important? Bhet has mouths to feed but men can raid." Bhet taunted Jih as he met his eyes. Jih absorbed Bhet's statement with the utmost severity. He recalled being in combat yesterday with some members of The Jagged Bark but couldn't wrap his head around their oath being broken. The Jagged Bark and The Elders were a long-lasting partnership he worked to maintain, but Jih remembered the disrespect that Tur had towards their traditional allies. Jih reasoned that Tur's treatment of their own was the final push to cut ties. Jih's attention was brought back to their conversation as he heard Bhet's words.

"Meat for sixty." Bhet said with a smug expression. Bhet knew that the oceans were barren, and that the jungle seemed to lack the game he was searching for. The game the three men played was a dangerous one as the stakes were high among all related parties. Jih and Kag stood to spare their band from elimination but if Bhet was unsuccessful in securing food, all his work would amount to nothing. Kag saw this as a lose-lose situation. If The Elders managed to secure the debt, their own people would starve to death. The answer to not complying with their demands was obvious and painted a larger target on their backs for another raid.

"Days? People? This is much meat. Details are needed." Kag questioned, his mind calculating what kind of game they would need to start looking for.

"We will give until next quarter moon for meat." Bhet said, his mouth salivating at the thought of that amount of meat being dragged over by The Elders in exchange for their lives. Bhet doubted such a demand could be met but to see The Elders squirm to do so was its own reward on top of the paltry sums they would get as tribute.

"Seven days? Impossible, we do half-moon instead. This will be one month for demand." Jih shot back quickly, shattering Bhet's fantasy.

"Fine. Half-moon. Perhaps no death, food for life." Bhet said, shaking his head in agreement to the terms.

"This is bleeding buffalo Jih[12]." Kag said with anger in his voice. Jih agreed with Kag's sentiment, but he could not back out now that he was this close.

---

[12] A bleeding buffalo is a food source that rather than butcher for meat immediately, is instead kept around and used for its blood. The creature eventually dies and is slaughtered for meat and so the intention is still the same. Is death by a thousand drops of blood what The Elders hope to accomplish?

"Bring big game only. No Sarudeu or Smir-Tamdeu.[13] This Bhet insists or there will be punishment." Bhet added on with a grin as he continued to shift the deal in his favor. Jih's anger leaked over his body at what he agreed to but there was no other choice. Jih nodded his head in agreement and the two shook hands. Kag sat as the witness for The Elders while the others would account for Bhet.

He insists? Kag thought as he watched Jih shake hands with Bhet finalizing the terms of the agreement. Jih could only figure out how he was to inform The Council of the debt they now owed. This was the price of the peace they desperately hobbled together to achieve. Jih hoped it would be worth the effort. As Jih rose with Kag in tow, Kag moved towards the outskirts of the village while Jih remained.

"Bhet. Jih has question to ask. Why did you attack us?" Jih asked as Bhet's brown eyes met his. Jih hoped to find some sort of rationale from Bhet's mind. He recalled Dran's objections to gathering stockpiles of meat or anything else that could have stuck out from the other bands of Sundaland. Jih was a logical person that always searched for a root cause, but Bhet was an agent of chaos and difficult to understand.

"Why not? You are no different than anyone else." Bhet commented. His answer unnerved Jih, as simple random chance was infuriating on its own. Jih couldn't control chance, luck, or fate. All these factors have decided to work against his favor and now it happened once again. Jih heard all he needed to say and stared at Bhet briefly before turning to meet with Kag. Bhet had his fill of The Elders and dismissed Jih to join Kag.

"Bhet grows tired, and you must hunt. Make your leave. We will arrive in one month." Bhet ordered, while his men moved to return the spears that Jih and Kag placed down earlier. Jih was surprised that he would be allowed to return with his weapon, but they made good on their word. He and Kag were escorted back to the shoreline and now were left to their own devices to begin the trek home. Jih walked with silence as Kag caught up to Jih's quickened pace. Kag placed his hand on Jih's shoulder in support as he greeted him.

"Brother, Kag must ask. Will we visit Hyu again on our return? The Neck-Shells may have found her. Kag wants to check." Kag asked as he stopped his pace. He almost winced as he felt a cold sensation come over him. He could tell that Jih wasn't handling things well.

"Kag can. Jih will return home. There is nothing to do." Jih mentioned, not offering to say anymore on the matter. Kag could detect Jih's walking changed as Hyu was brought up. It was at these beaches that Jih learned to swim from Kag and Hyu who dumped him in the water. It was a grueling process that took many hours, but he became one of the strongest divers they had, much to the admiration of the other children. He had much to be grateful for and it was much to process. Kag planned to visit his sister's resting place regularly, but Jih refused to do such a thing. Though they only buried Hyu some hours

---

[13] Sarudeu or Smir-Tamdeu are words that refer to types of local deer in the area that are common meals.

ago, Kag wanted to return for Jih's sake. To Kag, it felt as if Jih's immediate attempts to repress Hyu's memory just made him worse off.

"When you are ready, you know the way." Kag said to Jih who remained silent. Kag changed the topic of discussion to something more at hand, Bhet and his insane demands for meat.

"Kag fears the deal will not be met." Kag said with much worry in his voice. He looked above him to attempt to figure out the time and reasoned by the sun's position there was still plenty of time in the day.

"Yes. Jih knows this. It was intended." Jih added with a small chuckle as he kicked a nearby rock where it was picked up by the moving tide.

"Kag does not understand. You shook on bad deal?" Kag interjected, as he gave Jih room to continue speaking.

"For time Kag, we have one month to prepare. We must plan our attack." Jih asserted carefully, as he tried recalling what was within reach.

As Jih kept walking, he absentmindedly kicked another small rock in the direction of a king cobra that raised its head up from the sand. Left on their own, king cobras were rarely aggressive and slinked off when threatened but were still treated with the same severity as a tiger. Snakes inspired great fear among The Elders as they provided injuries that none knew how to treat, and death was absolute. Rainforest animals rarely found themselves out by the beach but with recent human activity their patterns were altered significantly. With a heavy tug, Kag dragged Jih back some distance while the two of them stared at the snake. It didn't move as it absorbed the sun's rays but looked in their direction.

"We have few warriors for task. Tough kills to be had for big game." Kag mentioned.

The two slowly retreated backwards to give the snake a wide berth before descending further towards the water. The beach was wide enough for more than one creature to make its way, and the king cobra could have all the room it wanted. Jih and Kag kept their movements slow, retreating to a different path that led them further from the outskirts of their camp. The two took a deep breath as the sights of home gradually took shape. The smoke and industry of home filled their senses as they returned with a heavy heart from their expedition into Neck-Shell territory.

"Nagpu is small, yet it kills many big things." Kag said, as he reminded Jih to watch his feet on occasion.

"This gives Jih an idea." Jih commented as he and Kag found themselves in the vicinity of camp.

Jih watched as the other members of his band continued to labor without rest. As overworked as he was, Jih looked towards the shadows that hung over the open village. The sun shone high over them as another calm day was promised but their home remained bustling with activity. The day was still young and there was much to do. Jih was to report back to The Council and Kag needed to attend to his duties at the medical tent. Now that Hyu was gone, Kag would need to fill both roles and the difficulty of that dragged on him. Before this though, they both took a small breather back at Jih's home to talk again in secrecy. The two stood outside the ruined state of Jih's home. Kag placed his hand on Jih's shoulder in support of him. Jih gave a nod and pointed to the ground for the two to sit.

"Kag has special knowledge. Kag works with plants that fix problems, some cause them as well." Jih explained as he picked up a nearby stone and looked at it with a satisfied expression. Jih hardly considered himself a schemer, but his look of satisfaction was known to Kag. Jih felt as if he could have some power in his life return. The two met each other's gaze as Kag nodded in understanding.

"Yes. Some plants can be..." Kag's voiced trailed off as he saw that Jih was ready to reply. The two shared a synergy that only decades of knowing one another could give.

"Poisonous. Grind poison from plant and Neck-Shells will fall." Jih said flatly, as he finished Kag's sentence.

Jih looked at Kag whose pupils expanded upon realization on what Jih was asking him. Kag thought of his supplies and wondered what could do the job. While Kag was focused on healing, he occasionally received requests by Vut to poison the blades of weapons for the Hunting Team. He avoided leaving his material in the tent for long periods of time as children were curious and couldn't tell the difference between those and the safe ones. Jih and Kag calculated the plan as they traced the movement of their fellow band members. Logistics to meet Bhet's demands was going to be difficult if Tur stood in the way. Jih hoped to enlist the Stoneworking Team for their efforts, but Kag had other ideas.

"Their lust for meat will end it all." Kag commented, as he let out a small grin. Kag had reason to smile again as he imagined the screams of the Neck-Shells dying. If anything was to be done, Hyu's death would be avenged from the Neck-Shells, and they could watch Bhet's empire crumble before his eyes.

"Kag, we must keep this secret until it is time. We will serve tainted meat to Bhet." Jih concluded as he and Kag stood again before making their leave. Kag nodded in understanding and looked Jih over once more before rushing off. Jih waited for some time until Kag vanished into the crowd of people going about their day. Jih walked through the length of the village to The Council's tent and noticed the varying states of rebuilding that went on around him. While the rest of his band already focused on moving on, Jih found himself at a crossroads as he was now only comforted by the past.

Jih returned to The Council who were once again sat outside as their tent continued to be repaired. Tur leaned on his walking stick as he directed young builders under his watch. They were situated over a pile of gathered logs that were turned into chopped wood that reinforced the stakes used to prop it. The other members of The Council talked among themselves while Jih remained unnoticed except for one. Aab sat on the periphery of the group as she secluded herself from their activities. She raised her right hand and motioned for Jih to come forward. Jih's eyes drifted to Tur who remained unmoved from his duties but was prompted by Aab to speak. Though Tur was the definitive leader of The Council, Aab was more than capable of carrying the burden of information.

"Jih has returned. Tell us, what is your news?" Aab commented as she looked behind her. She was beside herself at the state of The Council and held a rational mind much like Jih. She was aware of he and Tur's animosity but saw it best to keep Jih on side rather than ostracize him at any given turn.

"Jih has made deal with Bhet. This will be hard to do. The Elders will give meat for sixty by the half-moon." Jih explained as he stretched his arms. He waited to see Aab's response before talking further.

"Aab understands this will be difficult. Yaan or On-Takom is our best choice.[14] This gives us one month to prepare. Aab will direct Hunting Team to build smoke pits. The meat will hold when it is dry." Aab proposed as Jih nodded. Aab wondered how likely it was that the conditions of the tribute would hold. Jih held out his hand in reassurance to Aab's distant expression.

"Bhet has his sights on other lands. We are useful to Bhet for now as an early raid will give him no food." Jih reasoned to Aab who nodded but kept some concern.

"The Council will answer on this. Jih, you are one of us, but you hold hurt in your eyes. You must rest." Aab mentioned as she took Jih's hand with grace. Jih nodded in gratitude as he lowered his head to Aab. He stood by and met a glare from Tur who turned around before Jih made his way back to his home.

---

[14] Emic word for rhino.

Standstill

Jih obeyed Aab's orders to rest but he couldn't until his home was fixed. Jih stood at the front and looked at the sorry state of his home. Two walls completely collapsed and exposed his dwelling to the elements. His roof made of thatch was burnt in the raid and only a few tufts remained. Bani removed some of Jih and Hyu's belongings to store in her tent after he left to give Jih room while he worked on repairs. Jih was unsure of where to start but saw that the Woodworking Team was busy at work with The Council's repairs. Jih traversed through the village as he made his way to a community pile of assorted resources at the northern end. Jih scanned the pile for anything of interest and met two recently carved long strips of wood for his purposes. He bent over and lifted as hard as he could. Jih felt his muscles strain as he attempted to lift the wood and started to second guess himself. Jih considered himself a strong man as he took labor seriously but found that this strip of wood was wedged under a large rock. Jih attempted to use the force of the wood to flip the rock over but was unable to do so. He gritted his teeth as he noticed his efforts made a slight crack in the wood. He then attempted to slide it out by rotating it slowly and nodded in satisfaction. Jih scooped the block of wood with two hands and dragged it along the ground to the front of his home. Once he arrived, he quickly placed the first down and retrieved the second in the same manner.

Jih lacked the finesse required to make sophisticated things from wood as his experience was best suited for stone. Jih weighed his options as asking Tur was out of the question and the Woodworking Team was occupied for the time being. Jih wasn't comfortable using his new status to take over people's time and saw himself in a much different light than others. Jih closed his eyes and attempted to visualize the stake that he needed. Jih realized his tools failed to do the job and searched for a nearby axe. He quickly found what he needed from a nearby neighbor who wouldn't mind theirs being missing for a few hours. Jih returned with his new axe and swung it in his hand as he admired the heft behind it. Jih wasn't used to using a specialized axe for woodcutting and was amazed at how much easier it was to hack off the pieces he wanted. Jih crouched over the long block of wood and worked his way down with the axe. He attempted to shield himself as best as he could from flying pieces of debris. After a couple of hours, Jih managed to make a stake that was slightly longer than the ones used to support his home but felt it would work with some adjustments. The second stake took less time to construct as Jih felt more comfortable in his form.

Jih maneuvered carefully through the exposed skeleton of his home and dug a small hole with his hand to secure the stake into place. He lacked a large rock to anchor the piece but did his best as the first was put into place. As Jih ran to grab the second stake and secure it, the first misaligned much to Jih's annoyance. Jih looked to see that the remaining stakes were reinforced with fibers and were tied to the other. Jih realized the distance required was a two-person job, but he attempted to do it on his own. Jih took a small pile of wrappings to use as his bindings of choice and eyed the space between the two stakes. Jih's fingers were cumbersome for the wrappings as he constantly struggled to tie the knot on the two stakes to keep them together. Jih's annoyance with his inability grew quickly as he nearly made a hole. With a stretch of luck, Jih managed to tie the skeleton together. His knots were much less tight than that of Hyu's and while Jih stared at the knot in an attempt for it to stay together it unraveled all the same. Jih repeated this motion for some time until it practically wore the fibers completely thin, and he had to start over. Jih could feel the light bits of rain come over him and sought to improvise as he grabbed an assortment of discarded furs to use as his roof. The furs were layered on top as Jih stretched them out along the edges of the stakes. A few heavy rainstorms could spell the end of his structure, but it would hold for now.

Jih retreated into the refurbished remains of his home and closed off the entrance with a flap blocking the way. Jih felt somewhat secure as his body dried past the opening in his home. Jih attempted to resurrect the campfire that was in the central hearth when he and Hyu first built this home together. In the small bits of darkness from his side of the tent, Jih felt around and found two pieces of flint sticking out the dirt. Jih hit them together and timed his strikes perfectly for the first amounts of sparks to fly off from impact. The fire in the hearth struggled to survive and needed more to last. Jih took a small portion of leaves from Hyu's former bed to use as kindling for the fire as a flame rose to illuminate the room. A low layer of smoke dispersed through the dwelling before leaving the top. Jih coughed and rubbed his eyes as the smoke cleared. The small flame grew and could now stand tall to protect its summoner once more. Now that there was time for him to process things on his own, Jih's thoughts focused entirely on Hyu. His memory of the event was hazy as his mind had already tried to suppress the raid done by the Neck-Shells. Jih stared at the fire and turned away. Fire was his protector and life giver, but it trapped him and the other members of his band. Jih ignored all calls for his aid as he curled on a bed of leaves. The only thing that Jih had left of Hyu was the necklace that he wore. Left alone without the comfort of any, Jih's eyes watered, and he sobbed profusely.

No reason to live, yet none to die. Jih thought.

Jih isolated from the rest of the band while he mourned. An existence without Hizo was painful but he felt prepared. The life of a child always kept the death of their parent in the back of their minds. Although Jih wanted more time with her, he accepted her death for what it was. Hyu was unexpected and some of her goals were hardly met. Jih felt immense guilt for her fate and lamented the times he did not deliver as she wanted. Jih couldn't change death, but every missed opportunity felt like a punch to the throat. Life for The Elders continued without pause. Jih only left his home to relieve himself and barely acknowledged the passage of time. He ignored hunger and thirst often as he felt himself withering away. The kind hearts of Kag and Bani noticed the little activity from Jih as they went about their duties. As soon as they could, either one of the two would leave Jih small bits of food and water. On occasion, Bani could see a shaky hand grab a few pieces and sip some water but not much else. She or Kag would always tug twice at the entrance to signal Jih that sustenance arrived.

Kag and Bani were conversing outside of their tent, carrying supplies as they were stopped by an errand boy of The Council. He wore red face paint that differentiated him from the others. Kag recognized the boy from his gait as one of Tur's favorite troublemakers. On the days Tur felt lazy and chose to seclude himself from village affairs, he entrusted a small group of children to deliver news to him back at The Council's tent. Bani raised an eyebrow as she adjusted her head to greet their new visitor.

"Bani is speaking to Kag, what do you need of us?" Bani questioned the child. Bani could tell something was off as they normally didn't get visitors. It was hard to hide on her face, but she wondered if the situation had to do with Jih.

"Do you know where Jih can be found?" The boy asked as his eyes met Kag's.

Kag took a deep breath and concluded that Tur was looking for him to do something. Jih wouldn't acknowledge anyone, not even Kag, and knew this request would not be heeded any time soon. Jih's inactivity was a topic of concern among The Council who hadn't seen him for some time. Jih remained in mourning for one week while Kag and Bani continued to oversee Jih. Bani wasn't privy to the inner workings of The Council and Kag's understanding was also limited, but he knew that not showing up to duties would obviously have consequences. Members of The Council were held to a different standard than others and although Jih wasn't treated as such all the time, there were expectations. Kag was prepared to defend his friend in any way he could and chose to stall for the child.

"Jih is out hunting. He will return with pelts, Kag is sure of it." Kag said with a grin as his eyes moved to Bani. Bani nodded slowly in support as she backed up Kag's statement.

Kag had always waited outside each morning for Jih to venture out of his home so the two could proceed on whatever adventures he planned the night before and today would be no different. He decided that prodding Jih to leave the tent would be in his best interest as people were looking to figure out where he'd been. A cover story wouldn't matter much but he was willing to pilfer a few furs to sell the image to anyone with questions.

The easily swayed child left Kag and Bani for the moment as the two placed their supplies on the ground. Kag knew they needed to act quickly before Jih could get himself into any further trouble. As the two made their way to Jih's home, they could feel the den of sadness that culminated around them as the outside of his home was hardly maintained. Bani could feel a cold breeze come over her as she prodded Kag to go forward.

"Will today be the day?" Bani asked with some worry in her voice to Kag. Bani crouched down and attempted to look inside of Jih's tent for any sign of life. She looked somewhat discouraged as she looked at Kag.

"Kag does not know about Jih. It has been one week." Kag said, patiently looking at the flap that was the entrance to Jih's home.

Jih could hear the voices of Kag and Bani talking some distance away from him, but he didn't realize they were at his tent. Jih hadn't registered how much he'd miss in the world, but he shook himself awake upon hearing that he'd been this way for a week. Jih gave himself a small breath to calm himself down before he started the slow crawl out of his tent to face the open. He inched towards the entrance, seeing streaks of sunlight peek through the animal hide flap. At first his arms emerged, but he dragged himself forward as he was assaulted by the rays of the sun that had practically stunned Jih upon exit. His vision clouded up as he put his hands above his eyes. All he could see was the happy smiles of Kag and Bani close ahead of him. Jih pushed himself off the ground with some difficulty as he was still light-headed from not much food.

Kag gave Jih a hearty hug as he shook him tightly. Kag's smile changed slightly as he noticed a particular scent was present on Jih. He knew he hadn't bathed for a while. Three days was considered the acceptable amount of time in between baths and a week was excessive. For cases when a hunt was particularly bloody, many sought to bathe as soon as they were able. Jih understood his situation and quickly detached himself from Kag in embarrassment.

"Brother, go to ocean. Jih needs to bathe." Kag leaned in for a closer smell and shook his head.

"Choose the river instead." Kag said with a hearty laugh as he got a small grin out of Jih, just as he was hoping for. Although the ocean and river were both suitable places for a bath, The Elders considered the ocean a communal bathing area where Jih's smell could offend others, while bathing in the river past their camp was more private. Bani handed Jih a small stone made from pumice to scrape the noticeable amounts of dirt off his body. Foragers from the Hunting Team would often bring these back as Sundaland was home to a series of volcanoes and these were found to be incredibly efficient for keeping clean. The trade network between the bands also found these from time to time so most adults kept one for themselves.

"Jih should move quickly. Tur has been looking for you. Make yourself presentable to The Council, Kag and Bani gave you some time." Bani voiced with urgency in her voice as Jih nodded his head.

Jih retreated as fast as he could from his home with his camp vanishing behind him. In his haste, Jih's hair had gotten caught on a free tree branch. He tugged hard to remove it and discarded the piece of wood to leave it on the ground. Jih knew the lay of the land incredibly well, so it took little time for him to find the familiar sound of flowing water. The path to the river was also carved out with the work of axes as trees in this section were favored for building material. The slow flow of the river was comforting to his eyes. He chose a particularly deeper section of the river and carefully placed his pumice stone on the bank. He stripped down and dunked himself in the water first, before grabbing the pumice stone and using it to wipe off the dirt that accumulated on his skin.

In the heat of the day, it felt like a warm bath. Jih palmed the stone in his hand as he let the current wash off the remaining dirt. Despite laying in his own filth, Jih noticed his beard lacked any considerable growth as he looked at his reflection in the water. His hair grew fast when he was younger, and he often had to shave.

Jih headed back to shore and shook his body as splats of water hit the soil from the bank. He grabbed his clothing and gave it a large dunk in the water. His buffalo hide was heavier than usual as it filled with water but was clean. Jih eyed a spare hand-axe was on the ground and decided to pick it up while he let his clothes dry. He could tell this was made by a novice, but he knew for his purposes this would suit him fine. Jih looked up and noticed he took refuge under a mango tree.

"Jih has food in teeth. Jih will fix..." He said to himself as he felt around in his mouth with his tongue.

Jih realized he also hadn't brushed his teeth either. The smell of mango filled Jih's nose as he realized he was close to a ripe few. He would have to take some back to Kag and Bani in gratitude for their aid. He reached and snapped off a tree branch. He bent the ends as well as he could and used his recently found hand-axe to scrape off the bark until small strips remained. Jih then used the exposed twig and lightly brushed it against his teeth while he took a handful of river water further away from where he bathed. He washed out his mouth with the water and scraped carefully. Teeth-cleaning twigs, especially from mango trees, were a popular choice among adults. [15]

He gave a smile to his reflection in the water, satisfied with his look for the day. He discarded the twig with a flick of his wrist as he redressed himself. The clothes were still somewhat damp as they clumped on his body. Now that Jih was presentable, he took a deep breath as he prepared for the verbal lashing, he would undoubtedly receive if Tur was involved. Jih followed the path of the river with urgency to find an alternate route to The Council's communal home. Jih noticed the scent of fresh smoke filled the air and he knew that their meeting would be starting soon. Jih hardly received any official instruction, but the chaos of the last few events left him without guidance on the process. Tur made it clear on the day of his initiation that Jih's ascension among them was not of respect but for obligation to one of their fallen. Jih noted their absence outside and saw the repairs of the tent were finished. He hurried his pace and stepped forward through some shrubbery that rattled as he did so. Jih rushed to the entrance and in a single motion, tugged the flap to signal his arrival and entered inside. Each member of The Council turned their heads as he entered. The Council were sat in a circle as they surrounded a lit fire that illuminated their faces. Tur sat at the far back of the tent and pointed a finger at Jih. His expression was filled with scorn on his arrival.

Jih sat down and was immediately assaulted with questions by the less senior members of The Council. He held his hand out to silence them as he was beginning to

---

[15] Mangos contain a compound known as mangiferin that is inherently anti-bacterial. Other twigs were selected for the job due to a high amount of fluoride. These aided in killing microbes responsible for bad breath, plaque, and other dental related issues. Jih's teeth also benefit from the diet of the time with little to no sugars.

speak. One of Jih's biggest annoyances was being cut off before his thoughts could fully form. Aab and Tur kept quiet as they waited to hear Jih's defense of himself. The fire that surrounded them crackled and sputtered as the wood withered away.

"One week! How could Jih leave us?" A woman questioned sharply as Jih nodded his head.

Jih hated how the topic was framed. He attempted to keep his emotions under control as he met the eyes of others. Jih compared their clothes and noticed he was the only one who wore the clothing of an herbivore. More than ever, he felt like a cornered buffalo as he sat in a tent filled with predators waiting to sink their teeth into him. The heat of the tent caused Jih to sweat some as he hoped for a breeze to relieve him. Jih's eyes met his ravenous questioners as they waited to catch him off guard or make another mistake to capitalize on. Jih understood their game well in attempting to get onto Tur's side as leader. Jih could hardly be any closer to these people, they were separated by a Recognition Hunt and did not respect each other as equals.

"Jih buried Hyu and rested." Jih explained with exhaustion in his voice. He hoped this explanation would be enough, as it was perfectly fine for other adults to mourn their lost ones for some time before going back to their tasks. The Council held as they considered themselves above the fray.

"Jih apologizes..." He added on, his voice trailing off as he was insincere. Jih's gaze turned to Aab and Tur who remained neutral in their expression.

Jih felt that he didn't owe any of them an apology for his feelings regarding Hyu's death. Kag carried more fiery rhetoric that Jih censored in the presence of the others. Aab shook her head in thought. She was the one that recommended Jih rest in the first place and saw no ill intent behind his actions. She understood that Hyu was an important component of their structure and responsible for the welfare of older adults such as herself. Aab lost her own partner in the early days of The Elders before choosing Tur and she understood the pain that came with such things. Tur debated the validity of this in his own mind. Tur knew he couldn't directly attack Jih on something like this so openly, so he decided to prod him by evaluating his performance.

"We have responsibilities Jih. You were not present for repairs after deal was made with Bhet. The tent you sit in now was done by Tur. The Stoneworking Team was not aware of your absence, and we are behind on worked stone." Tur huffed as he cited his micromanagement of the Woodworking Team as his achievement. The ravenous younger members of The Council silenced themselves when Tur spoke as speaking out of turn would label them a problem all the same. Jih remained vigilant as he knew his team was far more prepared than Tur had any knowledge of.

"Aab spoke to Jih and said it was fine. If Aab perished, would she not be mourned Tur? Jih has done nothing wrong." Jih countered as the old man's eyes tightened.

Jih's expression soured as the rules of acceptable behavior seemed to change whenever needed and were now suited to fit Tur's ceaseless vendetta against him. While each member of The Council was considered the most skilled in their field, Jih rarely saw communication with their respective teams. Jih always found himself entrenched in the grunt work that the Stoneworking Team provided and was lauded by them all. He knew that if they questioned his absence, it was for a good reason.

"These are lies, The Stoneworking Team has surplus of material. We make two tools per person; age does not matter. If Tur bothered to ask them, it would be known. Jih understands what is happening. You have always hated Jih, and you waste our time with baseless claims. Admit it Tur, your true thoughts are hidden. Jih has apologized for being absent and is ready to work. We must address Bhet." Jih stated as Tur remained unmoved. The rest of The Council looked at one another where their attention came to Tur. Tur tugged at his leopard print and accepted Jih's provocation. He let out a low laugh that unnerved the rest as he called for their attention. Tur cracked his neck where the sound filled the tent.

"You wish to know what Tur truly thinks? You are a failure brought by fate. An omen of disappointment and misery." Tur stated, as Jih was visibly offended. Aab looked at Jih with concern as she held a conflicting view of that to her partner.

"Jih fails? You are the one who made us lose alliance with The Jagged Bark. Jih does not know what you said to them, but Bhet mentioned he brought them here. Neck-Shells took our ally and made them an enemy. We expected aid and they arrived only to cut us down. The death of Hyu and all lay on you." Jih spat with rage.

A few members of The Council looked in shock at Jih's reveal of this information. The mystery of The Jagged Bark's betrayal made more sense to them as Tur was the only one who kept in contact. They were aware of the emissary's presence in camp but didn't address outside bands as this was Tur's responsibility to represent them. Tur felt the dynamic change as for once, the eyes of The Council lay on him. While Tur held absolute authority at the head, the scale of violence enacted during the raid soured the opinions of many, including his most loyal defenders. Tur rarely sweated as much as he did now. Jih stared at him with judging eyes as Tur rubbed his leg and the dirt. Tur coughed as he shook slightly in a mixture of genuine rage and embarrassment. Tur hated challenges above all else and a direct attack on his leadership meant all-out war.

"Tur has as much control over The Jagged Bark as one does wind. They were never good enough for us and they figured it out. Now they scramble like Denmey to bite at our legs until we bleed." Tur said as he attempted to wrestle control back to him. Tur hoped to deflect off his criticisms and point back to The Jagged Bark as a container for their hatred. Jih looked for justice for Tur to admit his role in Hyu's death while the advantage remained in his corner.

"Tur has done nothing to save us. We have burned bodies of those who will not return. There must be justice for this. The people mourn and depend on us. We must give them something." Jih commented as his eyes met the other members of The Council and stared at Tur.

"Hyu died for The Council. That was her duty. This is what fate gave for her. She was robbed of her destiny for something far greater. Do you know what it was? Tur knew of it the day she was born, outsider." Tur said with disgust.

Jih stewed in anger at the hypocrisy of Tur's words. Although Hizo was accepted with open arms, the love that Tur had for Hizo stopped only with her. Tur had always had it out for Jih as long as he could remember and Tur was always one step ahead of him, always cementing his grab for power. Now that he had it, he wielded it with a mighty fervor over others. Tur saw Jih being nominated to The Council as a favor to honor his late instructor's last wishes and nothing more. He doubted his qualifications on all counts and as soon as he had a chance, he opted to get rid of Jih. Tur worked to find reasons to oust Jih but nothing truly stuck until he noticed the fallout of Hyu's passing and decided to capitalize on this opportunity. Tur was mortified by Jih's crumbling decorum and lack of respect. He clasped his staff and motioned to hit Jih out of disrespect, something that was done to him many times as a child, but now Jih was much larger. Jih's eyes followed Tur's hand as it remained still and did not move. A few confirmatory nods from other members of The Council agreed with his words. One man patted the ground with his hand and quickly spoke.

"Jih speaks falsehoods against Tur! He should be punished!" An eager man shouted, interrupting the two's discussion. While Tur supported the measure, he retained a neutral expression as he received mixed looks from the others on how to proceed. The man spoke out of term and would be handled afterwards.

"There is no time for these games Tur. Jih made pact with Bhet, and we must hurry to meet demand. The Council is weak, Bhet has single arm and yet we cower. Use numbers to get meat we need." Jih said, his anger visible as he rubbed his forehead in annoyance.

"Tur told Jih to make peace. This is but a simple break. Ever since you came here, you could never follow directions. You have stood in the way of all that is important to us. Chak would never fail my instructions. Hyu would be alive because he was destined to be with her, and he would protect her. It is because of you, both no longer live. Tur can no longer walk with Chak." Tur said as he huffed air from his nose. Jih's voice became strangely calm as Aab studied his face. Jih carried anger that reverberated throughout his body. He lacked a weapon but desired nothing more than to silence Tur. Jih momentarily lost his composure but realized that Aab's eyes were on him and watched with fear. Although Jih was furious, he respected Aab's compassion during his weakest moments.

"Jih is not Chak. Chak has been dead for over twenty-five years. Get over it. You have told Jih to move on from Hyu, you must do the same." Jih commented as his voice trailed in disappointment. He closed his eyes and took a deep breath as he felt near his breaking point.

"Tur knows the story. You watched as Kwiekyaan tore him to pieces. You killed my son!" Tur yelled with fury in his eyes as he stood in rage. His own clothing was disheveled as the two men stood opposed to one another. Jih was tired of explaining himself and being painted as a murderer against an act of nature. He was only a child and would have joined the same fate if he hadn't acted as he did.

"You can join him." Jih stated while the rest of The Council looked in confusion.

Jih felt himself filled with an indescribable fury as he was triggered by Tur's shouting. Jih reached over and clasped his hands on Tur's throat and choked him. Jih hadn't realized how easy it could be. In all the years of knowing him, Tur was an unshaken mountain and was nigh untouchable. Jih could feel the vitality leave Tur's body as he was now brittle and bitter. Jih lost all control of himself as he let his darkest desire take over. It was one thing to denigrate him in front of The Council or insult the fallen memory of Hyu, but Tur's mention of Chak hit harder than anything he could have imagined. Tur's reverence of Chak was an encapsulation of their relationship of almost the last thirty years. Jih couldn't stand the pressure of being compared to Chak his entire life. Tur meddled often and withered Jih down to a husk of a man but would no longer stand for it. Jih was expressionless as his hands were fixed on Tur who gasped for air. The other members of The Council immediately sprung to action and shoved Jih away from Tur. Jih attempted to punch his captors but was pinned down by three of the men.

"Jih...will be put to death for this." Tur said as he coughed into his arm. Aab stood quietly as she took Tur's arm and comforted him. Her eyes of sympathy melted as Jih met her gaze. In just one moment of rash action, Jih ruined his entire life. Assault on any member of The Council was met with punishment which usually resulted in death. It was unknown what to do when one of their own committed actions against them. Jih knew that while The Council didn't respect him, Jih was a known man among The Elders and held a level of respect that the people would not allow for such punishment.

Aab walked to Tur while the other women stood at the corner of the tent with their eyes painted on Jih. While Tur's eyes were bloodthirsty and filled with revenge, Tur felt the touch of his partner and felt calm. Tur hadn't expected Jih to defend himself in such a manner and truly felt the grasp of death come for him. Tur remained resolute in that he now established control once again. Jih's outburst removed any doubt in his mind and Tur could spin any story that he chose where it was his word against Jih's.

"The legacy of Hizo protects you from the blade. Jih will be shunned instead." Aab said, her voice carrying throughout the tent.

Jih's expression gradually soured as he was worried. In some cases, shunning was worse than death. Those who were shunned had no contacts within The Council or in the band at large. It was an exile in all forms except physical. Those who were shunned were to survive on their own and were not inclined to participate in any projects. Their names were struck from the oral histories and were fated to remain in irrelevance. They could not take from the community areas or borrow tools or stricter punishments would be enacted. The shun could last as long as The Council saw fit, with many taking the ultimatum of it being the offender's life. The smallest children were taught early that to be shunned was one of the worst punishments.

Jih felt the anger fall out of his body as he heard the sobering words of Aab. His eyes investigated the fire as The Council surrounded it and put a quick vote to wholeheartedly to get Jih's punishment underway. Although Aab suggested the shun, she voted to abstain while all eyes remained on Tur. Although there a majority was decided, Tur was the leader of The Council and voted last to deliver the official sentencing. Tur eagerly raised his hand in support of the shunning. He basked in his victory with a smile of yellowed teeth that glowed under the fire.

"This was brought on yourself. Not only will you be shunned, but you will be exiled as well. Someone new will come. Leave in three days or Dran will kill you." Tur said as he grasped his staff and stomped twice on the ground to confirm his words and the ruling. It was understood by all that a new normal was established and the whole band would be aware of the changes in a few days.

"How can you be this cruel?" Jih pleaded to Tur who doubled down on his remark. Behind him, the rest of The Council nodded and clinked their various ornaments.

Tur gave him no answer and gave him a mean-spirited stare while the others followed suit. Jih worked steadily to build his reputation over decades and now Tur single handedly derailed everything he accomplished. Tur pointed to the entrance and let Jih walk away. Jih gave The Council a final look and left without a sound. Jih worked through much of his life to impress enough to get the admiration of The Council and the adults of his band. It was not only his dream to do so, but also Hizo's. As the two arrived as outsiders, Hizo always feared that Jih would never be accepted wholly. Jih applied all he had learned and was given that success. Although Jih had felt worried in the tent at his fate, there was a strange sense of freedom he felt knowing that he was no longer tied to them in this way.

Jih set out without delay to find Kag and Bani to debrief what happened. He set out with urgency as he felt his heart swell with adrenaline. The environment blurred around him as he rushed past a few children taking a short break. Jih almost overshot his destination as he stopped but could feel his momentum meet him. He practiced in his mind on how to deliver the news. Although smoke didn't rise from their tent, Jih knew the pair were home as he heard their voices. Kag and Bani were talking on matters not known to Jih as he tugged on the tent flap to announce his presence. Without another word, Jih was invited inside as the two looked at him in slight confusion. Jih usually announced his visits to Kag and Bani early and could tell secrecy was at hand. Jih spoke over himself and almost bit his tongue as he rushed. Bani prompted Jih to slow down as she saw the worry on his face.

"Jih is exiled and will not return. Jih tried to kill Tur." He stated flatly as he gave them a moment to soak in the news. Things would change quickly, and he felt they needed to be prepared. Jih didn't need to say anything more as he could already see the folds in Kag's face intensify. Bani looked confused, but Kag's face stewed in anger.

"This is unacceptable! Kag disagrees! Tur has gone too far." Kag asserted as he formed his hand to a fist.

Kag heard Jih's words but was hardly surprised at his statement. Tur was a problem for many and greater people than him reached their breaking point. Without any further mention, Kag knew already that Tur pushed him to act. He knew that Jih was virtuous in his goals for The Elders and had enough. While Jih had known to play the game, Kag was far more outspoken and knew his concerns needed to be heard. Kag's rage was rare, but when guided it was an instrument of power to wield. He got up to leave but was stopped by the strong hand of Jih on his shoulder.

"Kag and Bani. Jih has decided something." Jih said with defeat in his voice. Kag moved closer to Bani while he waited for Jih's response.

"Jih must go-" Jih said before Kag cut him off with a disapproving nod.

"No! Kag and Bani will speak to The Council!" Kag said, unable to imagine a world without his friend. It was well warranted; they'd been inseparable for decades and the stupidity of Tur would be the last thing that would come between them now.

"Bani agrees with Kag. This is not fault of Jih." She said sternly.

"Jih is no longer accepted here. Jih will find power rock to fix this. Problems here are beyond the ability of Jih." He finalized his decision to the others.

"Kag. Take over for Jih. Jih trusts you will do well." Jih said, giving Kag a tight hug. Kag was overwhelmed with emotion as The Council in just less than ten days had already torn his life apart with the death of Hyu and now Jih felt he had no other options left but to leave. Exile to a land strange and unknown was a pitiful existence and Jih was the least deserving among them. He stewed in anger as tears swelled in his eyes.

"What will Jih do? Power rock is very far." Bani questioned Jih as she consoled Kag. Jih had given it some thought but he proposed his solution to the two of them to see what their perspectives were.

"Jih will go north, Jih remembers that is where power rock flew. Jih will take the power and bring it home to Sunda. Jih will go for memory of Hyu, we wished to see it as one." He mentioned.

"By land? Do not walk, go by water. Kag and Bani will make boat for Jih." She said tapping her hand. Kag recovered his composure and agreed that going by boat would be best. The likelihood of Jih running into hostile bands was significantly less if he took a boat once he got past Neck-Shell territory.

The three came to an agreement as Jih pressed both tightly in a larger hug. Jih, Bani, and Kag talked about the logistics of Jih's plan for a few hours and Jih vented to them both about how the meeting came to pass. Kag and Bani looked incredibly angry afterwards, recounting it once more. After a few moments of silence among them, Jih left to go home while Kag and Bani talked to themselves.

"When will we begin? We should rest early." Bani asked Kag, rubbing his face with love.

"We wake early. Much time is needed for ocean craft. Kag will gather wood."

Jih's Journey: I

Dran awoke and her eyes were shrouded with darkness. She overslept and saw that her campfire died out the night before. The interior of her tent was bare as she slept on a bed of grass and had a small blanket of deer fur stitched together. She clutched it with care as she noticed an unusual movement from the entry flap of her home. Dran hardly got visitors, and this was a surprise to her. She lowered her head down and attempted to see who came to her tent. She planted her head on the ground and looked through the small space. She saw no footprints but noticed there was an object in front of her home that blocked her vision. Dran moved over to the entrance and used her left hand to lift the flap. Her eyes closed briefly as she adjusted to the morning sun. As she opened them, she noticed an axe with an obsidian blade. Dran lifted the axe up and opened her hand slightly to see that there was a covering on the wood. Dran recognized this as the executioner's axe used for the most heinous of crimes. As far as she could remember, she'd only seen it wielded once. The type of fur on it matched the nature of the crime although the outcome was always the same. The wood was tightly wrapped with a tiger's pelt and Dran knew murder was afoot.

Dran took the axe and carried it as she headed into the village. The productivity she was used to seeing was eerily silent as people were postured outside of their homes and socialized. It was a day of rest for The Elders, many were tired from working hard on repairs to their community. The Council thought it best to cancel work for the day to curb any negative sentiments towards them. Jih was the latest topic of discussion as The Council went to work on making him a public enemy. Dran heard bits and pieces of conversation involving Jih and his outburst with The Council and carried a look of surprise. Dran was stopped by a member of the Survey Team who recognized her. He was an older man that Dran recognized from her youth as her father was a competent captain for their group. The man's gray and white beard was bushy and hid most of his mouth as he nodded to greet her.

"Dran. You carry our axe. Jih has been marked, but you have three days. The story goes that his hands clasped neck of Tur and struck others like an enraged Tole. Go with caution." The man pointed as Dran let the axe hang from her hands.

Dran heard the story come from the old man's mouth but wasn't sure what to believe. She considered Jih to be a strict defender of the status quo, but a story like this doesn't get made often. She searched through the village square to find Jih and see what was truly amiss. She could see that practically the entire village was on standby as they ruminated discussion of the story. Each rendition of what happened the previous night grew grander in scope. Dran's efforts were stopped by her own forgetfulness, she needed to arrange the arena for an afternoon lesson for the children. She headed straight there without a second thought and started to build.

The Council's influence weaved through the camp like a snake as Jih received harsh glares from those that valued Tur's input. A town watch remained for the Neck-Shells or other raiders, but things finally calmed down. In just one day, Jih went from a rising star to a hated figure. Stones were thrown in his direction as members of the band called him a kinslayer and spat out other insults against him. Jih was powerless against the mob as he hung his head and tried to dismiss their jeers. Jih wasn't used to being hated to such a degree, and so their words of them weighed him down more than he cared to admit. Jih had few defenders now outside of his immediate circle as there were a few who agreed with his actions but joined the mob anyway. Jih felt the full effect of an exile as those who looked up to him now had nothing but their full hatred. Jih knew that low times were upon them. The community's piles of food started to wane in supply, but the people grew ever hungrier. The meat they did have was now reserved for the Neck-Shells to pick up at their leisure. Jih was responsible for this deal and was also blamed for their lack of food. The weather changed on a whim, and this provided unpredictable conditions for the Hunting Team.

Jih found resolve in Kag and Bani supporting him regardless of what happened. He felt honored that they would work to make the vehicle to start his quest, no questions asked. Kag urged Jih to use the time he had left to absorb all his home as it was likely he would not see it again for some time. Jih did as he was instructed while trying to avoid scorn from the others. Jih feared violence would come but he still had time before it came to that. Jih wasn't sure what to think of the lands that lay beyond. He remembered that his ancestors lived in those lands, and it would be up to him to reclaim them. As he looked up in the sky to note the troubling weather ahead, he found himself nearly tripping over a large rock propped on the ground. Jih hadn't realized it, but he walked through the southern end of camp to find Dran. She was accompanied by two eager students of hers that stared at their instructor. Dran didn't need to turn around to feel Jih's presence as he was a walking target. Dran knew this feeling well as she was often the target of unwarranted ridicule, but this was a special occasion.

"Jih." Dran's voice called out to Jih. She sat on the ground with her legs folded as she grasped a wooden spear and sharpened it with another piece of wood. It hadn't occurred to Jih that Dran would still talk with him after The Council's verdict, but she did anyway. He looked down to see her sharpening a wooden spear and replied.

"Dran. Jih is leaving, no need to cut head off." Jih mentioned, as he folded his arms. His eyes drifted to the axe in Dran's possession just a few inches away from her as she worked. Jih knew the axe as Hizo was the last one to wield it. He remembered the trail of blood that came with it and wouldn't fall victim now. Jih knew he was on a tight schedule but decided to explain his plan. He and Dran hardly talked but he found it freeing to express what he truly thought at any given point. Jih no longer needed to impress anyone, and his demeanor changed.

"Jih will find power rock." Jih explained further, watching as Dran lifted her head up in disbelief. She dropped her things and stood up, looking him directly in the eyes. She stared at Jih and slowly moved closer to him.

"Jih wears the clothes of Ker-Mah. It will be done for us both." He commented, tugging at his clothing.

Despite being exiled, Kag and Bani chose to view this as illegitimate and decided to grace Jih with some dignity of his status. Rather than go without furs of any sort, they cleaned his buffalo pelt as a parting gift. The smell of ginger and mango remained on his body as it was treated well. Dran quickly stroked Jih's clothing and moved her hand back. The leather was genuine and felt rough to the touch. This was a fine covering that would offer protection from the elements or a dagger to the side. Dran was aware that to find the power rock, Jih would be braving lands not known to their people and far out of anything they trained for. She imagined people much like themselves out there waiting to see who would come for them. She knew of Jih's experience with Bhet and talking with the leaders of other bands. Dran didn't know the details but felt it wasn't worth asking given the climate around him. Dran decided to see if Jih was serious about the endeavor. It was one thing to leave The Elders and find a new band to live in but another to go to their ancestral lands. Dran got up and moved the executioner's axe far from the others as she advised her students to stay put. Dran remained in understanding that the two echoed each other in situations. Dran's loss of Chak as a child was formative to her outlook on the world and hardened her. Jih now had to go through the same thing as an adult.

"Enter the pit Jih." Dran said, nodding to him to enter the arena for combat.

Jih pointed at the two students and Dran noted they would be observing. Dran warned Jih to not hold back, as she hardly sparred but remained a steadfast opponent. Jih gave an audible chuckle, but Dran's unmoving expression kept him on task. He raised an eyebrow as Dran knelt and placed a wooden spear in his hands. Jih grasped the piece of solid wood and moved it around with ease. It lacked the heft that he was used to and assumed she had to be joking. Jih was a well-seasoned warrior that was devastating with a spear. He lacked hand to hand combat skills, as his kind latched on to tools and made one their specialty. It was their duty to study every bump and crack on their weapons. Dran's skills were also especially sharp. As she was the bridge for the next generation to survive the Recognition Hunt, it was a task taken with the utmost importance.

"Show Dran you are ready. The world is hostile, and we must be prepared." She commented with spear in hand and oriented herself in position.

Jih knelt and adjusted position as he felt the soil course beneath his feet. Dran looked at Jih and evaluated her opponent. She knew that the clothing he wore had to be heavy and quite warm, but she would give no mercy to any opponent. Before starting, Jih silently held up his left hand, pointing up with one finger and then two fingers. 1 and 2 referred to the ruleset they would use for the duration of the sparring match. As it stood, ruleset 1 was very formal. This was often done for the entertainment of The Council, and to demonstrate for the younger children the potential of spear combat. It was intentionally structured in such a way that it could be timed to singing or clapping. They could only use practiced positions that were known by both parties to ensure the fairest outcome. Ruleset 2 differed as there was no formality attached, and all that mattered was nailing the killing blow. The person who initiated the sparring match agrees to the terms set by the challenger. Jih decided to opt for ruleset two, much to Dran's satisfaction for she wished the same. The terms of their duel went as follows, the first to nail a killing position would be the victor.

Jih and Dran stepped to the middle of the arena and turned around, their backs against each other. They were to take three steps in their respective direction before turning around to initiate the fight. Once the turn had been made, it was anyone's game from there. Jih and Dran counted down from three and turned, their wooden stakes positioned parallel to one another. The two stepped back further giving them a wide berth. Jih recounted the size of the arena as his eyes traveled to follow the oval shape. It was about the same size as when he was first trained by Hizo, and it only felt smaller now that he was an adult. The amount of room between the two was decent, but he would need to be efficient and not waste time. Jih reviewed his opponent and studied Dran's movements carefully. Kag was almost always Jih's sparring partner when they trained, and he used a rather unorthodox method with his technique. He only faced Dran a few times as a child, and the memories were hazy at best. He tried to remember her strategy as well as possible. Jih took the offensive and advanced towards Dran. His speed was quick enough for the wind to whip past his beard as he set himself up. Jih held the end portion of the stick in his hands and slashed to the side in a large sweeping arc as if he was cutting vegetation. He preferred a side swipe as the general reaction was to swerve to the left or the right of the coming target, even if he missed his mark, he could draw blood. Dran dodged, instead going for a lunge, where she advanced straight to Jih. He used the edge of his handle to turn the point of Dran's spear to the side, giving him just the moment he needed to recover. The wood let off a loud clang as the two collided.

Sweat accumulated on their faces as the sounds of clashing wood reverberated through the camp center. The adults couldn't bother with such a display but a few of the curious children made their way forward to observe but kept themselves hidden. They didn't want their role as onlookers to influence the outcome as bets were made. Dran embedded her stick in the ground and used that as a springboard to give herself a bit of a boost in outmaneuvering Jih. She used the weight of the wooden spear to propel herself and firmly placed her feet in the soil below. Dran landed with such power an imprint of her landing was left in the dirt. She ended up behind him for a moment and lunged forward primed to aim towards his back for the kill. Jih instinctively leaned forward, seeing the shadow of Dran's spear over his head as it touched the grass below. Countless times Jih practiced such a maneuver when fighting with Hyu. She often would raise her arm to crack her whip a short distance away and he would duck to spare its wrath.

The spear work of Jih's people was a dance given lethal form. As tools were an extension of one's personal spirit, their movements waved through the air in a calculated but free flowing manner. Jih felt this bond strongest when he worked with stone, and this is why he became a stoneworker. Jih hoped that by putting his best effort into making stone tips any one of The Elders could succeed. To the untrained eye, the two were flailing around without just cause but there was an intense battle of prediction. With decades behind them, the gap in skill was miniscule. The two searched for openings, with the distance between them serving to calculate the best chance for the win. Each imagined the movement of the ocean's current driving them forward as they struck one another, and just barely landed towards their objective. Jih sought a way to break Dran's concentration as she seemed unrelenting in her attack. Jih primarily focused on a defensive game when it came to his opponents, but Dran gave such force within her moves he was forced to react before she could.

The two locked eyes as the distance closed between them. Dran moved her stick around to try and distract Jih as she lunged forward, hoping to land a poke to the head. This was usually where the battle was decided, but Jih wasn't an easy opponent. Jih moved his neck to the side, narrowly avoiding Dran's dreaded double lunge where she feigned a stab, only to change direction. Jih's opponents throughout the years had different methods. As a boy, he knew that Kag relied on deception and trickery to get his opening, often talking to his opponent to goad them into anger before they knew he had already placed two lethal blows. Hyu tested the waters by seeing the extent of their range, making small wounds that eventually piled high to the culmination of victory. Her weapon of choice was not the spear, but she had experience. For the long-gone Chak, he only used raw power to get where he needed and it often worked, with many a child's spear broken apart.

When power failed, Chak would cheat to get his way. Jih remembered this feeling very well and was adamant about picking the strongest jungle wood for his own weapons. Dran held her wooden spear low only to rush it to where she anticipated Jih would turn. The wind of the wood cut through the stifling heat they generated and endured. Dran's stick brushed Jih's face as he slowed down. He knew that she had set patterns in which she attacked best. Jih decided to lay a trap for Dran as he intentionally left his leg open. Jih raised the spear over his head gradually as he repositioned himself. Dran took the opportunity to lunge forward, just as Jih wanted. He couldn't help but smirk as he soon knew Dran would make her mistake. What Dran didn't realize is that Jih pivoted himself earlier with his foot in the dirt. This gave Jih time to appear to the side of her and gave him a clear shot to the ribs. He tripped Dran who fell to the soil below, as she used her elbow to brace the fall. Dran saw Jih hanging over her with the wooden spear directed towards her neck as he slowly moved in position. With Dran having a free arm, Jih knew that she would not be able to wield her weapon properly and the victory would be his.

"Ha! You die." Jih said, noting the placement of the stick above Dran's throat. Dran's face had a grin on it that puzzled Jih. It was obvious he had won as after her fall; she would be unable to get up in time to attack again. Jih's eyes expanded as he noticed Dran's hands weren't on the ground as he thought. Dran had in fact once again gained control of her weapon. Although Dran was at a disadvantage, she wasn't going to lose entirely.

"Wrong. We die." Dran commented and used her free hand to point out that Jih had left his stomach open. All it would take was a lunge for him to be stabbed in the stomach, and he would die a slow and painful death. Jih took a second look and saw the opening she talked about. What a foolish mistake, the appeal of the sport had gotten to Jih, and he made a juvenile error. Jih assumed he emerged the victor, but it was a well-earned draw. Dran's two students patted the soil with their hands in excitement as they wished to be as skilled as either of them.

"Jih must practice more." Dran commented, as she saw Jih's extended hand. It was customary for the opponent that started the fight to get up on their own if they lost or tied, but Jih offered anyway. Dran took his hand and the two stood once again as equals.

"Yes Hizo." Jih said with some sarcasm, which prompted a rare smile from the often-irascible Dran. Jih was reminded that despite his skill, practice was always needed, especially now that they were older. One mistake could make all the difference. He needed to be ready for anything that came his way. He appreciated the impromptu match with Dran but had to get the rest of his affairs in order. Jih shortly made his leave but was stopped by a low call from Dran. As she turned around, Dran spoke to Jih once more, calling for his attention.

"Jih." Dran mentioned quietly.

"Hmm?" Jih asked, noticing a shift in tone.

"Dran is sorry for Hyu." She said, with a nod before letting him leave.

Jih said nothing more but nodded back to her words. While Jih remained an exile, Dran cared little about being told what to do as she had her own grievances with The Council. She would continue to acknowledge him as his own person. Dran and Hyu historically had low respect for one another on many things, starting as children for they saw the world differently. Hyu's sacrifice to save Kag and the child he was guarding made its way to her, however. The child was one of Dran's flock that was learning the art of combat and she showed great potential. Dran was grateful for this as she felt like a failure for the dead that were burnt and laid to rest. It was a burden many felt but couldn't express.

Jih left the arena with his pride intact as he left the camp boundary for a short walk. He looked at the decay on some of the trees with concern. Far off in the distance, a massive volcano let off large concentrations of soot. Jih wondered if these events were tied to the lunar eclipse embedded in his memory. The moon was in the sky while the volcano took land. In days past, the volcano was quiet and content. Jih knew that the land had some sort of sentience but to how much, he was unsure. The Council refused to investigate such matters as they were far too content with sending adults to risk life and limb for extravagant furs to collect.

"The grass withers like Mother." Jih noted as he knelt and rubbed a blade of grass between his fingers. It made a crunchy sound, something he hadn't heard very often. It appeared that the dry season came quicker and quicker each year. Jih's thoughts returned to the volcano that continued to spew soot and lava.

"The volcano spews hatred. The sky darkens and shows disappointment. This concerns Jih very much." He said to himself as he saw the sky lose its coloring with soot blown in the air in the distance.

Jih felt that the meteor's power would be the only thing that could suppress the ability of a volcano. Jih not only saw the validity of the meteor as something resolute, but he also saw it as the only means to rehabilitate his image and to return home for his friends. To prove himself in the eyes of his band, bringing back even just a piece would be enough to turn the tide and restore things to what they once were. Jih knew his time was up in this land and made his way to the beach where he knew Kag, and Bani would be working. Jih came by the beach to see that Kag and Bani had finished the boat for some time. He was surprised with how fast they worked, but Kag noted one was already made. He and Bani took it and made some modifications for longer travel. Inside the boat was a small basket made of wrapped animal skins with a collection of food to remind him of home. Kag scavenged along the beaches for coconuts filled with water to drink. Kag was unsure of how long he'd be by the ocean, but he packed enough provisions for one week. Jih looked at the boat and examined it. The hull was sound and rigid enough to tear through the current. Jih hung on the side of the boat for quite some time as he, Bani, and Kag exchanged words with one another. He was given a soft hug by Bani and a crushing grapple by Kag as Jih took a deep breath.

"Bani knows Jih will succeed." Bani stated as she retreated to Kag.

Jih entered the boat quickly as he didn't want doubt to cloud his actions. Jih knew that he needed to leave before he ruined anything else. Kag and Bani already risked so much to help him. He grabbed the oar on his boat and waved it in the water to test how well it pushed before he made the moves to leave. Jih made one final statement for the two of them before heading off.

"Jih will return soon. Kag and Bani, Jih leaves with love." Jih said, waving the two off as he paddled along the coastline. Jih gave them a final look back and paddled away, vowing not to turn his head again to see Sundaland until he returned victorious. The first paddles for Kag were harder than the others as he pounded sand with his fist. Kag was stripped of his friend's presence because of Tur, and he would need to pay. As Jih gradually disappeared, Bani left Kag to himself as she patted his shoulder for him to follow when he was ready. He took the time to himself as he ran his hand through his beard.

"Jih has left. Kag waits for his return." Kag said to himself as he rubbed his foot in the sand. He shook his head, promising himself that he wouldn't be emotional again as he knew this was important for Jih to do. Kag looked behind him as the village loomed in the distance. His home felt ever emptier, but he thought about his future child.

"There is much to do. Jih has left Kag with plenty. Kag will do this...tomorrow! Hehehe!" He said with a laugh as Bani looked behind her with a smile to see Kag in good spirits.

The Stone and Shell: II

Kag looked up at the roof of his home. He hadn't slept the past few nights as he kept himself up worried about Jih's safety in lands unknown. The time of the half-moon came quickly, he couldn't believe it'd been a month already since he and Jih set things in motion. The Council procrastinated on these endeavors, and it was up to the other adults themselves to pitch in for the efforts. For much of his life, Kag knew that The Council was highly important, and should not be questioned, but his opinion of them has soured incredibly as of late. Kag rightfully laid the claim of Hyu's death and Bani's endangered child to be The Council's fault. They were warned time and time again about the Neck-Shells being a problem, but now were forced to enact a huge debt for the veneer of peace. Kag's life was ruined from The Council's callous decision making and now he would be given a chance to set things right. Kag knew that to secure power in The Elders was difficult and for that he would need help.

Kag woke up to the sound of Bani shifting around on her bed of leaves and fur. He felt relief that at least one thing in his life remained the same. Kag decided to honor Jih's request and attempt to sell himself to The Council on picking him as a successor. Kag lacked any real stone tool experience as he worked with plants than any other material, but he felt with a strong attitude and a nice smile he could ease his way in. Kag left Bani to her dreams while he set out on his own. Kag emerged from his home and let out a big yawn as he looked towards the sky to find the sun's position. The branches of the tree above him obscured his vision but saw that the activity in the village was bustling as usual. Kag left without a trace as he followed the path of the river to reach The Council's tent. He looked above it and saw smoke from the opening to indicate they were home.

Kag ventured forth and barged through the flap of The Council's tent. Kag was a routine visitor when it came to prescribing herbal medicine for The Council who had varying ailments that came with age. Tur ate copious amounts of ginger that Kag processed to ease back pain and inflammation, and Aab ate turmeric for her heart. Kag knew the concerns of the others, but Tur and Aab were well taken care of. He lowered his head to meet the eyes of Tur who looked quite confused, as the remaining members talked among themselves. As Tur's expression changed, so too did the others as they directed their attention to Kag. Kag knew he was an uninvited guest but counted on this spontaneous gesture to aid him.

"Kag? Tur has not asked for you. Why does Kag come?" Tur asked, propping himself up with his walking stick. Tur had a fragile ego and surrounded himself with avid followers, but still resented their feeble attempts at fealty. Tur's opinion of Kag differed from that of Jih immensely.

Tur wore an elaborate clouded leopard fur that draped over his body, the newest of his increasing demands. Kag prepared for this moment in his mind a few times and encouraged himself not to fumble in front of The Council now. His eyes met the gaze of Aab who had stopped with her needle and thread to read Kag's emotions. He also bore the mark of a tired and frustrated man, but he came willing to do the job. She was open to hearing what he had to say. She extended her arm to the soil and gave it a soft pat out of respect for Kag to sit down. Compared to the others, she admired the dedication of the medical field and the prosperous conditions that Hyu and Kag once produced. They were truly competent, and now Kag was given the burden of responsibility to handle solely on his own.

"Kag takes over for Jih. Kag is experienced, ready to serve." Kag explained as he hit his chest with a mighty thud. Kag saw that Tur studied him closely and waited to interject his reply.

"Jih has abandoned us? He left earlier than expected." Tur joked with feigned concern, tugging at his chin. The others looked around and started to whisper among themselves as they were unsure of how to operate. There was no known precedent for a member of The Council to leave their post and to have a replacement.

"Kag has different experience than him, this is true." Aab noted, prompting a few nods from her subordinate members. She looked over Kag who looked at the group with a large smile. She couldn't help but accept his presence. Tur noticed this and agreed that Kag could prove useful outside of his immediate needs.

"Kag will fit. Good student and quick learner." She added, with little signs of dissent from the others. With the decision made almost unanimously, the last vote fell to Tur as the most senior leader. He nodded and took his seat and moved to accommodate Kag. Kag offered a smile that the others accepted, but he was quite bothered. He had his personal grievances with The Council at large, but especially Tur. Kag couldn't stand to look at his smug expression. As far as the work was concerned, Kag felt his tasks would be easy to complete. The hard part of striking a deal with the Neck-Shells was already conducted by Jih, and The Council was notoriously lazy in the band. They spent the latter half of the day discussing things of little relevance, while the real problem solvers were the working adults.

"Kag. Jih had tasks to complete. Will you do them?" Aab questioned. Offering this as a question was a light formality, if someone higher on The Council's hierarchy ordered something, it would be done efficiently. Kag hardly imagined these tasks would be strenuous on him as he gave a smug expression.

"It will be done. What must Kag do?" Kag mentioned as he braced himself for whatever strange requests that would come his way. Tur opened his hand out to the other members to speak their piece to Kag.

"The Hunting Team complains. Address them." One man ordered Kag, as he saw Kag using his fingers to keep track of the tasks asked of him. He gave Kag a judging look but nodded his head, prompting the person next to him to speak next.

Complaints? About what? Kag thought. He hadn't bothered to think about what the other adults were doing as his job as a healer kept him isolated from the daily business that was placed elsewhere. Jih used to be his lifeline for gossip as making stone tools was often a group activity, and he had a front row seat to what happened that day.

"Give meat total for last hunt, ensure it is separate for Neck-Shells and The Elders. The half-moon comes tonight, and we must be ready." A woman informed Kag as he absorbed what was being asked of him.

"Kag must make hand-axes, big need for project." Another man mentioned the demand to Kag. He gave a long stare at the lining of the structure that housed them as orders were being given to him. Kag had very little experience making hand-axes and with lithics in general. Most of the time, he just used whatever Jih made for him as a base with some modifications for his needs, but the process was usually lost on him. When it came to picking up the stone, he could imagine what he wanted to make, but the execution was horrid.

"Anything else Kag must do?" He asked with an exasperated sigh. His response garnered a few chuckles from the younger members, but Aab and Tur glared at them. Kag was volunteering to do their busy work and should be grateful for it.

"Visit Dran. She has bothered The Council many times. Handle it." Aab ordered, as her face was unmoved from her current threadwork. Kag already felt overwhelmed, but his mind categorized what tasks were most important, shelving the hand-axes for the last thing on his mind. He knew that he'd need a hand with those, but who would be willing? Tur was the last one to speak, this time pointing at Kag directly and moving his finger to touch his chest.

"Kag must find successor. Kag cannot work alone. Pick child that shows promise to your work." Tur said as he grabbed his staff.

He lifted it up and slammed it twice on the ground to cement his words as lay of the land. Kag wanted nothing more than to hit him on the head with it but knew to bow out gracefully. Kag was committed to playing the long game. He gave a nod repeating the tasks to The Council that he was given. Seeing that it was well within his memory now, Tur dismissed Kag from the tent for him to begin his duties. Kag decided to go in the order of the tasks he was given, this would probably be easiest. He hadn't kept track of how much time had gone by, but he assumed that the morning hunt would most likely be concluded by now before the next party would set out. Before Kag would begin his day, he decided to take a quick stop home to check on Bani. The path to home was dull as his fellow band members rotated to take naps. He quietly crawled into his hut where she appeared to still be sleeping.

"Bani hears Kag." She said, her tone showing she had been awake for some time.

"Kag has much to do. Are things fine?" Kag asked as he moved towards her and gave her a tight hug.

Bani inquired of how the meeting with The Council turned out, and Kag happily reiterated all the tasks he had assigned. When Kag reached the task of making hand-axes, Bani's face scrunched up. Although she arrived relatively late at Kag's life, it was already well known by her and through Jih's stories that Kag was an awful toolmaker. She chuckled at the idea of him perched over for many hours to make something.

"Kag works hard. Bani will make hand-axes. How many are needed?" Bani offered to Kag as she tickled him in the stomach. Kag laughed as he tried to calm himself down.

"Unsure. Just many." Kag mentioned.

Bani nodded and brought herself up from the bed and looked at Kag. She leaned in to rub her nose with his and she dismissed him to start the day while she looked for suitable stones to start the process. Bani left her home shortly after Kag and looked around the camp for suitable stones as she kept her ear low to the ground. Jih's exile was old news by the time Kag had taken over his duties, but what she did hear was the growing amount of discontent among the adults. The Elders were once again stretched thin and the pile of meat they had as offered was miniscule. The best minds of their day attempted to find ways to preserve the meat longer and settled on heavily smoking it to last three days. Two men were arguing with one another over something in the distance. Bani recognized them as members of the Survey Team where they located ideal areas for hunting parties to forage.

"What troubles you both?" Bani asked as her voice barely carried over the two snarling at one another. Bani raised an eyebrow at the two men.

"We are on Survey Team. No new orders have been given." The first of the two men asked.

"Bani, you are in good spirits. What can be done for you?" The second asked as he lowered his head in respect. Bani returned the gesture in kind as she addressed the two.

"Bani requires good hotspark for hand-axes. What can Bani do about this?" She asked, waving her hand at the solution coming to mind. The second of the two men pointed to the eastern end of camp. Bani nodded in agreement as this was in the direction of the Stoneworking Team's domain. Bani reasoned they would be able to produce Kag's order by the end of the day and with her help, even earlier than anticipated. Bani's attention was put on the two who argued as she hoped to guide them in the right direction.

"We do not know to go north or south." One of the men answered her. Bani nodded as she heard the source of the two's quarrel. She rubbed her hands together in thought as the gears turned in her mind. The problems that they were talking about seemed to be administrative in nature, which is what she guessed before.

"Well, north is beach. This is Neck-Shell territory. Until things change, we should look to south instead for food." Bani asserted to the others.

"Yes, but Vut said nothing! We must find more meat soon. There is not enough for the demands of Bhet. Berries though are in good supply." The other man explained to Bani. Bani took this into account and followed the dots. If there was a hold-up on the delivery of meat, the rest of their band would lag as a result. Pelts were constantly shuffled in and out for various uses, and Bani remembered the large debt the band was now stuck into paying the Neck-Shells at the risk of annihilation.

Kag took himself to the southern end of the camp where the hunters would be meeting. The southern end of their encampment was far less developed than the rest of the village. Kag saw the morning Hunting Team sitting on the floor and talking among themselves as they didn't bother to address Kag. At first glance, the haul was impressive. There was a bounty of giant tapir and a cut of water buffalo, but something was amiss. Kag took a smell and contorted his face as the meat was clearly scavenged. Depending on the quality of the meat brought back, the smell could be offensive to some not used to the freshest finds before cooking, and the drafts would waft potential stench away from camp. Kag stood over them and raised an eyebrow over the group of four who rested. Kag was confused about why activity ceased. The pile of meat seen here wouldn't be fit for a dhole to eat, let alone to give as an offering.

"You block shade of Vut. K-Kag, why is Kag here?" Vut said as he looked up to see Kag standing over him.

Kag looked at Vut who worked steadily up the ranks and enjoyed wearing deer fur. Vut and Kag hadn't interacted much in the years past their initial Recognition Hunt but gave each other mutual respect as survivors of the ordeal. While every adult hunted to some degree for their own personal meals, the stockpile they held was maintained by a dedicated team who went out twice a day before resting for nightfall. Although the hunting party was trained to recognize potentially useful plants, gathering plant material and berries was the responsibility of the Survey Team.

"The Council sends Kag. Complaints?" Kag asked Vut as he prompted the others to get up. One of his apprentices, a teenage girl, came closer to Vut as he ordered her to grab her spear. She held it and Vut grabbed it. He bent the wood with little effort and let the cracking sound of the spear speak for itself. The other two adults looked at each other, returning their gaze to Kag. They hadn't expected The Council to move on an issue and address anything, for their complaints fell on those who cared not to listen.

"Does Kag see problem?" Vut asked with an annoyed tone, pointing to the ground as splinters accumulated in the soil.

"Dran makes spears... Talk to Dran." Kag said with an anxious tone to his voice. Although he had only just started things, he already imagined a line of people waiting outside him and Bani's tent with their problems instead of The Council's, which was their actual job.

"Spears for children! The wood breaks quickly, Tur and Woodworking Team makes better quality wood." Vut complained.

His apprentice had a sullen look on her face as her spear was broken for a demonstration after she worked hard on her project. Kag patted her on the shoulder and promised that better wood would come. He wasn't sure how well he could keep it, but he would try. He wondered what was wrong with the trees that the spears were being sourced from, but then he remembered it was once again the Neck-Shells' fault. Despite living near the beach, a significant portion of jungle wood was theirs for the taking as they had a population entirely geared and trained for combat. Sneaking into the forest to acquire better quality wood was a high risk, and many felt uncomfortable doing it, with the last raid fresh on people's minds.

"Yes, Kag hopes to fix. Kag must know, how much good meat is there? This smells terrible." He inquired with a worried expression.

Kag needed to be sure that enough meat was allocated for the Neck-Shells but more importantly that everyone had enough to eat. Bhet's demands were outrageous and Kag knew he couldn't meet this in any sustainable manner. Kag weighed his options in case he and Jih's plan fell to ruin. Attempting to move the entire band was not feasible as the Neck-Shells would most likely pursue and cut them down. Their allies were tattered to pieces, either living in the uncontacted parts of the jungle or now putting arms against them in alliance with Bhet. Kag put his head into his hands as he knew that he was trapped. Vut held out his hand to Kag, stopping him in his place. He wanted to make his appreciation known, even though Kag already was in a rush to get moving.

"The Council has not sent person before. Vut will help." Vut commented as he lifted his hand to get the rest of the Hunting Team to follow his instructions.

Kag instructed Vut to separate the meat into two piles based on the demands agreed upon by Bhet. Vut snapped his fingers as he watched his two assistants scrounge out a pile of animal skins for the meat to sit on. He looked at Kag with a confused look on his face but followed through on ordering the others to start moving the meat just as Kag requested. The two watched as the pile grew. Vut looked at the rising ratio and then back at Kag's whose face was unchanged. He urged the crew to continue until Kag lifted his hand to stop. The total meat given was almost a ninety-ten split. Vut's face was in dismay as he looked to Kag once more to ensure this was the accurate amount. Kag reiterated to Vut the specific parameters given to him and advised to take members of the Survey Team with him for extra support.

"Vut must understand this. No Smir-Tamdeu of any kind? Only big kills by half-moon, which is tonight?" Vut reiterated as he let out a nervous laugh. He was joined by the other members of the Hunting Team who shared their leader's worried expression. The rains weren't generous, and they would need to penetrate deeper growth to find the promised prey.

Vut couldn't promise anything and was at the mercy of the jungle, but he understood the assignment and wished to live another day. Kag nodded and Vut broke apart from the group as he went back to his home to sleep before the afternoon hunt. With that task done, Kag massaged his forehead as he mentally prepared himself to visit Dran. On his travels, he bumped into Bani, who was busy looking over two pieces of stone she debated bringing with her. Kag's face filled with glee seeing Bani as an oasis to the growing desert of problems.

"Bani, you are not resting?" Kag asked, looking down at her stomach. Bani nodded her head no, reminding Kag that she promised to heed his requests for hand-axes. She held a small basket that was filled to the brim with stones.

"Kag must find Dran. The Council has problems. Where can Kag find her?" Kag commented as he panted slightly. Bani frowned as she could see exhaustion on his face but knew he was doing his best.

"Dran was by beach. Near...the spot. Bani is curious on why this is. She should be home now." She said, seeing Kag off with a wave before returning to her duties.

Dran and Hyu never got along, but she reserved a special distaste for Kag long since they were young. Dran's residence was a fair distance away from the other clustered homes. She wasn't a remarkably friendly person with adults, but she adored her role and gained the unwavering support of the children that graced her arena. Kag approached Dran's hut and peered his head through the open flap inside only to see her staring back at him with judging eyes. She was unusually close to the entrance as Kag instinctively backed away. Although he felt unnerved, Kag couldn't help but look at the arrangement of things inside her dwelling. She had an unusual collection of branches that were snipped off at the ends and arranged perfectly in order of size in the center. To the untrained eye, these were just random, but Kag was aware that these were all from different trees that were whittled down to their most basic form. Dran was using these as reference material for her weapon construction. Jih recalled that each type of wood held a different feel for the weapon and Dran incorporated this into her teachings. The animal skins that made her blanket were folded and placed in a corner, with the rest of her space empty. Kag rarely bothered to do such things with his bed, only swapping out furs when they became itchy.

"What does Kag want? Dran is busy." She asked, her voice visibly tired. Kag wasn't sure what she meant by busy, as she was sitting on the ground with her legs folded.

"The Council sends Kag." He explained, seeing her disdain grow before him.

She rolled her eyes at their mention which prompted Kag to reconsider this task. Vut had already been let down by The Council's inaction to do anything, so he could already imagine her reaction. Kag felt his leg be tugged by something. His first reflex was to kick, but he soon saw it was a small child who wanted to leave a present for Dran. Kag looked down and moved slightly to the left for them. The child rolled a small stone past Kag to which Dran gave a small wave of thanks to the young boy. Kag was surprised she found herself among the company of children in the vein they once idolized Hizo. She held little regard for her own mistakes and that of others but was exceedingly kind to the young. She noticed Kag was still standing in the entrance as he was not properly invited in, and she slowly motioned for him to sit down. Kag entered without delay and prompted her to explain further.

"The Council said there is problem...?" Kag asked, wondering what he was about to get into.

"Yes, Dran has gone fifty-seven times." Dran stated smugly to Kag who couldn't hide his expressions at all.

"W-What?" Kag said in utter disbelief. He couldn't imagine asking someone more than twice to do something, but fifty-seven times? What kind of person was this? Kag found it difficult to imagine even having that many problems, let alone the same one. He closed his eyes and reopened them, giving himself a mental reset from what he heard.

"Vut says wood is fault of Dran. Dumb and untrue. Woodworkers bring back bad wood." Dran commented, pointing at her branch collection.

"Woodworkers bring bad wood? Tur would not like." Kag commented in mockery as he imitated Tur's dry tone.

Dran let out a small smirk at Kag's impression of Tur, it was pretty good but still needed work. Kag's mind was starting to shape the origin of the problem. If the wood was faulty, Dran's weapons for the children were inadequate and for Vut's case, the Hunting Team had drastic consequences with unreliable weapons in battle. The inability to bring food not only of course endangered their group's needs but made supplying the Neck-Shells debt even more difficult. Kag sought to find the root of the problem instead and went to address the woodworkers.

"Jih was right. Tur should die." Dran said, blowing her nose in protest hearing his name. Kag was curious about her hatred of Tur, as she wasn't particularly close to Hyu or Jih, for that matter who had a much longer history with him from his perspective.

"Dran!?" Kag said in shock of her openness on the topic, although he completely agreed with her.

"World is not fair. Hizo gone before Tur." Dran muttered, as she folded her arms.

Kag nodded in agreement but kept quiet on his true thoughts. Now that he had everything he needed, Kag made his exit from Dran's home. He looked behind him to still see her looking in his direction as he left. Luckily for him, the woodworking area made itself known with an intricate trail of shavings that littered the ground below not too far from Dran's residence. He noticed a few of the adults were eating some berries as stripped logs piled behind them. Kag was called over by a woman who sat on the floor while her comrades passed around pieces of meat on a stick. She offered Kag one to which he graciously accepted, and they ate together. As he swallowed his food, Kag brought up the purpose of his visit.

"Kag hears there is bad wood? The Council-" He asked, opening the discussion to start.

The ones that were still eating stopped and glared at their leader and then back at Kag. A collective sigh filled the pit as the words of The Council brought up an assortment of mixed reactions, with most trending negatively. Though they were respected highly for tradition's sake, The Council's recent publicity was not great. Leaders always have their shortcomings and in the case of The Council, choosing to actively ignore its people was only going to make things worse. The group held a particular grievance towards Tur as he hardly showed any rooted effort into his own team except to order them around for renovations to their tent.

"The Council asks for too much." One teenager said, speaking for his superior who was still chewing her food.

"Explain to Kag." He pressed, looking for more details on the situation. Kag leaned in closer to listen to the young man's response. Kag grabbed a second skewer of meat but chose to save it for Bani instead.

"Wood needed for big project. Tur is head woodworker. Tur cannot find good wood." The teenager explained, noting Kag's almost subconscious reaction of anger as Tur's name was brought up once again for a problem. For Kag, hearing that basically every problem boiled down to Tur again was truly a sign of the times.

"Tur can also not be found. Is he in the tent?" One woodworker jeered, prompting a laugh from the pair.

"Neck-Shells own good wood. Too dangerous, but Tur says go gather anyway." The woman said, shrugging her shoulders. She put her arm over her student in concern of his safety, citing to Kag that the axes they had were not suited for combat, but to carve specific woods instead.

"Jih and Kag have made deal with Neck-Shells and evil Bhet, jungle will be safe once more." Kag asserted as he slapped the ground with his hand. He gave the group of woodworkers a large smile that did little to break their skepticism.

"Jih is gone. And Kag believes Neck-Shells? They will come tonight and dine on our food." Another chimed in, using the end of their stick to pick a piece of meat out of their teeth.

Kag couldn't help but laugh as he shook his head no. He informed the group that there was a plan to deal with the Neck-Shells once and for all, but that trust was required in time. He knew that the words fell flat when it came to anything promised under The Council's mark but felt that he had enough personal rapport to enlist their trust. To bring the point home further that he was on their side, Kag decided to take matters in his own hands.

"Kag is serious about this. Do not work until change is met. They will listen then." Kag ordered with a surprising amount of confidence.

The woman looked at Kag with a sense of confusion, but she wasn't opposed to a day off, or under the terms Kag suggested, until The Council decided to address matters again. She wasn't sure if this was a blessing or a gentle way of saying she was now out of a job. She offered her hand to Kag that he shook with satisfaction. Kag's day was going better than he anticipated. The last thing on Kag's list was both incredibly simple and complicated. Tur's orders of Kag finding a successor were the last thing in his mind as The Elders were fortunate to constantly have at least someone shifting between responsibilities as they saw fit. The Elders operated under an apprentice system, where the young that passed their Recognition Hunt would be classified as adults but would still be inexperienced. To be integrated into society proper, these newly minted adults often jumped around shadowing and working in the field with experienced adults to learn the various crafts. The smallest among them would join in these endeavors as it was never too early to think about your lifelong occupation.

All adults had a job of some form, and the accompanying students they have would learn from them until eventually deciding to commit to a particular skill. Kag and Hyu talked briefly in the past about getting a student under their wing, but as the two operated as distinct halves of a whole, Kag felt he couldn't adequately train a student in the same manner as the other adults. Those that were picked by members of The Council, such as Jih, Kag, and Hyu however, weren't given an option to move career choices, and were trained fully in their master's craft. Kag hadn't thought about the medical tent in some time, seeing as his day was hectic. He decided to see if there were any patients that needed his presence before searching for a worthwhile child. Kag's eagerness to help everyone nearly came at the cost of neglecting his primary task. His pace quickened as he noticed a group of children that lingered outside. Kag initially thought someone was hurt and needed aid but saw there was a curious look on their faces.

"Sit. Kag will be ready soon." He ordered, as they talked among themselves. He frantically looked around the inside of the tent for something of value to show. Kag tossed around dried animal skins as he lifted them up. His search was frantic, but his eyes looked to the corner of the room where he noticed a small sack. Kag quickly grabbed it and struggled to make a lesson plan on the spot.

"Kag teaches plants. Two leaves, same color. One is very poisonous, other is tasty. What must be done?" He asked, holding two leaves by the stem very carefully, as a few of them peered in closer to look at them between Kag's hands. For demonstrations sake, these were the same leaves but with different variations. Kag was met with silence, as the group uncomfortably stared at him for the answer. Kag let out a small smile, hoping to entice the others to say something but they held their ground.

"If same look and unable to tell... Do not eat either. Mistakes with plant are deadly." Kag explained as he lifted a finger to catch their attention. He received a few nods and lectured on the various types of plants that were common in the area, as he noticed soon most of them got up to leave and go in a different direction. Kag was annoyed, but he understood. He wasn't the best teacher for things, and plant studies to the fresh and new could be considered very boring. It wasn't active like hunting or scouting roles, and it was not productive in the sense of woodworking or stoneworking. In a twist of fate though, one decided to stay and learn more. A small girl, who Kag noticed hadn't bothered paying attention at all the first time. She was around six years old and had long hair that covered her eyes. She tugged at a blue flower woven into her hair as she looked up at Kag.

"Naza does not like crowd." Naza spoke quietly and introduced herself.

The two continued their discussion, but this time, Kag framed it as a conversation to understand the youth's perspective. Naza held a quiet voice that was barely audible to Kag and relied more on nonverbal communication. As the two conversed, the frame of Bani appeared in the corner of Kag's vision. She lovingly clutched a hand-axe and shook it a little to get Kag's attention. She already dropped off the goods in front of The Council's tent. Although Kag felt beyond overwhelmed with his new duties, he felt some semblance of normalcy after Hyu's passing. The work continued to come, but many hands make light work. With his house in order, Kag's actions were centered now on getting revenge against the Neck-Shells, just as he and Jih had planned. Kag looked up to the sun and saw he had some time to rest. His eyes grew heavy as he dismissed Naza for a nap before handling business. Kag swiftly headed home and yawned on his travel back. The familiar sight of home was warm and welcoming. It provided him with just enough peace to calm his worried mind.

Kag's nap was brief but enough to recharge his senses. Not much long after, the time was due to get things started. Kag quickly exited the tent and ran towards the village center hoping to ensure that his plans made earlier were put to fruition. Kag moved past a group of people to find Dran in rare discussion with someone else. Kag took center stage as he tapped her shoulder and interrupted her conversation. Dran seemed somewhat relieved as she hardly was one for small talk and wasn't sure how to handle it.

"Dran, have you seen Vut? Is the meat here? The meat for Neck-Shells. Half-moon is upon us tonight and we must be ready." Kag mentioned as his voice grew more frantic. Dran was taken aback slightly as Kag was usually more grounded than he currently sounded.

"Kag needs big game and Vut has not delivered." Kag said, pulling at his own hair. Stress was not an emotion Kag carried lightly as he could always feel wrinkles developing on his face. The mention of the Neck-Shells made Dran lift her head to look at Kag in solidarity. Dealing with The Council was one thing, but the Neck-Shells was another issue entirely. She curled her hand into a fist as her desire for vengeance was strong.

"Right. Deal with Neck-Shells, Dran remembers." Dran repeated. Dran never considered peace being an option would be the case. Jih's rage at the death of Hyu was well known and something she could empathize with. Although the two had not been complete friends, Dran felt empathy to Jih's plight, and the death of any member of their society was tragic. For those that survived the attacks of the Neck-Shells, the hate for them ran deep, especially for their generation who now led. They survived many dangers of the jungles, only to be cut down by people worse than themselves.

"The Council forced our outcome. Meat for sixty given on half-moon. This is the day." Kag explained. He detailed the encounter he and Jih had with Bhet, noting her reactions as she worked out the details in her mind. A few nosy onlookers watched as the two continued to talk.

"So Kag now needs Dran to fix problem, yes?" Dran questioned as she turned her nose at him. Dran was going to help regardless as she had personal stake but enjoyed watching Kag squirm to get the words out.

"Vut hunts well but help is needed. Kag needs much meat." Kag commented, waiting for her to offer a solution. Kag tempered his expectations as he knew it was a tall order to give.

"Dran was to take the young out. There is On-Takom north of here. Will this do?" She asked, lightly tapping Kag's shoulder to follow her finger. Kag nodded but held up his fingers in response. Dran lifted her eyebrows as she waited for Kag's reply.

"Kag needs two to be slain." Kag mentioned while he met Dran's shocked reaction.

"Two? This is difficult Kag. Dran will help Vut obtain meat, they headed in that area. We will meet them there and work as one." Dran recalled to Kag as she witnessed their leave from the village earlier. Dran looked to find herself willing participants for the hunt. Kag had his doubts on the young brood but had no other choice.

"Kag knows. Your warriors are...fresh. Can it be done? Time is limited." Kag commented, trying to keep count of the experienced adults they had around other than themselves. Those that he had in mind were busy and wouldn't spare the expense needed for such a job. The teenagers that were bound to have their Recognition Hunt soon could be of use to Dran as she came up with a plan. One rhino was a tough fight to have, but two? He felt the odds were truly stacked against him.

"Can, yes. Will? Dran does not know. Neck-Shells truly need two?" Dran asked again, her voice hoping in vain for Kag to say the opposite.

"Neck-Shells will not eat all. It is a test, but we must have it." Kag warned her. He nodded, affirming her question. He braced for her decision, only to have a sigh of relief once he saw her return the nod. She extended her hand, and the two shook in confirmation.

"It will be done. What will Kag do?" She inquired. Dran noticed a pair of teens that broke off from their parents wandering through the village aimlessly. Dran clapped her hands to get the attention as their heads turned. The two in the distance heard their summons and made their way over to her and Kag. They lowered their heads in respect to the pair.

"Kag has job to do. Bring meat and Kag will say more." He commented, keeping his plans secret much to the inquisitive Dran's disappointment. Seeing that things would develop on schedule, it was now time for the next stage to begin. Kag looked at the sun's position in the sky, he had about 6 hours left to do his part and meet the Neck-Shells with the meat as promised. The rest of the band were now aware of the peace agreement through communication from The Council and have steadily prepared for it. Kag walked by to see foliage trimmed as the boundaries of their village expanded. Bits and pieces of branches fell while children cleared the debris to make room for the two parties. The Elders were unaware how large the contingent of Neck-Shells was but made special accommodations to host the first arrival.

As Kag made his way back from meeting with Dran, he chose to stop by Jih's tent. He entered Jih's abandoned home and grabbed some dried animal skins that were left over. Kag peered into the low light of the home and found a knife and a small pouch filled with rocks. He emptied the pouch, cut the dried skins into pieces, and wrapped his hands gently around them. Kag figured these would serve as makeshift gloves as he did so. Kag scooped the pouch and left for his destination at the beach. Kag remembered the poisonous plants in the medical tent, but they were withered by now and sought a fresh source. He left Jih's tent and eyes then turned to the direction of the beach at the north end of the village. He walked with great haste as he headed through the ever-familiar stretch of forest that opened towards the sea. The smell of salt filled his nose as he looked in the direction of Hyu's grave. He took a quick smell of the seawater and approached as the sand once again settled between his feet. He carefully extracted a few of the hazardous plants from the vines that long reached the floor. Kag was unsure if the poison from these plants could enter through the skin, but it never hurt to be careful. Hyu had always made a great effort to not disturb the plant life, but Kag figured an exception could be made. Kag carefully picked each seed and a couple of bundled leaves as he carefully scooped them into the pouch. With his bounty of plants placed into the pouch, Kag made his way back to his workstation. As he continued his trek, Kag surveyed his handiwork carefully. He acquired castor seeds and leaves which contained the deadly compound ricin inside. Four to eight seeds were enough to poison a man slowly, but he acquired about twenty of them, along with the leaves that also in small doses could leave devastating effects.

Kag intended for Bhet to die but was happy to include the rest of the Neck-Shells. Kag moved quickly to get things started but couldn't afford a rush job. Kag was in dismay at the state of the tent, Hyu usually kept it clean when she reached her boiling point. As Kag lectured earlier, mistakes with plants could be deadly and he needed to stay focused. He moved aside a small piece of wood to use as a bar, while he grabbed a large rock to smash the seeds and leaves. Kag upended the pouch and watched as the seeds and leaves rolled out. Kag held his breath tightly to not take in any dust as he processed the material. His goal was to break down the materials to make a fine powder that he could sprinkle on top of the prepared meat and to pass off the mixture as a seasoning, much like how the Neck-Shells lather their meat in fish oil. This all hinged on Dran and Vut's success in bringing the meat he desperately needed. He bid his time for a few hours, making the powder as fine as he could. He carefully placed the processed powder back in the pouch. Bani made sure to do her part as well in gathering large leaves from the jungle that would serve as the container for the meat. Although the Neck-Shells were simple brutes in their eyes, she knew that Bhet's ego needed to be fed. Presentation mattered just as much as meat. It took around three hours, as the sun's rays waned to night, but he was met with a fortunate surprise. Kag looked to see a few fires getting prepared for night, and saw figures returning, dragging back sizable chunks of meat with a rug underneath. Kag felt relieved as he saw Dran's and Vut's familiar faces. He approached the hunting party and offered his thanks.

"Strong warriors, Kag thanks you." Kag mentioned, extending his hand to the teenagers who timidly shook his hand. Kag was relieved to see a massive pile of meat just as he told Vut. He didn't question the means of how they gathered it so quickly. Dran and Vut with their combined teams managed to isolate a rhino and bring it down. The carcass of a slain elephant filled the rest of the deal. It wasn't everything he hoped for, but it would pass Bhet's demands. Vut saw that the problem was fixed, and he gave Kag a nod before returning to his own affairs. Dran stuck around as she was curious on what Kag prepared for in her absence. She dismissed her students with a small hug, proud of the work they achieved today. Kag kept his voice low as she leaned in.

"On-Takom is fresh. Yaan less so, but one can eat." Dran commented. She then gave Kag a glare, noting that her work was done.

"Kag made poison. Neck-Shells will eat tainted meat." He explained to her. Her eyes widened in shock but returned to her usual neutral expression. She was unsure of how viable the plan was, but she remained impressed at Kag's and Jih's ingenuity.

"We are not strong for conflict, but for this, much death will be had." Kag mentioned, having entertained the futility of a full-on attack again with the Neck-Shells.

At once, the smell of the meat filled the village center and people prepared to cook it as well as they could before their arrival. The lights from the fire illuminated the village as Kag directed people to grab firewood and prepare a large bonfire. Some of the Stoneworking Team contributed to the added heat by sharpening sparks of flint to heat the wood at higher temperatures than by rubbing sticks alone. Dran watched with some impression on her face as the role of administration felt easier to Kag than expected.

"Poison will bring balance. Will they eat?" Dran asked.

"Yes, Neck-Shells will." He said with a look over the cooking meat.

The smoke filled the village center as many rubbed their stomachs in hunger. Kag grabbed extra firewood while others camped in front of one of the open flames. The Neck-Shells were barbaric but of course would turn down any rotten food. Dran nodded, finding Kag's answers sufficient for now. The sound of a man yelling with his hands cupped sounded throughout the camp, signaling that something was about to unfold. Making a rare appearance, The Council retreated from their long tent and huddled closely to the western side of camp where the Neck-Shells would be meeting. Tur led the others through the village center as a young boy carried a torch to light the way for them. Kag obscured his plan to poison the meat as he knew there was no chance for approval. Bani arrived with the large leaves and placed them a short distance away from the fire where men continued to haul the warm meat. Kag waited until all the meat was prepared and made a smart decision. He took the large leaves and separated the stacked meat into two distinct piles. He took about one third of the meat gathered to use as safe food while the other two thirds of the meat were aligned with the powder. To not raise any potential suspicion from the Neck-Shells, Kag also used berries to sweeten the meat's smell and make it delicious. Kag gave special instructions to Bani to keep the meat exactly as he set it before. Kag found himself caught in a rush as The Council made their way, with people stopping their tasks to pay respect.

Kag was unsure if he should accompany the group but made his presence known. He studied their clothing and was surprised at how intricate their dress could truly be. On the other side now, Kag never thought much about their presentation. Kag noticed that for this they wore special ornaments held together by fibers around their neck. Their signature pigments glistened in the waning light as fires increased in volume. Tur took a deep breath before gathering the attention of those in the camp by slamming his staff down in the soil four times in quick unison. As children, they were trained quickly to adhere to the stick when an important announcement was made. It always amused Kag how quickly everything came to a stop once the stick's sound was heard. Even where it wasn't audible, seeing the reaction of others was more than enough.

"Tur has made deal with Neck-Shells!" Tur announced, his voice booming through the camp.

While it was Jih and Kag who did such a thing, he instead took credit for himself. Although there was audible joy from many, there were several adults much like Kag, who did not take the news kindly. They were more interested in what they considered to be justice or vengeance rather than complete capitulation. Kag pretended to have a smile on his face as he made his way to The Council. He lowered his head in respect and Tur spoke to him with Aab by his side. Kag saw the smile of Aab and was compelled to answer. Aab guided Kag over to her and noted his efforts in organizing. Kag observed Aab and saw that her cheeks were bloodied with the mark coming from a sharp knife along with her red pigment. She wore an enchanting leopard pelt to match Tur's that draped over her shoulders. Kag noticed in her other hand, she clutched an object with resounding strength for her age.

"Kag has shown great potential today. Those you have helped come and thank us for our glory. As you sit with us, you must wear this. We do not have furs for you yet, but this will do." Aab said as she slowly presented a bead necklace. Kag felt them with his fingers and realized these were made of rhino horn.

"Kag. Take your place with us." Tur mentioned, gesturing to the other members talking amongst themselves as they were guided to meet the soon to arrive Neck-Shells.

Kag's mind was entranced by such an intricate article of clothing. Rhino horns were exceptionally prized for their use in ivory for tools, but to make them for something like clothing was a display of obscene wealth among their people. Kag caressed it within his fingers and savored the touch. He couldn't wait to show Bani but remembered to ground himself. The Council were not his friends, and no amount of jewelry could change that outcome. He remembered the plan that he and Jih agreed on and death would come today. Kag was struck back to reality as he heard an order given by Tur.

"Kag will serve food. The party arrives soon." Tur ordered.

He directed the other members to sit patiently, as the group folded their legs in spots they designated for themselves. The peace arrangements would be made within both sections of the leadership. To Kag's knowledge, only Bhet led the Neck-Shells, which was different from the multiple leader system of his own group. Who would he bring to represent him? Kag nodded his head and returned to the piles of meat. Kag looked at the rhino's corpse and decided to cut away the full horn to hold as his own trophy for the time being. Not only did Kag wear the ivory necklace, but he held the horn in his hands. He then dragged them along to the ground to the center as he did so. The other members of The Council watched Kag with much intent as he worked diligently. When it came to the matters of hosting a delegation of any kind, people took this with the utmost severity. Tur gave Kag a nod of acknowledgement and motioned for him to come forward. The space where Jih would have sat was now empty, and he was directed to sit there as his chosen substitute. Kag gulped in his throat at the pressure but remained calm. The moment he waited for arrived, the camp fell to silence. The Council sat further ahead, while the other adults including Bani and Dran sat some distance away from them, their eyes trained on the movement that came from the brush. The children who had been so helpful previously retreated into their tents and made no sound. With the last bits of sunlight gone, the half-moon arrived and shined where only the sounds of insects and the last call of birds filled the silent village. Kag was surprised as the Neck-Shells were punctual but arriving much earlier than he expected. His eyes narrowed as the familiar boom from a conch shell announced their arrival far beyond their visibility.

A contingent of Neck-Shell warriors moved into the light and carried weapons but dragged them along the ground. Their shells clinked against their bare bodies in a cacophony that filled the forest with sound. Their torchbearers slowly revealed their presence as a looming light followed them. They moved forward, scanning the area for where the meeting was to take place. Their eyes saw The Council waiting patiently in their multi-colored arrangement and fancy furs. They locked eyes with the group and Kag, while Bhet was the last one to make his appearance. Bhet had a turtle carapace strapped to his chest that he wore proudly on his body, while he lifted his one hand to signify that it was indeed him. Bhet's eyes glanced over to see Kag, who he remembered being part of the initial negotiations. He glared at him before returning to the matter at hand. Tur saw it best to lead by example and stepped forward. With the eyes of his village on him, Tur couldn't falter and show weakness. Between the two parties was the stack of meat promised as Tur hung on with his walking stick.

"The Elders welcome Neck-Shells." Tur opened, gesturing to the display that Kag had carefully prepared for them.

"Bhet sees much meat. The Elders listen well." Bhet mentioned, forwarding the conversation straight to business. His first impulse was to take a bite as Kag predicted, but he decided to act differently.

"You are the one known as Tur, yes? You will take first bite." Bhet ordered as he pointed at Tur.

Bhet wanted to ensure that the meat hadn't rotted in the time of hunting until their arrival. Bhet also considered making Tur do it to show dominance. Bhet gave a sinister smile as Tur stood his ground. Tur hated being challenged openly among his own people, let alone by an outsider such as Bhet. He looked behind him and saw the faces of The Elders behind him who only wanted peace. Kag took a small sniff in a slight panic as he wondered if his ruse had been figured out somehow. Bani matched eyes with Bhet, trusting Kag to keep his resolve. There was no reasonable way for someone as dull as Bhet to know the meat was tampered with, but he couldn't be too careful. Kag took pride in his abilities and calmed himself down. He remembered placing the meat piles into two distinct pieces, and he placed the better of the two next to The Council. Tur acknowledged Bhet's suspicion with some hesitation but proceeded. He took a hearty bite of the meat and as he swallowed, massaged his stomach which satisfied Bhet and the Neck-Shells for now. Tur retreated backwards with a scowl on his face as Bhet and the others advanced. Kag watched with glee as the Neck-Shells scooped the meat in droves, their stomachs fattening out as they ate with much fanfare while The Elders watched in silence. Their own stomachs growled but not an inch would be given to them. Kag held the rhino horn close to him as a trophy, and Bhet noticed Kag's admiration of his trophy. With food filled in his mouth, he demanded it as tribute. Bhet found it amusing as he could not only demean Tur but also insult Kag's standing as well.

"Give horn to Bhet." Bhet demanded as pieces of meat fell to the floor.

Bani shook her head as their gluttony was beyond disgust. Kag felt a surge of anger that receded on the fact that he knew the day was won. The moment that Bhet scooped his single hand into the meat and swallowed the powder, the game was over. Kag complied, knowing that he would get back what he wanted in due time. Bhet gave the orders to pack whatever meat they couldn't eat in one sitting to return back as the others waited. The Council and Bhet's court negotiated terms for the next shipment of meat to be delivered, this time with an even higher demand attached. While The Council sheepishly accepted, Kag sat with a smug face. The meeting ended quietly as people gradually dispersed. Kag waited with Bani, while Dran watched further away seeing the Neck-Shells leave in the distance.

Close to home, Bhet felt an odd sensation come over his body. It stopped him in his tracks, as he grasped his stomach with immense pain. They now digested the mass amounts of tainted meat given by Kag. He and the other Neck-Shells looked at each other, as some started to cough violently. Blood hit the sand beneath their feet as they crawled over, inching towards the children that remained behind. Their eyes were filled with tears as the adults before them withered, clawing at the ground like wild animals for water. The adult Neck-Shells were trapped in a prison of their own bodily fluids. The irony of being at the sea where not a drop to drink was around didn't evade the Neck-Shells in their final hours. The seagulls and vultures come morning would gorge on their beach-bound bodies. The surviving group left were given a choice, to fill the lost ranks or scatter in the winds by choice or by blade.

A Mother's Love

Jih's travels on the road took him to the southern border of China where a new and aspirational group lived in these lands. Dawn was coming quickly as a village filled with raging fires subsided under a mist that permeated through it. A young woman slept inside her hut and heard the noise of three others as she slept. She felt an intense thirst and woke up looking for something to drink. She exited her home and headed towards a storage tent just a few steps away filled with woven reed baskets that stored rainwater. She lifted one up with two hands and drank profusely as bits of water fell on her and the grass below. As she drank, she heard the faint sound of footsteps until they stopped. Behind her, she felt a hand on her shoulder and quickly turned around. A look of relief came on her face as she recognized the man before her.

"Sadal, you're eager to start the day, aren't you? You have grown considerably in your efforts to lead, and it is remembered." An older man addressed her with a sly grin. Sadal and the man rarely crossed paths directly like this but she savored every moment to hear his words.

"Ronkalk, you always manage to sneak up on me like that. That's a rare skill at your age." Sadal said as her voice carried through the quiet village.

Sadal had every reason to be proud of herself. At her greatest strength, she was twenty-one years old and full of energy. Her skin and eyes were a deep brown with determination inside them. She stood at a towering 5'4, above many of the women who barely breached 5 feet. Her face was weathered with experience but had a youthful glow that was admired often. Her hair was dreaded and kept at shoulder length, maintained often by a knife she kept in her clothing. She wore her kills with pride and custom-tailored her outfits accordingly to befit her status as a Master Hunter. All her people valued the hunt, but Sadal took it to a professional level. People looked up to her, and she felt happy to be needed but Sadal was hungry for more. Ronkalk could tell she was waiting anxiously for something new to do since they'd settled in this area. He gestured to the water bucket and grasped it from Sadal to drink himself before placing it down with a hard thud.

"I have a special assignment for you today if you are willing. You are one of my best hunters, but rest is always needed." Ronkalk said with a warm smile.

Sadal lowered her head in respect to her band's leader and locked eyes with him. Ronkalk held a dark brown face, and like Sadal, carried dreadlocks that poured down his upper body. The origin of his hair was gray while black remained. A burly man, underneath his grass coverings was a chiseled chest and stomach filled to the brim with scars that marked his placement as leader among their people. His face was rough from years of travel but was calm and understanding. Ronkalk considered himself a man of the people and grounded himself to further his vision. Although he had access to them, he spurned fur and often dressed down like the common folk. He had both the raw strength of leadership and a sound mind to wade through untested territory.

"A task that befits a star of The Broken Bone. There is Weypeu in this area, and the land must be cleansed. Our priests have prepared plenty of powder for battle if extra is needed. Make a team of your choosing and report to me when things are settled. I scouted the area myself once and saw that there was at least one that holds a den with a waterfall. It's the dry season so it will most likely not have a cub. This is a prime spot for settlement, but we can't hunt in peace with this present." Ronkalk explained as he saw Sadal's eyes light with fury.

She was excited to equip her throwing spears and charge once again at the enemy. Sadal preferred to destroy rather than create, where cleaning the land was a welcome and often sought activity for specialists. Land cleaning was the pinnacle experience of her culture's hunting, killing the tiger would restore spiritual balance to the environment and required the utmost precision to do well. Those who died during a land cleaning tainted the soil and the land would be empty and considered uninhabitable. Her band had great plans, numbering around 160 people. They sought to control the region from the beasts and hunt the strongest among them so that the future could be secured physically and otherworldly. A constant but fair struggle against the offers of nature and it was an honor to do so. Her people's overall population was small but many of her kind chose to stick together making large enclaves where they were. Organizing themselves with those they viewed as lesser was not an option. Her people were direct and didn't take kindly to being taken advantage of. Their strength came from years of betrayal at the hands of others. Loyalty was above all else the greatest quality they valued. Adopting the name from their enemies in years long since passed, they referred to themselves as The Broken Bone. Sadal felt a strong sense of community with such large numbers, but on an individual level, not all was what it seemed. The Broken Bone consisted of four bands that merged for large scale operations and lived a two day's travel from one another. Her specific band was known as The Painted Hand.

"Everything will be fine with me. Your training has earned me many trophies." She gestured to herself and spoke with confidence. She hoped to reassure Ronkalk's worries, as true respect wasn't something he gave out easily. Ronkalk's rare expression of joy was enough to fill Sadal with further pride.

"It's seen on your face. Make me proud, Master Hunter, for failure is not our way." Ronkalk concluded as he made his way. He stopped short as he noticed Sadal hadn't moved and was waiting to ask a question. Ronkalk nodded and let her speak freely.

"Before I leave, can I take Deeso with me? She's been wanting to join us for clearing." Sadal questioned, her voice straining a bit with excitement. It was some time since she worked with her sister, and her impatience was obvious to Ronkalk who was far more reserved.

"Only you and other Master Hunters may carry the powder, but I understand your enthusiasm. It is known that you Wanderers like to stick together. Deeso is with the weavers today once she wakes. She tends to sleep late but it's better to be well rested for the day ahead. Tired hands make many mistakes. See to your family and that they will be aware you will be gone for some time. Before you make your leave though, I have a speech to give later. Be present for it." Ronkalk ordered.

Sadal was left by Ronkalk now to her own devices. Sadal's first instincts were to go home but she remembered the state her home was in. Sadal originally built her hut for two, but it housed four counting herself. Aside from her and Deeso, her partner Nurzan, and young son Brab lived there. It was a tight squeeze with all four of them placed together and Sadal valued the open space of the village. Sadal also felt the atmosphere was unpleasant at times as she and Nurzan argued constantly. Deeso was only two years younger than Sadal, but she didn't want to leave a bad impression on her and tried her best to keep the ideal family alive. Sadal went on a walk to clear her head for the mission. She admired the intricate design of the huts that surrounded her as they were adorned with various decorations. These were short but wide structures with wooden stakes that came in the ground and tied leather around them. These varied in size but were individualized to the builder's tastes and their respective family that dwelled within them. Those that came from a proud hunting background displayed the polished skulls of their kills. Decorations such as shell beads or floral patterns from gathered flowers also accompanied the entrances.

Sadal could never grow used to any village layout as The Broken Bone were highly migratory in their fanatic pursuits to clear the beasts from their land. Homes were built and constructed in the blink of an eye as each village was built with a standardized plan orchestrated by Ronkalk in relation to the new environment. A family could pack things away at a moment's notice and each one had a net to hold their belongings in. She recognized that the outskirts of swamps weren't desirable as she found herself swatting away mosquitoes that drifted in. As the day matured, Sadal watched as more of her band woke up and started their tasks. The Painted Hand hosted around fifty members and was the largest of the four groups. Dedicated workstations were set up throughout camp, but people rotated in their duties. Sadal was fortunate to have steady work as a Master Hunter, but others were not as fortunate. Sadal traversed between two huts and smiled as she saw a growing pile in the center of the village. Each settlement of The Broken Bone hosted a circle outlined in the ground where victorious hunters would place the skulls of dangerous predators inside as a testament to their mastery of the area. Once the circle was filled, a ritual was held to thank the spirits for their prowess in battle. The circle was littered with the remains of hyena and dhole skulls with the occasional leopard. Sadal hoped to donate the tiger's skull for the circle and the pelt for herself. The call of the fighting pits at the west end of camp rang to Sadal's ear as she wondered about spectating a match. Visitors from other bands wishing to prove themselves would enter here, but a good fight also solved in group issues.

Sadal could only delay the inevitable for so long as she circled around to find herself back amid her home. Sadal performed many roles, but the most important one to her was her role as a Master Hunter. Sadal was no stranger to growing responsibility, but she carried it with pride in her endeavors. In times of trouble, she thought of home and the various forms it held, but even this would not keep her grounded. Home brought its own challenges to the young woman. Sadal entered her home to see Deeso carrying Brab while Nurzan hardly reacted to her arrival. Sadal looked over him first. Nurzan held a bare face as he caressed his chin. His skin matched Sadal's but was slightly lighter as most of his work was done indoors. Nurzan's eyes were gray which contrasted from the sea of brown around him. In the early days, Sadal remembered Nurzan as kind, but lacked the ambition she craved to support her. They were but two lovers who rushed to build a family, and Sadal felt weighed down by their choice. Resentment built over time between the two and things broke apart.

"You're home. Welcome Sadal." Nurzan said bluntly as Sadal grunted in response. Nurzan was an expert weaver and could never be seen without fibers to turn into string. His work consumed him as he thought this was better than the alternative of having to address his problems with their relationship.

Sadal turned her head and walked over to Deeso to give her a tight hug and a kiss on the forehead. At nineteen, Deeso looked to Sadal as her own flesh and blood. Her face was dark brown, and she wore her hair in tight brown curls on her head. She wore simple clothing, a coverall of deer fur that Sadal made for her. Absorbed by Ronkalk's band in the same manner as Sadal, the two shared a friendship bonding over their foreign entry into the warrior culture before them. They were indoctrinated to love the hunt, and the challenges that came with such a life, for being one of them was no easy feat. Much sacrifice was made where only those with a certain aptitude could prove useful to the group. Deeso pretended to be happy at the energy of the room for the sake of Sadal's child, but her feelings were far more complicated. Deeso knew that Sadal was lying to her about her happiness but found it impossible to convince her otherwise. Deeso took great care to not injure Brab as she stepped closer to Sadal. Deeso had a growing pile of supplies close to her that she had in mind for Sadal's quest. She knew that it would be soon and prepared ahead of time.

"Deeso, I'm going to hunt Weypeu for Ronkalk-" Sadal said as Deeso got up and pressed herself onto Sadal. She was beyond excited that Sadal could complete her goal of claiming a tiger for her kill.

"We've been waiting for this for so long Sadal. To hunt Weypeu is a beast that fits your status. I will fill your pack with whatever you need." Deeso said with a big smile on her face.

"Speaking of need..." Sadal mentioned, her voice trailed off as she looked at her son Brab.

Sadal held a guarded nature when it came to her son. Brab was a beautiful boy and was freshly weaned. His face was a carbon copy of Nurzan but held his mother's eyes. Brab's birth was a complicated matter as although Sadal gave birth without much difficulty, there were dark tidings predicted. Sadal was a woman of faith and understood the importance of the priesthood and their messages. The priests affirmed her initial thoughts and marked the newborn child as an omen of terrible things to come, the day he was born. Sadal remained respected from her hard work and great efforts, but few touched the child. Deeso held a much different perspective and shunned the words of priests and often looked after Brab, being more of a mother than Sadal. Sadal and Nurzan didn't converse much as the demands of Ronkalk grew ever greater.

"I'm sorry Sadal, I can't take care of Brab today, Ronkalk has me out with the weavers and you know how much patience that requires. Besides, your young warrior should learn from his mother about the hunt! It's never too early." Deeso said to Sadal as she gently scooped up the young boy and placed him in Sadal's hands. Deeso turned her attention to Nurzan and pointed with her finger as she dreaded having to spend this time alone without Sadal or Brab to keep her company.

"Understood. I'll take Brab for a few days while my team and I deal with the Weypeu in our area. We'll all sleep better when I finally put that beast to the spear." Sadal said with her hand curling a fist. The young Brab watched his mother and wiggled his fingers. He briefly formed the same gesture before attempting to eat dirt once more. Sadal awkwardly rocked Brab in her hands while Deeso gave a warm grin. Motherhood was challenging for Sadal as she was mostly absent for clearing caves and other areas on Ronkalk's behalf.

"I can watch my son." Nurzan interrupted as he received a glare from Deeso and an apathetic response from Sadal.

"Do you want to take Brab then?" Sadal asked, her voice breaking slightly as the two locked eyes.

"No. On second thought, I don't. I can't be distracted right now since Ronkalk wants a gift made for Stobai. Do what you want with him." Nurzan said as he waved his hand to end the discussion.

"Then what was the point-" Sadal said, as her anger started to rise at his comment.

"How about this Sadal. You get everything set up for Ronkalk's needs and I will spend some time with the boy. When you're ready, I will have your pack prepared and his clothing changed." Deeso commented as Sadal gave a small grin to her. Deeso scooped up Brab and carried him up with her arms as the boy made a funny face that amused her.

"Thank you Deeso. We'll hunt soon, I know you've been wanting to do that." Sadal said as she bowed her head before making her leave.

Sadal couldn't help but be thankful for Deeso. Any day now she was this close to losing herself to anger and looked for any method she could to ground herself. Sadal looked to the village center to see who would make her contingent of warriors. Ronkalk worked ahead and made a summons for warriors willing to test their stone at Sadal's command. Many answered the call, but few held Sadal's specific criteria. Sadal's eyes drifted to a group of ants that marched by carrying a piece of decayed fruit as she likened their structure to her own. The Broken Bone were a group of powerful ants that swarmed the enemy until they were defeated. She continued her pace until she was stopped by a man that she brushed shoulders with. Sadal lifted her head and scowled.

"Oh Sadal, seems you can never keep track of where you're going." The man derided as he stared Sadal down.

"Don't make me laugh Zulag. Ronkalk trusted me to take out the Weypeu. Go on and sharpen your knives or whatever you do." Sadal taunted.

Sadal and Zulag had a lengthy history, both were Master Hunters and competed often for Ronkalk's approval. Zulag wasn't the biggest fan of Sadal, but his main rivalry was with Deeso who constantly found her way to meddle. Zulag was the nephew of Ronkalk, and the de facto leader primed to be the successor of The Broken Bone. In their society where might was right as law of the land, decrees of blood relation were seen as skeptical choices to make. The strong were who did the decision making. Compared to Sadal and many others though, Zulag was no slouch. He was twenty years old and kept a well-toned body. He had a higher view than most as he stood at 5'9. His skin held patches of white discoloration on his otherwise tanned skin. Some think he was cursed by a spirit, while others believe it was a punishment for sins done by his ancestors. His face was often adorned with a red pigment that drifted down his cheeks and appeared as if his eyes were bleeding. He had a thick beard that was well trimmed and hair that was loose rather than tightly packed like the other men. He wore clothes constructed from dhole skins, and the head served as a hood to keep the rain out and served as camouflage. While many wore an assortment of grass with light processed leather, he chose to wear furs for status. It didn't matter to him if he constantly sweated from the heat, only that he looked better than everyone else. He was used to giving orders rather than carrying them out, but his aunt and uncle put him to task. Although his relatives have urged him to find a partner within the band, he was more concerned about cementing his place.

"Right. You're gonna take on a Weypeu all on your little lonesome. Oh, I've seen your team. They can hardly catch a Perkaku let alone anything dangerous. A stiff breeze-" Zulag mentioned as Sadal interrupted him. Zulag's voice betrayed his appearance as it was hardly as gruff as the man before her. It wasn't high pitched, but it sounded off for who he was.

"Spare me your complaints, the jungle is full of Weypeu. I'll bring back the biggest of them and you'll all see that skull on the mound." Sadal huffed as she gestured with her head. Zulag ran his hand through his beard as he let out a hearty laugh before choosing to leave the conversation.

As Sadal reached the northeastern end of the camp which stored their weapons for outer travel, she looked at the assortment of people at her disposal that waited outside. Sadal was aware of the land Ronkalk spoke of and assessed what would be best for travel. Sadal and Zulag both felt a slight detachment to those that served under their command as Master Hunters. Although Sadal enjoyed her role, the amount of people in her collective band meant that the teams were always different for big hunts. She didn't get to grow close with those that accompanied her, and she felt disconnected as she had to learn all new names, their stories, and every little other thing they decided to throw her way only to die in front of her. Sadal rightfully assumed the job would break down a lesser woman than her. Ronkalk's leadership style forced his band to rotate roles so that each one could be proficient in the other's occupation. He believed it was the best way to build group rapport, but Sadal also considered it a practical reason for a viable replacement when something bad happened. She became jaded with the constant rotation but vowed to never let it compromise the mission at hand.

As hunting leader, she ran a strict unit, with a dedicated plan made well in advance using their knowledge of the surroundings. She looked over her team, who wore leopard fur and pigmented stripes as makeshift camouflage. They carried small torches to provide light, and to cover themselves in smoke to ward off mosquitoes while masking their scent. On their person were small sacks that hung on the back, filled with rations and tools. Sadal's specialization was the throwing spear, which she launched by hand with deadly efficiency at her target while the others preferred to use axes or knives. They were extensively shortened down and were light to carry. The lethality came from the sharpened points and the speed at which they could be thrown. Sadal ordered one of the axe wielding members of her strike team to carry spears like her own for extra ranged coverage. With her team made, Sadal remembered that she needed to visit Ronkalk and attend to Deeso to collect Brab.

Spread throughout the camp was the sound of industry as people worked on various tools and tasks of their own. A day in their shoes was always busy. Ronkalk sat on a stump some distance from his home, marked with the skull of a leopard in front, a kill he made on his own. A warm fire greeted Sadal as she made her way towards him with her team. Ronkalk's face was inviting and kind as he looked with approval at her team composition. She always felt as if she was intruding on an important matter. This was something she internalized greatly due to her status. Sadal was previously an outsider to this group, but quickly rose to become a prominent voice among her community. People in the community like her are labeled as Wanderers, outcasts that were without a band of their own for one reason or another. Some were accepted openly given the right story, while others were viewed as a curse under the varying views of superstition. On their person, they had an engraved mark cut into them, usually present on their hand, shoulder, or back. Sadal's was on her dominant left hand and Deeso carried one as well.

Ronkalk felt the former when it came to Sadal, as he saw Wanderers as a means to expand the vision he had for his people. His grand vision of peace and security. Outsider perspectives were important, and he could put them to work just as any other. He was often seen testing tools of his design, made by one of their expert crafters. Ronkalk held a pair of bolas in his hands as he watched them sway back and forth. He brought his attention to the group of people in front of him and addressed them.

"My respect for your quick thinking is well earned." Ronkalk answered, holding his hand out as a sign of acknowledgment. She nodded and graciously returned the gesture.

"Are you concerned about them? Their experience is variable, but I trust you can line them well for this. As Master Hunter you hold first claim for the kill. Your team is to support you in this endeavor." Ronkalk mentioned, placing his hand on her forehead with a friendly tap.

"Not at all. It's just one more thing for me to do." Sadal responded with confidence in her voice. Sadal had always been her own person and knew how to say no with ease, but when it came to Ronkalk, something compelled her to go above and beyond.

Ronkalk helped himself up from the stump and waved his hand over. A man with a horn carved out of a water buffalo's everyone to listen to his words. The sound reverberated through the camp. Speeches were rare for Ronkalk, as he much preferred to talk to people as individuals. Ronkalk spoke with a power that grinded everything to a halt. Deeso's head turned as she heard the horn and quickly shouldered Brab while Nurzan followed. She sat quietly on the outskirts, just barely picking up his words, while she looked to find Sadal in the crowd. Ronkalk raised his fist into the air that the others followed before lowering them.

"Members of The Broken Bone, I come to bring you in good spirits. Do not lose yourself now that we have gotten so close. In my day, I would have never imagined the lengths we overcame together. When I was young, the land around us was grassland and now we contend with forest and swamp. The beasts are mighty here. The trail has been difficult, and we have lost a few on the way. It would seem in our haste that we have forgotten where we come from. Our roots. I will remind you of that today. When we came from the west, we faced a life of toil and misery. It was through my legacy of the ancestors before me that the path was given to us. Life is cruel, and so are we, but this is not forever our fate. We are to build a new path, to purge the predator, clear the land, and achieve a lasting peace. This is the message I received when I took control and it is one, we will accomplish as one. The priests have made it so."[16] Ronkalk spoke with gusto.

Sadal and Deeso watched in awe as he spoke, the power that boomed from his voice was truly something to behold. Ronkalk captured an audience with ease as he could unite any to his common cause. His war against the beasts was a goal that appealed to many, but his drive and organization was something unmatched. Deeso felt they were on the verge of a golden age with Ronkalk at the helm of leadership.

"It was this wetland that I saw a great settlement to be had. But before we build and make our way, there must be more to be done. We have run into a problem. The Forest Seekers have not been hospitable to our kind, and they are a thorn in my side. [17]

---

[16] Sadal and her people are Modern Humans. Originally her people were from the far reaches of the west, boldly walking through from Africa to settle among the many lands that made up South Asia. Modern Humans in the archaeological record have been detected to have lived as far as modern-day Laos, Cambodia, Vietnam, and Southern China. There has been increasing amounts of evidence regarding earlier wave dispersals during the Paleolithic and her people were among them.

[17] The Forest Seekers were the name given to the local population of Denisovans that lived in the areas they wished to settle. Generally, a peaceful and sophisticated group, they offered little resistance to incursions on their territory until recently, with one group in particular causing trouble for Ronkalk's scouts and the other Modern Human bands.

We have tried everything, but the path now has led us to violence. They say we desecrate their way of life. They see the predator as not their equal, but their superior. It is a weakness." Ronkalk stated, as his eyes were trained on the crowd who talked among themselves.

"If you see one, kill one. The time for negotiations is over. I have delivered my word, see to it that it is done. I will do my part and I expect you all to do the same." Ronkalk demanded sharply.

Ronkalk's speech was closed off with the sound of rhythmic patting of the ground as people pounded it in respect. Sadal was enamored at such a display of power as Ronkalk once again reinforced why he was the boss. Even if Sadal's home life was starting to wear itself thin, she could trust Ronkalk would lead them through anything. Sadal felt invigorated once more and made her way to Deeso to retrieve her gear. Deeso returned home to quickly pack Sadal's bag. She was a master at maximizing space as she fit some scavenged provisions and secured the small Brab in the same pouch. She spit on the baby's forehead for good luck as she closed the pouch just enough so he could breathe well but stay secure. Deeso propped up three of Sadal's throwing spears that maintained its sharp edge for the hunt. Deeso carefully attached the powder bag and reinforced it with a knot as a small bit of gray leaked from the top. Deeso was confident in Sadal's abilities that she'd only need two, but more could be made on the hunt. She was excited to see that Brab's first hunt to witness would be a creature as mighty as a tiger. Sadal approached Deeso with a smile as she saw her sister point to a full pack with food and the young Brab in tow. Sadal gave Deeso a long hug before carefully securing everything. She looked back at Deeso once more before meeting the rest of her team on the outskirts of their village. The road to the region where they were going was a two day's trek, which was the average fare for a big hunt. Her company of warriors stood at the ready, the teams were often small to keep needs for supplies low. A group of five were present with a smile on their faces. The tiger was a hunt of great challenge, one that was surely needed after the scores of small game they were consistently preying upon. With Sadal and Brab, their crew was seven.

"Is everyone ready to go?" Sadal asked, already knowing the answer.

The two-day trek was by all accounts dull. The conversation they did have was focused on the specifics of the plan to clear out caves for tigers and other logistical concerns. Their names were not exchanged, save for Sadal's who was recognized as the leader for the expedition. As they reached the deeper section of the rainforest, Sadal noted the location. A small river not too far from their location led to a large lake, undoubtedly full of fish and other marine resources that fed the tiger. A waterfall opened to the mouth of the lake just as Ronkalk told Sadal prior. Caves opened in wide chasms that were thinly guarded by vegetation, but the cave they were looking for was well in view. Although the smell of the tiger hadn't reached their noses, its handiwork was evident. Sadal instructed the group to take off their packs and leave them some distance from the cave. Brab was kept with the rest of their gear as Sadal prepared for battle. She held two of her throwing spears in her hands as she waited for the others to get into position.

"The Weypeu is not present. I saw it by the entrance, but it evades my vision." One of the women commented as she strained her eyes to make out the view in the distance.

Sadal's pupils expanded with a sudden shock of realization. Just moments ago, she too thought she'd seen it soundly from a distance. It would be impossible to mess this up. She reasoned, a few spears to pierce the brain or throat would be all they needed. A prepared tiger was no easy feat to take down, but with the proper planning the day could be won. Her face was riddled with anger as she had forgotten one important detail to consider. A reluctant and new mother, Sadal found herself dealing with the responsibility of rearing a child she had no real experience with, while balancing her role in the band as a Master Hunter. Brab, who hadn't made a single sound during the journey on her back, made noise some distance away from them. Sadal couldn't tell if the boy was hungry or anything else. Brab's harsh cry behind Sadal exposed their position early and the tiger began its hunt. The group noted the injured paw it had, its normal prey would be too much of a risk, but for humans, it would be more than a match. By chance and ill-fated opportunity, Sadal had damned her comrades to a trap that would prove impossible to get out of.

"Sadal!" One of the men shouted as the tiger unsheathed its claws. Sadal had little time to react to save her comrade as she grasped her first throwing spear. The tiger let out a distinct snarl as it sliced the man's chest clean open. The soil was tattered with piles of blood and exposed viscera. A feeling of dread settled among the others as they withdrew their knives and axes in a panic. The tiger's speed was unlike anything they had anticipated. This tiger wasn't a bombastic animal, choosing to instead hunt in efficient silence as it made short work of the team. Injured or not, the tiger's frenzy was enough to exhaust them. Sadal ran another one of her spears as she reached past Brab. She frantically adjusted her grip before releasing. She grew further panicked as every second she wasted would mean one second closer to death.

The first one she launched haphazardly, which briskly touched the tiger, scraping some of its fur. That mistake would not be repeated. She retreated some distance while the tiger was locked on another one of her hunting party, the tiger quickly biting the neck of the poor woman underneath. Her head was promptly severed from her neck and blood pooled out below. Her head rolled a short distance. Sadal's throw from about twenty feet away was a direct hit, piercing the back leg of the tiger. It found it difficult to move and could only claw in desperation now. One of the men who attempted to rescue the tiger's previous victim tackled it with the utmost ferocity, slicing away at it to no avail.

Another one of the men deserted, leaving Sadal alone with one hunting partner and a tiger still filled with anger. Sadal joined the one who attacked the tiger, holding her spear with one hand and attempted to jam it into the flailing tiger. Although she had been spared a gruesome mauling by the tiger's claw unlike her comrade, her arm was knocked backwards by the force of the tiger's resistance. She let out a harsh scream as she quickly left to grab another spear and aimed for the head. Sadal curled her body as she tossed with an intense ferocity. This throw was a direct hit, one of the few times she had managed to get a shot clean into the eye. The tiger which had multiple spears pressed into it and stab wounds finally fell over. Its body landed with a thud that was obscured by the grassy bottom below. The animal's hide was in terrible condition, but it didn't matter now it was slain. She walked towards the corpse and looked at the tiger's throat. She used her knife to slit it and drink the blood. This was to gain the strength of a dangerous predator after the kill and was reserved for the toughest of battles. As she recovered, she looked at her last comrade who was barely breathing. Sadal looked at the man as he slowly nodded and understood his fate. Sadal slit his throat as a mercy and surveyed the scene around her.

While she gained her composure, she felt a sharp and intense pain that the adrenaline of battle suppressed. Her arm to her knowledge was broken from the moment she connected with the tiger's force. It hurt to move, and her face held back tears that were daring to flow. Tattered furs, flesh scattered in the soil, and the marks of blood splattered along the ground made for a site open for scavengers to make their way in. Her comrades lay dead at the hands of unforeseen events. It wasn't meant to be this way, for the day started out simple enough, but life doled out punishment with no remorse. Her camp was a two-day travel from the incident, and help would be no use now. Sadal looked to the sky and thought about the priesthood's premonition that marked her for bad luck. This omen followed everywhere she went, and she realized what the common cause was. Her gaze turned to Brab who was nestled inside her pack.

"My arm. My arm is broken. No, not like this." She said as she tried to guide herself through the pain. Sadal's eyes were filled with rage as the words of the priests grew louder in her mind. Her rage took over as she could only see Nurzan in Brab's face.

"This is your fault. I never asked for any of this. You were a bad omen. I could have left you home, but then nobody would take care of you either!" Sadal said in regret. Her voice reverberated throughout the acoustics of the nearby cave. The priests of her people viewed the baby as an apparition for terrible tidings, but Sadal chose not to listen. It was clear she should have.

"You are why my arm is broken. The arm that kept me and everyone else alive. I can't feed myself or you. You will not survive, and I will not risk it." Sadal said as she looked at her fingers and her hand.

Sadal dislodged Brab from her pack as he blocked her supplies. Deeso only packed food and a small bit of fibers for first aid. In dismay, Sadal weighed her options. She would have to run away once again. To abandon everything for the second time wasn't something she could accept lightly. She couldn't bear the disappointment of what she did. Failure of a cleaning brought a punishment that only death could relieve in the eyes of her people. The shame of her fallen comrades' deaths and the land rendered unusable due to this were consequences she couldn't bear to bring home after Ronkalk put much trust in her. She failed to guide them to work as one and knew as leader, she bore full responsibility and the punishment that would follow for their deaths. Sadal couldn't bring herself to deliver the news either to the affected families. Their rage, their tears, all of it, she was unprepared to handle. Deeso would understand that this brief cowardice would be the correct choice. She made a vow to unite with her once again when times were different, and she could come up with a defense for her actions. In Sadal's right hand, was a rock that she grasped with a tight fury. As she looked at Brab's face, tears swelled their eyes and let out another piercing cry that rang her ears. It was here Sadal made her decision.

"I failed because of you!" She shouted, her hand wavering slightly, before slamming the rock on their face with incredible force. Sadal was delirious as she was overwhelmed with fatigue and ranted about her relationship with Nurzan. The deaths of those she surrounded herself with flashed through her mind. The child's head popped back as she did so. Blood leaked from the child's face. Sadal's rage blinded what was left of the stress she endured. She continued to strike Brab with the rock, each hit more devastating than the last.

"I never wanted you!" She added, her voice echoing as it reached the acoustics of the cave near her. The crying continued for a bit longer until her hands filled with blood as the job was done. No noise came now as Sadal looked at her handiwork in a fit of rage. That day, the child learned a mother's love was conditional. Sadal looked at everything around her and could hardly breathe as she was surrounded by death and took her son from the world.

"Tired hands make many mistakes." Sadal said to herself as the words of Ronkalk rang in her mind.

Meeting of Minds

Now that the adrenaline from her encounter wore off, Sadal was faced with the reality that she was now truly alone. She looked with horror at the crushed face of Brab. The boy was innocent but suffered for the ills of the father. With his death, Sadal saw that there was no return and this life needed to be put behind her. Sadal was a skilled survivalist from a young age, but her injury made her a vulnerable target to the many dangers of the jungle. Sadal once survived out in the wild on her own and now she'd have to do it once more. She lifted herself up using the wall of the cave as support while she used her free hand to balance. Sadal scooped her pack and left the place to ruin. She held her broken arm and picked a direction at random to go in. Sadal chose her movements deliberately as she nursed her injury. She needed to find aid as she lacked the knowledge to set her arm. She was a warrior for combat only and was healed back at camp.

"What is there for me to do? I can't go back home now, and some of the Forest Seekers would kill me on sight." She asked herself aloud.

Past the claimed territory of The Broken Bone and a few other bands, they contended with Forest Seekers that occupied these lands. As an elusive and generally peaceful bunch, they kept to themselves, but patches were valiant defenders of their territory, making settlement difficult past the wetlands. On her travels she took note of the wildlife. She heard the familiar grunts of bearded pig and rubbed her stomach as she was starting to get hungry. She remembered what little rations she had left in her bag, but these grew stale. A black eagle watched Sadal as it was perched up in a tree. It let out a harsh cry as Sadal looked towards it in awe. It was one of her favorite animals as it was able to soar unsurpassed by any other creature. She felt with this sighting, the winds of change were upon her. Deer droppings aligned the jungle floor as the rushing sound of another river nearby filled her ears from the otherwise silent wilderness. Sadal felt a sense of unease as she looked behind her. Her head perked up as she heard another noise northeast of her. It didn't match any of the animals she noted and so she figured the noise must have come from another human. She weighed her options and decided to move closer to the source of the sound. As it reached her ear, she could hear that someone was trying to get wood from a tree.

She positioned herself carefully to avoid the brambles of the nearby bushes and peeked her head out to see some figure in the distance. She noticed that it was a man, but something was unusual about him. He was holding some sort of large rock in his hand as he was getting strips of wood. He seemed to look at the pieces of wood and threw them aside as if he was testing the quality. His clothing was odd, just a loincloth and a covering of buffalo hide that was on its last legs.

Where are his clothes? Did someone steal them? He's not a Forest Seeker but I can't tell who he is at this distance. I should go closer and see what happens. She thought.

Sadal was aware that the man was foreign as he hacked trees with reckless abandon. Forest Seekers were fanatical when it came to the treatment of trees, and none would dare strip one for wood in such a manner. While the man continued to hack away at the tree, she decided to reveal her existence. She picked up a rock and tossed it a short distance as it landed with a thud. Sadal watched as she heard saw the man stop hitting the tree and turn his head once more. His face was different as he had a rough forehead with a brow ridge that contrasted with her smooth one. Sadal was puzzled as she'd never seen anyone like it. Sadal silently moved from her previous position to bring herself into view.

"You! Come here but keep your distance. I must ask you something!" Sadal shouted as her voice called out to him.

The man looked up from his work as he saw Sadal in the distance, yelling something to him. He looked behind him, wondering what this woman was shouting about. A look of realization came to him as he realized he could understand what she was saying. He was aware they spoke the same language, but the delivery of her words confused him, he could only gather about every third one.

Jih is confused, this one talks strange. Jih hears her words, but they are odd. Jih thought as he advanced closer to Sadal.

Jih spent about a week wandering alone in the jungle and was terribly lost. He lacked a reference for where to go past north and was trying to find any of his kind for directions. His only guidance was to look to the sky, but in the dense jungle this was an effort made in vain. He hated to admit it, but he was lost. He thought that he would be welcomed by his people, that he assumed would live here, but this was not to be. As Jih heard Sadal's voice, the questions in his mind now were limitless. How much was The Council hiding from him all these years? He felt that he would only run into members of his own kind, but things have changed since the stories he heard as a child.

Jih picked up his spear and walked to Sadal. Jih continued to move closer to Sadal who slowly backed away, trying to keep a respectable distance. Sadal threw another rock she had in her hand in his direction as she pointed to an arbitrary bush that she used as the boundary.

"I said stay back! I know you can hear me." She yelled at him.

Jih continued to go forward but looked at his spear. Jih assumed that Sadal saw this as a threat and attempted to deescalate. He slowly dropped it to the ground in hopes that would ease the tension as he tried to make sense of what was happening.

"Jih asks for aid. Do you know of power rock and where it can be found?" Jih asked Sadal.

Jih looked at Sadal's reaction and gathered she had the same sentiment about being able to understand each other. Jih found it incredibly frustrating that although he could grasp some context, he was otherwise lost. Sadal's lack of a reaction prompted Jih to try again, but this time extend his arm out in a handshake instead. Sadal, however, wasn't buying his peaceful claims. Although she initiated contact with Jih first, Sadal saw anything as a potential threat, and this was instilled within The Broken Bone's training and her upbringing as a Wanderer. She hoped to assess his abilities and evaluate from there. She noticed that Jih's spear was some distance from him and decided to go on the offensive. Her eyes looked to the ground and back at Jih who remained still with his hand out. Despite having a broken arm, she felt plenty capable of making her point across. She adjusted her stance and ran towards Jih.

"That was your first mistake." Sadal commented under her breath.

She attempted to rush Jih by checking him with her uninjured shoulder. With Sadal barreling towards Jih, he noticed that she looked very different from the people he interacted with and still had so many questions. Sadal didn't look like Hyu or Dran. Jih noticed that Sadal was injured in some manner and kept his guard low as he was unsure why she was rushing towards him. Jih felt he was in control as Sadal was unarmed and twice her age from his estimate. She elbowed Jih in the ribs, while he responded by swiping at her legs with his foot and tripped her to the ground.

"Stop!" Jih yelled at Sadal who continued to thrash around in defiance.

He took a kick to the stomach as he stood over her. He grabbed her leg and bent it backwards, causing Sadal to grit her teeth. Jih pressed himself against her and used his body weight as a counterweight until she at long last stood still. As Jih restrained her, Jih looked towards her arm. Although Sadal considered it broken, Jih noticed it was just sprained. Despite her experience as a big game hunter, Sadal had little experience with human anatomy compared to that of animals. Injuries in her profession usually ended in near-instant death, and she only knew her throwing arm was unusable. Jih had seen Hyu fix injuries like this and could reproduce the effects in his sleep. In one corrective movement, he aligned Sadal's arm back to normal while she let out a scream in pain. Sadal's tone changed as she realized she had a better feeling in her arm. It still hurt and needed to be supported by a sling, but she would be able to heal properly soon. Jih then stepped away to give her room. While Jih was close to Sadal, she sniffed the air around him which prompted a raised eyebrow from him. His scent was unusual, as it was not what she was typically used to. It was obvious this man was a foreigner, but from where? Her attention turned towards her better arm as she got herself up.

"What...What did you do to me?" She asked in surprise.

Her question remained unanswered as Jih left Sadal shortly after and picked up his spear to walk off. Sadal, not one to be unanswered, decided to go after him. She followed Jih through the rest of his walk as he looked over his shoulder at her. Jih did his best to ignore Sadal as he was focused on his mission, but the realities of the jungle made his efforts incredibly difficult. He frowned in frustration as he marked trees to try and guide himself, only to see the same ones again. For Jih, who knew his own jungle like the back of his hand, this was torture. Jih reasoned that Sadal was a native of this area at the very least and could offer him some guidance if he asked nicely. Jih stopped to rest on a nearby log as he chewed his tongue in thought. Once he left to hit the trail, he looked behind him only to see Sadal rush towards his direction with no signs of stopping. He put his hands in his face as he wiped some of the sweat off it and let out a small sigh of resignation.

Here she comes again. She follows Jih like young Tole. He thought as he saw Sadal coming into his vision once again.

"Who are you? Do you have a name? My name is Sadal." She asked.

Sadal continued to stare at Jih with wide eyes as he wasn't sure what to make of her. Jih was confused as the first thing Sadal did was attack him and now, she attempted to befriend him. Jih gave a small laugh as this reminded him of some of the youth of his home. Jih figured his travels would have him go alone but now this young woman with him was an extra element to consider. He wondered if she knew about the power rock as well but had no idea how to demonstrate that to her. He decided to humor her and see what she could gather from his words.

"S-Sandal?" Jih repeated to himself as he shook his head. He had a feeling that wasn't her name but would learn to pronounce it in time.

"Jih searches for power rock. Do you know of this? It came in sky for many moons." He commented to Sadal as he pointed in the sky, which was obscured by the high tree growth.

Sadal followed his finger up and Jih noticed her face was puzzled much like his own. She hadn't heard the voice of his people before, but to her ears it sounded rough. Sadal waited for Jih to explain further, as he slowly grabbed a rock while still pointing to the sky. She watched him closely as he moved the rock across his face. It took a moment for her to realize, but she nodded as she was able to guess what he was talking about.

Is he asking me about when night became day and the sky filled with fire? Our priests noted this event, and we had a feast for it. The meat was tasty. Sadal thought.

Jih watched with curiosity as Sadal picked up the rock and repeated the action as she nodded in support. She did know about the power rock! Jih's perspective on his unrecruited traveling companion lightened up as he could see their goals were aligned, as much as he cared to consider anyway. Although the sun's rays barely shot through the dense canopy above them, Jih knew he had been walking for what seemed like hours. His stomach rumbled as he hadn't eaten for some time much like Sadal's. He noted her condition, and Jih knew that at least for now he'd have to do the hunting. Jih shrugged his shoulders and knew he couldn't get rid of Sadal, so if she pulled her weight in time, he would take her along.

"I can see you're also hungry. I will do what I can." Sadal mentioned.

The two settled on making camp at a clearing while the day was still fresh. Sadal worked on getting a small fire going as she broke off branches within her reach. As she was unable to use her left arm, she instead stomped on the small branches and used the force of her foot to crack them. She amassed some rocks as well to retain the integrity of the fire while she watched Jih closely. He was surveying where he could possibly find something to eat. In the patches of grassland and jungle where he lived, it was simple enough to just run-down prey and corner it, but here Jih needed a new strategy to adapt.

He ignored Sadal as he picked up his hand-axe and his spear. Walking some distance, Jih noticed a riverbank not too far by. He continued to mark trees so he could trace his steps back after a kill was made.

Jih was happy at the turn of events as he knew animals would have to come by a river to drink and for him it was a matter of waiting. Jih looked at the ground and saw that the dirt was quite malleable due to its moisture. He decided to build a trap by unearthing an inhuman amount of soil to capture whatever got stuck. While he waited, he wondered about Sadal. Not particularly her, but the circumstances that surrounded him meeting her. Jih questioned if she was an anomaly or if there was a whole group of people like her. Sadal's situation reminded Jih of Bani as he found her in similar circumstances where she was alone in the wilderness and was left for dead by her band before joining with him. He wondered if this was the same situation with Sadal, as he treated her wounds. In those days, it was Kag who offered the best treatments, having an assortment of powders to use as pain relief but Jih could only do the basics. Jih rubbed his stomach as he hoped to capture a deer or a pig so that the pelt could be used for later.

Jih admired his handiwork as he surveyed his trap. Jih exhumed dry soil using his hand-axe as a shovel and cast it to the side while he moved mounds of mud from the riverbank. He hoped that under the right amount of weight, the prey would sink in his trap, and he could kill it. He eyed strange fruits that were hanging not too far from his location. He placed his tools downwards and slowly climbed up the tree, shaking it just enough for the loose fruit to fall on the ground. Jih then hit the fruits at the base of the tree, exposing the seeds and he tossed them around the mud hole he created. Jih sat waiting ever so patiently for his handiwork to come to fruition, and eventually fell asleep as nothing seemed to come his way. A loud flapping noise jolted Jih awake as he looked through groggy eyes to at long last find something pecking away. A wild jungle fowl with black and red feathers appeared to him. It had a mouth full of seed and turned its eyes to Jih before eating more of them.

"Poulji. Small one." Jih complained as he grabbed his spear.

Jih moved slowly and stopped short as he felt the eye of the jungle fowl on him. Jih took great care to not make sudden moves that would end up in a chase. The animal seemed to not mind Jih's presence as he inched closer and stabbed it directly through the back. The animal made little sound as he ejected the spear and grabbed it by the tail, while blood pooled from its body. The jungle fowl's neck went limp as Jih hoisted it over his shoulders. Jih debated looking around for another animal to hunt, but he decided against it as he felt he needed to get back to Sadal, so one would have to do it for now. While Jih made his way back, Sadal had plans of her own. Her travels took her not too far from the campsite as her ears alerted her to the sound of an injured animal. As she went in that direction, she could see that it was a sika deer based on the pattern of its fur. It was evident the deer near her was someone else's claim, but it was in such a bad way it remained alive. She saw a dart sticking out of it and removed it. She took it on herself to end the deer's life quickly and decided as she was the one to place the killing blow, it now belonged to her. Sadal noticed a lack of antlers and saw that it was a doe, so it was light enough for Sadal to drag on the ground back to camp.

I found this fresh morsel not too far from here, but I'm going to let him think I hunted it. That should be funny to see. Sadal thought as she strained a bit. With both of her arms she could drag bigger prey with no issue, but she had to reserve her strength since she was still recovering. She cut up the remains of the deer as much as she could with a knife she kept on her person while she prepared. Sadal resisted the urge to eat immediately as she realized Jih hadn't come back yet.

Jih returned with the chicken and some berries in hand and gave Sadal a glare as he was met with a cunning grin from her. Jih tossed the chicken on the ground and ate a berry while he lowered his hand for Sadal to grab one. Jih looked at the deer and back at her, puzzled on how Sadal found it. The deer was visibly a fresh kill, so it ruled out finding an old carcass to scavenge from.

"What, are you not gonna pick out the feathers?" Sadal asked in annoyance as Jih yawned. Jih looked at the cut pieces of deer meat that Sadal processed earlier as he rubbed his stomach again, emphasizing his previous statement. Sadal got the message as she gestured towards the piles of meat that were next to her.

"You said you were hungry, so eat." Sadal commented as she picked up a piece of the raw meat, holding it to Jih's face. Jih slapped her hand away as he pointed at the fire while Sadal held the meat in her hand.

"Right, I should cook it first. I get carried away sipping the blood." Sadal mumbled as she watched patiently, waiting for the deer meat to cook as she threw it onto the campfire.

The smoke of the fire filled the surrounding area, and the scent was pleasant. Sadal ate her meat without much cooking attached. Jih waited far longer for his meat to be prepared as he feared having tapeworms, a common illness for his people. Jih looked at Sadal as he finally removed his food. He took some of his scavenged berries and squeezed them over the meat as it cooked for a few more minutes. The smell of the juice caused Sadal to lick her lips as she stared at Jih for a piece while looking at her food. Jih rolled his eyes and ripped off a small piece for her to eat. The two ate happily until their stomachs were full and sat back, taking a moment to absorb their surroundings. For the time being, Jih now had someone he could rely on. Before Jih and Sadal slept for the night, Sadal broke several branches, and she scattered them around their campsite. If an animal large enough to break the branches approached, the noise from them would allow the two to know that they were compromised and in danger.

When Worlds Collide

Jih and Sadal slept soundly by the small fire they kept going throughout the night. Unknown to the two of them however, they were under the watchful eye of the Forest Seekers who had an axe to grind regarding the previous day's events. Their mastery of the environment was unsurpassed, as a group of eight converged on the two with not a sound made. Sadal's trick the night before worked well for the inexperienced, as she laid branches out to look as if they were natural rather than planted, but the Forest Seekers were one step ahead. Some held small daggers in hand, while the others held hollowed out bamboo tubes at their side, blowguns that launched carved darts at amazing speed. The Forest Seekers convened at Jih and Sadal's campsite. A man carrying a club looked with disgust as a lit fire remained between the two of them. He kicked dirt that suffocated the fire as smoke dispersed through the camp. He looked behind him and was given the signal to proceed. With a mischievous grin, he hit the ground beneath them and waited. Jih clawed the air as he woke up in surprise. Jih noticed the group carried strange weapons and decided to play it safe, leaving his spear on the ground. He slowly moved his arm over and nudged Sadal with his leg as he kept his hands up to show he would not put up any resistance. Sadal's reaction was less animated as getting up for her in the mornings was difficult, but her normally foggy vision straightened out as she was at the business end of some angry people.

What should Jih do? Jih thought as he saw another group of people that looked completely alien to him. He noticed they wore a strange arrangement of leaves and animal skins on their bodies. Others wore straw much like his people as well but were far more intricate in design. Their clothing served both as functional camouflage and a personal statement regarding their connectivity to the environment. Jih's vision was fixed on the group as he noticed they were much shorter than him.

"You stole something of ours. It was not for you to take." One of the men stated, pointing his dagger at Sadal. Jih saw this and moved to close the distance between the two of them. Jih found that his words were far easier to understand than Sadal's. Jih remained vigilant as he saw that Sadal and this other group shared a history that he was unaware of.

"What are you talking about?" Sadal asked, her tone increasing in annoyance. Her expression soured as she realized what he was referring to. She turned as her vision shifted to the pile of deer meat left behind them.

"This can't be about the-really? There's several of them, get over it." Sadal said to the man.

Sadal glared at the group while she shifted her eyes to Jih to see his reaction. The silence from the Forest Seekers confirmed Sadal's questioning. She found it difficult to obscure her rising laughter. How inept did they have to be to not just hunt something else? It made no sense to her. To Sadal, the Forest Seekers were cowards who attacked from the shadows only to vanish again when real danger came.

"If you cowards could actually kill the prey and give it a good death, perhaps I would be more thoughtful next time." Sadal chided as she raised her head to address the other voices from behind. The remaining Forest Seekers were visibly angry and swayed back and forth to ground themselves for battle.

"Thunderfeet have no self-control!"[18] One woman yelled, attempting to get the others riled up. Sadal bared her teeth at the other Forest Seekers who shook their weapons to intimidate her. Sadal and Jih both realized that their interests lay elsewhere past slaughtering them as they were still talking.

"Eshe! Come forward. You are needed, we have two in our hands." The man holding the wooden club spoke. He backed away as he continued to orate.

His voice boomed throughout the forest as the other Forest Seekers shifted in a line. The group kept their weapons in hand but slowly dispersed to make room for another. The sound of the hornbill was one that Sadal heard often while foraging, but it carried an unusual call as it did not live in a flock. Jih looked up and saw a hornbill that landed on an accompanying branch a short distance to the left of the pair. Jih figured animals had some sort of intelligence but could never be sure what they were truly thinking. This one was special, and it held a tight bond with its tamer. It was named Thornback and belonged to a powerful person. The hornbill was not one animal that could be easily made to submit, but it watched at a distance studying the scene before it. A woman about 5'2 was visible to both Sadal and Jih as she stepped through and looked at her prey. She carried a jagged knife in her hand that she manipulated between her fingers as she stepped forward. She flicked her hair to the side, clearing her vision to see her bounty in front of her. She wished to reclaim stolen pelts and to find answers about the new arrivals in her region.

"I am Eshe. My job is to speak with outsiders. Why are you here Thunderfoot? Did you not see our last message in these woods?" Eshe introduced herself, as she heard the laughter of a few of her comrades behind her.

Eshe held her hand up as the time for humor was for later. Eshe incorporated a strong image to outsiders as she and the rest of her people would not be rolled over so easily. Eshe took personal strength in the vitality of the forest that she guarded with her life. The message that Eshe referred to was a small group of Thunderfoot skulls shined with animal fat and placed at the bottom of trees along the roads they walked. These served as a warning to any outsiders that these lands would not serve their purpose and

---

[18] Thunderfoot is the derogatory term that Denisovans call Modern Humans due to their loud movements in the jungle that scare their food away. Denisovans are another species of archaic human that inhabited Southeast and East Asia throughout the Middle Paleolithic. They are a recently discovered species as not much is known about them, but their DNA is a part of many world populations today.

any attempts to enter would only result in death. Eshe's group was hardened to combat, and words were secondary.

"You don't scare me." Sadal taunted, trying to get Eshe's attention while she remained unmoved. Jih turned his head to try and figure out Eshe's motivations as he processed her words. Eshe's voice was quiet but could pierce through the ambient sounds of the jungle. She spoke with purpose as her words were masked with secrecy. Jih could tell that she had this position of leadership for a while, given how quickly things turned. Sadal wanted nothing more than to strike Eshe down and could only stew in anger as her arm prohibited her from fighting effectively. Sadal looked to Jih and hoped he could be of some use if things became hostile. A group that size was beyond her ability but to die in battle was an incredible honor no matter the opponent.

Eshe was an accomplished woman leading a small group of Forest Seekers throughout the jungle. Her face was brown with an inquisitive look on her face as she studied her two new captives. She wore an outfit made of leaves and had black long-flowing hair that flowed just past her shoulders. At thirty, she saw that the only way to deal with Thunderfeet was to take arms against them. Peace was exhausted time and time again as attempts to negotiate were cast aside. Their beliefs of the forest and its sentience were mocked by Thunderfeet that callously burnt their lands and harvested their trees for wood. Eshe once followed the path of peace that many Forest Seekers chose to do, but she broke away from this and chose to have a more direct impact. Her decision was controversial, but her wit and vision appealed to those that reached their limits.

"My intent is not to scare you, silly Thunderfoot. It is to educate you. You have stolen life from the forest, and it must be returned." Eshe threatened.

"Well, maybe if you actually killed it, I would've considered it. You all are terrible hunters. This is about an animal you wanted to kill in the first place. Besides, I thought you all were supposed to be peaceful; I assume those blades are for a ceremony?" Sadal mocked. Jih gave Sadal a glare as it was clear she certainly wasn't helping the situation.

"Bound the Thunderfoot with rope and cover her mouth. She offends me with her shrill voice." Eshe ordered as she waved a hand to get things started. Sadal kicked as two Forest Seekers tried to grab her, but she was pressed to the ground, and she was bound, albeit briefly. Eshe didn't see Jih as much of a threat, as on closer glance he wasn't an identifiable Thunderfoot like Sadal.

"Why are you doing this?! Sandal has done nothing wrong." Jih burst out in anger to Eshe, where a few Forest Seekers stopped their movement as they heard Jih speak. Sadal looked confused as she noticed their pause but continued to try to get herself out of the bindings now placed on her.

"What do we do with this one?" The man asked, pointing his dagger at Jih.

"Take his weaponry on the ground. If he resists, cut his throat-" Eshe commented as she stopped in place. She studied the reaction of the others and realized that Jih also sounded very different from Sadal. She raised her hand to the other person that had rope handy to bound Jih. One Forest Seeker man took Jih's spear and held it towards him as he held a serious glare. Jih felt embarrassed that he was now held hostage by his own weapon but had no choice but to relent.

"You intrigue me. Keep the Thunderfoot under watch but tie the hands of this one. He is too large to be carried, so I will have him walk instead. My mother will decide what is to be done with you." She ordered as Jih complied at spear point. His hands were bound to face opposite directions so that he couldn't get his way out. Eshe wasn't worried about Jih escaping, as it was evident, he hadn't been in this area before.

Eshe observed Jih with intrigue and focused on his face. She placed the back of her hand to her forehead and compared them with one another. Jih's was much more pronounced than her own, and it was not as smooth as the Thunderfeet's. He was different, and Eshe was unsure on how to proceed. As Sadal was bound by the legs, she was carried by three men as she attempted to squirm while Jih looked back at her a few times. As he was unarmed, and incapacitated himself, there was nothing he could do other than watch. After about twenty minutes, the outline of Eshe's village appeared to the group. This was not Eshe's original home, but one of many on their long rotation as the season would unfold. Forest Seekers were migratory like all, but their town structure differed from most groups. Villages were stationary but the people themselves left when it was time to move. The Forest Seekers carried a sense of collective ownership where structures would stay in a continuous cycle where another group would pick up what remained after a move. They believed that parts of the soul of people could be placed in the things they built, so leaving portions of what remained was a sign of welcome for the next group to live there. At heart, they were philosophers who questioned why things were how they are. Despite an almost aloof nature, they were not ignorant by any means. Their villages were kept hidden well, as the smoke from their fires vanished in the forest fog. They were not to be found unless they wanted to be.

A large group of Forest Seekers waited by the entrance of their village marked with two large stakes in the ground. The crowd waited in anticipation for Eshe's return as she was on campaign for a few days. The feeling was mutual for her as she longed to return with a suitable prize. Jih and Sadal marched in and observed with different reactions. Sadal was given a look of disgust as she frantically tried to get out of the men's grasp. Sadal confirmed every piece of propaganda given by Eshe about Thunderfeet and she couldn't be happier about the outcome. Sadal heard jeers from the group as they raised their hands in the air in smug satisfaction. Jih was an oddity that received less fanfare as he looked into the eyes of others. He studied their dress and was reminded much of The Jagged Bark before their betrayal. Some Forest Seekers went without clothing almost entirely, while he saw a mixture of intricate leaves and feathers that dazzled the eye. Jih favored animals with muted palettes for his own clothing but couldn't deny the quality put into those designs. Eshe's ideals were hard to convince others to emulate so she often felt she needed to impress to keep her ideology alive. Eshe took the gracious celebration of her people with stride as she continued to usher her party inside.

Eshe waved to her people but returned to relay orders to her comrades. Eshe called for Sadal to be put in a small hut away to be put for questioning while Jih remained still. Jih felt a tug on his arm as he was jostled by his Forest Seeker handler and glared at him. Jih noticed out of the crowd a younger woman approached. She was guarded in her nature, but her face lightened on seeing Eshe. As Eshe ordered Sadal to be placed away, she was hugged from behind and turned around. Eshe's expression brightened as she was familiar with the warm touch around her stomach. Eshe had to balance the life of a hardened revolutionary with the development of her village and valued connections. Eshe turned around and saw her partner Akma. Akma wore more elaborate wear as she had a single draping long coat of deer fur that flowed behind her, and a necklace made of bones.

"Akma. I have returned. Is my mother awake?" Eshe asked happily as she took Akma's hand. Akma thought and nodded.

"Yes, your father went to go find some flowing water for her to sip on her orders. It seems you have caught another Thunderfoot, and you have..." Akma said, as she looked at Jih who was in awe at the structures built by the Forest Seekers. Jih couldn't stray far, but he studied the camp layout and was curious about where Sadal was being held.

"This is why I need her. I found that man there, but he lacks the Thunderfoot ferocity I am used to. I have my perspective on his nature, but I must know more." Eshe explained. Jih broke out of the man's grasp and gave a glare as he saw Eshe staring at him. She nodded her head as one of her comrades went and forcibly grabbed Jih to return to her. Jih wanted to look for Sadal, but he saw that he would need to deal with Eshe first before doing so. Jih found himself face to face with the two women and spoke out.

"Do you understand Jih? Jih has many questions." Jih asked as Akma tapped Eshe's arm.

"I will answer whatever you have to say, but there is something that must be done first." Eshe explained to Jih.

Akma shot her a look as Eshe agreed to take Jih to her mother. As the three walked, Jih observed The Forest Seeker way of life. Jih noticed right away they had no work schedule that he could see. People worked on things as they chose and supported each other in their endeavors. Forest Seekers slept on the ground in the shade and gorged on fruit. Jih noticed many that lacked the use of stone and instead entertained themselves with wood. Jih saw this as a feeble material to work with but found himself comparing their work to Tur's. He noticed that even Forest Seeker children could reproduce designs that rivaled Tur's expertise. He heard music that played through ornate wooden flutes that occupied a small central part of the village. The melody was soothing to his ears as he continued to look around. Jih saw Forest Seekers moving in and out of their homes. He saw they had two home designs; one was a large structure made with packed thatch as a roof and a rounded base with rocks. These were held up with wood and walls made of packed mud. Jih wondered how such a composite build of materials held but they remained sturdy. There was a flap on the front that would indicate if someone was home or not. This was for families to live together, while another home was far smaller and was for individuals. They were low to the ground with an open mouth to crawl in. These had beds with leaves that also found their way to the roof. An intricate network of tied branches built up the skeleton of the home and were also found to be scattered throughout. Jih noticed that children often slept in these while adults took the larger homes.

Two homes? One for adults and for children? They seem to be separate. Jih thought and laughed aloud at the prospect.

For the first time in a while, he thought about Hyu. Hyu was responsible for helping births and children of The Elders were born in the same tent as their parents. A separate tent for children would have been a blessing from the world itself as she attempted to guide new parents on the expectations and care for a newborn. As his mind drifted, he nearly tripped over an exposed tree root as he looked to the ground. Back home, things like these were removed from their camp, but Forest Seekers integrated the jungle and forests they inhabited into their village design. They considered the forest a living organism that they structured their society around. Where stumps were common from deforesting trees back home, he saw that there was no work of this kind anywhere to be seen. Jih approached the large house that Eshe, Akma, and her parents lived in. He noticed it was built into a tree and had a tree branch that cut through the mud wall. Eshe's mother lit a small fire that was dug into the ground, rather than on the surface like other groups. The Forest Seekers thought they respected the power of fire the most and chose to keep them low so the chance to burn something was lower. Needless fires were also doused without question when they slept as fire could only remain in control under the eyes of a watchful person. She invited the trio inside with a warm smile as Eshe entered first with Akma behind. Jih raised an eyebrow but as he was escorted inside, he sat with the three women on the opposite side of him. Eshe opened the conversation.

"I found this one with the Thunderfoot we have captured. Mother, you have seen things beyond my range of vision. What do you know of him? He looks different." Eshe commented as she gestured to Jih. Jih looked offended as he looked at Eshe and the old woman in front of him.

"Where is the loud one? Where is Sadal? Jih must know if she is safe." Jih asked, his concern returning to Sadal. His question was ignored, as Eshe's mother looked over Jih and heard his voice. Her face scrunched in thought as she realized something. Eshe and Akma looked in anticipation as Jih grew impatient. He had his fill of the elderly dealing with The Council.

"Eshe. This is an incredible turn of news. This man...must be a Stone Breaker. I remember when I was very young, my mother said she had seen a glimpse of them. As you know, The Stone Breakers are-" Eshe's mother continued as Jih turned his head. He was trying to parse what he could understand of her, but his eyes lit up as he heard the name of home.

"Hm? This is job of Jih. How do you know this?" Jih interrupted with a look of confusion on his face. Jih heard this moniker and thought about their use of the title. As a Stone Breaker, Jih was the highest qualified stoneworker among his band, it was a position to be upheld and took years to master. For these people, it seemed to be the name they chose for any of his kind.

"Yes mother, I am aware of the legend. But how can we be sure?" Eshe commented. Jih folded his legs as he watched them discuss. Jih wasn't used to being such a centerpiece of attention.

"I agree with Eshe. After The Great Vanish, we have yet to see a Stone Breaker in many generations. The tales of your mother could just be hearsay." Akma commented. Akma's role was important as she was the oral historian for their people. Serving as the understudy of Eshe's mother, she was able to keep a good deal of knowledge, but not everything was still known to her.

"Let us ask him then. Your name, can you give it to us?" Eshe's mother asked.

Jih was exasperated now at their question. Jih ignored the fact that he mentioned his name earlier but assumed none of them listened to him. He chose his words carefully and slowly as he tried to explain his position to the others. Jih held little respect for his captors as he was now bound against his will and spoken about so casually. He found it to be incredibly disrespectful but needed more answers. He straightened his posture and tried to save face.

"This one is named Jih. What is...The Great Vanish?" Jih asked with additional confusion. He was also concerned about the use of the word vanish; its use was never good.

"When we first came to this land, people like you were here. We were ignorant and did not know anything. When we came, we had no voice. You opened your throat to us and gave us a voice. We got our language from you, this is how you understand our tongue, you all showed us the way. You taught us to use the material that comes to build our homes, and you told us what animals were safe. You built them with tools made from stone. When it came time to pass, The Great Vanish, your people told us above all else to ward the forest, otherwise we would surely perish. Everything comes from it." Eshe explained, as Jih tried making sense of everything. Jih recalled many stories he was told from his early days, but none mentioning the presence of others such as this.

"Jih has question. Eshe speaks of past. These events have happened before. Where did Stone Breakers go?" Jih said with skepticism in his voice. Jih assumed that his people remained on this new landmass but his isolation in the jungle was hard to argue against. He wondered if these past events correlated with his band's refuge in Sundaland. Jih saw no reason for Eshe and the others to lie about such things, it lined up with the orders they were given to never go past the northern jungles.

"Stone Breaker, show us how you make your tools. If you know the ancient ways, we will take you in as our own. Consider it forgiveness for your treatment by the hand of my daughter and her warriors. This is your right." Eshe's mother stated, as she grasped a rock for Jih to use.

Jih sat as he gestured to his wrists that were still tied together. Eshe withdrew a small knife from a loop in her clothing and looked at Jih with some hesitation. She met Jih's eyes as she reached over and cut the fibers. Jih looked around for another rock. He recognized the workhouse stone of flint. Jih took her order with the utmost severity as he went to work producing a hand-axe. Years of practice led to this moment as Jih could produce one in just twenty minutes. He displayed his hand-axe as he gave it a tight grip on the side while Eshe looked at her mother who nodded in satisfaction. Unknown to Jih, his expertise of The Old Way that he spent years perfecting, was already considered outdated among the Forest Seekers. Not many worked with stone, but the ones that did used far different methods than his. Eshe looked at the evidence before her and gave a grin, now that it was shown that Jih's origins were true. She saw Jih in a new light on account of his heritage, and opportunity struck her. It was through her blind luck that she was able to find a living Stone Breaker that could be of use to her and her ambitions. Eshe recalled Jih's previous treatment and gave him a warmer grin as he looked at her still with some suspicion. Jih wasn't aware of the legends around his people, so seeing this reverence of those like him was confusing.

"Stone Breaker. You honor us with your presence. Your people have done much for us and now I can extend that gesture. Your legacy speaks for you, but as one man, you have much to prove still. You have many questions, and I can help you however I can. Though, I must ask you to do something for me." Eshe said to Jih.

"What will Jih do?" Jih said as he rubbed his hands together. His eyes followed Eshe's movements as he walked by.

"We will discuss this in private." Eshe commented to Jih as she prompted him to get up. As Eshe waited for Jih to accompany her, her attention was briefly interrupted by a man who whispered in her ear. He was waiting for some time to give Eshe the news as he was incredibly forthcoming with the information.

"The Thunderfoot has revealed her name and her intentions in our land. She goes by Sadal and was hunting for food and got lost. Our efforts for anything else though have not gone well. Two are injured, we will try again." He said with a sigh as Eshe gave him an affirmative pat on the shoulder.

Jih accompanied Eshe to a small area on the outskirts of the village where the two could discuss important matters without interruption. The distant sound of children playing slowly faded away until they were silent once more. Eshe sat down first and folded her legs. Her eyes glanced towards the ground where Jih made his way to sit down. The two were silent as they met each other's gaze, but Jih let Eshe speak first. As far as he was concerned, he was still a captive despite the sudden change of respect.

"I try not to worry Akma with my affairs. She is often concerned about my vision. As impressive as this is, Stone Breaker, this is not normal. My people do not have leaders in the same way that the Thunderfeet do. We are disorganized, and not one person or group holds control. Asking someone to do a task requires much persuasion." Eshe explained further as she saw Jih about to interject.

"No special name. Jih will do." Jih said, lifting his hand up at her comment. Jih preferred to be called by his own name, for he found the title something he did not truly earn. Jih held pride in his abilities but wished to rid himself of The Council's influence. Eshe would abide by his request in private but would classify him as Stone Breaker to any who perceived him.

"Jih it is then. Now, you need to understand something. While you are here, you are my guest, but my hospitality has limits. The Thunderfoot you travel with, her name is Sadal. She is not like me. The Thunderfeet have caused us great pain over many years. They have killed my kin, burnt our forests, desecrate our way of life, and there is an effort to kill us all. My goal is to unite my people to beat back the Thunderfeet. They are a small group but live in large areas of our territory. Some say they can bring them to peace, but I know better." Eshe explained with a pound of her fist as a clump of dirt engulfed her hand.

"These are bad things, Jih has experience with people who do this. What can Jih do?" Jih asked, coursing his fingers through his beard in thought. Eshe's description of the Thunderfeet reminded him much of the Neck-Shells, but the one named Sadal seemed to be fine. He would have to inquire further into the matter. Jih knew that Eshe had an agenda that needed to be met and wondered how far she was willing to go.

"Perhaps you can tell others of your kind to support me? There is a village of yours I am sure of it." Eshe stated with excitement.

"Jih is not able to return home." Jih said flatly as he briefly considered the scenario of making his way home and attempting to tell his friends about the strange people that lived in forests to the north. Jih figured even if he wasn't exiled nobody would support his words. Jih's goal first was the power rock and anything else to get there was secondary. Eshe didn't bother to ask the details and expressed disappointment at his words. The burden of leadership was heavy as she had a dedicated following but expanding these efforts has been difficult as of late.

"There are a few camps nearby that are willing to hear what must be said. You will accompany me today and speak in support of me. The word of a Stone Breaker holds sway for those who respect our ways."

"Why does Jih understand Eshe better than Sadal?" Jih asked with some confusion as he was able to follow their conversation much more closely.

"The Thunderfeet are new to this land. Their voice echoes yours, but it is not the same. We all share the same tongue but the way we say our words is closer to your ear. Thunderfeet have experience with my kind and understand our words better. You will learn in time. Monkeys can learn new skills, Thunderfeet are just as close." Eshe explained as she paused to look for Jih's reaction.

Jih laughed at Eshe's comment. Jih hardly agreed with her but getting on her good side seemed to be the way people got things done here. Much like the social dynamics of home, he would have to appease her ego, but not in a heavy-handed way. For Jih to be of any real help to Eshe, he needed to understand how this society was run. The burning questions that Jih had on his mind, Eshe was willing to answer. Eshe stood up and pointed with her finger out towards the outskirts of their camp where they would go. Jih nodded and began walking as Eshe did.

"So, there is no Council here? Who gathers food? When do you rise? How does anything get done so late?" Jih asked with interest as it was hard for him to grasp his mind about how the anarchist nature of the Forest Seeker life managed to keep them as stable as they presented themselves. It was unheard of for people to thrive without the tight control he was used to seeing. Jih looked at the trees that made up where they were going, rarely did he see any marks on them, and wondered how they gathered their material.

"We wake when we choose too. There are always things to be done, and we have much time to do them. Jih, have you thought about why you must wake so early?" Eshe asked as Jih silenced himself to think on Eshe's question. As they drew nearer, Jih felt it was best to respond to her probe.

"There is wisdom in structure and discipline. You must prepare for dry season or starve. Jih has seen people fall to less." Jih commented as he crossed his arms. He shook his head in dismissal as he couldn't imagine wasting the day in the same manner as them under normal circumstances.

"Making things is your art, but this art requires blood. If you make something for the sake of it alone, does it make you fulfilled? Are you able to enjoy what you make before having to do something else?" Eshe inquired as Jih's eyes looked to the ground. Jih held personal pride in every tool he made, he felt it was his purpose to do so but his tools were made in service to others. Jih had no room to innovate past his own experimentation as Tur's demands were immense.

"While the light is high, we will go meet two groups at a neighboring village. You will say nothing to the others until it is time. I want your presence to be a surprise. We have people who represent our interests, the ones who speak with outsiders. I hold this position and we meet to talk about what we have seen. It is something that is voted on." Eshe commented. She stopped walking as she cupped her hands together and blew with her lips to make a low whistle. This was to call her hornbill who often resided some distance away from Eshe.

Jih saw the bird's shadow gradually descend as Eshe extended her hand out. The animal's claws were careful to avoid the fleshy portions of Eshe's hands as she gently massaged its feathers. Jih looked into the eyes of the hornbill with some suspicion. He was familiar with them as his travels with Hyu led the two to collect the eggs of many birds, but Jih only knew to duck from them rather than see them as calm beings. Eshe sensed Jih's unease and spoke to calm his nerves.

"Thornback is a messenger of the forest. His soul is tied to many, but only I can call him. It is a special connection we share Jih. The Iru watches over us all and it would seem he sees you as well."

Jih rarely saw anyone have such a bond with animals in such a way, let alone a bird. The orangutan was an animal that Jih's people respected, it had an awareness that made it different from other animals, and it was seen as taboo to do anything negative towards it, but a bird was outside the norm. Eshe gave Jih an opportunity to touch Thornback. Jih reached his hand over, only to stop as the bird darted its head and scrambled its neck before calming down. Eshe opened her lips and blew a small stream of air onto the bird, soothing it as Jih rubbed. The importance of such an event was lost to Jih but Eshe remained in good spirits as she saw the bird's acceptance. He placed his hand back to his side and the two continued. Thornback left Eshe's grasp and flew at a distance watching the pair. Jih saw a mass of foliage in his path to cut down and lifted his hand-axe, but Eshe held out her hand to stop him. She guided his path to look below, and Jih noticed an assortment of logs and rocks. Eshe explained that to obscure the exact locations of their settlements, directions were not marked as obvious as trees, but instead determined by logs placed along the ground.

"Jih. Pay attention to my words. Here we come to a crossroads. The village we are supposed to be going to is on the left. The right leads out to the further woods. We tell this by the logs here." Eshe said, taking a knee as she flipped over a log that was piled with a few others. Two lines in the log means they are accepting visitors; three lines means they have goods to trade. The logs return to the soil when we leave." Eshe narrated as she ran down the knife marks on the spare bark. There was no mistaking the two fresh lines that went down the front and back ends of the log.

"Eshe trusts Jih with this knowledge?" Jih inquired as he attempted to remember Eshe's instructions. She nodded and understood that Jih seemed to be overwhelmed. Eshe wanted to have Jih's defense of her vision as heartfelt as possible, so she felt extending the knowledge she was given would be best to do that. This was also information he was entitled to as a member of the Stone Breakers; it was as tactical as it was in adherence to the old ways and the respect that followed.

"Yes. This is your right from your heritage as much as ours. We will approach soon, so say nothing until I do." Eshe told Jih.

Eshe and Jih lingered around the entrance of the village for some time until a member of the hosting party approached them with a hearty grin. He was an older man who used a walking stick to get around but held some stride in his step. He wore no fur but instead wore a grass covering with multicolored feathers on them. Jih looked at the construction of this village, noting some key differences from Eshe's home. All the buildings were arranged in a semi-circle while Eshe's lacked structure to begin with. Jih followed Eshe's instructions and kept quiet while he observed the two in conversation.

"A guest! How unexpected. Eshe, we welcome you as always. Have you eaten?" The man said, giving her a tight hug.

Eshe nodded and patted her stomach; she always had enough room for a good meal. The older man guided the two to the village center where a few other Forest Seekers were sitting down and eating their meals on top of animal skins that covered their legs and feet and served as plates. Jih looked in surprise, he hadn't given it much thought. When food was dirty, Jih wiped it off or washed it with water. Eshe and Jih sat close to one another, some distance from the main group and were given the customary skins. Eshe quickly equipped hers while Jih stood confused as he tried sticking his leg in, only for it to come out the other end, and missed entirely. He observed a child wrapping the animal skins around his legs and feet and copied their movements. A small depression in the skins formed where the food would be emptied into, and then subsequently scooped out for eating.

"I hope you like Poulji." Eshe said as a young child ripped portions of meat and distributed them to the various Forest Seekers that ate with glee. Although many were separate in their individual endeavors, many often chose to congregate together when it came to eating. Jih appreciated the camaraderie that came with group meals like these. He would usually eat with Hyu or his Stoneworking Team when they had the time to do so.

"Jih knows this word. It is favorite food." Jih said as he sniffed the meat.

"Yes. Eat as much as you like. Prosperity like this is just one of the benefits of working with me." Eshe said as she scooped a piece of chicken into her mouth as Jih did.

The two ate and exchanged brief inklings of their past. Eshe learned of Jih's fate within The Elders, and the loss of Hyu. Both things she did not feel qualified to give her perspective on. Jih learned much about Eshe's plunge into leadership and the challenges that came with it. It wasn't something she wished to take on her own, but it was a task that needed doing like any other. Eshe felt her crusade against the Thunderfeet was of self-preservation. She saw their incursions of them as meetings first marked with curiosity and interest. This was not to last, as sometime later, Eshe felt an uncomfortable and horrid silence when the forest tasted the blood of her kin. As the meal came to an end, some stayed because they wanted to hear Eshe's speech of unity, while others went back to their own tasks. Eshe saw that the camp's stomachs were full and ready to listen to her proposal. Eshe got up and prompted Jih to follow her. Jih folded his arms in indifference as he did so. Eshe stood and locked eyes with the two representatives, two men roughly around her age. Their distance was a well-traveled way, with a week between locations. Eshe didn't want to leave any of them empty handed. The old man that gave Eshe such kindness, raised his walking stick in the air and stomped it on the ground.

"Eshe, daughter of Khoet and Enza will speak to us today. Her issue is regarding the Thunderfeet presence in the area. You may speak when you are ready." He announced, slowly sitting himself back down.

"I ask all of you, including our host village, to listen to my call. The Thunderfeet are a problem. They are small now, but their goals and ambition are dangerous. They seek to replace us. Some see the animals we hold sacred as harbingers of evil to be destroyed. Yes, we fight Onpeu and Weypeu when the time comes. The Forest is not one entity, but many fighting for control. Some are good and in our best interest-" She said, as her gaze briefly turned to the old man.

"-While others seek to keep us divided further than we stand today." Eshe continued.

Eshe looked at the audience. Some members of the village hadn't seen Thunderfeet before. She saw some concerned faces, which is what she wanted to see but others were more steadfast in their approach. They heard stories before, but stories were meant to scare children. Jih was moderately impressed at Eshe's ability to capture the crowd in such a way. He sat back and wondered how Eshe would deal with dissent to her words. Would she use reason to turn their minds, or would she boil down like Tur? Jih was bound to help Eshe regardless as he needed to bide his time to find Sadal, but his enthusiasm depended on Eshe's response.

"Have any of you seen a Thunderfoot?" One of the representatives jeered, prompting a few laughs from the crowd. Due to the disorganized nature of the Forest Seekers, Eshe's encounters with Thunderfeet came off as a hard sell. Few rarely experienced what she saw, and many were quick to believe they didn't exist to begin with. The Forest Seekers have occupied the land since time began as far as they were concerned and inherited their place in the world from The Stone Breakers.

"You are the same one to mock me, when I have also witnessed a Stone Breaker. One of whom has traveled this way with me. They have returned to confirm my words." Eshe said, giving Jih a hearty jab with her elbow. Jih returned an annoyed glance at her and waited as he saw that the representative had more to say. Jih wasn't expecting to be put up to the plate so early.

"Impossible! The Stone Breakers have become one with the forest after The Great Vanish. Surely you insult us today." He commented and stood up to prove his point further.

"Eshe is correct, Jih has returned to this land. The Thunderfeet are raiders. They take and will burn everything." Jih added on, now looking at the man who stepped up. Jih could tell that the person before him reminded him of Chak, a blowhard who had something to prove and everyone needed to know.

The heckler's statement crumbled apart as Jih stood in the flesh. He was speechless, but there were other points that needed addressing. There was no denying that Jih's existence was true. He ran his foot in the soil and gave a glance to the other representative who ran his hand through his beard as he observed the situation. The growing crowd observed the scene with interest as they tried to get a glimpse of Jih.

"Well Eshe. If you are willing to invoke the Stone Breaker in your words. I will do so as well. How could you think of breaking The Vow? It is known that they told us to never harm another human for our blood taints the growth of the forest. The Stone Breaker named Jih, what do you say of this?" The man said as he waved his hand to Jih.

Jih attempted to come up with a retort but fell flat. He was unaware of the details of legends surrounding his own people and felt exposing his ignorance would endanger Eshe's standing. Jih saw that Eshe was preparing to make a statement of her own and would support whatever she said. Eshe looked around in faux confusion at the man's statement. The crowd remained silent as the two exchanged a war of words.

"I have kept The Vow. The Thunderfeet are no more animals than the Mulku or Vatki. They can be slain and any traitor to the forest must be burned. That is what we decided. Your defense of them gives me pause. I will only say this once. We need to come together and bring the fight to the Thunderfeet. They have been here for five generations; we number over 500." Eshe replied with a sly grin as she captured the crowd once more. People that were involved with their own tasks turned their heads to listen now.

"Eshe, we are not warriors. If these Thunderfeet are as dangerous as you propose, what chance do we have?" The other representative mentioned.

"We know the land better than anyone else. I would like to say it would be easy, but with our blowguns and the gifts that the forest provides, we will have a chance." Eshe mentioned. While the two representatives were apprehensive at her words, the old man heard plenty.

"Eshe, our bands have remained close despite years of separation. You will have whatever resources you need. The world must be safer for the next generation. I have not seen a volcano, but I am aware that it is dangerous." He mentioned as he helped himself up.

Eshe sat with victory in her eyes as she gained the alliance of at least one person. She wanted more, but greed was not something that she was inclined to get as a character trait. To cultivate a following of armed resistance, Eshe needed to meet people where they were. The crowd dispersed as the other two representatives promised to give a response to her in a month's time. Jih stood closely by Eshe as he absorbed the scene before him. Eshe placed her hand on Jih's shoulder and whispered into his ear.

"You did very well today, Jih. Keep doing this and I may just help you. A bed will be made for you to stay, but you will not leave until I say so. You and your Thunderfoot companion owe me a debt." Eshe said as Jih felt a cold rush on his back. The word debt was one that Jih wanted to wipe from his memory.

Eshe waited by the entrance of the village as she waited for Jih. He was approached by the old man who lowered his head in respect to Jih and held his hands. Jih couldn't hide his confusion on the matter but felt his expression was sincere and repeated the gesture. Jih looked behind him and followed Eshe. The two walked in silence as they entered dense undergrowth once more. While Jih's thoughts were simple, Eshe's mind raced at the scope of her plan. She was used to conducting raids and holding the occasional captive. This plan was much more now as Eshe knew there was only so much rhetoric alone could give for her people's freedom. Where would the weapons be made? Her people had basic stone tools aside from their blowgun technology. She needed a steady trail of supplies and people to work them. She also needed to build more forces if she could stand a chance to the organization of some of the Thunderfeet bands she's heard of. Eshe rarely wore stress on her face, but the prospects of success were both invigorating and terrifying. It would be a long walk home.

A Lost Soul

Deeso felt like an outsider in her own home as she woke up to Nurzan staring at her. For the past three days, while Sadal was out on the tiger hunt, Deeso was stuck having to do work she felt was beneath her. Out of everyone in The Painted Hand, she despised Nurzan the most, and had to share a tent with him. The man was hunched over a pack that he filled with thread. Deeso was at her wit's end as he didn't engage in any conversation regarding Sadal. It was clear to Deeso early on that only Sadal tried to keep up a facade of their relationship and continued to wonder why he didn't just leave them be. Nurzan took zero interest in Brab after he was born but was excited about the prospect of a child. Deeso knew the routine and quickly settled into the expectations for today. Deeso looked at the walls of their home that were decorated with the pelts of Sadal's most prized hunts. Deeso arranged them in order of importance and left a large spot prepared for the tiger to hang up as victory.

"You have nothing to say of Sadal and her victory over the Weypeu? Surely, you'd want to make the pelt into something nice for our home?" Deeso asked as Nurzan stopped briefly. He lifted his head to stare at Deeso and then continued rifling through his pack.

"There's nothing to talk about. Bring your things and come with me. It's Ronkalk's will that you must go. So, let's go." Nurzan said as he left the hut.

Nurzan resented Deeso for several reasons, the most relevant one is that he found her judgmental and only considered her a sacrifice to be with Sadal at the time. Nurzan also found himself dissatisfied with Sadal and her needs but felt trapped. Sadal was one of Ronkalk's treasured Wanderers and Nurzan asked him for permission to make a new life with her. Ronkalk allowed those in The Broken Bone to unite out of love rather than obligation, but Nurzan was aware of their special connection. He feared retribution and coaxed Sadal to break things off as well as he could. Nurzan had little patience for those that were inexperienced and detested Ronkalk's rotation system for his weaving means. He didn't see himself as a teacher but an unappreciated artist instead. Deeso's inexperience irritated him highly.

Deeso found Nurzan and a few other weavers quietly starting the day in a clearing behind their home. She sat down and looked at a pile of materials in the center of the circle. She saw three distinct piles of stripped bamboo, hemp, and reeds that were collected and kept in well supply. One weaver nodded to Deeso and slid her a bone needle on the ground to wrap around string to get started. Deeso shared the same sentiment as Nurzan towards him. Deeso considered him dead weight and nothing more. He was unappreciative of her efforts in cooking and maintaining their tent's hygiene. The work of caring for Brab was thankless in the times Sadal was missing. He didn't attend festivals or participate in the fighting pits and stewed at home in anger. Ronkalk assigned her that week to the weavers as extra help. Ronkalk was preparing to court another band and needed baskets to contain the bounty of meat and fruit. She hated weaving but understood its necessities. Her fingers constantly struggled to slip through the loops, and she became frustrated with her reed baskets often collapsing in on themselves due to uneven distribution. It was not a skill she took with any pride, she wanted to emulate Sadal instead. Like her, Deeso found her way into The Broken Bone around the same time, and the two considered each other siblings. Deeso's life starting out was not pleasurable. Before she left her own band, it was known that she was born as a pariah among her people, as she was born under a solar eclipse. For many of her kind, the sun was seen as the ultimate giver of life, and for Deeso's untimely birth, this was a bad omen. The priests who oversaw the process noted that due to the sun leaving during her birth, it was a sign that she was to live a life full of hardship and misery. She lost the universe's favor before taking her first breath, and this was a sentiment that would follow her for the rest of her life.

Her attitude towards the supernatural was one of utter disdain, but she held her tongue around leadership and those she couldn't trust. Deeso didn't believe in curses, but she felt punished for having to deal with those below her intelligence. She was without purpose, but through her hardships and friendship, she gained people she could trust with her life. The wetlands they inhabited during the wet season were something Deeso considered dreadful. The irritating hum of mosquitoes was enough to keep her on edge in addition to the worry that continued to fill her mind. Deeso spent many hours concerned about Sadal's whereabouts as she continued to finish one basket. Nurzan and the other weavers were on their fifth. The weavers were responsible for making two types of baskets with different uses. Coil baskets used a carved piece of wood as the base and were built on by tying pieces of bamboo together and threaded into place with string to hold the shape. Each layer was sewn into the top of the other and the track could be shown. Coil baskets held water and were suited for long journeys as they were sturdy and incredibly packed together. Lids to hold these in place were also made to accompany them. Reed baskets were made of jute and were more utilitarian as they could be made in just under an hour. She was unsure of what form she wanted to make and struggled immensely. Her hands were sweaty, and she constantly had to rub them on her legs to keep her grip on the loops.

"You should leave." Nurzan said to Deeso as he remained uninterested in offering help.

The other weavers were also anti-social and cared little for distractions. They saw it was best to not get involved with personal grievances. Deeso found herself dissatisfied with her work and decided to dismantle it to spite Nurzan. Two of the weavers looked up and frowned at Deeso's behavior but understood the learning curve. Deeso returned home and got her axe. She looked at the blade that dulled from a lull in battle. She lifted it and swung in her home, just barely hitting the hut's wall. To cope with her anxiety, Deeso left and joined a few other members by one of the few toolmaking circles scattered throughout camp. She needed to do some maintenance on her axe and felt listening to other people's problems could put her at ease. Deeso approached and watched as the group's circle moved a bit for her to fit right in. Deeso kept her ears peeled on the conversation, while she held her hand out for a sizable rock. Her wish was granted as she weighed the massed stone placed in her left hand while she reached for a nearby antler to start.

Deeso's technique was more advanced than that of the Old Way used by Jih and his people.[19] This started out with a source stone, usually made of flint or limestone that would be shaped by applying careful strikes towards the edges of the rock. Deeso preferred to use antler than other material as the strikes were softer and more suited for her needs. Deeso hit her rock carefully watching as flakes piled around her. She grabbed a nearby leather bag that was empty. With some work done from one end, she noticed that her rock was in the shape of a turtle shell, with a flat bottom and a sizable hump on the top. Deeso dislodged the old blade from her axe that was rugged and worn. It was hardly a prized weapon in this state, and she looked to her new construction. She used the dull blade to split the construction down the middle and flake off points to keep the new blade sharp. She placed the new blade into the wooden void left by the previous one. She slammed the wood tightly and lifted the handle to ensure it was a perfect fit. She watched as the group passed around a prepared stone core and made blades from its construction.

"Not bad." She said to herself as a fledgling tool smith in the making. Deeso pocketed the remaining larger flakes in the small bag to keep for later. Deeso eyed the group that sat before her. They took their time at the tool area; it was one of the few places they could socialize as working on their tools was personal and didn't require teamwork. While she didn't feel close to them, she was at least tolerated.

"Pass me some hot spark." One of the men asked as Deeso and a few others ferried some prepared flint to him.

"You came at a good time, Deeso. We've been talking about Sadal and the great hunt." He added on, as he waited for another in the circle to begin speaking. The conversation among the people picked up as they took breaks working on their tool construction.

"It's been at least three days." One woman said as she ran her finger through the soil.

The atmosphere was tense as Master Hunters almost never ran late past their expected return date. There were four Master Hunters within the Painted Hand that led teams to clear out predators while hunting for food was done by all members. Those that were infirm to hunt live animals often operated in scouting positions or harvested fruit. The only two Master Hunters of relevance to Deeso were Sadal and Zulag. She was aware of their rivalry, and that Zulag long wanted to secure the tiger hunt for himself. Deeso smiled as she knew Sadal worked hard for the honor and Ronkalk finally acknowledged those efforts. Deeso's good feelings though eroded as there were doubts growing among the ranks.

---

[19] Deeso uses a technology type called Mousterian technology, it's a stone knapping technique that developed around 250,000-300,000 years ago during the Middle Paleolithic period. Neanderthals, Modern Humans, and Denisovans use this as the gold standard for their tool construction and is what Deeso learned how to do growing up!

"Did they fail? This is very unusual." The same woman asked with some concern in her voice.

"Sadal? No, there must be something better coming." One of the men assured the group who seemed to have mixed opinions of their friend's prowess. He patted Deeso's back with a hearty thud as she nodded in agreement. Deeso put her tools down as she was entrenched in the gossip surrounding Sadal's expedition.

"Sadal always tries to impress. She once took some hunters to get Smir-Tamdeu, and we ended up with a whole On-Tokam instead!" Another woman chimed in with a small grin.

"Better than a Weypeu? Even Ronkalk has yet to claim a Yaan. The old man is losing sight of his vision and Sadal was not qualified. Nobody's perfect. I have been saying that for some time now, but she always seems to think so." Another man said, breaking his silence on the matter. Deeso decided to intervene on Sadal's behalf while she couldn't defend herself. Deeso's expression was irate as her head whipped around. She addressed the cantankerous figure before her as he was well known for speaking on topics that weren't his business.

"She is a Master Hunter for a reason. [20]A title you lack Ututar. It's a hard-earned honor. I would suggest you learn some respect." Deeso shot back with a glare as Ututar sucked his teeth in response.

"To be blunt, you children have no idea. The walk from when the land was hot and dry was a true test of our might. Zulag's forces took a similar route to Sadal's to oust a bothersome pack of Denmey, perhaps when he returns, we will see if they crossed paths?" Ututar suggested with a grin that irritated Deeso.

Ututar was in his mid-30s and a generation ahead of Deeso and the others that made up their stone circle. He constantly used his age as a cudgel against dissent. He had a large scar on his cheek that he cited as a battle wound in his early days against a lion. Ututar was an outspoken critic of Ronkalk and his policies as he felt they weakened the integrity of the band's structure as a collective. Deeso shared no interest in his vision and was a Ronkalk loyalist to the point of willing to risk her own life. While there was resentment against Ronkalk for a string of bad decisions in the past, nobody could imagine a future without him. Ututar gave Deeso a smug grunt as he looked onward at the camp around them. After some time, a low bellow came from a man who played a horn. Deeso recognized this sound for announcements from Ronkalk but was also used to signal the return of Master Hunters. In the distance, Deeso could see the outline of figures trickle into camp. They moved slowly and were exhausted with strife evident on their journey. As Deeso and a few other members of the band went to greet them, Deeso's expression soured further. The returning team was Zulag's while Sadal's remained unaccounted for. Deeso started to worry as people were clamoring for their loved ones. Sadal led the team but there were others who relied on her leadership to bring them home.

[20] Master Hunters in The Broken Bone are distinguished warriors who have taken down large predators in single combat. Their responsibilities involve clearing the land for settlement and providing food for their large numbers.

Out of the growing crowd, Deeso waved her hand and jumped to get the hunting party's attention. Zulag's eyes had bags underneath them as they marched continuously without stopping to make it home. Deeso looked into his eyes and knew that something was amiss. His usually cocky attitude was far more reserved than usual.

"Zulag!" Deeso yelled out as she went to greet the returning search party. As she approached Zulag's field of view, his already tired expression became worse. Zulag wasn't fond of outsiders to The Broken Bone that she and Sadal once were, and Deeso resented him as his position of third in command came from nepotism. Although Deeso could hardly stand Zulag, he was the only potential source to figuring out Sadal's fate. She needed to know what happened for her own sake. Sadal took Brab with her and both lives were at risk.

"Deeso, I wasn't expecting you to be here." Zulag said coldly as he was taken aback by her presence.

One of Zulag's responsibilities as a Master Hunter was to inform the family of any deaths and bring back what they could for burial. Zulag's distaste for Deeso leaked out of his posture and other unspoken words, but this was about professionalism. Zulag looked over Deeso and nodded his head for her to follow. Deeso carried a confused look on her face as Zulag set off some distance from the growing crowd. Deeso looked behind her as she saw other members of his hunting team empty their packs.

"Come. I haven't told my uncle this yet." Zulag said as he walked some distance away from the other members of their band. He didn't bother to look behind him as Deeso caught up with his fast pace.

The two convened in a lesser traveled area of the village and were able to talk in private. Ronkalk's home loomed in the distance, but he was not home. Zulag looked to make sure the two weren't followed as he was aware this was a sensitive manner.

"We've been talking about what happened with Sadal's hunting party. What do you know-We've?" Deeso said as she was interrupted by Zulag lifting his hand up. Deeso became frantic as she couldn't wait to hear the news. Zulag took a deep breath.

"After I cleared the Denmey pit, we searched for any stragglers. I realized the extent of their territory matched where Sadal was ordered to kill the Weypeu. We searched the area to see how it was disposed of. The Weypeu was slain, and the corpse was there, but what I saw was unexpected. Her team was torn to pieces by the beast. We found parts of them and brought them with us. The land was unclean, and the powder was missing. Sadal didn't deliver." Zulag said, as he rubbed the back of his neck.

Deeso felt weak as a sudden feeling of nausea fell over her. Zulag watched as Deeso supported herself on the side of a nearby hut wall. She couldn't bring herself to believe Zulag's words, but with the amount of detail and his tone of voice, this had to be the truth.

"Are...Are you saying Sadal fell in battle? Where is Sadal's body? Do we have it? I want to bury her with honors." Deeso asked as she saw some of the other members of the search party looking for the next of kin to bring the unfortunate news. Deeso's eyes watered, but she held hope that young Brab remained. Zulag couldn't help but hide his apathy much to Deeso's face as he turned around to answer her question.

"That's just it little Deeso. The one you're looking for is gone. I couldn't find Sadal's body anywhere." Zulag huffed.

"I am aware of that. I just want her home. Was she..." Deeso questioned, her tone increasing in severity as her patience was running thin. Death among The Broken Bone was as common as rainwater that fell from the sky, both to their own and those they fought against. It was something they all accepted as an inevitability, so mourning came at the manner of death as opposed to death itself. Had Sadal died in a dishonorable way, it would be a great sadness.

"Eaten? No. No trace. We tore its stomach to see if she was eaten and nothing was there. Her tools were gone as well." Zulag retorted. Zulag hardly entertained Deeso, but it was worth mentioning to provide extra context to the situation.

"And what of-" Deeso mentioned, as she stopped herself. She couldn't bring herself to utter the question, but Zulag understood what she was asking. Zulag folded his arms and looked to the foliage above him before looking back at Deeso.

"There was something in the cave though. A boy? He was killed. The wound wasn't from the Weypeu so I wonder where it came from. I have that body if you want to bury it with honors." Zulag said with a grunt.

Deeso covered her mouth with her hands in disbelief. Deeso saw herself in Brab, as the child was marked a bad omen by the priests. Though the boy couldn't talk, she felt they had a special connection from a shared origin. Deeso naturally ignored these testaments and did her job as best as she could while Sadal balanced her responsibilities. She couldn't comprehend such a thing happening, as she assumed Sadal taking the baby out on the hunt was to bond with the child as the birth mother. It was common practice among their people to take infants on smaller hunts as they believed they were able to learn new skills from birth and the earlier, the more efficient, the warrior would become. Deeso curled up her fist and jettisoned it straight to Zulag. His quick reaction time just barely made it in time to keep him guarded from injury.

"How...dare you accuse...Sadal." Deeso said, with her breathing growing heavy. She felt as if she couldn't move and had nobody to talk to. Nurzan wouldn't have reacted in any meaningful way, and she had no allies anymore.

"I just say what I see, nothing more. Quick punch. I thought you were going to kick me instead." Zulag countered and he gripped Deeso's wrist tightly. She was able to pry herself free without much difficulty as she twisted his arm causing him to let go.

"I hope you die in your sleep." Deeso mumbled to herself.

"Yes, many do and many more will. Get used to your future leader." Zulag taunted with some disgust in his voice. He ended the conversation and left in the direction of Ronkalk's home. Zulag heard some rumbling from the hut and knew his uncle was home. He took a deep breath as he made his way to tell his uncle what had transpired. Deeso watched Zulag wander off and had much to mull over as she evaluated the scenarios that led to Sadal's disappearance.

Zulag's face held a frown for he had felt his uncle wouldn't take the news well. Ronkalk stood outside his home and carried his young infant in his arms. Zulag watched as Ronkalk bounced him in his arms, the love of an uncle was never the same as the love of a father. Zulag solemnly approached the proud leader. Ronkalk kept his gaze on the village but felt Zulag's presence coming closer. Zulag remained silent and waited for his uncle to finish. Ronkalk turned around and opened the discussion by extending his arm out.

"Your aunt is visiting Stobai on my behalf, so it's just us and the child today. Boy, are you willing to speak now, or will you stand to bare me more shade?" Ronkalk teased as he gave Zulag a smile.

"Uncle, I have news for you." Zulag said with some hesitation in his voice. He gave him a wide berth but was invited to come closer.

"Well Zuzu, I wait with great anticipation." Ronkalk said with a cheery expression on his face.

Zulag wondered what kept his uncle in such good spirits. He reasoned it must have had something to do with his cousin in his arms. He gave his cousin no mind and met his eyes with Ronkalk's. Zulag hid his embarrassment as his nickname came from his inability to say his own name as a child. Ronkalk raised his head at Zulag and studied his nephew's face. All it took from Ronkalk was a bit of prolonged eye contact to get what he wanted.

"It's regarding the hunt. The Denmey were killed with ease and the pelts are brought home. We found that the extent of their territory overlapped with where Sadal was sent for the Weypeu. My team arrived after the fighting and found that it was...bloody." Zulag said as he waited for Ronkalk's questions.

"How many were slain?" Ronkalk questioned as he ran his fingers through his beard.

"All, except for one. We have buried the rest and told our members of what happened." Zulag answered.

"The most likely to survive was Sadal as she shares your rank. Sadal was on the raid, but her return was not known to me. She has no family, other than Deeso, Nurzan, and the young Brab. Who did you tell this news to before me? This is a sensitive matter." Ronkalk questioned Zulag in an investigative tone only a parent could give as he waited for a response. Zulag stayed quiet as he decided to ignore the part of his uncle's question and powered forward instead.

"That's just it uncle. She's gone." Zulag coughed.

"What do you mean by gone?" Ronkalk asked as his tone grew more serious.

"There was nothing left of the body. There was no powder present at the site either. The Weypeu's stomach was empty, so she wasn't eaten. The baby she had was also found dead. I saw that he had a rock embedded in his forehead, tell me what you think it means." Zulag asserted with confidence.

Ronkalk raised an eyebrow at what Zulag was alluding to but remained conflicted on the matter. Desertion was a serious accusation. Murder was another case entirely, but infanticide was practiced among their people in grave cases. It was known by him that Brab was a target of the priests and wondered if this was connected. Ronkalk ultimately feared the secrets of his band's structure leaking out would weaken his position of leadership. Sadal was given much respect for the amount she worked to achieve her role. It was rare for Ronkalk to give personal access to any member of the band, let alone a former Wanderer. He took her input with the utmost severity, but Zulag's claims were also ones he considered. Despite some tension that rose between Zulag and Ronkalk regarding succession, Ronkalk considered him an incredibly close confidant as a close born family member was quite rare to have.

"This sounds to me like Sadal was attacked by our enemies, but the sign of no struggle clouds this claim. Sadal is a skilled warrior, and her pursuers would easily be thwarted." Ronkalk commented as he stood to look his nephew in the eye. Zulag nodded, waiting for him to finish. The trust Ronkalk held in Zulag was immeasurable as Zulag had to earn his current position as a Master Hunter just like everyone else.

"I will muster up a search party. The old ways have told us we must kill deserters. If this is to be the case and my claim is incorrect, I will enact a rule of mercy. I want Sadal brought back alive so that she can explain the details of her leave. This is an unusual circumstance, and I must know if foul play occurred." Ronkalk decided, much to the disdain of Zulag. As strict as his uncle was, Zulag was taken aback by such a suggestion. How could an exception be made for Sadal when she committed something so egregious?

"I don't want to speak out of term-" Zulag said, his voice almost cracking as he did so.

"Then don't." Ronkalk retorted. He then added on, with the lecturing tone that Zulag had long since associated with a scolding.

"My reasons do not need explanation as my will is resolute. As you are my nephew, I will allow you this. There are practical reasons behind every decision I make. Yes, I am contradicting the warrior code established by my grandfather. Sadal, like yourself, is a Master Hunter. We have many people who rely on her to bring food besides killing the beasts. She must be kept alive. She will be punished, but she will not die by our hands." Ronkalk mentioned. Zulag looked to the ground for the moment as the word "punished" hung over him for a few moments. He didn't envy those who were disciplined by Ronkalk.

"Now then, as this is an urgent matter, I want you to get the band involved. Go to our horn player and gather everyone and then meet me here. You were looking for an opportunity to lead, go forth and do so." Ronkalk said as Zulag nodded in acknowledgement to gather the attention of the others.

Zulag wasted no time in getting the camp ready for Ronkalk's orders. Zulag arrived to find their announcer resting under a tree. He lowered his head and glared at the man as he leaned back and watched the wind blow through the trees.

"Ronkalk has something to say. Gather everyone." Zulag ordered, as the man got up to signal the group.

Zulag watched him head in the direction towards the summoning horn while he went to join Ronkalk. The sound permeated through the wetland drowning out the sounds of the frogs and insects that made up their surroundings. Ronkalk saw his will was fulfilled and cracked his knuckles as he prepared to speak. Those that heeded the call placed down their weapons and other pieces of interest to listen. Activity throughout the camp ceased as all gathered to convene in the village center. Ronkalk delegated most of his orders through Zulag and occasionally another helper which prompted some concern. Ronkalk speaking meant the issue was beyond their current power and something serious was amiss. Deeso wiped her eyes as she cleaned herself from weeping in her home. Her eyes were red but filled with determination as she looked to hear the words of Ronkalk to give her courage. She made her way past the other homes around her and joined a line of people to sit by. Ronkalk waited for people to pool in and situate themselves on the grass before he spoke.

"By now, the news is known. Sadal is missing and likely in the hands of our enemies. They could be our kind looking to ransom her or the Forest Seekers where she is being tortured. We must find her. I will form a search party and I will ask for volunteers." Ronkalk spoke as members of The Broken Bone remained seated. Zulag noted a slight hesitation among them and moved forward from his uncle. Zulag saw an opportunity to invigorate and inspire the people and walked forward to offer his theory.

"Sadal has deserted us. She was not taken. She left us. We will make her pay." Zulag added on to his uncle's words. Zulag could see some already hesitant faces in the crowd starting to get restless.

He hoped to get a crowd going by appealing to their base and bloodthirsty desires. If Sadal truly deserted, many of The Broken Bone were able to elevate themselves as Sadal was an incredibly skilled opponent. This reaction was exactly what Zulag was hoping for. He reveled in it as Ronkalk gave Zulag a look of interest. Ronkalk hadn't expected Zulag to be so brazen, but the winds of change kept going. He noted that Zulag never spoke aloud when he gave a speech. It was clear Zulag was trying to convey he was ready for more responsibilities. Ronkalk decided to ignore this for now and proceed with what he planned to offer to his community.

"Which one of you will come?" Ronkalk asked, his voice coming off as warm and inviting. His eyes darted to Ututar as he stood up. Ronkalk was delighted to see a strong warrior offer his services. Ronkalk was aware of Ututar's criticisms and found that he could kill two birds with one stone by inflating his ego with an important task and getting rid of him for the time being. He extended his hand out in respect to the volunteer and gave a smile. The expression of content in his choice turned to one of confusion as he did not step forward as was customary.

"I will do no such thing. This is a waste, just like everything else you've done since coming here." Ututar sneered as he attempted to turn the tide of the crowd against Ronkalk.

The color of Zulag's face vanished as he heard Ututar's words. He wasn't expecting such a bold declaration and was intrigued. Ronkalk's position was well respected, and anyone would have felt honored to fulfill his will. Zulag was aware there were contenders who sought to not only unseat Ronkalk but threaten Zulag's bottom line of inheritance. He kept himself quiet as he let Ututar dig himself further into a hole.

He's as good as dead. Zulag thought as he remained perfectly still. Ronkalk bellowed out a small chuckle. Ronkalk was amused and let the man continue as he eyed the crowd who remained motionless.

"Your decisions to put us somewhere with no game have brought doom. I share favor with the priests, and they agree with my decision." Ututar spat as he attempted to subvert some of the crowd over to him.

"Priests, I respect your aid. Does Ututar speak for you?" Ronkalk asked, as he received nothing but silence.

The priesthood was an integral part of The Broken Bone and inserted themselves in events where applicable. While Ronkalk and some members didn't see eye to eye in private, they were united in the public gaze. Ronkalk would receive no open challenge or questioning to his edicts. Ronkalk received no words from the various skull wearers that hid their expressions. He nodded happily and noted that the right choice was made. Although the priests may have operated in deception behind his back, Ronkalk knew that the power within him still shined bright and true. It would be suicidal to challenge his authority.

"Are you sure you want to challenge me?" Ronkalk asked one last time. He spoke with finality in his voice as the intent to kill was on his mind.

Deeso sat some distance from Zulag and Ronkalk and noted that the man who spoke now was the one she crossed paths with earlier at the fire pits. She gave a look of disgust at Ututar as he sullied Sadal's memory in front of her. She was curious on how far the man was willing to go to prove a point, going against Ronkalk's decision making. Despite some setbacks, Deeso was content with how things were run in The Broken Bone.

He can't be this stupid. Zulag thought. He coughed as he saw that Ututar agreed to Ronkalk's goading of him. Zulag was compelled to grab branches from the nearby trees and set. The others that saw such a challenge done in the past went to work as they also went to grab branches. Zulag pushed the ground as they placed these branches in an oval to build their arena. Smoothed stones were then placed down to mark the boundary line.

"We will do this as our ancestors have then. They will build. We will watch. The line is made of branches and rocks. We fight to the death." Ronkalk mentioned to Ututar.

Ututar scoffed at Ronkalk's explanation as if he was an ignorant child, he was well informed of what his treachery would mean. Deeso scoffed at Ututar as she felt there wasn't much of a contest to be excited about. She looked up to the sky as the sunset was upon them. She stood up to get a better view of what was going on as she saw that fires were lit for the two combatants. All around her, the darkness of the night was put at bay. The camp was set alight as the two fighters were surrounded by a wave of heat where the fires simmered. Ututar was not a Master Hunter like that of Sadal or Zulag, but he maintained an important position within The Broken Bone. He trained the children to fight with melee weapons and was a ruthless teacher in his role. He was forceful and brutish, but you could be sure that your survival was in good hands. Ronkalk hated having to run through new people and get them acclimated to such a crucial task, but he couldn't be disrespected in such a way. It would all fall apart if he were to crack now and allow this to go unpunished.

With the preparations complete, Ronkalk was the first to enter the ring. It was understood by all parties involved that combat with fists was the method for dealing with these disputes. Ronkalk was disrobed by Zulag, revealing his scarification as the current leader. He certainly defied the odds being a strong fifty years old. He heard the jeers all before, but it would matter little. His body was in powerful condition, for underneath some situational body fat, he held a well preserved six pack and powerful thighs. Ronkalk's punches were said to give mountains fear as he could break a boulder itself.

"The gray on your hair tells us all we need to know." Ututar commented.

At an established thirty-five, he was not the youngest of men himself. Ronkalk offered no retort this time, as he was already focused on the kill. Ututar was also in an impressive physique, with his role keeping him quite agile to contend with the likes of the children full of energy. His students watched closely and held a good bond with their teacher but adhered to the rank of Ronkalk as leader. They made no affirming noises but also watched in silence. Deeso watched the scene intently and determined that she knew Ronkalk was forming a plan. She watched him scan for any weaknesses. People don't get to his age by accident. She remembered an adage she had heard while traveling. "Fear the old for they have survived much."

Without much fanfare, Ututar began his rush inwards to attack Ronkalk. He elbowed him in the jaw, and disoriented Ronkalk as a tooth became loose in his mouth. Ronkalk removed his tooth with little issue and remained on the defensive. Zulag watched intently with conflicted emotions. The love for his uncle was strong, but the desire to finally be recognized as the leader of The Broken Bone gnawed at him from the inside out. His disdain for Ututar was evident on his face, but the resentment towards the child his uncle produced leaked onto him as well. How could he do something so selfish at his age? He analyzed his uncle's fighting style and was curious that he was only taking hits without retaliation. Ronkalk saw an opening as Ututar went for a kick this time. He missed entirely as Ronkalk maneuvered around him and cupped his leg under his biceps. Restricted to just one leg, Ututar manipulated his current leg trying to pry it loose from his grip as Ronkalk pushed him away and caused him to tumble to the ground. Ututar went for a series of jabs this time, with each one of them landing their mark. Zulag's concern grew slightly as he noted the blood that pooled into his uncle's mouth. Deeso kept a calm expression as she was tracking their movement. The moment that Deeso waited to see finally come to fruition. As Ututar went for a left hook, Ronkalk's reflexes doubled in speed, where the man's hand completely eclipsed Ututar's fist. He squeezed tightly as Ututar could feel the pain pressing down on him. His fingers cracked; the noise audible quite some distance as the men continued to slug one another. A loud crunch sound was heard as Ututar's fingers completely folded in on themselves. Every bone in his left hand was now utterly smashed to pieces, but the adrenaline kept him going.

Ututar's free right hand now did double duty as he used his left arm and right hand as a springboard to get up and change position. He gave an affirmative kick to Ronkalk's stomach that caused him to cough intensely as he was disoriented. He looked towards the mud below him and knew what needed to be done. Ronkalk's past life was wrestling, a field where he maintained control of his own space; it was now that Ututar needed to be put there. He chose to bait Ututar and had his left side exposed for another direct jab. As he did this, he morphed his arm around his while using his free left leg to completely trip Ututar, and he hit the mud with a resounding thud.

Ututar's head rang for a minute as he tried to get his bearings but was met with the massive mountain that was Ronkalk. The weight that he had been disparaged about for some time became an asset as his grip on Ututar was absolute. His back withstood the frantic kicks of Ututar, and Ronkalk was free to do as he pleased. He whipped out his thumbs and jammed them straight into Ututar's eyes, his force unwavering as tears and blood spilled onto his hands. For Ututar, he couldn't have picked a worse day as his eyes gradually morphed to darkness. The heat of the fires surrounding them filled the air as well. While blind, Ututar still had plenty of fight as he clawed at Ronkalk's face like a wild animal. Ronkalk returned the favor kindly with fists attacking Ututar's face and sculpted it as if he were an artist chiseling marble. Ronkalk looked to remove Ututar's teeth as his jaw was dislocated by the man's pure strength. His lip was split open and bled profusely as he laid in the mud. His punching continued as the tanned skin on the man gradually reddened. In his bloodlust, Ronkalk ripped the man's ears clean off, while focusing his punching again on Ututar's forehead. The crack of the man's skull rang as Ututar was flailing for his life.

The onslaught was relentless, as under the setting sun, he felt a further rage fill within him. Any semblance of what remained of the man now was mush as he pried open his jaw. Zulag noted Ututar died some time ago. Ututar's body ceased to move and Ronkalk kept going. The head of the body was nigh unrecognizable, for the ground was littered with brain matter as he slammed him into the hardened mud. Ronkalk took a simple breath and noted his handiwork. He eyed his injuries, which were more than he anticipated. He slowly got up and took a moment to breathe. To the crowd that observed the body, they were utterly horrified at the man's transfiguration. Zulag shook slightly as he walked over to wipe the blood off Ronkalk's face with some spare animal skins. Ronkalk then spoke, against the behest of Zulag insisting he get rest.

"I ask again. Who will go?"

Deeso saw Zulag's shock and shared the same expression. Ronkalk's words brought back to her reality as she was moved by such a raw display of power. The hostile words of Nurzan that told her to leave the weaving group came back to her. Deeso decided to take his advice and act on her own accord. Deeso's love for Sadal was absolute and she would sacrifice anything to see her again. She doubted Zulag's claims of desertion but vowed to strike down any who harmed Sadal. Deeso also saw this as an opportunity to test her abilities and prove to herself that she had a role worth having. She saw the opportunity and rose on her own to stand proudly. Deeso wasn't afraid of the wilderness, her desire to bring death to Sadal's captors filled her with rage. She felt the stare of others as she stood in the growing darkness.

"I will go." Deeso said, prompting some of the crowd to finally break their silence.

There were looks of confusion, as Deeso was not particularly notable in anything. Her tools were rudimentary, she lacked the reputation of a great hunter like Sadal, and she had ill favor with the priests. Ronkalk looked at Deeso with intrigue on his face. As leader, Ronkalk was aware that she possessed a skill that was ill-appreciated among their people. He decided to test her and ask a question.

"You are close with her. How can you...be trusted to bring...her home?" Ronkalk questioned, his breath still waned as he recovered from his injuries.

"That's why I am best suited for the job. I know everything about her. I will find her, and I will make sure she is kept alive." She said, as she kept her eyes pointed directly on Ronkalk. Although the gawking eyes of the crowd didn't help any, she felt compelled to undertake this task now. Deeso thought about her potential allies for such an endeavor. Nobody came to mind as helpful to her cause.

"This is acceptable. You have my blessing to go. I can't send only one though, there must be more." Ronkalk said after much deliberation.

Zulag darted his head in complete disdain as he heard Deeso's voice across the crowd. He narrowed his eyes as he made out her figure through the campfires. Zulag couldn't help himself but to meet Deeso's claim. Zulag debated the possibilities for him regarding Sadal's disappearance. If Sadal was truly captured by the enemy and his suspicions were wrong, he could prove himself in battle and eliminate an enemy that would threaten his succession. If his theory of Sadal's desertion was correct, he had free range to kill off his hunting rival for good and have the best kills at his disposal. Zulag saw nothing more than a chance to elevate his status and had the skills to pull off the job. Not one to let a moment like this go to waste, Zulag decided that his talents could be best used somewhere else while he waited to inherit. His mind couldn't understand his uncle's logic, as Deeso offered nothing of value to him on the surface. Zulag was aware that Ronkalk wasn't getting soft with age as he defaced a man before his very eyes. He knew there was something hidden about Deeso's abilities and wanted to see if his uncle truly could see beyond as he claimed.

"Sadal's shadow has finally come out." Zulag mumbled.

"Uncle, I will go as well. I hold to my theory that Sadal betrayed our way of life and I can hold that one to stay on task. I am a Master Hunter and I am aware of all the tricks of the trade. If it comes to pass our enemies have captured her and I am wrong, I will admit that. Sadal and I will bring death to the foe and her legacy will be cleared." He said and pointed to Deeso who shot an opposing glare at him.

"Zulag, I admire your efforts in volunteering. I approve of this venture. As I sit here, I realize I have kept you too close to camp and to see the outside world like your father once did will be good for your growth. You are not suitable to lead, and I will name my son to inherit instead." Ronkalk noted as he ignored gasps from the crowd.

"W-What? B-But he's an infant." Zulag said as he coughed into his arm.

Zulag couldn't believe what he heard. That punch of dialogue hit Zulag harder than any spear to the chest ever could. All his planning and scheming to convince Ronkalk he was ready for a position of power now meant nothing in the hands of the entire crowd that witnessed this. Not only was Zulag personally embarrassed, but his status was also put under question. People talked among themselves in conflict; Zulag was expected to be the heir apparent from his displays of competence, but Ronkalk naturally thought differently, giving his young son the mantle instead. Many disagreed with that decision seeing that Zulag was a proven adult, but the fate of Ututar is one all wished to avoid. Their tempers were tamed by crushing dissent, but this was one more notch in many mistakes.

"I am tired. I will rest. I will not spare more than four for this journey. Come to me tomorrow with your decision then." Ronkalk ordered Zulag and Deeso.

The crowd vanished as they took Ronkalk's need for rest as a sign for them to do the same. People picked up their tools and slept under the stars or returned to their homes. With the sun just about down, a few fires remained to keep away predators. Zulag glared at Deeso once more before he returned to the shelter where his family slept. Zulag struggled to deal with the reality of his stripped title and now had to return home to Ronkalk alone.

As for Deeso, she had a new lease on life. Sadal's choice to desert without her, if true, was a hard blow to their relationship and established trust. If Sadal truly suffered, Deeso always opened herself up as a resource to talk. She also felt responsible for the many who would struggle to find food without Sadal's leadership. Deeso had her doubts on Sadal's true fate, but if she really was alive, she needed to know. Deeso walked home but saw a lone flame flicker on the outskirts of the village. Deeso's desire to see Nurzan was minimal, and she decided to take the long way home. She continued her walk and found a lone woman sat some distance away at a fire. She was heating some sort of meat with a skewer. Deeso's stomach growled as the smoke reached her nose. Although she avoided eating at night, the pain was too much to bear so she sat down. Deeso noted the strange markings on the woman before her. Her mind raced as she remembered who she was looking at. She was a member of the priesthood and wore green pigment on her face. Deeso held little respect for priests but something about her nature disarmed her. Deeso had her opinions but decided to remain civil with the woman. It was clear she was an outcast in some form, much like herself. Her eyes fixated on the meat once more.

"Can I have some?" Deeso asked as the woman silently broke off a piece of meat for her to chew on. The food was delicious, incredibly so, to her starved stomach. Deeso noted that the woman hadn't asked her name. She looked nervous as she was unable to start a conversation of her own. She lifted her neck to Deeso and pointed to a harsh scar underneath. Deeso heard the rumors around the fire pits but hadn't bothered to see for herself. She chewed her food and swallowed.

"You are Cikya..." Deeso whispered.

Cikya nodded, hearing her name. Her eyes drifted to the soil as she wasn't used to being acknowledged by others. Only the sounds of the crackling fire filled the air as the two women looked at one another. Deeso noticed this and adjusted the tone of her voice.

"I am Deeso." She said as she introduced herself with pride in her stance. She waited before speaking further as she looked around for any eavesdroppers. Deeso's recollection of Cikya's fate enlightened her to take care with her words. Deeso then took her attention to the crown of bones fixed onto Cikya's head. It was a mortal sin to remove them now that they've been honored this way.

"I never agreed with what happened to you. You stole because the need was there, and the weak were punished. That is their fault, not yours. They also tell me that you were given a blessing. As a second chance for a life of ill-gotten gains." Deeso summarized as she raised an eyebrow.

Cikya nodded again, this time with a more forlorn expression on her face. Deeso saw an opportunity arise as she remembered Ronkalk's orders for them to find additional members for their search party. In one conversation, Deeso could tell that Cikya had something to prove and so she offered the best thing she could, her friendship.

"Shamans, priests, Seers, whatever you call them, they and I disagree on many things. Will you still help me?" Deeso asked with feigned innocence in her voice as she moved her foot around in the dirt.

Cikya smiled and formed a fist to slam into the palm of her other hand. Her eyebrow raised some concern with the person who would be one of her new partners, but she appreciated her presence, nonetheless. Respect had to be earned but for Deeso she didn't ask much. The real task would come the next morning.

A League Of Their Own

As Zulag was no longer in Ronkalk's good graces, he stewed in rage at how he was cast out and seen as unfit to lead. Zulag was unable to sleep as the events of the previous day replayed in his mind over and over. It just didn't make sense. What was he doing wrong? His mind thought of his younger cousin who was sleeping in the arms of his uncle. As the first to rise, Zulag took a stump as his seat and waited to meet the others as agreed. He felt that his partners would be unreliable, and this journey would be his own instead. Zulag watched the morning sun as he sat by himself for a few hours. The night before, Ronkalk mentioned that Zulag should meet Deeso at the southern end of camp. To his surprise, Cikya came forward into his vision. The white of her bone crown prompted all attention as it stuck out to some onlookers. She yawned and covered her mouth, but she was awake. In her hands was a large staff built from wood that she carried around. She was fit, just like many of her group, but this was her weapon of choice. She wore a small backpack that had a small dagger inside and some bones. Zulag was visibly uncomfortable seeing Cikya at first but decided to put his mind on other matters.

"I knew she wouldn't be here. Turns out her volunteering was simply a-" Zulag mumbled to himself as he turned to see Deeso approach. He gritted his teeth at the sight of her and didn't bother to give her the satisfaction of a greeting. She also held a small backpack, but her axe was tied to her upper leg with a string. She positioned the handle to face her and the blade towards the ground to avoid injury.

She gave Cikya a wave and barely acknowledged Zulag, only nodding her head as the three sat in silence. Within minutes, the frame of their leader showed up as he dragged the carcass of a pig behind him. Zulag could always rely on Ronkalk to provide with the morning hunt. Ronkalk cleaned up considerably from his previous injuries the night before, but the damage done to him was still apparent. Zulag moved quickly to receive his uncle, but Ronkalk held his hand out as Zulag approached him. One of his lower teeth was missing as he greeted his new search party, and the swelling on his cheeks was still noticeable. Ronkalk looked at the others before speaking.

"That was a good tooth. I will miss that one." Ronkalk opened and broke the silence right on time.

"I thank you all for volunteering. I wish to find closure on Sadal's disappearance from our group and ensure her safe return. There are few I respect in this world, and she is among them. Zulag, I need you to reinforce our defenses before you depart. Speak to those who are responsible for the watch, I fear the Forest Seekers may have plans beyond my knowledge."

"Yes uncle. Did you still need-" Zulag said as he was cut off by Ronkalk.

"I have it handled. Fill my will and return soon." He ordered Zulag, watching as he placed his stuff down before moving towards his next objective. Now only Deeso and

Cikya remained. The two looked at each other, unsure of what Ronkalk had in store for them.

"Deeso. I want you to accompany me for a brief task. There is a camp nearby that has sought contact. I am to speak with them, but first we must wait. I've given them a gift and I plan to sweeten the deal with some more." Ronkalk mentioned. Ronkalk looked up at the sun and yawned. He hoped to be more energized for his duties, but he just hunted a pig.

"Have you seen Nurzan around? You live with him, so I presume you know his location. He and the weavers should be giving us a basket full of meat soon." Ronkalk mentioned as Deeso turned her head to him.

"I have not." Deeso said sheepishly.

Cikya pointed in the distance to see two men carrying baskets. She deduced this was Nurzan and an assistant of his that headed towards them. Cikya leaned against a tree as she watched the two. Cikya's opinion of Nurzan was low as he was at best a bore, and at worst, a complete curmudgeon. Cikya wouldn't miss his presence much as she thought about her choice to join Deeso and Zulag. Nurzan prompted his assistant to place the first basket filled with fruit. Ronkalk inspected the bounty and nodded while Nurzan placed the second basket filled with meat. Nurzan waited patiently as Ronkalk assessed the strength of the basket. Ronkalk gave a look of approval that Nurzan took as dismissal as he returned to his task. Before he left, Ronkalk called for his attention. He noticed Nurzan's behavior was strange when it came to Sadal. Those with a tight bond would have jumped at the helm to avenge her but Nurzan sat among the crowd and remained quiet.

"Before you run off, I must ask. I have not seen you weep or make any sort of demands of your leader to solve the injustice put on you. You pleaded with me for her hand once, and I used my influence to present you worthy of her embrace. You seem to be in high spirits with the absence of Sadal at hand. What's your secret to balance? Are you confident at the strength of my nephew and his companions?" Ronkalk asked. Nurzan felt a cold sweat down his back as he heard his leader's questioning.

"Screaming against the will of the spirits won't bring her back." Nurzan answered as he had his feet turned to face a new direction. He stared at Ronkalk with soulless eyes.

"It's true that you were never really a warrior, it's our gift to be in tune with your emotions. Make your leave until I call on you again." Ronkalk said with a derisive tone. Sadal kept her grievances private, but Ronkalk could tell that there were issues below the surface.

Ronkalk placed his hand on Deeso's left shoulder as he pointed in the direction of the baskets. He picked one up with one hand, while Deeso held the second one close to her body. This was the opportunity she was waiting for. She couldn't wait to smirk at Zulag and rub it in his face as she treasured personal time with their leader. Ronkalk gave Cikya no orders, as he looked her over with disinterest. Ronkalk then turned to guide Deeso towards his goal for the day. The two carried the baskets of food and Ronkalk directed their movement carefully through the outskirts and forest that followed. Deeso felt a rush of emotions she couldn't explain as she accompanied Ronkalk. She kept herself quiet and absorbed the sounds of the road and early morning beyond them.

"Converse with me Deeso. It's not often I get to speak to the concerns of the youth. Zulag has different responsibilities than someone like yourself." Ronkalk explained as he cracked his neck.

"Since you mentioned it...Why was Zulag spurned leadership? I understand this to be private, but it was done in front of our band." Deeso asked. Although she was well composed on the surface, internally her mind raced intently. She knew that she was taking a very big risk asking such a question. Deeso was the last person to care about anything regarding Zulag personally, but she conceded that he was seemingly liked by some people and at the very least knew what he was doing. Her question evaluated Ronkalk's decision making, and she feared that it would be viewed as her being out of term.

"I have no need for secrecy so the truth can be spoken. Zulag is competent and ambitious, through natural talent and with my mentorship. This is known, but in his heart, there is a desire for power that I cannot control. Leaders serve best when placed into situations beyond their abilities, and alter their surroundings to make it work, instead of creating a problem from nothing." Ronkalk stated.

Deeso nodded, not envious in the slightest of Zulag's position when it came to having to follow in Ronkalk's footsteps. She matched his stride as well as she could, making sure to brush foliage out of the way in advance for Ronkalk. It was an unneeded gesture but one that came from respect. Ronkalk decided to offer a question of his own to Deeso as well.

"I saw you in the fighting pits last week, but the question escaped me at the time. Your opponent Bheyra, we will discuss her. She is a fierce foe, a Wanderer like you were, and you bested her in battle during a Blood Feud no less. It was a difficult match, and you had clearance to take her life as she dishonored you. Why did you refrain?" Ronkalk asked as he adjusted his grass covering. Blood Feuds occurred when an opponent disrespected the other to a degree where only the field of battle served as the remedy for the insult. An opponent in a Blood Feud is allowed to be killed, and it's a spectacle that many chose to witness.

"It was taught that loyalty mattered above everything else. Bheyra is one of us." Deeso commented with pride in herself.

"Animals can be loyal Deeso, but there is more than that with you." Ronkalk mentioned, urging her to go forward.

"Losing is often considered a sign of weakness. Weakness should not be culled, but cultivated, for us to do well. A Weypeu only walks as well as the weakest leg. Killing Bheyra means we lose an extra hand to make tools or to bring home food. There's no reason to do it. If people die under us, it should be for the right reasons. Everyone started from somewhere, even you Ronkalk." Deeso further explained.

Ronkalk let out an unusually jovial laugh as he nodded to Deeso's words. She felt terrified when she saw his face but was relieved to see that his emotions were genuine.

Deeso imagined herself often in the background compared to Sadal, but to hear Ronkalk's words was a great boon to her confidence.

"I am interested in your perspective. I was much rasher when I was younger. If I had someone like you who waited and listened before striking in my circle, we would be in a much better place. The group we are to visit just a short walk away now are a band who have concluded their long walk from the west as well. They are new arrivals. I sent out Zulag in my stead to establish contact, and interest was made. Our band has operated with the balance of four for quite some time, but a fifth entrant allows me to make big plans." Ronkalk said as the path gradually opened now to a clearing in the forest. There was a definitive road that was maintained by knives to cut down foliage and ash was present on the ground. The smell of burning wood filled the air, and it was here that the two would wait.

"They will do a group vote on whether or not to accept us as their new masters. Regardless of the outcome, I am proud of the work all you have been doing to clear the region. I have counted many Onpeu slain and Denmey are next on the list. We can never get rid of them all, but it's a start." Ronkalk mentioned as he extended his hand out towards a man who waited as the other band's representative. Ronkalk and Deeso placed their respective baskets on the ground and waited for someone to collect them.

Deeso estimated their walk took about twenty minutes from the vicinity of their camp, so not much time was wasted. She nodded at Ronkalk's words, hearing the explicit words of pride from him was something that she would hope to cherish for the rest of her life. Their associate guided the two who arrived as guests to a predesignated spot. The two sat in front of an open flame where the leader of the opposing band stood with his council shortly behind him. The outcome of the vote was already decided ahead of their arrival, but for display purposes, the group deliberated as was customary in front of a guest. This was to validate the seriousness of the endeavor. Ronkalk rose to meet him and noticed that in his hands there was a small object clutched. Ronkalk entrusted Zulag to provide an offering of a necklace forged from the teeth of dholes as a sign of solidarity between the two groups. He was prompted to open the man's hand to see the very same necklace, and found their offer was rejected. Deeso covered her mouth to hide her expression as she noticed Ronkalk stood very still.

"I accept the result. But I must ask why." Ronkalk said, his voice unwavering in the confidence of his people and his vision.

"While we are in agreement on some things, we instead choose to pursue peace with the Forest Seekers that inhabit these lands. Our numbers are small, and raiding is not for us. For this, we reject your proposal. Our vision is opposed to yours, Ronkalk." The man said with his arms folded. Ronkalk forcibly grabbed the necklace back in a show of strength. The two glared at each other as they stood apart from one another. Ronkalk studied his opponent's build, and while he was taller, he lacked muscle. This representative wore flashy clouded leopard fur that covered his body. His look was complimented by an array of red and white feathers that surrounded his wrists. The tension was remarkable as Ronkalk waited with the other man. Neither one wanted to be the first to break. Ronkalk decided to extend the conversation just a bit further.

"I see. The Forest Seekers choose to destroy us. They do not see us as potential partners, we are viewed as a problem. An obstacle to be destroyed and to be fed to the wilderness." He said before getting interrupted.

"You place your vision prematurely. Do you not view them the same way?" The man countered. The time for negotiations was over as far as Ronkalk was concerned. Ronkalk decided to leave this band with a word of warning to redefine their current relationship.

"Your decision is your own, and it will be respected under my leadership. That said, if one of my members is harmed with your affairs with the Forest Seekers and I hear of it, I will rip you apart myself, with ease and glee like the blades of grass beneath my feet. Are we in agreement?" Ronkalk said as he showed his teeth to the other man. The two bumped chests into one another in a show of force.

"It would be best if you made your leave. The Broken Bone will be remembered in the days to come." The other man stated as he and Ronkalk slowly retreated to their original positions. Deeso stood and held a disappointed expression on her face as Ronkalk approached her.

"These are parts of leadership nobody tells you about. Rejection happens to us all, even me. Don't be saddened Deeso, this was my mistake to make, not yours. We will make our return to camp. By now, Zulag should be finished and the two of you can start with my blessing." Ronkalk professed.

"There's also Cikya." Deeso pointed out Ronkalk's omission.

"Yes...the three of you." Ronkalk said, correcting himself.

The two continued their discussions regarding various things, where Deeso arrived back at camp to see Zulag and Cikya converse about something. Converse was a strong word to use considering Cikya's mute status. Zulag would speak and gauge his responses based on Cikya's expression. Deeso raised an eyebrow, as this was the first time, she hadn't seen Zulag scream at someone. There was a past hidden between these two she would have to find out later and to see if this would endanger the structure of their team. Ronkalk had no words for Cikya, with his attention instead focused on Deeso and Zulag.

"Deeso, remember what we discussed earlier." He said, waiting as if on cue to see the obvious reaction from Zulag. Zulag noticeably sniffed the air at Deeso's mention, prompting a small chuckle from his uncle. Zulag was nothing, if not incredibly predictable, and this made amusing circumstances when the time was right.

In an unusual display of affection, Ronkalk grabbed Zulag and held him tightly for a hug as Deeso and Cikya watched. Ronkalk spit on his forehead for good luck. Zulag felt his chest cave in slightly with the amount of force his uncle was giving him. He then gave him a small kiss on the forehead, much like he did to his younger cousin. Zulag groaned at Ronkalk's expression, but he couldn't help but feel thankful despite his anger. After everything, they were family at the core. He knew that bringing Sadal home would invalidate Ronkalk's complaints, and that things will be back to normal.

"Come home alive Zuzu." Ronkalk said as he watched the three walk off until they vanished into the undergrowth.

With their goodbyes said, the trio moved to head away from camp, or at least they would have, if Deeso and Zulag could decide on where to go. The outline of their main camp was still noticeably behind them as the two argued over the possible direction Sadal could have gone while Cikya slumped against a tree. She twirled her staff around as she had no opinion of the matter.

"She went north. We need to go through camp and head through the cloud forest. There's plenty of places to hide out there and those who hold criticisms of Ronkalk's rule. It's possible that one of these subordinate leaders may house Sadal to manipulate us." Zulag proposed as he cupped his hands over his eyes to get a better look at their surroundings.

"I think Sadal went west, Zulag." Deeso countered.

"West? Are you out of your mind? Why would she go west? Our allies live to the north and it would be more likely she would have searched for someone up there for her to take refuge. They may have her captured as we do to all deserters." Zulag stated, his annoyance clearly visible on his face.

"Zulag. Out west is hostile territory, there are Forest Seekers everywhere. Think about your line of thinking here. Everyone in our band knows what Sadal looks like. Our allies would have taken her in, but it's the responsibility of the other bands to bring people back. We saw no contingent arrive with her bound or dead. She would have returned by now." Deeso asserted, sharing the same tone of irritation. Cikya looked at the two of them and rolled her eyes. She was willing to try anything at this point to get things moving.

There's a river out west. Perhaps she found someone with a boat to aid her escape. It would be much quicker than walking the entire length of the forest. Cikya thought. She walked over to Zulag who looked at her and waited for a response. She tapped her foot on the soil which left a distinct footprint underneath as she did so. Cikya made a flowing motion with her arms as she tried to get the two's attention on the matter. Zulag struggled sometimes with Cikya's expressions, but he generally understood much quicker than most members of the band.

"Cikya...What are you implying? Wait. I know that sign. The river. You think Sadal went towards a river? None of us can swim." Zulag mentioned, his expression becoming further confused. Cikya nodded her head but held up a finger to his face.

"Oh, there's more?" Deeso questioned. Cikya nodded and cupped her hands together in the shape of a dugout along the river. She grabbed her staff and pounded it on the tree in agreement with Deeso. West was the direction she settled on as well. Zulag saw he was overruled and decided to relent but made his distaste known.

"Fine little Deeso, we'll go investigate your claim to the west. If you've wasted our time though." Zulag said as he snapped a tree branch.

"I've heard it all before Zulag. Let's move." Deeso said, her voice devoid of emotion.

On the trail now, the group walked for about an hour and a half, as hunger overtook them. Deeso lifted her hand for the group to stop and check supplies. Zulag and Deeso both a had surprise on their faces as they looked at their backpacks. They felt somewhat heavier than before, but the two hadn't given much attention to the matter. While Zulag and Deeso were busy, Cikya used her free time to stuff them with dried meat and various fruits to eat. The rewards of home were hardly one to be wasted and they needed every advantage they could get.

"How did she know I liked Valai? I like spitting out the seeds." Deeso asked herself as she peeled a banana to eat, while Zulag enjoyed a mangosteen. Zulag knew that Cikya could be thoughtful, but he didn't imagine a bounty quite like this.

After eating, the three continued on their travels and noted some of the wildlife. A fireback looked at them through the brush and emerged from it. It was male with gray plumage and a black tail that contrasted from the sea of green around them. The bird flapped its wings as the three advanced on its territory. Zulag sensed an opportunity for fresh meat and took out one of his signature throwing knives from a loop in his clothing. He rotated his arm and launched it with incredible force, embedding it into its chest. The bird briefly flapped around before bleeding out. While not exactly the noble kill he was looking for, he figured the extra meat could be good use. He used the knife to rip apart portions that he felt were worth keeping and gave Cikya the spare feathers for her to carry. The trio continued their pace, as Zulag hacked branches out of his way with a knife while Deeso and Cikya ducked below. Zulag stood a head taller than both, so he was often face first into freely hanging foliage, leaving behind a small trail to follow him. Deeso used her axe to hack away thicker undergrowth that impeded the group on their travels.

"Zulag, you're going too fast for Cikya and I." Deeso pointed out, noting the different length in their strides.

"Then walk faster." Zulag commented, not bothering to look behind him as he moved even quicker to spite Deeso. She scowled at the back of his head and waited for Cikya to catch up. Cikya's staff dragged behind her as she attempted to quicken her pace, but after being on the road for what seemed like hours of unchanging scenery, she was at her limit for the day. Cikya took her staff again, and this time loudly banged on a tree to get the two's attention again. Zulag's expression of annoyance lost all color in his face as he reflexively looked up. Deeso looked in the same direction and backed away slowly. An industrious buzzing sound radiated in volume as Cikya continued. She looked alarmed as she noticed Zulag's expression.

"Cikya, stop! You're going to make them angry." Zulag said, pointing up to a bee's nest that was nestled high above them. Cikya made a surprised face as she saw her error and quickly found the motivation to run just a bit more.

"The river is up ahead. This seems to be a spot with a road highly traveled." Deeso noted, pointing to how the foliage was manipulated by human hands.

She took a deeper look at the rainforest's soil which became muddier as they approached the river that Cikya mentioned. Although she generally chose to keep this to herself, Deeso had experience tracking animals when accompanying Sadal on her hunts. While Sadal was able to locate the prey once she got sight of it, Deeso was able to map out an environment in her mind with ease and trace an entire case behind it. Not one stone was left unturned as she was prepared to smell dung, look at claw marks, and she could even give a rough estimate of how old the animal may be depending on its gait. She was a natural. She stopped Zulag by holding her arm out. He gave an annoyed grunt, but he waited to see what she had to say.

"Just a moment." Deeso said and waved for Cikya and Zulag to come closer as they shoved one another for a look at the space.

"Alright. Now what?" Zulag said, begrudgingly accepting the possibility that the river theory may have held some weight.

"Look at the ground. Before we arrived, there were footprints. It's hard to guess, but I would say maybe a few hours. If these are the Forest Seekers who Sadal may be in contact with, we will need to be careful. She could be injured when we grab her." Deeso assessed. Based on her probable injuries with the tiger, Deeso assumed that Sadal wouldn't be too far from their location. The site of the tiger attack according to Zulag was about two days' travel and they anticipate being able to meet up with her in a couple days walking in a singular direction.

I heard the Forest Seekers tie leaves to their feet to hide their tracks, so I'm not sure. Cikya thought as she shrugged her shoulders. Zulag shook his head at Deeso's statement. He caressed his beard as he weighed the evidence.

"No that can't be it. Forest Seekers are way more careful not to be found, it's the only thing they're good at. This is one of us. If we head in this direction, we can probably find a camp, or at least somewhere for us to work off of." Zulag proposed while Deeso stayed silent.

"I'm sure if we can find and capture one, we can ask about Sadal's location. We are new to this land, and so there aren't many who look like us. We can work backwards and see what we find." Deeso answered. She carried surprise on her face as she received a supportive nod from Zulag.

Deeso and the others had no idea how to find a Forest Seeker village to begin with, given the amount of effort made to keep them hidden in the undergrowth. Their people tended to uproot and convert trees for use and make distinct spaces, but the Forest Seekers integrated the design of the jungle itself into their home structure. One could walk through a settlement and not have the slightest idea. Deeso and the others were unaware of the logistical capabilities of Forest Seekers and hoped they had at least a working knowledge of other bands in the area.

"I'm making camp, Cikya's clearly tired. Go chop some wood." Zulag ordered Deeso as he headed off in the direction, he had his mind set on earlier.

"Zulag, we have some daylight left. We should keep going." Deeso commented going in the other direction as she felt her shoulder be grabbed by Zulag. She reflexively lunged away and shot him a glare, as Cikya folded her arms standing next to him. Cikya pointed to her ear, prompting them to listen. A large flowing sound could be heard within the relative silence of their environment.

"The river is...bigger than I expected." Deeso commented as the sound of the rapids amplified as they got closer to the river. Deeso saw that they needed to find an alternate route but didn't have enough time in the day to do so. She decided to get started on gathering firewood. It was going to be a long night as she felt restless.

"This river is too big for us to wade through. So, until we find a way around, or a way across, we'll make camp here." Zulag mentioned, already going ahead to set down his pack.

He took it upon himself to stretch his arms out and relax while Deeso hacked wood. Zulag took the portions of fireback meat he saved and skewered them with a nearby twig as he waited for Deeso. Deeso lobbed cut blocks of wood in Zulag's general direction. She wore a sly grin, as she watched him scramble around to pick up the pieces like a monkey attempting to gather fruit. Cikya tried her hardest not to laugh at the sight, but failed to do so, as she reflexively massaged her throat. The pain was worth it. Zulag constructed a campfire with the collected wood and the three sat with one another. The bits of smoke and heat carried through their makeshift dwelling for the day. Zulag dumped his pack out and stuck the fireback meat over the fire. Deeso and Cikya did the same with their dried meat and ate happily. Deeso sat opposed to both Zulag and Cikya. Zulag remained rugged as his beard was thick. Deeso's eyes looked at Cikya now that she had time to rest. Cikya was unmistakably beautiful with a slim frame that befitted her status as a priestess. She wore two deer furs bound together with a leather strap and wore two accompanying ones over her wrists and forearms. Her hair flowed downwards and was cut short just as the opening of her clothing revealed her scar. Her brown skin glistened with vitality as she ate a piece of fruit. She hardly did work outside of rituals, but Deeso made sure she would pull her weight just like Zulag.

"We have a lot of ground to cover tomorrow. I will take first watch." Deeso said between chews. With no complaints, Cikya and Zulag slept quickly as the day exhausted them more than they anticipated. Deeso herself also felt tired, but she didn't trust her new companions in the same way. Perhaps in time she could get a good night's rest.

The New Arrival

A low amount of smoke filled the campsite as their fire withered. The previous night for Deeso was uneventful as she took watch. Deeso rubbed her eyes and face as she tried to get a sense of her surroundings. The first look at her comrades saw that they were awake grooming themselves. Zulag used a sharpened rock to shave some of his beard while Cikya shook her wet hair. Deeso grabbed a few spare sticks and rubbed them together to reignite the gentle fire between the three of them. Once the flames were lit, Deeso started out her day with a few stretches so that she remained limber. As she stretched, Deeso watched Zulag shave himself. His eyes drifted towards hers and he recoiled in annoyance.

"What are you looking at?" Zulag said to Deeso while he carefully ran the sharp rock in a straight line. He took a small sigh of relief as he cut his hair without a mistake. Deeso noted his concentration and decided to break it.

"It would be easy to move it just a small bit and cut your neck. I'd be more careful." Deeso mocked with distaste. Her stomach rumbled as did the rest of her partners. Deeso remembered her backpack that Cikya stuffed with some extra food before they set out on their journey. Deeso walked over to the bags and hoped to get a reaction from either Zulag or Cikya.

"Is there enough to eat?" Deeso asked as she pointed to the leather packs, they used to store their belongings. Between the three of them, there were enough rations for another day's work, or two if they ate very little. There was hesitancy on their part to gather some fruits as there was a valid fear of accidental poisoning. They were after all great hunters of game, not plant collectors.

"I got us food yesterday. Either you or Cikya can handle it. I have better things to do." Zulag said, as he dedicated much time to grooming himself.

"Zulag, I took watch yesterday. You get the food with Cikya while I sleep." Deeso mentioned while Zulag bit his tongue in annoyance. She decided not to address the issue anymore as she grew tired. Deeso curled up on the ground and willed herself to sleep.

Deeso and the others were on the search for an agreeable Forest Seeker to interrogate but their efforts wouldn't be in vain. At the tail end of a raging river, two Forest Seekers traveled in search of food and precious bamboo. The bounty of the forest was plentiful, but they searched far and wide for material to bring back for building. They weaved through the jungle growth freely and required no blade to find their path. A boy walked with his father as the two carried baskets down a clearing in the growth. His father pointed at the trees in awe as he waved his finger through the air. He hoped to instill a sense of pride and respect for the natural forest in his son around him.

"Ozul, do we know what this one is?" The proud father asked his son.

Ozul looked up at the foliage above him while his father stood proudly. Ozul was young, only twelve years old. He had short brown hair caked with sweat that flowed down his neck. He had a large nose that accompanied an anxious expression that he carried as a frown. His eyes were a deep brown and looked worried regardless of where he was. He wore a tan leather covering over his body that fit through his head and down to his legs. His eyes absorbed everything; the bugs that crawled on the ground, the birds that perched in the trees and the movement of shadows. The world gave much to him and like that of his ancestors, he hoped to understand the natural environment around them. The first step for Ozul was to accept the reality he was born into. His father told him early about the legacy he carried from The Stone Breakers, but Ozul felt he wasn't ready. Ozul moved with fear in every step as he was terrified of the various dangers of the jungle. He strapped himself close to his father as he was still anxious. Ozul looked at his father and realized he hadn't answered his question. Ozul often found himself locked in his own thoughts.

"Mangya! This fruit is very tasty.[21]" Ozul said with a smile.

"You collect the fruit over that way, I will return shortly." Ozul's father ordered.

Ozul was a rule follower and trusted the systems that he grew within. There was one thing though that he hoped to accomplish on his own, regardless of what anyone else would tell him. His mind was set on producing his own blowgun. The blowgun was integral to the identity of Forest Seekers as it encompassed the ultimate bond with nature and was inherently sustainable. Many Forest Seekers lacked organized fighting like that of Thunderfeet or the legendary Stone Breakers but instead preferred to attack from a distance using the environment. His group was peaceful and only carried weapons in the event they crossed paths with dangerous creatures that inhabit their environment. Ozul's attempts were thwarted in the past, but he hardly gave up. He shook the tree's branches as asked and watched the best fruit roll into his woven basket. He held his ear close to the wood and tapped it with his fist. The wood was quite pliable for darts, but he wished to make his blowgun out of bamboo if he could find the material. He filled the basket up to the brim and dragged it behind him as he waited for his father. Ozul picked up a small branch and tossed it around while thinking of eating the delicious fruits.

"One will be fine." Ozul said with a whisper.

Surely nobody would notice one that went missing. He looked around, despite knowing fully well it was just him out in the wilderness. He stuffed the mango into his mouth and chewed it with satisfaction. He exhausted the fruit's contents and threw the core into a nearby bush. Ozul was aware that fruit and other organics would return to the soil and feed the land once more. True to his word, he had enough willpower to stop there. His pace quickened as he grew anxious. Ozul looked to the sky to see how much time passed but the sun's movement was obscured by the canopy above. Ozul reminded himself that the spirits of The Stone Breakers guarded these forests and would ensure safe passage for both him and his father. Ozul felt a gaping feeling in his chest as he was uncomfortable

---

[21] Emic word for mango.

with the still air. Legacy or not, Ozul's anxiety got the better of him as he abandoned the basket to look for his father. He picked up the tree branch again and made noise to alert anything around that he was present.

"Father? Where did you go? The trees do not answer, so you should..." Ozul said quietly to himself.

His travels led him to a difficult section of the jungle, even for someone of his stature. Ozul was surrounded by thick brush that he needed to run through head on. His exposed arms and legs were scratched by brambles and thorns, but he ignored it all as his search became more frantic. Each vine bent to Ozul's will as he powered through to find his father. Ozul remained obscured in the bush as he spotted a figure in the distance. His father was attached to a tree holding an axe to get fruit. His sense of relief was interrupted by a familiar low growl. Ozul shifted his head around to get a better look and knew that a leopard was nearby.

"Of all things today...Why the Onpeu?" Ozul asked himself quietly.

Ozul's eyes were confused as the cat came into further view. This leopard was black compared to the typical yellow he was accustomed to. He had difficulty tracking the animal's movement as he remained in the bushes to hide himself. He saw his father reach into his pack and tossed fruit at the animal to get it to leave. Ozul found this strategy was fine for getting rid of more docile creatures, but a leopard only saw this as a challenge as he could see its claws were extended.

You will only make it angrier! Ozul thought as he tried to figure out how to alert his father without exposing himself.

He picked up a small pebble and hurled it through the bush hoping to divert the creature's attention. Ozul heard the slither of a snake moving towards him in the bushes and had no choice but to step out. The leopard turned its attention to Ozul but walked slowly as it remained in control. Ozul saw that the leopard evaluated the risk of attacking them both and hoped to keep it that way. Ozul's father's disapproved of his son's actions and climbed down the tree to grab a rock. It was too risky for him to run across and grab his son without setting off the leopard, so he chose to divert the leopard's attention. He threw a rock and hit the leopard squarely on the head. Ozul saw the rock make its mark as he turned to see the wave of his father.

"Run Ozul!" He shouted.

The leopard's attention shifted to the shouting man and another outburst caused the leopard to pounce towards his father. Ozul could only watch in horror as his father attempted to shield himself from the beast. He quickly moved his axe in the air and attempted to swing at the creature. His face was filled with fear as the leopard approached him. The leopard snarled and swiped at his legs and ripped off a section of flesh. His father bashed the creature aside the head with his axe. He was powered by adrenaline, but the material broke apart due to poor condition. As he lacked a weapon, he curled his hands into a fist and punched in sheer desperation. The man's flesh fell apart as his arms were eviscerated.

As this occurred across the bend, Deeso was woken up from her early morning nap by Zulag and Cikya. The two found a fork in the river low enough for them to cross and scouted the terrain ahead. She squinted her eyes as she looked up to see Zulag's face. Cikya stood next to their field packs as she waited for Deeso to get her bearings.

"Is there a reason you're in my eyes?" She asked, rubbing dirt from herself.

"Quit sleeping and grab your axe. We have work to do, great tracker." Zulag said as he forcefully passed Deeso's backpack to her. Deeso opened it and dumped the few contents left inside to grasp her axe.

"I think you forget who leads here. You need to be reminded." Deeso commented. Her voice carried a disgruntled tone as she gave her axe-holding arm a steady swing away from the others.

"Who made you the leader? I think it's obvious what-" Zulag scoffed as Cikya stomped her foot down trying to get the two to focus. Zulag extended his hand out to Cikya, letting her know that he was now listening.

"I'm awake now, so what prompts this move?" Deeso interrupted Zulag, as she looked to see Cikya waving for their attention.

I haven't hunted with people in a while, I hope they can get what I'm trying to say. Cikya thought as she made a stance. She tried to emulate a leopard as best as she could much to Deeso's amusement.

"Cikya found Onpeu tracks not too far from our camp. It would be wise to take care of it." Zulag commented, as he pointed to Cikya made snarling expressions while she clawed the air. Deeso held in a small laugh as she saw Cikya's accurate depiction, but she took the news seriously.

The trail they were hoping to track Sadal on was cold, and Deeso feared for the worst. Deeso and the others hoped the presence of this animal across the river could lead to some potential settlements. Leopard pelts were valuable, and they hadn't bothered to bring anything for negotiations on Sadal's whereabouts. The extent of the leopard's territory was evident to the three of them as they looked for markings on the ground. Zulag struck ahead first and kept his ear low to the ground to listen for anything out of the ordinary. He turned his head to see Deeso waft air towards her nose as she took in the surroundings. Deeso was aware of the various ways that animals marked territory and looked for any discrepancies.

"Scratched log over there, and some...dung as well." Deeso said quietly, scrunching up her nose slightly at the smell. From the expression on her face, Cikya could tell that the dung was fresh and that their target was not too far away. While Deeso always maintained a sharpened axe, the weaponry of Zulag and Cikya were more eccentric in their nature. Zulag carried several knives on him that were light enough to be thrown with ease. They were sharpened on both edges to the point where just gracing the blade would cause bleeding. He always carried one on his person, with the others held together by a small leather strap on the inside of his clothing. Cikya carried a staff made from a long heavy block of hardwood. Normally seen as a walking aid, it could prove essential for combat when needed.

Zulag waved his hand forward for the others to join him as they kept quiet. Far in the distance, they heard the muffled sounds of a leopard attacking something. The three put their heads together as they evaluated the prospects of the plan and where to head from there. It was clearly distracted attacking something or someone else for the time being. Although each one could take out a leopard on their own, the three coordinated their efforts based on their training.

"I hear it. There is one Onpeu, certainly an adult." Zulag commented, while the other two nodded in affirmation.

"I suggest Cikya distracts it. I will go towards the back, and Zulag, you will take the front." Deeso suggested to Zulag who already had his hands on his assortment of knives.

"Why the back? A better kill could be had with us both at the front." Zulag asked with some skepticism in his voice. He kept his voice low so as not to expose their position as they planned.

"My arms aren't as long as yours. Onpeu pounce towards the prey. I will strike its ankle instead." She answered. Zulag thought it over and shrugged his shoulders.

Cikya, who knew her role well, was already one with the details. She ran her hand down her face to wipe away sweat before going forward first. She kept a slow pace as she advanced towards the increasing sound of the leopard's roaring. She dragged her staff behind her and left a distinct line in the soil for Deeso and Zulag to refer to later.

Cikya came across some small rocks and scooped them into her free hand. She inched closer to the sound of the leopard and raised her hand to throw. Only a short distance away now, her concentration was broken as she saw the leopard attacking someone and a petrified child unable to move. She was bewildered at the sight, as she expected the creature to be alone but went to work. Cikya launched the rocks in her hand in the leopard's direction. She heard the pained screams of a man and could only feel bad as she quickly figured the boy and man were related in some way. Two rocks hit the leopard's backside and paused the assault of the creature. Its head turned away to address the new threat in its area and looked at Cikya. Cikya held her staff out with two hands and took a stance as she swayed from side to side. Her eyes locked with the creature. She gradually moved in a circular motion towards the leopard and kicked up mud and dust to blind it. Ozul turned his attention to the dancing woman that appeared within his vision. He was beyond confused at what was happening but saw this as an avenue to escape. He retreated further into the treeline and climbed a tree to hide. Although he was aware of the leopard's ability to climb trees, he couldn't help but observe his new saviors down below. Deeso and Zulag saw Cikya in the distance doing her part, while the two glared at one another before getting into position. Zulag went to the left of where Cikya was and withdrew a knife. Deeso stayed out of the leopard's line of sight for the moment and remained still. The distraction by Cikya proved to work well as Ozul's father was left with his wounds.

Deeso propped herself behind a tree and took a deep breath as she readied her axe. Cikya slammed her staff on the ground and baited the leopard into turning around to pursue her. She ran quickly as the leopard pursued and slid some distance into the mud before veering off into the bushes. While the leopard was dead set on attacking Cikya, Deeso jumped out and swung her axe at the leopard's hind leg. While not the ankle that she wanted, she certainly wounded the beast. The leopard's movement ground to a halt as it struggled to move with an injured shin. She retracted her arm just quick enough so that she wasn't hurt by the recoil of the reaction.

Zulag hated to be outdone by Deeso and took his killings seriously. He saw that the leopard turned around as it attempted to return to Ozul's father. A fallen target was an easier meal than the active human attacking it. Zulag ran out and quickly curved his arm to launch a knife. The throw was silent as it was jettisoned through the air. Zulag's accuracy was superb as he hit the leopard right in the eye. The leopard frantically clawed around as its vision faded. Dust and mud splattered them as it panicked. Deeso continued to assist Zulag as he avoided the leopard's claws to use another knife to stab it directly in the head. Cikya returned to grab her staff and struck the leopard. She grinned with glee as she did so. Unable to deal with multiple assailants at once, the leopard was unable to recover and gradually succumbed to multiple wounds on its body. To be sure that the leopard was truly dead, Zulag withdrew his knife and cut at the leopard's neck until its head was severed from its body. He then offered the head to the other two as they all scooped up a small bit of blood and licked it. Their red tongues confirmed the kill was complete. Unknown to the others, Ozul climbed down the tree and slowly made his way over to them.

"Is anyone hurt?" Deeso asked as she assessed their conditions.

"Only my pride. I had to use two knives instead of one." Zulag commented. Outside of the context of the hunt, Zulag and Deeso couldn't have been more opposed to one another. As it stood though, their team was effective and to ensure Sadal's safe return, everything would need to be dedicated to the victory. Cikya celebrated their hunt with a small clap, but her attention turned back at the man who laid before them.

"What is it, Cikya?" Deeso asked with a raised eyebrow. Cikya motioned for Deeso and Zulag to come forward as they saw the man they saved. His face and arm were torn apart by the leopard's claws. He somehow remained alive and struggled to speak. Zulag looked at the man and his face soured.

"He's not one of ours." Zulag remarked as he turned up his nose at the man.

Deeso raised an eyebrow, but her surprise was noted as Zulag was correct. Deeso was as disgusted as Zulag. To her, these were the people that took Sadal away from her, and it was frustrating she needed one of their own. Zulag emulated his uncle's thoughts on Forest Seekers and saw them as an ungrateful people for what they were trying to achieve.

"Look at his face. He's a Forest Seeker. Look at how he bleeds to the ground below. This is the threat my uncle told us all to be prepared for?" Zulag questioned with disgust as he crunched a leaf below his foot.

"M...my son..." Ozul's father said, as he raised his non-flayed arm to point to the clearing. Deeso turned around as she saw the man feebly lift his hand up. She saw nothing and assumed that he was hallucinating.

"Leave him, we got the hide we wanted. I'll carry the carcass back to camp. We'll strip the fur once we arrive. Onpeu fur goes for a lot, and we need food." Zulag commented. Deeso agreed with Zulag and urged Cikya to rest before they left.

Deeso and Zulag peered out into the deeper brush and looked to retrace their steps as they caught their breath. In the distance, the lone and shy Ozul, was just barely visible to Cikya. While Deeso and Zulag were content to let the man bleed out and die, Cikya was more sympathetic. She picked up one of Zulag's spare knives and stuck it in the throat of Ozul's father as an act of mercy. As she got ready to leave, Cikya noticed Ozul's return. She panicked and quickly hurled the knife to obscure her actions. Ozul ignored the three of them entirely as his father was lifeless. Ozul held him tightly as his father's blood leaked onto the ground and onto his clothing. He rummaged in the man's pocket and withdrew a small carved elephant tusk with holes in it. Deeso gave no reaction as she pointed for Zulag and Cikya to follow in her direction. She stopped her movement as she heard a faint sound reach her ears.

"You killed the Onpeu." Ozul said with a newfound resolve in his voice.

Ozul repeated himself as he assumed he wasn't loud enough for them to hear. Zulag carried their leopard's carcass and walked off as he intended. Deeso stopped and turned around as Zulag continued his pace. Cikya stayed with Deeso and gripped her arm to grab her attention. The two watched as Ozul dragged his father's body towards a tree and left him there. While Ozul felt sad for his father's physical passing, he knew that he would be safe as bodies would be reclaimed by the forest, and it was here that his corpse would stay. Cikya noticed Ozul's struggle and went to help, only to be stopped by Deeso's grip on her.

"Forest Seeker. This kill is ours. Go somewhere else." Deeso commented to Ozul who nodded in understanding.

"The pelt is yours. I have no need for it. You saved me and I want to help you in return." Ozul said, as he saw a puzzled look on Deeso's face.

It was beyond their imagination to wonder why nobody would want a pelt this valuable. Deeso yelled for Zulag who reluctantly turned to see what the problem was. Although Deeso claimed her role as the leader, she felt it was necessary for all the group to be engaged when talking with others. Cikya studied Deeso and could tell she was having some conflict in her mind as she attempted to rationalize what was happening.

"If you see one, kill one. The time for negotiation is over." The words of Ronkalk sounded to Deeso in her mind.

Deeso had no problem taking the life of the enemy as she's done in the past, but for some reason her hand could only hang over her axe. Deeso had in mind the idea of capturing a Forest Seeker, but one as weak as Ozul was only going to be trouble from her perspective. Killing him would be easy, but Deeso found herself paralyzed as she looked at Ozul who stared at her in gratitude. Deeso had a soft spot for children as her love for Brab clouded her hatred. She hadn't imagined what the boy looked like if he was grown but imagined him to be a sweet soul. Ozul's innocent demeanor was disarming all on its own.

"I thought the two of you were done here. Why are you wasting my time?" Zulag asked Deeso and Cikya. His eyes slowly turned to Ozul, and he quickly deduced the conversation topic.

"No. End of discussion. Forest Seekers are beneath us; I shouldn't have agreed to the previous plan. I expected this from Cikya, who can see the souls of all and feel pity, but from you Deeso? What about our original plan?" Zulag said angrily.

"It wasn't my idea. The child feels indebted to us." Deeso said back, ignoring Ozul standing next to her. Ozul gazed at the ground as he overheard the discussions of the three Thunderfeet among him. He had nowhere else to go and was stuck in a hard position.

"Well, he can go somewhere else as far as I'm concerned. That thing couldn't protect himself or the father." Zulag said with a callousness that irritated Cikya. Cikya interrupted Zulag by standing in front of him and making obscene gestures.

"Now's not the time to argue with me Cikya." Zulag said with much irritation in his voice as he made attempts to ignore her.

"She makes a good point actually." Deeso said with some tiredness in her voice.

"We are in unfamiliar territory, and this child knows a lot more than we do about the land. We've been looking for someone to help us and it's all the better if we don't need to attack someone for it. It can be to our advantage. If we find any other Forest Seekers, he will follow. They are elusive, but seem to trust their own, which means they will trust us." Deeso reasoned with Zulag, as Cikya nodded in support of her words.

Ozul didn't see any real way out of his situation other than seeing what could be done with these people. The jungle was a harsh place, and he needed allies or whatever this situation was, to stay alive. He was surprised to see Deeso's expression change from anger to acceptance as the two locked eyes.

"It is noble of you to want to help us, Forest Seeker. We are enemies but we don't have to be for now. There's something else you want from us as well, I can tell. Nobody does anything without giving back. I consider myself a reasonable person, we can always make a deal." Deeso said.

"My father is gone, but there is family of mine to the west. Take me there and I will take you through the forest. A life for a life." Ozul proposed. He was willing to let everything go so that he could get what he wanted, which was safe travel. He knew he didn't have the experience to deal with anything like the leopard he just faced, but with three bodyguards at his side, he could have a chance.

Zulag festered over Deeso's reasoning with a growing rage. As sound as it was, he couldn't bear to give her another win but relented. He kicked the dirt in frustration and withdrew one of his knives to Ozul.

"Fine. You can come with us since you're somehow useful. Annoy me and I'll slit your throat." Zulag threatened Ozul who stayed silent as he nodded.

"What is your name, Forest Seeker?" Deeso asked, crouching now to meet at eye level with him. Cikya mirrored Deeso's stance with a smile which prompted him to speak.

"Ozul. My name is Ozul." Ozul said with the bow of his head.

Ozul made his way back to camp with Deeso, Zulag, and Cikya. He studied them closely and tried to understand more about the makeshift alliance he managed to find himself in. As a quiet boy it took great effort for him to make conversation with others. Ozul knew his place among them. His eyes went first to Deeso, who moved with purpose in each step she took. He was unsure about how to feel about her, something bothered him on the inside that not everything was what it seemed. Zulag was like any other bully that he'd seen before, and he had many growing up. He was used to threats and thoughts of inadequacy that came with his jeers, but it was from a foreigner this time rather than his own kind. Ozul wasn't afraid to admit he had a crush on Cikya. He could tell she was kind from the moment he saw her. He also noticed her condition of being unable to speak, and while he was curious, knew better than to pry into some random person's affairs. In such a short life, Ozul was surrounded by loss as many of his community perished in the jungles. While Deeso, Zulag, and Cikya had their stuff laid out, Ozul started from scratch with nothing more than the clothes on his back and the instrument with him.

Zulag and Cikya stripped the leopard's carcass to obtain the black fur while Deeso dealt with Ozul. Zulag held his knife carefully and opened the leopard from the stomach onwards. He held his breath while Cikya guided him with her finger as the first cut was crucial. As he did this, Cikya held her hand into the open stomach and slowly removed organs out. She tried to minimize as much blood leaking as possible. The trio intended this hide for trade, so Zulag needed to account for symmetry and quality of the hide as he and Cikya worked on it. Cikya grasped the intestines and made a disgusted face as she did so. Cikya was aware of the processes involved with making her meal or clothing but was spared more of the brutish aspects as a priestess. Zulag cut deep with the knife and used his hands to remove pieces of the skin. Sinew from the spine and legs were prized and Cikya removed these as they could be used for thread. Back at their main camp, Deeso and the others would have hung the skin but lacked the building material to do so. As they stripped the leopard, Deeso started a fire while Zulag kept a lasting glare on Ozul. Deeso folded her hands into each other as she motioned for Ozul to sit. Ozul distanced himself from the rest as he fixed his posture. Zulag used his knife to make multiple wooden stakes from nearby branches. Cikya held the bloodied pelt as Zulag placed them through corners of the fur. Ozul heard the words of Zulag as he and Cikya worked to clean the fur and make it presentable.

"Cikya, take one of my knives and scoop the brain out. There should be a strip of wood from this morning. Mash it hard on there with a rock and let it sit near the heat. We'll take the guts and rub them there." Zulag ordered.

Deeso found she needed to talk above Zulag and Cikya as they worked. She raised her voice and snapped at Ozul to grab his attention. Ozul whipped his head to answer Deeso's call.

"Ozul, was it? For this to work, I must ask you what you're able to do. Everyone must contribute." Deeso asked, as Ozul responded with a silent nod. Ozul felt this was a reasonable question to ask and so he answered the best he could.

"I am unable to kill great beasts like you all, but there are things that one can find helpful. I can make rope and other useful tools. My father...taught me how." Ozul explained to the three of them as he held his special instrument.

Ozul explained that with a cut down carved ivory tusk of an elephant, he hollowed out holes that could allow him to twist fibers together through the space when needed. The antlers of deer could also be used, but elephant kills were considered especially powerful sources for these tools. Deeso rubbed her chin in thought as she nodded in understanding. With a dedicated toolmaker in the group, the three of them could focus on gathering information regarding Sadal's whereabouts and food. Zulag shot Deeso a look as she brought Ozul up to speed on their current objective.

"We're looking for someone that looks like us. Her name is Sadal, and we have good reason to think she may have been taken by a Forest Seeker village. She's a very strong warrior but I fear she may have been captured. Your people have not been kind to our presence in this land recently." Deeso explained as Ozul nodded.

"Oh. Well, our villages are often hard to find. I would suggest we look down river to find this person to start. People often look for food there and word spreads." Ozul replied, seeing an opportunity to impress them early.

Ozul was aware at least in his stretch of jungle that he knew about the resentment towards Thunderfeet. His own opinion was variable, but they could be reasoned with. Deeso looked beyond the trees to her as she heard the word river; they were trying to avoid water travel as much as possible. Swimming was not a skill prioritized in their training, as much of The Broken Bone's history led them to deal with open grasslands and dense forests away from deep sources of water. Cikya watched closely as Deeso grabbed the last bit of their rations. While Deeso was talking to Ozul, Cikya got Zulag's attention in the meantime. She rubbed her stomach and pointed to their bags seeing that they were just about out of food. Zulag nodded to her complaint and agreed they would move soon.

"Deeso, do we have anything to clean the hide while Cikya waits?" Zulag said as he interrupted her conversation with Ozul.

"Go by the river and scoop up some water if we don't have any. The fat should do the job though, Sadal and I have done it many times." Deeso commented.

Deeso remembered Sadal's passion of making clothing for herself and others. Deeso wore a design made by Sadal and she preferred to use brain matter as her material to tan a skin. Crushed and heated fat from the brain settled into a pelt with ease and made it more agreeable to work with. While other hunters often left their heads to rot, members of The Broken Bone carried the heads with them in case they were unable to reach camp. Due to their highly migratory nature, it wasn't a guarantee to find tannins from fruit, but the kill always had a brain. After the skin was lathered in fat, the material remained soft and pliable. The worst part about skin preparation was the length of time it would take to fully dry. Zulag and Cikya hoped that the skin would be prepared correctly because otherwise the hide was raw and would hold less value. If done correctly, the processed leather would change color and be soft to the touch. Raw hides also had their purposes such as floor decorations or building material. Predator meat wasn't very tasty, but the pelts they acquired would fetch a high asking price if they could find a village to do trade in and there would be plenty to eat.

"We've got at least four hours until this pelt is good for trade." Zulag mumbled to himself.

"In that case, we should scout ahead and see what we can find for now. We kept our place well hidden, so there's little to worry about." Deeso decided as they would return to sleep that night.

With plenty of daylight ahead, they obscured the location of their valuable hide and ventured out as a group. Ozul was the smallest among them, so he lagged due to the length of the others' strides. Deeso and Zulag used their respective weaponry to slice through foliage much to Ozul's chagrin. The forest and its respective treatment to all else trumped his shyness, and he was not afraid to voice his displeasure with how the plants were being treated.

"There are other ways around than to do that. The vines feel what you do, and you will not like it." Ozul complained lowly to no avail.

Deeso guided the group to the river that she scouted by earlier and remembered the strip of land they used to find their initial kill. Ozul held out his hand and knew of a previous village that he and his father visited. Deeso and the others stayed a respectable distance from the river's flow as Ozul cut ahead of them. His face was ready to deliver on what he promised.

"We will need to cross. Come here-" Ozul mentioned as he saw the three of them not move an inch further as the roar of the river increased in volume. Ozul dipped his feet inside as the mud gushed between his toes. The sounds of the others he expected were not present. He looked confused and it soon dawned on him what the problem was. These mighty warriors he found himself with were lacking something he thought everyone knew how to do.

Luckily for Ozul, he saw that jute grew further inland from the river's boundary. Jute served as an essential part of the Forest Seeker toolkit, the butts of the plant were used for cloth and the fibers had great absorption properties. Deeso watched as Ozul ripped pieces of jute with careful precision and placed it under water. Ozul watched as the fibers unraveled from the root stems that he yanked out of the ground. Unlike the general foliage that Ozul had issue with being cut, there were sections of the forest that were seen as acceptable to use among his kind. Working plants were seen as spiritual gifts, and not using them was the greatest insult. He used his father's tool and pushed the fibers through and coiled them together long enough to take hold. He held the tied pieces with his teeth as he roped them through his fingers with precision. The grooves inside guided the rope's direction as Ozul concentrated on binding the fibers together.

"Jaat is what I use to make my things." Ozul explained as he silently worked while the three of them watched him. Zulag had his doubts about the construction and decided to make that known to everyone else. He walked over to get a closer look at Ozul who was putting the finishing touches on the fibers and pushed him aside as he felt the rope in his hands.

"What kind of lousy junk did you make? This looks like it'll fall apart in seconds!" Zulag groaned as Ozul looked towards the ground. He raised his fist to Ozul but decided it would be a waste of time to reprimand him further.

"I was not finished yet...Please wait." Ozul pleaded as he made large knots that bound the rope together.

After some time, Ozul had a working rope ready to be made. Ozul's plan was to swim the length of the river with the fiber rope and secure it to a large rock for the others to grab. He attempted to look for the least deep portion of the river as he tied a coil and stuffed a good deal of it into his mouth. He used his free hands to swim the length of the river, which wasn't too far for him or the others. On the other side of the river, Ozul was watched carefully by Deeso and Zulag.

"Can he seriously not lift that rock?" Zulag complained, getting the attention of Deeso. Cikya found herself distracted by birds in the trees as the two talked.

"I'm not sure what you expected from him, Zulag, Forest Seekers are weaker than us, he's also a child." Deeso snapped back, already tired of his complaining. Deeso saw that Ozul was looking for a large rock to use as an anchor and she yelled across, hoping her voice would carry over the expanse.

"Ozul! Tie it instead to the base of the tree if you can't lift the rock!" Deeso suggested, as she received a small nod from him.

Ozul massaged the bark in an apologetic manner as he placed his rope around the base of the tree. He then ran the length of it again with a secure knot and emerged with the tightened rope for the others to grab. Deeso gave Ozul a small nod of acknowledgment while Zulag defiantly held his head in the air. Cikya clapped at the success of their group having means to ford the river. The three held on tightly to the rope now used as a balance as they walked in unison towards the other side. Ozul was already back at the other bank and watched them patiently. He didn't think drowning was possible at the height they were, Zulag was visible some distance in the water while the women hung on tightly to one another. The three quickly hoisted themselves to shore and were happy the ordeal was over. Ozul collected his construction and the group continued onward.

Ozul's prediction to go down river managed to come off successfully as he could already make out figures in the distance. Some Forest Seekers, a few years older than Ozul, were playing by the riverbank. Along the edge of the bank were small baskets made from bamboo filled with berries and other assorted fruits. These teenagers were workers but took a much-needed break to have fun. Deeso watched them with mild curiosity as they tossed small spheres made of clay at one another. The group wore an assortment of grass skirts and feathers that flowed in tandem with the wind they made. The boys favored white and black feathers while girls chose blue and green. She studied their movement as they attempted to either dodge or catch the spheres. She looked to Ozul for an explanation, and he felt obliged to give one.

"I see you looking at them. That over there is Mudball, one of our favorite sports. Every kid plays it.[22]" Ozul said with some resentment in his voice.

"What is the purpose? Are you good at this game Ozul?" Deeso asked to which he nodded no.

While Ozul had the energy of any other child, he lacked the raw athleticism shown before him. He wasn't as coordinated as the others, and this has led him to some embarrassing games from his earlier memories. Ozul was more technically minded, so he could form effective strategies, but put into practice, he struggled immensely. Deeso gave Cikya and Zulag a look as they returned glances to her. The game appealed to their competitive nature, and they needed time to kill while their pelt was processing. The first step of their plan was they needed to find a Forest Seeker village and now they had an opportunity at their disposal. Cikya raised her eyebrows at the sport. She watched the Forest Seeker teens contort their bodies to reach all sorts of lengths. Cikya stretched her body and tried to copy these same poses as she heard her bones crack. Deeso pointed to the group in the distance. She saw the group had some coordination, but like all Forest Seekers lacked discipline and this was something she hoped to exploit in the game. This was not without any good reason; any member of The Broken Bone was subject to drills of many kinds their entire lives and practiced until failure was laughable.

"This sport seems easy to perform. We don't have anything like this back home, but we should ask them to play a game. Wagers are popular for us so they may agree." Deeso suggested to the group. Ozul decided that it would be best if he sat out but would participate if needed. Cikya seemed interested in the game and jumped up and down. She placed her arm around Zulag to make him excited as well. Zulag was not as easily convinced.

"And have them witness my amazing prowess? It wouldn't be remotely fair. We could just-" Zulag said, getting interrupted by Deeso.

"If we don't get what we want, then we start smashing heads. Zulag, we must be patient. Nobody will tell us anything about Sadal if we just go in and stab the first person we see. Did Ronkalk teach you nothing about playing nice with others?" Deeso said to him

---

[22] Author's Note: I got the idea for the game by reading a research article about clay balls that were found in the depths of a cave, some theorize these may have been children's toys once upon a time.

while Cikya gave Zulag a small grin. Zulag's face reddened in anger at her comment, Ronkalk's passing remarks were still a fresh wound.

"So, none of you have played before and you think you can take these people?" Ozul asked with some worry on his face.

"Sure, with you not slowing me down anything is possible." Zulag shrugged, much to the annoyance of both Deeso and Ozul.

Deeso stepped forward and the others followed suit until she was close to the game that was wrapping up. The Forest Seeker teens laughed at one another until the figures of the four appeared to them. They were quiet as they attempted to make sense of their new visitors. Whispers piled among the boys who were unsure of what to do with their new situation. Zulag gave a snarl to those that looked him over. He flexed his muscles in intimidation while he caught the eye of a few curious Forest Seeker girls. Out of everyone present, Deeso saw that their attention soon shifted to her and broke the silence.

"We would like to play Mudball." Deeso opened, as the Forest Seeker teens looked at each other in disbelief.

Deeso was met with more confused stares that slowly morphed into glares. Ozul tucked in his lip as he sensed the tension brewing. While he was more approachable to Thunderfeet in general, it seemed Eshe's sentiments were further than he realized.

"You all are Thunderfeet, no? Find someone else to entertain yourselves." One of the boys said, as he folded his arms.

"You all seem to know each other quite well. Why not a fresh set of opponents? Unless of course you fear we are better than you all." Deeso replied to the teen. Deeso saw a couple of Forest Seeker girls sitting on nearby stumps surveying the group with some suspicion. Ozul went forward and decided to speak.

"These are-I was escorting these Thunderfeet. They have resources for trade." Ozul said, as he tapped Deeso's arm. The boy sized him up and noticed Ozul's small size compared to the others. Ozul gestured to his companion's backpack and gave it a slight shake to emphasize his point.

"You happen to be a guide, yes? Surely then, tell these Thunderfeet your time is being wasted and get out of our river! We have better things to do." He responded to Ozul.

Deeso felt testy as she already saw that the reputation of her kind already soured relations. She was annoyed, but knew Forest Seekers were ungrateful people for the service she did in keeping their precious forest safe from hostile predators that saw them not as loyal followers but as meals. Ozul knew he was on borrowed time and needed to think quickly. He waved to the other Forest Seekers for attention as he spoke.

"W-Well...actually I have an idea." Ozul proposed, catching the eye of some of the silent onlookers.

"W-What is it?" One of the girls eavesdropping on the stump replied, as she mocked Ozul's higher pitched voice. Ozul frowned at the display as a few others joined and laughed but decided to keep going.

"How about this? We will settle it with Mudball. I and these Thunderfeet here have a black Onpeu pelt in our possession. If victory is yours, you can have it. If you lose, you take us to your village." Ozul proposed.

Deeso gave Ozul a glare, as she and the others worked hard for their pelt, but she was impressed at his ingenuity. She watched closely as the boy thought to himself and then shook heads with his comrades. While leopards were considered important to the Forest Seeker environment due to their nature, the practical element of such a luxurious fur was alluring to all.

"They speak the truth. I saw a black Onpeu last week patrol our area. It housed a spirit that led my mother astray, if they killed it, it is a gift from the forest and the soul can travel elsewhere. On that alone, we can entertain them with the game of our people." One teenage boy mentioned as he shrugged his shoulders.

"Our village? What-Of course, this should be easy enough. We get to defeat some Thunderfeet and give our village a prize? An offer not one gets often." The boy said to his friends as Ozul observed them patiently. He could tell from their conversation that the offer was a good one. Ozul evaluated his three allies and noted they would have enough potential to last in the field but would need to know the rules first.

"Alright. You have a deal. As usual, we will play three games. Normally we have a bigger team, but we can make this work." He said as he looked them over.

Deeso turned her head to Ozul as a reference for the rules. They got this far just off bluffing and appealing to their ego, but now they needed to perform, and the three were at a complete loss on what to expect. Deeso, Zulag and Cikya made the team that would be competing while Ozul was to keep score for their team, and one of the Forest Seeker girls on the stump kept score for the opposing team. Both teams met in a small huddle while those that kept score began the ball making process. Ozul gathered clumps of clay and took great care into making each ball as round as he could. He tossed it lightly, hoping that it would maintain form before moving to the next. The balls for the sport were made with clay from the river and remade each round. Mudball has ten balls that vary in size from the smallest that can be hurled with ease in one hand, to the largest that require teamwork to toss. The goal of the game is to hit your opponent with the ball and remove them from the game or eliminate their supply of balls on the line. Catching a ball will remove an enemy player from the game. As Mudball is a sport made by Forest Seekers it combined both mental and physical strengths. These ten balls are the only balls that can be thrown in play and as the game ends once they are all expended, they cannot be lifted again for reuse. In times of close matches, some groups would idle for minutes at a time, hoping to find a strategy to get the other group to break first.

"What do you think we should do?" Deeso proposed. She knew that she couldn't exactly ask Ozul for help when the game was about to start. She turned her head to see that the others didn't need to talk things through since they had much more experience. Zulag decided to give his input. His eyes were poised to look at the line and saw the dramatic size difference between the clay balls.

"So, see those small ones there? I'll run and grab as many as I can. You and Cikya can back me up." Zulag said lowly as he moved his head to see if the other team was eavesdropping.

"Zulag, they're just going to hit you if you take too many." Deeso said, with Cikya nodding in support of her statement. Cikya looked at the ground and noticed that their section of the boundary was a lot damper than the other side. She figured this would be important to consider later when they needed to dodge. She felt the mud on her ankle and gave a small frown but was determined to win the game.

Ozul and a Forest Seeker girl stood up and clapped twice. The first match started, and the players were in position. Although Deeso expected a sport like this to have fanfare, Mudball was a tactical game where the crowd chose to watch in silence and predict which teams would win. In a mad dash, Zulag instead went for a larger ball rather than the small ones that were laid out on the line. He wasn't expecting the slimy feeling of the material but held a tight grip as his nails dug into it. Deeso looked at him with bewilderment as he completely disregarded his previous plan. One of the boys grabbed a small ball as he lunged forward. He hurled it towards Deeso as bits of mud touched the rest of them. She dropped herself quickly, taking mud in her face and hair, but shook it off as the first ball was a miss. With nine left in play, Cikya was able to grasp two of decent size while Zulag held his remaining large ball. Zulag strained as he picked his target, one of the boys who found himself teetering the line as they moved around.

Why is this so heavy? Zulag thought as he attempted to hurl the large clay ball some distance. He studied the pattern in which balls of similar size were launched and noticed that it landed at an arc that differed from the smaller ones. Ozul watched Zulag fall for one of the oldest tricks in the Mudball strategy guide. The larger balls weren't meant to be thrown directly at your opponent; it was a trap to be caught so that the thrower would be placed out of the game. Victories with large balls in play were rare and often required a lot of patience to manage.

Cikya tossed Deeso the other ball in her possession. Cikya threw one where she landed a hit on one of the boys in the ankle. He winced as he wasn't prepared for the hit and briefly massaged it. He grumbled at his loss while Cikya gave him a wink. Deeso's ball came at a miss, and she hid her frustration. At least though, they had an inherent advantage to start out. While she commanded the team, Zulag saw that Deeso was about to be hit by a ball. He pushed her out of the way and palmed one of the smaller balls. He caught it with a smug grin as he looked at the boy on the other side. Ozul stood up quickly and pointed to the boy, directing him to the sideline. Zulag then threw it on the ground, leaving one of the boys remaining. Zulag and Deeso thought victory was at hand, but there were still more balls at play. The boy who spoke with them the most was highly skilled, as he performed a dance that irritated Zulag immensely.

"You can't just brag when the match isn't over!" Zulag yelled from across the field, as in his anger, he noticed that Cikya was pelted by a mudball. She shook her head and walked over to sit down. Irritated, Zulag grabbed what balls were around and chose to launch two back towards the boy with both clear misses while his teammates were laughing at his display.

"Zulag, you throw knives! How in the world are you missing?" Deeso asked him as she instinctively jumped backwards.

The boy feigned his throw and projected he would aim for Deeso, but instead hit Zulag in the shoulder with a remaining mudball. Zulag rubbed his shoulder as he felt the impact of the clay hit him. Zulag kicked up some soil but made no further outbursts as it was down to one other and Deeso. Deeso was left with a large ball that she had trouble throwing, and it was for naught as the boy beat her to one of the last small balls and tagged her. The first match concluded with a victory for the Forest Seekers by elimination. Ozul frowned at the outcome but was surprised at how animated his new company was about it. Zulag grumbled as the second game was to start as soon as Ozul and the others made the next batch. The match started the same, where the boys rushed to grab their respective balls of choice, while Deeso, Zulag and Cikya were left with the spares. Zulag was determined to try something different. He was made a fool, and this wouldn't stand to happen twice.

He's going for the large ball again!? Deeso thought as she tried to provide cover for Zulag by waving attention to the boys who attempted to target him. Deeso rolled along the ground and took a moment to wipe some dirt off her clothing. She ducked as a spare clay ball flew in her direction.

Unknown to the other players, Zulag wanted himself to be a target. Despite being a blowhard, he had an attention to detail that went unnoticed. Ozul was quite verbose in his explanation of the rules, and while Deeso and Cikya listened for what they couldn't do, Zulag listened for what was possible in the confines of the game. Players needed to be hit or waste their current balls. Zulag lifted not the largest ball, but one of decent size. He couldn't use it to throw well, but he instead used the ball as a shield. He instantly broke apart the smaller balls that collided with it. Ozul hadn't seen anything like it and nodded happily while the other Forest Seekers were annoyed. Deeso saw this display and followed suit. She snagged a smaller ball and landed a hit on one of the boys in the knee as he massaged it and got into cover. Two of the boys ran into the line and saw that in their haste to target Zulag, their balls were expended. While the opportunity to catch the balls was still possible to win, Deeso anticipated this by purposefully making her throws as difficult as possible where dodging would be the only course of action. Cikya followed Deeso's instructions and made short work of their competition. With all players in, and all the balls expended, Deeso and the others took the victory!

A small breeze carried over the river and cooled down the group as they wiped sweat off themselves before getting ready for the third game. A tinge of desperation fell upon the Forest Seeker boys who thought they'd win unopposed. With the stakes as high as they were, there needed to be some serious strategy changes. The groups huddled together, and the balls were made once more. Deeso noticed that this time their opponents decided to meet and come up with a plan. She gave a small grin as this meant they were now taken seriously. As the teams got into position and played once more, Deeso and the others now had to change strategy seeing as Zulag's was copied by their opponents. One of the balls Deeso picked up was heavier than normal, and she felt something was off. Ozul himself watched with curiosity as well, the throws that they made weren't nearly as effective. Ozul assumed at first that they were tired after playing two straight games, but on a second glance he had a heavy frown on his face as he realized the deception at hand. As he saw Deeso, Zulag, and Cikya return to his side one by one and the other Forest Seekers celebrating their victory, Ozul interrupted them, kicking some mud in their direction.

"Wait. You stuffed these with rocks! That is cheating." Ozul complained to the boy as he held up one of the half-destroyed balls, revealing the content inside. Zulag lifted an eyebrow as he felt Cikya's hand on his shoulder.

"Yeah? And what are you going to do about it?" The boy said, pushing Ozul to the ground. Deeso and Cikya were surprised to see such aggression among The Forest Seekers towards their own kind. Ozul picked himself off but decided not to escalate things. He kept his head down and retreated behind the others. Zulag wasn't sure who he should be annoyed at more, the teen's desperation to win and not play fairly or Ozul's weakness for not defending himself.

"Since you cheated, this cancels our loss and makes us the winner." Deeso commented, as she crossed her arms and shook her head in disappointment. Cikya went to work picking some of the mud out of her hair and Deeso's as well from their previous games. Despite the cheating fiasco at their hands, Deeso found the game could be adapted for play and training back home. The mental aspect is something that could surely be appreciated by Ronkalk, but she would most likely have to add some additional rules to keep the process honest and fair.

"Who do you think you are?" One of the Forest Seeker girls stated. She approached Deeso from the stump as the first boy nodded in agreement with her.

"No, it does not-" The boy said as Deeso punched him in the face. Cikya nodded in approval as she looked over the teen's condition. His mouth and nose were bloodied. His followers were too shaken to do anything other than stare at him helplessly. Ozul's head peered out as he saw the scene before him. He felt joy at seeing fate turn so quickly, but he was reminded of the brutality of his new companions as well. This is something he would need to figure out how to accept in due time to survive and find his family.

"Yes. It does. Now take us to your village before this knife of mine cuts more than that pitiful strand of hair on your chin." Zulag said with a laugh, pointing towards the boy's grass pants.

The other Forest Seeker teens returned to work not saying another word as their hatred of Thunderfeet grew further. For Ozul, he felt conflicted, after all he tried to be nice and have a game with his peers, but they chose to shun him anyway. This happened everywhere he went, and he couldn't understand why. He hoped that people would eventually understand him, but that day was a long time coming.

On The Trail

As Eshe worked to consolidate power among the other Forest Seeker bands that were nearby, Jih followed her in kind and the two delivered the same speech with mixed results. Eshe wanted to push more and more, but Jih was tired of the charade they did. His goal remained ever present in his mind, as meeting Eshe was a setback to the meteor. Jih debated leaving in the dead of night a few times, but the land was alien to him, and he felt some sort of responsibility for Sadal who was forced to do menial tasks around the camp as he watched closely. The two spent time with one another as Eshe allowed them to interact when she didn't have any plans. Jih would visit her and give small gifts of food. Sadal was ready to leave as her injuries were finally healed. Eshe announced to her small pool of growing supporters that she was to go on a campaign, this time to capture another Thunderfoot spotted in the area. Jih finally had enough as he put his foot down.

"Stone Breaker, I ask of you one more-" Eshe said, her voice stopped by Jih's angered expression. Eshe's protectors moved quickly to her, seeing Jih's still tone change dramatically. Eshe wasn't worried, with a simple flick of her hair disarming them as they stood by waiting for orders.

"Jih has helped Eshe with all tasks. Eshe will now help Jih." Jih said curtly to her.

"I suppose you have. I would have liked to see you in battle, but you are worth more to me alive than injured like the Thunderfoot, or dead like many of your kind. What is it that you want?" Eshe asked, as she rubbed some dust off herself.

"Sadal must come with Jih. Jih must know where power rock is. Who saw the sky alight?" Jih questioned.

"One thing is simpler than the other. My father witnessed the sky that night, and the Panmarat spoke to him, saying to go west. As for the Thunderfoot, I better have good fortune to replace her." [23] Eshe said as she ordered one of her guards to let Sadal go free and back to Jih. This was a payment she decided was equal to Jih's help.

Sadal was brought back to Jih with a scowl on her face, but he felt comforted seeing that her sling was removed. Her arm was fully healed now, and the real fun could begin. Jih's small smile soon left however as Sadal approached him, her finger poking him in the stomach. She had an axe to grind with Jih regarding her time under Eshe's eyes and ears.

"Who do you think you are helping her?" Sadal questioned with anger in her voice.

Now that Eshe let them go free, Sadal and Jih were left to their own devices. Sadal and Jih had gotten a better understanding of each other, literally and figuratively during their stay with Eshe. Eshe reminded Jih that despite Sadal sounding strange at first, their tongues were closer than she realized. After extensive conversation, Jih was able to extract the differences in Sadal's speech to a considerable degree. While he still struggled on

---

[23] Emic word for Banyan Tree. In real life, the Banyan Tree is thought to be a place of worship and communication with the spirits too!

occasion, he could grasp the majority of what she was saying. With the Forest Seeker tongue recognized by Sadal's ears, Jih's adoption of the dialect made significant strides on her end. Jih spoke with his own idioms that eluded Sadal but for the things that mattered, they had solid communication. Jih couldn't do much under his internment as Eshe's prisoner. She held them hostage for two weeks as Jih performed various tasks on her behalf and used him to elevate her status among the other Forest Seekers who were skeptical about what she had in store. With the unwilling endorsement of The Stone Breaker called Jih, she held much more weight, and in exchange served as the bridge for the two to learn off each other. Sadal and Jih had a rocky friendship starting out. There weren't others to trust other than themselves, but their differences kept them distant for some time. Sadal felt slighted by Jih's perceived friendship with Eshe, to her it was aiding the enemy she long prepared to do battle against. Jih's loyalty was hard to determine, and Sadal found this could be a liability for her as the two traveled together. Jih naturally felt that he lacked agency under Eshe's watchful eye.

As Jih left with Sadal, he couldn't help but feel he was observed by Eshe and the other Forest Seekers. He looked behind him, and thought he saw the outline of her while Sadal pressed onwards. Jih told Sadal that they were to go west, but the idea of how far west was, that took time to figure out. Sadal didn't bother to answer Jih as she was still annoyed at him. The roads of civilization gave way again to tracts of unmarked foliage that the two cut down with their weapons. Jih arranged earlier for Sadal to have her weaponry returned in the event they were set free. Jih also remembered being watched over as his methods of The Old Way were examined. Jih knew that Eshe was resourceful, and there was no doubt in his mind that perhaps she was trying to understand more of the Thunderfoot arsenal and how to combat it. Jih remembered that Bani understood Neck-Shell technology exceptionally well, perhaps she also had this gift. Jih looked to mend the rift between the two of them as best as he could. In the limited amount of time they shared, Jih grew attached to Sadal more than he cared to admit. They held a shared experience as outsiders to the Forest Seekers and Jih needed Sadal's input on finding the meteor above all else.

"Sadal. Jih has asked if you are alright. No answer was given and Jih begins to worry. Answer Jih now." Jih said with a gruff tone.

"I'm not dead, am I?" Sadal said sarcastically to Jih as he rolled his eyes.

The vast jungle hardly made an easy path for either of them. Sadal grew frustrated as her knife failed to hack away the thickest of pieces of foliage. Jih attempted to find another route forward as he signaled to Sadal to follow him. Sadal remained close and looked up as she heard gibbons above them. Their loud calls bothered both Jih and Sadal as they ran into a patch of forest with less noise. The air was calm again, but Jih heard laughter in the distance. Jih assumed that this area of jungle was isolated as there was little work done in clearing the land. Through the underbrush, four men emerged in the distance wearing a variety of grass coverings and jewelry made with bone. Jih recognized them as some sort of hunting party with the weapons they were carrying. Jih looked at the figures as he held his spear close to him. He could tell by their gait alone that they weren't Forest Seekers. Sadal ran forward of him, stopping shortly thereafter as she lifted her hand up to Jih for him to freeze in place. She moved her ear to listen closely as Jih covered his mouth. Sadal peered through the foliage and examined their dress. She turned around and shook her head knowing what needed to be done.

"Either help me or stay out the way Jih." Sadal whispered to Jih.

Jih felt a wave of slight relief as Sadal's anger towards him subsided for now. Jih held a look of exasperation as Sadal ran off with no visible plan. As most injuries in combat were fatal, Jih took great care in deciding when and how he'd enter combat. Sadal's rush to the enemy was completely reckless in his eyes but he had to support her. It was obvious she recognized these men, but from where? Jih grumbled at Sadal's display but chose to follow her lead. He found cover behind a tree and waited, where only a few strands of Sadal's hair were visible to him. Not too far from Jih, Sadal sat ready and primed with one of her throwing spears. She also kept a small knife wrapped in her clothing for close encounters. The four men sniffed the air around them and noticed something was amiss.

"You smell that? We're far from alone." The middle of the four mentioned.

To Sadal, it was obvious this one was the most experienced, so this would be her target. She looked back at Jih's direction, wondering how it was so quick for them to get caught. She inched closer until she felt she was comfortable enough to land a solid blow. A small breeze carried through the forest where the sweat on their backs dripped to the leaves below. The crunch of Sadal's foot allowed Jih to tell where she was positioned, as he wondered what she planned to do next. Jih looked at his spear and assessed its condition, seeing that he would need to use it soon. Jih waited for Sadal's signal and prepared himself for battle.

"For Ronkalk!" Sadal shouted, as she stepped from the brush and in one swift motion, hurled her first throwing spear. Jih nodded with satisfaction as Sadal skewered the guy clean in the stomach. His skin ruptured as there was blood that drained out from his exposed flesh. He attempted to remove the vessel out of his body but was powerless to do so. As the three men saw the spear launch into their friend, they knew right away they encountered a professional. This wasn't just some crazed hunter either, but one of their sworn enemies from The Broken Bone. The other men scattered as Sadal went towards the kill, dislodging the spear from the entry wound to throw again.

"Where are the rest of you!?" Sadal yelled out; her voice stifled by the volume of plants that were surrounding her. She heard nothing until light footsteps gave way to another one of the attackers attempting to get the jump on Sadal as he swung wildly with his axe. Sadal rolled along the ground just in time to see her adversary. She scoffed at the attempt, as honor in combat was what she valued most. An even match of strength could be had, but he resorted to simple trickery.

"Attacking from behind? Nothing else I would expect from The Mud Forged." Sadal said to herself, as one of the men advanced towards her with an axe in hand.

Sadal dropped her throwing spear to the ground, as it was too awkward to use up close. She took the knife from her clothing and held the handle with her left hand as she attempted to move the man's arm away from her. She saw an opening and swiped at the man's legs, much as how Jih brought her to the ground some time ago. Sadal's adaptability to learn techniques, even ones used against her with great effect, were incorporated into her fighting style. On top, Sadal was able to get an opening as she dodged the swing of the axe by moving her head closer to the man. The two collided heads, and while Sadal was dazed, she quickly recovered and jabbed the knife into the man's neck. She reveled in the rush of the battle as she hoisted the knife out through a pool of blood.

While Sadal and the other Mud Forged were engaged in combat, Jih went over to her to provide support. He was stopped, however, by one of the others. He took his knife and lunged at Jih who quickly held his spear parallel to him to absorb the blow. Jih used the weight of the wood to bring him to a stop. Jih grounded himself in a stance with his feet and kicked the man in the torso. Jih assessed the impact would be enough space for him to move without issue. Jih knocked the wind out of his opponent before jabbing the spear into his throat. Jih normally fought in silence but felt compelled to join Sadal's yell as their two voices rang in unison through the jungle. As a gift, he learned to craft throwing spears that Sadal mentioned to him based on her description. Two were equipped in her field bag that Jih looked at with much pride.

Jih saw that the men in question were people who looked like Sadal. Jih decided to refer to these people as Thunderfeet for now, much like how Eshe introduced Sadal. This display was enough to justify the name in his eyes with ease. They lacked the gracefulness he was used to seeing among the Forest Seekers but noted their formation tactics echoed the ones he learned at home from his mother. Jih hadn't fought with this much ferocity since his last blows of combat with Hyu at his side. It was a rush like no other. Sadal was hardly his partner with decades of understanding but the two made an effective force in combat. Sadal looked behind her to see the outline of Jih in the distance as she triumphantly lifted the man's corpse below her. Jih did the same as he groaned from the blood that came all over him. Jih found that through the fighting one of The Mud Forged managed to escape and ran in the opposite direction. Sadal knew right away that he was looking to find reinforcements and couldn't let him live. She took a deep breath as her gaze turned to Jih.

"One more remains and escapes us. We must find them, yes Sadal?" Jih asked as Sadal gave a crafty smile. Jih laughed as Sadal sniffed the air with bloodlust apparent on her face.

"Well now! It seems your hatred runs deep as well. Good, these people are scum and deserve nothing else to them. It's clear to me you aren't one to run. We had no plan and now this is what we'll do." Sadal said with some satisfaction.

Sadal's opinion of Jih improved considerably as she expected to kill them all on her own. Jih and Sadal gave each other a nod of mutual support as they prepared to pursue.

The two talked with one another as they attempted to reach the running man further from them. The trees and grass weaved by their vision as they remained with their eyes peeled.

"Why does Sadal hate them?" Jih questioned, clearly seeing Sadal's zeal towards eliminating the people that attacked them. Defending oneself was a simple endeavor, but Sadal initiated the attack on these people.

"They are one of The Betrayers. Before I left home, we were taught the stories of our people. The Broken Bone had friends before we came to this land. There are three of them. One of which we wiped out already, but two remain. These are The Mud Forged, The Onpeu's Legacy, and The Worn Web. The Worn Web weaved a plan to take power from us and claim the best hunting lands for themselves. We had balance in the land, but greed took over and our goal of removing the beasts was not popular. They failed to see our greatness and the vision we worked to achieve. Ronkalk was young then... The Mud Forged were the last ones of these to break ties with us and we've since vowed their destruction." Sadal said as she pointed to the right.

The two changed direction as they kept up the pace. The sound of the man keeled over in exhaustion hit their ears. He let out a horrid cough as he hit the soil. Jih and Sadal emerged from another bush as the man from The Mud Forged begged for mercy. The outline of their village was just a short walk away and Sadal couldn't be happier. Jih trained his spear on the man as he attempted to plead once more.

"Please...Spare me. I'm this close to home. My furs and everything else are yours." He pleaded.

Jih raised an eyebrow at the man's claims. The pair were essentially broke with nothing of value aside from the clothes on their backs. Pelts for information made a good bargain. The deal was enticing, but Jih wondered how much the truth was compared to the desperation of a man at death's door. If he lived, he and Sadal would be in greater danger and understood the necessity of the man's death. Sadal laughed at the man's sniveling as she kept an eye on Jih.

"Make me your captive, I can weave-" The man said as Sadal's face noticeably grew angrier as she heard the word weave.

"No, you spare me. You know what your people did when you took arms against us. Ronkalk doesn't take captives and neither do I. Does Krukzig still live, or has he gorged himself to death on Teen-Sa?[24] Doesn't matter to me, you won't answer either way. Jih, end it now." Sadal said as she waited.

Jih took no time in inserting the spear into the man as he stared at the camp in the distance. He didn't make a sound as he remained motionless. For Jih, it wasn't personal, it was about survival above all else. Jih grabbed a few leaves from a nearby tree to clean the blood off his spear. The Elders believed that entering a camp with a bloody weapon was a bad omen and clouded intentions of meeting. With violence begetting violence, Jih

---

[24] Emic word for honey.

didn't want to immediately have fingers put against him and Sadal. The pair decided to walk around the man's body and make their way to the village from another entrance.

Jih was unsure of the proper way to enter a Thunderfoot village and looked to Sadal for any reference. He hoped that Sadal could control herself for the time being as they worked to get any sort of information. As the two waited for their arrival, Jih noticed that the camp was woefully small. There were only about eight tents present which was a far cry from his own home or his stay at Eshe's. The Mud Forged had three separate camps spread throughout the landscape, and this was the smallest settlement of about twenty people. Jih noticed that there were baskets with honeycombs stored inside and assumed this was a worker's camp as they looked to bring resources back home. Jih found honey to be a food to consume within a couple hours, but he noticed that Thunderfeet stockpiled the material. Under the correct conditions and free from moisture, honey had an indefinite shelf life that lasted even past smoked meats. Honey was also an invaluable food for the elderly and children as it could be consumed without teeth. The Thunderfeet innovation with their tightly woven baskets and lids contained honeycombs that could be broken apart later for consumption. Jih noticed that a large amount of smoke dispersed through the camp, and this was used to calm bees that nested in the outer areas. Jih recalled his experiences with gathering honey for Hizo and these memories were not pleasant. He and Kag dared one another to stand underneath an active hive with a torch while one stuck their hand inside.

Jih and Sadal let themselves in as only a few kids seemed to be present. They were unaware of Sadal's status as a member of The Broken Bone and gave both mangoes as a greeting. Jih wasted no time eating as he also told Sadal to do the same. Now that Jih had a moment to think, he recalled the details of Sadal's story from earlier. All these twists and turns seemed to center on one thing, the need for power and resources. The Neck-Shells were Jih's only real frame of reference of an enemy faction, so he thought of them often for power dynamics. The Neck-Shells were raiders that bullied the weak and his people became weak because of this, but for Sadal's, they turned their circumstances around into something worthy to be respected or perhaps feared. Jih was unsure of how to feel about this, but he knew that Tur and The Council robbed his generation of a real chance to lead.

"Home, there is The Elders. Our leader is Tur. Tur is terrible leader and many died. Supplies are needed, but Tur wastes time with pelts. Pelts only Tur and The Council keep." Jih said, offering a noticeably short summary to Sadal. Jih's expression changed as he made himself angry again.

"So, what's the problem? Why not take a dagger to his throat for all to see? He clearly is unable to fight. If he can't claim his own pelts, there's no use for him to be around." Sadal laughed.

Experience for both The Elders and The Broken Bone was an interesting endeavor. Jih's entire society was built on the importance of inherited knowledge where those with the most attained status and the decision making were relegated to them. Those of high ranking in The Broken Bone certainly had worthwhile knowledge, but leadership was open to be challenged and encouraged to do so. Jih shook his head wishing it were that simple.

"Jih almost did, there was great and powerful anger. We use words, that is not how things are done. Jih would have been put to the axe, but Mother saved Jih in death." Jih explained.

Sadal looked visibly confused as Jih went into further detail how his leadership system worked. The Broken Bone had subordinates that all answered to Ronkalk, while maintaining their own bands. She didn't understand the need for such cloak-and-dagger politics when a strong hand is what people responded to best. She shrugged and knew that some people were just different and that was about all she could say on the matter.

The two were met with some strange looks but were given no mind otherwise. Jih and Sadal continued to talk among themselves until commotion from the exterior of the village rang to their ears. A few adults returned with a bounty of fruit and meat at hand. Sadal held her hand out to Jih and got up as she kept her knife in her hand. She eavesdropped on their discussion and found that the bodies of the slain were discovered earlier. She turned to Jih and nodded her head. As Jih got up, the remaining adults of The Mud Forged emerged into the camp in surprise at their new visitors. The wounds on the bodies match the entrance of Sadal's knife and the two feared another conflict to occur. A woman with club held it trained on the two of them as one man of The Mud Forged came forward. Jih stared down both while Sadal opened conversation.

"Whatever you're thinking didn't happen. You should put your club down now." Sadal mentioned as the woman glared at them both.

"You're not one of our allies. Why have you come to this camp?" She asked as she looked at her companion for support.

"The rest of our hunting party has fallen, and reinforcements won't arrive for another three days. Let us rebuild in peace." The man stated bluntly.

"My friend and I are looking for something far to the west. Are you aware of the time night became day? Do you know where the meteor landed? Tell us what you know, and we'll make our leave." Sadal said as Jih nodded.

The two looked at one another and felt in their heart that Sadal was the one who killed their hunting party. They lacked the strength to fight back as they were exhausted from the hunt. Neither of them witnessed the meteor shower that night but knew that Krukzig was a witness. His tale spread far past their lands as they were bothered by other pilgrims in the past. They humbly pointed the pair in the direction out of their camp. Their fear was apparent and figured that appeasing them would be easier to survive another day.

"Our jungle obscures the view of above, but our main camp two weeks out from here witnessed it. We have our leader who did so and at least one priest. Talk to them there out west." The man replied to them.

Sadal looked at Jih to see if he accepted their story. Jih was convinced that west was truly where they needed to head. He heard the directions independently from both Eshe and these random Thunderfeet, it couldn't have been simple coincidence. Jih attempted to thank the man but stopped short as he realized his odd sounding voice would cause them more confusion in a tense conversation. Jih and Sadal backed away from the pair as they wielded their weapons and gave space between them. The two walked backwards away from the encampment until they were once again left alone. Jih spoke to Sadal as they continued their path.

"Those Thunderfeet and directions of Eshe were the same. West must be where we go. Jih does not know how far yet." Jih exclaimed as Sadal agreed with him.

Two weeks on the trail to Krukzig's encampment wasn't an exciting prospect but Jih and Sadal hoped to make good time. As they were left to the elements, Jih looked over the state of his clothing. Jih was no stranger to a bloody battle, but he liked to keep clean when he could. Jih knew that the two of them needed a bath, so he would be the first to find a river to clean off. Dried blood was also an invitation for the more dangerous predators to come by, so it was in their interest to get it removed. As the two continued to walk, Jih smelled the air around him. He sniffed his body and cited the blood that was on him from earlier, but there was a much worse stench that floated around him. He couldn't wrap his head around it, but the smell practically stunned him and inhibited his thought. His eyes scanned the ground for carcasses that rotted in the sun, but there was nothing to be found. It wasn't the smell of dung either, but his eyes practically watered at seeing Sadal. He looked over her to see visible patches of dirt on her skin as Jih stared at her. Sadal picked at her teeth with a spare finger as she noticed Jih came to a halt.

"What? Why have we stopped moving?" Sadal asked.

Jih and Kag were close, so it was easy enough to say that Jih needed to bathe himself, but it was considered rude for newer people. Jih realized that Sadal hadn't been given a bath practically the entire time that they were with Eshe, but it only became apparent when she ran around and exerted herself. His nose was blind for their travel but now that he had a chance to experience it for himself, the time was nigh. Jih lifted his finger and faintly heard rushing water. The rainforest was full of creeks, streams, and rivers so Jih was free to pick whatever he wanted.

"Jih wants to look for game by river. Will you help Jih?" Jih said as he guided their pace towards a riverbank. Sadal's backpack was in shoddy condition, so she saw it as a perfect opportunity to find some fresh pelts to make things for her and Jih. She was delighted at the endeavor and encouraged Jih to go forward.

"I wonder what we'll find today..." Sadal questioned out loud as Jih remained silent. Jih pointed forward as the brush opened to a hefty riverbank where water leaked out. Sadal saw no trace of any kind of deer in the distance, but she remained vigilant.

"Oh-by the river? Jih, let's find another way around." Sadal said, as she quickly realized they would need to cross water.

It was unknown to Jih, but Sadal was unable to swim, and she had a tremendous fear of water, to the point where it even affected her grooming habits to a large degree. While practically all members of The Broken Bone couldn't swim, Sadal's inherent fear of water was all her own. Jih saw that Sadal was looking to run in the opposite direction. Before she could do so, Sadal felt herself lifted. Jih figured while they were here, they could get some water on their bodies. Jih wanted to clean off and figured prey would arrive all the same.

Oh-Is he going to carry me over? That's thoughtful of him. Sadal assumed as she covered her eyes with her hands in fear.

Jih walked into the muddy bank with Sadal in tow. She waited for Jih to step over before they were to reach dry land again, but she felt that he was going deeper. Jih hoisted Sadal up again as she frantically tried to get out of his grasp and heard the rushing water.

"Wait- Please no!" Sadal screamed into his ear as she kicked Jih frantically.

Jih found a particularly less shallow portion of the riverbank to carry Sadal as he toughened out the injuries. Jih was at his wits end with Sadal's smell and forcefully dunked the two of them under the water. He hardly felt proud doing so but even children knew to bathe occasionally. He did this once and already saw visible improvement as the water washed away some of the layered dirt on her body. The water that flowed off Sadal's body changed color as she resurfaced. Jih stuck out his tongue in disgust and met an annoyed but clean Sadal. Jih nodded happily at the outcome although he saw that Sadal was upset. Sadal broke away from Jih and sat at the end of the riverbank. Jih picked up a smoothed rock that looked good for cleaning.

"Why would you do that?! I hate water!" Sadal yelled in anger towards Jih.

"Sadal. Please clean." Jih said, as he tossed her a stone. Sadal folded her arms as another came in her direction. Sadal threw it back at Jih who dodged by moving sideways. She moved herself to where only a small amount of water could touch her toes and looked at Jih as she slowly rubbed a rock on her skin. Jih didn't seem impressed, but he was at least satisfied with the bare minimum offered by Sadal. Anything past three days was pushing it, but two weeks was egregious. Sadal's scent would do more to scare off animals than running at the prey with a lit torch.

"What, do you want to watch or something? I'm doing it!" Sadal yelled at him, which made Jih laugh. Her temper reminded him of Dran, and this made him laugh harder as he missed his friends but could see traits he valued within Sadal.

"And my outfit! It's completely damp! How am I supposed to deal with this?" Sadal added on as Jih left her to her privacy.

Once Sadal finished cleaning, it was time for the pair to keep going. Their eyes settled on a flattened area of the jungle that was devoid of tall grasses. Although it had been some time since Jih and Sadal camped together, they already made a routine where the first thing they did was construct a fire for the night. Jih was fed before they left Eshe's encampment, so he didn't feel hungry, but Sadal was a different story. Sadal rubbed her stomach, and Jih looked up to see that his fortune was good.

"Angya tree." Jih mentioned, as he guided Sadal's eyes.

He grabbed his spear and knocked off two large jackfruits that fell to the bottom, just in time for Jih to catch one. The other rolled to the bottom and slid past them both. He gave Sadal the fruit who looked at it with some disinterest.

"Why are you excited? There's no skill in finding fruit. I wanted game, but fruit is passive and dull." Sadal said as her stomach took over her decision making, and she ripped portions of the fruit. As she chewed her food, she spoke to Jih.

"You owe me you know. For what you did back there." Sadal said as looked at Jih's expression. She knew he thought about the water, but her eye was on something more important.

"Remember Forest Seekers like Eshe aren't to be trusted, but she just happened to be right this time. You take the first watch." Sadal said as Jih shrugged and closed his eyes to take a nap before nightfall.

Welcome Home

As Jih promised Sadal he'd keep watch that night, he regretted his decision soon after as a wave of exhaustion came over him. Jih drifted in and out of consciousness as the excitement of the day wiped him out. His nap hardly did much for him. The sun was setting and Jih continued to fuel the fire. He felt he had plenty of energy still, but his age caught up with him at times. Jih thought of the existential questions that came to mind with meeting both Eshe and Sadal. What happened to his people? If the world was his own as The Council taught him and everyone else from very young, why were these others not mentioned? Jih concluded that The Council chose to lie to him for their own selfish desires. It seemed reasonable enough, it was an answer that filled a lot of problems. They claimed to have infinite knowledge of the world around them, so things that came as a surprise to Jih was deception on their part. His tired face turned to a scowl as he was marred by the thought of Tur and how not a word could be trusted. Jih gritted his teeth as he slept.

"Tur...took life from Jih." He complained to himself.

Jih's eyes shot open as he heard a familiar yelp past what was left of their fire.

"Denmey again..." Jih added as he felt around in the darkness for a rock.

Far in the background, hyenas yelped over the remains of a deer and their sound filled his eardrums. Sadal slept like a stone, with only the light lift of her chest as a sign she was breathing. Jih looked at her in awe of how she could stay asleep with the symphony of animals around. Jih grasped a rock and flung it to the infinite expanse of darkness that was the outer foliage. For Sadal, the sound of hyenas was something she screened out long ago, but Jih struggled to do the same. Their camp was a rough construction, but a large fire brought warmth and security to the pair. Jih and Sadal's sleeping positions were comfortable but tactical, as they faced opposite directions from one another. The noise subsided and Jih found it difficult to stay awake. Jih drifted to sleep with a spear in hand. Jih was a light sleeper and rarely rested well, but when he could, he often hung on to good memories. Hizo taught this skill to all her students to keep calm in stressful situations. Her teachings continued to support Jih every step of the way.

Jih's dream was simple in its construction. His world was an open cave by the side of the ocean. When he was young, it was an escape for him where he could always get the advice of Hizo, and as an adult he would see Hyu there. In life, Hyu found this amusing. It warmed her heart that Jih always had her in his mind. Now it was the only place he could see her. Jih found himself back on Sundaland, a much healthier and vibrant looking one than the place he left before. It was strangely empty, save for one person and a bounty of life at the sea. Jih wore different clothing as his pelts from his time in The Council were removed. He wore an outfit woven with plant fibers and brush instead. Not his personal style, but he went along with it. Jih felt the sand in his feet as he saw a figure standing alone next to some supplies. He made his way over as a gentle wave called him. Hyu was at the end of the beach with a net and spear in hand. She watched the movement of the water. Jih froze as he was unsure of what to think. Hyu's hair swayed in the wind as she turned around and Jih remembered her vibrant brown eyes. Despite what Jih initially thought, Hyu didn't seem confused or bothered to see him. She looked at him with a smile and handed him an extra spear. Hyu pointed to the water, she looked at all sorts of fish that made their way towards the ends of the shore.

"Hyu must cook Peymin for Bani. Will you help Hyu catch them?" She said, giving Jih a look before laughing.

"Jih must cook Peymin for Bani. Hyu is bad at this." Hyu commented, correcting her previous statement. She could tell that Jih had a lot on his mind, so she offered the floor to him.

"Jih has seen much recently. There are others besides us you know." Jih said as he copied Hyu's position, the two holding spears one-handed above them, ready to strike at any moment.

"Hyu knows, remember the tiny Osa?" Hyu mentioned as she made a small splash along the water that got a fish's interest. She impaled it happily as it struggled for a few moments before the water reddened. She used her free hand to detach the first fish and put it in her net.

"Mmm. That was some time ago." Jih said as he felt his face.

Jih stood in silence as Hyu looked him over, it was clear that Jih was sitting on information, and she had to know what it was. Jih looked at the fish and glared at one swimming on its own. His stare compelled the fish to swim towards him. It treaded water as it looked up at him and was ready to be stabbed. It was clear that Jih knew he was in a dream, but it didn't matter to him for now.

"Jih has new friend, the one named Sadal. Jih is unsure of what to do with her." Jih remarked, breaking the silence between the two.

"What else is there to do? Sadal has come with Jih. Be there for her where no one else has." Hyu guided as she placed a supportive hand on Jih's shoulder.

"When it is finished, bring her to our people. If she is strong, another for fighting pit of Dran!" Hyu added, mocking Dran's tone of voice as Jih nodded in agreement.

Jih laughed harder than he felt he had any right to, but he knew his time here was not long. He decided to go to the matter at hand and Hyu recognized this. She waited patiently just as she did for the fish.

"Jih went to look for power rock like we once said. What should Jih do now? Jih had plan but now Jih is lost." Jih offered to Hyu to give her input.

"Hyu has thoughts. Hyu must hear what Jih thinks. Explain to Hyu." Hyu responded as she leaned in closer to Jih. Her large hair enveloped a part of his arm as it flowed over.

"Jih must go west, this is known. Sadal agrees with Jih. How far west we do not know. What should we do?" Jih explained.

"There are places the ancestors have gone before. Remember our stories and you will find your way. It is hunt for Sarudeu but only much bigger." Hyu said confidently as she rubbed Jih's head with affection. Jih was happy to hear Hyu's input, even if it was the back of his mind justifying the fact he and Sadal were terribly lost.

"Jih. Hyu has favor to ask. Can you do this?" Hyu added, rubbing noses with Jih. The two separated and Jih stepped back as he answered her.

"Yes. What will Jih do?" Jih asked.

"Let Hyu go." Hyu said as her voice invaded Jih's ears.

Jih covered his ears and sheltered himself from the horrid sight. The color of Hyu's skin receded from her body until she was a faint gray, and her pupils were devoid of all life. Her smooth skin hardened until she was no softer than a spear point. Her body still stood and slowly bled as the liquid seeped into the sand beneath. Jih saw bits and pieces of her flesh fall apart. Fragments of her hair fell towards the ground and hissed at Jih like cobras. The water and waves stopped moving entirely and were no longer under control. The sky blackened as a volcano rose out of the sand and launched debris and ash for miles around. Jih felt himself cough profusely as his eyes watered. Each panicked breath brought more pain onto him as ash entered his lungs. Jih keeled over and coughed blood as he looked at Hyu. Her eyes were empty and only revealed the sockets where blood seeped out. Jih watched as Hyu fell to the ground and remained lifeless afterwards. The apocalypse that Jih hoped to avoid for his people was realized in his mind. Although Tur caused suffering in his life, there was more to it than just one man. Jih knew that the power rock would not just save his band, but now perhaps all of Sundaland too. He was then ousted out of this world.

All that was around him now was an endless supply of darkness as he realized their fire lost its volume. Jih reignited the fire with a new path given for him. Jih's bloodshot eyes opened fully once more, and he took watch for the rest of the night. There would always be another chance to catch up on some rest. The morning gave way and Jih slumped over, having passed out again from exhaustion. Sadal stood over Jih as he snored. She had a frown on her face as he slowly came to. Jih looked up to see her arms folded.

"Yes?" Jih asked, as he tried to inch away and give space to Sadal.

"You are terrible at keeping watch. You fell asleep! It's the middle of the afternoon. Not only did I hunt, but here, I made you something." Sadal said with some irritation in her voice.

"Sadal lives another day." Jih said as he shrugged his shoulders.

In the hours that Jih was asleep, Sadal made two backpacks for her and Jih to hold extra equipment for their travels. For Sadal, backpacks were a common occurrence, but for Jih, this was cutting edge technology. Jih hovered over her like a small child in awe at what Sadal made. He hadn't seen anything like it. He marveled at the design where the two straps fit onto his back with ease. Sadal was a diligent toolmaker in her own right, as she enjoyed working with the pelts of her fallen prey to make all sorts of productive tools. This most often extended into personal expression through various outfits, but this expanded into other areas as well. Using a fully grown Sambar deer, she was able to use much of the animal's stomach space as containers for the two of them and knitted fur around it. Animal bladders and stomachs would be emptied and dried out in the sun. She sewed the straps on with sinew ripped from the muscles of the deer and used a bone needle to set it in place. Sadal hoisted her backpack with one shoulder with ease and jumped up and down to test the tightness of her build. Jih carefully approached it while Sadal could barely hold it together as she was puzzled by Jih's reaction.

"I saw you were using Jaat to tie your weapons to your back at Eshe's encampment, so this is much better. That is what Forest Seekers use. We use backpacks. When you want to close the backpack, stuff this end inside it and pull tightly." Sadal said in a judgmental tone as Jih nodded at her words.

"So much space for tools!" Jih said with genuine surprise on his face. Jih placed his hand into his backpack and felt around the interior. Back in Sundaland, practically everyone carried extra goods in reed baskets that were cumbersome, and hunting parties were often large to carry all the tools. He knew the Hunting Team back home could only dream of having this much convenience.

"Jih thanks Sadal for...backpack." Jih said as he put it on, and emulated Sadal's prior movements.

Sadal watched with some pride in her craftsmanship as Jih admired her work. Although Jih figured the matter was over, Sadal brought the topic of Hyu back to discussion. She took a deep breath through her nose and pointed her finger at Jih.

"By the way, I couldn't sleep because of you. All I heard was you talking about some person named Hyu. What is she, your daughter?" Sadal asked, as she rubbed her hands on her legs.

"Kag has child that is coming. Jih does not have one." Jih stated as he looked through her hide backpack that was sprawled out on the ground.

"You didn't answer my question Jih." Sadal countered, with her eyes narrowed at him.

"Hyu was special to Jih. Many years were spent together." Jih mentioned, as he decided to keep some privacy to him.

"Hmm. I'm sure it hurts to have left such a perfect life and be stuck with me, yeah?" Sadal said to Jih. Jih folded his arms at her comment as he looked towards her. Jih was hardly one to enjoy a spoiled life despite the status given by his mother. Jih worked hard for everything he was given, including the relationship he had with Hyu. It wasn't easy as he and Hizo had their arguments and to be the eye of Hyu's heart required effort.

"Not all was perfect. Love requires time and patience to build. Jih and Hyu worked hard to build life worth having. Patience that people can lack." Jih explained as he eyed Sadal.

Jih could tell Sadal was hurt over something as he studied her reaction. Sadal looked back briefly on her life with Nurzan, she knew she wasn't happy prior to leaving. Sadal could tell from Jih's inflection alone that he held more care for Hyu than life itself. She wished to ask what being happy was like to Jih, but she decided not to pry further for now. She put her hand on Jih's shoulder and looked into his eyes with understanding.

"Wish I had that. I do have someone special though, my little sister Deeso. I miss her a lot. I hope to find her soon and explain everything that's happened." Sadal commented with a low sigh.

"Kag is brother of Jih. This Deeso will understand if your words are fair." Jih said supportively.

"Deeso's a sweet soul, but I know even without me she'll manage and get home back to the way things were. She always finds a way." Sadal said to him.

"Jih, I think what we should do next is go and try to find another village. We know my people live in these forests as well. We'll need a fresh source of information for the meteor. We can find it that way. Krukzig is our enemy and if we find him, we must kill him. Are you ready for that?" Sadal added on. She pointed vaguely in the distance as Jih collected some of their spare belongings.

The message weighed in Jih's mind as he gave a slow nod. For Jih, the only goal that mattered was finding the power rock. Jih felt the ends justified the means as he settled into combat with Sadal. He looked at his new backpack and gripped it tightly. With this, Jih felt ready to take on more of the great beyond with Sadal at his side.

Fool Me Once

Two men worked side by side wielding large stone axes at their helm. The forest was vast and teeming with life. They gave a low whistle as they worked and surveyed the landscape. They were fixated on finding the perfect tree. The two bore holes into the bark and stuck their fingers inside to smell them afterwards. These two were Thunderfeet that found themselves unaffiliated with any band. They were Wanderers and wore their rank with a sign of honor rather than shame that many groups had. Unlike Sadal, who wore hers on her left hand, theirs were made on the back of their bare shoulders. The pair's respective builds were large and exuded strength. They easily topped six feet and walked as giants among the other inhabitants that lived in this area. On top of their heads were two helmets made from the skulls of long killed water buffalo. The first of these men was named Nezzall, who was slightly shorter than his older brother but with a stockier frame. Nezzall had dark brown hair in the form of dreadlocks and a covering of deer fur. On his back was a large pack filled to the brim with objects tied down with fibers. His older brother Dronall wore his hair short and kept a more muted expression. He chose to look as plain as possible and kept short hair. He carried a large bag that was strapped to him with a leather strap. To those that saw them, they were known as The Buffalo Brothers.

"Brother, how goes the search for the sap we wanted? I crave its taste." Nezzall questioned Dronall as he kicked one of the trees next to him. He extended his hand out for a mangosteen to fall into his hands.

"I'm beginning to think The Forest Seekers lied to us so we would leave their village. These trees are barren!" Dronall complained with annoyance in his voice. He and his brother looked over the number of trees they had carved into, numbering over twenty at this rate with no sign of the precious nectar they were searching for.

The Buffalo Brothers prided themselves as men of exchange and lived to trade goods for the things they found interesting. Unlike other traders however, The Buffalo Brothers simply did the minimum amount of effort to get the maximum return. With their intimidation and cunning, the two quickly made an operation out of their trades as scammers. They focused on mass production and made tools quickly as possible to boost their personal name but counted on people choosing quantity over quality. They would dazzle with a varied selection and gather far better items than they dared to dream. It took talent to make a hardy tool but even more to make a convincing fake. Their faces were obscured, and their identities couldn't be tracked. For them, it was a perfect system. The Buffalo Brothers were wise to the environment that they were in, and when it came to business, didn't share the bias that other Thunderfeet had towards Forest Seekers. They had items of value and were seen as customers just like anyone else. The two hardly dealt with complaints but had procedures in place to deal with those as well. Dronall or Nezzall would take over with the approach deemed necessary. Both were quite charismatic and could talk their way out of most situations. Dronall used speech lathered with honey, while Nezzall preferred a more pragmatic approach with a heavy axe.

"Hey! You-" A voice shouted from the brush.

Dronall realized that a perfect trail was left behind by their work on the trees. Their marks of scratching the trees for sap was the easiest indicator of their movement. It took a moment for him to recognize who it was, but it was a Forest Seeker woman who they exchanged with some hours ago. Dronall groaned under his breath at the sound. His eye moved towards his brother as he nodded in understanding. They reasoned this woman followed them the entire way there. This type of tenacity only meant one thing; they wanted a return.

The Forest Seeker woman had a blowgun in her hands as she stepped out in clear view interrupting the two. She wore yellow feathers in her hair that stuck out from the sea of green that surrounded them. At her side was a small bag filled with darts and other tools from her travels and tied to her person with jute. Dronall turned his head to address the woman and gave a nice smile. Nezzall didn't react as he knew his brother had this situation handled. He studied the two's reactions and noted their size difference.

Look at how puny she is! That blowgun may as well be made from twigs. Dronall has a sharp tongue and I know he can handle it. I'll wait and see what happens. Nezzall thought as he propped next to the tree.

"You gave us a bad deal! This is not what we agreed on!" She said, as she stomped her foot in the ground. Nezzall tensed his fist around the axe, but Dronall eased his concerns with a light touch as he stepped forward.

"You must be mistaken. For a woman as radiant as yourself, we would never violate the deal we made. Why if I were-" Dronall said. He held back his laughter as he noticed her face contorted with anger.

"I want my axes!" She shouted angrily.

Dronall's smooth approach didn't carry over well, so it was time to use force Nezzall reasoned. He let loose a smile that pointed the woman's attention to himself while he gave cover for his brother to think of a plan.

"These axes? We can't allow that. The quality is too good." Nezzall commented, as he hit the tree.

Pieces of wood splintered to the ground and visibly angered the woman before them. The Buffalo Brothers were aware of The Forest Seeker's beliefs on trees, but they didn't care. They were looking for the rumored life-giving sap and if the directions they were told would have been true, so many more trees would have lived.

"And the most important rule of exchange...is no returns." Dronall said. He walked towards her as she reflexively moved back, now held in place by the trees she valued the most. Her eyes fixated on the buffalo skull as Dronall stepped closer.

She gave a harsh whistle that offended both Dronall and Nezzall's ears as they looked towards each other. The realization hit them as Nezzall immediately ran towards Dronall.

"Grab the bags! We need to go!" Dronall yelled as he heard a whirring sound beyond his ears.

A cacophony of darts filled the air as Nezzall crawled towards the ground and scooped the other bags that remained. One of the darts hit Dronall on the head, but his skull cap deflected the direct impact. It protected him well as a tiny crack was made in the piece. Unknown to them previously, this woman was far from alone. Six of the Forest Seekers from her camp followed a short distance and were hidden from their prying eyes. Dronall pushed the woman to the ground as he helped his brother carry the goods. They weaved through the thick brush as well as they could, using their size to get themselves through tighter areas. Their strong builds barreled through the foliage as branches cracked beneath their muscles. Their arms had scratches on them as they did so, but anything to avoid death. The roads they went on were well traveled by the Forest Seekers. They were aware of paths revealed themselves with the arrangement of logs on the ground. The Buffalo Brothers trained themselves to know which paths were correct, as some were led intentionally to problematic areas or dead ends. With everything in mind, the two had a strange respect for The Forest Seeker lifestyle, using deceit and trickery was all part of the game.

Dronall's objective was to find an area where they could cool off and lay low for a while. The darts' sound only intensified as he saw the shadowy outline of his brother hoisting the bags while they ran. He made a small noise and cupped his hands to warn Nezzall that he was going to change direction and the two followed suit. The pair split up temporarily to divide the Forest Seeker war party after them before reconvening. Nezzall won out with the move by arriving at an abandoned campsite. He took a deep breath and searched around him for any signs of life. The two had intricate knowledge of their village structures and found that camps like these were not commonly made by Forest Seekers. This camp had to have been constructed by one of their own. It had the essentials, a tanning rack in disrepair, some outlines for beds and a fire pit. Nezzall secured the perimeter and returned the noise to find that Dronall was not too far from his location. He emerged from an opposing end of the brush with a triumphant laugh as the two walked to one another and bashed their heads together in a satisfying move.

"We should be fine here for now. I had to drop some of our stuff to lighten the load, so this bag is empty." Dronall commented, as he tossed his brother the empty bag.

"I have an idea. Fill this with whatever you can around here, someone is likely to come to our point and we can begin anew." Nezzall reasoned as he reinforced the old campfire with some spare pieces of wood.

Behind them lay a meticulously carved path of forest that served as the roads of exchange, and now they sat at the crossroads. All they needed to do was wait for someone to arrive. Dronall followed his brother's instructions and looked to find suitable material. He laughed to himself as he found just what he was looking for. Jih and Sadal traveled around these carved roads and were filled with questions.

"How are we supposed to find anything here? I said we should look for a village but that was some time ago." Sadal asked, her voice carried through the forest as she looked around cluelessly.

"Eshe said to find log on bottom with markings. Jih sees many logs, this is not helpful." Jih complained, as he echoed Sadal's concerns.

The smell of Nezzall's lit fire filled the two's noses as smoke meant that food was being prepared nearby. Sadal led with her sharp nose as she dragged Jih along with her. The two nearly tripped over each other in a rush. She gave a slow nod as she realized what Eshe meant by marked logs. Her eyes scanned the log and found incisions made in it that formed symbols. She furrowed her brow in confusion as she nudged Jih to take a closer look. Jih pointed in the distance to find that there was a camp nearby and two strange men inhabited it. Jih's eyes scanned the outline of the camp and saw that they had large backpacks and knew they were Thunderfeet.

"Dronall, look!" Nezzall said, getting his brother's attention as his gaze met the two figures.

Nezzall jumped and waved his arms to signal that they were friendly. Dronall already started their routine as he took an assortment of goods from another pack and laid them out along the ground. He crossed his arms as he studied the two who didn't seem to have much that they wanted but decided to hear them out. Sadal's pack was filled with various things she looted off the bodies they killed after they left Eshe's encampment while Jih's own belongings were sparse. Sadal was more than relieved to see that the camp they found was inhabited not by Forest Seekers, but two men that were of her own kind. She noted their unusual headgear but imagined they were powerful hunters like herself to fell water buffalo and wear the kills with such pride. She held her hand out to Jih first as she knew his voice would confuse the two men and addressed them first.

"Do you two belong to The Broken Bone?" Sadal asked with some hesitation.

Nezzall looked at his brother in confusion, he hadn't heard of any sort of group with that name before. Although Jih and Sadal were quite far from Sadal's home by now, she reasoned that eventually some consequence would come from her desertion. Ronkalk was a man of indomitable will, and she knew that he would search for her. Sadal knew she was an incredible warrior among their people and her "death" would not be accepted so easily. She remained skeptical of other Thunderfeet that were not easily identifiable. Dronall massaged his chin in thought but addressed her concern. He noticed the tone in Sadal's voice had some slight worry to it but saw that only meant an opportunity could be struck.

"We all run from something. Tell us your name. And of your...companion there. I am Dronall and my brother Nezzall is over there. We are traders in these lands." He gestured to the wares on display.

Sadal felt her backpack had some items of reasonable quality to trade, most notably, her shortened throwing spears that stuck out the back. She carried around four at any given time but was willing to part with half her stock for something of value. She had a few looted knives that were also stored inside. Sadal wasn't willing to give up any food, but she barely had anything on her person.

"Sadal. This is Jih." She said flatly as Jih turned with his name called.

"We aren't interested in trading. We need directions." Sadal commented while Jih nodded in confirmation of her words.

"Well now, we can't just...give you this for free. Say, how about between us, we do an arm-wrestling match? If I win, you'll trade something, and I can answer your question. If you win, I will give you something in addition to your question." Dronall raised to Sadal. He could see Sadal gave some thought to his decision, as she loved a challenge and to show off her ability. Jih was less accepting of the proposal but shrugged to see the outcome.

"Alright, you have a deal, Dronall. Jih, see when his arm touches the ground. I don't trust his brother to be fair. Two out of three?" Sadal asked, offering her hand out to him.

Dronall happily accepted the wager, and the two shook. Nezzall looked for a suitable location and pointed out a nice area of flat land for the two to have their match. To account for their height difference, Dronall laid flat on the ground and arched his back to match. Jih moved his head to the side and looked to verify there was no foul play. He gave a nod to the two of them who prepared while Nezzall and Jih looked at each other in silence. Dronall's arm was quite the mighty tree trunk as it stayed resolute past Sadal's initial pushes, but he felt his wrist contort. Sadal was filled with stamina that allowed her to keep her grip despite having barely graced the ground a few times. The turn of battle shifted in Sadal's favor as Dronall's wrists gave out. He chalked it up to his exhaustion earlier from chopping wood. Sadal won the first match with a decisive press to the ground as she gave a charming wink much to Nezzall's annoyance.

"Dronall, you seriously can't lose to her!?" Nezzall interjected in shock.

"Arm wrestling is a game of tactics, not just pure strength brother. I was unaware of my opponent's skill and that was my mistake. Have resolve in me." Dronall commented to Nezzall who remained silent again. The other two matches were hard fought, but Dronall won out in the end with Sadal practically cupping her own hand in exhaustion.

"Fine, show me what you have. I can part with something." Sadal was annoyed at her performance.

Jih looked over the various things on offer. Dronall noticed Jih's curiosity towards the colored rocks on display and decided to offer those first. Although Sadal gave an annoyed tone, she felt that she could at least change her circumstances depending on how well negotiations went. She would get directions either way, so anything else she left with could only be a gift.

"You were a mighty opponent, Sadal. Someone as capable as yourself might be interested in these. Do you walk the path of the spirits?" Dronall inquired as he lifted some precious rocks to her. Sadal looked at Dronall and at the rocks with some suspicion but was willing to hear him out.

"What's so special about these rocks?" She asked as she reached her hand over. She felt them in their hands and noted their smoothness and the sheen they emitted under the sun's rays that pierced through the treeline above them. Sadal carried quartz in her hand but was told by Dronall these were jade instead.

"These are our finest leafstones, gathered by the rivers in this area. Note how smooth they are and the shine among them." Dronall mentioned as he looked at Sadal's eyes fill with wonder.

"Sadal, this is crystal[25]. Crystal shines light when held in hand. Leafstone is green and soft to touch.[26]" Jih explained as he locked eyes with Dronall.

Dronall struggled to understand Jih completely, but he gathered that Jih knew what he was talking about. His patience was running thin as he tried to preserve the ruse. He could tell from one look at Sadal that she was a prime hunter and likely had great offerings for them to take.

"You certainly have a Weypeu's heart. Though, I see you're looking at our collection. We have all sorts of things. Perhaps you would like this?" Dronall said as he picked up a quartz rock in a different color. He smirked as he gave it to Jih to hold.

"This is still crystal. There are many colors. Are you new at this?" Jih said with snark in his voice.

"Well, this is some of the best hotspark blessed by the priests themselves. Do not mind the color, the process of blessing changes them. Notice their shine as the sun calls upon them." Dronall said with the utmost seriousness.

Sadal removed her backpack and displayed some of the knives she had earlier. Nezzall gave an affirmative nod as Jih extended his hand out. Dronall guided Sadal's wandering eyes to more products he wished to sell. Although Jih had his complaints, Sadal saw value in having accessible flint.

"What do you want for the rocks? I have tools for combat and for hunting." Sadal questioned as Dronall looked in thought.

"Depends on what you have. Pelts are the standard for trade, but we take tools as well." Nezzall stated as he looked over the three.

Jih and Sadal's eyes turned to the offering of rolled up pelts on the ground. Pelts were the foundation of economic trade among the various bands. Pelts not only were used as a means of exchange but could be used for clothing needs or for decoration. All groups knew of this system and held different values attributed to them, but some beliefs were universal. Common animals such as deer were considered low-value pelts while the most highly sought after were from dangerous predators such as tigers. Pelts from exotic lands or from underrepresented populations were given a much higher value. Pelts were also immune to saturation as they eventually expired and needed active hunting to be restored. Pelts set the value for trading items as well where tools, food, and other services could be leveled against them as a standard.

---

[25] Emic word for quartz.
[26] Emic word for jade.

"If not stones, perhaps our pelt selection may be better for you. We have the usual common fare, but we do have oddities. This pelt here is Bher. I'm willing to part with three of your spears for it." Dronall mentioned as he lifted the bear's skin.

Sadal recognized most of these pelts, but some were of unknown origin. Sadal was a Master Hunter for many years and was sufficiently familiar with the biodiversity in her environment.

"What kind of Bher?" Jih asked as Sadal also had questions.

"Just Bher, this comes from where the land is dry and hot. A luxury item like this doesn't come often in our collection." Nezzall stated with a grin.

"Right...This is an unusual color. Was the kill not healthy?" She inquired, as Dronall gritted his teeth.

The two brothers watched as Sadal looked at the unraveled animal skin. The hair was soft to the touch, but the skin itself was rough and her expression changed. She looked at the pair with growing skepticism but reasoned that the rest of the selection was better. Nezzall hoped his brother would come up with a suitable response. It wasn't known when another source of materials would come by again, so they had to do this right. Dronall saw it best to intervene on his behalf.

"Secondhand trades can be unreliable at times. Though I can assure you our offers are top quality. It lived a powerful life and was hunted with honor." Dronall said, as he placed his hands on Sadal's shoulder. Keeping the deal alive was the only objective. In a very bold move, he decided to lift his buffalo skull to expose his true identity. He always performed this action to show that his words were sincere and revealed a larger portion of his face.

Jih's going to find us out if I don't do something Nezzall. You better distract him while I focus on Sadal. Dronall thought as he tried his best to ignore Jih and talk to Sadal further.

Dronall's options were running thin and the two would be at an impasse. He decided to offer another idea instead that he hoped could seal the deal. Jih hadn't bothered listening to what Dronall and Sadal were talking about, but his opinion of the two tradesmen before him lowered considerably. While Nezzall wasn't looking, he picked up a knife that was dull and the wrapping holding the blade to the handle together practically fell apart as he did so. What sort of craftsmanship was this? Jih's patience wore thin as he was intentionally being ignored now by the brothers.

"Well-How about this. I have an offer here you may like. Give us three items of your choosing and we can share the contents of whatever remains in the bag you choose." Dronall commented. He gestured to the two bags that were in front of him and Nezzall, shifting his position to the one that Sadal eyed the most. Her gaze was on the full bag that was well behind them.

"Move to your right. I want that bag." Sadal said as she took out her throwing spears and laid them out.

"Oh-That bag?" Dronall said, his face showing a clear sign of relief as Sadal pointed past him to the third bag.

Dronall couldn't believe his luck as he stumbled on such an opportunity. Sadal's face couldn't hide her smile as she felt she had negotiated a prime price. She practically rubbed her hands together in glee as she saw Nezzall struggling to lift the bag. Someone as strong as him lifting it with difficulty meant the bounty was surely a well-rewarded one.

"That bag there is quite heavy and contains an assortment of supplies. For three items, it's yours. Even Nezzall struggles to lift such a bounty. You will always remember our generosity." Dronall explained as he noticed Jih glaring at him.

"I'll take the bag!" Sadal said happily, before being interrupted by Jih who grabbed Sadal's shoulder.

"Sadal! We need these to catch food!" Jih exclaimed, his voice practically pleading with her to not go through with the deal. Jih was close to ripping his hair out as he saw Sadal's main supply of bringing food wasted away on something that she had no idea the contents of.

"Jih, I have it handled. I can make more spears. It's a deal!" Sadal said to Dronall.

Ha! I got you right where I want you. Dronall thought as Nezzall stepped forward to bring the bag that Sadal requested. He placed it down with a satisfying thud that was audible to the four of them. Sadal gave Jih a smug expression while Jih blew air from his mouth in indignation.

Ha! I got you right where I want you. Sadal thought as she ignored Jih's insistence on bothering her while she was getting them much more needed goods. Sadal couldn't believe her luck with such a deal.

"Before we agree to the deal, you must remember that there are no returns in the art of exchange." Dronall and Nezzall expressed with the utmost severity as they stood up extending their hands to her.

Sadal and Jih agreed with the statement and shook hands with both brothers. Now that the exchange was made, Jih and Sadal finally were able to get what they came for. Jih grabbed the bag and held it for Sadal while she explained their issue. Nezzall lifted Sadal's spears and examined their craftsmanship while Dronall kept his eyes on Sadal.

"We are lost, and we've been searching for the direction of the meteor. Know anything about that?" She asked, as the two brothers looked towards each other.

"Easy. There are traders we have connection to where the land is dry and hot. Go there and they have seen the sky. No trees to block the path like here." Nezzall stated as he was impressed with the given bounty.

"You will want to stay on the western path. We ran into hostile Forest Seekers there, but there are those who are willing to speak. They saw the sky those nights. Be careful though. They speak in riddles so you must be clever." Dronall explained as Sadal nodded.

Jih and Sadal left shortly after with the news given to them by The Buffalo Brothers. West lined up independently with each source they've gathered from their travels so far and they knew they were on the right track. Nezzall felt relieved as he tapped his brother on the back. The two packed up their things and rested. They soon looked over their new spoils, Sadal's throwing spears for a mystery bag. On the road again for some time, Sadal's excitement couldn't be contained. She commanded Jih to put down the bag he was holding so she could see what she received. Jih stretched his arms and watched Sadal closely as she unraveled the layers on top. Sadal moved quickly and used a spare knife to open the top of the bag. Jih couldn't break it to her that once he carried the bag himself, he understood what happened, and so he waited for her to figure it out.

"Huh, they could have cleaned this before giving it to us." She said as she noticed some dirt sticking out of the mouth of the bag.

She stuck her hand inside, hoping to feel an assortment of things but all she could feel was one thing. Her face of excitement morphed into confusion and then outright fury. She obsessively ran her hand in the inside of the bag only to find that the contents were just dirt. She traded some of her best hunting weapons for a bag of packed dirt. She grabbed the heavy bag with both hands and turned it upside down. She dumped the dirt with Jih watching it seemingly have no end as it piled on the forest floor. Sadal gritted her teeth in anger as she kicked the dirt and launched a stick at a tree.

"When I see them again-" Sadal screamed at the top of her lungs only to be interrupted by Jih's laughter.

Jih was laughing to the point of tears in his eyes as Sadal stewed in anger. His anger at the situation dissolved long ago on realizing Sadal would just have to learn on her own. Without any other words, Jih made their camp for the night as he continued to laugh.

The Rumor Mill

Kag sought to prepare for war against Tur with the Neck-Shells now no longer in the picture. It was weeks since their removal from the region, but the fear remained in those who waited for a call from The Council. Despite their sheer ineptitude to take leadership, many of the band still saw them as the arbiter of policy and operated on stagnation. People performed their jobs as expected, but with no clear guidance on what to do, morale started to waver. Kag made a great effort to sow seeds of dissent as he was angry with the treatment of others under Tur's leadership. Kag sat with a few disgruntled adults as he asked their opinions on administrative matters. It was a slow workday without many orders given as some abandoned their tools and socialized instead. Kag kept his ear to the ground on rumors spreading throughout the camp and hoped to capitalize on conversation.

"Kag saw food pile is low, what is happening?" Kag asked as he rubbed his stomach.

He sat in a small circle on the ground with six other adults that shared a collective look of worry. Kag could tell that his concerns weren't the last they've heard recently. As a member of The Council, Kag applied extra pressure to get what he wanted. He eyed the circle and wondered which one of them would break first. Secrecy among adults of The Elders was common as upsetting others was seen as disrespectful to the collective, but nothing got done without communication. His attention was grabbed by a woman who wore binturong fur.

"Hunting Team has not given much. We scavenge what we can from deeper jungle. It would be best to ask them. We must feed our families Kag." She stated as Kag nodded to her concerns.

Kag and others noticed that smaller amounts of food were making their way to their meat pile than usual. Berries and other greens were also low in supply. Kag was aware that with the influx of children taken from the defeated Neck-Shells, more food would be needed but this conflicted with earlier reports he heard.

"Kag understands concern. Kag has heard other things. Scouting Team says season for hunting is good. On-Takom and Perkaku have been seen north and east. Are they wrong on this matter?" Kag questioned.

The Scouting Team was seen as incredibly reliable in their assessment of the landscape. If there was plenty of game to catch why is there so little meat had? Kag felt he needed to have a conversation with the Hunting Team and understand their new approach. He understood that hunting rhino was a difficult endeavor, but tapir should be standard fare. He and Bani conversed about the topic often. The Council truly had their heads in the sand over how things were going.

Bani knew Kag was trying to distract himself from thinking about Jih with work, but she felt that he had the drive to make meaningful change as well. Bani recognized that although Kag had good rapport on a personal level, the members of their band were fickle in allegiances. Bani needed to find strong allies for their efforts to unseat Tur and his malicious intent. Bani decided to walk towards the safer shoreline thanks to the extinction of the Neck-Shells. Bani soaked in the waves and the smell of salt on her nose. She thought about her developing child and how she needed to be proactive in securing a better future. Would the Neck-Shell children be able to adapt to their ways? She knew that the move to eliminate the adults was calculated and brutal, but felt it was beyond justified. They gave no mercy in taking Hyu away and countless others with justice now finally served. Bani stood by the edge of the water as she turned her view to see someone a short distance away.

Dran bathed in the ocean as she turned to see Bani offer a gentle wave. She enjoyed her alone time as much as anyone, but no ocean was private. She nodded her head in acknowledgement of Bani. Dran typically wasn't one for conversation, but Bani's eyes were inviting and kind. She evaluated how her relationship with Hyu went, and so she was willing to try something different. Dran soured her friendship with many over the years and had few she could trust. Bani and Kag held a flair of optimism that could withstand insults with ease. Bani could even get Tur to have a conversation with her as she absorbed information.

Bani intended to just walk to clear her mind, but opportunity struck as she saw Dran there. They hadn't talked much, but she knew that they both shared a friendship to varying degrees with Jih and that Kag once thought of her as important as well. Her thoughts of The Council were also incredibly well known, and an outspoken ally would make all the difference. Bani sat down on the sand and waited for Dran to swim over to her.

"Bani has plan with Kag. Will Dran help?" Bani asked, as she wiped away a piece of seaweed that drifted towards her. Dran weighed her options as she knew what Kag was up to. She could cast Bani aside like everyone else or take a different path.

"That depends. What is plan?" Dran inquired, as she swam closer to shore.

As Kag acted in Jih's absence for The Council, she saw him constantly trying to micromanage things, but wondered how well that was really going. His expression worsened each time he emerged from their space, and she knew Tur had to be ruining his life, just like everyone else's.

"There are demands to be made. Kag and Bani thought much on this. We have three for now." Bani said as she held up her hand.

"1. Recognition Hunt will change, all children will know animal for hunt. Not just leader. Kag tells the story very well of what happened to you all." Bani said as Dran nodded. She knew the Recognition Hunt was something her students weren't looking forward to, the prospect of dying at The Council's whims were a bit more present among them than when she was a child.

"2. The Council tent must be in main village. They are best skilled and must be present. It is a waste otherwise."

"3. Tur will no longer be head of The Council." Bani said, counting down as Dran raised an eyebrow. Bani noticed Dran's skepticism on such demands. They were quite reasonable, in fact Dran considered it almost tame to ask, except for the last demand.

"Tur is stubborn like Ker-Mah. Far more than Dran, how will he leave?" Dran stated, both out of curiosity and a minor test for Bani to see how well she and Kag have thought things through.

"Everything will stop. No new furs for The Council. Trade will fall and people will be restless." Bani said with a thinly veiled laugh.

Dran nodded at the vision. She knew that above all else, The Council coveted many furs and to stop the influx would turn some heads. Furs were an essential part of life for everyone, but Tur and the others particularly favored luxury furs. The Hunting Team's duties grew substantially as they were required to bring a processed set of furs once a month for The Council members, with their demands growing more eccentric as time passed on. Clouded leopard furs were the most recent request that caused stress among them. The Hunting Team skipped out on subsistence meals as they were stretched thin searching through longer tracts of jungle to find these animals.

"The Council is run by age. Tur is leader, Aab succeeds Tur. This is the order when he leaves. Will Aab be better than Tur?" Dran reminded Bani.

Dran additionally informed Bani that The Council operated on seniority, and as Kag was the newest member in Jih's stead, his power was certainly limited. This didn't mean change was impossible, however.

"Bani knows this is not easy. Will Dran work with Kag and Bani?" Bani questioned as she extended her arm.

Dran considered her input on the situation as her agreement to work on this issue. Revenge was a great motivator for her as she was already ruined socially after her failure to fully defend their camp. She remembered the long-winded verbal lashing given by The Council for a situation she had no control over. Beyond that, Dran deeply cared for her community despite setbacks and people's low opinion of her. After she took over Hizo's position, she vowed to make sure that The Elders would be safe from any threat. This she felt also extended to threats from within.

"Dran must ask Bani something in return. Why stop at Aab? The Council corrupts all it touches. There is more that can be done." Dran said as she locked eyes with Bani.

"Bani knows and wants more, but there are limits. Things were different where Bani is from. This...does not work but we will do what we can. Aab is old and fickle. She will hear our words and bend." Bani stated as she picked up a twig to emphasize her point. Dran carried a rare look of surprise as she was shocked to hear Bani with such intrigue.

Far away from their discussion, Tur opened the flap of The Council's abode. Tur looked forward as the wind went through his hair and he felt ready to survey his kingdom. At his side was his hearty walking stick that announced his presence with an ever-imposing figure around it. He scrunched his eyes as his vision adjusted. He cracked his neck and held his hand up to the sky as he could smell rain in the distance. As he walked alone towards the main village, the lazy activity of The Elders changed almost immediately. Although Tur technically shared power with the rest of The Council, many only heeded he or Aab's directives. Tur was greeted by a young child who lowered their head in respect as Tur looked onward. He gave a glance with an authoritative grunt and nothing more as he continued his march. Now in the arrangement of tents, he looked over with satisfaction on his face as the ground was kept impeccably clean of tree roots and other debris. For Tur, a meticulously clean space was the foundation of order. He listened to the sounds of productivity of the various teams at work just as he envisioned. The onlookers who witnessed Tur ceased their discussions in quick haste as they didn't want to have his ire.

The silence Tur enjoyed was broken by the malicious compliance of the Stoneworking Team who were Jih's former co-workers prior to his ascension to The Council. Taking a break longer than usual, the group worked with a noticeable pile of flakes that leaked past their usual area as they chewed on tapir meat skewers. Jih often prepared these as they were a traditional favorite to hold in your mouth when processing stone for hours at a time. Tur's head darted at their sounds that carried over in the distance as their voices were audible from the wind. He decided to see what the disturbance was as he looked to the sky. The day was far from over as there was much more to do. His vision for The Elders had a grand scope and laziness except from his own accord wouldn't be accepted. As he walked closer, Tur's old ears picked up the sounds of the Stoneworking Team and an immense frown came on his face. Tur's popularity was mixed, as many adhered to the social structure and respect of The Council but had personal animosity for his irrational decisions and callous nature. The Stoneworking Team had the biggest grievances when it came to Tur. Their leader was personally exiled by Tur without any regard to their feelings or workload and made their distaste evident by leaving buffalo dung outside their tent.

While the other members of the Stoneworking Team were embroiled in their conversation, they made no reference to Tur approaching them. Their conversation carried on as normal as Tur stood in silence looming over them. Tur surveyed the scene as he noted the midden piles were spreading into the vicinity of the main camp. He was also concerned about the quality of the stone tools being made. The complaints from the Woodworking Team entered his vicinity, and it was with these stones that their work could begin. The few times Tur cared about his leadership position of this group; he often took out his frustration on whichever team that entered his range of vision. He hardly held enough experience to dictate to the Stoneworking Team how their hand-axes and other implements should be built, but he felt his life experience trumped it all.

"What is it you are doing?" Tur finally questioned as he looked down at the other adults who were sitting on the ground. One man hurried himself to stand up and address Tur but was paralyzed by the man's glare and remained still.

Tur picked up a flake and tested its quality. He used a surprising amount of strength for his age and crushed it sufficiently as he let the dust settle between his hands.

He glared at the others as the rest of the Stoneworking Team looked at one another to decide who would answer his question. He lifted another rock with scrutiny as he pointed to the worked ends of the pieces.

"That is rubbing stone[27]. This is not for tool Tur. It is used to sharpen material. The Jagged Bark used to trade us for it." A woman explained as it was clear that Tur had really no idea what they used.

She was hardly sure he could tell the difference between flint and obsidian. Tur grumbled and decided to accept this excuse for now as he looked on the ground to notice the statement seemed correct. The next target of Tur's criticisms was the workspace itself as he brought up the number of middens present.

"Tur. There is little need for you here. We have it handled, Jih gave instructions." A shirtless man commented as he folded his arms.

"Oh? Jih left you instructions. Tur does not see him here. Do not mention him again or you will join him in exile. Tur sees three piles. Make pile tall and fat, do not spread further." Tur dictated as he spat on the ground.

"The piles are to tell which is which. Much more work is had with one pile to separate and remove." The woman answered again as Tur demanded they begin moving the massive piles further away.

"Do you not have eyes to see? Follow will of Tur. Remove them. Now." Tur demanded as he stomped his walking stick.

Tur placed his walking stick on the ground and pointed to the length that he deemed acceptable so that there was a clearer separation. She nodded to the rest of her circle who started the long process of using animal skins to sweep up portions of the pile and move them further into the brush.

"The Council knows best. Do not question for work keeps us happy." Tur added on with a smug expression.

The other members of the Stoneworking Team kept a mental log of the various things Tur instructed them to do. Tur watched with satisfaction as he saw the Stoneworking Team hack away bushes to expand their work area as requested. Before he departed, Tur looked towards the beach where Bani and Dran conversed. He shook his head and continued to peruse through the main village.

Dran hadn't imagined the circumstances would align themselves to where she'd be working with Kag and Bani so extensively, but their goals aligned and made for a good partnership. Dran had access to the children through her work and used her rapport with them to learn about camp events.

Bani and Dran continued to converse while Kag saw himself embroiled again with the affairs of the Hunting Team. This was yet another time where the meat was running low, he had to say something. Kag moved forward and noticed that there was a lull of activity present. He didn't see himself much as a lecturer, but he knew he needed to do

---

[27] Emic word for talc.

something to get them into gear. One of the teenagers that was an understudy of Vut lifted his head up to address Kag.

"Kag has question for you. There is no trained adult here, very well. Why is the meat low? Scouting Team tells Kag much game has been seen but little meat is here." Kag asked as he saw a concerned look on the young man's face.

"The Council says to find Onpeu skin. No other animals should be hunted." The teen replied much to Kag's confusion.

"Onpeu has terrible meat, why hunt this animal?" Kag asked out loud as a look of realization came upon him.

He noticed that Tur wore a particularly brightly patterned fur instead of the usual leopard pattern. Kag tugged at his beard in thought. Without delay, Kag made his way to The Council's tent and made his way inside. By now, Tur returned home ahead of Kag after making his rounds. Kag entered to see Tur sat down in the middle of carving something on a piece of wood. Kag cared little to ask what the man was doing, as his rage clouded him entirely. Tur was so sure of himself that he didn't bother to raise his head to greet Kag at all. He felt the wind of Kag's arrival on his skin as he grabbed his staff. He slammed it on the ground for Kag to sit.

"Kag. You are done duties already?" Tur questioned.

Tur gave a nod of satisfaction in his pick. From Tur's perspective, Kag was reliable and didn't bother him with his problems regarding Bani or anything else that didn't need his input. The Council was supposed to be open and accessible to all, but many grew tired of offering advice to a group they felt were ungrateful.

"Tur. Kag spoke with Hunting Team. Why are they hunting Onpeu?" Kag questioned Tur as he finally turned himself around to address him.

"Onpeu looks nice. Tur wanted it and Tur shall have it. Simple as that." Tur commented with a yawn.

"People must eat! Onpeu is dangerous. This killed father of Jih! Our Hunting Team is not fully trained!" Kag said, as he raised his voice at Tur. Tur lifted his hand and closed it in a tight fist as his eyes pierced Kag's soul.

"You speak of the shunned Kag. There is no such mention of him." Tur warned as he pointed a finger.

As far as Tur was concerned, he saw plenty of capable hunters. The Hunting Team and all teams operated under the orders of The Council. As leader, Tur felt he could rule and direct the respective teams with impunity. Nobody would challenge him openly and the other members of The Council often agreed with his proposals. It was not lost on Kag that the others wore more extravagant furs as well compared to his own or Bani's grass. Kag grumbled as he saw that all managed to benefit under Tur's direction except for the people that mattered.

"Those who are hungry will hunt. Tur will not have laziness." He commented with a cough as he pounded his chest. He sniffed the air around him.

Kag was astounded at Tur's ability to ignore the obvious. Tur looked at his skin which felt rough. His bones creaked as he adjusted his neck and relighted the dying fire in the tent. Kag patiently waited for Tur's death daily as he entertained the man's ramblings. Tur coughed once more and pointed his finger to a small pile of leaves that stored some crushed turmeric.

"What does Tur want?" Kag said. He waved the harsh smoke from the burning fire as he let out a small cough.

"Come closer. These old bones need to be rubbed. Rub Tur as Tur eats Mun-Ca." Tur ordered Kag as he braced his position.

Tur threw out his shoulder on the rare occasions he overexerted himself, one of the many challenges that came with old age. Kag was not as skilled as Hyu, but he was aware of the fix to the problem. He also knew exactly what he could use to serve as a muscle relaxant as well but lacked the motivation to get these. Kag looked at Tur with some disbelief in what he was asked, but his voice carried with the utmost severity. Kag moved over one of the leaves with the crushed turmeric and watched with disgust in his eyes as he watched Tur happily scoop the solution into his mouth. Although Tur had surprisingly healthier teeth than others his age, chewing could be difficult for long periods of time, and he'd rather have someone else do the legwork for him. Kag feared the prospect of becoming so old that he could not last in the state that Tur was in but felt he would age gracefully with all his faculties.

Kag moved and unconsciously hovered his hands near Tur's throat, only to rest them on his shoulders. Kag blew out some air in his nose in complete disbelief at what Tur requested him to do. He couldn't tell if Tur wanted to humiliate him or if he trusted him enough to do such a task. Kag gently moved Tur's arm, stopping for a second as he heard a small grunt come from Tur as he finished. Kag's face was expressionless as he looked to treat Tur no differently from any other patient he's received, but instead of any light-hearted jokes or the promise of a flower afterwards, he did this in near silence. Kag was unsure of how long he had to do this for Tur. A massage done well should take no more than ten minutes if he was lucky, but Tur loved to hear his own voice. Kag heard Tur inhale as he broke the silence asking a question that weighed heavily on the rest of The Council.

"Bani is with child. Is she healthy?" Tur inquired, as he felt Kag's grip tighten with her name mentioned.

Kag had few words to say to Tur willingly, let alone under duress. The ideal of respecting authority to its utmost extreme proved to be a hard life to live when it was someone as insufferable as Tur. Kag knew how Tur truly felt about the various adults. They were seen as disposable to keep the structure of The Council alive, but there was more to it than that.

"Yes." Kag said, his answer deceptively short.

Kag was unwilling to divulge any details about Bani's pregnancy to Tur, for the last thing he wanted was any sort of bad omen to come across them. If anything were to happen, Kag knew he wouldn't be able to control himself and his emotions. Kag would finish what Jih started just like with the Neck-Shells.

"This is good, more are needed. Many of your group did not have. Dran is now too old, Hyu is dead. Others are disappointing to Tur. Their children may not pass Recognition Hunt. Tur may see a Yaan this time." Tur stated with a laugh as he stretched his back while Kag deepened his grip on the massage. His statement of an elephant was no coincidence, he remembered Jih's fear of elephants well into adulthood and mocked him for it behind closed doors.

The older members of The Council were concerned about leaving enough of a legacy behind with the changing demographics. Now that the Neck-Shells were out of the region, The Council was focused on rebuilding their numbers, and wanted a strong successive generation. The adults that The Council relied on however were a mixture of the middle aged, and those barely older than teenagers. Those most likely in the band to start a brand-new family of their own were taken in the raid or lost a loved one and had to start anew.

"Neck-Shells are gone. This was good fortune by Tur." Tur said, giving himself a laugh that Kag could only look at in irritation.

"Yes. It certainly was your doing Tur." Kag egged on, with his comment completely going over Tur's head. It was natural that as the highest-ranking member of The Council, he inherited all the praise and dispersed all the blame to Kag or any other lower ranking members.

Kag continued to rub Tur until his slow hand raised up and urged Kag to stop. He took great pleasure in wiping his hands in the dirt, preferring its grasp over having to touch Tur's body.

"Kag, things are changing quickly. Tur sees opportunity for more furs. The old Neck-Shell territory. Sightings of Ma-Turun[28]. They are returning. Order Hunting Team to search for them." Tur ordered Kag. Tur was unaware of the plot against him, but he was aware of his friendship with Jih. He decided to rope Kag's thoughts back into the fold by offering him more information and with it, more furs for him and Bani.

"Kag. There is much to know about The Council. You will hear of these things in time. Follow directions and you will do well."

Before Kag left, Tur stood up, this time not needing the staff and looked Kag in the eyes for a few moments. The two paused, as Tur clasped his arm on Kag's shoulder and gave him a hearty thud. This was the closest to a thank you Tur could possibly give. Kag moved quickly through the pleasantries and exited the tent. His frustration was continuously evident as he made his way to the Hunting Team to finally give them new orders. Kag made his way as expected, but he stopped and realized Tur wasn't going to check any time soon. Instead of going to the Hunting Team, he made his way home to talk to Bani. The heat of the tent filled as fresh leaves were placed on the going fire. He crawled

---

[28] Emic word for binturong.

through the opening of his home and saw not one but two people. To his surprise, he saw Dran inside as well. The two shared an awkward glance before addressing the rest of their problems.

"Dran...?" Kag asked as his eyes turned to Bani who gave him a small grin.

"Dran is here, yes. Are you dumb and blind?" Dran said, as she pointed for Kag to sit down.

He shot Bani a look of confusion as he was being ordered in his own home but decided to let it go as he sat down. Kag was unsure of why Dran was here, let alone half the time, but he gave Bani the floor to speak.

"Kag. Dran knows everything. She will be with us. What news do you bring?" Bani asked.

"Kag does not bring good news. Tur has told Hunting Team to go after Ma-Turun. We will starve because of him. What will we do?" Kag asked, already anticipating Dran's response.

"What will you do? Dran or Bani has no power over Hunting Team. Somehow, you do. Order them to do something else." Dran proposed.

Kag sighed, he was aware of that prospect, but he thought about reaching out to Vut to see what could be done. In the past, Vut was far from a rule follower as he was close with Dran and her league of troublemakers as a child. Now though, Kag hoped to harness this energy for the right reasons.

"Kag will go and reach out to Vut when able. We have worked together before, one more job will do us well." Kag mentioned as he leaned the two in further to plan.

Two Steps Forward

In the heart of Iraq, a band of The Aligned[29] prepared for a celebration. It was a cloudy day where they were spared the harsh sun's rays. The sound of industry rang through the camp as decorations were prepared. Furs were exchanged and a bounty of meat and fruit was piled high at the village center. This band numbered sixty people and comprised all ages. Everyone was expected to contribute from the youngest child to the oldest adult. All were working except for a group of fourteen young women that were exempt from the preparations.

Every two years, young women between the ages of fifteen to eighteen of The Aligned were expected to leave home and start their own lives. These women would travel in groups together to scout out terrain and built communes of their own out in the grasslands before finding a band they felt was worth joining. Each home in the village that had a daughter leaving was marked with a painted object of importance outside. One of many traditions, The Aligned valued these objects with as much care as their families. The Aligned were a risk-averse group and were efficient builders of their homes. These structures were built on a plan often passed down from generations. Their homes echoed that of Thunderfeet in the area, with a wood skeleton and animal skins as building material. The Aligned set themselves apart as they favored a more rounded top, and a flap in the back to control temperature. These features were prioritized to withstand shock damage from harsh winds. There was also a flap of animal skin hoisted on the front that served as a door. The Aligned additionally used less decorations than Thunderfeet. They felt that superfluous material was better for tools or used to personalize their indoor space.

Two members of The Aligned stood outside their family home and looked at their painted piece of carved wood. It was lathered with ochre and believed to channel the spirits for a safe journey. Both were raised with the belief they held a special position in the world. They were the intermediaries between the ancestors they called "The First" and that of their Thunderfeet counterparts known as "The Youngest"[30]. These two onlookers were twenty-year-old twins named Narro and Trekkal. Narro and Trekkal, like most twins, claimed to have a powerful connection with each other. Narro stood a small bit above his sister at 5'2, with a burly muscular frame and a large beard. His black hair was tied back in a ponytail with some spare cloth. He wore a gazelle pelt that stood out with a distinct reddish hue from the others around him. Trekkal always carried a mischievous

[29] The Aligned are what we call Neanderthals today. Neanderthals are a species of archaic human that were found to have occupied Europe and the Middle East during the Middle Paleolithic and died out around 50,000 years ago. Neanderthals have been found to be just as capable as their Modern Human counterparts with both interbreeding events and similar tool traditions and cultural phenomenon such as dedicated burials of their dead.
[30] The Youngest is a nickname for Modern Humans citing their inexperience in their lands due to their recent arrival and exposure to their culture. While Modern Humans and Denisovans have bloody feuds against one another, Neanderthals are generally neutral and will trade with them.

grin on her face as she ran her hands through her black hair that flowed down past her shoulders. Her hair glistened as it was well fed with fish oil, and she stood at 5'0. Trekkal sought to match her brother and wore a gazelle pelt with a more muted brown. Although her clothing masked her appearance well, she was well toned with muscle from swimming in the rivers they called home. Both of their skins held a delightful tan that stood out past the dull gray in the sky above them.

The last wave of their band was to leave today and Trekkal was a special case of the village. Trekkal missed her initial leave of the village when she was eighteen due to sickness and pleaded to stay with her family instead. Their family was loving but felt a crawling sense of shame as they worried about Trekkal's lack of conformity. Narro ignored these complaints as the most supportive of her decisions. He decided to take it on himself to equip her for her leave now that she was ready to move on. Narro held a wooden bowl with white pigment. He stuck his fingers in to get a good wipe and moved towards Trekkal's face. He looked to his left and saw the other women comparing their weapons for the journey. He noticed an assortment of clubs and short spears. Trekkal carried a sling and held little desire to deviate from her approach now. Ranged weapons were used among their people but carried far less prestige.

"Stand still Trekkal, I need to finish putting this paint on your face. I know it stings on your skin." Narro said as Trekkal squirmed.

"Why must we use the color white as opposed to any other? Oh-You all are making me leave everything behind! I have so much to do here." Trekkal replied.

"Do you not remember? It is one of the teachings given by The First. Trekkal, this has been a long standing tradition of our people. As for the duties you ignored, I took care of those as well. I can always visit you sister. Try not to bite the heads off your companions." Narro grinned as he answered her question.

"Brother, you mention tradition. Are you not also upset with what you are expected to do?" Trekkal questioned as she saw Narro shrug.

While the women left, young men in The Aligned were encouraged to build their own tents within the confines of the band's territory with the intent to start a family. The politics behind tent construction was a complex endeavor. The Aligned believed in having a strong connection with a partner that they called their "One", for they were born as halves and sought to find the person who would complete this union. It was a decision not taken lightly, so young relationships were often superficial and casual due to the rampant perfectionism expected. Those that were single built a family sized tent but lived alone to signify they were ready.

"You get to see the world for what it is. I must build a tent and wait for someone to come my way. Not exactly what I call an adventure, but the routine is easy." Narro commented.

"I worry for you sometimes sister. I clean, cook, and make our clothing. What do you do other than play by the water?" Narro said with a laugh that hid his concern.

Trekkal rubbed her hands together as she could tell Narro had doubt in his voice. She knew her brother more than anyone else as he could hardly hide his thoughts. Narro yearned for something greater than a homestead and Trekkal wanted to start life on her own terms. Trekkal looked back at the group that was honored and she was proud to be among them. She was treated well by her companions and had many friends growing up, but she felt something else drove her. She gave a mischievous grin and looked at Narro.

"This life bores me. I can tell you are too. I know you must be thinking about when the spirits flew across the sky. We saw it all on the way here." Trekkal mentioned.

Narro lifted his head, as he was always surprised by Trekkal's shift from playfulness to serious and thoughtful conversation. The assortment of the camp's homes lay in front of them. Narro watched as smoke left from the back of various tents to air out before closing once again. Narro's answer to Trekkal was interrupted by the arrival of their parents. The pair's mother held the remains of a doe in her hands while she was assisted by their father and uncle. The three wore deer pelts and were greeted by Narro while Trekkal remained quiet. Their uncle didn't stay around long, but he was a trader and brought various goods from his bag for the others to see. He advanced with open arms and grabbed his niece and nephew.

"Trekkal and Narro, you have grown so much. Let me hold you once more. You know, I have a story to tell you. Let me share it while those two skin our kill!" Their uncle said as he held them close. Narro and Trekkal both hugged their uncle warmly while their parents watched with approval.

The three sat on the ground as the pair stared at their uncle with a gray beard and strong muscles. He'd seen much of the world and continued to travel. The pair grew up with many stories and wished to have their own to tell. Trekkal knew that it would be a very long time until she'd see her family again, so she decided to stay and listen to one of their uncle's tales. He described watching a group of The Youngest encounter a Mahaku with no survivors to tell the tale, other than himself of course. As their uncle described the horrific scene before him, Narro and Trekkal had different reactions.

"It gave a mighty yell and ripped apart the group with no care in the world. It vanished and only a pool of blood remained, and that is what happened. None of our kind of course, they were a group of The Youngest who went fishing without a rod or harpoon at their side!" He said with some annoyance in his voice. Trekkal smirked at the tale while Narro looked fairly upset at his sister.

"Trekkal! Why are you laughing? Someone died at the hands of one! A Mahaku is no laughing matter, you know this[31]." Narro commented with surprise as he shook his head in protest.

"The Youngest think they know everything until they come face to face, and they freeze, serves them right. Better them than us. A few shattersticks[32] will do nothing to

---

[31] A powerful creature in Neanderthal legend.
[32] Neanderthal slang for throwing spears favored by Modern Humans. These are usually single-use weapons and therefore cheap in quality and break easily.

deter the Mahaku and the desire for blood. The spirit rewards stupidity with death." Trekkal scoffed at Narro's concern.

Narro disagreed with his sister, as he chose compassion over coldness but acknowledged that The Youngest could be foolhardy when important matters were at hand. He hoped that her opinion of them could change in time. There was an uneasy peace between the two groups who traded on occasion and occupied the same areas for hunting. The Youngest overall were less numerous than their own kind, but their large settlements dwarfed them entirely. Narro and Trekkal's mother took a break from her work to address her children. She knew that Trekkal was crafty and would come up with any way to delay her destiny. She folded her arms and gave her a stern talking to in front of Narro and her uncle. A few onlookers observed and chose to eavesdrop on their conversation. As she spoke, word of their dysfunction spread quickly.

"Trekkal. You pleaded with us to stay last time; you will not be left behind once more. At twenty, you already embarrass us. There is a band just down the river that would happily have you. You are always welcome, but you must leave us. I am not trying to be hostile to you." Trekkal's mother said as she pointed at her.

"I was sick in those days from a terrible rain! Surely you must believe me, and what will you do when I am gone? Surely you would die of boredom with just him." Trekkal retorted back as she grabbed Narro.

"See? You would miss me so much; you would actually perish!" Trekkal said as she squeezed Narro's cheek.

Narro offered a small smile as he felt sandwiched between pleasing his sister and his mother. He could feel his back sweat as he met his mother's eyes. Trekkal frowned as she saw her mother's face remain unchanged. Trekkal watched as her mother's eyes met the glances of adults carrying offerings of goods to the village center. The spread of gossip through the camp from onlookers filled Narro and Trekkal's parents with further embarrassment. The Aligned were a proud people and cared for their standing. Narro was often enough of an overachiever to be unmentioned, but Trekkal was always a point of contention.

"Trekkal. I want you to go talk with Stelo. She will give you your blessing like everyone else. Once we have our feast, it will be time to leave." Trekkal's mother stated as she pointed to the other end of camp.

Stelo was one of the first women to arrive in the band decades ago and established herself as the main leader. Stelo held the position of Seer which was the head priest. The Aligned's society valued the role of spiritual matters highly, much like Thunderfeet and Forest Seekers, but priests were seen to be more important than even leaders who proved their worth through hunting or combat. They didn't seek knowledge for its own sake in the same way as Forest Seekers but sought enlightenment and self-actualization through their place in the world and the spirits that made up their surroundings. In her late 60s, she was among the oldest of their band. Stelo was resoundingly healthy for her age and defied the prognosis of their best healers. She was blind and had silver hair but remained

248

sharp as ever. The priest's tent was oriented on an east-west alignment to match the movement of the sun. The ground where the priest's tent was located had special symbols carved into the ground with stone tools. Stelo was outside enjoying the breeze as she turned her head to hear footsteps approach her.

Trekkal approached the priest's tent with her head hung low. She usually bumbled around camp with reckless abandon but took her faith as seriously as any other. Trekkal admired Stelo and looked at her assortment of shell jewelry. Stelo was wrapped in it from head to toe as she wore auroch leather for clothing. Trekkal's presence was known and Stelo guided her forward. She waved her old hand as she reached out in front of her. As she was blind, she determined people of her band by just the touch of their face. She could tell with just a few moments of thought who came to address her. Trekkal stood on her knees and leaned in towards the old woman. She felt the delicate hands of Stelo run across her nose, forehead, and cheeks. Stelo received requests for blessings throughout the year, but Trekkal waited until the last moment. Blessings were always given as asked and the process was a simple formality.

"Stelo. This is Trekkal. I was asked to take your blessing for my journey. Will it be given?" Trekkal's voice softened as she asked.

Although Trekkal approached Stelo with confidence, she felt sadness come over her. It was a sudden rush of emotions as she held back her thoughts and tried to compose herself. While it was true that Trekkal was a slacker, she had an inhuman amount of resolve for things that took her interest. Trekkal saw this as her chance to prove everyone else wrong about her.

"Ah Trekkal. Yes, I remember when I still had my sight. You were always around to listen to my stories. It appears you have one on your face and I can tell from your voice. You sound upset, there is a great sorrow in your words." Stelo observed as she straightened her posture.

"I hear their words and how they think I am stupid. My mother looks down on me because-You always understood me best. You always took me at my word. I am not a failure; I never have been." Trekkal said as she studied Stelo's expression.

"The sickness took many, and although you are well, it is inside that may still remain ill. Trekkal, to see the world is a good thing. Limiting yourself to the comforts of home does not allow for growth. These people are set in their ways." Stelo said as she was stopped by Trekkal.

"Well, Stelo, that is what I wanted to talk about. I do want to leave but I want to do something different. My mother told me to come here and get your blessing. Do you remember the night that the sky was alight? Every night it fills my head with dreams." Trekkal asked as Stelo's expression changed.

"Of course. I never saw it myself, but I felt the presence of the spirits. I understand now. That was some time ago and it has yet to leave your mind, we are cut from the same cloth. I understand what you ask of me, let me give you my answer." Stelo concluded as she shook her head in agreement. Stelo grabbed Trekkal's hand as she did so.

"Be my eyes Trekkal and tell this old woman what fell from the sky that day. I want you to feel it, and if possible, bring it home to us. You have always listened to my stories; it is time I heard one of yours."

With these words, Trekkal hugged Stelo tightly. For Stelo, it was a win-win situation. Trekkal got the push out of the nest she needed while the hope of finding such a powerful object gave Stelo hope. She sought to inform the others of her decision as an aide assisted her. Trekkal walked with caution as the frame of Stelo came behind her. As the two conversed, Trekkal observed their weaponsmith retouching some last-minute implements for the gathered party. He looked in Trekkal's direction and shrugged his shoulders as he remembered Trekkal's use of a sling. There was no need to apply the knowledge of their people. The smell of burnt honey filled her nose as beeswax was used to improve various resins made from local trees. The other women that talked among themselves noticed Trekkal walking with Stelo. One wearing a bear pelt waved her over and got the attention of the others. Although Trekkal's status was a point of contention among the older adults, Trekkal shared popularity as a role model despite her lazy personality. The group saw her as the fun aunt to be mentored by and reminisced on the good times they shared together.

"So it is true, you are coming with us? Bozah remains on the outside, it would mean the world for you to see her again!" She mentioned as Trekkal gave a warm smile. Trekkal rubbed her arm as she gestured to Stelo.

"You all look wonderful." Stelo said, as she received a few groans from the group.

"Trekkal will not be coming with you. I know you were looking forward to her joining but another calling has come for her. The meteors that come from the sky converged on a day with high activity from the spirits. It is no coincidence. I have decided in my feeble age to defer this message to Trekkal on my behalf." Stelo explained as she gathered the attention of the others.

Stelo orated as loud as she could for her voice to project. For those in the vicinity, Stelo's words reverberated through their ears as it was seen as a sign of respect to remain quiet when Seers spoke. While Stelo spoke, some of the adults were discontented with such an egregious break of tradition. They cited favoritism on Stelo's accord and grew jealous that none of their daughters were chosen for such an essential task. The atmosphere was tense among the resentful as their stares pointed daggers at Trekkal and the rest of the group.

"Trekkal. If what Stelo says is truly your fate, we wish you luck in finding the meteor." One of the women said. The others were happy to see Trekkal find a purpose she was well suited to doing.

Once Stelo finished speaking, she heard the murmurs of others that upset her. The Aligned valued honesty above all else and hated secrecy. Narro and Trekkal's parents observed with intrigue as they heard bits and pieces of conversation in their vicinity.

"Why would it be Trekkal who has the favor of Stelo? My daughter has-" One voice grumbled as he ran a flint knife across another stone.

"What band would take her? She has no skills-" A woman said as she made some modifications to a piece of clothing. Stelo broke the rising discourse with a swift raise of her hand. The wind blew her hair as she slowly set it down. Above the roar of the plains surrounding them, she yelled with gusto.

"Are we The Youngest? I hear your doublespeak under my ears. Enough! You all have chosen your path in life, accept what you have made and let them go. I will have no more of this. I have given Trekkal a quest to fulfill under my will. A celebration will be had, and they will go their separate ways. Who wishes to challenge me?" Stelo threatened as she waved her hand in the wind.

"Your sour attitudes taint a wonderous feast. Be the ones I raised you to be. You all know better." Stelo scolded. Her back was to the others as she turned around.

Stelo took a deep breath as she exerted herself and felt around for something to reorient her balance. With a stern talking to, the rest of the events planned went as scheduled. Trekkal gave an embrace to the group of her friends, and she set out for home. In the distance, she saw Narro carrying a basket.

"Narro! Narro!" Trekkal shouted as she ran towards him.

"I see you managed to get your way, no need to tell me. Allow me to pack, the least I can do is escort you out of our territory. I remember it was due east. We will head there!" Narro said with certainty in his voice.

"Narro, this will be fun, you know that!" Trekkal said as she scrambled over to give her brother a tight hug. Trekkal sunk her head into Narro's shoulder and the two rubbed noses. For The Aligned, nose rubbing was seen as platonic instead of romantic, but this wasn't often known by other groups they interacted with.

"Have you considered what I said? You could come with me." Trekkal said lowly as she met her brother's eyes.

Narro entertained the idea in jest about leaving but Trekkal was resolute in her desire to do this. It was something that he'd never seen before and couldn't be prouder. With some light convincing, Narro agreed that change for his life could be worth pursuing. Trekkal and Narro talked to one another about the logistics of the plan and most importantly, how to deliver the news to their family. Narro settled on compromising his moral code with a small omission of the truth. He did plan to escort Trekkal out of their territory as promised, but he never said when he would return.

"You know, this could be good for me. I could find my One any day now." Narro commented as he saw the barely obscured laughter of Trekkal. He glared at his sister who shook her head at his words.

"Narro, I thought we were trying to be honest with each other." Trekkal joked as Narro's face blushed.

"I already went ahead and packed your things. You really need to keep better track. I placed your sling and your chiseled rocks in your pack already." Narro mentioned as Trekkal brought him up to speed on her conversation with Stelo.

Narro was always practical in his thoughts, and he wished more than ever to oblige Stelo's wishes. A journey like this could take a long time and his heart could not bear the failure to find this object before Stelo's eventual passing. He knew the sky was set alight for many days and that this and Stelo's words were no mere coincidence. This was an opportunity from the spirits at hand, and the fact that he and his sister were given this opportunity was no accident. Narro and Trekkal's parents returned with Stelo in tow as they were told of her fate. Stelo stood between both parents as she was guided by a tug on her clothing. Their father remained quiet but looked emotional as he understood the changing circumstances. He tugged at his necklace while their mother spoke.

"Narro-" She said as she was interrupted by her son.

"I will make sure Trekkal makes it safely. I have always been the responsible one after all. I will return soon." Narro said as their parents nodded without a second thought.

"But not too soon. The world is dangerous but vast. Try to enjoy it." Stelo said as she cupped the air with her hands.

Stelo left a sly expression as she could hear the rebellious elements within Narro's voice. Narro took this as a sign for a hug and held the old woman tightly before letting go. Narro looked to his bag that was outside of their home. He passed it to Trekkal before running off into the distance. Trekkal grasped the bag but was confused at Narro's retreat.

"Narro! Do I look like I was made for labor? Come on, grab your bag!" Trekkal shouted, as she gestured for Narro to return.

Narro gathered his strength and retreated behind the tent of another home. Narro remembered this was the location of a buried bone pendant belonging to the ancestors. He closed his eyes and felt a few tears go down his cheeks. He gave penance to the spirits as he wished for safe travel for them both. Narro was just as ignorant as Trekkal at what lay outside and needed every avenue of protection. The spirit pantheon was one of many aspects to life in The Aligned, but their nature was still mysterious. After some time, Narro rushed across camp to return home. His eyes were dry now but slightly red. He practically huffed in exhaustion as Trekkal gave him a pat on the back and handed his belongings over. Luckily for the pair, there was plenty of daylight left for them to officially start their adventure.

"I had to hold that for five minutes. Do we have everything we need before we leave? Were-Were you crying?" Trekkal asked with a playful tone.

Trekkal embraced her adventure to the fullest, and only took some core raw materials and her sling. She left her beloved fishing tools behind for another member of the band to use as she could make her own. Narro anticipated Trekkal's barebone approach and kept a steady supply of food and aid. He also held some raw material from the weaponsmith for his own needs.

"I should have everything I need for another club. The last one-" Narro said before getting interrupted by Trekkal.

"Another club? A bit traditional, yes? Narro, we have so many other options." Trekkal said as she stuck out her tongue in mockery.

Narro nodded in disagreement and pushed Trekkal forward. She gave a laugh that intensified as Narro clutched his backpack. He placed the single strap over him. With a final goodbye to their old life behind them, the late starts that were Narro and Trekkal looked to head east just as Stelo instructed. The first two weeks out on the trail were uneventful for Narro and Trekkal as they found little to do. In the long stretches of open plains in neighboring Iran, game was plenty but capturing a meal was difficult. The animals in this area used quick bursts of speed that evaded the two. A few camps of their people dotted the landscape behind them, but these would be the last ones for a while. Narro and Trekkal traded at one of these, so their backpacks had some spare food to last a while. All around them was a vast field of high grass and sloping hills that seemed unending. The air was calm as the ambient sound of insects flew. The sun's rays were harsh as the glare met both Narro and Trekkal's eyes. As they walked, the pair stopped and felt a strange presence. Narro sneezed as some dust flew up his nose and saw that there was a mass movement of animals in the distance.

Trekkal was about to say something to her brother, only for him to turn around with his hand over his mouth. She raised an eyebrow but saw the fear in Narro's eyes and followed suit. Narro and Trekkal crouched along the ground and held each other's hands as they moved through the high grass. Narro led quietly while Trekkal clutched her sling. Although inexperienced, these two were able to detect the presence of lions from a far distance. These fearsome creatures owned the plains and took its pick of the prey while competitors could only watch in pure jealousy. Narro and Trekkal were aware they were on the menu as well.

Narro and Trekkal were unsure of how far these animals could hear, but knew their hearing far exceeded their own. The harsh moan of a gazelle alerted other herbivores that converged on a small stream. They stampeded in all directions as a cloud of dirt and dust filled the air. Trekkal tapped Narro's shoulder and confirmed what he saw in the distance. Narro lifted his hand up and opened it outwards as Trekkal counted on her fingers the amount he seemed to have seen. The animals that dispersed ran in five separate directions, each with a lion chasing after them. Trekkal knew that while the lionesses hunted, a male remained behind and the last thing they wanted to do was infringe on its current territory.

Trekkal stood out of the thicker grass around them and popped her head out to scan the surroundings. She groaned quietly to herself as the yelping of hyenas in the distance picked up in volume. They were scanning for any stragglers that would have gotten trampled in the previous stampedes, but their trail ran cold. Trekkal's eyes widened as she saw something that took her interest. She saw a porcupine chewing bark on a fallen log and pointed for Narro to head towards it. Trekkal looked at a rip in her clothing and realized she forgot to trade for a needle to repair her clothing. Narro shook his head in disagreement and gestured at his arm, seeing as he would only have a club to do combat. Trekkal rolled her eyes and moved her hands to signal to Narro that all he needed to do was run quickly and bash it over the head. Trekkal was willing to launch a stone or two as well.

Narro decided to oblige his sister's request. While the porcupine was usually nocturnal, it was common knowledge they would leave their dens to sunbathe on hot days. Narro saw the animal chew bark without a care in the world, while Trekkal stared at him. Narro slowly moved over and froze as the animal stopped chewing and looked in his direction. He remained still as the creature shook its behind and raised its quills to intimidate Narro. Narro retracted his club from his backpack and assessed its condition. It had a solid wooden handle and a stone cudgel on the front. Narro slowly lifted a fallen branch and placed it in the vicinity of the creature's vision. The nose of the porcupine puckered at the sight of the paltry offering, but the log was quite stale.

Good little Mulku. Come to my hand. Narro thought as he looked ahead.

Just as Narro expected, the porcupine moved its way over to the branch that was thrown out towards it. With a slight sigh, Narro hurled his arm and slammed his club down hard on the animal's head. The impact stunned it entirely and with a second mighty swing from Narro, blood and bone fragments leaked onto the soil. The animal collapsed and writhed around before dying, as Narro reduced its skull to atoms. Trekkal looked up to make sure his scene didn't catch the attention of the remaining lions and she gave him a nod of approval. She carefully approached the back of the animal and withdrew a knife she would use to get a couple of needles. In a pinch, the flesh of such a creature could be used for some traditional recipes for sickness, but it was better to hoard the needles and the pelt itself for trade. Narro looked to pocket the pelt for himself, but Trekkal moved in front of him. She stuck her butt out in his direction as she skinned the animal. She left the corpse to rot as the quills were gathered. The meat spoiled quicker than most and was not worth the effort to carry. The sound of the herds vanished and quiet scared them both. For Narro and Trekkal, this was seen as unwelcome news as the lions now met their prey. Narro and Trekkal watched as a troupe of macaques caused mischief for the male lion that rested under their tree.

The monkeys happily enjoyed their time in the tree as they picked figs to eat, but a few mischievous ones threw the remnants at the male lion. The first fig was ignored, but the second fig would be the last. The lion reared up and placed his weight on the tree and knocked the macaque off the branch. The animal's life flashed before its eyes. It kicked up dirt and triggered the male lion as it eviscerated the macaque into a confetti of meat with a strong roar. Narro and Trekkal took this as a sign to run as fast as they could now that the male was agitated and looking for a fight. The lion's attention was stuck on the tree and disregarded the two humans running away in the distance. One of the lionesses pursued them and watched carefully. Narro and Trekkal continued their run. Narro outpaced Trekkal by a fair bit, as he saw patches of higher grass fade to simple open grassland. He could see it stretched for miles. Trekkal was a slow runner and didn't practice as she rarely tracked down prey to hunt. She looked behind her to see the frame of the lioness emerge through the grass and quickened her pace. Narro didn't bother looking behind him as the lioness made its way. It cut across and strafed around them a noticeable distance to let out a roar of acknowledgement. The intent of the animal was to observe rather than maim this time. Its hunger was satiated with blood of the animal it attacked just moments ago.

The lioness stood silently as it watched the two scurried away before returning to the others. Their pride had seen The Youngest and knew danger was present with their shattersticks. One of their own was slain before and two men were killed in retaliation. It hadn't occurred to the pride that there were differences between the ones that walked on two feet, but this lioness saw something unique. Now that Narro and Trekkal were far away from the pride, the two stopped to recover. Narro and Trekkal breathed heavily to another as they grasped hands, thankful they survived. Narro looked to the sky and acknowledged the spirit's role in keeping them safe. While the two were able to defend themselves against a threat, running often was the best choice. Choosing to be a hero like The Youngest they ridiculed would only have them end up maimed or worse. Trekkal took a deep breath and then spoke.

"I will never do that again!" Trekkal said as she looked around.

"Never do what? Run from a blood lusted Kalpeu and live to tell the tale?" Narro mentioned, with his heart still racing from the endeavor.

"No, stay quiet for that long! I had to hold in the biggest scream!" Trekkal said with a laugh, as Narro nodded to his sister's comments.

"Just how far east do we have to go?" Trekkal inquired as she took out a hunk of dried meat, cutting half for Narro to eat. It was second nature as the twins shared everything.

Fool Me Twice

Narro and Trekkal were walking along the open plains of India for some time as the relentless sun shone high above them. The two were able to make significant ground in the region after constructing a boat and riding along rivers. Now in East India, the two couldn't believe how much differed from home but still stayed the same. Narro narrowed his eyes as he scouted for any fragment of shade he could find but came up short. Trekkal stood behind her brother and used him as a source of portable shade. Despite the beauty of the landscape before them, the two faced dangerous animals and they were strangers in an even stranger place. The two found that their kind was completely absent from this area. Trekkal noticed that two factions claimed this space as home. She was unsure of how to feel about Forest Seekers, she only knew them through legends. Trekkal resented the presence of The Youngest who were quick to take up refuge in space she felt belonged to her people. The two were curiosities to settlements that peppered the landscape. As Narro and Trekkal were not visibly The Youngest or Forest Seekers, they were a neutral party.

"We have been walking for who knows how long and not a soul to help us." Trekkal spat in annoyance.

Narro twitched in annoyance as he heard Trekkal's comment. It was her stubbornness that led them to such a situation to begin with. Although lacking in encounters with their own kind, there were people here worth asking directions for according to Narro. Forest Seekers and The Youngest were the stewards of this land and he felt Trekkal's distrust of outsiders only led to their ruin before the adventure could truly begin.

"Trekkal, we passed a camp earlier, but you refused to let us go inside." Narro noted with a smug expression. Trekkal shoved Narro slightly with a pout as she triumphantly shook her head in agreement with her decision.

"You know fully well why I refused. The Youngest are not to be trusted. Did you not listen to our parents?" Trekkal mentioned with a scoff.

She heard the familiar sigh from her brother as he offered a counter to her question. Narro turned around and leaned his forehead into Trekkal. He grabbed her by her arms and lightly shook her.

"Sister, we are adults now. This adventure is for us, not for them now. You do remember this, yes?" Narro commented with an exasperated tone.

His anger at his sister was dulled by the gaping pit that was his stomach. The berries and moss they found previously were barely holding them by as the desire for meat was strong. Trekkal fished when she could, but the waters were fast flowing, and it was hard to get a line. Camps near The Youngest had spare food to trade, but they lacked anything of significance to bother with the endeavor. Narro stopped abruptly in the middle of the plains with his twin doing the same. Narro looked behind him and had a defeated look on his face as he looked around on a swivel. All he could see was what looked like an infinite expanse of grass with some patches that varied in height. He didn't want to admit it to his sister, but they were lost. The directions that Narro remembered expired in his mind. The pair improvised as they said words of encouragement to each other along the way.

"Why have we stopped?" Trekkal asked Narro as she could now feel her feet starting to press in pain. The rhythmic movement she had going managed to dull her nerves long enough but walking for as long as they did was a tiring endeavor.

"I am unsure where to go now. What we were told by Stelo seems to not line up with what is before us." Narro explained with much resignation in his voice. He knew he had to come clean, but his mind was preoccupied with absorbing everything they saw and their vision faded quickly.

"What do you mean? Everyone saw what happened that night, the meteor is very important. You told me that we needed to go east." Trekkal said, as she chewed her tongue in annoyance.

"Well, the priests see things we cannot, but I am confused. I remember her words. She said to go east, and we will find a cold land. As you can see, not very cold." Narro commented, as he wiped sweat off his face. He braced himself for the impact of Trekkal's response as his eyes widened, realizing the extent of their situation.

"Stelo did not see where the meteors went, you took the sole words of our blind Seer!? We are in the middle of nowhere!" Trekkal said, as she grabbed Narro by his shirt and shook him frantically in anger.

Narro could only let out an awkward grin as he realized the gravity of his mistake. She let him go and pushed him away. Trekkal gritted her teeth and threw a rock at the ground. She attempted to calm herself down as she tried to nail a familiar landmark but struggled just as much as Narro to get a foothold on their location. She sat down in frustration and turned away from Narro as she wiped sweat off her forehead. Trekkal shut down as she felt Narro's hand on her shoulder. Narro took this opportunity to set up camp for the two to rest while they figured out a new strategy.

The Buffalo Brothers found themselves in East India as well. Their trade networks were vast, and this patch of scrubland housed valuable pelts they sought to collect. Dronall could often secure secondhand pelts but found that their luster was lost after exchanging hands. Both brothers were fed up with paltry returns and decided to put their own efforts to the test. The pair wore extra protection than usual, and wore thick boar hides on their body. The two wielded stone axes as they surveyed their hunting area. Dronall wanted to slay a sloth bear as their pelts were in demand this season. The sloth bear was responsible for the deaths of Forest Seekers and Thunderfeet alike, so a fresh pelt would make them kings on the market. Dronall and Nezzall were guided by a Forest Seeker under their employment. Dronall negotiated for his tracking services by pawning off some quartz he mentioned was from their ancestral homeland. Neither brother knew where it was from, but their silver tongues convinced the young man to help these two out. The young Forest

Seeker from the plains had no knowledge of the jungles to the east. The Buffalo Brothers used this as a perfect cover story.

"And you were saying that these rocks are embedded with spirits from the ancestral homeland? Quite the distance." The young man said as Dronall nodded.

"Indeed, my brother and I are well known traders. You were lucky to find us when you did. Someone else would have gotten such an object." Nezzall said with a sly grin.

"Well brother, they say that Bher is in these lands. What do you say Forest Seeker." Nezzall proclaimed as he gave a hearty laugh.

"You have my word on the ancestors. This patch of land holds the Bher you seek. It is an errand for fools, but I will tell you the truth. I have seen it rush towards Kalpeu with reckless abandon." The Forest Seeker man stated as he scratched his gazelle pelt.

"Are we to trust his words? How are we supposed to know our source was correct?" Dronall asked his brother. Nezzall said nothing as he pointed to a growling mass that headed towards their location.

While The Buffalo Brothers prided themselves on swindling, they were adept hunters and provided on their own. Others of their kind were less tolerant of their antics and Forest Seekers provided the perfect launch to start over. After their escapades with Jih and Sadal, the brothers chose to lay low and separate themselves from the action that was going on. The Forest Seeker man distanced himself from the brothers as he remembered the terms of their agreement. He would receive half now and half once the corpse was back to camp. He watched as they marched with gusto and taunted the bear before them. Dronall ran up first and sighted the enraged bear. He waved his arms around and immediately got himself into position as the sloth bear raged towards him. Nezzall ran quickly past him with his axe as he attempted to strafe the bear as it ran downhill. Sloth bears offered no warning prior to an attack, so The Buffalo Brothers had to react quickly.

The sloth bear advanced on Dronall with intense speed as it raised its paw at him. Dronall quickly rolled on the ground as the bear came to a slide. Dronall and Nezzall evaluated what areas of the bear to strike as they maintained distance. The two were situated across from one another as they faced opposite ends of the beast. Dronall studied its frame, the bear's eyes stared directly back at him. It was a small bear and was likely still a juvenile but was more than a match for their skills. On its head were two large black ears with a long snout and a tufted mane that protected its neck. Dronall was aware of the bear's tough fur that would make any direct attacks from the back utterly useless. He needed to get in close but dreaded its long sickle-like claws. Nezzall scouted the terrain and noticed they were on an incline. He hoped that he could use this to their advantage.

Dronall egged on the bear as he yelled to make himself appear larger. Dronall retreated as he saw the bear rear up to intimidate him further. Dronall swung with his axe but missed as he heard a snarl from the bear. It kicked up dirt as it sped its charge once more towards Dronall and barreled ahead. Dronall quickly attempted to scale the incline while he noticed Nezzall was downwind. The Forest Seeker man waved to Nezzall as he hid behind a nearby tree and relayed the directions Dronall pointed.

"Brother! I have made the Bher stand! I'm thinking that if one of us goes in while it's upright, the other can charge in and slice the heart in one fell swoop." Dronall yelled.

Nezzall nodded as he tried to close the distance between the two. Dronall adjusted his helmet and made a valiant charge towards the bear. He let out a roar as he charged and collided with the bear. He stuck his axe in the bear's neck and fell to the ground. He rolled away as it remained embedded in its neck. The bear was enraged and clawed at Dronall. Dronall excelled without a weapon, but unarmed combat against a bear was certain death. He rarely felt panic but felt his heart rate magnify. The bear stood as it let out another roar. Nezzall saw his opening as he launched his axe with accurate precision and landed it straight into the chest as blood poured. The impact of the axe pierced the bear's chest with a harsh thud that knocked its center of gravity. Within seconds, the enraged animal depleted so much blood it lay still. Dronall got up as Nezzall returned to him. The meek Forest Seeker man was surprised to see the kill done so quickly but their teamwork and connection showed.

"That was risky Nezzall." Dronall stated as he dusted himself off.

"Yes, but it worked brother. Now go on then, lift the rear. Forest Seeker-earn the rest of your keep." Nezzall ordered as he called him forward.

The three men quickly skinned the corpse and left it to rot while they headed towards camp. The Buffalo Brothers kept their space well-maintained as it served as their front for trading. The Buffalo Brothers inhabited this area for some time and filled four large backpacks with an assortment of items from their travels. The Forest Seeker slept under the stars while Dronall and Nezzall shared a tent. Nezzall's packs carried the surplus items they would use for trade while Dronall carried the spoils of what was gathered, along with their food. As the party arrived, Dronall quickly went to a backpack left out in the sun. He opened it and grabbed the remaining quartz. The Forest Seeker accepted the rocks and nodded in agreement at a job well done.

"As we agreed. The rest of your rocks for the Bher pelt. We will be in this land another season and may ask for your aid again." Dronall said as he dismissed their guide.

As the brothers took a moment to catch their breath, they looked over their haul. The demands of the two changed often as they discussed their goals. Dronall pointed to his wrists and sought to construct bracelets of rare materials by any means necessary. They noticed that village leaders in this area carried them as a mark of prestige and saw the value of being perceived in this way. The Buffalo Brothers wanted a steady supply of trading partners in settlements past random people found on their travels. Dronall and Nezzall held a vision where they could scheme to their heart's content and have the ear of power at their side. It was possible to forge a bracelet that caught the eyes of others, but it was far more satisfying to earn it through wit. Dronall went over to the collapsed piece of kindling that was their campfire. He took a moment to reignite it while his attention turned to a log.

As he did so, Dronall noticed a man with many wares on his person in the distance. He was one of their kind and a fresh face from the usual Forest Seeker clientele. While they weren't keen on trading off the fresh bear pelt just yet, their desire for bracelets sated their curiosity. He noticed such an object on the man's wrist and rubbed his hands together with a devious smile. Dronall called for his brother's attention and received a nod of approval. Nezzall noted that the man walked with authority, he was a certified trader as well as themselves. Negotiations would be interesting as they walked a fine line between barter and interrogation. The Buffalo Brothers usually dealt with the uninformed but someone who had an eye for trade was different.

"Hold on now, I see someone in the distance. Another trader? How excellent. Let's address them. They'll have an idea of the land here." Dronall mentioned as his brother's head turned.

"You! Come friend or trader, my brother and I have wares to exchange with you, if you're so inclined." Nezzall opened as he prompted the man to come forward.

The man hesitated but shrugged his shoulders and decided to enlighten the two brothers. He could hardly disguise his curiosity regarding their strange headwear. While The Buffalo Brothers made themselves a pariah in some places, they were just as obscure as anyone else. The man didn't know what he was getting into, but he had tricks of his own. At once, Nezzall gathered the goods they felt acceptable to trade while Dronall addressed the man who stepped into their camp. He looked around and observed the place. Dronall noticed he was a man of means as he wore a leopard pelt that stood out from the usual deer or grass he was used to dealing with.

"I am Dronall, and this is my brother Nezzall. Welcome to our encampment, you will find our selection here. Everything except the Bher pelt is for trade. My, that is a lovely bracelet. Could you tell me your name?" Dronall asked as he locked eyes with the trader.

"I choose to remain anonymous. We're here to trade, not socialize." The man said conflicting with Dronall's amiable tone.

"Very well. Nezzall, bring out the rocks." Dronall mentioned while Nezzall hoisted up a backpack and dumped them into a neat pile. Nezzall sorted them by color and stood by his brother as the man watched.

Nezzall studied the man's movements and noticed to match their collection he brought out some pelts. He noticed a few obscure ones and looked behind him to see what would match the value. He placed his hand on Dronall's shoulder and whispered into his ear as he pointed out the amount on offer. It was a generous deal for one individual to carry on their own and carried some slight skepticism. Nezzall proposed that a ruse was taking place, but he couldn't figure out what it was. Dronall played it cool and kept his gaze on the pelts on offer. It was entirely within the realm of possibility for the man to have a good trading season and he didn't want to isolate a potential partner.

"May I? This is Ma-Turun? Very far from these lands if I recall and kept in such good condition. What's your secret?" Dronall asked as he placed his hand over one of the furs.

"Do you doubt my wares are good quality?" The man asked defensively.

Dronall asked his question genuinely as even the best practices that he knew of could kill a pelt's quality depending on the change in temperatures. Dronall understood his brother's concern though as he realized the man's quickness to defend himself. He raised an eyebrow underneath and decided to inquire further. He wanted to see how he reacted under pressure and to test Nezzall's theory.

"Not at all. I would just like to inform you that when my brother and I make a deal, there are no returns in the art of exchange. This is understood by all parties before we continue?" Dronall commented as he flicked his fingers.

"Of course." The man stated as he tugged at his covering.

"That is an impressive collection. I would say almost one of a kind." Nezzall interjected as he walked closer to the trader.

Dronall picked up a pelt and felt it in his hand. It felt exceptionally soft to him, but Nezzall remained unconvinced at the man's sincerity. Dronall passed his brother the pelt while the man watched. He started to sweat and cited the growing rays of sunshine that beat down on the three men. Nezzall looked at the pelt with a precision that puzzled both the trader and Dronall. His fingers ran along the inside of the hair and felt something unusual. Nezzall's eyes widened as he felt a tiny gap. He stuck his finger inside and slowly ripped apart the pelts to reveal there were two. The brothers paused and stared at the man. Nezzall realized that these were counterfeit pelts, where two or more pelts were stitched together to make it appear as if the killed animal was larger. The asking price of a pelt depended on the species, but factors such as weight and location also factored into the value of the trade. Dronall was livid and was impressed at his brother's sharp eyes. Although Dronall prided himself as the brain of the operation, his younger brother had his moments.

"I must admit, you nearly swindled my brother and me. We are experienced in the art of exchange, and yet such a simple trick went beneath our noses. Sewing low quality furs together to match a pelt, not bad." Nezzall said as he used his arms to rip apart the seams. Nezzall chewed his tongue as he waited, eyeing the man before them. Although his composure was calm, Nezzall could tell the trader was quite startled that his ruse was found out. This had to be a tried-and-true method for him to do it with such boldness.

"We don't take kindly to amateurs. I would suggest you give us your pack and you can make your leave." Dronall chimed in, as he cracked his arms for a stretch.

"You said it yourself. There are no returns in the art of exchange, right? You grabbed my pelt-that-that is confirmation you wanted it. You can trade me for a needle to get those furs repaired. You've made a mess." The man stated with an angered expression as he tried to suppress his nerves.

"Hardly, checking the product is part of the game. You can choose to dance around it all you like. Bold words to claim. Is your life worth your pride? We offer you a chance of mercy, and yet you wear the pride of an Aroc." Dronall stated with venom in his words.

"Nezzall. Take your axe. Slice him from top to bottom and I will take the loot." Dronall ordered as his brother nodded and lifted his axe with ease. For those smaller, an axe of this size needed to be held with two hands, but Nezzall's physique could handle it with ease.

Nezzall approached with his axe at the ready and the pair could tell the man was not made for this life. He quickly threw his pack and leopard clothing from his body as he ran for his life. The sniveling of the man was audible from a far distance as his vision clouded from tears and embarrassment. He'd gotten this far off his wits and his bracelet alone, but in the face of professionals he fell flat. The two brothers watched as he scrambled along and sniveled away in fear. The physicality of the two men were enough to cause many to tremble before them, but they knew nothing better than the fear of another conman.

"He's heading towards the low grasses, if not us, the Kalpeu will surely get him. What a pitiful little man. Nice stuff though." Dronall laughed as he turned to face Nezzall.

"With that out of the way...how shall we begin the rest of our day today? Ah, let us stretch." Nezzall said as he removed his skull cap. Dronall admired his brother's physique citing how well he took his advice into account. Dronall joined Nezzall in his exercises and scanned their camp for where to start.

"A good kill we made on that Bher, didn't we? The pelt is in excellent health, and we didn't have to kill anyone. That's a good day for me, but something tells me you have another plan." Nezzall said as he limbered by stretching his arms out. He held himself in position for a few moments before his attention was caught by Dronall's reply.

"Well, now that you mention it. We are low on food." Dronall said as he walked towards the log and lifted it up. He held his breath before dropping the piece to the ground and repeated the process.

"Cerbho makes good eating, why don't we go for one? [33] Now-hear me out. The fat can be used for fire. As for the ivory? We can use it to court a village leader. All it takes for us is to catch the eye of one the camps and we have it made. Imagine us at the top, all the food we could want, pelts as high as our tent." Nezzall said with a grin.

"I'm hardly a settled man brother, but you have a point. A Cerbho? We would be a pair of fools to do so. Let's do it." Dronall said with a hearty laugh as he gave his brother a handshake. The two men flexed their muscles as Nezzall gave his older brother a grin.

"A pair of fools indeed. Though, I believe I may have the answer we're looking for. Let's find another pair of fools to help with this task. Do you think the boat by the river is still there? Ours was destroyed on the way here." Dronall asked as he received an affirmative nod from Nezzall. All was according to plan, now they just needed some help to do so. The two equipped their skull caps before leaving camp and hit the road.

The small camp that Narro and Trekkal made was built with stones in an oval shape while their fire was situated right in the middle. Campfires made by The Aligned were

---

[33] Emic word for hippo. Hippos had a much larger range in the Paleolithic with populations as far reaching as Southern Europe!

built in this manner as it was a good omen among their people. For the birds in the sky and spirits in the invisible plane, this meant a safe place to land. Narro and Trekkal were in a staring contest with one another as Narro slowly raised his finger to point to two figures that headed in their general direction. Trekkal refused to admit defeat but heard laughter that broke her concentration. She reached into her pocket to reveal her sling. Narro and Trekkal looked at each other as they noticed two of The Youngest approach them. Dronall made his presence known with a hearty wave and a friendly smile. Nezzall was shortly behind him with a bag filled with supplies. Trekkal came forward with sling in hand as she raised her arm to the two men.

"Ah a lady with such beauty and toughness. Surely you would like to help us?" Dronall opened with a sly grin.

Trekkal backed away expecting some sort of trick to happen upon her. As a young girl, she remembered when one of The Youngest pulled a prank on her by placing a snake in her backpack as a surprise. It was a harmless one, but it further cemented Trekkal's dislike of the group. Narro couldn't help but laugh as Trekkal shot him a glare. She wasn't interested and walked away while Narro refused to leave. Narro was amused at their sight, and the helmets on their heads caught his attention.

"We are new arrivals, but we wanted to see if you want to-" Nezzall commented as he was nudged by Dronall to choose his words carefully. He scanned Narro and Trekkal's belongings scattered through the camp and his eyes pointed to Trekkal's newly minted fishing rod on the ground. Dronall followed his brother and retained his expression.

"Go fishing?" Dronall added as he finished his brother's sentence.

Trekkal stopped, as she would drop anything to go fishing. Although these men seemed to be genuine in their words, she refused to associate herself with them. Trekkal was conflicted, her principles said to leave them alone, but the prospect of beating them at their own game was enticing. She rubbed her stomach and felt extra practice in these waters could be useful.

"We would be happy to accept. I am Narro, and this is my sister Trekkal." Narro explained.

Dronall raised an eyebrow as he noticed Narro approach him directly. Narro leaned first but realized he was using the wrong greeting. He gave an awkward smile and extended his hand out to the two men while Trekkal kept her arms folded. She grabbed her equipment and addressed The Buffalo Brothers.

"You lack a rod, why is that?" Trekkal pointed out, raising a supportive look from Narro.

"We prefer to spear with our boat. Have you been on the water yet? It's just a short walk away." Dronall explained.

Trekkal could offer no counter to his statement and remained quiet. Narro came closer to Trekkal and placed a supportive hand on her shoulder.

"Would you two happen to know where exactly we are? I know you said you were new, so I must ask. Perhaps one of your kind gave a message. Are you also searching for what was in the sky many moons ago?" Narro asked.

At first Dronall looked confused, but Nezzall quickly reminded him of the pair they came across who were looking for such a thing earlier. Nezzall mentioned Sadal's insistence on finding the meteor and the other two people they met on their travels to this region. Dronall massaged his chin in thought and wondered if they could trace the knowledge of those wanting to know about the meteor for their trade.

"Yes! This meteor, we have information for you two. We ran into someone else looking for such a thing quite some time ago. They were heading west from where we were at the time. She was one of our people. Now of course, nothing comes for free. Come with us and help us...fish." Nezzall explained with a stifled laugh.

Narro was utterly demoralized by Nezzall's news. He took a moment to calculate the directions, going west from their position now meant they would have to backtrack all the way to their home once again, and then figure out where to go next. Aside from the journey back, the embarrassment was life-ending on its own. The four left the camp and made their way to the river. As promised, their walk was short as they maneuvered through thick grass that wrapped around their feet. The river was murky with the water filled to the brim with slit in some sections. Narro noted that the river's course seemed to go on for far longer than they anticipated. He thought about how the two of them could potentially use the river to get themselves home much faster. Nezzall commandeered the present boat by placing himself in it as they stole it from the current owner. Dronall kept a steady lookout while Narro and Trekkal exchanged glances. An assortment of tools was present on a small patch of grass by the mud, but the most important tools were a net and a few long spears with thicker points to serve as harpoons.

"We will use the boat of course. It can fit all of us." Nezzall explained and prompted them to quickly join him in the vessel.

"What kind of Peymin are we getting?" Narro asked as he was not as well acquainted with the various types as his sister.

To Narro, fishing just meant finding whatever would hit his rod or what he could spear from the river, but Trekkal was far more specialized in her endeavors. She was already imagining what kind of rough fish could be found that dwelled in such murky conditions compared to the clear streams of home. Dronall laughed as Trekkal gave the man a glare. She situated herself and quickly took her fishing rod with her. She felt the material of the boat and was quite impressed with the construction. The inside was tightly woven together for breathability, but the exterior was reinforced with wood that made it highly resistant to bumps that would easily be a problem within the rapids found in this area. It held a banana shape with two respective ends that curved up, giving a bit of cover, and was powered by oars. There was enough room for it to hold a crew and associated objects for a time out on the river. It was not sea-worthy, but Trekkal thought with some modification it could easily accommodate those conditions.

"Ah, Narro. You have quite the build to match our own. Will you help me steer?" Dronall asked as Nezzall grabbed one of harpoons.

Narro nodded and sat himself in the boat next to Trekkal and took the large oar. Dronall took the opposing side of Narro and the four with a slight push were now on the water. Trekkal took advantage of their slow movement and was the first to cast. She lacked bait to get her catch, but she managed to get a hit on her line anyway. Despite the low visibility, the fish here were generous. The river itself flowed quickly, but the fish were slow and offered little resistance. Trekkal nabbed herself a catfish and gave a smug expression to the three men as she worked to double her efforts. Nezzall hooked a fish that appeared at the top with his harpoon. He pierced it straight through, placing it on the boat while Narro kept his eye on the river's flow. Little talking was done between the four as Dronall kept his eyes peeled for their actual target. The river's flow was sporadic as the slow current boosted in sudden shifts of speed while Narro and Dronall tried to compensate by turning the boat sideways. It was a hard workout for the two, but they managed to keep course. As they continued onward, Trekkal noticed that the river opened to a wider range. Dronall used his oar to stir up some bubbles at the bottom of the boat while they brought attention to themselves.

"Hey! Stop it, you are scaring the Peymin away!" Trekkal shouted in protest.

Narro tapped Dronall's shoulder as he pointed to see a group of hippos situated at the opposing end of the river. The hippos were packed so tightly they effectively dammed the river and made it impossible for their boat to fit through. If they chose to go further, the river would move them directly into the herd.

"We need to go back. We have two Peymin already." Narro said with much worry in his voice.

"Go back? This is what we came for! Brother, pass me a spear!" Nezzall said excitedly as he grabbed a throwing spear.

Nezzall gave a mighty yell and attracted the hippos to their position. It didn't take much for their attention to be raised as they were extremely territorial, but they were still enough distance away to not be any problem. Trekkal's face turned red with rage at their clear deception. Fishing was one thing, but they didn't sign up to take on a hippo, let alone an entire herd of them. She and Narro were now stuck to the mercy of nature and the two men they were with. Dronall slowly inched the boat as much as he could while keeping a respectable distance from the hippo herd that sequestered itself. He recommended to his brother that they attack a calf for ease of use, but Narro suggested they find an adult as the herd would not be as vicious in defending the injured.

"Oh! I see. Since we are just trying to get one of these Cerbho, how about I try?" Trekkal taunted her intentions and confused The Buffalo Brothers.

Trekkal was visibly annoyed and yet she was the first to take initiative in attacking the hippo. Narro quickly grabbed her shoulder as Trekkal was literally rocking the boat and making it harder to stay on course. He took a worried breath as Trekkal strained her neck in anger.

"Sister..." Narro said, attempting to calm Trekkal down. Narro could tell she was clearly upset and while he shared the same sentiment, he remembered the environment they were in. Any mistake now was just going to be a bigger problem down the road.

"You want a big kill to bring home?" Trekkal said with a faux cheery tone.

The Buffalo Brothers nodded happily but shared slight concern in the back of their minds. She withdrew her sling from her pocket and lifted a hefty rock to launch from the boat. The color from Narro's face vanished as he quickly realized the extent of how petty Trekkal could truly be. She rotated her sling to get a good angle; the three men ducked hoping to dodge her swing with their bodies hugging the wood as she did so. She landed a direct hit on a hippo, causing it to submerge to avoid the further barrage as it blew bubbles at the top.

"I missed that time. How about another?" Trekkal said as she launched another stone, this time just barely missing as it bounced a few times.

Narro saw that Trekkal had no means to stop, and he grabbed her as the hippos were clearly upset. Nezzall launched spears wildly at the herd and managed to stab the submerged hippo where a pool of blood filled. The murky water left a distinct trail of red that permeated through the dirt and silt of the river. He formed a fist and triumphantly raised it in the air as he drew first blood. He took another spear, but this time missed entirely as the boat rocked back and forth.

"Dronall, easy with the oar will-" Nezzall said, getting interrupted by the growl of a hippo that appeared in the back of the boat. They were so concerned with the herd in front that they hadn't considered there was any on the sides. The hippo opened its mouth and clamped down hard, practically submerging the boat almost instantly. Trekkal barely escaped the jaws of the hippo as she felt her heart jump out of her chest.

Narro quickly grabbed Trekkal by the arm as the two hit the murky water. He hoped that in the chaos that ensued it would be The Buffalo Brothers instead of them. The Buffalo Brothers scattered from Narro and Trekkal as they took hold of each other as well. Dronall used the oar to slap the hippo and hoped to draw its attention elsewhere while Narro and Trekkal sped for the coast as quickly as possible. Swimming against the current was a struggle but the two managed to touch land with relative safety as they ran into a small calf resting. They picked themselves up from the mud and ran as fast as possible with the mud on their bodies falling off. The mother hippo sighted Narro and Trekkal and pursued. Nezzall threw his last spear into the mud and gave a sigh of relief as it stuck into the hardened dirt despite the current. He held out his hand for his brother as the two used the spear as a point to orient themselves towards the coast and reached the shoreline. They made no attempt to recover their losses as they ran as fast as they could back to camp.

"Perhaps we were too greedy, brother! A story to tell on the roads to come!" Dronall said, panting heavily as he received a nod from Nezzall.

Narro could only follow the sound of Trekkal's frantic screaming as they advanced through the brush with the sound of the hippo competing with her. He couldn't tell if she was screaming out her frustration at The Buffalo Brothers or her fear of being mauled by the hippo. Trekkal ran quickly while the hippo's sound gradually vanished. She gave no time to look for her brother, who luckily appeared out of the bush some distance from her. Trekkal gave Narro a smirk at the outcome of their adventure. Trekkal turned her head and encountered two people who seemed just as lost as she was. The first was an older man wearing some furs who stared at them for a moment, while his younger companion matching his dress, held a throwing spear and walked into view. Trekkal then heard him speak.

"Sadal! Come with Jih. Help is needed." Jih said as he pointed his spear at Narro and Trekkal who stood before him, struggling to catch their breath.

Trekkal saw the business end of Jih's spear as he gave a judging look towards the pair. Trekkal noticed Jih's still expression and quickly sought to defuse the situation. Trekkal gave Jih a small smile that caused him to lower his spear to his side. She seemed to pose no harm. Sadal had come by catching up to Jih and stood in front of him. She scanned the two strangers before her and noted that they were especially strange. They looked nothing like Forest Seekers, so at least she considered them not a problem.

"About time I had something worth doing. What's the problem? What needs to die?" Sadal asked, as she cracked her fingers.

Narro looked at the two of them and lifted his hands up. He decided to be truthful with his new arrivals. He gave Sadal a curious look and turned his attention to Jih with a puzzled look on his face as he heard his words.

"Listen everyone, I know we just met but you do not want to go the way we came! Someone made a Cerbho quite angry, but we should be fine for now." Narro explained and glared at Trekkal who had issues of her own to air out.

"Wait a minute! This was all your fault Narro! If you actually listened, we would be on the right track for the meteor instead of being lost. How did you know to go this way anyway? Oh right. I remember now." Trekkal huffed in annoyance.

Trekkal gave Sadal a closer look and could see she was one of The Youngest. She retreated slightly but Jih intrigued her. Sadal shook her head at the two's fighting. She wasn't sure who they were or where they came from, but the mention of the meteor got her full attention. She tried to reign the conversation back to the task at hand.

"That's not important right now, what's this about a Cerbho in the distance? I might need something a bit stronger than my spear." Sadal said with some concern.

Sadal was trained to take on dangerous predators, but she lacked any experience in taking on a hippo. She dreaded the idea of approaching the creature with a weapon as precise as her throwing spears. The entire creature's thick skin would laugh off her blade. Jih decided to keep his attention on the discussion of the meteor.

"Did this one say they know of power rock?" Jih said, pointing at Trekkal.

Narro and Trekkal smiled, much to Sadal and Jih's confusion. Narro and Trekkal glanced at each other and noted Jih's voice sounded strange. It wasn't one they had heard from a living one of his kind before, but his dialect rang in their ears. Narro gave his sister a nod and knew that good fortune would come. Jih and Sadal were looking for Krukzig's encampment as he was the last person they remembered to have a clear witness, but ended up in the land that was dry and hot instead. While their efforts came up short, the pair figured the two in front of them were able to help find an answer.

"Why, yes I did. I am Trekkal and this is Narro. Now that you have been graced with my presence, your adventure can actually start." She said with a smile, as she ignored Sadal.

"No... Are you one of The First? We thought you all vanished! [34] This makes everything worth it." Narro said as he slowly inched over to touch Jih.

Jih raised an eyebrow at Narro and Trekkal's strange reverence of him, as he's never seen anything like them before. Jih already experienced this type of admiration when meeting with Eshe and her group, but now these new people also felt this way? Jih considered himself fortunate, as he remembered Sadal attacked him when they first met. Jih recalled the stories of the lands that were dry and hot. The concept was almost alien to him as living in the rainforest was the normal way of life for many generations. Stories past the environment of the rainforests were among the earliest of The Elder's oral histories.

"This again? Jih is very much alive!" Jih commented with some irritation in his voice. Sadal interjected, as she was clearly being ignored in the conversation.

"I don't know Jih all that well, but you two seem to just have everything figured out apparently. We have something we need to do-" Sadal said as she matched eyes with Trekkal.

Trekkal's face scrunched up at Sadal's tone of indifference. It was clear to her she didn't understand how important this was for her and Narro. Trekkal took a deep breath and stepped closer to Sadal. She studied her frame and scoffed in irritation.

"Oh, I see. You are one of The Youngest. Typical, you know nothing of legend or our ways." She said, as she placed her hand out for Jih to grab.

"Nor do I care. Why is Jih so important to you? I found him first, get your own." Sadal stated as she slapped Trekkal's hand away and pointed her spear at them.

Trekkal's opinion didn't change regardless of Sadal's behavior. Their connection with The First was a long and monumental process in her and Narro's upbringing. The Aligned kept the tradition of The First alive through song and dance. The priests channeled spirits in the dialect that Jih and the others of his kind spoke through and were familiar with his cadence. As Narro and Trekkal were devout members of their faith, they spent much time with Stelo and were able to pick up the sounds of the dead. Narro and Trekkal were overjoyed to find that their answers were called for in flesh. Although Jih was physical, he represented a gift given by the spirits of The First to guide them on their journey. Jih noticed Sadal's mood and attempted to speak with her. He knew this was a

---

[34] Much like Denisovans, Neanderthals have their own legends regarding ancestral species such as H. erectus or H. heidelbergensis and call them The First given their age and experience as a species. Neanderthals respect The First to a considerable degree and have their language structured based on theirs as well.

tense situation for them both as their encounter with Eshe left them with many questions and the realization that they could only trust one another. Like Narro and Trekkal, Jih and Sadal were also completely lost on where to go next, and it came to pass that help was hard to come by. Jih could only see that cooperation was the best way forward.

"Sadal, we are lost. Let us work as one." Jih commented, as he extended his hand out for the others to grab in solidarity.

While Trekkal motioned forward, she was stopped by Narro who held his club out. Trekkal saw he was armed, and she grabbed a stone on the ground to load into her sling. The grass in the distance shook as Jih and Sadal watched the undergrowth. Both held their spears to their bodies as they backed away slowly.

"We need to move! Wait, friends. Hold on-I hear the Cerbho again. Arm yourselves now!" Narro shouted as he waved for the others to retreat.

The Competition

After Jih and Sadal avoided a close encounter with the hippo, the two looked at their present company. Trekkal looked at Jih with a nice smile while Narro shared a similar grin that unnerved him slightly. Jih nudged shoulders with Sadal to open a bit more and make sense of their new guests. The arrival of Narro and Trekkal couldn't have been stranger to the eyes of Jih and Sadal. Two strangers from the bush brought a hippo, they certainly had a story worth hearing. While Sadal was ready to move on, Jih had other thoughts. Jih swat a fly in his direction as he turned his attention to Trekkal. Compared to Sadal's slenderer frame, Jih saw that Narro and Trekkal were quite stocky with more square faces and thick muscles, especially for their legs. Jih worked especially hard to maintain his frame, but for them it was a state of being.

"We are safe, so Jih asks again. Power rock, you saw this, yes?" Jih said, as he pointed to Trekkal.

Trekkal stuck her tongue out and turned her head. She chose to shift the blame to Narro in typical twin fashion. Narro patted mud off his body while Sadal looked him over.

"Well, yes. Our Seer told us we needed to go east and find a land that was cold. We figured out the first part but the second seems to have eluded us. Narro failed to tell me that he forgot this." Trekkal huffed as she prepared herself for his rebuttal.

"Of all the-Trekkal! You are the one who decided not to visit any other camps! You know how close we were to starving?" Narro fumed in annoyance to her.

Sadal's patience ran thin as she stopped to address what Trekkal mentioned. A look of surprise came on her face as she was sure Trekkal got the directions wrong. She needed more context before she could come up with anything else. She shared a glance with Jih as she tried to clarify what they heard.

"East? Where are you from? Everyone has told us to go west." Sadal commented, shaking her head as she was trying to make sense of their directions.

Jih shook his head at the parallel discussions going on that were overwhelming to any outsider. He stuck his head into his hands and heard the audible sounds of his stomach. The sentiment was shared by the others who were also hungry. Jih's eyes scanned for something edible, but the environment of the open plains was a stark change of pace from the jungle where food practically ran towards them. The paths of the jungle weaved for all to arrive at the same place, but the plains were wide and open. It was going to be an adjustment for both Jih and Sadal.

"Jih thinks we must look for food." Jih commented as he rubbed his stomach.

Sadal agreed with Jih, she couldn't think about anything else on an empty stomach. If she was going to be stuck with these two, an extra hand on the hunt could be useful. Sadal and Jih had a perfect system when it came to hunting. Sadal used her ranged weapons to bait prey into positions where Jih would be lurking with a lunge to the extremity. She wondered how her approach would work with a team of four.

"Well, since we are all friends here, how about a wager? We need to get food and feed ourselves, we should make it fun!" Trekkal proposed much to Narro's complaints.

Trekkal looked over at Sadal with suspicion. Sadal laughed at the prospect; hunting was what she was born to do. Trekkal narrowed her eyes as Sadal did so.

"Jih and I will easily-" Sadal said, herself stopped by the interruption of Trekkal.

Sadal scoffed at her juvenile demeanor. Sadal saw that she practically curled her arm around Jih's as Trekkal stood in front of him. Trekkal moved herself close to Jih while she stared at Sadal. Trekkal turned her nose at the prospect of working with Narro or anyone else.

"I will take Jih. You can take my brother." Trekkal said while she motioned for Narro to move closer. Narro shrugged his shoulders and turned his head to Sadal, as he waited for her reaction.

"You know what? This will be a good opportunity to learn what's around here for me to kill. Whoever can bring the most food before sundown will be the winner then. We'll build a camp over that way." Sadal said, pointing underneath a large tree in the distance.

She offered her hand to shake with Trekkal, but she folded her arms much to Sadal's irritation. Narro looked over Sadal and gave a gentle wave. As far as Trekkal was concerned, the competition had already begun and so she was determined to get started.

"Come Jih! We have food to catch and a game to win! The Cerbho should have forgotten about us by now!" Trekkal said with glee in her voice.

Jih didn't agree to play the game to begin with, but he shrugged his shoulders and decided to play along. Getting something to eat was all he cared about for the moment. He was unsure where Trekkal led him, but he noted that the direction looked like the one where they were running from the hippo previously and gripped his spear tightly. Jih found the humor in being dragged alongside the Indian plains by Trekkal who seemed unable to finish a sentence without going onto a new topic. Trekkal brought up names and deeds of people who he had zero context on and left Jih to sit with a permanently confused look on his face as he tried to piece things together. Jih found it hard to wrap his head around it. Sadal was a talker as well, but there was some sort of structure paired to her. Jih brought an important topic to Trekkal's attention as she stopped in place.

"What will we hunt? Things here are very fast." Jih asked with some concern.

Now that Jih was next to Trekkal, he realized just how tiny she was. She was short, shorter than Hyu, Dran, and Sadal for that matter. Jih wondered how she was able to run down the prey without tiring herself out. Jih guessed that she was around the same age as Sadal, so she was full of youthful energy with time to burn. For every stride Jih made, Trekkal walked twice that.

"I am not a fan of running either. We are going for Peymin, their environment is easy to find, and they are easy to catch. To the river we must go!" Trekkal said with a cheery voice.

"Peymin? You know of Peymin? Sadal hates water." Jih said, as his face lifted with genuine joy. It'd been some time since Jih was able to find a kindred spirit when it came to the water. He smiled and saw there was hope after all in his new companions.

Sadal was left with Narro, with the memory of Jih and Trekkal walking off burned into her retinas. Although Narro had a disabling personality, Sadal was suspicious of the random man now dumped at her feet. Narro yawned but gave her a small grin, much as he did to Jih previously. She pretended not to notice. Sadal decided to evaluate her prospective hunting partner so that she could come up with a plan for them.

Hmm. He has a good build, strong shoulders, he must be a good hunter much like myself. This can work, with that club of his, he's bound to fight at close range as opposed to mine. Good. Trekkal seems to not have had a day of discipline in her life, so I certainly have the better deal. Sadal assessed. Sadal decided to further assess her partner's skillset by asking Narro for a starting idea of where to go.

"Narro, I assume you've been here as long as Jih and I. What have you been able to find here to eat?" Sadal asked. She folded her arms and waited patiently, her inexperience in the plains was something she hoped to fix shortly after with a satisfying hunt.

"Well, there is fruit found by some rivers. I have seen Retōdeu around here, but we must be careful to not spook any. 35" Narro mentioned. He moved his arm out and let Sadal lead the way as it was clear to him, she had some sort of plan.

Sadal frowned at these offerings as none of these offered any sort of challenge. Hunting gazelles was a fool's errand in her and Jih's eyes. Much faster animals could beat them to the punch, and they'd receive nothing for their efforts. As the two walked, Sadal's eyes turned to see a large bird in the distance. She was vaguely familiar with them. She heard a few stories of them around the campfire but hadn't hunted one herself. She let out a laugh as she felt this was going to be an easy hunt with her throwing spears. A female giant ostrich stood tall and observed the surrounding grasslands. The ground was bare save for the clustered nests that were scattered around. Sadal saw imprints in the dirt left behind by the weight of the creature as it walked around without a care in the world. Narro stood closely to Sadal and watched the bird's movement with her. It ruffled its feathers as its head turned. The bird called out in hopes her mate would hear her call. Ravenous hyenas waited in the wings to find themselves an easy meal, but a giant ostrich was an incredibly difficult challenge.

"How about we go for something with a bit more...meat on it." Sadal said, tapping Narro's shoulder as she pointed to see the ostrich of interest guarding a few eggs.

Narro gritted his teeth as he tried to remain calm. Narro was far from a noble hunter, but he was a good team player. If Sadal had a solid enough plan, he would do what it would take to make it happen. Narro saw that the ostrich was his height just sitting down, let alone from standing. The ostrich made another call as Narro spoke to Sadal.

---

35 Emic word for gazelle.

Sadal's mind was already made up as she hoped to use the spoils of the kill for her own devices.

"You want to go for the bird or the eggs?" Narro asked, as he deduced Sadal's intentions.

"Whichever comes quicker." Sadal teased, as she ran ahead in the direction of the bird's nest.

Narro stood alone as he watched Sadal run off. He was hesitant as she clearly just ran off base instinct but maintained a close distance. The ostrich was immense now that Narro took a closer look. He was apprehensive about going for such a large animal with only two people. Sadal found it particularly strange that the animal had little reaction to their arrival, but as she saw its size it was easy to see why. The ostrich didn't see these humans as worth the trouble as it sat. Narro met up with Sadal and looked at her and then at the ostrich.

"Well, what do we want to do? We are in a staring match between us and the bird." Narro said to Sadal.

Sadal ignored Narro's question and ran up towards the bird. She made an angry expression and yelled at the animal only to see it turn away in irritation. Sadal was rightfully annoyed herself as she was not seen as a legitimate threat by such an animal.

"This is a lot bigger than a Poulji. No matter!" Sadal said as she withdrew one of her throwing spears from her pack.

Now that she had what she needed, Sadal gave her pack to Narro to hold as she went up towards the bird very carefully and gave it a large kick in the rear. The ostrich's head turned around with a sudden speed and drove fear into Narro's soul as the bird rose. Sadal saw Narro's face, and he ran away with an intensity she'd never seen before. Narro immediately ran in the opposite direction as he held Sadal's pack. The bird got up and pursued Sadal with a cloud of dust shortly behind. It blindly barreled towards her as it practically trampled the ground below and any unfortunate creatures that happened to get in its way. The ostrich's eyes were filled with rage as it swiped with its toes.

"Grab the egg!" Sadal ordered Narro as her voice carried over the distance while she attempted to find some way to evade the animal.

Narro worked quickly to relocate the nest before the male ostrich returned. He was aware of the animal's sharp claws that even made lions reconsider. He thought Sadal had truly lost her mind. Narro saw the brood of eggs, they were massive, and he was unsure of how to transport them. At the very least, he knew he wouldn't have to worry about the egg breaking. He positioned himself to scoop the egg and took a deep breath as he practically strained to carry it.

Why is this so big? Narro thought as he tried fitting the egg into Sadal's pack. He threw out some superfluous material for it to fit, the stitches and seams were practically bursting but it held. He fixed his posture and ran in the direction he saw Sadal last. He hoped to reunite with her quickly as he noticed the bird's ferocity only increased over time.

Sadal's endeavors with the bird were a feat of their own. The ostriches' legs allowed it to quickly overtake Sadal, where it swiped at her with its foot and flapped its wings. She jumped out of the way just in time as she felt the wind of the ostriches' speed run through her hair. Sadal knew she had no way to reliably outrun the creature, so she needed to make it not worth its while. Sadal was breathing heavily as she saw the ostrich's gait. With a massive gap between its legs, Sadal felt she could easily fit through it. Sadal took advantage of the animal's speed and fell to the ground and used her throwing spear to stab its exposed belly. Sadal's spears were not made for thrusting but as she was able to use enough force, the animal bled in the chaos. Sadal's spear shattered as it collided with the bird, but with enough time she was able to get away. Sadal rolled away and saw blood pool out from the bird as the spearhead remained embedded. She hoped that Narro was able to follow through on his end. In the chaos that ensured, Sadal rushed forward as she waved her location to Narro. Narro looked in the distance to see a faint figure he found was Sadal and continued. Narro could only hope that Trekkal was having a better time than they were.

Jih and Trekkal found a stream not too far from their earlier location. Trekkal made a great effort to avoid the hippo herd that caused her and Narro such grief before, but she noted this was part of the same system. She knew this was a popular spot as not only did they find a boat here, now destroyed by The Buffalo Brothers, but there were further signs of human activity. Throughout spots on the river, there was an arrangement of stone tools left behind near the river's edge. Flakes were left behind, but some tools were left for some reason. It didn't matter to Trekkal which bands owned what tools, she looked around and saw there was a chance for her to use something instead. Trekkal smiled as her eyes found a net close by, this was going to make things much easier. Jih saw her excitement as she grabbed the net and some other tools, but he looked unimpressed.

"Trekkal. This is stealing." Jih mentioned to Trekkal as she scooped up a random person's net. Trekkal looked at Jih with a mischievous grin on her face while she continued her actions.

"Jih, this is borrowing. I plan to return it. Maybe." Trekkal said with a wink.

Jih nodded in slight disappointment at her words as he put his hand to the water and felt the temperature. In the heat of the day, the water was a refreshing prospect. Jih looked at his spear and the various flakes on the ground. He took a moment to rub the sharpened flakes onto the point of his spear, hoping to refine its edge as it would need to pierce through the fish that swam by. He took a step back from the water's edge and looked carefully for a dry patch of grass. He removed his pelts to grab his spear but was interrupted by Trekkal.

"W-What are you doing?" Trekkal asked in slight confusion as Jih stripped down and removed his clothes. Jih walked towards the water and shivered slightly as he felt the water that covered a significant portion of his body. Jih hadn't expected the water to be this deep, but he looked with much intensity to find a fish as he raised his spear above his head. Jih's spears were suited for land animals rather than fishing, though he assumed that with a little creativity, he could get a few fish to bring back.

"Jih is getting Peymin. What is Trekkal doing?" He asked as he turned around to watch Trekkal stretch out the net.

Jih hadn't seen much in terms of net technology, many of his kind used harpoons to impale the fish they wanted to grab and then placed them on a raft back to shore. In his younger days, he and Hyu also enjoyed spearfishing in the water for all sorts of creatures. Trekkal's words fumbled briefly as she saw Jih's physique which was in great form for his age. The constant workload of The Elders kept everyone in great shape. Much like The Broken Bone who ran constant drills to practice, labor was given as the most important thing anyone could produce and it was done with pride. Great works and constant projects kept The Council happy and reinforced a communal sense of importance. This was also taken into personal health as well.

"Oh-what? Jih, we use nets to gather Peymin. If that way works though, go right ahead. Let me know what you find!" She said, dipping her hand in the water close by.

Trekkal kept her ear low to the ground to find some sort of bait to attract fish as she would hold the net towards the shore and wait for something to arrive. In his excitement, Jih forgot the most boring part of fishing, which was waiting for something to come his way. While he could go hours without saying a word, he could tell that Trekkal was practically bursting from not being able to say anything. Jih motioned his hand for her to talk downstream while he waited with his eyes poised on the water. Trekkal served as a lookout for any predators or angry hippos.

"How did you get here?" Jih asked, wondering about the strange course of events that gave him and Sadal two new companions. His thoughts drifted to Sadal on how she fared with the newly arrived Narro. He let out a small chuckle as he already knew that Narro surely was going to be put to work. From his demeanor, Jih could tell that he was more of a gathering type, but this was fine.

"Oh! Narro and I ran into these men that wore strange skulls on their heads. Skulls of the Ker-Mah-" Trekkal said, stopping short as she was interrupted by Jih's scowl. It was clear to her that he had some history with these men as well.

"Jih knows of these men. Sadal did not listen to Jih, we were made fools." He commented flatly.

"You know, they probably still have camp here. I know there are a few camps of The Youngest around here they probably have tried to swindle just as much. We should give them a visit. Get some revenge?" Trekkal proposed with a smile.

Jih let out a low laugh as he thought of giving the two of them a piece of his mind. He didn't think they needed to die for it, but maybe a broken finger or two would be a good lesson to not mess with people's pelts. Their efforts at the water were for naught, but Trekkal decided to pocket the net she borrowed, stuffing it as well as she could into her pack. Jih dressed himself again after not being able to land his mark. She remembered easily where the camp of The Buffalo Brothers was. Her sense of direction was usually terrible, but with a motivator like revenge, she was quite capable. She grabbed Jih's wrist and pulled him forward as she pointed out to the familiar clearing where she and Narro met with them just hours before. She sniffed the air, noting that there was a particular smell. For whatever reason, Dronall and Nezzall were not present. Trekkal assessed that they were once again on the move, probably bothering some other villages for supplies. She took advantage of the moment with great pleasure as she saw some of their belongings present as well. Jih recognized the smell as he looked at Trekkal. The smell of smoked fish filled their noses as a bag filled with the stuff was present. Jih decided to serve as lookout while Trekkal crouched and grabbed as much fish as she could before stuffing it into her own pack.

"Jih, are you not mad? Go on, break something!" Trekkal urged Jih as she gestured to some things left over. Jih looked at the two's skin tanning rack constructed from dead wood. With a smug expression, he kicked it over as it fell apart.

Jih looked towards the bounty of stone left behind and took the good stuff for himself. Trekkal threw around some sticks from their burnt fire and smeared mud on their straw beds. Jih gave a gruff yell as this would be good enough of a warning. He urged Trekkal for them to move back quickly to where they agreed to meet Narro and Sadal before none was the wiser. Trekkal was happy, she got to cause some well-deserved destruction and got a delicious meal from smoked fish. She was salivating at wanting to eat some.

Narro met with Sadal and looked at her slumped over in exhaustion on the ground. Sadal rubbed her face with the back of her hand and stuck her tongue out in disgust. She hadn't expected such a workout from hunting an animal like an ostrich. Far from gentle giants, she found that the stories weren't accurate and needed a far better storyteller at the helm. Sadal looked up at Narro as he held out his hand to hoist her up in support. Narro gave a small grin as he gestured towards Sadal's pack filled with the coveted egg. Narro and Sadal returned with the bounty in hand. He checked her for injuries and was impressed that Sadal had no more than a few friction burns from her time with the ostrich.

"Where did you learn to do all of that?" Narro asked as he envisioned her rolling around. Narro stopped his train of thought as his attention was drawn towards a particular group of rocks. Sadal looked quite confused, but she was sure Narro had something in mind. She wasn't an expert stoneworker like Jih, so she thought that Narro could see some utility out of these pieces.

"Sadal, this here is some of the best Muupasi I have seen yet in this land[36]. The Forest Seekers say it provides a delicious meal. We have something similar at home, but nothing like this. Cook it with some fat and you will be living happily." Narro said. His smile vanished as Sadal looked woefully unimpressed. He carried a few of these lichens in his hand and stuffed them into his bag.

---

[36] Emic name for moss and various lichens that Neanderthals like to eat.

"I learned these things from my home, The Broken Bone. We hunt the beasts because they plague this land and deprive us of safety. Muupasi is no such beast. It's below me, and if you're going to be with me, it is also below you as well." Sadal said, her judgmental tone carried over to Narro's words. Sadal decided to let him keep the bounty for his help in securing the giant ostrich egg. Sadal felt it would be incredibly difficult to somehow surpass her triumph.

As expected, Narro and Sadal arrived under the large tree to see Jih and Trekkal waiting. Trekkal waved her bag filled with smoked fish while Jih raised an eyebrow at what Narro and Sadal had. Narro revealed his bounty of moss and grinned with pride. Trekkal looked at her brother while Sadal and Jih matched eyes with one another.

"You...brought Muupasi?" Trekkal said laughing loudly, as she pointed to Narro. Jih followed suit, moss was often considered something they forced children to eat in hard times. He hadn't considered anyone would have liked the taste. Trekkal's laughter came with an increased satisfaction as she saw Sadal's face clearly angered by her partner's performance. Sadal sat back and listened to Trekkal's laughter for some time until she had enough. She coughed and prompted Narro to reveal what they collected.

"Well, I brought this egg. But I almost chipped a tooth trying to open it!" Sadal commented, as Narro carried her pack and revealed the giant ostrich egg that rolled to the ground with a satisfying thud.

Sadal flicked her hair at the two as Jih and Trekkal saw just how heavy the egg was. Sadal tried opening it with her nails, but Jih held his hand up stopping them. He had just the tool for the job. Going into his pack, he withdrew one of his hand-axes, and slammed it into the egg, where some of the yolk splattered onto the four who licked it off their bodies.

The wake of Jih's and Trekkal's raid on The Buffalo Brother's camp wouldn't be unnoticed. As luck would have it, Dronall and Nezzall returned sometime later in a rage to see their camp was ransacked. The two brothers looked at each other and were quick to blame the other one for their misfortune. They assessed the damage, lamenting at how their beds were also now ruined. Dronall quickly checked on the status of their tanning rack as the sloth bear pelt's success rode on it.

"Brother, you left out the food. I'm sure Denmey or another creature took advantage of our absence." Dronall proposed. He stretched out his arm, and heard a satisfying pop sound, well needed after their antics with the hippo.

"Makkak most likely, they are quite curious and clever here." Dronall added on, as he saw the handiwork of missing food and debris present in what remained of their campsite.

"The stone is gone too! Those must be some smart Makkak." Nezzall said with a flair of sarcasm as his brother glared at him.

"What?" Nezzall said with a shrug as the two went back to work once again on cleaning their camp.

Jih and the others laughed in the distance as they established camp for the night and worked on eating their good meals. Jih and Trekkal told Sadal of their tale in enacting revenge on the Buffalo Brothers' encampment, much to her approval. Despite being strangers just mere hours ago, Jih and Sadal felt better than going alone. If one was injured, much as Sadal was when they started their travels, it was going to be that much tougher to get to where they needed to go. Narro and Trekkal served as a good buffer, and their skills were useful for the journey. Jih's knowledge of plants paled in comparison to Kag, but he knew enough. Narro and Trekkal's travels were helpful in providing extra context to the material he found while foraging. Sadal and Trekkal had a tense relationship, but the two stuck together and defended one another anyway. Jih wondered how the rest of their journey would take hold.

A Day In The Rain

Jih and the others built a large tent to wait out the storm that brewed over their heads. Walking in a storm for the rainforest was easier than the plains, there were at least large leaves and foliage to take shelter. The group built theirs from several animal skins and wood scavenged from the outer forests. Those who didn't plan had ill favor when the rains fell, and they could only sit cold and wet. A small fire was placed in the middle of their tent where the four occasionally opened the flap to let the smoke leave. Dinner was just finished, a nice meal of smoked deer leftovers.

"How about a story to pass the time? I am far from tired though the rain is quite dark." Narro said to the curious eyes of Sadal. Narro turned his head to her but looked towards the ground instead as he ran his finger in the dirt.

"I think a story would be wonderful! That said, it better be a good one. I am not one to sit through anything boring." Trekkal said as she clapped her hands. Trekkal shook her wet hair, and some of it slapped Sadal's face. Sadal was open to the idea of talking about her accomplishments.

"Well, we are all accomplished here, Sadal certainly is. How about this, we should...say our first hunting story." Narro said with a grin as he knew she would speak some on this matter.

Narro hoped to eliminate some of the awkwardness that came with their partnership and learning something new about their allies couldn't hurt. Jih prided himself as a good storyteller, so he cracked his knuckles and offered to tell his story first. Jih raised an eyebrow as he saw the young faces that were his companions stare deeply at him through the low light of the fire. The thunder that accompanied the rain sounded off as Jih spoke with purpose. His story was brief, but it was one he felt proud of.

"First hunt was with Mother many years back. The rains were gentle that day. Hizo told Jih to wake early and bring nothing. No hand-axe or spear. Hizo was missing and Jih had to find her in forest. Jih searched for some time and saw footprints. Jih went on his own and found Hizo with Sarudeu. The Sarudeu was injured and there was much blood. Hizo told Jih to finish kill with his hands. Jih stood over it and clamped hands onto the neck. Jih squeezed and watched it lose air until death. Jih saw Mother watching over his shoulder. Hizo made sure Jih felt the power of life and death." Jih said as he raised his voice to win the challenge of competing with the thunder above.

Sadal held her hand out to interrupt Jih's story, while he turned his head to address her. Narro and Trekkal watched silently and studied the two. Jih had a feeling that Sadal would have counter his claims of a story while he waited for her to speak.

"Well, that's not very sporting, where's the excitement? The risk? Your mother tracked it and couldn't bring herself to finish?" Sadal teased Jih as he explained his first hunt that he could remember.

"Hunt was not sport Sadal. Hizo taught Jih death, it comes for all." Jih said, as he slowly moved his hand above the fire and gave an affirmative squeeze in the air. He mimicked how he strangled the deer as he made a cracking sound from his mouth.

"Jih, I liked your story. It was very short but an important lesson for us all." Trekkal said, as she purposely undercut Sadal with a mischievous grin.

"What was that? Trekkal, start your story!? Of course, I will." Trekkal said as Narro grumbled a bit to himself.

"I was at a river as a young girl, and I saw the flow-" Trekkal said, as Sadal felt compelled to interrupt much like Jih's. Her hand patted the ground in irritation as she knew right where Trekkal's story was heading.

"Am I the only one who knows what an actual hunt is?! Going to go after Peymin is not hunting-" Sadal complained, her voice muted slightly by the ongoing rain. Narro's eyes shifted to his sister who took the challenge of Sadal's words with ease.

"Yes, it is. Peymin are animals, and I killed it." Trekkal interrupted, while Jih conceded that Trekkal was correct with a nod. Trekkal continued her story without any other interjections from Sadal who stood quiet instead.

"I lacked a rod then, so I took a really large stick and spent all day sharpening it to a point. I looked down below and saw it swimming, this one had a grayish color, and it blended in with the murky water. I made a small bug my special friend for the day, and that gray one ate it. Oh, I was so mad! Sometimes, they look up and come to the water to see what is on the surface. Little did that Peymin know my sharp stick pierced their gills. I then found it fun and kept doing it until a pile sat by me." Trekkal mentioned.

"Is that how that went, surely I remember something slightly different." Narro said with a laugh. He teased Trekkal as he ran his hand through his beard. He decided to offer the next short tale.

"My hunt was truthfully quite dull, as these things tend to be. I was with our uncle." Narro said, as he instinctively pointed his finger to Trekkal who ate dried fish. The crumbs from her mouth rolled down her clothing and fell to the ground with every bite.

"I was around perhaps ten years of age. Usually that is when we do things, he told me that he wanted me to find this Digha[37] that was bothering him along the way. They say that they taunt you on the hills and mountains. I believe that, have you seen how they climb? Anyway, I took the offer from my uncle and scaled the hillside." Narro mentioned as he raised his hands up to emphasize the scale of the climb.

"And you did not look down, because you were afraid of heights!" Trekkal interjected, as she knew the story well. Sadal gave a warm smile at this tidbit of knowledge that Narro clearly wanted to keep to himself as his face was filled with embarrassment.

"Yes... I met the Digha, and we did battle briefly. I tripped on the hill and the foolhardy animal thought he could charge me. I turned and rolled to the ground, but it mistook a step and fell to the ground. I was just a bit quicker, and I used my club to knock

---

[37] Emic word for goat.

it out and then I smashed it until blood and bone came out." Narro said, as he rubbed his arms, now with a tiny bruise as a reminder of that day.

Jih prompted Sadal to speak, who despite her interjections of the previous stories seemed to be a bit reserved when it came to hers. Sadal had some hesitation in her voice that Jih noticed. He shot her a look of concern, but it was dismissed by Sadal who got her resolve together. It was clear to Jih that something sensitive happened which made it a harder topic. He was somewhat perplexed however, as hunting was Sadal's lifeblood. What could have happened?

"Well, the first real hunt I had was a bit different from all of yours. As you may know, I'm a Wanderer, or I was. I left my home for the first time; I was ten much like you were Narro." Sadal said, the tone of the tent grew somber as her delivery continued.

"My home was not great. Like you, I have wounds but from my earlier life and when I took the chance to leave, I decided to do so in the dead of night. I stole a knife from my parents and left with the furs on my back. I traversed the jungles for many days alone, only surviving based on what I saw others doing. Many saw me, but none offered to help me. I was not given the mark yet on my hand, but people could tell. I survived off berries and bird eggs." Sadal explained, embarrassment evident in her voice from her perspective of being helpless. Jih noted her abuse as a child and thought how this led to her decision making.

"It wasn't until I saw an animal bound up in rope with small rocks on the ends of them, that I had gotten a chance at some meat. I hardly remember what it was now, perhaps a Sarudeu. Nobody was around, and so I picked up a rock and went to crush the poor thing, but I heard a voice and was startled. A man looked towards me, and I defended the dying animal as well as I could, using the dagger I had. I wanted to steal the kill, this was before I knew the honor of the hunt, and it was one of my biggest shames. The man laughed at me and knelt to meet me in my eyes. For some reason, I felt no compulsion to stab this person, like the many who saw me as lesser. His voice told me that everything was going to be fine, and that I had the will that he was looking for. I wasn't sure what that meant, but he seemed nicer than anyone else, so I decided to go and deal with whatever consequences would come from it. This was Ronkalk, he understood me from the beginning. He knew what I truly wanted and desired from this world. Little did I know, I would run into my younger sister Deeso that day as well." Sadal mentioned as she felt the warmth of the fire over her hands.

"Deeso is like Kag for Jih." Jih supplied with additional commentary.

"I went with Ronkalk, he didn't take my hand, instead he let me pick a direction where I wished to go, and he would follow. It seemed beyond my understanding, someone of his age and status following someone around of my own making, but he was a parent as well. It was an opportunity to learn already. I picked that we go to the east, far away from where I left before. I didn't know in those days I had found my way into the claimed territory of The Broken Bone, anywhere I picked would have been safe. As it would turn out, I spotted a Smir-Tamdeu and after being reassured, I was told to go after it with my dagger. It bounced off with its small legs from the tree with a speed that shocked me, but I kept going." Sadal's hands went to her canteen as she sipped some refreshing water and spoke again. A few droplets of water fell down her face below as the pattering of rain continued above on the surface of their tent.

"Then, I found it. The Smir-Tamdeu was injured, as some girl a bit smaller than me grappled the animal and slid across the soil. It took a resounding amount of strength, Deeso and I are two years apart, so she was eight when this hunt happened. She was bleeding slightly, and yet challenged me for the kill. I accepted, I was angry at my parents, and at the world. I curled up my fist and I hit her. She wrestled me to the ground, and for whatever reason, I found myself unable to get up. She kicked me and I coughed hard. I took a few hits and returned until we tired each other out. Then Ronkalk, after some time saw our bout, and said to us both..."How about one more?" " Sadal concluded with a small grin.

Jih gave a heartfelt grin and patted Sadal on the shoulder. It was a good story that explained a lot about her morals and what truly mattered past the facade. Jih had his own thoughts on the matter surrounding Sadal, and many things he knew or predicted already, but Sadal's life prior to joining The Broken Bone was a complete mystery. The group of four continued to share bits and pieces of their collective heritage.

A few weeks from the plains in neighboring jungles, Deeso and the others made their way continuing in the vague direction of westward since they started their expedition. They were following the Forest Seeker rumor mill of a powerful woman making waves through their ranks. Deeso's first thoughts rightfully led to Sadal, but Ozul mentioned that one known as Eshe was someone to keep their ears about. Ozul was familiar with Eshe's plight against the Thunderfeet. Though the boy was young, he remembered two years past that Eshe first came to his people that happened to occupy a neighboring village from Eshe's on their migration. She talked a great deal about finding her way with violence to oust the growing problem from their lands. Ozul didn't see it this way, for about eight out of every ten people, eight were of his own kind. The fear was not justified.

Much like Jih and the others, the four were pinned down with wild winds and a horrific storm waging above. They constructed a makeshift tent out of tree branches and used large jungle leaves as a buffer from the intense rain above. A small fire was spared the brunt of the devastation thanks to Ozul's quick thinking by digging a small hole in the ground. Deeso looked up and saw that there was a slight leak in their structure. This leak caused the occasional drop of rain to settle in her hair, and then slowly drip to the soil below. Zulag stepped outside to add another leaf to their floundering structure and returned with drenched clothes as he shook his head to dry off. Although grass was comfortable and easy to wear, it lacked the warmth furs had when the skin was cold. He leaned in closer to the fire.

"Well, I'm bored. We have nothing to do. Can't hunt anything out here if you don't want to get lost." Zulag complained while Ozul and Cikya shrugged their shoulders. The pair looked at their equipment that was soaking wet outside.

"I always like to tell stories. We could talk about something- " Ozul said. His eyes turned to Cikya who gave a small wave with her fingers while Ozul looked embarrassed at seeing her eyes.

Right. I keep forgetting that. Ozul thought.

"Oh, a hunting story? We do have a good amount of those, it's in our lifeblood after all-" Deeso commented, as Zulag interrupted.

"Finally, something interesting! Oh, there's so many. But my first? Let's go with the first one I actually care about." Zulag stated with pride.

"My first hunt I went for an Onpeu, pretty simple stuff. This is the animal we use to initiate those into The Broken Bone. Deeso had to do it and so did Sadal. Anyway, I was tired of everyone insulting my skin, so I decided to take on the beast for myself. [38]" Zulag said. Ozul looked closely to see Deeso's reaction and used her as a barometer for how much Zulag seemed to exaggerate.

Ozul felt somewhat bad as he saw his eyes gravitate towards Zulag's discolored skin. Like the others except Deeso, he followed a path of spirits as well, and was unsure of what to make of his markings. They only seemed to have a social hindrance, but when you relied on others to survive, it could be just as debilitating as any other illness.

"I took a few knives with me, crafted them by myself, and set out to find the creature. Here's what happened. I left the outskirts of camp right before the first meal of the day, can't hunt on a full stomach after all. Ronkalk had no idea I left, which is how I usually solve problems. The Onpeu's scent was downwind, and I could see it was lingering around, waiting for something to show up and steal its prey. Scavenging is beneath me, what are we, Denmey?" Zulag said with a hearty laugh that was accompanied by a sigh from Deeso. Zulag scoffed at her response and kept going.

"I looked up and I saw it. This Onpeu had its meal in a tree, just waiting for an opponent to challenge it. I offered myself and the animal climbed down the tree. I saw its claws extend out and I knew the battle was accepted. It swiped at my feet with a foolish lunge as it quickly got punished by a knife I launched into its side. The hit was dull, but it was enough to know that I was not one to go down easy." Zulag said as his eyes darted across their shelter.

"And then what happened, Zulag? Did the trees sing to you as well? Did the sun's light move just one bit closer to block its vision?" Deeso sarcastically chimed in.

Cikya nodded her head and wagged her finger at Deeso. Storytime was rarely meant for interruptions and that was something Cikya took seriously. Deeso preemptively rolled her eyes while Cikya's glistened in the light of the fire. Zulag got up and

---

[38] Diseases such as Zulag's vitiligo were hardly understood and were seen as markings of those falling under bad tidings but through great feats, these were overlooked. Being the nephew of the leader also isn't a bad starting point either!

demonstrated his pose with much fervor. He hit his head slightly on the roof of their tent as he was the tallest among them.

"And then! The Onpeu jumped towards me, mouth ready to lop my head off, but my knives were just a bit faster. I rolled out of the way, just in time and I placed two that landed their mark. One in the eye, and another in the throat. I watched it beg for life as it thrashed around in its own defeat. I was too weak then to drag the carcass myself, but I got some help, and we brought it back. At a certain range, getting hit by my knives means you're dead, no doubts about it." Zulag said, finishing his story to the small clapping by Cikya.

Ozul didn't have much of a past to tell, he was after all only twelve years old, but he did have one hunt he was proud of. In the days before his blowgun, he used his father's axe to hunt, much like that of Deeso's, but hers was in much better quality. Ozul sheepishly felt the supportive touch of Cikya, urging him to go next. Deeso didn't object, she was curious to see what Ozul had to offer and after Zulag's animated display, a tale more grounded was something she sought to listen to.

"I hunted a Sahroh[39] last year, I went on others, but this was without my father. I looked-Yes...Zulag?" Ozul said, as he saw Zulag slap his hand on the soil to interrupt.

"You hunted a Sahroh? I thought you all didn't eat meat. Your Vow or what's it called." Zulag questioned while Deeso raised an eyebrow.

"Zulag, we went hunting together last week. I eat meat. The Vow is the promise we made to ourselves and The Stone Breakers to not taint the forest with the blood of others such as us. I am not allowed to slay humans, but the animals that come are a gift from the forest." Ozul explained, hoping to put this topic to rest.

"Right..." Zulag mumbled, as he let Ozul continue.

Cikya nodded her head and hit Zulag lightly on the head for interrupting while he shot her a glare.

"Well, I was supposed to go and deliver some berries to the next village over, but the call of the Sahroh had other plans. I only saw a glimpse of the tail, but I had a need to place my basket down and go hunt it. Sometimes, we have animals in the forests that represent physical spirits wanting to tell us something. I saw the Sahroh had a message for me, and I intended to know what it wanted." Ozul explained by picking up a stone and moving it as a visual aid.

"This animal had a message for you, and yet you chose to kill it?" Deeso asked with some skepticism in her voice. She was unsure of what to make of what Ozul was talking about. If this animal was so important, why go through the motions of slaying it?

"It was through the chase that I learned what was important. The creature stopped at the base of the Panmarat and rested, as if to signal for me to hear the words it had to say. When it was done, the creature returned to a feral state, and I killed it there. It was a

---

[39] Emic word for serow.

hunt with purpose as it led me somewhere important. The meat was just a small gift." Ozul said happily.

Deeso and Zulag kept quiet. Cikya scooted herself closer to the fire as she shook her body. She prompted with her hands for everyone to come together, giving her some room. As Cikya was mute, she had to get creative with her storytelling. She stretched and posed, as she acted out her story. Deeso and Zulag shot each other a glance as they attempted to figure out her display, but Ozul noted that Cikya was rotating her arms, mimicking a bird's flight. As a priestess, Cikya had to do very little hunting and so her experiences were not as dramatic as Zulag's or Ozul's. Cikya was depicting her hunt at night, looking for an eagle-owl. She pointed at the fire, and held a stick in hand, showing that she was carrying a torch as she walked by searching for it. Cikya rarely was a night person, but she heard the call of the owl that was keeping her from sleeping.

Past the village where The Painted Hand was, she saw the alluring orange place her into a trance as she held her torch. In those days, she was just an initiate into the priesthood, and lacked her usual face paint. In her hand were a few rocks that she picked up, as she hoped to encourage the owl to leave. She crouched low with the light of the torch carrying over. The owl's head turned and stared at Cikya who remained still. Her footsteps were loud, and the owl had her certainly matched, but it remained quite curious. The owl howled and while she sat back, it flew closer in a warning to her. Cikya took this warning with zero care and launched a small rock at the owl sitting on the branch and in a panic, it flew into another tree and fell to the ground as it hit its head.

"Yes!" Cikya shouted, her joy emulated by the present Cikya with stretched and prideful arms.

Deeso was the last one to tell her story, as she remained quiet for the others to settle down before they realized she hadn't spoken. Deeso had a soft voice, so they had to be quiet for her words to carry along the cracking of the fire.

"I was very young. At eight years old, it is one of my earliest memories. Like Sadal and Bheyra, I am a Wanderer. The mark is on the outside of my hand. I had to leave after events beyond my control forced me to look elsewhere." Deeso said, her words evident to Zulag that she was being cryptic about her reasons for leaving. They were her own and nobody else bothered to pry about it, but it was something to note. Deeso found it still difficult to fully trust her companions despite the time they've had on the trail. She was a very private person, and the abridged version of her story would hopefully be suitable.

"It was a hard life; I was on my own and I had nothing but the furs on my back. I didn't know how to make tools either. My first axe came from a man who died of exposure, and I learned quickly how to use it. I spurned the help of others. I didn't trust them and their intentions with me were questionable at best. At one point, I was incredibly hungry, and I would have eaten anything to survive. My luck changed the day I found a Smir-Tamdeu, and I pursued it. My long hair got caught in the brambles and I used my axe to cut it down. I saw the creature and tackled it to the ground, holding it there. I didn't know how to wrestle then, but the ground called to me. I struggled with the beast to hold it down, but then my luck changed when I saw her." Deeso said as her face turned to a small grin.

"The girl who would become my sister. Sadal was there, running towards me. I challenged her for the right to the kill, after all, it was mine. She came towards me, and I got a punch in the face. I spit blood and then with all my might, I jumped into her, and pushed her to the ground. I flailed almost helplessly, but in the time that it took for us to have our bout... I was stopped by a man's voice. It was earth-shattering, as if time itself stopped. I saw his eyes and the dreadlocks on his head. The man looked at me on top of Sadal, with a fist poised. His voice grounded me, and I could no longer move. Ronkalk spoke to me, and he said, "How about one more?" " Deeso stopped speaking as she looked at the others. Zulag bit his tongue, Ronkalk was selective in his presentation of stories, he wasn't aware to the extent he was involved with both Sadal and Deeso's entrance into The Broken Bone, but all he saw were two outsiders trying to get their way.

"For the first time in my life, I felt like there was something more than the struggle to survive. Our fight against the beasts. Our fight to live and have greater peace and security. I found this through Ronkalk, and I hope to find that with you all one day." Deeso stated with a tired feeling in her voice. The night was late, and she was tired. The rest digested these words as they exchanged a few glances before nodding off.

A Debt To Pay

While Deeso and companies' search for Sadal's whereabouts ended up cold for some time, their fortune would soon change. Deeso communicated to the others on her travels to find food, she scouted out the presence of a few camps that were connected much like their own back home. She was certain they were her kind, which came as a great relief to Zulag and Cikya. Ozul was apprehensive on the matter, but he was aware that not all Thunderfeet camps were the same. Some even welcomed the idea of peace and cooperation, which he was thankful for and willing to try. After heavy rainstorms bombarded the four, they were quite damp and cold. Ozul took it on himself to prepare the fire this time as he used his hands to make a small depression in the ground and threw refuse material in that he lit carefully. Cikya observed the design choice but saw that the earth insulated the flame and stabilized its direction. A breeze wouldn't cause it to spread outwards and set the loose leaves on the ground alight.

Deeso hunched over the fire and held her arms out to dry off before speaking. As she shook the water off her body, small drops of water spattered the fire and caused smoke to come out. She gave a slight cough and backed away. She rubbed her eyes, realizing much like a moth she went too close to the flame. She gathered the attention of her team as she folded her legs to sit.

"Those camps not far from here, we should go make contact with them. Something tells me that they would have come across her at some point. It's been some time since we found our own to meet with." Deeso mentioned as she met the eyes of Zulag.

Zulag gave a small grunt as he thought over her words. Zulag wasn't opposed to contacting these other villagers. Seeing other Thunderfeet in a sea of Forest Seekers was quite appealing but he had some apprehension he felt worth mentioning.

"Any idea what group this is? We do have enemies aside from Forest Seekers you know. If I need to go into combat, we should be prepared for it." Zulag commented.

Cikya nodded in support of Zulag's statement. She passively counted on her fingers the amount of people who have sworn revenge on The Broken Bone or cast down a curse on their leader. For Ronkalk, it was something to joke about, for many failed to achieve the success he created with his leadership. For Zulag, it brought nothing but immense worry as he would have always had to keep an eye out on those who have a target on him and his uncle's back. Zulag figured with as far they were, any enemies would have been long behind them.

"I saw nothing that would give me pause. Will we go or stay? Sadal gains more ground by the day, so I suggest we do something. It's an hour away." Deeso commented, while the others thought to themselves. Ozul looked at his growing pile of responsibilities, including making more rope for the group to use. It wouldn't make much sense for him to leave with all that was to be done, but Deeso willed it so.

Without much objection, the four left some of their supplies behind to take the hour walk to the camps that Deeso mentioned. They were armed and prepared, except for Ozul who walked behind the three. He continuously checked behind his shoulder to make sure they weren't being followed, either by Thunderfeet or his own kind. Ozul peered through the treeline and looked for distinct patterns of vines and grasses that Forest Seekers wore. At this point, Ozul knew that enough saw him as a traitor for dealing with Thunderfeet, and he needed to be vigilant of this. He felt trapped as he didn't fully trust the three people he traveled with just yet, but his options ran out.

Unknown to Deeso, the camp she stumbled on was the network that belonged to The Mud Forged. While not as mobile as The Broken Bone, they settled in areas of the forest and chose to clear out distinct pathways by doing controlled burns and smoothed paths of dirt with heavy rocks. These constructive actions brought the ire of Forest Seekers as well, so they were no stranger to combat. Jih and Sadal originally were looking for Krukzig's base camp but ended up finding the plains instead. Sadal was able to sight members of this group from previous travels while hunting, but Deeso didn't have this experience. She led the group into enemy territory and had no idea. Cikya looked around and saw the organization of the path below her. The land was cleared significantly where just small patches of dirt were the roads that led further out. She noticed on the greenish bark of trees there were handprints with brown and black coloration that seemed to mark areas. She saw Ozul's scowl as it was clear that the trees were uprooted in the process. He took great care to rub the exposed roots before catching up with the others.

Why does this look...? Something seems unusual about this place. Cikya thought as she examined the handprints.

Zulag gave little importance to the matter as they stepped in the camp's boundary. There were no sentries or any sort of guard present, so one could just easily weave in without issue. Zulag kept his mouth pursed as he looked around and noted the strange symbolism much like Cikya did. It took a moment for him to realize where he was. Krukzig enjoyed a bountiful region where there was plenty to hunt, and these strange symbols were offerings of gratitude to spirits that dwelled in the forests. The Mud Forged didn't prioritize hunting dangerous game like The Broken Bone and took a generalist approach to their lifestyle. The camp was surrounded by an enclave of thick forest that cushioned it from the rain while sparkles of sunlight tore through the canopy. Deeso found an opportune time to enter the abode. She announced her presence by cupping her hands together to yell and waited for some time. The camp wasn't empty, as she saw smoke lift from fires. There was an ambient rustling some distance away until her greeting was returned. Deeso was answered by a gruff older man answered who appeared before them carrying a club. He wore an assortment of feathers wrapped tightly on an armband and red paint on his face. He wore little other clothing than leaf wrappings on his feet and a loincloth. His eyes looked at the group of four. Ozul hid behind Cikya as Deeso addressed the man.

"Why have you come here? You don't look like Forest Seekers or looking to cause trouble, so we can open our camp to you. If you deceive us, then your fate will be sealed." The man replied.

Deeso's attention turned to Ozul as she nodded her head for Cikya to move out the way. Ozul felt a slight sting of betrayal as Cikya moved and all eyes were on him. Deeso gave Ozul a small grin as she figured out a way to smooth things over with the occupants of the camp. Zulag wanted to skip the formalities and get on with it, but he was interrupted by Deeso's speech before he could do so.

"We have a captive, if that's where your interests lie. My friends and I are looking for information. Can we come in?" Deeso asked as she turned a question into a negotiation.

"You want furs for him?" One of the men asked, as he pointed to Ozul.

"I am not for trade!" Ozul said, with visible offense as he instinctively moved towards Cikya.

Deeso struck Ozul with the back of her hand as she glared at him in front of the man, partially to keep up appearances and because she was annoyed at his outburst. The man nodded in approval as Deeso kept Ozul in line, while he attempted to remember what she requested.

"Information hmm? We had someone ask one of our people for information some time ago. Word takes time to travel but I remember it was something about a meteor? Krukzig witnessed this in the sky." He asked as he looked at the four of them.

Zulag's head turned on a swivel as he recognized the name Krukzig. His expression changed as he clumped his hand into a fist. The gesture went unnoticed as Zulag remembered quickly to keep his cool. Zulag felt an utter sense of disgust with Krukzig's name. Zulag locked eyes with the man.

"I know what that is. I remember hearing about it from the priests back home after hunting. I didn't think anyone was actually looking for it, but it's said to have a powerful spirit. Do you think she would be searching for this?" Zulag commented as the man nodded.

"A woman who looks like us, did you come across her recently? Her hair is dreaded, last I remember, she is twenty and most likely injured. She should be carrying throwing spears." Deeso inquired. The man rattled his head in thought and lifted a finger.

"We sent scouts some way from to our work camp some time ago, but they've yet to return. Shouldn't be long now though. You should talk to our leader. He will know more." The man said as he directed the four in the direction of an open tent some distance away.

The man prompted another one of the camp guards to bound Ozul's hands together with rope as he was Deeso's captive. Deeso, Zulag and Cikya walked as guests in Krukzig's encampment while Ozul was prodded along with a club at his backside. Ozul resisted as hard as he could to avoid shaking with fear. His eyes scanned the camp and looked at the mixture of people that were gathered. Much like his current company, Ozul mostly only saw Thunderfeet in their warrior occupation and was genuinely surprised to see various innovations in their camps. A woman was hunched over with a small child as they made fur cufflinks as decoration for others with thread. They prioritized fashion as much as efficiency when it came to defeating the foe. The first guard and his comrade that watched over Ozul were curious about the new arrivals. The guard in the back looked at Zulag as his mind turned in thought.

"Though, I must ask. Where do you come from? Who speaks for you in this group?" The guard next to Ozul asked.

"We are from The Broken Bone. Who are you?" Deeso asked.

The man's sudden change of personality startled Deeso as it was clear she made a grave mistake. His expression angered as he spat to the ground. He then gave a jovial laugh, but Deeso knew this was artificial. Her hand idly sat near her axe while she could see Zulag and Cikya out of the corner of their eyes waiting calmly. She knew that fighting in the heart of the camp would be a problem, so she hoped to choose her words carefully. Deeso was met with a second chance to adjust her response much to her relief.

"You amuse me young woman. Those interlopers were dealt with before. Their stupidity to come to my soil and my people. Ha! Now tell me, who are you really?" The man asked as they saw the frame of Krukzig in the distance.

Krukzig was a burly man with a large stomach and a patchy beard with gray that took a life of its own. The top of his head was bald and smooth to the touch. His eyes were hazel in color that contrasted from the sea of brown before him. He had a strong smell of honey and had mud lathered on his neck and arms to cover himself from the sun. He wore no covering as his chest was bare but wore a grass skirt. Krukzig sat on a throne of his own making with a log and small stump to serve as his chair. One woman came by and placed down a basket filled with honeycomb. A stack that survived the journey from the work camp awaited him. The first of many baskets was torn into by Krukzig who tossed the lid aside as the bounty came to him. His eyes looked at a stack of honeycombs. He broke these apart and ate the deceased larvae as well as the honey that came by. The woman who previously carried the basket stopped her task as she noticed the new arrivals approach her location. The others gave little interest to her, but she retracted slightly at the sight of Zulag. Krukzig gave no reaction as he continued to eat. The woman withdrew a knife from a pouch in her clothing. She looked to be about the same age as Krukzig but was in far better condition.

"You! Step forward!" She said as she pointed to Zulag.

She was armed with a blade that was weathered with experience. Deeso held genuine surprise at her reaction while she looked to see what Cikya thought. Although Zulag hadn't met eyes with Krukzig before, he knew the stories of him well. Krukzig was one of the few remaining people to know Ronkalk from boyhood, he was once a good friend but now a sworn enemy. It was both divine intervention and through pure grit that Krukzig lasted as long as he did. Zulag assessed the situation before him and raised his arms slightly as he stepped away from the other three. He didn't make any sudden moves as he locked eyes with Krukzig. Zulag found it hard to hide his disgust as honey slipped down the man's lips.

Mud Forged Territory, I should have known. Little Deeso led us right to a trap, now it's up to me to get us out. Zulag thought as he closed his nose in disgust.

The guard at Ozul's back glared at Zulag. He placed his hands off Ozul as he raised his club in the air. He waved to get his attention but was only going to be met by the sound of his voice.

"The son of Ronkalk! I should have known! The scouts said your skin was cursed by an Onpeu's spirit. It's uglier than I could have foreseen." He said in disgust.

"I'm his nephew! Your scouts couldn't track a Yaan if they tried!" Zulag spat back in annoyance at the man. Zulag slowly reached into his clothing as he glared at the woman who held a knife towards him.

Krukzig had enough of a spectacle before him to make his appearance known. He helped himself off his makeshift throne and approached boldly. He let out a large bellow as he rubbed his stomach. His crazed eyes stared at Zulag, and the memories came flowing back to him.

"Ah, I know who you are. This is Zulag, son of the cowardly Aralic and foolhardy Chindi. My quarrel is with your uncle, boy, so state your business in my camp." Krukzig mentioned to the growing crowd as he gave a grimace towards Zulag.

Krukzig was a hospitable host to those he viewed as friends or resources. Zulag was locked out of the first option, but the team could prove useful for his goals. Krukzig decided to test Zulag some as he felt comfortable in his position. Cikya reached the same conclusion earlier as Zulag did without giving any confirmation to the fact. She looked behind her and saw that a few armed and curious eyes converged on their position while Deeso was none the wiser. Cikya found it unusual that nobody stripped them of their weapons but carrying culture differed from settlement to settlement. She found herself in a difficult position as tapping Deeso's shoulder to alert her would cause further suspicion from Krukzig, so she braced for the consequences that would come.

Although Deeso and Cikya swept under their noses, Zulag's appearance was unforgettable. Their scouts covered large swaths of territory for weeks at a time. Krukzig was aware that The Broken Bone remained in the periphery of their lands, and he knew some details, but not everything. While Deeso's brain worked overtime to come up with a solution to get the group out of danger, she was interrupted by the call of another man who alerted their attention. Deeso, Cikya, and Ozul could only sit and watch the shouting match that was to unfold between the two. Decades of tension between The Broken Bone and The Mud Forged piled up with skirmishes that happened on occasion but never a concentrated number of forces placed on one another. The Broken Bone outnumbered The Mud Forged by sheer membership but not by much. Ronkalk's approach of absorbing Wanderers made it socially unacceptable among some groups to decide to work with him and his cause, and their backing went to The Mud Forged instead. Krukzig had a solid operation with plenty of allies to spare.

Zulag wasn't sure what to approach first as his face reddened in anger. The disrespect of Ronkalk or the honor of his parents that was violated before him. His fingers twitched as he preemptively curled a fist. He could feel the hairs on his skin rise as his target could only scowl towards him. While Zulag knew he needed to ask about the meteor and Sadal's whereabouts, his mind could only fixate on his festering hatred for Krukzig. One of the few things Sadal and Zulag shared was a complete disdain for The Mud Forged. They both felt it was their right to inherit Ronkalk's quarrel with them that only death could relieve. Zulag demanded answers that could be relayed back to Ronkalk on his return.

"How are you still alive? You left my uncle to die when he was but a boy and the things, they did to him! Unspeakable!" Zulag yelled with such fury that even Deeso felt unnerved. Cikya looked at Zulag with concern while Ozul attempted to free himself amid the chaos unfolding.

"I was but a boy as well. What happened to Ronkalk was from his hubris. These events are older than the two of you put together. The raid fell through and the strong made use of the weak. It happens to everyone. Get over it. This I told your father as well, the sniveling coward he was." Krukzig taunted as he gave another laugh that filled the camp.

Deeso and Cikya kept themselves occupied as they were entrenched in the dialogue of their discussion. The standoff between the two was palpable as they exchanged words. Deeso wondered how two people who loved to hear themselves talk could have a discussion, but she was interested in hearing what Zulag had to say regarding Ronkalk's past. Ozul made a small incision into his bindings with his teeth.

"I'll rip your tongue from your throat! My father died in battle against Kalpeu! Back when we lived where the trees were sparse, and the land was hot! [40]" Zulag yelled at the man. The rage within his voice was palpable as Zulag surged with it and struggled to keep it together.

"Did he? Why, I remember those days better than you. But what do I know. The Broken Bone is behind me now." Krukzig stated with a burp.

Krukzig smiled as Zulag was as easy to manipulate as Ronkalk all those years ago. Zulag was practically vibrating from anger. Cikya looked away as she heard Zulag's reply to Krukzig, this was something that both Ozul and Deeso noticed but chose not to address.

"Now that my memory returns to me, there were three scouts that died to claim Teen-Sa. They were struck down by the enemy with weapons that flew through the air. Sound familiar? I see your knives and how they work. The guilt of our dead lies on your faces. I see that now." Krukzig stated.

The scouts Krukzig referred to were defeated at the hands of Jih and Sadal, but the blame now rested on Deeso and the others due to their historic rivalry. News traveled only

---

[40] As there are no true terms to define areas of the world yet, the different groups recall traveled areas by accounting for the temperature and various factors in the environment. When the trees were sparse and the land was hot refers to India's plains at the time.

as fast as one could go, but a survivor left alive returned with the honey and gave Krukzig the news just two days before. Deeso was once again caught off-guard as she was painted for something she didn't do. This was not something Deeso expected to come across but like every situation, she felt she had a plan. She waited patiently as her hand slowly moved to her axe.

"We didn't-I've had enough." Zulag said, as in a single motion he reached into a loop in his covering and launched a throwing knife into Krukzig's direction.

In a panic, Krukzig used his arm to take the hit of the knife while Deeso and Cikya sprang into action to quickly reach formation with Zulag. Deeso's fingers at long last grasped her axe and she swung wildly. In her haste, she remembered Ozul's bindings and set him free. Ozul was paralyzed with fear as he didn't want to violate his principles but knew something needed to be done to ensure his survival. Zulag's mind was set on killing Krukzig. Rather than launch another knife, he used his body weight to tackle the man to the ground. Zulag took a hearty punch to the face as his head recoiled from Krukzig's meaty arm.

"If I can't kill the uncle, the nephew will be just as fine!" Krukzig spat in disgust.

Zulag removed the knife from Krukzig's arm and jammed it into his throat. He slowly dragged it across as blood pooled to the ground. Krukzig attempted to wrestle Zulag off of him in a blind rage. Bits of grass crunched as Krukzig grasped the dirt and moved to stuff it in Zulag's mouth. Ozul witnessed the scene and strangely felt compelled to help Zulag. He placed his body weight on one of Krukzig's free arms and prevented him from attacking. Ozul took The Vow seriously, but the life of Zulag was at least in the moment worth more than that.

Deeso and Cikya's attention turned to the few fighters that The Mud Forged had at their disposal. While Cikya's main duty was a priestess role, Ronkalk instilled everyone with combat training, and she could contend with human opponents as well as their usual predator hunts. Cikya used her staff to keep the enemy at a distance while Deeso took advantage of her opponent's exposure to slice their body with her sharpened axe. Bits of flesh and blood fell to the ground as the few warriors attacking the four were cut down. Deeso's attention went towards the woman that held them at knife point earlier. She lunged at Deeso as Deeso ducked to avoid the first strike. She lifted her arm up and let the gravity of the axe accentuate her strike as she knocked the knife out of her. As the woman scrambled to recover her weapon, Deeso swung low and hacked off a large portion of her wrist as blood seeped everywhere. The woman let out a scream of terror before falling over numb. Deeso silenced her screams with a chop to the throat as she heard the familiar crunch. She used her foot as a support to remove her axe and moved to the next target.

Ozul dove low and used himself as a weight to ground those he targeted while Zulag cut them down with his knives. Those of The Mud Forged in this camp that remained shook in terror at Zulag whose fiber and vine clothing were saturated in blood. Deeso and Cikya stood at his side and glared to accompany him in true visage that The Broken Bone symbolized. Their hands and faces were caked with blood as they hacked the survivors to bits that begged for mercy. Members of The Mud Forged who would have run otherwise converged to recover their fallen as they sought to grab help from the other camps. This was a futile endeavor as Deeso and Cikya were quick to end the lives of those who failed to evade their grasp. Zulag didn't see the need to torch the camp, he wanted it left standing as a reminder of what happened. Zulag stood and surveyed the damage of the camp that once held around thirty people. Once the armed resistance was taken care of, it was a simple matter of removal. As he watched Cikya and Deeso help themselves to the food stored, he rested his foot on the corpse of Krukzig, and saw that he finished what his uncle started. Ozul watched in horror as he saw the infirmed and other groups fall flat to the ground until only exhaustion from Deeso and Cikya served as a reprieve. These were people that were their own kind, Ozul shuddered to think what happened to the Forest Seekers they went into combat with. He felt disgusted having helped with their demise.

"Why do this? This trail of bodies. Would it not have been better for you to capture him instead? He had information we needed." Ozul asked.

It was mind boggling to Ozul that this much death was needed to make a point, a clear schism in their views of the world. Zulag stepped closer and gave him a grasp on his shoulder. Ozul tensed up immediately which gave Zulag a small grin of satisfaction. He leaned in close and spoke into his ear. Zulag pointed out and explained the intricacies of why they conducted themselves the way they did.

"Ronkalk doesn't take captives. Captives are a waste of resources. One must kill them all or let them scatter like Toles into the jungle[41]. You may fear that they will become stronger, but we strike so that retaliation isn't to be feared." Zulag explained to him.

Ozul's face turned from shock to a frown as he felt guilty in assisting in the murder of these people. He couldn't look any of the others in the eye, especially Cikya. With the calm of the air now and the smell of blood hanging over their noses, there was something that needed to be addressed. Although the release of emotion and destruction of the foe brought satisfaction to Zulag, Deeso, and Cikya, Ozul was quick to remind them of the question that eluded the four once again. With the death of Krukzig, their plan to ask about Sadal's whereabouts now died with him.

---

[41] Emic word for dhole.

The Sound of Silence

With not much ground left to cover after their murder of Krukzig and scattering The Mud Forged, Deeso felt it was necessary for the group to rest after a hard day and to come up with a plan. The group was going to continue going further west as Deeso's original theory of river travel seemed to line up with what they had found so far. There were no complaints on the matter. Cikya kept watch the following night and was restless. Ozul often ended up taking over as he was nocturnal to begin with, but given the last few days, he was exhausted. Ozul was slumped over as he fell asleep on a pile of furs. Deeso looked at her weapon as she reached for a block of wood, her axe handle was loose, and she would need to haft on another in due time. As she weighed it in her hand, Cikya returned the glance. Deeso had a burning question to ask, and she felt after they've known each other this long it was time.

"I have to ask this Cikya. Why are you wearing that on your head? You keep it on for combat and when you sleep. It has to hurt." Deeso inquired as she noticed Zulag frown at her comment.

Deeso was legitimately curious as she saw Cikya's normally cheerful expression turn forlorn while Zulag protectively went to soothe Cikya. Deeso was surprised at the gesture but held her opinion to herself. Zulag usually offered a glare to Deeso for a remark he found stupid but his concern for Cikya trumped it above all else.

"You really don't know, do you?" Zulag said with some dismay in his voice.

Deeso nodded, as she saw she was in too deep to go back now. She felt it was good for the team to truly understand one another. Deeso knew the rumors, but now she would have the source. Zulag gave a look at Cikya who agreed, Zulag was to serve as the mouthpiece where Cikya's gestures would fail to tell the story. Zulag sat down and folded his legs.

"Get comfortable. It's a long one."

Two years prior to their current adventures, Cikya served as Zulag's mentor. They knew of each other before, but Cikya was picked by Ronkalk out of the many priests to be Zulag's personal teacher. The older priests offered their services to Ronkalk, but he had a specific vision for Zulag, and found someone closer in age to connect with him easier. While Zulag shadowed Ronkalk often, he had many duties of his own that needed to be performed. Cikya's role was to serve as the bridge for Zulag to convene with his spirituality, an important element Ronkalk considered was necessary for any successor. Hunting and fighting were important tasks, but these were things that Ronkalk asked of anyone. Ronkalk made it a priority for Zulag to be in touch with his emotions and encouraged vulnerability as these were part of the requirements to make a rational leader.

Cikya lounged about in the dirt as she sent Zulag on an errand to retrieve some animal teeth some time ago. Her sessions with Zulag were often on the intersection of the long roads between The Broken Bone camps, so these were well traveled areas that kept an open line of communication. There were wide open spaces where Zulag could hear all sounds of the forest as he attempted to contact the spirits. Zulag's frame came into view and clutched a small object in his hands as he looked to see Cikya.

"You're really keeping yourself busy aren't you." Zulag greeted Cikya. She gave a half-smile to Zulag as she tapped the ground for him to sit.

Cikya moved over slightly and folded her legs for him to sit directly in front of her. Cikya was overjoyed with her job, mentoring was the easiest thing she's ever had to do. Zulag touched the ground as he copied her movements and the two sat across from one another. Cikya looked down at Zulag's hand and beckoned him to open it.

"You found all the teeth I requested? [42]" Cikya asked, as Zulag unveiled a small bag.

It came with an assortment of animal teeth that fell to the soil below. Zulag didn't understand the intricate natures regarding the priesthood, but he respected their authority and influence far more than his uncle did. He made sure to keep a steady count of the various creatures on Cikya's list, some much more difficult than others.

"Yes, do the reading. I've been waiting for some time." He answered, as he crossed his legs to sit down and watch her go. Cikya rubbed her stomach as Zulag heard it. His own also felt quite small. The Broken Bone was in hard times with two bad months of foraging gone awry. Tensions were high with the other bands that threatened to dissolve their union had Ronkalk not fixed things soon. The pressure weighed to a large degree on he and Zulag's minds.

"There hasn't been much to eat. So, finding the teeth was difficult." He added on.

Cikya nodded as her hands felt the texture of the various teeth. There was an assortment of predator and prey species that Cikya could call upon. Her goal as instructed by Ronkalk was to give Zulag a vision into the future, the perspective of his life path. For any leader of The Broken Bone this was important. Ronkalk's vision from the priesthood is what inspired him to unite the leadership under The Painted Hand to begin with. What would be Zulag's destiny?

Although Zulag preferred to meet his teacher in a more secluded location, it was often that other members of The Broken Bone would stop by to chat. At the age of twenty-three and a responsible adult, Cikya was already popular without her priestess status being counted for. Cikya was considered beautiful by all as she was approached by men and the occasional woman through their travels. She spurned them all in any serious capacity for she enjoyed her power far more but had fun where she could. Her voice was distinct and could pick up a good tune. She spent most of her time on charms and jewelry making, some for her occupation and others for enjoyment. She gave a small wink to a few admirers who practically swooned over her as she flicked her hair. Cikya loved the attention as she gave them a bit of hope only for them to be hopelessly crushed later. Zulag groaned in annoyance at the onlookers and threw a rock in the distance.

---

[42] Divination with the use of animal bones is a long-held practice by many cultures around the world, and it's no surprise here that the priests of The Broken Bone use this as well!

"She's a priest! Get over yourselves." Zulag warned the other men who left with some anguish on their faces. He turned his attention back to Cikya who huffed her nose as she snatched the bag from him.

"Alright. Let's see what we have. I like this, this is good." Cikya said to herself as Zulag watched with a raised eyebrow. Cikya held up a finger to the impatient Zulag as he attempted to reserve himself. Cikya scooped up the array of teeth and rotated them in her hands. She closed her eyes and dropped the teeth to the ground. She gave the spread time to settle as she waited for the ideal time. Cikya's eyes tracked the movement of the sun that would provide context for her interpretations.

"These teeth are arranged like so, here represents stability. You will have a strong core with you. As there are multiple teeth, this is to represent your council. You will not lead like your uncle does, but in your own way." Cikya explained as she aligned them in a way that caused Zulag to shake his head as she manipulated them.

Zulag stayed silent as he evaluated Ronkalk's performance as of late. The swamps weren't desirable past all the bugs and diseases. The region they picked was barren and supplies were incredibly low. Zulag weighed the impact of Ronkalk's desires and felt going his own path was a goal worth pursuing.

"And what else?" Zulag questioned as he stirred in position.

Cikya continued to look at the teeth. This time, Cikya took great care to make sure the rays of the sun were present over the bones. She lifted them slowly and analyzed the cracks in the bone. She ran her finger down them and felt the grooves left behind. Bone reading was Cikya's specialty, so she took great care at this compared to anything else. Teeth compared to other bones were especially important as they could be used to infer the health of the recipient for the reading.

"Well, there is excitement to be had. Something will inspire you to act in the weeks to come. There will be a strong test of your will but by the end you will be honored in the way of our people." She added on, as she saw Zulag's cheerful reaction. It's what he had been anticipating for some time, some good news.

"Is there anything else I should know!?" Zulag asked with impatience as his mind raced.

"Well, since we're here." She said leaning into him.

She burped in his ear and gave a small laugh as Zulag glared at her. Although he was angry for a short moment, it gradually vanished as he also laughed. While some of the other priests disagreed with his decision, Ronkalk was steadfast in his choice to pick Cikya. On occasion he would eavesdrop and observe Zulag's progress with none the wiser. Ronkalk knew that stuffy teachings wouldn't reach through to him and his nephew would be no different. Cikya held enough experience in her endeavors to take on a student with ease.

"I would avoid Poulji of any kind until I hear again. There is a spirit that takes its worldly form and will bring demise to us if we are not careful. I am unsure how to root it out, so until I receive a new vision, stay sharp." Cikya warned with a serious tone in her voice.

"Is there anything that troubles you, Zulag? You seemed to be in thought when I brought up Ronkalk earlier." She noted, as she saw him tense up. Zulag took a small breath, although he tried to remain calm, his body betrayed him.

"Yes actually. I haven't agreed with many of his decisions lately, and my aunt and he are thinking of having a child. It confuses me, a child at their age. They also want me to find someone within the band. You see my problem. Ronkalk tells me that it's necessary to secure my legitimacy for the other members." Zulag stated with a worried expression.

"Well, what's the problem? There's many to pick from." Cikya asked, placing her head on her fist. She looked up at Zulag and studied his appearance, he bothered to keep in track with his hygiene which was already a step above many.

"I have no options, Cikya. I appreciate my devoted followers, but there is no challenge in that. They all just want to access my uncle through me." Zulag huffed in annoyance.

Devoted followers...? Oh, he means the initiates. I shouldn't tell him they're supposed to follow him around. Cikya thought with a short laugh as Zulag narrowed his eyes at her expression.

"We have four bands to pick from and you aren't related to anyone other than your uncle. Though, let's make things interesting. If not local, how about a Wanderer?" Cikya suggested, mostly to stir the pot as she could already tell his reaction before he spoke.

"Taking in Wanderers is the worst thing my uncle has ever done. We ended up getting Sadal and her shadow, not to mention a few that are just entirely dead weight. Now we suffer from too many mouths to feed." Zulag laughed.

Cikya raised an eyebrow in interest as she heard Sadal's name. For what she knew about Sadal, she knew that she and Zulag were the same rank, and she was certainly capable. Sadal was a promising warrior from the day she arrived and could have any partner she wanted but entertained the whims of a humble weaver. Her choice intrigued Cikya and had to get Zulag's perspective on the matter. She pressed further in wondering his reasoning.

"Sadal has the ego of a boulder-" Zulag explained before he got cut off by Cikya.

"Sadal really is an odd one, isn't she? Out of any in the village, she picks some boring weaver. Nurzall? Nurzan, his eyes are soulless. That man doesn't love her. I just know it." Cikya protested as her eyes met Zulag's. Zulag adjusted his posture as he wondered what Cikya was alluding to. Zulag was opposed to Sadal in every sense of the word. Their rivalry as Master Hunters started when both were sixteen years old and Zulag felt he needed to overachieve to keep Ronkalk's good graces.

"He pleaded with Ronkalk to give his blessing as if that would help. She can do whatever she wants. I think they're perfect for each other in my opinion. A match so terrible made from two miserable people, it'll clip her wings and she can come down to the soil like the rest of us. I tried hunting with him one time, just to see how he works, and he immediately walked in the other direction once we found the kill. He can't commit to anything, let alone a relationship. Why do we keep him around?" Zulag ridiculed as he lifted his head in disdain.

"Hey, if you don't want her, she's mine then. Sadal, that's a woman after my affection." Cikya moaned as Zulag carried a look of disgust.

"Cikya, she doesn't bathe. Are you really that desperate?" Zulag said with a cough.

"All the better. I want to smell her with the blood of the enemy on her bare shoulders. She doesn't have to say a word about the hunt. Her hair is immaculate, her body, oh-her body! Her eyes are brown as soil and her voice is a warm flame. Zulag, she's powerful and I want her. You must understand where I'm coming from. There are good men out there that I've entertained, but have you seen them here? Dreadfully boring, but she's a challenge. A woman like Sadal needs to be loved with care like a flower. My wisdom is beyond your years, I'll be waiting when that stick hut of a pairing blows in the wind. Give it time." Cikya said with a sly grin as Zulag raised his hands in defeat.

"As I was saying, Deeso has the personality of a block of wood. You may ask, what about Bheyra? Well, she just frightens me. Not suitable for what I want." Zulag mentioned as Cikya kept a count on her hands. Cikya folded her arms and darted her head to the side as she investigated Zulag's expression.

"Don't give me that look, I am aware the priesthood is not allowed. They have to leave it." Zulag scoffed at Cikya.

"Well, your aunt taught Ronkalk and look what happened after..." Cikya said with a grin that unnerved Zulag to the core. She laughed as he could see him squirm in his stance.

"Relax, I like the quiet ones. You certainly can talk your ear off. You also need to fix your clothing when you can." Cikya said as she pointed to a rip in Zulag's grass skirt.

He looked down and sighed in annoyance as he was waiting for the chance to find some fur coverings for his legs. All the fur at this time was used for bedding. He ignored the urge to scratch mosquito bites that piled up on his lower legs. He forgot to apply balm to his legs, and it was a decision he regretted. Cikya looked up to see the movement of the shadows in the foliage above them. She saw that as their reading and gossip of the day was finished, Zulag needed to attend to his regular duties. The two lowered their heads in respect to one another as they stood up as one. Cikya dismissed Zulag to go about the rest of his day as she saw a figure not too far from them previously emerge from the covering of a nearby tree. He peered his head prior to their initial discussion but respected the confidentiality of a spiritual reading. On his face was white face paint, this man was of higher status. Cikya turned to address him and lowered her head in respect.

The highest of the priests in The Broken Bone and some other groups of Thunderfeet wore red face paint, while white, green, yellow, and those without paint made the other rankings. Cikya earned her keep for some time, enjoying the benefits that having green pigment could offer. Cikya became part of the priest order when she was seventeen and at twenty-three years old, she was a solid green rank. If Zulag were to be a successful leader as many hoped, there was conversation for her to reach white ranking someday. For now, though, she could order the yellow initiates and the curious around to do her errands while she worked on her own endeavors. It was a good system she hoped to exploit for all it was worth.

"I know you're here." Cikya said, as she saw another priest come forward with a small stone in his hand.

"I kept myself hidden as is customary, but I have things that need to be said." The man's voice said.

Although Cikya had been an accomplished priestess, she was still very much learning, like that of her pupil. She opened her arm out, inviting her superior to sit with her. He took Zulag's former place but on his face was an expression of disappointment.

"You hid a portion of the reading, Cikya. You can't coddle the man anymore. He is eighteen and has been a man for some time. Does he know the truth?" He asked, his fingers touching his bare chin.

"The truth? You mean that his life will come to ruin because the wind went another way? Zulag is capable of any challenge thrown in front of him. I've seen it, he is gifted and while he is arrogant, he respects our ways and heeds my wisdom." Cikya argued in good faith for Zulag who couldn't defend himself.

"And of his father?" The priest asked as he looked behind him to ensure secrecy.

"Ronkalk told me not to say anything." Cikya said, her eyes looking towards the ground.

"I'm sure Ronkalk has a different opinion of the matter. You are his teacher, not his sister." The man said as his tone lowered in severity.

"Zulag would have known by now if that wasn't the case, no?" She said, giving a fake grin to her superior.

He stewed his foot in the dirt, as Ronkalk's rage was the last thing they needed before the large ceremony would take place. Cikya and the rest of the priesthood worked extensively to gather materials despite recent hardships. It was in the planning stages for a few weeks and would involve the other leaders of The Broken Bone and their associates' bringing representatives with them to meet Ronkalk. Zulag's stress to Cikya on his lack of a suitable partner was his fear of being paired off against his will to secure an alliance. The priesthood was under a lot of pressure trying to memorize the dances for another band to be entertained.

"Speaking of Ronkalk...There is another matter to discuss. He has found out about your raid on the food supplies. It honestly should be of little concern; priests are a special group, and we require more to be able to do our work. It will blow over like all things do for us." The man continued onward. Cikya felt relieved at the news.

Cikya's affairs were not just of concern to the priesthood that she belonged to, but also Ronkalk. Although she assumed her deception was well hidden, this was not the case. To stay from starving, Cikya left in the middle of the night and took scraps of food from the allied bands of The Broken Bone. Her plan seemed to be a solid approach, but hard times were on everyone. Cikya was caught and identified by her green colored face paint, something in hindsight she realized she had been so foolish to not remove. It was only a matter of time before there was retribution to be had. Cikya assumed that her rank would give her a light punishment or some extra duties that she already was responsible for but there were other ideas.

The two ended their discussion and left their separate ways as they went back to the camp. She took a moment to survey her surroundings. People were dejected and tired, and barely scraped by to survive much like herself. From an outside perspective, Cikya was incredibly selfish in her endeavors, but the priests were revered and given such priority first so they could maintain balance within the spiritual aspect of life that guided them forward. With her, they could at least have some motivation to keep going. Not wanting to see this any longer, she turned in the direction of her home. Cikya had particularly interesting circumstances in her life. As an only child, she was fortunate enough to have both of her parents still living. Cikya lived alone however as she was distant from her mother who wanted nothing to do with her after she joined the priesthood. Her father was part of a hunting team for a different band of The Broken Bone and so the two didn't interact often.

She approached her home with much relief as she had a busy day. The Thunderfoot home of the swamps was much like that of The Aligned, with a rounded base that formed the appearance of a tent. Cikya built her home to compensate for the unusually soft terrain. The structure was held up with carved stakes pressed in the ground that were bound together with fibers and rope made from string. In colder areas, these were built with only furs, but in the swamps, they used a mixture of packed fibers and animal fur as the covering. Resources were hardly as generous as the open, so whatever could serve their function would do nicely. Cikya displayed some of her charms in the front of her home. She entered a quiet space and laid down on a bed made of leaves to rest for a few hours.

As Cikya slept, two men stood outside the tent and clapped loudly to startle her awake. One was Zulag and the other was a man she hadn't seen before. She put her head out ready to yell in annoyance, but her expression changed as she saw Zulag with an unusually solemn face. She wondered if something happened to him after she did the reading for him.

"Ronkalk wishes to speak with you." Zulag said as he and his associate guided Cikya.

Cikya remained undeterred but second-guessed herself as she moved forward. Zulag knew that Cikya had questions, but he ignored them all as he led her to a further section out in the swamps. Cikya recognized the route as this was a training area where the young and new recruits would be drilled. Though instead of the bustle and sound of productive students, some members of the priesthood, the representative leaders of the other bands and lastly Ronkalk were present.

"Zulag, why all the secrecy?" Cikya asked, only for her question to be answered in just a moment.

Zulag and Cikya walked in on a conversation between Ronkalk and the head priest for the proceedings, his white face paint visible from far away. There was a red priest among their ranks who made no sound as he watched patiently. Cikya felt a rush of pure fear come on her as a red priest rarely made their entrance to The Broken Bone or associated with the lower ranks.

"Ronkalk, she is a priest! Have you no honor?" The priest with white-face paint said with a frantic tone of voice.

"I have more honor in one finger than you have in your entire body. Cikya didn't steal from me. She stole from another leader. I will not look weak, and I must save face for this to work. I have my role, and you have yours." Ronkalk proclaimed as he approached the priest and pressed his body onto him.

The head priest lowered his head down now, hoping to save some face while he turned to the rest who looked dismayed at the state of Cikya. Zulag broke away from her as the man accompanying them both and prompted Cikya to walk over to the other priests. They embraced her with a tight hug while she squirmed wondering what was going on. Zulag approached Ronkalk and looked into his eyes with a heavy amount of contempt for his uncle's actions. Zulag already had some questions regarding Ronkalk's decisions as of late, and this was the tip of the iceberg as far as he was concerned. Ronkalk and Zulag had differing opinions of the priesthood's importance that often led them to clash in discussions, but here Zulag could only take orders. Ronkalk prioritized general spirituality over the structure of the priesthood while Zulag adhered to the special hierarchy. Zulag recognized the other three leaders of the allied bands who judged the scene with an almost surgical position at what was to unfold before them.

"I did as you asked. She's here." Zulag stated to him.

Ronkalk gave Zulag a hearty pat on the back and an understanding nod. He decided to go further than he originally asked of his nephew. Ronkalk felt it was necessary to give Zulag a test to see how much he truly learned. He unsheathed a knife from inside his grass covering and gently handed it to Zulag. Zulag's face was filled with anguish.

"Zulag. I want you to do this. I trust you and as my successor, there are things that we must do. The burden of leadership is heavy and requires that consequences be fulfilled for foul action. Will you prove this to me?" Ronkalk asked calmly. Zulag knew the answer that his uncle was expecting, but he chose to ignore this instead.

"No!" Zulag said strictly, causing Ronkalk to slap Zulag.

He had never been hit before even for much more outrageous outbursts, but he had enough social awareness to know the other chieftains were watching. Zulag's face reddened with the impact that reverberated throughout the discussions being had. He composed himself to not embarrass Ronkalk any further but refused to partake in Cikya's punishment. It was beyond him to do such a thing.

Ronkalk's eyes were red as he spoke. It was clear he didn't want to do this, but given the circumstances behind what's happened, it all would fall apart if he were to falter now. The priests who had embraced Cikya so passionately before were now prompted by the authoritative glare of Ronkalk to move forward. The pigments dripped to the soil below as their faces were filled with sorrow for their companion. Tears filled their eyes, and their voices hung low. The red priest's pigment remained as he continued to observe from afar. Cikya let out an impassioned whimper as she was dragged against her will forward. Her respect for Ronkalk, which was fanatically high, came crashing down. She was too fraught with shock to let out a scream or even resist. Her eyes peered over to the knife in hand, and she felt great sorrow. She was to be slaughtered for something that she'd seen as trivial, but Ronkalk always had a reason for what he did.

"I will do it myself then. You will watch." He said to Zulag, as he snatched the knife from him. Ronkalk stood solemnly as the priests that dragged her, weighed her down to the point where she couldn't bother to kick.

"Cikya. You are being punished for stealing Stobai's food. This food would have gone to children, to our sick, to our elderly in the bad hunting season." Ronkalk explained, his voice steady through the process.

"Ronkalk, you can't be serious..." Cikya pleaded, as she felt her arms and legs weighed down by her fellow priests.

She had enough sense to not embarrass Ronkalk further by resisting, but all the same she felt an utter sense of dread and terror upon her. Close by were the other respective heads of the band that The Broken Bone consisted of. Cikya locked eyes with the three, two men and a woman who watched to see how Cikya approached death. Ronkalk closed his eyes and breathed through his nose as he grasped the knife in his right hand. Cikya recognized the knife as one of Zulag's that they made together a week prior. Everything with Ronkalk was planned down to the last detail. She always hated that about him. He pressed down decisively, with the flesh ripping from the very sinews and sliced her throat clean across, as Cikya released a bloodcurdling scream that deafened those closest to her. Blood fell out of her in volume as she flailed involuntarily while Zulag watched in horror. He never felt lower than today. Cikya didn't bother calling out for Zulag, she knew that nothing could be done with him, and she feared they would both share the same fate. Cikya felt as if she were a slain deer, as the blood pooled out and she lost consciousness. Her screaming had shut off all at once. In the last moments before she fell through, she tried to call out something, but she was unable to. Cikya was now mute, and she realized this as nothing came out. In the process of slicing her throat, Ronkalk paralyzed her vocal cords, and she was now trapped in her own mind.

With the damage done, Ronkalk threw the knife to the ground and turned around to face his partners within The Broken Bone who were satisfied with the display seen. The three nodded with blood given, but Ronkalk wasn't finished. He dismissed Zulag, while letting the priests handle Cikya's body as was tradition for the deceased. Zulag refused as he walked some distance away to eavesdrop on Ronkalk. Zulag needed to know what happened to bring Cikya this way. The red priest walked to the scene to get a closer glance at Cikya's fate. The red priest studied her wounds and made a small hum with his mouth. While the lesser priests were distraught, opportunity struck the mysterious figure who looked on her.

"Stobai. Stay." Ronkalk ordered, as the two men who led the other bands began their trek home.

She waited as instructed, and as the area emptied, it was just Ronkalk and Stobai. Stobai was a woman who was a few years younger than Ronkalk but maintained a commanding presence as leader of her respective band. She had dark brown skin and matched his height. The sides of her hair were cut short while she had two large braids that went down her shoulders. She wore a freshly processed binturong pelt that glistened in the light. She looked at him with some confusion as everything had gone as expected. Zulag watched behind a tree as he remained hidden. He kept his breathing completely still as he took in every word of their discussion.

"Is this enough for you? Do you want the blood of my nephew as well?" Ronkalk asked, his hands now drenched with Cikya's blood.

Stobai shook her head, unsure of which direction to nod. She held a slight ring of anxiety course through her as Ronkalk's words saddled upon her like a heavy weight. Although the four bands grouped together, Ronkalk was ultimately the one who was the de facto leader of the group. It was Stobai's band that Cikya had stolen from, and so the blood spilled was the debt paid in full to her. Ronkalk stared at her as Stobai made her way back to her camp as well. She didn't answer Ronkalk's question because she felt any answer wouldn't solve the problem at hand. This was a wise decision.

Zulag heard enough and made his way to his family's tent. His eyes were filled with tears as he mourned the unjust death of his teacher and friend until he tired himself out. Unknown to Ronkalk and Zulag, Cikya didn't pass on as they expected. The red priest extended his shriveled arm to signal to the others what was to be done. The priests in all their incredible odds gave blessings to Cikya as they carried her away. Rather than bury her in the pits, they quickly went to work in trying to deal with the wound. It was a split-second decision but one that proved to be quite clever. Ronkalk left such a clean cut that it was simple enough to pad the gushing blood and apply what they could to save her. A bowl of water was thrown on her to clean the wound and what they managed was wrapping animal skins around as a bandage to stem the flow. In some cases, crushed berries could also serve to slow blood flow, but Cikya was unable to eat. Cikya was a valued member of their community and the priests looked out for their own, regardless of how dire times were. She was kept far away from the main camp and out of the reach of Ronkalk for the time being. It took a lot of time but four days later, she arose anew and at the bottom of her feet was a crown made of bones. The chance at redemption and a new life began.

Deeso could only feel numb as she heard Zulag's conclusion of what happened. He spoke with such genuineness in his voice it was unbelievable to witness. She disagreed with Cikya's punishment when she heard about it, but to understand the logistics behind it was truly stunning. She stared at the soil in thought only for her concentration to be broken by Zulag.

"Pass me some hotspark would you? I need to make a fire." Zulag said as he held out his hand.

Building Bridges

Ozul was slumped in the corner, with his head in his arms and a pile of furs. He was exhausted having worked through the night on rope and tools for the others, but if one saw his eyes, they were stained with tears. He spent some time crying as he missed his father. While death was an inevitability accepted by all groups, Forest Seekers believed in a form of reincarnation. Just like the villages they constructed, where the soul would rest, this also came in the form of animals in their environment. Not all animals were seen equally, for there were plenty of game to be hunted and tools made from them. Dangerous animals like the tiger though were considered half-animal and half-wretched human souls who deviated from The Vow and lived a life of evil towards others. While not pleasant, defending oneself against these creatures was understood as restoring balance. The travels of battle against the various people that Deeso and the others took issue with weighed heavy on Ozul's mind. While he learned to accept his current company, Ozul was beside himself accepting the cost of blood that came with such things in the forest.

Ozul didn't directly claim any life yet, but he knew that the time would come eventually to defend himself. He took The Vow as seriously as any other Forest Seeker. Throughout the night once he addressed the demands of Deeso, he worked on a project of his own. Ozul searched for the right material to make a blowgun, the signature weapon of his people. The rejects were gathered around him in bits and pieces. In respect to the forest, most of his blowgun designs were constructed from deceased trees and the wood was not ideal. He knew he needed to find a good patch of bamboo which was harder to find than one realized. Deeso was usually the only one to announce her leaving while the others tended to just vanish and reappear. Ozul saw his opportunity to take his leave as the three were discussing tales of their homeland he cared little about.

He borrowed one of Zulag's knives as a tool for his own devices, while he brought some spare rope and a bag for anything he hoped to scavenge along the way. Deeso's soft spoken voice vanished quicker than Zulag's until the forest reclaimed these sounds. His eyes were poised to find the presence of bamboo which often clumped together past the regular undergrowth. He walked around for some time, with his head on a swivel to make sure he wasn't being followed as he grasped the knife. In earlier days, Ozul wouldn't have bothered grabbing anything for combat, but he saw the use of a deterrent. Ozul heard a large cracking sound as he looked around in confusion. He looked above him, and he saw a man poised with a spear as he gripped the branch.

"Why are you up there? The Panmarat would work better without you on it." Ozul questioned. He rolled his eyes, seeing as this was another Thunderfoot who sought to use the trees for their own aims. He was grateful this one didn't start a forest fire.

"This is a trail for forest Yaan, don't you understand? I will wait hours for a prime meal." The man said as he scratched his eye.

"You want to...kill a Yaan. From up there with that tiny spear? [43]" Ozul asked, his voice skeptical of the man.

The man grunted, quickly placing his hand against the trunk as he almost slipped. Ozul saw his camouflage and was impressed with the amount of thought put into it. The man wore an assortment of leaves and green pigment to disguise himself. Ozul couldn't help but smirk at the foolish man's antics. He was aware of what a forest elephant could do, depending on the one he just happened to find.

"You look like someone who gets left behind. I saw some of your kind due north of here. Probably left about twenty minutes ago. You can probably catch them if you hurry. Come back this way and you'll see my glorious bounty!" The man said to Ozul as he shook his head.

Ozul at first dismissed the man's words, but the prospect of going north sounded interesting. It was possible he could find others of his kind looking for bamboo as well, where safety in numbers is always a good thing. Ozul studied the winding paths and decided to go for it. Ozul stayed low to the ground as he wanted to be sure that his profile was low. The man's words were correct as he could see the outline of footprints in the softer mud. They were slightly larger than his own, which indicated these were children. Ozul felt slight hesitation in himself as he remembered plenty of times where he was bullied for just being different. He came to find the sound of light-hearted laughter. It was a big group, about six kids in all that were foraging for various supplies.

Ozul peeked his head out of a bush and spied on a few of them. His first observation was of a burly teenager who carried a large amount of wood in his hands. Trailing him was a girl about his age, her focus entirely on her companion. In her bag though were cut bamboo shoots. He knew that he was close. He gave himself a deep breath and slowly walked over and signaled his presence to the other group. He hadn't realized he carried Zulag's knife in his hands as he did so. One of the other Forest Seeker kids looked at him and pointed.

"Wow! That could strip a Tole clean! Did you make that?" He asked, causing the others to look at Ozul.

"My name is Ozul. I took the blade from a Thunderfoot, and no one is the wiser. It cuts well, do you want to hold it?" Ozul asked as he gently offered the blade in his hand. Ozul was nervous but saw the look of impressed faces of the others. The group didn't need to know the details, just that he stole the knife from a Thunderfoot, which was technically correct.

Ozul's small tale got the children talking among themselves as the entrant of Thunderfeet into their lands was a hot topic. At least two of the other kids were aware of Eshe and her growing crusade against the Thunderfeet. Their opinions were mixed, they hadn't experienced them personally but knew other people who had their complaints.

---

[43] Believe it or not, climbing a tree and waiting to stab an elephant along their designated trails is a strategy seen by the Bashimunina of Zambia. While bizarre to Ozul, the idea would be to stab the elephant directly in the head or shoulders with minimal injury.

These were adults though who seemed to not value the child viewpoint as much. With Ozul though, they could get the truth.

"So, Ozul. I want to know about those Thunderfeet you have traveled and seen." The girl with the bamboo shoots said.

"Are they intelligent?" Another one of the Forest Seeker children asked.

Ozul wasn't used to such questioning, let alone positive interaction but he took it in stride. Rarely did he get to say how he truly felt about things. He looked at the curious kids before him and gave a nod. Ozul gave it a moment and disagreed with the idea. He held in a chuckle as he looked at the brown eyes of the others that waited for his response.

"No, not really." Ozul said with a smug grin.

"The woman named Eshe visited a village that my friend is from. People say things but the truth must be known. I heard she says that Thunderfeet can do magic. Is this true?" The girl replied to him as she kept her eyes trained on him.

"I have seen a priest. She does things with her hands and sometimes it works. I am not an expert though, Thunderfeet seem to have different spirits than we do." Ozul explained further as the other kids exchanged responses with one another.

"The blade is impressive, but do you not have a blowgun?" The wood carrying teenager asked. Ozul frowned and nodded his head at his question. Ozul was looking for bamboo to begin with, but his initial searches ran short.

"I was hoping to find some Augmarat to use. I know this is a big ask, but may I take some?" Ozul requested.

As it stood, the bamboo patches seemed to be in this group's foraging range, it was considered bad form for outsiders to use it without permission from the village. These were all measures the Forest Seekers took to maintain balance in the environment. The kids looked among themselves while Ozul sat back in anticipation. He knew it wasn't likely he'd get the answer he was looking for, but he was quite surprised at their response.

"Normally, we would not do this, but you have told us more about the Thunderfeet than any of our adults. Come with us, and you may take some for yourself and do repairs for later." The wood-carrying teen commented to Ozul.

Ozul walked accompanied by the other Forest Seeker children who sighted out the bamboo growth. He walked with respect, but the excitement on his face was too difficult to conceal. He moved his hand down the bamboo stalks feeling carefully for the right ones until he chopped down the base using his knife to do so. He decided to take three stalks for himself, one for the first try, a second in case he made a mistake, and a third for repairs. Once he finished gathering the large stalks, he now began the process of chopping them and was fortunate enough to receive a helping hand or two in the process. Ozul was surprised how much cooperation truly made things easier. Ozul decided to stay for a little longer as they exchanged stories and he was brought up to date on the latest village gossip, not that any of it ultimately mattered to him. It just felt good to interact with his own kind that didn't immediately consider him a traitor for working with Deeso and the others, or bullied him outright. As the day started to wane, Ozul gave his farewell to the nice group and hoped he'd run across them again sometime. Ozul had a fantastic memory as he could trace back his steps quite easily. He couldn't help but laugh as the man was still on top of the banyan tree with his spear. He looked noticeably more exhausted but made a valiant effort to stay put.

"Still up there?" Ozul asked, as he heard a groggy sound from the man.

"Oh, it's you. Did I miss the Yaan!?" He said with some anger in his voice. Ozul wasn't sure whether to lie to the man or not, but he decided to take some pity on this one.

"No, you still have plenty of time." Ozul said as he made his way back home, with the path closing off behind him.

Deeso, in the far distance, lifted her axe as a sign of warning against the potential trespasser only to find that it was Ozul who jumped up to make himself more visible. The last thing he wanted to do was accidentally get mistaken for someone else. Cikya gave a gentle wave to Ozul as he returned safely. Zulag said nothing as he was embroiled in an argument with Deeso.

"Where have you been? I need more Jaat rope for tomorrow. Zulag spent it all on the last hunt." Deeso asked him as her tone grew impatient.

"Oh, of all the-Ozul, don't listen to her. Deeso's lying out of her teeth. She's the one who thought lassoing a hog was a good idea." Zulag scoffed, himself quite wiped out from the day's events.

Ozul nodded to Deeso's words and knew that he would be working hard through the night once again. Now that he had secured his bamboo however, the time would come to work on what he valued the most. Not all days were good, but some good could come out of the day.

All It Takes Is One

The seeds of Kag, Dran, and Bani's plan matured before their very eyes. Before they could go further, they needed to attack the heart of Tur's operation. The Council's demands for furs spearheaded by Tur were causing all sorts of logistical problems. Dran and Bani walked through the camp and cited all the problems that broke down because of Tur's gross mismanagement. There were far too many to think of in one sitting but held them as ammunition for further questions. Kag was at his wits end as the sick needed bone marrow to assist their healing process. Meat from the Hunting Team was best suited for his needs on the scale that people could get injured. Feeding a group as large as The Elders required the utmost strategy and given their choice to take in the population of Neck-Shell children this became incredibly difficult.

It's often said that people are three days away from anarchy and for The Elders, this is something Kag wanted to avoid at all costs. Kag originally visited the Hunting Team a few months ago and they complied in some fashion. Kag noticed though a larger than usual influx of luxury furs that once again endangered their band's integrity. Kag mobilized Dran and Bani to join him as they confronted Vut on the disparity. The three made their presence known and stomped their feet on the ground loudly. They stood in front of Vut's tent as they waited for him to come out. Vut, like many of the Hunting Team, had to sleep to build up the energy again for two big hunts a day. He was woken awake by their noise. Vut noticed a faint shadow appear out of his tent as he inquired about what it could be. Vut gave a sigh as he opened the flap to find the troublesome trio before him.

"Why are you three here now?" Vut asked, his exhaustion evident on his face. Bani felt slightly bad seeing the man's expression.

It was well established the three were trying to stir up trouble among the ranks. Vut didn't agree with their methods, but he noticed The Council's demands were becoming unreasonable for different branches of their band and somebody had to do something. Vut enjoyed the stability of his job and found it hard to fight against the rising tide and was firmly in the middle. It was one thing to find the occasional luxury fur here and there at The Council's request and he felt great honor doing it, but the group were more suited to hunting deer than they were at killing leopards.

"Kag talked with you earlier Vut. Kag said to stop hunting for furs and hunt for meat. We require food, why do you go against the wishes of The Council?" Kag asked with an irritated tone.

"Tur said otherwise. Vut has good job that Vut enjoys doing. People depend on Vut for the things they need, furs are one of these. Kag challenges this by putting everyone else against Tur. Why should Vut and Hunting Team listen to you?" Vut questioned.

Kag knew a wind of resistance would come as he had to explain his positions well. Kag now felt bold enough to openly challenge Tur's claim to leadership but knew he needed to angle it well. Due to the nature of his work, Kag was in a more intimate setting with Tur and noticed a pattern of behaviors that seemed unusual. At first, Kag thought nothing of it, but even some basic tasks started to cause him issues.

"What is last thing Tur ordered to you to kill? Weypeu? Do you feel your team is ready for such a challenge? Of course not, you have those still learning." Kag retorted.

Vut grumbled, he wasn't particularly excited about scoping out a tiger's den to grab the furs at Tur's request. He understood the importance of the fur economy as much as anyone else, however. He saw scouts leave to go and contact other bands deeper into the jungles for trade. As The Elders failed to recover their relationship with The Jagged Bark, Vut assumed the furs were used to rebuild their established relationship.

"Where do you think furs go Vut?" Dran asked with a sincere tone of voice.

"To trade, to work, whatever else they are needed for. Vut cares little for it, Vut has a job to do." Vut said as he raised his hand.

"They hoard them in The Council tent. There is a pile of wrapped furs that are made into clothing by some of your team, but they never leave camp." Bani noted as she studied Vut's face.

"Ignore anything Tur orders. We will starve if you do not hunt food!" Kag said, as he gave Vut a strong pat on the back.

Vut glared at Kag as he bit his tongue. Dran raised an eyebrow as she waited for Vut to make his decision. His eyes looked to the direction of The Council's tent and then back at the others as he weighed his decision. Tur's and by extension the rest of The Council's authority was law above Kag as he was the newest member. Vut also felt that Kag's increased interest in wanting to oust Tur was to boost his own credibility and try to scrounge to the top like the others.

"Vut sees your ambition Kag and does not agree. Tur brought you into the fold and this is how he should be treated?" Vut remarked.

"This is not personal matter Vut. Kag is healer and Tur is not sound of mind anymore. Kag can prove it to you." Kag mentioned. While his expression was neutral, Kag figured he could use his position and knowledge of medicine to secure Vut's loyalty in this manner.

"Tur said The Council will be speaking soon. Join us." Dran ordered gruffly as Vut relented.

Vut valued the time he had to sleep with the rigorous demands of their hunting schedule but joined the trio as they headed to the village center. Activity bustled with people stopping their tasks to prepare for the speech. Tur's speeches were more frequent as he tried to suppress any resentment gathered from their antics. The teams were usually kept separate with their duties but one by one started to bridge their concerns were administrative instead of individual. A few adults were already present and excited for a break as impromptu speeches rarely came by. Skepticism lay heavy on his face, but he was willing to at least hear them out. If Kag was proven wrong, Vut wouldn't stand in his way, but he wouldn't have his support either.

Tur and the rest of The Council arrived in plain clothes. To some of The Elders they were nearly unrecognizable without their pigments and ceremonial garb. Tur and Aab remained the most decorated of The Council as they both shared leopard print clothing. Aab waved to the growing crowd with a slow rise of her hand until she paused all at once. The purpose of this meeting was a simple checklist of achievements they worked to accomplish and to uplift the workers. Tur grasped his walking stick and stood proudly as he spoke to the others.

"Workers of The Elders, we have come together once more. Tur has seen great works from you all. We have beat back Neck-Shells and taught the next generation how to live as one of our own. This is a good day. Tur has sent scouts to build connections with other bands. Tur and The Council ask all of you to work together as one and complete our goal. We want to bring peace to our land." Tur opened as his eyes drifted through the crowd.

Vut remained with his arms folded as Tur continued to speak. Nothing seemed out of the ordinary and Kag's words seemed to be simple slander. Vut held this position until he heard the next words to come out of Tur's mouth.

"Tur h-h-h..asd...has..." Tur stated with pride in his voice. Tur quickly held his hand to his forehead and felt a hazy fog come over his vision. He took a deep breath and oriented himself back to the attention of the others. Tur continued to speak and outline the layers of his plan with the rest of The Council.

Tur spoke with the utmost authority in his mind, but the rest of The Elders could only sit in silence. The air was uncomfortable and the adults that observed felt claustrophobic as they watched Tur's words slur on themselves. A small bit of drool exited Tur's mouth and slipped down his face as he continued to speak without noticing in the slightest. The Council seemed unaffected, but Kag wondered how much they were concerned about his condition. Kag reported to both Dran and Bani that Aab was more suited for some of the longer tasks done outside their knowledge. Dran and Bani shared a look of surprise as they weren't aware of just how bad this was. Kag kept a still composure as he knew this was happening already behind the scenes. It was now that Tur started to really show the effects of his degeneration before the rest. Vut was horrified at the state of Tur as his eyes met Kag's for just a moment. He couldn't imagine taking orders from Tur in this state. Tur could send his team to their deaths and have no conscious reality of his decision.

The rest of The Elders suffered from this speech for another fifteen minutes. An overwhelming sense of dread filled some of the adults as they recalled laughing at Kag's words. There was a large contingent of the band that still respected The Council's hierarchy but were unsure of what to make of this. Vut's decision was made for him already. As the adults dispersed back to their tasks in silence, Vut watched as they were escorted by two younger men back to The Council's tent. Kag looked at Vut with his hands clasped together and saw that he realized what was truly at stake. Vut had his dignity but could admit when he was wrong. Vut approached Kag and agreed to defer to his instructions. He left the group shortly after as he needed to catch up on rest for the time to hunt was sooner rather than later.

Now that Kag had Vut on side, he took Dran and Bani to their usual meeting place of the medical area where nobody would come to bother them. Kag chose this area due to its isolation and the ability for him to multitask while Dran and Bani continued to operate on the outside. By now, Kag organized a system where Naza would complete tasks that Kag left out for her once she was walked over by her parents. The quiet Naza worked on processing fibers close by as she overheard their conversation.

"The Council will notice furs have stopped coming. Should we fear them going against us?" Bani assessed as she looked to see the conditions of their own clothing.

Bani and Dran wore coverings made of grass which were easy to maintain, but Kag's furs fell apart as he neglected to keep up with his appearance while running around to do tasks. His beard was scraggly and unkempt but what concerned him more were the noticeable tears in his clothing. They hoped that by keeping the supply of luxury furs low The Council would be forced to address their concerns. The stockpile of pelts at their disposal changed as often as the wind blew which made this endeavor realistic in scope.

"Bani will make repairs Kag." Bani noted, as she lifted his tattered deer skin pelt. He gave a smile to her that was met with the same kindness.

"Vut is handled. Now what do we do?" Dran inquired of the others. Bani and Kag looked at one another before returning their gaze back to Dran.

"Dran has arena lesson, yes?" Kag asked as he scratched his head.

Dran looked above to see the direction of the sun. Her eyes squinted with the faint rays, but she saw that the time was fast approaching. Although The Elders kept a distinct amount of structure with their workdays, appearances by The Council pushed everything into disarray. She hadn't had enough time to get all she needed prepared.

"See what adults think and come back to Kag and Bani. Speech of Tur must still hang on their minds." Bani proposed to her.

Dran gave an affirmative nod and left the two to their devices as she made her way for the next lesson. Dran recalled what today was and to her relief, she realized nothing on her end needed to be made. She gave the children an assignment of their own to do outside the arena. While Jih taught promising stone workers the more advanced techniques to lithics, he wasn't above reminding them of the basics. In his absence, Dran now did this alone, and her lesson today was to teach the young how to repair their tools. Each one of her students was given a rock to modify as they saw fit and to return with it the next meeting.

As Dran was the rare generalist of their group, she had to wear many hats. Along with the camp defense and for combat, her role falls under general life skills. For many children, Dran is the one who taught them how to start a fire on their own, or what sources of water were good to drink aside from their parents. Dran made her way over to the arena to see a bunch of bright-eyed faces staring at her. Dran found this slightly unnerving, as she remembered distinctly wasting plenty of time until Hizo's lessons started. Perhaps this group just really enjoyed learning.

Naza remained tying fibers together as she held her worked rock close to her. Kag and Bani continued to talk but their eyes drifted from where Dran ran off and back to Naza. Kag tapped Naza's shoulder and pointed to the other end of camp where the rest of her cohort was meeting. The young Naza who was always late due to Kag ran as fast as she could, wanting to hear the next lesson. She dropped her wrapped fibers on the ground in a huffed sweat, although there was no need to rush. Kag gave her a wave as he watched the young child run through camp as a cloud of dust came behind.

Dran scrounged around and looked beneath a pile of refuse she left behind to hold various things. She had a few cores brought by her that she was going to use to demonstrate what makes a good tool and then how to improve on it. As Dran lifted her head to address the crowd, the tired Naza breathed heavily as she settled into the group. While Jih could talk at length about the various stone types in their native Sundaland, Dran was more focused on what can be produced efficiently. Dran sat down and folded her legs while the others followed suit. She waited for the attention of the others as she lifted one rock with her left hand and lifted a smaller one with her right. Dran smashed the two together as loudly as she could, drawing a few onlookers. She exaggerated her strikes so that large flakes could be shown off. A few of the children that sat closest used their elbow to shield themselves from the debris. She dropped the two rocks below and looked at the growing pile.

"Much like to make fire, these are flakes. Hotspark is best but others will do. Flakes can be used for new tool or-" Dran said, her eyebrow raised as she saw an already eager hand to intervene. She nodded her head at the young boy to speak.

"Jih did this better!" He complained as another kid nodded in support.

A few of the younger children covered their mouths and pointed at the young boy. Jih was shunned and mentions of his name would only bring punishment on those who did it according to The Council. Children were spanked and reprimanded for it while adults had far more serious consequences. She glared as some of the other students covered their mouths in reference to Jih's name being uttered by her. They started first with the young who followed the rules of any adult that were asked.

"Jih is not here. Dran is teacher, listen to Dran." Dran said as she demonstrated her point by taking the larger flake and smashing it against the ground. She gave a small grin as another piece of stone broke off with some force.

"This tool is broken! How does one fix?" Dran asked, as a few faces looked among themselves. A timeless endeavor was finding the one student willing to answer the teacher's question.

"Naza says to scratch small flake on big one." Naza pointed out, as she received a few nods from the older students.

Dran nodded, a smaller flake could be useful for whittling down an edge or sharpening a point if needed. There was something else though that Dran was looking for.

Dran held a stone with her left hand while she used her right hand to point freely to the various dimensions that could be used to make a tool.

"There is something else, big tool can change form. Much like clouds in the sky, tools with the right force can be different." Dran explained as she pointed to various areas where a tool could be morphed into something new before exhausting it entirely.

Tool repair was easy to learn but hard to master as many of the children only saw a tool for its primary use and shelved it away, a wasteful habit for an inexperienced mind. She received a few nods, as the lesson continued. Dran herself didn't teach very long as she knew the children were better off applying their skillsets than listening to her talk and she knew they grew bored easily. Dran watched as they compared designs of their tools with one another and let them experiment with materials to further work on their tool. There were fragments of bone, wood, and various rocks sourced from The Stoneworking Team to help facilitate the lesson. She thought about how her peers taught when the time arose. Jih often spoke past the children's heads that came to him as he found little to do with them but the ones that could follow well, learned well. Hyu would talk often and give long stories that the children listened to but often left more confused than before and Kag was Kag. He tried his best but somehow, he managed to get the attention of just one. Vut, to her surprise, was the most effective teacher. Everyone on his hunts came back alive, which was the metric for a good lesson when your target could injure you in the process. Dran took her job seriously but could only do so much.

As Dran let the children play in the arena with some of their tools, she decided to follow through on what Bani proposed. She sat back and left briefly to listen to the concern of some adults who seemed to have dissatisfaction on their mind. Her curiosity led her to hear the complaints of the Stoneworking Team who did their operations today not so far from her. Dran noticed the refuse present and saw they were clearly overworked. They were in discussion over a serious matter regarding their numbers and capable workers.

"Tur should have spoken to us. We lost two. He is gone and the other died in battle against Weypeu. Did he forget to tell us?" One woman complained, as she looked over her shoulder to make sure she was not eavesdropped on.

"It was a foolish hunt-" A man commented as he tossed a useless stone into the bushes.

"Yes, but if he had good tool, he would be alive." She replied to the other man's voice.

"The one that is gone could work bloodstone. Many hurt themselves otherwise." She alluded, as she found a loophole to mention Jih without uttering his name.

"You question decision of The Council? Tur has led us well. Be grateful." The man commented as he went up to start separating the rocks into distinct piles as Tur reprimanded them for before.

"This decision is to be questioned. Others should as well after what we saw today. That is all to be said." She said as she lifted another rock and tossed it behind her.

Dran couldn't help but give a small grin at their words. How could they have missed such an important group? Although Jih was a member of The Council, he didn't shirk his stoneworking duties prior to being inducted. He held a close rapport with his team, though he did not consider them friends in the same way as he did for Kag and Bani. She slinked away and turned her head to watch the kids some more until they were exhausted. Once they went away to do as they pleased, Dran's next goal was to find Bani and tell her of what she heard. With the stopping power of the Hunting Team and the legitimate grievances of the Stoneworking Team, the trio hoped to build up a strong case to oust Tur from power.

The House Always Wins

Now finding herself in India, Eshe made her way with a band of followers behind her. Long after her encounter with Jih and Sadal, she decided to follow her father's vision and head west. She was motivated by the vision of a grand network of interconnected bands that shared information with each other as fast as time could allow to strike and make a united front against the Thunderfeet. It was known that other Forest Seekers like herself moved throughout the continent, and it was likely for her to find more allies here as well. The Thunderfeet came from somewhere, and she reasoned correctly that they came from the west and pooled into the jungles. Her crusade had her visit camps dispersed throughout the jungles where she spoke about her experiences with the Thunderfeet and with such conviction about her tale with The Stone Breaker named Jih. While she kept her ears to the ground on news of the meteor for its astrological significance, this was of little strategic importance for her efforts to clear the lands.

Eshe and her warriors sat waiting in a bush as their eyes centered on a camp some distance away. The camp seemed to have mixed occupation with both Forest Seeker and Thunderfeet inhabitants. The land was tailored well to accommodate the stringent spiritual requirements of Forest Seeker life. Eshe saw the trees were healthy and without marks. She realized that some of these inhabitants were Thunderfeet who were attempting to adapt to their ways. This was an unusual situation for Eshe as she couldn't imagine the groups building together in such a manner, but it was something worth investigating. She hoped that this show of harmony wouldn't dissuade her revolutionaries from the goal.

"Should we raid this one Eshe? I see some of our kind here." A woman said with some hesitation on her face.

In the months that followed, Eshe's leadership went virtually unchallenged as this was the first time there was any meaningful effort to organize the Forest Seekers. She believed in practice by presence, where participating in raids herself, her message would resonate stronger, and it proved to be effective. She saw the onlookers towards her as she spoke quietly.

"We are liberators, we will slaughter the Thunderfeet and offer freedom and a better life to those that choose it. If they resist our ideas...let them go. If they are violent, cut them down." Eshe said as she closed her fist to end the discussion.

Eshe gave a low whistle as she called Thornback to retreat further into the treeline. The call of the hornbill always announced her presence, but for the element of surprise she needed to remain quiet. She called forth some of her forces, about twenty for a raid this large, where they would assault the perimeter with their blowguns and attack whatever defenses lay there. Two of her closest confidants carried torches on them to burn the structures built by Thunderfeet. As they believed part of the soul went into the things they constructed, Eshe would not only erase the Thunderfoot's physical presence, but their spiritual one as well. In her eyes, this served as a complete reversal of events.

Without hesitation, Eshe gave the orders for the plan to be executed. The village that she attacked was two camps that coalesced through the jungle, using portions of cut down forest as roads to travel between the two. Both were integrated with Forest Seekers and Thunderfeet in them. She went forth and withdrew her blowgun. Her lips touched the device and blew, her first dart being a silent one. Unlike a few of the others, she didn't need a tracking dart to figure where her shots would land, which took large amounts of practice to do. Her first target was a Thunderfoot woman carrying a basket of goods foraged from the forest. Inside were branches and other gathered materials, no doubt cut from the trees Eshe valued as sacred. The woman let out a scream as she withdrew the poison dart but fell silent as the village scrambled. The Forest Seekers that occupied this space knew quickly that one of their own orchestrated the attack. They were dumbfounded as they saw that The Vow was violated by their own kind, but self-preservation won out. They scrambled on their own, and a cacophony of wooden darts whizzed through the village center. Eshe and some of her forces stayed behind trees to return fire until they exhausted their supply of darts. The Thunderfeet armed themselves with axes and short spears. One runner in the chaos went at breakneck speed to the other town to alert their new defenders that their area was under attack. He hoped in the run it would take to reach the other camp it wouldn't be too late.

The Buffalo Brothers enjoyed the benefits of leadership in a tent, their signature skulls hung on a wooden pole and some string not too far from their location. After their near-death experience with the hippo, they decided to move back eastward for a time. The market called for their influence, and they delivered. They managed to deliver the sloth bear pelt at a high value and gained an assortment of blessed gear from a local settlement on their travels. The two brothers retained their skill at deception and fooled poor villagers into thinking they were mighty warriors to defend their settlement.

For the brothers, this place was easy prey. They sold themselves well as warriors ousted from a faraway land due to their immense skillset. With their frame, gear, and intimidation, they were able to play the part well and rebrand their image from simple swindlers to warrior heroes that other Thunderfeet could only hope to admire. These camps were desperate and the Thunderfeet in this town had no grievances with them unlike their antics in the west. Gorgeous women of both Forest Seeker and Thunderfoot variety answered the call of The Buffalo Brothers, food was gathered for them from the jungle and all the pelts they wanted were theirs. For them, they had it made, but they were utterly bored. The Buffalo Brothers didn't imagine success to be so bitter for them. Their loving arrangement came to an end as a young man approached their tent. The brothers quickly donned their helmets and boar skin reinforced clothing as they heard the footsteps come closer. Nezzall stayed quiet as he and Dronall exited their tent to see the disturbance.

"We are under attack! Some Forest Seekers from somewhere have come. We need your aid now!" The young man yelled at the two.

Dronall looked at his brother and thought about what he said. Although he and Nezzall firsthand experienced hostile Forest Seekers, the two were skeptical of the man's claim. Dronall studied his dress and saw it was disheveled as the man was clearly in a rush.

"Forest Seekers attacking their own? Brother, this seems like deception to me. What do you make of this?" Dronall proposed to Nezzall who nodded in agreement to his brother's words.

Nezzall cracked his knuckles as the young man gulped in fear. Nezzall went over and placed his hand on the young man's shoulder and pressed down. Nezzall was more than ready to lend a helping hand as Forest Seekers were much smaller than themselves. As giants, he and his brother were expected to intimidate the enemy with ease.

I didn't expect us to have to actually do anything when we agreed. These people all have their own weapons. What kind of trouble are we getting in? Dronall wondered as he looked at his brother addressing the man's concerns.

"Leave it to us to take care of these raiders. After all, we need to earn our keep, yes?" Nezzall said, slowly lifting his skull cap, just enough to reveal a smile that could put any at ease.

The two ventured forth vowing to bring defeat to the foe and peace to the village. Dronall and Nezzall favored fighting hand to hand with human opponents more than anything else and so they decided to go as they were. The two charlatans rushed through the brush as quickly as they could and pushed aside anyone else that happened to come in their way. While the idea to drop and run at the sign of danger was appealing, they assessed the risk and reward about defending the settlement. They arrived at the scene to see the scene as Forest Seekers were attacking denizens of the village with knives. Dronall quickly waved over his brother and focused on their efforts on two running towards the town center.

Nezzall curled up his hand to a fist and punched a Forest Seeker in the face. He used his strength to grip their arm and contort until they yelled in severe pain. He used the skull of his buffalo helmet to bash their head in. The sharp horn pierced the man's head and caused him to bleed. Dronall defended his brother from a stab from behind from a Forest Seeker woman as he used his leg to trip her to the ground and knocked her knife to the floor.

"Quite the mess we've gotten ourselves into, wouldn't you say brother!?" Dronall said as he lowered his head and charged into a Forest Seeker while he saw more Thunderfeet moving into the area from the previous village. Reinforcements were surely welcome as fighting soon lost its luster to the pair.

"Exciting surely! Consider this, less people means less we have to share! The bounty is ours for the taking." Nezzall commented as he looked through the bushes to find more Forest Seekers in the distance.

Eshe hadn't anticipated the combined efforts of the Thunderfeet and Forest Seekers to put up such a resistance, she almost felt betrayed seeing how well their tactics complement one another, but she was far from a loser in this battle. She ordered her torchbearers to go forth and set alight the residences of those in there, regardless of their affiliation. They made their way to the second camp undetected and found that it was evacuated. The words of the young man warned them ahead of time, but their homes and valuables were torched.

In the same breath, part of Forest Seeker fire management was a strong mastery of mud and soil to restrict the spread of such things. The torchbearers worked quickly to accumulate mud, concealing the worst of the flames to the structures below. Eshe chewed her tongue in anger as she saw that she couldn't complete her full objective. They would rebuild, and she would return once again.

The Buffalo Brothers contended handily with their Forest Seeker opponents, offering support to the steadfast defenders. When word spread that evacuation of the camp happened, they saw some of these same fighters leave to find their families. With a stalemate evident, Dronall and Nezzall could read the room and saw that with the torched settlement, there also went their rewards and glory. The two brothers took the opportunity to steal bags of their own and were on the run once again, with the glory days behind them. In the relative safety of the chaos, they were assured that nobody would question their absence after a while. Their skulls made them marked men but their desire to hide their identity stayed strong. The two were out of breath and ran quickly with the burning settlement still fresh on their minds. They needed to come up with a new plan but were more than happy to start over. The two brothers were addicted to the chase and wanted nothing more than a chance to try again.

"Well brother. It was good while it lasted. We must start anew." Dronall assessed as he stretched his arm and checked himself for injury. He gave a grin to his brother as he got a playful jab to the side.

"We mustn't grow fat and happy at the top, for it's always about the climb to glory once again. As they always say, there's always another fool." Nezzall said with a mighty laugh as the two shared a piece of meat together.

"Do you know where we will go from here?" Nezzall asked as he scratched his head.

"Oh yes. I have a feeling our mysterious guests arrived due north of here. This attack was no simple raid, there was planning, and they used fire to send a message. It's clear to me now they must want something different than usual. Let us seek them out and bolster ourselves with their endowment." Dronall said, with a sly grin as the two schemed with one another.

After a week of laying low, it was time for the Buffalo Brothers to enact their grand scheme. They scoped out the perimeter of one of Eshe's satellite camps located not too far and eavesdropped on the tales of the elusive Eshe and concluded that their attackers must have been organized by her. Dronall and Nezzall hoped to achieve their original vision of having the ear of a powerful leader but maintain their autonomy. The situation for them now was to figure out how to get close without being directly hostile. Nezzall lingered on the outskirts and listened to a few men who were busy skinning deer. While he cared little for gossip, the topic of interest caught his eye.

"The Jaat is in low supply this season. I fear we may not have enough tools for the job. My blowgun needs repairs, but the plant has been used up. What can be done?" The man said, while he saw his companion nod.

"Right, I hear that some of us can work stone. Perhaps this could be useful to us, but there is a problem of finding good hotspark in lands we do not know. I was with Eshe from the beginning. I heard her and The Stone Breaker. I left everything behind to follow but we need more." The other man explained to his friend.

Nezzall nodded with a nice smile on his face, as he heard all he needed to know. While his brother was more focused on negotiations, Nezzall also had a silver tongue and was good at making people like him, even hostile Forest Seekers. He took a moment to prepare himself, his favorite persona being a man that's lost his way and stumbled upon the village by accident.

Nezzall moved himself into the Forest Seeker camp carefully, slightly exaggerating his movements as he was met with a strange look by the two men in discussion. They quickly realized that Nezzall was a Thunderfoot, and they withdrew sharpened sticks as a deterrent.

"Leave us Thunderfoot, before you are cut to pieces! We do not follow The Vow. Our strikes are deadly." The man said as he threatened Nezzall. Nezzall looked at the man in confusion, his body language evident that he was clearly lost in some way. Now that he had their attention, he needed to bring them in. Dronall watched patiently from the shadows seeing his brother's prowess.

"Oh, this happens more often than I thought. I came from a village that was attacked some time ago. Can you tell me where I should go?" Nezzall said, his tone surprisingly disarming. The two men held their sharpened sticks as they saw the buffalo skull on his head. They weren't sure what to make of this. They could see that Nezzall was unarmed so for the moment they kept the advantage.

"Are those your knives? Shouldn't you use stone for that?" Nezzall added on as he directed his attention to their items in hand. The two men looked at one another, it was clear that something was going on, but they weren't sure what.

Nezzall took their delayed reactions as a sign to make the sale as he and Dronall always practiced. He held back his laughter as he offered his services to the men before him. As he waited, Nezzall evaluated the size of the encampment and tried to scope out who held the highest status.

"I was a trader who made stone tools. Even the Forest Seekers here know where to find such material. You seem new. We could work something out, some meat there for our tools?" Nezzall proposed. The two men remembered Eshe's policy strongly of not wanting to deal with Thunderfeet, but supply issues were a serious concern. Information was more valuable than pelts in a land that was unknown.

The two men looked at one another and mulled over the proposal. From their perspective, they had everything to gain and nothing to lose. The man before them was unarmed and practically begging to make a deal. Any punishment that would come from Eshe later was small in comparison to the opportunity brought for them. They also thought of being able to extort information of Thunderfoot camps out of Nezzall as he was a trader who would travel to other areas.

"We want a sample of your work." The man concluded.

Nezzall sweat a bit, seeing as he had nothing to sell the ruse, but a quick idea came to mind. Nezzall pointed upwards to the helmet that he wore on his head. The buffalo skull he wore was adorned with intricate grooves placed on it as the two men looked closely at it. Their skull decorations were practically the only thing the two brothers put effort in aside from their ruse. The two men nodded in satisfaction and placed their sticks in the dirt. One remained to watch Nezzall while the other went to locate Eshe's inner circle.

Eshe was on a walk with Akma as she hadn't had much time with her since really going into her dream of ousting the Thunderfeet. The pressure was immense as Eshe needed to bring tangible victories for her followers. She looked into her partner's eyes and was beyond grateful she joined her despite being miles away from their home region. Akma's logistical mind also assisted in gathering supplies for a growing force constantly on the move. On occasion she woke up at night with a cold sweat, as her tactics slowly echoed that of the Thunderfeet to assert herself in the region. The burden of administration weighed heavy on the young woman who sat on a log with her hands in her head in thought. Akma tapped her shoulder as Eshe looked up to see one of her many eyes and ears that moved between potential camps of interest.

"We have something to tell you Eshe. One of our followers had contacted Thunderfoot traders who seem willing to give us supplies. What should we do about this?" A man asked as he was accompanied by another scout.

"And you refused to cut them down because?" Eshe said, her tone sharp as this meeting cut into her personal time.

The other woman with him was silent as she casually gestured over to the lack of suitable tools for the terrain. Eshe saw what was presented to her and nodded in understanding. Eshe got up from the log and walked over and decided to give these mysterious people an audience. There were some fights she knew she couldn't win on her own. After some time, Dronall and Nezzall waited proudly as they saw the Eshe of legend herself appear. They noted the appearance of the hornbill that accompanied her, and truly saw she was someone of great renown. From their perspective she seemed short, but like any customer, they were there to do business and do it well. The two brothers loomed with their helmets as they watched her turn to address them.

"I was informed you two are stoneworkers. Is this correct?" Eshe said coldly as Nezzall tapped his brother to speak for the two of them.

"Only the finest. We were informed of your goal, and I would like to say we share no ill-will towards your kind. We were ousted by another group and could care less what you choose to do. That said, my brother and I were going to a village to do trade but seeing as our partners are now dead or missing, you will be our point of contact." Dronall said, as he lathered his words with honey to smooth the deal over. Eshe was aware of such Thunderfoot pleasantries hiding their true intentions as she glared at the two men before her.

"What are the terms you wish to make?" Dronall said, stretching his arms out. Nezzall took a mental note as he waited for Eshe to speak.

"What we need are stone tools. I want two sets of knives made from stone for a group of thirty. Can this be done? We have very few capable workers. Hotspark is preferred, but other stones will do. These must be sharp. What do you want as compensation?" Eshe asked, as she raised an eyebrow at the two of them. Nezzall nodded his head in agreement, recalling everything that Eshe stated previously. The two knew this would be a tall order to make, but they assured Eshe that they would move mountains to make this possible.

"What do we want? The only thing that matters to us is pelts. We will take half now and to sweeten the deal, provide you with information on where to find sources of your own material. This is agreeable. Nezzall and I have a schedule to keep as we are in high demand, but we can deliver this to you in one month. To prove our severity in the matter, take my bag as proof. No further trades will be made until your request is filled." Dronall said with a sly grin as Eshe absorbed his speech.

Eshe was rightfully annoyed at The Buffalo Brother's demanding half directly, but she was exhausted and relegated some of the collection as collateral to make the deal go smoother. The two brothers were quite happy seeing binturong and serow pelts among the exchanged pieces which Nezzall quickly pocketed. The two of them couldn't believe their luck this time. This was by far one of their greatest scams to fill.

"Of course. A perfect deal for a lady as refined as yourself." Dronall said. Although he felt zero attraction to Eshe personally, he often layered extra compliments depending on who he was dealing with. For those he could not figure out, he often just went with the safe approach of affirming their appearance.

"Oh! I see you are spoken for. She is a sharp one to make a deal with us." Dronall said, as he looked at Akma who gripped Eshe's hand. Nezzall looked back at Dronall, stopping him for just a moment before the two shook hands. How could they forget their most important rule?

"Before we agree to the deal, you must remember that there are no returns in the art of exchange." Dronall and Nezzall expressed with the utmost severity as they stood up and extended their hands to her.

Eshe grabbed their respective hands to shake, and the deal was made. The other Forest Seekers gave encouraging glances to Eshe as she showed true leadership. From their perspective, if they could harness Thunderfeet technology for their own ways, this was one extra step into aiding their fight against the enemy. The two bowed their skulls to Eshe, ceding faux respect to her obvious position in authority. She found the gesture strange but welcome. The two men then left to scheme once more.

Darts In The Wind

Deeso and the others walked as one to an atmospheric place that was a fun spot for Forest Seekers to converse. The group had a few days of bad luck hunting and were caked with dirt. The mud beneath their feet caked onto every surface as they kept their balance on loose vines and guided one another. The shadow of the foliage above their heads continued to track them as a distinct change in temperature was felt on their skin. Ozul gave a small grin from the back of the line as he realized they were close. Hot springs were considered places of healing among his people. The rest of his companions had no complaints. The four decided to move their camp close to the spring for easy access, with more dense forest further ahead for foraging. The four weaved through an assortment of bushes to see dry rock with pools of water. They saw mist hover over pools that felt warm to the touch.

"Good find Ozul. I'm glad to see this was correct. Remember, you and Zulag have to hunt today." Deeso stated to both.

Cikya had a remarkable eye for fresh fruit, so she accompanied Deeso every so often. Deeso and Cikya were productive the past few days and were tired, so their gaze went towards the boys whose turn was coming up. The four took no time to strip down and claim their springs. They chose to bathe at the same time with some separation. Ozul and Zulag were situated at one spring in discussion with one another while Cikya and Deeso said nothing to each other. Ozul stepped in first and felt instant relief as the dirt off his body melted. The pool was the deepest and warmest in the center. Zulag and the others stayed close to the first ring to not fall in. Ozul saw the reflection of Zulag peer over his shoulder in the spring.

"Don't think I didn't see you looking Ozul..." Zulag said with a sly grin as he slowly lifted his hand to grasp the back of Ozul's head. He smugly pointed a finger in the direction of Cikya and dunked the boy's head under water. Zulag was tall enough that he was able to be stable in the water, while Ozul struggled a bit to maintain height. Ozul gasped for air as he glared at Zulag.

"You know you are unable to swim, yes? I should push you in the center and see what happens." Ozul said, as he coughed into his arm. Zulag chuckled at Ozul's words, he was finally starting to fit in.

"Can't say I blame you, she's more refined than my knives. A bit old for you though." Zulag teased as he tossed Ozul a rock to wipe dirt off his body.

"It'll be our little secret. She'll never know. Just us pals." Zulag taunted Ozul as he saw the boy's face hide away. Ozul cleaned himself and enjoyed the heated water on his skin. He attempted to change the conversation to another question that was on his mind.

"Zulag, I must ask. Not that I was looking but..." Ozul said with a tinge of embarrassment.

Zulag was confused at Ozul's statement as he looked around and wondered what he possibly had to say. Zulag looked down at his body and gathered what Ozul was afraid to mention. He scoffed at Ozul's insistence but decided to oblige his curiosity.

"I get this all the time. It's a ritual to prove our manhood after you've passed our trials to be an adult. Women get their ears pierced and we get that done to us. I couldn't walk for a week. Never mind that it looks different, it works all the same. Trust me. [44]" Zulag said with a smug expression as he continued to wash himself.

"Have you seen any Sarmpa around here recently?" Ozul asked as he splashed some warm water on his face.

Zulag frowned at the thought. He and the other members of The Broken Bone considered snakes to be low, there was no real honor in killing them as they lacked any appendages that were useful for their needs and were much too dangerous for any sort of showmanship. Snakes were avoided at all costs and rooted out of their settlements. Zulag gathered that Ozul had some use for these outside of his skillset or was just looking for a death wish.

"No. I hate them." Zulag said in irritation.

"No matter. I have what we need for today, I just wanted to make more of them." Ozul said as he kept his surprise hidden.

Sometime later, the two finished up and headed back to camp, while Deeso and Cikya decided to stay longer in the spring. Zulag hoped to at least bring home a few deer by the end of the day. He equipped a good deal of throwing knives in his pocket and strapped the rest to his body with jute rope to his leg. He tossed a spare in Ozul's direction that he barely caught between his fingertips. Ozul was prepared with his blowgun and had a few darts ready for hunting as well. Zulag seemed stumped on where to go, but Ozul already had a direction planned. He held out his hand to Ozul and stopped him.

"Where do you think you're going? We need to figure out where our route is." Zulag ordered.

Ozul pointed out a direction that compelled Zulag to follow. Ozul had been this way before, he recognized this path as an apparent trail for forest elephants. Ozul looked up in a vain hope to see the Thunderfoot man again at the top of the tree but he was absent. Ozul shook his head and assumed he gave up the hunt. The environment spoke for itself as there were trees that were off-center. These trees were uprooted by the trunks of elephants. While Ozul was concerned for the health of the trees, it didn't carry the same rage as when human hands altered their flow. Forest elephants were seen as titans of the forest responsible for forging the first forest paths that the Stone Breakers used to build their communities. Ozul saw something faint in the distance, and he ran towards it while Zulag lagged behind. Zulag had never seen Ozul run that fast. Zulag returned quickly to find Ozul carrying a rock with his additional weaponry as he was engaged in combat with a pit viper. Ozul's back was against a tree as he saw the animal on the ground and baited

---

[44] Circumcision is an ancient practice found among various African hunter-gatherer societies, it's highly likely that The Broken Bone would have kept up this practice as well.

it to rise. Ozul tossed a rock squarely at the animal's head with the flick of his wrist. He disrupted it for just a moment as he used Zulag's knife to stab it directly in the head.

"Ozul! Get away from that!" Zulag yelled to Ozul as he ignored him.

Ozul collected his kill with ease and pressed carefully on the animal's head. Ozul sought to cut it off by the neck and used the blade of the knife to open the animal's mouth. He took out his darts and squeezed the exposed fang, smothering the tips and placing them back in his bag after letting it dry. Ozul had a proud expression on his face that he obscured quickly once Zulag walked by.

"You don't listen at all, even someone like you should know Sarmpa are dangerous." Zulag scoffed at Ozul.

The two started looking for food and Ozul rubbed his hands together in excitement as he heard a low rumbling sound. It was the sound of a herd of elephants grazing in a clearing in the forest. Their rumbles carried through the forest growth. Trampled shoots of bamboo were present near them as well that Ozul thought about picking up.

"Zulag, I found what we are looking for." Ozul said, as he pointed happily towards the elephants. Zulag looked at Ozul and looked past the elephant herd in their path.

"I don't follow. You mean the Yaan over there? Come on, be serious with me." Zulag asked as he tried suppressing a laugh. While Zulag was a blowhard when it came to the field of battle, he at least had the foresight to know when he met his match. An elephant was above his pay grade and there was no shame in that.

"Yes. If you allow me to show you." Ozul said calmly as he withdrew a dart laced with the viper's venom. Zulag knelt to Ozul's level and placed his hand on his shoulder.

"You really think you can take out a Yaan with that thing huh? You know what, I'm in a good mood. Entertain me and I may make it worth your while. Over there, why not go to that calf." Zulag said, with a vainglorious expression, as he knew in his heart that Ozul was just talking a big game. Zulag was ready to leave once the two had their fun agitating the forest elephants to find a more manageable meal.

Ozul nodded his head in disagreement, he felt for his darts that a calf would be a complete waste of his ability. He decided to make his way towards one of the adults, and just to add insult to injury, he went for a bull elephant that had its trunk busy with a tree. Zulag watched as Ozul walked over calmly with some suspicion. He took two darts out, each laced with the viper's venom and loaded one into the blowgun. He blew harshly with his first and landed his shot. The target wasn't so difficult to hit. The second dart came with the same delivery onto the elephant's rear end. The thick skin of the elephant barely registered the two darts, but Ozul launched them with enough speed to break the skin. Ozul returned to Zulag who watched with little excitement as nothing seemed to happen.

As the elephant was a mighty creature, the dose of the venom took its time to work but soon Ozul would have a mighty bounty on his hands. The elephant attempted to grab the branch it was eating from but continued to miss as its vision blurred. The elephant's sight vanished first. It hopelessly flailed out into the abyss of darkness until it felt a searing pain course through its body. In its haste, it ran into a tree and made a loud collision that

Zulag covered his ears for. The other elephants nearby were unsure what to do, the mothers attempted to shield their calves from the raging male.

Ozul wished he could paint caves for how much he wished to preserve Zulag's expression of surprise as he saw the devastation unfold beyond him. The other elephants sounded to each other and slowly retreated from the male who was beyond saving. They formed a protective circle around the young while keeping this distance. The elephant thrashed around for some more before it fell flat to the ground, burdened by its own weight. The elephant landed with a small accompanying thud that collapsed a nearby tree. Ozul anticipated a few other elephants would return to mourn their dead as he'd seen them before, but the venom made the animal so deranged, they prioritized their survival instead.

"You will need your knife." Ozul said with a proud tone in his voice as Zulag silently walked over to the deceased elephant.

Zulag looked over every angle of the elephant to ensure that it was truly dead. He returned to find Ozul perched on top of the kill and saw him give a gentle wave. Ozul plucked out his two darts and tossed one to the side. The darts used by Forest Seekers were reusable, a testament to their care of keeping their environmental impact low. The first dart he used was damaged beyond repair, but the second one remained useful. Ozul would have to apply this one again with venom.

"What..." Zulag said in complete disbelief of what he witnessed.

Ozul gave Zulag a strong pat on the back as the two skinned the elephant's carcass. Their packs practically burst at the seams with meat. Zulag and Ozul worked to extract the tusks as ivory was a great reward to capture. With this bounty they would be able to negotiate for a week's worth of supplies at the next camps. An observer hid behind a tree and watched as the two talked with one another. This was a Forest Seeker who was in his early 20s much like Zulag. He carried the disdain for Thunderfeet that seemed to be more common as time passed. For Eshe, he would have been a prime fighter. His face carried disgust as he looked at Ozul and then Zulag.

"You think you can kill a Yaan on our land and get away with it? You were given no such passage. You traitor and that Thunderfoot of yours." A voice stepped forward.

Zulag looked up and gave no concern as he continued with extracting the tusk. Forest Seekers were below him, and their idle complaints meant nothing when he could end the man's life in an instant. He decided to let Ozul handle the situation. Ozul made the kill and now it was his time to defend it. Ozul looked uncomfortable as Zulag noticed Ozul's hesitation to address the situation. He hadn't considered any onlookers would be present, but the kill was along a well-known elephant trail. In times of strife, Ozul often sought to find a diplomatic solution. This was supposed to be the way of their people, but the ideal and reality rarely agreed with one another.

"The forest gives us all a bounty, for nobody owns the land. We can share if this will help. There is plenty of meat to give." Ozul offered the young man with a shrill voice he found difficult to control. Zulag rearranged his backpack as he offered his perspective.

"Ozul, this was your kill. Tell him to get lost." Zulag said with irritation in his voice as he focused on gathering more meat.

The man walked towards Ozul with a seemingly understanding expression, but Ozul was punched in the stomach instead. Ozul learned quickly that some people were beyond convincing. Ozul's body reverberated as he felt the punch and took a knee. He coughed profusely and felt betrayed once more, as he barely held down his breakfast from earlier. Ozul grinded his teeth as his hand touched his stomach.

"You think meat can fix what was done here? You enable the Thunderfeet to pillage our land. Traitors must be burnt!" The man yelled again.

He waited for Ozul to rise once more so that he could punch him again, before moving onto Zulag. Zulag knew that this Forest Seeker couldn't possibly stand a chance against him, so he decided to stand behind Ozul instead. Zulag figured the boy needed a little motivation to become as hardened as the others. Despite being put off by his weakness, Zulag saw there was some potential that needed to be brought out.

"Ozul! Punch him back now!" Zulag yelled at him.

Zulag got up and curled his hand into a fist as he hoped to energize Ozul. If things became too bad, Zulag would certainly intervene and end it with ease. While Ozul was generally passive, he didn't want to have the ire of the others once again when he went back. Zulag was perplexed by how Ozul could take the life of an elephant with ease but struggled to stand up for himself. Ozul's dedication to The Vow was strong, but Zulag saw that this was going to be a problem later. He hoped to fix this issue before it would cost his life in battle. Ozul didn't dare look behind him as he knew Zulag was glaring at him to act. He picked himself up and begrudgingly leaped onto the taller man and tackled him to the ground. Ozul used his elbow to put some separation between him and the man present. Zulag watched with interest. Ozul's entire body shook with dread as he felt ashamed of what he was doing. Ozul withdrew his knife that Zulag gave him before and pointed it directly at the other Forest Seeker slowly. His eyes teared up as he quickly realized the only way he'd be able to get respect was by force. Everything his father taught him about kindness and good works started to fall apart.

"Not so tough with a knife to your throat, are you?!" Zulag said with a laugh to the Forest Seeker.

Ozul didn't have in him to end the man's life, but he did leave him with a punch to the jaw. Ozul thought this was enough, but Zulag decided to have some extra fun. Zulag took the spare rope he originally brought from his backpack and walked over to the scrambling Forest Seeker. He let out a sinister smile as he forcefully wrapped the man's hands together and pinned him to a tree.

"Stand up." Zulag said as he pointed his knife at the man.

Ozul looked at Zulag as he walked behind him and kept his gaze on the man. He was going to use the man as target practice. Zulag threw the first knife that landed just above where he stood. The man shook in complete and utter torment as he felt the wind whisk between his hair. Zulag was toying with the man as Ozul was aware he could land a moving target with ease. Zulag propelled a knife to the man's foot and caused him to yell in extreme pain. Ozul looked away as another knife entered the man's shoulder. Ozul didn't understand the need for such cruelty but as the pain of his punch continued to ring in his jaw his thoughts went elsewhere. Zulag relished in the man's panic as he tried to summon the spirits of the forest to defend him. His screams grew louder as he attempted to block out the pain. Zulag was a devoted man to the spirits but was turned off by such desperate zealotry. Zulag saw the job was done as he decided to walk over and take the man's life. With a quick insertion of his blade, the man bled out quickly with a punctured artery.

"What? He was getting annoying." Zulag remarked as he withdrew his knife from the man's throat.

The two sat in silence as Zulag let Ozul collect his thoughts while his stomach rumbled. Elephant meat was a strong source of protein and cooked easily when the kill was available. He was looking to get things moving quickly and signaled the time to head back to camp before any dangerous scavengers bothered showing up.

"People that disrespect me deserve to die. You are with me by association, so remember that. I'm sure Deeso will tell you the same when you hunt with her." Zulag remarked as he looked at Ozul who wiped away a residual tear from his eye.

"I remember, there's something you all do to traitors in your people, right?" Zulag asked.

"He yelled at me earlier. We are supposed to burn them when they violate The Vow. This is so that their ashes will not go into the forest and be reborn." Ozul recalled to him.

"Was he a traitor?" Zulag asked as he gestured to the corpse.

"No. He just hit me, but he did not violate The Vow. There was no intention to kill me." Ozul explained.

"You don't know that for sure, but if he was? You would burn him?" Zulag inquired as he listened in between Ozul's words.

"I would." Ozul mentioned to him.

Zulag nodded his head in acknowledgment of Ozul's statement. While Cikya and Deeso continued to see Ozul as a hapless child, Zulag felt he was ready for more. He conjured a plan in his head for later to truly test Ozul's commitment to his words.

"That was a good Yaan kill, was it not? Do not worry, the venom vanishes when the creature dies. The meat is good." Ozul said, trying to change the subject with Zulag as they walked back with their bounty.

Zulag decided to table the issue for later, he would talk to the others about how to properly use Ozul as a member of their team. Zulag had to admit, out of all the creatures they could have killed for food, an elephant was a choice hard to beat.

"Come on. The girls won't believe this one." Zulag remarked as he patted his backpack and held a portion of the massive elephant tusk.

The Initiation

Ozul dreamt soundly in his bed of leaves with a fur blanket. He slept with some comfort as after being on the road for some time he became somewhat acclimated to his new friend group. He had plenty of time to think about his situation. He was originally terrified of Zulag and felt nothing but unease with Deeso. Cikya was warm and kind to him from the beginning and this is something he valued as he thought of her often. He slept at the base of a thick tree, a short distance away from the other three who slept close to the ongoing fire. The chaos of the last week made them tired, and their rest was well warranted. Cikya went to gather more kindling for the fire, while Zulag followed Deeso's trail as she was towards the river's edge.

Deeso sat by the river's edge and piled a small collection of fish next to her. She used an empty bag to gently scoop water and drain it out onto the soil. This was a slow method for capturing fish, but it was enough to gather slow enough creatures. The taste of elephant meat from Ozul and Zulag's previous hunt wasn't appealing to her, and she opted to get her own food to prepare. As fishing required the utmost concentration for Deeso, she was irritated as she heard footsteps come near her.

"Deeso!" Zulag yelled to grab her attention as she tried to ignore him.

Deeso reached over and looked at her catch as she attempted to focus but heard Zulag's voice intensify. Her eyes watched the shadows of the sun on nearby plants and knew it was far too early for his shenanigans. She yawned as she continued about her business while Zulag caught her attention. He practically stood over her as she remained hunched over with her task.

"Zulag, I'm busy." Deeso asked as she stripped a fish with a knife.

"The kid's had it easy for some time now. After yesterday, I saw something though. If we push him more, he can be useful to us. We got into a fight yesterday and he actually defended himself." Zulag said as he decided to goad her further.

"Nothing is stopping you from talking to me, so speak. I won't leave until you do." Zulag demanded in annoyance. He let out a small grin as he heard an annoyed sigh from Deeso.

"He fought back and didn't run away?" She said with some confusion in her voice.

"Exactly right. Him making rope doesn't bring food home. I do. We do. Cikya does. But there's something there." Zulag mentioned, his voice increasing in pitch as he got worked up.

"Killing isn't their way, remember?" Deeso said as she hoped to end the conversation.

"Given what we've seen lately, I'm starting to think that's a lie. He said he wants to help us, well, what do we do? If any of us get injured, we're down a person and that will make the whole thing fall apart." Zulag reasoned, as he waved his hands around him.

"You have a point. What do we do?" Deeso questioned.

Deeso was rarely one to support Zulag's statements, but she was incredibly logical. If it was possible to train Ozul to get comfortable with the grimmer realities of their journey, then she would do whatever it took. Ozul's hesitation to kill others proved to be a strategic disadvantage when the time called for it. She recalled having to keep an eye on Ozul during their battle at Krukzig's encampment. The increased efficiency of her team meant greater odds when it came to surviving to find Sadal. She needed to be at her best in order to stay strong for her sister. She relented and allowed Zulag to explain the breadth of his plans.

"That's the easy part. When you're done, come meet me further upriver. I'm going to have Cikya distract him while I take some rope." Zulag commented, as he looked in the distance.

Zulag walked back in the direction of camp and his face instantly frowned as he saw Ozul still asleep. His gaze turned to Cikya who had concluded amassing extra wood for their fire. She was perched next to Ozul and gently rubbed his head as he slept. She looked up to see Zulag and waved her hand over for him to join. Cikya always tried to get him to do something out of his comfort zone. It was a quality that irritated many, but the sheer lack of care exhibited by her was something Zulag found impressive. It was a special kind of resilience that her positivity always shined through. Zulag wondered if it was the blessing she was given, or more accurately, she saw what despair led to and decided to reject it outright. Cikya got up and met with him as he approached. She noticed Zulag was about to yell in an outburst as he always did but was met with her hand over his mouth. Zulag was too puzzled by the action to react and stood until Cikya brought her arm back down.

"Cikya." Zulag said, his voice less loud this time. Her eyes perked up as she heard her name being called. She lifted her eyebrows with a slightly sarcastic grin and moved her hands, prompting Zulag to speak further.

"I need some rope. Did he make any for us?" Zulag asked as he noticed their packs were moved from the previous night.

Cikya nodded and grabbed a sizable coil to hand to him. Her expression was a bit confused as she tried to guess what he needed it for. They agreed they didn't need to cross any bodies of water for at least another day while they rested.

"Don't worry about it. Just keep Ozul where he is. Deeso and I have a job to do." Zulag said with his voice trailing off.

He looked behind him to see Deeso returned with Cikya giving her a small hug. She didn't understand why this happened every time, but she was always given a warm embrace by her friend. Sadal, by comparison was much less touchy, but always had good words to say. She smiled and forgot that this was how Cikya expressed such things with her condition. She grabbed her axe instinctively as he made his way outside the camp. He went with a fast pace to the upper end of the river and stopped, as he waited for Deeso to catch up. Deeso felt disgusted as her hands and forearms were marred with blood from the fish. Slightly out of breath, she looked up at Zulag.

"You dragged me out here for what exactly?" Deeso said through lapsed breathing.

"This is a good one. I saw some Forest Seekers down the road a while ago. We're going to capture one of them and bring them back to camp. Ozul said yesterday that he would know how to deal with those who come against us. I want to see if that's really true." Zulag said with a smug grin.

"Why would we do that? That is extremely difficult. Remember their blowguns?" Deeso questioned. The last thing she wanted to do after a previous confrontation was to be at the end of those tubes. The sound of the whizzing darts was a fresh memory in her mind from her and Cikya's last venture into the deeper forest.

"We're going to have Ozul learn what death is." Zulag said, turning his left hand into a fist.

"How so?" Deeso replied with an exasperated tone.

"Easy. I saw some of them capturing water. We're going to wait and ambush them. Consider this just revenge for that attack you and Cikya dealt with." Zulag mentioned to her. Deeso nodded in approval, it was embarrassing for the two of them to be put into such a situation to begin with.

"We are the masters here in this land. Let's see if your idea holds true." Deeso commented.

The two of them waited in complete silence as Zulag hoped to test his theory on the Forest Seeker drinking patterns. On schedule, a young man approached carefully. He looked around and cupped water to drink. The two observed as he quickly gulped it down. He had a basket on him that was tightly woven and filled to the brim with fruit to bring home. Zulag and Deeso were ready to strike as he was distracted. They assessed that a village wasn't too far from their camp, but the location remained obscure. Deeso took the rope from Zulag's hands as she watched him rush over and tackle the man to the ground. She used her axe to split the coils into two distinct halves.

"Huh?" The man asked in confusion as he was overpowered by Zulag. The man hopelessly kicked in the dirt as he tried slapping him away. Deeso sprang into action with the rope as she pinned the man's feet down and quickly wrapped the cord around his ankles. She gave it a secure tug as he thrashed around further under Zulag's grip.

"Are you done yet?" Zulag asked with irritation in his voice.

Deeso ignored his question and moved to the side of him to show she had finished. The man's hands were flailing around as he attempted to dislodge Zulag from him. With a good amount of force behind her, she kicked the man in the head and rendered him unconscious. Zulag gave a quick look up at her in concern.

"He's not dead, I just knocked him out so I can bind his hands." She explained as she held the other rope.

Zulag got off the man and dusted himself off. Deeso wrapped the man's wrists together and bound them tightly. It would take a master to escape the knots she made.

Now the real issue was getting the body back to camp without any suspicion. Deeso listened for the sounds of others through the forest but could only hear the idle chirping of birds.

"Are we alone?" Deeso asked as she looked over her shoulder.

She couldn't make out anyone that was a part of the treeline, but she was well aware of the Forest Seeker's prowess at using the environment to keep themselves hidden. She didn't want to lead the two of them into another trap that was unavoidable. Zulag shrugged his shoulders as he didn't hear anything either. He went to work and grabbed the front end, while Deeso was left to grab the feet. A look of disgust filled her face as they carried the body back without issue. The two arrived back at camp to notice that Ozul was missing. Cikya sat looking at a figurine made by him while they were out hunting for food a few days prior. She tried drawing the figure's likeness in the dirt with a tree branch but got frustrated as she kept messing up.

"Where is he?" Deeso asked Cikya, as she answered by pointing in the direction opposite of them.

Ozul left to gather fibers for more rope, but also kept an eye out for wood where he could. He carried a small knife from Zulag's collection, one that he hoped would not be missed. The two dumped the unconscious body a short distance from the fire as they looked to see what caught Cikya's attention.

"What's that supposed to be?" Zulag asked, snatching it from her hands.

He manipulated the small doll in his hands while Deeso attempted to get a better look at the object. He passed it to her, and Deeso couldn't help but be impressed by the craftsmanship. The figurine had etched hair much like her own as she held her hair to it and saw that he amassed similar pieces of wood around the same size near his sleeping area. Cikya pointed to the man on the floor and inquired what they were doing with a captured Forest Seeker. She could guess, but she waited to see if her prediction was correct. It had been impossible for them to find one of their settlements, even with Ozul's assistance. It was likely they would interrogate this man on where he came from.

"Our little project for Ozul when he returns." Deeso explained as she kept her eye on the figurine. As Cikya gathered what Deeso alluded to, her face showed some anger. She nodded her head in defiance but was shut down by Zulag.

"You coddle him too much. This is important, and it's the only way he can try to be one of us." He countered her.

Cikya frowned as she was overpowered but couldn't come up with a defense of her own. Zulag grabbed a torch and waited for it to light from the fire. He heard mosquitoes in the distance and wanted smoke to waft through the camp. Ozul returned sometime later with a bushel of bamboo that he placed gently down in the space where he slept the night before and turned to address the three of them looking at him. Ozul noticed their unusual silence as his attention shifted to the still person.

"Who...is that?" Ozul asked, pointing to the restrained man who lay unconscious. His eyes narrowed as he figured something was going on, but he was trying to remain calm.

"We found someone who's got some explaining to do." Zulag commented as he held the man by a clump of his long hair, slapping him awake with a loud hit.

"Were you attacked? Are we being followed?" Ozul asked, his tone picking up in interest as he spat out multiple questions.

Ozul looked at Deeso's arms and hands marred with blood and grew concerned. He met Cikya's eyes and saw profound sadness on her face that confirmed his judgements. Ozul knew his survival was dependent on his allies and acted accordingly. Deeso didn't see herself as a master of improvisation, but she could provide compelling evidence to manipulate Ozul for her needs.

"We were going to ask this man for directions on Sadal's whereabouts, but he attacked us instead." Deeso lied.

Deeso held back a smile as her plan worked as expected. Zulag noticed her content expression but nudged her to speak. He was aware that Ozul valued his judgment the least, but he also had his role to play.

"See that singed torch in Zulag's hand? That man tried to burn me with it. Think of the destruction that could have caused." Deeso explained to Ozul.

Ozul frowned as the man looked at him. He noticed that he was one of his own kind and his tone of concern changed to one of complete scorn. It was instilled from birth that the forest's importance went beyond all else, this was not something to be taken lightly. Just yesterday, he was attacked by another Forest Seeker who saw him as an enemy instead of someone worthy of sharing their respect. His patience wore thin as he was tired.

"Fire should not be used like that, it is dangerous. You do not have the same connection to the forest as I do. Why do you care what he does?" Ozul asked Deeso.

Deeso was slightly surprised to hear such an inquisitive response, but she thought about an answer to this as well. Deeso knew that Ozul craved acceptance more than anything else and it mattered little where it came from. Behind his resolute expression was a sad child looking for affection. Deeso appealed to his ethos as she understood elements of Forest Seeker unity in their brief talks with one another. She prioritized companionship in her words and acceptance of who he was.

"It's because we care about you, Ozul. You are one of us, and it's important we rely on each other. Cikya knows this, and she trusts us, as does Zulag. Do you not trust me?" Deeso asked as she ran her foot in the dirt.

"Let me go!" The man yelled as he frantically tried to get himself out. He was pressed down by the weight of Zulag's foot on his back.

Ozul knelt next to the man and spoke to him. He decided to take Deeso's judgment to heart and reasoned he would hear what the man had to say before he decided anything.

"The forest is important to all of us. Why would you do something like this? My friends told me that you attacked them for a simple task. You had the option to say no and go your own way." Ozul expressed in a judgmental tone.

"Your friends? You traitor! How could you go against us?!" The man yelled at Ozul, coughing up dirt from his dry mouth.

Ozul massaged his face as he remembered the wound he got yesterday when he was hunting. Ozul felt a tinge of rage course through his body. He recounted how each time he tried to see with reason, he was shut out and considered irredeemable. Deeso shot Zulag a look of satisfaction as this was a result she hadn't expected. The man's outburst was now the wedge she would have to put Ozul against him and in turn trust their group more. For her, it was a win no matter the outcome.

I have seen everything I need to know. Ozul thought.

Instead of attempting to remotely defend himself, the man chose to attack his standing. This could only prove to confirm his guilt on the matter in Ozul's eyes. He remembered his father's words regarding forgiveness and tried his best to uphold the importance of that legacy. It was one of the few things Ozul kept in mind before he fell to the brink of despair.

"I forgive...you." Ozul said through gritted teeth. There was a moment of silence where the man stopped yelling as Zulag grabbed his head and planted him in the mud to silence him.

"Ozul. Do you really forgive this man for what he did? If we let him go, what will stop him getting others to attack us? Think about what they call you. Your goal to find your family is hardly worth being called a traitor. What will you do to find them?" Deeso asked with as sincere of a tone she could muster. Ozul thought and shook his head.

"No, my mind has changed. I do not forgive him. He knew the rules and broke them anyway. He attacked you both without cause." Ozul said lowly to himself.

Zulag heard this and withdrew a knife from his clothing. He gently tossed it to Ozul who didn't react as it landed to the side of him. Ozul slowly walked over and punted the man with his small left foot. He did this a few times until his eyes looked towards the torch in Zulag's hand. Zulag backed up and gave him an interested glare as he wondered what was happening. He hadn't noticed, but the man was wearing a mixture of animal skins and jungle leaves that were sewn on. Ozul with tears in his eyes, took the torch from Zulag's hand and loomed over the frantic man. The man's eyes widened as he spit out blood from his mouth and attempted to roll away. Ozul rested the torch on top as the flames quickly enveloped the man's clothes. Ozul set him alight, and the resulting flames spread to the rope. Although he was now technically free, the man was now in too much pain to do anything rational. He let out a horrific scream that amplified in volume as his flesh melted from the tinderbox he wore along his body. Patches of his skin darkened as he attempted to roll around in the dirt to douse the fire, but it was far too late for that. Zulag was taken aback by the action as he lifted his eyebrows in shock. He was impressed that Ozul truly meant every word he said. Zulag already held an elevated opinion of Ozul after his impressive elephant kill but he could see that with enough of a push he could truly be a strong warrior. Deeso's reaction differed from Zulag as she was pivotal to influencing Ozul's decisions. She saw that she could mold him to a stronger ally but would need to be sure he could be kept under control. She covered her nose with her hand to obscure the smell while she watched the man burn and Cikya looked away entirely. Cikya wasn't sure if there was anything that could justify such a horrid death.

Ozul knelt again and calmly watched the scene before him. While averse to violence, the burning of traitors and those that violate The Vow was considered as normal as breathing. For Ozul, this was life as it was, but Deeso, Cikya, and Zulag felt they awoke something worse than they anticipated.

"Traitors are to be burned. This is part of The Vow." Ozul said lowly to himself repeatably as the charred corpse of the man remained there.

The Battle of Bull Run

Jih was awake as he heard Sadal banging rocks together. He let out a dissatisfied groan as she disturbed the peace and quiet, once he finally got away from the chaos of the jungle. Aside from the raving hyenas every so often, life on the plains wasn't so bad. While Jih was content supplementing his diet with he and Trekkal's efforts at fishing, Sadal grew tired of the sparse subsistence the group had since their time together, and she felt it was time for a change. They needed a large and successful hunt under their belts, but it wouldn't be easy. Their campsite was sparse, with just a few beds made from grass and a campfire as they chose to sleep under the stars. Their tools were lined up by Narro in order of age with Jih having the first and Trekkal the last. Jih found it amusing that Narro thought this much regarding detail.

Jih watched as Sadal punched and kicked the air with some confusion evident on his face. Sadal was shadow boxing to limber herself up for the day's events and she often imagined a target that she was up against as she continued to march in place. Jih shook his head and sat on the ground, content to do nothing for a while longer until he got hungry. Jih's concentration on relaxation though was interrupted by the concerned Sadal. Sadal was getting testy and needed to come up with something to occupy her time.

"I understand that we've had some issues recently getting food. Today this will change because I have organized some drills and training for us to do. This is how we do things in my people." Sadal said, as her head turned to the still very much asleep Narro and Trekkal. Sadal's gaze turned to Jih who attempted his best to shield himself from Sadal as he didn't want to work either.

"Sadal, do you fight spirits?" Jih asked as he mockingly imitated her pose. Sadal rolled her eyes at Jih's comment.

"Well, if you have room to talk, why not give me a partner? Give those old bones of yours some practice." Sadal said to Jih.

"Jih fights with tool, not with hand. If Sadal uses tool, Jih may consider. [45]" Jih said with an egotistic tone.

Sadal took Jih at his word as she walked over and grabbed two spears that Jih made, his primary and a spare to have just in case. Jih looked at Sadal with some suspicion, he hasn't seen her use a long spear ever in the months he's known her. Unknown to Jih, members of The Broken Bone were proficient with various weapon classes to be prepared for the hunt, but they chose a specialization afterwards. Sadal had

---

[45] Authors Note: As someone who has practiced martial arts for a long time, coming up with different methods of fighting for the various groups in Jih's Journey was fun to do. Stone Breakers struggles with fist combat but their utility for tools makes them deadly when armed. The Aligned prefer to use their strength with targeted strikes in heavy punches. Forest Seekers mostly prioritize disarming movements and footwork while Thunderfeet have the closest to standardized fighting techniques using a mixture of punches and kicks.

plenty of reason to be confident against her opponent, but behind Jih stood a connection with his weapon like no other, and years of experience as old as herself.

"Is Sadal sure of this?" Jih asked, as he caught the spear that Sadal threw in his direction.

Sadal nodded and perceived that Jih's reluctance was trying to avoid embarrassment from their skill gap. Jih went to remove the stone tip of his spear, but Sadal held her hand out and stopped him from doing so. She wanted the full experience as she was trained, they would just need to be careful. Jih was apprehensive but agreed to the terms as they stepped forward. Jih held his spear mid-way out while Sadal clutched hers very closely to her body. Jih was puzzled at what form she appeared to be using but saw her the same as any opponent. Sadal had a devious expression on her face as she hoped to exploit Jih's shortcomings to her advantage.

As the two discussed what they considered a valid kill, Trekkal arose with drool over her face as she made out the amorphous blobs in her eyes that were Jih and Sadal. She saw their weapons in hand and reasoned they were sparring. Narro still rested, but he was jostled awake by the constant moving of Trekkal.

"Oh-brother, take a look at this. It would seem the eye of your interest as of late is going against Jih. I hope she gets brought back down to the dirt like the rest of us. A He-Uku, Sadal is not." Trekkal said, pointing as Narro groggily rubbed his eyes.

Jih turned his head to see that Narro and Trekkal were awake, so their show would have an audience. With the openness of the plains, their arena was massive in scale, but they hoped to keep their movements contained in their camp. Jih and Sadal took their separate positions and counted down from three to begin. Jih held his spear in a defensive position as he circled around and kept a moderate distance from Sadal's position. Sadal saw this slowness as indecisive and proposed to rush Jih while he contemplated his next move. She ran forth and extended her spear to swing wildly. Sadal's doctrine instilled into her was to bewilder the opponent with bold strokes to obscure your true intention and then go for the kill. For an inexperienced spear fighter, this would be more than enough. Jih knew this was fluff as Sadal's leg position told him what he needed.

Sadal lunged forward as Jih sidestepped towards her. Jih positioned himself clockwise to her position and was able to place himself parallel to Sadal. He took the opportunity to reverse grip the spear in his hands and held the point towards him and used the handle to swipe at Sadal's feet. When she jumped just as expected, Sadal felt this presence and rolled accordingly to save face, but she dropped her weapon in the process. The spear rolled as it hit the grass below as Sadal went to grab it. Jih decided to add insult to injury by kicking the handle of the spear out of the way much to Sadal's anger. The two began again and much like before, Jih was able to quickly break through Sadal's movements.

Narro and Trekkal could only watch in shared embarrassment as Sadal continued to hit the ground as Jih placed his kills on her with brutal efficiency. Jih could tell that it was starting to get to Sadal but continued as Sadal goaded Jih to keep going until she could figure out his strategy. Sadal felt her anger rise as she felt mentally locked into the same drills that Jih saw through and sprinkled elements of randomness to prove a point.

"Sadal. This is not fun for Jih." Jih said, as he once again tripped her with the same maneuver.

He saw the prying eyes of Narro and Trekkal watching, where Trekkal gave a small wave to Jih while Sadal stomped her foot in the ground. Sadal had an internal crisis, while she's lost battles before, this just seemed egregious. As much as she respected Jih, she felt betrayed by her teachings. By the third match, Sadal was furious as she gritted her teeth in annoyance.

"How do I keep losing?! I was taught by some of the best warriors this land has been graced with. Why do I fail now?" Sadal voiced in frustration as she was puzzled on her loss.

"Jih was taught by Hizo. Never forget this." Jih answered with a slight smile as he saw Sadal's face carry a disgruntled expression.

"I guess we can consider this part of your training complete...for now." Sadal said to Jih before she turned her gaze to Narro and Trekkal.

"What does she want?" Trekkal complained as she saw Sadal waving them over. Narro got up and left immediately to see what Sadal wanted while Trekkal made her way over at a slower pace.

Jih, Narro, and Trekkal stood around while Sadal moved to begin her first lesson. She knelt to the ground and looked up at the three of them who put their attention to Sadal. Sadal coughed and patted the ground. She instructed the group to watch her movements closely.

"In my hunting here, I've noticed that the prey seems to find us quickly because there is no foliage for us to hide in. For this, I recommend we stalk our prey by crawling towards the ground. Not only will this obscure their view, but your scent won't carry over to the prey either." Sadal mentioned as she waited for the others' reactions.

"Sadal, perhaps your strategy does not work as well as you think. Consider, my fishing has kept us fed." Trekkal said smugly to her. Trekkal gestured to the bag held with dried fish that was her doing. The evidence was hard to ignore, but one heat wave could reduce the amount of water that Trekkal depended on.

"This comes straight from Ronkalk who lived in these lands longer than you've been alive. My strategy has kept Jih and I alive before, you two seem to just fail upwards. This should yield us better fruit than your Muupasi." Sadal expressed, her finger pointed at Narro and Trekkal.

Trekkal shot a look at Narro from the audacity to imply a foreigner such as herself could survive on the plains like her people. She stuck up her nose at her comment. Sadal moved into position as a small cloud of dust materialized around her body and she rolled around, stressing the importance of keeping your scent to match the environment. Jih raised his head in suspicion, he remembered having to apply mud to hide his scent when hunting rhino, but he didn't need to roll in the ground like a hog for that.

"Is she serious?" Trekkal asked Narro as the three of them watched Sadal crawl along the ground echoing instructions. Jih scratched his head but also knelt to the ground and rolled around just as Sadal did.

"We can at least humor her, try to pay attention Trekkal." Narro said, his gaze evident not on Sadal's tactics, but somewhere else. Trekkal saw this and gave a light punch in the arm to her twin. Narro followed suit and got himself acquainted with the grass for a short while until he and Jih got up again now that their scent was masked.

"I am not doing that. I can throw stones through the air that kill things for me. That is why I have a sling." Trekkal complained in indignation. Sadal shook her head as she decided to continue onwards with her speech.

"When you get up and find the prey, you'll want to chase in a serpentine formation so that you will confuse the target. The animal may be as smart as us in trying to find a way to fight back-Yes Jih?" Sadal said, pointing to Jih who raised his hand.

"Sadal, what is serpentine?" Jih asked, prompting a laugh from Trekkal.

"Like a Sarmpa, Jih." Sadal explained with a stumble as her train of thought was stopped.

She made a movement with her arms to emphasize her point that Jih nodded in understanding. Sadal ran around their camp in such a manner which gave Jih a look of familiarity. Although he recognized the technique, he hadn't bothered to match it with Sadal's words. Sadal grabbed one of her throwing spears and explained more details about the logistics of the hunt with weapons. She raised her throwing spear up and emphasized its placement in her hand and the orientation of her wrist.

"And remember, the most important thing when you release is wind. This will change your throw's direction." Sadal said, reiterating verbatim the words she remembered from Ronkalk years ago.

"Sadal, Jih and I do not use throwing weapons. How does this affect us?" Narro inquired as he scratched his beard while Jih agreed with his question.

"You will learn in time. Use rocks to stun your target at a distance and then punish it harshly. Doing this reduces injury when dealing with aggressive prey. In The Broken Bone we eliminate the most dangerous game, and every advantage is needed." Sadal stated with a big grin on her face. Jih offered no counter, he didn't have anything to argue against such a practice. This was a tactic mostly done by children who couldn't hold larger weapons yet but integrating it even as an adult could prove useful.

"We're going to do some exercises next to-" Sadal said as she turned her head to await Trekkal's next snarky comment.

"Exercise? I can excuse the strange crawling, but I can lift twice of you. Look how strong I am!" Trekkal flexed her arms to her heart's content while Narro and Jih looked at one another.

"You know what? I've just had enough of you. I came up with tips to keep us all together as a unit. We're going to go on a hunt, and you know what we're going to bring back? A Ker-Mah. Get in line and get focused." Sadal said as she looked at Jih and Narro who moved to grab their weapons. Trekkal turned her nose up at Sadal but slowly withdrew her sling from her clothing to show Sadal she was ready for some time.

The four left their camp in preparation for the hunt that Sadal wanted to take. Narro saw plenty of other eligible prey as they advanced over the plains, but Sadal's goal was a buffalo to bring home. From what he and Trekkal could tell, water buffalo tended to congregate in large groups near deeper rivers. Finding their target would require them to go along the edges of streams. Their hope was to find the prey undisturbed by hippos that caused them a great deal of stress before. The water buffalo could be found by their smell long before you could get sight of them. The dry plains gave way to more lush patches of green grass and mud. The smell of buffalo dung pierced through everything else and was a slap in the face for those new to the procedure. Jih plugged his nose in disgust at the smell of them but observed them digging holes in the mud for water with their horns. Jih looked to Sadal to see what they should do next as they placed down their packs on some grass close by.

"I hate their horns, they remind me of those irritating Youngest that Narro and I dealt with some time ago." Trekkal spat in annoyance as she pointed into the herd.

Narro sighted ahead an old female that seemed perfect for their efforts. He hoisted his club with his hand above him and signaled to the others. Narro was more than happy to contribute to the team, his excitement invigorated Jih's initial apprehension.

"Over there! See that Ker-Mah? If we can get it out of the mud, we should be able to get something to eat." Narro proposed to the others.

Jih and Trekkal had no opinion of the matter, but Sadal was the holdout as she wanted a stronger fight for the kill. Given the circumstances behind them though, she noted the depth of the mud where the animals were staying in the marsh, and she became nervous. Although mud was earth, what lay below was rising water that would come in as the flow of the tide changed. Jih was aware of Sadal's fear of water and decided to take the initiative for her to stay on land.

"Jih will go in mud first and scare Ker-Mah. You three will corner beast." Jih said, as he gave Sadal a passing glance.

Jih left forward with his spear quickly, his pace suddenly slowed as the mud sloshed up to his knees. At 5'7, Jih was the tallest of the group and he hadn't anticipated how deep it was. He trudged slowly towards the buffalo that hadn't acknowledged Jih's presence while Sadal, Narro, and Trekkal followed along the riverbank. Jih's feet sloshed at the bottom of the brown abyss below. He looked behind him and saw the other buffalo that seemed content to roll around in the mud. He lifted his hand and started to make noises with his mouth attempting to catch the animal's attention. He took a deep breath and flailed around only to stop when he wasn't noticed.

Trekkal saw that Jih's attempts to rustle the buffalo wasn't working as well as he planned. She looked at her sling and put a few rocks in her hand. She estimated the distance and tossed a rock first to test. She watched it sit at the top of the mud until it slowly lowered down with a tentative expression on her face. Trekkal knew that if they weren't careful, it would be a difficult endeavor to get out of the mud. Narro studied the terrain as he attempted to predict where it would exit but his concentration was stopped by a yelp from the animal. Narro turned to see Trekkal launching rocks at the buffalo which caused it to stir around in the mud. Jih turned his head and frantically moved to signal Trekkal to stop. Trekkal interpreted this as a sign to keep going while she gave a raise of her fist as encouragement. Jih listened to the buffalo's yelps that eventually got the attention of the others that started a mass movement. Narro watched as the other buffalo stirred in place and started to rile each other up. He realized quickly that a stampede was imminent if the aggressive males didn't get to Jih first. Jih found the mud layered on top of him and made it more difficult to move.

"Trekkal...What did you do?" Narro asked as he grabbed his sister's arm.

Sadal noted that in the chaos Trekkal created she would have a golden opportunity to lay some direct hits on the animal now that they were distracted. She moved as close as she could to the edge of the bank without touching the water. Jih looked behind him to see the rapidly increasing number of buffalo that were panicking. He attempted to get himself further back to the bank but was met with another accumulation of mud. Jih felt twice as heavy as he sank lower. His eyes could hardly hide his panic as he looked for a plan. Jih remembered how he and his friends sunk an elephant in mud during their Recognition Hunt, and he wondered if the same principle would apply in his situation. His eyes scanned for pockets of higher elevated land in the middle of the marsh.

"Jih is stuck in mud! This will take much time." He yelled out, his voice barely hanging over the sounds of the buffalo.

Narro luckily heard his concerns and devised a plan. He tapped Trekkal's shoulder and prompted her to grab one of Jih's spare spears. He was hoping to use the wood to weave a path for Jih to get through the mud and back to the bank. Narro hoped that if he could lay it on top before it sunk into the mud, he could propel Jih forward.

"Sadal! Jih is stuck! Can you help me make a line for him?" Narro asked as Sadal nodded in acknowledgement.

Sadal ran to her backpack to see if she made any rope but saw there was no jute or sinews for her to use. Trekkal thought to herself as she watched Narro and Sadal discuss solutions on how to get Jih out. She overheard their discussion and clapped to get their attention.

"I know how we can get Jih out of the mud. This happens all the time for Peymin hunting. We will hold hands and stand in the lesser heavy areas of mud. See? Throw a rock to see what sticks and what does not." Trekkal said, extending her arm out to explain where she saw some pockets were more water than mud. Narro looked at Trekkal and gave a grunt of satisfaction with the idea and urged Trekkal to continue.

"I can grip onto the club Narro has. Sadal, you have the longest arms so you will go and give Jih this. Jih will grab the wooden end, and then we tug out with our strength!" Trekkal pointed to Jih's pack where one of his spares were.

Narro and Trekkal were happy with the plan and Sadal begrudgingly agreed. For now, she hoped to table her disdain for water for the time being in order to help save Jih. Narro served as the anchor for their human chain and held the thick end of his club out while he waited for Trekkal and Sadal to get into position. Trekkal hopped in enthusiastically and tried as best as she could to grasp Narro's end while she held her hand out for Sadal. Sadal was practically shaking as the water got closer to her. She closed her eyes and passively felt around for Trekkal's grasp and barely held back tears. Narro frowned seeing this display while Trekkal called out for Sadal.

"Over here! Grab my hand. Do you have the spear?" Trekkal asked while Sadal nodded. Despite her grievances with Sadal, Trekkal couldn't help but feel bad seeing her like this either. Sadal cringed at the sounds of the mud and rushing water that was going by as the buffalo continued to rampage.

"A little too close." Trekkal said, pushing Sadal back as the two collided with each other. Sadal held Trekkal's hand in a vice, barely letting her have circulation as she held out the spear in a long way.

"Jih! Can you come to us!? We have a spear for you to grab!" Sadal yelled; her eyes still closed as she attempted to block out her surroundings.

Jih looked over and saw the opportunity at hand. He took a deep breath and mustered his strength to lift his legs up and move forward. Narro cheered him on as he got progressively closer to Sadal. Jih trudged forward and felt himself weighed down further by the mud, but he pressed on as he did so. With just enough of a grasp, he was able to latch onto the tail end of his spear. Sadal gripped it with enough care so that she could avoid accidentally stabbing herself. Trekkal saw that Jih was in Sadal's grasp, and she urged Narro to tug. Narro retreated backwards, while Trekkal did the same with Sadal. Jih did his part as well, using the force of the other three to jettison himself through a particularly deep pile of mud. Jih was able to walk back on his own now that he was closer to shore. The difference on his person was night and day as his bottom half was caked with mud. He knew the first thing he needed to do was take a bath.

As for the buffalo that remained, their luck soon changed as it met them along the shore. Sadal opened her eyes as she touched land, and hugged the bank as she did so. Trekkal ran towards the buffalo again and propelled rocks at it with her sling, while Jih used his recovered spear to jab it with much fury. Seeing them work together filled Sadal with a sense of pride as she looked up to see Narro with his hand extended. He pulled her up and ran to join the others, just in time. Narro saw the old buffalo headed for a charge as he braced for impact. As this was an old female, he didn't need to worry about being gored by their horns which had long since fallen off. He swung with his club hitting it squarely in the face as it turned direction to kick them. Jih and the others hit the ground immediately to dodge the assault before them. Sadal grabbed her throwing spear and rushed past the others, as she launched it directly into the animal's stomach. It let out a low bellow as in the process of attempting to dislodge the spear, it impaled itself much to Sadal's satisfaction. A pool of blood filled the ground as the animal collapsed from its own hysteria. The four gave themselves congratulations on a job well done. Jih left shortly to grab his hand-axes for the group to start butchering the meat. A buffalo was a heavy endeavor and bringing back the whole corpse would attract scavengers, so taking the most desirable parts was preferred.

Jih started to work on butchering the meat while Trekkal hovered over him for a few moments as she eyed what parts would be worth bringing back to camp. Jih gave a sigh of relief as he was just happy to be back on land for the time being. Trekkal gave him a tight hug and was pleased to see him safe. Narro looked at Jih's hand-axes and addressed Sadal as he did so.

"Wow Sadal, you went in the water for the kill! This was very impressive of you to face your fear." Narro said with a warm smile as Sadal looked away in embarrassment.

For an impromptu hunt, Sadal was glad to have had success in both reinforcing group tactics but also for her own personal growth. Though she continued to fear the water, for her friends, she was able to attempt to do what she could to save their lives. The only way their journey could hold was if they worked together, and above all else, she hated being a hypocrite. If she couldn't bring herself to work within the group, what would all her training as a Master Hunter go towards?

Monkey Business

Jih, Sadal, Narro, and Trekkal had known each other for a few weeks along the Indian plains, and after much practice had sound strategies to secure food. Given the amount of time spent on hunting, they finally were able to rest for a bit as they had a surplus to last a few days. Trekkal found a few other camps of notice along the landscape, and although she held little trust in The Youngest, they would be the best chance to find out details about the meteor. Forest Seeker settlements were found to be slightly more accommodating to the group but those were sparsely found. Sadal and Narro went as friendly faces to the Thunderfeet that lived in the area. The two left Jih and Trekkal alone to make contact and trade for any stone that could be useful as repairs were needed for their tools.

Jih looked behind him to see Trekkal grin with glee as she moved towards him. Although he was informed by Eshe about his role in the world, Jih felt quite uncomfortable with the extra attention put on him by yet another group of people.

Trekkal is staring at Jih. Can she stop this? Jih feels strange. Jih thought. He decided to return the smile to Trekkal albeit with much less excitement.

"Jih is tired. Do we have beds to sleep?" Jih asked her as she scratched her head.

"Well, Jih, we could just sleep on the ground. Narro usually makes our beds, but we can look for suitable grass. Our last ones broke." Trekkal said as she looked around the landscape.

It had been some time since the four decided to camp longer than a day's worth of walking as they tried to remember the right way to go. Landmarks aside from settlements or rivers were sparse. They were lost and felt as if they saw the same places repeatedly. The plains greatest strength of the wide expanse was also their greatest weakness. Jih frowned at the mention of sleeping bareback on the ground. He was blessed to not have terrible back problems, but at his age was not looking forward to them starting now. Jih usually tried to sleep sitting up, while the others curled over when they lacked a bed.

Jih agreed and the two decided to leave their stuff in pursuit of grass. Their now empty camp was one of many prime spots open for foraging, not for humans that came by these lands but some just as crafty. A particular troupe of macaques that sat around in nearby grasses were comfortable with the increasing human presence. From their perspective, the larger animals that competed with their sources for food were prey to these mysterious figures that walked on two legs. The human tendency to gather resources in designated spots also meant a reliable lunch for the days when foraging was not ideal. While primarily focused on gathering fruits, a few pieces of meat never hurt.

As very social animals, macaques numbered about twenty-to-thirty at any given time in this area and held quite an appetite. Two scouts of the troupe noted that Jih and Trekkal left their shelter for the time being, and although it was unknown when they would return, it would be the opportunity they were looking for. The matriarch of the troupe smelled the area as she let the others know it was safe to enter. The macaques rushed to the camp and ravaged through the food bag that belonged to the four. A glorious bounty of nuts, berries, and roots gathered by Narro was now in the hands of these animals. Not satisfied, they stole Sadal's smoked meat as well. They tossed the bag around wildly and took bites out of what they considered edible.

Trekkal's fishing tools were ransacked, as one of the macaques played with the fishing rod and ran the string through its mouth. It ripped the string and bent the stick as it was trying to get its hand from being untangled. Jih's hand-axes were tossed aside in indifference. They continued this for some time before they had their fill and retreated out once again towards the open grassland.

Sadal and Narro talked to each other as they compared their hauls from their earlier visit. Sadal gave Narro a look of interest as he carried the stone with ease. Their trip towards the other camp was about a half hour's walk, but with carrying their supplies the return trip would take longer. Their backpacks were filled to the brim with material, and they cupped some in their arms as well.

"While you can't hunt that well, I'm glad you decided we should go to that camp Narro. How did you know we'd find such good stone here?" Sadal questioned.

"After you told me how The Buffalo Brothers tried to hand you second-rate stone, I had to be careful. Thankfully though we can use this to get ahead. My club could really use the repair." Narro mentioned with a grin on his face.

"Yes, not to mention their priest saw the sky that night. We've been heading south when we need to go west. Let's fix that as soon as we can." Sadal said as she walked past their camp.

"Sadal, where are you going? Camp is right here." Narro said as he knelt to place the stone he was holding on the ground.

"This isn't our camp. Everything's all out of sorts! Wholly unorganized and improper." Sadal voiced, as her eyes scanned the arrangement of things on the ground.

Sadal locked eyes with Narro who remained still. He watched as Sadal recognized their belongings. She was filled with anger as she saw that it was indeed their camp, just in an even worse state. Sadal's thoughts first went to Trekkal. Trekkal was the most unorganized, as her belongings were normally scattered around compared to the other's attention to order. Jih and Trekkal were also absent, and she would give them a piece of her mind once they returned. At the same time Sadal and Narro were searching for the culprits of the attack on their camp, Jih and Trekkal were at their wit's end searching for the material they needed. Jih withdrew a hand-axe and cut some reeds that they found alongside a small spring. They were different kinds, but Jih decided to just pile them together to see what would stick.

"Trekkal, have you found grass? Jih should have paid more attention to Kag..." Jih mumbled while he compared two sets of reeds between the other.

Jih furrowed his brow in indecision over which reeds would be best. He could barely tell the other apart aside from their texture. Jih was aware that the plants in his jungle environment would be different than the plains but grass by bodies of water were everywhere. His eyes turned to look at one and the other. He gave a sigh as he knew Trekkal could hardly help his efforts and relented to his limitations. His knowledge of plants paled in comparison to Kag, and Jih thought of him spouting off all there was to know as he often did.

"No Jih. Nothing is here. These are all so small! Have you seen them? Here, take a look." Trekkal said as she clumped some of the reeds together in her hand. She walked over to Jih and held them close to his face. Jih sneezed and wiped his nose with his arm.

"Jih has decided. We should return and check on camp." Jih commented, while Trekkal nodded in agreement. She tossed the remaining useless reeds back onto the ground and wiped her hands on her knees.

The way back for Jih and Trekkal was shorter than Narro and Sadal's back to camp as they didn't go as far as planned. She had a craving for a snack to boost her energy while Jih still remained quite tired. The two walked side by side as they found their way back in the general area of camp. She noticed the outlines of Narro and Sadal in the distance and waved to receive a response back from them. She nudged Jih to follow as they returned. Trekkal shot Jih a strange look as she noticed that Sadal was looking for something along the ground with Narro copying her movements. Trekkal raised an eyebrow as she watched the two more. Her head turned to the interior of their camp now, as she headed towards Narro's bag.

"Who took all of our food!?" Trekkal yelled as she immediately noticed the empty rift inside.

She lifted the bag and attempted to shake it. She heard nothing inside the bag as she saw that their gathered meat was scattered around, and the fruit was missing entirely. Trekkal frantically looked to see if anything was remotely saved, and all she saw were a few bite marks on some of the meat in addition to Narro's completely barren fruit bag. Trekkal massaged her stomach in hunger. Sadal was not amused as she tapped her foot to get Jih and Trekkal's attention.

"Nice of you to join us. Jih, Trekkal, can you tell me why you left camp? Who came here and stole our food?" Sadal demanded as she glared at the two of them.

"Hold on, Jih was the one who suggested we leave. I trust him way more than you. We had everything under control. Things just went apart when you two came back, so clearly this is your fault." Trekkal said, attempting to deflect the blame onto Sadal. Sadal sidelined Trekkal entirely as she waved her hand off to dismiss her but walked up to Jih and gave him a hard poke.

"Oh-So this is your fault Jih!" Sadal accused Jih.

"Yes Sadal. Jih clearly threw the food and destroyed camp for amusement." He said with grit in his voice as he grew annoyed at Sadal's blaming.

Jih, Sadal, and Trekkal argued with each other for a few moments while Narro cleaned up some of the mess. He ran his hand through his hair and his ponytail bounced slightly as he did so. Jih grew annoyed with the discourse. He looked at some of the damage and assessed what may have happened. The bites of the meat were small and Jih saw that his tools remained, a human wanting to raid would have bothered picking them up.

"This was not human. Jih thinks Makkak did this." Jih proposed to the others.

"Back home, there is Arancu-Onru. He is lazy and does not do this. Makkak though is cleverer." Jih mentioned as he described the animal's behaviors.

"Well, I'm not going out again for another hunt, we can figure this out tomorrow, so I hope you like eating bark." Sadal scoffed as she sat down and folded her arms.

Jih took a deep breath and thought of a plan. Jih wanted to test his theory by placing some bait to see if the monkeys he had in mind existed. This would line up with the practices he'd seen before. In Sundaland, the crab-eating macaque was a common sight for his people. The Elders often gave them pieces of food as thanks, for their diet interfered with the diet of The Neck-Shells who also searched for crabs to eat. The Neck-Shells caught wind of this practice and would place down food that served as bait to kill them, so for the macaque, it was often a risk for reward.

"There was some Muupasi I sighted some time ago-" Narro offered as he received a glare from Sadal. Narro chuckled at Sadal's reaction and went back to cleaning up as Trekkal assisted this endeavor.

"Sadal, why must you be this way? We have so much daylight left!" Trekkal complained to her. Sadal decided to bait Trekkal and see how she would respond.

"Sure, why don't you go then!?" Sadal yelled out to her.

"Now wait hold on, did you not say you were the best of us? Surely a novice such as me would mess everything up." Trekkal teased, as Sadal bit her tongue in anger hearing her words placed back to her. Jih gave a small chuckle at their exchange as he sighted a tree in the distance. He walked over and nudged Sadal to accompany him as he explained his idea.

"Sadal, Jih will need bait. Use spear to hit the fruit." Jih asked of her as the two looked up at a tree with figs. The sun's rays made a few of the brood particularly hard, but there were plenty of edible ones left. Jih hoped to accomplish two things with this, finding out his theory, and if the food was edible, to secure a snack for him and his friends.

Jih thought about climbing the tree, it was easy enough, but he noticed that the bark was particularly rough on first touch with his hand, and that his feet would surely be damaged. Sadal realized she forgot her belongings and raced back to grab them. She returned with two of her throwing spears as she tried to find the right distance. They were about fifteen feet in the air and dangled high. She scratched her head as she was trying to figure out how to do this. Sadal was used to throwing her weapons horizontally rather than vertically. Jih stood underneath the fruit he wished to find and pointed upwards. Sadal walked back some and ran, while Jih ducked as the spear ended up in his direction.

"Sadal! You almost hit Jih!" Jih voiced with rising anger.

"This is a bit different; I'll try again but you should move next time." Sadal said dismissive of Jih's concerns.

Jih moved a significant distance from the tree this time and watched Sadal's form as she started her throw. Sadal's second attempt didn't fare much better as she got closer to her mark, but the weapon was too heavy for it to hit. The arc was impressive as it soared upwards but struck the ground. Sadal gave Jih a shrug but kept silent as she realized what they needed to do.

"You know. Trekkal's weapon could probably do the job. The stones are light, but much force can be used. I just have to hear about it for the next week that she actually did something for once." Sadal said to herself as Jih turned to her.

Jih agreed, as he remembered the utility behind Trekkal's sling. He gave Sadal a pat on the shoulder as the two headed back to camp.

"Short hunting trip, I take it?" He asked, seeing Jih and Sadal return empty handed. Trekkal was sitting closely to Narro and drew figures in the dirt with a stick.

"Trekkal. Jih and I need your help with something. Your weapon can hit the fruit high. Jih can't climb the tree and my spears-" Sadal said before getting interrupted by Trekkal.

"Oh, I see. Did you try crawling on the ground first with your stomach so the fruits will not see you?" Trekkal mocked Sadal as she recalled Sadal's earlier hunting lessons. Narro laughed at Trekkal's words as he urged Trekkal to get up and help.

"Trekkal, we need these fruits so come on and do what needs to be done." Narro said through suppressed laughter. Sadal shook her head as Trekkal meandered along to grab her sling and some rocks to hit the fruit.

Narro was left to guard what little of what remained as Jih, Sadal, and Trekkal returned to the fig tree. Trekkal spotted a few fruits and loaded her sling. She watched with glee as it made the mark. She proceeded to get as many as she could while Sadal and Jih watched the bounty accumulate at the bottom.

"This arm is tired. Good thing I can use both!" Trekkal said as she looked at Sadal who rolled her eyes.

Jih scooped up the fruits that he separated for the group and for the monkeys. Trekkal gave Jih a happy wink while she watched him grab the figs to the point where some were falling out of his grasp. Jih nodded his head for Sadal to grab some sort of storage that he could use to hold the pieces. Sadal came back shortly with her hunting bag and opened it while Jih placed a large portion of the figs inside. The ones that he kept for himself were to be used as part of the plan. Jih nodded and called over Sadal and Trekkal, bringing them in close.

"Jih has plan. Jih will place fruit in circle like so-" Jih said, as he demonstrated to the two in a careful manner.

"Then we will see if it really was Makkaks that attacked our food!" Trekkal said happily. Sadal sighed, for her it didn't really matter much what attacked their food, but that it was missing in the first place.

"Perhaps we could eat them instead." Sadal proposed, to which Trekkal massaged her stomach, but Jih shook his head in protest.

"Makkak is bad for body. Hyu knew more, but we must stay away. Jih will see where they come from. Makkak has food to eat, and we will gather ours later." Jih mentioned to Sadal who nodded, accepting the outcome of this plan.

The three returned to Narro as he stood proudly of how he arranged their camp. Jih gave him a large pat on the back as thanks, while he placed the figs in various spots along the campsite. After some time, Jih moved a few of their belongings further away from the camp and ushered them all away, while Sadal and Trekkal informed Narro of Jih's master plan. They sat some distance away where they could see any potential arrivals to their camp.

"Denmey..." Trekkal called out, her voice trailing in disinterest as she looked around to see what animals would be close. Sadal shook her head as she watched Jih stare intently with precision focus.

"Ker-Mah that way. Good eating for later." Sadal said, pointing her hand out to the far distance where an amorphous blob with horns grazed in the distance from their vision.

"It could be worse, imagine if Jih left out meat instead! A Kalpeu and their friends would come to visit us." Trekkal said, teasing Jih who remained unmoved by her words.

"Jih, the others may not believe in your plan, but I have seen many things. The wisdom of The First will win out certainly." Narro commented in support of Jih. To his muted surprise, a small group of macaques scouted out the area and took to the bait just as he assumed.

"Ah-ha! Jih knew it was Makkak!" Jih said as he cupped his hands over his eyes to see the macaques return to the scene of the crime.

The troupe happily stuffed their faces with the figs as Jih grabbed his spear and ran over. He gave a mighty yell that scared the animals as they scattered in many directions, hoping to not meet a violent end by the two-legged beast with the sharpened stick. While Jih was happy to see that his idea was correct, the matter of finding food was still an issue for the four. The day waned, and while they decided to eat their remaining supply of figs, the desire to claim a large meal once again was a challenge for the next morning.

A Distant Land

The stifling weather of India's open plains proved to not be well suited for the jungle dwellers that were Sadal and Jih. The group prepared camp at the base of a tree where the dense foliage above gave a reprieve from the harsh rays. Narro and Trekkal fared better, but they also were affected considerably. Morale was low and food, although bountiful, was difficult to capture once again. The slow buffalo made way to fast antelopes that evaded their grasp at any turn. Sadal felt her head and she knew that a fever was coming. Jih wasn't in the best state either, a constant downpour of rain weathered the pair considerably. She felt weak and coughed into her arm as she lay underneath the makeshift tent, she constructed for herself. She rested on top of a bed of grass and her head was supported by some spare animal skins. Her nose was stuffy, and she felt miserable. She reached out her arm and waved it around, as she tried to get Jih's attention. Jih hoped to ignore Sadal for the time being as he looked for somewhere to find fresh water, but he knew she wasn't in the best condition to be left alone.

Not wanting to take any chances, his eyes looked towards some spare cloth that Sadal traded one of her spears for. Jih grabbed it and wrapped it around the back of his head reminiscent of a bandana. His nose and mouth were lightly covered. He'd seen Kag and Hyu cover their mouths in different ways many times where they worked, either by hand, or a piece of fur to avoid stench. Jih observed Forest Seeker healers wear masks carved from wood and trusted their abilities. Jih knew that smiles were contagious, but so were diseases that came from those who coughed and sneezed. He remembered how as a boy, some of the other children were sick all at the same time as their communal living meant if one person wasn't strong enough, the rest would soon follow. Jih hoped to avoid Sadal's bad air that she produced. He looked over Sadal with a raised eyebrow who gave him a small grin.

"Jih...Come here. I won't hurt you, but clearly I am not well." Sadal said, holding back laughter as Jih inched closely to her. Jih took a knee and looked over her. He grew slightly concerned with the amount of sweat that was present.

"Tell me a story. I'm bored." Sadal asked Jih. She tried to punch him in the arm but was too weak to muster a hit of any significance. Sadal coughed more and patted herself on the chest to suppress it as well as she could.

"Have those two come back yet?" She said as she spat out some phlegm.

She wiped it into the dirt with her hand and the rest on her clothing. Jih found it difficult to mask his disgust. While not a squeamish type, he was particularly paranoid at getting diseases at his age. It worried him as his mother had similar symptoms to Sadal before one day she was gone without a trace.

"No. They are still hunting." Jih responded, as he folded his legs and prepared to tell Sadal the story she wanted. Jih thought long about what kind of story would be worth telling, for he had many at his disposal. With Hizo still fresh in his mind, he decided to tell Sadal a story from when he was her age.

"Jih had mother named Hizo. She was sick, but lasting sick." He explained, his tone evident to Sadal that his mother died of the illness. He stood up straight and cracked his neck before speaking loudly for Sadal. Although Sadal's eyes were closed, she motioned for Jih to continue as she listened, and attempted to imagine what was before her. Jih hadn't bothered to tell this story to anyone before, those of his band that were aware didn't need it retold.

The Elders moved their camp to the far eastern stretches of Sundaland[46]. Although the terrain was uniform with rainforest, there was a much higher elevation which often made the group run out of breath quicker. Jih was twenty-two and traveled carrying a small basket of supplies in his hands behind Hizo who looked at him with a warm smile. She was proud of how well Jih was flourishing with his training just about complete. Now an excellent stoneworker, Jih could truly contribute to the group. In his basket was a steady supply of hand-axes that he was exceptionally proud of. The two walked among the sixty that made up his band in a line towards the familiar clearing where the camp was last constructed. As The Elders only moved location every couple of years, their former camps were often reclaimed by vegetation. Hizo recognized the foundations of the training center she constructed some time ago, as the rocks remained but moss grew over them. Other placements looked familiar to Jih as the head of line stopped and realized they reached what remained of the old camp. Tur was delighted to see that the local varieties of wood lacking in the west returned in great bounty to their new eastern dwellings. Jih and Hizo watched as the rest of their band dispersed to start their tasks. Jih felt the strong hand of his mother on his shoulder.

"Mother. Will we hunt today?" Jih asked, receiving an affirmative nod from Hizo.

Although Vut and other members of the Hunting Team were responsible for bringing food, this area wasn't visited as often as their usual location that bordered the Neck-Shells. The routes were not as well known, so finding suitable hunting grounds could prove dangerous if they were not careful. They spent their time sharpening their weapons and tested them on nearby trees. Jih, however, was impatient and hadn't eaten for some time. Not too far ahead, Hizo gave a warm laugh as she could hear the voices of Hyu and Kag bickering among themselves. She practically considered them her own children aside from Jih with as much she was around them.

"Kag buried something here once. Is it still there?" Kag asked with some intrigue to Hyu as she could only roll her eyes at her brother's questioning.

Kag shrugged his shoulders as he tried to remember what he placed in the ground for some time. He reasoned that if he couldn't remember it, surely it wasn't that

---

[46] Eastern Sundaland was part of a region that now makes up modern Borneo and the subsequent islands that were back then bridged together along with the rest of the mainland. The forests were less sparse overall due to higher altitude, but growth was still very common due to moisture from the nearby Kapuas River.

important. Jih and Hizo built their home easily as the foundations were still left along with the remnants of some processed wood. They placed the skeleton that would make up their walls and decided to revisit the project once they got some food into their systems. Jih was somewhat concerned about Hizo, but he tried to hide it as best as he could. He remembered seeing his mother suffer from periodic shakes that would stop anything she planned to do for the day. It was some time ago, but not long enough for it to leave Jih's mind. She was in good spirits today and was eager to spend some time with her son.

Hizo told Jih to get anyone interested to join them on the hunt, and he naturally gravitated towards Kag and Hyu who dropped any opportunity to come for adventure. Hizo gestured in the direction of where she thought to have seen a glimpse of Dran, but she wasn't present. Although Hizo had friends of her own that she hunted with, she cherished the time she spent with Jih, Kag, and Hyu out on the trail. She delegated tasks for them to accomplish on the hunt as they took point. Hizo's target was a Javan rhino. She took her position as leader seriously and charted out a course for them to take once the prey was sighted. Jih and Kag were to use their spears to corral the rhino into a position where it would be unable to advance, while Hyu would act as a support with her whip.

The rhino's hide was thick, but even a small scratch with the barbs on it would be enough to send the rhino into a frenzy. Hizo gave herself the hardest task, which was the actual kill itself. For a direct hit, she would want to pierce the brain or have it bleed through the eyes. If she could avoid it, she'd want to claim the rhino's life without too much resistance. Stressed meat didn't make for good food. The Council found use for the horn beyond her understanding and knew that the meat would be well appreciated by the Hunting Team who ran into difficulties on the walk. Hizo's memory was sharp as she remembered a few local streams that ran concurrent to the river. If any animal were to converge there, that would be the spot to go.

The four traveled quietly, where Jih carefully cut away vegetation with his hand-axe while Kag's eyes were focused on locating the kill. Kag noted a few plants that he would need to study the properties of, as he needed to restock on some with antiseptic properties for the wounded. As they were away from the Neck-Shells for some time, they had little worry of raiding, but injuries were more common around these parts. In older years, Hyu and Hizo spoke on occasion to each other, with Hyu mostly nodding respectfully to Hizo's words and guidance. Although Hizo treated her and Kag with immense kindness, Hyu always felt a slight divide between the two when it came to Jih. Hizo spoke often of legacy and how to maintain it through the ages as she was proud of her heritage. Hizo respected Jih and Hyu's union but both abstained from children. This made Hyu wonder if there was any hidden tension between the two due to this decision. While Jih was close to his mother, there were times when the two didn't talk at all despite living in the same hut together. Hyu still shared a hut with Kag but wanted to build a new home with Jih. Jih often tried to dodge the subject wanting to avoid conflict with his mother. Hyu felt it wasn't her ground to speak on the matter to Hizo, and Jih was not open to her about this. Hyu's thoughts were interrupted by Hizo's movement coming to a halt.

As Hizo trained them to fight since they were children, she only expected the best of teamwork to come. She held her hand up and gave a closed fist as a signal for the others to look ahead as their objective was close. Their descent down the hilly foliage led to the stream that she remembered. It was the rainy season, so the stream filled up past their ankles as they sloshed around in the flowing water. This provided an excess amount of mud that piled up.

"Down here. Rub mud carefully and hide your scent." Hizo said, as she urged the others to wipe mud down on each other.

Although this wasn't standard practice, Hizo knew that the wind that came from the fast-flowing stream would make their scent apparent. Mud was a miracle covering as it obscured their scent and made most of their skin impenetrable to bugs that otherwise would impede their objective. She took a handful and applied it to herself. She moved her attention to Jih and gave him a loving grab on the cheek as she rubbed mud on him.

Down on the far end of the stream, the outline of a rhino sipped happily from the flowing pool. Jih waved the others forward as they took opposing sides of the stream and stalked their prey quietly. A bellowed grunt from the rhino signaled it knew something was coming, but their eyesight could only reveal so much. The four took advantage of this and got themselves into position just as Hizo envisioned. Hyu crawled low on the ground, retracted her whip, and struck the animals' bare back legs. The crack it made through the air startled the rhino and left it vulnerable. The bewildered rhino led a charge towards a tree while Jih and Kag waited with spears on opposing ends to trap the animal. Kag gave Jih a wink as he let out a triumphant grunt, where Jih joined him and bewildered the animal's senses. The two stabbed wildly at the rhino as it prepared for another charge. In the fighting, Kag dropped his spear below and was unarmed.

The rhino thrashed around and Kag tossed rocks to divert its attention away from him so he could reclaim his weapon. Hizo, as daring as she was, took her spear and went straight for the right eye. She jammed it in tightly and watched her handiwork as the creature bled before her. A large amount of blood burst out at once and littered the mud below as the rhino quickly bled out. The impact from the speed at which she jammed the spear thrust her forward and she struggled to keep balance as she fell over. She evaluated her weapon and saw that it nearly cracked in two with the exertion she placed on herself. She wiped her brow and breathed heavily as she saw the others were also exhausted. They weren't yet acclimated to their new conditions. The four celebrated their victory with a short cheer as Hizo admired the quality of the kill. Jih looked at his mother with pride while he heard Hyu and Kag bicker once more. Kag and Hyu argued over who would carry the meat, with Kag losing out as Hyu handled that duty last time.

While Jih tore off sections of the rhino to pack, Hizo let out a pained expression as she lifted her head. Her vision stifled as she was held by Hyu and Kag who ran to carry her. Jih dropped his hand-axe to assess his mother's condition and was puzzled as she just landed the killing blow on a rhino just moments ago. Jih thought perhaps his mother was feeling faint from lack of food, but there was more than that. He gave Hyu a concerned look as this wasn't the first time this happened. Jih remembered his mother being strangely absent-minded a few weeks prior and he had to repeat the same instructions that she told him just moments ago. Kag and Hyu were stumped on where to begin.

"This has happened before, yes brother?" Kag asked with concern as Jih nodded.

"Yes. Hizo fell to ground in hut before." Jih noted as his head turned to hear Hyu offer her perspective. Kag looked to Hizo who tried her best to suppress her shakes as her fist clenched the dirt. Kag held her steady while he looked up at Hyu. Kag's eyes scanned the perimeter for copperleaf in hopes a quick salve could calm her nerves.

"Hyu has thoughts on what should be done. Did Hizo eat bad food? Worms in stomach cause bad shakes, requires bitter drink to heal. This may be head worm? [47]" Hyu proposed.

They suggested Hizo get rest to clear her head as she was overworked due to demands from The Council. While this was true, Hizo had a tumor that developed in her head for some time but the effects of this only arose in the last six months. She was particularly quiet about her condition, as she held immense fear of being treated. She felt that the medicine was just as painful as the injury, and as she was able to work most of the time, there was nothing to make a fuss about. Kag suggested taking a piece out of Hizo's head to relieve pressure as a joke, a gesture that only scared her further. Hyu shot a glare at Kag who awkwardly smiled, as he realized his delivery could've been better. While Kag and Hyu were trained, their teacher remained the primary caregiver and they were the one that Hizo would trust with these affairs.

"Jih will return Hizo to camp." Jih said as he took the unconscious Hizo in his arms.

Jih and the other youth of his group didn't have any sort of strength training like that of The Buffalo Brothers or of The Broken Bone, but the regimented exercise of the hunt was more than enough to build muscle and keep it on. This strength enabled Jih to last as he carried his mother uphill, while Hyu and Kag worked to get the meat sorted. Sometime later, Jih found himself in the company of Hyu and Kag who shared his concerns. Out of breath, he barely made it with Hizo back to the boundary of camp. Tur, who had been talking to a member of The Council about his plans, noticed Jih in the corner of his eye and dismissed himself early from the conversation.

"What did you do?" Tur asked as he saw Hizo's state. Jih grew annoyed as Hizo's condition was no fault of his own, but he assumed that something was amiss.

---

[47] Medical science in the Paleolithic was at its infancy to put it lightly, but there is traditional knowledge kept by the groups in Jih's Journey and in real life instances evident through the archaeological record. Tapeworm epidemics were something sought to be eliminated and, in many cases, agents used to reduce inflammation have been found in coprolites and were represented in strontium analysis. Modern hunter-gatherers have an assortment of herbs and other compounds to assist.

"Hizo fell. This has happened before. She has said nothing." Jih explained, his voice venomous to Tur's questioning. All that mattered now was getting Hizo the treatment she needed if that were even possible.

"Take Hizo to tent, Tur will summon healer." He said pointing to the other end of camp. He quickly made his rounds to find Kag and Hyu's teacher, an older man who had a bounty of fruit to eat as he was informed of what happened.

Jih placed Hizo at the mouth of the medical tent and looked over her before returning to the half-finished hut that they started. He sat for about an hour, as he watched Hyu and Kag go towards the medical tent until he saw Tur arrive in his direction. He picked at his skin in utter disinterest, but it was apparent Tur had good news. Hizo was revived with water and time. She remained weak, but she was able to leave a message of dire urgency. Tur clapped to get Jih's attention as he watched Jih raise his head to listen.

"Hizo sends Tur for message. Come with Tur now." Tur stated as Jih got up without further delay.

Jih and Tur made their way to the tent where Jih broke from Tur's sight almost immediately. He lifted the entrance flap and saw the immobilized Hizo resting on a bed of leaves. The tent was barren as there was little preparations made other than her presence. A few spare coconuts were empty as their contents were poured into Hizo to hydrate her. She briefly lost some control of her body and was turned manually to face visitors. Her eyes darted up to see Jih before her. Jih hesitated to touch Hizo in fear of injuring her, but her eyes gave Jih warmth that allowed him to touch her.

"Mother!" Jih yelled in hysterics.

"Not so loud my son, Hizo is right here. It will only take some time before we hunt again. There is something Hizo wants from Jih. Can he give it to Hizo?" Hizo asked with a small grin.

Jih nodded without question. His desperation for a cure would have him search the ends of the world if it was required. Tur's shadow lingered outside the tent and eavesdropped on their conversation.

"Jih will look for white flower. It is called Moon Orchid, flower of much beauty. Hizo heard of such things when she was young but never saw it. Will you find it? Will you see if it is true? Hizo does not know more than that." Hizo asked with a cough.

"Yes. Jih will go when sun is high tomorrow." Jih said as he placed his hands on Hizo's stomach.

"Jih. Moon Orchid is not cure for healer. You are my legacy. One day you will outlive Hizo in years and death will come for you. Live the way life has set out for you. The choice of your destiny is the greatest gift Hizo can give." Hizo stated.

"Jih knows death will come. It is only a matter of when." Jih said as he looked away from Hizo.

"Remember our first boat ride? We held oars together and it was difficult to go against water. Our shoulders hurt for days. Much like water, death flows where it chooses and Hizo has made peace. It could be tomorrow or many years from now." Hizo said.

"What will Jih do when Hizo is gone?" Jih asked, as his eyes were on the brink of tears.

"Live? Hunt? Work stone? Jih will do what he always has. Hizo has survived to see Jih grow and live full life. Many others are dead and cannot say the same for their children." Hizo reprimanded Jih. Jih hugged Hizo as she rubbed his head with a smile.

"Go with love Jih. Hizo will be with you always." Hizo said as she felt a wave of exhaustion.

Jih saw this as his means to leave his mother to rest. He lowered his head in respect and left Hizo to recover. He exited the tent and saw Tur lock eyes with him. Jih could tell from his expression alone that he was aware of Hizo's condition just as much as he was. Jih knew of their shared importance to Hizo, and for the first time in ages, he decided to ask for Tur's input. Jih humbled himself briefly as he called for Tur's aid.

"Tur, this Moon Orchid that Mother talks of, does Tur know where this is?" Jih asked as his voice reeked of desperation.

"Moon Orchid is not found here, but..." Tur mentioned as he closed his eyes in thought.

"But?" Jih replied as he waited for Tur to finish his statement.

"Tur has heard of land across ocean. Many flowers on coast where those dare to find it." Tur suggested to Jih as he gestured to a direction beyond their lands.

Tur was undoubtedly a master woodworker, and he was willing to collaborate with Jih on a project for this. His plan for Jih was to make a boat that could brave the ocean so that Jih could voyage to retrieve the Moon Orchid. Tur rarely had much to say towards the younger generation, but he held a close friendship with Hizo and respected her dearly. Although Tur was not yet a member of The Council, he held significant favor with them and would use his influence to mobilize most of the band to help with his project.

"Tur will make village build boat. Many hands make light work, and you will leave tomorrow morning." He said, anxious to gather the attention of the adults that were reconstructing their homes.

Jih nodded in approval and agreed that this would be the best way to move forward. Tur went to work right away, and gathered the wood he would need to apply his ideas. Jih had never seen Tur with such drive before and despite his personal issues, appreciated the effort to save Hizo. Jih left to return home to plan his route for the next day. Jih turned his attention to see Kag come in his direction. Jih gave a wave and greeted his friend as he saw the outline of Hyu appear sometime after.

"Brother, what has happened? Nothing good comes from Tur." Kag asked with a slight grin, propping himself up against the wall of Jih's half-done hut. The wall caved in slightly as he leaned in and Kag gently pushed a wooden stake back into position.

"Mother has given Jih orders. Jih must find Moon Orchid. It is white." Jih explained, with some doubt in his voice. He shot Kag a look to defer to his expertise on all things plant related and needed to know if it was true.

"There are many flowers that Kag knows! Color is white?" Kag questioned as he tried to remember what plant would be most useful for Hizo's condition. He recalled the incident where Hizo fell unconscious and already drafted a plan of action.

"Yes Kag, it is white. Jih needs to know all there is." Jih replied.

Kag's expression was blank as he gave a shrug, it wasn't something he was particularly solid on. This gave Jih some worry as he stuck his head into his hands in distress. While Jih was having a moment, Kag turned his head as Hyu made her entrance. She gently stepped in front of Jih and squatted. She stared at him with wide eyes as she did so. He lifted his head up to see the warm face of Hyu looking at him. She gave Jih a tight hug and the two rubbed noses.

"Where will we go?" Hyu asked, as she interjected into the conversation.

Jih pointed ahead as the two turned around to see the rush of production. The denizens of The Elders carried long pieces of bark that were stripped together and placed on a raised platform with cut pieces of wood. It was a remarkable construction, with each worker chiseling away an essential piece for the boat. Tur personally worked on the hull which he considered the most important piece. He measured out a long sturdy piece of wood by using smoothed rocks as an estimate. As people came to seek his approval, Tur pointed his finger and dictated instructions with vigor in his speech.

"Tur has power. Not good for us." Hyu said with a slight laugh as she wrapped her arms around Jih.

Jih nodded in agreement and saw how well fitting it was for Tur to bark out orders to the rest of the group as he worked. He was primed to be part of The Council; it was his goal since the day he was born. Prestige and wisdom were admirable goals on their own, but what Tur craved above all else was power. He couldn't get respect in the way Hizo did, so he hoped to one day reinforce that another way.

"Island to the east. We must go and find Moon Orchid." Jih reiterated for Hyu. Kag noted that the endeavor might need an extra hand, but it was difficult to find anyone willing to leave their post. Tur had only told Jih, and he assumed that he would go alone, but the boat was large enough to accommodate far more. Jih decided to take the initiative and ask around for anyone willing to help, as Kag and Hyu already pledged to drop everything to help Jih. Their loyalty to him and their love for Hizo would see them through any challenge, including finding a place they'd never seen before. Hyu and Kag waited by Jih's tent and talked as they watched him look for eligible people to come on their short trip.

While Jih got many sympathies regarding Hizo's condition from the members of his band, he wasn't getting any takers on the offer. The hollowness of people's statements was enough to put anyone on edge. Jih grew frustrated considering all the things his mother did for their community, even arriving originally as an outsider. His efforts were for naught as he circled around. Although a few plucky teenagers offered their services, Jih would feel guilty and face the wrath of any parents if their loved ones got injured or worse. It simply wasn't worth the risk. As Jih reached the outer boundary of camp, he gave an audible sigh as he approached a tent that was already complete.

Ever industrious, Dran had already finished setting up her tent and waited patiently for Hizo's orders. Alone after the death of her father in a scouting accident, Vut's family took her in due to their friendship, but she remained ever distant. She served as Hizo's understudy, as she learned the ways of the combat arena and the various responsibilities that she would carry on in the present. A small fire lit the enclosure as smoke billowed from the top, indicating that she was home. Jih pulled on the flap of fur that served as the door for her tent. The flap shot up and Dran crawled out of the entrance of her home to look around. She locked eyes with Jih and shot a glare. Dran took one look at Jih and lowered the flap.

"No." Dran commented, as she retreated further into her tent.

She turned around and brought her attention to more important matters, like her assortment of branches she enjoyed collecting.

"Dran...please. Listen to Jih." Jih pleaded outside her tent, his voice exasperated as ever. Jih already regretted bothering to ask Dran for help, but he was desperate. He heard no response come from her, but he decided to continue anyway.

"Hizo is sick. Jih must help fulfill her will." Jih said, as his ears heard a faint rustling sound.

And Kag likes this one? Surely there is someone better. Jih thought as he waited.

The flap opened again, and Jih was given a small invitation inside. He knelt and crawled into the entrance of Dran's home and sat up. She sat a respectable distance from Jih as she studied him closely. She was trying to deduce if he was lying, but Dran's expression took him at his word. Jih was many things, but he always delivered things straightforwardly. This was one of the few traits she appreciated regarding Jih. When she heard of Hizo's condition, it was incredibly difficult for her to process. She was preoccupied with the recent move and hadn't checked on her mentor in a few days. She felt incredibly guilty. She reached over to Jih and gave him a small hug. Jih's body tensed up entirely as his eyes expanded slightly in surprise at the gesture. He wasn't sure Dran had a heart to begin with, but as he looked around her tent, he noticed the various quirks about her. She collected tree branches that she could talk about in length, and the inside walls of her tent were decorated with a green pigment, something that took noticeable effort. Jih was more comfortable with expressing himself while Dran kept two separate lives. She prided herself on being a cool and calm person, often unaffected by such things. She and Jih's friend groups couldn't be further apart, but age made strange situations. They relied on each other more often as the demands of older adults forced them to put aside their differences. Jih left first with Dran coming behind him.

The two walked quietly, not saying much to one another as Jih saw Hyu and Kag still waiting outside his tent. He offered a small smile to the two, knowing that this would be a controversial pick no matter how he sold the idea to them. Hyu shot Jih a look that meant they would talk later as she attempted to be civil to Dran. Dran glared at Kag who gave a greeting of his own by emulating Jih's smile.

"Dran." Hyu said, her tone curt as Jih returned with Dran walking beside him.

"Hyu." Dran said as she didn't bother to acknowledge Kag at all. Kag gave a cough where Jih hoped to save the moment by informing them all the plan he formed in his mind.

Jih went over the details and after a few moments they shook hands and agreed. Jih went to work finding material to make hand-axes and other implements while Hyu accompanied Kag to see what plants he could forage for injuries. Hyu wished to prepare bandages and looked around their stock for any spare skins she could wrap around. Dran left to return to her tent and slept. She knew that she would fulfill her end of the bargain by arriving on time.

"Hyu will make supplies. Make sure Dran shows on time Jih." Hyu warned with suspicion in her voice as she watched Dran walk off.

The next morning, a young child stood over Jih and lightly kicked him. He held his fingers to his lips to keep quiet. He arrived under the orders of Tur and was told to follow. The others were already awake and ready to go as Jih quickly gathered his things that he could fit in his hands. The walk was longer than Jih anticipated, but the familiar smell of the Sundaland shore took root in his nose as he got an early wave from Kag. Tur stood by with a prepared boat as promised, with his arms folded in judgment upon Jih's arrival being last.

Hizo was too weak to go accompany Tur, but she gave them a warm message that encouraged the four to start on their quest. Jih nodded, as he heard Tur explain the importance of this endeavor and how grateful she was for everything. They piled into their boat; a large vessel made from solid bark that housed them quite well. The feature Tur was proudest about was the hull and the accompanying oars that came with it. Most seacraft were not built in such a manner, but the currents of the east were fierce, and no mere raft would be able to contend with this mighty canoe. For a project that took less than a day, the boat was resoundingly high quality.

With a small push, the boat rocked slightly as they were beginning to reach the starting current that would drive them out to sea. The water was a delightful teal color and seemed infinite to the eyes of the four. Dran obsessively checked the directions of the boat and made sure they were heading east as Tur instructed. They continued to move forward until Sundaland slowly faded behind them. Kag and Jih rowed for some time in relative silence, but Kag couldn't stand it much longer. He had something he wanted to ask.

"Kag has question for group." He said with a smirk on his face.

The four sat on the ends of the boat, where Jih and Kag would steer as it was responsible for Hyu and Dran to scout the sky for birds. Birds meant land was somewhere nearby, and they would accomplish their goal. He laughed as he heard an audible sigh come from both Dran and Hyu as there was no escaping his sense of humor.

"Is spear the handle or point? Discuss while Kag rows." Kag asked, as he looked around and saw the faces of his friends churn in thought. Dran and Jih spoke first giving it little time to consider as they both have more intimate knowledge with stone working.

"Spear is point." The two said in unison while they waited for Hyu's answer. Hyu shook her head as she disagreed with the two.

"Spear is handle. Long wood makes spear. Short wood makes dagger." Hyu said as she stretched out her idea with her arms.

"Wrong. Point makes spear. Curved point makes axe. Handle can be anything." Dran countered, as she elbowed Jih expecting him to back her claim.

Although Jih hadn't known Dran too well, much of his issues with her stemmed from Hyu who had a much different image of her painted. On occasion he also felt Dran's wrath as a child, but this was not his fight to wage. Hyu and Dran saw the world in very different ways which made them opposed to one another from the beginning, but Jih hoped they could find more in common.

The island of Flores was a six-mile journey along the water, so their travel time with the combined power of Jih and Kag was shorter than expected. Daylight was at its prime in the air as they headed towards a strip of the coast with their boat. Jih and Dran lifted the back end of the boat, while Hyu and Kag pulled backwards to park the boat in the sandbanks. With that done, the four found that the island was much like Sundaland, complete with beaches and tropical foliage. If anything, at least they wouldn't be homesick. Jih took to the boat one last time to take out the small number of supplies they brought for the voyage, including their chosen tools. Jih, Kag, and Dran all used spears while Hyu stuck with her whip and a small dagger for closer encounters. Unsure of where to go, the four walked down the massive coastline before them. Occasionally, one of them would look back and track their progress, as a long line of footprints refused to vanish behind them.

"Island is quiet. Kag does not hear anyone else." Kag observed as he kept his ears open for the sound of anything out of the ordinary.

Kag saw the outline of a volcano and raised an eyebrow wondering how much of a concern that would be. In the past, he heard from Hizo and Tur stories about when these would erupt and cause ash to fill the sky with much death. A grim story, they were often told this to remain in good behavior, because only the bad were hexed by a volcano. Jih stopped Kag as he pointed to the ground and saw that there were other footprints aside from their own.

"People are here. Feet are small, perhaps these are children?" Jih asked as he received nods from Dran and Hyu. Their footprints practically engulfed the ones they saw before them. Hyu hoped that she would be able to ask them for a general direction on where to go to find the flower.

The four walked for some time and noticed that the island was home to particularly strange animals. Kag scouted a stork along with its mate that pecked at the ground. It lifted its beak up as it sighted the group and opened its mouth letting out a harsh call. Kag was taken aback by just how large the animal was, it was taller than all of them. He'd seen storks before, but none this big. Jih and the others wondered if other creatures were also this way.

"Vatki is large! Jih, look over there! [48]" Kag said to Jih who nodded in agreement.

The two studied the creature's appearance with its long pink legs and yellow beak as it flapped its wings in a strange display. One of the storks flew in the direction of the others and Jih felt a tug at the back of his shoulder as Kag laid to the ground. The two shared a laugh together with their faces full of sand. While the two were enamored over the size of the large storks, Hyu's gaze turned to see a creature idling in the sand for some time. It was a Komodo dragon that remained uninterested until its head turned to look at Dran. Hyu could see the color drain from Dran's face as she also locked eyes with the creature noting its size and tail that dragged behind it. To Dran, the animal before them reminded her of a snake as its tongue exited its mouth, and she opted to avoid finding out if it shared the lethality.

"Those are claws to avoid. It eats meat, we are meat." Dran noted as she extended her finger out towards the beast.

Her words fell to a crowd that none could hear as Hyu sprinted ahead. While Hyu avoided the creature, she peered into the distance to see another Komodo dragon, but this time, there was a strange mass surrounding it. On a further examination, she could see that young children were engaged in combat. Hyu waved to grab the attention of the others before setting off on her own.

"We must help them! Hyu will go now." Hyu pointed in the distance.

Jih and Kag gave each other a look but noted that this would be their best chance to find what they're looking for. Reactions were mixed to Hyu's insistence to help these new strangers. Jih and Kag were willing to help Hyu, but Dran had thoughts of her own. She gave a low grunt as she reminded the others. She kicked the sand in protest as she got the attention of Kag and Jih.

"We need to find Moon Orchid! Stay on task Hyu!" Dran yelled out to her.

Hyu ignored Dran's warning as she inched closer to study how the Komodo dragon fought. She saw that another Komodo dragon heard the fighting and approached, making the match uneven. There was a group of about six focusing their efforts on the first creature. As Hyu ran ahead to deal with the problem herself, Jih turned his head to see her vanish. Jih dragged Kag with him as they ran past Dran.

"Follow Jih! Hyu has gone to fight." Jih said, as he raised his spear to meet with her. Hyu stood some distance away as she got herself into position to fight the Komodo dragon.

---

[48] Emic name for stork. On Flores, giant storks about 6-7 feet tall were common in this period!

She found herself involved in the fray, where she noticed the second of the Komodo dragons turned to pursue her. Hyu raised her arm and cracked her whip, touching the ground next to it, as it didn't react to the sound of her attack. She observed the speed of the lizard as it ran towards her. Hyu ran quickly to the side of it, and landed a hit, but the tough skin wouldn't do much without a strong penetrating weapon. Hyu looked to see Jih arrive quickly with his spear, as he swiped widely and hit the creature's tail. As it started to bleed, Hyu saw her opening and aimed for the tail wound, causing it to sting the creature a great deal.

Dran arrived shortly after with Kag and kicked sand at the animal in an attempt to blind it. She jumped to the side and used her spear to land a solid hit on the beast, but her spear point fell off as it was embedded in the creature. Kag let out a loud yell and bewildered the animal by using his intimidation to ward it off. Unable to successfully kill the animal, their assault was enough to make it retreat as they recovered their strength. Jih saw that Dran's spear point broke off with the Komodo dragon's scales, so they would need to avoid engaging with these creatures at all costs. A short distance away, the children they witnessed earlier were still in combat with the other beast.

The Komodo dragon whipped its tail and tripped a girl to the ground. She managed to get away just in time before she was bitten or gored by the sharp claws. It was clear to their onlookers that an expert was among them. Jih raised his eyebrows in shock as the Komodo dragon took a bite of one of the children's arms. It had a low bite force, but the amount of venom that excreted from the bite was enough to practically cause instant death in targets this small. The boy fell over where he stood. There wasn't much blood left. The Komodo dragon's claws severed another young girl's arm clean off as she screamed, where the cry was audible to the four watching.

"What...What has happened? He just fell dead! Jih does not understand." Jih said in shock as Kag shared his expression, with their mouths agape. It didn't take much for Kag to decide that a better route was possible than to deal with these lizards as Hyu decided on their behalf.

"Kag has plan!" Kag announced triumphantly, while Hyu and Dran looked onward waiting for Kag's instructions. In his haste, Kag rushed to make his way back to the boat before hearing Hyu scream at the top of her lungs.

"Kag! You come back here right now!" Hyu shouted, prompting a worried laugh from Kag.

"Sister, Kag was getting help!" Kag said with a cheeky smile.

What the four saw to be children were full-grown adults. These were members of the group known as Stumps, a nickname made by Kag for their short stature and brown skin much like their own. [49] Jih noticed that these people were pointing in their direction as they came up to them. Jih couldn't help but be impressed at such a young age they did

---

[49] Stumps or Homo floresiensis, are a species of human known for their incredibly short stature. At an average of three feet and six inches tall, these people were faced with overwhelming odds, with everything seeing them as potential prey.

such a kill. Given how they approached it, this was not a Recognition Hunt, but instead a routine one done by clearly well-trained individuals. As they approached Jih his expression changed to one of pure surprise. He saw that their faces looked aged, older than himself or anyone else. A woman among them with her hunting companions that survived the ordeal above the bleeding Komodo dragon stepped forward and was caked in blood. She shook as the excess blood dripped into the sand.

"You are new. Avoid the Nalinata when you can." The woman said to Jih.

She introduced herself as Osa, with her hunting companions tending to their wounded. Jih remained stunned at their appearance, and slowly extended his hand that Osa accepted kindly. Osa and her hunting companions were in their early 30s, about a decade older in age and it showed. Osa gestured to the rest of the group and introduced them. She was surprised at the height of Jih, and the others that far exceeded their own. Jih and the others were respectively stunned that others of this island differed from their own and that they could understand them.

"Hyu, these are not children. This one has beard!" Kag said, pointing to the man standing close to Osa.

Kag compared the thickness of their respective beards. As he heard Osa address the others, Kag couldn't help himself as he felt a bout of laughter spout out. The mystique of their foreign nature vanished quickly. Due to their size, Osa and the other Stumps had high-pitched voices that sounded humorous to Kag. Jih found this amusing as well, but he kept it more hidden than Kag ever could.

"Our leader is missing. We must find him. Will you help Osa?" She asked, as Hyu was happy to help answer for the group. Dran folded her arms in annoyance as the last thing she wanted to do was involve herself in the affairs of people she just met, but Hyu practically already made new friends by talking to them.

"Hyu accepts. We will help you find leader. Tell us what happened, and we will do all we must." Hyu said while she looked to Jih who nodded in support. Dran was itching to get back to the matter at hand and interrupted Hyu's further statement.

"Moon Orchid. Do you know of it? It has the color white." Dran asked as Osa's companion tapped Osa on the shoulder and reminded her of the flower that Dran was referring to.

It went by a different name, but she was certain that based on their description this was what they were looking for. It grew around the boundaries of their village, and she was willing to part with it given she received the help she wanted. The four looked at each other with some confusion at their new circumstances, for their entire lives they were told that they were the only people out there, and yet, this wasn't the case. Hyu organized a small huddle among them as they were unsure of what to do with this new information. Jih dragged Kag over as the four talked among themselves while they weighed in on helping Osa. Osa stood patiently with the others of her kind as she did so.

"The Council should know of this." Hyu said with some fire in her voice.

"Kag agrees. Stumps are strange ones, but we speak the same tongue. There are questions and The Council is hiding something." Kag commented in agreement with his sister.

"They will deny it. If this gets us flower for Hizo, let it be done already." Dran resigned as she broke the circle.

Hyu ran forward to give their decision while the others waited. Jih looked at their tools to see what they were using to take down such terrifying opponents. As they were visitors to this island, he wondered if there was anything worth retaining from their neighbors. Jih observed the three were carrying sharpened spears made of wood but lacked stone tips. The length of these weapons was practically the same height as them. The smell of dung was in the air and Jih noticed this as he examined their weapons more closely. The tips were smeared with dung to fester in the wound and cause infection in the prey.

While germ theory was a concept not grasped by them, there was an understanding that agents such as these would interfere with the healing process and enhance the severity of injury. Osa herself carried one of these spears, but also had specifically carved pieces of wood tied to her grass skirt. These were throwing sticks that on their own could kill small game but were used in their hunting of the Komodo dragon to disorient them long enough for a stabbing in the extremities such as their underbelly or eye. Fighting the Komodo dragon was especially heinous, as unlike a dhole or other animals, one bite would guarantee death. Osa and her core group had to be exceptionally careful, and they lost plenty in the past.

The voice of Sadal broke Jih's concentration as she interrupted him with an assortment of questions. While Jih was appreciative she was paying attention, he felt his flow was stifled. Sadal was insistent on continuing to do this as she saw Jih stare at her and not give a response. She tapped the ground as Jih spoke, and his eyes looked directly at her. A small plume of dust filled her nose as she sneezed, and Jih retreated as he waited for another to come from Sadal. She sneezed again as Jih anticipated and wiped her nose. Sadal was raring to get Jih's input as she called his attention. Jih lifted his head and worried something was further unwell with Sadal as he watched with concern. Sadal's smile set him at ease as she spoke.

"So, you're telling me that there's big lizards that could open their mouths real wide and take a bite out of you?" Sadal said as she opened her hands to match the size.

"Yes. Jih does not lie about this." Jih said with a slight yawn in his voice.

"Wow, I would love to hunt one of those. Venomous too you say?" Sadal asked with her voice elevating in excitement.

"Can Jih finish story? Only Jih knows what happens." Jih said, as he hoped to reign in the conversation. Jih tried to remember where he left off. Jih was a patient man but had a low tolerance for being interrupted for something not important. He looked behind him as he spoke, with still no trace of Narro or Trekkal.

Much like Jih's home with the Neck-Shells, Osa's group had a rivalry of their own with another band from the island. They had a singular leader who was captured, along with their young infant. Osa and her people raced to find any solution to bring the two back safely but their attempts at raids were thwarted. With the new arrivals however, Osa figured a deal could be made. Despite her joyful appearance, Osa was not yet willing to expose the location of her village to new arrivals. She urged them though to set up camp in a much more sparsely populated area so that they could keep in close contact and venture out when the day was new. Osa gave her new potential allies a wave and a vow to arrive once again in the morning to collect them.

Kag took advantage of their free time and voiced he was hungry, as he hadn't eaten anything since before they left Sundaland. He gestured to go fishing while Hyu accompanied him a short distance away. Hyu guided Kag to stabbing fish with whittled sticks while Jih was left alone with Dran. Jih watched as the two gathered fish and took a seat in the sand. Jih scratched his legs as he felt his grass skirt catch on his behind. Jih turned his head to meet Dran's as he saw her sitting close by him.

The two held an awkward silence as they only shared a few select moments together on good terms. Their relationship was complicated as Jih felt in a tough position from his personal feelings and the respective influences of both Hyu and Hizo. Hyu's opinion of Dran was well known, but Hizo prided Dran as her star pupil and forced Jih to interact with her. Dran's thoughts were about Hizo and in the calm of the waves, she felt herself break down. Her nose sniffled as she wiped it with the back of her hand and put it in the sand. Jih remained quiet as his eyes tracked the movement of the water. The thoughts of Hizo's words remained in his mind as he wondered what his destiny would hold. Jih could hear Dran's voice quiver slightly as she spoke. Their eyes didn't meet one another as they talked.

"Dran is sorry Jih." Dran uttered quietly as she could hardly construct the words.

"Hm? For what? Dran has no reason to apologize." Jih stated as he continued to stare out to the ocean.

"For everything. The years have been hard for Dran, Dran did not make things easier for you." Dran said with guilt evident on each hanging word.

Jih shook his head at her words, while an apology was welcome, he knew his was given by the wrong person. Chak's apology never came but his death was more than enough justice for that. The crux of his interactions with Dran were always stifled, and while he suffered from bullying as a young boy, it was hardly the worst. Jih's eyes drifted to Hyu and remained absorbed by her energy.

"These words are meant for Hyu, your wrath on her was greater than on Jih. You speak these words to Jih as you fear what she will say. Is Jih correct?" Jih said as he nodded at Dran's silence.

"Why did you come here?" Jih asked, as he turned his head to face Dran.

"Dran came for Hizo. Hizo saved my life, and this is all that can be done for her. You could use help as well." Dran mentioned, as her finger pointed at Hyu and Kag who remained in eternal argument among themselves. Their conversation was audible to the two of them, much to Dran's annoyance and Jih's amusement respectively.

"Hyu will cook Peymin-" Hyu said before she got interrupted by Kag with a laugh.

"Sister, you are tired. Let Jih cook instead! It is edible that way." Kag said as Hyu shot a glare. Kag lifted his hands and kept a smile on his face as he went to gather wood to build a campfire.

"Jih asked many, but you came. This will be remembered." Jih stated, as he pressed his finger into the sand. He got up to leave Dran by herself.

Jih went over to see Hyu while Dran occupied herself grabbing branches to use for kindling. In no time, Kag returned with a steady source of wood from further inland, some of it was rotted but would burn easily as he made a heat source. Jih quickly went to work as the chef of their party and was sure to rub the fish in the wood so that the smell would carry onto the meat as it cooked. Once the fish was prepared, Jih sat happily as he watched his friends eat and took a bite of his making. Just like his mother taught him, timing was everything when it came to cooking on the campfire. The atmosphere was tense around the campfire as they discussed possibilities for the next day but chose to retain a positive outlook.

With the sun setting and a full stomach, Jih found himself wiped out from the day's events and rested his head on Hyu's lap. Dran made herself a blanket of sand that remained warm through the night. Kag chose to sleep close to the ocean and used the sound of the waves to keep him asleep. The only one fully awake was Hyu who hummed her stresses away, being concerned for Hizo's health. Jih could hear bits and pieces that would stay with him always.

As Dran slept, she heard a creature walk by. Her face furrowed as she twisted in her sleep. The animal's cries were loud enough to rouse Jih. Jih was a light sleeper and had trouble staying asleep as Hyu rubbed the back of his neck. Although she tried to soothe him, it was doing the opposite. Dran awoke to find a giant rat gnawing a fruit close by her as she was startled. She let out a growl as she punted the rat with her foot and hurled the animal some distance before it ran off. The rest of the night went off without any issues. Hyu and Jih were awake early, as Dran and Kag lagged behind. Hyu went over to her sleeping brother and slapped Kag awake, with the imprint of Hyu's hand still on his cheek. The brief sound carried through as Jih gave a small chuckle.

"Harder next time Hyu! Kag could feel nothing!" Kag joked with a laugh.

"They are here." Dran said with her voice audibly groggy as she saw the outlines of Osa and a few of her comrades come out to the beach. She came by and jumped in excitement while the tired four made their way over to her.

"Osa has idea! Tall ones will help us beat the foe." Osa explained to them. Jih nodded his head while Kag once again tried his best to not laugh at her voice.

Osa took their hands and manually guided them along the coast. Their trek across the way would take them into the hands of their rivals. Although Osa was not aware of her new friend's combat prowess against humans, she figured through their size, they could break through the defenses set up for them. Small snares were tactically placed in the undergrowth that filled the larger sections of the jungle. These were meant for animals but could just as easily trap one of Osa's company.

"Watch your step. Traps are present." Osa warned them, while two of the other members of her group pawed at the ground and looked for signs of disturbance.

Jih studied the placement of these snares that Osa identified and saw that these could be good to replicate back home. These traps for creatures of unusual size were something that he hadn't been used to seeing but he appreciated good construction. Osa guided them through large tracts of swampland, taking care to point out the elephants that fed on the local grasses. Jih shook as he heard the growl of the dwarf elephant warn them of their territory. Although much smaller than what he witnessed before, Jih still felt terrified. Hyu held his arm tightly in understanding, while Kag attempted to keep his mind busy. Dran was in awe of how Jih could face a tiger or a rhino with little issue, but an elephant, especially a small elephant, made him no different from a child.

Jih sighted a concentration of smoke that bellowed above the bushes, and Osa nodded showing that this was where they needed to go. Osa held out her hand while her two companions scouted the perimeter. The usual scouts that patrolled the area were absent, it was clear that they were out on a raid which would be perfect for their group to arrive. Jih and the others stepped in to see the village and looked around. Kag nearly tripped over one of the homes constructed by them. The Stump home was a strange construction, with half of it on the surface, and the other half dug into the ground but aligned with dense jungle leaves that served as a cushioned bed.

"Osa was stopped before! Not this time." She said, as she cupped her hands to yell towards the seemingly empty village. She tossed her throwing stick some distance as it landed with a small thud to the ground. Hyu knelt down to Osa's level to ask her a question.

"Hyu understands pain of Osa. What can Hyu do?" Hyu said with rage in her eyes.

"Osa must look for leader. Tall ones must help her." She said as she frantically looked in the homes and poked her spear around.

Kag waved the group over as he saw a small man bound and gagged in one of the homes. He was doused in a white pigment meant for captives. Kag held out his hand as he instinctively knew Jih would be behind him. Jih passed Kag his hand-axe to cut the man free as he was weak but was able to get up. Kag reached inside and cut his bindings. He looked distraught as he extended his hand for the man to grasp on. Osa and her companions ran towards the man with much happiness as they shook him happily. Osa leaned her head in to hear the words of her leader and nodded. Her face was filled with regret as she heard the details of his capture. The raiding party that caught Osa's leader returned, with the men shocked to see Osa and her group, complete with the tall ones that accompanied her. They were flustered but rushed towards them, attacking with short knives. At first, Jih and the others were afraid of what was to happen, but he quickly realized how significant their size difference was. He and Kag's spears kept them corralled at a significant distance, while Hyu took enjoyment in whipping at their feet, and watched them dance in a panic. She gave a satisfied grin as she turned to see Osa raise her spear above her head in a boastful expression.

"Osa wants blood. Finish it!" Osa told the four of them as she launched a throwing stick at the opposing group and knocked one person unconscious in the head. Though their captured leader was recovered, the child was sacrificed and Osa earned half her victory.

Jih looked at the others with a shrug as he kicked the man in the stomach harshly with his foot while the others soon followed. Osa looked on approvingly as the man suffered before her. He twitched as he was stunned on the ground, while Dran took a wooden spear to pierce the man's body and gave the blood that Osa craved. As simple as the endeavor was to them, it meant the world to Osa and her people. Sometime later, Jih and the others were escorted back to the beach by Osa. She waved over one of her companions who held four white flowers in his hands. Although Jih and the others requested only one Moon Orchid, Osa was generous enough to give them four. Jih echoed Hyu and knelt to meet Osa at eye level.

"Jih thanks Osa. Hizo will be happy for this." Jih said as he looked in the direction of their boat.

Jih's expression was filled with embarrassment as he realized their boat was in terrible condition. Osa shared this and gave the group a look of confusion as she saw the state of their boat that was left on the sandbanks. She knew that this was how they arrived on her island, but she was confused about how they would return, for there were only so many resources around.

"Kag! Our boat is ruined!" Dran said in dismay while Hyu inspected the watercraft. She could see that there were hand-axe marks made on the pieces with scraps of wood taken. It was structurally sound enough to maintain a rough shape, but on the water, they would surely sink and must swim back.

"The enemy works fast and took your wood. Osa can be faster." Osa commented.

She held their hand out for the four to wait. One hour passed and the sound of many grateful hands from her village came by as they hauled a large raft to hit the water instead. Repairs to the boat were beyond their ability, but they could travel across back to Sundaland proper. In the distant past, they scouted the eastern coast to see what was of value.

Osa noted that the size of the largest raft they had was tailored to her people's size, so they would have a tight squeeze. Hyu sat on Jih's lap while Kag sat next to the two. Dran furrowed her brow at the prospect of sitting on Kag's lap who gave a dumb grin in response, while Osa attempted to give herself a bit of room. Dran would have rather attempted swimming the distance than bother with such an endeavor. Hyu chuckled as she urged Osa to go, much to Dran's chagrin.

Dran begrudgingly arranged herself to sit at the edge of Kag's ankles and gave a smug expression as she did so. The raft was uneven, but Osa could make the trip. Their travel time was short, especially since the route was well known for them. Osa dropped them off a short distance from the sandbank as their bottoms were wet. She waved them off and began her paddle home. The four with their Moon Orchids returned to their home as fast as they could. Jih ran ahead of the others to return to he and Hizo's tent while Kag, Hyu and Dran, watched him in the distance. Kag shot Hyu with a look of concern that was returned. Jih noticed that his home was worked on more than last time, which indicated to him that Hizo was working on it while he was away. He was filled with hope that Hizo found the energy to continue. Tur finished the construction while they were gone. Along his way, Jih was stopped by Tur. His face looked tired and weary. Jih knew something was amiss as he received no comment from Tur denigrating him.

"Jih..." Tur said as he looked away from the impatient Jih.

Tur was filled with many emotions but couldn't bother to look Jih in the face. The pain of Hizo's death was too much to bear and he let Jih go without any more to say. Jih shook his head with irritation at Tur's interruption, set on his goal to bring the flower back. He took a moment to take a deep breath and entered his home.

"Mother! Jih returns with-" Jih said as he looked inside to see nothing but an empty home. Jih's belongings were present, but nothing of Hizo's remained. It was as if she never existed at all. An empty hut meant complete death, for many believed that portions of the spirit could come into their tools. Jih kept some of Hyu's possessions in present life as he believed she could still be found. The small pit in Jih's chest opened as he knew what transpired while he was gone. Hizo was gone and she passed on to somewhere where he couldn't follow. Hyu followed behind Jih and heard subdued sobs as she obscured her entrance into the home as discreetly as possible. Her worst fears were confirmed by the sound of her lover's sadness. She held Jih with a tight hug.

Although Jih didn't directly witness this part, he was given a secondhand account by Hyu who heard this directly from Tur. While Jih was gone, Hizo was beyond help. She arranged for Tur to do a mercy killing just hours ago. Tur questioned Dran about their expedition on the island and the existence of the Moon Orchid. Dran informed him of everything she witnessed including her encounter with Stumps. After he heard the mission was a success, he debriefed with The Council in their own abode. He entered through the signature flap as The Council was in intense discussion.

"Your entry was not announced." An old woman said, as she stopped Tur, but nodded her head allowing him to speak anyway.

"Tur brings news. Hizo has died." He said, as his voice wavered with mixed glances of concern from The Council.

Due to their close friendship, Tur knew for some time about Hizo's increasingly worse condition but kept up appearances for show. She and Tur planned for Jih to not be present when it was her time to go. Hizo felt it would be better if she was remembered in strength. One member of The Council let out a gasp in complete horror. From The Council's perspective, Hizo was in great health, and the circumstances were not entirely known surrounding her death. Tur quickly assured them that Hizo's death was natural and foul play was not to be considered. Hizo was an essential part of their structure in keeping the band well trained against enemy threats and now they felt lost. Tur held his position for one more piece of news.

"Hizo was important. Neck-Shells will be problem later." One man said as he tugged at his beard.

"Tur has more to say. There are others, different from us. What do we do about this?" Tur inquired. He held his breath as The Council looked at one another, with almost knowing glances.

"There are rumors. This will stay that way. Does Tur understand?" The old woman said, as she gestured towards an open spot where the group sat. Tur eyed the opening carefully and nodded. His proof of loyalty would be more than enough to secure himself a seat in The Council. He left without a sound.

"That...was so sad!" Trekkal said, her eyes visibly red as her nose sniffled. Jih turned around, startled as he had no idea how long she'd been eavesdropping on the conversation. Sadal was now drifting to sleep, tired from her fever, but her eyes leaked tears as she heard Jih's words. Narro waved at Jih as he showed some fish that the two caught. It was a relief to Jih that they now had some food, and that their new friends could certainly carry their weight.

Self Reflection

Dran sat alone in her tent as she tried to keep herself calm after a long and infuriating day. Though the Neck-Shells were history, The Elders rarely forgot anything. In a tight-knit community such as theirs, the best achievements were spoken about for years to come but the worst failures in the same vein. The trio faced many challenges as members of The Elders spoke against their crusade to oust Tur from power. The pressure also mounted on the Hunting and Stoneworking Teams for associating with them as well. Dran often heard her own failures week after week in the gossip of onlookers as she went about her duties.

Bani expressed concern to Kag in previous conversations that she hadn't seen Dran for a few days and started to get worried. She would've visited herself, but she was wrapped trying to mediate another conflict brewing within the Hunting Team. Kag was happy to take any excuse to not interact with Tur and took the time out to go and investigate the problem. He found himself at Dran's home and the drape was on the entrance. Kag looked at Dran's tent and saw no sign of life, but he wasn't entirely convinced. He took to the ground and looked under to see feet. In the low light that came through, his prediction was correct. Kag knew it was no secret that the rest of The Elders decided to make Dran the target of discussion once again. What was unique this time was Dran's reaction to it. Kag knew Dran as the biggest defender of her actions and lack of care for the thoughts and pitiful gossip of others. Her outright disappearance from public life came as a shock to him. Dran didn't carry the burden of the past alone, Kag and Bani were under scrutiny due to their association with Jih. Kag also found himself ridiculed due to his comedic nature, but he cared little about it.

"Dran, Bani asks for you. Will you not come?" Kag asked, as his voice reached Dran's ears.

"Not now. Leave Dran alone, Kag. Are there other things you must do other than bother Dran?" Dran said to him as her voice tapered to silence.

"Dran is upset, for what exactly? Words of many have always meant little to you." Kag goaded Dran.

Dran bit her tongue as she mulled over Kag's words. Despite Kag's demeanor he was particularly skilled in getting what he wanted out of people. It made sense that Jih really did see him as a viable replacement for leadership past their friendship. While Jih might have walked away, Kag was increasingly persistent and pointed with his statements. Dran's silence hung with both for some time before she spoke.

"They talk of things not understood. Dran protects The Elders and then questions how Dran does it. Dran has been blamed for many things." She said, while Kag voiced his approval, happy to have gotten an actual response from her. He knew that there was more to her initial statement and questioned further.

"Is it about her? Many have said things to Bani, but none have come to Kag. All of it is dung of Ker-Mah." Kag replied as he gave ample time for a response. Dran's silence said it all as he then wondered what brought this up now.

"Is this guilt you feel? At a time like this? You had many years to make your peace. Your words do not honor my sister Hyu. Why be upset now? You made life hard for many, this is true. The past will not change but your help is needed. Tur is our problem and is much worse." Kag said with brutal honesty.

"Dran has killed many with failure. All those people." Dran said as she dismissively shook her head at his words. Dran worked herself up into a loop of self-doubt as she shook silently from anxiety.

"It took time to figure this out, but Tur is the one who broke our peace with The Jagged Bark." Kag dropped on Dran as he heard an audible gasp.

"What?" Dran asked in surprise.

It was evident that Tur was involved in the intricate nature regarding the alliance with other bands, but Dran was not involved in the inner workings of The Council. She could only operate on what limited exposure she had. Dran thought there were other factors at play as The Jagged Bark aligned with The Neck-Shells. She knew that Bhet reached out to them for alliance but saw this was a matter of pure greed over anything else. As Kag explained it, she pieced together that Tur conjured an unequal relationship that compelled The Jagged Bark to act in their self-interest. While The Jagged Bark could have opted for neutrality, Tur's sins were egregious and had to be acted on.

"Jih spoke to their scout and Kag remembers that he was denied the right of the ancestors. It was Tur who soured our alliance. When Bhet struck, our pact fell through. Your plans to keep our village safe depended on them and they did not come. Have you thought about why?" Kag said as he inhaled before speaking again.

"Hyu blamed Dran for many things. Some were just cause, others not as much. Kag knows Hyu does not blame Dran for what happened to her. Kag saw it himself and Dran was right about Neck-Shells. They ignored your words. Hyu saved Kag, which she chose on her own." Kag mentioned, as Dran really wasn't sure how to respond to this.

"B-" Dran said, her voice emitting from the tent until Kag cut her off.

"Listen to Kag for once." Kag said as he waved his arms in annoyance. The frustration in his voice was evident as it was filled with exhaustion.

"Kag knows mistakes were made. Some cowered and stayed behind. Their voices are loudest. Dran, Kag forgives you. Kag has for long time. Death comes for all. It came to Hyu and Dran must forgive Dran now." Kag mentioned.

Dran knew that Kag forgave her deep down. After all, they were working together to dismantle The Council's image and credibility. Kag was one person, but her thoughts drifted to Jih and his soulless eyes on that day. There was nothing but an abyss in her as she couldn't unsee it at night.

"And what of Jih, hmm? Jih sees Dran no different than Weypeu. A thoughtless beast with an insatiable hunger." Dran said as she rubbed her hands in the dirt next to her.

"Kag does not speak for Jih. Kag knows though, Jih is kind and understanding. When he returns with power rock, Kag knows he will say the same." Kag mentioned as his eyes drifted to the ground.

Much like Jih at first, Dran avoided the subject of Hyu. Dran's doubts of Kag's words subsided, but she decided that for her to center herself once more, she needed to give her former adversary a visit. She waited for some time until the footsteps of Kag were long gone. Dran was appreciative of his efforts and behind the self-doubt, she worked steadily to help Kag's vision. One of his primary goals was to rehabilitate Jih's image so that he could be forgiven if he were to ever return. The Elders cared through acts of service. People knew of Jih's importance as a stone worker and his craft was honored but the lies that Tur and The Council weaved were powerful and painted Jih far differently than those that knew him personally.

Dran found herself poking around Jih and Hyu's old home and looked for anything of note left behind. Many of Jih's early possessions were torched but there was a surprising amount of goods left behind that were borrowed by others. Kag restored Jih's home and returned his things in the hope that he would eventually come home. Dran mostly found a few reject hand-axes made by Jih, but other objects caught her eye. Kag restored the home to its former glory after Jih left as a small parting gift for his friend's return. She looked around some more and saw a strange arrangement of leaves. She raised an eyebrow and decided to move them away. It was unusual, but this was one of the few possessions left that Hyu held. Dran saw that it was part of a hide of a giant pangolin. It was spared devastation from Bani who borrowed and returned it. Dran's hand curled into a fist as she bit her tongue in annoyance.

"Kavagol..." Dran said to herself.

She knew this was certainly Hyu's work. Even in death, Hyu had to be perfect. Dran hardly bothered going with pangolin kills, spears were hardly effective against it, and there's rarely any use that she could find. The meat had an acquired taste, and the effort was better spent with much larger creatures. Hyu's whip could get into the crevices of these creatures with ease and bring the kill home. The pangolin was valued for its armor and to have ownership of it meant protection would be provided in times of hardship. Hyu thought ahead and gave Kag and Bani the pangolin pelt as a sign of goodwill for the help and blessing of their developing child. As Bani and Kag held the pelt, their family survived, but Jih and Hyu weren't afforded such luck.

Dran's thoughts of Hyu carried over as she left. She decided to take a walk to the beach and finally give herself some closure. Dran made her way to the beach where she'd seen the others go before to visit the patch where Hyu remained. She sighted the poison vines and maneuvered them carefully and quickly obscured herself as she did so. She turned her head and saw the clump of dirt not too far from her location. She looked above and saw an arrangement of great flowers. No matter what her thoughts were, Dran knew this was a beautiful spot.

Dran sat alone at the grave that by now had moss and other coverings over it, but the mound's shape stayed the same. Her hand reached over to touch the smoothed stones, but she stopped herself. Dran's hand hovered over the grave. She knew she didn't have the right in life and wouldn't have it in death either. Although the knowledge of her true location was concealed by Jih and the others, Dran deduced it for herself. Dran occasionally found herself lingering near Hyu's grave at dusk. Bani was aware of Dran's movements here, but she said nothing about it. Bani knew that Dran was a particularly tortured soul and needed to work things out on her own. In the back of her mind, Dran had significant regrets regarding how things went between them. Dran was alive, and Hyu was no more, with no resolution between the two. This wasn't the first time Dran dealt with death. Her relationship with loss evolved throughout time. She lost Chak who was her first love, her father who cherished her, and lastly Hizo herself. Hizo prepared her to deal with both deaths and her own passing, but the death of Hyu was something else entirely. Hyu was someone she always imagined would remain a thorn in her side until she wasn't.

Dran closed her eyes as she breathed through her nose and absorbed the sounds of the sea. She remembered what was put behind her long ago. It was the first anniversary of the Recognition Hunt, and she remained in the tent while her father was outside. Dran clutched Chak's bone necklace while she was wrapped in a bundle of fur. The shadow of two figures were in intense conversation as the low light of the fire filled the room with warmth. Dran recognized these outlines to be her father and Hizo in discussion.

"Nelk, you have anguish on your face. What is wrong?" Hizo asked as her voice wrapped around their home.

"Hizo. Can you talk to her? Dran has done nothing in one week. Nelk must seek new territory for Tur and Woodworking Team. One woodland is never enough, is it?" Nelk said as he placed his hand on her shoulder.

"Hizo can try. The young do not understand us very well." Hizo said with a shrug.

Dran heard the laughter of her father and Hizo. The two often talked to one another on the long expeditions orchestrated by The Council. Hizo was always a helping hand and accompanied those in need. Dran turned her head and looked to the entrance of their home as Hizo tugged at the flap to signal her entry. This was done as a formality as adults could enter homes that children occupied without their consent. Dran waited for the inevitable as a burst of light entered the tent and Hizo's face occupied it. She gave a bright smile that Dran ignored as she flipped over. Hizo took it on herself to sit at the edge of the tent and waited quietly until Dran turned again to address her.

"Why are you sad?" Hizo asked as she saw Dran's eyes water.

"Do you not know what today is? It has been one year. Chak was hero of our people, and he is gone." Dran said as she met Hizo's gaze.

Hizo held a look of embarrassment on her face as she forgot the significance of today. She didn't speak to Tur as she always did, and she hadn't realized he and Aab were absent. Hizo understood the absence of Chak and his importance to The Elders, but deep down she held little care for him. Hizo was a master at obscuring her emotions, but the Chak she knew as a trainer compared to his public image was hardly the same. Chak was a powerful force but driven to a destructive and toxic ego by Tur's interference. Hizo found it difficult to care for Chak as he was a harsh bully to her own son, but his outlook hardly matched the collectivist mindset the group attempted to instill in the others. Hizo saw herself usually as the voice of reason, but she had her biases and wasn't afraid to make that clear in the company that mattered. Hizo's love for Dran superseded her disdain for Chak, but she couldn't bring herself to lie to the young woman in front of her. She moved close to Dran and placed her hand on her head. Dran continued to clutch the necklace as she was soothed by Hizo's touch.

"Chak was powerful yes, but death has meaning. Heroes are not perfect and have flaws Dran." Hizo mentioned to her.

"What is meant by this? Chak was killed by Kwiekyaan because it did not recognize his power. Everyone knows this." Dran huffed in defiance.

"Kwiekyaan knows no master, Dran. The stories say differently. With only one life to live, Chak saw you as twigs between his teeth. Twigs to clean his mess that he refused to solve. Dran told Hizo of shell weapon given to him as a prize. What did he do? Did Chak thank you?" Hizo asked as she felt Dran's skin get cold.

Hizo remained silent as she listened to Dran's steady breathing. Tears came from Dran's eyes as the cracks of the flames were audible. Hizo's shadow rose as she fixed her posture, and the flames contorted its image. She continued as she felt it was important to tell Dran who she knew Chak as. Dran was young and had her entire life ahead of her, it would be a waste to mourn someone in such a manner who didn't deserve it.

"Chak took it as his prize. He felt he deserved it, just like the lives of others. If raiders come, Hizo will die for it. Chak sent you and my son to do it for him." Hizo stated with a calm voice.

Dran ruffled the furs over her head as she tried to block out Hizo's words. Hizo closed her eyes and realized she needed to taper her words a bit more. It was rare she let out her true feelings, but Dran was as much a friend as her mentee. Hizo knew that one day Dran would succeed her, and she needed to be prepared for all the realities of adult life.

"Tur and Aab are sad because Chak was their job and they failed. You are young and have much to look forward to. You deserve to be treated with kindness. If companionship is what you want, there are others." Hizo mentioned while she rubbed her chin.

Dran groaned as she heard Hizo's voice. Hizo lifted her hand and gave a gentle laugh that soothed her. She couldn't help but have a mischievous look on her face. Hizo considered herself above the drama that went on among her students, but she was enthralled as everyone else.

"Kag is foolish but has good spirits. He will make someone very happy. You need someone grounded, like my son." Hizo said with an intentional cough.

"Dran, you are worthy of my blood. One day consider these words. You may mourn for Chak as you see fit, but life moves forward. Hizo misses Frir every day but lives for Jih. You and many others are our future, we must think of it. Be leader that Chak could not." Hizo said as she looked over Dran.

Dran's face was littered with disgust that made Hizo laugh further. For Hizo, she was happy to get her point across. Life was filled with change and that was something she needed to learn one way or the other. Hizo knew Dran had the potential to be a legend of her own and far exceed the pride held in Chak. Hizo sat with Dran until she fell asleep and lingered for some time before leaving the tent.

In the present, Dran looked up at the canopy of branches above her. Dran remembered how she treated Hyu, Kag, and to a lesser extent Jih. She was far from an innocent person. Hyu always bothered her from an early age. Dran hated the social climber that Hyu set herself out to be. She felt it was inauthentic that Hyu knew everyone in the band as well as she did. Dran felt there was an ulterior motive she could never grasp as Dran spurned Hyu's offering of friendship. Dran had a very small knit group of people she was loyal to but otherwise didn't bother with basic pleasantries. Dran and her set of friends tormented Jih and the others for some time in the years after Chak fell in battle.

As her friends died off from disease, battle, or other causes though, the desire to make enemies grew less appealing as more were buried in the soil below. It took her time to realize allies were what you needed to make it in this world. Dran held a mixed view when it came to Jih. Jih was quiet and didn't see himself enamored in the bubble of the others aside from his proximity to Hyu and Kag. Dran saw potential with his almost limitless work ethic, and being the son of the beloved Hizo wasn't bad either. Despite her reservations about being tied to Hyu and Kag, Dran felt a kindred spirit to some degree and spoke to Jih as an equal to join her and the others in their antics. Hyu was furious at such an invitation and drove a deeper wedge into their already volatile rivalry. It was one thing to reject Kag's unwanted advances which was taken with grace, but another to impede directly on her and Jih, and getting him involved in her circle.

Hyu and Hizo sought Jih to enter The Council for how important it was to them both. While Hyu was incredibly kind and sensitive to the needs of others, she did have a dark side as well. Her capacity for forgiveness could be limited, which wasn't extended on Dran. Hyu had her line in the sand that Dran crossed long ago. Hyu truthfully found Dran abhorrent for years. After their adventure to the island of Flores, Jih decided to let the past go when it came to Dran. He appreciated that out of the many he asked to help, she bothered to show up and do something important for his mother when the time came. Hyu appreciated this as well when life was difficult to adjust without Hizo's presence. Hyu's approach softened enough to tolerate Dran on the occasional outing, but no further.

Dran sighed as she was her own greatest critic. Kag was quick to forgive Dran, accepting that mistakes, even those that couldn't be undone, didn't mean she was a terrible person. These were kind words from Kag, but only made her feel worse as she knew she wouldn't be able to muster that kind of strength for herself. To take her mind off things, she evaluated how the condition of The Elders was going.

Like the rest, Dran's remained stressed at the thought of Tur who remained in power and seemed to rule with impunity. She could feel her heart race with intense anger as she tried little to suppress violent thoughts. Tur was the source of many problems for Dran, even earlier than his issues with Jih. Although the old man was slowly chipping away, the damage of Tur was felt by them all. Tur felt she had no place to go and would end up being a waste of space in the band. Dran refused to listen to anyone's teachings for long and found little enjoyment with shadowing others. Tur himself offered his knowledge of woodworking to be passed on to Dran. Dran spurned all of these until she was plucked by Hizo who seemed to understand her better than anyone else. Dran recalled the first time she was assigned to shadow Hizo from Tur, she didn't bother showing up at all. Tur scoffed at the gesture, especially as he and Hizo were very close and never forgave her for it. For some reason though, Hizo chose to ignore Tur's advice on Dran and give her another chance. Hizo knew that Tur spoke from the perspective of a bitter adult who didn't have to understand the youth perspective, and her life changed when she saw her in her tent.

Dran wasn't sure what Hizo wanted her to do as she was quite capable already, but she showed up ready to learn. Dran learned the various tools that Hizo implemented into their strategy, and passively taught Dran some of Tur's woodworking that she used to make training weapons. Hizo organized these testing woods into long strips that she would look at, a habit that Dran emulated to this day to a more refined degree. Dran and Hizo were a strange duo that turned heads, as the problem child was doing something useful. Hizo was cognizant to some degree of Dran's problems with the others her age, mostly through her talks with Jih, but she remembered the strain that both she and Hyu had with one another. Dran was one to never ask for advice, let alone help, on a task. She was humbled graciously, but with kindness, as she attempted to duel Hizo once much to young Jih's amusement. That was a mistake she'd never make again. In time, Hizo grew to be Dran's closest thing to a friend she had besides her dwindling group. Dran spoke plenty to Hizo and told her many things. Hizo kept these secrets to her grave. Hizo once gave Dran some advice, the same she told Jih. The very literal Dran didn't understand her adage for many years, but it was a matter of looking at things differently. Everything had a purpose behind why things were. She didn't ever think she would be working together with Kag and Bani to overthrow Tur. It was beyond her to imagine that Jih, the favorite golden child, would've ever been exiled. It was her time to act for the right reasons instead of just for herself. Dran got up from her place in the dirt and ran her hand across it to remove her imprint. She gave one more look at the mound that accompanied her and gave a sufficient nod. Dran saw that night was coming soon and she would need to return, as the last few moments of sunlight vanished. Dran did her best to conceal her visit as she did.

Dran was unsure why she went through such lengths to hide herself. There was no shame in honoring those who passed. Others had their own ways of processing the harsh realities of their life, either done in the privacy of their tent or in the deep jungles. Dran dusted herself off and walked quietly to the sight of a few low campfires, while there were a few sentries out to keep watch for predators. In the distance, Dran saw the wave of a torch and looked with panic until she realized who was there.

"You must be tired; it is getting late." Kag's voice called out in the growing darkness.

Painting In The Rain

Jih and the others sat in a circle looking over their tools. Weapon maintenance was as natural as breathing for those who wandered this world. Jih lifted his spear and saw the quality of the wood degraded after much time. He massaged his beard and looked around for a suitable replacement, but trees were few far and between out in the grasslands. He wondered how others managed to keep their implements up to date. Sadal's throwing spears were smaller than his spear, and she could produce more of them with the same amount of wood as one of Jih's. He would have preferred to find his own wood, but the likelihood of them finding another village seemed to increase. After the past couple of days without a sign of life other than themselves, Jih was certain they could find not only directions to stay on task for the power rock, but a trader with the wares he looked for.

"Jih has question for group." Jih asked and looked up to see the three's heads rise at the sound of his voice. Sadal moved her hand, prompting Jih to speak further while she realigned her clothing. Trekkal put her head in her hand and looked at Jih, while Narro ran his finger through the soil.

"Are there spare furs? Jih must trade for wood. Good quality." Jih explained as he gestured to his spear that fell apart from repeated use. Jih replaced the heads of his spears often with many of them being removed from use or a misdirected hit on the prey, but even the handle came with a shelf life of its own.

The three looked at each other while Jih waited patiently for a reply. Trekkal was the first to trudge around her belongings and felt around her backpack. Her face perked up as she felt she had something to loan but only withdrew a piece of fiber she worked on. Trekkal scratched her head and looked inside seeing that she clearly used up what she acquired. As Trekkal mostly focused on fishing, finding pelts for use was often a secondary concern.

"All I have is string. Sadal? Narro? How about you?" Trekkal said with some slight embarrassment in her voice. She gave Jih an awkward smile that he returned with a knowing nod. Jih didn't expect much from Trekkal, but he kept a good face as his eyes turned to the often more responsible Narro and Sadal.

"How do we keep running out of pelts? We go hunting almost every day!" Sadal said in dismay as she received glares from the others.

As Sadal was often industrious with her clothes making, she differentiated herself extensively while the others wore more simple attire. She wore a composite of pelts that stuck out with dhole and sika deer patterns on her body. Narro gave a small cough as his eyes diverted to Sadal before looking away. Jih and Trekkal got the hint as they raised their eyebrows at her.

"What? Are you all saying what I think you're saying?" Sadal tried to deflect in protest.

"Well Sadal, have you looked in a puddle lately? Your outfit is worth at least a month of meat alone! Look at all the dots." Trekkal shot back across to her.

"Feel free to hunt your own, I manage mine and I run down the kill." Sadal huffed.

"Sadal looks like Tur. Come, Jih just needs a small piece." Jih said with a sly laugh.

Narro shrugged his shoulders to Jih's raised eyebrow. He looked around him and saw nothing of value in the expanse they sat in. Narro turned his head to address Jih's question.

"Only the clothes on my back Jih. Sadal, how are you not warm in that? Tole fur is heavy." Narro asked with a confused look as he wiped some sweat from his forehead. Trekkal covered her mouth and tried to stop herself from making another quip, but she failed.

"Anything for Sadal to wear less clothes, huh Narro." Trekkal mumbled as she got a hard shove from her brother in feeble protest. Sadal shook her finger at the two while she noticed Jih getting ready to do something.

Jih stood up first and picked a direction at random for the group to go. Their last directions to head west were running stale so they improvised where they could. Jih anticipated seeing other travelers who were looking for the power rock much like himself, but it seemed that wasn't the case just yet. The rest followed suit as they started another day of walking. Trekkal winced as she felt her legs, she was exhausted from a previous day of wandering around aimlessly to curb her boredom. Narro looked back at her and shook his head, they needed to cover some ground before taking another break.

Luckily for Trekkal, the clouds overhead started to paint a different picture. She looked up and saw that rain was on the horizon, but she was unsure when it would fall. In the jungle, rain was a minor hindrance as the canopy blocked the harshest weather and many people carried large leaves with them to stay dry. Out on the plains, rain could be devastating as there was nowhere to shield yourself from the elements other than tents of their own making. A light rain was often no issue to the weary traveler, but nobody wanted to be caught drenched and cold. Narro also noticed the rain coming and realized that any wood they did happen to find would be difficult to make a fire with. He tucked his lip in thought and stopped the others.

"The clouds are filled with darkness overhead. I sense a bad rain is coming. Trekkal and I know that caves in this area are common, so we should go there!" Narro offered to the group. Jih gave no complaints, waiting out a storm was fine as there was plenty of game to return when the waters were filled. He could then get the furs he needed for trade; it would just be a bit longer.

With their altered travel plans to avoid the rain came the search for a cave. An hour later, the open plains led to large jutting cliffs that were present along the landscape with some openings to caves. A Forest Seeker village was present some distance away, but the population on the plains differed from the jungles. Their core beliefs still valued the jungle and its principles, but they lived a minimalist life. They used stone tools, rather than wood or bamboo and lacked blowguns. They instead used rope from fibers or animal sinew and ambush tactics along the plains to secure food. This was a curiosity for any onlookers such as Jih and company. The Forest Seekers in this land also differed in their practices than the jungle variety Jih and Sadal met. While clothing was hardly gendered, Forest Seekers in the plains and The Aligned held more nuanced views past the typical binary. Narro noted to the others he'd seen about four genders that were differentiated by paint on their faces and specific materials on their bodies. He wasn't aware of exact nuances, but it echoed some villages of his own people. Trekkal found their appearances intriguing and wondered how much this related to their spirituality.

"Oh! Just our luck." Narro mentioned, as he sighted the small presence of the camp. The camp in question only numbered about twenty people, a far cry from the numbers they were used to. Jih noticed the group were Forest Seekers and tapped Narro's shoulder, as he remembered Sadal's hostility to the group.

"Sadal! How about you and Trekkal look for shelter before the rains come? Jih and I will contact the camp. If you hear a scream, come running." Narro mentioned, as Sadal looked to see Trekkal hovering behind her.

Sadal lifted her hand in resignation as she was strapped to Trekkal while she watched Jih and Narro walk off. Their outlines were still visible in the distance as she waited for their return. Sadal looked around and scouted for any signs of life that she'd need to eliminate with the help of her comrades. Trekkal was far less enthusiastic about the endeavor but quickly trailed behind Sadal to not get lost.

"We have nothing to trade Narro. How do you know we will be accepted?" Jih said as he pointed to his empty pack on his back. Narro nodded in agreement.

"Certainly not, but a good smile can get you anywhere. We need directions to shelter and all else will fall into place." Narro insisted. The two grouped outside of the Forest Seeker camp and lingered. A few of them looked at each other in confusion.

"Are you lost?" One of them asked, their voice audible to Jih and Narro's ears.

Jih looked them over and studied their dress, or lack thereof. What he assumed to be men and women were shirtless, only having their bottoms covered with fur trousers. He saw their faces covered with different pigments that glistened in the sun just as Narro described. Jih picked up a strange scent that entered his nose. He stuck his tongue out in disgust and gave a closer look at the source of the smell. Their exposed skin was covered with a translucent salve forged from animal fat that was on their skin. This retained heat for the colder nights and cooled them off in the day. The Forest Seekers here didn't carry coverings for parasites like in the forest and were freer in their dress.

That one looks like Eshe. Jih thought.

"Yes, we are actually very lost. The rains come soon and we need shelter. Where can we go for this?" Narro questioned.

"What is this on your face?" Jih said, pointing to a younger man's face pigment. Narro shot him a look to mind his manners. Jih rolled his eyes at Narro's gesture, he had a question and he wanted it answered.

"We get that often from visitors, it is fine. We stay in the caves in these lands. Sometimes there are Bher present, but we make a deal with them. Thunderfeet in these lands make their own way, but we use what the spirits have left behind." One of the men answered. The young man that Jih questioned pointed to a few assorted bowls with the solution used to paint his face. The Forest Seekers in this land used it for all sorts of purposes, but cave painting was also popular.

"What do you mean? You mean Kal-Bher. I have yet to find Kal-Bher in this land. 50" Narro commented as he looked at Jih.

"Jih knows of Bher. It climbs trees and eats Teen-Sa." Jih said as he received a look of confusion from Narro. A woman with a shaved head who was close by gave a laugh at the two of their questions.

"These Bher are not what you think. They are small, but they are fast and even Weypeu reconsider attacking them." She mentioned as she sat on the grass next to the others.

"You can have what we have left from these bowls, we try to keep our belongings to what one can hold on their own." The man said to Jih and Narro. Jih happily accepted the gifts of surplus pigment while Narro gave a glance at Jih. After some more discussion of the happenings in the land, the two set off to reunite with Sadal and Trekkal.

"They probably went this way. Let us look for an open flame." Narro said, as he pointed to the assortment of depressions in the cliffs. Jih figured they didn't spend too long at the other camp, so catching up to Sadal and Trekkal would be easy enough. Long before he could see them, Trekkal's voice carried over the emptiness of their surroundings.

"Jih has found them." He said with a slight chuckle as the two continued their walk. Sadal and Trekkal made the fire using some spare branches and the ground was dry enough to keep steady. The two sat together on the opening of the cave and tested the acoustics by seeing who could clap the loudest. Sadal clapped twice and waited for the sound to reverberate back to her while Trekkal took a deep breath and made a large boom sound. Sadal bit her tongue while Trekkal gave a cheeky smile to her clear victory. She shook her palms as they were slightly red from the impact. While the two continued, Jih and Narro were running as fast as they could to avoid the ongoing storm that moved its way through the plains. The sky opened with glorious thunder that seeped across the sky as far off in the distance the other Forest Seekers returned to their caves. Jih and Narro couldn't make it in time as they felt water bombard their face and shoulders. Jih's hair covered his face and Narro's tightly bound ponytail flowed as his wrappings ran loose.

---

50 Emic word for Cave Bears.

The two prioritized the bowl of pigments as they returned. Jih and Narro arrived with their bowls of pigment much to the surprise of Sadal and Trekkal.

"How was contact? I see you both are unharmed, though very wet." Sadal noted as Trekkal immediately moved over to look at the bowl.

"We did not ask about power rock." Jih said with annoyance as it was uncertain if he would find these people again.

Jih placed the bowls that he held in his hand to the left side of the cave wall. Jih approached the fire and warmed himself up as he stepped aside and shook his body to get the rest of the water off him. Sadal moved slightly out the way as she wanted to avoid her hair and clothing from getting wet. Narro took the time to tell everyone his plans for the bowls of pigment while Jih turned around to hear him. Cave painting was a fun tradition among The Aligned and was used for story telling but also depicted all sorts of things in life. Sadal was aware of painting done with handprints, but she hadn't tried her abilities yet at depicting something she wanted to make.

"Well, since we have some time before we can go again, all of you take your hands and dip it inside." Narro offered, as he already saw Trekkal took her fair share with her hand.

"It is time to paint! If you wish to change the color, just throw some dirt on it." The two said happily, while Sadal and Jih gave each other a glance before looking at the bowl.

Jih also knew of the practice, but Sundaland proper had few caves that he could find, his people preferred to carve on seashells instead. He went to the left wall of the cave with his bowls of pigment and waited for the others. Jih found that this cave was occupied by others besides themselves as there were depictions of other animals that he could vaguely understand. He looked at the pieces and noticed their exaggerated forms which brought a sense of slight distaste to him. Jih was hardly a critic, but he found it ill prepared to relay information which is what he considered to be the function of art. Narro and Trekkal by comparison enjoyed art for the process and cared little for realistic proportions or anything of the sort.

"For those who do not know, all you need to-" Narro said as he saw himself get interrupted by Trekkal.

"Slam it on the wall!" Trekkal said, while Narro nodded in agreement. She left a large handprint on the cave as she did so.

"Narro, what is this?" Jih asked as he pointed to an image of a water buffalo on a nearby wall.

"Oh Jih, do you not see this is Ker-Mah? See the horns? We have hunted those plenty already." Narro said with a laugh.

"No-Jih knows this. Jih means this." Jih expressed as he pointed to a series of dots that were placed on the animal's stomach. Narro was impressed at Jih's eye for detail that others seemed to ignore. Jih noticed that these were arranged in a line while he motioned for Narro to get a closer look. He closed one eye and examined the sequence of dots on the buffalo's image.

"I believe The Youngest use these to keep track of time. We have a different system." Narro said to himself as he looked over at Sadal.

"Mmm. Jih uses the moon to keep time. Moon is always present for things when Jih needs it. Growth and movement of animals works just as well." Jih explained while Narro nodded.

"I bet you can make something better Jih, come grab yourself some from the bowl and let us see your skills." Narro said as he clapped his hands.

The four went to work on their masterpieces. The sounds of the group talking to one another reverberated from the walls of the cave only to vanish with rain drowning it out. Narro was the most skilled and chose to depict the open flame that illuminated their room. He used his handprints to layer on top of one another as he did so. He picked up some dust and decorated the outer edges as well, making the appearance of hazy smoke. Narro picked up a piece of kindling from the fire and rubbed it against the side of the wall. He used the burnt ashes from the fire to simulate the cracks of the material. Trekkal remained secretive of her drawing but worked on an elephant on the right side of the cave wall while Sadal made a small hunting scene. Jih made simple shapes as he took his time, in thought about his life back home. He used a circle to represent himself, while Hyu was a triangle, and Kag and Bani were squares. Jih gave a small square below as he remembered that Bani would have given birth soon.

When it came to abstract art, Jih lacked some of the finer elements that came to fruition with the others, but he worked as hard as any. Jih looked over his piece happy with the results of what he made, while the sound of Trekkal laughing filled the cave. Trekkal wiped away a tear while she worked on the final piece of the puzzle. She called the others over, and then Jih heard the laughter of both Narro and Sadal. Jih was desperate to know what was so amusing as he turned his head around and walked over to the others. He looked at it with a raised eyebrow while the other three barely kept their composure. Jih saw that it was a drawing of an elephant.

"Yaan is terrifying! This is not amusing. Yaan is dangerous creature." Jih said with his arms folded.

"Jih...look at what Trekkal did..." Sadal said, as she wiped her eyes in between laughter. She pointed to the elephant's penis which extended much further than the animal and had a face with a smile on the top. Jih just looked more confused at the three of them. Jih took a moment to study the design and raised his eyebrows in understanding of what he saw. Jih gave a small grunt as he examined it a second time just to be sure.

"That is too long." Jih bluntly stated as he turned his head, and his eyes traced the length of Trekkal's drawing.

Narro could barely contain himself as he grabbed onto his sister in laughter. Jih's seriousness with the painting at hand made it even funnier for the three of them. Jih shook his head at the three, he remembered being young once, but chalked it up to the age gap between them. Jih waited patiently to show off his proud drawing, citing the pieces and who they identified with. Jih chose to speak about Hyu as much as he could now that he truly respected his companions. It was the best way for him to bring her into the world and to keep his spirits high. On occasion, he could feel a warm presence on his shoulder.

"Tiny square is for little Kag. Or little Bani? Jih does not know." Jih explained, as he saw Trekkal trying to make sense of his drawings.

The group went through the other's pieces and Jih remarked with pride how Sadal drew the four with their numerous hunts. The group's stomachs rang as they once again felt the pangs of hunger. The storm still raged on through and the thunder would scare off any approachable game. Narro saw this and got the group to huddle closer to the lit fire and try to sing. If all went well, the next bounty would be glorious.

Skipping Stones

Out of the three of them, Jih bonded with Narro the least at this point. Like himself, Narro wasn't the most talkative, but Jih appreciated his attitude when having to do tasks. Unlike Trekkal, who came up with various excuses or tricks to try and get her way, Narro accepted the reality for what it was. While Jih took it on himself to reach out to those in need from time to time, Narro took it a step further. He felt some strange burden of responsibility to not only care for his twin sister, but the wellbeing of those he came across. His parents instilled in them both from a young age that using your various strengths to help the weak was the best course of action in this world. This type of thinking was a far cry from the philosophy that Sadal was given from The Broken Bone, and to a lesser extent of Jih's upbringing as well. Jih sat at the campfire watching the movement of the flames while Narro tirelessly whittled away at a piece of bone with a small rock. He was occupied trying to improve on his flute-making skills, as rejected attempts piled behind him. Narro noticed Jih's boredom was apparent as he didn't know how to occupy himself without anything to do. He decided to get up and talk.

"I was looking to get some wisdom from one of The First." Narro said with a slight grin as he gave Jih a strong pat on the back.

Jih let out a cough and nodded as he got up. As they were in the middle of a grassland with some rolling hills, it was easy to get lost in the vast expanse. The smoke from their campfire made a good guide for them to return home. Trekkal and Sadal were out hunting for a few meals which gave the other two time to relax. Their walk took them to a depression in the ground that was a small pond after days of rainfall. It was easy enough to walk around, but Narro had other plans.

"Have you skipped rocks before Jih?" Narro asked as he picked up some sizable pebbles.

"Jih will win this game." Jih said as he carried Sadal's competitive streak.

"I was thinking more of a friendly game." Narro commented as Jih gave an understanding nod.

Jih took the first pebble, and it skipped three times before sinking to the bottom while he smugly waited for Narro's attempt. He raised his eyebrows, confident of his stellar form. Jih had all the reason to be sure of himself, he long practiced along the beaches where he grew up. Narro's first attempt trumped Jih's entirely. It made its way to six bounces before losing steam and hitting the bottom. Jih wasn't impressed at his performance. Jih held a competitive streak and hated to lose, this was something he and Hyu shared. Jih tapped his foot as he waited for his turn to throw again and the two continued.

"Jih has seen better." Jih commented as he held his tongue from saying anymore.

Jih folded his arms in disappointment at his own performance. Jih hadn't seen anyone skip rocks so effortlessly since his late mother who he failed to emulate. The two continued skipping rocks until they threw about ten each with varying degrees of success. Although Narro hadn't bothered keeping score, Jih certainly did, and he extended his hand out to him. Narro looked at his hand and his eyes returned to the unwavering position of Jih.

"Jih? Can I ask you something?" Narro inquired. Jih gave a nod and found a dry patch of grass to sit on as he waited. His head turned to Narro as he looked at him directly in anticipation.

"This is complicated but, I was wondering if you could help me with..." Narro opened with, his voice trailing off as he waited.

"Boat is complicated. Problem of Narro not so much." Jih said with a warm smile.

"Yes...Well. It regards Sadal. I want to know how to impress her." Narro said quietly, despite there being nothing around them. He sat down as his hands clumped a small part of the soil.

Jih laughed as he was somewhat confused about what he was hearing. He looked again at Narro to confirm his expression, but he could tell that he was indeed serious. Jih was looking for an opportunity to level with Narro, but he hadn't anticipated something of this caliber was the discussion. Jih's laughter subsided as he thought of what to tell Narro. Jih knew that Narro was a serious man and wouldn't bring up a topic like this lightly unless he had a plan in mind. He had his thoughts but didn't dwell on such matters as his focus was towards the power rock. Jih decided to take this new information to reexamine his perspective and pondered about Trekkal's jokes on the matter. He originally only saw it as simple teasing but could connect the dots that they were starting to spend more time with each other. Jih didn't know where to start when it came to Sadal's relationship past. He remembered her prickly reception to Hyu in the early days in her travel with him. He could tell that there was something she was hiding, but she kept that hidden away.

"Sadal does not impress easy. Has Narro thought this through?" Jih asked as he'd rather stick his head in the dirt.

"Yes Jih. You traveled with her for some time before you met Trekkal and I. What would you do in my situation?" Narro asked, hoping that Jih could give him an answer.

"Sadal likes big and dangerous game. Narro, you should hunt very big animal." Jih explained as he stretched his arms out, to emphasize his point further.

"Trekkal refuses to help me. She does not trust Sadal, or any of The Youngest for that matter. We have argued many times. Have you seen her Jih? Sadal has nothing to hide from us." Narro said with a sweet tone to his voice.

Jih could only shrug his shoulders as he was at a loss. Sadal was certainly a talkative type, but Jih imagined something as sensitive as this wouldn't be handled well. She wasn't equipped to handle these sorts of matters; it was obvious to Jih she was emotionally stunted from her work as a warrior. He stayed quiet until Narro opened with another question. Narro wished to ask Jih about his relationship with Hyu, he figured it would prove to be a point of comparison for his attempts at a budding relationship with Sadal. He also saw how lively Jih could get with her memory and enjoyed seeing this side of the stoic man before him. Narro had an exceptional talent at getting anyone to break their barriers and approach him with a kind heart.

"Tell me about Hyu. What did you do for her?" Narro asked with a raised eyebrow. Jih's expression changed as he realized what Narro was asking. It was something he remembered quite well. Narro stretched his body out as he listened closely to Jih's tale.

"Jih got lucky. Jih helped Hyu with idea and she never left. Listen to words of Jih and these may help you." Jih said with a chuckle.

"This was simple. Hyu needed to find Stingmin, big Peymin with pointy tail. Jih held breath and swam down to bottom. It was struck twice by the spear and bled out. It took time, but victory was had. The Peymin did not matter, what mattered was that Jih was there to help. Hyu had dream and a goal in mind, Jih was there to help fill it where her brother could not." Jih explained.

Jih stood up and made a triumphant pose to Narro as he completed his tale. The wind picked up behind him as his gazelle fur waved with it in a complimentary fashion.

"Jih is finished. You may clap when you are ready." Jih stated with a big smile.

"Jih, the Stingmin slayer! This sounds like a real legend to be had." Narro said, with a loud clap as he and Jih shared a laugh.

"So, for Sadal, I should ask what her dream is? There must be more to it than that. I would have done that ages ago." Narro interjected.

"Sadal is...complicated. There are things Jih knows and things Jih thinks he knows." Jih admitted as he shrugged his shoulders.

"I was thinking of offering her some sort of meal, warriors must be reached through their stomach and that could be all the difference. We have tried hunting many things in these lands, but everything is too fast. If I could find a way to combine both, then I may have something." Narro declared.

"Sadal values contribution to team, she hunts, you clean. She makes clothing, you find materials. Do these things and she will appreciate you. Jih remembers talking of Hyu to Sadal early on, and she grew angry. Jih thinks this was disappointment in her own life. The one with Sadal did not give equally, and she grew resentful." Jih examined.

Jih raised a finger as he looked to Narro once more.

"Remember, love requires sacrifice. Narro is young with long life, if you think it is worth it, you must give." Jih warned.

"Of course, I would do anything to make this work." Narro commented.

Jih held a hesitant expression regarding Narro's eagerness. Jih was aware they approached relationship building in a different manner than his own people and needed to mind these differences. Sadal had a lot of maturing to do in his eyes. Narro's boredom long since left as he was enthralled by the rest of Jih's stories. It was both entertaining and something worth learning from. Enough time passed for Trekkal and Sadal to have filled their duties for the day as they made out two figures in the distance. They recognized them as Jih and Narro who were in deep discussion on something. Trekkal narrowed her eyes as she focused closer. She waved over to try and catch their attention but saw she was ignored. Jih looked in the distance and saw a small figure ahead, but his attention was brought back to Narro.

"But really Jih, what should I do? I have no pools of water to perform miracles." Narro asked Jih as his eyes looked to the ground. Jih felt slightly deflated from Narro's question but placed a hand on his shoulder. He was going to offer his services to help him woo Sadal even if it killed him. He was well experienced in keeping Kag's head on straight and figured someone as well natured as Narro would be great under the right guidance.

"We will start small. Talk to Sadal, use your words, and see what she thinks. We are in strange lands, there is plenty to discuss." Jih stated.

"Alright, in exchange for this advice, I have a joke for you." Narro mentioned as Jih lifted his head.

"What do you get when you cross a Denmey and a pack of hunters?"

"Peace and quiet." Jih guessed as he gave his thoughts.

"A feast for the ages you can smell for miles!" Narro said as he slapped his leg at his own joke. Jih remained utterly confused.

"Jih does not understand, what is this humor?"

"The point of the joke is it is exactly the opposite of what you would expect. Denmey meat tastes terrible!" Narro mentioned while Jih tried to understand the irony of the joke. As he thought about it, he could see how that would be amusing to some, but it was lost on him.

"Your sister is better. Jih is glad you told this here instead of to Sadal." Jih smugly stated which prompted a laugh from the pair.

"What are those two doing over there?" Trekkal asked as she chewed on some pine nuts. She nudged Sadal and pointed as she saw Jih and Narro laughing together.

"I haven't seen Jih like this, well...ever. He always takes himself so seriously. Seems your brother has some sort of talent." Sadal commented as she took a nut from Trekkal's hand while they walked back to camp with their packs full of goodies.

"Jih can tell us all about it when he plucks all these feathers!" Trekkal laughed as Sadal gave her a nice pat on the back.

It Stares At You

A Thunderfoot sat at the edge of a large pool of water. The Forest Seekers saw this as a pristine place where one could communicate with the various denizens of the forest undisturbed. This area was cleared of their presence some time ago. He dipped his finger in the water and observed the movement of the fish within it. He sat with his legs folded and took a deep breath as a slight breeze carried over the water. The sounds of birds chirping in the canopy above sang a great song. He chose to remember a time that he once thought was better.

It was an unusually hot day. Two boys ran across the grasslands in search of their home. The first boy struggled to meet the speed of his friend who outpaced him. The first of the two boys' feet were blistered from days of walking. His stomach was emaciated as he ate nothing and could only think of home before he was left behind once again. His wrists were a dark red and resounded with pain. He was bound so tightly that the coils embedded into his skin. The second of the pair retreated further from his view as he continued to run. His wrists were also bound but in a much freer fashion. The pair's hair was shaved, and they wore clothing that was ripped apart. A pack of lions settled underneath one of the few spots of shade left. The first boy met the eye of these lions and gave a look of hatred towards them. While he grew to rightfully fear these creatures, they also served him well. The presence of lions was a deterrent for lesser willed bands to make incursions on their territory.

The boy limped by as the lions watched in utter boredom. He looked to the sky to see signals made from smoke and knew that home was close. The limp turned into a run as he ignored the pain and was happy to see familiar faces once more when he arrived. An old man who wore extravagant cheetah fur sat on the edge of the camp in thought. Under his crossed legs was a rug made with the same material. His eyes met the growing silhouette of the boys. The faster of the two continued his pace as his destination would take another hour. The first boy stopped and fell to the grass. His eyes closed as he hit the ground knowing he had returned to safety. When he came to, he absorbed the scale of his village. There were usually at least 100 people here, but most were gone. The boy realized he returned on a special day. There was a feast coming with great expectations, so most of the adults were busy and out to find good meals. All capable hunters that day found themselves trying to kill as much as they could bring back to spare and wouldn't return for several hours. The band was hosting allies they hoped to have on board for a great vision one day. Violence scourged the land and bloodshed was not productive. There were more acceptable ways to go about life and this feast would be the great uniter. This was a feast that also celebrated their bounty, for the rains were good and the lions were lazy. The old man called the boy forward and looked him over. He chewed on a branch to keep his jaws strong, at his age, his teeth could fall out at any moment.

"Boy, you come to me, beaten and bloody. I was promised victory, but defeat is all I smell from you. I knew you weren't ready." The old man spat with disgust at his grandson. The boy could only nod his head in embarrassment as he hoped to make amends. Loss in the field of battle wasn't something to be taken lightly and the old man felt slighted to witness such circumstances.

"I returned after I was left behind. What can be done to fix this dishonor?" The boy asked and took a knee as he lowered his head.

For his attempt at forgiveness, he was only met with a harsh strike to the back with a staff. His back was already marred with injuries and one more strike practically made him fall over once again. He held his composure long enough to nod in respect to the old man. He knew that in time things would be different, but he wasn't sure when.

"It's an embarrassment and a stain on our people, Ronkalk. Return to your dwelling and I will speak to you later. Untie yourself." The man ordered Ronkalk.

Ronkalk was dismissed with nothing further. Ronkalk thought he did everything he could to the best of his ability but was punished for it all the same. After all he did to prove himself, he would never be worth it. He knew matters needed to be taken into his own hands, but recovery was the most important. He weaved his way through the clustered homes to find the tent where he and his sister resided. His eyes filled with tears as he recounted his capture and conditions of internment.

"Chindi...please help me." Ronkalk said as he stumbled through the tent.

Chindi ran over to the bloodied Ronkalk and held him in her arms. She pressed him against her body and the two remained still in a tight embrace. Ronkalk's red eyes looked up to match the protective gaze of his sister. Chindi was three years older than Ronkalk. At fifteen years old, she was steadily taller than him and took a knee to match her brother. She had long black hair that was packed together into braids and wore two shell spools in her ears. Ronkalk looked into her eyes and saw the dark brown that matched his own. She wore a cheetah print covering like their grandfather. She scanned Ronkalk's injuries and knew they were dire but would heal in time. Chindi's eyes noticed that blood leaked down his leg and his clothing was torn apart. Chindi couldn't hide her changing expression as it morphed into fear and disgust at the fate of her brother. Chindi took her knife and quickly uncut Ronkalk from his bindings and blew air on his wrists. Chindi assessed Ronkalk's fate, but she asked for her brother's input on the situation to be sure. Capture in battle was a shameful display among their people and the politics around it were damaging. From Ronkalk's perspective, his torture and abuse to be used as a set piece by those who could instead provide support, enraged him. Chindi shared these sentiments but was responsible for keeping the peace among them.

"Brother, what happened? You were missing for days. You are bleeding, do you want the sleeping leaf for your wounds?" Chindi asked, as she could feel the anger emanating from his body.

"Krukzig and I went to avenge our kin who fell in the east. We were too weak, and I was held for three days. I crawled as far as I could, but I was too tired to return. They dragged me. I broke away when the others left but..." Ronkalk explained as he declined to speak further.

"My hair...it was shaved. It must grow all over again." Ronkalk said as he felt Chindi's hand on his head. She saw that he was clearly upset but knew that these issues were something he worked out better on his own. Chindi reprimanded Ronkalk as she was supposed to but could only do so much.

"This was the job of our warriors to do, we are the leader's grandchildren. We must set an example, but I understand. The old ways of waiting for the spirits to do things makes me tired, action needs to be had." Chindi said as she locked eyes with Ronkalk.

Ronkalk propped himself off Chindi as he slowly fixed himself to sit in their tent. He wiped his eyes and his sniffling stifled as he was comforted by a nice feeling. Ronkalk forgot how soft the bear skin flooring of their home was. He rubbed his hand against the floor while Chindi rummaged in a nearby basket for a sleeping leaf to administer to Ronkalk. She quickly clutched it in her hands and held it in front of Ronkalk. Ronkalk opened his mouth and chewed as he felt a slight numbness take over his body.

"We should give our grandfather a visit. He should see the new pelt I've been working on. We can wait until you rest though." She said as she looked towards him.

"We can go now. I'm sure he has good words for it." Ronkalk replied impatiently and tried to get through the conversation.

Ronkalk's eyes drifted to a short blade by Chindi's bed. She used this to cut strips of meat but used it to also cut the edges of the fur. Chindi was relentless when it came to covering every inch of the tent as she tore them to the seams. Ronkalk drifted his leg over and grabbed the end of the blade with his foot. Chindi turned her head and looked towards Ronkalk. Chindi helped up Ronkalk as she scooped a rolled-up pelt that she prepared for the ceremony.

The two walked just a short distance away to the entrance of their grandfather's tent. Chindi looked at Ronkalk and saw his attempt to conceal the blade. She decided to stay silent instead of calling him out for its purposes. His back was turned as the two entered. Chindi observed her grandfather's callousness as he shouted obscenities at Ronkalk's lack of respect and decorum. The effects of the sleeping leaf overtook Ronkalk as he felt time slow down for him, but his thoughts were already made. In one fell swoop, Ronkalk withdrew Chindi's knife and lunged towards the man in an indescribable rage.

"Ronkalk! Chindi, help me at once!" The man shouted as Ronkalk tackled their grandfather to the ground.

The old man with such power over them, felt like raw bone to Ronkalk's touch. He swung with a fanatical rage that beat the man's teeth out of his jaw as he struggled to come up with any words. The grandfather feebly fought back against Ronkalk's strikes as his punches barely had any effect. Ronkalk continuously stabbed the man in a frenzy as blood pooled over his body. Chindi watched as her knife entered her grandfather countless times. Ronkalk felt this was due retribution for his treatment after being held by the enemy. He suffered an unimaginable price for the honor of his people, and this was only met with scorn. Chindi could only watch with a dead feeling in her eyes. She kept up appearances as well as she could, but her feelings were shared, any love she had was lost some time ago. While Ronkalk acted off pure emotion, Chindi was more manipulative as she had the eye and favor of the people. Chindi waited for the opportune moment to wrestle control of their band, and now Ronkalk's actions set things in motion. She would have to explain this to their parents and the rest of the band for that matter, but that would come later. All she could think about now was the new cause.

Ronkalk's last thoughts were of Zulag and how his quest to recover Sadal was going. He retrieved deserters before, sometimes on his own as well. Ronkalk felt that with Deeso's competence to guide him, despite their hostility, they would see the job done. Ronkalk remembered the small Sadal and how much she'd grown since their fateful meeting. The question of her disappearance burned in his mind. Ronkalk thought perhaps he'd done something wrong but was unsure of what to do. Ronkalk's meditation was disturbed by the steps of another. Ronkalk turned to see who would make such an effort to find him. One of the priests of the red rank spoke out to Ronkalk. Ronkalk was generally bothered by the white painted priests who were often finicky in their allegiances and were incredibly irritating. Ronkalk held little patience for squabbling at the top. Even for Ronkalk, a red priest was considered a serious inquiry to be had and so he would listen until he felt slighted. He didn't recognize this voice, but the priests were keenly aware of all the inner workings of the other bands within The Broken Bone and their various projects. Ronkalk was a popular subject as of late.

"Ronkalk!" The red priest called out as he made his way over.

Ronkalk bowed his head in respect, an honor he barely reserved for anyone else. Red painted priests were often the role given to the handicapped as their perceived injuries were seen as a sacrifice to the greater spirits, and their interpretations of events were considered much stronger than the others ranked below. A red priest is who assessed that Zulag would have strange markings on his skin, but the spirits still gave him considerable favor. His face wore a wooden mask which was painted red, and one arm was smaller than the other. He wore the pelt of a sun bear that glistened in the sunlight. There were only six known red-painted priests, and Ronkalk's band was prestigious enough to have two of them, it was something he worked very hard to manage. The red-painted priests lived in isolation from the greater priesthood but offered their knowledge just as much as any other.

"Priest. What news do you give me? Have we finally found Aralic?" Ronkalk asked with false hope in his voice.

The red priest was confused as to his question. At this point Ronkalk's hopes of finding those that left The Broken Bone was a herculean task. The priest had a heavy defeated tone to his reply.

"Ronkalk, it's been twenty years. Why are we still doing this? Why send out the occasional scout? Aralic is gone and I believe he joined the spirits." The red priest sighed as he looked through the slits of his mask.

"I have never received an answer on why he left. Like Sadal, he was one of the best. He was my friend once. He is the father of my nephew. Those don't come very often." Ronkalk commented. He waved his hand to the priest, ready to hear the next trivial complaint that would come his way.

"I come to you out of respect and have not called the other band leaders. We have concerns about your wasted efforts on the search for Sadal. Zulag would be useful for our needs, but you have sent him out. We need to move and take decisive actions against the Forest Seekers. Our scouts tell us they seem to be working towards some sort of goal. We are not sure what." The man said as he informed Ronkalk of the priest's perspective.

The priesthood stood in a very precarious state of being, some leaders of The Broken Bone saw them as religious consultants only, while others chose to involve them in strategy for hunting and conflict with other bands. The lines were certainly blurred, but at least for Ronkalk, he saw them as a subservient arm under his leadership. Red priests were a disruption to this dynamic as Ronkalk was forced to divulge all he could out of obligation.

"Concerns? Yes, I see. Concerns are what Ututar had as well. Ask him about your concerns and hear his words." Ronkalk said with venom. The priest was visibly shaken, as he heard the details of Ronkalk and Ututar's confrontation.

"Your threats can only last as long as your luck Ronkalk. Both seem to be running out. The other bands say things that come to our ears. I would look behind you when you walk, a dagger comes among you through the bushes." The red priest stated as Ronkalk huffed in defiance.

"I trust she will be brought back safely. After all, my nephew knows how important this is for us. Things will return to normal, and we will begin anew. It came to me in a dream. They will emerge victorious, for I have taught them well." Ronkalk said in response to the red priest's inquiry regarding Zulag.

"I recommend that we arrange a meeting with The Forest Seeker leadership to get information. We priests are seen as unaffiliated to hostiles unlike the rest of the band." The red priest said as he raised his hand to Ronkalk.

Ronkalk laughed and shook his head at such a remark. The idea of sitting down with Forest Seekers on any given terms was an idea as ludicrous as when Chindi recommended it to him years ago. Their goals were completely opposed to his own vision of the world. Compromising the safety of his people was a fate he would never be able to give up willingly.

"The Forest Seekers are a thorn, yes, but the beasts are our primary concern. This is our livelihood. Sadal's failure to kill the Weypeu in a clean manner still has lowered morale. We must watch for the movement of these other creatures. My respect for your rank is as infinite as the trees in this land, but you don't know what you're saying. The Forest Seekers have no leadership. You can ask one what color an Onpeu is and they would debate on the issue like rabid Denmey." Ronkalk gestured as he pointed to the rest of the foliage that surrounded them.

"The color is yellow, by the way." Ronkalk said, with humor in his voice as the priest's body language further stiffened.

"We have heard that a woman has been visiting them and trying to rile them up in arms. This should be the cause for you Ronkalk. It's one thing to work on a boat but another to threaten our way of life." The red priest argued with conviction in his voice.

"I've yet to see a problem. I have already stated that Forest Seekers are to be attacked on sight. We have exhausted peace. Your idea will run into ruin, they can't differentiate us from The Mud Forged or anyone else for that matter. To be practical, a Forest Seeker decides to eliminate our enemies for us, ones that we have struggled to wipe out for some time. I will say it again, our mission is to get rid of the beasts, but I understand your concern. I will modify our training to deal with Forest Seeker attacks. Do you know if they use any sort of formation or tactics not seen before?" Ronkalk asked, as he only received silence from the priest.

Ronkalk knew that the priesthood was disconnected to the daily realities at hand. It came to be no surprise that even the most informed could only do so much without experiencing it firsthand. The red priests have already sacrificed much in the spiritual battle and were masters of their domain but could only observe in the physical plane. It was up to the red priest on how to decide communications would end. It was expected for leaders to be subservient as a formality to the red priests, but Ronkalk was well respected to use the tone that he did. Ronkalk ruled with such esteem even after his actions regarding Cikya that infuriated the lower ranks. The two nodded in respect with their conversation.

"We will find you again when there is more to know. My leave will begin shortly. Heed what I have told you or you will pay for it in time." The red priest commented.

Ronkalk covered his eyes as was customary. The location of where red priests lived must be obscured from leadership, as only the priesthood would know where they made their shelters. It was seen as a violation for the unaffiliated to enter their space otherwise. Ronkalk attempted to hear the man's leave as he stepped away into the deeper woods. After some time, Ronkalk opened his eyes to find him gone without a trace, just as the priest intended.

"I hate that they make me do that." Ronkalk said to himself.

House Edge

True to their word, The Buffalo Brothers worked on the intricate process of blade-making that would support their humble business endeavors. Although the pair said they needed a month, their work time was far quicker than that. As a pair of procrastinators, the two waited until the last minute to do what Eshe required. It was easy enough to take their paltry sum of pelts and run with no delivery, but Dronall and Nezzall did adhere to verbal agreements when it suited them. They knew that Eshe was relentless and would hunt them down if she was given nothing in return. They were only given half but hoped to receive what they agreed on. What separated a good con from any run of the mill scam was giving a glimmer of hope.

"The load is heavy, as you travel with no bag on your back. Let's make this deal so you can retrieve yours that you left behind with that Forest Seeker witch." Nezzall mentioned.

He adjusted the strap's placement on his bag and flexed his muscles. Dronall gave his brother a nod in agreement as they left a small fire at their camp. The Buffalo Brothers found an area of interest just a few hours travel from Eshe's location. The pair searched for workable stone to produce the weapons as promised. The two carried axes they looted off some poor saps who found themselves dead from exposure. The brothers found they were more suited for chopping wood, but they could be modified to serve as picks to extract stone.

Their travels took them to what appeared to be a lake, but on further examination, they noticed the presence of sand rather than mud. Dronall kneeled as put his hand into the sand and gave it a hearty smell. Nezzall tapped his brother's shoulder and the two scouted out their ideal location. A few mounds of dirt not too far off in the distance that was lightly covered with some grass. The pair walked around the hill and unearthed layers of soil to unveil various rocks buried under the dirt. Dronall lifted his skull cap to get a better look, while Nezzall stood close behind him. The two focused on a small deposit of silcrete.[51] The pair pocketed the core for themselves and would mass produce the order that they agreed to give Eshe with the remains. Dronall put his arm around his brother's shoulder as he felt the tannish-colored stone with his other hand. He raised his eyebrows in satisfaction as he grabbed his axe and attempted to mash a portion off.

"Two for ourselves, finest quality blades to admire, let us make the Forest Seeker witch's haul with the flakes that come from behind." Dronall said with a laugh as the two mined for the stone in synchronization. The material was difficult to work on its own on-site, the two needed to return to camp for the next phase of their plan.

---

[51] Silcrete was a highly sought after tool material in the African Middle Stone Age, where sourcing efforts for the material could go up to a range of 200 kilometers away from other sources of workable rock such as quartz indicating a preference in some way. Heat treatment was a technique projected to be used as early as 164,000 years ago by Modern Humans to alter composition before tool formation.

After some exhaustion, the two were able to separate the clumped silcrete from the rest of the material. Nezzall stuffed the core in his bag and strained a bit as it was heavy, even for someone of his strength. Dronall reassured his brother that the effort was truly worth it.

"Let us return before we catch the ire of the Onpeu." Dronall warned as the two headed back to camp.

With camp now in sight, Nezzall strained as he placed the bag down that was filled with their other supplies. Dronall overlooked their bounty and snapped his fingers for Nezzall to get some material for a fire. Nezzall raised an eyebrow as he pointed to the ongoing fire currently made. This stone needed to be heat-treated before they could do more with it. Dronall recounted the instructions while he guided his brother's attention again.

"Good start, but a bigger fire is needed than the small one we have. Keep that one for light when we wake. Let the other grow, I will dig and place the rock underneath. We will sleep and then once we wake, it will be ready. Do you understand brother?" Dronall asked Nezzall as he shrugged his shoulders in response.

Dronall dug a medium-sized hole with his hands and placed the block of silcrete inside for the next fire. Dronall grabbed some extra branches and looked around for other material. The two were aware that different temperatures from the fire could be produced depending on the species of tree used. He took a piece of nearby chert and set it alight as the two listened for the crack of dirt.

The two slept for six hours, their afternoon now turned into night. The large fire that Nezzall built still raged on as the two awoke and went to work. Dronall doused the worked flame and exposed the stone which darkened in color just as he planned. Nezzall approached and reflexively grabbed the stone. He yelped in pain as he turned around to see Dronall glaring at him. Dronall nearly held his breath as he hoped the core would remain stable.

"Brother, did you assume the stone would be cold?" He said with a worried chuckle as Nezzall waved his hands around to cool them off.

Nezzall sunk his hands in the loose dirt and felt instant relief. He looked to see Dronall walk over to a pile of refuse some distance away. Dronall wrapped his hands in pelts to form gloves and slowly walked to the stone. He crouched down and picked up the object while the heat dispersed through the fur. He looked over and saw various cracks in the stone and was impressed with their prowess. Dronall turned to hear his brother as he approached holding chisels made from chert.

"Hold on, brother. I have an idea. Take the flakes we make and mark incantations on the blade." Nezzall said with a devious grin. Carvings on weapons were a common belief to make them hold stronger powers for the user.

"Why? I'm not a priest." Dronall said with a dismissive tone in his voice.

"Exactly. If we tell the Forest Seeker witch, we imbued these with magic, surely our haul will be greater. As you said, in the art of exchange, information is the most important.

The Forest Seekers believe in the realm of spirits much as we do. Eshe's crusade is against our kind, let her believe this magic will help her in battle and watch her hopes be dashed!" Nezzall stated as Dronall could only agree.

The two continued their labor through the night with the occasional mischievous bout of laughter, it was rare they had such enjoyment. The finished product was certainly notable as it glistened in the low light of the fire. The blades were flattened out on one edge and of an acceptable length. They were incredibly thin but sharp to the touch at the point. The handles were made of wood and reinforced with some animal sinew to serve as fibers. At first glance, these were a fine construction, but were at best suited for ceremony. A hard hit from the side would practically shatter them to pieces. To sell the presentation further, the pair wrapped the blades together in deer fur.

The pair idled for some time until the day started. The two took their offerings back to Eshe's encampment and waited. The call of their entry was announced to Eshe who was busy over yet another task. She prompted one of her associates to grab the remaining pelts they agreed to give. One of her men came by with Dronall's bag he left behind along with their reward. Dronall's eyes looked at the wrapped-up bundle and salivated at the offering. In the center was a small glimpse of a tiger's pelt. Nezzall saw this as well and knew the mark of the tiger was unmistakable. Eshe was unaware that such a valuable pelt was in the bundle, but some of her associates thought to show off their prowess to the lowly traders at their camp. The war against the Thunderfeet was both physical but also a game of wits. Eshe came by some time later as she looked to see a wrapped-up bundle in their hands. She would need to investigate the haul given to her before they could leave. The brothers remained motionless as they peered underneath their skull caps to see her approach.

"Are these the blades we agreed to?" Eshe asked with a raised eyebrow as she looked at the folds.

"As we agreed previously. Our end of the deal is on the soil below." Dronall mentioned, as he slowly unrolled the blades. Dronall spoke shortly and lacked his usual charm when it came to Eshe. Eshe found it hard to hide her surprise, as she was moderately impressed. She picked up the blade and felt its sharp touch.

"Be careful. It can slice a Peymin with ease." Nezzall added.

"What are these markings? Are they damaged?" Eshe said to the two as she noticed some strange etchings along the hilt.

"Our special touch. We have embedded magic into the blades. Convening with the spirits is something we both share." Dronall commented as he and Nezzall nodded.

Eshe shrugged as she held no real knowledge on Thunderfoot spiritual matters. She turned her head in judgement but a few of her associates took to accepting this as a sign of good will. Eshe assessed the blades while the pair waited silently. Their skulls obscured their deceit. Eshe's knowledge was wholly inexperienced when it came to using stone tools and she assumed that sharp tools meant powerful ones. She raised her hand to make the final decision as leader and called for the pair to be rewarded.

"Give them the pelts and his bag back." Eshe ordered as they scooped up the bundle. Dronall sorted through the collection and gave a satisfied nod. The two shook hands and went off and left Eshe with their new collection.

Three days later, Eshe wanted to test out her new weaponry on fresh targets. She watched the newest of her recruits stab the air and enjoyed seeing her words put into practice. Her vision soon shattered like the tools she traded for. Eshe heard a cracking sound as one of the knives broke. Eshe watched with interest as two people sparred with the techniques she learned on her travels. She watched as their blades collided and shattered to pieces. The pair had confused looks on their faces as they went to Eshe. At first Eshe attributed this to just a rookie mistake, but another of her initiates came with the same problem. Eshe quickly deduced that the batch was bad. She curled her hand into a fist and pounded on the ground in annoyance.

"The stone is sharp, but it breaks easily and is useless. Where are the Thunderfoot traders? It has been three days, not much progress was made. We must get a return." Eshe demanded of one of her associates.

"We gave them a Weypeu pelt." One of her associates voiced as he braced for Eshe's reaction.

"You gave what!? We need to fix this!" Eshe shouted at them.

She was rarely made a fool of, and this thought would stay with her for quite some time. She attempted to calm herself down and take a walk in the forest to collect herself before coming up with a plan. Eshe and the other Forest Seekers were surely had by The Buffalo Brothers who could only laugh with glee, but Eshe was not one to be trifled with.

In The Bush

Zulag was awake first and roasted some deer meat over a roaring fire. Deeso, Cikya, and Ozul were asleep on beds of leaves. As the meat cooked, the smoke wafted to their noses and their eyes opened one by one. The forest floor was comfortable enough for Zulag to lay back on a layer of leaves and never touch the soil below. It was Zulag's turn the previous night to keep watch, so he remained awake and took some time to himself once daybreak struck. Zulag was hasty and quickly snatched the meat. He took a small bite and found the meat was a bit raw for his initial taste. He stuck his tongue out as he was impatient and wanted to eat.

"Dekdeu meat. Now this is for refined taste such as mine. I'm tired of Zemaii all the time." [52] He groaned to himself and decided to place it back on the fire. A cloud of smoke from the fire filled their campsite and shrouded them in the smell of cooked meat.

Zulag turned around to see the rustling of the others. He met eyes with the three who had their view pinned on Zulag's meal. Ozul's eyes were the biggest as he drifted from Zulag to the cooked deer meat. Deeso bit her lip as she absorbed the smoke. She noticed that the wood Zulag picked for cooking left a smell that enhanced the flavor.

"I'm not giving a piece! Get your own or get lost." Zulag threatened as he raised a fist at them.

Cikya's stomach rumbled as she looked through her pack to find just a few pieces of fruit worth scavenging. She tapped Ozul's shoulder and offered him a small piece of a banana which he graciously accepted. He chewed it happily as it settled in his stomach. Ozul frowned as he looked at the conditions of their camp. Aside from Zulag's personal morsel, they once again searched for a big meal to bring home. It was hard to concentrate being an hour from starvation every day. Deeso hoped to distract their concerns about food by mentioning Sadal.

"Well, do we have any leads on Sadal? I'm one of the best trackers we have, and the trail has gone cold. We've been improvising so far." Deeso said as she absentmindedly bent a twig in boredom.

"Do I have to do everything around here? I thought you had the nose of a Denmey." Zulag complained, much to the sound of Deeso and Ozul who sighed in annoyance at their lack of progress. Zulag grabbed the more cooked deer slice and stuffed it in his mouth.

"I heard some Forest Seekers talking about some woman named Eshe during my hunt. Maybe she's their leader or something? I don't know." Zulag said through his chewing. He coughed as he regained his breath. Ozul lifted his eyebrows at the mention of the name.

"She travels around with some of her people, fighting against the Thunderfeet. I remember three years ago; she came by to our people looking for warriors to fight. It was

---

[52] Emic word for turtle.

not our way, so we declined, and she was very angry. As you all killed the Thunderfoot named Krukzig, it would seem we should find her." Ozul noted with some severity in his voice.

"I can see why. You all are pathetic. You roll over like a hog in mud to anyone who glances at you the wrong way." Zulag scoffed while he saw Ozul's frown.

"Then why is it that your kind has come here? According to the stories of your own people, Zulag, you are exiles. Undesirables from the land that was dry and hot." Ozul said defensively as he quickly held his arms up to cover his face as Zulag stood up in front of him with gritted teeth.

"Deeso, are you going to take such disrespect from him?" Zulag said with a tang of judgement in his voice.

"Zulag, he's just a kid. I can't punish him for telling the truth. Didn't you pay attention to what your uncle told you?" Deeso reasoned. Zulag shook his head and shot Ozul a glare. Cikya tapped Deeso's shoulder, grabbing her attention as she took a long stick and slammed it against a tree.

"Yes Cikya? Did you need something from me?" Deeso asked as she turned her head.

Cikya heard of a few local Forest Seeker boys trying to summon Eshe in the same manner of a spirit to channel. Cikya's travels by the river showed her that they intended to leave a sacrifice to attract her or her followers. She struggled to figure out how to communicate this though, but pointed to the soil where she drew some hints.

I hope you can decipher this. Cikya thought as she started to draw.

Deeso motioned for Zulag to approach as he observed the attempted drawings on the ground. He scratched his head, as he was confused by the vague imprints Cikya made. She wasn't an expert at drawing by any means, so it was difficult.

"Does it have to do with Eshe?" Deeso asked, as Cikya clapped her hands with glee.

"Great Deeso, asking the real hard questions. Cikya. Do you know how to find her? This is what we're actually looking for." Zulag asked, hoping to end the guessing game as quickly as possible.

Cikya pointed to Zulag with her finger and grabbed his attention. She gestured towards where his face paint used to be and then to her own. She was trying to hint that it was ritual in nature much like how they acquired their face paints. Cikya felt Deeso wouldn't get it so she looked to see if Zulag could answer.

"My face? What does that have to do with anything? Cikya, I know you used to speak in riddles but..." Zulag commented as he scratched his elbow.

"Zulag, it's not your face but what's on it. She's trying to tell us there must be something else." Deeso noted, which gave an impressed expression from Cikya.

"It's a ritual. They use a ritual to summon Eshe. But Eshe is just a person, no?" Zulag questioned as he looked back at Ozul.

Ozul watched the three closely as he looked through his bag of supplies. He had some knowledge of the ritual from his interactions in this area. It was a small legend among the younger kids, mostly just to try and scare each other. Some adults who were tuned in, operated as pretenders to Eshe's legacy, both to inspire their own groups and for the thrill of adventure.

"You know, we could have probably just asked Ozul since he knows who she is, Zulag." Deeso said, putting her hand to her head in frustration. Cikya nodded and confirmed that Zulag was correct.

"Sounds boring. Not interested." Zulag said. He was tired after doing watch the previous night, so if anyone was to explore this inquiry, it would be Deeso.

"What? This could be what we need to help us find Sadal! What if she came across this Eshe? She would be seen as the enemy, and they would have gone into combat. If this is her territory and she's as powerful as the legends say, there's no doubt that she would know." Deeso asserted with some concern in her voice. Zulag couldn't resist as he saw the perfect opportunity to disparage Sadal.

"If Sadal is as amazing as she touts herself to be, we won't have much to work off of. I'm sure she'll say some story about how she threw twenty spears before one hit the ground just like my uncle likes to say." Zulag said as he mocked Sadal's voice.

Deeso raised her hand in anger to strike Zulag in the face. He didn't move as it impacted his face but left a small sting. Zulag rubbed his stomach in laughter as Deeso continued to stew in anger.

"It really is too easy with you little Deeso. One of these days I might like one of those slaps!" Zulag taunted her.

Deeso tuned out Zulag's mockery and looked at Cikya and Ozul. She decided that to find Eshe, she'd need Ozul's eyes of the forest. She nodded her head and gathered for his attention. Deeso hoped to address both their food insecurity as well as find information she needed on Sadal's whereabouts.

"I'm going to go hunting. Ozul, come with me." Deeso commented as she waved her hand.

"Me?" Ozul asked, with his mind still on his pile of materials.

Ozul was still hard at work on an upgrade for his blowgun build but took a small knife with him for protection. Deeso raised an eyebrow at him as she motioned for him to follow. Her curiosity about the ritual and its success was something she wanted to see for herself. Ozul was the means to an end, and she intended to use him as bait for such a project. Ozul wondered why Deeso wanted to travel with him. Out of the three, he found Deeso the most disturbing to be around. Zulag was offensive and mean, but the two started to have more common ground. Ozul took this as a sign he was slowly being accepted by him. Cikya was warm and kind to him from the start, but there was something ultimately unreachable with Deeso. It was true that she allowed him to join their operation in the first place, but it felt misplaced in some way. He also felt a great sadness project from her and there was little he could do.

"What will we hunt today?" Ozul said, as he put on a slightly more positive tone than usual. He usually hunted for things alone or was paired with Zulag, so having Deeso instead was an interesting change of pace.

"I'd like to get a Smir-Tamdeu but I'm not picky." Deeso said, as she noticed Ozul's attempts at small talk.

Ozul trailed behind a bit, as he left a reasonable berth of space between the two. Deeso noticed this and turned her head to look at Ozul. Ozul felt a tinge of fear come over his body as the pair settled. All he could hear was the ambient sound of birds that flew overhead. Deeso let the silence hang for a bit, as she knew Ozul was a curious one and wouldn't be satisfied with just that.

"My actual goal is I want to find one of your kind and ask them how to find this Eshe." Deeso mentioned.

"I see. I have two questions. What will you do if you find her? And you do not have to answer this...but why is Zulag so mean to you? I get me, everyone finds a way to be mean to me, but you have done nothing wrong." Ozul asked as his eyes looked towards the grass. Ozul made sure he took great care to avoid stepping on flowers.

Deeso was expecting the first question, but she hadn't anticipated the second. She paused as she felt sweat go down her hand and she gripped her axe in a vice. She felt the heft of her weapon with a smug satisfaction. Her eyes met Ozul's as he leaned to the side of a nearby tree. She didn't have any expectations on what Eshe would be like but found her appeal to leadership among Ozul's people intriguing. Deeso let out a smirk to him as she imagined herself with Eshe in her grasp. The fear in Eshe's eyes as she raised her axe. All of it was another way to prove herself and the means she would go to find Sadal.

"I plan to ask her some questions. Afterwards, she will die by my hand. Nothing will take Sadal from me." Deeso stated while Ozul gave a small gulp in his throat.

"And Zulag?" Ozul added on, as he still waited for his answer.

"The Broken Bone is my only home now. I was kicked out of two places before I was found. As you know, Zulag's uncle is our leader, and he is the one who took Sadal and I in. Zulag distrusts me as much as he does you, and yet he depends on us both to save his life." Deeso said, with surprise in herself as she laid out the events of her life with such clarity.

She stretched out the palm of her right hand and pointed to long healed scars that were on the outside. She gestured to her Wanderer's Mark and watched Ozul's reaction. Ozul gently caressed Deeso's hand and looked at his own. His were rough but from making tools. Ozul looked up at Deeso's face and saw that it remained smooth with youth, but her hand was weathered. Deeso's hand carried her entire experience.

"My hand no longer bleeds because I have purpose now. Ronkalk gave me that purpose. Let's find food." Deeso said as she waited for Ozul to let go.

The hunt for the Smir-Tamdeu was a slow one, as Deeso made soft sounds to try and attract the animal. Ozul held his small knife close to him as he scanned the low brush for one to approach them. He studied Deeso's movement as he looked around for any hidden surprises. There were a few times he caught some of his own kind in hiding and kept it to himself as to not alarm the others. Despite never being in such an environment, she walked with poise, much like Cikya did, but had a certain roughness to her that was hard to emulate. A small deer jettisoned from the nearby bush at breakneck speed and the pair pursued the animal. As Deeso ran, she saw that Ozul climbed a tree to get a better vantage point. She was confused at his strategy and wasn't aware that Ozul had practically mapped out every route the animal could go already.

"I know where you will go. He was running parallel which means that there's the direction of a river nearby. I must be correct." Ozul said to himself as he carefully climbed down.

Deeso ran ahead of Ozul who maneuvered carefully through the brush. Thanks to his mental mapping, he was able to catch up to Deeso with relative ease as she hacked away portions of vines with her axe to keep visual on the prey. She looked surprised but ultimately focused on the goal at hand. There was clearly more to this kid than he let on and she wanted to learn more. Above all else, Deeso valued competence in her allies. She realized that Zulag was correct in pushing Ozul to do more. It was no substitute for hunting with Sadal, but Ozul remained engaged. There was a lot at stake from Ozul's perspective, he felt he needed to perform above and beyond to improve his standing among his friends. His breathing grew heavier, but he ignored the pain of his lungs to focus on the target. He turned his head as he heard the amorphous voice of Deeso through the line of plants that separated them. Deeso decided to test Ozul and offered a nudge to see his full potential.

"Hey Ozul! How about this? If you catch the little one, I'll wash the clothes next turn!" Deeso yelled. Although she wasn't visible, her voice carried over loud enough to take.

"That is a wager I can accept!" Ozul yelled in response.

Deeso diverted to the left and was out of Ozul's hearing range. As he predicted, the deer arrived at the river and attempted to ford the current. Ozul watched as the poor creature tired itself out as it swam against the grain. He hopped in with the knife in his teeth as he extended a hand to grab the animal's leg and use the combined weight of him and the deer to stay steady as it moved around. Ozul was excited as his grip tightened while the two went downstream. The rapids slowed until he was at a far slower section of the river. Ozul withdrew the knife and quickly stabbed the deer while blood filled the water. Ozul dragged the meal out as marks of blood trickled down his back. Once on shore, Ozul realized something was missing. He had no idea where Deeso was and needed to be sure nothing happened to her.

"Deeso? Deeso!!? Oh no..." Ozul said, as he shook in worry.

"To go back alone would be out of the question. I must find her." Ozul said as he proudly hoisted the deer's carcass over his back.

Unknown to Ozul, in Deeso's excitement, she misjudged a branch in her haste and knocked herself out unconscious by running into a tree. In the moments that followed

Deeso hitting the ground, she was slowly dragged away. Sometime later, Deeso could make out the sound of a few voices. As sight returned to her, she found that she was wrapped and bound, much like she originally intended for Ozul. Deeso planned on trailing Ozul's potential captors to find their location but was now completely lost. She groaned as her head hurt but looked over herself. Her clothing was undisturbed, and she felt nothing transpired while she was unconscious. Deeso eyed the structure of the camp she was held in. It barely resembled her own as it was wholly unorganized.

These are the worst kidnappers I've ever seen. Deeso thought as she now noticed her predicament.

Deeso was attached to a large stalk of bamboo among many that were embedded in the ground. Her axe was in view, some distance away. She gnawed at the wrapping around her wrists and found they were made from plants and were easier to break. After a few tugs, they ripped with ease, but Deeso stayed quiet as she wanted to identify who captured her. She grabbed her axe and noticed that it was some sort of work area, with an active fire going so that her captors couldn't have been far. Deeso saw a few baskets filled with gathered fruit. She positioned herself behind a thick tree and waited. Her eyes drifted to a knife that was left near the campfire and deduced it was part of the sacrifice. Deeso heard two voices she recognized as Forest Seekers as they were frustratingly soft to her ears. Deeso listened and pieced their voices through the sounds of birds in the distance. She found the pair to be a younger boy and a girl. Ozul sounded different than them and she prepared herself for combat.

"What do we do when we find her? If Eshe is real." The boy said to his companion.

"Of course, she is real. We just need to see if she is here, as opposed to somewhere else. Have you not heard her call for our people? She left behind a feather of the Iru." The girl said as she looked at their campfire.

As they waited for more arrivals, there was a brief pause that turned to silence as the two entered the interior of the camp. Their pace quickened as they realized something was amiss. Their gaze was fixed on Deeso's shed wrappings on the ground and the lack of her presence at the bamboo stalk.

"She has escaped, we are missing the most important piece." The boy mentioned. Deeso could tell the boy was worried but tried to not arouse suspicion to his companion.

"Did you not tie the knots like I asked?" The girl interrupted as she sniffed the air around them.

It was evident that they could smell Deeso's sweat from their own and knew she was still close. The Forest Seeker girl grabbed a nearby wooden staff and felt around with it between various bushes for clues. Deeso kept her breath held as she observed. She felt compelled to leave, but she needed answers about what they were doing to contact Eshe. Deeso turned her head as she heard a noise that sounded vaguely like the call from Ozul. As Forest Seekers were silent in their travels, the moment Deeso lost sight of her briefly, she was unable to find her. Deeso was soon confronted by one of her captors. Deeso heard a sweeping sound that cut through the air as the girl raised the staff behind her to strike

Deeso. Deeso made quick work of her opponent's weapon with the sharpened stone of her axe as it degraded the wood to bits. Deeso quickly rolled on the ground where she outmaneuvered her opponent and slashed her back. The wound wasn't as deep as she wanted and so she ran again. This time she slammed her with enough force to fall to the ground. Her face contorted slightly as she hit the ground. Deeso winced as she hurt her shoulder doing so but finished the job with brutal efficiency. Blood soaked the ground and bloodied Deeso's bare feet as she stomped on the kill she made. The girl's companion abandoned her while she was occupied with Deeso, but another boy came by through the thickets as he heard the ongoing commotion. He grew into a panic as he saw Deeso was out of her restraints.

"W-Wait!" The Forest Seeker boy shouted clutching a basket of fruit as Deeso ran towards him at breakneck speed.

She jammed her axe in his bare chest, and caved it open with the sound of cracked bone that filled the silence. The blood from his chest leaked out, as his body spasmed involuntarily and revealed bits and pieces of bone. Caked with blood, she dislodged her axe from his chest and took a swing at his neck. She hacked it off with the same care given to a deer. His head barely hung to a loose tendon in his neck. She finished lopping his head off with another mighty swing. The boy's head rolled onto the soil. It leaked blood that pooled as sinews and the exposed flesh of the boy's body was now exposed for the world to see. She was exhausted now but filled with enough adrenaline to keep going.

"Who's next?!" Deeso shouted aloud.

Deeso wasn't really one for huge displays of prowess like that of Sadal or Zulag, but pride was an emotion she felt just like any other. As she calmed down and realized she needed to locate Ozul, she fell to the forest floor. She hit the ground and put her hands over her head in a panic. By now, Deeso was used to the sound of whizzing darts but there was just one. The dart protruded from a nearby tree a short distance from her. Her eyes scaled the tree past the dart and looked up to see a few birds had made their home above her, but one was a hornbill that called out in a harsh cry. Deeso lifted an eyebrow as she saw a lone mango in the campsite. Deeso wasn't sure of what to do with this but felt compelled to investigate. She knew that Forest Seekers used their environment to try and confuse their targets. Her eyes scanned the bushes for anything out of the ordinary. Eshe waited on the outskirts and knew she needed to intervene. Two of her kind fell before the Thunderfoot's rage and it was time to take manners into her own hands. Eshe was silent as she stalked behind Deeso with a knife. She wore a special line of clothing that blurred the light around her with varying tones of green over her usual outfit. It was bound together with string and made with tightly strung leaves and clumped grass. While the interior was warm, it provided no compromises for stealth.

Eshe took a great deal to obscure the sound of her footsteps. Large jungle leaves were tied around her feet and left no trace for trackers. It was a simple technique that led itself well to the environment around them. Deeso felt the touch of Eshe's hand breach her shoulder as she made herself fall to the ground to avoid the woman's lunge. Although

Deeso only saw a masked green figure, she could have sworn she saw a grin come from underneath. Deeso knew this adversary before her was someone far more experienced than her previous opponents, and she knew she needed to try. Deeso slipped out of Eshe's grasp for the moment as she ran towards Deeso in a strange zig-zag formation that she found hard to keep track of. It dawned on her that it was some sort of camouflage, one that could be removed with some thought and planning. Deeso remembered the campsite they were at, where the lit fire was still warm. Deeso dodged Eshe's attempts to confront her as she rolled to grab a piece of smoldering wood. She baited Eshe to come forward as Deeso tossed a burning piece of wood that caught onto the surrounding leaves.

Eshe was forced to reveal herself as she threw her slowly burning cloak behind her. Without hesitation, she lunged towards Deeso haphazardly swiping with a knife made from stone. Deeso was unaware that Forest Seekers made them on their own. Although she had intimidation on her side, Deeso realized Eshe was still an amateur. Her arms left her exposed and her position gave itself not much room to evade. Deeso closed the gap between the two and made it impossible for Eshe to retreat without Deeso catching her. The skill gap was obvious when it came down to it. Eshe was someone who was inspired to fight and so she did for her people, but for Deeso, combat was as simplistic as breathing. She swiped with her axe and drew blood from Eshe's arm. Her intent wasn't to immediately kill her like the others. She hadn't revealed herself as the one she was looking for, but Deeso felt she was the one. Eshe strong-armed Deeso in the stomach and attempted to pin her to the ground. Deeso found the folly in Eshe's movement as she was an experienced grappler. From the earliest days in The Broken Bone, she watched Ronkalk's matches against the various leaders who offered challenges and took to the ring herself. She used her legs to subdue Eshe and placed herself on top while attempting to reach her face. Deeso poked Eshe's eye causing her to block her arm and pushed Deeso off her.

Ozul moved his way through the bushes out of breath as he saw the fight between Deeso and Eshe. Ozul ran forward as quickly as he could. He jumped and tackled Eshe by keeping his tight grip on her leg. The two rolled on the ground while Eshe kept her hand steady for a quick recovery. She shook Ozul off as much as she could, but he hoped to stay grounded. Eshe kicked Ozul in the face as her attention returned to Deeso.

"Foolish child! What do you gain from stopping me when I am so close?" Eshe yelled as she looked for an opening with space between the two.

"I am trying to save your life! She has more skill than you." Ozul answered, as he placed himself between Eshe and Deeso. In frustration, Deeso threw her axe that Ozul maneuvered out of the way but injured Eshe on the leg. She wouldn't be running for a while.

"Ozul! When we get back-" Deeso pointed at him as he held his ground.

"Whose side are you on anyway? You helped me slow her down and now you stand in my way." Deeso said with irritation.

Ozul placed his head down and walked to retrieve Deeso's axe. The two didn't look at one another as their attention was pinned on Eshe. Eshe also shared Deeso's annoyance as she got a better look at Ozul. Her face was riddled with anger as she could see he was one of her own. Sympathy for Thunderfeet was betrayal in her own eyes, but she waited to see what would come of this. Deeso chose to address Eshe as she saw it was clear who won the fight now.

"I can see that Sadal would have made quick work of you. My concern has been eased about her safety. Which brings up a question-" Deeso asked as she looked at Eshe.

Deeso was interrupted by what sounded like pained laughter coming from Eshe. The name was all too familiar to her. It was a while ago, but someone as notable as Sadal was one that couldn't be forgotten so easily. Eshe nursed her wounds and looked over the body. The taste of defeat wasn't known to her and she realized just how deep her problems started to become.

"Of all the days...You Thunderfeet are so predictable. I remember seeing one of your kind named Sadal. As loud and as inconsiderate as the rest of you people, a blight on the land. I had the means to kill her, but out of respect for The Stone Breaker she travels with, I did not." Eshe said, not bothering to crawl away. She stalled for time as her followers would arrive soon.

Ozul and Deeso shared drastically different reactions. Deeso's confirmation of Sadal in meeting Eshe filled her with an unyielding sense of conviction and confidence in what she was doing. It was her who told them to go west and now the culmination of their decisions led to this moment. Ozul's eyebrows were raised as Eshe invoked the Stone Breakers. Ozul was in belief like many that Stone Breakers were a long-gone people, but she spoke with such conviction there was truth to her words. If Sadal was able to get the eye of Stone Breakers, it meant this was an exceptionally gifted person and they would need to be careful. The power of the Stone Breakers was an incredible legacy to uphold and was dangerous in the wrong hands.

"What do you know? We have been looking for some time for this person." Ozul asked as he interrupted. Eshe shot him a glare that unnerved his stomach as he did so. She decided to offer the young boy a test of her own. Was this just a lapse in judgment or is there more to the picture?

"You are misguided, helping this one Ozul. You would be better working with me instead of working for her." Eshe offered. She gave a small laugh and knew the compromising position she was in, but perhaps via Ozul she could reign herself the victor. Eshe blew some dust from her nose and spoke again.

"I see it on your face Thunderfoot. Torturing me will not give the information you seek. We have a mutual interest and so I will give you an audience. In two days meet me due south of here. There's a tree marked that shows a clearing in the forest. Come in the dead of night, my forces will not see me convene with Thunderfeet like this. I will be waiting." Eshe said as her interest turned to Deeso.

"We will go. Cross me and the entire forest will watch as I burn everything you hold dear. I will arrive and kill you myself. The boy will not get in the way." Deeso threatened.

Ozul didn't bother answering her inquiry as Eshe's reputation preceded her. Ozul was logical and it took little time to consider his options as she was unknown and hardly worth the risk. He reluctantly stood by Deeso, as more rustling from the bushes was heard. A few of her men arrived to obscure their leader from view with blowguns at the ready. Eshe's raise of her hand and calm demeanor relaxed them as they moved aside. They noticed her injury and carried her away as the two were now left to themselves. Deeso anticipated another fight, but it would seem for now they had a moment to relax.

"Who does she think she is? Making demands like that?" Deeso asked as she spat on the ground.

"You got what you asked for. We need to go. I left the Smir-Tamdeu on that branch over there." Ozul said as he pointed in the distance. Deeso stopped for a second as the two walked.

"How did you find me? I figured I was quite far from you." She questioned as she stretched her arm out.

"It took a bit of searching, but I found this nice boy gathering fruit and he pointed me-" Ozul explained. His voice fell flat as he realized that his benefactor was clearly killed by Deeso.

Ozul's eyes surveyed the damage of the camp from Eshe and Deeso's confrontation. His gaze fell to the boy who was decapitated by Deeso's hand. He looked at the mutilated body and held back a few tears. Someone that was kind to him was now cut down without his knowing. Deeso shot him a look, but they continued forward as Ozul went to grab the pelt and hoist it over his shoulders.

"What?" Deeso asked in confusion as Ozul's statement stopped.

"Nothing, we should get back to camp." Ozul said.

"That was a hollow threat, yes? About you burning down the forest?" Ozul asked Deeso, as he received no real answer from her. Deeso gave a small chuckle and ran her hand through his head. Ozul kept his thoughts to himself.

The way home was a quick route as they followed the direction of the river and headed upstream. Zulag's words filled their ears, and they knew they had made it just in time. Ozul placed the mouse deer carcass down and immediately went back to work tinkering on his blowgun designs while Deeso strolled in. Deeso looked at the pair while her attention sat on their meal.

"Ah, our little man finally brought us something to eat!" Zulag teased as he looked at the kill. He stuck his hand in the deer's mouth assessing its health and saw that the deer was cut down in its prime. He and Cikya looked at Deeso with a slightly confused expression as she looked disheveled and massaged the light bump on her head.

"What happened to you?" Zulag asked, normally not concerned with Deeso's whereabouts.

"I was kidnapped by Forest Seekers." Deeso mentioned, as she tried her best to obscure the circumstances behind her injury.

"Kidnapped? I don't believe it." Zulag questioned with some skepticism as Cikya raised an eyebrow sharing the same opinion as Zulag.

"She tells half the truth. It was correct she was taken, but only after she knocked herself asleep by running into a branch." Ozul stated as Cikya and Zulag burst into laughter. Cikya strained a bit in pain as she tried to suppress her emotions.

"More importantly though, it is because of Deeso we located Eshe. She wants to have a meeting in two days. This will help you find your friend Sadal." Ozul added on, with his gaze focused as he used a small stone to cut segments of bamboo. The concept of a meeting between Eshe and the others sounded like a mind-numbing experience to Zulag.

"Sounds boring. We have to sit and talk about why the leaves change color instead of crushing some skulls. Did she have any demands?" Zulag asked. Ozul nodded his head no, while Deeso stripped the deer's flesh. Cikya helped in the process where she could. She skewered the deer clean with a sharpened stick and grabbed one of Zulag's knives to cut sections of the meat for the four of them.

"Hey! Cikya! That's my knife, I just cleaned that!" Zulag said as she stuck her tongue out at him and continued working.

As the meal was small, cooking was quick and Cikya passed out the sections of the deer. As Ozul claimed the kill, he was to take the first bite. He took the right leg for his own, and the rest followed suit, while they ate in silence. Their stomachs for now would have something to sit on. Deeso intended to take Eshe at her word just as they agreed.

With two days passing, Deeso knew this was an unusual break from routine as they normally left at dawn but chose to meet at dusk. She remembered Eshe's instructions, to head south and look for the tree that marked a clearing in the forest under the cover of night. She tried to rouse everyone awake. Ozul was more nocturnal than the others, having worked steadily through the last nights on his project that was now finished. He sat quietly as he always did and clutched the fruits of his labor with a rare look of satisfaction. A medium sized tube of hardy bamboo with a wood covering that fit over it for protection. This was his new and improved piece. His eyes looked over to Cikya who greeted him with a quick nod of acknowledgment. Deeso grabbed a few spare pieces of wood and tied fibers around them that burnt. She prepared torches for the four of them as smoke dispersed through the area. The four weren't sure what to expect, with the mysterious Eshe's expectations unknown. Deeso expected heavy resistance to befall them if negotiations went south. Eshe was going to give them an audience, but it was likely they would be in deep pockets of fighters all around them. She saw the impatience of Zulag who stomped his foot in anticipation.

"Some of us have things to do. Are we going or what?" Zulag asked as he tied his throwing knives to his body with some loose string.

The outline of his shadow expanded as he stood up from the ongoing fire that projected onto the surrounding plants. Zulag looked at Ozul and saw an expression that he wasn't used to seeing. He walked over to Ozul and noticed his new blowgun and had a rare sign of interest. Zulag remembered the power it had in killing the elephant and wondered what new changes Ozul gave it. He snatched it from Ozul's hands and studied it.

"Zulag! Give that back, now!" Ozul pleaded with him.

Zulag kept Ozul away from him as he took his sweet time admiring the detail. He couldn't believe something so well designed made for the purpose to kill came from someone as timid as Ozul. The wood even had etching made with a bone needle. As Ozul tried to get back his weapon, Zulag teased him by holding it above his head as he jumped for it. Ozul kicked Zulag in the shin. He just barely caught the piece before it fell to the ground. Zulag couldn't be mad, the kid was finally learning how to stick up for himself.

"This will save all of us some day." Ozul commented proudly to the three who looked towards the path they needed to take.

"Remember Weypeu hunt at night just as well in the day. Stay close to me." Deeso mentioned as a warning to Ozul.

The four walked in silence as their torches flickered through the night. Their gait was slow and deliberate as they walked as one. The air was still and only the ambient sounds of insects, and a few low growls accompanied them. The way to Eshe's location was deceptively short but had a variety of winding paths, each seemed more inviting than the other. Their torches illuminated the way as the growth unraveled in their presence. Cikya looked around and noticed that the paths of the forest seemed to weave exactly towards where they needed to go. The very roots themselves didn't impede their feet below. Ozul reminded the group that the most obvious trails were ones that were often used to trap or elude unsuspecting travelers from their villages. He tapped Cikya's arm and pointed to the logs below that were given incisions underneath. In due time, they arrived at what they believed to be the place. Deeso looked around and saw that there were multiple trees in the torchlight. She scratched her head, as she tried to make sense of what kind of sign to be looking for. Zulag sat back and watched Deeso stumble around for some time to his amusement until he decided to speak.

"I'm guessing it's the one with the knife in the center." Zulag stated flatly, which gave a hushed laugh from Cikya.

Deeso heard a rustling from the bushes shortly after and the frame of various Forest Seekers came into view. They brandished blowguns and clubs as Ozul met eyes with a few of the others. While Deeso and the others carried torches, the Forest Seekers before them wore clothing with white feathers that illuminated under the moonlight to reveal themselves. Zulag gritted his teeth as he anticipated a backstab but saw that they didn't move an inch. He tilted his head and attempted to see the person that all this effort was for. Eshe appeared to them and waved them forward all the while her escorts herded them towards her. Eshe arranged a location for them to speak. At a certain point, Eshe held out her hand to them and prompted them to stop. A lit campfire and mats with expensive furs were visible, this would be where they would talk things out. Eshe made sure to demonstrate her power and status to the group before her. Deeso nodded and she looked at the others as she placed her axe to the soil below. Cikya surrendered her staff, with Ozul following suit with his blowgun. All eyes were on Zulag who painstakingly removed the various knives he had in his clothing and on his body. These were collected by a representative of Eshe's.

"These will be returned to you after we have discussed things." Eshe told the group. Zulag bit his tongue in annoyance, while Deeso shared the same sentiment.

"I agreed to your terms. My friends and I are unarmed, and we've come to your place, now surrounded with weapons. Did you think I was lying?" Deeso asked as she saw another Forest Seeker look over her.

Eshe looked Deeso over with some interest. Her mind was still fresh from their encounter. Cikya looked at Eshe's clothing fairly impressed with the arrangement of leaves and fibers that blended Eshe into the grass around her, these were some ideas she hoped to incorporate into her own dress for hunting.

"To the matter at hand then, you have given us an audience and you know of Sadal. What will we do about this?" Deeso asked as she looked behind to the faces of the others behind her.

Eshe prompted them to sit while she stood, and looked over them as if they were mere children. The flames of the fire moved around making its own wind as the four sat across her where she folded her legs and sat down.

"I prefer material benefits for my people, and you want information. We have a common interest. I am aware of your prowess in the battle, but as for the others, is this something that is shared among your group?" Eshe commented, as her finger pointed to Zulag who sat next to Deeso. Deeso rolled her eyes as she looked over him.

"Being humble isn't his specialty." Deeso commented, as Zulag glared at Deeso.

"There is a way you can be of use to my movement. There is a problem. They are of your kind, called The Buffalo Brothers. Two men that wear the skulls of the Ker-Mah. Other groups have been surprisingly charitable given my aims, but like a creek in the dry season, our patience runs thin." Eshe explained to Deeso.

"What have they done exactly?" Deeso asked with some concern.

Cikya gestured to her own crown of bones at Eshe's comment describing The Buffalo Brothers. She put her hand into a fist and shook it, showing she understood well what Eshe was asking them to do.

"That matters not to you, should it?" Eshe responded, as her hand tensed up.

"I just want to know. This is how I can help you best." Deeso stated calmly, as she noticed Eshe's annoyed tone. Although Deeso herself held a sharp tongue, her skill in defusing tension worked greatly in her favor.

"You seem to be in good shape considering what happened before." Deeso noted Eshe's wrapped foot. She knew the axe wound she inflicted would take some time to heal. How was Eshe walking around as if nothing happened?

"The sleeping leaf when chewed strengthens the body. As for which one it is, you will have to find yourself Thunderfoot." Eshe taunted her, as her eyes looked to Ozul. Eshe continued her speech as she set the scene for the rest.

"These men whittle down our forest bit by bit for junk. They desecrate our way of life and hunt our food for sport. They are a mockery of everything we hold dear. Not only does their presence offend me, but I was foolish in having to deal with them. We agreed to a deal, and I was swindled." Eshe said, with resentment heavy in her voice.

"Oh, I see what's going on here. Sounds like a personal problem, many of you Forest Seekers have attacked us on sight on our quest, so why all the talk? If you hate them so much, why don't you do it?" Zulag interjected into the conversation as he decided to pay attention again. Deeso shook her head at Zulag's outbursts, there was no way she was going to allow his interference to interrupt locating Sadal.

"I consider myself a reasonable person. We can always make a deal." Deeso said, as she hoped to extinguish the energy that Zulag exuded to Eshe.

"It could be done, but then you have nowhere to go. This can benefit us both and I prefer to keep my hands clean. I am currently injured." Eshe said, with a shake of her head as she addressed Zulag's outburst.

"Eshe, can you promise that if we do what you ask, you will help us? We have risked much to come here." Ozul said, as he finally mustered the courage to say something as Eshe and Deeso continued to talk.

I hope you know what you're doing, Deeso. I've put a lot of trust in you to get us this far. Finding her wasn't an easy task, even with Ozul's help. This seems simple enough. We convince these two to stop their actions, and we can get moving. I doubt it'll be a hard fight. After all, there's four of us. Cikya analyzed the situation.

Deeso felt the affirmative touch of Cikya on her shoulder as her teeth glistened while the movement of the flame went over her face. Zulag crossed his arms but kept his gaze on Deeso as she continued to negotiate with Eshe. He studied her body language as she spoke and wasn't sure what to make of it. At the very least, he knew that they weren't going into another trap this time. Deeso extended her arm out in a confirmatory handshake to Eshe who returned it. They shook as the heat of the fire bound their agreement. Deeso stood up now and nodded her head for the remaining three to follow.

"Ozul, we move now." Deeso said, as she reminded him to stay on task.

Eshe had other plans as she called forth one of her guards to hold Ozul. She had her eye on Ozul for some time since negotiations started and she overrode Deeso's commands.

"You three will go do my bidding. Retrieve my pelts and I will tell you everything I know about Sadal and her location. Return these broken blades to them. The Buffalo Brothers were last camped out west of here towards the land that is dry and hot. My scouts say it should take about six hours by foot, there is no river. The child stays with me as collateral. There are things we must discuss." Eshe said as she looked into Ozul's eyes. While Deeso hated having her authority overridden, she let it go as the information about Sadal's location was more important than anything else.

"Return their weapons. Now that we have made our agreement, they should be on their way." Eshe ordered one of her guards as the trio extended their hands out. One guard entrusted Zulag with a bag filled with the blade fragments from Eshe's broken supplies.

"Please return safely..." Ozul said, as his voice trailed off to a whisper.

With Deeso, Cikya, and Zulag off to accomplish their goal for Eshe, it was only Ozul that remained. Ozul watched as they walked as one into the night with torches in hand. Ozul was guided forward by Eshe and the guard at his side. It was some time since he interacted with so many of his group, but the familiar sight of leaf tents and straw constructions was a well-earned comfort for him. Eshe reached her hand out for Ozul to grab, but he kept his hands to himself. He was guarded as he saw potential problems in the group he was now left with. Ozul was prompted by Eshe to walk through her current base of operations. While there were a good number of people that slept, some were awake to see Eshe's return with Ozul. Ozul envied those who called this camp home after sleeping in pitiful shelters that barely kept out the rain or just under the stars. Eshe turned around suddenly and Ozul bumped into her. The feeling was awkward as he backed away quickly.

"Ozul, how old are you?" Eshe said as she crouched to meet him at eye level.

"I am twelve, soon to be thirteen. I was born in the dry season[53]." Ozul said as he crossed his arms.

"That is the cusp of when I recruit, but I know you seem to have different loyalties. I have a question as you are currently in my stead." Eshe gestured.

Ozul gave no response as he was under Eshe's control. Ozul observed the affairs of the Forest Seekers loyal to Eshe as the light of the moon shone through the camp. He saw them discussing strategies with wooden tools, much like how he saw Thunderfeet practicing. Eshe was proud of her growing influence and that she could trust actions to be done without her direct interference.

"Will you come with me?" Eshe asked, as her tone masked her intent behind the question.

Eshe and Ozul walked together as the visage of Eshe's base camp gradually vanished. The vines and brambles of the jungle unraveled themselves for the two Forest Seekers. The two stood in darkness until a man came forth holding a torch for the pair. Ozul's expression changed as he could feel something ominous was in the air as Eshe slowed her gait. She stood and gently lifted a large leaf for Ozul's space to occupy next to her as they approached a clearing. There was evidence of a skirmish that occurred with uprooted soil and trees stripped of their bark.

---

[53] Every group in Jih's Journey has a method to track the passage of time and to age themselves. Forest Seekers age themselves with the dry or wet season depending on their birth and add depending on how many they've experienced in the memory of others.

"Your entire story is spoken from your face. I know the life you have lived. Your timidness killed these people Ozul." Eshe commented, as she gestured towards a few corpses laid bare by trees.

As Forest Seekers didn't bury their dead, they were in varying states of decomposition as the forest gradually reclaimed their bodies. Stab wounds were evident on a few, as well as the marks of scavengers who clawed and bit at their exposed flesh. Although Eshe wished to shock Ozul with such brutality, he was wholly desensitized from the death he witnessed. His travels with his allies were enough to bring any true fear he once had into something trivial.

"The Thunderfeet only take and leave a path of ruin. It is clear to me we misunderstand each other, and this is why I fight. I will give you a bed of leaves to call your own, food and a community, should you make your choice. What have those three given you? They see you as lesser and you will never be one of them. Aiding the Thunderfeet, you are responsible for violence against your own people. I can change this Ozul." Eshe said with authority in her voice. Ozul gave no reaction as he blankly stared at the bodies.

"Why are you with them? You are clearly disrespected and not valued. The one known as Deeso orders you around with no cause. You are a tool to them." She spat in anger to Ozul. Eshe waited for Ozul to absorb the scene before them and made their way to camp once more.

It was some time until the two spoke again as Ozul chose to make his responses very carefully. While Eshe thought Ozul thought nothing at all, he knew better than to mouth off before forming his statements. While night still surrounded them, more of their people awoke. Ozul remained quiet as he saw a woman peer in the distance towards the two of them as her shadow rose over the moving fires. Akma saw that Eshe was busy with a guest, and she went to work quickly getting food for the two to eat. Eshe waved over Akma to join them both. Ozul stared at the pair as they rubbed noses in front of him. Ozul looked and saw the love the two shared and wished he could have his own someday. They wore matching necklaces with shell beads. His attention changed back to the matter at hand.

"I know nothing of those people you showed me. You say I am a tool...Am I not a tool to you also? Our goals are different." Ozul said sharply as Eshe gave no counter to her statement. It was true, Ozul was a tool for her own devices, but she felt a sense of curiosity with the one that walked with the others. If anything, Eshe wanted to understand why the call to help them, even after such treatment.

"When my father and I were attacked by an Onpeu, those three chose to save me. I saw none of your warriors or anyone else come to save me. The trees show us many things." Ozul said as he noticed Eshe's painful expression. There was nothing she could offer to counter that statement.

Akma held two bananas to eat as she rubbed her stomach with a warm smile. Ozul's eyes matched hers as she looked away. The normally polite Ozul said nothing as Akma gently placed it into his hand and Eshe's before retreating. As far as Ozul was concerned, he wasn't going to be won over by something as simple as this.

"And another thing." Ozul said, as he munched on the food he was given.

"How can you say that I betray my people? Your words are filled with hypocrisy as you send Thunderfeet to do your bidding. You traded with them. You chose to meet us at night to hide your actions. The Vow is something we all know and with your desire for revenge, you flood the forest with blood." Ozul assessed. He saw Eshe's look of surprise, as she hadn't seen it this way, but she could understand how those among her ranks could certainly have questions with her recent actions.

"You invoke The Vow. This is something I take as seriously as any other, but there is something to be said. The Vow was made by the Stone Breakers because they wanted to provide peace to the forest. We strive to be peaceful, but you mistake peace with pacifism and subservience. Peace is about balance and sometimes violence is required." Eshe said as she spat out banana seeds.

"These are opposites. The minute blood is exchanged, the cycle repeats itself. There are better ways for us to move forward. But these ways, I am unsure on how to reach them. I am but a child, I hope a solution will come." Ozul said in response to her words.

"I asked you Ozul to drop your weapons with your Thunderfoot allies when you came to my camp. Why do you carry a weapon?" Eshe proposed to him.

"I carry my blowgun because it is a staple of our people. I use it to hunt and provide for my friends." Ozul said, before getting cut off by Eshe.

"Your friends, hmm? You also use it to defend yourself, much like how I carry mine. You have been attacked, and you have fought back." Eshe explained as she shrugged her shoulders.

"I defend myself from the spirits that see me as no different than a piece of meat. My defense does not involve attacking Thunderfeet camps who have done nothing to me. I can see your words, and where they hold meaning, but I do not agree." Ozul touted as he felt his statement was final. Eshe took a deep breath, and saw that the two were at an impasse, but rather than be met with aggression, she saw promise. Ozul was a moldable mind at only twelve years old.

"I have had many speak against me and my dream, but this was because of cowardice, ineptitude, and other emotions tied to lesser minds. I see your criticism comes with wisdom in your words and yet we remain at odds. You are only twelve, we will see what comes. The movement will always be open if you choose to change your mind. My parents still remain, and therefore, I do not have your perspective of being an orphan. With this, I have decided to teach you some things that your father cannot." Eshe said to Ozul who raised an eyebrow at her statement.

Akma watched as Eshe and Ozul walked together, this time to a hut that held a few items of interest. Ozul looked and saw the familiar looking dress that Eshe wore in her fight with Deeso. Eshe took out a spare one that was tailored to her size and held out in front of Ozul. Eshe looked above and noticed in their talk that the night gradually started to wane. The moon was high, but she felt the comfort of the sun would come.

"This is our Leaf Walker. Akma, my love, made it herself. Her hands are very good at this but mine are not. The design is very simple. You layer leaves of many different types until it is dense, much like a bush. You take Jaat and bound it to a rope and poke a small hole through it with bone. This connects the chain. There is much time that must be taken to construct one of these correctly. A rush job will only be as effective as wet firewood." Eshe instructed Ozul as he absorbed the information.

"You mentioned some time ago that you talked to one of the Stone Breakers, did you not?" Ozul asked Eshe, who confirmed her words with a slow nod.

"Yes. The Stone Breakers seem to be stoic people. His name is Jih. I held him and Sadal captive for some time, a foolish mistake when I did not know his origin at the time. His story touched me deeply, there is much to be said of him. Assuming the job is done by the others, perhaps when you find Sadal, you can hear his words and expand your mind." Eshe said, as she decided to give him another set of belongings. Ozul was given a larger bag than the one he normally carried, this one made from the stomach of a serow.

Ozul sat on the boundary line of Eshe's camp with his new bag as he stared out in the treeline waiting for the others to return. This is what he did often when he awoke after the others left for a hunt. Sometimes a part of him hoped they would never come back, but he only felt this way when he was frustrated. Ozul found it difficult to see where his place in everything was. Eshe's words weighed on him more heavily than he anticipated. He stood alone for some time, until he felt the hand of Eshe touch his shoulder.

"Tell me about your father and the life he lived."

Can't Get Fooled Again

Deeso, Zulag, and Cikya walked for hours as they left to fulfill Eshe's request. The moon long since passed to the early morning dew as the last bits of forest opened to the plains. Deeso took in the wonders of the wide expanse. The change in temperature was drastic as she felt the heat of the morning beat down her neck. She was used to the confined nature of the forest but thrived in the vastness of it all. The color change was stark, the bright greens and subdued browns vanished to have a yellowish-brown color as the soil below was tanned and dry from the sun's rays. Deeso looked back at Zulag and Cikya who looked tired. Cikya massaged her stomach as she was hungry and shot Deeso a look as she shrugged with all of them having eaten their previous rations.

"Weapons check. Do we have everything we need? I anticipate we use our words. Eshe was kind enough to return our weapons, but we shouldn't need them. They seem more like simple-minded raiders than anything else." Deeso mentioned as she examined the head of her axe.

Deeso assumed that a simple threat would be enough to get their point across and there'd be little to worry about if they were just sincerely traders. She held her hand out to stop the other two before they continued to walk further. Deeso wiped the sweat off her forehead before speaking.

"The directions Eshe gave us weren't the best, but we got there. Take a look at this place. I see smoke in the sky, this must mean people are near." Deeso explained as Zulag and Cikya nodded in agreement.

"We should make a plan first." Deeso mentioned, as she prepared to hear Zulag's gut level response.

"Easy, we kill them, get the pelts back and take them for all their stuff is worth. Eshe's only rewarding us with information, but we need to eat. They're supposed to be traders, right? They'll have something good." Zulag reasoned. While Deeso wasn't above stealing from those who couldn't defend themselves, she didn't want to risk the pelts being damaged in the process.

"That can be our second option. We will convince them to take the knives as Eshe planned." Deeso mentioned to them.

"Yeah, I can see why even Forest Seekers wouldn't want this garbage. My knives are leagues better than this." Zulag said as he shook the rolled-up bag of broken blades.

He held his ear up to it as the sounds of the bad stone clanged together and he shook his head in disappointment. Cikya looked around as she wouldn't be much use for talking. She would've preferred to stay behind and look over Ozul, as her trust in Eshe was razor thin.

Dotted across the landscape was plenty of activity as animals were bountiful and the open atmosphere around them made seeing from a distance far easier. The three wandered out and took notes of the various landmarks that were around. Herds of gazelles marched proudly as they nibbled at shrubs and eyed the new arrivals. Clustered camps were seen throughout but there was one that stood out from the rest. It was none other than their target, The Buffalo Brothers. They had a modest establishment with three heavy packs dispersed in a small circle, while a few small tools were put into a pile. Their beds consisted of a pile of animal skins as they laid out under the stars. Nezzall and Dronall took turns drinking a hearty gulp of water with a canteen made from an assortment of deer bladders. They made a habit of constructing their camps out of the forest boundary to catch any potential strays that went too far out.

"Dronall, this is a good spot. We have a decent travel time between the camps, and I think we may have a potential customer soon." Nezzall stated with a sly grin much to the enthusiastic laugh of his brother.

Dronall cracked his knuckles at the prospect. His eyes widened as he placed his hand over his eyes to get a better glimpse at something in the distance. He could see the movement of what appeared to be people on the horizon. The first customers of the day were always a welcome omen to have.

"Not just one, I see three who have knowledge in the art of exchange. Look, they have goods of their own in multiple bags." Dronall said as he got his brother's attention.

The Buffalo Brothers sighted three figures at the vicinity of their camp and prompted each other to quickly wear their skull caps. Nezzall did a clean sweep of the camp and made it presentable while Dronall gave an intoxicating smile as he stared them down. Deeso, Zulag, and Cikya headed in their direction with Nezzall jumping up to wave his arms to invite them over. Cikya pointed to see the obvious display and noted how eager they were for a fresh set of new faces. Zulag looked around at the site and wasn't impressed, but he feigned some interest.

Looks like we're at the right place...Their hats are quite strange. Cikya thought as she followed the other two's lead.

"Welcome to our camp! I take it you have heard about us from the other settlements not too far?" Dronall opened happily, his tone glad to see that more Thunderfeet were settling in the area. Although the Buffalo Brothers happily did business with anyone who was willing to trade, Forest Seekers didn't often offer such camaraderie.

"Yes. Your reputation precedes you. We have something to trade for you." Deeso mirrored as she matched his tone.

She urged Zulag to step forward and he shook the bag. Dronall wasn't sure what to make of it but seemed excited. Dronall anticipated a bounty of bones in the bag as he rubbed his hands together. He knew that priests in the area would trade an arm and a leg for high quality ritual bones. His eyes peered towards their pelt collection and wondered if the trade was worth it. Zulag placed the bag down and unveiled the tools that made a small pile. Dronall raised an eyebrow at the trio in confusion as he saw the pile of fragments grow in volume. It was clear to Deeso he recognized the haul before them.

"Well? Are we going to trade?" Deeso insisted, as she teased to her axe.

At first, Dronall looked to his brother with slight concern. Zulag reached into his clothing and showed off a knife. Dronall admired the quality and was assured that there was more material to be added to the deal. Nezzall's attention was on Cikya, and it was obvious to all parties involved. Cikya scanned the camp and noticed the unusual energy that emanated from Nezzall. She couldn't see under the skull cap, but his body language said everything. Nezzall usually helped the sales pitch, but he hadn't bothered to address Deeso or Zulag. Cikya noticed his juvenile expression. She gave Zulag a subtle tap on the back to let him know she was leaving for the moment while he watched Deeso and Dronall discuss.

"The first rule of exchange is we don't do returns. Once a deal has been made...it is final." Dronall said with some severity.

"Well, we are new people. So, let's see what you have." Zulag suggested.

Dronall scoffed under his breath at Nezzall and lifted a finger to keep Deeso and Zulag waiting. Dronall reached his hand inside to show the assortment of items he offered from his backpack. It was an impressive haul with various trinkets that were of moderate interest but the two kept their eyes peeled for the most important piece. Deeso's eyes peered to the wrapped-up bundle of pelts located right by and saw the glimpse of tiger stripes. Deeso was fortunate that The Buffalo Brothers hadn't parted with them yet and she formed a plan.

"What do your eyes see? You speak with wisdom beyond your years, you know." Dronall said as he attempted to butter up Deeso with compliments.

Dronall waited patiently as Deeso reached over and figured out which item she was most interested in. Dronall smiled from ear to ear as her hand hovered over objects. He leant his ear in as he attempted to hear Deeso's whispers. Dronall studied Deeso's face and tried to look for objects that would appeal to her interest. Zulag remained irritated at the prospect. Deeso knew exactly what she was looking for, but she needed to sell the appearance of a well-meaning customer.

"These pelts here. Weypeu is it? They are nice, but they don't belong to you." Deeso said as she pointed to the bundle. Dronall looked at Deeso with some suspicion. Under the guise of his skull, Dronall's expression tightened. Dronall hated a comedian above all else, as Deeso's words were concerning.

"Ha! I didn't take you for a trickster. What do you mean by that? Clearly they are mine and my brother's." Dronall said as he folded his arms in indignation.

Cikya knew she'd be little help with negotiations, so she decided to put her other talents to use. She carried her staff with her and nodded towards Nezzall who left the conversation to talk to her. Nezzall had complete confidence that his brother could handle the more complicated matters of exchange. Nezzall was perpetually distracted by his romantic endeavors while Dronall handled the shrewder manners of business. In slightly more privacy, the two walked over to the other end of their camp. Cikya gave him a nice wink while she kept a steady glance on Deeso and Zulag.

"I bet you have a stunning voice..." Nezzall teased as he ran his finger down Cikya's forehead in a flirtatious manner. Cikya gave a slight grimace that gave him pause as he looked closer to see the scar that was on her throat. He raised an eyebrow, but his expression remained with a grin.

Come on you two...Make the deal while I keep him distracted. Cikya thought as she gave Nezzall a fake smile that made him even happier. Cikya had a feeling that Dronall would catch on to their plan so she hoped they would make the exchange and could leave quickly.

"These aren't yours. These pelts belong to Eshe. You will give them back to her, and we will give you these knives that you've spent so much time making." Deeso said with sarcasm attached in her voice.

"This knife in my hand? That's how you make one of these." Zulag taunted Dronall as he lifted another one of his by the point.

She knows! Dronall thought as he realized their operation was exposed and by a Forest Seeker no less.

Dronall let out some air out of his nose in a laugh that concerned both Deeso and Zulag. Dronall towered over them both as he lowered himself to reach her level. Dronall walked over as Deeso looked up to see the man's irate face. Dronall reached over and in one fell swoop, slapped Deeso harshly across the face. The impact of such a blow nearly toppled her over as he let out a bellowing laugh. Deeso shook with anger that reverberated through her body. Zulag shot Deeso a glare as the validity of his second option grew more relevant by the minute. Zulag vibrated with rage at Dronall's action.

"Ha! You amuse me. Tell that Forest Seeker witch we will keep the pelts and our knives then. We could kill you right now for such insolence." Dronall scoffed.

"You should give our stuff back before we just decide to take it." Zulag said as he escalated already high tensions. Dronall saw a direct threat and decided to step past Deeso. Zulag had no choice but to look up at the man before him due to his height.

"And will you make good on that threat, Onpeu spots?" Dronall teased Zulag with venom in his voice and pointed to his skin. Nezzall, who was uninterested before, turned to see his brother face Zulag.

"Eshe-hm? If you work for her, you're our enemy. I'd hate to scar your friend's beautiful face." Nezzall stated as he flexed his muscles for Cikya.

A thick tension filled the air while the five of them remained still. Deeso cast the first stone and used her axe to bludgeon Dronall in the ankle. She was filled with rage from her disrespectful slap. Her objective now was to cause as much chaos as possible. Zulag was surprised to be beaten to the punch, but he reacted accordingly. Nezzall quickly left Cikya to assist Dronall in attacking Deeso and Zulag. Cikya was insulted as she wasn't seen as a threat like her comrades but thought to use this lapse in judgement to her advantage.

Cikya was torn whether to help Zulag or Deeso, but she chose to help Deeso. Deeso ran past Dronall and rushed towards Nezzall with her axe and swiped wildly as the man dodged. In the time that the fighting started, The Buffalo Brothers were unable to grab their weapons. Nezzall kneed Deeso in the stomach and prepared to punch her while she was on the ground. Cikya ran behind him and jumped forward. The impact of her collision crashed him towards the ground and allowed Cikya to hold her staff over his neck. Nezzall was on the ground and let out a gasping sound for air as he felt the constriction on his throat. Cikya released all restraint on her body and made herself deaden towards the ground. She hoped to use the weight of the staff to crush his windpipe as she held it over his throat. Nezzall broke out of her grasp and took a deep breath of air. He tossed her aside and called Dronall to him. Dronall abandoned his combat to meet his brother and the two stood side to side. They lowered their heads and charged forward with their skull cap's horns pointed directly at the three of them.

Nezzall swept at Cikya's legs and tripped her to the ground. He curled his hand into a fist and was ready to cave her face in. Nezzall was stopped by Deeso, who used the full extent of her weight to shift Nezzall a few inches away. Nezzall's punch hit the air and his arm was exposed. Deeso bit the man's arm before clutching her axe again. Cikya breathed a sigh of relief and picked up her staff and used it to keep distance between the two. Cikya maneuvered her staff around and reflexively hit Nezzall as he got within her attack range. She decided to take his idea of going for the legs and kicked up some dirt to blind him. The wind of the grassland settled some dust to reach his eyes, and he had no choice but to wipe them. Deeso rushed behind with her axe and embedded it deeply into Nezzall's back before removing it. Nezzall's wound was deep but he was still able to fight. Cikya slid along the ground dodging Nezzall's frantic punches as she used her staff to hit him directly in the back of the head and shattered a portion of his helmet. Bits of the skull helmet reached the ground while the back of Nezzall's head was exposed.

Dronall was left to contend with Zulag. Dronall grabbed Zulag by the neck and choked him. Zulag quickly realized his reach wasn't enough to hit any vital area of Dronall's body. His breathing stifled and he needed to think quickly. Zulag decided to quickly jump upwards, not to loosen Dronall's grip, but to grab his knives that were tied to his side by string. He formed his fingers around the knife. At close range, his knives were a sure hit as he withdrew one and immediately launched it into Dronall's exposed stomach. Dronall yelled in pain as he extracted the knife, but now had a weapon of his own to use. Zulag took a deep breath as he was released from Dronall. Dronall called for his brother but received no answer. Blood pooled out slowly as Dronall was giving himself a moment to breathe as he thought of what to do next.

The Buffalo Brothers relied on their core strength to get through much of their problems, and while they were certainly cunning, they lacked the pure militaristic training that the three held. Dronall held the knife in his hand and pushed back while Zulag unleashed another one. Dronall used the knife he extracted to block the throw with excellent timing while he lunged towards Zulag. Zulag hit the ground narrowly dodging Dronall's stab attempt. He got up quickly and kicked Dronall in the privates causing him to lower as Zulag wailed on his face with multiple jabs. Fighting in The Broken Bone was meant to be honorable, but the only thing that truly mattered was victory. Honor was meant for those who were respected. He quickly finished his assault with a kick to the face. Zulag knocked off Dronall's helmet and exposed his beaten face. Zulag's own hands bled from punching bone, but it paled in comparison to Dronall's injuries.

Dronall reflexively looked for his brother who fell at the hands of Cikya and Deeso. Zulag kept his arm tucked around Dronall's throat, with a knife resting securely on it while he pointed him in the direction of Nezzall. The concussive damage from Cikya's staff was enough to disorient him long enough for Deeso to come behind with a stroke of her axe. She landed the killing blow on his neck as it shattered his clavicle. Nezzall convulsed on the ground as he sustained heavy damage from the combined assault of Deeso and Cikya. To ensure the kill was certain, Deeso swiped again ensuring that his head was properly severed from his body. She made sure that Dronall watched as she hacked it some more and reveled in the man's tears.

"F-Fine! T-Take the pelts back! You crazy people!" Dronall yelled with heavy breaths as he pleaded for his life. For Dronall, to see his brother writhe in pain as he died was unbearable. Their hubris was the blueprint to their success and now their downfall came.

"Let me go! Please! Take it all!" Dronall added as he tried to wrestle himself out of Zulag's grip. Dronall tried to make a last-ditch effort to lower their sense of security for an attack, but Zulag wasn't having any of it.

"An Onpeu doesn't let prey go." Zulag said as he jammed the knife into Dronall's neck while he desperately clawed at Zulag.

Dronall fell short as he bled on Zulag's clothing before hitting the ground. The three looked at each other and put their eyes towards the pelts. While the ground was caked with blood, the bounty that came afterwards was pristine. Zulag shook as much blood off him as he could and attempted to pick up the pelts. Cikya assisted him in doing so. Deeso walked over with her axe towards Dronall's corpse and used her axe down to chop a section of his body off that she personally carried as a trophy.

"Are you...taking his hand?" Zulag asked Deeso as he sorted through the various goods left behind.

Zulag decided to mutilate the bodies of Nezzall and Dronall, using his knife to detach Dronall's head. He moved the disembodied masses and switched their positions, so that Nezzall's head was now on Dronall's body and vice versa. He took a moment to admire his handiwork. Cikya in her own twisted humor walked over and closed the eyes of the two men as their bodies now rotted in the sun. She turned around and wondered if there were any witnesses that came by.

"Eshe would want proof that they were dealt with. So, I took his hand. The one he decided to disrespect my presence with. Grab the heads and wrap them in those bags there. It will be a gift for her." Deeso stated while Zulag and Cikya nodded.

"I could use a wash. We should go." Deeso said coldly.

Deeso and the other three returned to Eshe's encampment with little else to say as they walked off the blood that now saturated their clothes. Deeso noticed that she and Ozul were in an intense discussion over something and waited. She held up her hand to signal to Cikya and Zulag to wait. Through the thick of the woods, one of Eshe's guards recognized the trio. They heard a short series of whistles and were given entry. Ozul tapped Eshe's arm and pointed for her to turn around. Eshe saw that the new arrivals were present.

"Is it done?" Eshe asked as she saw Zulag holding the pelts that were wrapped up.

"Cikya, the bags please." Deeso ordered as Cikya opened the bags containing the heads of The Buffalo Brothers.

Cikya dumped them out and used her staff to roll them towards Eshe. Eshe was speechless as she didn't realize the extent of what would be done to get her belongings. She anticipated a job well done, but nothing this good. Eshe took a moment to compose herself. Eshe left Ozul to investigate and raised her eyebrows. Eshe was rarely impressed, but she couldn't hide her reaction this time. She was unsure if she should be concerned or satisfied that they bothered to go as far as they did. Two more dead Thunderfeet to add to the pile. Deeso nodded her head with satisfaction. Zulag walked over and returned the rolled-up bag of pelts.

"Everything's in there. Not a drop of blood on them, but we took a few prizes from the camp." Zulag said with honesty as he passed the wrappings to her.

"My pelts are returned, and The Buffalo Brothers are dealt with. Our deal has been met, so I will give you what I know about the location of Sadal. She walks with The Stone Breaker to search for the meteor in the sky many moons ago. My scouts have found that they have gone northwest of here. For those of us who know, The Stone Breaker is a rare occurrence. One of his people have not met us in many generations. Those who know our legends will know and there you will find him. Take the route you took to The Buffalo Brothers, and you will arrive with a few days of travel. The land is not like here, where it is wet, and trees are everywhere. Sadal is in the land where the grass is dry, and the land is hot. This is all I know." Eshe said as she gave Ozul a nudge to join the others.

Ozul got up and walked over to the embrace of his friends. He held his hands to his side as he looked back at Eshe's village before they continued their search for Sadal. With one last check, he looked to see that Eshe once again retreated into the shadows. He wondered if they would ever cross paths again.

A Day of Rest

Deeso and the others followed Eshe's directions to the letter. Much to their shock, Eshe truly meant every word. At long last, they reached the Indian plains in full. Deeso found herself restless as she anticipated finding Sadal soon but minded the condition of her team. She looked back to see discontent among the ranks as they sat in camp. Deeso only experienced swamps and jungle, so she appreciated the openness of her new surroundings. Any threats could be seen from miles away, but the opposite was certainly true for anything wishing to do them harm. Their camp was more organized than that of Jih's and the others. Deeso kept her belongings folded neatly in spare skins, and the rest in her respective backpack. The others did the same as it was easier to keep track of their things. Deeso often kept the others in line with her plans and working attitude, but even she had her limits and morale weakened with two failed hunts. The creatures were more agile than they were expecting from the forest, and their old strategies to trap game fell short. A new direction was needed if they were to thrive instead of just surviving off gathered roots and berries. She sighed to herself as Zulag yawned behind her. She turned around to see Zulag who had a look of frustration on his face.

"Go on. I know you're going to say it. Deeso you're not pulling your weight enough, all I do is-" Deeso commented in annoyance. While she prided herself as a great tracker, Deeso took the failed hunts as a personal failure.

"Actually, I know exactly what's the matter." Zulag said with his eyes closed.

"We've lost favor with the spirits. This place has a different presence than back in the trees. That must be it. We get close and then all of a sudden, the prey gets a burst of speed, and we can't catch a thing." Zulag added on as he gestured to the expanse that surrounded them.

For Zulag, the land taunted him in whatever way it could. The hunt didn't offer good sport, in fact it was exhausting as they chased gazelles only to see the clouds of dust behind them. In their travels they had found the remnants of some camps, and he could only wonder how people managed to live here for long bouts of time. Deeso found it hard to contain her laughter at Zulag's response.

"Anything to avoid saying you made a mistake of course. Tell me, what are these spirits saying right now?" Deeso mocked as she waved her hands around.

"I don't expect someone as simple as you to understand. This doesn't concern you. This is something that needs an expert." Zulag said as his gaze averted to Cikya.

Ozul and Cikya were busy maintaining the fire as they saw the figures of Zulag and Deeso approach them. For Ozul, there was no forest around to be burned so he had no qualms about a large fire out in the open. He and Cikya were previously busy collecting bones that she found were interesting for various purposes. The marrow was a good source of nourishment where it could be found, but she had other plans for the bones.

These were often used to maintain her crown that she wore but assisted in rituals she performed for their group's wellbeing.

"Oh-No food again I see." Ozul mentioned as his glance reached Deeso and Zulag who seemed hopeless.

"Not exactly. We seem to run into the issue where nothing shows up and the things that do, we can't catch." Deeso explained.

Deeso and Zulag had their hands full trying to get all sorts of prey to bring back. Scavenging was out of the question as the corpses were too rotted with the heat of the sun. The antelope that inhabited the plains taunted them with their deceptive bursts of speed. The birds that occupied various trees were difficult to grab as she and Zulag were unable to attack them with the weaponry at their disposal. She could only wave her axe around, while Zulag's throwing knives landed flatly on the ground once more. He could hit a moving target with ease, but a flying one, not so much.

"Have you tried leaving out bait?" Ozul questioned as he laid down on the grass.

"That would require us to have food to spare Ozul." Zulag said to him as he took a seat at the ongoing fire.

While Deeso was about to speak, she was promptly cut off by Zulag who left to address Cikya. Ozul quickly moved away from Zulag and found himself near Deeso. Deeso gave him a look over and Ozul moved to keep a respectable amount of space between the two of them.

"Cikya. I want to perform the Hopping He-uku with you. I'll start gathering materials. Do you think we have time?" Zulag said, as her head turned to hear his instructions.

Deeso put her head into her hands and rubbed her temples upon hearing Zulag's request. Deeso thought the two of them performing song and dance was ridiculous as she gave Ozul a worried look. Cikya got up and looked at Zulag with a look of curiosity as her eyebrows were raised and she tilted her head upwards. She moved her finger and noted the sun's trajectory. It was still early, so there was much time to prepare and get the arrangements set. Cikya moved her arms against her body in a confused manner and tapped Zulag's forehead with her pointer finger. Deeso studied Cikya's expressions and wondered what Zulag would get out of it.

"Yes, I still remember everything. After all, we've done it before." Zulag answered.

"The Hopping He-uku? What could that possibly be?" Deeso asked with genuine ignorance in her voice. Zulag shot a look at Deeso in utter contempt as he tried to dismiss her words.

Cikya frowned at Deeso's question, she considered it an embarrassment to not be in tune with such things, but she was aware of Deeso's disdain towards the spiritual.

"This is why people don't like you. You should know this. The Hopping He-uku calls upon the spirits to guide us towards fresh game. The soul is recycled. It requires a sacrifice, and so this is what we're going to do. I'd use you but I might get struck by lightning." Zulag said to Deeso as he pointed at her with ire in his voice.

Deeso looked up to the sky and saw not a single cloud was in the air. Ozul watched quietly and joined Deeso in looking up at the sky. Ozul wondered about the strength of Cikya's abilities and if she could truly summon prey for them to eat. It was a better plan than trying to work around their limitations. She spat towards the ground at his comment and was about to retort only to be stopped once again by Zulag interjecting.

"I can't concentrate with your mouth flapping in the wind, Deeso. Go somewhere else. Cikya and I have work to do." Zulag said as he turned his back to her.

"Yes, trying to take in the sun's light like a flower is truly hard work." Deeso mentioned with a derisive tone. She was more than willing to have the two waste time while she came up with an actual plan for them.

Deeso took her light backpack and tapped Ozul's shoulder to follow. Ozul noticed he was summoned and was compelled to see what Deeso wanted with him. Ozul still reserved some fears about the last time he found himself stuck to Deeso. He gave Cikya a small wave good-bye that was returned with kindness, as she and Zulag discussed the logistics for the ritual. As Deeso had no interest, she chose to walk instead with Ozul being her companion. In an earlier hunt with Zulag, Deeso mapped out much of the region already and remembered a river not too far out. Hippos were present but those were much further downstream than where they were going. Deeso touched her scalp and groaned at the state of her hair. It was a mess, and it was something that she neglected for quite some time. She felt the bits of dried blood and dirt that came with such a vigorous task of providing for the group.

Deeso walked with purpose while Ozul kept up with his feet moving quickly to catch up to Deeso. She generally enjoyed a quiet walk, but noticed Ozul was primed with questions. She took a deep breath and waited for the excited child to say more. Deeso found this particularly interesting as Ozul was generally gated off from the others. He didn't seem to fit in anywhere. Ozul above all else loved silence, but he hated silence when it came to interacting with Deeso. Ozul always found himself tripping over his words and made a conscious effort to remain calm.

"Why do you always hunt with Zulag? You two fight a lot but it just seems odd." Ozul questioned.

It was a genuine question on Ozul's account, although he had his thoughts on the group dynamics that he kept to himself, even from the prying eyes of Cikya. Despite his often-formal demeanor, Ozul was very much still a child and was curious about topics he knew he shouldn't poke with a stick.

"It's wise to hunt in pairs. I do gather with Cikya from time to time, but Cikya is unable to call for help if we get separated, and Zulag and I have the most experience. I am a tracker, and he is a Master Hunter. This is how it works." Deeso mentioned in response to the stifled smile of Ozul. Ozul shook his head in understanding but there was something he just couldn't shake. He decided to shelve it for now and just try to figure out how to get out of this situation.

I can never figure her out. It is beyond difficult to understand her unlike the others. Ozul thought as he noticed the smell of dung filled his nose.

Ozul pinched his nose hoping to block out some of the smell but was relieved to know this meant an animal was nearby that they could possibly encounter. His eyes turned towards the river that Deeso directed them to, and he noticed an assortment of plants that grew along the banks. Deeso walked in front of him and looked into the water. She chose to lean in and dunked her head under water for a few moments before resurfacing, her entire face was now soaked. Deeso watched her shadow with glee as her hair sprang up with moisture which surprised Ozul. Deeso sighted a small patch of trees that grew close towards one of the river's mouths and chose to rest underneath it. The dense shade was a relief to both parties as they surveyed what was around them.

"Ozul. Come and braid my hair." Deeso commanded as she waved him over.

Ozul looked over the wet mess that was Deeso and tilted his head in a bit of confusion. Although Ozul did have experience with such a task, he wondered how Deeso would know. He hadn't been able to do Cikya's hair on account of her bone crown that was never to be removed. Ozul's knowledge of plants allowed him to recall some properties that would be useful.

"You trust me to do this?" Ozul asked with the insecurity in his voice evident to Deeso. She didn't answer but just gave him a small grin in return. Ozul moved towards Deeso leaning in slightly as he sat on his knees.

"Is there some way you wanted this done?" Ozul asked her.

Deeso shrugged her shoulders and let him decide what her new look would be. Ozul wasn't used to such complex decision making, but he had an idea in his mind and set out to do it. Ozul knew he needed some supplies before starting. He looked to the ground to find a small branch that suited his needs. He broke off the ends into multiple sticks and would use these to wrap around segments of Deeso's hair. Ozul was aware that mud under the right conditions could be used as an agent to keep the consistency of his design together. Ozul saved a small strip of string from his pocket for last. Thunderfeet hair varied wildly compared to his own people, so he hoped the methods that he knew would work for Deeso's texture. Ozul decided to make cornrows for Deeso as he'd seen in other Thunderfeet but with tighter coils[54]. He held a branch in his mouth as he parted her hair and slowly worked. The two sat in silence for some time. As Ozul braided, he continuously wiped his hands on his legs. Braiding took hours and he dreaded the prospect of a job not done well. He sweated profusely out of nervousness as he recalled his role about his situation. Ozul was briefly distracted as his thoughts caught up to him. The words of Deeso thawed the freeze on Ozul who stared at the back of Deeso's head.

"In the past Sadal used to do my hair, but we're looking for her. You will do it for now. Your hands are delicate enough to work string." Deeso noted.

---

[54] Cornrows are one of the oldest known hairstyles known to man. These have been found to be depicted on figurines from the Upper Paleolithic.

"Do I scare you, Ozul?" Deeso asked as she could feel Ozul's hands subtly shaking as he continued to work with her hair.

"N-No, not at all Deeso. Why would you ask such a thing?" Ozul said as he attempted to hide his fear. Ozul tried to distract himself with the job at hand but his anxiety was crippling.

It was an ill-fated attempt to do so as Deeso could tell he was clearly lying. Ozul witnessed firsthand Deeso's proficiency at cutting down opponents and people that she considered a problem. Ozul was a pacifist among warriors who sought the best and most challenging fights, it was madness. He couldn't forget the few Forest Seeker children he befriended that were subsequently murdered when they first found Eshe. The memory was fresh and despite having now known a life of violence himself, he was horrified of becoming like all of them wholeheartedly. Ozul also didn't want to become a problem for Deeso.

"I can assure you I'm only as scary as you make me out to be. Everything I do is for our safety and to get Sadal back to us." Deeso said as she closed her eyes to better hear her surroundings.

"Tell me more about this Sadal you all are after. I have heard the campfire stories, but who is she really?" Ozul mentioned. He calmed down as he knew that Sadal was a safe topic for Deeso. He knew the love for her was genuine.

"Well, where do I begin? My sister is why I'm alive today. I want to help her, but that isn't possible until we find her. Unlike Zulag and Cikya who were born into our band, Sadal and I came later." Deeso stated. She adjusted her position as Ozul caught his fingers in her hair. She winced slightly as he pulled but said nothing further.

"I was very young when my parents left me to die. Most Wanderers are by circumstance but for me it was destiny. I was cast out because the sun and the moon fought each other when I was born. I was around eight years old when the secret of my birth broke. My knowledge was little, but I endured. I found myself in a new community who gave me my Wanderer's Mark on my hand. Though after two months, I was kicked out again because they found out about my birth. A trader from my band recognized me among them." Deeso explained.

"I found Sadal not long after. Her life wasn't great either. They didn't want her, and she came bruised. It seems silly now, but we fought over a dead Sarudeu. The meat was too much for us to hold, but I won! It was the only time I ever won. What I didn't know is that she was already in the care of Ronkalk. He is someone worth dying for." Deeso said with a slight laugh.

"And this life you chose? Did it make you happy?" Ozul asked, breaking his silence as he looked at the start of his masterpiece. It wasn't too different from what Deeso had before, but it was rejuvenated.

"Happy isn't a word I would use. I feel I have a purpose. Life in The Broken Bone is not for the weak-willed. Sadal and I had to pass many tests to meet what Ronkalk had wanted. We became fast friends during such trials, and she became my sister not long after. Every day we drilled early in the morning and did everything as a team. "Deeso, make me a knife!" Ronkalk would say, and I would do it very quickly. I was not as skilled as Sadal at hunting, so I could never make it to a Master Hunter rank, but I supported her where I could. She has given me more in this life than any." Deeso expressed as she envisioned Ozul's nod.

"What separates me from Zulag, Ozul, is that I worked to get to where I am today. He was simply born into greatness as the priests who kiss his feet say, but he will never be as worthy as Ronkalk. He must live with that truth." Deeso stated with a smug voice.

Ozul let out a nervous laugh as he agreed with her but wasn't sure how to process this information. All he could see was that she was part of a community where they were probably far more bloodthirsty than her and hoped he never came across them. Deeso's interest in talking about herself wasn't as exhaustive as one would think. She had other interests in mind as well that she wanted to keep private as she enjoyed the time of isolation with Ozul. Deeso was particularly enamored with the subject of Eshe and how she cultivated power. Deeso was able to defeat Eshe easily in battle, but she saw her ambition in uniting the Forest Seekers under her leadership as a desirable trait. Deeso wondered if in time with her own maturity, she could one day serve with distinction as a leader of The Broken Bone, or perhaps, her own band entirely.

"What did you and Eshe discuss?" Deeso asked as her voice grew quiet.

Ozul's face scrunched up a bit as he thought Deeso would've forgotten about it, but he recalled it quite well. Much of her words weighed heavy on his mind. Ozul and Eshe's ideals collided with one another, and while Ozul wanted to save face for the rest of his kind, he felt compelled to answer Deeso with honesty. Ozul's relationship regarding Eshe was a difficult one for him to come to terms with as he thought more about what would be best for his own destiny.

"Well, when you all were "trading" with The Buffalo Brothers, Eshe blamed me for the deaths of our people. She said my weakness was what killed them. I have never met any of them! What did they do for me, other than make fun of me or call me a traitor?" Ozul screeched as his voice cracked slightly.

"She was right. She was also wrong. Your weakness didn't kill them, but you all lack community and structure that makes it difficult to organize-" Deeso said as she got interrupted by Ozul.

"I did not finish. She asked me to join her. She said I could be made better. She gave me knowledge of her special clothing. The one that lets us walk without a trace." Ozul mentioned. Deeso nodded as she remembered this clothing. She hated to admit it, but it caught her off guard just long enough to touch her. It was a resourceful tactic.

"We also talked about The Stone Breaker. The one that Sadal travels with." Ozul said as he gave Deeso a tap on the shoulder to go look at her reflection in the river. As the two walked over, he continued speaking.

"Eshe did not reveal this to you out of distrust, but The Stone Breakers are the ones who willed caring of the forest to us. Thunderfeet have no such legends to my knowledge.

Before the Great Vanish, where the trees reclaimed them, one night we were silent and without a voice. The next morning, they gave us one better than their own. The Stone Breakers were selfless in any endeavor, and though we do not understand everything, their return of even just one means something big will happen. In short, I will not allow you to harm him. I must understand what the one known as Jih wants." Ozul said with the utmost severity he'd given so far. Ozul's devotion to the forest and to The Stone Breakers outweighed practically all fears. Deeso saw her reflection in the water and nodded with a satisfying review of Ozul's handiwork so far.

"As long as we get Sadal back. Thank you Ozul. We should return to the others once we finish up." Deeso said as she pinched Ozul's cheek.

About eight hours later, the walk back to camp was a quiet one as Ozul mulled over the new information he gathered about Deeso. She saw that Zulag and Cikya were in a trance-like state and hopped in step around a pile of bones. She tapped Ozul's arm and pointed as they remained in an indescribable chant. It was a complicated maneuver as Zulag hopped backwards while Cikya hopped forwards. The two chased each other but never touched one another. Deeso noticed that there were scratches on their arms, as these were small notches where blood would exit on top of the offering.

"Have they done this the entire time instead of finding food?" Deeso complained to herself.

She didn't bother understanding as the two continued their dance for several more minutes. Deeso and Ozul felt tired as they were mesmerized by their movement. Deeso wondered how Cikya and Zulag still had so much stamina, but they were powered by their beliefs and felt invigorated. She nodded off to sleep only to be awoken a few hours in the dead of night later by Cikya who gave her a warm smile as she clutched her backpack. The crackle from the large fire illuminated the plains as their shadows traveled across. In an amusing move, Cikya raised her eyebrows with a sly expression. Deeso wasn't sure what to expect from Cikya's plotting but was surprised to see the girth of the backpack. Her expression brightened as Cikya slowly dumped the contents out to the ground for Deeso and Ozul to start processing through the night. The bounty was various kinds of turtle meat and assorted bird eggs. Deeso was in complete shock while Ozul was just happy to finally see some new food, he didn't care how they got it. While Deeso and Ozul slept, Zulag and Cikya found a camp to do trading with. Zulag spun an amazing tale on how they went further down river to find turtles prime for the taking and saw Deeso's face darken in anger. Deeso hated to be outdone by a ritual she considered to be ridiculous, but at least she got her hair done well.

Old Man, New Tricks

After a long night of keeping watch, Jih stretched his arms out and took some time for himself to work on his tools before sleeping. Jih was soon joined by the others with work of their own to do. Jih made it his responsibility to make sure everyone remained capable of combat and their tools were up to par. While Jih knew how to work the techniques demonstrated by Sadal and Narro in their tools, Jih still stuck with The Old Way. Jih was stubborn as his tools were a piece of personal pride and considered them an extension of himself. Jih and Sadal previously gathered many stones together for use. The four took respectable space from one another as they sat in a circle and worked quietly where only the ambience of the plains was heard. Stone working required concentration, so Jih remained quiet when he worked but Trekkal loomed over his shoulder.

"It would be great if tools could never break. Imagine, something that was very sharp, and we only had to do it once?" Trekkal said as she watched the others work.

Jih groaned as he heard Trekkal's comments. He couldn't think of anything to occupy her time and when her imagination ran wild, everyone knew she'd keep going. Sadal shared the same sentiment as she silently grabbed Jih's attention and rolled her eyes. Jih gave a small chuckle as he saw her expression before returning to his tools. As Trekkal used a sling for combat, she didn't need to work stone in the same way the others did which often led her to coming up with ways to stave off boredom. She peeked over the shoulders of the other three and hopped between them.

"Could you be any lazier sister? Do not take that as a challenge." Narro complained as Trekkal watched the three of them.

Narro found a way to keep Trekkal engaged by passing rocks as needed. Jih looked at the others with a raised eyebrow as he was wondering why they needed so many. Jih's experience taught him well to have a minimalist approach for his stone tool construction. Jih felt his beard and looked to see the rock he shaved with was dull and needed to be sharpened. Jih felt a new rock placed at his feet by a happy Trekkal who gave him a small grin as he looked up. To add on to his dwindling collection, he sought to make another hand-axe. Jih constructed a hand-axe with relative speed and a subsequent spear point from another rock in the time it took for Sadal to produce one for her throwing spears. As Jih worked, he got another look from Sadal who remained curious at Jih's efficiency.

"I never realized your points looked so odd. Narro, come look at this." Sadal said as she called over Narro. Narro sat next to Sadal as the two watched Jih closely.

"Jih, you are done already?" Trekkal asked as she rested her head on his shoulder. Trekkal turned her head to the piece that Jih had in front of him, but her face carried a look of confusion on it. As Jih only used The Old Way for his individual tools, she was surprised to see that what he was doing was something she'd never seen before.

"What? Why are you all watching Jih? Do you not have tasks to do?" Jih complained in annoyance.

"Is it...supposed to look like that?" Trekkal asked again, as her gaze matched Narro and Sadal's.

Trekkal stuck her finger in her mouth in thought. She saw there were considerable differences in the girth of the tools among other things as she held Jih's hand-axe. She also noticed that the spear point was heavier on one side rather than the weight completely distributed through the piece.

"Jih has made tools your way many times. The Old Way is what Jih learned, and this is what Jih will use." Jih stated defensively.

"Well, Jih, our way's better. We're not just talking about looks, this is important for combat you know. Now, if you can't make them yourself, we can take over." Sadal said as she was interrupted by Jih.

"Are you challenging Jih? Jih is master stoneworker, there is no better." Jih huffed.

"I was being nice, but if you insist, I can tell you everything I see wrong with it!" Sadal grinned as she laughed at his comment.

Narro and Trekkal decided to stay out the growing spat between Jih and Sadal. Jih felt slighted as he was an expert on stone. It was what he trained his entire life to do and now he was being shown up by someone half his age from his perspective. Jih was rarely a conceited person, but his stone tools were the gold standard back in Sundaland. He had to be the best no matter the personal cost. Jih yawned at the others and got up with his tools. Jih secluded himself somewhat further as the three watched him move. Trekkal massaged her stomach that made an audible noise as she looked around her bag to see what she had. Narro frowned at Jih's reaction but understood his frustration.

"Sadal, we have no food! We should probably go grab something to eat." Trekkal said as Narro nodded in agreement.

"Think you can last on your own Jih?" Narro asked as he received no answer while Jih worked.

Jih gave a small grunt of acknowledgement at the others leaving while he worked on refining his craft. Jih heard their voices gradually fade into the distance and he was left alone.

Sadal, Narro, and Trekkal were out with their gear as they drew a line in the sky with their fingers. Jih kept the fire going high for their return in their absence. Sadal intended to have some more personal time with Narro but didn't mind Trekkal accompanying them. Their travels took them to a small piece of outer woodland where an axis deer with white spots on its fur was visible. It chewed on some spare leaves from a nearby bush as its free eye drifted towards the three hungry humans. Trekkal dangled her sling and launched a rock towards the deer. Sadal eyed the arc of the rock and saw that it struck it directly in the head. The deer attempted to run forward but was disoriented and tripped on itself. Trekkal lifted her arms in victory and shouted at her accomplishment.

"Excellent throw sister!" Narro clapped as he watched Sadal run over.

"Sorry Sadal, next time you better-" Trekkal teased while Sadal's pace increased towards the collapsed deer.

The impact of Trekkal's rock caused the deer to bleed but it soon recovered its stance. The deer attempted to run through the thicket while Sadal looked back at Trekkal with a glare.

"It's getting away!" Sadal yelled as she chased down the deer with her throwing spear.

Sadal was able to keep an easy lead on the deer from the blood trail that led to a clump of bushes where the animal was cornered. She lifted her arm and launched a spear through the undergrowth that silenced the beast's suffering. Sadal called out for them both to approach and mind their step as some of the plants had thorns. Narro and Trekkal approached Sadal to see Sadal's spear sticking out of the hindquarters of the animal. Trekkal's grin was replaced with a smug expression from Sadal who saw it as a competition between the two.

"Alright Trekkal. You know the rules, I killed it, so you take it home. Narro, why don't you make yourself useful and use those muscles of yours to help?" Sadal said as she playfully squeezed Narro's arm.

"Oh and mind the antlers!" Sadal added on with a cheery tone that irritated Trekkal.

Narro helped Trekkal hoist the deer from the bushes as the two dragged the deer back to camp. As the three progressed back home, Sadal saw a lone hyena approach them. She raised her arm backwards to grab her throwing spear but paused as she saw something inside its mouth. She saw a human head wedged inside its mouth that bled with a trail behind it. Sadal was less than impressed as Trekkal stuck her tongue out in disgust. Narro protectively stepped in front of Sadal as he dropped his half of the deer. He held a club in his hand as he locked eyes with the creature and saw it was satiated for now. Hyenas always waited in the wings to find where the next good meal was, but this one could see it was outmatched for the time being.

"Better him than me, we should get going." Trekkal commented as she pointed to the accumulation of smoke in the sky.

Sometime later, the trio returned with victory in hand. Sadal rubbed her stomach as she debated already taking a bite into the fresh kill. Narro hoisted the deer up and placed it by their campfire while Trekkal got skewers prepared to cut the meat. While the other two were busy, Sadal cupped her hands and yelled to Jih.

"Jih! We got food! You going to help us or what? We did our part, time to cook!" Sadal said with a grin. Her expression soured slightly as she yelled again and heard no answer.

"I think he's mad at you Sadal. He hasn't moved from that spot in hours." Narro said as he nudged her gently.

"Jih...I can see you're a bit upset. I didn't think you'd be this mad about me making fun of your tools. Are you going to cook food for us? I went and hunted this meat here!" Sadal said as Jih turned around and focused back on his crafting.

Though the smell of cooked deer was appealing, there was more important business to attend to for him. While the others could cook, Jih's expertise was by far the most preferred. Sadal nudged Jih gently as he turned his head to see three empty mouths staring at him.

"Jih has hotspark prepared. The fire will be hot and good." Jih said before going back to work.

Narro gave an audible sigh as it came down to the three of them to figure out how they wanted to prepare the deer. Sadal was visibly annoyed as this wasn't the response she was expecting, but it was clear Jih was preoccupied and showed no signs of stopping. At this point, Jih took practically all the rocks they sourced this morning for his own devices.

"Great, now we will starve! Sadal barely cooks as it is, and Narro always has the middle cold! How do you do it?!" Trekkal said in dismay as she looked at the two of them and the food.

"Sister, I see a solution here. You can cook if you complain about our methods." Narro proposed, while he heard a hushed laugh from Jih who remained centered on his task.

"Wait, let us reconsider me working on anything." Trekkal commented with a sly grin as Narro and Sadal both glared at her.

Trekkal was hardly one to work, let alone when dinner was involved. There was always some way she'd end up burning the surrounding area or making too much smoke to near the fire as the meat cooked. Jih did his best to drown out the bickering of the other three who were quick to devolve back into children over how to best cook the deer meat at their disposal. To his surprise, dinner was left uncooked, the other three dipped into their supply of gathered berries as they were unable to find a solution that worked. Jih groaned to himself as he silently left his task and prepared the meal and took his project with him. He worked as he rotated the cooking deer meat while the other three sat in silence. Jih turned his head and glared at the others who could only offer awkward smiles in response. Jih called over to the others once food was made. While Jih and Sadal ate with their hands, Narro and Trekkal used a stone blade as a utensil to cut the meat. Jih ate quickly and returned to his work. The hours waned as Jih had a growing pile of rejects stacked up next to him of all sorts of tools. It was Trekkal's night to take watch, but she overslept. She was woken up by the sound of Jih banging rocks together once again. Trekkal rubbed her eyes after a yawn to see a shadowy figure still hanging around at the same spot where Jih sat. She rolled over on the ground. Her hand grabbed a bundle of sticks from the void that came from the fire with low light and her range of vision increased as the kindling burned. Jih finally spoke after much silence.

"Trekkal must be awake, it is her turn to watch. Jih saw nothing for now." He said while Trekkal groggily nodded and sat herself up in a struggle to stay awake.

Is he seriously still working? Trekkal thought.

"Jih, just remember we care about you. If you are tired, please sleep. We have more years than you." Trekkal said with a sweet voice that carried over to his ears.

Jih's eyes were practically bloodshot as he hadn't gotten any rest from the previous day. Trekkal's eyes surveyed the stones and she saw that each one was practically perfect and yet Jih rejected them anyway. Jih gave a grunt in acknowledgement, he didn't need to be reminded that he was older than everyone else. For Jih, Trekkal's insistence to go to bed reminded him of his mother who told him to slow down. In those days, he worked hard to prove himself to the onlookers such as Tur and those that relied on him and his tools. Jih felt that abandoning The Old Way was a severance of his people and tainted the memory of his last instructor, but he understood the importance in wanting to have the best to protect his friends. He hoped to drown out his dependence on the style until it was as second nature as breathing.

The overzealous Jih fumbled around in the intermittent flickers of light from the campfire and looked for more rocks now that his personal breakthrough had been made. Jih made not only a new spear point, but a hand-axe, two burins, and a racloir, all reproduced with the utmost skill for himself. Jih looked over his collection with pride. The tear dropped shaped hand-axe was his all-purpose tool, and he preferred these over carrying a knife like that of Sadal despite their weight. Jih's creativity was limited, but he allowed himself some room to experiment with the alternative tools in his possession. Jih lifted the first of the two burins and noted the sharpened and chiseled edge with a smooth bottom that snugly fit in his hand. He narrowed his eyes and gently poked the top with his finger to ensure it was done correctly. Jih remembered that Narro used these to engrave his weapons with designs that appealed to him, and he wanted to make something of his own for his spear. It was delicate work, but Jih knew with enough time, he could make something fitting of his status. The latter racloir allowed Jih to process hides more efficiently to help Sadal in making clothes. It was smooth to the touch. He collapsed on what remained of his work and slept soundly until the afternoon. He woke up to hear his friends once more and Jih's bloodshot eyes saw the others using his tools just like any other. Sadal wasn't one to apologize, but she saw Jih's desire for recognition with his tools and in the middle of his nap, decided to try them out with workable results. Jih gave a small but satisfying grin as exhaustion took hold once again, but this time he could rest easy as he accepted the utilities of what was new.

Woodwind

Jih and the others found themselves in a strange predicament. The week's events were plentiful and there was nothing but time to kill now. While moving was a possibility, the group stayed on a steady track for a few weeks. Their feet burned with the amount of ground covered recently and they wanted a few days to absorb their new surroundings. While the plains seemed ever infinite, this patch of land was an oasis from the close calls on the way. Food was plentiful and the predators were distant. Jih hadn't expected their group to be so productive, but his mental checklist was completed. He was happy to enjoy the silence as their group sat at camp, but the stifled noises of an irritated Trekkal caught his attention.

"I am bored. There is nothing out here, and the last people were some time ago." Trekkal complained as she played with her hair.

"For once, she makes a good point." Sadal commented as she clipped her long fingernails down with a rock and a filer made from bone.

Generally, the tasks that came with their lifestyle were enough to do the job on their own, but personal expression remained important. All took some modicum of care to their personal hygiene, Jih and the others of his kind often bit their fingernails, a habit considered rudimentary but effective. He was a quick learner and adopted Sadal's method, as he didn't enjoy the taste of dirt on his tongue.

"Speaking of people, we should come up with a name for our group. Every band has a name, and if we're something, we should, right?" Sadal mentioned as she studied her fingers. She wasn't particularly satisfied with the way her nails were done, Deeso usually took care of that duty, but those days were behind her. Sadal gave Trekkal a look and turned her head away as Trekkal folded her arms at such a request.

"At home, we have teams for duties. Jih was part of Stoneworking Team as leader. We could be Exploring Team. Not like Scouting Team, they must return to camp." Jih said as he met Trekkal's shrug.

"I sense boredom on our faces. Be still friends, for I found something interesting in my travels. It took all my meat, but we can hunt again." Narro commented with excitement.

Narro ran his fingers through his beard with a satisfied look on his face as he retreated away from the group to check his new pack left on the ground. Over the past few days, Narro negotiated with a wandering group of Forest Seekers who were traveling in the area and brought an assortment of things with them. Although Sadal considered Forest Seekers a group to attack on sight, Narro and the others didn't see it this way. He found a kindred spirit among them to trade with and got some items. With his good nature, Narro was able to make it happen.

"You traded all your meat for what exactly?" Sadal asked, as she looked to Jih who shrugged his shoulders.

"Oh no..." Trekkal commented as she saw Narro rummaging through his pack as he debated what to keep and what to throw away. She gave a resigned sigh and rubbed her forehead as she knew exactly what Narro was going to do.

Rather than bring a few objects back at a time, Narro dragged back the sack with some noticeable effort. As he was the strongest of the group, his pack was filled to the brim. The group's packs were individualized to their personal tastes. Trekkal kept a small number of stones in her pack along with various fibers she would find to be of use for later. Sadal's eyes were kept on replacement rocks for spear points, while she looked to find light wood that wouldn't be too difficult to throw. Jih kept a very minimalist approach to his bag. Spare components that he could use to construct a spear or supplies for injuries could be found in his bag. Jih shot a look at Trekkal and Sadal as Narro silently removed some seemingly unrelated objects.

Narro first unveiled a turtle shell that came from a juvenile but was a worthy addition to the pack. His signature instrument of the flute was next and was crafted from bone as opposed to wood. He treasured the feeling of bone due to the reverberations as he blew into it and used it as feedback. The horn of a deceased ram was next, and there were two holes he hollowed into the piece. He needed to be sure there was one to blow into and the other was where the sound would come from. He hadn't tried to use it yet, but he had a decent theory of how the acoustics would work and hoped that the sound would pick up. The last instrument was something he'd never seen before. He remembered the Forest Seeker trader describe the object as a "Spinning Ker-Mah"[55]. He saw that it was crafted from wood and string, and the device generated its noise from manually spinning in the air.

"Oh right, the big game hunter I envisioned you being is but an idle music player." Sadal commented with a dismissive tone in her voice.

"Oh Sadal, why the long face? I have something for you, but not yet. Come friends. I have much to show you. Pick whatever you like. The flute is mine to use." Narro prompted the three to come closer.

"Roped into playing music again. Fine, just give me something different this time." Trekkal commented as she grabbed the bullroarer quickly and left Sadal and Jih to decide which ones they wanted.

Jih looked over his options and slowly reached for the turtle shell. He was drawn by the color and lifted it towards his ear. Jih looked at his instrument with a raised eyebrow but raised his hand to get Narro's attention. He looked at the turtle shell with

---

[55] Bullroarers are a musical technology that consists of a weighted airfoil (a thin rectangular slat of wood about 15 cm to 60 cm long and about 1.25 cm to 5 cm wide) attached to a long cord. Depending on the length of string and the size of the wood, different noises can be generated and are used for long distance communication! The earliest known surviving models have been uncovered in the Upper Paleolithic about 18,000 BCE.

some curiosity as he flipped it over and blew into it. He wasn't sure if it was supposed to make a sound or if he needed to do something else to make it function.

"Jih has shell in hand. What will Jih do with this?" Jih questioned Narro while he tossed it in the air. Jih was surprised with how light it was, once the turtle itself was absent.

"Yes Jih! This Zemaii shell right here. I want you to hit it and put it to your ear. It will make a noise when struck." Narro explained as he found his attention quickly grabbed by Sadal.

Sadal was left with one option as her eyes gravitated towards the ram's horn. It was the largest object there and it was certainly the most interesting compared to a simple turtle shell or the object left for Trekkal. Sadal imagined the appearance of the creature that used to have this horn and felt a spirit from it still dwelled inside. Sadal felt the girth of the object in her hands and was satisfied with the heft. A powerful warrior such as herself could only have the biggest instrument to match her energy.

"Narro! How does this work?" Sadal asked, as she placed the ram's horn up to her eye to see the holes. Narro quickly ran over to help Sadal while Jih was content with his instrument.

"This is a horn. You place..." Narro explained as he pointed to the end that was where she needed to blow. Sadal nodded her head as she absorbed Narro's words, but her eyes shifted to something in Narro's possession instead.

"What do you have in your hand? Why is mine different from yours?" Sadal asked him as she placed the horn on the ground and pointed at Narro's flute. Narro smiled and was happy that the others bothered to join in the first place.

"This is a flute. Do they not have instruments where you come from?" Narro asked with some disbelief in his voice as Sadal's question seemed to be quite sincere in its delivery. Trekkal chuckled as she watched Narro position his flute for Sadal.

Jih's eyes turned to the small shell in his hand, and then back at Narro who gave him a small grin of encouragement. Jih shook the shell and lightly tapped the back. His eyes opened wider as he felt the sound and the vibration of the turtle shell. Jih continued to tap the turtle shell and alter how hard and how frequently he hit the material. Jih was no stranger to music, but much of what his people produced was done through oral tradition or clapping and stomping on the ground. Narro's attention turned back to Trekkal who looked highly confused at what she was given.

"Oh brother, what about me, Trekkal? The most important thing in your life?" Trekkal interrupted as she called Narro over to her. She seemed confused as she was unsure of what exactly to do with her instrument.

"Oh, this works much like how you swing your sling. Figured you would pick the instrument that required the least amount of effort." Narro mocked as Trekkal kicked some dirt in his direction. Narro gave a small clap to get their attention. His demeanor shifted somewhat as he saw the attention of his friends put their gaze on him. Narro took a deep breath and rounded them all up to take some space close by from one another.

"Perfect, now that we all have our instruments. Let us make some music. Sadal, why not start us out? Do whatever comes to mind." Narro proposed as he saw Sadal's expression turn happier.

Although Sadal hadn't been given much help with her instrument, she figured it out easy enough. She took a deep breath and blew the horn as loudly as possible. Her cheeks expanded as the noise reverberated throughout the plains with nothing in sight to hear it other than them. Narro physically recoiled at the sound that came through as he attempted to correct Sadal, but she was having too much fun to listen. Jih blinked twice as he was startled by the noise that was generated from the horn. Trekkal was in her own world and didn't bother to acknowledge it as she hummed to herself. Sadal inhaled deeply once more and blew into the horn once again, while Narro clapped his hands to make her stop. Sadal smiled as she took this as applause for her performance and admired her instrument.

"The echo from this one is strong. I like it." She said happily. She raised an eyebrow at Narro who practically cuffed his ears.

"Did I not do the task well?" Sadal asked as her she frowned.

"No! It is very loud. Loud does not always mean better." Narro retorted as Sadal shot him a glare.

Trekkal continued to give little attention to Sadal's performance with the horn. The wood of the bull-roarer that Trekkal raced in the sky gave a mighty woosh. Trekkal spun around wildly and gave herself ample room to experiment with as the sound waves filled her eardrums with a nice hum. She closed her eyes and truly felt connected to her instrument. As Trekkal continued to spin with it, she also took the same direction and teetered close to the others. The target of her unintended spinning was Sadal; she was hit directly on the cheek, and while she didn't bleed, it left a noticeable mark on her face. Sadal stopped blowing the ram horn and tugged at the string which made it collapse to the ground. Trekkal turned her head to see the source of her sound stopping came from Sadal and she bit her tongue in annoyance.

"You hit me on purpose!" Sadal yelled as she put up her fist.

"What are you talking about? Did your Master Hunter senses not tell you an object was coming your way? This is not my fault." Trekkal pouted indignantly as she turned away from Sadal.

"Don't turn your back to me!" Sadal yelled, as Narro quickly stopped his flute playing to mediate the situation.

"Sadal, it was an accident. Trekkal, your mood does not help things." Narro stated meekly, as he could already see the two personalities brewing for a shouting match. He looked over to see Jih still enamored with the turtle shell while ignoring the others entirely. At least one person appreciated his attempts at bonding.

"You're taking her side? You can see she was clearly in the wrong." Sadal spoke in anger.

"Yes! As he should, I am his sister after all." Trekkal huffed.

"I think we should take a short break. I have been thinking of songs for all of us, but the one for Sadal is finished. It lacks lyrics, but I think you will understand what it conveys. I call it The Rest of A Warrior." Narro said as he stifled the discussion between the two.

Jih looked at Narro with intrigue as he overheard him addressing the others. Since the day Narro was open about his feelings towards Sadal, Jih gave extra attention to their dynamic. A song in Sadal's honor was unorthodox but he was curious to see how well she'd take it. Ballads of victory were rare among his people, but they were known for it. Narro sat on the ground as he closed his eyes and play his flute. The sound was grating to everyone's ears, Jih wasn't sure if Narro's skills weren't as he advertised, or that the instrument was made from bad bone. Narro's body moved with confidence as he swayed with the wind that enveloped over the plains. Narro built his sound based on a select pattern exhibited with his fingers. Sadal felt compelled to whistle along with the rhythm of the music. While Sadal generally enjoyed more upbeat music, the soft tones resonated with her ears. She felt a warmth come over her as she was glad to hear something that was in her honor. While Trekkal was quick to offer her feedback, Sadal stayed quiet. She watched Narro carefully with interest. Effort among all things was attractive to Sadal. The memory of her treatment by Nurzan steadily remained in her mind, but Narro had the opportunity to make new memories. As soon as Sadal let herself be immersed in Narro's song, the song was over, and she heard Narro's voice bring her back to reality.

"I would like if we could play as one, but that seems impossible." Narro said with frustration.

"Our team has stayed strong for a hunt; a ballad should be easy." Sadal commented as she hugged Narro.

Sadal felt invigorated by Narro's song and mobilized the others to get their instruments. While the group practiced, they started to harmonize as their sounds led to different tracks that played along Narro's base melody. Narro briefly opened his eyes to see his friends playing along and closed them once more as he was satisfied with the turn of events before him. With a life full of violence, both physical and emotional, the times of coming together were few and far between. Narro savored every one of them and he hoped the others did as well.

The Thrill Of The Kill

Deeso scratched her head in thought as she looked at the state of her traveling party. Without any sort of direction, they looked up aimlessly towards the movement of clouds, but Deeso didn't allow herself to have such luxuries. Deeso was busy as she tried to come up with plans to close the gap on Sadal. Every time she felt that she was getting close to finding her, there was some other obstacle in her way. Deeso mulled over her interactions with Eshe and how her tale related to Sadal's struggle. Deeso was aware that Eshe had contact with Sadal in months past, and while she didn't believe everything of her story, there was enough nuggets of truth to go off. The Stone Breaker myth yielded results as there were those who heard of Jih and his travels. Whispers by the campfire of their antics with the now deceased Buffalo Brothers were discussed as their impact on trade was important in this area. The meteor was also something discussed among Thunderfeet in this area, though she held little patience for superstition. She had leads on both counts and didn't know what to think, but she felt that some time to clear her head would be good. Deeso looked over at Zulag and called for his attention.

"Zulag, do we have a count for furs?" Deeso asked as he let out an audible grunt.

"Same as last time, but I can check again. We haven't caught anything worthwhile for trade." Zulag said as he got up. Zulag dusted some dead grass off his clothing as he opened their respective backpacks to do a count.

While Zulag labored, Ozul enlightened the group on his observations on how Thunderfeet in this area killed crocodiles. Zulag debated the venture as he overheard Ozul's claims, but his rightful apprehension of the water kept him from taking the plunge. Deeso's eyes met Zulag in disbelief but decided to let Ozul finish his tale.

"My kind do not approach the Vatmaraku. It is a terrible creature, but I have seen Thunderfeet do it. Now, they use a big stick to find it under the water. They then take a log and have it crunch down and use great force to turn it over and poke it. It requires many to do so." Ozul said as he held back a sneeze.

"They use a log? That should crack right in half!" Zulag asked in disbelief while he worked. Ozul nodded his head in confirmation while Cikya emoted a horrid expression on her face at the thought.

"Yes, I saw it myself! They use thick wood. There are not many trees but the ones here are hardy." Ozul defended himself. While Ozul spoke, Deeso grabbed a few furs off the top and was stopped by the glance of Cikya who held her hand out. Cikya was concerned as they needed to keep an emergency supply of furs handy but relented as Deeso stared at her.

"Just in case. I feel the moon may be visiting soon. [56]" Deeso said flatly as Cikya nodded in understanding. Cikya passed her a few extra furs while Deeso retreated a bit and dressed herself.

"I'm going to go hunt and see what can be brought back. My hunt shouldn't be too long, just a few hours." Deeso mentioned, as Zulag got up to accompany Deeso.

"Alone this time." She added on, while Zulag set his knives down.

Zulag was perfectly fine with taking a break, but Cikya and Ozul were a bit less convinced. Their concern weighed on their faces but knew Deeso would press on anyway. Deeso emptied her backpack and ate a few small berries as a light snack before setting out on the plains. As she walked out on her own, she lifted her hand up to wave good-bye for now. The other three remained at camp and watched Deeso walk until she was no longer visible. Cikya urged Zulag to leave and follow Deeso just in case, but he argued against it. If Deeso insisted on being alone, that was her choice.

At the same time, just an hour away, Jih looked for Sadal as she "borrowed" some spare flint from Jih's backpack. He was asleep and hadn't realized Sadal left when he wanted to light a fire to cook breakfast. Jih looked over to see Narro sleeping, and his head turned to Trekkal.

"Trekkal. Have you seen Sadal? Jih needs hotspark for our food." Jih questioned. Trekkal was daydreaming about something she'd already forgotten but was brought back by Jih's voice.

"Huh? Did you want me to do something about it? She left some time ago. No idea where she went." Trekkal said as she opened her arm to the vast space of the plains where they sat.

Jih sighed in annoyance, both at Sadal's action and Trekkal's response. While they had no rush, Jih was anxious to cover more ground and they could only do this together. They could come and go as they pleased, which was acceptable, but at least one person had to be aware of where the other would be at any given time. Sadal chose to ignore this protocol as the demands of the hunt spoke louder. Sadal was fixated on hunting a boar that found her interest. As far as prey animals went, a boar was an acceptable kill for Sadal's skillset. She knew that it provided a great bounty of meat, and the fat alone could be used for lighting and heat. She thought about chiseling down the tusks into something for Narro as a thoughtful gesture from the ballad made for her. She noticed the tracks earlier and looked for the best time to find it. While not the most adept tracker, Sadal could tell from its gait and dung that it was likely headed towards a water source. It was a suitable opponent that would stand its ground when challenged and wasn't a suicidal endeavor such as taking on lions who only attacked in groups. She crawled along the ground as the visibility of the plains was a detriment to the hunter.

---

[56] Hunter-gatherers not only menstruate much later in life than in settled communities, but less often as well. Many modern hunter-gatherer women don't menstruate until about age 17 or higher and their caloric intake affects this too. To deal with this, many seclude themselves or wear a diaper out of animal skins much like Deeso.

"Since everyone's complaining but not getting any furs..." Sadal said to herself as she hoped to hear her prey in the low ambient clicking of insects.

She wiped her head and although she was warm, there was no sweat on her hand. Sadal shook her head and knew she was clearly dehydrated by now. Sadal could tell that if she was thirsty, her prey out on the trail was as well. She looked for the direction of the wind that a stream could go. Sadal slowly acclimated herself to the call of the river. As far as she could remember, she was about an hour's travel from camp.

Deeso thought ahead and found herself at a stream with tall tufts of grass that could engulf a person. Far from the shade of a strong tree, it was still a welcome reprieve from the sun. Deeso swatted at a couple flies and yawned as the waiting started. She noticed a few tufts of loose hair that stuck out from the rest of the ground. She knew her target was a boar from the hair alone and that it rolled in the ground at some point to mark territory. Her plan was simple, wait at a safe area for prey, and she stayed until something came by to be home by nightfall.

"Everything has a thirst. First thing I need to do is fill my own water while I'm here." Deeso commented as she rummaged through her backpack to extract a small canteen that she made for herself.

Deeso smelled the inside of the bladder and stuck out her tongue in disgust. In the dry heat of the plains, it smelled horrid, but the water would hold. Deeso drifted off to sleep in a weird bout of exhaustion and exposure from the sun. Her nose twitched as she slept, but she was rustled awake by the sound of a snort trudging through the mud of the stream. She recognized this as nothing more than a hog in her vicinity. Deeso's adrenaline surged and woke her up as she saw a large stick course through the air and land some distance away. She raised an eyebrow and recognized that it was a throwing spear. The origin was naturally human, but she was unsure if this was an enemy or some other hunter that just happened to have the same idea. Deeso grabbed her axe and reasoned she was under attack as she always prepared for the worst.

The sound of the boar loudly squealed and gave Deeso the perfect opportunity to get ahead of her mysterious competitor and cut them down if need be. Deeso rushed out of the tall grasses and quickly darted her head around and made sure to not lose the trail before it was too late. Deeso stopped as she heard a feminine voice in the distance that sounded familiar.

"I missed! Don't think you can hide from me!"

Deeso's heart raced as she recognized that it eerily sounded like Sadal, but she had to be focused on the prey at hand. As it turned out, Sadal and the boar were a package deal. Sadal was visible to Deeso and just barely as the boar goaded her in the distance. Deeso's eyes couldn't help but tear up. Deeso looked at Sadal and studied every detail on her face. She was in awe that after all this time, Sadal was just as she remembered, but somehow even more amazing.

Sadal's battle with the boar persisted as she looked to see a figure in the distance. Her eyesight wasn't as good as Deeso's, so it took a moment for her to figure it out, but by her gait alone, Sadal felt something was right. Her travels and sacrifice were everything she hoped for. Now Sadal could tell Deeso everything that happened to her and the new life she lives.

"No, it couldn't be!" Sadal said as she saw the familiar gait of a figure in the distance.

She ran over quickly and nearly tripped over herself in the process. Her eyes teared up seeing the outline of Deeso in the distance. A short while later, Deeso's outline was whole. Sadal observed Deeso and noticed she changed significantly from her last days at The Broken Bone. Sadal wasn't sure about Deeso's trek to this land, but she knew that something was different. Not having to exchange any words, it was clear they needed to track down the escaping boar before it was done. The two women ran at breakneck speed towards the boar who gained a sudden bout of courage. It dug its heels into the soil and snorted. The animal charged in the direction of Deeso, just in time for her to roll out of the way. Deeso hoped to serve as a distraction for the boar so that Sadal could get a clean skewer, but the boar was a persistent creature and saw through their ruse.

Sadal and Deeso were used to the challenge of slender but powerful creatures like the leopard, so landing the decisive blow on a boar was harder than expected. Deeso ran with her axe parallel to Sadal as she moved quickly to catch up. She bit her tongue slightly as she turned to change course. Deeso attempted to corral the boar between the two of them before the boar decided to retaliate. Sadal left with three throwing spears, and she wasted one that broke trying to kill the boar by surprise. She heaved with a mighty throw and nailed the boar on its hind quarters. The boar managed to eject the spear by thrashing around. Sadal ran to retrieve the bloodied spear so she could throw it again. The boar ran towards Sadal with a surprising amount of speed as Sadal rolled along the ground. Deeso gave Sadal a supportive nod as she successfully recovered her spear.

Deeso taunted the boar as she threw a rock at it and kicked up mud to draw attention. The creature was enraged and headed towards Deeso. Sadal looked surprised as she saw Deeso maintain her stance but extended her arm forward. She launched her axe at an arc and waved over at Sadal to throw once again. Deeso missed intentionally as the boar avoided the first projectile, but it was to provide an ample throwing angle for Sadal to exploit. With a sufficient grunt, Sadal propelled the spear through the boar's head, and it was stopped in its tracks. A satisfying crunch sound was heard as it sufficiently shattered the boar's skull. Deeso nodded as Sadal remained efficient as ever, a true compliment to her skills. Sadal removed the spear with brain matter and flesh on the wood. She tore into the animal with her spear and exposed the viscera. Sadal watched as blood pooled in the ground. She ripped out the stomach and tossed it to the side while her hands soaked with blood. Deeso grabbed the head of the boar and examined it for the animal's health. She was impressed as the two managed to kill one in its prime. Sadal revealed a small knife from her clothing and cut the throat of the pig. Deeso and Sadal both knelt at the kill and scooped the blood from the torn throat. Although this practice was reserved for predators mainly, a worthy herbivore could be given this offer as well.

"Where'd you learn to do something like that? I never saw you use that technique before!" Sadal said with surprise in her voice. Sadal opened her arms and gripped Deeso closely. She pressed Deeso against her body in a warm embrace. Deeso rubbed Sadal's back and was happy to see the two reunited.

"Oh-I have been practicing new ways to hunt with my axe. Zulag taught me that throw." Deeso noted as she accompanied Sadal while she retrieved her remaining throwing spear.

"Zulag?!" Sadal spat out in disbelief.

Deeso gave a small chuckle, there was a lot that Sadal needed to be updated on. As for now though, the shock of seeing her waned as she was at equilibrium. She reflexively put her hand to Sadal's face. Deeso was happy to see the visions that plagued her at night were nothing more than delusions that could rest.

"Don't get me started. I'll let you in on something since it's you. I give him a hard time, but my opinion of him has changed recently. It's more favorable than starting out." Deeso said as she pointed to the boar haul.

Sadal dug into her backpack and withdrew a spare flint knife. The two shared the meat and were happy to see that there was plenty to bring back home to their respective parties. Sadal and Deeso were quick to build a fire and used the tall grasses from the stream as decent kindling to cook the meat. The two roasted pieces of the boar as the carcass was put to rest some distance away from them. The two split the tusks as the ivory was good. Deeso found it unusual that Sadal needed such a large quantity of meat for a single traveler, but she chose not to question it for a far more important matter was at hand. Deeso's eyes looked at Sadal's hair now covered with soil and blood from the kill.

"Sadal, your hair is such a mess! I know a good river to get you cleaned up." Deeso offered to Sadal who nodded in between chews of the pork.

Deeso knew Sadal's fear of water well, so she reassured her safety as the two neared the stream. Deeso cupped her hands as tightly as she could to hold water. She scooped it up and watched it all pour over Sadal's head. Deeso couldn't help but smile as Sadal gradually became cleaner over time.

"Same as before? I don't have my tools, but some twists should work." Deeso asked with a raised eyebrow as she noticed some stale blood on Sadal's head.

Sadal nodded and the two sat together. Deeso began the long but rewarding process of twisting Sadal's hair as she always did. There was a comfortable silence between the two for a while, but both knew that the question would come up eventually. It was in this intimate setting Sadal and Deeso had their most intricate of conversations, and this would be one such time. Sadal felt an overwhelming feeling of sadness come over her as she kept her true story hidden for so long. She hadn't anticipated the feeling of touching and seeing Deeso again but now home was here. She braced for Deeso's question.

"Sadal. You have always been honest and your heart equally as so. Why did you leave us? There was good cause to believe you perished in battle. There were lies spoken about you, but I refuted them all. I would like to know. I grieved for you and Brab for days in my mind. Nurzan didn't, of course." Deeso mentioned.

Sadal took a deep breath as she felt Deeso's touch.

"Deeso. You deserve the truth more than any. That day, I asked Ronkalk for you and your experience to come with me, but you were with the weavers. I was told to clear out a Weypeu which was no easy feat. I went out to the land our scouts said to clear and I led a team that was ill-equipped, but Ronkalk willed it anyway. I brought my son with me that day as no one could watch him. His very being was cursed and I should have listened to our priesthood. His crying brought dark tidings to us as the Weypeu destroyed us piece by piece. Some scattered to the winds never to be seen again, while others died not with honor, but suffering and pain. If you were there that day, you would have died in this way. I saw no other option but to kill my son and the dark tidings would escape us. I was the only survivor, and I couldn't provide for Brab. In the end, I chose your life over his." Sadal said as her voice dryly stated everything that happened. This was something she kept deep inside her and trusted nobody with. Sadal felt a damp feeling on her shoulder as she remained still. It was the tears of Deeso that came from reddened eyes. Sadal knew her pain, but she dared not look Deeso in the eyes as she continued.

Deeso felt a sense of nausea come over her as she attempted to keep her composure. She was confused as Sadal's failures were never known to her. Her thoughts came to the lives of those that perished in the tiger attack. Deeso was aware that Brab grew in a broken home, but never anticipated that his downfall would be the result of it. Sadal couldn't admit it even to Deeso, but she saw the hatred of her union with Nurzan in Brab and stress took over.

"You-You killed Brab?! How could you do such a thing!? Why would you do this?" Deeso said to Sadal, the physical shock was far too much for her to stand and she hit the soil.

"I ran because I failed. You know as well as anyone else that failure for us means death. This is what we agreed to when we stopped being Wanderers and joined The Broken Bone, remember? I made my choice as a mother. Brab lived and died before he could speak, and he was cursed. Why would I leave him to a life of pain and misery? This was a mercy as if his father had him...I fear he would have been a monster and hurt others beyond my control. It was better this way." Sadal commented as she hugged Deeso.

Despite such terrible news, Deeso still felt a calming presence at Sadal. Deeso inhaled some air through her nose and calmed herself down. Her eyes were blood red as she shielded herself from dust. Deeso knew she had to look at the situation rationally and accept the losses at hand. All that mattered was the mission, and she just succeeded in finding Sadal and making sure she was safe. She tried her best to keep her composure.

"Nurzan was a horrible man to you and broke you in ways I could never imagine. I have not hunted Weypeu before but all I care now is you are safe. I forgive you. You are my sister, and nothing will change that. It's not up to me anyway. Ronkalk is the one who wants you back. He also wants you back alive. This is a rare act of mercy, and it must be respected." Deeso said as she still clung to Sadal.

"Wait...So the reason you're with Zulag is because?" Sadal asked as she figured out what was happening. She stood up and separated her grasp from Deeso. Sadal stepped away, with a frown on her face, as she did so. Sadal didn't want to draw any conclusions just yet, but she felt a grave feeling in her chest.

"From the perspective of the rest of our people, you deserted. Ronkalk asked us to find you. This is a rescue." Deeso said as she extended her hand out to Sadal. Deeso's voice was calm and grounding, while Sadal felt more uneasy.

"What do you mean by us? Deeso, I was honest with you, and now you need to be honest with me. Am I in trouble? What is happening?" Sadal asked as she actively resisted the urge to ball her hand into a fist.

Deeso stood with her arms at her side as she saw Sadal start to fall apart in front of her. She held her hand out again and urged with a small grin for Sadal to come closer to her.

"Why are you raising your voice at me Sadal? I have already forgiven you. You violated Ronkalk's will, not my desires. I have always only wanted you back safe." Deeso explained as she tried to calm Sadal down. Deeso's voice quivered slightly as she looked at Sadal's rising anger. She lowered her voice and attempted to soothe her.

"I'm not alone. There is Zulag, Cikya, and we have Ozul as well." Deeso explained, as she decided to narrate the origins of how her team came to be. Deeso expected Sadal to be proud of her, particularly with her escapades against their longtime enemies The Mud Forged. Deeso's expression wavered as all she could see was disappointment from Sadal.

"Ozul? That's not a name of our people. That is a Forest Seeker. Deeso, those are our enemies! How can you accuse me of breaking Ronkalk's will when you do the same?" Sadal said with rising anger in her voice. Sadal felt she was right, Deeso did change, and it seemed to be for the worst. She expected Deeso to fully support her as she always had, but their philosophy put a wedge between the two women.

"He is one, yes. There are compromises to happiness and the world is more complex than I have seen. The blood of many rest on my hands to find you Sadal. I am glad that you are safe, but now we must go back. We have tracked you for about seven months now if my timing is accurate, working tirelessly to find you. There was much sacrifice." Deeso said, waiting for Sadal to grab her hand just as she imagined in her head. For Deeso, everything she did to get Sadal back was out of obligation and love for her sister. She felt honor-bound to do so, and for the answers to burning questions she could never find out otherwise.

"You what? How did you find me?" Sadal said, as her tone held both a sense of urgency and utter curiosity.

"I ran into the Forest Seeker leader known as Eshe. We made contact and after some negotiations, we came to an agreement. I followed her instructions and here we are."

Deeso said, satisfied with her planning that yielded the success she desperately craved. Sadal spat at the ground at the thought of Eshe and her internment. If it'd been better days, she would've brought the enemy to heel and her head as a trophy for Ronkalk.

"I can't do this in good faith. I've bloodied myself again and revoked our oath. The Broken Bone is not a life I live anymore. I respect and adhere to the warrior code, but there is nothing left for me." Sadal said as she revealed her left hand to Deeso. Deeso covered her mouth in shock, she felt a shake come upon her as her skin grew cold despite the heat of the day. Deeso attempted to make sense of it all, but she felt sick instead.

"Someone forced you to do this. I don't know what lesser people you find yourself with now, but we are your family. Sadal. I want you to come home. Please." Deeso said, her voice in clear denial as she grew more upset at Sadal's actions.

Sadal saw that there was still an opportunity for the two to see eye to eye. Sadal reasoned that if Deeso could see that her life was changed for the better with a new purpose, her sister would understand at least. Sadal's hopes in the meteor correlated with Jih's excitement as they got closer to their goal. She hoped that if this meteor truly possessed powerful abilities, she could use it to augment herself with immense power that could bring victory against any foe. The tiger humbled her approach and she needed to find a new source of strength to achieve her full sense of self.

"I know this may come as a surprise to you, but I'm on a journey to find the meteor in the sky. You remember that night when everyone looked above and saw the sky alight? This will fix everything Deeso. You must understand why I'm doing this. I want you to help me, I really do. You can come with me instead and leave them behind." Sadal offered with a grin to Deeso whose expression vanished as she heard Sadal's reasoning.

Sadal knew historically that Deeso was skeptical about the affairs of the spiritual realm, but she hadn't expected such a response to come from her. Deeso was quiet and walked over to Sadal and gave her a tight hug. Sadal patted her back as she felt Deeso's movement and thought Deeso was crying as she rubbed her back. Deeso's tone though was far different. Deeso was laughing at Sadal's reasoning for her new purpose in life.

"So-So you leave everything behind, people who depended on you, to starve, for a rock? A rock that you have no idea where it is and-you want to tell me that this is more important than the nine years we've spent together?" Deeso said with a laugh.

She felt it through her core as she looked towards the ground and rose to see Sadal's face turn to a scowl. Deeso reached over to grab Sadal by the hand, but she was met with Sadal slapping it away with force. Deeso was bewildered, she hadn't ever seen Sadal like this before.

"If you want to really help me Deeso, tell Ronkalk and everyone else I'm dead. You won't come with me, so this is where we part ways. I can't come back; this is the only way forward. I deserted in more ways than one." Sadal said as she folded her arms.

Deeso's laugh now was more of a nervous tic than actual humor of the situation, but Sadal didn't see it that way. As Deeso went to grab Sadal one more time, she used both hands to push Deeso away from her. Deeso was pushed with enough force that she found herself on the ground, stunned at Sadal's reaction. Sadal looked over at her with disappointment as she packed her remaining stuff away. Deeso sat on the ground, her eyes empty as she saw Sadal's figure storm off in the distance until she was no longer visible. Sadal was so angry she didn't bother taking meat with her. Deeso pocketed the rest as she played the situation over again in her mind. She knelt to the ground and pounded the soil with her fists as once again, the spirits she loathed so much interfered in her life again to make her miserable.

Sometime later, Deeso returned silently with a bounty of meat to Zulag, Cikya and Ozul. Zulag was busy running a knife in the spaces between his fingers while Ozul watched with mild curiosity. Cikya was repairing clothing as the frame of Deeso with a full pack and goods in her arms showed in the distance. The three were quite happy but gave her a look as they saw Deeso was visibly upset in a way they've never seen. Deeso dumped the meat on the ground and sat down, watching the three dig in like ravenous dholes.

"What happened to you?" Zulag asked, as he took a bite of the cooked boar meat.

"I found Sadal." Deeso said, while the other three looked at each other in confusion. Zulag chewed his food and swallowed quickly. Ozul looked around the vicinity of their camp, he hadn't found any sign of another settlement in his time foraging after Deeso left.

"And where is she? I don't see her bound in rope or here with you." Zulag replied as he tried to make sense of Deeso's announcement.

"I let her go. I'm going to sleep now." Deeso replied to Zulag, but her eyes were still poised on the soil below.

"You what!? Deeso, you can't be serious right now! This is our chance." Zulag yelled as Deeso remained unmoved by his anger. Any feeling Deeso had was long gone now, and only a husk of a woman remained.

"Deeso...Are you sure you want to sleep?" Ozul asked as he received a pat on the back from Cikya to keep quiet.

It was clear that Deeso sleeping would be best for the group. She plopped her head on the ground quietly and turned her body away from the others. Once Deeso's still body turned to sleep, Cikya who was still awake looked over at a few furs that remained. She folded them gently as well as she could into a square and lifted Deeso's sleeping head so that it could rest with comfort. A good night's sleep was needed, as for tomorrow the real work would begin.

Just Checking In

The fight Sadal had with Deeso was heavier on her mind than she expected. She spoke a great deal about her sister to the others, and how proud she was of her, but there was an emptiness inside her that took root as she weighed her response in her mind. Sadal looked behind her and saw the determined face of Jih as they ran in unison tracking the call for antelope on the plains. Sadal originally wanted Narro, but Jih volunteered instead. Jih was looking for an excuse to spend some time with Sadal as he was concerned about her behavior recently. While Narro and Trekkal seemed oblivious, or at least, not willing to engage with the matter, Jih was a different story.

Sadal was determined to find something to bring home as Jih accompanied her for a routine hunt for antelopes. They traveled for about an hour and marked specific trees to keep track as the hunt grew to a close. Sadal ran quickly where Jih met her speed as she watched for the animal's movement. The antelope made a small yelping sound as it sighted Sadal's increased pace. It was slower than most, being an old male but still had some life left in it. She jumped up and launched her arm forward. Her eyes tracked the arc of her weapon as she saw the shadow of the spear converge with the antelope. She hoped her spear would land a direct hit, but it missed entirely. Jih yelled to scare the creature as he maneuvered a further distance for it to approach Sadal once again. Jih looked with hope that Sadal could bring the kill home but was slightly disappointed at the outcome. Sadal missed twice on what any other day would have been a clean shot to the side. With the amount of practice they all did, killing antelope were second nature to the group. In a silent rage, she tore apart one of her throwing spears by the handle and stewed in anger. How could a simple herbivore make such a mockery of her? Her thoughts of Deeso clouded her mind once more.

"The wind mocks me as well!" Sadal yelled to Jih in the distance who turned his head to her statement.

Jih nearly fell to the ground as he slid on some loose mud. He grabbed the handle of his spear and lifted his foot to scrape off some mud. He let out a sigh of relief as he turned to Sadal. Sadal gave no reaction as she was consumed with her own thoughts. He raised an eyebrow in suspicion towards her. Jih noticed Sadal was erratic for a couple days now, and she wasn't one to make mistakes like that often. He assumed it was a fluke, but his expression changed somewhat as he saw Sadal unusually bothered.

I pushed her. I thought I pushed her on the ground, but I just pushed her away entirely. She laughed at me. Sadal thought as she looked in the distance.

Sadal's eyes were strangely fixed on a termite mound. She watched the movement of the termites until she felt the hand of Jih on her shoulder. Jih looked into Sadal's eyes and saw that all was not well. Jih decided it was best to call the hunt early and focus on rest instead.

"Sadal. We should head to camp." Jih said as he pointed behind them.

"Jih, we didn't capture anything. I never return empty-handed. My honor won't allow it." Sadal commented with some annoyance in her voice. Jih shrugged his shoulders at her comment. The antelope lived to see another day now that their talking separated them far from it.

"We have smoked Peymin. There is enough for two days. Rest." Jih countered back in a parental voice that echoed Hizo.

The two walked a short distance until Jih veered off the path and found the shade of a large fig tree. He wanted a reprieve from the sun and decided to fold his legs and sit down. Jih looked at her deeply and held his head up on the palm of his hand.

"Sadal. What is happening?" Jih asked. He'd seen Sadal plenty angry before, but never enough to destroy her own weapons. Jih was proud of his stone tool work, but Sadal took her weapons with the utmost pride as well.

"I've had a lot on my mind recently. I met with Deeso some time ago." Sadal said as she saw Jih's eyes look at her broken throwing spear. Jih tried to recall when he last heard of Deeso, and he remembered that there was a time where Sadal left the group without telling anyone. Jih assumed this is what she was referring to.

"Deeso. This name is familiar to Jih, sister of Sadal! Yes, Jih remembers this. Is this not good?" Jih asked as he gave her an opening to speak.

Sadal paused and chose her words carefully. She didn't want to cause any alarm to Jih or the others about what transpired, and she wanted to keep the origin of her first travels as tightly under wraps as possible. She feared being cast away and having to start over once more. Sadal felt that by helping Jih find the meteor, she could also clear her conscience and find a new path from the life she left behind.

"Well, we talked about many things. She wanted me to come home with her. I said it was better for me to help you instead. I believe in your cause for the meteor. She wasn't happy with me, and we ended up yelling at one another." Sadal said as a short synopsis of their argument.

"I didn't tell her when I left home, and she was quite angry about that." Sadal added with a slightly concerned laugh that Jih matched. Sadal's eyes averted Jih's gaze as she did so.

"Do not blame yourself, she acts with passion. Deeso may be mad now, but she understands Sadal. Power rock is very important." Jih answered Sadal as he considered her words.

Jih hadn't thought about it at first, but something started to generate in his head. He and Sadal traveled far from when they started, with months now behind them. If Deeso was truly Sadal's sister and the two happened to run into each other, how could that happen? He remembered Sadal was alone when they first interacted with each other, and then their time with Eshe, as they were hidden away from the world. He went practically everywhere with Sadal when they were first together. He recalled not hearing a word about the two interact before until today.

"Deeso is mighty warrior to brave journey alone. Braver than Chak! We have traveled a great deal." Jih mentioned as he gauged Sadal's reaction.

"Who?" Sadal said, as she scratched her head.

"Someone Jih knew long ago. Deeso can teach Jih many things. After all, she knew where to find Sadal." Jih said, his tone more evident that he knew something was up.

Jih knows Sadal is hiding something, but what is it? There are things that make no sense. Deeso is younger than Sadal and not as mighty, but braved rivers and jungle all her own? There must be more here. Jih thought.

Sadal panicked slightly as she could see through Jih's words. Jih's sympathy slowly turned into skepticism as he thought about the circumstances possible for this to happen. There had to have been a conscious effort by Deeso to find Sadal's whereabouts. He remembered her tales on how the two hunted together as one, but now it would seem that Sadal was their prey. Jih didn't think anything malicious from Deeso would occur though. She was just a lost woman looking for her sister, he would do the same thing for Kag. What intrigued Jih more was what made Sadal leave The Broken Bone to begin with. Why did she need to leave home without telling anyone? Jih was open about his shunning and the politics that ensued by Tur to do so with her. Her privacy was her own and Jih wouldn't pry, but there were questions brewing in his mind.

"Sadal. If you are upset, tell Jih. Jih has lived long and can give help. Narro will tell you what you want to hear. Jih says what you have to hear." Jih teased Sadal with a small grin as Sadal matched his as well. Jih kept his cool regarding Narro and Sadal but was secretly a glutton for gossip as he heard bits and pieces of the other as he worked with them.

"We have rested enough, we should go. Trekkal probably left food cold again." Jih grumbled as he got up and extended his hand to Sadal.

Jih helped her up with his hand and kept his grin. In the back of his mind though, Jih had a much different perspective on Sadal. He valued their friendship more than anything, she was his first traveling companion, but he seemed slightly hurt as well. Jih knew that Sadal wasn't giving him the entire truth about Deeso, but it was enough for now.

That was too close. Sadal thought as the two walked back to camp. Sadal felt that this wouldn't be the last time she would come to see Deeso. Although Sadal was quite forceful with her, she felt that she had the opposite effect of what she wanted. Rather than convince Deeso to let her go free and do as she asked, she instead pushed her further. Deeso was born with a tenacity that few could match. Her drive to get anything done, especially when powered by spite, was a powerful motivator. Sadal felt that by disrespecting her in such a way she now made not only her, but the rest of her group a target. From her perspective, Deeso and her group traveled for months looking for any sign of her. They must have left a wake of destruction in their path as Deeso thought she was hurt and in danger. Sadal needed to take precautions while attempting to figure out how to resolve her emotions.

Sadal and Jih returned to camp with the happy eyes of Narro and Trekkal looking at them. Jih appreciated their usual optimism that served to balance he and Sadal's somber outlook on occasion. Sadal volunteered to take watch as the other three looked at her. Jih raised an eyebrow at Sadal's gesture as she decided to completely ignore what he said earlier.

"Sadal, Jih said to rest. Let Trekkal do watch, she has been waiting." Jih said with a mocking tone as he turned to see Trekkal grumble.

"Now hold on Jih, if she wants to do my part, why not? The watch is getting done either way." Trekkal said with a smug grin on her face.

"That is not fair Trekkal. We have talked about this already, taking watch is important and you being lazy is not an excuse." Narro reprimanded her.

"Oh, always here to save Sadal in her time of need. Can you not just let me relax and sleep? The Denmey have kept us up all night you know." Trekkal replied with scathing resentment in her voice.

"What does that have to do with anything?!" Sadal shot back to Trekkal as the two glared at one another. The tense space made between Jih and Sadal already crumbled now that Trekkal added to the mix with her antics.

"If all of us have been awakened by the Denmey, that excuse also falls short. Can you believe yourself? Jih-" Narro said as he was taken aback by a large sigh from Jih.

Jih and Hyu never wanted children but in the blink of an eye, Jih now had three to take care of. Though all of them were in their early 20s, Jih saw no difference in how they bickered from the children back in Sundaland. After some bickering among the four of them, Jih relented and let Sadal take watch as she wanted. As he looked through his bag, he kept his eye on her and studied her closely. With the waning hours of the sun towards them, Jih asked Sadal one last time if she wanted to take watch again. She nodded in agreement and Jih took to his tent to sleep. He peeked through the flap of his tent and watched Sadal again. She withdrew tree branches from her bag and spread them throughout their camp. Jih remembered when camping with Sadal the first time in the jungle, she used the same method to keep them informed if anyone hostile was present. Branches were hard to come by in the plains, but she made do with the small amount. Though the two struggled to communicate early on, Jih now wondered if those branches weren't for enemy Forest Seekers, but instead to alert her to someone tracking her down.

Sadal felt relieved at the sounds of snores from her friends. She looked up at the night sky and saw a few stars while the campfire continued. She looked for streaks in the sky to check for direction. Narro taught her some of the basics of astrological navigation that he and Trekkal relied on to stay the course. Sadal took a deep breath as she dragged her finger in the darkness. She didn't want to hide who she was, and what happened, but she felt it was better this way. She needed to think about the possibility of seeing Deeso again on less than friendly terms. It wasn't an inviting proposal that came to mind.

"I'm sorry everyone. We just need to cover more ground tomorrow." Sadal said to herself.

A Hard Truth

Cikya and Deeso didn't hunt together often, but when they chose to do so, it was always worth mentioning. After a streak of successful hunts, the two watched with glee as Ozul and Zulag were hunched over with their tools. The pair were on skinning duty for some time, so Deeso and Cikya looked for ways to relieve their boredom. Ozul and Zulag worked to try and rip some skin off the bones. Ozul never worked as hard as he did with Zulag, who took any sign of slacking personally. Deeso was content to nap in the sun, but Cikya had a burning desire to do some walking and explore outside of hunting. She grew anxious as she saw others taking the day in stride. She noticed the movement of people convening in sections of the grasslands heading towards something of interest. Cikya had her eye on a Thunderfeet settlement for some time and wondered what the news was in this area. Cikya gently nudged Deeso's leg with her foot.

Deeso opened her groggy eyes and looked to see Cikya made a sign with her hands. Deeso recognized this as a clear cry for help and decided to take pity on Cikya. Deeso knew that Cikya felt restless as it'd been some time since she really got to do anything fun. Deeso looked at her alternatives to spending the day with Cikya, which mostly consisted of watching Zulag and Ozul work. Deeso emptied what remained of her pack, except for her trusty axe and a few dried pieces of meat they saved from yesterday.

"Cikya and I are going to go forage. Any requests?" Deeso asked as she equipped her backpack and prompted Cikya to do the same.

Deeso's call was unanswered by the industrious Ozul whose arms were practically blood red from handling the various animals they managed to capture. Out of the terrain of the forest, Ozul wasn't nearly as protective of the wildlife that existed and hunted with more vigor than seen before.

"Zulag, I need another. This skin is done. We will build a rack later." Ozul said, as he extended his arm out for the next small animal for him to rip apart. Deeso stood a bit longer as she turned her head to Zulag, who also seemed busy.

"Huh? Oh, you're serious? If there's any Salimpu[57], bring some back. The sun is harsh on my skin." Zulag said as he concentrated on sharpening one of his knives to make a cleaner cut.

Cikya looked at the pile of skins that Ozul lorded over and took two dry ones for trading. Although their initial plan was to turn these into clothing, Cikya wondered if they could be used for extra material instead. Without much delay, the two were off. Cikya seemed quite excited to travel as she bounced around Deeso. Deeso and Cikya enjoyed a low maintenance friendship as the two held mutual respect but on the surface seemed to have little in common. Deeso was one of the few people who respected her on her own merits, despite her objections to the priesthood. Despite being the oldest, Cikya found

---

[57] Emic word for Centella otherwise called Indian pennywort.

Deeso to be easily the most mature of the group and often put much of her trust in her actions. She was impressed enough by her negotiations with Eshe to find Sadal. Deeso normally enjoyed the silence, but her own thoughts plagued her sometimes. Her travels with Zulag made it so that she always had to address whatever came to mind, but not so much here. Cikya clapped her hands twice and gathered Deeso's attention as she turned her head.

"Yes Cikya? What is it?" Deeso asked with some slight confusion.

Cikya imitated the fast flow of water as she gestured to her mouth. She reached into her backpack showing her canteen which was empty. Deeso snapped her finger in thought as she remembered she came across a stream at some point further on the way.

Deeso and Cikya walked with no clear aims in mind although they made a promise to the others to forage. Nothing seemed particularly appealing for the two to grab. After an hour and a half venture from their initial walk however, their fortune changed. Cikya reminded Deeso of the village she scouted earlier and gathered the outline of people in the distance that belonged there. The river that Deeso remembered was populated as she saw a group of women close by the waterline. They appeared to be weaving baskets from reeds and wore strange clothing not seen previously by either of them. Deeso took a moment to narrow her eyes as she needed to discern if they were her kind or Forest Seekers. On a second glance, it was clear that they ran into fellow Thunderfeet. The two continued to walk and Deeso shot a look at Cikya who appeared content with the presence of these people. She offered a wave that was returned in the distance. A few of them carried clubs that they used to defend against raids on their lands. On Cikya's insistence, the two approached and made contact.

"It's good to see others of our kind here. We thought you were Forest Seekers at first." Deeso said and introduced herself as Cikya also greeted them.

Deeso raised an eyebrow as she saw the woman before them looked somewhat distant. From their perspective, both Deeso and Cikya carried weapons in their pack, so they weren't a threat. Deeso assessed there was another reason why they were guarded. Deeso was astute and reasoned there was some sort of social violation she and Cikya made. For Deeso, this was one of the most irritating prospects of visiting established villages and preferred the smaller company of distant working camps.

"Outsiders come to our stream and the first thing they want to do is take our water. We have always weaved here. If you want to use it, you'll need one of these." The woman mentioned pointing to her wrist. She and the others clinked their bracelets in a warning. Deeso gave Cikya a look as she was interrupted. She was confused about what this meant.

"This entire river is in your band's territory? It seems a bit difficult to keep safe given the size." Deeso questioned with skepticism in her voice. Deeso was willing to talk things over, but she was already not a fan of their introduction.

Is this what they consider fashion? Cikya thought as she noticed their ostrich eggshell bracelets[58]. She nudged Deeso and pointed with an unimpressed look. Deeso wasn't sure what to think about their dress, she mostly just threw on whatever was clean, but she knew Cikya had an opinion. Much like Sadal who made her own outfits from processed pelts, Cikya also had an eye for fashion. Her fixation on charms for her craft and personal expression made her a harsh critic as she thought of the inconsistency of the armbands before her. Cikya knew she could do much better given the opportunity. Cikya noticed that a few of the women had small sections of their face and lips that were different colors. She waved her fingers to one of the other women in preparation for a magic spell. Deeso gave a small nod as her attention turned to one of the women holding a club in her hands.

"My friend wants to know if you're in the priesthood. The markings on your face show such things. We have something like this back at our original camp. I imagine you are too busy guarding your precious stream to be involved with such things though." Deeso said with immense sarcasm dripping from her voice.

One of the women in the group placed her club down and walked up to Cikya. She reached over to touch her hair and the crown of bones that sat on top of her head. Cikya reflexively slapped her hand away with a scowl on her face. It remained important that the crown never leave Cikya's head as it was her chance at redemption. Her slap didn't help things as the others were dubious about the onlookers. Deeso eyed the others and looked for any sudden moves as she instinctively stepped closer to Cikya. The affected woman retreated slightly as her attention turned to someone else.

"Our bracelets come from the birds that tear Kalpeu apart with their toes. The egg is large and powerful. It's a rite of passage among our people to carry them. Outsiders try to reproduce them but only end up dead. Which will you be?" Another woman questioned as she looked over the two.

"We are running low. Perhaps if you can acquire an egg of such a creature, we will make you the bracelets so that you can use our stream and the goods it-." She added on before turning her head. Cikya looked at the water and saw some bubbling. She nudged Deeso and they decided to move further inland.

"You know...You are right. We are but humble visitors to your precious river. Enjoy the Vatmaraku that's about to surface." Deeso smugly commented.

As if she willed it herself, one of the crocodiles hoisted itself on land, and prompted the others to retreat briefly. The animal opened its mouth and let out a large splash as it rolled in the mud. The creature slinked back into the water without a second thought, only to remind those who truly owned the river and its resources. Deeso saw this as an opportunity to leave the somewhat irritating ostrich bracelet women, but Cikya wanted an adventure. The others followed Deeso's and Cikya's lead to go further inland as they

---

[58] Ostriches may be surprising at first, but these birds were found throughout Eurasia thousands of years ago. Their tough eggshells are the perfect material to make beads from, and said beads make beautiful jewelry and other crafts!

discussed more of the terms. Deeso remembered Zulag's request and figured it could be possible to find things for herself as well with their network.

"Do you have things to trade in your home camp? Something worth our time other than hot air is welcome." Deeso questioned.

"Of course, I'm an expert weaver and we have some Yaan tusks that are freshly polished. Some of our men will be returning with plants gathered downstream, you're free to talk with them if you need those. If you have something, maybe we can talk. But you're not getting anywhere without one of these." She commented as she jostled her wrist.

Cikya nudged Deeso to agree to the terms that they stated. A bird compared to the other dangerous game they usually encountered seemed trivial by comparison. How hard could hunting an ostrich's egg be?

I can't believe I'm doing this. Deeso thought as she grabbed the attention of the women who were still looking at the crocodile.

"We accept your terms. The nests will not be far away if they are as common for all of you to wear. Will you be at this river again in a few hours?" Deeso questioned.

The woman who offered such terms nodded smugly and knew that the call of the ostrich was powerful. With the crocodile back in the river and unbothered, a few returned to their positions. Cikya saw another scoop up clay and patted it with their hands to apply on their faces. In this band, the use of clay as a cosmetic was common for both sexes. The river was a constant supply, and the distribution of clay was often placed along the face and lips in random patterns that fit the wearer.

It hadn't occurred to Deeso as she walked with Cikya in tow, but the pair had no idea how to fight an ostrich. Deeso was aware of ostriches from stories and her observation on the plains, but if a lion struggled against them, how would she fare? Cikya shared the same perplexed look as Deeso as she ran through a few scenarios in her mind, with all of them involving the dangerous talons. Finding the adult birds was easy enough, but looking for their nests was going to be a harder quest. Deeso reasoned they would need to be stealthy and not make any sudden movements. Cikya looked to the sky and saw tufts of smoke that indicated the way back to the previous camp once they achieved victory.

"These birds are strange for they don't fly. The Poulji is small and jumps in the air but this isn't one of those." Deeso said to herself as Cikya agreed with her statement.

They came upon a flock of ostriches that were clustered around some small grasses where a few nested while the others passively grazed. They needed to collect two eggs. Sadal and Narro previously had their hands full trying to deal with giant ostriches before, and while they succeeded, it wasn't easy. These ostriches were smaller but far more agile and yet remained just as dangerous. Deeso saw a perfect opportunity in some small grass to find a nest, but the neck of an ostrich arose and turned to stare at her. Cikya had her backpack poised to scoop the eggs of any unsuspecting bird, but it took time for Deeso to act. Deeso was a considerable distance from the mother ostrich that looked to defend itself valiantly. Deeso stepped forward as the ostrich stared at her. She felt slightly unnerved with its gaze unmoving. The bird remained completely still and Deeso wondered if such an animal could hold its breath.

Why are their eyes so large? Deeso thought as she knelt and picked up a stone.

Deeso threw a rock directly at the bird that caused it to rise and flap its wings. She was hoping to aim for the head and knock it out directly as she'd seen others attempt but failed miserably. It bolted straight for her with a surprising amount of speed as she started to run in a serpentine fashion. Deeso's eyes scanned the plains as she looked for any loose branches or rocks that would trip her as she ran. She felt the wind of the dust pile up as a backwind from the ostrich obscured Deeso's vision. Her eyes watered as she saw the amorphous blob of the ostrich approach her and let out a harsh call. The amount of space between the ostrich and her shrunk dramatically as she waved around to signal to Cikya to bag the eggs. With around ten eggs in the nest, Cikya could have her pick of the litter for her needs. Not far from Deeso, a wandering pack of hyenas were disturbed by the ostrich's call. The group snarled and ran out to defend their territory from the new invaders. Deeso's torment by the ostrich was saved by the pack that ran past her for a much more filling lunch. The ostrich decided that Deeso wasn't worth the effort as a few hyenas collided with the ostrich. Deeso turned back to see the animal kick one of the hyenas well into the air with its legs. Cikya salivated at the sight of the large eggs as she scanned the landscape for the mate of the ostrich and wondered when it would return. Cikya saw Deeso's expressions and moved quickly to scoop the eggs in her empty backpack. She was surprised by the weight as they were about three pounds each, but she managed to grab six. She took great care in making sure the eggs would be secured and waved to Deeso to point where she would be waiting.

I still hate Denmey, but this was helpful. She thought as she ran out of breath trying to catch up to Cikya.

All the effort was worth it as she saw a bright smile from Cikya's face when she withdrew an egg for Deeso to hold. Deeso weighed it in her hand as it felt solid. She instinctively dug her nail into it but found nothing would budge. She reasoned that the clubs the other women held were probably used to break the eggs into fragments that made up their bracelets. The two came back to a few moderately impressed faces, as Deeso placed two eggs carefully on the ground.

"We got six, but two should be enough for now, no?" Deeso asked as she backed away slowly.

Cikya tilted her head up and extended out her wrist and prompted Deeso to do the same as their part of the deal was through. The eggs were collected by another one of the women carrying a club and she smashed them to pieces of varying size. The process after collecting the eggs was simple, a sharpened rock or bone would be used to make a hole in the center of the pieces and rope was used to connect them. A knot was tied at the top to condense the pieces together, but an intricate design could take hours.

While Deeso and Cikya waited for their bracelets to be made, Ozul and Zulag remained back at camp. With the last of their skins just about finished, the two looked to rest. Although they made great efforts to keep themselves isolated, Ozul noticed a gradual movement of people across the plains over the time they've spent working.

"When do you think Deeso and Cikya will return?" Ozul asked Zulag as he wiped his hands on a spare skin. Ozul felt anxious as he vibrated with worry.

"Why does it matter to you? You're not having fun skinning? We've got one more to go and then we're good for today." Zulag scoffed as he heard Ozul's question.

"Well to be honest, no. It is very tedious but necessary. Have you noticed that there are people around? Some group has been lingering for a while. Should we be concerned?" Ozul asked with worry.

"I remember Cikya saying there was a settlement nearby, we shouldn't need to worry. They're probably just out hunting; not like we have anything else to do out here." Zulag asked as he stretched out on the grass.

Zulag fell asleep while Ozul worked silently on the last one. By now, Zulag was used to Ozul's background noise as he kept himself busy, but he was eerily quiet. As he woke up, his eyes widened as he saw a group of four men get closer to the borders of their camp. Ozul kept his lip tight as he stared at them and watched their movements. The group were armed with clubs and short throwing spears that stuck out of their backpacks. One of the men pointed in the direction of their camp and continued forward. Ozul noted their dress, the one who seemed to be the group's leader, wore a brown loincloth with leopard fur that draped over his shoulders. He came with followers that wore grass that suited the environment. Their hair sprawled out wide and natural as their faces donned red war paint. Ozul was uncomfortable as he saw their pace advance towards them. Zulag gave no reaction as he couldn't imagine anyone would attempt to come towards their camp. Ozul grabbed his blowgun while he looked to Zulag to see what to do. Zulag kept his cool as he could tell much of their display was for intimidation only. Zulag attempted to remain disinterested but was interrupted by the leader of the men who called out to them a short distance away. The man's voice carried over the distance as Zulag turned his head to address him and his followers.

"You have a lot of furs out there, are you traders?" The man asked with a deep voice.

"No, we just had a good season. I'd suggest you look elsewhere." Zulag replied.

"Oh, well I'm sure you have plenty to go around. Those pelts are a fresh hunt you say. Outsiders hunting in our lands isn't something we take kindly, so we'll take those." The man replied as they headed closer to their position.

The men in question weren't aligned with the settlement that Deeso and Cikya were in. They were simple raiders that took whatever they pleased. Zulag could tell from their demeanor alone that the man that addressed him only wore his status as a farce. A man to hunt a leopard doesn't just telegraph their attacks to the enemy. Zulag withdrew one of his knives and waited patiently for their opponents to reach him. Zulag turned his head in surprise as he saw Ozul was proactive and blew a dart that flew past one of the men. The group converged on Zulag and Ozul with increased speed as they let out a wild yell.

Zulag was on the offensive as he quickly dispatched one man with a knife thrown to the stomach. He used his shoulder to check him to the ground and the two fell with a harsh thud. Zulag withdrew the knife from the man's wound and subsequently stabbed him in the neck. Blood pooled to the ground as he prepared to rise and face the next challenger, the man with leopard fur. While Zulag was engaged in combat, one with a club headed to him from behind. Ozul was a target as valid as any and needed to react quickly as the last man headed towards him. He loaded his blowgun and felt sweat on his hands. Ozul had to defend himself, but if he failed, Zulag would be vulnerable. In the past, Ozul helped the others fight by keeping others from attacking, but it was clear he needed to kill these men. Ozul thought of his devotion to The Vow that he kept amid the forests with the utmost dedication.

The Stone Breakers told us to keep the forest safe from the blood of others. We have left the forest. I must act now. Ozul concluded.

Ozul took a deep breath and decided to strike back, as he blew his wooden dart to pierce the man's skin. The man used his arm to block the first dart but yelled in agony as he gritted his teeth through the pain. Ozul reasoned that to protect himself and the innocent past the forest, blood could be spilled by his hand. He quickly loaded another that landed with precision as he blew. Ozul saved his poison darts for animals and used his whittled wooden ones for combat to deter humans. The second dart went through the man's forehead that stuck in pain as the man attempted to dislodge them. Ozul took advantage of the man's stagger and grabbed one of Zulag's spare knives on the soil. He quickly moved to thrust the blade into the man's stomach. The smell of human blood and viscera was disgusting to the young boy, but he powered through and succeeded in defending Zulag. Zulag felt a strike from behind as he turned around to see him faced with the two men. Zulag dislocated the jaw of the leopard skin wearing man as he punched with a powerful jab. He used his legs to trip him and used his weight to keep him pressed on the ground. As he placed his hands on the man's throat, he saw Ozul slash the legs of the other attacker and watched as he bled out from a sliced artery. Zulag's attention was brought back to the man in question as he listened to the sound of his breath whittle away. Zulag looked at one of his discarded knives close by and quickly grabbed it. Without a second thought, he lodged the knife into the man's throat and stood up. The two were covered in blood, but safe for now. Zulag looked at Ozul as he picked up the man's leopard pelt as a prize for himself.

"Go clean yourself up. I'll take the bodies away from camp." Zulag said as Ozul nodded.

After some time, Deeso and Cikya were presented with completed bracelets put on their wrists. Deeso felt no sense of emotion towards it but looked back to see Cikya filled with glee. She put on a smile to ease her friend's concerns. The image of Cikya's happiness was enough to give Deeso some relief from the tension on her mind.

"Showing these will mark you as an ally in our land. We were about to get more clay if you want some." One of the women said, as her tone changed to be far warmer.

Deeso and Cikya watched as some scooped the clay into baskets and packed it together into clumps. Strips of clay were cut with stone knives and wetted with water as it was rubbed into the face and upper body. Cikya missed her priestess face paint and had an idea as her eyes drifted from Deeso to the clay. Cikya gave a mischievous smile as she leaned over towards the riverbank and scooped up some clay.

"No-I-Cikya..." Deeso said as she saw Cikya gesture towards a pile of clay in her hand that made a squish sound as she moved it around. Cikya already decorated her face in small circles and under her eyes. Deeso sighed as the last thing she wanted to do was adorn herself with clay. It wasn't for a terrible reason; mud was difficult to get out of her hair, but Cikya was mindful and applied the clay onto Deeso's cheeks and chin.

Deeso peered into the reflection of the water as Cikya's head appeared behind her own. She placed her head on Deeso's shoulder briefly as the two looked at the water. Cikya knew she wasn't a substitute for the void Deeso felt with Sadal but their age gap of almost six years was something she considered to be important. Cikya considered Deeso to be a surrogate sister and would do what she could to keep spirits high during their adventure. For Cikya, the road to redemption held many paths but suffering for its own sake was a terrible way to live. She knew that she could have fun along the way and felt she deserved it. Their concentration was broken by some interesting conversation that went on. Cikya was a gossip regardless of if she could orate or not and was primed to listen in while Deeso had her eyes on an insect crawling along the ground.

"Can you believe what happened? This is only rumor from my brother, but there is reason to believe that our allied daughter rejected the offer made by the ones to the west. We have been trading partners for some time now and this will hurt relations." One of the women packing clay together with her fist spoke to the rest of the group.

Deeso's ears perked as she listened into the various bits and pieces of information that came their way. She was hoping to find some semblance of Sadal out of their words and to see if she or her companions underwent the same challenge. Most of the information at hand was useless to her, but she was intrigued by a line of discussion between two people.

"We really needed that stone, as our hotspark is low quality. What was the problem? Were the eggshells not large enough?"

"Far worse than that I'm afraid. A no show to the feast held. No, they had to say she fell in battle against the bird to save face! In reality, it seems she ran to the arms of the Forest Seekers."

Cikya's face contorted a bit as she heard this piece of information. Deeso noticed her reaction and narrowed her eyes at Cikya and knew something was amiss. After some time spent drinking water to recover, Cikya checked on the remaining eggs that were still quite hardy. No doubt they'd make a tasty meal after a long day. The two walked for some time with some glee on their face but something seemed to stay on Deeso's mind. She knew Cikya was hiding something and hoped to address it quickly.

"Cikya. Can we talk about something?" Deeso asked as Cikya nodded.

"It's about Zulag. We talk sometimes out on the hunt." Deeso said as she adjusted her backpack. Cikya stopped short and raised her eyebrows in faux surprise. Cikya had her own theories regarding the two for some time now that she kept in the back of her mind. She rubbed her hands together, and anticipated some important information, but she wasn't prepared for what came next.

"He talked about some of what living here was like for you both. He also mentioned that you've been avoiding him for some reason. Did something happen between you two? I remember that after we were at Krukzig's encampment you barely looked at him for a few days. It's not that I care, but if our team is going to be resolute in the search for Sadal, I want no problems. Problems aren't good for us. You understand this right, Cikya?" Deeso mentioned.

Cikya's expression spoke for her as she wore heavy guilt on her face. When the group made its way to the plains, Cikya and Zulag did spend time together, but in much lesser amounts. This region was one of The Broken Bone's ancestral homelands, this is where Ronkalk and Aralic spent a good deal of their lives. Zulag and Cikya were also born here a long time ago. Zulag recognized that this place was the foundation of their band and was reminded of memories carried by their people. While Zulag felt pride, Cikya was reminded constantly of the secret she kept from Zulag and the others as she was a scholar of the oral histories of their people. It was one of the many duties Cikya had in the priesthood, but what good was remembering an oral history now when you couldn't speak? The connection was hard to gather at first for Deeso, but she and Ozul managed to find it had to do with the true fate of Zulag's father. Cikya always attempted to divert the topic to something else. Deeso and everyone else was told he died in battle, but the circumstances surrounding it loosened quickly when the details were examined.

"Ronkalk said we have to be honest with ourselves first." Deeso added on, as she saw Cikya's face.

Cikya nodded but snorted some air out of her nose as she saw the irony in such words. She debated with herself as she slapped her head in stress. She emoted with her hands to Deeso who was trying to figure out what was happening. Deeso resisted the urge to touch her face as the clay was still hardening. Deeso was familiar with the story given to her, but Cikya struggled to sign the rest of the story to Deeso. She powered through and revealed the truth. Deeso stood quietly as she studied Cikya's face to see what she regretted and what she understood. Deeso's conversations with Cikya rarely focused on the deep intricacies of what she valued, and this was an eye-opening experience for her. There was a sense of relief on her face after mentioning the details to Deeso who could only stand by as she thought about everything that happened. Cikya shrugged her shoulders at the end of her tale while Deeso looked concerned.

"So, Zulag's father left when he was born. We have no idea why, and Ronkalk took on the responsibility to raise Zulag after his mother passed. Did I get this right? Ronkalk also told you to keep this a secret?" Deeso asked, while Cikya's slow nod confirmed the words. Deeso was mortified, as this was a real scandal on their hands. Sadal's leaving of

The Broken Bone was controversial enough, but at least her desertion was common knowledge.

"So that grave then somewhere? Oh..." Deeso said to herself.

Cikya made a sign where she brought her hands together and kicked up dust and indicated that it was a story conjured from the soil. From what Cikya could understand, Ronkalk didn't want the story of shame to befall Zulag as he ascended to leadership as he already faced the battle of his skin condition with other things. Ronkalk also felt personally hurt by the dismissal and decided it would be best to establish that Aralic died with honor and could be remembered fondly as someone in better years. This didn't stop Ronkalk from sending the occasional scout to find a man with a similar build to what he described.

"We need to tell him the truth." Deeso stated while Cikya immediately nodded her head in disagreement.

The two remained in intense discussion with one another as Deeso's voice picked up over the field. Ozul jumped up and down to signal that they were near camp. Ozul and Zulag saw their new attire and weren't sure what to think, it was certainly new. Deeso ordered Cikya to get things started while she took care of the ostrich eggs.

"Cikya has something to tell us. Right, Cikya?" Deeso nudged her in the back while Cikya tucked in her lip.

Cikya took a deep breath that Zulag raised an eyebrow at as he sat with his legs folded at the campfire. Ozul's eyes looked as large as his stomach as Deeso took out one of the captured eggs.

"Well, what is it? Is it about your clay? It looks nice, you even got Deeso to match with you." Zulag asked as he looked at her face.

Zulag could see that she had a sad expression on her face and felt something must have gotten her upset. He shot a quick glare at Deeso, but his tone changed as he noticed her look matched to Cikya. Cikya shook with fear as she grabbed Zulag's attention. Ozul stared at Cikya, and she couldn't help but turn away briefly before settling herself in for the emotional rush to do it once more. She gathered Zulag's attention with a sniff from her nose and lifted her hands. She depicted the land's importance to their people and specifically the connection that Ronkalk and his father shared. Deeso looked at Zulag and could only feel terrible as his face contorted in thought. Past grievances aside, she knew very well how harmful deception could be as well as anyone. She extended her hand out and prompted Deeso to explain anything left unanswered.

"Zulag. Cikya acted on orders from Ronkalk to do this. Please..." Deeso said, her voice losing volume. She and Ozul could watch now that the truth was finally revealed.

"I thought you were family! How could you agree to this? How long did you know? How long?" Zulag yelled as he drowned out Deeso's pleads. Zulag lost all feeling in his legs as he felt tired.

Cikya recoiled in horror as she felt her body tense up at Zulag's rage. She'd always known his anger as an inseparable part of his personality, but this anger and wrath was placed on her and her willingness to agree to keep the lie for so long. As his teacher, she felt shame behind her decision, but was too far in to change course. She opened her eyes and regretted that decision as past the teary red eyes of Zulag facing her, she could only see the visage of Ronkalk appear as an apparition in his place. The memory of the knife hitting her throat caused her to hyperventilate. Deeso was frozen in concern as she wasn't sure how to react. It was apparent to Deeso and Ozul that Cikya never really got over the circumstances of her injury, she only knew how to hide it away for so long. Cikya felt a heavy weight come over her as Zulag's words ran through her mind. She attempted to ground herself as she felt a ringing sound in her ears.

Zulag witnessed Cikya form into a ball, and his rage subsided as he threw a rock in the distance while the watchful eye of Deeso remained fixated on him. He knew he couldn't blame her ultimately, for the sin fell to his uncle. Cikya was only given this knowledge when she agreed to be Zulag's mentor, if it wasn't to be, Ronkalk would have died with it. He just didn't understand the purpose of his uncle's interference in something so important. A lot of decisions made by Ronkalk he didn't understand. Some were virtuous and good for the order, but this Zulag felt was targeted and personal. His day hadn't gone that well to begin with after they left. Zulag found it difficult to find suitable stone to replace his now broken knives from hours of skinning and from fighting off raiders. Cikya's sobbing was the only source of sound. Ozul occasionally looked at Zulag only to meet an annoyed glare in which he turned away, his back to the campfire and plains.

"What do you want?" Zulag said to Ozul. Ozul had little to say on the customs of the Thunderfeet surrounding him but was aware these are things they valued. Ozul gave Zulag a harsh look but understood his pain. As Ozul watched his father die in front of him, he could only imagine Zulag's mourning process and the veneration of his legacy through a bunk story. With this gone, the questions of his abandonment and all else could potentially consume him alive. Ozul kept watch and waited for the others to sleep before he inched over to Cikya, who was still awake.

"Oh. This is for you." Ozul said as he tapped Cikya's shoulder. She looked at his hands and gently opened them to see a wooden whistle. Her eyes went from the whistle back to Ozul and she grasped it gently. It came with a string attached woven from plant fibers that could hang around her neck with a tied knot.

"When you need one of us, blow this and we will come. I know things are hard right now, but they will get better." Ozul explained with his quiet voice over the low fire. Cikya nodded happily and gave Ozul a tight hug for some time before she attempted to fall asleep.

The Gift

Zulag woke up the next morning and surveyed the camp as he noticed stillness in the air. His eyes were dry after the tension of yesterday's conversation filled the team with dread, but the morning subdued them for now. Deeso was missing while Ozul and Cikya remained. Zulag stretched and found a small bundle at his feet. This bundle was wrapped in some spare deer skin and a slight scraping sound was heard as he reached over and steadily unwrapped it. The bundle was a carved set of six throwing knives that were extensively well crafted. He looked first at the handles and examined them more closely. The handles were bone rather than wood which gave them a more definitive arc as he weighed them in his hands. In the jungles, wood was incredibly common and mostly lightweight. Bone was a far more reliable choice when it came to his needs. As bone was denser, he would have to compensate for the trajectory change but, they will reach their destination regardless of wind. Bone use was much more common in the plains for Thunderfeet and allowed all aspects of the corpse to be used after hunting. The blades themselves were also symmetrical, a detail that Zulag highly appreciated.

These are good. I would have added a curve to the handle instead of keeping them straight, but these will do. Zulag thought as he studied the collection once more.

Zulag pondered the origin of such a gift and looked to see where Cikya was slumped over. Cikya didn't sleep as the stress of yesterday's events affected her heavily. Her eyes, much like Ozul's, had bags under them and while the adrenaline of her fright vanished, she wasn't her usual perky self. Cikya stayed withdrawn and drew little attention to herself. Ozul tried to reassure her, but she ignored him. Zulag looked at his gift and made his way to Cikya who was still curled in a ball. He loomed over her and tapped her gently, where she shifted and stood up. Her eyes remained red from her extensive crying the night before. She shook with a rush of anxiety over her that magnified as she heard Zulag's voice.

"I didn't mean to scare you. Thank you for this gift Cikya. I'm sorry, yesterday was a lot." Zulag said, as he opened his arms for a hug that she took happily.

Cikya gave him a small rub on the back as she did so. While Cikya was happy to see that Zulag was no longer angry at her for her deception, she couldn't help but look confused. She peered past Zulag to see an open collection of knives. She was unsure how they got there as she was preoccupied with her own thoughts the previous night. He noticed Cikya's confusion on her face and correctly reasoned she wasn't the one behind such a thing. His attention shifted to Ozul.

Ozul slumped to the side of his bed after keeping watch. He played with one of the wooden figures he enjoyed crafting. This one was of a dhole, with the paws packed tightly together and the ears slumped over. Ozul made it originally from a horizontal block of wood that he cut.

"Ozul. Did you make these?" Zulag asked with some skepticism in his voice. Although Ozul made tools for the others often as part of his responsibilities, Zulag had almost never seen him work with stone in any capacity.

Ozul shifted positions in bed to turn his head and face Zulag. Ozul nodded no as he had little experience with lithics. He knew Zulag's impulsive nature, and while Ozul tried to be coy, it was better to just tell him right away.

"Deeso worked all night on them. I found some of the bones though when I went foraging when you took a nap before." He said as he looked in his backpack to find a snack. His pack held some berries from yesterday that would make a good breakfast. He placed a few in his hand and walked over to Cikya who stuffed the berries in her mouth and ate them quickly. Her mouth oozed some red as she wiped it away with her hand, much to Ozul's joy. Ozul tucked his lip in as he saw Zulag's face grow angrier. He knew it was futile to stop him once he got annoyed so Ozul sighed as Zulag stormed off.

"Where's Deeso." Zulag said as he met Ozul's glance.

"She is by the lake to the west. She wanted not to be followed as she was meditating." Ozul said quietly as he knew Zulag would ignore his instructions anyway.

Deeso was at the edge of a lake much as Ozul promised. Although she couldn't swim, she found the allure of the water calming. The stream's flow was slow as the sounds of a few small bubbles occupied the space. Deeso was accompanied by the ambient sound of insects that chirped on occasion in the heat of the day. Her eyes were closed, and she took a deep breath with her nose as she tried to focus. Although she stayed up all night laboring, she wasn't tired. Her spirit was restless, and she hoped that through meditation, she could ground herself better for the days ahead. She attempted to clear her mind of the encounter with Sadal, but it consumed her still. Deeso chose meditation as it promoted self-improvement above else. She inhaled again and held it in as long as she could before she exhaled. The sound of heavy footsteps reaching her ears caused her to roll her eyes as she knew it was Zulag's.

"Why did you make me those knives?" Zulag asked, visibly annoyed at Deeso who refused to turn around.

"I'm busy meditating." Deeso commented as she hoped to dismiss Zulag.

"You don't walk the spirit path, what are you trying to contact?" Zulag asked with genuine confusion.

"Ozul recommended I try it. Occasionally, he gives a good suggestion. I don't walk the path, so this is how I achieve enlightenment. I find what's inside, if there is anything." Deeso pointed out.

"Do I look like I care? Answer my question." Zulag scoffed even louder, as he broke her concentration.

"You cared enough to come here and disturb my peace." Deeso said coldly as she opened her eyes. She met a deafening silence from Zulag as he practically bit his tongue in annoyance. Zulag sat down and copied her position mockingly, as Deeso studied him.

"Is that all you came to say?" Deeso questioned.

"Well, I wanted to say thank you, actually. The knives were good, not as good as mine, but good." Zulag mentioned.

"I didn't think about it until recently, but I realized something. I recalled about what happened with you and Sadal. I don't say this often, but I was wrong. Not in general but about you. I assumed when we first started, I'd have to do this journey alone, but I think I looked at this the wrong way. When I struck Krukzig, you and Cikya handled the rest of them without a second thought. That's the fundamentals of a good team. You didn't ask questions, you just did it. I knew I was going to survive." Zulag mentioned as Deeso shrugged her shoulders.

"Krukzig insulted our leader, it would have been cowardice not to do so. The Mud Forged are our enemies." Deeso commented. Deeso wasn't sure what to make of Zulag's statement but let him continue.

"Yes, he and Ronkalk's history goes far, but that's not why I struck him down. He insulted my parents. I grew up on these lands before we walked to the land that is wet and hot. You didn't have to help me there, but you did anyway. It's appreciated." Zulag mentioned as he pointed out various rolling hills in the distance.

"What does this have to do with Sadal?" Deeso asked with skepticism in her tone.

"You don't think I know how important this has all been? You have something that sets you apart from Sadal. I can't say I'm surprised but what did you expect? Sadal and I were the same rank. We know the stress of the battle differently than everyone else, but we have a responsibility to keep up. My uncle always favored you both as his prime Wanderers. His project to make his words successful. What does that mean for me? I was always put at the backside. For Sadal, this meant she could never be told no. When Sadal got the Weypeu order over me, I was furious. My uncle didn't respect my abilities and handed it to her. Sadal is skilled but she's not used to failure. Ronkalk told us that every warrior needs to be able to harness their emotions for the hunt and I've failed many times, but that's how you learn. When we faced The Buffalo Brothers, we were threatened but you kept your composure and we succeeded. You know how to stay calm. Now we're here in the land that's hot and dry because Sadal couldn't." Zulag mentioned to Deeso.

"What happened with Sadal from the beginning? You told us you two argued." Zulag asked, as he gave a slight cough.

"I told her we came all this way for her. She told me it would be better if I went back and told Ronkalk she was dead. She pushed me to the ground. Everything we had, she was willing to give up for a rock that may not be there. Rarely have I felt such sorrow." Deeso's voice wavered as she recounted what happened between the two of them.

"It's not just a rock, Deeso. My knives and your axe are just rocks. The spirits guided us here so we can do what we need to do. That said, I won't argue on Sadal. She was always full of herself, and it would come to pass that she'd step on anyone to get her way. Even you. I'm just honest about it. The question now is, what do we do about it?" Zulag questioned as he wondered what her response would be. It was obvious to them both that letting Sadal go was not something they could truly do if they wanted to solve their problems.

"We're going to continue onwards and follow her until she decides to give up. Failure isn't an option and Ronkalk trusts us. I will not betray him now." Deeso commented. Zulag couldn't offer up any counterpoint, as he himself didn't respect traitors or broken promises.

"What of Ozul? The kid saved my neck yesterday during the raid. He killed two guys too, not bad from someone who was scared of his own shadow once." Zulag mentioned as he scratched his beard.

"What about him? At one point I considered leaving him behind, but he is on our team, and I am a woman of my word. We promised that we would take him to his family, and I intend to deliver. As for where they could be, I have no idea and I'm not going to tell him either. He did his end of the deal, as he got us through the forest and continued to help us find Sadal." Deeso mentioned.

"Yeah. Family. Believe it or not, you've inspired me a bit. After we bring Sadal home, I'm going to find my father and get answers." Zulag said as Deeso was visibly surprised at the scale of such a venture. Deeso was aware that Zulag had virtually no information to work from. She found it was easier to find the magical sky rock Sadal preached about than a man missing for over two decades.

"You are? Do you think Aralic will give you what you seek?" Deeso asked.

"My uncle can hardly be trusted now. I don't know what to think, but I want to know what happened and why it was so bad enough to leave me like this. He could be dead now for all I know, but I won't know otherwise." Zulag grumbled.

"Anyway, I hope you know what you're doing with this." Zulag said to get up as Deeso remained sitting on the ground.

"Zulag, to answer your first question. After what happened yesterday, I felt bad. I know what it's like to be disowned by your parents. You weren't given a chance at all, it would seem. From what Cikya told me, your entire life has been a lie up to this point. I always knew who I was. All of us trust Ronkalk to make the right decisions, but even he is human. You also said your tools were worn down and there was no good stone to be found. We must have the best tools to find Sadal and bring her home safely. So, I found stone." Deeso mentioned as she alluded to her Wanderer's Mark.

"A Dreamwalker you aren't, but I appreciate the insight." Zulag mentioned while Deeso's face changed at the mention of the word dream.

"Since you're here. I had a vision some time ago and I wanted to know what it meant. Cikya offered her perspective, but I want to know what you think. Until recently, you sat at the means to inherit power. What does this mean to you?" Deeso offered as Zulag weighed her request.

"Describe it to me." Zulag stated.

"Well. I was in a forest, back when the land was hot and wet. I carried a torch with me in the dead of night. The sounds of the forest surrounded us on all sides, but I kept my strength within me. The flames of the torch shone brightly and guided my path. We walked through leagues of mud, many were tired, but I convinced them to keep going. They listened to my words, and I saw something beautiful on the other side. We headed up a large hill that jutted high, perhaps it was a mountain. I pressed onward and saw a valley below as the wind blew my worries away. It was a place much like this, devoid of the predator. We could build without interference from those we saw as lesser. It was a good life." Deeso mentioned.

"We?" Zulag inquired.

"Yes. We-There were others besides me. Behind me, there was a group of people who depended on me for something. They were not our people, but something else. I don't know what compelled me to leave The Broken Bone but I am older in this vision. My face remained the same, but my stride changed as I marched with purpose. I had a strong right hand, someone who reported to me, but I'd like to believe they were an equal in my eyes. Leadership requires competence and a good heart to be done correctly. I have both, but not always." Deeso remarked.

Zulag's expression changed as he heard Deeso orate the mechanisms of her dream to him. Zulag hadn't anticipated doing an interpretation of anyone's dream, especially Deeso's, but he found the opportunity to use his training and took it. Zulag decided to change his outlook on how he was going to respond to her claim. At first, he was going to offer his usual snark but an expression of vulnerability in this manner was interesting and exceptionally rare. Zulag also appreciated the fact that Deeso, despite everything, pushed for Cikya to admit the truth regarding Aralic to him. Deeso's desire for justice was mighty and she was willing to jeopardize the status of her friendship with Cikya to accomplish it.

"From what you've told me, a spirit has guided your intentions. Though you don't walk the path, the interests of both parties align. It would seem you leaving and taking this group with you is what it wills. The animals of the forest are dangerous and yet they didn't pick off the children or the elderly that would have been with you. All made it to the promised land of the land that is dry and hot. It's rare that a land is empty and untested, but not impossible. This could be a gift from the ancestors, much like how our leadership must climb the highest tree and grab a He-Uku feather to possess a key aspect of their strength." Zulag explained while he studied Deeso's reaction.

"Spirits this and spirits that. I appreciate the honesty, there will be more clarity on it, I am sure. If we didn't need you, I'd have you thrown in the lake and watch you drown." Deeso added on to Zulag with a slight grin on her face. Deeso felt it was a cruel irony to have her fate be guided by a supposed spirit as she didn't see herself as a zealot as she painted Sadal.

Zulag mulled over her words as he walked off. Deeso didn't give a response and chose to watch Zulag head back in the direction of camp. She looked at her reflection in the water that distorted with the rare breeze. She returned to meditation and saw that a path opened for her to achieve her goals. The time to be upset was over and instead action must be taken. With a clear mind, she had much more planning to do.

To Begin Again

Deeso was out with Zulag once again on the hunt. The open expanse of the plains continued to be their greatest adversary as they wandered around. Deeso evaluated her potential hunting partners and wondered how it came to be she always found herself with Zulag. The practicality of the matter came to mind. Ozul was inexperienced and while Cikya was certainly competent, communication over longer distances wasn't viable with her. Their strengths worked in tandem with one another, Deeso's tracking skills determined much information about the creatures they looked for while Zulag was adept at pursuing and making the kill. Much like Sadal, he was a Master Hunter after all.

Their hunts together at first were silent. Deeso could plan and study her surroundings, while Zulag got to stretch his legs and throw his knives. Most hunts took only a few hours, but their current journey led them to more than a day's travel. Hunts like these grew boring without much to do, and the two talked further. Deeso decided to take a different approach and lean into the strengths of her team instead of walling herself off in isolation.

"You really want to find Ozul's family? There are many Forest Seeker bands around, and many more that want to kill us thanks to Eshe." Zulag stated accurately as Deeso nodded to his word.

"I told you both, I made a promise and I intend to keep it. He helped us get out of the forest and find Sadal as we agreed. I found her. As for what we do now, Sadal is easy, we will follow and ask for the meteor she seeks. It was a night that many saw. The tales of this Stone Breaker are ones that get told as well. Ozul's family will be far more difficult." Deeso commented with a wave of her hand.

Deeso rested her head on her backpack and stared at the clouds with the grass beneath her. Zulag grumbled to himself as his eyes focused on an animal coming into view. It was a hyena, one of the many thousands they'd come across at this point. There was no escape from their presence. Deeso remained unbothered as she knew Zulag would handle it in her stead. She looked at the shape of the clouds and managed to correlate that the shape often came with weather.

"Ah-What are you doing here?" Zulag yelled at the hyena that came by scrounging around their resting area for any instance of food. Zulag yelled at the hyena and kicked up dirt in its direction. It growled in turn but changed course as Zulag grabbed a knife from his clothing and launched it. The knife landed on the animal's paw. It ran around in pain as it dislodged the knife to the ground, only to run off in a scattered panic, and left a small trail of blood behind.

"We could have killed and eaten it. Where there's one, there's plenty more to be found." Deeso said in annoyance to Zulag as the hyena ran off now.

"Are you serious? These things eat their own dung. They're the lowest form of life! Not worth any sort of pursuit. I know you're hungry but have some standards." Zulag complained as he threw a rock in the direction of the retreating hyena. With their last chance of food behind them now, Deeso felt her stomach rumble. The two were exhausted, with visible marks of deprivation on their eyes.

As Zulag returned, he saw a strange mark on Deeso's hand that differed from her Wanderer's Mark. The wound looked fresh as he focused on it. Without saying anything, Zulag assessed the injury and cut off a portion of fur from inside his backpack. He grabbed Deeso's wrist and bound the fur around the open cut. He snapped for Deeso's attention as she looked at the bandage.

"What happened to your hand? You usually don't get bites." Zulag questioned.

"A Tala with child bit me before we departed our last camp site. With all my luck in the world I was caught unprepared, but it's minor. Cikya wanted some bones for a ritual on our return. The animal is dead by my hand." Deeso explained.

"What did it look like? They know to fear us. Was there drool out of its mouth? [59]" Zulag questioned, with a slight sigh of relief as Deeso nodded no in response.

Deeso was grateful for Zulag's cooperation, but felt a whole bandage was woefully unnecessary despite the occasional twang of pain as she moved her hand around. The two ventured forth once again as there was nothing of value where they rested. Deeso wasn't one to be homesick, but it was a comforting thought from time to time. Despite the recent things she learned about Ronkalk, she still found him a source of great admiration. Leaders were allowed to be flawed. Deeso thought was a prime opportunity to get more knowledge into the inner workings of the band.

"How did it come to be that Ronkalk runs The Broken Bone the way it does? There are four, but it's clear he is the one everyone defers to." Deeso pondered.

"He's private on the details, but here's what I know. Before Cikya and I were born, The Broken Bone lived in these lands and the four bands have had a connection that has been eternal. Ronkalk "inherited" his position from his grandfather-" Zulag stated as he noticed Deeso stopped moving.

"Kalpeu has been through here. Should we engage?" Deeso asked, as she interrupted Zulag's tale.

"Where? How can you tell? I see no trees to scratch like the Onpeu." Zulag noted. His nose flared up as an unusual scent hit his nose and he looked around. Zulag stuck his tongue out in disgust.

"The urine smells different than others. The males use urine, the females rub their paws on the ground from what I have seen. That rock over there is strong and coated with it." Deeso mentioned. She tapped Zulag's shoulder to look closer at the rock that was visibly distinct from the others around it.

[59] The presence of rabies is a disease that has very visible tells and for creatures that act unusual in their behavior, this is noticed by the various denizens of Jih's Journey. This is an important thing to look out for when on the hunt as one bite certainly means death.

"Hmm. Normally I'd say yes, but Kalpeu hunt as a pack. We're just asking to be torn apart without Ozul and Cikya to help us." Zulag answered while Deeso agreed. The two went on further, and Zulag once again answered the question proposed to him earlier.

It came as a surprise to Deeso that the two shared more views in common than thought previously, a fact that irked her slightly. She decided to change her attitude on the matter though as agreeing with her opinion meant she was right all along, just as she intended to be. Zulag came to notice that the "block of wood" he once described Deeso as had some definition. Now no longer in Sadal's shadow, he found her to be far more grounded, a respectable trait that reminded him of Ronkalk. With everything they've been through, they understood each other much more clearly. Things changed a great deal since the first days of leaving The Broken Bone's camp.

"Ronkalk's rise to power wasn't welcome by all. From what I understand, he struggled at first as my mother Chindi was due to inherit by being older. In the past, rule by might was not how we did things. Many wanted blood for his actions against the cruel man. He decided to prove himself as a leader by organizing a great hunt for the Kalpeu." Zulag explained.

"This doesn't seem different from what I expected-" Deeso said, interrupting Zulag once more.

"Oh, there's more. When the hunt began, the leaders left with a small few of their hunters by their side. The hunting season was bad that year, and the beasts grew ravenous even fighting one another. Ronkalk had Stobai as his tracker in those days. She was quite young. My uncle intentionally led them to odds so stacked against them, that defense was impossible. The Kalpeu were slain, but what really brought them to their knees was a horde of ravenous Denmey. My uncle watched those who went against his vision torn to pieces by those foul creatures. All according to plan. He and Stobai went back and spun a great tale of their death in battle. Ronkalk picked those who supported him to lead the other two bands and gave Stobai a position of her own." Zulag said, with a smug expression on his face while he recalled Ronkalk's great deeds. Despite their tension, it was beyond clear that he admired Ronkalk more than any other.

Deeso lifted her eyebrows in shock. Just when she had Ronkalk figured out, there was always a deeper layer. It was just one of many more feats that added to his legend. Zulag and Deeso looked at each other as smoke rose far in the distance. A camp nearby could be good fortune for them both or a fight at hand. A woman nearby who carried a basket with fruit was close by. The bounty was impressive and gave them an idea as they felt their empty packs and stomachs.

"We should take her stuff. She's unarmed, and I'm sure lightening the load wouldn't hurt." Deeso pointed out, while she watched the woman's gait. Fruit was far from an honorable food as there was little challenge in acquiring it, but food of any sort was welcome by now.

"Not like we have all day, let's get to it then." Zulag mentioned as he cracked his knuckles.

"Actually, we do." Deeso remarked with humor.

Deeso and Zulag withdrew their respective weapons as they calmly approached the woman hunched over with the basket. She was one of their kind. It was fortunate she wasn't a Forest Seeker as the two would've cut her down. She turned around, to see Zulag standing in front of her with the knife, and the hilt of Deeso's axe to her back. Powerless to stop them, she lifted her arms and dropped the basket to the ground.

"We want your fruit basket. You can scream if you want, but we'll kill them too if we must." Deeso mentioned as her eyes scanned for helpers. Zulag raised his knife at her but noticed the woman's slow slump as she attempted to pick up some of the jackfruit that fell. She was pregnant, a fact that was also apparent to Deeso as she recognized this within Sadal before. Zulag gave Deeso a look as she silently made use of her eyes to guide Zulag to the woman's condition. Deeso kept her axe trained on her. The woman lamented as she saw Zulag put more fruit into his backpack but was puzzled as he stopped to a certain point and chose to leave half.

"These are supposed to be Angya?" Zulag asked as he looked at the basket. It was clear that this woman didn't know exactly what they were looking for, Zulag swore in his youth he saw jackfruits that could almost require two men to lift.

"Food has been hard for us all. I can see this is why you choose to do what you do. We cannot wait for the biggest of them to grow." The woman said with disappointment in her eyes.

Zulag nodded to Deeso who gave a light shove for the woman to retreat, now that they had a not as mature bounty. Deeso was certain she could remember the direction with smoke, but prepared themselves for a fight as it was clear the woman here would warn her group of their actions. Much to their relief, this camp wasn't affiliated at all with the woman in question but were an entirely different group of Thunderfeet. Deeso and Zulag stumbled upon a celebration of union with two leaders of the band moving into the same tent together. The two hung on the outside and waved, which signified their presence into the camp. Zulag tapped Deeso's arm and reminded her to put her axe away while he obscured one of his knives. The men were organizing an event of some kind, while the women, much like Deeso had seen before, were busy applying clay onto all visitors that came. The pair were greeted by one person who gave them two hearty scoops and rubbed it in their faces. Zulag noticed that the color obscured some of his skin markings while Deeso was less than thrilled.

"You must be among some of the visitors that we have been waiting for. Is that Angya I, see? A pleasurable offering for our leadership." A woman said while she pointed to the two's protruding backpacks. Zulag shot a glare at Deeso who wasn't sure what to say, but she decided to roll with it and nod in agreement. Deeso decided to follow Cikya's mantra and try to take things as they came.

Zulag received a few stares from onlookers but returned quickly to their duties as he looked around and saw that they had clearly found the wrong place. He hoped to find a trader so they could bring something back but now they were stuck here in a place with random people he couldn't care less about. The men carried and placed rope down in long strips along the ground with tight ends. Tug-of-war was a fun display of strength for the band, and in the context of union was especially important. In this group, it was the job of the young couple to place their bets on the winning team and good fortune would go upon them.

Deeso prompted Zulag to take off his pack while she moved the two some distance away where the two could keep an eye on their belongings. Zulag took out a piece of their bounty and cupped it in his hands as he saw there was a growing pile of donated foods and other offerings. His eyes expanded as he saw an assortment of bone, eggshells, and a few luxury pelts. Whoever this was for was certainly important, and this was something not primarily done within their group. Those in The Broken Bone of course took great joy in the hunt themselves and the removal of the beasts was its own reward. Deeso looked at some of the women's adornments and noticed they lacked eggshell bracelets, the piece of clothing she and Cikya risked their necks to get. She gave a small laugh to how trivial things like this were, it was only by sheer chance they ended up finding that band with that set of rules. She saw the young couple who wore bone necklaces around their necks.

"There is a game to be played soon you know. Would you like to take part?" One of the men tanning a cloak from jackal skin called out to Deeso. He could see she stood out like a sore thumb, which was fine as she was a visitor after all. Deeso turned around and saw the man stare at her for an answer.

She nodded and turned to see Zulag eating something. She went over and her eyes immediately focused on his hand. Zulag just barely finished stuffing it in his mouth as he heard Deeso's voice.

"Where did you find that!?" Deeso asked frantically.

"One of the clay women is just giving them to people that look hungry. I have no idea what it is, but it's tasty. They have a hearth some distance from here. Here." Zulag said while Deeso stuffed a piece in her mouth ravenously as bits fell to the ground. She stuck her tongue out as the meat was especially dry and had a somewhat salty flavor, but anything to eat was worth it.

This camp had a population of fifty people, with visitors from affiliated groups making their rounds and providing gifts. While some were focused on cooking food, the younger group were restless, trying to keep themselves occupied. Deeso observed some of them playing tug-of-war with no strategy, and already thought of a plan to win. Of all things, Deeso enjoyed games that required a lot of mental strategy. On the surface tug-of-war seemed simple, but there was a lot more than that. Zulag also watched the event in question and massaged his arm. The lack of food atrophied his body a bit more than he would've liked but remembered playing the game extensively in training. With the formalities under way, Deeso remembered the man who asked her about playing the game, and with Zulag in tow, returned to him.

"Oh, welcome back. I take it you and your partner there will go for my team?" He asked. Deeso nodded while Zulag gave no response to him.

"What's exactly the point of this game? We've played before but this was to train, not for this." Zulag questioned. The man raised an eyebrow at Zulag's statement.

"That man there with the necklace around his neck is to be the next leader of our band. As the closest male kin he has, he will bet on our team, and we will deliver a victory. I'm not sure what his partner will choose but let us hope it's us. A portion of the pot goes to us to give them good fortune." He explained to him.

Zulag's eyes looked to the larger pile of goods, and he found all the incentive he needed to participate. He rubbed his hands together and waited until the lines were drawn. A woman in the center cupped her hands and yelled to grab the attention of those with their own tasks. Zulag turned his head to look for the place where their new team member would be meeting. The man waved them over, and Zulag looked a bit dismayed at their team of six, two of which were far older but still determined. Deeso wasn't sure what to expect, but the group talked among themselves for a bit as they took a middle rope and positioned themselves. The man that invited them both served as the anchor, while Deeso and Zulag took the occupying spaces in front with the rest of the team secured in their placements. A small boundary line in the dirt was marked with a piece of wood.

Let go a little bit, grip, and then pull hard. Deeso thought as they looked at the other team. Her eyes met briefly with the couple they were performing for who looked back with curiosity. As Zulag stood taller than Deeso, he was able to get a better view of their opponents as he tilted his head to see them. He looked slightly discouraged but felt their skills would win the day. The first event took off with the opposing team favoring a quick pull, as Deeso practically felt Zulag on top of her where they lost balance. Zulag's hands were burning as he and the anchor attempted to return the rope back to normal.

"Deeso, lean into me now while I put my feet in the ground." Zulag ordered as she gritted her teeth trying to keep the rope steady.

Her bandaged hand absorbed some of the burn, but she could understand the others' pain quite well. Deeso did as instructed, stopping just short of feeling Zulag's sweat that accumulated on him. Zulag's presence was unusually comforting as she focused on her goal. The man at the anchor slowly raised his arms and shook the rope slightly to position it better in the other's hands. Deeso saw the opportunity and prompted Zulag to grab again, this time to put his left leg ahead of his right. Deeso let go for a short moment, which Zulag observed as odd but realized quickly she was trying to use the force of the other end of the rope to improve their standing. Zulag scooped a bit of dirt with his hand and used it to put a better grip on the rope as it hung straight in a stalemate. The anchor geared up for a small retreat backwards as the rest of the team followed suit. Using their combined force, it was a slow victory as the feet of the other team slowly made their way past the boundary. The other teams also performed admirably, while Deeso and Zulag watched, happily taking the time to soothe the visible marks on their hands from the tight ropes. With the final event in the game taking place, Deeso and Zulag took their previous positions and fought hard in the field as one with the rest of their team. The four separate teams that competed in tug-of-war each had a sense of pride in their achievement in entertaining the leaders before them. They discussed quietly among themselves which performance they liked the most. Deeso noted that the woman of the pair looked in their direction, most likely due to how close the performance truly was. A blowout was far from entertaining but matches of closely defined strengths were always exciting.

The man that served as their anchor looked smugly at his comrades and waited for the confidence to be given. With a decisive point from the two, his gambit surely paid off. Their bet was picked with their injection of visitors and their diversity that could prove to give a better showing. Deeso and Zulag were given necklaces of their own as part of their victory, but these were humbler beads to put on compared to what the two leaders wore. As promised, a portion of the meat was given to Deeso and Zulag who happily placed it in their packs along with the spare jackfruits they kept with them.

"This was...fun. Thank you for hosting us and the bounty found here, but we must-" Deeso said, getting cut off by the man on their team.

"Will you two not stay for the ceremony? It is short, but as the winners we must be involved. The pair must jump over our rope as we hold it." The man asked with a cheery tone. He chose to ignore Zulag's insistence on getting the two to leave. It was well warranted as they were already a full day's travel from where they last made camp with Ozul and Cikya. Their mission to gather food was now secured, and they needed to make use of it before it was spoiled.

Deeso begrudgingly accepted and saw that it was bad form to make enemies of people who've given them such hospitality. She and Zulag took one end with the man, while the rest of the team took the other rope and held it low but tightly. The couple adorned their faces with a white pigment as they walked together and saw the rope held by the victorious team. Seeing such a display was moving for those involved, although Deeso and Zulag remained stoic onlookers. It was difficult to wrap their heads around such a display, Ronkalk rarely gave large ceremonial displays like this within The Painted Hand or within the rest of The Broken Bone for that matter. Zulag informed Deeso that ceremonies for their group were a duty given to the priesthood, but since she didn't care for such things that they slipped by her without notice. After the couple celebrated, a large feast was given for those in attendance and the opportunity to feed themselves further came with much excitement. As they gorged on food for themselves, Deeso and Zulag overheard a conversation regarding the movement of a large group of people. A few younger members of the band gathered in a circle not far beyond them. Their words picked up to the pair's ears as they continued.

"Gathering this meat was a strange endeavor. I found some Forest Seekers on the trail walking around aimlessly. They seem to be lost, which is unusual. Perhaps they came from another land instead." The man said as his friend nodded in discussion.

"Really now? People move all the time, what makes you think these were different?" A woman said as she bit into a jackfruit.

"Well, Forest Seekers are in these lands, but they wore different dress than the ones we have witnessed. Something to consider, they wore necklaces made with feathers. The ones I've seen don't bother with decoration." The man commented in response.

As Zulag chewed his food, he shot Deeso a look as she nodded in acknowledgment of the fact. Ozul's statements about his family no longer existed in a vacuum but were now an actual reality for the two of them. If they could meet up with this group of Forest Seekers, Deeso can meet her end of the deal that she promised. After a short and relatively smooth good-bye, Deeso left another jackfruit behind as an offering and the two made their exit. With the winding path of the still celebrating camp behind them, Deeso scratched her face, as her dried and started itch her skin. The hunt was always full of surprises. Deeso decided to debrief some on all they witnessed at the camp while they walked. She hoped to be back by the next dawn, if possible, but getting lost was just as likely. She made a mental note of the environment around her and hoped to come across the lion's marked rock to remember their way back.

"You did well out there when it mattered. Victory was assured and we got ourselves something to eat." Deeso said, while she tightened the strap of her pack. She looked him over as he shook his saturated hair. Zulag felt disgusted as his beard felt unkempt, and the first thing he needed to do was shave once he got back to camp.

"Of course I did. Though, it could have been worse, that was a smart decision of you to grip the rope like you did." Zulag replied. Deeso raised an eyebrow, but nodded at the thing that came across as some attempt to compliment her.

"Now, do you remember what direction we went?" Zulag asked as he opened his arm to the vast stretch of nothingness that awaited.

A House Divided

Ronkalk was on the hunt himself once more as he felt the pressure of leadership weigh down on him. Sadal and Zulag's absences as Master Hunters started to show its toll on the group. Master Hunters weren't just experts at hunting the large predators that impeded on their proclaimed lands, but they were those who could source the best places for prey as well. At his side was Stobai, the one who served as his tracker in years past and was ready to enact her former duties once more. The two hunted together when they could, both to get away from it all and the call of nostalgia for a better time. Now with families and work of their own, it was rare for them to do such things, but the time called for all hands-on deck. Ronkalk had four Master Hunters in his retinue that he could call, so he operated at half capacity. Ronkalk had hopes in the next batch as he remembered another Wanderer who was ready. Bheyra would start her test soon and fill the void that Sadal left behind.

"Ronkalk, it's an honor to be by your side again. What will we go after?" Stobai said as she waited for an answer. The ambient sound of birds in the trees filled the air as the two stood.

"We need to bring Sarudeu home, but if there are any Denmey, we must take care of them. They are a plague everywhere we go." Ronkalk said with a sigh. Stobai nodded, she approached Ronkalk and noticed he seemed upset about something.

"Sarudeu, you know this brings a Weypeu. Do we have the strength today for such a kill?" Stobai questioned as she looked at her bag.

"I know what it brings. This is what we will find." Ronkalk said. He withdrew his bolas and clinked them as he carried a club in his other hand. Ronkalk generally liked to use his fists, but this time, he wanted to use something with more power.

Ronkalk nodded his head for the two to move as Stobai withdrew a knife she would use. The two set out on their journey with the visage of Ronkalk's camp behind them. It was a familiar walk, as this was the one where he waved off Deeso, Zulag, and Cikya quite some time before. In the absence of camp politics, Ronkalk was able to speak freely about the state of the world and his affairs in a much more casual manner.

"Stobai, I trust you among the many. Before I begin, your travel here went well? It's a last-minute task that wouldn't be given if not needed." Ronkalk mentioned.

"The trek is two days but when the call is given, I will arrive." Stobai replied, as she braced herself for the conversation to come. Stobai was aware that the other members of The Broken Bone seemed to call Ronkalk's decision making more openly than in recent years. She held the utmost faith in him, but criticisms were not unfounded. After all, Ronkalk was but one man.

"It is appreciated. I have heard things from the priesthood that concern me. My conflict with the Forest Seekers has taken much of my time, but I hear there is dissent among the ranks." Ronkalk said.

"You use the word "my" when it is supposed to be ours, Ronkalk. We have slain Forest Seekers when the opportunity arrives. Your vision is followed but yes. Dissent has arrived. There are some who challenge your decisions as of late." Stobai mentioned while she held her hand out to stop Ronkalk. She sniffed the air and looked up to see a troupe of gibbons that pinned their eyes on the two. Ronkalk let out a laugh, he always appreciated the eyes of the apes.

As the two continued onward, they saw a rush of brown go through the treeline. Ronkalk and Stobai crouched as they looked to a source of mud. The two scooped the mud and applied it carefully on their bodies to mask their scent while the gibbons nearby continued to swing from tree to tree.

"This decision making, wouldn't have anything to do with my nephew, would it?" Ronkalk mentioned to Stobai as he pointed in the distance where he saw the blur of brown once more.

"Yes. Many are dissatisfied with your choice to make your infant son your successor over Zulag. He is capable and by casting him out, people have spoken about this. It doesn't bode well-" Stobai commented as she bit her tongue.

"And your opinion? You tell me of others, but you are your own person Stobai." Ronkalk asked while he bent a nearby branch.

"I don't understand you sometimes. That is my opinion. Why not cut your losses with Sadal? You search for her by sending one of your best hunters." Stobai complained with a sigh.

"As you know, leadership is not just hunting. There is more that he lacks. I didn't do it because I am crazy, I did it to send a message. If he went down the wrong path, he would become his father, a fate I wish to avoid. Besides, Sadal is as much family to me as Zulag is. I trust my nephew will bring her back safely and we will discuss what is to happen on her return." Ronkalk said. Stobai paused, she hadn't really considered that part of his logic.

"And what will happen?" Stobai questioned.

Ronkalk kept his silence as he wasn't sure just yet. It was a complicated matter that required much thought. The two paused, with the search for faint footprints taking precedent over their current conversation. As Ronkalk scanned the forest floor and had no leads, he heard another question brought up by Stobai.

"You mentioned Zulag's father. Are you still searching for him after all this time?" Stobai questioned with some disbelief. Stobai was one of the few who knew the true fate of Aralic, a reward for a long friendship. Stobai was aware of the great deal of pain that was given when his name was uttered, though she knew of it, she censored herself out of care for her friend.

"You and the Red Priest have both labeled me as a pariah for this search. I know he is alive. I want an answer for why he left us, just like Sadal. He walked with us and my sister is dead because of him. She lost the battle, and he left us in disgrace." Ronkalk said with disgust in his voice.

"If I would know any better, he perhaps took refuge with-" Stobai mentioned before she was interrupted by the sound of a creature in the bushes.

"Sarudeu!" Stobai pointed as the two started their pursuit.

Despite their age, running up to the deer was no issue as the two briefly separated in the thick of the foliage to pursue their meal. The deer let out a loud bellow as it heard Ronkalk head towards him. Ronkalk readied his arm and gave a mighty hurl of his bolas as the deer vaulted over a log. They wrapped around the hind legs of the deer, and it slammed onto the forest floor as it thrashed around attempting to wrestle itself free. He ran over and lifted his club. He slammed down hard on the deer's legs and caused it to yelp in pain as a satisfying crunch was heard. Ronkalk held a smug look as he knew the hind legs were surely broken. Stobai emerged some distance away with her knife as she ended the animal's suffering quickly with a quick slice of the throat. The two went to work dragging the deer's corpse before none were the wiser.

The deer's girth made it difficult to travel through some of the denser patches of forest, so the two worked instead to move it through some of the clearings. The problem at hand though was that their usual route seemed to be blocked by three cave hyenas that saw an easy opportunity from the two. Ronkalk shook his head as they seemed to inhabit every environment they've found so far; he was surprised at their adaptability but remained ever insulted by their presence.

A few hyenas yelped loudly at the two as they intruded into their space. Ronkalk let go of the deer while Stobai followed. The hyenas evaluated the situation and haphazardly ran towards the food seemingly dropped at their footsteps, until one lost all sight. The mighty club of Ronkalk swung wildly towards it and knocked it out cold. The other two hyenas began their assault, centered on Ronkalk while Stobai ran behind one of the animals and grabbed its hind legs. She braced and gritted through the pain as she felt the claws scratch her legs while she stabbed the beast. Ronkalk's face was filled with rage as he did battle with the hyena. The last living one jumped at Ronkalk, laughing as it did so. Ronkalk was infuriated as their sound mocked him. Ronkalk lifted his arm and the jaws of the animal ripped apart his clothing as he attempted to shake it loose. The hyena's jaws were incredibly strong as it bit through the leather and gave Ronkalk just mere moments to recover. He felt the weight of the creature press him to the ground as the animal reared up to bite him. Ronkalk applied a sufficient kick to the animal's testicles that gave him just enough time to give one swing that knocked the cave hyena out. Ronkalk considered himself lucky as only his clothing was torn apart but he remained fine. He lifted his club and smashed the cave hyena's skull in with a mighty roar of his own.

"I await the day you all vanish." Ronkalk said as he spat on the corpse of his enemy. Stobai took no time as she lifted the hyena's corpse out of Ronkalk's direction before he walked further. The two walked back to hoist the deer carcass.

"Now that that is done, we should discuss further. Ronkalk, there is a plot against you by the other two band leaders. They have kept tight lips on the matter, but I hear things that disturb me. They feel the region here is barren and that we are not going as offensively as hoped against The Forest Seekers." Stobai opened as the two caught their breath.

"It is one thing to say there is dissent, but another to say a plot. Which is it, Stobai?" Ronkalk questioned as he waved to her to grab the back end of the deer carcass.

"To me Ronkalk, they are one and the same. One can't exist without the other." Stobai said as she adjusted her clothing.

He and Stobai resumed their duties and carried the sambar back to the boundary of camp. While many continued their duties, Ronkalk noticed that there was some discussion going on as he entered. This was caused by another young upstart, a man who seemed to have forgotten the fate of Ututar. As he didn't make himself as flashy as the other leaders, Stobai included, he often blended in with many until his face was shown and respect was commanded. In the mentality of might makes right among their people, competition was encouraged and alliances for the young were quick as they saw to take advantage of the power vacuum. Ronkalk and Stobai decided to listen in on their discussion. Ronkalk saw he wore bear fur over his shoulders and knew he couldn't have hunted it. Bears were wiped out in these lands for some time, it was an imported good.

"Zulag is finished, back my claim for Master Hunter and your stomachs will be full." He mentioned, while he sat back and listened to a few of his admirers. Some of the others offered their theories as well. Ronkalk saw this as simple posturing between rivals and nothing more until another statement was echoed.

"And what of Zulag, hmm? His father left him, and here we are dealing with his issues. Leave to find Sadal? In his foolishness, he left us without another Master Hunter. Sadal was weak, and it's because of her as well that we starve." He said, as felt a foreboding presence behind him.

Ronkalk looked at Stobai who also shared a look of shock. This was confidential information, who exposed something like this? Ronkalk knew better than to point the finger at Stobai, there was a greater power at play, and he felt it had to do with the priesthood who argued with his decision making. Ronkalk stood silently as he inched closer to the discussion. Unlike most leaders, Ronkalk often participated in discussion as a listener so he could best evaluate how to organize things, there were things he did not agree with, and others that were excellent suggestions. He decided to break his silence and make his presence known.

"Who are you to will such falsehoods into being?" Ronkalk answered, while the group of six looked to recognize their leader. A harsh chill went up their spines.

Fueled by the need to impress his followers, the young man's foolhardy nature didn't realize he fell into the belly of the beast. Stobai held her ground as she watched to see what Ronkalk would do. She hoped for the group's sake that he used his temper out on the hyenas they faced earlier. Ronkalk took advantage of this fear as he captured their attention.

"I know this feeling well; you speak from jealousy. You spit lies about my nephew so that you can feel large. Do you feel like a man speaking on things you don't understand? Master Hunters sacrifice many things, and not everyone is able to do this. Zulag left us because he believed in a cause greater than his own ambition. He could have refused but he did not." Ronkalk replied to the young man. Ronkalk knew every single person's name, their parents, and their loved ones in each of the four bands that made up The Broken Bone. It was the thing he prided most, so his message was for all of them.

"We respect you Ronkalk, we always have, but Zulag is not you. We must be honest with ourselves. You yourself couldn't see him as the successor, why should we? You trained him and yet you made it known in front of us all, there is something else missing." The man countered as he received a few nods from his followers.

"I'm not sure what you mean. My actions require no explanation, I give it to you all because I see it as such. There is much more in this world than you will ever know. I have heard the rumors; I wear the scars of Denmey on my arms. I have brought a Sarudeu twice my weight at twice your age." Ronkalk scoffed with disgust.

"You say we speak of falsehoods, but the lake reveals the same face. And that of Zulag's father, you lie to us you know. We know deception is at hand, and yet you treat us as children." The man said.

Stobai coughed to announce her presence as well. The few that heard her lowered their heads in acknowledgment of a fellow leader. Ronkalk was often turned off by the rigid atmosphere generated in some of the other camps, but occasionally, he needed to remind people who was the boss. Ronkalk gave a heavy sigh, he had to defend Zulag from the jeers of others when he was young due to his skin. Ronkalk instilled in him the confidence he needed by training in the arena to handle himself. Never did he feel that he would now have to save face regarding his father as well and his own leadership decisions.

"You want the truth? I can give it to you." Ronkalk said as he extended his arms. He grabbed the young man and pinned him against a nearby tree. One hand was on his throat and the other was on his body. A few of the followers stood motionless as Ronkalk did his antics. He leaned in close to the man but spoke loud for any onlookers to hear. Ronkalk tightened his grip on the young man's throat.

"When I was a younger and stronger man, Aralic left The Broken Bone. It's been about twenty years now, longer by now. I've sent your mother to look for him once, and every day I wait for his return, so I can remove his head from his body and wear his skull as a necklace and place his body on a stake. I stood by Chindi's side for two days and watched her spirit go in the ashes of the wind. The shame and dishonors were so great, I made an announcement for everyone that he died in battle against a pride of Kalpeu. The priests confirmed my statement, and a grave was dug. We put shells and dirt for the mauling that was supposed to be so great there was nothing to bury. This was to preserve our honor. A farce for the greater good. Imagine what I can do to you when I feel like trying." Ronkalk said, his gaze unwavering as color vanished from the young man's face. He was so petrified with fear that he couldn't offer even a slight rebuttal. Nobody else interfered as well, Ronkalk had them right where he wanted them.

Ronkalk released him to the ground where he fell with a thud that shook the others. Ronkalk had enough experience to differentiate between rendering someone unconscious and choking to kill, but for now, he would let them stew on which decision was made. Without another word, he looked to Stobai and the two left.

"Stobai. Before you leave, there are two things you must hear." Ronkalk ordered as he dragged the deer pelt to their storage tent.

"I will call a meeting with the priesthood so we can discuss the Forest Seeker situation. Bring the traitors as well. Also, go and talk to her. It's been a while and she could use the company." Ronkalk said, pointing to the tent where his family lived. Zulag also stayed in this tent prior to him leaving with Deeso and Cikya. Stobai looked in the direction of Ronkalk and nodded. Ronkalk held his hand out to stop Stobai for just a moment longer.

"Thanks for today. It was fun." Ronkalk said as he nodded and went off to handle some other business that required his attention.

Who Tells It Best

Back at Sundaland, months of deprogramming in The Elders finally started to take root. The dissatisfaction of The Council compounded with Tur's increasingly worse condition. Tur still went out and gave speeches to elevate his position as the battle of ideas quivered against his favor. Tur was often accompanied by other members of The Council who acted alongside him and amplified his voice but found their popularity waned as they stuck by him. Tur remained a sharp adversary as he feared his journey to irrelevance. The Council became more draconian in its edicts as Tur operated with malice. Tur even attempted to disarm the population and decreed that only scouts and hunters could hold weapons in camp, but this was ignored. Kag sat with pride as Tur morphed into an enemy of the people, but there was something else that bothered him.

While the Neck-Shells were long gone, and Tur drove himself into quicksand, Kag faced his biggest battle yet. The insult of Jih's shunning still hung over Kag and a select few who viewed the action as unjust. Although Hizo was gone for many years, people still spoke highly of her to this day. It was only right for Jih to receive such veneration as well in case he never did return. He hoped that by telling stories about how Jih was beneficial for the group, this would turn public opinion and win the minds of the people. As Kag asserted himself as a member of The Council, people looked past his joking exterior and took him as seriously as any of the other members. Bani was tasked with addressing a crowd of supporters to their cause and offered her perspective of how Jih impacted their community.

Bani looked quite satisfied at how things were turning out. Despite being now heavily pregnant, Bani still made efforts to go around and do tasks much to the dismay of Kag. She was accompanied by a younger man who guided her around as she found some other tasks a bit more difficult with her state. She made her way to Dran who was already delivering passionate fervor to the crowd of ten. Dran and Bani were close by now, and so Dran offered a smile to her friend as Bani set herself down.

"We will take spears and axes to The Council! Their heads will be on these pieces if they do not listen!" Dran declared as she nodded her head to the approval of clapping and stomping in the dirt.

"Tur does not care about you. He never has. Tur sees you as resource to be taken away. Will we let him continue? We must be wary. All The Council is tainted. Kag sacrificed this, so we may be better led." Dran spoke.

"Dran has called Bani to come and speak. We must tell them what happened with Jih. His importance to us and why he must return." Dran added in clear defiance of the shun.

"Bani is outsider, or at least she was once. How did you come here?" A person asked. Bani escaped most questions of her origins due to Kag's position, but she was prepared to meet any skepticism with grace.

Dran wasn't present when Bani initially came to The Elders. She had a hard enough time with her position of teaching the children than to bring any attention to any new adults that came by. It was only until after the Neck-Shell raid that Dran was truly skeptical of new arrivals in the band. Although she and Bani were good friends, Dran remained curious about her origins, it was something she didn't bother acknowledging for some time. Bani felt her stomach as she closed her eyes but brought her attention back to Dran and the others. She spoke with a softness that could lull one to sleep if they weren't careful.

Bani was from an area of Sundaland considered the north from The Elders' perspective. Tur and the other adults early on considered the north an inhospitable place at the behest of The Council who decided that sending scouts in these areas was a fruitless endeavor. Between rampant tiger attacks and hordes of mosquitoes that carried malaria, the north was considered a lost cause though brave foragers still made the occasional trip. Some speculated that the Neck-Shells originally came from this cursed region as well. Bani was lost in a dense patch of forest without clothing. She was caught in a harsh rainstorm that ruined her clothes, and the remains were tattered as she ran from a charging rhino some time earlier. All was not lost as she saw a citrus tree filled with mandarin oranges. She hadn't eaten for some time, and she was quite hungry. Bani reached over and nabbed a piece where she could.

"Dewtatu always finds Bani." She said to herself with a small grin.

Bani also saw an opportunity to be made with the present wood. She checked around her and used a stone to scrape off some wood so she could make a handle. It was a crude compromise, as she attempted to use the same stone to brute force her way into making an axe. After some time, she had a functional tool in her hands. Bani was annoyed given her current limitations, but she was desperate to have something. She swatted at a flying mosquito that was headed towards her. She gave a small grin as it torpedoed to the ground with the back of her hand and the whining noise stopped. Bani continued onward for some time, unable to really determine any direction of where she was going. She couldn't find a stream or anything to use as a marker. She stopped short as she heard a sound that was too rhythmic to be animal in its nature. Bani kept her blunt instrument close as she popped her head through a bush. The man that Bani saw heard a rustling sound, she assumed undoubtedly from her, but she saw that he looked up instead. She saw a man wearing an outfit of palm leaves and fibers tied together.

"All this for one feather. How does Hyu know difference?" Jih said in frustration as he picked up a stick and attempted to throw it up towards the trees where he could see a nest of some kind. He backed up as he did and tried to adjust his throw.

While Hyu was an adept climber of trees, Jih was not as daring at times. He often tossed branches at the top to see if anything awaited him. He continued this for some time until he felt a presence behind him. It unnerved him, and he turned around, taken aback at the nude stranger who appeared from the bushes. Jih looked Bani over and saw they were in rough shape. He looked past her to see if she was followed. He backed away slowly to give Bani some room. He hadn't expected to run into anyone out in this area for people rarely ventured this way.

"What happened to you?" Jih said with some suspicion. Jih remembered rumors of the northern jungles having unreasonable hostiles, but these were just rumors. He had a hand-axe prepared for any issues, but he felt that this person in front of him could be reasoned with.

"Bani has nowhere to go. Bani needs a bath and some balm." She said to Jih as she scratched her arm. Jih shook his head as she told the young woman not to scratch bites from mosquitoes. Bani reflexively already opened a few of them from her scratching.

"Muucu bites, disgusting creatures. This requires Marubaat[60] for treatment. Kag makes remedy, Jih will take for healing." Jih said as he looked over Bani's arm.

"Jih searches for Iru-Uku feather. Do you know this bird?" Jih asked the naked woman in front of him. Jih normally never went this far when foraging, but Hyu requested he find a feather and some eggs for her collection. The hornbill was indecisive on where it chose to nest, and after Jih found difficulty going to the usual places, north was where he ended up going.

Bani knew of the hornbill, but she hadn't seen any in her travels. Jih decided to call off his endeavor for now to get Bani back to safety. Jih shed his palm covering and put it over Bani instead so that she would have something to use as clothing for the time being. The two continued to travel through the jungle undeterred, as Jih always made a path for himself with his trusty hand-axe, marking trees so he wouldn't get lost.

In time, the two eventually found their way back to The Elder's campsite where the sounds of industry flooded Jih's ears again. For Bani, this was somewhat overwhelming at first, as the lifestyle of her people was far laxer. She could have been a Forest Seeker in another life, where appreciating doing nothing was normal and welcomed. Jih was met with a few curious eyes, but not much else was said as people returned to their tasks for the day. Jih looked in the direction of The Council's tent but sought first to find Hyu and Kag. Jih practically dragged Bani along, grabbing her wrist as he knew she wanted to immediately start looking around as all newcomers did.

"Work keeps us happy. This is what The Council says anyway." The voice of Hyu said as she made conversation with one of her patients.

It was a young boy who injured himself scouting and he refused to work anymore. His arm had a sizable wound that appeared to be a scratch, but it was some time before he was able to get it treated. Her eyes met with his as she used her finger and pressed down to assess what the boy's pain threshold was. Hyu knew that no reaction to her poking around was a bad sign. Hyu often experimented with the bodies of the deceased before burial, dead tissue looked the same to her on both living and gone subjects. Hyu was alone at their medical area as she sent Kag out to get some last-minute ingredients for a resin to hopefully restore their condition.

---

[60] Emic word for Indian Copperleaf.

"Hyu! Jih returns." Jih announced his presence to her. Bani took one look at Hyu and was smitten by her kindness. Hyu moved her head to see Jih and then Bani, and back to Jih. She raised an eyebrow at the two of them.

"Hyu welcomes Jih. No feather, but you bring a woman? She wears what Hyu made for Jih." Hyu said with a sly grin as Jih knew what Hyu was alluding to. He nodded his head profusely at the mere thought of being unfaithful.

"Jih found Bani in north. Muccu bites require treatment. Is Kag here to give resin?" Jih asked as Bani scratched again. Hyu was waiting on Kag to fix her first patient, so she decided to look at Bani.

Hyu stepped up, she was a head taller than Bani as her hair flowed down her shoulders and touched Bani's arms. She narrowed her eyes at Bani and ordered her to open her mouth. Jih looked at Hyu with some confusion, but he realized he hadn't seen Hyu do this before. She looked inside as best as she could to see if Bani was healthy.

"Does she have worms?" Hyu asked Jih as she saw a confused look on her love's face. Jih shrugged his shoulders. He hadn't thought to ask anything about that at all in his travels with Bani. She asked the same question to Bani.

"Bani does not think so?" She said as she rubbed her stomach with a small grin. Her tone was playful as she found the question a bit odd to ask, but she saw that it was no laughing matter for Hyu.

"Yes or no." Hyu said flatly, as both Jih and Bani reflexively straightened their posture.

Bani nodded her head no, much to Hyu's relief. A worm outbreak was difficult to quell once someone was infected as it could spread easily among the various prey they hunted for. Adult worms were visible to the naked eye in stool, so Kag and Hyu were able to isolate people with difficulties and attempt to treat them. Hyu decided to take Bani with her for the moment as Jih looked at the young boy who stewed in his own thoughts.

"Outsiders must be welcomed by The Council. You will stay in tent of Kag for now. Say nothing. Jih will return later." Hyu said lowly to Bani. Hyu left shortly after while Bani sat at the tent of a stranger. Hyu left to collide with Kag as he found her. Bani could hear their exchange outside the vicinity.

"Sister! Did you need something?" Kag asked in confusion.

"Hyu will explain, apply resin to the boy. Jih brought a new arrival. She is housed here for now." Hyu mentioned as she nodded her head. Bani saw the shadow of Hyu explain the details.

Bani didn't personally witness the rest, but she was able to piece together what happened next while talking with the other three afterwards. Kag looked bewildered but nodded at Hyu's words. He worked ahead of time to make the bandage needed so he applied it onto the boy who screamed loudly. Kag was not one to ease into things, slapping on the bandage much to Hyu's annoyance. The three discussed how to handle the Bani situation. Kag felt blindsided having to now house a new arrival and Jih thought how to approach the matter to The Council. For Bani, the only thing that mattered now was getting to know how things would go. She waited in Kag's tent for some time as Hyu stuck her head inside. Hyu looked at the tired Bani with a small smile.

"Hyu welcomes Bani." Hyu mentioned with a smile that stretched from ear to ear.

Bani had more to say, but the concentration in her story was broken by tremors in her stomach. Dran got up from the circle and addressed her. Her energy was expended so she gave Dran room to talk instead. Bani crunched in pain as she felt physically weak.

"Bani, speak to Dran." She said to get Bani's attention.

Dran could tell she looked dehydrated and waved someone over to bring a basket of water. Bani just waved her hand to Dran which gave a sigh of relief. Dran herself felt quite warm as well, so she could imagine how Bani felt. The crowd remained moved by Dran's service to others and Bani's account on Jih's humility. Dran decided to lift Bani carefully and take her to her and Kag's home to recover. She figured a distraction would be helpful to keep her mind steady and preserve the health of the child.

"Like Bani, Dran has stories of Jih." Dran said with slight embarrassment, as she decided to skip some of the more hostile parts of their earlier relationship.

Dran spoke highly of her time with Hizo to Bani as she slowly walked with her. Bani was never able to meet Hizo, but it was clear by how everyone talked highly of her that she was a woman of high esteem among her people. Dran and Jih were both sixteen at the time. Dran awoke in the tent that belonged to her father. Dran was given little direction as she found it difficult to place a niche where her talents could truly shine, but something drew her to the arena. Although she and Jih had a negative relationship due to his proximity to Hyu and Kag, Hizo saw great potential in Dran and harnessed her energy into something productive as a promising student. Despite being considered adults, many of the students still returned for refreshers from Hizo. She massaged her stomach in hunger and looked to see if the Hunting Team brought anything worth her time. Nothing but berries this time.

Dran's head turned as she heard the voice of Hizo not too far in discussion with the deep sound of Tur accompanying. Many of her generation never understood how someone as amazing as Hizo could honestly find themselves in Tur's company. Hizo and Tur talked often, but the discussion they were having was one of extreme interest to Dran. Like many young people, she was curious about the inner workings of The Council who remained mysterious despite her distaste for the group. Dran decided to eavesdrop on the conversation and pretended to be engaged with looking at something on the ground.

"Hizo. Consider the offer of Tur." Tur said with a friendly smile as he placed his hands on Hizo's shoulder. Tur was highly interested in attempting to secure a place for himself in The Council. He made occasional offerings out of wood to sway favor with them. Tur also thought highly of Hizo's skills and was trying to also sell the case for her to be considered a member. Hizo and Jih were once outsiders, but Hizo worked exceptionally hard to integrate her and Jih into the ways of The Elders. Her spear skills were unmatched to what they had before, and with the concern of other groups and fragile alliances, defense was a priority.

"The Council is where you belong. Furs for Hizo and the young Jih. This is what is deserved." Tur said to Hizo.

Hizo debated the offer seriously, she respected her autonomy above all else. Hizo recognized that entrance into The Council would be enough to finally put to rest some scant claims that Hizo and Jih didn't have the best interests of their group at heart. The oral histories that The Elders prided themselves on led to many being skeptical of outsiders. Hizo knew how important this was personally to Tur also. She was grateful as Tur and Aab were accommodating to Hizo and Jih when they first entered The Elders. She felt that she owed Tur at least a chance to prove the investment in their friendship was worth it.

"Hizo is unsure. The Council has many heads. Not all of them agree." Hizo commented to Tur. Hizo flicked her hair as she saw Tur was nodding in agreement with her words.

Tur laughed; he understood as much as any that this was the case. He felt someday soon though he would weave into his rightful place. He wished to have his closest friend by his side as he did so.

"Tur has told The Council of performance. Hizo should do one for them. Let your work speak for itself." Tur mentioned while he met Hizo's expression with a smug grin.

Hizo covered her mouth in shock. She hadn't bothered to train anyone for a performance of any scale, and she was taken by surprise. Tur hadn't gone to The Council yet, but he planned on doing it shortly and told Hizo to prepare.

"Tur suggests you find best students. Does Hizo have these?" Tur asked with some curiosity. Hizo gave it some thought but nodded her head with a smirk on her face.

"There is one. The one named Dran. She has Ker-Mah spirit, but it can be quelled. Dran learns quickly and defeats the foe well." Hizo stated with pride.

"This will require two. Do you have another?" Tur asked. He had a relative idea of what she was looking for but was curious about what she would display in the arena. Tur had a low opinion of Dran but knew Hizo's link with the young woman and kept his tongue silent.

"Hizo will take Jih. Hizo has plans for them." She said while Tur suppressed his distaste of the idea. Tur's expression had caution written all over his face.

"Jih? He has skill yes, but in..." Tur said, before getting cut off by Hizo.

"Jih is son of Hizo. He will do it. He inherits my legacy." Hizo said sternly to Tur. Tur could do nothing more than nod as Hizo was the expert in this situation. Tur's disdain for Jih had early roots, he considered many of the children to be irritating troublemakers but understood that children were needed to keep society moving forward. He tried, but his didn't last to adulthood.

Dran heard enough as she recalled Jih's name being mentioned. She scoffed as she knew Jih would have Hyu and Kag behind him as he always did. Dran didn't have anything personally against Jih that she could think of recently, but the two irritated one another. Dran's respect for Hizo gave a begrudging tolerance of Jih that was difficult for Jih to return. She saw Hizo walk off and realized the time. Hizo would be waiting at the arena for Dran to arrive. Dran rushed over to the arena, out of breath to meet Hizo who gave a casual stroll. Hizo gave a small conversation to a few people who asked how she was doing, and she turned her head to see Dran rushing and shoving a few others out of her way. Hizo laughed at the display and decided to let Dran catch her breath before starting. Hizo caught Jih at a good time, for his training with Illol was cut short due to her feeling ill. She waved him over as he walked by carrying a carved stone in hand. Jih walked over and hugged Hizo tightly as he always did, and the two walked over together. Dran narrowed her eyes as she saw Hizo with another figure, this being Jih in the distance. Although not audible to Dran, she could tell that Hizo and Jih were talking about something. She figured this would be the presentation she overheard. As Jih and Hizo approached though, Dran picked up Jih's reaction to hearing his mother's words.

"What?!" Jih's voice rang in her ears.

Now that Hizo and Jih made their way to the arena, Dran sat on a log seeing that mother and son were still in discussion. She attempted to look disinterested, but she was nosy as any other. Jih normally had such a neutral expression on his face, so seeing anything else was intriguing.

"Jih. This is important for Hizo." Hizo reminded Jih, placing her hand on his shoulder firmly but calmly as she took a deep breath.

"Jih does not dance, and Dran is awful." Jih complained, while he saw his mother's face change.

"Jih, Dran is present." Hizo said sternly, as Jih turned to see Dran looking at the two of them. She glared back at Jih who looked away in annoyance.

Jih walked over into the middle of the arena with his arms folded, while Hizo raised her hand for Dran to join. She got up and walked over, keeping her look only at Hizo. Dran had to pretend that she didn't eavesdrop on Hizo's previous conversation as Hizo reiterated the details of what was expected. Hizo knelt and grabbed a wooden spear roughly the size of her that she manipulated in her hands.

"Does Jih and Dran remember spear rules?" Hizo asked the two, lifting two fingers with her hand. Hizo took it on herself to remind them of the differences. Rule 1 was the ritualistic aspects of spear combat, while Rule 2 was the unregulated ruleset most used. It was the first set of instructions any child learned in the arena when handling weapons.

"Jih and Dran will perform for The Council in three days. Hizo has thought of something to do. Hizo will demonstrate this." Hizo reiterated while she set herself into position.

"Yes mot-"Jih said, getting cut off by Dran who chose to speak louder than Jih.

"Yes Hizo." Dran said quickly.

Jih glared at Dran while Hizo took a deep breath and danced in a strange and rhythmic motion that the two studied carefully. Although Hizo was performing with her spear work in silence, it was traditionally accompanied with chanting and some form of music as well. Jih and Dran studied different parts of Hizo as she danced, her legs in particular, as she continued to perform. The act in all took about five minutes, but it seemed to have lasted much longer than that. Dran looked confused as she questioned the ease of the task. Dran held a look of overconfidence that diminished slightly as she saw Jih's face look not as excited. She would soon know why, as Hizo explained that there would be a sizable crowd accompanying The Council and that their movements had to be perfectly synchronized for it to be considered complete. Hizo gave some time for Jih and Dran to collect their wooden spears and position themselves as the two repeated Hizo's movements, first as separate entities to understand the various movements involved. Their first attempt together was stopped by the glare of Hizo that compelled them to start over once again in silence.

"Again." Hizo said to the two of them as they took some distance and attempted to mirror the movements. Jih and Dran got a bit more progress this time, before once more Hizo shook her head. Hizo saw that while they did manage to do the first set of movements correctly, they failed to communicate as a team which prompted them to start anew.

"Reflect Jih. Jih will go left, Dran will go right." Jih commented, his voice devoid of emotion as he signaled to her to follow suit.

Jih was the first to speak, as he figured out his mother's demands quickly. Out of the corner of his eye, he saw Hizo give a subtle cough. Hizo continued to watch the two for some time and then left, seeing that the two of them were starting to coordinate. Dran and Jih practiced and gave blunt corrections to each other. In the bushes not too far from the two practicing, Kag and Hyu watched the two from a distance. Hyu waved her hand, to catch Jih's attention as he nodded his head no, while Dran looked behind her briefly. Hyu's hand went into the bush again just in time while Dran returned to Jih's expression.

"Stay on task Jih." Dran said sternly to him.

As the day waned, Dran and Jih chose to conclude their training. Hizo spread the word that the performance would be done in three days' time which led to an insurmountable amount of pressure between the two. Dran took Jih's idea of reflecting him literally in the days that followed, as there wasn't a waking moment where she wasn't near him. Wherever Jih decided to go within reason, Dran was right behind him.

The day of the performance for The Council was upon Dran and Jih as they once again went over what needed to be done. Dran had gotten so good at imitating Jih's moves; she could even replicate his yawn. Hyu stewed in anger as she watched Dran and Jih practice, waiting for a time that Jih would finally be free to adventure again with her and Kag. She understood that this was for Hizo, but she was going to be mad about it. She and Kag sighted out an early seat for the display since The Council stopped all work for the day. Hizo hadn't slept the past night with the pressure of everything being so stressful. Hizo summoned Jih and Dran to the arena once more as she sat on the log present. She was clearly bothered about something, as she felt uneasy about Dran and Jih's connection with one another. While Hizo knew no punishment of course would befall her, she feared the social consequences behind her failure. Not only would she have failed The Council and Tur, but herself in this endeavor as well. Hizo had a strong image she worked to maintain and instilled this in Jih as well.

"The dance starts at sunset. Are Jih and Dran ready?" Hizo asked the two. Jih nodded and went into position, but Hizo lifted her hand. She didn't want to see what was done prematurely, she wished to see the authenticity of everything they worked for just like the rest would in time. Hizo advised the two to get rest as they would have to expend a lot of energy.

Jih and Dran awoke out of their respective tents and silently walked over to the arena. The camp of The Elders was quiet as only the sound of birds chirping their last calls in the distance could be heard. Dran turned her head to see a large crowd before her. The only ones not present were the few who remained on watch for any attackers that would come for a raid when the camp was distracted. Hizo looked different, wearing pigment along her face that had a green color as she was to speak to The Council. Lit fires were present in the four corners of the arena while Hizo stood in the middle, as two spears of equal length waited for their respective wielder. A small murmur came across the crowd as some fought among themselves to get a better view. The Council were always the last to arrive at an event, with the way cleared for them in advance. They looked down on the others as they were showered with admiration and love. They took their seats and Hizo took this as the signal to begin. Her eyes scanned the crowd, and she saw Tur's face among them, nodding in solidarity.

"This is to honor The Council. Hizo is grateful for their kindness." Hizo opened. She was a natural as she was used to speaking to a large group at any given time for her occupation. Hizo's words could make even the smallest space feel grand in her presence. The Council nodded in acknowledgement of Hizo's words as she called forth Jih and Dran.

"In the art of spear, there are two ways. Today will be way one. Jih and Dran, show us your gift!" Hizo orated to them as she slowly retreated from the arena. A few older men that sat on the cusp of the arena yelled in sync and made a harmonic tone as they slammed the soil with their hands. Bits of dust were visible as the dry grass was struck.

Jih and Dran grabbed the spears and, as customary, stood back-to-back. The two raised their legs up to make large strides in a circular motion that circumnavigated the arena. Their spears poked out into the crowd, barely reaching the faces of those that stood close enough. They stuck out their tongues as well, making various expressions of anguish and fear that came with the severity of spear work. Once the first rotation was done, it was then performed counterclockwise. They then stepped again into the center, but this time stood some distance from one another. Dran was to swipe first at Jih's legs, where he jumped, and then Dran did the same. The two then swiped at each other's heads, the wood just barely colliding with one another as they ducked.

Hizo watched with the utmost patience as she recalled every step she did as the two performed them without pause. A smug but satisfied expression could be seen on her face as even Tur, as doubtful as he could ever be, seemed to hold his tongue at the display. Jih and Dran then clinked their spears together, the noise synchronized with the chanting of the men as clapping from the crowd started to rise in volume. Clapping was not part of the plan, but Jih and Dran made do with what they had. The two placed their spears in the ground and jumped back and forth, changing position a few times and they grabbed their spears once more. For Hizo, this was the conclusion of what she offered to do. Her face was filled with surprise, as there was more than she expected. To impress Hizo, Dran made an interesting decision. She hoped to add one more maneuver to the formula that Jih begrudgingly accepted but executed without issue. The two gained speed and tossed their spears at an arc, rolling on the ground and quickly extending their hands to grab the other's respective spear right before it touched the ground. The dust settled as they went into position and stood back up in the center of the arena. For Jih, this only meant making his mother happy for the time being, but for Dran this meant everything. Dran's face rarely showed joy, but she couldn't help but give a small smile to Jih with a job well done.

Dran finished her story with Bani now resting as her back was elevated on the wall of her and Kag's home. Bani found it uncomfortable to be directly flat and so she used it to support herself. Dran peered out the flap of the tent to see Kag returning shortly and the two parted ways until the next day.

A Fresh Start

The culmination of their planning finally came to a head. After many months of careful planning with Vut's Hunting Team and getting the support of Jih's former Stoneworking Team, Bani was ready to organize a full strike. She and the others decided long ago the killing blow of Tur's operation would be to cut off The Council's supply of furs. This was done through a change in priorities to the kills made by the Hunting Team and with the bonus of the stoneworkers choosing to ignore the requests for scrapers and other implements to process these kills. With two vital arms of The Elders now against The Council, resentment took hold over other adults who found themselves having to fill in duties not normal to them to keep things moving. In Kag's stead, Bani kept the peace as he was preoccupied with trying to restore an alliance with the remaining survivors of The Jagged Bark. With Dran gone to assist Kag in this endeavor, she was trusted with this work alone. A small pang in her stomach grew as she held her hand into the wall of her hut. These were like usual, but she could tell this occurred in a timelier fashion. It was time for her child to be born.

Delivering a child was a dangerous ordeal as the stakes were incredibly high. It was only through sheer luck and determination that Bani would survive and the child as well. Often only one would emerge to see a new day out of the ordeal. As new children were born only every so often, it was an important affair in The Elders. Tur kept his watchful eye over Bani on occasion during her pregnancy and when the time was near, a few volunteers stood by. As Bani was also Kag's partner, she enjoyed some of the benefits that came with The Council position and was given a special rug made from clouded leopard skin to rest on. Bani's tent was entered without permission as Tur's helpers were to assist her in the birthing process. Hyu and Kag were responsible for this task when they were both healers, but things became more complicated with Hyu's passing. Two of their strongest men hauled a log to balance Bani; she had to give birth standing up as this was considered the natural position. The baby would be pushed and gently fall on a bed of leaves to be protected.

Bani understood the responsibility she had and attempted to clear her mind. If Bani was lucky, labor would only take about ten-to-twelve hours. She felt slightly discontented with having to do this alone, but she knew there were greater forces at play. Bani held her breath as she attempted to ignore the presence of others around her, and she pushed. Prior to giving birth, members of The Elders were often given a diuretic using crushed ginger beforehand to smooth the cleaning process and the idea of ingesting material afterwards would ruin balance. Bani hadn't eaten and felt lightheaded as she stood by to close her eyes. She felt the prying gaze of others and the pause of village activity as they waited patiently for news of the birth.

Kag looked up at the sun's position through the treeline and saw that the day was waning. He waited on Dran to finish the last bit of the speech before their return to camp. Much was discussed between the two on their return. With the defeat of the Neck-Shells, The Jagged Bark could once again recruit and build their numbers up. A great political victory was assured and would certainly boost Kag's credibility among his peers. Kag's thoughts were of home, it'd been a two-day trek in the jungle, and he needed a bath. He and Dran were covered in mud to ward off mosquitoes that The Jagged Bark used as a natural defense to deter outsiders from approaching. The Jagged Bark moved further inland into the jungles to hide from hostiles but had yet to approach others about their return, so they were sought out. Although they kept an intricate knowledge of their environment, the shifting patterns of the jungle occasionally turned the two of them around.

"Dran, how much longer?" Kag asked, his voice reminiscent of younger days as he grew impatient.

"Dran has answered this already. She does not know. Stop asking." Dran grumbled and leaned against a tree. She instinctively checked it for the presence of bees nesting nearby.

Kag shrugged his shoulders and proposed they search for the smell of salt and follow the coastline back to camp. Dran had no other suggestions and decided to follow suit with the idea. The two walked with some sense of direction to go south and while Dran learned not to doubt Kag nearly as much, she still had reservations. Kag stood with a smug smile as the crashing sound of waves eventually came to their ears and Dran huffed in credence to this. The walk to The Elders camp was unusual as the sentry that often took watch was strangely absent, a young child took the reins in their stead. Kag gave a concerned look to Dran and their pace increased in speed as they made their way to the center of camp. Kag turned his head to see a growing number of people in the direction of his hut. His first thoughts were of Bani. Kag moved past the others with Dran barreling her way as well. Kag heard the strained sounds of Bani and thought she was injured but stood agape as he entered their home to see Bani was giving birth.

He quickly moved to support her and grimaced at the lack of preparation given for the birth. Expectant mothers were often given something to chew as pain relief during birth, but Bani was given no such thing. The others could only stand in awkward silence as Kag reprimanded them. His focus, however, shifted back quickly to Bani who was close to giving birth. Kag guided Bani as he'd done with other women in the camp before and gently waited until the child was finally born. A small lump of a boy emerged from Bani as tears swept down the new mother and father. Kag cut the umbilical cord with a hand-axe, this was far easier than using their teeth for a task. Kag looked to Bani to see what name she'd given the child. The two hadn't come up with one, as they were primarily concerned with their work on dismantling The Council, but naming was one of the most important things to be done in The Elders. Traditionally, new parents took the child to The Council to be named after the phase of the moon they were born under. Kag, Hyu, and Dran were named this way but given their current animosity, Bani decided to take the initiative and come up with a name on the spot.

"This one is named Cren." Bani said weakly as she took a moment to recover. Kag signaled for someone to bring them a bucket of fresh water to keep Bani hydrated amid the sounds of the crying baby. The remaining helpers sought to clean up the bodily fluids that leaked from Bani as best as they could while the rest of the band breathed a sigh of relief for Cren's health.

A couple of days later, Kag, Bani, and the new baby Cren sat in their home. Cren attracted the attention of all with his large brown eyes. It was easy to get sidetracked, but business still needed to be handled. Bani held Cren to her breast as she fed him and got up to join Kag for the last phase of the plan. Bani ignored all calls for rest as she was powered through grit alone. While Kag and Bani adjusted to life with a new infant, Dran organized the Hunting and Stoneworking Teams together for their strike. The group counting themselves numbered around twenty-five people, more than enough to cause a rupture in the group of seventy that made up their band. Bani shook Cren lightly to lull him to sleep while Kag addressed the others that gathered around the village center. Kag looked among the crowd and saw that the ever-tired Vut was part of the proceedings.

"We will go to The Council tent and give demands. We will not leave until they are met. Do we agree?" Kag asked as he received nods from his supporters. A few nosy people took their eye off their tasks to see Kag addressing some people.

The group made their way known as they headed in the direction of The Council's tent. As the group walked, they saw the prying eyes of others watching them as they did so. Dran could tell that not many were loyal to Tur directly, but The Council was such a respected entity it was practically forbidden to discuss such actions against them. What mattered now however was that they moved as a united front. Dran was the first to sit patiently as the others filled in the ranks and sat in front of The Council tent. On the inside, the quiet but observant Aab noted shadows moving along the tent but said nothing as the others idled.

"Our furs have run aground Tur, it is time to collect." One of the members of The Council stated, his gruff voice echoed the concerns of the others as he showed an outfit with relatively little wear on it. Tur gave a low laugh as he shook his finger for the younger man to wait his turn.

"This is correct. By now, the morning hunt would have ended. A fresh set of furs will arrive." Tur commented.

Tur used to leave the comfort of the tent to go and address the Hunting Team directly from their workshop, but in recent years has instead had them deliver a processed set for them right to their door. While the group wore clouded leopard furs this time, the fashion demand held their hopes high for a slain tiger. For Vut's young and overworked teenage crew, this was far too much of a challenge. Tur gave a smug look to the rest of The Council as his he stuck his long arm out and palmed the air to signal to onlookers to drop the furs as was always done. Tur waited for some time and his expression gradually grew sourer as the rest of The Council questioned what was happening. On the outside, a few other curious adults saw the earlier movement to the tent of The Council and decided to investigate. While some were previously opposed to Kag and the other's insistence on the matter, the opportunity to voice their complaints with the support of others seemed to be popular. Other adults soon followed and the initial twenty-five grew to add another ten members. Tur opened the flap of their tent to see what the delay was. Vut often had to come up with various excuses to conceal his actions of intentionally disobeying orders as Tur's thin patience severely eroded. The group of thirty-five that sat outside the tent of The Council saw Tur's face emerge as he looked at them with a scowl.

"Why are you here? Get back to work." He spat with disgust in his voice as he looked to find Vut or members of the Hunting Team in the crowd. A few quickly lowered their heads and got up, but the glare from Dran caused them to reconsider their movement.

"Tur. Kag and others have demands to be met. We will be listened to." Kag said as he grabbed his attention.

For his age, Tur's head moved quickly on a swivel as he heard the voice of Kag close by. Despite his declining position, Tur felt a second wind of energy. He used this not to better himself, but continued to attack those that he deemed as lesser. Tur decided enough was enough. His anger mustered him the strength to walk through the crowd and some dispersed as he radiated a harsh energy that carried through the soil. Kag stood up to meet Tur with a still look on his face as Tur gave a hearty laugh.

"Kag, this display brings amusement to Tur. Like a child who did not get biggest slice of Poulji. You have no standing." Tur said as he noticed Kag's still expression. Dran unveiled a hand-axe from her clothing as did the rest of the Stoneworking Team with far sharper edges than their own. Tur's eyes slowly affixed towards the others as he saw the writing on the wall.

Tur scowled at the growing resentment beyond him and invoked the oral histories that they treasured. To make use of the dead in Kag's eyes was a cheap move, his friendship with Hizo was remembered fondly and he was able to pull the wool over the eyes of many who held doubts regarding his leadership. Kag groaned at this but decided that two could play this game. Hyu's influence was ever lasting as she was popular among their camp. Kag looked at a young teen who joined the growing circle and noticed his previous injury with an impressive scar. He was one of the last people Hyu attended to before her passing. Kag called him forth and brought everyone's attention to the shy teen.

"Show your arm. Hyu mended this for you, yes?" Kag asked, as he absorbed the pause of those watching.

The teen nodded and a woman rose to show her foot, Hyu and Kag treated her foot with a salve after an accident with fire. One by one, other members of The Elders rose and highlighted areas where Hyu's hands touched them both metaphorically and physically.

"Tur thinks you are ungrateful. He thinks you are to be thrown away. Hyu was healer and not protected under leadership of Tur. Well, is he right?" Dran said with intent to incite the crowd fan the flames and get people angrier. It was working well as some talked much to Tur's stoic face that cracked under pressure.

Tur turned his back on the crowd and retreated into his tent. By now, it was obvious to the rest of The Council that not all was well. They discussed what to do as Tur nodded his head in disgust at the munity beyond him, but Aab slowly raised her hand for her to have them address the crowd.

"Tur, they are armed. What have you gotten us into?" Aab questioned with a low whisper as she looked through the slit of the tent to see the still very hostile faces standing outside. A few adults made their point more known with carried spears in hand.

Aab opened the tent and ventured out to face the crowd. She was seen as the most stable of The Council and her word was respected as much as Tur's who only ruled higher by seniority. The other members of The Council stood quietly as they each stepped out with their clouded leopard furs shown. Most of the adults quickly looked at their own clothing of grass and furs that were in varying states of decay as they glared. The exploits of the Hunting Team were exposed by Vut. The disparity between leadership and the collective was obvious. How was it fair that they had to mend one outfit for weeks at a time, but The Council got a fresh new set of clothing whenever they deemed necessary?

"Aab understands. There are mistakes that have been made. What do you want?" Aab questioned; her tone visibly shaken as she quickly imagined the hand-axes before her covered with blood. It would take a great deal of maneuvering to get out on top and she realized that concessions surely needed to be made. The other members of The Council looked to Aab for guidance on what to do while Tur sat quietly.

"1. Recognition Hunt will change! All children will know animal for hunt. Our children must be prepared." Dran said from the crowd. A few of her young students looked at her with some confusion as their time hadn't yet arrived but it would be soon.

"2. The Council tent must be in our main village, not separated from us all. You are supposed to be best skilled and must be present. It is a waste otherwise." Bani said. People instinctively lowered their voices so that Bani's could carry through the crowd.

"3. Tur will no longer be head of The Council. This is the compromise; our argument is in our spears and hand-axes, made by Bani. Things can get much worse." Kag said as he counted down with his finger. Kag and the others offered the three demands that the rest had asked for all this time. The first two were reasonable, but asking for Tur's immediate removal from power was a step that was controversial.

"Agree and we will work again." Kag said, much to the affirmative grumbles of the other adults who had enough of the current paradigm.

Kag hadn't seen himself as a leader at first, much as how Jih carried his own insecurities. With Bani and Dran at his side, he grasped his hatred of Tur to turn into a weapon to punish The Council's gross mismanagement of the band, and most importantly their involvement in Hyu's demise. It was here Kag hoped that the shift in loyalties would be enough to see the day. Dran raised an eyebrow and paused as they deliberated. Four other members of The Council stormed off in protest at Aab's choice to address the matter.

The very act of defiance among them was beyond their realm of acceptance. Tur now stewed with his arms folded at the crowd. Aab offered no call for the disgraced members to return to her. She knew she was outnumbered and meekly nodded her head, in acceptance that she would succeed Tur immediately. The angered man lashed out to yell, but his voice was already drowned out in irrelevance as they looked to Aab for the next decision to be made. To cement this as final, Kag stepped forward and with the support of everyone else around him, he extended his hand to Aab. Despite everything, Aab loved Tur with her heart but knew that this was an unwinnable battle. To preserve her life and everyone else's, she agreed to the demands as presented.

"It will be done. Aab takes over for Tur. Your point has been made." Aab said as she paused before raising her hand to shake.

As Tur saw the transfer of power conducted, he slinked off to gather what possessions he had to isolate himself from the rest. Although Kag had only wanted Tur to no longer be the leader of The Council, Tur couldn't fathom having to be subordinate to anyone else and instead decided to abdicate entirely from The Elders. With this met, Kag and the others could start to build a new vision into what The Elders was truly meant to be. It would be another matter to resolve the issue on Jih's shunning, but for now, Kag enjoyed this victory for some time to himself as he took the young baby Cren and hoisted him on his shoulder to give Bani a break. Now that the home front had won, it was time to be a father.

Mushroom Madness

Narro and Trekkal were out foraging in the outer plains of Iran while Jih and Sadal were on skinning duty for the last big hunt. Narro and Trekkal couldn't be happier that new skins were made as their clothing started to itch and their spares fell apart. They originally found two axis deer and were excited to wear the spotted patterns. Chores were a common duty that needed to be done to keep camp order and everyone had the ones they were best at. Jih floated around for various tasks and was responsible for maintaining and producing tools, while Sadal liked to process hides to suit her creative endeavors. Narro liked to organize the camp's resources into collective piles for use as a clean space was a clear mind. Trekkal preferred to forage over just about anything else as staying still was difficult for her. Narro studied the horizon while Trekkal quietly shuffled through her backpack as she looked behind her for any signs of being followed.

"Roots...boring...a few feathers..." Trekkal said to herself as she felt various things with the back of her hand. Trekkal watched her brother with interest as his attention was focused on something.

"These rolling hills and slopes feel familiar. Are we in the land of our people once again?" Narro said while he focused further on a land formation with large rocks embedded into it.

"Do you not recognize where we are? Not like we walked past these already or anything on our first time Narro. That was your fault." Trekkal recalled.

As the two walked in the direction back to camp, Narro let out a gasp as he noticed a clustering of dark brown and yellow mushrooms grown on a log. Trekkal felt the back of her head grabbed as Narro gripped on tightly with his palm.

"Hey Trekkal. Are those what I think they are?" Narro asked as Trekkal lifted her head to see where Narro pointed.

She gave him a confirmatory nod as the two laughed mischievously and scooped up the collection of mushrooms into her bag. Trekkal rubbed her hands together in excitement, a bounty of fungi was always a good snack on the road, but these were special. Trekkal figured at this point of the road, it was time to let Jih and Sadal know how things worked around here. To celebrate their long friendship, Narro and Trekkal decided to incorporate hallucinogenic mushrooms into their stew of the night. The use of these mushrooms was an important practice by The Aligned as these were used to convene with the spirits. Outsiders were rarely given such permission to use these without the approval of a Seer, but many were also ignorant of their properties.

With not much discussion on the matter, the two picked them out of the ground and smelled them to make sure they weren't mistaken. Narro and Trekkal were experienced in the art of mushroom collection and often traveled on the spiritual plane themselves back home to search for answers and for the sheer fun of it. The two returned to see Jih and Sadal in discussion on what to do regarding the skins they processed. Sadal built the bowls for tonight's dinner herself as Jih refused to work the wood.

"Jih thinks we should trade skins. Hotspark is low Sadal, these clothes can last another day." Jih huffed as he eyed the spares.

"I think we should repair our clothing instead, look at our skins! They're run ragged! This is what we agreed to Jih, hotspark can wait." Sadal said with some resentment in her voice as she noticed the arrival of Narro and Trekkal. She saw Narro evaluated the situation and stopped her discussion as he gave a laugh.

"So, Trekkal and I are going to prepare the stew shortly. To be clear, these mushrooms have properties that let us talk to the spirits. Are you willing to do this journey?" Narro asked as Trekkal gave a curious look to the two.

Jih had little experience with spiritual matters, but he decided to humor the twins in this endeavor. At this point, Jih questioned most things in his life and decided that perhaps something like this was worth pursuing. Sadal gave her consent as the last thing she wanted to do was make herself the odd one out. She found that in the excitement of her travels, she found herself unaligned with her spirits and decided to give herself clearance on the matter. She gave her nod and Trekkal happily grinded the mushrooms in her collected backpack for the stew. Narro took bits and pieces of their dried deer meat and crushed them into a powder with a stone. Jih and Sadal sat back with a shared expression of skepticism on their faces as they were eventually given the concoction. Jih gave a smell and while it offended his nostrils, he took it back in and swallowed with a harsh feeling at the back of his throat. He stuck his tongue out in slight disgust as Narro and Trekkal then stared at Sadal while they joined her. Sadal noticed that the effects they proclaimed weren't immediate, she seemed fine above anything else.

"You will need to wait some time, let it sit and begin to absorb what goes on around you." Trekkal advised Sadal.

After about twenty minutes, Jih noticed that although no wind was blowing, the grass started to move on its own. He paused as he evaluated what was happening. Jih skipped out on breakfast and so the effects of the concoction were much more immediate for him than Sadal. Although Sadal saw nothing visually, she felt confined to her position where she sat. Her entire body was weighed down and she slumped over.

"Trekkal...Trekkal! Trekkal!" She said, as she attempted to lift her hand and course through the air.

Trekkal gave a laugh as she and Narro finished their bowls. With their body type and experience with such things, they had better control regarding how to navigate their space under the influence. Narro trudged over and looked at Sadal who attempted to crawl along the ground but remained unmoved. Trekkal looked around as the four were isolated from anything that would bother them. Her attention was poised on Jih who seemed to offer no reaction as she witnessed what appeared to be soulless eyes. Jih was placed in an almost trance-like state of being as he noticed the allure of the wind on his face. Jih's sense of touch was elevated beyond what he was used to, as he attempted to sit up straight, he could feel the growth of his hair. It was a slightly unsettling proposition to have. Jih looked up at the sky and was taken away by the vast emptiness above him. If it were night, he would have seen a variety of constellations and outer stars that they used to keep track of the seasons. All he could see though was faces in the clouds, one of these reminded him of Hyu as he sprawled out his body. Narro decided to join Jih in his cloud watching endeavor as he summoned a resounding amount of strength to point to the sky.

"This one here. It is soft like a ball made of skins. Look at how it goes. Clouds are the spirits that tell us the weather. That big one there is filled with darkness in the center, this means rain will come. Hopefully this will be after we leave this place." Narro said to Jih who gave a simple grunt in response.

As Narro and Jih discussed with one another, Trekkal looked over at Sadal with a bit of worry. Sadal's breathing quickened as she rubbed her hands in the grass. Sadal's anxiety took hold and soon lost control of herself as she hyperventilated. As Sadal closed her eyes, she saw a distorted image of Deeso for a short second. Trekkal looked to Narro as she nodded her head to him, and he lumbered over to address Sadal. Sadal shook harshly but felt the warm hand of Narro grasp her own and she felt calm. Sadal's thoughts which were occupied previously with all sorts of contingency plans for an emergency or encountering an angry Deeso were now slowly replaced with an utter feeling of nothingness. It was a feeling of zen that was alien to her and caused some slight worry in her face that was seen by the others. Much like Jih, Sadal always had to be doing something for her to feel as if she had control. Trekkal stumbled next to Jih and guided Sadal and Narro over to her. Trekkal rolled along the ground until she bumped into Narro and gave a small giggle as she saw Sadal copying her movements as strands of dry grass got into her hair. Jih remained unmoved as he turned his head to ask the others a question.

"Narro says clouds are spirits. Jih is confused, are these everywhere?" Jih asked with a curious note in his speech. Narro and Trekkal gave Jih an affirmative nod.

"More or less. We can never be too sure where they are, but we know they have the potential to make great change. Narro and I always make sure to leave a little bit of food for them as they must eat like us. Being a spirit is tough work, at least that is what our Seer tells us." Trekkal said as she slowly lifted her head to look at Jih.

"Jih understands. If spirits must eat, they must do other things. Do spirits die? Where do they go?" Jih asked as he was trying to make sense of what was given to him.

The existence of an afterlife wasn't something Jih thought about much, The Elders rarely gave much attention to what religious matters were, but the idea gave him comfort. Life was seen as harsh and filled with work, an opportunity to reinvent oneself after death was thought provoking. Jih wondered what he would have done if working rock wasn't his calling. Jih knew of rituals for the deceased among his people as it wasn't uncommon for members of his society to be buried with these in mind. There was a tradition done for the various work teams that would honor the life of the recently departed. Jih knew that if he perished in the Neck-Shell raid instead of Hyu, he would have been buried with a crafted hand-axe from each of his fellow stoneworkers and given proper rites as a member of The Council.

"That's quite the topic to bring up Jih..." Sadal said with some surprise as she wasn't prepared for a discussion on mortality as the four stared up at the sky. Sadal could feel the warmth of the sun on her skin. Under the influence, this was magnified as she could feel her pores open and release sweat. She'd never given any conscious thought to the action but now her brain power was dedicated to this instead.

"Do they not discuss where people go when they die in your culture, Sadal?" Narro asked, as he was eager to hear her response on the issue.

"Huh? Oh. I'm not a priest, so they know more, but Ronkalk mentioned that our souls get recycled into some place where we must hunt our greatest adversaries in life. My greatest defeat was at the hands of a Weypeu, so I will see this when I return to the soil. After this hunt is completed, we may rest as accomplished warriors to be called upon in battle for the next generation. If I ever have descendants, I wish to be a guardian with the aspect of an Onpeu. Powerful yet majestic all the same." Sadal mentioned with pride in her statement.

"Very interesting. We have something similar-" Narro said as he was interrupted by Trekkal cutting him off. She slapped her hand in the grass.

"Are you just going to tell Sadal about The Land of The Dead like that? One of our most guarded secrets. She may be our friend, but she is still one of The Youngest. How do we know she will keep it a secret?" Trekkal huffed as she moved a piece of hair from her eyes.

"Well, Trekkal, you just brought it up. It would be bad form to not explain it now." Narro said with a smug grin while Trekkal's face reddened at her error much to Sadal's stifled laughter on the issue. Trekkal stayed silent as she let Narro explain The Land of The Dead. His description of it always gave her a small tinge up her spine despite having intricate knowledge of the topic for some time.

"The Land of The Dead is a place that is...uncanny. One can hardly tell the difference between this place and where we are sitting and looking at the sky. The spirits linger here and are able to reach out to us this way. It is an open field with no trees to speak of. The grass is gray like the eyes of the blind and there is no wind. The only sound is you wandering around to find another lost soul. We have lived a long time, and we will live for much longer. In the time where we learned from The First, the Land of The Dead was a barren place, but now there are plenty of us there. They say when our people are all gone, the land will be restored to its former glory with full color and our people will finally know peace. Only Seers have been able to access The Land of The Dead in our memory, but there may be other ways." Narro said as he saw everyone remain silent.

"This land. Can Jih find Hyu there? Hyu could survive home, she will thrive there." Jih said as he lifted his eyebrows attempting to imagine the scale of such a place.

"I am unsure. I know this is where our people go, but much like how this Eshe mentioned The Great Vanish, we had this happen to your people as well. It is likely Hyu would have joined them even from far away. You just have to be dead first." Trekkal voiced, addressing Jih's question.

"Big risk for Jih." Jih said as he ran his finger through his beard.

Trekkal couldn't help but laugh at Jih's response as she sat back in the grass and watched the motion of the clouds. Trekkal twirled her hair in her fingers as she mulled over their answers. Few times like these were special, she didn't have many she considered close with aside from her brother. An incredibly social being, she had many acquaintances but very few friends. Sadal sought to ask a question of her own as the atmosphere grew silent.

"I have a question for everyone. If you had a different role than what you'd do now, what would it be? As in, if you could pick something else." Sadal asked.

"I think I could be a Seer one day. To help others like me who seem to be looked at as stupid. Back home, Stelo and I had a good connection, she made things easy to understand. She was one of the only people who ever did..." Trekkal mentioned as her eyes looked to the ground.

"Sister, you annoy us, but to put yourself down like this helps nobody. You contribute in your own way and that is perfectly fine. For me, I think I would be an herbalist in the same way of your brother Kag, Jih. I lack a set job in the way that Trekkal does, but plants are interesting to me." Narro mentioned as he looked at Sadal's reaction.

"Jih was made to work stone, but if not. Jih would be builder. Homes are important for many people and The Elders are big band. Jih can make shelter, but shelter is not home. These are two different things to Jih, but some disagree." Jih commented.

"Mine should be easy, all I've ever known was the hunt, but if I could make clothes full time, that wouldn't be the worst thing in the world. My people lack a word for it, but you all wear my best after all!" Sadal said with a laugh that was joined by the others.

For some time, the group enjoyed their stupor that went on for hours. All good things come to an end as their grip on reality became stronger once more. Jih and Sadal weren't used to the coming down from mushrooms and expressed pain in their expressions as a multitude of thoughts once suppressed now came in full force. Jih felt groggy as he remembered all his current tasks to do, while Sadal's guilt caught up with her. Sadal involuntarily teared up and quickly wiped her eyes while Narro and Trekkal gave each other a subtle look. It was evident that Sadal saw something during her vision that caused the issue but decided to not bring it up again.

"Sometimes these things take us by surprise as well." Narro said, hoping to relieve Sadal's frown while Jih grumbled to himself slightly. After drinking some water, the two felt better and were in awe of how quickly the day went. Time seemed to have no effect on them until much later.

"Have something to coat your stomach. Take some of this meat." Trekkal offered Sadal as she lifted her hand over. Sadal waited but took it and stuffed the morsel in her mouth happily giving her a nod.

"Some Peymin caught by Trekkal yesterday. Boiled to perfection!" Narro commented as he gave a small smile to them both.

"Jih and Sadal thank Trekkal for food." Jih said as he shot Sadal a look. Of all things, Jih strived to be polite when he could afford to be. Sadal shrugged her shoulders and in-between chews gave her thanks. She coughed slightly as Jih patted her back for the fish to go down smoothly.

For Narro and Trekkal, Jih and Sadal were two strangers they hadn't imagined would come across their way, but the prospect was an exciting one. In the time that followed their encounter, the twins expanded their circle of trust, one that did not come easy. The Aligned took care of their own and could be wary of the outside, but the two found merit in their new companions. With the rest of the west now ahead of them, Narro and Trekkal prepared to hike through home once more and enlighten their new friends on the wonders and fears of the new horizon.

Trekkal and The Baby

Now fully in Iran, Jih and the others went through a large tract of wilderness to see a few small settlements in the distance. Their plan, once all awoke, was to contact anyone who remembers the night the sky was lit. Trekkal woke up first and found herself on the whims of no one as she had all the time in the world. She looked at her bag and one of Jih's spears and the wonderful idea of fishing came to her mind. She decided to fish in the traditional way of her people by stabbing blindly into the water and seeing what stuck. Trekkal found her peace whenever she was near water. She hated silence, but the soothing sound of rapids awoke something in her. Trekkal hummed quietly to herself as she walked away from camp until the small structures they made vanished behind her. Trekkal sat at the edge of the riverbank with her eyes focused on the water. She took great care to hit the surface of the water and alert the fish that some insect happened to land by. Trekkal remembered the plan, she just needed to do some fishing and grab a quick snack before nobody was the wiser. What Trekkal didn't expect however was for her concentration to be broken by a harsh cry. Seemingly abandoned in some grass by the riverbank, a baby was nestled in wrapped cloth. She looked up at the sky and watched the clouds roll by. In The Aligned's culture, undesired children were often left out to the elements to expire in peace.

"I-Is that a baby?" Trekkal asked herself as she attempted to keep herself focused on her task at hand. Trekkal's ability to focus, however, was often dismantled quickly and now the child was her greater interest. She awkwardly held Jih's spear as the weight surprised her but kept it at a ready position as she decided to step forward and check to see if she was correct. Trekkal parted through thick grass that Trekkal's eyes darted to the ground to see a small baby with its gaze fixed on her. Trekkal decided to scoop up the trusting baby in her hands. She sniffed her, and slowly moved her around to figure the baby was a girl.

"We should take you somewhere safe. I do not want you either, but you should have a chance to live." Trekkal said, unconsciously as she gave a higher-pitched sound to the baby. Trekkal held Jih's spear with one hand, while she cradled the baby back to her original spot where she fished.

"She...really looks like me. We share a nose and everything." Trekkal said, as she held the baby's face over the water to closely look at her new companion.

Trekkal used her finger to trace the outline of the baby's face and matched it with hers, so she knew that she was finally back in the land of her kind. Forest Seekers were a strange curiosity and her issues with The Youngest certainly hadn't changed much, although she warmed up considerably to Sadal. Trekkal held the baby in her lap and used her legs as an anchor while her head turned to see something walk further down river. It was a large animal, one she couldn't recall or at least bothered to remember until now. It had antlers on top of its head but was much larger than a deer. It held a spotted covering on its body and had a long tongue. It resembled a distorted giraffe to Trekkal's mind. She saw the animal walk to the edge of the bank and slurped water with its long tongue attempting to wrestle the mud as well. Trekkal was bewildered at the strange beast before her while she took her attention to the baby at hand. She was unsure of what to do now, but she studied this animal in detail. The strange hybrid looked at her and moved its antlers in the dirt. Trekkal interpreted this as her challenging the animal's territory and decided that with her new companion, challenging it wasn't a wise move.

"You must be the Marivapa![61] No, there were no mushrooms in my food. This is real. Come to me strange creature. Just like the legends have said, you have...antlers but you also have spots?" Trekkal asked herself in confusion.

Trekkal backed away slowly into the grasses and decided to house the baby inside her backpack. She made no noise as Trekkal tightly secured the child behind her and kept walking. Trekkal retraced her steps, and the pair made their way back to camp. Unknown to her, this baby was far from abandoned. She was left behind on purpose by her parents as they were out hunting. As Trekkal found herself with an extra mouth to feed, the parents that returned were in dismay. They split up hoping to reunite by nightfall with their lost one.

Trekkal returned to the others where the baby started to cry now that she was in an unfamiliar environment. Trekkal attempted to stifle the baby's crying by covering her mouth, but it was loud enough to wake others. Jih's eyes shot wide open as he heard a baby's wail. He got up and opened his tent flap and saw Trekkal with a baby in hand. He wiped his eyes and hoped he was seeing things. Jih yawned as he hadn't anticipated an early start today and was hoping to sleep in.

"Trekkal, what is that?" Jih said as he pointed to the baby she was holding.

"Oh. Well, I went to go get Peymin and I found this little pebble! Look at her. She was left to die and I simply could not let her go. We said yesterday we would go to some of the villages close by. Let us return her there." Trekkal said as she attempted to reason to Jih.

"Jih. I have an important question to ask you." Trekkal asked as she shook to calm down the screaming baby.

"Yes Trekkal, Jih can help. What is your question?" Jih asked now that he was more awake. He wasn't prepared for what Trekkal was going to ask him as he was processing the arrival of the new baby.

"Have you seen an animal with antlers and spots? It was very large, and I saw it by the river-Jih, I am serious! This thing was hard to describe. It walked around with a long tongue as well." Trekkal said in response to Jih's expression of disbelief on his face.

"Let them sleep, will you come with me Jih? We have to find her home." Trekkal mentioned.

---

[61] Emic word for Sivatherium.

Jih was happy to see Trekkal take charge for once, even if the task at hand was only because it centered her current goal. He decided to bring something to attention with Trekkal as he noticed his spear was missing but was instead in her hand. Jih thought her form with a spear was awful, but it couldn't be as bad as Narro's.

"You took spear of Jih without asking." Jih noted as he noticed Trekkal's vice on it. A flush of embarrassment came over her, Trekkal remembered Jih and Sadal had more hard lines when it came to personal property.

"Did it serve you well? If yes, all is forgiven." Jih said with an affirmative nod much to Trekkal's relief. Though Trekkal rarely found her actions worth apologizing for, she rarely sought to upset Jih as she took his minor scolding with the utmost severity.

Jih and Trekkal set off as the sound of the baby continued to ring in the pair's ears. Jih tried to concentrate on the route they were taking but couldn't focus. He decided to try his own approach to making their travels quieter. Jih knew that the baby attracted the wrong type of attention from onlookers and her harsh cry would be enough to warn animals from a mile away. Jih groaned as he glared at Trekkal and grabbed her out of Trekkal's backpack himself. Jih felt slightly uncomfortable as he felt the baby struggle around as it cried further. He hadn't realized just how soft their skin was. Jih's thoughts immediately went to Kag and how he was adjusting to life as a father.

"Jih, what do you plan to do?" Trekkal asked with concern in her voice.

"Jih has seen Hyu do this many times. Observe." Jih said as he tossed the baby up gently. He repeated this motion a few times, each increasing higher. Jih's eyes expanded wildly as he barely caught the baby on the third throw. Jih gave a slightly hushed laugh but was happy to see that the excitement gave her enough of a thrill to smile instead. Jih placed the baby back in Trekkal's backpack.

Jih and Trekkal continued onward as Trekkal moved ahead of Jih. The baby was now asleep, and the pair could hear themselves think. Jih kept a low voice as he approached Trekkal, and she nodded to confirm his words. She stopped short and saw a small village that was populated by some of her kind. There were about ten tents in all that housed only one person. Trekkal noticed it lacked some of the other functions of home, but she reasoned the baby must have come from somewhere close by like this one. She had half a mind to tell off the parents for their behavior but kept her tongue still for now. Trekkal held her hand out to Jih as she advanced closer and gave a gentle wave. She saw a woman hunched over some fibers and met her gaze. Trekkal noticed the woman was younger than herself but had a mature composure about her. Jih followed close behind and his eyes scanned the town.

"Who are you?" The woman asked Trekkal.

"I am Trekkal, and this is my companion Jih. Did you happen to leave a baby behind?" Trekkal questioned as she met a confused look on the woman.

"Baby? I do not recall if anyone was with child before they came here. We have been out on the plains for six months now and have not met a man out here. Wait- Trekkal? Would your band happen to know someone named Bhisal? If you are who you say you are, you have been talked about for some time. Welcome to our camp, sister. I am Veluh, from The Empty Eyes." Veluh mentioned as she waved her hand for she and Jih to join them.

Veluh wore a necklace with a single bear claw on it while her arms were covered with scratches on them. She wore a covering of deer fur that was strapped together to the back with fibers and a skirt of grass as she approached the others. Jih noticed her necklace and pointed to his as well with a nod. The two were welcomed by a small group of just seven women left that stopped their duties.

"In our culture, women that are old enough, leave the band to find a new home. The intent is to find your One in a new village, but it serves as a good experience to see the world for what it is without the comforts of home. Some people manage to do both without ever leaving." Trekkal explained to Jih as she pointed to a couple that held hands. Jih gave a curious nod as he continued to look around.

Jih and Trekkal followed Veluh as she gathered the others' attention. Trekkal saw a varied amount of activity as they were led through the small encampment. Two were skinning hides while one woman's responsibility was weaving fibers. Trekkal reasoned the rest of the band were out hunting for something in the meanwhile. Trekkal and Jih both received gentle waves as they labored over their tasks for the day. Trekkal noticed a slenderer woman among the others with her face buried in a basket. She wore her hair in a long single braid that draped behind her as she peered up to look at Trekkal. Her face lit up immediately as she recognized Trekkal. Trekkal remembered Bhisal as somewhat of a wallflower, but she seemed to flourish here compared to back home. Her smile remained white with youth. She was a minimalist when it came to clothing and only had a layer of fur trousers held together by a few strands of tightly woven fiber. Trekkal and Bhisal looked into each other's eyes with happiness. Bhisal's eyes were a hazel color that shone differently from Trekkal's brown.

"Bhisal!? Are you with the others from our troupe?" Trekkal called out to her.

"Oh! Trekkal, come to me. It has been so long! Have you found the meteor that Stelo wanted? When you find her, I am sure she will be filled with joy!" Bhisal mentioned as she hugged Trekkal. The two appreciated their respective warmth while Jih yawned.

"Unfortunately, we are taking a detour. I spent the last half year far east of here and saw nothing. A new direction might be better, but we came here on account of the little one on my back. They are not mine." Trekkal started to clarify.

"Ah-I see. Let us see this small one. Oh, hmm. None of us have had children, but I think the village due west of us has them." Bhisal explained as she gently handed the baby back to Trekkal.

"Aw, thanks anyway. I had a feeling that was the case, our camp is situated between both, so we will pick up the rest of our party and leave as one. Please, send my blessing to the others, for they are missed terribly." Trekkal said as she placed her hand on Bhisal's shoulder. Trekkal gave a satisfied nod as she realized Bhisal's gained strength since they last saw each other. Life on the plains was tough work to begin with, but to excel required great effort.

"About that. We had a much larger group when we first left, but some died to raids or injury on the hunt. Our strongest ones went to gather Peymin further upstream, but it has been about two days. The rest of us worry but what can be done about it?" Bhisal complained.

"The last thing I wish is for you to worry. We are surviving out here as well as anyone else. Thank you for believing in me Trekkal. I hope to be in these lands for another season before moving onwards. We may cross paths again." Bhisal mentioned.

Trekkal lowered her head in respect to Bhisal as she tapped Jih's shoulder to move on. The two said their good-byes with the goal in mind to keep moving and find the baby her home. Jih observed Trekkal closely as the two walked by. Despite having told many unrelated stories about her life, Jih barely knew much about Trekkal, the real one anyway. Trekkal was an icon all her own as she instilled confidence in those that she worked with back in their original band. While her age was seen as shameful for jealous older adults, Trekkal was seen as a repository of knowledge. She was spoken highly among those that survived. For her people, she was patient and could break down things well. Trekkal and Jih set their destination back to their camp as the next village was close by their own. Jih occasionally checked the baby's condition as they walked back to camp. Trekkal stormed in and clapped her hands.

"Sadal! Narro! Get up! We have things to do!" Trekkal shouted as Jih held a hand up to his ear.

Narro got up to the sounds of the other two causing noise, while Sadal remained asleep. Narro gently nudged Sadal awake and backed off quickly as he heard grumbled speech coming from her. Narro approached the others and immediately raised an eyebrow in suspicion.

"It would seem you are with child." Narro joked to Trekkal who rolled her eyes at his humor.

"I have not forgotten the plan, once Sadal wakes, we should-" Narro said, getting interrupted by the sound of Sadal picking herself off the ground where she slept. The four now gathered in the center of camp.

Sadal's eyes drifted to the baby and then back to Trekkal as she had a confused look on her face but said nothing else. She didn't think Trekkal was pregnant ever, but the baby looked so much like her it was uncanny. Jih could see that Sadal was still trying to figure things out, so he filled in the blanks for her.

"Sadal, Trekkal found baby by river. We went to previous village, but no parent was found." Jih mentioned.

"Yes! Would you like to hold her, Sadal? I feel you are great with children." Trekkal stated as she slowly handed the baby to Sadal to hold. Sadal cupped the child with no emotion and stared blankly into her eyes. Sadal felt uncomfortable and quickly gave her to Narro instead while Jih laughed at the sight. It seemed just like Hyu, Sadal also lacked maternal instinct as well.

Narro carried the baby for some time as the others took their weapons and a bag of furs with them to this village. It was another small community of about thirty of The Aligned. Trekkal was delighted to be in the company of her own kind once more as Jih and Sadal looked at one another. By now, Jih was aware that his people seemed to be missing everywhere but back home, but a small part of him still hoped to find a kindred spirit out there. It was a humble place, two constructed hearths were where most of the activity took place, with large tents housing some, while others rested under the stars. Trekkal ran ahead of the others, in her haste, almost forgetting the baby she decided to take responsibility for. She snatched the child from Narro's grasp and got the attention of a few people at the first hearth who looked at her with some confusion.

"Hello! I am Trekkal, and I found something that belongs to one of you!" Trekkal mentioned as one of the men looked confused. Jih noted their shared looks of confusion and wondered if the child was an orphan at this point. Two villages at this point seemed to turn towards this line of thinking. Jih couldn't bring himself to abandon the poor thing but feeding five was going to be a struggle all on its own.

"Did anyone lose a child?" The man asked as his comrades looking around for anything.

"The youngest one we have is five years of age. My One is with child but they are not born." Another man responded to him. Trekkal's face sunk as she realized nobody seemed to have a claim on this baby as she thought. Just how far away were these parents? Trekkal looked behind her at Jih's impatience and remembered they also needed to get directions for the meteor's location. Narro stepped forward to help address the situation.

"Thank you for your kindness. We will keep searching for this lost one on our own account. There is a question we must ask if you can help us?" Narro opened up.

"I suppose I can be of help. What must be done?" The man asked as he wiped some dirt from his hair.

"Which one of you remembers when the sky was alight for several days?" Narro asked as he saw Jih's expression change.

The man held his hand up to the others as he walked back to his tent and dragged his son who ran his finger through the dirt, a plucky eight-year-old who happened to have a remarkable memory. Though he seemed to lack focus in much else, there was one task he was good at. Jih's expectations were small as he looked over the child. Jih looked at the boy and then up at his father, he could hardly hide his distaste that they trusted their oral record to someone so young. Children were dumb and would often add events that never happened just to sound more interesting.

"Boy, tell them of what happened to us." The man said as he folded his arms.

"Can I go play?" The kid asked as Narro offered a gentle smile.

"In fact, we can play together. My friends and I want to hear your amazing story first. Not often does someone like you get to tell it to new people." Narro said as he knelt. The young boy folded his legs while the four listened to his tale.

"The sun set and blood from Smir-Tamdeu was on the hut. A big day was coming for us. At first there was nothing, but then! It came. Fire lit the night sky. The first of many. The rocks in the sky flew very far. There were many large rocks that landed." The boy said, making a blowing noise with his mouth.

"The sky was set on fire for three days. First very red and then a deep blue that led to black. The mountains have seen all. On the last day, the biggest one landed, there." The child said, finishing his story as he got up and pointed in a direction indicating northwest.

The details were vague, but he was at least able to give them directions. Jih and the others looked confused. He combed the young boy's account and focused on the largest of these rocks. Though Jih had no doubt the smaller rocks were still powerful, the largest is what he would need to fix home proper. There was still the matter of the baby at their disposal. Trekkal covered the baby's mouth as she started to cry again. She could tell she was hungry but there was nobody who could feed her.

"Trekkal, where did you find the baby again? Perhaps the parents returned back on their search." Sadal offered as a point of advice.

"I found her hidden in a patch of grass by the riverbank we passed on the way here. Should we go back?" Trekkal questioned as she received nods from the other three.

Trekkal grumbled to herself as her tale of the mysterious Marivapa was up in smoke and Jih's skepticism grew larger. Her only witness was a baby, so she was stuck defending herself. Sadal's hearing was the best of the four and her head turned as she saw two Thunderfeet were mulling about in a frantic search for something. Sadal watched the scene unfold and she turned to Trekkal.

"Trekkal, I think those are the parents." Sadal prompted her by the point of her finger.

"What do you mean? They look nothing like her." Trekkal said in an irritated tone.

"It would be unusual for one of The Youngest to rear us in such a way, but it is possible. We should see, the other group here does not seem likely to accept her." Narro commented, as he felt uneasy about asking the previous band to take another.

Trekkal grasped the baby and walked over on her own. Her mind was surely made up but she was willing to at least listen. Narro decided to follow while Jih kept himself close to Sadal. Trekkal held the baby forward and slowly walked over where the supposed father came over and shouted for his partner. On closer inspection, the two were clearly hunters with a sash around them with a bag sewn on that stored some meat. They both wore no covering and had a grass skirt bottom.

"She is found! She was in care of one of The Aligned, thank you! Thank you!" He shouted to the running woman as he turned to give Trekkal a large smile.

Trekkal was hesitant, she needed a question answered before she was willing to give the baby over.

"I found her alone by a riverbank. Why was she placed there? In our way, this means you are trying to get rid of the child." Trekkal said with a scrutinizing glare. The father of the pair had a look of anguish on his face.

"My partner and I are hunters. We placed her in a bundle so that she could be safe upon our return. It's hardly practical to bring the baby on the hunt where she could be injured. We didn't see it that way, but there is understanding." The man commented. His partner arrived and gave Trekkal a hug as she snatched the child away in the same breath. She was relieved to have her return.

"She is safe and well. A little hungry, but I didn't expect you to feed her!" She said with a slightly amused tone. The two looked at one another and decided to give Trekkal a small reward for her kindness. Trekkal was about to say more but was interrupted by Narro's appearance.

"We are happy to return-." Narro said. Trekkal stomped on his foot and gave a fake smile to the two of them.

"What my brother meant to say was that we could use some extra meat. If you can spare it for our trouble..." Trekkal said.

"For her, anything. Here, take this Tala carcass we found earlier this morning. Not exactly what you asked for but for the life of our little one, anything is worth it." The woman said happily.

Trekkal offered a small nod as thanks. She watched them leave for a while before returning to the others.

"I am proud of you sister! A whole conversation with The Youngest! Truly." Narro said with a hearty laugh. Trekkal didn't share his sentiment, she felt slightly empty, but she had to admit it was a nice pelt. Trekkal was conflicted on finding the identity of the baby's parents. She seemed to have a good life with those that cared about her, but Trekkal's personal animosity for The Youngest clouded her judgment.

"Who will teach her the old ways Narro? They do not know it." Trekkal said with distaste.

"That is for them to decide. I am sure they are familiar enough with our people to find someone who can. Things are not always as they seem you know." Narro said, trying to cheer her up.

Trekkal sighed as Narro's face frowned from her reaction. Narro felt he had the last trick up his sleeve to make his sister happy as he always did. As Narro and Trekkal collected Jih and Sadal, the four walked back to their camp reflecting on the strange events of today.

"So, one more time, tell me now about this animal by the river bank. It had antlers, stripes, and it was very large, yes?" Narro asked again. Sadal was busy trying to visualize how much meat it would bring home. Her mouth salivated as she was getting hungry.

"Spots! I said spots Narro! You also forget the long tongue, that is very important you know! The feet were like that of Ker-Mah as well!" Trekkal said as Jih let out a laugh of his own. Although Trekkal's mystery creature still evaded them, her passion for such a topic stayed with them as they went back home to rest. Trekkal vowed to find the mysterious Maripava once more and prove to the rest of the group that she was telling the truth.

Shell Shocked

Unusual for his behavior, Narro was the first to wake from the fire. Sadal kept watch that night while the other three of them soundly slept just as she wanted. Jih volunteered but Trekkal's insistence for Jih to relax forced him to enjoy a good night's rest. Jih remained suspicious of Sadal's zeal to take watch but couldn't argue against it. Sadal couldn't sleep that night as much weighed on her mind. The thoughts she had about Deeso loomed over her once again. The air was still, and she coughed as her throat felt dry. She shook her small canteen that was once filled with water. Sadal turned around as she heard the shifting of someone behind her. She felt relief as it was only Narro who poked his head out behind her. Narro looked at her with a slightly weird expression on his face as he noticed how jumpy Sadal was.

"How was the watch yesterday, Sadal? Third time this week. I believe I am finally next." Narro asked her, his voice low as to not grab attention from Jih or Trekkal.

"We are alive. Nothing happened." She replied with her back still facing him. She sat with her legs crossed and surveyed the endless plains in front of them. Grass went on for miles all around and the squish of mud as the march from the fresh rains were enough to make one squirm.

"You have been working very hard lately. I just appreciate you wanting to keep us safe." Narro commented as Sadal gave a pause in her words. Narro approached Sadal and gave her a calming rub on the back. It was enough to have her drift to sleep, but she knew there were tasks to do for the day. Sadal found Narro's touch comforting as the two strengthened their bond often.

"I thought it was the dry season but clearly the spirits had other plans." Sadal complained at her wet feet. She found a dryer patch of grass and attempted to dry herself off by rubbing them harshly on the ground.

"Not too far north of here while I was foraging yesterday, I found a band of my people with many goods. We should go to them." Narro mentioned with slight concern in his voice. He let out a small cough as he kept his distance from Sadal who appeared to not react at all to his words. The last few days were rough with constant rainy weather making the others feel lousy, but they continued making progress.

"I don't have any other ideas, so we will go with yours. Wake the others and take us there." Sadal ordered. Sadal heard no movement from Narro and spoke again with a much more personable tone.

"Please." She added with a small smirk not visible to him.

While Narro went about his duties, Sadal prepared a few small bags filled with dried meat they prepared some time ago. Although hunger was evident on the party's faces, opportunities for hunting would come again soon, and this meat was shelved as an offering of good faith. Narro gave Jih a hearty pat on the shoulder for him to get up. He stirred but awoke and rubbed dirt out of the corner of his eyes. Trekkal was the last one to get up and so would face the penalty that he saw fit.

"Wake up sister." He said, with a swift kick in the behind as she frantically skirted around.

"Stop doing that! You make me think something bad will happen." She remarked as she wiped drool from her face.

"Will we pack?" Jih asked as he gestured to the objects on the ground left scattered around.

"We will spend another day here, but for now we will be visiting a settlement up north. It should be about an hour from here. Grab your things though." Narro explained to the three of them, with Sadal giving a nod in confirmation. The group took a few moments to fill their packs and went towards their route.

Narro's instructions were followed to the letter and the group came across a small settlement of The Aligned that welcomed their kind with open arms. The layout of their camp held a few larger tents that displayed items for trade on patches of fur while smaller ones were dispersed further out to serve as individual homes. As these were highly mobile traders, they lacked more longer lasting features to their settlements. Narro noticed the lack of worked piles of stone and the small size of a hearth in the distance. Today was a day of leisure for them as the tasks were long complete and food was in plentiful supply. Trekkal and Narro surveyed the scene with much enthusiasm as they did so, finding comfort with their kin. Jih and Sadal as outsiders gauged how to feel on the reactions of the previous two.

A large man looked in the distance as his eyes perked up upon seeing the figures walk towards his encampment. His outfit was assorted with multiple layers of fur that dragged behind him as he moved over to greet the new arrivals. He carried some rope with him as he did so. Trekkal noticed an ample number of containers in progress, mostly woven from scavenged reeds and some made with wood and animal hides. The objects in them were random but were oriented between a few of the others that inhabited the camp. She could overhear discussions of various things, nothing though about the meteor. It was to be expected, they'd been on the road for some time now and the news that would have been shocking gradually faded into irrelevancy. Some people though like themselves were fixated on it and could provide essential context to their mission.

"Sadal. These seem to be good people. They are traders, so we must have something of value to give." Narro commented, his eyes fixated on the bag of meat in her hands.

"Jih, Trekkal. You two look around and see if there is anything we can trade that will be equal to our meat. Some bones go a long way, I could use a new flute." Narro added with directions for the two of them.

Jih nodded and patted Trekkal to follow him as the other two made their way towards a seemingly bored man whose eyes were glazed over. He looked at the two that were left and decided to satisfy his curiosity.

"You must be looking for something, yes? I have many goods." The man said, hoping to get their attention over the others around them. Narro took the lead in the discussion. He imagined things would go smoother operating with one of his own kind.

"Yes. We are looking for the meteor. Do you remember that night?" Narro questioned as he gestured to the sky.

"The big one? You are not the first to look for it. Some with the time to spare have come to us many moons ago. They were strange types, somewhat flighty with high pitched voices. I had never seen so many, but they travelled as one. I have what you seek, but our people trade for what we want." The man replied with a yawn.

"I have meat to trade." Sadal mentioned with a small bag of dried deer in her hands. It was certainly appetizing to the rest of her party that hadn't eaten breakfast.

"This will not do. I have a better idea. We should play a game instead, are you interested?" The man asked with a sly grin as he studied Narro and Sadal.

"A game? Are you a child?" Sadal retorted quickly to the man's demands. Narro gave Sadal a slightly worried look as he could see she was tired. Perhaps there was something correct to Jih's almost parental complaints.

"We are one to grow old, but not grow up. You Youngest are so worked up. Entertain me and I will deliver." The man said with confidence knowing that they had nowhere else to go.

"Hold on. Before we do anything, what is your name? Your band? How are you to be trusted?" Sadal questioned, holding out her arm to stop Narro from moving closer. The man let out a hearty laugh. He found Sadal's testiness typical of her kind, and with a smile introduced himself officially.

"Straight to business. I am known as Khok, and our band is called The Cracked Dawn. As you can see, we are quite bored. The fact we let you walk here, and do as you do, means we are no threat to you." Khok mentioned as he flexed his muscles. Khok approached Sadal and leaned in. She immediately recoiled at the gesture and backed away.

"No, none of that. What are you doing?" Sadal asked, her words pointed as Khok seemed shocked.

"Oh! Surely you must know we rub noses as our greeting. I assumed he would have told you. I mean no offense." Khok commented, while looking at Narro who returned the greeting without question. A moment of silence came from Sadal as she begrudgingly extended her hand out instead. Khok raised an eyebrow as he returned the greeting and awkwardly shook.

"I am Narro, and this is Sadal." Narro mentioned and introduced themselves properly to Khok. The other members that accompanied Khok stuck to themselves but looked back occasionally at their new visitors. Some offered a gentle wave with their baskets.

"Now then. You are my guest, so I will have you offer an idea first. This is exchange." Khok explained as he tapped the dirt for the two of them to sit down. Sadal was the first to sit down with Narro following suit. She held her face in her hands as a wave of tiredness fell over her. She needed a way to keep herself awake.

"If a game is what you want, I would like to do a race. It invigorates the senses, and the terrain here is flat, so the run would be fair." Sadal mentioned as she looked behind where Khok was sitting.

"Running is not part of our way." Khok said with a laugh as he massaged his stomach. Being traders, his group ate well with the amount of game that came into their vicinity. Khok looked over at Sadal and studied her carefully. Practically every inch of her body was suited to running both long distance and for sprinting. Compared to Sadal's frame, he was far from a runner and knew that in any serious capacity, he would easily lose.

"I have shells. These shells are all the same type, however there is a mark underneath that will be the one to use. I will show you them." Khok demonstrated as from the vicinity of his bag, he withdrew colored shells. They were a collection of shells gathered from freshwater gastropods that Khok found interesting. He received a strange look from Sadal but ignored it as everyone had their hobbies.

"I am unsure about your choice. You control the shells and their flow, how will it be fair?" Narro asked with a stroke of his beard in concentration.

"Your friend here can watch me with her sharp eyes. Do you trust the one named Sadal? This is simple, a game of chance where everything is equal." Khok said with a smile. Narro nodded at the explanation that Khok gave, finding it sufficient for his liking. It seemed logical enough and with Sadal's sharp eyes, she would be able to find any wrongdoing.

"Now nobody is to enter empty-handed. My friend, what do you have to offer?" Khok asked with his hand extended. Narro looked at his pack and rummaged through it to withdraw a flute.

"Sadal, let me offer this first. This is my flute. I carved it out of Cerbho ivory. It is old though." Narro mentioned. This is one of the first flutes he carried from his time in India when he first met Sadal and Jih. Along the way he found a deceased hippo and made quick work to get the ivory before none was the wiser. Khok didn't need to know he scavenged it. Narro saw Khok's look of approval as he placed a heavy hand on his shoulders and clamped hard. The man's eye studied the construction and happily took the piece without issue.

"Cerbho, you say? Well, quite the tough kill. I accept this offering." Khok commented as he arranged the shells.

"I assume you are playing first, Narro?" Khok asked with an unassuming grin on his face. Narro nodded and placed his hand down to signal he was ready.

"Go ahead, win back your flute and get us what we need." Sadal said with a warm smile that gave him some encouragement.

Narro watched intently as Khok moved the shells. It was a bewildering speed that he wasn't prepared for. Sadal was dizzy as he spun the shells for a very long time. Khok treated a game like this one as an endurance test as he hoped to break the person's concentration. Narro felt his eyes dry as he held back the need to blink. He knew that if he did, he'd lose sight of the one he found. Khok's movements were a blur to his vision. Narro knew this man was here to win and so he debated his options carefully. He looked to see for any sort of inclination of where the marked shell would be, but he remained frozen in his choice. He replayed the movement in his mind and remained indecisive for some time. The pressure was immeasurable as Khok smiled at Narro waiting for his resolve to crack. Khok kept his eyes trained on him as Narro attempted to decide what to pick.

"Narro...You have to pick something eventually." Sadal said with some annoyance in her voice. Khok watched Narro's reaction with glee as he sighed in resignation and picked the middle shell. The mark was missing. Narro got up this time and switched positions with Sadal.

"Better luck next time Narro. Sadal, what do you have for me?" Khok asked with the same grin on his face.

I want to knock his teeth out. Sadal thought as she gave him two halves of her broken throwing spear from her pack. Khok raised his head to look at her with an initial frown on his face as he wasn't expecting a broken tool.

"The wood is from a strong tree. You can haft it to make a better spear." She explained to Khok. He looked it over and shrugged his shoulders. Narro sat and focused intently on the movements made by Khok. He couldn't wrap his head around how he was doing this. While Sadal considered her choice, Narro waved for Trekkal to come forward. Jih relaxed by a tree as he watched Trekkal return to her brother.

Sadal's lack of sleep had gotten the better of her as she struggled to keep track of the shells. Her choice was the furthest left of the three, and she hit the ground in frustration as this one too was not the marked shell. A small mound of dirt was left behind from her outburst. She stewed in anger for some time as she saw Trekkal approach the game. Sadal reasoned Trekkal liked to goof off so playing games would be natural to her, but Trekkal's reaction wasn't what she expected. Trekkal lifted her nose up at the sight.

"I hate this game. Not playing." Trekkal commented as she saw Khok with the shells on display.

"Trekkal. You must participate. Sadal and I both lost to Khok, and we have one more chance, otherwise we have to start from scratch again." Narro said sternly to her. Trekkal rolled her eyes at Narro's comment, but knew he was right.

"I can always take the clothes off your back if you want. Yes, young one. Can you succeed where your friends have failed?" Khok asked.

Trekkal noticed the belongings that were piled up next to him and she realized that they had to put something as collateral for the game. She took off her pack and placed it on the ground and took out some smoothed stones from the river. Their value was best as sling ammunition, but Khok appreciated the aesthetic value. The moment Khok stopped moving the shells, Trekkal picked the first one without any thought, which prompted intense anger from both Sadal and Narro. While Sadal and Narro were meticulous planners, Trekkal sought to use the element of randomness to her advantage. Khok's movement was basically impossible to reasonably predict so it made no sense for her to try and left the choice to random chance. It was a calculated risk, even if Trekkal looked incredibly disinterested.

"Trekkal! How could you just pick something without any thought whatsoever?" Narro said with much annoyance in his voice. Sadal said nothing as her expression became even angrier, both at their situation but also at Trekkal who didn't take an ounce of seriousness in the matter. Khok let out a hearty laugh as he eyed his new collections.

"You know, this is where the last group like you gave in. They offered me Jaat which saved me a good trip. Though I remember there were four of you. Have him come forward." Khok proposed as he looked at the other three.

"Oh, he isn't..." Sadal tried to explain as she saw Narro waving Jih over. At first Jih ignored Narro's wave, but as he kept doing so, he decided to approach. Sadal looked somewhat worried as she knew Jih was getting discouraged over the past few days but said little about it. Khok's normal joking expression changed to a more neutral one as he studied Jih closely. There was a certain type of seriousness that fell over his face.

"What is this?" Jih asked, looking at the three of them and more closely at the miserable faces of Narro and Sadal.

"We're playing a game. This man here knows where the meteor is, but we have to win. We used up all our chances Jih." Sadal explained to him. Sadal's mention of the power rock inspired Jih to go forward.

"Jih will play this game." Jih said which prompted a strange look from Khok. Khok noticed Jih spoke differently than the others and wondered if his suspicions were correct.

"Before you make your pick, you must offer me something of value for what you seek. Choose wisely." Khok said to Jih.

Jih folded his arms and remained silent as he considered what he had to offer. He looked at the assortment of goods by Khok's side. Sadal gave a spear, Narro gave one of his many instruments, and Trekkal offered smooth stones she picked up from the river. Jih looked at his pack, which mostly had just basic implements for first aid and working rocks for tools. Jih took Khok's message of something valuable to heart and took off the necklace he wore. Khok raised his head at Jih and was curious about what was on offer.

"Jih will give this necklace." Jih said as he opened his palm gently to Khok. Jih chose to give Hyu's necklace as an object he thought was of equal value to the power rock. Sadal held a look of shock on her face as she attempted to stop his actions.

"Jih, you don't have to give that to him. It's important-" Sadal said in a low voice to him.

"It is simple, but well crafted. The claw is also unique. I accept." Khok said as he clutched it in his fist. Khok let out a hearty laugh that wasn't reciprocated by Jih. His eyes were trained on Khok as he already looked to see where his opening would be. The shells rotated with a speed that would bewilder anyone, but for Jih, he remained unmoved.

"Jih, make your pick." Khok mentioned while running his hand through his hair.

Jih looked at the shells and back at Khok who remained with a judgmental expression. Jih noticed something was off and he decided to lift his head up from the shells to look at Khok. Jih waved his hand slightly and prompted Khok to come closer. Khok was expecting a clean house but was met instead with the quick hand of Jih gripping onto his finger. Jih reached over and grabbed Khok's wrist with his left hand and placed his right over his index finger. Jih bent Khok's finger back as he let out a grunt in pain.

"W-What?! What are you doing! My finger!" Khok yelled as he got the attention of the others in the camp who turned their heads with concern.

"Jih! Stop! You are hurting Khok! He will not say anything now!" Trekkal said as she attempted to shake Jih.

"No! Khok cheats. You are lucky Jih did not cut it off." Jih replied with a slam of his fist into the dirt as he left an imprint on the ground. Jih pointed with anger at Khok as the two met eyes. Jih showed his teeth to Khok in rage, he hated cheating in any sort of game. If the rules were broken, this generated disorder and Jih resented this above all else. Jih valued control and sought only to lose due to his lack of skill rather than any externalities that would affect the outcome.

"Jih, I saw it with my own eyes. Khok is crafty, but he is playing fairly." Narro explained to Jih. Jih shot him a glare as he pointed to Khok's folded leg where a spare shell was barely visible under his furs. Jih knew little how to perform the art of sleight of hand, but he'd seen it done enough times to know when he was had.

Sadal said nothing as if she had known, she would've easily done the same thing or worse. She raised an eyebrow curious about the outcome before her. Khok remained quiet as he wanted to see if the others would go against each other while he could, but at the expense of the rest of his hand decided to come clean. Jih turned his hand to a fist as he threatened to punch the Khok before him as he raised his hands to defend himself. Jih sensed the man's weakness and decided to lower his hands down as he stared at Khok.

"Please! I was just having some fun. No, he is correct. I did cheat. I should have never doubted the wisdom of The First. I should have known better. The old ways have not been forgotten." Khok coughed as he sheepishly looked at the others.

"Well, seeing as you deceived us, I will take our stuff back." Narro stated with some annoyance in his voice. He quickly moved to scoop their belongings back, with Trekkal's face filled with glee as her precious rocks were returned.

"How did you know Jih?" Trekkal asked with genuine confusion.

"Kag likes to cheat, Jih has seen it before." Jih mentioned with a huff. Jih remembered playing this game often as a child when waiting for training to start. Khok had gotten plenty of others with his antics, but Jih quickly learned to spot deception.

"Khok, tell Jih where power rock is." Jih demanded as he watched Narro give back their things. Jih placed the necklace over himself once more and tapped it to secure it in place.

"I do not have the information you seek personally, but there is one I know who has been trying to piece together everything that happened. Please believe me!" Khok said to satiate the rising anger of Jih.

"Well, we're waiting." Sadal said as she bit her tongue.

"There is a man named Fahlrit. On occasion, he sends someone looking for ochre and we do business. He used to be a hunter but now is a painter. He has been trying to depict that night in art or so the story goes." Khok mentioned.

"Where does he live?" Jih asked as he looked behind him to see the others carrying the same annoyed expression.

"After the accident, I can hardly imagine he goes far. Go west about two hours from here. You will find a small patch of trees and some caves. His people live in that area." Khok explained as he let out a yawn.

The exchange afterwards was brief and the four decided to cut their losses and keep the smoked meat they originally offered. Jih gave a small laugh as he heard the tales of the other three who were swindled by Khok. Jih decided to cook them a nice meal when they returned so that their spirits could be high once again. With the new knowledge gained by Khok, Jih and the others decided the next task on their list was to find the one known as Fahlrit.

Painted Skies

The next morning, the four sat by the fire as they looked at one another in thought. Jih gnawed on an acorn and spit it out in disgust. The search for Fahlrit was on everyone's mind but they weren't sure just how to do it. Trekkal looked around for any notable landmarks to map their current progress but was met with emptiness once again. She scratched her back while looking at the rest of the group talk among themselves briefly. With the idle conversation of the others shortly dying down, Jih decided to bring the focus of their talk to the matter at hand. Jih hoped that Khok's directions would hold and that they could find Fahlrit before nightfall.

"We must find this painter. Jih hopes he can remember that night." Jih said to the others as his gaze met Sadal's. He saw that Sadal was ready to speak with a plan, and he leaned back with interest.

"Khok gave us a vague direction to go, so we should probably make our search wide. We'll all start from the same place but branch out like a tree. If we hear or see nothing, we will return to our original location and make our way back to camp. What do we say to that?" Sadal asked of the others. She turned to Trekkal.

"That seems fine. I remember Khok saying that there is a woodland nearby. We can find more supplies while we are out. The trip is two hours, so I am unsure if we should just pack our stuff now and use a cave for shelter or just stay here." Trekkal proposed. She felt the touch of Narro as he rubbed her back in acknowledgment to her statement.

"Perhaps once we explore a bit more, we can find some smoke in the sky. This will let us know where his people are, and we can follow it to Fahlrit." Narro added on. Narro and Trekkal had a vague idea of what to expect, their native Iraq echoed the landscape here with not much difference. The Aligned in their area would either use rock shelters or tents of their own making to build their communities.

"Khok said that Fahlrit had some sort of accident, I wonder what happened? We should probably quicken our pace, so we are able to make it in time." Narro mentioned with some concern in his voice. Sadal gave him a small grin, she appreciated Narro's limitless kindness for those he'd never met before.

Jih got up hearing everything he needed to know and grabbed his spear and backpack before heading out. He stood at the outer part of their camp while the others took somewhat longer to get into gear. Whenever Jih felt he was one step closer to the power rock, all bets were off. He was bursting with anticipation to get things started but the routine came first.

"Jih! You forgot to brush your teeth!" Trekkal teased, as she pointed to a visible piece of crushed acorn left in his mouth. Jih covered his mouth with his hand and ripped the small piece out before tossing it to the ground below. He would find a suitable twig later.

After their morning tasks were done, the four decided to leave some of their stuff to show that the camp wasn't abandoned. They proceeded to go in the current direction that struck their interest. Sadal took a moment to scan the horizon as the wind blew through everyone's hair. Sadal looked to the sky for signs of smoke, but they remained clear. Sadal observed the movement of animals that would be good to hunt on their return.

"Nothing all around us once again." Trekkal complained.

Past where the four walked, the appearance of tents that haphazardly dotted the landscape now vanished behind them back to the expanse of nothing awaiting them. A few hyenas gnawed at the carcass of a gazelle and yelped towards the group as they turned to give an annoyed look of disgust and kept walking without saying a word. How were these things everywhere? The four stopped their pace and looked around to see any landmarks they could find. Jih noticed a rock protruding from the ground that was in the shape of a thumb and copied its position with his own. Jih and the others agreed to meet at this odd rock in due time. Sadal sighted the presence of a long low-flow stream that seemed to lead everywhere. There was a large hill that overlooked much of the plains they walked on and a moderately sized woodland that matched Fahlrit's directions. The four agreed to step towards this direction and set off with little time to spare.

Jih was the first to go and saw the outline of trees in the distance. He looked to his left to see some scratched pieces of wood. His pace quickened as he remembered the mention of woodlands by Trekkal, he had to be close. The second part of this was a cave with grass that grew on the surface and bottom of the entrance. He weaved through the woodland and peered through the lines of trees. A large brown figure appeared in the distance and shuffled its way around. His route took him to the territory of a hungry cave bear that was too busy clawing at a tree to bother with him, at least for now. Jih took the miracle with the utmost severity.

Large Kal-Bher. Jih should go elsewhere. Jih thought as he quickly ran away in the other direction.

Jih scratched his head wondering if he should attempt to go back into the woods but decided that was far too much of a risk until the bear was well out of his range. He was rightfully apprehensive from when he and Sadal encountered a sloth bear who was anything but slow. Jih thought of the others and how they were doing.

Sadal looked to traverse a nearby hill so she could get a better vantage point. She kept her body low to the ground to keep herself balanced as she felt the rapidly increasing steepness of the hill. Along the way, she saw a goat effortlessly scale the hill. It let out a small yelp as Sadal glared at the animal, she felt as if it was somehow mocking her as it watched her lose balance. Sadal felt herself slipping and slowly slid down the hill much to Trekkal's amusement who watched below seeing the outline of Sadal in the distance. Sadal had enough control to keep herself from rolling downwards but she was on a steady decline. Sadal decided to goad her new goat adversary by throwing a rock in its direction. She stood up to hurl it and yelled across hoping to catch its attention.

Narro decided to go off the beaten path and search for the smoke that was in the sky just as he told the others before. He decided to go to the stream and follow its direction, as he figured that the band that lived nearby needed a source of freshwater that they could come to. Narro's gamble paid off as he looked to see evidence of people having worked this area before to some degree. He saw a small midden of worked bone fragments and pilfered through it for his own needs. A few long pieces could be useful for engravings for ritual needs or to fine tune the next flute he wanted to make. Narro noticed that this stream also led right to a section of the woodlands that Jih previously entered but was much further away. Narro walked in to see that some of the terrain was certainly worked, the trees had bark that was stripped for tannin and others. On closer examination, Narro recognized these as birch trees[62]. He was aware that these trees were important for making handles and he knew that an expert stone worker must have been among them. Narro looked next for the caves, these were harder to find than most, but he stumbled on a new sight. The smoke he thought to find led himself into a new village inside the woodland where there was a group of The Aligned who were resting. Narro approached carefully, and made his presence known by giving a small wave as he stood by the trees. He was given a look of scrutiny but was allowed inside.

"Why do you come here? Hm?" One of the men asked Narro as he sized him up. Narro raised an eyebrow, they were about the same build and while the last thing he wanted to do was fight, he cared much for his friends and would do whatever it took to help Jih with his goal.

"I look for Fahlrit. A man named Khok sent me." Narro explained. Narro took a step back as he noticed the man's face change dramatically upon hearing his name. There was an air of confusion on Narro's face as he processed the man's reaction.

"You. You want to see Fahlrit? What business do you have with him?" The man said with his eyes pointed to the ground. It was obvious to Narro that the topic of Fahlrit was somewhat of a hard-hitting topic, but he needed information.

"He remembers the night the meteors flew across the sky. Khok told me he was painting it. I would like to ask him about what he saw. That is all." Narro answered as he offered a small grin.

"He lives about twenty minutes from here in a cave. We have tried to have him come here, but he crawled up himself and refuses to leave." The man explained, as he acquiesced to allow Narro to go further.

Narro took the man's directions and found himself at the promised location. Narro looked hesitant as he had an immense distrust of caves after he and Trekkal accidentally disturbed a cave bear. He felt his fear was somewhat irrational as his band knew he was clearly living there. Narro threw a rock down the long chasm and waited for a response of any kind. Much to his shock, a rock was thrown back at him, almost surpassing his speed.

---

[62] Birch bark tar was a staple in Neanderthal tool production as this process was used to haft stone to their wooden handles, rather than wrapping them tightly with fibers as Jih or Sadal do for their tools. Birch bark was more reliable, but this could be done with pine resin or hardened beeswax as well!

"Hello...?" Narro answered. As it was still daylight, a good portion of the cave was visible as a man crawling on the ground noticed the figure standing at the mouth.

"Who? What do you want?" The man replied, visibly annoyed at the presence of his visitor. Narro noticed he was missing a leg as he attempted to support himself along the wall. He seemed to be in relatively healthy shape otherwise. Narro thought the man reminded him much of Jih, with a rough exterior. They looked to be about ten years apart, perhaps a grim look into the future to come.

"Well, I came looking for you actually. You must be Fahlrit, the painter? Khok sent me." Narro mentioned rubbing his stomach.

"That man truly has a Sarmpa stomach. He owes me a great debt of six pelts and has sent the likes of you to quiver for him. Yes, I am Fahlrit." Fahlrit mentioned as he sat himself on a rock and looked at Narro. He studied him closely and saw that he meant no harm.

"Well, better you than the cannibals I suppose." Fahlrit added on with sarcasm dripping from his mouth. Narro gave a nervous laugh at the man's attempt at a joke. Cannibals? Those were but simple stories told to him and Trekkal as children to stay behaved.

"It would appear so. But why are you out here alone? The Youngest are the ones to oust themselves from the world like this. You have people concerned for you." Narro asked. The Youngest were a proud group of people to the point of self-sabotage, thinking they could rough it out on their own. Narro knew his people though thrived on connection and no matter what would have people to call upon in time of need.

"I live in a cave to be away from others. You are ruining that now. There is a troublesome group not far from here to bother instead. My relatives, the ones who told you how to find me I am sure." He added on as he gestured in the opposite direction.

Narro, always insistent on making a new friend, looked at the man again, this time at his hands. They were an unusual reddish color, and the walls too were covered with attempts of artwork in varying quality. Narro found a kindred spirit in Fahlrit as a fellow painter. Narro hoped to find inspiration for his own works through the avenues of another aspiring artist. He analyzed the lines of his hands and saw there was intentional design considered with his ochre application.

"Your fingers, is that blood? No, you have a gift for art. Much like myself. I see the ochre." Narro pointed. He gave a small grin as the wall the man placed seemed to have finally eroded.

"It is true. I do have art in my blood. But what is it to you? My masterpiece is not complete. I need something to finish it." Fahlrit huffed as he waited for Narro to reply.

"A masterpiece is great from start to finish. That is why master is first in the name, no? My name is Narro. Perhaps we can help each other." Narro countered, seeing the man's brow furrow. Although Trekkal prided herself on her wit, Narro was no slouch either. Fahlrit begrudgingly invited him into his space and pointed at the various animals he depicted in his cave. Narro observed patiently as he went over what inspired each piece.

He saw engravings on the walls with a series of dots and lines that enhanced his composition.

"I used to be a great hunter, until that-I refuse to say the name." He said with venom in his speech and pointed to a strange animal. It appeared to be a cat but wasn't that like that of a lion or leopard. Narro wondered what possibly could have caused such animosity from such an encounter. Fahlrit sat idly by while Narro offered his commentary, most of which was nothing but praise for his attention to detail and how different portions of the drawing changed appearance by the sun's rays entering the cave.

"Mahaku? Those are real?" Narro asked in genuine surprise, as Fahlrit shot him a glare.

"Of course they are! They ruined my life! You have probably seen one before but did not put the two together. Many say that the spirit and the animal are one and the same. This I found out on my own..." Fahlrit mumbled. Fahlrit took his attention to the matter at hand once more regarding his paintings.

"If you want to really help me Narro, I will answer any question you have if you can get me some Tiratcai. I need to crush these so that I may fully capture the light that came from these woods." Fahlrit explained to Narro. Narro seemed stunned at such a trivial request. He nodded happily, having expected him to take down some mighty creature or something else, but gathering grapes was an easy errand. All he needed to do was figure out where they grew and they'd be well on their way.

"A deal can be made between us. I will return soon with the goods you asked for." Narro said happily as he agreed to Fahlrit's terms and made his way back to the rock with the shape of a thumb as promised.

Jih and the others were waiting by the rock as they went over their failed attempts to find Fahlrit. Trekkal noticed that Narro hadn't returned yet, so she felt that perhaps he was successful. Her thoughts on the matter were interrupted by Sadal.

"Do you think Narro ran into trouble? I could go look for him, and maybe bring back something to eat in the meantime. I have a score to settle with that Digha that mocked me earlier." Sadal said as her eyes looked back up at the hill, where a few more goats were happily grazing.

Jih pointed his finger as he saw the shuffling gait of Narro approach them with a large grin on his face. Trekkal's intuition was correct, and she ran to hug her brother. Jih let out a sigh of relief at Narro's return. The group quickly united with one another as Narro paused to update everyone on the next phase of the plan. Trekkal studied Sadal's reaction as she went to embrace Narro with a tight hug.

"Your One was asking for you." Trekkal commented as she attempted to mock Sadal's voice. Narro suppressed his joy on the matter.

"Did you find him? All our searches were barren." Trekkal asked as she turned her head to see Jih and Sadal offer shrugs of their own to support her statement.

"Yes, I found the one named Fahlrit. Strange man, but he does have the information we seek. I need to go find Tiratcai and bring them back. This should be pretty easy." Narro said as he nodded for everyone to make their way home.

"Jih remembers forest near camp. Narro should check tomorrow." Jih recommended as they walked by. The others nodded as they kept a small list of duties that needed to be done. Jih needed to make containers for their gathered materials and found birch bark to be pliable enough for storage needs. He saw that some of The Aligned in this area made baskets with the material and an idea hatched in his mind as a project for later. Jih hoped that with everything coming into play, they'd make some real gains on just figuring out where the power rock landed at the end of it all.

An Unlikely Ally

Narro took the task from Fahlrit with the utmost severity. For his key to the puzzle regarding the meteor, all Narro needed to do was grab some grapes so Fahlrit could complete his masterpiece. Narro was vaguely familiar with Iran's terrain that reminded him of home. In past years, his band may have even found themselves here at one point in their travels. Narro went to pick up some extra supplies and he saw Sadal was working on building a tanning rack. Generally, she processed her furs on the ground, but decided to do something a bit more involved this time. She furrowed her brow as she saw Jih standing over her, who passed the occasional rock for it to keep balance. To Trekkal's eye, it seemed that Sadal was making it way more complicated and quietly chuckled to herself. Narro shot a glare at his sister who has always seemed to remain unhelpful for Sadal's projects.

"Sadal, I am having trouble looking for Tiratcai. Have you seen any on your travels this morning?" Narro asked as he gestured to the carcass she had her hands in.

"Kind of busy, Narro." Sadal said as she tried her best to dry a stripped pelt. She shook her hands that were caked in blood. Sadal groaned as her construction was clearly crooked. Jih suggested making a hole in the ground for the larger sticks to stay straight. Sadal was losing her patience at the endeavor.

"Jih only makes suggestion." Jih commented with a shrug of his shoulders in response to Sadal's visible annoyance.

"Well, I will be off then. Just needed to grab some food since I may be gone for a while." Narro mentioned as he walked past Trekkal to take some mushrooms she foraged for.

Narro left with little fanfare as he looked back at his three companions before setting off. Sometime after Narro left, Trekkal carried a slightly forlorn look on her face. Trekkal felt a special connection to Narro and while she was quite self-centered, she carried deep concern for her brother's safety. Trekkal didn't want to ask Sadal as she was still busy with her project, but Jih remained free. Her voice called out to the resting Jih. Jih was sprawled out on the ground and looked at her.

"Jih? Could you go follow my brother? We are never apart that long, and I fear something will happen without me." Trekkal asked out of concern.

"Does Trekkal have broken leg?" Jih asked, his tone filled with sarcasm as Sadal coughed in laughter with a piece of meat in her mouth. Jih chuckled as well but decided to stretch his legs. Jih got up and looked to grab his pack and spear. He looked to Trekkal and hoped for her to point the way. With nothing left to be said, Jih departed as well, hoping to find something of value for later.

Narro's travels took him to an open woodland where herds of aurochs made their way. His mouth salivated at the thought of one of these giant cattle being hunted by Sadal and cooked by Jih. Narro remembered that he had some spare salted fish left over from Trekkal's last haul but decided to save it for later. It was a nice reward as she found her way across a small band of their kind who were practically giving the stuff away. He knew it was a fruitless endeavor to hunt one of these large animals alone although he could take a hit or two if it came down to it. Narro made a mental note of this spot to let the others know later. Narro penetrated the deeper sections of the forest with caution as he kept his ears open for any dangerous creatures. He looked up in the trees and hoped to find any semblance of the grapes that Fahlrit described. Narro searched for grapes, he tried to remember what they looked like, but he seemed to come up short every time. Narro's eyes went to the ground and noticed bundles of sticks that were ritually broken and dispersed in the area. The sticks were arranged in a small circle and spaced out a few feet. Narro walked with care as he knew that this forest was maintained to some degree by others of his kind. He hadn't grown up near woodlands, so he was unaware of what spirit they were trying to invoke. The forest was full of bounties though and Narro hoped to collect and then some.

Narro was walking towards a trap, and he had no idea what to suspect. He saw that this was an offering to the forest's spirits as located along certain points of the path, there were small scraps of meat and withered bone left behind. Nourishing the spirits that kept bounties plentiful was a serious endeavor for many. Along this trail, Narro saw that the forest was in different states of use. He raised an eyebrow and looked closely to his surroundings. Narro's hand touched the bark of a nearby tree and took a deep breath. He noticed that the trees around him were cut down or stripped of their bark for various things. It was evident that this was meant to restore balance, as the wood was harvested, and the spirit was starving. He looked down and peered at the distance to see a body at the far end of the path.

Narro ran towards the body in a panic to check the person's condition. He saw that their eyes were closed, and they were bound by some sort of rope. The body was a teenager's, several years younger than himself, but the evidence was undeniable. Narro quickly looked around him for any sign of danger as he knew this was human sacrifice at hand. Human sacrifice was considered the purest form of giving to spiritual feeding, humans were the closest that embodied the spirits and would help them become whole. While this idea was known collectively among The Aligned, human sacrifice was unilaterally seen as a terrible practice and wasn't something that earned much respect. Narro ripped the animal sinew with his nails and teeth. He removed the teen's holdings and tried to slap them awake. Narro heard a rustling noise through the forest and withdrew his club from his pack as he did so. Two burly members of The Aligned made their presence to him known. Narro studied their dress, one was shirtless and instead wore gray body paint in the shape of handprints over him, while his companion wore bear skins that covered some of his face and shoulders.

"How could you? What are you-" Narro said, as he was immediately challenged by the two men.

The two decided to attack Narro as they could offer no explanation that didn't incriminate their position. Narro wielded his club, and struck the shirtless man in the face, leaving a nasty wound as he bled. Narro gave a victorious grin as he readied himself for another attack. Narro was willing to do whatever he needed to defend the innocent and sought to defeat the two men quickly. Rattled for a moment, the shirtless man's companion stepped in and assaulted Narro. Narro was punched in the face, and his club dropped to the ground. Narro tackled the first of his attackers and bashed his head against the ground. The soil left a remarkable imprint each time as Narro pressed the man to the ground. While he was doing this, the bear skinned man withdrew a large rock and rushed towards Narro. The shirtless man pressed Narro closely to him and hugged tightly to hold him in place. His arms were locked in a vice as he attempted to thrash out the way. Narro turned around and braced for impact as he saw his attacker rush towards him. Narro was hit over the head with the rock and rendered unconscious for the time being, as the bear skinned man helped his companion. The men worked quickly to bind his arms and Narro joined the pile for the sacrifice.

In his quest to follow Narro at the behest of Trekkal, Jih had his hands full as well. Jih approached the woodland further south than Narro. His eyes darted to the movement of a hare that locked its gaze on him. Jih pursued with spear in hand and followed the trail and ended up at the vicinity of a campsite. It was in a prime location, under the cover of birch trees to shield from the rains and just far enough from the exterior that one could hunt from the plains with ease. Jih peeked around behind a bush and noticed a lit fire. He moved ahead and observed that it was well-lived in with multiple hafted tools in various states of progress. Jih nodded in respect to the craft. He noticed drying pieces of meat that were skewered over the campfire. It was a large bounty of hare that Jih felt nobody would miss if he took a bite. Jih looked around him to make sure nobody came around and helped himself to a small strip. The hare was delicious, and he looted a single cooked piece. It was just enough for nobody to notice, Jih hated someone that took an entire bounty but felt someone should have left their food guarded.

As Jih finished his meal and grasped his spear to continue looking for Narro, he heard a rustling in the bushes. He moved forward and held his spear to protect himself as he saw the outline of a human. As he came closer into view, Jih saw a short but powerful man. He had a massive beard that covered his mouth and wild hazel eyes that stood out. The man wore deer pelts over his shoulders and tied around his waist that made him well camouflaged.

"I do not believe that was yours, little man." The man commented as he held up his club to Jih. Jih remained silent as he couldn't defend his actions reasonably. Jih attempted to walk away but was stopped by the rush of the man's footsteps.

"Your drive to survive is impressive. You will make a great sacrifice!" He yelled to Jih as he turned to face him in combat.

Jih's spear met the heft of the man's club as the two collided. Jih sought to make the kill quick as he relied on keeping the opponent at bay to search for a weak point. The man was hardly an experienced fighter from what Jih could tell. His movements were sporadic and kicked up a fuss while the state of his camp imploded as the two fought one another. Jih leaped backwards with his spear to dodge the man's massive swinging arm as he felt the wind from the potential impact hit him. Jih grimaced at the thought of one of those hits connecting to him. Jih gave a smug grin as he realized the opening left under the man's right armpit. Jih forced the spear inward and heard the man's yelp of pain as he did so. Jih figured this would be the end as blood poured from the man, but he was sorely mistaken. In the same breath, the man took a deep breath and found his resolve. He used his left hand to grasp Jih's spear and shook it while Jih at the far end strained to hold it in. Jih was in complete awe at the man's strength compared to his own. Jih held his spear with two hands, but just one was needed for him. An amateur of The Aligned was still enough of a challenge for him to take on. Jih realized he needed to wear his opponent down carefully before landing the kill.

This man is massive, Jih must be careful. Where will Jih strike? His legs? No, look at them. They could crush Jih with ease. Jih thought as he felt a genuine rush of fear.

The man's burst of strength dislodged the spear and it fell to the ground. A large stream of blood trickled down the man's side but was undeterred as he barreled towards Jih. Jih felt his back pinned against a birch tree as the man clasped his hands on his throat. Jih desperately attempted to punch his way out but saw that his fists barely did anything to the man's thick skull. Jih was struggling to breathe as he quickly felt the life drain from him. He used his left hand to grasp a low hanging branch and quickly lodged it into the man's eye. The man yelled out another scream as he reflexively let go of Jih. Jih quickly moved to recover his spear and leaped into the man's backside with his spear embedded inside. Jih retracted it once more and stuck it into the neck of the man until he fell silent. Jih sat at the campsite to recover his stamina as he reflected on his fight. Jih hadn't needed to try that hard in some time and while he kept confidence in his skills, The Aligned were mighty opponents. He was fortunate that Narro had such a kind soul. As Jih recovered, he saw the woodland was a wide expanse and his search would take some time. Narro would have to rely on the aid of another as Jih weaved his way throughout the forest.

Alone on the trail, Zulag ventured out to forage some food out in the expanse. He looked to feed himself, but also harvest some wood. He heard along the rumor mill of camps that he and the others looked around that there was a forest which was blessed by spirits that The Aligned revered. Deeso naturally took zero value in spiritually charged wood, but anything was better than nothing. Deeso and Cikya made their complaints known with the handles of their weapons starting to lose quality and a suitable replacement was needed. Given Deeso's tenacity and tracking skills, their group was never truly too far behind Sadal. It was a patient gauntlet, inquiring about the meteor and following the advice given to them. As Sadal searched for the meteor with Jih, the trail became increasingly clear. At their best, they could only be a day behind, but were normally a few days out from their location. Today was fortunate for Deeso and company, as they were in the same area and had no idea.

"Get more wood...get more meat." Zulag mumbled to himself at the growing list of foraging requests given to him by Deeso. He spat at the ground as he looked around. Zulag was far from an expert on wood, the handles for his knives were often made from antler or other bone.

"We could have Ozul done this instead, I know nothing about wood!" Zulag complained to himself as he attracted the attention of a grazing auroch that looked in his direction. Zulag raised his fist at the beast before him but paused to think as he saw the animal's mighty horns.

Zulag sought to distance himself away from the giant horned cattle, but he noted that the meat would probably be delicious if they hunted as a group. He perused through the woodland, marking trees with his knife so that he wouldn't get lost. Zulag's eyes found their way to the ground, and he saw an odd bundle of sticks. Zulag thought nothing of it and grabbed some that could be used as kindling. Zulag raised an eyebrow as he saw more of them and realized quickly that they led in a specific direction. Given his knowledge of the area and personal background, there was some sort of spiritual energy that reverberated here. His curiosity led him to follow the source of these strange sticks. He hid himself behind a tree and used it as cover to survey the area.

He raised an eyebrow as he saw two bodies present. Zulag looked around and saw that he was alone. Zulag looked to loot them for anything of value and assumed at least one of them was dead, but it was far from the truth. Zulag looked over the two bodies, the first was the teen's body who was cold, and then a man around his age. Zulag saw the struggle on his face, he had wounds that were fresh and saw that he was bound. It was obvious what was happening here. Zulag jeered, it was his first thought to blame the man before him for being so stupid to fall into such a trap, but he realized that he followed in likely the same manner. Zulag hated being a hypocrite above all else and he used his knife to release the bindings of the man if he was alive.

"Surprised? It seems you have quite the Sarmpa stomach. You Youngest have no respect for what we hold dear. How will our forest grow when you mark things with that pitiful blade?" A voice called out. Zulag looked around for the source of the voice. He imagined the only ones to have such tenacity were Forest Seekers, but there was shock on his face. Zulag saw a man with body paint in the shape of gray handprints and his bear skin wearing companion. He saw that the first of them was injured and assessed the unconscious person's injuries. He came with the reasonable conclusion that the two must have fought. Zulag was no stranger to fights that outnumbered him, and this would be just another one.

"Oh, this one is certainly strange. He has the marks of an Onpeu, and the frame of one as well, look at him! So thin and puny!" The bearskin wearing man laughed as Zulag's expression angered considerably.

"I can make that smile of yours last a lifetime." Zulag threatened as he brandished his knife towards the two men.

The two Aligned decided to toy with Zulag, where the first man spectated as he nursed his injury. He let out a few derogatory jeers at Zulag's expense and cheered on his comrade. Once they'd had their fun, Zulag would be added to the pile of bodies for their ritual. Zulag took to the offensive and made his way towards his opponent. He tossed his held knife and lodged it directly into the man's skin. The hit landed with ease and caused some visible drops of blood to eventually pour down his leg. Zulag closed the distance and balled up his hand into a fist to strike his victim. With as much strength as he could muster, he punched the man squarely in the jaw. While Zulag expected the man to be knocked over as expected, Zulag hardly received any feedback from the man at all. His face could hardly hide his surprise. Zulag dodged the man's punches with a quick duck and instead resorted to footwork to nail his target. He kicked him squarely in the stomach and caused him to cough. Zulag snickered at the prospect, The Aligned were simply too slow. The problem of The Aligned though was that where speed was lost, there was instead significant strength. Kicks were risky as the leg could be grabbed and balance was disrupted. While Zulag managed to land his hit on the man with another, his hand grasped Zulag's foot and caused him to fall to the ground. Zulag's eyes expanded slightly as he realized the vice his foot was now in as he winced in pain from getting crushed. Zulag was dragged by his ankle with ease by the man wearing the bear skin.

I take back what I said earlier, sending Ozul out here would have gotten him killed! Zulag thought as he found himself dragged in the dirt.

Zulag gritted his teeth and fiddled in his clothing for the few knives he had with him. He threw a spare knife into the back of the man who released him, but Zulag could already feel the pain coursing through his upper body. His fur covering was basically scraped off from the friction. Zulag attempted to tackle the man to the ground with his bodyweight but found he could only cling on like a helpless dhole. This puzzled Zulag strongly, but he realized that he was suited to fighting his own kind and Forest Seekers. The Aligned were a whole different beast on their own.

"I grow tired of this weak display. Make it quick." The observing man commented, his comments infuriated Zulag further as he bit the bear skinned man's shoulder.

Zulag was flung off the man's back like an insect as he hit the ground with a thud. Zulag felt as if something cracked in his body, but he seemed fine. He took an exhausted breath but took another fighting stance as the man before him ran towards Zulag with the intent to kill. Out of the corner of his eye, a nearby shape grew larger and larger. Narro rushed to save Zulag by slamming the man with his shoulder and the two collided to the ground. Narro hadn't bothered to acknowledge Zulag at all, but when he came to, he noticed that he was unbound, and his first thoughts were on revenge and engaged in combat. Narro was determined to make things right. He dislodged his assailant's club with his own hand and broke the man's wrist. Zulag observed as the two fought and took a second to catch his breath. Narro scooped up the club for himself and wrestled with the second man. Narro felt his grip strengthen over the other man considerably as he continued to crack his hands. His opponent worked through the pain as well as he could.

Narro separated from the man and grabbed the club with satisfaction. It wasn't his own, but the substitute worked just as well. Narro heaved with a heavy yell and dislocated the man's jaw entirely on a successful hit. A rush of blood and broken teeth littered the forest floor as the man was stunned and yet continued to fight. Narro held him back with a mighty punch to the throat and slammed the club on the back of the man's head. Bits of brain matter and bone splattered throughout as Narro gleefully turned him to mush. By the time Narro was done, the man before him had a caved in head and forehead. If Zulag hadn't witnessed it himself, he would have thought an elephant crushed his skull.

Zulag took due advantage of the situation. The painted one rushed over and grabbed one of Zulag's spare knives for his own devices. He pushed Zulag to the ground and launched the knife with utmost power that paled in comparison to Zulag's throws. It beelined for Narro's right eye and landed its mark. Narro screamed in incredible pain as he convulsed on the ground while the bear skinned man lay beaten. Blood pooled out of the wound and down his body to soak the soil below. Zulag saw this and grew enraged as he used his last remaining knife to attack the shirtless one before him. He used his cunning and natural talent to slice bits and pieces of the man and took great care to avoid hits where he could. Strands of skin and muscle swayed with the movement of his body along as blood pooled. Zulag continued his assault with each stab growing deeper past the point of no return. The few times the man's fist collided with Zulag, he felt as if he would be knocked to the ground. Eventually, Zulag's speed gave him the advantage. He took the opportunity to slice the man's throat in full and caused him to bleed out.

Zulag was nowhere near in any pain as Narro was for the time being, but he certainly sustained some damage. He walked with a slight limp now that the pain in his foot and leg coursed through his body. His primary concerns were on Narro, after all, it was his knife that caused the man a great injury.

"Hold on, this is going to hurt a lot, but I can save this." Zulag said to Narro who lay still.

Zulag carefully held Narro down and slowly extracted the knife. He tossed it aside, seeing it as tainted goods and he would make another one. Narro was in so much pain, his muscles practically shorted themselves out and he was once again unconscious. While he was out, Zulag looked at his already tattered clothing and decided to make a makeshift bandage. He removed what remained of his upper shirt and tied the fur ends together. He stuffed as much as he could into the open wound and wrapped it around Narro's head. While Zulag's first thoughts were to just leave, he felt a resounding heaviness over his body. He would need to rest before he could make his move. Perhaps in that time, the man before him would revive once more. Zulag closed his eyes and rested to later get a small tap on his shoulder. Zulag lifted his head to see Narro looking at him with an extended hand. Zulag felt a slight sense of relief at Narro's condition but wasn't envious of his injuries. He found it slightly difficult to look him in the eye but powered through it.

"I didn't need your help by the way. But...thanks." Zulag said begrudgingly as he looked at Narro's hand.

Zulag decided to grab it and felt himself propped up with some force with Narro's grip. He studied Narro's build, far stockier and more filled with power than his own slenderer frame. Zulag bit his tongue, knowing he learned a great deal from his fight with the others. Now that he had a moment to relax, a particular smell came to his senses. Narro noticed Zulag looking towards his bag, and he gestured towards it.

"Is that salted Peymin in your bag?" Zulag asked Narro who nodded hearing his words.

"Yes, would you want some? You seem a bit famished." Narro commented as he used his hand to hold the bandage over his injured eye.

"Not exactly my first choice, but I know someone who really likes the stuff. I'll give you a knife for it." Zulag proposed to him. Narro shrugged his shoulders, he was willing to part with some of his belongings for free.

"Have some on me. You did save me after all." Narro mentioned as he looked over Zulag who folded his arms. Narro went over and scooped a large chunk of the goods into Zulag's bag. He was certainly grateful. The two stood a bit in silence, Zulag was far from one to participate in small talk, but he did feel he needed to ask a question.

"Are you able to make it on your own? I carved a path earlier, but we can stick together until we find the grass once more." Zulag asked. Narro put his hand on Zulag's shoulder and put his concerns to rest.

"My camp is not far from here, but I appreciate the offer. My companions are probably missing me right now!" Narro said with a laugh that was returned with a more muted chuckle by Zulag.

"Right. Good luck then." Zulag mentioned as he scooped up the goods. He looked back at Narro before retreating into the forest with his limp. He would have quite the story to tell, and he dreaded the berating from the others from not bringing any wood.

Jih arrived on the outskirts of the woodland exhausted and covered in blood himself from his previous encounter. Jih looked around him as he still found no sign of Narro, but he noticed another man exit around the same time. Jih planned to go over and ask for directions. Jih found the man looked to be in relative shape, but his expression changed seeing his injury. As Jih got closer, he realized that this was in fact Narro. Jih called out for Narro who raised his hand and waved over. Jih could only cover his mouth in surprise now that he saw Narro's injuries in detail. Narro went through a lot in his ordeal and would need to be looked at once they arrived to camp. Narro arrived quickly to meet with Jih and the two looked at one another.

"You seem to have had a day. Jih, how bad is it? My injury?" Narro asked as Jih could only grit his teeth and gave an awkward reception on how to deliver the news properly. There was no feasible way for what was left of his eye to be saved, and the wound could grow infected if it remained. Jih swallowed his spit, knowing that the eye would have to be removed once they returned to camp. He was far from the doctor that Hyu was, but he would be able to at least save Narro some grief.

"Jih is surprised you are still walking. There is much blood." Jih inquired as Narro thought to himself.

Narro propped himself over Jih's shoulder as the two made their way back to camp. As for Zulag, he returned to camp to see the bored faces of Deeso, Ozul, and Cikya playing a game tossing sticks to pass the time. Ozul frowned as he saw Zulag appear, and his pointed finger prompted the attention of Deeso and Cikya. Although in decent condition, the rest of Zulag's clothes were tattered, his entire upper portion was missing, and he had friction burns along his back.

"Are you alright!? What happened?" Deeso asked as she assessed Zulag's health. Her voice carried a sense of care that was unusual to the others as she looked over him with concern.

Zulag laughed as he saw Deeso's response. It was clear she was taking her role as their self-appointed leader seriously by looking through her pack for any sort of aid. Ozul pointed out to Deeso that he extracted some bark from poplar trees that he saw The Aligned used from time to time for pain relief. Ozul advised Zulag to chew the bark as much as he could stomach.

"I decided to be you for a day and stick my nose in other people's business. I saw combat with one of The Aligned. They are tough. Seriously, if we need to fight them, use your axe, any weapons. Don't bother with hand-to-hand, they will rip your arm off." Zulag warned the three of them as they nodded to his words.

"Your foot is unwell, I can fix it, but it will hurt. Please tell me you will not hurt me before I help this." Ozul asked nicely of Zulag. He mumbled and let Ozul do what he needed to do.

"Oh and Deeso. There's a snack for you in the pack. One of them helped me out in the woodland." Zulag said through strained breaths as Ozul cracked his ankle.

A short time later, Sadal looked up to see the return of Jih and Narro. She looked concerned as she saw Narro's injury and already scrambled for any sort of aid. While Sadal's first concerns were to treat Narro's wounds, Trekkal had a different response. Trekkal was the first one to get up as she barreled past Sadal and practically knocked Jih over as she gave Narro a hug. Narro was happy to see his sister, but his expression changed to a slight frown when he saw Trekkal looked incredibly angry.

"Narro! What-What happened to you?!" Trekkal mentioned with her hands flying around puzzled.

"I tried to save someone and-" Narro said as he was interrupted by Trekkal.

"You always have to save everyone, but never yourself! When do you ever think about me? Your sister. The most important thing you have." Trekkal said while Jih could only glance at Sadal who looked at the ground.

"Trekkal." Sadal intervened, her mouth stopping short as Trekkal turned around.

"And what? Were you going to do something about it? You run him into danger all the time!" Trekkal said to Sadal.

"Jih came to grab me, but before that I was saved by one of your kind Sadal. He had strange markings on his body, much like Onpeu marks. I did not tell him this though, that would have been rude." Narro mentioned. He looked slightly concerned as Sadal felt a bit of sweat come to her forehead, hearing Narro's depiction of what happened to him.

No, there's no way he could be talking about... Sadal thought as Narro explained everything. She tried to keep herself calm, but Jih could tell much like Trekkal, she was clearly bothered by something. When Narro was situated, he would have to figure out exactly what that was.

"Jih will fix Narro. Sadal, Trekkal, build us shelter. We will be here for some time." Jih ordered with a rare authoritarian sound as the two complied with his demands.

Training Day

Cikya was the first to wake from their group slumber as Zulag rubbed his eyes while taking watch that night. He groggily moved his way over closer to the group and moved some of their equipment out the way. She gave a small clap with a happy expression as she was excited for today. Just a few steps from their camp was an area that was cleared by the previous inhabitants that was the perfect size for their devices. Cikya, Deeso, and Zulag planned out a training day to refine their combat skills at Cikya's request. Deeso and Zulag both agreed that a refresher could be useful, with some close calls on their hands after dealing with the occasional raid and Zulag's battle with The Aligned. Originally their training required them to do hand to hand combat which worked for them and Forest Seekers but was not performed well with The Aligned. She saw that Deeso and Zulag had their respective weapons already equipped to them and Cikya waited for Ozul to join them. He stayed asleep, but it wouldn't be this way forever.

Cikya got the attention of Deeso and Zulag by placing her staff down. She repeated the notion, and watched closely as the two removed their respective weapons and placed them down with hers some distance away. They turned to address her as she was ready to start the first of their exercises. Cikya stomped her foot down on the soil and shook in place. As Cikya was the oldest, she decided to dictate today's session much like how she taught Zulag. Now she had an extra two students on her hands. Cikya stretched out her arms and Deeso and Zulag followed suit, the three took deep breaths as the slight cracking of their bones filled the otherwise silent surroundings.

Cikya took to the ground and adjusted her body for push-ups that the others followed. Cikya specifically formed a fist and dug into the earth, making a flat surface out of dirt for her to grasp on. The Broken Bone's exercise structure had developed far ahead of other bands with a general understanding that multiple exercises targeting muscle groups were ideal. The benefits of exercise though could only go so far with a limited knowledge of techniques. The three did push-ups until exhaustion and took a moment to recover as sweat accumulated on their bodies. Zulag felt the brunt of it as he was still recovering from his previous injuries but muscled through the pain. With a smirk on her face, Cikya rose now and held up her fists and punched the air. Zulag instantly knew what she meant, sparring was something that he didn't get to do as much as he was mostly busy with Ronkalk's various errands, but he participated in the fighting pits when he could. Deeso was an adept wrestler inspired by Ronkalk's exploits. While she struggled to have a decent fight on top, she was far more formidable on the ground once she managed to get a hold of her opponent.

"You want to spar?" Zulag asked Cikya who nodded in agreement, but moved her head to gesture to Deeso who was going to challenge instead.

Deeso was looking for an excuse to let out some steam for a while and she found it would be much easier to dole it out on Zulag. The Broken Bone valued combat above all else and had dedicated rules to the endeavor. Sparring was a normal agreement between two parties, their fists were covered with animal skins to soften the blow and would be stopped at the observer's discretion. Cikya returned in a short moment with some soft skins and rope that the two would use to bind their hands together. To soften the blows, Deeso and Zulag wrapped these skins around their hands and opted to not aim for the face, or any particularly sensitive areas. Deeso and Zulag locked arms at the behest of Cikya who nodded to officiate the sparring match. Cikya felt that although they needed to reinforce their weapons training, reviewing the basics of fists would improve their form dramatically.

This should be fun to see. Cikya thought as she watched intently. She clapped twice starting the match and backed away as Deeso and Zulag got into position.

Zulag extended his hand and immediately punched Deeso in the nose as the match began. Deeso shook her head in anger. Zulag couldn't help himself as he felt his reaction take over for him. Deeso was blindsided by the hit as she let out a snarl in response to his actions. Deeso sniffed the air and noted she could now smell a bit better after her nose was clogged up from dust.

"Zulag!" Deeso spat in annoyance as she kicked up dirt.

"What? Oh, right. No hits to the face, honest mistake." Zulag said, trying to obscure his laughter.

Deeso looked at his violation of the rules with disdain and decided to go about her own way instead. She backed up and this time, went to kick Zulag in the shin. He gritted his teeth as he felt some real pain, especially after his beating from before, surely enough to rival Deeso's hit to the nose. He knew he deserved it, so he couldn't be too mad. Zulag's reach was both a boon and a curse as he had to lean in close to be able to grab Deeso who skirted around him. She sought to trip him up by swiping low, but Zulag was able to see this, and jumped to reposition himself while giving himself brief relief to his sore leg. Deeso took a deep breath and she saw that Zulag had to expend a lot of energy for that maneuver having just woken up. Zulag decided to bait Deeso into grabbing him close, so he could slam her to the ground and pin her for Cikya to declare the win. Deeso ran towards him, but rather than stop short for a jab, she decided to rush towards him.

You've lost this one. Zulag thought smugly as he realized that she continued to run towards him.

Deeso lowered her head and headbutted him in the chest, causing him to exasperate and fall over. Deeso's body took the impact of her collision with Zulag, toppling both to the ground. Deeso took advantage of the momentum with Zulag's body weight and worked to grab Zulag's arms and pinned them to the ground. She used her feet to grasp the back of Zulag's head and clasped his face with her ankles. Although Ronkalk himself enjoyed the spectacles of combat, it was reinforced early into training in The Broken Bone to achieve the victory as quickly as possible so that matches were short if well experienced.

Zulag was clearly tired as he found it difficult to dislodge himself from Deeso, where Cikya saw a clear winner and decided to call it. Cikya laughed to herself as she found humor at the compromising position the two found themselves in by the end of the match. Zulag scoffed at Cikya's immature expression while she left. Cikya's attention turned to the last member of their group who remained undisturbed.

"Deeso. The match is over. You're still on top of me." Zulag said with some irritation as he turned his head to see his throwing knives where he placed them earlier.

"Huh? Oh." Deeso loosened her grip and pushed Zulag away from her as she got up to go reclaim her axe.

Cikya looked over the sleeping lump that was Ozul. In her hands was a small basket filled with river water that she had. She placed it down and took a moment to dunk her head in and cool off before lifting the remnant of this and chose to dump it onto him. Ozul still didn't move, his exhaustion was apparent as his eyes practically were filled with bags underneath.

Wake up. It's time to train. Cikya thought as she pinched Ozul's cheek. The startled Ozul looked over and hid himself, embarrassed that his wet hair obscured his vision. He turned his head to see Deeso and Zulag talking about something, and he looked back at Cikya.

"H...Huh?" Ozul asked, barely registering that water was thrown on his face.

"Am I supposed to be doing something?" Ozul asked, while Cikya nodded her head yes. She gestured to Ozul's blowgun and darts that he protectively placed his hands over.

"You want me to...do what you all are doing? With this?" Ozul said, rubbing his eyes as he pointed to see Deeso and Zulag already practicing independently with their weapons.

Cikya nodded in agreement to his words as she took a twig and blew on it, imitating his blowgun. While Ozul didn't feel like participating, he learned quickly that this was Cikya's idea, and that for him to be included she must have had faith in his abilities. Ozul walked over with his blowgun and kept a few darts handy that he finished crafting the previous night. While making his way over to the training area where Cikya patiently pointed for him to go, he could overhear Deeso and Zulag's conversation.

"Deeso, you keep twisting your wrist when you do-" Zulag said, getting interrupted by Deeso with her pointing her index finger at him.

"What about it? Don't tell me you're upset from losing." Deeso answered, her arm swaying as she stopped swinging her axe. Zulag huffed in annoyance and shook his head in disagreement.

"No-You should curve your foot instead and keep your wrist straight, it centers the throw better. Your axe has a larger arc than my knives do." Zulag explained, as he took out one of his knives, noting that the handle made from bone had a curve for it to flow better through the air.

"Look who's awake." Deeso said as she tried this time to have more force. She hoped to have the axe propel forward but it fell flat. Zulag was right, it was too top-heavy, and a new handle could make all the difference.

"Oh, so you've decided to finally step up and train with the experts. Alright, let's see it." Zulag judged as he watched Ozul take a knee. Ozul stuffed the first dart into the device and left some ample space as he placed it in his mouth.

Ozul saw nothing but low brush around him, but his eyes were poised to a decayed tree trunk. Dead trees felt no pain and so this would be an acceptable target. He blew with great might as his cheeks expanded slightly and the dart was released. Deeso's head turned upon hearing the dart. She and Zulag recognized the sound with ease as it was something they encountered often, but never considered that Ozul had darts of this caliber. His weapon generally made no noise at all.

"So that's where that sound is heard from. Zulag and I have had some close calls with those on the hunt when the land was wet and hot. The sound always comes from these?" Deeso questioned. Ozul didn't bother answering her as he loaded in a second dart. Deeso hadn't realized Ozul shot off darts twice, but Zulag and Cikya watched closely.

"Why do you look confused? Yes, we use many darts with this. I have loud ones, my wooden ones, and my poison ones. The loud ones are so we know where to aim, otherwise it is silent. If you were being attacked by those, that was a warning. I usually have a good sense of direction, so I know where my darts go. The others seem to want to avoid attacking you." Ozul explained with a yawn.

"Well, one thing is for certain. Use whatever you can against The Aligned. They will crush you with ease. I wanted to send you instead to go get wood but that was a really bad idea." Zulag said as he stretched his shoulder. Ozul reflexively put his stuff down for the moment and sought to massage Zulag which at first made him slightly uncomfortable but felt like much needed relief. How was he so good at this?

Zulag felt he was preaching to the choir as they were all aware of The Aligned's stocky body type that differed from their own, but he also made note of some of the limitations he found to exploit. Deeso and Cikya took note, it was unlikely they would have to see combat with them again, but in the situation that it did, these tips would be invaluable. No matter how strong someone was, they could only get stabbed so many times and live. As ranged combat in general were the domain of Thunderfeet, Deeso, Zulag and Cikya felt secure in their place against these much more formidable opponents. As for Ozul, any target for his blowgun would be taken down if it meant a threat to his personal safety. The worries of the road weathered him down considerably, although he showed great compassion as a young child, it was much easier for him to switch this side of his personality.

"I will keep practicing." Ozul commented as he nodded in the middle of their discussion.

He continued to practice for some time while the others maintained a similar schedule. The group looked to each other to see who would handle the duties of food, and

Ozul sighed as he started a small fire by rubbing two sticks together along with some kindling. He shook his hands and coughed as the smoke rose above. Each of them stuck their meat with one of Zulag's knives and held them over the fire as it cooked.

This wasn't so bad. Cikya thought.

Running of The Bulls

Ozul and Cikya decided to gather supplies in the early stretch of the dawn. Deeso and Zulag slept silently as Ozul shuffled around and dumped things of little use out of his backpack. It was his idea to leave the camp for today as he was hoping to get some materials together for a special meal for the group to enjoy. As the group often discussed, leaving in pairs was the best way to cover their backs. Ozul walked over to Cikya and lightly poked her in the arm. Cikya shuffled around with a mound of messy hair. Cikya forgot she agreed the night before to help Ozul. She willed herself and shook her hair as she saw the bright-eyed boy stare at her.

Oh right...I forgot. My head hurts from yesterday. He's looking at me. Smile Cikya. Smile. Cikya thought as she nursed herself from a tired night of song and dance at another camp. She gave Ozul a small grin and a nod to acknowledge that she was ready to go whenever he was.

Ozul looked around a bit more, took his blowgun and some darts with his bag, and the two were off. Cikya could always count on Ozul to pick up the slack as she cleared her mind, she knew that he practically worshipped the ground she walked on. Due to being extremely observant, he often offered ideas of some use to her, one such involved her staff. Cikya used one of Zulag's knives to sharpen the end of her staff to a sharp point so she could have a makeshift spear when the blunt end wasn't effective. The two walked from the open field to a more secluded woodland that had dense trees. Ozul was unsure on how to receive this, these weren't the jungles of home, there was no banyan tree to find or any creatures particularly familiar to him. While he was open to finding deer meat, he wouldn't mind something more exotic. In the distance he saw a jackal and shook his head in annoyance, these were animals with great fur but made for terrible meat.

Cikya watched Ozul check the roots of the trees. Ozul pressed himself against a Persian oak and pushed his face into the trunk. She saw he was smelling the bark and looked immensely puzzled. She decided to copy his motion, watching to see what exactly he was looking for. It was a strategy among his people to smell the bark of a tree as it was a way to tell if it bore fruit or anything else. The oak tree dropped acorns as Ozul climbed up a small part and shook the branch. Cikya gave a surprised look as she saw some of the acorns drop to the ground and she scooped them up. While Cikya remained low to the ground, her eyes darted to a small grove of mushrooms that grew at the base of a tree a few steps away from where Ozul was. She diverted her stance and decided to make her way over to them.

"Are you sure you want to eat that without cooking? I have never seen it before." Ozul said as he scratched his head.

Cikya turned around in surprise, she didn't expect Ozul to be so quick. She didn't make a sound as he moved. She hadn't eaten in a while and these mushrooms were as good as any she presumed. Cikya offered one to Ozul who shook his head no, as he wanted to wait until later to eat. Cikya ate the mushrooms and the two continued on their way. After some time, Cikya saw the trees of the forest meld into themselves, and she saw the light call her towards the entrance. Ozul was dedicated to his acorn hunt and his focus was steady on that task. Cikya found herself in the middle of the field and plopped to the ground as she absorbed the sunlight above her. Sometime later, she saw the amorphous head of Ozul and his hair. She lifted her arm and rubbed his cheek.

"Cikya! Cikya! Hello...?" Ozul said, straining his voice with worry.

Ozul frowned and saw that Cikya was unresponsive. Ozul attempted to carry Cikya, he was still weak, but made a steady pace as he looked around and slowly dragged her back to camp. The walk wasn't too far but in the heat of the day it was tiresome work. Ozul came back, his forehead dripped with sweat as he took deep breaths moving Cikya. He plopped over to the ground in exhaustion but was in the relative safety of their camp. Ozul woke up much later to the familiar bickering of Deeso and Zulag, but it seemed different to his ears. Zulag was carrying a dead gazelle over his shoulder. He got up, betrayed by the limits of his body, and looked over to Cikya who still seemed distant.

"I see you two are back. How did the hunt go?" Ozul said with a groggy voice.

"Hunting exceeded my low expectations, but ultimately still disappointing. It is better when you communicate with your partner." Deeso commented, her eyes pinned on Ozul, but gestured to Zulag who sat down and scratched his back. He gave an audible sigh of relief as he did so.

"Well, if I had better directions, things would have been a lot smoother. Don't you think? Pointing and saying, "Here seems good" really isn't that helpful." Zulag said with an irritated expression on his face. Zulag looked over Ozul with a tinge of concern as he saw him unusually low of energy.

We are still talking about hunting, right? Ozul thought as he turned his head back to Cikya. Ozul noticed Deeso's expression as she looked past him.

"What happened to her?" Deeso asked with some slight concern as she looked up at Cikya who lay still but watched the clouds move in the distance. Zulag got up and raised an eyebrow at the sight.

"Oh, well we were gathering some plants while you two were asleep. I... wanted to make you something as a thank you for all your hard work. I found her like this in a field and had to bring her back. We could not find any meat." Ozul explained as he looked at the small gazelle slumped over Zulag's shoulder.

"How long has she been like this?" Deeso questioned Ozul.

"Well, I brought her back right when I heard you leave to hunt, so this should be about...six hours if I am right. We left at sunrise." Ozul mentioned as he kept good track of the time. The now sober Cikya darted up as she saw Deeso and the others. She let out a small sneeze that announced her presence as she received a quick hug from Ozul.

I'm going to need more of those mushrooms. I saw everything! This will be useful for my visions. I need bones so I can see what they tell me. Cikya thought as she turned her head to see a traveling group make their way with a fresh kill.

Deeso studied Cikya's reaction and grasped her axe as she saw a small group of The Aligned linger a short distance from their camp talking to one another. Deeso remembered Ozul and Zulag's testimony on how they dispatched the first set of raiders at their camp. She found that the land had plenty to offer and thought they saw their group as weak. She shot a glare at them, but her demeanor calmed a bit when she saw they were essentially unarmed. Deeso looked at Cikya's enthralled reaction with her friends and felt relief.

"Friends of yours?" Deeso asked as she saw a group of The Aligned wave in their direction as Cikya stood up. Cikya gave a wink in acknowledgment.

Maybe if you made some more friends of your own, you'd be in a better mood. Cikya thought as she gave Deeso a nice grin. Zulag found the entire situation hilarious and gave a laugh contrasting from the more concerned Ozul and Deeso.

"So, these things made you that way for hours, and let me guess, you want more?" Zulag asked with a mischievous look on his face. He knew his teacher better than anyone and was well aware the priesthood made their strongest interpretations in an altered state of being. Cikya nodded her head happily as she brought her arm around Zulag's shoulders.

"For ritual purposes... Since you're back on your feet, let's go find them. What do these mushrooms look like?" Zulag asked as Cikya clapped in happiness.

Deeso grabbed the gazelle off Zulag and threw it to the ground. Ozul went to work without a word and grabbed a spare knife to strip their kill. Cikya led Zulag along the trail that she remembered Ozul taking her but this time their travels were accompanied by a herd of aurochs that stomped around and grazed through the field that led to the woodlands. Cikya tapped Zulag's shoulder as she emoted her thoughts to him.

"You want to talk about that now? Even when you can't speak, you're a gossip." Zulag said with the smell of dung approaching his nostrils. He nearly gagged at the smell, no matter how often he found himself nose-blind, auroch poop just broke all expectations. Zulag held out his hand to stop Cikya's advance as the two neared the herd. The aurochs did nothing to acknowledge their presence now, with only a few curious calves taking heed.

"Say...I know you want to find those mushrooms you ate, but it's been a while since you've hunted big game. What do you say? Sure you're not rusty after watching Ozul?" Zulag proposed as Cikya placed her hand into a fist and pounded it in her open hand. She nodded and the two went to work. Zulag crawled along the ground some distance away while Cikya went alongside him. Cikya wondered on occasion how Zulag was able to crawl as he did without accidentally injuring himself with his knives.

"Let's avoid the ones with the large horns. An On-Takom this is not, things can get out of hand quickly." Zulag reminded Cikya. Cikya nodded, she remembered hearing tales of the great auroch hunts her new Aligned friends mentioned to her and wondered if the rumors were true, or if this was hearsay.

Zulag spotted a young female that seemed to stray off some from the herd. He sighted the larger males busy ramming one another with their horns while the calves observed. He pointed to Cikya who nodded in agreement. Cikya looked at some of the debris on the ground and noticed a few large sticks. She wanted to make a torch that could be used to divert some of the larger auroch away from their target. Zulag continued his crawl, the auroch's skin was hardy, so he needed to land a solid extremity and wait. The auroch would eventually bleed out, even if it took hours. Zulag heard Cikya hacking away with rocks as she continuously applied friction to make enough sparks that ignited the wood. She only needed one torch for the job and decided to blow out the rest quickly. She held the torch and attempted to cup the flame with her hand so that the wind wouldn't extinguish it. Zulag reached a close enough range and launched his throwing knives. He launched two in rapid succession and embedded two into the hindquarters of the young female that yelped in pain. Zulag slowly crawled back but increased his speed as in the panic of the young female, the males stopped fighting and centered their attention on the apparent threat. Cikya noticed the rush and attempted to defend Zulag as well as she could. She ran over, and offered her hand to him as he got up and set off without delay. Zulag ran with such speed, he was unable to stop himself as the momentum of him nearly knocked Cikya over as they collided. He panted quickly but looked to see that the knives made their mark as the blades remained in the cow's skin. As the young auroch thrashed around, Zulag's blades fell to the ground.

A large male not seen by either of them charged in their direction. The speed of the auroch surprised them both as it quickly neared the pair. The two briefly separated and took two directions to run from. The auroch previously targeting Zulag decided to change course and rush to Cikya. Cikya waved the torch around as she felt a surge of adrenaline. She attempted to stay calm, and guided Zulag with her hand to maneuver around so they could meet each other. In Cikya's haste to get out the way, however, she slipped on loose grass and dropped her torch. Cikya quickly reclaimed the torch and attempted to stomp out the growing smoke, but the wind was her enemy. With the fire now engulfing some of the tall grasses that made up the field, the cattle were spooked into a stampede as a heavy sound of multiple footsteps matched the sound of a brewing volcano. The noises of the animals were so loud that Zulag and Cikya could hardly hear themselves think. Clouds of dust filled the air around them as Zulag coughed in disgust. The two retreated into the forest to hide as the cattle were now scattered to the wind with fire behind them. The plan now was to claim the mushrooms that Cikya sought and return to camp in one piece.

A couple of hours away, Jih and the others were invested in deciding whose turn it was to watch Narro as his injury healed. Narro's condition was not ideal. He could barely stomach down food and felt nausea every time he stood up. Though he was able to at least clean himself on his own, there still required someone to pour fresh water in the wound and change out the bandages. Jih did the last two days of Narro duty, so he looked at both

Sadal and Trekkal. The pair were indecisive about who would have the responsibility and Jih was at the end of his patience. Trekkal was still visibly upset from Narro's display of bravado and refused to talk to him. Sadal kept her thoughts to herself.

"Are you still angry with Narro?" Jih asked Trekkal, as he immediately regretted his statement.

"-and another thing!" Trekkal yelled, as Jih let out a large sigh. Jih decided to turn his attention to Sadal instead who hadn't contributed to the conversation.

"Sadal, will you watch Narro? Jih must go trade for bandage. Trekkal, come with Jih. We must talk." Jih mentioned to her as Trekkal blew air from her mouth. Jih saw this as a time to give Sadal a bit of a reprieve from the hostile atmosphere that brewed between Narro and Trekkal.

"You want me to watch Narro? I don't know the first thing about healing. What if something happens and you're not there?" Sadal questioned, with some concern in her voice as she looked over at the closed tent.

"You would be great at watching him, Sadal. Somehow, you always seem to be by his side anyway." Trekkal commented as she kicked the dirt and collapsed a small anthill in the process.

"Useful as ever Trekkal." Sadal said as she turned her back to the two. Sadal changed direction to the tent where Narro was sleeping. She nodded her head to agree to keep watch over him while Jih and Trekkal were to conduct trade as Jih instructed. Sadal waved the two off and stood outside the tent for a while.

Trekkal and Jih ventured forth from camp to see the vista of large plains grasses sway once again in the wind. The two found their campsite faded into obscurity as they continued to walk. Jih turned around and traced the sky with his finger to make sure Sadal maintained a strong signal for them later. It took little time for Trekkal to emit her true thoughts on the situation to Jih. While she talked with Narro often on their outings, her opinons of Sadal were not a popular topic. Trekkal looked immediately for support regarding Sadal in Jih as she grabbed his attention. She tugged at some loose hanging cloth on his shoulder. Jih remained still as he folded his arms in irritation and sought to lecture her.

"Can you believe her Jih?!" Trekkal pouted as she kept her eyes scanning the expanse beyond them.

"Trekkal, Jih has said this before. Narro helped people, this is good thing. The past cannot change. We must be better." Jih said as Trekkal sighed from the lecture she received.

"No Jih, not about that. I think something is odd with Sadal. All of The Youngest are crafty and should not be trusted. I do like Sadal, but there is something...different about her. You know what I mean?"

"Jih came to same conclusion some time ago. What does Trekkal think?" Jih noted as he kept his prior talk with Sadal quiet. Jih was curious about what Trekkal observed and chose to think. As far as he was aware, Narro and Trekkal didn't know about Sadal's meeting with Deeso.

"Sadal has said practically nothing to me about her former life before she met you. There are only bits and pieces from our stories around the campfire. I know much about Hyu and Kag. Sadal is an empty rock wall." Trekkal said with some slight sadness in her voice.

"Narro thinks I am being unreasonable, and sometimes I am, I want to give Sadal a chance. Sometimes she is great, and it is as if we are truly in the same band, and other days I never understand what she does. Is that wrong Jih?" Trekkal added on.

"Jih does not question past much. Sadal hunts, fights, and crafts as we need. You are sister of Narro. If Narro is happy, you must be happy. He would do the same." Jih voiced as he reminded her of the direction they needed to travel.

Jih paused as he saw a large dust cloud in the distance rise. He hadn't remembered dust storms being part of the weather in this area, but upon closer examination the hulking shape of enraged aurochs converged in their area of the plains. Trekkal was one step ahead as she grabbed Jih by the wrist and ran quickly. Jih wondered where this great burst of speed came from Trekkal when they needed to hunt something. Jih gathered that the aurochs were much like the water buffalo of home and India where they were powerful herd creatures that operated as one. He saw their pointed horns that were incredibly sharp and their black and brown coats. The two rushed to safety and took temporary refuge in a small inlet in the ground as Jih peered over slightly to investigate. Jih felt a tug at the back of his neck as Trekkal advised him to stay low. The raging aurochs continued onwards and let out small yelps that told lesser creatures to leave.

"Who in their right mind would set these Aroc off? We only go after the old or the very young..." Trekkal stated with annoyance.

After the dust settled, the pair made their way to the village Jih mentioned where they needed to go. Trekkal noticed a few of The Youngest were present in the camp that she looked at with disdain while Jih opened the negotiations. At first Jih felt uncomfortable with his status when he met Narro and Trekkal, but he could see the utility in having good relations with those who recognized who he was.

"Jih has goods for trade. We need bandages for injured friend." Jih mentioned as he felt a few stares come on him.

A few of The Aligned sat by a central fire as each looked to the other to address Jih's question while Trekkal stood by his side. One of them got up and went to her tent and handed a small bundle of fibers to place in Jih's hands. Jih studied her dress and noticed she wore clothing in the same style as Trekkal. He wondered if this was a shared trend among her people or just a coincidence. Jih noticed that the woman wore an auroch pelt that covered her stomach and noted its luster as it stayed pliable regardless of exposure.

"One of our own is injured, this requires nothing." She said as she gave Trekkal a nod. The pair thanked her for the kind gesture and set out on their way. She turned around to the other members of The Aligned with a slightly confused expression as she made a double take on Jih, but by then, the two were gone. Jih was taken aback slightly at the gesture, even his own people rarely did such deeds out of the kindness of their heart. There was much to learn for him still.

Jih and Trekkal made their return to camp. Trekkal noticed Sadal was missing and soon grew annoyed but noticed Jih walking towards the tent where Narro recovered. Jih opened the flap and stuck his head inside, moving slightly as he did so. Jih did his best to shield the light from the outside with his body as he observed. He found that Sadal was resting close by Narro while on a second glance, he saw that his dried bandages were replaced. It seemed that Sadal took care of this while they were away. Jih quietly placed their collected bandages at Sadal's feet for when she awoke and closed the flap. Trekkal sat herself at the fire bored while she looked at Jih's expression to see that all was well. She felt a great weight off her shoulders but was still bored. There was a bit of daylight to burn, and she wasn't tired.

"Jih, can you tell me a story about your home again? I want to know more about this Dran person. What happened after the Teemba incident with Hyu? Did they really nest in her hair?" Trekkal asked innocently. Jih laughed, as it had been years since he remembered such a time. Trekkal had an amazing memory when it suited her.

"Jih will tell story. Grab something to eat." Jih said to Trekkal. Trekkal happily listened to Jih orate about his times in Sundaland until the sun went down and the two fell asleep.

The Cheetah Girls

As Narro was busy healing from his injuries, the others were forced to wait as Jih directed. Jih was able to successfully remove Narro's eye with a thin knife of Sadal's after knocking him out once more with a special concoction. Sadal and Trekkal emulated the design of one of the traditional tents of The Aligned and gave Narro extra space he needed to recover while the rest slept under the stars. Throughout the morning, the skeleton for another tent was slowly built by Jih and Trekkal in case of coming rain. Sadal found herself bored with little to do as she did her skinning for the day already and was waiting for another pelt to dry out on the tanning rack before she could work it. She slowly drifted to sleep but her eyes picked up as a cloud of dust built up in the distance. Sadal's eyes barely registered the blur but she was invigorated and needed to tell the others. Sadal felt her blood pump as the hunt finally brought something worthy to her. She looked around to see Jih and Trekkal virtually unfazed as they were tying wooden pieces together.

"Did you see that?" Sadal said with some excitement in her voice as she waited for the other two to lift their heads.

Jih's eyes scanned the perimeter of the camp and saw nothing was out of the ordinary. Trekkal didn't bother to acknowledge Sadal's comments as she was fixated on making a tight knot for the string. Jih looked at Sadal and wondered what she was looking at. His eyes weren't as good as the others for his age. Sadal heard a gazelle in the distance. It was dodging a fast-moving animal that propelled itself from its own speed. Sadal's eyes widened as she saw a cheetah in the distance. Unlike the other cats, Sadal noticed that this one didn't announce its presence with a roar but instead let its speed speak for itself. She tapped Jih's shoulder and pointed where Jih narrowed his eyes, and saw the creature that Sadal talked about. The cat was still and panted to catch its breath while the two watched.

"Oh, Jih sees creature. Smaller than Onpeu, is it dangerous?" Jih asked with an inquisitive tone.

"Jih, I wish to claim this creature. Its blood will quench my thirst and I will obtain its power. The pelt looks like it will gather a high trade. Also, the dots look great with my necklace. I can see it well." Sadal commented as she was practically jumping with excitement.

"Jih can help with-" Jih said, stopping his thoughts for a second as he saw the cheetah gain speed once more to attack the gazelle that just narrowly avoided death. The chase between the two seemed eternal, and Jih couldn't wrap his mind around how Sadal was going to begin to hunt such an animal. The plains were vast, and she had no option for cover to surprise it either.

Jih's brain short-circuited as he practically saw the cheetah teleport from one location to the other. It was as if its feet barely touched the ground. After processing this information, he saw Sadal offer a hand to him and he started to laugh. There was no possible way Jih could get to this animal with its bursts of speed. Jih was fine taking on larger animals that were slower, but he felt as if his lungs would burn trying to catch up to it. Jih felt his bones creak at the thought of attempting to run down such an animal any longer than he already did.

"Jih has run far, but Jih is old as well. Take Trekkal, she could use a break." Jih said with a laugh as he turned to see Trekkal stick her tongue out at his comments.

Trekkal pouted slightly at the prospect of running, something she only did for survival, but she decided to indulge Sadal on her potential trophy hunt. Trekkal was still mad at Narro and refused to speak with him for some time as he healed. Trekkal found herself frustrated with tying knots for string and decided to take a break. Trekkal also saw it as an opportunity to confirm her suspicions regarding Sadal or if she just happened to extrapolate again. Jih figured he could get some time to himself as he occasionally popped in on Narro to assess how he was doing. The biggest concern for Jih was making sure the wound on Narro didn't grow infected, as he was unsure of what to do at that point. Sadal grabbed a set of her throwing spears and stuffed them into her pack where they stuck out of the back more so than usual. Pack making wasn't a uniform practice, so on occasion, even the experts made mistakes. Trekkal got up and shook her hair before settling herself to the outer edge of their camp. She waved Sadal over and talked to her briefly.

"I already have my sling, worry not, we can find rocks on the way." Trekkal said.

Jih waved them both off on their adventure. Sadal gave a muted wave while Trekkal offered a more jovial one with a smile attached. The two set off while Jih started some of the other busy tasks he put off taking care of Narro.

Sadal was unsure of having Trekkal as a partner for this one, but she decided to give her a chance. Sadal explained her hair-brained scheme to Trekkal to catch the cheetah that she was able to keep track of. While Deeso was originally Sadal's tracker, she figured Trekkal's eyes to find fish in murky water could be enough to help them see the day through. Trekkal wondered how they were going to hunt such a creature. She'd seen a few cheetahs in her travels as a young girl, but never seen anyone bother to catch one. Trekkal remembered that cheetahs had a very particular way with their hunting, by paying attention to the direction of their tail, they could predict their traveling direction.

"So, now that you have the plan, we're going to go and do this. It might take all day." Sadal explained to Trekkal who tried to suppress her annoyance. Trekkal's eyes scanned the plains for the yellow blur that ran around, but she saw nothing else.

"So how does it move?" Trekkal asked, prompting an annoyed reaction from Sadal who stopped in disbelief.

"Did you not listen to me this entire time? I just told you...It goes very fast and then it must take a break to rest. It does not run as long as the Kalpeu does. Didn't you see these creatures here in your lands?" Sadal asked.

"Sadal...I am aware of that. I want to know, what direction does the tail of it go? It uses the tail to change direction. Like how we favor hands, some of them have a direction they often use to hunt." Trekkal said smugly as Sadal bit her tongue.

Sadal found it difficult to hide her surprise at Trekkal's statement. Sadal only focused on the speed but realized there were other factors to account for. Sadal hadn't considered Trekkal's point, but it certainly made sense. Sadal was impressed, she felt Trekkal sometimes just coasted along for the others to do work for her, but she certainly could contribute when needed. Trekkal looked to the ground and saw a small indent in a mud puddle where the cheetah ran through in its pursuit.

"It dragged the tail along the ground here. The mud is wet, perhaps we can use this to find what we are looking for." Trekkal said as she prompted Sadal to take a closer look.

"We'll have a more obvious trail soon if we can find the animal that was injured. Do you recall if it bled?" Sadal asked, while Trekkal tried to answer her question.

Their pursuit was relentless as they ignored the delightful meals that accompanied them on the open plains. The two were not the only ones on the hunt, cheetah hunts were a popular activity for young couples, particularly for The Youngest who compared the patterns found on the pelts. For those that had the aptitude, finding and collecting all the known variants gained a lot of reputation which went far. Even members of The Aligned that were sympathetic to The Youngest participated and enjoyed the practice. Sadal and Trekkal would have to most likely compete with other groups wanting to find their cheetah. Compared to more hostile wildlife, the cheetah was somewhat easier to hunt but these were also prey for lions, so one had to be careful.

"Over there!" Sadal shouted as the two ran, where Trekkal's pace sped steadily to match Sadal's.

Sadal saw in the corner of her eye an injured antelope that was well on death's door. It had claw marks on it, but the cheetah was absent. Trekkal feared that a larger predator may have made it leave but to her relief she heard something far more irritating. She sighed as a band of hyenas laughing in the distance waited to scavenge anything else in the wings. The sign of a claimed animal was one positive sign that they were heading in the right direction.

"Denmey, always wanting to waste the time of everyone." Trekkal commented, as she nodded to Sadal for the two to keep moving.

"From what I remember, you left home to find the meteor because you wanted to see it with your own eyes. Didn't you have something to do before you left? Jih worked stone for his people, I brought home the game and purged the land of the predator. What did you do?" Sadal asked Trekkal in between breaths as they ran.

Trekkal raised her eyebrow in confusion as she looked at Sadal.

"What do I do? I do whatever I want. I choose to fish and look great doing it, you are the one that seems to place so much work on yourself." Trekkal retorted with some snark in her voice.

Although Sadal meant that question with genuine intent, Trekkal interpreted this as something different. While fishing was her calling, it wasn't taken in the same way as a weaver or tanner would be. She was unsure of what she was truly meant to do, and it was one of the few questions that really bothered her. She recalled her conversation with Jih and the others in the past and her connection with Stelo. The priest's life seemed inviting, always in an altered state of consciousness to interpret things in the sky, but she needed to concentrate to fish. Hunting for hours without reprieve also was dreadfully boring, so the path of a hunter like Sadal wasn't in her vision.

"I have wanted to figure that out for a while. Everyone tells me what I should be good at, but this takes time to know." Trekkal admitted to Sadal in earnest.

Sadal nodded; it wasn't uncommon for anyone to feel this way. In the early days of hunting in The Broken Bone, she paled in comparison to the greater hunters that have long since fallen in battle. It was through Ronkalk's encouragement that she kept practicing until she could claim a leopard on her own and excelled above the rest.

The two rested and caught their breath but saw something appear in the distance. It was the precious cheetah they had searched for. Sadal admired its blackened fur, as this was a patterned king cheetah that was sure to turn heads. Now that they had a visual on the animal, they needed to play it carefully. Sadal and Trekkal minded their scent that would possibly alert the creature, but the breeze that showed up was downwind. Sadal and Trekkal figured the best thing to do was get as close to the animal as possible once it tired itself out before rushing it down while it rested. For getting the best pelt, Sadal reminded Trekkal that the cheetah needed to die quickly. Although they didn't plan on eating the meat, it was believed that if the animal died without some dignity, it would show later.

While the two readied themselves for battle, Sadal saw some rocks that were thrown in the air. Sadal grew angry as another hunting pair had gotten there first to ruin their plans. The cheetah ran away again, but Sadal remembered the direction to head towards, and hoped they would get a second chance. Sadal despised those that intentionally broke a hunt without consent. It was an unspoken code of honor. Sadal paused the search as she would need to deal with these people and their disrespect. Sadal noticed those responsible were two of her kind who already had cheetah print of their own, one with a reddish hue. She was furious, to be so greedy, and take advantage of the legwork done by her. The couple looked to see Sadal walking towards them and Trekkal trailing behind.

"Sadal...come on. We can still find it." Trekkal said as she tried to ease Sadal's mood. She too found The Youngest interfering to be annoying, but they already went so far.

"She and I have traveled for hours to hunt this creature. Go somewhere else." Sadal said with much anger in her voice. The two people looked at Sadal and Trekkal, and looked around, wondering who Sadal was addressing in jest.

"As if you can lay claim to a single creature-" The man mentioned as Sadal listed off everything she knew about the animal. It was clear she did her research well and intended to finish what she started. The heat of the day put sweat on their faces that dripped down as Sadal wiped her face dry.

"But I suppose they are right. We already have a pelt of high quality, look at its luster-" The man said to his partner who was less convinced. The woman gave her perspective on the matter and addressed Sadal's complaints.

"Success is hard to match, I understand that much. How about I give you this pelt so you and your partner will have something to share? We have seen its black hue, this bounty will be a prize for our love and our people." The woman offered, infuriating Sadal to the point of palpable anger. The last thing Sadal wanted was to rely on someone's charity. The hunt was what she was meant to do, and it was a great insult to her character.

"She wishes." Trekkal scoffed as she watched Sadal curled her hand to a fist and punched the woman straight in the jaw. The man pushed Sadal back and scooped the pelt, hoping that it could remain as it was before touching the mud below.

Sadal glared at the pair while Trekkal moved a bit closer to Sadal, wanting to leave not for their safety but for the others'. The couple weighed their options and decided to leave as the woman spit a bit of blood. Though the desire for revenge was palpable, they did have a prize they still needed to keep. The four glared at one another until eventually they vanished out of sight, but certainly not out of mind.

"One thing Trekkal is when you see disrespect, you stomp it out quickly. If you are with me, we will not be embarrassed in such a way." Sadal said sternly to her. Trekkal could hardly care about what values The Youngest held dear, but she did show concern for Sadal of course. The two continued on the path to at long last have their rematch with the king cheetah.

The cat stretched out, and rested in the heat of the afternoon as it finished a meal. It saw Sadal and Trekkal far before they could see it, but in the animal's well-deserved pride, it managed to evade all threats. The heat of the day betrayed its full stomach as it was forced to remain stationary while it cooled off. These people came closer to the cat's vision as it willed itself to get up but was still exhausted. In time, Sadal and Trekkal met the cheetah, and it watched its own demise as a rock flew at breakneck speed and hit it well in the face. It was stunned, seeing the ground distort as it tried to get its bearings. The cat saw a sharpened stick hit its paw and blood poured out. The pain was tremendous as it attempted to lick its wounds in agony. The first one of Sadal's throwing spears. It called out in a low purr in the distance, but it too was silenced as the second spear skewered the brain.

"Ah, there you are my sweet. Go on, do that thing you do. You made the kill." Trekkal said as she nudged Sadal forward with her elbow.

Sadal and Trekkal looked at each other happily as they finally landed the prize they yearned for. While Sadal intended to have made a full display with the cheetah pelt, Trekkal certainly earned her fair share and had a few ideas. Sadal knelt to the corpse and ripped its throat to drink the cheetah's blood while Trekkal watched in utter confusion. Although generally done for dangerous animals, Sadal valued the cheetah's speed and strategy the two underwent to make the kill. Sadal hoisted the remains of the cheetah over her as she and Trekkal made the long walk back home.

Date Night

It had been two weeks since Narro got himself into trouble. His helpful attitude left him permanently scarred, as he was blind in his right eye. Trekkal remained stubborn and refused to talk to him after his act of bravado. Narro didn't care though, someone needed his help, and he was happy to provide. His optimism was a shining beacon for the group that otherwise could get caught in their own self-doubt and worry of the outside world. Narro himself was getting used to the constraints of his new injury, he hadn't expected much, but was moderately surprised with how well he got on to begin with. Narro used a club as his main weapon, so he didn't require the range of view that Sadal or Trekkal needed to land their targets. He lay in his shelter that Trekkal begrudgingly made for him as he recovered and looked to see a shadow linger on the outside.

"Oh, now you wish to speak to me Trekkal? I guess you got hungry and want me to find food?" Narro teased, as he saw the tent flap open to reveal Sadal's head pop in instead.

Sadal's face was easily identified through the now bright rays of light that entered inside. He was taken aback as it was unusual that Sadal entered a tent without good reason. Trekkal had no excuse and was just nosy, while Jih stumbled in occasionally to make his greetings. Sadal was hoping to catch Narro alone for a while but hadn't the time to do so.

"Ah, there you are Narro. I was looking for you." Sadal commented with a small grin.

"She's still mad by the way." Sadal added with a snarky laugh as she saw Narro sigh in dismay. She sat down and her eyes peered towards Narro's single-strapped backpack. She hadn't bothered to look at his craftsmanship before, but Sadal and Jih preferred the double-strap design for their equipment.

"How are you feeling? I've been out hunting the past two days with Jih and I wasn't able to talk to you. I do worry about you sometimes." Sadal asked as she looked to see the pitiful expression on Narro's face.

"Welcome to the new Trekkal Tent. She wanted me to call it that since she made it all on her own." Narro commented with a snort that Sadal returned in kind.

"I can tell." Sadal said, looking at the haphazardly placed wooden stakes and animal skins that was Narro's recovery tent. She was afraid to touch it as a stiff breeze in the open plains surrounding them would be enough to break it entirely.

"Step out in the light so I can see you. Jih's kept you hidden away." Sadal commented as she stepped outside waiting for Narro to crawl out. He'd taken a few glances of the outside world on his own but nothing substantial. Always one to impress however, Narro had a few things stored in his bag for such an occasion. By now, it was well known among the four of them that Sadal and Narro had a shared interest in one another, much to the chagrin of Trekkal and fatherly teasing of Jih on both accounts.

"I have something for you." Narro commented as he reached into a pack.

"It's not Muupasi, is it? I still can't believe that was the first thing you decided to hunt for us. It was cute of you though to think that was a mighty meal." Sadal teased as she awaited Narro's gift.

"This is a flower. For you. It came with thorns, but I took them out." Narro said with a smile.

Sadal lifted an eyebrow and grasped the flower to look at it. She didn't recognize where it came from but felt her stomach was empty. She opened her mouth and ate the flower in front of Narro's eyes. Narro found it hard to hide the look of devastation on his face as Sadal continued to chew. He was brought back to reality by her statement.

"This wasn't very tasty but thank you." Sadal said as she stuck her tongue out.

You...did not...have to eat it... Narro thought as he took a deep breath.

"As for Muupasi...never... I have something else for you. Try not to eat this please." Narro said, quickly shifting a pile of moss he gathered into another corner of his backpack.

The object he was looking for was a small dagger he forged in his spare time while healing from his wounds. It was an intricate weapon, with a handle made from antler. Narro sent out Jih to collect things on his behalf when foraging and he vowed he would return them in kind. The flint was whittled down to a multi-layered smoothed surface that was finer than what Jih usually produced for his needs. Narro could tell that he'd been watching the others closely and replicated their sharpening techniques to eventually surpass them.

"I wanted to give you this." Narro said, as he carefully hid the blade between his two hands.

Sadal looked at his hands and locked eyes with Narro. She was unsure of what to make of his strange gesture, but she opened his hands and clutched it close. Narro knew what made people happy, and a fresh new knife to boot was always a welcome gift. Sadal gave Narro a tight hug before letting go as she admired her newest hunting tool. She studied every detail of it, down to the incisions made with the very bone Narro usually reserved for improving his flute-making abilities. Sadal made the decision right then and there.

"Come Narro. I want to test this knife, see if it's really earned a spot on my belt." Sadal gestured with a wave for him to follow her. Narro followed her but stopped for a second.

"Will I not slow you down on the way? The first time I have been on two legs and have not lost my stomach." Narro remarked.

"Narro, don't flatter yourself. You were slow already!" Sadal said with a laugh.

Narro gave Sadal a slight glare as he soon followed her. Trekkal was adjusting her hair as she looked at her reflection in a small puddle of water. She tossed her nose up at the sight of Narro. The two gave each other a quick look before addressing Trekkal. She hummed to herself while Jih slept on a makeshift pillow some distance from them. While Sadal still had plenty of energy to burn, Jih was quite tired from the day's ordeal.

"Sadal." Trekkal said to her. Trekkal slowly turned her head to address Sadal only while keeping Narro in the dark.

"Where are you taking my foolish brother?" She questioned as she patted the ground next to her for a comb. Personal hygiene was important among the group, but Trekkal took it to a whole new level with the amount of maintenance she did on her hair. Sadal was known for styling hair, her own was dreaded thanks to Deeso's work but Trekkal had some tricks of her own.

"I heard you can use oil from Peymin to make it stay. The small strands that refuse to stay low you know." Sadal suggested, as she messed about with her own hair.

"Well yes Sadal. I distinctly remember myself telling you this some time ago, only for you to bring it up again! Typical of your people. Anyone who knows the art of Peymin, knows the oil has great properties. Take the dumb one wherever you like, just make sure you bring back something worth our time. In fact, feed him if you want. You think being only able to see half of the things would make you more grateful for what you eat." Trekkal grumbled as she massaged her stomach. All this talk of fish made her hungry, but there wasn't a flowing stream for miles. She would have to settle with some gathered fruit and the leftover meat until there was more that could be found.

"Trekkal, I can see fine-" Narro said lowly but was quickly silenced by Sadal. It was clear Trekkal had some steam to blow off, so that was for Jih to handle. For now, it was just going to be them out on the infinite plains around them.

Sadal decided to pick their travel direction by tossing a stick in the air and Narro guessed the direction it would land. She took a stretch of her arm and launched it as high into the sky as she could. It was a game she played when she was younger with friends and for the quick learner that Narro was, he enjoyed it much as well. They decided to head southwest to see what lay ahead. The greenery surrounded them for miles ahead as temperatures were warm and the sun was nice on their skin. Sadal enjoyed the relative silence with Narro for a few moments as she turned her head to face him.

"Sorry for the deception, but I didn't want to hunt for once this time. I actually wanted to talk with you alone. It's been a while." Sadal said as she rubbed Narro's arm. Narro let out a small grin, but he remained focused as he wanted to be sure to be able to answer whatever Sadal asked of him.

The two walked together and pointed at various animals they'd seen before, but also new and exciting ones to explain to the others back home. For Narro, they were among the outer ends of his homeland, to see his people's land flourishing happily was a fulfilling sight as he knew better days were ahead. Narro filled Sadal's curiosity as he spoke about various legends that his people shared. Sadal was ignorant of most of these, but she remembered a few commonalities between them. After some walking, Sadal stopped to give Narro a once-over as she thought for a moment. All that accompanied them on the long walk was the sound of a few antelopes grazing and making bellowing calls.

"What you did back there to get your injury. Why did you do it? All I saw was you return to me hurt." Sadal asked, her voice dropping some. Narro was taken by surprise, he imagined he articulated everything about the situation before, but he realized that he only did this with Trekkal. Sadal was now in the middle of a series of misunderstandings between Narro and Trekkal.

"I can tell you what I told my sister. Someone needed my help. Simple as that." Narro explained with shrugged shoulders.

"But you were outnumbered, I don't understand. Why go into a conflict that you can't win? You would have died if not for that mysterious person who saved you." Sadal interjected and stopped short of saying too much. She knew from Narro's description of events that Zulag helped Narro rather than be the opportunistic person he was and kill him for his own aims. This situation was something she still needed to wrap her mind around, but this meant that Deeso was somewhere still searching for her.

"Yes, and I would do it again. We support our own kind no matter what. It is a loyalty thing. Trekkal thinks the world is built of those who only serve for self, but I think differently. You have to help each other because the world is so cold otherwise." Narro said as he decided to rest his legs and sit on the ground. He patted next to him for Sadal to join him.

"Loyalty..." Sadal said to herself as she felt the presence of Ronkalk's aura behind her. She looked up and saw they sat under the shade of another fig tree.

Sadal sat close to Narro and looked into his remaining eye. Sadal was grilled by Jih under a fig tree some time ago, but Narro's questioning was filled with innocence to a fault. Sadal reflected on what loyalty truly meant to her. Loyalty is what kept The Broken Bone strong and bound to its own destiny, rather than be the subjugate of another. Jih had done Sadal a service above and beyond what was required, and for this she felt a bond could grow between them. This is how she decided to make her way with Jih to join his quest for the meteor. As she thought about Deeso and her strict interpretation of loyalty, she felt immense guilt come over her that was visible to Narro. Narro approached and cupped Sadal's chin in his hand with a small smile to try and change Sadal's expression.

"Deeso is loyal. My little sister. That's what kept us going during the tough years. I hope we can see eye to eye again." Sadal mumbled.

While trying to come up with the words to address Sadal's statement, he instead was out of words entirely as he felt the delicate touch of Sadal's hands.

"Narro, mark my hand. Use the knife you made for me." Sadal said with a smile, revealing the top of her hand to him. He was incredibly confused, why would she want herself to be maimed? Why would he be entrusted with this? It was known that Sadal was left-handed and so she did everything with this in mind, the pain would be unbearable.

"Before I met you or Trekkal, or even Jih. I had a life of my own making but at the crux of it was someone else. I said this was it, but I have decided that is no longer my path to go. I may keep some of the old ways, but it's time for me to do something different." Sadal explained as she gestured to her hand.

"Yes. That old life of yours. You only tell us so much, but I remember hearing words from Jih on occasion. A man named Nurzan? What happened there?" Narro asked as he lifted his arm and attempted to grab a branch with a fig.

Sadal froze slightly as she put that in the back of her mind but knew that she would answer Narro with some honesty. Sadal decided to let go of the fact that Jih opened about this detail without her permission. Her attention that truly mattered now was Narro. She felt a warm energy radiate from him that put her at ease. She still thought about the song made for her as its melody played in her head when she slept. Sadal studied Narro's movements and noticed something awry. Sadal knew that those with eye injuries had difficulty with depth perception. Sadal gently guided his arm an inch closer and at last he broke the branch off.

"Before I left The Broken Bone, Nurzan asked for my hand. I agreed, there was something about his humble nature at first that made me happy. I require a lot of room to do what I do and a lot of patience. It was a union that worked as it required little effort to maintain. The same man always waited for me with a nice meal on my return. A Master Hunter's job was no easy task, I had to be away often to make the land safe for my people. I was nothing short of a hero. Nurzan received a glowing approval from Ronkalk, and I wanted to be on his good side. It all worked out for a while as all I wanted was a simple life where I could be appreciated. One day though, the love I wanted seemed to break apart. It just didn't make any sense to me." Sadal stated with a pause. Her words faltered slightly as her gaze left Narro's to the soil and then back to his single eye.

"When I walked in the hut after a long day, I would talk with Deeso often and that lifted my spirits high. I didn't get this with him. He was an expert in his own right and never held ambitions for hunting like me. It wasn't jealousy, but I can't figure out what it was. Deeso thinks it was to control me, I didn't believe her at the time. He would just look at me with these horrid eyes. I tried everything to keep things as they were. People looked at me and I know they talked about me. I silenced them and defended Nurzan, and for what?" Sadal kept herself grounded as she felt her voice quiver.

"I remember the effort to make me feel special, it was an intricate basket made from the finest fibers and sinew. I treasured it dearly, always used it for my tools, but one day... I went without it and he yelled at me. His voice was filled with poison. It wasn't just in the privacy of our home either, it was out in our village center. I wasn't sure what to do. I never take disrespect, but Nurzan was my love or that's what it was supposed to be. I froze and had no response. I walked home and blocked it out of my mind. It was embarrassing to my legacy that I worked so hard to achieve. This happened more often than you'd think. Remember I told you about my hunting rival, Zulag? The spoiled leader's nephew and I locked eyes during the whole exchange once when Nurzan berated me in front of a few others. I wasn't sure what was worse, being exposed like this for the sham of a family I was trapped in or seen as inferior to him. For some reason though, after that, Nurzan never yelled at me again in public. Perhaps those incidents were connected. Either way, my treatment at home just grew worse."

"It was scary how quickly he turned from someone filled with genuine respect and love to something horrid. I felt like an invader in our own space. Nurzan would arrive and when it was only me in our tent, I just felt suffocated. I was trapped in a never-ending cycle of being miserable. Like a dark cloud, he only brought bad tidings on us. We had a child named Brab, and I thought Brab would be our answer to fix our lives and the tension in our home. It only made things much worse. I was told that Brab was cursed by the priests, and he brought a bad omen on our home. Deeso cared little for the words of the priests and was the mother to our boy. I would ask Nurzan to watch Brab and the air between us was cut dry. I felt like a bloodied Ker-Mah that couldn't feel the relief of death. The simplest exchanges made me filled with anger but my feet boulders. I couldn't move. I couldn't do it over again. The Broken Bone was my home and so I dealt with it until I couldn't." Sadal explained.

Narro kept his silence as he knew that Sadal wasn't yet finished explaining her past. Narro felt overwhelmed with emotion as he imagined Sadal's suffering. He felt especially touched that she was comfortable enough to reveal this information to him. His heart felt rage was an emotion that wasn't going to be helpful, Narro needed to be kind and understanding of Sadal's situation.

"I wanted to tell someone for a long time. Deeso knew, but she was my sister. What was she going to do? I couldn't tell Ronkalk, his time was too important to be wasted." Sadal mentioned as she looked to Narro.

"And what happened to your son Sadal? Is he still with this man?! How could one be so callous to you?" Narro asked in stifled anger.

"I left him behind. It was the only way I could ensure there was a better path. I haven't mentioned it to anyone, and I would like to keep that to myself. But now you know what happened." Sadal said with a large sigh of relief.

Sadal felt slightly guilty as she left out the details regarding Brab, but that was her business only. She needed to look to the future and truly find out what life she was going to leave for herself. On her left hand was a small incision in the shape of a circle from years past, whereas a young girl, she received the same mark. It was to designate her status as a Wanderer. A resurgence of the mark meant that it was time to go once again somewhere new. Sadal's life in The Broken Bone was over. It was something she had considered for a long time after she ran away but couldn't bring herself to do so. She couldn't bear to ask Jih to do it, not out of any inherent distrust, but she felt as if she was under the guise of a judging parent.

"I want you to understand that things won't be easy. This life with me will take work Narro. I will disappoint you, I will make your life much worse, but you still say you want to be with me? You want me to be your One?" Sadal asked.

"All I have ever done was work, but with you, I can work and live. Sadal, we are a band with Jih and Trekkal. More importantly, you and I are a team. I want to be your One more than you could imagine." Narro said with a warm grin.

"With this mark, all my commitments are now gone. Which means..." Sadal said, intentionally leaving a void for Narro to fill in. Narro withdrew the dagger silently and complied with Sadal's instructions as her hand tensed from the blood that seeped through. Narro gave a pained smile as he was beside himself on how such a barbaric ceremony was considered normal.

"For all your profound wisdom, you sure are a smooth stone Narro." Sadal said with a clench of her teeth as her hand leaked blood out. Narro still said nothing as his eyes met the ground. He was too nervous to move as he thought he was going too hard with the dagger. It worked effectively and cut through the flesh with ease.

"I start anew. No title, no rank and...no partner. I have at least one of these now. Come Narro, a new life waits for us both. I could use a bandage too." Sadal said as she let Narro lead the way back home.

Lessons Learned

Now that Narro was fully recovered from his escapade, he went out for a hunt on his own. It was a nice feeling to be back in the land of his people. His mind raced about the task at hand given to him to Fahlrit some time ago. He was worried that Fahlrit had forgotten about him after the two weeks he spent in recovery but persisted nonetheless with the task. After some time of foraging, he saw a tree that held grape vines and he pocketed a generous amount in his bag. Narro had a small grin on his face as he finally got what he was looking for. Narro had good reason to be happy, he and Trekkal made up, and she was attached to his hip once more.

For whatever reason though, she chose to stay behind and instead comb the rivers for more fish as usual instead of joining him to work with Fahlrit. He also thought about Sadal's rather odd display of affection. Not much around was worth his time. Alone, gazelles far outpaced him, and his stomach would not spare another meal for deer this time either. His travels took him to the familiar woodland where he was received by the man who held great sorrow at the mention of Fahlrit. Narro shook the bag of grapes to show that his quest was finally fulfilled. Narro noticed this once again, but decided to not bring attention to the matter as he made his way to the opening of Fahlrit's cave. Narro noticed a lit fire with some strange meat cooking. He also noticed a bag with assorted objects inside, so he knew Fahlrit was present.

"Fahlrit...?" Narro answered.

There was a slight pause between Narro's words and the grunt of Fahlrit acknowledging that his name was mentioned. Narro's voice echoed through the cave and reverberated slightly. Slowly but surely, the man came on the ground. Narro entered the cave and without a second thought, chose to support Fahlrit by quickening the man's pace towards his usual rock. As Fahlrit was placed down, Narro gave him a wide berth to stretch.

"I was getting to you. People your age can never wait, can they?" Fahlrit remarked with snark in his voice.

"Oh, you have returned. I assumed you got eaten." Fahlrit mentioned as he assessed Narro's condition.

"Seems I was half right. Given your eye and all. What happened to you? Did the tree fight back or something?" Fahlrit goaded.

"Well, I have returned! With what you asked for..." Narro mentioned as he slowly approached Fahlrit and withdrew the grapes as he requested. Narro held a smug expression that Fahlrit chose to extinguish with some glee in his delivery. He looked at Narro up and down with some shock given his recent injuries in battle. He figured a man of his build would hardly run into trouble, but even their own kind could be felled by a beast.

"My apologies Fahlrit, but things got complicated very quickly. I just hope that you can-Are you eating those?" Narro asked, his voice raising in severity. Fahlrit nodded with a snide expression as he scooped up the grapes and ate happily.

"I grow hungry. When you were recovering, I had someone else do what you asked me. These are not for the tint I need as my masterpiece is complete." Fahlrit gestured at his rendition of the meteor shower. Narro absorbed every detail, with white streaks arranged in a formation to represent the meteor's trail, while more abstract paintings filled in other crucial details of what occurred.

"Now that is finished though...Say. You seem like the build I am looking for. How about a Yaan hunt, hmm? The boys and I have been planning one for a while. This is for an important reason. I can tell you whatever you need to know on the way." Fahlrit mentioned.

"Of course, I would be happy to help you Fahlrit. It is the least I can do for your quest. Now as for that meat there..." Narro asked as he rubbed his stomach.

Fahlrit crawled over and guided Narro closely to the bag. He withdrew a hunk of meat that was covered in a gelatinous cover that Narro looked at with slight disgust. On a second look, Narro realized that the meat on the stick and the one in Fahlrit's hands were one and the same.

"Here, have some meat. What, are you not hungry? The meat is fine. We have only had it for a week now." Fahlrit pointed as he passed the meat over to him. Narro couldn't hide his distaste at the prospect.

"Meat for one week? How can you stand the smell? Smoking it keeps it held for a few days, but..." Narro said as he sniffed the meat.

"You must be new to this. A good Yaan hunt can keep us fed for a month. The fat you see, keeps it from going bad. Smells like dung if you do it wrong though. Quit your bellyaching and wait for a properly cooked piece." Fahlrit lectured as he held a finger to tell Narro to wait his turn.

"We usually eat Aroc where I come from, so my surprise is a bit..." Narro remarked with a bit of shock.

"A dull and often uninteresting meat, it fills you, sure, but do you live when you consume it?" Fahlrit asked Narro.

"Do you always entertain those that visit you with such profound statements?" Narro replied in jest.

Fahlrit grumbled at Narro's statement. Fahlrit attempted to reach over and grab a knife just out of reach. Fahlrit was a frustrated man for reasons beyond Narro's current understanding, but Narro looked to the obvious and decided to comfort his sorrows. Narro gently moved over the piece to him and watched as Fahlrit grabbed it. Much like The Youngest he disparaged, Fahlrit had a streak of independence that only amplified after his injury where even kind gestures were looked at with the utmost suspicion.

The two ate the meat silently as Narro took in their surroundings. Although the taste was hardly what he anticipated, the meat was edible, and he was excited to see what the hunt could bring. Narro lacked any grand hunting experiences in recent memory that were all his own, and he couldn't wait to tell Sadal. Once the two digested their food, Fahlrit looked up to the sky and tracked the sun's trajectory. He cracked his knuckles and started to crawl. Fahlrit was stopped by Narro who stood in front of him. Fahlrit had a bag of supplies he kept handy for his plan of the big elephant hunt.

"You said it yourself. I can only see half, and you are unable to walk without help. Why not work together? Your friends will be happy to see us as one. You can be my extra eye, and I will be your leg. Climb on." Narro proposed as he waited while Fahlrit shrugged his shoulders and decided to do so. It was awkward at first, but having much less weight than anticipated, he was an easy carry for Narro.

"Just what is around here to hunt? I saw Retodeu but they are much too fast for me." Narro asked his new companion.

"As I mentioned, a herd of Yaan have found their place here for some time. The water flows well here and not much attacks them in the day. This would be good game to hunt, and you will not have to swing your club." Fahlrit replied as he passively spoke into Narro's ear.

Narro was confused at the man's insistence, but he let it play out. If Fahlrit truly saw combat with a Mahaku and survived, his words were to be listened to. As the two descended from Fahlrit's cave, Narro noticed Fahlrit gave the camp of his relatives a look of disgust as they went down. Narro and Fahlrit continued to go through the woodlands as they made small conversation with one another. Narro looked up and saw the beauty of the trees that outlined their surroundings. The vista of changing leaves was something that he hadn't seen often.

"You know, my friend Jih would never have done this. He harbors a deep fear towards Yaan of all kinds. It eludes me but I am sure there is something I am missing." Narro mentioned.

"He respects the Yaan well, for they are compassionate creatures but also vicious when the time comes. It was perhaps he faced the latter end of that." Fahlrit remarked.

Narro agreed with the man's words. He knew that Sadal was informed about Jih's experience with elephants and reasoned it wouldn't be too hard to get out of her.

"Your people did not give me the warmest welcome, but they seem kind. Tell me about them, where do you come from?" Narro insisted, as he hoped not to pry too much into Fahlrit's privacy.

"We have gone by many names, but we are now called The Red Cloak, for as you guessed, our use of ochre. I mentioned I was a great hunter some time ago. There were two more besides me, my One named Evdic and my younger cousin named Jarzill. Now there is only me. My hunting buddies are from two other bands to the south. For them it was a three-day trek, so it is best we keep them entertained." He mentioned with a stiff delivery.

"I know a great hunter as well. Her name is Sadal. Given what you told me, I imagine the two of you would be good friends. I think in time she may be truly my One, but we will see." Narro noted much to the gruff laugh of Fahlrit. Narro was lovestruck, he loved his friends and sister more than anything else and much of his thoughts centered around Sadal. It hung in the air like misty fog.

"Sadal. That is a name of The Youngest. What makes you say we would be good friends hmm? Is it my charming personality or my infinite breadth of knowledge?" Fahlrit said with a cough.

"Well, both of you are hunters. In her band, everyone is expected to hunt predators like Weypeu or Denmey to clear the land for the next generation." Narro stated with pride in his newfound love.

"You mean to tell me; they hunt these things on purpose? My band and I enjoy the hunt as much as anyone else, but we stick to those that eat grass. The ones that see us as lunch are not as appealing." Fahlrit commented.

"I am just making jokes. That is good to hear, let us hope your village is more careful with your One than my own." Fahlrit added on bluntly which gave Narro a surprise as he paused.

"What do you mean?" Narro asked, as he stopped walking.

Narro was surprised that Fahlrit was so forthcoming with this information but realized that what he needed above all else was a friend. Narro kept himself quiet as he let Fahlrit air out his frustrations and provide some extra context onto the state of being. Fahlrit clamped his hands on Narro's shoulders as a rush of anger flew over him. The experience was something one could never get over but it remained ever raw for Fahlrit as he felt himself to blame as well.

"You heard me. Those Sarmpa stomachs will never live with the fact they killed Evdic and caused Jarzill to leave. They pity me because of my injury and see me as an idle child to be taken care of rather than the man I am. With the death of Evdic, I am cursed and there is only one solution for that-I am getting ahead of myself, those hapless fools took them both from me the day we went to hunt the Mahaku. Ah-It was not long ago, perhaps two years now. Our leader called us forward to claim the land and as the best hunters it was our call to do so. The Mahaku was a bothersome creature that made trade difficult." Fahlrit explained.

"Who? Jarzill is a unique name, but Evdic sounds more like us." Narro questioned.

"Evdic is-was-my One and Jarzill is my younger cousin. I took it with pride, a stupid mistake, but felt it was one that needed doing. We went as far as we could go, out to where the land was open and warm. A hulking gray spirit we knew of that caused problems. We knew about the Mahaku from legend-" Fahlrit commented as he whispered into Narro's ear.

"Nothing prepares you for the real thing." Fahlrit voiced as his words hung over Narro's ears. Narro felt the color vanish from his face as Fahlrit described in more detail what happened that fateful day.

"Our scouts said only a team of three were needed. No, you must take this as seriously as an angry Yaan, a band is needed to kill such a beast. My sweet Evdic was not one for that brutal work, he had the heart of a tracker, but fought with honor like any other. When you see your One ripped to pieces in front of you, there is not much to say. Have you ever felt so powerless that all one can do is scream and hope it ends? Anger consumes you and nothing more can decide. I held an axe, but I was filled with such hate, I kicked the beast and lost my leg for it. Jarzill was born differently from the rest of us, hence his name, but I never saw him that way. He was a kind soul." Fahlrit mentioned as he tried to suppress his distaste.

"I am sorry for your One Fahlrit...Did Jarzill also pass?" Narro asked with a low voice.

"Oh, I sure hope not. It has been some time since I have seen him last. Not much to say but, my cousin Jarzill showed much promise to succeed even me until one day, he started seeing strange visions after our encounter with the Mahaku. It was destiny he was to instead be a priest, which is just as high an honor. Others did not see it this way. Our Seer had told us not to be alarmed, but he took this vision with the utmost importance. His face was marred by the creature, and he was so embarrassed he hid his face from the world. I chose to hide my very existence in that cave. He carried on for some time, but he took a mushroom for healing from our Seer and one day vanished without a trace." Fahlrit explained.

"This is interesting. I have yet to see anyone become a Seer through such a tragedy since our leader Stelo and her journey. Did he happen to see some sort of animal come to him?" Narro questioned.

"No animal, this was under unusual circumstances. Before that though, I knew that his soul changed. The bright and cheery cousin I loved grew into something far more sinister. These visions he had, he said that there was an insatiable hunger that needed to be fed to a spirit. It was a lone spirit that ranked above all else. I trusted the vision of my cousin and so I had everyone hunt for all sorts of game to match what he saw but nothing worked to suit his demand. He said he needed something purer, and I heard him mutter the name of a man under his breath. I feared Jarzill meant to find man as his prey, but when confronted on it, he went north for a new purpose. He was always fascinated with the sky and where things came from. So, if you see any one of those people I am unfortunately related to, they carry the shame of that day and the death of my One on their hands. It a shared burden but I bear the brunt of it all." Fahlrit continued as he pointed to Narro the clearing from the woodland that led out to the open plains once more.

As Narro listened to more of Fahlrit's tale, this grand hunt had much more finality to it than anything else. Narro could see why his band members gave him such discomfort when Fahlrit's name was mentioned. Something was not well with him after the accident. Narro took Fahlrit's words to heart. The death of a person's One would only bring misery and pain of unimaginable force. Without the proper guidance, the influence of the curse could project onto an entire band. Collective guilt was a scary proposition and one many bands sought to avoid. It was no surprise that many were hesitant to build such a connection, it wasn't an easy ask to do. His thoughts were interrupted by Fahlrit's words again.

"Near us is a chasm that ends with a sharp drop. Are you following? The clumsy beasts will be crushed under their own weight, should we scare one to take the plunge. Food for days, supplies even longer. Let us use this tree to hold our things." Fahlrit explained as he latched himself off Narro for the time being.

A group of The Aligned in the distance were busy preparing some sort of construction with digging sticks that was visible to the pair. Fahlrit announced he and Narro's presence with a mighty yell that carried over the distance. It was returned in kind as Narro awkwardly repeated the yell back. There were a few confused looks, but Narro was accepted all the same. Narro noticed a force of about eight people, a large task for a hunt that seemed simple in its execution. Narro introduced himself to the others and while he thought he was strong, Fahlrit's friends dwarfed him in muscle mass. As they were from a different band than his own, Narro didn't recognize some of the importance of their dress. He did notice that all of them had their faces smeared with red ochre while his was bare.

"Are you aware of the plan young one? Fahlrit has entrusted you with this ceremony?" One of the men asked as he examined Narro's beard.

Narro attempted to hide his surprise at the wording of ceremony. He wasn't sure what spectacle could be brought for a routine hunt, but he decided to take it in stride. Narro nodded and watched as the rest of them worked to prepare. Narro noticed that multiple sticks in the ground were placed in a distinct pattern and were coated with animal fat. The objective was to cast them alight with a torch once they got the attention of one of the straight tusked elephants. The smell was enough to disorient them and the light of the flaming torch would dissuade them or so they hoped. Narro's gaze met the lumbering herd of elephants some distance away, but they needed to be lured over. Narro noticed that the soon to be lit sticks marked a pathway to guide the elephant to the end of the chasm below. This was a survivable drop for man, but for an elephant would spell doom.

With this in mind, their task was now underway. Narro went to collect Fahlrit and returned to the group who greeted him with the utmost warmth. Narro listened intently as Fahlrit gave plenty of context to the situation to Narro and kept him included. To complete their plan, they needed to find an eligible elephant, but which one out of the plenty could they pick from? The group schemed together and sighted a straight-tusked elephant with a bum leg. An ironic choice from Fahlrit that he found amusing. The animal's loss was to be their own gain. Their prey chewed grasses some distance from the others as it struggled to keep up. Fahlrit advised Narro to take him towards the chasm to examine the route. The chasm that Fahlrit mentioned was visible to them where it was safe enough for someone of their stature to slide down with ease but became a nightmare for the elephants. Down below were some bones from previous attempts that validated this as a tried-and-true method. The rest of the hunting party waited patiently for Narro to return to position with Fahlrit in tow.

"Fahlrit, what is your will for this plan?" One man asked as he gave Fahlrit a slow nod of understanding.

Narro examined the men and saw a mixture of weapons at their disposal to finish off the elephant in case it survived the fall. A few of them swayed back in forth in excitement for the rush, but Fahlrit seemed to have their attention the strongest.

"Narro, let me down here and I will crawl to the prey. I will count to three when I am ready. Once I have neared the Yaan, you will join the others and set the stakes alight. Take this with you. Not exactly hotspark, but it should make a flame with enough force." Fahlrit said as he reached around for some rocks. He tossed Narro two pieces of stone he couldn't directly identify. He held up his fingers and prompted Narro to do his part of the plan.

Fahlrit crawled towards the elephant and held up his hand. One of the men rushed past Narro to scoop Fahlrit up as he gripped on his back. Fahlrit and the other man remained silent until Fahlrit counted down in his mind and then loudly screamed at the top of his lungs and gathered the attention of a few other elephants. Their interest was piqued by the strange humans before them but not enough to do anything, just as he anticipated. Fahlrit reached to the ground as he was carried to scoop up a few rocks in hand. He pelted the elephant and caused it to blow wind into his face of the two men. Fahlrit felt the rush of battle course through his body once more and the vision of better days filled his mind. For just a moment, he imagined his beloved Evdic and cousin Jarzill at his side again. As Narro watched this unfold, he followed the lead of the others who maintained their positions to surround the point where the elephant would be corralled. Fahlrit and his guide goaded the elephant to go on the chase and it succeeded. Fahlrit could feel the vibrations of the elephant catching up with them as he yelled for Narro to focus.

Narro watched as the others ran over to close the distance and took the initiative. He grasped a spare torch set on fire and joined in making noise while he waved it around. The combined efforts of The Aligned men rushing the animal with spears and waving fire was a devastating combination in most situations. Their weapons could hardly do much now as they were broken off inside the animal's flesh, but blood pooled to the ground all the same. This set the elephant into a rage as it clearly had seen the impact of a bad fire on the plains before. The rest of the herd watched and ushered the calves away while a curious male looked to see what would happen. Narro ran as fast as he could and used his torch along with the others now to light up the other stakes. The wind blew the smoke into the elephant's direction, and made it panic more as the group directed it towards the cliffside. Their plan worked almost too well, as the elephant reared up, and placed extra weight on the shaky foundation. Narro ran as fast as he could, and launched his torch ahead of him to give it one final push before it reared over. The elephant let out a mighty shout that lowered in volume as it fell to the ground and practically combusted into pieces from the force. It landed to the ground with a solid thud as it turned to chunks of meat that were skewered by the bones of its own ancestors.

The meat was spread around but left a remarkable display to add to the pile below. Narro covered his mouth in shock at such a plan working out so well, but Fahlrit knew his method was foolproof. Fahlrit directed the others to cut the meat while he looked with satisfaction over his kill. The two traversed down the slope carefully to meet the prize of their victory. Fahlrit pocketed what meat he could, and willed the rest to Narro as he finished fastening bags to hold meat. Narro couldn't believe the extent of meat they had gotten from the kill. With just one, they were well on their way to having a surplus of meat for weeks. Fahlrit and Narro watched as those of their hunting party brought two sleighs to hoist pieces of the meat. The pair started the long process of stripping sizable chunks of meat with their respective axes and filling holes in the corpse as they did so.

"A tusk for you. One for me. This is a bounty for our loved ones that we shall share. This Sadal, you told me about, she will be quite impressed. Not very often do we get such things." Fahlrit commented as he did his best to carry what he could in his hands, while Narro strapped the rest to the sleigh. It was a grueling climb, but the rewards were certainly worth it as Narro wiped the sweat off his forehead. Fahlrit's friends lingered and gave their best wishes to him.

"You honor us Fahlrit, the glory was shared by us all. Evdic stands with us still. I hope your journey is met with happiness. The meat will be taken to your band as soon as we are able to cook it." One of the men said as he nodded to wipe a tear from his eye.

Narro made his way back to Fahlrit's cave, where the two rubbed noses with one another in respect to the craft. Narro lowered his head in acknowledgment that the hunt was complete. By now, Narro realized that the hunt in question was a last hunt and braced himself for any further requests. Narro felt a resounding urge to help and give a vain attempt to see Fahlrit change his mind. Narro understood the validity of the endeavor, but he was unsure if he was willing to do the same for Sadal just yet.

"I want you to go lower into the valley and tell the others I have left an offering for them. Can this be done?" Fahlrit requested as he pointed to the arrangement of small tents in the clearing. Though his tone regarding the ones he called family was still sharp, it had a more protective tone this time. Narro was relieved to hear such good words come from his friend. Narro felt the embrace of his clan was what he needed the most after what seemed like a long time of isolation.

"I could take you with me, it is no trouble at all." Narro offered. He saw his arm grabbed by Fahlrit who nodded no.

"Who will be left to work the meat? Take your reward and head home once it is done." He replied with a grin as he dismissed Narro shortly afterwards. Narro nodded but vowed to return with the clan in tow.

Narro did his due diligence, and returned to the village as he met eyes with an older woman that called forth for the one he spoke with before. He approached gently; his back saddled with plenty of meat as he saw another man with a spear held out towards him.

"You again, what do you want this time?" The man asked, his tone judgmental of Narro's presence among them.

"I have hunted with Fahlrit. He tells me he has given an offering for you." Narro explained. The man put his spear down and hugged Narro like one of his own. Narro held a surprised expression on his face at the man's response but returned the greeting in kind.

"You...what?" The man replied as he turned to a few of the other members of the band who shared his surprised expression. Narro noted his disarmed expression, it was clear that the others hadn't considered Fahlrit's opinion on matters. Due to his disability and the events that happened surrounding his loved ones, the band pitied Fahlrit, but failed to address his real needs.

"We will make our leave right away! It has been hard to have him do, well, anything." One of the women admitted within the group.

Narro nodded and followed the others up to the foot of the cave. He looked over the small group of ten, led by an aging priestess who took much pride in their endeavors. She and Narro talked about many matters of what laid beyond their mortal vision, and he felt enlightened. Narro spoke of their cunning hunt with much bravery and gusto. Narro realized that despite their icy exterior, Fahlrit came from a community that loved him but didn't understand him.

Alone now, Fahlrit saw the fruits of his labor and looked at himself. Fahlrit made peace with the life he lived and was able to join his friends for one more glorious hunt. He still felt like a burden to his band, but in killing a straight tusked elephant, he was able to relieve the many starving stomachs below. It wasn't an easy decision but moving him around wasn't practical. Their band stayed for weeks at a time, and he could feel that his band was waiting his life out. Contrary to his own feelings and the band's guilt around Fahlrit's condition, he was cherished, and they felt happy to have him around, but Fahlrit couldn't be convinced otherwise and the curse from losing his One and the mysterious fate of his beloved cousin remained a stain on his conscience.

I hope you are real, and that I can see you again in The Land of The Dead, Edvic. I did a good job but with you, I will be great. Fahlrit thought.

His masterpieces were now finished, as he made a small memorial for the current day. The stranger named Narro gave him some light. He took a sharpened biface to use a makeshift knife and made it quick as he slit his throat. He deceived Narro, as he was more than willing to give him the entire brood of the elephant's meat, but he had to look out for his band as well. It didn't take much for Narro to realize the scope of what happened as he arrived. Narro stood silent as he met the others. Fahlrit's family didn't move as they stood in sadness over the corpse of their beloved hunter-turned-painter, now with a masterpiece in a pool of his blood. He didn't die as sad or miserable as one would have believed, but through Narro and his friends he was able to recapture some of the joy he once felt on the field of battle. His intent to take his own life was present for some time as those around him were unsure of how to help him. The curse of losing your One could not be removed and when the bond was broken, this was seen as the only way. Fahlrit felt he did a service for the rest of his band who hardly deserved such treatment as the curse would die with him. Fahlrit decided that he needed a way to do this with honor and the great elephant hunt was carried out. As this was achieved, he chose to leave the warmth of The Red Cloak. He decided now that he had reached the zenith of his glory, it was his time to go and start a new life.

Narro chose to let the family mourn in peace, himself retreating while holding back his own grief. It felt strange, he only knew Fahlrit for a short amount of time and yet felt an incredible energy come over him. He refused to look back because he knew he would fall apart entirely if he did. He pressed on with the meat in tow and walked for some time before the usual sounds of his friends put his heart at ease. Sadal and Trekkal were arguing over a matchup between a cave lion and a cave bear. Jih sat drinking water from a leather flask and waved to Narro as he arrived in camp. Narro placed the assortment of meat he gathered down while Jih raised an eyebrow at the size of the haul. Narro stretched out his body and was relieved of the weights that were on him most of the day.

"I'm telling you Trekkal, a Kal-Bher would easily win against a Kalpeu. The hide is too thick." Sadal said, stretching her arms out to prove her point.

"No! You are wrong, a Kalpeu is much more agile, it would avoid the Khal-Bher. Jih, we need you to weigh in." Trekkal said through chews of berries in her mouth.

"How many Kalpeu?" Jih asked, closing the flask now, and tossing it to the side of him.

"See Sadal! He asked how many Kalpeu because they always hunt in packs. Therefore, in this situation, the Kalpeu would always win." Trekkal huffed as she gave a big grin.

"We have one Kal-Bher, so there is one Kalpeu. That's how it works, Trekkal." Sadal said as her voice increased in volume. She blew some air out of her nose and knew fully well Trekkal attempted to get a rise out of her. The two continued to go at it while Jih put his face in his hands as he looked at Narro who seemed noticeably upset.

Narro nodded at the scene and went into his tent. Jih knew Narro wore his heart on his sleeve, and gave a fatherly nod to Sadal and Trekkal, and watched to see which of the two would go first. Trekkal saw an opportunity to spend some much-needed sibling time with Narro and looked to follow his pace.

"We will talk about this later." Trekkal said, pointing to Sadal as she left her to accompany her brother. Although he said nothing, she laid down on their grass mat floor and held on tight to his back and was there for comfort as Narro was slumped over.

"You did great today, whatever happens we are here for you." Trekkal whispered over the ambient sounds of Jih and Sadal outside in discussion.

Narro said nothing as he felt his sister's touch and subsequent snoring afterwards. Narro thought about Fahlrit's fate and about Jih. The loss of Fahlrit's One caused him to take his own life, but for Jih, the loss of Hyu invigorated him to undergo the journey to find the meteor. Narro was perplexed at the choices made between the two men but saw that both paths worked best. Narro gave a small grin as he looked at the wall of their tent. He learned that day that he couldn't save everyone.

Time For Action

Back at the main camp of The Broken Bone, Ronkalk dressed himself for a meeting with the other band leaders that made up their organization. As he felt he needed to assert his authority after news of the apparent plot against him, Ronkalk donned a tiger pelt that draped behind his back like a cape. Their meeting was to be supervised by a member of the priesthood, Ronkalk had no doubts his mental opponent of the red priest would want to stick his nose in his affairs once more. Ronkalk resented this portion of the priesthood as his power had no grasp in that realm. The priesthood often sent a representative who attended the gathering of the four bands that made up The Broken Bone to serve as mediators. Ronkalk and Stobai ran their respective bands the longest, but the other two bands generally were more volatile in that they rotated leadership a fair number of times.

The time was early as Ronkalk left his home quietly while his partner and young child slept. He was received by a young man who would serve as his guide, not that Ronkalk needed one. He was honor bound to carry his weapons and other items on his behalf. For appearances, however, he allowed such a gesture to be offered. To the young and impressionable, much like how Deeso accompanied Ronkalk, time with him was considered otherworldly. This feat could only be surpassed by the priesthood and associated spirits. Ronkalk's guide led him to a small enclave in the forest where a sizeable pyre was lit as he locked eyes with Stobai and the two other leaders of The Broken Bone. Ronkalk looked impressed as he and Stobai chose to wear the same animal without coordinating. One of the accompanying men known as Jacrod spoke out to Ronkalk's apparent late arrival.

"You're late." Jacrod answered, as he met eyes with Ronkalk.

Jacrod was a thin man who got by as an influential trader. He excelled in acquiring prestige goods that turned the heads of many, but this didn't save his personality. Ronkalk knew Jacrod as a cantankerous individual, he was as paranoid as they came with the state of his band in recent shambles after an attempted murder in the night. Ronkalk wanted to feel bad for him, but in the back of his mind, he felt he deserved it. Leadership was about compromise, and he tried his best to keep a civil tone when addressing the other leaders. Ronkalk rarely wore such luxury furs, but today he hoped to send a message. He scoffed at the other two leaders who wore leopard and binturong furs. Impressive in their own rights, but these failed in comparison to the tiger fur. Ronkalk felled this one himself in his leadership of a hunting team.

"You answered my call, you will wait for my arrival." Ronkalk said as he looked at the others. Ronkalk bit his tongue as he waited for the arrival of whichever priest decided to make their entrance known to them.

Just as he predicted, his intuition called out to him that there was someone present. By this point, Ronkalk could tell very easily when the red priest he came to verbal blows with would arrive to ruin his day. Today was one of these times. Ronkalk turned around and saw the others slowly lower their heads in respect. Ronkalk followed the same as the familiar mask showed up through the trees.

"I have two red priests for our band. Why does the other one never come?" Ronkalk questioned, as he turned his head to address Stobai and the others.

"She has far more important things to do than listening to you all squabble like children. This, I find amusing." The priest said with a stifled laugh. He used his longer arm to signal to the others to begin with the proceedings whenever they felt ready.

"Let us start. I ordered Stobai to make this meeting happen. There have been concerns from all parties-" Ronkalk opened with his eyes meeting the observant gaze of the man in the mask before continuing his statement.

"-regarding the Forest Seeker presence. I have gotten reports from scouts that they seem to be looking for stone and other material. They normally work with wood and use ambush tactics against their enemies, but they seem to be attacking more boldly these days. Does anyone have anything to say on this matter?" Ronkalk concluded by opening the floor to the others.

Stobai raised her hand, it was customary to do so, but Ronkalk nodded his head and allowed her to speak. In theory, they all shared the same rank and so discourse flowed freely whenever it was possible. Ronkalk imposed raising hands as a system of dialogue so that one could build their thoughts before speaking to the rest of the group. Time was precious and wasting their arguments on unnecessary outbursts wasn't a popular move.

"Our band The Sleeping Sarmpa has its hand in rumors. I sent one of my-" Stobai recounted as her eyes turned to see Jacrod cut her off.

"Rumors, hearsay, and doublespeak are not one for action. We need to move now. Ronkalk, you've been sitting on your hands because of this Sadal situation. I am tired of it." Jacrod interrupted. The red priest who observed watched Ronkalk with intrigue and wondered how this would unfold. His job was to report back all the current details for the priesthood.

"Stobai didn't finish her statement. I understand your need to rush but rushing into battle without good information leaves you picking the quills from a Mulku out of your rear. We know you make a good show of your rear, but do not embarrass me, or yourself again in front of our priest." Ronkalk commented.

"As I was saying, I sent out a few gatherers many moons ago who have finally reported information to me. They are gradually being united over this cause championed by one. We know this "leader" is a woman with the name of Eshe and that her forces have razed a village of both Forest Seekers and our kind. This is a strange development, but it proves the validity of the mission, they have issues to be exploited just like us. Oh, and Ronkalk, one of the Forest Seekers they questioned, reported that they were attacked by an odd-looking man with knives that flew through the air. I'll let you be the judge of that information and who they are referring to." Stobai said with a small grin.

Ronkalk and the others operated on months-old information and secondhand accounts when it came to the movements of the Forest Seekers, but they were crafty enough to make predictions on what to do and react accordingly. Ronkalk nodded with some pride in Stobai's words. He needed a well-earned win after the last couple of days and hearing the news of Zulag reportedly alive and well was one such thing.

"Thank you Stobai. Very thorough as always. I ask you, next Vichi. What is your opinion on this situation? You sit at the hand of where your father sits. It escapes me why he chose to leave and spurn our meeting but no matter. You are in this meeting with the three of us, your opinion as next in line is just as valid." Ronkalk explained to him.

Vichi was the sixteen-year-old son of the previous band leader who belonged to The Shattered Stone. He wore the binturong pelt that was an ill-fit for his body as it was his father's. He always found it amusing how close their original band name was to that of The Broken Bone they all identified with. Vichi emulated Ronkalk and Jacrod's expression of massaging their chin, but he lacked a beard to which brought amusement to the other three observers.

"My father mourns our mother and uncle. They died in combat against a Forest Seeker attack." He said with some shame in his voice as the other three closed their eyes and gave a heavy nod. The young boy felt honored at the sight, and he spoke again. He felt the flow of anger course through him, and vengeance was on his mind. Vichi hoped the sentiment carried on with the rest of the band as he continued.

"I think we should send more than just scouts. As you said before, the beasts are what we need to focus on. We can't do this without Forest Seekers getting in the way. We need to be on the offensive. If the Forest Seekers fight among themselves, we can take advantage of the chaos and sweep in." He said, as he waited for a response from the others.

Stobai and Jacrod nodded in support of the young man's plan, the time to act was now and with the information they received from Stobai's intelligence, there was an opening. The three looked at Ronkalk for the final decision. Ronkalk took a deep breath and as he evaluated the evidence, he knew the case was clear. He prepared a response in his mind ahead of time.

"We are all warriors who have devoted our lives to the removal of the beasts. You all agree with my vision. To keep our goal in mind, to provide peace and security for our people, we must go hard. I will use what I can spare. With two of my Master Hunters gone, I must put more time into gathering food to keep our population up and well fed. We also need to figure out what to do with The Mud Forged or any other lesser bands that may interfere with our plans. This will come later, but I approve our plan to launch strikes against the Forest Seekers. Start controlled burns along the heaviest sections of fighting. Do it in the dead of night so they can't run away." Ronkalk said, giving an affirmatory nod. With the meeting ending, Stobai and the others rose, but Ronkalk stood still. There was one more matter that needed to be addressed.

"You were not dismissed. There is something else that requires our attention. It was brought to me by Stobai that there was an attempt to wrestle power from me, a plot as she put it. Which one was responsible for making this happen? Surely it was not I or Stobai." Ronkalk mentioned. Jacrod felt his throat tighten and his eyes slowly drifted to Vichi.

"Vichi. You are not responsible for the sins of your father, if they come to pass, but I must know from you, what has happened?" Ronkalk questioned him. Vichi knew better than to obscure anything from Ronkalk, so he kept his head low and spoke the truth.

"One month ago, I was summoned by my father. He spoke with Jacrod about his issues with Zulag. He did not see him as legitimate to take over, nor your son. He proposed that he would succeed you and wanted me to carry it out at our next band gathering." Vichi said, his palms becoming quite sweaty as he heard Ronkalk's next question.

"And did you agree, Vichi?" Ronkalk asked with a raised eyebrow.

"I did. He was my father." Vichi stated. He knew the gravity of his statement and chose to refer to his father now in the past tense. Though he was alive, Vichi felt it wouldn't be this way for long now that everything was revealed.

"Ronkalk...it's not what you think. I said no. I spurned his advance. Stobai always had it out for me. She always did." Jacrod said, attempting to defend himself. Ronkalk held his hand up and closed it into a fist to silence the sniveling coward before him.

"Thank you Vichi. All of you may go now, but Stobai, I must speak with you." Ronkalk said as he dismissed the rest. Out of the corner of his eye, he still saw the red priest lingering by as though he needed to be dismissed by him as well. Ronkalk couldn't order him around, so he operated with business as usual. Stobai waited and lowered her head in respect to Ronkalk as she waited for his words.

"Stobai. Take the boy with you, have your people make him a meal. You have a daughter around the same age. Bring him into the fold, make him of your own, we will need his sharp mind in the battles to come." Ronkalk whispered into her ear.

"It will be done. You will keep the fool around?" Stobai said as she looked to see the frightened Jacrod make his way back to his own camp.

"Jacrod is weak, and he amuses me for now, so I will let him stay. Treachery of this scale, however, will not exist as long as I am leader. Vichi's father will not to live to see another night, my honor has made it so. If he mourns his family, and yet still plots against me, he will join them." Ronkalk said to her in confidence as he saw the boy offer a small wave in the distance.

In the drop of a hat, Ronkalk lost all respect for the man he hunted and scouted with, refusing to utter his name and only by extension his relation to Vichi. Ronkalk waved back to Vichi and set Stobai on her way. The red priest who observed everything slinked off into the shadows, ready to prepare the priests for a funeral.

Fun In The Sun

In the heat of the morning sun, Trekkal fumbled around in the grass of their campsite. She felt its unusually dry texture as she ripped a portion of it between her hands. Trekkal looked at the rest of her team sprawled out in the ground in varying states of exhaustion. It was too hot for anyone to sleep or do anything remotely productive, even for Jih and Sadal who were far accustomed to the warmth of the jungle. The four were dripping in sweat because the region had an unexpected heatwave. Their furs that were suited for the open plains now ran them too hot. The animals around them hadn't bothered moving, the dholes and hyenas were far too busy panting and fighting among themselves to be any danger for now. They hadn't anticipated an intense heat wave with no trees to cover the sun's harsh rays. The rivers ran low on water, and the amount of water in their packs were all but gone. Trekkal's travels the previous day to find water took her to a few isolated homes lived in by her people. She was accepted by their kindness and was informed of a very large body of water about an hour out from them. It seemed to be a popular place as she found the company of a few fellow fishermen and they talked about the different types of fish that were in the area. She knew she had to get there early to find the best spots. Getting the best catch was one thing she hoped to get above all else.

"Good morning, everyone. I have a fun day planned for us!" Trekkal said, wiping sweat from her forehead.

"And by fun, what do you mean exactly?" Narro questioned with a shake of his drenched hair.

"More fun than teaching us how to play music." Trekkal said. She received a small smirk from Sadal who fixed her face as Narro glared at her. Jih stretched his arms out and laid back slightly, he was as hot as the others, but kept his mind focused on the beaches of home to keep himself mentally cool.

"There is an ocean? No, wait. Not an ocean. Uh-" Trekkal commented with a tug on a strand of her hair as she tried remembering what she talked about the night before.

"So, you don't know what we're doing?" Sadal interjected; her patience lowered steadily as time went on.

"No! It is a large body of water, but not an ocean, a sea actually. A very specific difference." Trekkal explained as she raised her finger at Sadal.

She prompted everyone to get up now to the direction she was pointing, which was northwest. Sadal frowned at the sound of the sea, her fear of the water was well known by now, and still she avoided it whenever she could. For Jih at least, the sound of water of any kind was an absolute blessing. He was caked in sweat as he moved his head back and forth trying to generate any sort of wind to cool off.

"Jih, bring our packs but leave our tent up. We are going to stay here and come back later." Trekkal commented as Jih nodded.

Trekkal voiced her desire to fish once more, and Jih strapped on his backpack and carried Trekkal's in his hand. For fishing, Jih knew he needed to bring a few things with him. He watched as Narro stuffed some things into his pack while Sadal decided to leave her throwing spears behind and took a dagger instead just in case.

Sadal shrugged her shoulders in confusion as she met the stares of Jih and Narro. They were just as puzzled as she was while the three followed Trekkal's bizarre directions. Trekkal remembered the way to places using strange idioms that only made sense to her while the others were forced to guess what she meant. Trekkal recalled her route with accuracy however, the grassy plains below their feet gradually morphed into pockets of gravel and dirt that increased in volume. Trekkal noted that they were walking on an incline which matched with the fishermen's directions from the previous day. Jih could smell the familiar feeling of salt hitting his nose. It wasn't as strong as the oceans back home, but there was a faint scent attached. Trekkal stopped and prompted the others. They arrived at the southern end of the Caspian Sea. This region was well known for its shores lined with steep cliffs and outcroppings overlooking the water. The group looked and saw there was a long way down.

"There is a cliff here at this edge, but the downward path should be a nice walk for us. We will need to go down carefully." Trekkal warned as she spotted a depression that seemed to lead its way down the cliff. Trekkal carefully started to descend on the incline.

Trekkal nearly lost her balance as her left foot graced a rock. She groaned as it felt rough on her skin but didn't cause any bleeding. Trekkal looked up at the other three who descended much slower down the slope. Jih didn't want to end up rolling steadily down the hill for who knows how long. Sadal latched onto Narro as she wanted to ensure she'd have insurance if she fell. The four carefully voiced to one another potential holes in the terrain that could disrupt their balance.

"I am just fine! For anyone that cares." Trekkal joked as she kicked the rock further down the path so the others wouldn't run into it.

The others followed Trekkal's instructions as she guided them and kept a steady pace. Jih had the hardest descent ahead of him, as he was carrying two packs. Jih felt his legs buckle slightly under the stark change, but he managed just as well by tightening the strand of Trekkal's pack to his body and used it as a counterweight. To his surprise, the pack held steady though he was a bit concerned about the contents inside.

As the group made their way further down the slope, they noticed right away there was a distinct shift in temperature. Sadal could finally think straight as she cooled off gradually, but her hair was another matter. Like Trekkal's, Sadal's hair looked different from the drastic change in humidity. The last person to work on her hair in any serious capacity was Deeso, and that option was long gone now. She could attempt to see if she could fix her own hair later, perhaps using the sea's water as a mirror for her reflection. With everyone accounted for, Trekkal guided the others to a much gentler slope that gradually opened out to the spread of sand and water. Jih dropped her stuff to the ground. Trekkal absorbed the sound of the waves that hit the sea and closed her eyes in pure bliss.

She felt the hand of Jih on her shoulder as he nodded in understanding of what needed to be done.

"Do we have the net, Jih?" Trekkal asked with a grin, as from the look on his face, Jih clearly forgot to bring it with him. He offered a disarming smile, one that he learned from Kag that was used often to wiggle his way out of a problem.

"I brought it Trekkal. Jih already had a lot on him." Narro interjected. He gave Jih a strong pat on the back saving him from an earful from Trekkal. Jih returned the gesture as it was highly appreciated. Trekkal noted that now she had everything she wanted to start the day.

"Sadal, I take it you will not be joining us?" Trekkal teased as she gave Sadal a smirk. Sadal folded her arms and lifted her head at Trekkal's comment.

"I'll make my own fun. You three can enjoy the water. Maybe I'll go hunt one of those...things. What are they exactly?" Sadal commented, pointing at a seal that beached itself.

Sadal felt the warm sand beneath her feet and crunched them, while she savored the feeling below. Narro took clumps of it in his hands and watched as it fell through his fingers. He was looking at the consistency of the material and noticed that it packed together nicer when wet. Jih held little enthusiasm for the beach he saw as lesser to the ones of home.

"Jih is not impressed." He noted, his eyes surveyed the beach they stood at.

Although it had all the offerings one would expect, Jih noted the distinct lack of palm trees and a typical cross breeze that came with the current. Jih was only exposed to the open ocean but understood immediately that the sea was closed off in some capacity. How large that was, however, he had no idea of. Relaxation as a concept was still hard for Jih to grasp, but he tried his best to take things in as he experienced them. His goal now was to see what Trekkal wanted to do. A deep blue chasm below them revealed a treasure trove of wildlife for the taking, and it suited nicely for their actual objective to cool off. Trekkal was quick to disrobe and head towards the water while she prompted Jih and Narro to follow suit.

Jih shot Narro a look as he noticed Sadal was wandering off by herself. Sadal, as she said before, saw herself face to face with the seal. The seal was the color of gravel and held innocent looking eyes that stared at Sadal. Sadal licked her lips as she saw the moving pile of fat as something worth eating and took a stance as she was ready for combat. She brought a dagger this time with her instead of her usual throwing spears as she assumed they would be too unwieldy for where they were going, and after that climb to reach below, she felt her assessment was correct. She made a growling face at the seal who looked at her with little concern and was happy to flop around. She ran towards the seal with her dagger out, only to stop short. Sadal saw there was barely any attempt to move. The seal saw Sadal's display of hostility with a roll in the sand as it moved a small rock towards her. Sadal was dismayed at her target; how could this seal be mocking her like this? Although she abandoned her official title, she was still a Master Hunter at the core, and only the most satisfying kills could bring her happiness. This was beneath her, and it was an ill-fitting kill for her blade.

She kicked the sand in frustration and decided to look for something else to do with her time. She had no idea how long Trekkal, and the others would take, so she waited in contemplation as she looked at the vastness of the sea, an entire range inaccessible to her. Jih noticed a prime opportunity for Narro and Sadal to bond further. His eyes shifted from Narro to Sadal who stood alone. Jih gave Narro a knowing stare as he ignored the call of Trekkal behind him. Jih gave a less than subtle cough as he gathered Narro's attention.

"Talk to Sadal, Narro." Jih stated as he took off his clothes, and looked to the direction of where Trekkal was heading out in the water. She shouted for Jih to come join her as she found something interesting.

"A little faster Jih! I know you are old, but not elderly!" She teased, sticking her tongue out at him.

Jih blew air out of his nose at her comment and walked into the water. He held his arms at his side and was ill-prepared for the cold temperature of the water. He put his head underwater and resurfaced, with his hair dripping water down his face. He looked over to see Trekkal treading water.

"I see you came alone. Narro decided to not join us?" Trekkal questioned as she saw Narro walking over to Sadal.

"Narro is with Sadal." Jih explained as he continued to tread with Trekkal.

"Of course he is." Trekkal said with evident annoyance in her voice.

Narro decided to take Jih's advice and made his way over to Sadal who sat alone at the edge of the water. He sat down next to her which made her smile. She rubbed his shoulders affectionately and rested her head on top of his. Although Sadal usually had something on her mind to say, she instead decided to just enjoy the silence that the two shared. She'd long grown used to periods without talking, as she made sparse small talk when leading her sections for hunting. Deeso was quiet, and while she and Sadal had engaging discussions, much of their relationship was too defined by mutual enjoyment of silence. Narro though was different, he was so used to living with Trekkal, silence was an alien concept to him, and he needed to fill the space. Narro rubbed the top of her head with his hand while reaching for a clump of wet sand. He then used both of his hands to pack it together and make a sizable mound.

Sadal watched intently and held out her hands. He passed her a clump of wet sand. Sadal lifted her eyebrows in surprise at the sand's malleable texture. It wasn't like that of clay or mud that she was used to, but something far different. She watched it pile up as she smashed it with her fist, and some of the wet sand sprayed onto Narro's face. He wiped off with a small grin.

"Not everything needs to be smashed, Sadal." He said with a laugh, as the two briefly locked their gaze on the other.

Narro remained ever humble, as his confidence on matters like these waned from time to time. He remembered back to when Sadal had shown him her Wanderer's mark, and how nervous he was being introduced to all this new information for the first time. Trekkal had been oddly very kind in keeping his woes a secret from Sadal, as the two discussed things often on their hunts together. Although the two enjoyed each other's company for some time, Narro still felt this shaking feeling of inadequacy. He was petrified of being compared to Nurzan despite being far better. Narro knew he needed to exceed expectations whenever possible and hoped to make that clear in his intentions.

"Look at them Sadal. They seem so happy out there." Narro mentioned while he felt Sadal's posture change.

"They are. Are you not happy here?" Sadal questioned. Narro bit his tongue at her question but nodded in disagreement.

"With you, even the tundra sounds appealing." Narro said happily in reassurance.

"I must ask you something. What does it mean to be your One? I know our previous talk and I mentioned that I would be this for you. I remember Trekkal talked about it. I know that we share a special bond as partners, but for you, it seems to be a bit more than that." Sadal mentioned.

"It is a cultural thing among our people. When you have someone, as in you love someone, our community calls this union a "One". We are born as halves first, and then find someone that fills in that half. This half is very important. To be severed by it once found, means you will be cursed at the least, or dead at the worst. Not to say that there is a problem being alone. Our priests have that vow and are the most important leaders we have." Narro explained as he packed the sand together now. In his mind, he envisioned trying to make a model of him and Trekkal's tent back at home. He broke apart a few nearby sticks and used those as the foundations for his sand structure.

Sadal's first reaction was to say "Does it matter?" but she knew that Narro's personality would never let him rest with such an answer. Given that was the case, she took a deep breath and decided to be completely open about her rationale, something she did for only a select few people. She could sense Narro's insecurity and wanted him to know that they were a team and would navigate together in the same manner.

"I thought about the importance of what that means and in regard to our future. When I first met you, I was already impressed. I had you figured out as a hunter who could possibly compare to my skills, which was a rare sight to be. Hearing you play music though, changed my outlook. I then noticed your arguments with Trekkal. While I wish you defended yourself more, the fight in you is present, but it shows up in other ways. You find random people and help them, even at your own risk." Sadal referenced, pointing to the eye patch that was a part of Narro's identity. Sadal felt the hard part of her words coming now and so she prepared herself, although she felt her voice could break as she was easily overwhelmed. The Broken Bone wasn't one to have such open dialogues on these topics in the same way.

"This selflessness and determination are why I admired my leader Ronkalk, but you take this further. There is a kindness that is inside you that dictates everything you see in the world. It's not bound by tradition or the ancestors, but simply because you see that it's right. No matter what." Sadal said with a single tear loose. Narro grabbed her tightly and rested her head into his chest.

Narro hearing Sadal emote like this was a shock to him, as the only person who rivaled in her presentation was arguably Jih. She was passionate when it came to such things as pride or anger, but her expressions of affection were often subtle. At the very least now, Narro had no doubts on where he stood with Sadal, as the two shared a loving embrace on the shoreline. He didn't need to hear the phrase "I love you" to know that their bond strengthened and Narro fully now had found his "One".

"Look at them Jih." Trekkal stated with venom in her words. Jih raised an eyebrow and wondered what Trekkal was alluding to as she saw the silhouettes of Narro and Sadal along the shoreline.

"They seem so happy, but I have this shaking feeling, something is wrong. Do you feel it too Jih? Sadal still seems to be a bit odd." Trekkal remarked as she turned her head to him.

"Jealousy?" Jih joked with a laugh. He wiped water from his eyes as Trekkal splashed a few times in annoyance.

Jih let out a small sigh of relief. For a good deal of their journey, Jih noticed the two's subtle connection and felt as if he were a conduit for their relationship to develop, just like he had done for Kag and Bani. Sadal trusted Jih, he learned early of some of her old life at The Broken Bone, and gained much ground with Narro as the two grew closer. He felt that Narro would be a good person to help Sadal grow, and while he had growing of his own left to do, he knew there could be comfort in making that assertion.

Trekkal looked below her and pointed at a small cluster of mussels that nested along the bottom of the floor. Trekkal looked at Jih with a bright smirk on her face. Lucky for the two of them, the shelf of where these were clustered wasn't that deep, only about five-to-six feet or so.

"I hope we have the same idea Jih. We should dive below and grab those shells. One may have a pearl. The rest we can eat." Trekkal suggested, with a rub of her stomach as she was hungry.

She swam over to Jih and ran her finger down his forehead, giving him a small bop on the nose with her finger. Her hair flowed through the water and floated on top as she moved through. Jih admired Trekkal's passion for the water and her boundless curiosity that came with it. It reminded him of Hyu, and he felt that the two would have been friends if they ever crossed paths. She could find pleasure in seeing something as simple as a piece of seaweed and be enthralled by its connection to the greater world. One such wonder of the Caspian Sea was the bounty of wildlife that inhabited the landscape. In the distance, Jih saw a porpoise surface for air. Jih was confused at the sight as he only imagined them as ocean creatures.

"Poramin in the distance." Jih said to himself as Trekkal followed his range of vision. She clearly had some disagreement as Jih raised an eyebrow.

"That is not what we call it. Does that look like a Peymin to you?" Trekkal huffed.

"Jih has been through this with Dran. Ancestors called it Poramin. We will call it that as well. It swims in water like Peymin but breathes air. What would Trekkal call it then?" Jih said with some annoyance in his voice.

"Well...I never really considered that before. The name just bothers me, there could be something better." Trekkal said as Jih splashed some water in Trekkal's face at her comment. Trekkal's eyes darted to the water as she dove underneath while Jih looked away. A few surface bubbles showed that Trekkal was about to resurface. Trekkal resurfaced with her hand clenched on a mussel.

"Look Jih! Look how she moves!" Trekkal said happily with a smile as Jih carefully held the mussel. It felt strange to the touch, as Jih looked at Trekkal while she nodded in support.

Jih swam out to shore and placed the first of many mussels there. Jih dug a small sand trap to hold their bounty while they collected them. He returned to where he was before and dove this time in unison with Trekkal as they gathered more mussels. Jih decided to keep going as he had an idea for a good stew to make for the others. Hizo prepared a good stew that came from oysters when he was a child, but after the Neck-Shells took control of the coast, he was robbed of one of his favorite meals. He hoped he could still recall it from memory as the others would surely enjoy it. The surface was filled with all sorts of anxiety and worry. For Jih and Trekkal, the ocean, or in this case, the sea offered a temporary reprieve. The silence that came below as they broke through the surface of the water together was euphoric to the ears. Fish took a respectable distance from the divers, happy for the moment their attention was on the mussels instead. Trekkal signaled to Jih underwater pointing to her hand and he looked around to see a few more for the taking. He descended and uplifted them from a small piece of wood that was anchored below. By the time they were through, they accumulated about sixty mussels total which was more than enough to feed a group much larger than themselves.

"Many shelled ones below. We have plenty, let us leave behind some for others." Jih said as he watched Trekkal attempt to eat one. Jih reflexively grabbed her hand before she could open her mouth.

"Jih will cook first. Bad stomach from Songkha otherwise." He warned her, much to her disappointment. If it were anyone else, she would have eaten four raw out of spite, but she relented to listen to Jih. Trekkal chose to stay in the water a bit longer as she held her breath underwater and reflected on her travels. Jih went ashore to clothe himself and rejoin Sadal and Narro.

Trekkal arrived late to find Jih already prepared an ongoing fire. Sadal remembered finding a turtle shell while the pair was busy that she offered to use as their bowl for prepping. Jih was telling Narro and Sadal about how his mother would prepare an oyster soup and how he tried many times to perfect it over the years as Hyu being his taste-tester, each time getting closer and closer. She sat down and joined the others and couldn't help but smile as the meal was cooked in front of them. The smell wafted into their noses and the group couldn't help but stare aimlessly as Jih used a branch to stir the melted concoction. Narro, Sadal, and Trekkal waited patiently as Jih held up his finger for them to wait. Jih grabbed the first oyster and cracked it open. He gave a grunt of approval as he cleaned the shell dry and chucked it along with the juices that came from it. Jih smugly stood proud as they dipped their hands into the bowl and sipping with delight. Jih ate a few more and enjoyed his handiwork. The waves of the sea crashed on the shore, sending a wave of salt through the air in their noses. As Jih and the others ate, he briefly saw the visage of his first friends as they were young back in Sundaland. He was the chef regardless of where he was. In Narro, he saw Hyu through his humility and selfless nature, Kag through Trekkal's carefree attitude and strong will, with Sadal echoing Dran by her silent but impactful presence with a job well done. He gave them a grin as he was happy to see that the mussel soup was delicious.

Staying Serious In Syria

Jih and the others were led by Trekkal's eager navigation and found themselves in the plains of Syria. This land was unknown to the four of them as they continued to barrel through high brush. Sadal lamented how cut up her legs were, and this sentiment was shared by Jih as well. Small droplets of blood accompanied each step she took in the process. Jungle plants had the courtesy of being poisonous but otherwise not grating on their skin while the high brush wrapped around their ankles. Jih consistently bent down to cut the grating material with his hand-axe while Narro and Trekkal were able to walk with enough force to drag them behind one another. Trekkal pressed ahead with speed as only the blur of her hair was visible to the three. She waved her hand and recalled an adage given to her by another village that spoke about this new area. Trekkal was invested in the idea as it seemed to align with their current travel plans but could also provide a new source of food and building material.

"Remember what they told us? Once the ground becomes water, we will find our answer. Just a bit more now! I have a good feeling there is some spiritual presence in this place." Trekkal shouted for the rest of the group.

Jih watched Trekkal bounce as she led with pride but lacked the same enthusiasm. His eyes scanned the horizon for signs of life and found nothing of value so far. Narro considered himself a trusting person but felt that Trekkal could be downright naive when given elements regrading spiritual manners. Sadal felt the ground's texture change beneath her feet as the moisture of the grass differed. She held her tongue and felt that Trekkal's theory held weight and that their direction made sense. Trekkal turned around to wait for the others and looked to see Narro's face filled with doubt.

"Trekkal...this is the last time we have you to guide us anywhere." Narro complained while Trekkal's face grew red.

"You say this as if coming across Jih and Sadal was not because you got us lost! I want to hear nothing of this!" Trekkal shot back while Sadal could only laugh in agreement.

"That was ages ago, Trekkal." Narro expressed with annoyance in his voice.

Jih continued his search and looked to the sky. He noticed a particularly odd streak of light in the sky. The presence of dense smoke caused alarm for him as he noticed the colors change from a dark black to a middling gray and back again. In the past, smoke signals were usually one color but multiple meant signs of distress. Jih knew that they were in trouble and debated with himself if they should be helped or move on. Jih placed a helping hand when he could but was inherently self-motivated as his focus was on the meteor above all else. Jih also evaluated the condition of his team and their livelihood. Jih was aware that they were dwindling on supplies and needed a stop by the river. To her credit, Trekkal's knowledge to pick out mysteries was impressive as the ground soon met the mouth of a river. Sadal swatted some bugs away as she tried to focus on what Jih was searching for.

"Jih sees cloud message. Look above everyone, we have people!" Jih pointed as he prompted the rest to look up.

"I say we go explore it. It's been a while since I had a good fight. Distress means two things, a predator, or a raider. If I'm lucky, it could be both." Sadal suggested as Jih nodded in support of her statement.

The grassy plains that they inhabited for much of their journey were now in low wetlands that spread throughout. They were accompanied by the presence of crocodiles and other animals that rested in deep pools of water and an interconnected river system. The four ventured through the marsh and carefully made their way to avoid detection by any hostiles. Jih made everyone evaluate their current weapons. In their haste to cover more ground, the group hadn't stopped to prepare spares for their weapons. Fights would be costly and needed to end with decisive action if they weren't careful. Trekkal noted the presence of worked wood that seemed unnatural as she looked at the ground. Narro kept his voice low as he looked around to see the source of the smoke in the distance. The sky filled with colored smoke from further distances. There was hardly a breeze in this area, so the smoke lingered as the group traced their fingers in the sky to some sources. In the spaces between open marsh, patches of high grass were found with the growth practically eclipsing the four in height.

"The smoke piles high up here. Keep your weapons steady. We have no idea what this could mean." Narro mentioned to everyone.

Jih nodded as Sadal and Trekkal scouted ahead. Jih pressed on, but he noticed that Narro was no longer moving. Unknown to Jih, behind Narro's back, a blade was poised on him. Narro attempted his best to signal to Jih that he could feel the blade's warm touch as it gained heat in the sun. Narro was hesitant to move as he wasn't willing to test how deep it could go. Jih noticed Narro's unusual silence and turned around. Jih withdrew his spear and silently shifted to the side as he attempted to see what caused Narro such grief. He could tell that there was something amiss based on Narro's visual cues, but with his body, Jih couldn't see past him. In the same moment, Narro felt the blade vanish and breathed a sigh of relief. His worry magnified when he realized that the next target would have been Jih. Jih stepped closer and saw a lunge from the bushes, a thin brown arm emerged with a long knife. Narro's back was free for the moment, and he quickly joined Jih as he saw that he stabbed the bushes with his spear. By now, it was obvious that someone was trying to attack them with some surprise tactics.

"This is Forest Seeker fighting. Jih has witnessed it." Jih noted with some derision in his voice. Although Jih enjoyed the status of being a Stone Breaker when he was with Eshe, his presence to Sadal painted him as an enemy by some Forest Seekers and he fought against them in their earlier travels. Jih wasn't a fan of the cat-and-mouse combat that the Forest Seekers employed. He preferred much more direct confrontations when possible.

"They invite us into the bush. It is a trap. Do not fall for it Narro." Jih said as he held out his hand to Narro. The two attempted to investigate the deep grass, but their assailant was well hidden as they waited on the inside overhearing their discussion. The hum of insects in the air filled their thoughts as they looked to see any sign of movement.

Sadal returned to hear the voices of Jih and Narro and left Trekkal alone to press ahead. She felt the need to check on Jih and Narro, only to arrive just in time with the two of them confused. Sadal assessed what the problem was but needed to be sure she was correct. Sadal hadn't imagined Forest Seekers in this land but combed the grass for their movements anyway. She remembered her training from Ronkalk and firsthand experience regarding their dress. She looked for irregularities of shadows that differed from normal foliage and the sign of any disturbances in the dirt. Jih and Narro raised their weapons as they heard a rustling of grass but only Sadal emerged.

"Why have you stopped?" Sadal inquired as she wiped sweat on her forehead.

"Jih found a Forest Seeker trying to attack us somewhere in this bush, but the grass is much too tall for us both. It is in their interest to have us separated so that we can be picked off. We are trying to root them out now somehow." Narro concisely explained to her. Sadal nodded and offered her perspective. Knowing Forest Seekers all too well, Sadal made an idle threat of burning down the bush and the very marsh itself. The Forest Seeker who lay in the grass couldn't help but offer a retort in a fit of rage.

"You insolent Thunderfoot! These grasses protect us all!" A feminine voice shot out from behind.

Sadal gave a grin of smug satisfaction as she knew their pride and dedication to The Vow was their downfall. Jih and the others turned around, they had no clue that the patch of brush they were looking at was no longer occupied. Jih also found that this Forest Seeker seemed to lack a blowgun, an interesting admission to make when attacking with the knife. They almost always favored using ranged combat over being close.

"A long way from home, Forest Seeker." Sadal teased lowly as she signaled for Jih and Narro to follow her into the bush.

While Sadal left Trekkal to find the others, Trekkal accidently stumbled into a camp where she noticed three men were in discussion and sat near a fire. She saw one that was smaller than the rest and was unsure if this one was actually a child. Two of them looked at each other while Trekkal ran off to try and get a better position. Trekkal took a page from Sadal and assumed that these were hostiles and hoped to separate as well as she could before joining with the others. Trekkal came equipped with her sling and found that running and shooting made it difficult to land a solid blow. The two men ducked to the ground as they noticed a rock fly in their direction. The pair grabbed their weapons and looked in the direction of the river where Trekkal dove without a second thought into the running current. The smallest of the three curled into a ball and put his hands over his head. Trekkal swam against the slower current as she looked to find her pursuers looking at her in confusion. As Trekkal looked at their faces, she noticed they were of her own kind but said nothing.

"She jumped in the river. Should we do something?" The older one of the two asked.

"Probably, yes..." The other mentioned with an irritated tone in his voice.

"The water becomes murky downstream! You will be running into Vatmaraku if you do! Be food for them if you want!" The younger Aligned man shouted as Trekkal's face visibly turned red in embarrassment at hearing this.

It could be a trick, but if they wanted me dead, they would have just said nothing at all either. I should probably try to reach the edge of the shore there when I can...I will keep my guard up for now. Trekkal thought as she attempted to find a bank in the river to place herself on.

Debris floated around in small volume, and she looked to grab these to reach the bank. Trekkal treaded water and looked to hear a voice that vaguely called for her. While she was just out of reach, she saw a fallen log carried over by one of the men and grabbed on tight. Using the jumpstart from the log and the mud below her feet, she was able to prop herself up to the other side. The older of the two men returned with a net but saw that Trekkal was already recovered. She held her sling out and kept her distance from the others.

"You ran off before we could say anything, but people do not swim in that water. The river is for rafts only." The man stated with some slight relief in his face. Trekkal's expression of anger vanished from her face as she realized her error. With a slight pause, Trekkal opened the discussion once more.

"I get we look a little rough, but we mean you no harm. We wanted to ask you something. We are looking for a girl, a Forest Seeker girl who may have been in this area." The first man stated while the one holding the net started his return to camp.

"I came here with friends of mine. Your camp is that way? I could wait there until they come along." Trekkal proposed as the first of the two shrugged his shoulders.

The three of them found their way back shortly after and gave Trekkal an opening to sit down. The pair placed their weapons down as a sign of peace and looked to see if she would do the same. After a brief silence, the younger of the two men decided to speak out. He figured that the best way to smooth things along was to introduce everyone.

"I am your savior by the way. The Youngest we have is named Emkak. Zoki just found Emkak one day and he never bothered to leave her. We like the little guy, but he also says very little. Nothing is wrong with him as far as I know but I go by Noshe, and here is Grak." Noshe said as he introduced himself and the rest of his comrades.

Trekkal looked around for the one named Zoki, but assumed they must have met up with Jih and the others. Noshe's finger pointed to a teenage member of The Youngest with slightly long fingernails and a thin frame. He wore very little clothing except for a loincloth and seemed to be immune from bug bites as he folded his arms and watched the movement of the fire. Emkak's eyes were dark brown, and he had a small afro growing that was maintained with cut sticks. Emkak's eyes briefly met Trekkal's in acknowledgement with a slow nod before returning to what he was doing. Trekkal folded her legs and sat down to stretch. She was asked a few questions and reiterated her story up to this point while the three gave their reactions. Some distance away, Jih and company were busy rooting out the troublesome Forest Seeker.

Narro ran ahead deeper into the brush and tripped over a rock. He saw the blade of the Forest Seeker woman approach him in a silent lunge. Narro punched her in the face, with her free arm taking much of the hit, as she maneuvered herself back within the foliage. He noticed that this woman was older and moved much like Jih did, not with much flash but deliberate and direct control. With some slight blood that ran down her face, she heard the footsteps of Sadal that powered through the brush. She lay low to the ground and grabbed Sadal's ankle. She stabbed the ground only for Sadal to jump back and kick her away. Sadal used her body weight to hang on the woman and pin her to the ground, where she concentrated her efforts on her throat. Sadal placed one hand on her neck while posed with her knife on the other as she felt her lower body tingle from a knee to her tailbone. Sadal attempted to stab her, but the Forest Seeker's arm was quick in her speed and knocked it aside. Sadal's knife fell to the ground some distance away. Jih was the last one to descend deeper in the brush, using Narro and Sadal's reactions to triangulate where the Forest Seeker was hiding. His ears picked up the struggle between Sadal and the Forest Seeker. He used his spear to signal his presence. After some time in a stalemate, Sadal saw the prodding of Jih's spear.

"Jih! Over here." Sadal said with some exhaustion in her voice as Jih nodded his head for her to step off and Jih took her place with his spear pointed over him. Narro eventually joined up with the others and saw that a hostage was taken.

"Take us to your camp." Jih demanded, as he noticed the Forest Seeker's eyes widened slightly upon hearing his voice.

She was one of the many who remembered the stories regarding The Stone Breakers. They truly had returned. Jih and the others, after some careful prodding, moved to the camp to see that Trekkal was fine and made friends along the way. Trekkal decided to bury any mention of her initial misunderstanding upon their return as she knew Sadal wouldn't be as forgiving in the matter. Noshe looked visibly upset at the state of the Forest Seeker woman and it was evident to Narro they knew one another well.

"You have Trekkal as a captive, we have this Forest Seeker woman here. We'll offer you a trade then. Your Forest Seeker who attacked us for our friend." Sadal said in anger. Jih walked next to Sadal and nodded.

Noshe and Grak waved their hands for Trekkal to get up. Trekkal hardly saw herself as a captive but decided to follow through on the theatrics. There was an awkward exchange as the two women crossed paths and joined their respective groups. While Jih and Sadal were quick to want to leave, Narro and Trekkal had other ideas. Narro noted that the four of them were running low on supplies and were unsure of where to go in their quest at this point. Trekkal heard bits and pieces about this group's adventure while they were busy but wanted to know more.

"You did attack us first, but we apologize for the condition of your friend. Say, could we ask you a question?" Narro asked the group. Grak looked over his friend's injuries and wiped some blood off her with a spare animal skin.

"You held me captive, and I receive no names from any of you. If we are on equal terms, then I shall start. I am Zoki. My companions here are Emkak, Noshe, and Grak." Zoki said with an introduction of herself and the others.

Zoki held long flowing brown hair with two large braids that went down her head. Her eyes were a light brown that reflected the others. She remained filled with adrenaline as she slightly vibrated. Her face was smooth but held a scar from the bottom of her left eye that descended to the middle of her cheek. Her dress varied from the others as she wore a covering of dhole fur that was held in place with tightly bound string. The group could tell she was the leader easily from her demeanor alone. Emkak turned his head to look at the new arrivals and said nothing. Noshe and Grak offered their hands out to Narro and Sadal who shook. For Jih, the two bowed their heads as Jih gave them a confused look on his face. Noshe and Grak heard the legends of his people from Zoki's tales regarding Stone Breakers and figured out they referred to the same people.

"Jih. Narro. Trekkal. Sadal." Jih said as he motioned for each to step forward including himself.

Jih gave the group opposed to them a glance. He noticed their group was compiled much like their own, with two of The Aligned and a Thunderfoot in the mix. The difference between their groups being each other's leadership. Zoki was a Forest Seeker which as Sadal noted was someone far from their ancestral lands much like his own. He wondered if she walked the path of the meteor or if there was another reason. Noshe and Grak looked like one another, as they were close in age. Jih was impressed as he noticed Zoki ran a tight ship and with not much effort, the camp cleaned up before their very eyes. Despite the initial hostilities created between both parties, Forest Seekers had the capacity to be forgiving and with Jih's status as a Stone Breaker, this was an important discussion to be had.

"So, what's your story?" Sadal asked out of curiosity to Noshe and Grak.

"Zoki found us with Emkak. Noshe is a bit older than me, we are three years apart. We had to leave our band however because our identity was exposed. It was an embarrassment for our people, and we felt it was best to join Zoki. See the world, you know?" Grak mentioned.

"What could possibly be so bad? Aren't you two brothers? You two look related." Sadal asked.

"No..." Grak mentioned sheepishly as his eyes met Narro in an attempt at solidarity.

"Cousins?" Jih questioned.

"We have an odd parentage. My mother, who is his aunt, was with child by our grandfather. They are related and not from another band. The man responsible to expose this to our band, the father of Grak, was put to death to silence the action. The father of

Grak is dead and the father of myself is his grandfather. It is...a situation." Noshe said flatly.

Jih and Sadal shared a look as they realized the extent of what happened, Narro and Trekkal felt terrible about hearing about the outcome. As the importance of keeping your One and the violation of this was paramount to an unforgiveable curse, it was an awkward situation for all those involved. They could only give their condolences to the pair.

"It is a pity. Though, now they find purpose with me. Our people are much freer about these things. To be held captive by such a permanent bond is interesting." Zoki added on as she watched Emkak stab a few ants to roast over the fire. She studied Jih's reaction as the words hung over them.

"Jih and friends search for power rock. Why are you in this land?" Jih asked as he waited for Zoki to allow them to sit down. Zoki sat down and gave room for the others to get comfortable. Jih and the others painted their attention directly on Zoki.

"Oh-that. I heard of it, and I know exactly where you should go. We hear such things on our travels around. When you go north of here, there is a large hill there that cries. When you see it, The Gorge will be waiting." Zoki mentioned, while Jih and the others seemed satisfied with the answer. Noshe and Grak looked at one another with some hesitation as The Gorge was not to be taken lightly.

"Mahaku lives there." The quiet Emkak orated to participate in discussion once more before returning to his own world. Jih and Sadal were unphased by the child's warning, but Narro and Trekkal knew this well.

"Jih and friends will do what it takes to go north. Power rock is our goal. Mahaku, cannibals, all stories that Jih is prepared for." Jih boasted proudly as he felt the warmth of the others.

"If you really must fight the Mahaku, allow us to make you something. This will be protection. The Mahaku you see, it has powerful claws that can rip anything apart. Emkak, can you show the others that trick you told me? There are plenty of Vatmaraku around." Zoki asked the young boy.

"This is the best part." Emkak announced to the group while Zoki gave a supportive grin. Emkak's eyes lit up as he stood up and was taller than the rest of the party. He stood and stretched his arms out while jumping in anticipation to get started.

"Oh yes, Emkak showed us a great way to get pelts for protection from the Vatmaraku. Come with us, we can show you. All you need is a good log and some patience. The jaws clamp on, you flip it over with enough strong hands and poke the stomach with a spear. We can get enough material to keep you protected." Noshe commented as Grak already grabbed a short spear for the purpose.

"The Stone Breaker and I need to talk about important matters. He should be prepared for his trip." Zoki remarked.

Jih and the others got up shortly to accompany them, but Zoki gave a small glare to Grak. Zoki had other plans regarding Jih that were more private in nature. She wanted to probe his interest in a few matters. Grak elbowed Noshe in understanding and gently prodded Jih to stay behind. Zoki gravitated towards Jih as she watched the others leave. Noshe opened with a story about their travels that got the interest of Narro and Trekkal while Emkak shot ahead. Sadal was the last to leave to join the others as she turned her head around in suspicion of Zoki before vanishing.

Jih and Zoki now stood alone at camp as they waited for the return of the others. Zoki turned her head in the silence and looked into Jih's eyes. She gave a small grin that Jih returned in kind. She set off shortly and nodded her head for Jih to follow. The ambient sound of the marsh accompanied the pair as they walked along the river. On their end, the water was clear and the two could see their reflection. On occasion, smog from other campfires filled the air and a mist floated by the pair. It was a calming place outside of the potential for crocodiles. Jih cautiously kept his distance from the river line while Zoki followed suit. Jih hardly found himself willing to start the conversation and was fortunate that Zoki decided to speak instead.

"So, all this for the power rock, as you call it? I am also far from home but you are further." Zoki asked.

"Yes. The power rock will fix things. It is a long story, and not one that would interest Zoki very much." Jih stated bluntly.

"I am interested, Jih. In you, your story, everything really. Though, I understand your need for secrets. It is said your people were mysterious. You could tell me, just a little bit, right?" Zoki asked as she positioned herself closer to Jih. She brushed her arm against his.

"You never answered question of Jih. Why are you here? If the power rock is not what you seek." Jih asked as his eyes studied Zoki.

"As for me, I had an...argument with my daughter and she ran off. What is a mother to do? Let the world punish her for a mistake? I was furious, but now I just miss her. I was part of a larger group of my kind traveling in the early days before I had to split off. As far as I am aware, they are searching for the ancestral home." Zoki said.

Jih nodded at this, he understood only the most dedicated could truly take the time out to find the power rock. For some, there were things of greater importance of course. He was quickly reminded of the fanaticism and fury his own mother would have had he made the same choice as Zoki's daughter to run away with no direction. Sundaland would have been ashes in weeks for Hizo's flock, but especially for Jih.

"Before I left, I served an important role. I kept the peace between the bands of the lands that are dry and hot. I sat in on meetings and negotiated the things that needed to be brought for us." Zoki added on as she waited for Jih's response.

"Jih did similar with group called The Jagged Bark. Leader of The Elders tore many years of partnership to ruin. Your patience is greater than mine." Jih commented. Jih felt his free arm grabbed by Zoki and said nothing further.

"Did Mahaku give you that scar?" Jih questioned as he pointed to Zoki's cheek. Zoki's wound was hardly fresh, it was one that was acquired early on her journey.

"No, it is a punishment for not learning how to fight Thunderfeet as well as I do now. Mahaku is much more dangerous than that. Be hopeful you do not cross paths with it when you go to The Gorge." Zoki mentioned.

"Your daughter. Children are dumb and do not listen well. You can only do so much. They must grow to make own mistakes, or they will resent you." Jih said with resounding confidence. Although he avoided any chance to be a parent, Jih could see some of himself in Zoki and how she would have wound up in such a situation. They were around the same age, give or take a few years.

"Ah yes, the infinite wisdom of The Stone Breakers I heard so much about. Please, tell me more." Zoki teased as she tugged Jih's beard.

"That was a joke." Zoki commented.

Jih felt a tinge of embarrassment as he looked at his reflection in the water. His beard was larger than he usually kept it. Jih mostly kept his feelings to himself, but he enjoyed Zoki's presence and felt warmth radiate from her. Her voice was high-pitched like all Forest Seekers, but it was a calming presence. The two sat down further inland. Zoki stretched her arms out and patted on some dry grass for Jih to sit. The two conversed about a matter of all subjects with time passing by without a care.

The things that mattered most to the pair were how people didn't understand their point of view, how it hurt sometimes to get up in the morning, and how grateful they were to have the support from their teams for their ambitions. The light in Jih's eyes opened as he felt a genuine kindred spirit in Zoki. Zoki chose to confirm her affirmation by placing herself onto Jih. Jih felt the weight of Zoki as she pressed down on top of him with a sly grin. Zoki and Jih linked hands and rolled over to a softer patch of grass. Jih felt Zoki's hand move along his body in a sensual manner that he returned passionately. While Jih didn't consider much of his physical needs in his travels, it was an appreciated gesture. The pair rubbed noses together in silence, only for Jih to feel a surge of anxiety come across him. Jih started to sweat but not out of passion. He slowly retracted from Zoki who couldn't put to words how she felt. Jih hadn't properly achieved the goal he promised for Hyu and felt a tinge of guilt course through the back of his mind. Jih knew happiness was something he would have once again, but his obligation and his own feelings of grief that he put off, came towards him in full force. Jih's eyes were red as he struggled to hold his composure. Jih kept his past on himself when it came to Hyu for outsiders. Jih hadn't thought about Hyu in a serious capacity for some time. The rigorous nature of the journey was enough to keep his mind at ease, but grief comes and goes. Zoki's warmth was enough to penetrate the wall that Jih made for himself to keep going and it threatened his entire psyche. Jih held a blank stare as his eyes met the soil. Zoki broke the silence as she looked up at Jih.

"Did I do something wrong?" Zoki whispered, as her words sat in his mind. Jih could only nod his head no as he felt the embrace by Zoki around his body in a tight hug. She wasn't sure what else to do but that. It worked for everyone else.

After some time, Jih got up and headed in the direction of camp with Zoki lagging behind him. The pair's expression brightened as they saw their respective teams having fun with one another. The group looked especially lively as they recalled the splashes of the crocodiles from the riverbank. Some fresh meat from their exploits roasted over the lit campfire while a bunch of skins were in varying stages of processing. Trekkal turned around and waved over to Jih.

"Look! Look! See how amazing I am with this?" Trekkal asked as she lifted her new clothing.

Jih was impressed, the armor wrapped around the chest and pressed against the stomach. The back was closed with a pair of loose fibers tied into a near impenetrable knot. The placement of the skin allowed for normal furs to be placed on top. Jih watched as Sadal tried various pieces of weaponry on it and made minimal impact. While she found it gaudy in appearance, its utility was unmatched.

Zoki gave Jih another look of longing before she returned to immerse herself in the discussion of the others. Jih sat down and placed his arm around Narro as he looked tired. Sadal was happy to see the gesture, but her attention was caught by an unusual piece in front of her. She pointed to a stack of furs hanging out of a bag on the ground.

"What pelt is that? I don't think I recognize it." Sadal asked as she noticed Grak's interest in answering her question. He walked over and scooped the bag with ease as he clutched it close to him.

"Oh. I come from the north, and this is a Wailos[63] pelt. Like a Tole, but somewhat larger and angrier. Not many of them, so this is a luxury for our people. I keep it for an emergency trade." Grak said with some pride.

"If you want, you can stay the night with us. The Gorge is not too far from here, but it is best to go in the early morning." Zoki recommended.

Jih looked to the others who gave a resounding nod of approval at the venture. The smell of crocodile meat was too good to pass up and there was plenty to go around with the making of their respective protection. Their meal was a humble exchange and the group of eight exchanged stories of their tales for the night before resting once more. In the early wakes of the morning, Zoki's group still slept, save for herself while Jih and the others were prepared to move on.

"Zoki will find little one soon. Be strong." Jih said as Zoki gave a nod in agreement.

She waved them off to see them head north as instructed until the four disappeared in the distance as thin sheets of light. Zoki stood alone and recounted her brief but enlightening experience with The Stone Breaker known as Jih. Her mind was on her daughter and the desire to see her smile. Zoki returned to her bed and closed her eyes, as her mind dreamed of the day she'd see her daughter once more. There was so much more she needed to explain and could hardly find the words to do so.

Susa...Please forgive your mother. Zoki thought before drifting to sleep.

---

[63] Emic word for wolf.

Not Too Long To Go

As the trail to find Sadal again ran cold, Deeso kept everyone on task in finding the Forest Seeker caravan that by now they weren't just a simple fabrication of Ozul's imagination, but real people that seemed to be somewhere. In between keeping her ear low to the ground on those who believed in the meteor's power and who remembered what happened that night, she also searched for this mysterious group. Deeso noticed that Ozul was looked at oddly by much of the population here which were her own kind and that of The Aligned. This worked into their favor as they would be able to find Ozul's family much easier as they stood out from everyone else. She remembered hearing wind of them some time ago and words of them still carried through here in this region.

Deeso turned her head to notice Cikya working hard while Zulag looked over her shoulder. Cikya crushed previously gathered pennywort leaves and used the last bits of animal fat to make a protective film for the group. Their travels took them to the lowland marshes that accompanied a long river system. Above all else, Cikya hated mosquitoes more than any sort of creature that attacked them. She took every precaution imaginable to deter their relentless onslaught. Deeso caught Ozul and Zulag having a short discussion on the situation while Cikya continued to work.

"So, you're saying they came through here. This sticky, awful, bug-infested swamp we find ourselves in. Are you sure they didn't just die along the way?" Zulag said as he received a glare from Deeso. Zulag shrugged his shoulders, the possibility was certainly realistic, but none that the rest wanted to think about. As for what to do with Ozul, that situation is something Deeso and Zulag spoke about at length with varying degrees to find some sort of solution once they found Sadal. For now, though, he would stay with them as agreed upon.

"Yes, that is correct." Ozul said with a nod as he wiped sweat off his forehead.

"Cikya works so hard for all of us. What is that she is making for us?" Ozul questioned as he turned his head to watch Cikya working.

"Salimpu...I'm fine with that, but the animal fat left behind smells like dung. I can only bathe so many times and still have the stench on me." Zulag complained as he turned to see Deeso lurking some distance.

"Zulag, the heat is awful, but would you rather be dealing with Muucu bites for days?" Deeso reasoned with him. As she heard a begrudging grumble from Zulag, she knew she was once again correct.

Cikya clapped as she was done and placed her solution in a makeshift wooden bowl she carved. It took significant effort to find enough material for the four of them, but she was able to make an effective solution for everyone. Cikya took a large swipe of the material for herself and applied it as such, and quickly went to do the same to the others. Zulag took it in stride, seeing it as it was no different than having her apply his face paint which was done before an extensive number of times. Ozul was happy to receive such treatment, while Deeso was somewhat wary. Cikya approached her with a slightly mischievous grin as she placed a large amount of her arms and rubbed it throughout Deeso's body.

"Cikya, I can-and now you're putting it all on me. I can rub it myself." Deeso said as she moved a little, not expecting Cikya to reach near her thighs.

Now that everyone was equipped for the day, Deeso and the others packed up their things as best as they could and left to find some sort of civilization. From Ozul's perspective, rivers were the pathway to life itself but not everyone saw it that way. He rightfully remembered that none of his companions could swim, and it didn't take long for him to remember their usual strategy to cross bodies of water. By now, the group was well acquainted with Ozul swimming across and laying a line for them to travel by moving along the rope. Ozul looked around, hoping to find something like jute in this area, but the material wasn't as strong as he'd like. Ozul went to grab some grass and did his best to try and make feasible rope, with his ivory piece to push them together. As he stood by, the rest of the group encountered a murky lagoon that had the water run an odd brown color. Silt from the outer banks of the edge obscured much of what was visible below. Ozul noticed the three looking closely above the water, trying to make sense of what lay below.

"I would wait before you ford this river. Can I have a stone?" Ozul requested, as Deeso felt around for a rock on the ground and tossed it in his direction. Ozul made a small whistle with his lips that mimicked a bird, and he gave the stone a mighty toss as it sank to the bottom of the water. Within moments, a crocodile emerged bitter at the false alarm that was given to them.

"My father always told me if the water was too dark to see, someone is living there." Ozul stated as he looked at the others.

Deeso jumped back and held her axe out at the reptile, knowing fully well nothing in their arsenal could take on such a beast. Although many found it to probably be a mighty hunt, if done correctly, the crocodile's domain was one they were unable to master.

"We should find another way around. I will need more rocks." Ozul said with a blank expression on his face as the four left the lagoon behind them.

Ozul looked around to see Zulag sadistically stabbing into the air as he attempted to kill flies around him. Ozul gave a small sigh but nodded in agreement as he did his best to ignore the onslaught of insects, but his concentration was surely breaking. Cikya folded her arms and attempted to huddle herself between the three of them as she ducked to avoid Zulag's wild strikes. Deeso offered no reaction as nothing seemed to approach her. The four continued on their search to find something of note, where the smell of burning wood and the subtle haze of smoke rose in the far distance. Zulag looked up and followed the trail with his finger, and he turned to see that there were multiples of these in the sky. Signals through smoke to communicate through the sky was a practice done out in the plains but made sense in the marshes as the ground was often considered inhospitable for long term settlement. Deeso realized that people who lived in this area used smoke to a variable degree to determine all sorts of communication rather than direct statements. Entire lines of hunting plans, offers for trade or meetings were done all with limited physical contact between those in the conversation.

"Why would anyone want to live here?" Deeso asked in genuine surprise as she observed the spectacle in the sky.

"Let's go and see what we can find over there. If anyone knows the way out of this awful place, it's one of them." Zulag mentioned as he started to walk towards the direction of the smoke signal they viewed earlier.

Deeso and the others decided to follow his intuition and head in the direction of the source. Sometime later, they came across a small network of huts that numbered around eight or so. They were ornate in presentation, with the most notable feature being a crocodile skull present at the base of one of the homes. Deeso nodded with some impression evident on her face, these weren't simple gatherers by any means. Cikya pointed to see two men were hoisted over a fire with a stretched-out pelt, holding it lowly over the fire and then releasing in one huff as the smoke billowed out to the sky. They coughed and ran their hands through the air to clear the smoke. Their eyes were hazy with soot but saw visitors upon them. The two stopped their duties and approached. Ozul studied their dress, fur coverings around the feet but much like their own bodies, wore a concoction made from pennywort leaves. They wore deer pelts that covered most of their body except for their heads.

"Welcome! New arrivals are...not common here. Are you lost?" One of the men asked.

The man tapped his associate to go into a nearby hut and bring out small necklaces. Zulag raised an eyebrow as he and Ozul were skipped, but Deeso and Cikya were happily offered some. He bit his tongue on the matter but answered for the sake of the group. Despite the humble abode at first, this settlement was vastly connected. This numbered around 100 people but was just one of many stops around the marshes. Zulag saw that small canoes were in various stages of construction along one of the huts. It was obvious to him that they used river travel to keep in touch with other ends of the marsh when smoke signals wouldn't do the job.

"Very." Zulag bluntly huffed.

"Can I have a necklace too?" Ozul asked with a small grin, as the two men looked at each other and back at Ozul. Zulag soon realized that these necklaces must have been garments that women in their band wore and were used to make them feel welcome.

"He's a boy, just no beard yet." Zulag said, giving Ozul a hearty pat on the back.

"Well, what is that you seek?" The man asked, as Ozul gave a slight frown to his request being ignored. Cikya happily added the necklace to her growing number of charms and swung it around her neck as she rotated in a circle, happy to hear the jingle. The two men smiled with satisfaction. The more vocal of the two continued to address Zulag's concerns while the other kept his eye on the quiet Deeso.

"We're looking to get out of here. Also, a group of people that looked like him came through here at some point. You see them or are we wasting our time?" Zulag said. His eyes narrowed as the other one tried to capture Deeso's attention for something most likely unimportant. Cikya gave a muffled laugh at Zulag's reaction that was quickly stifled by a tug from Ozul.

"If you keep heading north, and I mean, very far north, you'll find a place known as The Gorge." The quiet one mentioned, finally breaking their awkward silence.

"My friends' words are true, we hear tales of great and powerful beasts that rip and tear anything that moves." The other man responded as his friend nodded in agreement.

"The predators are a blight on the world, and we are here to return them to the ground. We will take on whatever comes our way. Tell us where to go. Can you take us to this place?" Deeso asked as she kept the necklace in her palm.

"Deeso, that is a big request to make of these random strangers. I would like to find this place as well, but we will have to do it on our own. Since when do Thunderfeet do things for free?" Ozul said, with a bit of surprise on his face as he spoke.

"Well, small one we can take the river up on one condition. You must settle our bet and give us the pelt of the creature you find up there. My friend thinks it is some kind of powerful Tala, I think the creature is a Bher." The man proposed to the group.

"That's it? You're willing to take us up the river in your...boat there just so we can kill something and bring it back to you?" Zulag questioned. Deeso shared the same sentiment as Zulag but if this is what was needed to get things started, they would do so.

Slim chance on us going back here ever again. Cikya thought as she tried to stifle her amusement at such a proposal.

Deeso offered her hand to agree to the terms but was stopped by the man as their customs were different. Instead of a handshake, lowering one's head at the same time was considered acceptable. Bowing to lower the head was done for a superior in their group but here it was done to solidify an agreement. With the terms met, the two men prompted the group to wait for a few moments and left them alone. The four idled for some time and heard a heavy grunt come by as the two men dragged a large canoe from another hut. Deeso noticed the craft was quite large as it made an indent in the dirt. There was some dried blood present on the wood as well. Deeso gave Zulag a slightly concerned look as she assessed the safety of the boat.

"My friends are unable to swim. Will you be able to help me save them?" Ozul spoke ahead as the two men returned.

"We have a big boat. This is for Vatmaraku we find on the banks. If this can hold such a creature, you four will be fine." The man answered Ozul. Ozul frowned as this wasn't an answer to his question, but there wasn't much he could do about it. As Zulag was impatient to leave, he helped the men drag the canoe to the riverbank.

"Oars! Yes, how could we have forgotten such a thing? One moment." One of the men said again, rushing to grab the oars. Cikya gave Deeso a worried look as she heard the man's response.

After what seemed longer than expected, the other man returned with a hunk of wood that looked more like a worked plank than an oar, but this would be sufficient for their needs. Ozul raised an eyebrow, Forest Seekers rarely used boats, but he remembered that an oar had a distinctly different shape than what he was looking at from his experience of working with wood.

These aren't oars at all... Deeso thought as she was quickly regretting her decision. She could see Zulag's derision of the two in the air and she was inclined to agree if their journey was going to have more hiccups. Deeso kept her axe close and looked to make sure everyone had their implements handy.

"This river is very smooth, and we will take you as far as we can before running aground but, then you are on your own. Remember our deal!" The first man said with a cheerful expression as he offered the boat to the others.

Deeso hesitated but got in first as she felt she should lead by example. As Zulag stepped in next, Deeso quickly gripped the side of the boat which prompted a laugh from the other man. Ozul quickly hopped on, his frame light enough to not cause a huge disturbance and extended his hand out to help Cikya onto the vessel. Though it was far from needed, Cikya happily accepted and the four turned their heads to meet the gaze of their navigators.

"We are in shallow waters; this is as low as we can go. It only gets deeper from here so stay sharp." The first man said, posing as the main navigator. He and the others felt a hearty push from the second man as they were moved by the current.

"So, tell us about yourselves. It's going to be quite the ride." The man said as he swatted away a few flies from him. The boat started to pick up speed but still not at a rate that Zulag was satisfied with as his eyes scanned the water.

"We don't do that." Deeso and Zulag said in unison, prompting a slightly confused look from the other.

Ozul decided to speak on their behalf and gave a summary about his current quest to find his family and how he came to know Deeso, Zulag and Cikya. Occasionally, the man turned around to steer the boat, but he was enthralled with how Ozul delivered his ideas. Cikya nodded happily whenever her name was mentioned, while Deeso and Zulag sat silent in agreement.

"A group of warriors to find someone lost, a noble and honorable goal, even if the methods are odd. What will happen if she does not want to be found?" The man asked, as he surveyed the land ahead of them.

"Nobody can deny the family we have waiting for her. It's been a long time. Is there anything we need to know about this area?" Deeso questioned, choosing to move on to a different subject.

She weighed her options quite some time ago on the fate of Sadal with Zulag's input, she'd walk back or must be carried depending on what happened. Problems such as these though weren't meant to be discussed in the presence of their strange hosts. Deeso noticed that there were a few temporary workshops along the shore where people would process fish and the hides of slain crocodiles. Her mouth salivated at the chance to get some of the meat for herself, if it tasted anything like salted fish she was in for a treat. The lead man waved at one of the workers and slowly drifted the boat over to make light conversation. Zulag had enough as he was irritated beyond measure to see their course change.

"Oh, come on! You see them how often? We need to get moving." Zulag complained at the man who ignored his outburst.

"We go with the current here..." The other man commented, attempting to soothe Zulag's anger.

"What are they doing anyway?" Deeso questioned aloud as she heard laughter come from them.

"We are asking for directions. This is not our usual route so we must ask for clarity." The other man explained as he pointed to the navigator asking a woman who carried a bundle of fish in her hands. The two nodded for some time and business as usual was here.

"It's good that you four are warriors, we may be running into trouble down river. We have some long sticks to ward off creatures from the boat, but if we are attacked, I hope you can defend us." The man added on as he looked behind him.

The river was a quiet journey for the group of six as they navigated their way past suspicious logs that looked like crocodiles and the occasional hippo that chose to make itself known. Deeso and the others kept their hands gripped on the boat as they saw the river's flow continued to change speed. Cikya was fast asleep, occasionally snoring as she would wake up in bursts of energy to find that nothing had changed. Zulag tried to entertain himself by counting the grooves in the boat and starting over in frustration when he lost count.

"I see some more smoke in the sky. What does it mean?" Ozul asked the navigator as he pointed upwards.

"Oh that's-" He said, pausing as he tried to interpret the message sent out.

Deeso gave the others a look of concern as the man's voice trailed off. She rustled Cikya awake to stay vigilant as she had intuition something bad was about to happen. Their navigator gave a silent nod to the other man to grab a large spear that served as a harpoon strapped to the side of the boat.

"What are you going to do with that?" Zulag questioned as he realized the size of the weapon in question.

The smoke above them changed color quickly from white to a hazy black-brown that picked up in volume. While not recognizable to the others, the navigator knew danger was afoot. As sections of their village were quite isolated from one another, this was both their greatest strength and weakness. In times of strife, the humble fishers would use smoke signals to relay the need for aid and use a canoe. The swamp-dwellers moved location with the wet and dry seasons, but unusual conditions have brought a larger influx of people than usual and the need for food grew larger. Raids by hostiles were rare but could be devastating in their delivery. At first there was nothing, but the smoke in the sky stopped. Unknown to the group of six, a raid had just begun. With a canoe of their own, a small band of about ten warriors traversed the river to steal supplies along the few tents camped out there. Their demands were simple as they filled their canoe with the hearty bounty of crocodile and fish meat. Some preferred to take trinkets such as the shell necklaces worn by women or priceless bracelets made of the same material. Those that fought were cut down with weapons forged from obsidian far to the north.

As the group continued to go down river, the devastation from these raiders became more evident as the navigator shared concerns with everyone else. This was the most recent occurrence of violence that happened. The burning smell of swamp wood filled the air and bodies were haphazardly laid out on the ground, nature already moving to take its course as ants swarmed and picked apart the corpses. In better days, those that were down river were given a nice wave or an attempt to trade before going back to their own duties. Far from heroes, Deeso felt compelled however to take a proactive stance on this as the life of their ferrymen were worth protecting. She urged the men to continue to row further until they grew tired. The six beached the canoe and Deeso looked at the others to step up and arm themselves. She withdrew her axe and pointed it at the direction of their guides.

"Your lives are worth our transport up this river. Do not move and we will look for these people." Deeso commanded the two men holding their large harpoon.

The group were equipped for battle, it'd been a while as they avoided fights with The Aligned when possible. The three's eyes looked to Ozul who was still hesitant but withdrew his blowgun. Ozul decided that the death of innocents was something worth protecting and so it would be done. Deeso stood low to the ground as she inched over to investigate what was going on. As the best tracker among them, it was easy to find their marauders were not far away, having dragged someone with a struggle in mind and with any misfortune, they would still be alive. These mystery people were lazy, and Deeso quickly gathered this was intentional. These humble river dwellers weren't particularly suited to combat and with it being equal access, they became a prime target for raiding. Though the river's bounty could feed all, it was easier to take from someone else. Deeso heard the familiar gait of Zulag behind her as his eyes scanned for anything out of the ordinary. Though the initial set of tents were ransacked, there was a small rustling sound that prompted the two's attention.

Cikya led a protective stance when it came to Ozul, practically smothering him as she held her staff out and poked into bushes. For a moment, Ozul saw a brief flash of movement from some high bush and left Cikya's watch. Ozul was the first to find one of these raiders, and noticed they wore white face paint much like how he remembered Zulag's markings. A woman lunged at him with a spear, with only having a few split seconds to dodge before he ran away. He lacked any true close combat skills but was adept with his blowgun. He quickly loaded a wooden dart and blew into it, launching it at speed and nailing his attacker in the stomach. She stopped and withdrew the dart with just enough time for the second to come by. This one was a miss as Ozul's hands sweat and he lost focus. He loaded in another dart as he hobbled away and kicked dirt into her face. With her arms raised to instinctively get the dirt out of her eyes, she exposed herself and much like a deer, was shot in the heart by Ozul's blowgun. Ozul didn't bother to look at the body and stepped over it as he looked to find any of his friends.

Cikya rooted around for Ozul and huffed as the boy was missing. Her thoughts led next to finding Deeso and Zulag, but she was stopped by two men armed with short knives. Cikya's staff gave plenty of distance between her two opponents as she rapidly shifted perspective to try and get the jump on them. Sweat from her forehead hit the ground as she carefully adjusted it to the middle and swiped low. She jumped back and realized this was only her fight to lose, not through just a skill gap, but through the range battle as well. Cikya took a big risk in baiting the two men to attack her as they hoped to overwhelm her by simple strength. Just as she hoped for them to do, Cikya quickly changed stances and used her staff as a counterweight as she kicked the first man in the shin before lifting her staff again to face the other. She gave a definitive swing that came across her attacker's head with enough force to cause a crack in her own weapon. He was unconscious and although not dead, he soon would be. Cikya dropped her staff and jumped on the other injured man and wrestled the knife out his hands. She was cut in the process and her hand slowly dripped blood. She winced in pain but used her foot to kick it away as she was knocked to the ground once more. She stretched her shoulder and picked up her staff. She charged it at the man's back. She knocked him to the ground and beat him repeatedly with the staff until a pool of blood seeped from his injuries. She took the collapsed knife and returned to the unconscious man and stabbed him in the eye. She gritted her teeth as she looked for something to fix her hand. Some spare furs off their bodies would do the job nicely.

Deeso and Zulag weren't concerned with the others that were killed by their team in battle but finding the person responsible for the raid in question. While it was possible for raids to be ordered independently, it was bad form for a leader to not be present at the scene itself. They were banking on slaying the leader to establish dominance and scare the other members into leaving them alone. Deeso decided that going for the big fish in the small pond had its own rewards. In their experience, a leader would often differentiate themselves from the others with a different color face paint than the group here that wore white on their faces.

"Kill the leader and they will rout." Deeso said to Zulag as they looked through a few overturned tents deeper into the marshes.

The two stopped as they saw a lone man sitting at the campfire. He was incredibly muscular and as Deeso questioned why he wasn't going to aid of his fellow villagers, Zulag quickly realized what they came up against. To their surprise, the leader of the raid was not one of their own, but one of The Aligned. Zulag remembered distinctly his last encounter with them that ended up not going as well as he'd hoped. Deeso was aware that their own people lived among them, but she never imagined they shared such tight bonds.

The idea of them living together in a community like this was unheard of to them. Although once antithetical, Deeso and Zulag's combat strategy was now complementary to one another. Each left an essential opening for their moment to strike. Zulag was hoping to slice the man's throat, but he felt some resistance from himself going with a direct strike. He would need to wear this man down before they could do anything. With zero hesitation, the man got up with surprising speed and barreled straight into Deeso knocking her over to the muddy ground of the marsh. She shook her head as she was bewildered with such raw power and realized she dropped her axe some short distance away. Deeso quickly recovered her orientation and grabbed her axe, determined more than ever.

"Deeso! Don't let him grab you or that arm is coming off!" Zulag warned as he launched two knives in rapid succession, one landing their mark on the man's ankle and another falling to the marsh grasses.

Zulag's knives made of simple flint did the job, but not nearly as well as he'd want. He grimaced at the man who now turned his attention to him. He wielded a club and swung with tremendous speed as Zulag attempted to dodge. He leaned back, and nearly fell to the ground in an attempt to do so. Zulag dropped to the soil and rolled to the side as he was just a second faster than the man's club that left a noticeable imprint in the dirt. Zulag's priority was disarming the man because he was even more dangerous with his club than anything else. He took another one of his knives and waited for the man's swing as he quickly stabbed forward and sliced the front of his hand open. A sea of blood filled his face as the man bled.

The Aligned man let out a harsh scream with the club making a sudden thud to the ground. Zulag resisted taking the chance to go in for punches and kicks as he usually did but remained on the offensive with his knife. Deeso ran up with a burst of speed and hurled her axe straight into the back of the man, who seemed to be distracted. His skin was exposed as he wore no covering and was an easy target. His flesh was torn as it was embedded into his shoulder blade but through pure adrenaline, he continued his assault. Deeso ran across Zulag and pushed him to the side to get him into a better position. As the delirious man charged towards Deeso, Zulag leaped onto the man's back and rapidly sliced his throat before a gush of blood came and the two fell with a hard thud on the ground. Zulag quickly withdrew Deeso's axe from the man's corpse, as shards of cracked bone were revealed. He held it towards her as Deeso approached him and graciously took her weapon back. She held her hand out to Zulag to grab and the two rose as one. The two looked at one another, now caked with blood and silently walked off to find Cikya, Ozul, and the way back to the boat.

Sometime later, Deeso and Zulag returned to see that Cikya and Ozul already found their way back to the boat, and the lives of their navigators were saved. Ozul sat in Cikya's lap as she pulled out dirt and bits of flesh from his hair while he awkwardly tried to stand still. The two navigators were in awe of their rescuers and set off once more to reach the land that hosted The Gorge.

The Gorge

Enroute to the base of the Caucasus Mountains, Jih and the others arrived in Armenia. The air was still as the four clutched their belongings and looked around for signs of life. It was empty, but not the eerie sort of way it was in previous times. Trekkal recalled the group's conversation with Zoki and her instructions to head north. On their travels, they heard word there was supposedly a priest who knew more of such events, much to both Narro and Sadal's skepticism on the manner. She told Trekkal the way would be clear when the ground shook and the spirits that lived in the hills shed their tears.[64]

"This has to be it. I remember it so clearly! Go to the hill that cries!" Trekkal said to the others as she received mixed expressions.

Jih looked around, trying to find what Trekkal mentioned but his eyes fixated on sloping hills in the distance. Jih saw that the top of these hills had mudslides that dragged boulders down in pairs and then understood the meaning of Zoki's message. Narro observed the movement of these rocks as well and wondered if there was a presence watching over their group as they continued to walk. Sadal took a moment to stretch as she spoke to the three of them.

"So, this is where we need to head to? If I remember correctly, this is called "The Gorge"?" Sadal asked as she let out a small sigh of relief as her bones cracked. Sadal hoped that once they reached the foot of the mountains ahead, there would be time to rest.

Though it was unpassionately known as "The Gorge", it was a long stretch of grassland and certainly wasn't barren. Far in the distance, tall mountains could be seen through the clouds as a looming reminder of their goal. Jih couldn't believe how close they were. Pockets of humanity made their living along these paths in sizable settlements, trading with one another and guiding lost travelers to various ends for compensation. Their occupations in these lands were seasonal and tied to the various prey species that made their home. The land was both occupied by The Aligned and The Youngest. At first there was some hostility between the groups, but cooperation won out in the end. The creatures of "The Gorge" humbled their approach and they worked as one. Jih remembered Zoki's warning about the creatures of The Gorge and the stress of how dangerous this region of the world truly was. Jih and the others evaluated their supplies and made sure to pack extra food on the trail for the goodwill of others. The gang kept their crocodile skin armor in good condition as they heeded Zoki's warning and hoped for the best. They felt safe from any human that would come, but the presence of beasts was its own challenge. Narro pointed out the outline of one of the settlements not too far from their location. He saw this as an opportunity to see what additional information he could find for the group, and to find resources to complete a personal project of his to make for

---

[64] Armenia is home to volcanoes and tectonic activity where the occasional tremor could be felt.

Sadal. The four walked in and absorbed the sights of the village. Jih studied their building material, with some homes constructed from packed mud and sticks, while elephant bones were also essential construction material. A small fire raged near the entrance of these and indicated that someone was home. Trekkal noticed that there was no distinct separation of this village between her kind and that of The Youngest. Their homes were blended as she could make out the minor but important differences between their constructions. The Youngest's mindset was more focused on presentation than functionality, as she noted the copious amounts of decoration.

"Not a common sight, is it? The Aligned and ourselves making a pact like this." A man said as he tapped Jih's shoulder. Jih turned around and noticed that the man was one of Sadal's people. The man gave Jih a strange look as he studied him but gave no further thoughts.

"Well, welcome. I take it you and your friends have seen much already. We have two other settlements we are in contact with if you wish to take the path. We are traders, but we hunt plenty of game as well." He explained further.

"Jih has questions for man." Jih said, seeing the man's reaction as he heard Jih's voice. The man was shaken, as he could understand Jih roughly, but something felt off. He scratched his head and looked uncomfortable. A woman holding a basket with animal skins overheard the conversation and approached, intrigued by their new guest. She interrupted the discussion as Jih turned his head to address her.

"Oh-You are different. I am Skozi. Talk to me or my One if you need anything. We hold this camp together." She mentioned, as Jih turned around to see Sadal and Trekkal peeking their heads into people's homes. He felt a parental embarrassment, these people deserved at least some privacy.

"Jih and friends must head north. Do you know of power rock?" Jih asked Skozi who looked at his dress. She couldn't nail what he was. His dress was like that of The Youngest, but his voice was rough like gravel. She understood him well but was also confused about the origins of this guest of hers.

"Well, there are many rocks. Some are larger than others. If north is where you need to go though, I would suggest you take some guides with you. The road is dangerous this season and new arrivals do not fare well. If you are unable to provide any trade, you should go back from where you came." She warned Jih. Jih shook his head, knowing that he would do whatever he needed to get closer to his goal.

"Jih has meat and tools to give. Jih will gather friends for guide." Jih mentioned as he looked at the others.

Jih gave a whistle that carried across some distance that he used to alert the others when help was needed. Sadal, Narro, and Trekkal found their way back to Jih who informed them of their next move. Skozi gave Jih a moderately impressed look as she saw how quickly they came to his call. Skozi led Jih and the others to a small section of the village that was distant from the usual activity going on. A small group sat before them as they were eating their lunch for the day.

"We have visitors who want to go north. From the looks of things, they have some pelts worth your labor." Skozi said to the group before making her leave. Jih turned around to see eager grins on their faces. Jih was surprised at their sudden birth of energy, but he also remembered being in his 20s.

"Check packs for supplies. We must make trade." Jih said to the others who placed their bags down and rummaged around.

Trekkal didn't want to part with some of her belongings but gave a defeated sigh as she saw the others making sacrifices of their own. Out of the main village's population of about sixty people, there were ten guides in all. Six were men and four were women. Seven of them were The Aligned, and the other three were not. Jih had no preference on who he wanted to accompany them, but he decided that at least three would be needed for the road ahead. Jih decided to let Sadal, Narro, and Trekkal make their choices while he waited. Jih's decision was a callous one as if things went south, he saw them as disposable compared to his own friends. Trekkal's choice was obvious, as she picked another one of her kind. A strong gentleman which reminded Jih much of Narro, except without being related to her. She gave him a small grin and Jih could tell her choice wasn't entirely strategic. Sadal felt homesick to a degree and picked one of her own to accompany her. This one was also a man who looked to be about Jih's age. Jih raised an eyebrow at the choice but shrugged, seeing as experience was always a good thing. Although he lacked the fanatic will of The Broken Bone, Sadal saw kinship in this one and thought some could be learned from him. He lived among The Aligned and wanted to know how he was received among them as she hoped to one day live with Narro and his family. Narro picked a woman of his kind as his choice, she seemed forlorn, and it seemed as if some brushed over her. Narro saw opportunity and wanted to make someone's day a bit better. Jih nodded, seeing their decisions and as he reached to open his pack he was stopped.

"We take half now, and half when you're safe. This is how we do things." Sadal's choice spoke.

Jih nodded, moving his head to Sadal to pour out some of her offerings that the group graciously accepted.

With the deal made, Narro, Trekkal, and Jih gave their portions as well before the larger hunting party set off. The outskirts of their village gradually faded behind them as they shared little words outside. Jih surveyed the land that they were walking on and tried to recall things that looked familiar to him. He felt that the guides were a good choice as "The Gorge" seemed to have no clear end or beginning past the village's boundary. The ambient sound of insects and the distant laughing of hyenas was enough to make anyone go mad as Narro expressed his distaste.

"Everywhere we go...we run into these things. Will they be underwater next? Perhaps they will sprout wings and go to the sky!" Narro complained, receiving a small chuckle from Jih.

Sadal screened out the other discussions that brewed to get more insight from her picked guide. Aside from Deeso and the occasional trader, she hadn't really had an in-depth conversation with one of her own in a while and she felt a sense of comfort as she did so. He could tell that she was eager to strike up a conversation with him as he felt her looking at him consistently. As the coast was clear, he let his guard down a bit. Sadal lowered her head in a nod of acknowledgement to the older guide.

"I go by Broll. The other two are Ticc and Figa. The burly man with the patchy beard is Ticc, and the quiet one is Figa." Broll explained to Sadal, as he adjusted the position of which he held his spear.

"So, what's it like? There aren't many of us out in these parts." Sadal asked Broll as her glance turned to Narro trying to strike conversation with Figa. She didn't say much to his cheery attitude.

"Hm? Oh, I fought The Aligned when I was about your age. I took a partner, and her sister!" He said with a slight laugh while Sadal looked confused. She was trying to recall what Narro mentioned before about his culture, but the one thing she strictly remembered was that every member of The Aligned had a One they considered to be their partner for life, and this is what she would be for Narro.

"That was a joke. The Aligned take their relationships very seriously. In fact, I had to claim at least two pelts of great creatures in order to prove my worth to the family." Broll narrated.

"What creatures were these?" Sadal inquired, she wondered if Broll came from a culture much like her own that sought glory from the most dangerous and rewarding bounties.

"Well, I took on many a Yaan, but my claim is surviving and bringing home a Mahaku pelt." Broll bragged with an exaggerated grin.

"Oh, have you? From what Narro's told me, these were intense and unkillable creatures." Sadal asked with genuine surprise on her face.

Trekkal gave a noticeable cough as she overheard the words of a Mahaku being mentioned. She shot a look at Narro who returned her glance with some worry. Jih hadn't bothered to pay much attention to their conversation, with his thoughts back in Sundaland. It was here that Figa broke her silence to suppress the foolhardy Broll. She overheard the conversation between the two and her head turned around with a smug grin on her face.

"You lie. You have never taken on such a beast. The Mahaku is a creature cursed by the spirits themselves. It is a vengeful beast and one we must avoid with great caution." Figa said, interrupting their conversation.

"Figa worries too much, but it is true Broll. You Youngest seem to exaggerate much of your accomplishments. Nothing is wrong with slaying a Kalpeu on your own, this is within your ability." Ticc shot at Broll much to the furrowed brow on the man's face.

The conditions were abysmally hot this afternoon and so the group stopped for a rest. Jih kept track of the time they spent on the plains by watching the sun's movement. They shared stories briefly and exchanged canteens made of deer bladders filled with refreshing river water before continuing their journey. Jih's head was in the clouds for a good deal of their walk, but he saw two hulking figures in the distance that brought him back to his senses.

Jih rarely had the look of genuine fear in his eyes, but this unnerved him far more than any tiger. Figa's head turned to see that her fears were indeed true. They had no cover and they found themselves in the middle of two titans that made their path the arena of battle. Two scimitar-tooth cats were engaged in combat over disputed territory[65]. Both were male, the slightly larger one was slower and took a slash to the stomach as the two fought. Dust piled on the ground as they swiped and gnawed at each other. They lunged at one another with great force, trying to outmaneuver the other to bite the neck. If it came down to it, these animals had no qualms about killing their own, but both males simply wished to send a message to the other. Their roars sounded for miles, and these were to be heard for all lesser life forms to not interfere. These creatures sported a medium gray that stood out from the tanned grass that made their home. Unlike other cats, these held complete supremacy of their environment, where camouflage wasn't needed. Scimitar-toothed cats were far different from the leopards and tigers that Jih and the others were used to. This creature was about the size of a lion but held no mane. At first glance, one could assume they were slender in nature, but this would be far from the truth. Its entire body was built with bulging muscle as its claws extended. It hit fast and it hit hard. It didn't ambush its prey from the brush and instead ran it down with the utmost persistence. It basked in the sweat and desperation that the prey had before giving the release of death. The two scimitar-toothed cats raged on for some time as the group was unsure of what to do. They tried going around but felt that this would indicate to the animals their presence. Figa proposed that waiting it out would be their best option. Trekkal was about to let out a scream that was covered by Narro pressing his hand quickly over her mouth while Ticc and Broll moved forward to investigate the outcome of the two titans fighting.

"Trekkal. Do you want to die today? Stay quiet and let them run each other out." Narro said through gritted teeth as he turned back to see Sadal placing down her pack and grabbing her throwing spears.

"Only those who wish to die tired would run from the Mahaku, so here's what we do. We'll have to fight if it comes to it. Can you all fight?" Broll spoke to their group. There was an exchange of nods in agreement, as Jih could only sigh in defeat at this.

"Yes. We can fight, can you?" Sadal asked, her voice annoyed at Broll's fabrication of his fighting prowess.

Broll gave a glare at Sadal, while in the background, the two animals solved their differences. The fighting ceased and an uncomfortable silence filled the field. Two fought and one remained in its territory. The victorious of the two smelled intruders in its land, and the injured loser licked its wounds and was strained due to its injuries. In no

---

[65] Homotherium latidens is one of the dominant predators of the Paleolithic and has one of the widest ranges as well, covering multiple continents in its wake.

condition to get its primary meals, there would need to be a substitute. It left the winning male's land without delay.

The dominant scimitar-toothed cat smelled interlopers in its claimed territory and was willing once again to fight. The afterimage of the cat could be seen in the distance and slowly increased in size as it ran closer to the party. For Broll, it was a battle of his ego versus his experience as he felt slighted by Sadal's words. He looked at his companions who nodded in step with him as they prepared themselves for a fight. Broll, Ticc and Figa all used melee weapons, while Sadal and Trekkal served as support with their ranged prowess. Jih immediately regretted not having a throwing weapon as he and Narro would also have to face the animal up close. The party braced for the fight as Jih and the others felt secure with their crocodile armor.

Broll led them out with his spear poised to aim downwards so that he could pierce the animal's head with a swift blow. Jih studied his form carefully but decided that his own would be better as he held the spear mid-level. He hoped this position would protect his vitals better from the creature's scratches. Jih knew that any animal could bleed given enough time, but he held his worries close. Ticc ran ahead of the others, with his spear in one hand and a handful of rocks in the other. The beast stopped short to assess the threat against itself before deciding that this would be trivial. The scimitar-tooth cat let out a terrifying roar that emboldened itself. Sadal planned to make a formation to attack the animal on all sides, but it was much too fast to consider such a thing. The groups defaulted to their own fighting patterns and vowed to help when applicable. The four of them were well experienced in hunting as a team, and this would be no different, except for now they were the ones being hunted. Sadal waved over Trekkal for her to come quickly while the cat took its time selecting its target. Trekkal felt her heart jump out of her chest as she carried her sling and some rocks. Sadal placed her hand in hers before speaking.

"Trekkal, I want you to aim for the legs of that thing if you can. Narro and Jih should know what to do, so just focus on that. If it comes in your direction, don't run, pelt as many stones as you can. Aim for the eyes too." Sadal said as she braced to join the others who began their advance.

"W-What do you mean stay here!?" Trekkal said, trying to contain her emotions. Sadal noticed Trekkal's panic and attempted to soothe her concerns.

"Be strong for us both. I'll return for you, sister." Sadal encouraged Trekkal before setting out on her own.

Trekkal looked into Sadal's eyes and nodded, understanding what needed to be done. She took a deep breath to calm herself down as she ran ahead some distance before rotating her arm to start releasing rocks. Trekkal focused and followed Sadal's advice as she looked for the right angle to throw. Although the scimitar-toothed cat was faster and could easily outrun her, Trekkal needed to be mindful as she had to stop entirely to use her sling properly.

Jih and Narro looked at each other, not needing to discuss the plan for action. Jih operated at a medium range with his spear work while Narro would have to dig in close with his club. While only having one good eye, Narro was impeccable at making his mark when he could. He scanned the creature's body as he looked for the best places to hit. Broll let out a scream in rage of his own as he charged the animal while Ticc assaulted with rocks. The scimitar-toothed cat retreated before diverting its attention to Ticc. Ticc dropped his rocks and braced with his spear as he waited for the creature to charge him. Mindful of his strength and bigger frame, he stuck his feet to the ground and focused. His eyes darted as the creature moved in his direction just as he planned. Broll saw an opportunity as he triumphantly ran forward to poke at the animal with his spear. He landed a few punctures on the animal before retreating off. Ticc whistled to Broll for him to return as he swiped the air. The cat darted its neck and avoided the spear as it did so. It lunged towards Ticc and pinned him to the ground as it extended its claws into his body. Ticc winced in immense pain as he attempted to punch the creature, its face unmoved as he did so.

Ticc was sliced into ribbons as the animal continued its assault. He could only scream as his fleeting strength failed to move the creature off him. It didn't bother to lop his face off and cease his shouting. His entrails leaked out onto the soil below as he was ground to dust by its grinding jaws. The animal's fangs emerged as its jaws opened, only for them to be concealed once more when the job was done. Its yellow eyes darkened to orange in the light as its face became clouded with blood. The scimitar-toothed cat seemed to have one weakness within its bloodlust, it remained fixated on maiming and mutilating its kill into nothingness with robotic precision. No other stimuli seemed to keep it away from its function as Ticc's body was strewn around while a pool of blood splattered the creature's gray hide.

As Jih studied the creature's sporadic movement, he made the callous decision in his mind that he'd need to sacrifice their guides so the others could get out in one piece. It pained him to consider this, but these were people they just met versus the ones he saw as family. With it distracted, he would be able to at least deliver some damage. Jih ran over to the scene and ignored Ticc's pained screams as he charged the back end of the animal. Small pockets of blood spilled from its hindquarters as it turned around quickly to face Jih. It swiped at him with its paw as the movement dislodged the spear.

Jih squeezed his stomach and jumped back. He heard his fur covering torn to shreds and his armor was broken entirely. It was an incredibly close call, and while the animal didn't land a killing blow due to these layers, it left a deep scratch in Jih's chest that steadily bled. Jih let out a scream in agony as he felt pain surge within him. The open air cut through his chest like a hot knife as he bit his tongue. Jih weathered the pain and realized he was fortunate, an inch closer and he would have been eviscerated completely. Jih felt a surge of adrenaline come over him as he tried to block out his pain and focus on survival. The cat ran again, this time directly towards Jih in another lunge. Jih quickly twisted himself to the side and made himself parallel to the cat rather than directly in front. With an increased burst of speed, the cat rolled to the ground as it worked to get itself back up. Sadal took advantage of the situation and pelted the animal with two spears, one that missed entirely and another that landed on the creature's shoulder. As it panicked, the spear embedded itself further into its body. Jih swiped at the enraged animal but overshot where its mighty paws broke his spear in half. Jih felt the end was near but saw the arc of another throwing spear make its mark on the beast.

"Jih! Follow me!" Sadal screamed as she caught his attention.

Jih attempted to run in her direction as the cat was stunned before getting back to its senses. Trekkal gave herself some silent praise as the rock she released from her sling struck the animal's eye, right as it ran towards their direction. She continued to launch rocks as she did so.

Narro saw that Figa was rushing towards the scene with her spear and he decided to join her as a united front worked best. As he went by, Narro picked up a heavy piece of wood along the ground that he grabbed while having his club in the other hand. Narro resourcefully used the block of wood to defend himself against the creature's swipe. It was a temporary measure as the wood splintered immediately but gave the opening he needed. He moved away just enough but hit it square in the jaw with his club as he heard a satisfying crunch and bits of blood pooled from its mouth. Figa additionally damaged its exposed neck as she attempted to get through the muscle. Broll noticed that she was struggling and pushed her out of the way briefly as Narro looked to Sadal to see if she was alright. The animal in its pained rage now put its entire weight on Broll. Broll attempted to punch the animal as it clamped on his neck and shook him violently to the point that his head was severed from the rest of his body. It revealed its cutting teeth as it crushed Broll's head inside its mouth for a bit before spitting what was left out. Brain matter gushed to the soil below as bits of bone were also crushed under the weight of the cat's jaws. His body became the creature's next target as it drank his blood.

Figa in a rage decided to tackle the scimitar-toothed cat itself in wanting to avenge her comrades. Narro called out for her to wait but Jih held out his hand to him. Jih saw no point in trying to stop her as she already sealed her own death. She managed to stab the creature in its exposed underbelly once more, making it bleed. This was a creature filled with inconceivable power and rage as it tore apart its prey, and Figa was no exception. Although the creature itself suffered significant losses of blood, it remained through pure adrenaline, a danger to those around it. It dragged her along the ground with her leg and tossed her some distance where she hit the ground with a thud. Her face and body were nearly stripped naked and brutally scarred by the force of the ground on her as the hides on her degraded into dust. She was still breathing, but practically unable to be saved as her skin was flayed from her body.

Sadal had seen enough death for today, with her throwing spear winning the day for them as it was this final one that jammed through its thick neck. The last spear stopped it from breathing as it contorted around, attempting to remove it until at long last it fell still. Surrounding the corpse of the cat were the strewn remains of Ticc and Broll. Figa was mutilated beyond recognition, yet she somehow remained alive for a few brief moments as her arm twitched. Jih knew she was well beyond recovery. Jih gave her a quick death and stuck a fallen blade through her.

"Jih! Are you alright? I see blood coming from you!" Trekkal said, her voice filled with concern.

Trekkal sat Jih down and he braced for impact as she washed out the wound with the water that remained from the deerskin bladder packs. Jih winced in pain as Trekkal looked to Sadal who rummaged thread from her pack to stitch together Jih's wounds. He winced in terrible pain as she slowly mended his flesh together. Jih was so numbed by his screams that he hardly felt anything as Sadal worked. Once her work was done, Sadal briefly left the group. Narro ripped off a piece of his clothing to use as a bandage that he wrapped tightly around Jih. Trekkal gave him a small kiss on the forehead to which Jih smiled slightly as he assessed everyone else. Jih slowly stood up and walked as he clenched his chest. Jih turned around to see Sadal move forward towards the animal's corpse. She took a knife to the creature's neck and drank as their foe was an astoundingly effective opponent. Narro lifted up Jih and carried him with ease as the rest continued onward to the nearest settlement with smoke in the sky.

Some hours after this, Deeso and the others too found themselves in "The Gorge". The group assessed from tales by locals that this is where Sadal would have been last. It was the late afternoon as the sun still peaked high, but dusk would follow it soon enough. Although Zulag complained, Deeso decided to enlist the aid of the guides as well. They were on the trail offering little conversation. The guides they had were two of their own kind and a member of The Aligned. They wore assorted clothing that matched their status as renowned warriors, with luxurious jackal and leopard pelt shared among them. Deeso found The Aligned to be a curious group of people to her, so she decided to add one to their retinue to study.

"Deeso, do we really need them? They're going to slow us down." Zulag complained as they were along the trail. Deeso heard Zulag's complaining since they arrived at the previous village. First, it was about giving them food, and then it was about taking the guides in general. She could only let out an annoyed sigh.

This place is spiritually rich, this much is clear. But...why? What is this place not telling me? Cikya questioned as she took in the surroundings of "The Gorge".

Ozul took her hand as his pace sped up to meet up with the others. Cikya looked over her party with satisfaction. Prior to their entry to this place, she placed a small white pigment made from crushed plants along their cheeks as a sign of good fortune. It was arranged in two small streaks that ran horizontally under their eyes. Zulag accepted it with graciousness, while Ozul was just happy to be included. Cikya debated skipping Deeso, but she felt that even if she didn't walk the path, there were forces interested in her survival. Deeso respected Cikya enough as her own person to keep the mark on her face. Cikya cared to listen well about the dangers of the animals that inhabited this land and called on a force of magic to keep them safe for the duration of their travels. She gave a steady breath as she heard something in the distance.

The party stopped short as they saw that a scimitar-toothed cat was in the distance. This one was far more depraved in its intent, for it didn't wish to merely defend its territory, but instead found a suitable source of food to recover. The animal saw the group of seven as the start of an afternoon meal. Unknown to them, this was no ordinary cat, but the loser of the previous fight with another of its kind earlier in the morning. The guides stopped short and looked among themselves. They urged them to stay low by signaling the need to duck and they complied. Deeso felt that the entire picture was missing here and asked for more information on what was happening.

"Why have we stopped?" Deeso questioned, gently pushing Zulag out the way to get a better look as their guides told them to keep their voices low.

"We have a problem. The Mahaku is here and it's not very pleased with us. It also looks hungry." The man stressed.

"And your point is?" Zulag interjected, wondering what all the fuss was about. Deeso shot a look at Zulag who had no idea what the creature in question was. Her glance then turned to Ozul who looked just as confused as she was.

"Mahaku. The One Who Maims." The Aligned man explained to Deeso and the others as his companions nodded. The name sounded imposing and a suitable challenge for their might. Even if the creature was injured, the name seemed to emit such fear from the guides. A creature of this caliber is what she knew she was born to hunt, and that sentiment was shared by both Zulag and Cikya.

"Regardless, a name is just a name, we are prepared to fight such a beast. It's actually an honor for our people." Deeso pointed out to The Aligned man. Zulag pounded his chest in agreement with Deeso's words, while the other two guides gave some nods and a laugh. They knew that just how dangerous this animal was and willingly throwing yourself into danger was a fool's errand.

"If you want to be cowards about it-" Zulag taunted, as he noticed the gaze of the guides staring at Ozul.

Although the other guides of their group had a working and affable relationship with The Aligned, their opinion of Forest Seekers was low. Ozul was an oddity among them, and they were distrustful of new kinds. He was also a child, which made it more of a liability for the guides to take care of him, but they received the food they were owed so they couldn't complain.

"How old is he?" The Aligned man asked with a raised eyebrow.

"He's old enough. What's it matter to you? Ozul, you're what, thirteen? He's a man already." Zulag countered towards the man as he pursed his lips in annoyance.

"The boy is weak, and he seems afraid of his own shadow. Not much help when we must fight such a creature. We should assume that this will be the case." One of the other guides commented as she bit her fingernail. Cikya's expression looked angry while she protectively grabbed Ozul's arm as he felt bad for drawing attention to himself.

Unfortunately for the group, the animal they hoped to avoid was well on the offensive. It practically salivated at the chance to find some fresh prey. Deeso mobilized the others to grab their weapons as she attempted to study the creature. The closest frame of reference she had was perhaps a tiger in its tenacity, but the build was different. She also knew that staring at it would just make it angrier. Ozul practically wet himself in a panic as he saw the creature's hulking size, his leg ran warm as he tried to keep focus. He felt embarrassed, but this was an animal well beyond his pay grade. Cikya nodded for Deeso and Zulag to follow her as she came up with a plan. She paired Ozul with one of the guides to stay behind, but Deeso had another idea in mind for him before she joined the fray. Ozul vibrated in anxiety as he was overwhelmed by the physicality of such a beast. He'd gotten comfortable with killing humans, but this was an entirely different scenario. Deeso noticed this and needed to keep Ozul's mind sharp for the battle ahead.

"Ozul, I want you to be our support while we're up there. You have made plenty of darts." Deeso voiced to calm down the visibly anxious Ozul.

"What are darts going to do against that?" He yelled back in a panic interrupting Deeso. Ozul's voice cracked astoundingly as Zulag and two of the other guides rushed forward with clubs hoping to bewilder the creature.

Zulag unsheathed his knives and rolled along the ground to try and find the perfect angle to launch his knives into the animal's flesh. They stuck their mark to which Zulag gave himself a grin, but it soon vanished as he saw that they weren't deep enough to get the job done. He debated jumping on its back while it was distracted but was advised against it as he saw The Aligned man try such a strategy. Zulag watched as the man was kicked to the ground by the creature's hind legs as it got up. As Zulag's knives weren't strong enough to deliver lasting damage on anywhere but the animal's extremities, he focused on doing recovery instead. As the fastest runner, he was able to pick up those who fell to the ground before the cat made its rounds again.

Cikya ran up towards him while Deeso took advantage of launching her axe directly at the animal's neck as it thrashed around. Cikya couldn't do much seeing as her staff would also break apart if it landed a direct blow, but she was able to strike it in the side. The fact the animal was injured was a boon to them, but it failed to sufficiently land the mark. It was only a flesh wound and now Deeso also had to run to grab her axe again. She ran forward while the other guide pushed her out of the way to get a better angle as she launched a spear into the creature's side. Deeso took advantage of the distraction to grab her axe but slipped over herself to the ground. Deeso's eyes widened as she dared to turn around and see that their opponent clamped its body weight onto her guide as she fell to the ground under its immense weight. The creature ripped off the woman's arm with ease and gorged on the flesh with an unending hunger as Deeso saw her gradually vanish into just a nub of a human being.

"Deeso! Grab my hand now!" Zulag yelled as she attempted to get up. She locked hands with Zulag as he dragged her to relative safety before rushing back to get Cikya.

Ozul decided to help as best as he could, his arm moved around inconsistently from the pure anxiety he felt. He dropped his first dart, but picked it up, and blew as hard as he could into it. The wind carried the dart further than he expected, but he missed the mark by a couple feet. The next few darts he had landed their mark but fell off quickly. It seemed as if he was just making it angrier each time he helped. He fiddled around in his bag and remembered the viper venom he got some days ago.

Wait, the poison! I have some. I just need to... Ozul thought as he tried to find a suitable distance to launch darts at the animal. Ozul marked these with different colored feathers normally, but in the case, there were no suitable birds, he opted for the color of wood. A bright colored wood was chosen for the darts that would be poisonous as he rummaged in his bag.

"Are you going to stand there and be weak or help me fight?" The man yelled at Ozul as he raised an axe and urged him to run forward.

Ozul's concentration was steadfast, but the man's yelling at him didn't do him any favors. The cat's gaze turned to the two who were a curious target as their strength was untested. It would be here that it would decide which to attack first. It ignored Deeso and the others as it ran towards Ozul and the other guide. Sufficiently annoyed with his situation, Ozul pushed the man to the ground and ran ahead of him as the cat clearly took his offering for the few moments before it would turn on him. Ozul felt awful about it, but at least he would live to feel awful.

"Y-Agh!" The man yelled as the animal sliced his back while he retreated.

Portions of his flesh were strewn throughout the ground as he fell forward, hitting the soil with a sufficient thud. The man's body was split apart as it chewed on what remained of his upper back. Ozul was so shocked he nearly forgot to fire his darts. As the creature gorged, he launched two poison darts that hit their mark, one on the shoulder and another right on the buttocks. The creature continued to mutilate the body with a rage leaving Ozul confused.

"I put enough to kill a Yaan! What is happening?" Ozul questioned as he started to move away towards the others.

"Ozul! It's him or us!" Zulag yelled at him as he ran towards Ozul to grab him. Ozul was light enough by Zulag to be carried well off the ground as he scooped Ozul up to regroup with the others. The four of them remained alive, and their Aligned guide was among the most careful of them.

The animal was now surrounded, as they pelted a multitude of objects against it. Cikya threw rocks hoping to stun the animal, while Deeso used hit and run tactics with her axe, narrowly avoiding retaliation from the creature. She was caked in sweat as her heart raced, the thrill of the kill gradually vanished as it was replaced with raw adrenaline to survive. Their remaining guide took his club and ran forward to press himself onwards to break the animal's paw. A crunching sound could be heard as he did so.

"Finish it!" The man yelled as he attempted to stifle the creature's movements as well as he could.

Ozul blew one more dart into the animal's neck as it thrashed around a bit longer. After what seemed like an eternity, the bewildered cat finally fell to the ground. The carnage was palpable as it laid on top of a pile of strewn body parts and shattered bone.

The four were especially lucky. To confirm that the kill was made, Deeso took her axe and carefully inched towards the creature. She reflexively jumped back but saw that there was no movement. She chopped at the animal's neck, almost struggling to cut the head due to its immense muscle, but she was able to get the blood to flow. Zulag and Cikya approached the kill and scooped up the blood as they did so. Ozul surveyed the damage but was called over by Deeso.

Out of their three guides, they had one survivor, the one that Deeso picked. Deeso felt a small sense of pride in her choice of for the journey as it was ensured her friends would survive. Deeso looked to see The Aligned man looked towards his dead companions and made a shallow grave for what he could bury as he waited for the others to go to the connecting village. It was a sobering reality, but the rewards of the hunt would be for him and his family.

"Ozul. Come here and drink with us." Deeso announced as she waved him over with her hand.

"You really pulled through back there. Good work, you did what you needed to do." Zulag said to Ozul in support of Deeso's words.

"This Mahaku. Do you think my uncle would have known of this creature? We should tell him when we return." Zulag asked Deeso.

"I don't think Ronkalk would have. We would have been taught how to deal with such a thing. Now we know." Deeso noted as she felt Zulag's hand on her shoulder.

Ozul looked at his free hand and the staring glances at the others. Cikya gave him a warm grin as her face was covered with the creature's blood. Ozul had been unofficially initiated as one of their own for some time since he took his first life, but he had never participated in the grand vision of Ronkalk that Deeso revered. He helped them take down countless herbivores, but the honor was reserved for far more compelling creatures. With his quick thinking, the dangerous Mahaku of legend, was finally quelled and the goal of clearing the land of dangerous predators to benefit her kind was forwarded. The only acceptable reward was to drink the blood with them as a trusted ally. The blood had a horrid taste to Ozul who stuck his tongue out in protest, but he scooped anyway and downed it much to the approval of the others. They drank a bit more and then gathered themselves, with Cikya assessing for injuries. As they walked longer for some time, Deeso looked at the ground and noticed a strange looking object was present. There was no mistaking it as she saw a curved stone that stood from the rest, and its size was immense. She knew this was the mark of The Stone Breaker that Eshe had mentioned and Ozul verified. It was one of Jih's hand-axes left behind in the chaos.

"We're coming Sadal, stay safe just a little longer." Deeso said quietly to herself.

Deeso and the others' arrival to the end of The Gorge met a well-earned rest stop as a small village that conducted trade was built in the interior right before the mountains. Their Aligned guide gave the group a nod to part ways after the rest of the meat was delivered as promised by Deeso. The group here treasured the mountains as a high point of spiritual energy, but also for the practical ability of keeping the weather consistent. She just missed Sadal by a few hours. Cikya took Ozul's hand as she noticed he was getting more strange expressions from onlookers. What Cikya interpreted as bullying was instead a look of familiarity. One of their kind that resided in this area approached them. He wore a jackal pelt like the others and came with good intentions.

"Is this one lost or left behind?" He asked, looking at Ozul. Ozul was confused about what he meant.

"So, you just happen to run into Forest Seekers all the time or are you trying to say something?" Zulag said with some irritation in his voice.

After their fight, his patience was minimal, and this was shared by most travelers who found themselves alive afterwards. The man sensed Zulag's anger and did his best to resolve the issue. He bowed his head in respect to the group who were less than thrilled to be questioned. The man pointed to Ozul and gathered his attention while the other three remained skeptical of his appearance.

"I noticed he looked familiar. About two-yes, definitely two weeks ago, I took a group of people like him up the mountain there." He mentioned with pride as he saw Ozul's face lit up. Deeso overheard the conversation and approached closer.

"Was this a large group? We have been searching for his family. This lines up too well with what we've been hearing." Deeso commented as the man shrugged his shoulders.

"It is possible. To my surprise, they also valued the importance of our mountain. They wished to stay up there and try to build a community much like the one we have here."

"Are you sure it was really them?" Ozul asked, he'd been burned before on this topic. Cikya rested her hand on his shoulder while listening.

I hope we find these people soon. Ozul has helped us through so much, he's earned the rest. Cikya thought.

"I recognize that weapon of yours. It's not one we see around here but one was given as a gift to our leader as passage rather than the usual meat. An exotic, but one certainly worth looking at." The man commented looking at Ozul's blowgun.

"Thank you for this. You say that we can find those who went through here up that mountain?" Deeso questioned as she looked up to see the vast landforms before her.

"Without doubt. Those who seek passage to the Far North must go through these mountains. As it so happens, I remember seeing the sky alight one night when the meteors flew. I saw it was past these mountains. The spirits here guided it home." The man said as Zulag stroked his beard.

"Right. Well, Ozul, it seems we're getting ever closer. When we find them...I hope it is everything you expect. It is not a replacement for your lost father, but to be with family is just as well." Deeso said as Ozul nodded to her words.

Ozul waited in anticipation of what was to come, and he felt nervous. For much of his young life, he was ostracized for being different and wondered if this really was the right decision to make. He remembered his father and his dying wish for him to join the others, it was what needed to be done. Deeso looked towards the mountain and her companions. The challenge of the climb would be hardly difficult for her, the real challenge is what she would do when she found Sadal once more.

Now She May Rest

Ozul and Cikya decided to take the reins on hunting this time as Deeso and Zulag were exhausted. Their system worked well, as they were silent much of the time but used gestures to communicate. Although Cikya could hear fine, Ozul felt it was better for him not to draw attention to the two as they looked for things. Cikya adjusted the string around her neck and held the whistle that Ozul had made for her long ago. She used it a few times during their journey when she got lost. The ability to contact each other for assistance over long distances was invaluable. The mountains to Cikya were certainly a cursed place; she heard from The Aligned that going there had an energy that was alien and unforgiving. Although she had these fears, she kept a brave face for the others as she remembered the job they needed to do. Ozul needed to get to his family in one piece, and Sadal needed to be brought back. It was the only way she could restore her place back at The Broken Bone, or so she thought.

They left early and allowed Deeso and Zulag to sleep soundly. Ozul held his fingers to his mouth as Cikya nodded happily. She wasn't sure what they were going to find, but the mountains yielded goats among other things of interest. She adjusted her crown and brought her staff with her. She recently made a new backpack to hold more things. She kept a few of Ozul's figurines in her pack. Ozul's admiration and affection for Cikya was a running joke among them as he spent the most time with her, but she didn't mind. Cikya kept them with the utmost care as she imbued them with protective magic. She tapped her knees ready to go as Ozul nodded. Ozul looked through his blowgun tube like a telescope to try and sight any prey that would be worth hunting. The sun's rays were bright and by keeping focused, he could see far better. He squinted and briefly moved it around. Ozul's focus was steadfast as he jumped in anticipation.

I wonder what's over here. Those two over there failed once again to find anything good. I haven't seen anything particularly enticing. Cikya thought as she looked to make sure Ozul was keeping up.

"I see...Oh! There it is! Cikya, come closer!" Ozul said, covering his mouth as he forgot he needed to stay quiet.

Cikya walked towards Ozul who remained pointing at the target. It was a ram grazing not too far from the hills that were adjacent to them. Alone, it should be easy enough to take down. Cikya signed directions to Ozul as he nodded. Ozul did the same, offering a slightly different approach. Cikya considered her options and shrugged in agreement.

"Ozul, once you start crawling, scare the ram and I will strike it with my staff. If I'm not close enough, use your blowgun once it climbs up." Cikya proposed to him in sign. Ozul reminded Cikya of the different darts that he made and to be very careful not to get them confused if she accidentally touched one. She nodded and rubbed the top of his head, prompting an awkward smile from Ozul.

Now that the two knew the plan, it was time for action. Ozul crawled along the ground slowly while Cikya walked casually towards the ram. The ram was a skittish type, but it lacked a fear of humans. She remained still and noted that this creature wasn't hostile. It wasn't a show worthy kill, but it would get them fed. The ram stared at Cikya briefly and then went back down to eating. She inched closer to the animal as she tried to guess its comfort range before she would be perceived as a threat. Ozul had gotten considerably close as he waited for a signal from Cikya to proceed. She waved her hand, which prompted the ram to look at her again, but it was enough for Ozul. He reared up and let out a yell, which caused the ram to go into a panic just as they planned. Instead of running towards the hill, it ran straight for Cikya.

Cikya waited for the ram to charge her as she rolled to the side, just barely clearing the horns. Their usual maneuvers were a bit more exhausting at the higher elevation, but she could still impress. Ozul loaded a dart and shot in its general direction, hoping to land a hit on the creature but he missed. He moved to load another. Ozul took a deep breath before running in her direction. Cikya stomped her staff on the ground twice before using it to divert direction and struck the animal's front leg as it came closer. The momentum of the charge caused it to fall over. She knew that attempting to crack the animal's skull would be impossible with the horns, so as the ram attempted to get up, she beat it as hard as she could with the staff. It let out a few pained cries as it frantically spun around trying to attack Cikya. Ozul loaded a poison dart and launched it with a direct hit into the animal's skin. It took some moments for the poison to act as Ozul waited. After he used the rest of his darts, he hoped they didn't run into anything else dangerous. With a final hit, Cikya settled it down and wiped the sweat that accumulated on her.

"Bit of a waste, but I think we did fine." Ozul said as he took a moment to catch his breath.

Cikya ran to Ozul and gave him a tight hug which he appreciated. Their hard work finally paid off, and now they could all be fed. Cikya looked at the deceased ram and felt around her empty backpack. She flared her nostrils in annoyance as she realized what had just happened.

"Forgot my knife. I'll send Ozul to grab it while I guard the kill." Cikya thought.

Cikya tapped Ozul's shoulder and told him to head towards the direction of camp. They were only about twenty minutes away, which was light work, even at a higher elevation than they were used to. Cikya looked around as she waited for Ozul to come back. She sighed internally as she saw a familiar face appear up on the hill above her. It was a dhole that was clearly hungry.

"These things again? Toles. Go away! This is our kill." Cikya thought, as she tried to scare it away by making a lot of noise and kicking up dirt. The dhole went away as she expected but noticed that there were now more that appeared. She counted four, which while irritating wasn't a problem for someone with her training.

The proud dholes descended towards Cikya and the dead ram. Although she felt she could be capable, she didn't feel like facing them alone. She decided to drag the kill as best as she could, but the ram was heavier than expected. Cikya's attempts to remove the kill was an ill-fated mistake, as the dholes growled towards her. More dholes converged on the hill with their eyes pointed towards her. Cikya, seeing she was clearly outnumbered, gave up the kill. She kicked it in frustration before walking off. Cikya found she was still being followed by those four troublesome dholes, but from a further distance. She tested this theory by standing still before she retreated and kept her eyes on them. The dholes continued to glare at her as she did so and closed the gap between them. Cikya knew that immediately running would cause them to chase her, so now she had to think of a plan. She remembered her whistle and blew. Ozul was on his way back from camp now, as he heard the familiar whistle. The echo of the mountain faintly reached his ears as he turned around. His pace steadied quickly as he wondered what Cikya could have run into.

"Cikya blew the whistle, I need to hurry." Ozul said as he was running back.

Cikya felt her heart jump out of her chest as she saw that after she blew the whistle, all twenty of the dholes now looked in her direction. The four dholes that were nearby pursued her and she froze. Cikya could only pray that Ozul heard her call, but what could he possibly do? Cikya ran in the opposite direction as the dholes started to chase her. She knew this was a fruitless endeavor, so she hoped that she could hold her ground while the rest of the pack was at bay. Although she spurned Ronkalk for his treatment of her, his words carried on in her mind.

When faced with odds that surround you, the path will open to the strongest. Give it your all. Cikya remembered the words of Ronkalk.

Cikya managed to find a new resolve as she adjusted her staff. She baited the dholes who attacked haphazardly and gave decisive blows. She hoped to prove that attacking them wasn't worth the effort of the hunt. The dholes lunged at Cikya, but one only managed to bite part of her skirt, tearing a portion of it to the ground. She could almost cry in sheer bliss as she managed to skirt the dholes and head towards Ozul's direction, running as fast as she ever could. She threw whatever she had on her, hoping to dissuade the animals. Ozul saw that Cikya was converging quickly on his location and was primed to go back and get help. There wasn't much he could do as he ran to Cikya and hoped to serve as a distraction long enough for her to come by.

Not too shortly after, Zulag awoke, his eyes practically sleep deprived as he woke up with the urge to urinate. He walked some distance from camp and relieved himself in the open as he could hear the faintest echo of a whistle. His expression perked up in surprise as he realized the source of the sound. Cikya blew the whistle again as she ran to Ozul, the two just moments away from one another. There was little time to waste as Ozul saw the dholes retreat.

"You made it! We need to go back now." Ozul said as he noticed that the dholes veered off course.

What Ozul failed to realize is that the dholes didn't vanish, they only changed their position to attack Cikya. Her second blow of the whistle sealed her fate. The two ran only for Cikya to see the same three dholes had met them on another hill as they called for their comrades to arrive. Without any way out now, the dholes lunged towards Cikya, and toppled her instantly while Ozul tripped over himself trying to recover. Cikya fought as hard as she could, but she knew her time was up with more dholes on the way. She shed her staff earlier so that it wouldn't weigh her down while she was running. A mistake that wouldn't have helped her one bit. She thrashed around and attempted to kick the dholes, but it was for naught as they bit into her. Portions of her flesh were eviscerated as she got Ozul's attention. Cikya gritted her teeth through the pain and realized she needed to deliver a message that only Ozul could deliver.

"Ozul...! My sweet boy! Tell Deeso...and...Zulag...I'm sorry!" Cikya spoke for the first time as she strained to get her words out.

Although she had a long way to go, Cikya's injuries weren't permanent as it was originally declared. She found that she could say simple sentences, but she hated how her voice sounded and chose silence instead. Her tone of voice was harsh to the ears but to Ozul it felt like a warm hug. Ozul's eyes were filled with tears and once again, he was forced to run from danger. A taller figure could be barely made out in the distance as he found it difficult to see. Those would be Cikya's last words. The dholes to Ozul, had taken great pleasure in causing her pain as she bled to death. Her right arm was dismembered at the socket and exposed bone and sinew where it now became part of the circle of life. A dhole chewed on it for some time before letting it rot in the sun. The other two dholes ripped Cikya apart, with her clothes scattered everywhere. A mixture of fur and blood soaked the landscape. Her flesh was torn from her legs, with claw marks down her stomach where blood pooled. Her left foot was now nothing more than a chewed nub. Her eyes were still intact but devoid of all life now. She was also disemboweled as her intestines were bit into.

"I heard the whistle-" Zulag said, his mouth agape as he saw the three dholes converging on something. He quickly looked to see that Ozul was alone and ran as fast as he could.

"Cikya! I'm coming, hold on!" Zulag said with utter desperation in his voice as Ozul pitifully followed.

Ozul grabbed his arm and shook his head while crying as Zulag stepped forward to see what remained of Cikya's body. The dholes that had surrounded Cikya's body now looked at their new target which was Zulag. He didn't breathe as he withdrew a knife from his side and launched with fury at the dhole that dared growl at him. The knife had pierced right through the dhole with ease. These were ones he forged from obsidian and were incredibly deadly. It was dead on the spot. Zulag yelled in agony as he ran towards the dholes that moved away with their fun now ruined. He threw another knife at the slower of the two dholes who now bled with their leg injured. Zulag withdrew a knife from the first dhole's corpse and walked over to the other dhole. He embedded the knife into the dhole's throat and decapitated it. He stomped on the animal's head repeatedly with his foot and threw it as far as he could.

Ozul could only watch in horror as he saw Cikya torn apart before his very eyes. He cried again, not only due to her death but that the death in question was his own fault. He thought what could have made the dholes want to attack and he realized that his whistle must have upset them somehow. He felt worthless and miserable. Even when he had the chance to save her, there wasn't anything he could do. If he threw himself in the ring, they would have both perished. Cikya already sustained enough damage from her wounds.

I loved them, and I killed them both. My father and now Cikya. Eshe was right all along. My weakness killed these people. Ozul thought. He let his tears flow to the soil as he sat down and crossed his legs. He put his head into his arms and lamented all that happened.

Ozul didn't dare approach Zulag now, but Zulag took the initiative as he absorbed all the damage to Cikya's body. He closed his eyes and cried himself. He hugged her corpse and noticed that despite all the damage to her body, her face remained relatively intact. He set her down and closed her eyes out of respect. The signature bone crown that never left her side remained on top. Once a symbol of the priesthood and all it stood for, Zulag crumbled as he was assaulted with a flurry of thoughts. Zulag took it upon himself to remove it, where a portion of Cikya's hair flowed down her body. Zulag had never once touched it, but upon seeing it, he was filled once again with rage. Not too far from his location was a boulder. He threw it against the boulder and watched the pieces shatter into bits.

"You are redeemed Cikya. Your student failed his master." Zulag muttered to himself.

"What happened Ozul..." Zulag asked, his voice very hoarse.

Zulag saw no need to blame Ozul for what happened. He was aware that his fighting prowess paled in comparison to their years of experience, and that it was evident that Cikya's selfless nature is why he remained alive. Although Ozul had since proven his worth to the group, he was still just a kid after all. Ozul attempted to explain what happened, where Zulag could only get the bits and pieces of what occurred before his eyes expanded on the dholes that dispersed back to the midst of their territory.

"Toles-So many-" Ozul said, unable to get the words out of his mouth. Zulag decided to walk over and placed a hand on his shoulder as he squatted on his knees to face Ozul at eye level.

"It's alright, they got what they wanted. I want you to go wake Deeso. There's something I need to do." Zulag communicated to him. Ozul was not worried as he still was armed with his blowgun, but he never felt worse. Though, before he left to do as he was told, he needed to tell Zulag the final message from Cikya.

"Before Cikya died, she spoke to me, Zulag." Ozul said, his voice quieter than usual. Zulag just barely picked up on what he said but nodded.

"What do you mean she spoke to you? What did she have to say?" Zulag asked as he looked at him with a raised eyebrow. Zulag felt great shame knowing that he wasn't there for Cikya when she needed him the most.

"I heard her voice Zulag. It was a waterfall that flowed with beauty." Ozul commented to her.

"What...? Only I know what she sounds like." Zulag said, his own voice now cracking as he started to cry again.

"She said to tell you and Deeso that she was sorry. I do not know why she felt this way, but that is what she told me." Ozul said, before going to give Zulag some space to himself.

After some time passed, Ozul returned with Deeso to find Zulag still in the same spot. Her reaction was more stifled than the other two, but she shared great sorrow in seeing Cikya's demise.

"Oh...Oh no..." She said audibly as she looked at every detail.

Deeso knew that none of them were invincible, and therefore she sought to live every day as she could, but seeing this broke a small part of her. Cikya sacrificed everything to give Deeso a substitute for the love that Sadal once had in her life for a sense of normalcy. She remembered the first time Cikya packed her bag with a banana, her favorite food that only very few knew of. Her anger towards Sadal increased tenfold. Cikya now lay dead because of Sadal's inability to come home the first time they asked, and one of their own had to suffer this terrible fate. Although Cikya died in battle, Deeso and Zulag knew that she struggled and died with immense pain from the state of her body.

"I will get a grave prepared." Deeso said, before being stopped by Zulag.

"We can't just dig a grave. There's something we need to do first. Ozul. You dig the grave. I need to do a ritual for Cikya." Zulag said to the two of them. Deeso gave it some thought, but she decided out of her bond with Cikya and respect for Zulag, she decided to participate further.

"What can I do to help?" She asked. Ozul gave a small smile as he knew it was a big deal for Deeso to touch anything regarding the spirits. Zulag was also surprised but gave a well-informed answer.

"Cikya's spirit needs nourishment so she can watch us for the rest of our mission. This is simple. I will use this knife to cut my arm, and I will cut your arm. She will drink until she is full and then we can bury her. When I was first her student, she gave me some of her vitality. I would like to return it." Zulag said. He asked Deeso once more if she was really willing to help. She extended her arm out and took the motion in stride. She was surprised how smooth the cut was not having worked with obsidian before. The two bled profusely and felt lightheaded while Ozul dug. He looked over at the two of them and went to camp to get supplies to heal their injuries.

Zulag and Deeso bled sufficiently and applied pressure on their exit wounds. Ozul silently wrapped their arms with some spare fibers from his bag and returned to his task. Ozul labored on the grave with love as his nails were whittled down to nubs from moving mass amounts of soil with his bare hands. Cikya was lifted gently by Zulag and given a final embrace before it was time to let her rest. Ozul decided to leave as he felt his emotions overtaking him again. It would be easier for him to go to camp instead while Deeso and Zulag finished preparations. The two sat in silence for some time. Zulag wasn't inclined to leave as he closed his eyes and sat at the grave. Deeso decided going back to camp wasn't worth the energy as she felt tired still. Zulag's hands were free, and Deeso decided to grab on tightly as the two mourned Cikya together. They held hands until the night came upon them.

In The Shade

Amid Cikya's death, Ozul was unsure on how to process his emotions. He internalized her death as his fault and nothing would change his mind. He slept alone the previous night with only the fire as his comfort. He couldn't find comfort among Deeso or Zulag who left him on his own since yesterday. Ozul observed the two traveled together more often over their adventure, but that was of little importance. At the base of the Caucasus Mountains, he knew that there was a crossroads ahead once they ascended further, but that was not for him to do. The three of them arrived earlier than expected, where any day now Ozul's family would hopefully be around as planned. The news of the surviving Forest Seeker caravan from the village at The Gorge once filled him with excitement, but now he was tired and just wanted a home of his own. He looked at the debris of stuff left behind from yesterday's events, evident of Zulag's rage at the world. Ozul's stuff remained untouched. Ozul sat alone and he decided to walk in whatever direction may come to him. Before leaving, however, his eyes turned to a log cut with Deeso's axe. Ozul added extra fuel to their fire to generate smoke. The smoke was visible from a vast distance as Ozul's face perspired from the sheer heat. He took some spare branches from Deeso's backpack that she left behind and cracked small ends of the pieces to use as a trail to find his way back.

The terrain of the mountain's valley held a mixed forest where trees clustered only to reveal sparse pockets of plains. The peaks of the mountain, for all their beauty, were topped with snow far above. Ozul saw nothing but gentle sloping hills patterned with trees, as he stood in awe of what he witnessed. At his side was his blowgun, he looked to find a snake that could provide him with the forbidden nectar he craved. Ozul remembered he needed to focus on what was important, aside from clearing his head, he needed to find out information about Sadal. Prior to Cikya's death, the four of them successfully managed to pinpoint her area and would search gradually for her as time came to pass. She was following the advice of those who came and went. Ozul and the others knew that in order to reach the meteor, they had to be somewhere in this valley. Ozul hyperventilated in worry as he feared that Cikya's sacrifice would be in vain if he failed to find Sadal.

Ozul's eyes were red as he could barely contain himself, his mind recycling the images of Cikya's mangled body, the dholes ripping her alive and scattering her entrails in sick amusement. Forest Seekers believed that nature had a right to reclaim what had sprung up from it, even their own kind, but the dholes hadn't bothered to eat her for sustenance. It was only for fun in his eyes. He had never known true hate until that day. He wiped his running nose with his elbow as he saw a goat perched on a rock. He studied the distance between him and the goat to figure that it would make a good target. He still had regular darts that with the right amount of wind would be able to get the kill before it would run off. He slowly crawled on the ground, unknowing that there was another among him.

For Jih, coming to the mountains was that of an ancestral visit he had no knowledge of. His people occupied this land long before his time. Below his feet were the bones of the ancients who lived a thousand lifetimes before Jih gave breath. He was walking for a few hours now with little success bringing anything home worth eating. He came across a few potential picks, but the competition with predators was something he wanted to avoid. Jih briefly lifted his fur coat and felt his wound. The brisk wind of the mountains came below as he felt it much cooler than he was used to. His wound healed better than expected, but Jih felt sensitivity from his encounter. Jih's thoughts also regarded his own mortality. He managed to evade death on many occasions through sheer experience, but he had a fleeting feeling his injury was the precursor for much worse to come. His confidence was broken in many ways, and it would take time to build again. His eyes saw a goat on a rock not too far from his position, and he decided to scale the hill to sneak up behind the animal as it sat. From what he could see, there was not a soul around.

Jih decided to take a page from watching Sadal and with enough force, threw his spear at the goat. He watched it flail around incessantly as he pursued the kill. The spear's flight was not smooth like that of Sadal's shattersticks, rather it was at a heavy arc where Jih launched it high, and it quickly gained speed as it reached closer to the ground. Although he infinitely preferred to run towards the prey, a new strategy had to be tested at some point. He was fortunate that it worked, but a failed attempt would leave him running to get his weapon. Jih concluded this had situational use at best but would be worth telling Dran about. Jih gave a sigh of relief, as the goat did him the courtesy of sliding down the hill with his spear sticking out. Jih removed the spear from the goat and dragged it behind him.

Ozul spoke quietly to himself as he noticed a figure managing to beat him to the punch. He debated blowing his dart at the man who stole his kill in frustration but decided that effort would be fruitless. He stood up and watched as the figure descended with the kill and walked off. Jih sighted this, and normally gave no mind, but he saw that the person in question was a child. While Jih often held little patience for children, something compelled him to look a bit closer. He was around the same age as when Jih first set out with his friends on their Recognition Hunt, and he saw something of himself in Ozul. Ozul turned around and Jih urged him to approach.

"Come closer! Jih will make amends." Jih addressed Ozul as he gently lifted his hand up.

Ozul heard Jih's voice and realized something important. Out of all the people in the world, he managed to find not only the Stone Breaker Eshe talked about in detail to him many months ago, but the knowledge that Sadal was somewhere near this man's camp. Ozul remembered his mission but was too awestruck to bother using deception against him. All he needed to know was that they were somewhere in this valley, and the rest would be up to Deeso and Zulag to find out. Ozul looked with some hesitation, but he complied with Jih's instructions. Jih took the kill to sit under a tree with a set of tools at his disposal. He removed his backpack and loosened the knot he tied to keep it packed. Inside he took out some basic implements to start a fire, and a hand-axe so that he could cut the meat. Jih couldn't leave empty handed, but he decided to give Ozul a lion's share of the meat, and a horn of the goat as it was male. Jih breathed into his hands and rubbed them together to make a bit of warmth. He noticed right away the boy's silence, much like his own, but there was something more behind it. Jih gave him a stare that unnerved Ozul slightly and forced him to speak.

"Why are you here?" Ozul asked Jih who seemed confused at such a question.

Jih pointed to the ground where the goat lay and gestured to the meat he was now primed to cut. Jih grasped his hand-axe and ran his finger down the side and ensured that it was still sharp. He pressed the hand-axe into the limbs of the goat. He saw that Ozul returned the stare at Jih, which emboldened him to give a more sarcastic response this time.

"Jih can ask same question. Tell Jih your name." Jih commented while he worked.

Ozul kept himself silent as he studied Jih closely. Ozul mouthed his name quietly as he couldn't bring himself to speak loudly, but Jih was able to decipher the boy's name through his lips.

"Sadness is on your face, Ozul. Speak to Jih." He said, his eyes unmoved from his task. He stopped as he waited for Ozul to say something before continuing.

"Someone close to me is gone and I am responsible...Does this feeling ever leave you?" Ozul asked, his voice fraught with worry. Jih was reminded of some of the younger children back in Sundaland who could barely look the adults in the eye after grabbing too much meat from the community pile, but this guilt was far more rooted in a serious cause.

"Guilt is a Weypeu. It eats even when full." Jih commented, as he gave Ozul another look over. He saw that the person before him was no older than about thirteen at this point. Jih also recognized that he was a Forest Seeker as he used Eshe as a frame of reference. Jih wondered if Ozul valued the grass and trees of the mountains as much as the jungle. For someone of his kind, he was far away from home. Jih saw this as something else they had in common.

Jih looked next to him and decided to give his hunting spear as a gift. He looked at Ozul's blowgun with worry as he knew that bamboo to replace it didn't grow in these lands. Jih had a few extras back at his main camp with the others, so he felt this was a sufficient gift to soothe some of the boy's ills. Ozul gave a slightly concerned look, but reached over and felt its touch. Ozul now owned a spear given to him by one of the Stone Breakers. He was in awe of the solid craftsmanship. It lacked engravings and although the blade looked simplistic from what he's seen of Thunderfeet construction, the weight of the spear from the wood was quite satisfying. It was unwieldy for his height much to Jih's amusement as he attempted to hold the weapon. Ozul dragged it along the ground behind him.

"Ozul will grow one day. Use the spear of Jih for great kills." Jih explained as Ozul quietly bowed his head in thanks.

"Have you lost someone Jih?" Ozul questioned.

"Of course. Countless. The most important lost was Hyu. Hyu was selfless and helped others. Jih saved many but failed to save her. Jih does not know her last words. This brings much shame to Jih." Jih mentioned while Ozul's head darted to him in response.

"And do you see this Hyu in your dreams? I have only nightmares now." Ozul asked.

"What are these nightmares?" Jih asked Ozul, as he was familiar with horrid dreams of his own.

Although Ozul had grown especially close to his friends, much of his internal thoughts were kept bottled inside, feelings of that sort of nature were not often discussed. In the times that they were, it regarded rituals that Zulag and Cikya practiced that Ozul had no knowledge of.

"I see her alive and happy. A great smile, she always had one-and then..." Ozul said with his words trailing off. Jih met Ozul's eyes and encouraged him to keep going.

"She begins to turn a dark red. There is blood everywhere that rises from the ground. Her limbs separate from one another and all that is left is screaming. Harsh wails that are a mighty wind. Her mangled body follows me every time I close my eyes. I-I gave her the whistle! The whistle that made the Toles mad!" Ozul said getting up now as he kicked the ground in frustration. He was beyond his own control as he sobbed once more and put his head into his hands.

"Everything has always been my fault! And it will always be this way. This is what happened because I broke The Vow! This is how balance is made. I can only be so happy and yet, it all comes crashing down." Ozul said, with his words reduced to a whimper.

Jih could only sit and listen as he gave an awkward expression while listening to Ozul's tale. He hadn't expected someone of his age to deliver such a vivid description of such a horrible thing. He gathered quickly that Cikya's death was some sort of hunting accident involving dholes. Inexperience was on his face and Jih felt no blame could be given for things that one did not know.

"Ozul. The world is cruel. There is a reason you live now. Honor her legacy and live well. This is what Hyu wanted for Jih. This one would want this for you too." Jih said as he gave Ozul a small poke that drew his attention. Past his tears, Ozul listened well to Jih's words. Living in fear and pity would do nothing to make Cikya's death better. There was nothing he could have done to save her from the dholes. Ozul's feelings of sadness receded into general emptiness with a hollow feeling coming over him. In time, he would grow past this as all experiences mold us, but for now, he needed to set things right.

"Jih has made camp west of here. Not far, if Ozul wants to come." Jih offered to Ozul. Ozul took this news wholeheartedly as he thanked Jih for his talk, but he remembered his obligation to the others.

"Thank you, Stone Breaker-" Ozul said as he was stopped by the hand of Jih. Just like how he conducted himself with Eshe, Jih quickly told Ozul to refer to him only by his actual name.

"Jih, it is then. Until next time..." Ozul commented awkwardly as he looked behind him a few times to see Jih still sitting by the fire for some time in thought.

Ozul bowed his head once more and took his gifted things with him. He wished that he could have asked Jih an assortment of questions that his people wanted to know for some time, but he hadn't announced to Deeso or Zulag that he was gone. He feared they would worry about him now that he didn't have Cikya to watch him. Now that Jih had given him the directions to their camp, it was only a matter of time for the two groups to converge and find Sadal once and for all. Ozul imagined the might of this confrontation and if he would have to witness this before his rendezvous with his family. Deeso promised Ozul that she was only concerned about Sadal and would leave The Stone Breaker known as Jih alone but a small piece of him wondered if this was really the truth.

Ozul's Odyssey

With Cikya's death motivating them to go just a bit further, Deeso, Zulag and Ozul sat and ate a small breakfast together, now emptier than usual. Deeso hadn't realized how quiet it would be without someone who made no sound to begin with. Just the day before, Ozul managed to run into Jih on his travels and get the information about his and Sadal's potential whereabouts due west of where they made camp. After delivering this information to the two of them, Ozul thought about what would happen next. Despite everything he could to support their goals, Ozul knew that he needed to think about what his future could be. If Sadal was taken alive and he joined them, where would he go? The Broken Bone would kill him on sight if he survived the venture back to begin with. Living on his own on the mountain was a terrible idea as well. Ozul felt his options were limited and decided to accept the offer to become part of these new Forest Seekers. Ozul found from that his first visit of them, they knew nothing of his father or the path he followed. It saddened him to find that the caravan he had searched for so long was a completely different group of people, but he knew it would ultimately be the best path for him to go.

"Deeso. Zulag. I made my decision. I am to go with the others of my kind here. They may not be my family, but they will give me a life for now." Ozul mentioned. The two of them realized early that this was the choice he was most likely going to make. After they finished their meal, Deeso got up and waited for the other two to get ready.

"I suppose that's it then. We found Sadal and now you've found...something. We will be in this mountain for some time after if you choose to change your mind. The Wanderer life is something that can be hard for people." Deeso said as Ozul looked at her.

Though much of their early relationship was transactional, she grew to value Ozul's input on many things. Zulag got up and equipped his gear for the day while looking at the spot where Cikya would have slept. Her death naturally hit him the hardest. Ozul rummaged through his pack and came across a few belongings, keepsakes he gathered throughout his time with the three of them. Ozul originally decided to keep Cikya's whistle for himself, but he figured it would have much better value for Zulag. He decided to remove it and stuff it in Zulag's bag without much reaction from him.

Zulag was quiet as he and Deeso followed Ozul's directions to find this party. Their walk was brief, as this new group of Forest Seekers made their distaste of mountain life known. They sat around mostly observing formations in the clouds and conjuring up stories about the faces seen on the mountain. The altitude change was also of concern to this group. Ozul was given some time to decide, and now that he was ready to do so, he was surprised saying good-bye would be the hardest part. The outskirts of the small Forest Seeker dwellings had most sleeping under the stars as reliable material could be hard to find. One of them, an old woman, saw in her silent observations from previous days that one Thunderfoot was missing from these lands, but Ozul was here. Ozul looked behind him to see some inviting faces, a first where he would not be ridiculed, or manipulated like that of Eshe. He looked at Deeso and Zulag before speaking.

"I put something in your bag before we left. The whistle that belonged to Cikya, please take it." Ozul said to Zulag as he nodded in agreement.

"Thanks." Zulag stated with a monotone voice.

Deeso hadn't bothered to say much, anything of importance that she had to say was used up quite some time ago. Now all she needed to do was focus her mind on her original goal. Much to her surprise, Ozul gave Deeso a tight hug that was slowly returned as she lowered her arms.

"When you find Sadal, I hope that the two of you find the peace you are looking for. It is a simple request to make. I hope you will not need your axe and knives to bring her home. She will understand what we have gone through." Ozul commented.

Ozul's eyes shifted to Zulag who folded his arms. The young boy smiled and decided to give Zulag a hug as well. Due to their difference in height, Ozul's hug of Zulag was mostly wrapped around his waist. As Ozul let go, he gave Zulag a small punch to the gut that caused Deeso to let out a rare laugh. Perhaps some of their teachings finally rubbed off on him. Deeso nodded and gave Ozul the space he needed to feel comfortable to finally leave. Ozul looked behind him and at his friends before making his way over to the interior of the camp. Ozul turned around as he thought he heard a voice. His eyes looked to Deeso first, but he saw that it was Zulag instead.

"Ozul, catch." Zulag said, with a throw of a spare knife to the ground beside him. Ozul crouched and picked up the knife. He admired its sheen and sharpness that only Zulag could give. He offered one last wave to the two before sitting himself near a campfire to listen to a developing tale.

Deeso and Zulag walked together and agreed that they didn't need to look back. Ozul was to their knowledge, safe and sound. Now that the pair were alone once more, the reality of their situation set in. Sadal was nearby and while they talked on occasion on how they imagined handling this situation, it was the topic of discussion for their walk back.

"Ozul's directions told us that Sadal's camp is to the west. I haven't found anything that shows her being here, but I'm inclined to believe him. If this is true, what do we do? We have no supplies for her. She could be injured or something as well." Deeso stated to Zulag.

"If we find her, and she decides not to follow us, we have rope left behind. She needs to own up to her mistakes and be punished as Ronkalk willed it. She can walk or we will drag her." Zulag commented.

"From what you told me back when the land was flat and hot, Sadal doesn't seem to be willing to listen. What are we going to do, if talking doesn't work?" Zulag added on, waiting for Deeso's reaction.

"That's just it. I dwelled on this for a while, and I fear that Sadal's delusions of thinking the meteor will fix everything will be our band's downfall. If it comes to pass that she attacks me or you...she will need to be killed. I thought I saw something left in her, and while I still feel this way, we must be realistic. I can't trust her if she won't put the safety of our people below something unproven again." Deeso stated coldly.

The two made their way back to camp, a segment of grass still fresh with Ozul's imprint from his body. Zulag went ahead and lit the fire while he took a deep breath. The pair evaluated their injuries and tried to think of a better outcome than what they had in front of them.

"Things will be different with her back, I thought I hated you, but it would seem you made quite a name with Sadal herself. I wasn't aware your rivalry was so extensive." Deeso joked, with her tone having some adopted optimism. Zulag could tell that it was false hope, but he decided to play along.

"I'm sure my uncle would just force me to have Sadal on my hunting team. Now that's a fate worse than death for someone like her." Zulag jeered as he looked into the campfire.

A large silence engulfed the two as the ambient sounds of blowing wind picked up. Zulag's eyes were focused on tracking the movement of the flames as he found them enchanting. Normally he would call upon Cikya to explain what he saw, but now he could only be left with his own inferences. Deeso's eyes turned to her axe, it was some time since blood of another human touched it. Like a hungry vessel, it called out to her, the call for violence. Deeso was a master of restraint, the last thing she wanted to do was take up arms against Sadal, but if it needed to be done, she would not be afraid. The pair briefly looked into each other's eyes, there was a synergy that was unsurpassed with months on the trail behind them.

"Zulag." Deeso commented as Zulag lifted his head.

"Remember in the land that was dry and hot, I told you about my dream? It comes and goes but I see it well now. The promised valley after the climb through arduous circumstance. The people who looked at me for leadership. The ones responsible for giving us the good life we crave. I see a collection of people like me, a band of Wanderers given purpose. No longer needing to move from place to place so often. One of acceptance and kindness." Deeso said, twisting a branch between her fingers.

"You haven't mentioned it in a while. What about it? Has the image gotten clearer for you?" Zulag inquired with curiosity.

"I know who should be at my side. A strong right hand to support me when things are tough." Deeso mentioned as she gestured to her Wanderer's Mark.

Zulag let Deeso's words hang as Deeso let him gather the significance behind her words. While their adventure started out as exceptionally contentious, the strength of their bond increased exponentially to the threats of the outside world. It was an amusing prospect as the two understood each other more than anyone else. Both wondered what would have happened if Sadal decided to stay and life remained as it was. It was a harrowing thought to realize that their growth came through such circumstances, but it was welcomed. Deeso broke the silence that hung over them as she felt her point was made.

"Do you have my back?" Deeso asked as the wind of the mountain coursed through the landscape. Their fur coverings were just enough to keep them from shivering. Zulag looked confused at Deeso's question, she was certainly still alive, so he assumed that he did his job well enough. Zulag nodded in agreement with her question.

"Of course I do." Zulag spoke with certainty. With Cikya and Ozul gone, all he had left was Deeso.

"Good. I knew you did, but I just needed to hear it. Tomorrow when we find her, we need to work as one, more than ever. Whoever gets in our way, we offer them two paths. One to live and one to die. We will see what happens." Deeso said, her eyes trained on the campfire as well. She turned her head and gave Zulag a small grin that was returned in kind.

Zulag looked at his bag and reminded Deeso of their low supply of everything. If they were going to accommodate Sadal, either willingly or by force, she needed to have enough to survive the long walk back. He dreaded the descent and having to backtrack The Gorge once more but would brave it all to complete the objective.

"I have not forgotten what you said. A good meal will be waiting for Sadal when she comes with us. Let's go hunt and skin every Tole we find. For Cikya." Deeso said with a small grin as she waited for Zulag.

"For Cikya." Zulag repeated solemnly as he prepared for battle.

The two walked away to pursue a target once more on the high mountains. Today was a day to gather supplies and do what was needed. After the emotional downpour of the past few days, a nice hunt would clear their minds. Tomorrow was the day everything would change for Deeso and Zulag.

Tears of Blood: I

Jih and Narro were sitting some distance away from camp, where with some small laughter exchanged, they started crafting new tools to use for the next hunt. A small pile of debris surrounded them as they worked. Sadal and Trekkal worked to maintain a fire. Their dwelling was under the face of a cliff that jetted out, so they were covered from the elements. To access the flatter areas, they only needed to take a brisk walk up a hill. Sadal could see her breath as the morning was cold and the clouds looked gray. She'd never seen snow before, but the clouds looked promising. She and Trekkal tied animal skins around their ankles to try and keep some heat in as they held their feet towards the fire and moved them away when it became too warm. Sadal had spent plenty of time with Narro and Jih, but she felt she had tried a bit too hard to avoid Trekkal once things with Narro had gotten more serious between them. Trekkal was aware of Sadal's relationship with Narro, but the two rarely addressed the topic at hand, even if it was well open. The two were close on all other matters.

Sadal looked around and absorbed the relative silence around her. She decided to grab her bag and stuffed a few throwing spears inside, and let the bag hang over her shoulder as she did so. Her eyes looked towards Trekkal who was bored as she rolled a rock around. Sadal went up behind her and gave her a random squeeze. Trekkal gasped as she turned around to see Sadal was the one embracing her rather than her brother.

"Lovely Trekkal. Would you like to go on a walk?" Sadal asked, placing her head on Trekkal's shoulder. Trekkal left a mess as always, where she was fiddling with some fibers. She always moved on to the next project before finishing, something that Narro was infuriated by often. Her bone needles of various sizes were also in disarray, and she felt uninspired to make anything.

"Yes. I could use the change. Are we here to hunt, or is there something else you had in mind? It has been a while." Trekkal mentioned, eyeing Sadal's bag on her back. Her view changed to the ground where her sling lay, and a few rocks she whittled down for ammunition. Like Sadal, her outfit had small loops to hold tools and she placed a small bag of sharpened stones inside.

"We should talk." Sadal brought up, her voice lowering even though they were alone.

"Talk? Is there something troubling you Sadal?" Trekkal said with slight confusion on her face. She got up and gestured towards the hill that she wanted to see more of. In her scouting, she saw that there was a spring with a sizable stream an hour out from their location. With any luck, there would be something to eat there and an opportunity to fill their canteens again.

"Jih always has his stories you know, and as for Narro..." Sadal commented, silencing herself as she didn't look at Trekkal. She anticipated the cold emanating from Trekkal at the mention of her brother.

"I am aware of what my brother thinks of you and your relationship. For a long time, I was mad, but I see you as family if you wanted to know. Not like I can get rid of you, big sister." Trekkal said as she gave Sadal a silly grin.

Sadal and Trekkal were only about six months apart in age, but their levels of maturity were certainly variable. She gave Sadal a hearty punch on the arm that came as a sign of relief to her. Sadal laughed nervously and twisted a bit of her hair but felt better. Trekkal allowed Sadal to lead the way. Trekkal's doubts on Sadal's sincerity evaporated some time ago in the forefront of her mind as Sadal and Trekkal grew exceptionally close over their journey. She recalled their synergy on the trail together and while Trekkal still held a distrust of The Youngest, she was more than willing to stick up for Sadal whenever it came up. Trekkal appreciated Sadal's encouragement of her own abilities.

"I've always wondered this, but I figured you would know. Do Peymin sleep?" Sadal asked out of genuine curiosity to Trekkal's shocked face. Trekkal hadn't considered that question before. The stream that Trekkal enthusiastically located had a small fog that carried over it.

The pair walked along the edge of the stream and Sadal reveled in Trekkal talking about her observations about fish. She lifted her head up to get a better view of what was swimming underneath. The water was especially clear that day, and she could see far to where the light reached the bottom.

"You should know this by now, Peymin live in all kinds of water. Some of it tastes like salt, others do not. As for when they sleep, I do not think they do. They would sink to the bottom." Trekkal narrated, pointing at a fish that seemed to be circling around for something. Sadal raised an eyebrow at the strange creatures that had webbed tails swimming in the water some distance away. She noticed a group of them were chewing wood and vanishing into the deeper recesses of the stream.

"What is that thing? Is it tasty?" Sadal pondered as she rubbed her stomach. Their supply of smoked food was starting to run low, and the opportunity to try something new was an exciting option. Trekkal noticed Sadal's excitement but kept her eyes gazed on the fish as she saw it blowing bubbles, which prompted Sadal to look closer.

"I have no name for it, but from what I see, it has brown fur, and they seem to build things that block their movement. I saw one run into a den made of wood earlier." Trekkal explained as she noticed Sadal's gaze.

"The Peymin also move from place to place during the season, like Yaan do." Trekkal added on.

"Where do they go?" Sadal inquired.

"I wish I knew. They seem to never get tired and just swim." Trekkal commented as she pressed onwards.

Trekkal stopped to notice Sadal wasn't to the side of her and wondered what made her stop. Trekkal turned to see Sadal making the face of a fish with her hands flapping on her cheeks like gills. She cracked a smile that prompted Sadal to go further. Her laugh was boisterous as she massaged her stomach from laughing too hard. The two laughed with such gusto that wasn't shown for a while. Their sounds carried over through the mostly empty land before them.

Sadal and Trekkal's laughter were cut short by what seemed like the yell of some person. It was long thought that they were alone but the two turned their heads to the source of the sound. Trekkal dragged Sadal with her, as she hoped to see what was going on. If they were injured, there was little they could do for them, but they had to try. To Trekkal, it seemed like they were in trouble. Some of Narro's spirit rubbed off on her in their travels.

"Hello! Are you injured? We can carry you to camp! We have little supplies but..." Trekkal offered and waved her hands out as she yelled. Although Trekkal was calm, she noticed Sadal looked uneasy and the gears turned in her mind.

"We should keep moving. I don't trust those people Trekkal. We don't know who's on these mountains and what they have for us. Remember, Jih's still injured." Sadal mentioned, which prompted Trekkal to nod in agreement and keep walking, this time in a slightly different direction to keep their distance.

"Sadal, you worried me just a second ago. Is everything alright?" Trekkal asked as she placed her hand on Sadal's arm.

"We need to stay focused. Just remain calm." Sadal said not looking at Trekkal. Although she had used that as a reply for Trekkal, it was reassurance for herself instead.

As the two started their slow way to the plains, Trekkal could make out what she heard earlier. To her relief, they were fine, but she saw that one voice was two. They were members of The Youngest, adorned with furs to suit the colder weather of the mountains. With a better frame of reference, Sadal knew who her mystery people were. It was none other than Deeso and Zulag. Deeso and Zulag had a rough week between the death of Cikya and Ozul leaving their party, they relied on each other as a team even more than they anticipated. They were exhausted and tired from fighting off all the mountain's hostile threats that came their way. Zulag's hands were in wrappings and Deeso appeared to be sleep-deprived. Much like themselves, Deeso and Zulag kept themselves covered in fur to keep the cold away. Deeso wore a warm down covering with brown goat fur while Zulag wore a well-crafted jacket constructed from the dholes he slayed in their time on the mountain after Cikya's death.

Sadal was dismayed at how they managed to find her. She assumed that Deeso got the message from their first talk, but it was clear this wasn't the case. Zulag's appearance was difficult to disguise, and therefore she knew why they were here. Their expressions looked tired but the strength of their partnership and commitment to the mission kept them going. Deeso lifted her finger and pointed in recognition of Sadal's gait. She was an excellent tracker after all, it would only be a matter of time before the two were reunited again. Ozul's words were true just as she hoped.

"Zulag. We found her." Deeso said in a low voice to him as he let out a small grunt in acknowledgement. The two pairs met on opposite ends of the plains for them to stop as one saw the other. Deeso and Zulag on one side with some space in between, with Sadal and Trekkal on the other. Deeso wasted no time in getting things started. She had sacrificed so much to get things started, and she was filled with anger.

"Sadal! We're here for you. Zulag and I must take you back. We have been this way for over a year now, and you've yet to find your rock. My patience is up." Deeso said as she adjusted her furs with the blowing wind. Her voice, normally subdued and quiet, carried much more weight. The gray clouds gave a gentle dusting of flurries as the four stood towards one another.

"Deeso. I told you to leave me months ago. Why are you here?" Sadal questioned Deeso. Sadal's voice quivered at her appearance as if she saw a ghost. Sadal remembered their last confrontation, on how she struck Deeso and pushed her to the ground in anger. She hoped to instead try and diffuse the situation another way, one that came to her with many months of experience.

Trekkal covered her mouth in shock as she witnessed the scene unfold. Sadal had talked at length about Deeso in such high regard. What happened between them that ended up making things turn so terribly? Trekkal wanted to give Sadal the benefit of the doubt, but the occurrences of her strange behavior started to make sense once more.

"We have a job to do, and on my life, I will make sure Ronkalk does not harm you. Sadal, I am your sister through and through. Everything I've done was to make sure you were safe." Deeso said, wanting to move forward but kept her place next to Zulag.

"Ronkalk, told us explicitly he wanted you alive if we could find you. He only wanted to know what happened. What really happened that day. Deserters are killed by us Sadal, these are the rules when you became a Master Hunter. My uncle respects you, not many earn that right, and you choose to squander it." Zulag said with a glare to Sadal. Sadal frowned at his words and formed a fist. She held it up and pointed at Zulag.

"Really? Ronkalk promised that I wouldn't be killed? That I would be simply punished? Like Cikya was punished? He ripped her throat out like a Poulji!" Sadal said in disbelief to the two of them. Deeso and Zulag shook their heads in anger at her statement.

"We've already lost Cikya. I don't want anyone else to get hurt. She died so that we could get to you. My friend died because of your selfishness. One of us fell in battle, isn't that important to you? Deeso said, her tone was increasingly annoyed with Sadal's comments.

"She was a thief, Deeso. I don't feel bad for her, but your hardship is something I can understand. You knew her better than I did." Sadal conceded while Trekkal looked at the two with a frown on her face.

Zulag was enraged at Sadal's dismissal of Cikya and gritted his teeth as he vibrated with anger. He felt the hand of Deeso on his chest pose as a small barrier. Zulag felt that

Sadal wasn't worth the effort as she continued to run her mouth. Zulag questioned his loyalty to his uncle's judgement, but he still held responsibility and a duty to the needs of his band.

"You have no right to talk about her that way! After all the people you left? We were starving then, and we're starving now. You would have done the same! We're both Master Hunters Sadal, this isn't an easy life." Zulag mentioned.

"To this day, I return to the soil, I owe Ronkalk everything for saving my life, but I will not give up my life. The new life I have. I have bloodied my Wanderer's Mark some time ago, and I no longer hold allegiance to The Broken Bone." Sadal said as she showed her hand up for Deeso and Zulag to witness.

Deeso took a deep breath as Zulag blew air out his nose. Deeso was distraught as the signs were correct. Sadal had truly left her old life behind. She could no longer appeal to Sadal's sensibilities through obligation, but instead through their personal bond. As Trekkal watched this, she felt a cold sweat come over her. The anxiety she felt from this interaction was enough to cause her heart to clench in the tension. While she trained her body on the others, her head slowly turned to Sadal.

"Sadal. I have many questions. Why is this happening? How long has this...been happening? What did you do?" Trekkal said, her face now upset as she was absorbing all this information Sadal obscured.

"Trekkal...now's not the time." Sadal said to her as she placed her hand across Trekkal's upper body and mirrored Deeso's movement for Zulag.

"Oh? Did she not know? Well, Trekkal. Sadal obscured this from you and your friends. We've been looking for her for months. I can see it's not only me you let down." Deeso said with malice in her voice as she saw Trekkal think about Sadal's strange behavior at times. Trekkal trusted Sadal intensely over these random arrivals, but Deeso mentioned the facts with such detail, ignoring it would be a fool's errand. She felt embarrassed and was exhausted.

"Come with us Sadal. I will not ask again." Deeso said with defiance in her voice. Deeso hoped to not have to involve Trekkal, this was a matter between her, Zulag, and Sadal as far as things were considered. If it came to pass that Trekkal got in the way, it was nothing personal. She decided that Trekkal would be offered the path of life or the path of death.

"Deeso. We are family. I want you to trust me." Sadal said, trying to ease the atmosphere by placing her bag of throwing spears down in front of her. She placed them down and attempted to show Deeso that conflict wasn't on her mind. Sadal felt that she at least owed Deeso a proper conversation, things did not end as she wanted before.

"No, you have done enough. Zulag is who I consider in my decision making now." Deeso commented as she nodded her head for him to come closer to her. Zulag reached into his clothing and grasped a knife as his hands hardened with the blowing wind.

"Hold on, Zulag? Him? You can do so much better Deeso." Sadal said with a pained laugh on her face that only soured Deeso's expression further. Humor wasn't Sadal's strong suit, but it was the only thing she could speak without bursting into tears. Although Sadal hadn't bothered to question their ties, Deeso's visceral reaction spoke volumes to her. There was a greater connection between the two than she realized, but the extent of that, Sadal would never know.

"You were always full of yourself Sadal. Nothing could ever be your fault, could it?" Zulag spat at her feet.

"I have seen enough. We are leaving, I have my thoughts on this but if you run at me, you both will die tired." Trekkal said as she broke her silence. She attempted to tug at Sadal's arm, but she refused to move. Trekkal feared rightfully that conflict was to break out. She knew how well Sadal could fight, and with two from the same group as her, she knew it would be incredibly difficult. She thought about getting help from Narro but still held a long shot they could air out their differences.

"This doesn't concern you Trekkal." Zulag commented, turning his gaze to Trekkal.

I've never seen her before, but why does she seem so familiar? Zulag thought as he observed the scene before him.

"Who do you think you are?! As if you can tell me what to do!" Trekkal retorted with a snarl.

"Bold words from the nephew of Ronkalk! You never truly worked a day in your life." Sadal yelled as she saw her gambit with the bag fell through.

Deeso pointed her axe at Trekkal, while she and Zulag dealt words to each other. She felt as if she still had control of the situation, but the stress was showing on her face. Despite the cold weather around them, she felt warm and shook her head. She spoke to Trekkal with pity in her voice as she felt bad for her.

"You're just finding this all out now and you are clearly overwhelmed. Walk away with your life Trekkal. This isn't something you want to get into. Sadal is my business only." Deeso said with sincerity in her voice.

Trekkal decided to adhere to Deeso's words, not because she felt like she should abandon Sadal but because she knew that she needed to call for help. She had no doubts about Sadal's combat ability, but she knew that she needed to get supplies to keep her steady once injured. Trekkal gave Sadal a look, to which Sadal nodded, in understanding of what she intended to do. Trekkal had gone a considerable distance while the three of them remained. Deeso gave a sigh as she realized her mistake in wanting to let Trekkal go free. Although she intended to do just that, a thought came to her.

"Zulag. I told Trekkal to run with her life, but I know she's not alone. The Stone Breaker still travels with them, and we don't know who else is with her. I want you to kill her. This isn't personal, it's just practical. Make it quick." Deeso said to him.

Zulag gave a slow nod of understanding. Deeso always had a surprise under her sleeve, this he learned to expect early on. Although he was more inclined to attack Sadal, he understood the importance of the request. Just as he was about to leave, he felt the touch of Deeso on his shoulder. Zulag assessed himself and while his hands were injured, he felt he was more than able to take Trekkal down and then set his sights on Sadal.

"Come back safe." Deeso said as Zulag ran off.

Sadal was stunned at Deeso's utter callousness before attempting to go after Zulag, but he was already too far away. Sadal stuck her head in her hands as she realized she practically sent Trekkal to her death.

"Deeso! How...How could you do this?" Sadal said in shock.

Zulag's mind already mapped out the entirety of his surroundings and headed in the direction that Trekkal was. Zulag's vision was better than Trekkal's and he kept in mind the vague outline of her in the distance. Trekkal took a moment to catch her breath, but her eyes expanded to see that Zulag was coming for her. It was evident that Deeso clearly changed her mind. Trekkal fiddled around in her bag and grabbed her sling to frantically gain momentum as she used her arm to hurl a rock down range. Both Trekkal and Zulag used ranged weapons, with the two hurling their respective weapons at each other. Trekkal outclassed Zulag when it came to range, so she was able to get a head start by tossing rocks.

"What was that?" Zulag asked himself as he couldn't make out the weapon Trekkal had in her possession. While not the fastest thrower in the world, she certainly made up for it in endurance as she kept a steady rate going.

I see now. She threw something at me with much force, but she has to wind it up which will make her tired. It's not a blowgun like Ozul's weapon. I just need to get in close enough to throw my knives. Zulag thought as he breathed heavily in a consuming rage. Zulag equipped his entire deck of eight throwing knives crafted from obsidian found at the base of the mountain. He admired its sheen as it was an incredibly hunting tool. The wounds were microscopic and would take a long time to heal which was perfect for him to test on a human target other than himself. He launched one knife, to see the range between him and Trekkal. It was a miss, but it was a planned one. Zulag stopped to pick up his knife.

"She has a limited number of stones. If I can have her exhaust them, she's easy prey." Zulag kept in mind as he continued his advance.

Trekkal undoubtedly knew that he was waiting for her to miss as he ran serpentine towards where she was heading. She couldn't throw and run at the same time, so having to gauge the risk was important. The first stone missed, but the second hit well. Zulag winced in pain, as the stone barely touched him but noticed he had been scratched quite hard, and blood poured from his leg. Trekkal had taken to sharpening her stones well enough to cut whatever target was close enough. If she had gotten a direct hit, she may very well have shattered Zulag's shin from concussive force alone. He knew this now and decided to respond with his own show of force.

Zulag remembered how he avoided danger before and laid low to the ground to recover, where Trekkal who hadn't looked back for some time lost sight of him. She remained vigilant and tossed a few rocks in the direction hoping to rile suspicion from him, but she heard nothing. Though the plains were open and devoid of foliage, Trekkal was so disoriented she couldn't see straight to begin with. The altitude of where they were at was as much a fight for Trekkal as Zulag himself. She breathed heavily and she felt compelled to look for water. Trekkal felt the impact of something sharp but didn't bother to notice as one of Zulag's knives embedded itself into her arm. The blade was so sharp that Trekkal's nerve endings didn't pick up she was cut. As a professional, Zulag could throw up to about forty yards with his knives, with lethality being much stronger the closer he was. For his special obsidian blades, all he needed to do was touch Trekkal and let her injuries do the rest. Trekkal felt some slight comfort as she could hear the river she remembered seeing with Sadal. She went to the water and splashed herself to cool down the sweat that had accumulated on her. She looked at her arm and pulled out a small fragment with a confused face. She hadn't noticed that one showed up.

"I need to get to Sadal. That Zulag guy needs to go." Trekkal said to herself as she looked at her reflection in the water. She dipped her arm underneath to clean the wound. Trekkal winced as she steadily bled and worked to quickly dress her wound.

Across the other side of the bank, she lifted her head up to see Zulag emerge from the bushes and toss a knife directly in her direction. Trekkal dove to the water entirely to avoid the throw, but she was weighed down by her damp clothing which made it more difficult for her to get out. He lobbed a few of his remaining knives at Trekkal as she attempted to swim back to shore, while Zulag maneuvered around the other side of the stream and found the least deep area to cross. He slowly moved himself across the water but once he reached the muddy banks, he ran once more. Zulag headed directly towards her now, as making her go to the water was an impromptu addition to his plan. Trekkal's rocks sunk to the bottom of the bank, all except for one in her hand. With a knife out in his grasp, Zulag dashed towards her, only for it to crack in half from a direct hit from the rock Trekkal launched. Zulag watched as his knife shattered entirely and took much of the force. Zulag ignored the pain and used his elbow to rush towards Trekkal and collided with her. He used his shoulder to knock her to the soil with his body weight, while his hands were placed on her throat.

"Just know it's not personal." Zulag said as he was starting to feel the effects of the blood he was losing. He shook his head and remained focused on the task. Trekkal could feel the life draining from her as she was stuck by both his weight and the pressure coming from her damp furs that had practically doubled its force on her. Her arm felt limp as she continued to lose blood herself. Trekkal realized that they were on an incline where the river was running.

She attempted to use her knees to uproot Zulag who remained with a tight grip on her throat and used the momentum to shift position. She took an exasperated gasp for air and withdrew a flint knife out of her pocket that she kept for backup. While a bit worn down, she reasoned it would still be good. Trekkal attempted to stab wildly but noticed the rock was not nearly as sharp as she hoped, with each bit of force requiring a harder amount to break the skin. She let out a scream and ignored the punches Zulag had given her to the face. Trekkal jammed the flint knife into his scapula. With the small window of opportunity given to her, she managed to garner enough strength to place Zulag's head under the water and used her hands to keep him down.

As a member of The Aligned, Trekkal came from a long line of stronger grapplers with a lower center of gravity, which gave her just the edge she needed. Zulag was just moments away from the surface, but he felt a heavy weight come over him as he was unable to get himself back up. The sounds of Trekkal's screaming resounded through the water as he felt himself drowning. His mind first drifted to Ronkalk, and how he failed the one thing his uncle told him to actually do. He also thought of Deeso and how things turned out between them through his journey in brief flashes. He recalled their last real conversation together, helping Deeso achieve her dream and dealing with whatever came of that. In a different life, perhaps things would've been better. Zulag didn't believe in reincarnation but knew he would find himself in the land of his ancestors. Zulag opened his eyes under the water and saw Trekkal's angered face morph and contort as he slowly lost consciousness. In the last moments before his death, he saw a brief glimpse of someone he'd never seen before. It was his mother. Trekkal held her position there for as long as she could, taking as many hits as needed until the body that gave her so much trouble remained still.

"The Peymin will eat." Trekkal said to herself as she massaged her throat and looked at her reflection in the river as blood from Zulag's remains corrupted its once pristine glow. Trekkal got up and slowly made her way back to Sadal where she had much to answer for.

Trekkal looked at herself and started to walk off in the direction of Sadal. She walked with a limp as she left a noticeable trail of blood behind her. Trekkal frantically looked around and was wondering where Sadal ended up. Trekkal struggled against all odds to do everything she needed to get to her.

"Ow..." Trekkal said as she limped.

While Zulag and Trekkal fought, the conflict between Deeso and Sadal had just begun. Deeso and Sadal stood opposed from one another as they stared into the other's eyes. Deeso was filled with contempt for Sadal as the pair instinctively checked their surroundings. Sadal knew that Deeso didn't want to fight despite her jeers. They remained in discussion, and Sadal vainly held hope that she could at least talk down Deeso to finally go their separate ways. The extent of Sadal's failures brought out to her were crippling to her psyche, but she could only see going forward as her only way out.

"Deeso. We can talk this out." Sadal said with her hands up as Deeso waved her axe around in a taunting motion.

"Talk? The time for talking is over. You really have lost everything we learned. I loved you, Sadal. I forgave you for everything. When you left us with no explanation, when I mourned your loss for days, and when you crushed Brab with a rock. I let it all go because I knew that you were important to me. We had a life together, it wasn't the best, but it was one we built together, and we could have made it work." Deeso said with her voice trembling.

"When we starved, I always gave you my food, so you could eat. When you were sick, I braved the jungles to find the medicine you needed. I'm the reason you survived and that is love. Love is sacrifice. Every time I went out there, I feared in the back of my mind, I wouldn't return to support you. I didn't do it for Nurzan, and you saw it all. I wasn't happy Deeso. Things were not going well for me, and I needed to go. I was given an omen and an opportunity to cleanse my mistakes. I love you too Deeso, but you are just one person. We trained to be strong, and I've never been prouder of you. For this though, it's just one life to the spirits." Sadal reasoned as she approached Deeso.

"Just one life? It's mine! Why did it have to be mine?" Deeso pleaded as she stepped away in pure offense.

"Sadal, I want you to pick right now. Me or the meteor." She added on with a broken laugh. Deeso knew the answer Sadal would pick at this stage, but she had to hear it one more time before she decided what needed to be done.

"Deeso..." Sadal said with no avail.

Sadal's eyebrows perked up as she heard a very low groggy noise in the distance that was Trekkal. In the stillness of the air, her voice carried out with not a sign of life anywhere else. Trekkal was on her last legs as she held her hand out to the back of Sadal far in the distance and fell unconscious. Deeso witnessed this and her face sunk low. With Trekkal's return, she knew that Zulag fell in battle. Deeso vibrated with anger both at herself and at Sadal. Deeso knew that because of her, Zulag would never get the answers he sought about his father, an endeavor she wanted to help with. Zulag was the last thing in Deeso's life that had some normalcy, and her antics with Sadal removed these as well. Now all alone, Deeso saw no other choice, but she wanted to see what Sadal would say.

"Trekkal has emerged the victor in this battle. Zulag is dead. Deeso, you need to give up or-" Sadal said, as she was cut off by Deeso's words.

"What are you going to do Sadal? Kill me like you killed Brab? Something we have in common; we're punished by your cruelty. I'm tired of having to try to believe you have good in you." Deeso stated with venom.

It was hard to maintain her own stoic expression as Sadal felt tears coming to her eyes, something that she had only experienced very few times. She felt a massive amount of guilt, not only for those she left behind as Deeso explicitly pointed out, but for her traveling companions. Her lack of communication put everyone's lives at risk. Trekkal survived her encounter, but had she failed to return, she would never forgive herself, and neither would Narro or Jih for that matter.

Sadal noticed that while Deeso had an axe on her person, she instead put it to the ground, just as she did with her throwing spears. Sadal's expression changed to confusion. This feeling was multiplied as she saw Deeso with a slight grin on her face. She raised an eyebrow as her eyes went from the axe on the grass and back to Deeso.

"You've put down your weapon. This means you concede." Sadal pointed out.

Deeso nodded her head in disagreement and let out a smile as her eyes were red with tears. Deeso detached herself from her surroundings as she focused on her targeted approach with Sadal.

"It's better with my hands." Deeso commented as she changed her position to a fighting stance.

Despite everything, Deeso still retained enough respect to fight Sadal on fair terms. It would mean nothing to just hack her to pieces with her axe like she did for many others. Sadal knew she exhausted all her options and did the same and took a deep look at her sister one last time. She knew deep down Deeso didn't want to do this, but she had nowhere else to turn. It took a moment of them locking eyes one last time before the first hit was done, this was from Deeso. Sadal's reaction time was just a few moments faster than Deeso's. Sadal was stunned as she felt the impact behind Deeso's punch. In the number of times that Sadal and Deeso sparred together, this eclipsed any power she ever gave.

"Deeso, please. You can still keep your life. You deserve better than what I have done to you." Sadal pleaded as she blocked Deeso's fist.

Deeso's intent to kill was apparent in her eyes as she saw Sadal as nothing more than an obstacle. The admission of Sadal's faults and acknowledgment of what happened was welcome, but far too late to serve nothing more than to fuel the cycle of rage. Deeso opened with a quick jab to the left of Sadal's face and landed a direct hit. As Sadal's face contorted briefly from the second strike of Deeso's palm, she reverted to a state of survival. Sadal's head tilted back, and she returned the gesture as she gave a powerful kick with her left foot to Deeso's stomach. Deeso let out a cough as she hissed at her.

"What did you think would happen? That I-I'd just come and leave it all? To-do, what? Hmm? Return to where I am unappreciated? T-To-" Sadal asked with a flurry of emotions distorting her speech.

Deeso grabbed Sadal's right arm and twisted. She hoped to break Sadal's arm but couldn't deliver.

"You always had a bad arm." She said coldly, as Sadal let out a pained scream.

Deeso's refusal to acknowledge Sadal's question enraged her further as she used the ground as a springboard to knock her off balance. She kicked her in the shin and caused her to wince in pain. Sadal knew that this would be a close match, being similar in build and having known her for so long. What Deeso didn't know, was the new techniques Sadal learned from Jih and Narro that she would employ to save her life.

"And you forgot I was left-handed." Sadal said as she punched Deeso squarely in the jaw with her throwing arm.

While her head was slammed to the ground, Deeso scooped a small amount of mud and threw it into Sadal's eyes briefly obscuring her vision as she ran behind Sadal and wailed into her back. She felt every punch as an unstoppable flurry filled with malice that became harder to resist. She could feel herself caving in on the pressure. The two interlocked their grip and struggled to gain advantage over the other. Deeso was unsure if she was being toyed with but decided to try and get an opening by manipulating Sadal's emotions.

"I hoped I could see why you wanted this thing so badly. Why was it worth all this death, but I couldn't and now it seems I never will." Deeso mentioned.

"If only you knew Deeso." Sadal said as she used a free leg to sweep Deeso to the ground and grabbed her by her leg.

Deeso kicked wildly, with one of the landed hits disorienting Sadal while she remembered where she was. Sadal's memories took her full attention now. She could see the smile on Deeso's face as they cleaned animal bones together and surveyed the land fresh for the hunt, but those days were gone now. In front of her was the next target of a long fight. Deeso rushed for Sadal and used the momentum from the air to topple her over to the ground as she reached for her neck. Sadal, among all things was tactical, and soon realized she now had home field advantage. Deeso had put her on top, hoping to rush for the throat, but Sadal was adept with her legs and quickly shot her knee up to Deeso and kicked her hard.

The force of the knee was enough to have her start coughing blood, but Sadal wasn't in the best condition either. She ached everywhere and felt as if she would need to rest for weeks. The two exchanged punches as they dodged with robotic precision, hoping to wear the other down before landing a hit. Deeso saw an opening and lunged forward. Deeso, fueled by adrenaline, poked her fingers into Sadal's eyes and she teared immediately. Deeso landed a few extra punches in Sadal's face as she felt her cheeks puff up and her eyes squinted. Blinded for the moment, she listened to Deeso's breathing and in one swoop, used her legs to confine Deeso close to her and her arms to wrap them around her neck. She was restrained, and as long as Sadal's strength held out, she was now in control.

Deeso bit into her exposed thigh causing Sadal to let her go as she got up now. Sadal's vision returned for the moment as she snarled in primal rage at her target. Sadal changed direction and headed eastwards while Deeso pursued her. Sadal's puffy eyes took her to a patch of a few trees that weren't too far from the clearing in the plains they were in. She hadn't considered it earlier during her walk but now it would be the best solution. Her vision darted to the second tree that was situated some distance away from her. She climbed it to a few feet suspended above the ground where she waited. Deeso snorted out of her nose as she recalled the times the two of them played hide and seek in the brush of the jungle. At a time like this, she was to be toyed with in such a way?

With the increased elevation, Sadal had a wider range to see. Deeso, who was relentless in her pursuit, made her anger audible to Sadal who knew she was approaching. She knocked on the tree's wood to give away her location as she jettisoned off her position into Deeso who was far too slow to react. She had hit the floor with a resounding thud and Sadal had restricted her in a tight hug, where her left arm was around her neck and her right had kept her body restrained. Deeso tried using a sharpened branch she picked up to get Sadal to relent, but to no avail.

"You...You win Sadal. I h-hope you find y-your p-peace." Deeso said through gasps as she felt her body weaken before her.

Of all the things said to her over the years, she decided to take what Ozul said instead. She didn't know why, but such a simple request resonated with her and her goal from the very beginning. She joined The Broken Bone because she believed in the vision of peace and security offered by Ronkalk. With this, she thought Sadal and her comrades would bring what she craved, but it seemed to her that she was wrong.

With no strength left to fight back, Sadal slammed her head against the tree's trunk. She bludgeoned Deeso to death while she ran out of oxygen. Deeso thought about what a waste it all was. Each hit removed just a slight bit of the background that Deeso could see, her once vast world started to cave in on itself. Dying in battle was the best thing she could have looked forward to, but even this felt dull to her with her current opponent. She saw herself one day being a true success, a powerful band leader in her own right, with a supportive right hand, and a child of her own to carry on the new legacy. These were all gone now. Sadal slammed Deeso so hard into the tree that a portion of her skull cracked, as blood and bits of brain matter leaked out from her head. After what felt like an eternity where she bled, Deeso was still and the tears from Sadal's eyes hit the ground. It was done.

Tears of Blood: II

Sadal looked over her handiwork and was filled with an intoxicating feeling of nausea. As Sadal looked over Deeso's remains, she walked over and vomited behind a tree. She felt disgusted with everything that happened. Sadal could hardly pull herself together. She recovered her bearings and looked at Deeso's corpse. Sadal promised herself that she would hug Deeso the next time they saw one another. She embraced Deeso's corpse for a few moments and then it was time for Sadal to move on. She debated burying her but felt it was better for nature to claim her instead, as she lacked the strength to haul the earth below to do so. She saw that there wasn't much distance between the river and the section of forest she was at, but during her fight it seemed a vast endeavor to reach.

Her breathing staggered as she looked towards her damage. It was remarkable that nothing was broken, but the pain surely reverberated throughout her body. Dark welts appeared all over her, and she felt at least two teeth were missing in the back of her mouth. She slumped along supporting herself with some trees until she got a steady footing on the ground. Her head was constantly on a swivel, as a weak person could make easy prey for any predators lying in wait. Sadal lamented the worst part of the day had just begun for herself, as she would need to confess everything that happened to not only Trekkal, but Narro and Jih who have been ignorant so far. Her stomach turned, Trekkal trusted her above any other of her kind she'd ever met. As Narro's One, she made a terrible mistake that almost killed her and his sister. As for Jih, Sadal gagged at the thought of betraying Jih's trust. She remembered a conversation the two had in private, she hadn't given the whole truth.

Trekkal was suspicious of Sadal for quite some time as they've been traveling together, but it was nothing that she could discuss with anyone at first. While often in her own world, Trekkal kept track of the various events that happened, and things started to make more sense. She noticed there were times when Sadal felt a growing sense of paranoia. At first, she thought this to be simple delusions of a tired warrior, but these concerns were very much real. Sadal would take watch more often, at first Trekkal took this as a nice gesture, she hated the noises that came from the dark, something she would never admit to any living person, and work in general. With extra thought attached though, these extra precautions and wanting to build camp near other groups made much more sense.

The formerly unconscious Trekkal felt a few loose rain drops on her skin. Trekkal felt as if she could rest on the ground, but she needed to find Sadal. In the silence that came by, Trekkal lumbered over to start her quest. Trekkal built a tight bond with Sadal over the months they spent together. Now, with two additional bodies to their name, Trekkal reached her limit. It still was all too much for her to recall in one swoop. She completely acted on instinct as far as she was concerned and hoped to block out the events from her mind for now. She took a deep breath and made her way to the edge of the woodland hoping that she would see Sadal out there. She had all hopes that Sadal would emerge victorious, but she held out her sling in case Deeso sought to finish the job.

Sadal limped over in the direction of camp and practically crawled on the ground as exhaustion took hold. She willed herself to continue onwards. If she collapsed here, everything would fall apart even more so than now. Sadal lifted her head up and saw where the first bit of their fight began. She saw her bag of throwing spears and Deeso's axe that remained. She crawled to the site and grabbed the axe as a trophy. Sadal turned her head and sniffed, it wasn't her body, but instead something else much worse that wanted to take advantage of the situation.

"Any...anything but you...Not now." Sadal said to herself.

Sadal heard the low growl of a puma in the distance that she was powerless to stop, but the familiar sound of a whirring rock caused it to heel and retreat elsewhere. In the distance, Sadal's blurry vision cleared to make out a bloodied Trekkal. Her clothing was ripped to pieces, and spots of her skin were darkened from Zulag's attacks. Trekkal swayed from blood loss and Sadal noticed an array of small cuts made on her body as well. Trekkal felt nothing as she made her way to Sadal and left a trail of blood behind her.

Much to Trekkal's expectations, the figure of Sadal appeared to her in the distance with a small wave. She let out a sigh of relief that led to a gradual souring of her expression as she got closer. Sadal raised an eyebrow as she eyed Trekkal but let out a small smile. Trekkal got closer and raised her hand. She immediately slapped Sadal in the face with what strength she could muster. Sadal's face was so numb it barely registered, but she felt she deserved it.

"I had my doubts you would make it." Sadal commented with a sarcastic tone. She knew Trekkal was angry with her, but hoped she could at least attempt to defuse the situation with humor much like Narro could.

"This is not the time for jokes." Trekkal argued with much conviction in her voice. Sadal stayed silent as Trekkal's face gradually reddened with anger. This was a rare occurrence as she rarely experienced emotions like these, so Sadal took them with the utmost severity.

"What is with your kind and fighting all the time?" Trekkal voiced in dismay, as she felt the wounds on her body. The adrenaline receded and the pain she felt from her fight with Zulag increased in intensity.

"Grab my hand. We need to go to camp." Trekkal said through an exhausted sigh of pain as she held it for Sadal to grab.

"I-" Sadal said.

"Grab it." Trekkal said, her voice curt in its delivery.

Sadal silently took her hand and the two stumbled together back to camp. While supporting one another, Trekkal took the opportunity to bring the conversation forward to what happened. Sadal took a deep breath; she knew there was a lot that needed to be answered for.

"I knew I was right about you. You and your doublespeak, fooling everyone. My brother and Jih trusted you. I trusted you!" Trekkal said, nearly slipping on some loose dirt.

"Why are you upset? They paid for their mistake in blood. We have killed, and we will continue to kill Trekkal. You must grow and understand that." Sadal said in a thinly constructed way to defend her actions. It was pointless to do so, but her nature made it almost impossible to take a verbal lashing like that without retaliation.

"Yes Sadal, my blood! Do you hear yourself? How could you try to blame me." Trekkal countered with obvious pain in her voice. Trekkal tried her hardest to hold back tears, not out of the injuries she faced, but for how much Sadal put the two of them through.

"You were there for this. They felt I dishonored them. Deeso sent Zulag after you to do her dirty work. I killed her for it." Sadal answered as she knew she had no real defense for her deception.

"This explains nothing. Why did you not say anything?" Trekkal commented as she twisted Sadal's arm out of anger. Sadal felt so empty inside that she gave no reaction to the already large amount of pain to her. Sadal lifted her head as Trekkal stopped to meet her gaze.

"It wasn't your problem. I had it handled. I told Jih...but not everything Trekkal. You don't understand. I never expected you to. I will tell you everything at camp. Jih and Narro need to be here too." Sadal pleaded with her.

Trekkal felt somewhat disarmed at the rapid rate at which Sadal's demeanor changed. It seemed to her that Sadal's own words were starting to erode her self-confidence. Against her better judgment, she decided that whatever Sadal had to tell her would be worth the whole group's input. With that in mind though, one question stayed on her mind. As the familiar sights of home came to them, she stopped.

"Was it true?" Trekkal opened, as her eyes looked to see the shapes of Jih and Narro in the distance.

"Was what?" Sadal asked weakly.

"You said we were family back at The Gorge. I called you sister, but when you say it...Did you mean that?" Trekkal added on. She noticed Sadal's pause and while she turned her head again to glare, Trekkal could only see tears come from her eyes.

Sadal said nothing as she and Trekkal finished their walk and practically collapsed at the sight of home. Their small tents were calling out to them. Sadal's vision faded again, but she was brought back by a scream. Jih was gathering some branches in the distance as he heard Narro rushing back to camp. Jih grabbed his spear and practically collided with Narro as he stood above in horror. He reached down and immediately went to Trekkal while Jih looked over Sadal.

"These scratches all over your body...What happened? What are these? I told you both that Jih and I would hunt this time! What game attacked you this way? I need answers! What? W-We need to stick together." Narro said, his words tripping over himself while Jih attempted to keep himself and Narro calm.

"Not what but who. Wounds are from tools." Jih noted, looking at Trekkal's cuts on her body. He looked to see that Sadal was not in great condition either, he lifted her up gently and saw that blood came. In the moments that followed, Narro went to grab Jih's bag and started to wrap them up with bandages.

"This is from bloodstone. Very sharp rock, Trekkal may bleed for days like Ker-Mah. Give her water and change bandage often." Jih said, looking at his own finger from an old cut.

Sadal tried to keep the attention of their injuries to themselves so that she could stay quiet, but Trekkal was far too persistent to let something like this go untouched. Mustering up what strength she had left, she forced Sadal to make peace with the group.

"Oh no, you have something you have to say, Sadal. Go on. Jih and Narro are here now." Trekkal commented, while Narro gave her a confused look.

"Trekkal and I were attacked by people I used to know." Sadal said, her tone still trying to disguise the amount of responsibility she had to contend with. Jih gave a knowing glare to Sadal, he had reason to believe early on that he didn't receive the entire truth about her situation to begin with, but there was nothing he could do until something happened.

"What do you mean? We have encountered many on our travels so far. Who could you have possibly run into?" Narro asked with genuine confusion.

"Back when you met Fahlrit, and we-You ran to one of my kind... one with Onpeu spots. His name is-was-Zulag. I told you about him. It wasn't just him either. There was also Deeso. The two of them, well, I guess they had more, but those two tracked me down for months." Sadal said, her voice trailing off as she attempted to fight the exhaustion on her. She fell lower and Narro hugged her gently and propped her up to speak while Jih looked over Trekkal.

"Yes, the bundle of joy, her beloved sister, known as Deeso, sent her special man to try and put my head on a knife. He was close too, but I was better." Trekkal spat in disgust.

"Trekkal-" Narro said, with a reprimanding tone in his voice. Trekkal willed herself to roll her eyes, but they just stayed blank.

"Narro. I am suffering because of your One and the stupid decisions she decided to make. I can have my fun." Trekkal countered.

"When I first met Jih, he found me after I had left my old life behind. It feels so long ago. There was a Weypeu that killed us all. I killed my son, for he was a bad omen, and this was needed to set things right. I have no regrets about that. This aligned me again with the spirits, but the physical world had other ideas. I had to leave Ronkalk and everyone else I cared about, for I was going to be killed for my failure. I was scared and alone. I tried to kill Jih the first time I met him. Deeso was worried and she risked her life to find me. When we first met the two of you... Deeso was following me through...Eshe. I hate that woman." Sadal said through gritted teeth as another surge of pain came over her.

Narro stood in horror at the woman he loved, he wasn't sure what to say as his face just stood blank. He gave Jih a look of judgment as well, how long did he know all of this? How could he find that this was acceptable? Narro kept a strong moral code, one that the others certainly had more flexibility on when it came down to it, but this was justifiable. Jih understood Narro's rage well, deception hurt anyone who did it, especially the one considered your partner. Jih knew Sadal the longest, so he was able to have a wider depth into why she acted this way. Jih could hardly cast a stone at Sadal, he recalled with ease that his own anger was the reason for his exile. A quick break in his psyche was all it took. Given that he was an exile himself, the sentiment made sense. Do what you can to support yourself and figure out the rest. Jih walked off to his bag to grab his canteen with water and gave it to Trekkal and Sadal to drink. Narro didn't move a muscle.

"When I ran into Deeso again...I was so happy to see her. I cared nothing for what she had to tell me. She wanted me to return home. By then, I had already left The Broken Bone behind me. That was when I decided in my mind to be with you Narro, my One. I-I didn't think Deeso would have taken my words so harshly but looking back...I was wrong. I pushed her to the ground and in doing so, I made my worst enemy. I destroy everything I touch. My sister of nine years, my little Deeso. I-I killed...her. She loved me, and I killed her." Sadal said, trying not to choke on the water.

"Trekkal. I'm sorry for Zulag. My feud with him goes way back and you were put into this through me. We were the same rank of Master Hunter, he was right, in that I left behind the honor that came with my rank and the plenty that starved. Being in Ronkalk's bad graces is something I avoided. Deserters are to be killed; this is what we agreed on. I hate him but he was just doing his job. He also gave Deeso a light in her eyes I had never seen before. I am tired. I want to sleep." Sadal added on, her face pointed to the ground so that she couldn't look Narro in the eyes.

"Sadal...You left all those people to die!" Narro screamed. He took a deep breath as his own voice shocked him on how loud he spoke.

"I value your passionate and kind heart. You are an amazing hunter, and your role was important. I can see why Deeso had the vigor she did. Aside from being your sister. I have killed many things so that Trekkal can sleep at night, and she has done the same for me. You not only lied to us, but you destroyed so many in the process. The loss is vast. I am your One and I will help you through this, but I need time. This will not be easy." Narro said, his voice shaking.

"Narro...please." Sadal said as she started crawling towards him. It was a hard sight to watch as Narro walked off while Sadal went his way. Jih was visibly uncomfortable as he witnessed the scene. He took a deep breath and decided the best way forward was to embrace forgiveness. He silently moved to Sadal and hoisted her up much like he did in the past and gave her a tight but comforting hug as Sadal devolved into crying.

"Be there for her, when no one else has." Jih remembered the words of Hyu. He broke his silence and spoke to Sadal.

"Sadal. Forgiveness and acceptance are the same. Regret is carried by many, Jih has so much. Your past will not change but there is more to do. You are young. There are many years left to be good, but you must put effort. You are allowed to improve." Jih said as he looked at Narro and Trekkal.

By now, Trekkal fell asleep out of exhaustion on her body. Narro took her to his tent and closed the flap behind him while he tried to sleep next to her. He looked over at her, with a slight sense of calm as she stuck her tongue out, clearly dreaming about something. She was badly hurt, and her bandages felt wet again. They would need to be replaced consistently for some time, so Narro hoped Jih would be able to find something. Sadal and Jih sat with the fire behind them. Jih remained unmoved as he gradually felt Sadal lighten in his grasp as her crying waned. She could only stare at the abyss of the mountain where she came and lost everything. A new day would hardly fix what happened, but the first step was forgiveness. Jih rubbed his hand on Sadal's back and held her close until the last bits of crying stopped. Sadal fell asleep to the low roar of the going fire. Jih was the last one awake and draped a spare pelt over her as she slept to serve as a blanket.

"The power rock will fix this." Jih said to himself as he took it on himself to take watch this night.

The Climb

Now that Sadal had recovered physically from her fight with Deeso, she still had some thinking to do. This took one month, and the group geared up to move from the Caucasus Mountains to Europe proper. Her friends had forgiven her quicker than she anticipated, as they were focused on the challenges ahead, but she still felt something was missing. In any case, Sadal felt she needed a change, but what would that be? She looked at her attire, having grown tired of the various deer furs that she accumulated, something far more fitting her status was much deserved. Although The Broken Bone was behind her, in her core she was still a Master Hunter. Sadal's record with cats wasn't what she intended to have. A tiger ruined her life when it started, she remained offended at how the scimitar-toothed cat humbled her, and how the puma had gotten the jump on her at her lowest point. Jih and the others huddled around a campfire, with the late fall turning into a harsh early winter.

The illumination of the campfire shone as a beacon of resilience to an otherwise blank abyss that stared at them. The snow's fall ceased for the day but there was bound to be more ahead. Narro took great interest in plotting the weather's course by studying the formations of the clouds. He'd gotten quite good at the endeavor. Jih saw that Sadal was quieter than usual as he loaded firewood on the campfire. He raised an eyebrow at her and noted her apparel. She carried alongside her not only her throwing spears, but nestled inside the bag was an axe-head that hung ever so gently from the bag. The trophy she carried from her fight with Deeso. Along the way, she saw a set of peculiar tracks and looked to pursue a beast. Though she saw that Jih wanted to talk with her, as he saw the withdrawn look on her face, and the almost delirious sunken feeling within her, she shook her head no.

"I'll be back soon." She said to the three of them. Trekkal rolled up a ball of snow with her hands and chucked it at Sadal's backside. Sadal stopped to laugh, the first one she'd given in some time as Trekkal stuck her hands inside her outfit to keep them warm.

"You better!" Trekkal said to her.

The moon's light gave way for the snow to shine brightly, and Sadal didn't need a torch to light the way. Her feet were wrapped with spare furs reinforced by string that sunk into the snow as she tried to follow the tracks of her mystery hunt. Sadal quickly noticed that she was on an incline that had been obscured by the amassed snow. She treaded carefully, her body just barely keeping in heat as she pressed onwards. The silence of the snowfall amplified Sadal's breathing as she trudged through.

The incline gradually became steeper as Sadal felt a harrowing wind blow. A mass of snow toppled down below and revealed a thin crevice where the daring would certainly have second thoughts. The tracks vanished as the snow moved, but Sadal remained vigilant. There were a few trees that were dusted with snow that stood out in the distance.

Sadal applied her knowledge that she remembered well. She deduced that her target was feline in nature from the footprints and knew that all big cats would mark their territory in various ways. She didn't smell urine, but she noticed strange markings along the ground that could have only been given by the cat's hind legs. This was the marked territory of a snow leopard, but Sadal wasn't aware of this just yet. She moved towards the tree, barren as it was and looked inside her pack. She muddled around inside and withdrew Deeso's axe. She used the axe to chop off some bark and make a sound that would carry throughout the territory. If the animal felt its space was being challenged, surely it would come and defend its claim? Sadal hoped her display with some time could be enough to lure the prey to her, whatever it may be.

Sadal saw that fresh snow accumulated again from the clouds. She remembered from very long ago, when Eshe asked if she heard of water that one could eat, the thing known as ice. It was clear this is what she meant, as curiosity got the best of her and she decided to take a small piece and stick it in her mouth. It wasn't very appetizing. She silently withdrew the first of her spears and stood perfectly still. Sadal stifled her own breathing, so that the fog that would come from the heat was at a minimum. Behind her was a series of higher mountains now decorated with an extensive array of snow itself that glittered in the sky.

Sadal saw a glimmer of gray appear out of the assortment of white and piercing yellow eyes stare back at her. Adjacent to her was her target, an elusive snow leopard. Sadal sighted the creature, noting its fangs and class and she reared for a fight. She tracked the animal with her vision and trudged through the snow at breakneck speed, only to see that this animal didn't seem to want to attack her at all. It distanced itself from her but kept its glare on her. Was she being toyed with? Sadal launched her first spear that flew with a resounding gracefulness as the sound of the snow blanketed the impact. The snow leopard bare its fangs and while Sadal braced herself for a worthy adversary, the opposite was far from it. The snow leopard was a nimble creature, preferring ultimately to avoid conflict with humans whenever it could. Much to Sadal's disappointment, it lacked the pure aggression of the other predators she seemed to find.

"What is this creature doing? Come, fight me!" Sadal yelled in frustration.

Her voice came with a resounding echo that filled the air, cutting through the stillness of the night. The snow leopard scaled a nearby hill as it heard Sadal's words. The snow leopard turned its head as if it was inviting her to follow. Sadal went to reclaim her thrown spear and placed it back in her backpack before she tried to scout out a path. The amount of snow that accumulated obscured her vision, but this was also the best thing for her. Sadal was light enough to walk on the packed snow, and she stuck her arms deep inside so that she wouldn't slip. In doing so, she was risking frostbite as her gloves could only keep in so much heat, but she was able to traverse up to the leopard's level. Her backpack moved ever slightly as the wind was harsh and Sadal's hair stuck to her face.

The snow leopard moved from Sadal, at a much faster speed this time, as it was running on a flat surface. Sadal realized this and got herself up to chase the creature as it left a puff of snow as it did so. Sadal took her spear this time and launched it, practically overextending her arm. The missile sliced a portion of the cat's tail, leaving blood in its wake as it continued to retreat.

I see now. This creature uses the environment to fight instead of its claws. This is a smart one. Sadal thought as she saw that the snow leopard was jumping away from distinct piles, Sadal echoed these movements, noting that these were deeper pockets of snow where she could get stuck and take longer to get out.

Sadal saw that the leopard ended up in the opening of a cave. To Sadal, it was clear that the animal retreated to its den. Sadal ran towards the cave where she tracked the remaining drops of blood and noticed that there was a tight crevice where the cat could move its way through. The snow leopard was able to fit in quite nicely as Sadal looked under to see a much larger chasm behind it where its home was. Sadal withdrew her bag and attempted to slide her spear underneath, where it ended up on the other side. A child could fit with ease, but a full-grown adult could have difficulties. The barrier to the further interior of the cave was a tight squeeze, Sadal however was slender enough to fit in the short space as she got herself through. Sadal stood up now and grabbed her spear to see the snow leopard reared up towards an incline. She launched the spear with much bravado and hit the animals' hind legs. Sadal's vision was low with the moonlight piercing through and illuminating the cave from an opening at the top. Sadal could only go off her now-adjusted vision and the sound of the snow leopard. It let out a soft roar as it bled.

Even in death, the creature's rage was more so at itself than at Sadal. It was a fruitless endeavor now and Sadal watched it go. The warmth of the cave dramatically felt better than the outside as Sadal moved her fingers, having feeling return to them. The snow leopard succumbed to its wounds sometime later. Sadal saw she had plenty of time, retrieved some of her other tools in the same manner she did for her spear. She extended her hand and slid the backpack through the opening. Upon the snow leopard's death, Sadal dragged the body as well as she could and used Deeso's axe to cut the creature's head off. She scooped the blood with her free hand and drank as was tradition in confirming the kill and scooped the brain matter for herself. She labored tirelessly to skin the creature with the opening of the night's sky gradually turning to dawn as she did so. Past where Sadal worked, there was a deeper cave system which worked its way further in, but luckily for her, a few open pockets revealed the way to the top. The snow leopard's den was expansive, but this was only one of many entrances to this cave.

One entrance she found was packed with snow, but it wasn't hard like the others. She hacked away at the snow with her spear, as more accumulated in its place. She dug out for some time, but the piercing veil of the sunlight reflecting off the snow attacked her eyes. She knew she was getting close. Sadal trudged herself out as she met the outside now, not too far from where she was in the entrance before. Now she had to remember how to get back. She climbed up on a mass of snow to survey where she went before and decided to trace her steps back from the visible cave's entrance, the bloody path of the leopard still showing true. She left the corpse behind but took the bloodied skin with her as she had it wrapped. Sadal descended from the path, taking great care to avoid the spots of heavy snow just as she did before. She then saw the tree which she had stripped of its bark and nodded. Her surroundings were familiar again, it would only be a matter of time before she returned.

Back at camp, Jih had prepared breakfast, reheating a few strips of smoked meat saved from a goat he was able to kill. He disliked their nimbleness on the mountains, but they were a good source of food. Narro helped as best as he could while Trekkal waited for the food to be done. There wasn't anywhere to fish up here. Occupying herself by piling snow, Trekkal noticed an unfamiliar figure walking in the distance. She glared, wanting to tell the others they had a visitor, but realized quickly from the gait, it was Sadal's return. Sadal gave a gentle wave to the group, her exhaustion still prominent, but much less so. Trekkal looked moderately impressed at the wrapped-up skin behind her and eyed the spectacled pattern of the snow leopard. She found a cleared patch of ground to rest the skin on for processing while she was given a large hug by Narro and Jih held out a stick with the reheated meat for Sadal to eat.

At long last, Sadal finally felt warm.

Dinner For Four

Descending from the mighty mountains, Jih and the gang noticed that the land of which they currently traveled was still. The soil was dry, and the grass was dead. Only the howling rafts of the wind out on the plains accompanied them. The river, always a useful guide, ran dry with little water to spare. This was unusual and the land bore no fruit to pick. Once plentiful, it was as if a curse was placed on this land. The expanse of the territory was as wide as an ocean, but deep as a puddle. There were, however, plenty of bones from the various creatures that were once stuck in this void much like themselves. Jih looked behind him as the imposing mountains looked over the weary travelers. He felt his pack was exceptionally light where their supplies were low. The last of their smoked meat went to their stomachs for breakfast, and while not hungry now, the feeling would return soon enough. Jih held his hand out to the others who briefly stopped their movement.

"Jih finds the air...cold. This is unusual to Jih. We must be careful." Jih mentioned.

Sadal raised an eyebrow as she was warm in her freshly acquired leopard fur. Narro understood the cold was not of temperature, but a horrible feeling that came on one's skin. To truly demonstrate his feelings on the matter, he clapped as the sound echoed through a field they found themselves in. The four looked around cautiously as their furs swayed in the wind. Jih and the others continued walking in relative silence, as exhaustion was apparent on all their faces. There seemed to be nowhere to provide adequate supplies to make camp and so they ventured forward. In the distance, Sadal noticed an unusual movement, it was a strange figure that was humanoid in its shape. She withdrew one of her throwing spears and prepared for battle.

"Wait, Sadal! That is a woman in the distance. Look at how her arms flail in the wind, she is unarmed. She is heading towards us, not a threat it seems." Trekkal pointed out grabbing Sadal's arm. Jih and Narro followed suit, hoping to figure out what they were looking at. She was one of The Aligned in clear distress that Narro and Trekkal worked quickly to address. Narro waved her down and placed his club down to show a sign of peace. He coaxed her over gently and offered the last bit of water in his canteen.

At first, the woman walked over with a slow gait but quickly ran to Narro, and practically knocked him over for the water. The woman's hands grasped onto Narro, who could only look embarrassed, as Sadal moved to quickly mediate the situation. She looked over the woman's condition and was puzzled at such a display. She wondered what could have made her act in such a manner. Her gaze met Trekkal's, and she shrugged her shoulders.

"We are offering you water, have some pride when you take it! Release Narro from your grasp now." Sadal demanded. She sharply adjusted her tone as she saw the amount of shaking that was evident on the woman. Her eyes were devoid of life as she tried to grasp the grass and scoop it into her mouth. She looked exceptionally pale compared to the others. Sadal gave Narro a concerned look as she placed her arm around him and reinforced her statement.

"Are you sick? You look much paler than us." Trekkal asked.

She eyed the woman over and saw that her furs were tattered and that some of her body was bleeding. It was clear she was attacked by some sort of animal, but what could be enough to induce such panic? Trekkal worried that they may have found themselves once again in the vicinity of the scimitar toothed cat's territory. The woman didn't comprehend her words, and only let out an ear-curdling scream in response. Jih covered his ears at the screaming woman and glared at the others.

"What band are you from? Can we take you there?" Jih asked, in hopes of ridding himself of the new arrival.

His words reached the woman whose head slowly turned to stare at Jih. He moved back slightly, clearly unnerved by what he witnessed. Her hand rose and feebly pointed north as she threw herself to the ground and clasped the soil. Jih looked at her and then to the other three who had varying looks of anguish and sheer confusion.

"This one points north. Will we go there and follow her guidance?" Jih questioned as he looked at the others. Narro shrugged his shoulders, while Sadal was quick to make her mind clear.

"Yes, it's clear she came from a place with others. We need to get food and if we have to fight something like a Mahaku again to get it, so be it." Sadal mentioned.

"I, for one, would rather go in any other direction than the one where the screaming woman came from. Does this not sound like a terrible idea to you?" Trekkal said in protest to her statement.

Narro had no chance to speak as Jih decided to make an executive decision in agreement with Sadal. He pointed north for the others to follow, using the logic that if there was one person, there were bound to be others who could have potential resources. The land to them was once again unknown, and given the landscape around them, barren of food. Knowledge could be more important than pelts in the event of a bad hunting season. Without further delay, the four set off once again to find a trail of nothing as they left the disturbed woman behind.

"Jih, I'm starting to think that going north wasn't the best idea. There seems to be still nothing here." Sadal observed as Jih continued to press on.

Jih held up a finger as the smell of burning wood hit his nose first. This had to mean a camp of some sort was nearby. He got the attention of the others to press on just a bit longer before they reached their destination. This was a camp inhabited by The Aligned, Europe proper was inhabited solely by them, so Jih and Sadal were once again in the minority. It was a small establishment with about five tents for a band of twenty people. A few sat outside and looked at the new arrivals. Their faces were unimpressed by Jih and the others but extended a welcome. Narro compared their dress, Jih and the rest aside from Sadal, wore goat skins while the rest held few scraps of clothing.

Jih and the others had little to offer materially, but for them it was fortunate that they just enjoyed their company. An older man with just a skirt tied around his waist and a gray beard prompted them to sit down. His arms were weak, it was clear he hadn't eaten in a while and the band were also on hard times. A few of the other members idly worked on their tasks for the day, and whittled weapons from bone for the mammoths that would never come.

"I take it you found nothing on the trail here? Many have chosen to leave this place behind, but we are different. Our tie to the land is strong and we know that with enough patience, the herds will return." The man said as he offered them a few pieces of stripped bark. Jih looked at the paltry meal and stuck out his tongue out in disgust, while the others had slightly more tact and nodded their heads no.

"What brings you here to this land? We do not receive many new visitors." The man questioned as he eyed the four strangers in front of him.

"We come with blessings from The First, our journey has us looking for the meteor that hit the sky. We have been looking for directions for some time, but a woman pointed us here to the location of your fine camp." Narro mentioned gently as he looked over the state of conditions.

"The First?" The man said as a pause grew over the others that overheard their discussion.

"You must be new. We speak none of The Plaguebringers and their ilk. As for your other thing. There are those who have bothered us in the past over such happenings. We want nothing to do with it. Their kind live further north you know. The land is colder there, and it must do something to their minds. One of them came by to preach and we took care of that." The man scoffed and spat to the ground as Jih glared at him. The meteor was a source of immense prestige and raw power, insulting it felt as personal as an insult to Jih's character itself, but he also viewed it as the interpretation of someone clearly ignorant.

"We are kin, so I must ask what did The...Plaguebringers do to your people? We have a much different opinion across the mountain." Trekkal questioned.

"What did they not do? Look at the state of our home. The only good thing they ever did for us was perish. Our home is cursed because they refused to find balance with nature. The Zaan are dead, the grass is dead, the mountains cry and it never ends." The man huffed as Jih narrowed his eyes at his words.

In the years before The Aligned were the only ones that settled in these lands, The Plaguebringers were members of Jih's people that lived here ages ago. The Plaguebringers were given this moniker as they were believed to have mismanaged the land to such a horrid degree that they killed off entire swathes of herds and made life difficult for everyone else. They were isolationists and stuck to themselves while The Aligned in this area stood alone. Jih understood that while his people were flawed like any, that this was beyond unfair. Jih felt that he wasn't responsible for the sins of those that came before him. Sadal reassured Jih that the label was just a word, and it didn't affect what their group thought of him. Jih decided to remain civil for the time being.

Narro perked up at hearing that there were additional communities up north who valued the meteor far more than the others. Despite the odd reception, Narro took an opportunity to smooth relations over while Trekkal yawned as she was tired. Sadal's eyes looked for anything of note within the small camp. She saw very little activity going on aside from a central hearth where the emaciated members of this band convened.

"Well, if you could allow us to rest, we would certainly make it your while. Is there anything you want from us?" Narro mentioned to the man. He massaged Sadal's back as he could tell she felt tense around these new people. She felt something was off but couldn't put her finger on it. Her gaze turned to Jih who remained glaring at the person in front of them.

"Now that you mention it, your presence is just enough. Visitors always provide something that helps the band grow. You can tell us what you have found past the mountain, maybe one of our followers will come." The man said with a hearty laugh.

Narro nodded with a laugh as well, which carried loudly through the camp and generated a few strange looks. He saw their new friend pointed to a spare tent where the four could stay for the night. Daylight would be up for some time, but their atrophied bodies made them quite tired. Narro saw that a few of the band were sipping some sort of broth that was being passed around, fresh from another hearth. Food was certainly scarce, but on occasion mushrooms scavenged from the furthest ends of these plains provided the bare minimum as the fungi were crushed and eaten with heated water. Sadal lifted her head in surprise as they too were offered some of this broth and took some. Trekkal awoke to the smell and sipped as they shared.

The man mentioned that the broth they shared helped sleep off the hunger pangs in between searching for meals. Narro was gracious, but only took a small portion as he found the taste not great while Jih refused entirely. Narro raised an eyebrow at Jih, it was far from him to be a particularly picky eater, but Narro knew Jih was a chef at heart and must have felt insulted to eat such ill-prepared food. Narro knew he already spurned the bark offered to them as well. The four took their slumber with great seriousness as they closed their tent flap quickly. Sadal and the others practically collapsed onto the grass below, not bothering to use their packs as pillows. Before closing her eyes, Sadal spoke to the others.

"We'll leave tomorrow morning and get back to where we need to go. If the north has more people who seek the meteor's strength, they may be able to find something to eat. People survive here, we will adapt." Sadal said and gave some reassurance to the others. Trekkal already drifted to sleep, while she fixed her position before nodding off.

Jih had insomnia for various reasons, and so it was much more difficult for him to fall asleep than the others. He huffed in and out of sleep as he heard chewing and some laughter that came from the crackling of the outside fire. It came to no surprise that they were clearly holding out on their supply of meat, this was reasonable to Jih as they were just visitors after all. Jih eavesdropped on bits and pieces of their conversation.

"The First...How people beyond the mountain revere them. Bah!" A woman's voice called out.

Jih frowned with anger as he heard the denigration of his people. Jih was treated with respect and admiration among Forest Seekers and The Aligned that acknowledged his legacy. Although he found it strange at first, he couldn't deny that it felt deserved after all he's been through. Jih recognized the man with the gray beard's voice in response to his companion. Jih grumbled lowly to himself as he remembered him as the man who despised the meteor. Jih recalled the conversation they held with their kind guest, and although it hadn't occurred to him at the time, he noticed that there were marks on the man's arms. These weren't injuries that would accompany a man who knew his tools well, they were remarkably more fresh than usual. Jih also noticed a subtle shaking present in a few of the people that sat at the hearth. It was an unnatural sort that contrasted with the feeling of the cold that permeated around them. In the darkness of the tent, Jih yawned and massaged his beard as he thought some more. Jih and the others hadn't found any game to speak of for miles. What creature would have possibly given him those injuries? He then considered the men who were sharpening weapons from bone. These were not strong enough to pierce the hide of an elephant and they were far too weak to defend themselves against a scimitar-toothed cat.

Jih drifted off to sleep and wanted to forget this line of thinking. He was silent and finally stilled his breathing only to be interrupted by a nightmare of that screaming woman and her eyes that Jih stared into. He remembered her direction and how she ran towards them. Her skin was pale, not because she was sick, but because she lost something. Jih tied it all together and linked that the person that ran towards them was in the same direction as the camp they were now staying at. Jih realized that she was pale because she lost blood and reasoned she was attacked by this group. Jih opened his eyes in realization before he drifted back to sleep from sheer exhaustion. He would have to communicate their next move as soon as he was able. The first advantage Jih had was the element of surprise.

The next morning, Narro woke up to find Jih missing from the tent. Narro's bladder was full, so he went to relieve himself. Narro walked away some distance from the village and urinated. As he did so, his eyes looked towards some middens of bone and small stone flakes that were piled up. Normally useless on their own, Narro liked to pick through them for small pieces of bone to work on his flute skills. He leaned in with his gaze fixed on a particularly larger midden. He made out bits and pieces of no consequence until picking through he saw what appeared to be a jawbone. Narro raised an eyebrow seeing that was strange as he remembered their quests for hunting weren't successful in any capacity. It wasn't a grave either, for these were much further away or in special places. Narro decided to touch the bone and realized that it was human. Another member of the camp called out to Narro, as the hairs of his back jumped on end.

667

"You are a curious one. Did you find something you were looking for? Your friend is waiting for you by the fire." The woman asked.

Narro looked towards the woman and gave a disarming smile. He had two options here, to either lie about his intentions or to play dumb. His gaze turned to Jih who stood by the fire and glared at the others. He was waiting for Sadal and Trekkal to wake before they quickly made their leave.

"I was just looking for a snack." Narro said with some slight humor that didn't carry over well.

Jih looked across to Narro who shared his knowing gaze of what these people truly were. At first, Jih thought to leave without raising any more suspicion, but his actions changed as he heard a loud scream. Narro and Jih ran over to find a now awake Trekkal who pushed someone to the ground. She grabbed her sling and swung it in a large circle and kept a few other people back. Sadal was groggy but came to as she quickly assessed what was going on.

"I saw what you all tried to do! I-I thought I was seeing things, but you tried to drag Sadal as she slept yesterday! Now you did it again! What is the meaning of this?" Trekkal spat in anger at the group outside the tent. She pointed her finger at a younger man with a scar down his face that drew attention.

Jih was confused as he thought he would hear their tent open but realized in his exhaustion that he fell back to sleep. Trekkal noticed their previously emaciated stomachs from the night before were now fat but far from healthy. Of all their luck, they found refuge with cannibals[66]. Their ruse was broken by their haste to eat, and the group's words were broken by the older man who accommodated them before.

"We wanted to do this quietly, you know. The soup you ate should have kept you asleep longer. You are our kin first and not our ideal choice. This member of The Youngest though is fresh and full of life. Her blood will bring back the Zaan." The man spoke as he rallied the others to come to him.

A silence fell across the crowd as Jih and Narro slowly moved their way over to Trekkal and Sadal. Jih frowned but had a smug feeling of satisfaction as he knew their intentions. Jih's only thoughts now were to protect his friends and get out unscathed. He searched for weakness in the ranks.

"Do you think we want to eat people? We do this so the Zaan can return. It is the only way. Your people ruined this land, Plaguebringer, and it will be her flesh that restores it!" The man yelled while pointing at Sadal.

Sadal was filled with disgust as she punched the nearest person she could find, square in the jaw. She exerted so much force in her hatred that her fingers hurt all over as she shook the pain away. Now that blood was spilled, there was no going back. Trekkal stood in front of Sadal and prompted her to duck as she propelled a rock at rapid speed,

---

[66] Cannibalism is a behavior that has been verified in the archaeological record and practiced by various human groups within the Paleolithic. These actions may have not only been for sustenance in hard times but hold possible religious or cultural importance for reasons currently unknown to us.

the impact of the throw downed a woman some distance away. Her femur shattered and she yelled in immense pain. Jih and Narro quickly took advantage of the ensuing chaos to retrieve their weapons and join the fight. If they were able, Jih wanted no one to be spared. He didn't come with bloodlust in mind, but he saw them as blights on the land much like how he and Kag eradicated the Neck-Shells like insects beneath his feet. Narro found himself quickly engaged with two warriors that tried to restrain him. He swung his club handily knocking one unconscious and the other's flesh was torn asunder as he disformed the other's face in. The work wasn't pleasurable, but it needed to be done. Those who couldn't fight panicked and attempted to grab the four to hold them down.

Sadal found herself in too close of a range for her throwing spears to be of any use, so she used close combat instead. She charged to one of the men with her shoulder and brought them to a daze. Sadal was aware of the strength of The Aligned but saw that their weakness in food insecurity was their biggest disadvantage. She moved to the side and raised her foot to kick her opponent squarely in the stomach. The man lost breath as she continued her assault. Sadal felt that she was grabbed by her hair as she went to do the finishing blow. She withdrew a knife from her clothing and cut a small portion off to free herself before centering her attention on the others. She slit the man's throat, jumped towards her next attacker, and delivered a large stab in the chest. Jih had a mission in mind, with his rage on the man who said such cruel things about the meteor. He was far from a devoted zealot, but he held great respect for the power that exuded from such an object, it would be criminal to not address it. The man saw this and attempted to ground himself, but with just a simple club of his own, he didn't offer much resistance. Jih moved to end the man's life effortlessly and used the length of his spear to trip him to the ground. Jih used his foot to pin the man's back to the ground and stuck his sharpened spear into the back of the man's neck. The man's skin broke apart with ease as the ground soaked with blood. Jih left to attack the others.

As the day went on, Jih and company found themselves caked with blood as their attackers dwindled quickly. Trekkal's assault with stones crippled many and made fighting back from their group's strikes quite difficult. A camp of twenty emaciated people and themselves soon were no more. Jih sought to have death to the last one for such vile actions and so it would be done. Reduced to nothing more than dust in the wind, the last of them was a sickly child left behind in a tent that was smothered by Jih. Jih saw this as an act of mercy so that they wouldn't have to starve any longer. The four gathered their thoughts as they saw the mountain of bodies that were left at their wake. While Sadal felt energized, Trekkal and Narro felt rather empty. The wholesale slaughter of these people was something they had to come to terms with, but keeping their family safe is what mattered most. Sadal started to loot the bodies for anything of value and noticed strange coverings on their feet. They were shoes that were a one-size fits all style. There were plenty for the four to wear and Sadal gathered them. Sadal and the others equipped their new footwear and felt much warmer. Jih looked at his shoes and saw they held a fur covering with a tanned hide that went around the foot and were fastened together by small coils made with sinew.

"Burn the camp. Denmey will not touch these cursed ones." Jih said to the others as he took a block of wood to light from their campfire.

Jih took this piece of wood and torched what remained of the homes. The others waited for the plain's grasses to catch flame and for the spread to take hold. Their directions now were to head north and find those who have witnessed the meteor directly. Narro pressed on in hopes that their journey would find good fortune for them to eat. He couldn't imagine having such a hunger that he'd be willing to eat any of his comrades.

As the group continued on their walk, Jih stopped as he picked up an odd-looking skull that was on the ground. He studied its shape and massaged his forehead and compared it to the other one. Jih's mind was more developed than the skull's that he picked up, but he recognized this as a mark of the ancestors. He looked at it and wondered if their words were true. Were the ancestors really this horrible? Although Jih held doubts on the most outlandish claims, he did feel there was something missing from the record. Jih thought about The Council and their deceit towards the rest of his band. The Council painted themselves as omniscient and without failure in the eyes of Tur. How could they have hidden such a dark legacy from them? Jih looked inward and considered all he's been through. Jih considered himself a good man and looked at the mess he left behind. It was brutal work but was justified as they were hapless cannibals. Nothing was going to stop his pursuit of the meteor now that he was this close. He dropped the skull to the ground and joined the others.

The Frozen North

The harsh winds of Northern Europe converged upon the proud settlement of The Aligned who dressed themselves tightly in warm furs. At the far reaches above, blackened ground from the meteor's impact was now surrounded by snow in the cold front that came in. Important to all but now considered a holy site by this settlement, it was no accident that such a community thrived here. It was built as part of the vision of one great man and a dream. One man that stood above the rest shrouded the meteor under a pile of animal skins. He placed his ear on the meteor, taking a breath of concentration as the heat from his mouth was visible. He closed his eyes in deep focus as he meditated. His followers slowly diverged on him as their capes of animal furs dragged along the snow.

"Jarzill. What does the meteor call to you?" A woman called forth as she clinked a necklace made of bone. She, like many others of their kind, waited for a message of some kind from their leader. Jarzill wasn't one to react to simple whims, when he spoke there was always a sense of urgency and deliberate motion at hand.

Jarzill identified as one of The Aligned, he was raised by them, and lived among them. His face was never shown as he wore a mask of petrified wood that obscured his identity. He was a towering 5'10 compared to the average of his group but inherited their strength. As a pure leviathan of a man, he was of mixed heritage, with his father being one of The Youngest. Though controversial to some, his charisma cooled down any suspicions that his loyalties lay elsewhere. Jarzill made the pilgrimage up north and lived as those beyond the mountains did. He disavowed the old ways of life and joined the others of this order who knew nothing else but sacrifice. When the meteor landed after a hunting expedition down south, Jarzill took his opportunity to cement power as an interpreter of its visions. Jarzill was one of their own through and through. He spoke with a diction that cut through the air as their voices carried through the deep wind.

"There is a hunger from her. She must eat so that she can recover from her journey. Meat of the Zaan fuels us, but there is more that must be given." Jarzill said as he lifted his head up to address her words. Jarzill waited as he looked over the reactions of those that followed. This group was close to Jarzill, but even as their leader, there was a separation of the life he had before he found the meteor. This past was mysterious and although interesting to some, it wasn't meant to be addressed.

"We will go to the south. Those who cannot walk will stay behind and guard our settlement. Those that are able, join me. It is time that the lesser bands understand what we guard." Jarzill ordered as a small contingent of warriors soon made their way to him. Jarzill held a small grin of satisfaction. Jarzill commanded them to walk single file to obscure their numbers in the snow above. Their footprints stepped in the snow as one to their goal.

The various bands here took little interest in other matters past their own daily needs. They enjoyed the gift of relative isolation, but this came at a heavy price as well. News among the bands spread at variable lengths, when times of great significance managed to capture the eyes of many, but in the blink of an eye, groups lived and died without having known any difference. At the front of one such village was a group of about twenty people, some of which used a rock shelter for their communal needs while building homes of their own. To the eyes of Jarzill, those who were not among his group were considered outsiders and ripe for his needs. The expedition took three days as they finally reached their goal. The warriors at Jarzill's disposal ate smoked mammoth meat to restore their strength as they looked at the settlement.

"Blood of the Zaan courses through our veins Jarzill. What will your will be?" One of the men answered as he withdrew a heavy two-handed spear that was strapped to his back.

"We must capture them live, to bring them without their spirit inside is but a hollow shell. We will mark them on our return." Jarzill ordered as he looked to see some shuffling around of tools needed for incapacitation rather than outright murder.

The right tool for the job was a smoothed stone that was rubbed against the ground for quite some time with an ivory handle. As wood was harder to come by in their area of the world, Jarzill's forces rationed the use of ivory for such things aside from their building material. The powerful ivory handle allowed for a devastating blow when needed, but also a light touch. It wasn't an exact science, but with enough practice the raid would be a success. Jarzill commanded his forces with thunder that surged through his voice as they stepped forward uninterrupted.

"Bring them out of their homes and to me! Offer them the choice to join or die." Jarzill said as he withdrew a club and led the charge. The other members, who were more concerned with their own group neglected to give any creed to the advance but one such boy sounded a horn that signaled their entrance. The able bodied of this village grabbed whatever they could to face off against the approaching horde. Jarzill's fighters were especially skilled as they ran forth attacking those indiscriminately in their way. While their target fought to preserve their lives, there was a special mission at hand for them. When it came to sacrifice, Jarzill held no favorite where any vigor would be acceptable for the meteor's immense thirst.

Jarzill sighted two from this village for his aims, a teenage girl who was busy tending to their wounded from a recent hunt and an elderly man who served as their Seer. The work was quick. As Jarzill looked through the slits of his mask to see the fighting going well, it was time for him to strike. He approached the girl with his club and barreled past the recovering people that lay on the ground. Jarzill made no noise as he attacked and used the ire of his wooden mask to draw the fear from his foes. She attempted to shield herself, but Jarzill wound his arm up and slammed her head with the club and caused her cheek to bleed. The impact from the club knocked her to the ground and was rendered unconscious. He would return for her later. The elderly Seer in the distance witnessed Jarzill's brutality but at his advanced age had little more strength than the person he saw fall to Jarzill.

The old man braced for death as he knew struggle his entire life, but he could only have been so lucky. Amid the chaos that ensued, Jarzill approached him with a single hand and choked him. The old man's breath vanished as he feebly tried to wrestle his grip. In time, the man grew still and Jarzill released him where he slumped to the soil. Organized chaos, two words that in most use were juxtaposed were how Jarzill handled his raids. With his objective for captive sacrifices met, he let the others run as they saw fit. Blood was drawn for the few who gave a large struggle, but each were able to bring down at least one.

As promised, Jarzill returned for the first victim of his raid. He dragged her by the furs of her clothing as she made a subtle line in the ground, while the old man was received by another of his followers. Once the fighting ended, Jarzill looked upon his handiwork to see a village cleansed of its inhabitants either through fire or clearance for sacrifice. His two prizes were bound with rope and dragged by hand for the entire trip back as many hands shifted the responsibility. The teenage girl awoke first to find herself hours later being dragged far away from what remained of her home. She had little comfort except to see that somehow, her Seer was also one of the survivors of this encounter. She wanted to scream and resist, but feared the worst to come if she did. As she saw the world upside down with her eyes opened, she attempted to whisper to the old man. One of Jarzill's followers noticed this and hit her over the head once more. Too obvious, she needed to be quieter next time. The old man pretended to stay unconscious as he held his pain on the inside. He had no idea where he was going but attempted to stay strong for the young that depended on him. His back ached with the pains of the road.

The next time the teen awoke was under the stars, in the dead of night and still moving. This time though she wasn't on the ground, but on some sort of wooden sled that was hauled. She wasn't only restrained to her wrists but bound to this vehicle as well. The old man's tired brown eyes met hers. He blinked twice, which gave her some confusion, but he signaled that two days had passed since they were on the road. His ropes were slightly looser than hers, and he was able to manipulate his arm enough to hold her hand for a brief time. The temperature here was much colder than they were used to, with their bare feet quite cold. The old man noticed that their captors were wearing shoes made with the hide of wooly rhino, impressive leatherworking indeed, if the circumstances weren't so dire.

The old man saw that their destination was finally reached. This was a settlement where there were more crazed people like the ones that attacked them. He studied their strange, adorned furs and looked for any sorts of patterns. He didn't think they were cannibals, as the trip was three days long and they surely would have been eaten by now, but something felt strange. He heard bits and pieces of the meteor being discussed. As a Seer, he was privy to this information already, but he was surprised at the fanatical nature that this band took to understand the secrets of the meteor. For them, it was a curiosity given by the spirits, but for these people, it was an obsession. He turned his head to find the teenage girl missing and strife was on his face. He closed his eyes as one of Jarzill's followers approached with a knife, but to his surprise, he was let go now within this village.

Jarzill sat alone in a tent with a small fire in the center. His hand lay on his spear as he nodded for one of his followers to release the binds on their captive. The teenage girl was bewildered at the events of the last few days but was finally given some room to speak. She massaged her head that was now bruised with multiple blows for her to remain unconscious. While her first desire was to murder Jarzill, she noticed that this had to be a test of some kind. She saw the man poised with his legs folded and his spear by his side.

"I understand your anger. The surprise of yours that you are still here. Let me answer what must be said." Jarzill said, his voice emanating from a nearby tent. The old man was quickly accompanied by another villager, and he said nothing as he tried to overhear their conversation.

"You-You monster! You all came and took my life from me!?" The girl said, her voice filled with hatred at the masked man before her.

Jarzill made no movements. He knew that his message wasn't a popular one, but in time, people would come to believe his visions and his words. He took a deep breath and spoke, his tone so disarming and enchanting that she was taken aback by such civility in his words.

"Tell me your name. You are part of a greater plan that the meteor requires. This is why you and the old man there were chosen for this. I could tell by his clothing that this was a Seer we have taken. Seers are special, but I am not bound by the rules of our people. There are greater forces at work. I offer you two paths. You may walk along with us or...you can return to the spirits. Make your choice." Jarzill commanded as he gestured to a dagger that lay between the two.

Despite the cold around them, the teen's hands started to sweat. She spent the last seventy-two hours being dragged off into the middle of nowhere from her perspective and now was offered the chance to live or die. She tried her best to not hyperventilate as she considered her options. As a survivalist through and through, the option of following the path as mentioned seemed to be the better of the two options. She knew that she didn't have the strength to be a raider but could offer some sort of chance for them as a healer. It would be important to use this time to escape. Only a fool could pick the latter option. She looked at Jarzill to see his eyes, but all she could see was cold and unfeeling wood.

"I...I will work with you. My name is Leta. Show me what must be done here. I am a healer. I was practicing until you came to our village." She said, her voice low.

Although barely audible, Jarzill nodded as he dismissed her with the point of his finger. The old man was next, and as he saw the young girl's expression, his own expression changed as his mind raced on what happened. As the old man eavesdropped on their conversation, he was aware of what Jarzill was going to offer him. He raised his hand to stop him mid-speech which gave Jarzill a pause.

"I know what you offered her. I wish to join the spirits. I have nothing of value to give you, nor would I want to. My time here is but a grain of sand now." The old man said with a scowl.

"Your knowledge is a gift to our understanding of this world. Are you sure you wish to reconsider?" Jarzill asked with a genuine curiosity of what this Seer has witnessed in his life. Jarzill valued knowledge as not only was it important for control, but he wished to understand the natural forces at work that allowed the meteor to enter its very state of being. He knew he was but only one man and would need the knowledge of many to bridge this together. The old man offered nothing more which saddened Jarzill, but his request was granted.

With a silent nod, Jarzill's followers took the old man away to the outskirts of their village. Jarzill called for the new initiate of Leta to accompany him and some of his followers as they started their ascent towards the landing site of the meteor. After some time, the group of people stopped short, and allowed Jarzill to walk first as his cape made from scimitar-toothed cat fur dragged behind him in the snow.

"Here is why we do what we can. This meteor houses a powerful spirit who will grant us knowledge of unimaginable things. She must be fed well, and I intend to be a good cook." Jarzill said, showing off the site to his new follower.

Jarzill held up his finger and watched the girl's gaze stare upon him. He approached the old man and placed two fingers down his forehead and ran them down the man's entire body as he stood in defiance. Jarzill reached deep into his clothing and wielded a dagger forged from obsidian. Obsidian was not natural in this area, it was a traded good far from the south, but was picked up as a trophy in battle in a village raid. Its clean cut was valued by Jarzill for the sacrifices that needed to be made. The old man was cut down in mere moments as Leta mourned her now deceased Seer. He leaked blood that painted the snow red as his frail body hit the ground with a small thud. In just mere moments, Jarzill cut down over sixty years of world experience in a single move. Jarzill made a point for her to absorb every detail before he spoke again.

"Do not be upset. His energy flows through the ground as we speak. His purpose was picked for his own and it will benefit us all. Another for the pile it would seem." Jarzill said, his tone unmoved by the audible cries before him. He placed his dagger back into his clothing, where the fresh bits still leaked from inside and left a small trail behind him in the wake of his leaving.

"If you are worthy, you will receive a message from her. You will come with me in one week. Be prepared." Jarzill ordered Leta as he called his followers forth.

Jarzill ordered his followers to build this new healer a tent of her own from great mammoth bone and a role of her own. For those loyal to him and his message, Jarzill could provide the resources needed to do great and amazing things. With the willing, this was the opportunity of a lifetime, and for the forced, this was a fate worse than death itself.

Snow Day

After their encounter with the cannibals, Jih and the others looked for a reprieve from their horrid ordeal. While the world was warmer, there was still the chance of unusual weather to show its face. Jih looked up at the sky to see that it was now once again snowing. For someone like Jih or Sadal who called the jungle their home, investigating the presence of where snow came from was an exciting one. Snow was seen in its present form on the mountain but here it fell freely as the four looked while their breath took physical form. Their feet were already sinking inside it and the few hills they saw were covered in the material as well.

"The clouds are filled with darkness but do not bring rain." Jih said as he looked up and felt a cold brush on him. He looked at Sadal's well-maintained snow leopard garb and how well it camouflaged her in the growing snow compared to the rest of them.

"Is there anything this stuff does besides make me feel cold? It makes terrible water but is fine in a pinch." Narro asked as he looked to see Trekkal's face focused on something. He tapped his sister's shoulder to grab her attention only for her to swat his hand away as she continued to watch.

"What are they doing up there?" Trekkal asked herself while she looked in the distance to see a few of The Aligned with a large hunk of wood at their side.

Trekkal noticed that the wood was cut and bound together with some sort of material. She and Narro knew of sleds and their ability to haul large pieces of meat but she hadn't gathered that they could be used for other things as well. Trekkal noted that the size of the sleds they were using but, were being used as seats for them to slide down the hill with increasing speed until they found a way to stop. It looked incredibly fun, and she wanted to ask if they could join in. Jih stepped forward but was quickly reminded by Sadal to remain silent so that his Plaguebringer mark wouldn't cause issue. She helped with this endeavor by stitching a small hood with some discarded skins over his head to hide his brow. From the face down, Jih looked indistinguishable from The Youngest to The Aligned.

"I want to do what they are doing." Trekkal said as she walked closer to the group.

Sadal was hesitant at the thought but as she saw Jih's curious desire to join Trekkal, she decided to follow along for the time being. The four made their way as they were buffeted by the increasing amount of snow. For the cheerful people in the distance this was nothing but a boon for them as their landing would be much softer than on the harsh grass below. Trekkal waved a few of them over with a happy expression on her face as two present looked at one another before addressing her. Jih saw an assortment of goods at their disposal in baskets lined with fur some distance away, this was a work break of some kind. Sadal watched the monotonous nature of them trudge their way back up the steep hill with the sled once more. How could this be enjoyable? Sadal's extent for what she considered entertainment would turn a few heads, but that question would be answered for her shortly.

"Visitors are rare on these sides of the mountains. Why are you here?" One of them asked, looking at the four of them with suspicion in their eyes.

Jih kept his silence as he didn't want to expose his status. He folded his arms giving a curt response. He felt he didn't need to advertise their business to this strange group. Considering the four were fresh from hostile outsiders, it was natural that Jih remained guarded.

"Well, we are looking for this meteor, would you happen to know anything about it?" Trekkal asked with some cheer in her voice. She was slightly startled as the woman that answered her, moved her face closer to hers at the question.

"You are also followers of the sky?" She asked as she examined the four of them. Narro gave a small wave to announce his presence and to enter the conversation. Sadal and Jih decided to let Narro and Trekkal handle this conversation for the time being.

"In fact, we are. We were curious about directions on where to go next. Our last source tried eating us. Surely you will not do the same. Right?" Narro said with a slight worry in his voice.

The woman gave a hushed laugh that unnerved Narro further while Trekkal decided to join her in laughter. She nudged Narro's arm for him to follow suit as she couldn't help but look back at the hill behind them.

"If you are patient and can wait your turn, we will let you four use our sled. I see it on your faces, many want to use our hill. The thrills of the wind in your face is anything our kind should enjoy. As for your request. If your words are true, you must know of Jarzill and his words. They speak to us and we carry his vision. This does not come lightly however, for a great sacrifice must be made for an audience with him." She continued to explain.

Narro raised an eyebrow as Jarzill's name sounded vaguely familiar, but he wasn't sure where he remembered it. The woman noticed Narro's reaction and held her fingers to her chin in thought as well. While the two conversed, Jih walked off and looked at the snow with interest on his face. He gave a childish grin as he felt the cold between his covered fingers.

"Whatever it takes for us to see him. This is an important matter. Our friend there- where is he." Narro said as he looked around to find Jih kneeling in the snow. He was making faces in it with his fingers much to his light amusement while Sadal attempted to drum up conversation with the other members of The Aligned.

"He searches for the meteor to find the answer on which he can save his people. You understand the perils of travel more than anyone else." Narro said in response.

"Jarzill will know more, but for now, you can help us claim the antlers of the Agharudeu[67]." The woman commented as she stretched out her arms.

---

[67] Emic word for Megaloceros or Irish Elk.

"Oh, that is a creature we have yet to see. Antlers hm? I would say after facing Mahaku, an herbivore is less of a challenge for us. Describe it to us, how can we help?" Trekkal asked as the woman communicated the endeavor.

"It is a powerful animal with a stature as tall as the trees that dot the forests of the south. You will see it and be enamored by the beauty it holds, only for it to charge and gore you. Bring us the antlers and we will give you what you seek." The woman stated.

Trekkal's attention span for the conversation dwindled further as she wanted to go slide with the others, so she gave a simple nod in acknowledgement and agreed to the terms. Narro and Trekkal soon joined Jih and Sadal who were nearing the top. One of the men present handed Sadal the slide that practically fell to the ground in her hands. It was large enough to support two people and was heavy, so she and Jih both carried it. As the two ascended to the top, Jih gave Sadal a look as she urged him to go ahead first.

"Ah, that is higher up than I considered it would be. Well, maybe we should. Oh, you're sitting down already." Sadal said as she looked to see Jih sit with his legs folded as he patted behind him for Sadal to sit.

While the two waited, Sadal awkwardly gripped Jih's stomach as she pressed against him for the sled. Although she would have preferred to ride with Narro, Jih seemed stoic enough to not cause a stir and she felt calm. Trekkal and Narro gave them a gentle wave as they were unsure of how to start their descent.

"Long way down. We will go with speed." Jih stated as he eyed how long their approach would be to the bottom.

Jih attempted to push the sled, but with he and Sadal's combined weight, it was too heavy for them to do it on his own. Jih gave Narro and Trekkal a look as he moved his head to come towards them and give a much-needed boost. Trekkal happily obliged, using her foot to give a strong kick to the two as they descended the hill. Narro could only give a mischievous grin to the pair as they slowly went below the curve.

"Tre-!" Sadal yelled as her voice gradually descended.

While it was possible to slide on this hill with just dirt alone, the snow made it a far smoother ride. The sudden change in speed was alarming to both as Jih instinctively tried to steer the sled using his body weight. Jih felt his very face be chiseled by the sudden gust of wind that struck him as he felt Sadal's nails dig into his skin. He wanted to close his eyes, but he was moving with such speed that this was almost impossible. Sadal's hair launched behind her as they floated through the air. The few members of The Aligned they conversed with earlier waited at the bottom, linking their arms together to act as a chain for those returning to land. Left to their own devices, Jih and Sadal would head much further than they anticipated. Sadal decided to take a change of pace as she realized how exhilarating the speed was.

"Let's go faster!" Sadal yelled loudly as she attempted to shift her entire weight on Jih while he turned his head around as best as he could to give a surprised expression to her.

Jih decided to oblige with this request, no matter how insane it sounded. He knew of boats constructed by Tur's vast knowledge that could take advantage of the current and he was envious of these, but the sled was a transportation tool not known to him. He wondered if these could have utility back home. Their design was simple enough to his logic, giant boards of wood tied together with fibers that could come from plants in his area but with the amount of foliage in his native Sundaland, the speed aspect would be far less useful than out on the open plains. Jih imagined the prospect of running into a tree at breakneck speed and wasn't fond of the image.

As the two reached the bottom of the hill, they gained so much speed that Jih lost grip of the sled entirely and with it, Sadal as well. The two barreled through the makeshift barrier the others made as the two crashed in a small hole in the ground and launched the pair some distance from the vehicle. Jih found himself in a face full of snow as Sadal landed shortly nearby with her face to the sky. Narro observed the sight from the top of the hill with his hand covering his mouth as he briefly looked to see if the two were damaged in any way before bursting into laughter.

"Going fast is fun, but learning how to stop is perhaps better." Sadal said as she wiped away snow that bound her hair together. She got up and walked through the snow to reach Jih. She held out her hand to Jih and although he was already halfway up, he grabbed it anyway as she gave him a strong heave. His shoes were stuck slightly as he jumped out to get a better footing.

"Jih will see how Narro and Trekkal do." Jih said to Sadal as he recovered the sled and hauled it behind him. Jih strained slightly as he moved it through the snow but could feel his muscles begin to feel strength again as he moved it towards the expectant crowd. He gave a sigh as he realized that he would need to haul the sled all the way back up the hill for Narro and Trekkal. He blew some air out of his nose as he felt the load slightly lessen as Sadal was behind him, urging him to climb higher as their shoes continued to march through without issue.

After some time, Jih huffed as he was short on breath while Sadal felt the same but put on a face for the two of them. Trekkal gave Sadal a slight look of concern as she raised an eyebrow but gave Jih a supportive wink. She was first to get on the sled while Narro sat down next as he placed his hands around his sister's stomach. Narro sat up straight and would serve as the anchor for the two of them in their descent down the hill. Narro and Trekkal were in sync with one another on their descent, able to control the speed of their sled as they collectively leaned back or forward. Trekkal didn't bother to keep her hands secure to the sled, instead waving happily to Sadal and Jih who watched from the bottom in slight jealousy on how they handled their descent with ease. As the sled was made for their body type, these two had a far easier time maneuvering the vehicle than Sadal or Jih. At the bottom of the hill, the two waited as Narro commanded the sled to come to a nice and prompt stop.

"Of course, you did it perfectly..." Sadal said with a slight grumble.

Narro could only give a happy laugh as he went to soothe Sadal's mood with a tight and gracious hug while Trekkal called for the attention of the others. Trekkal was rarely one to call team meetings, let alone one with a serious tone to her voice so when she spoke, many listened patiently.

"I did some talking and they know about the meteor. Not only do they know about it, but they apparently know where it landed too. The problem is...we need to help them hunt something. It is a big something and we will need to be prepared for it. This is no ordinary Sarudeu, we must collect the antlers for them. To find the one known as Jarzill, there will be a test for us." Trekkal explained as Sadal and Jih tuned into the conversation with their interest piqued.

Sadal scoffed at the request. From her perspective, hunting herbivores was just subsistence rather than any form of actual challenge. Trekkal reiterated the importance of the task while Sadal considered a few factors in her mind. She was aware that The Aligned were more durable in frame than she or Jih were and if this creature caused them issues, she should be somewhat concerned as well. Sadal remained confident however that her skill would surpass whatever threats came her way. She was trained by the best to hunt the worst and aside from the tiger, she felt any threat could be fallen by her spears. With a competent crew behind her back, she vowed to bring them exactly what they wanted.

"If what you say is true, then we have everything we need. Let's look around for shelter and get things moving for tomorrow." Sadal said as the other three nodded.

The Trial: I

While Jih and the others slept, Trekkal took it on herself to find the woman she made the deal with the day before. She exited their makeshift tent and walked shortly over to the small village where the expanse of nothing was dotted along with a few tents and a burning fire in the center that dispelled smoke into the air. Trekkal's face was remembered and the two held brief discussions with one another. Trekkal was unsure on how she would get everyone ready to hunt the animal they discussed before, but that was a problem for later. She lowered her head with respect, as she was a guest in these lands. Trekkal looked around to notice the strange markings on the face and hands of The Aligned that inhabited this place. This settlement was small, even by their standards, as there were only about ten people total. As they were an affiliate of Jarzill's will, they expected to receive supplies and aid for their devotion to his teachings, and more importantly, access to the meteor. Trekkal felt slightly uncomfortable with the sheer amount of devotion to someone who seemed to be but a mortal man, but the idea of one that could communicate with the spirit that inhabited the meteor was an interesting prospect. As Trekkal walked back to her camp, she remembered the words she was told.

"Remember, this animal does not accompany our steppe. You will have to go lower towards the edge of the forest. It will arrive there. Come back with the antlers or do not come back at all."

Jih felt a soft touch that he knew had to be Trekkal. She was always light when it came to Jih and reserved her more bombastic nature for Narro and Sadal. Jih awoke and started his morning routine while Narro and Sadal were more reluctant to awaken. Sadal's eyes were groggy after another night of nightmares. She tried to communicate that she was still plagued by the vision of Deeso's corpse. Her interest in the hunt would be a good distraction from the ills of her mind. Sadal prepared herself and hoisted her throwing spears in her backpack.

"I saw some of our kind use spears from bone here. Perhaps you can adapt this to your shattersticks." Narro said with a yawn as he looked over at the others.

Narro slept with his gear on the night before, so that he could easily get up and move. The way south to the edge of the forest was about three hours long. The group took note of their surroundings and used the snowy hill as a marker to find their way back so they wouldn't be lost on their return. Hunting a deer seemed trivial to both Jih and Sadal, but the size of the creature was something they struggled to guess from Trekkal's description. A small stream that opened to a lake was visible in the distance. With water, life could be found anywhere, and the growth of forest trees was visible.

Jih and the others took the end of this stream and followed it deeper into the forest. Jih took off his backpack and placed it near a pile of rocks where it joined the others. Jih noticed the presence of a snare not too far from his location. Other hunters were present in this valley as he took a walk around. There was a small breeze that carried through the boreal trees that braced together at the forest's entrance. Jih looked behind him to see the others combing through foliage, and each promised one another to reunite once the deer had been found. Jih headed straight as he held his spear. His eyes scanned the ground for clues and noticed a particularly large indent in the soil, a hoof print that was much larger than his own hand. He looked up to hear chewing. Jih was aware that deer ate a multitude of plants nearby, so he stayed low and attempted to hide behind a tree.

Sadal found herself close to Jih as she heard a low grunt come in the distance. She signaled to Jih, but he shook his head to indicate he didn't make the sound. Instead, the prancing motion of their deer came out to both their ears. At the edge of the lake, the giant deer towered over many. Sadal and Jih looked at the animal's antlers, almost thirteen feet in length, in pure awe. Narro and Trekkal eventually met up with Sadal and Jih to see that they stopped. It was true, the beauty of such an animal would captivate you. The ear of the deer twitched as it fed, and its eyes noticed the now still group of four in the distance. For this animal, it felt completely in control as the speed, strength, and knowledge of the environment put it at a better advantage than the bipeds with their sharpened sticks.

The deer's concentration was broken by the sound of another person leaving the bushes as it reared its head up. One of The Aligned that Jih was aware of, pursued the deer and held a spear of his own. The man came forward and decided to challenge its authority. The normally docile deer felt it was necessary to defend its claim to the land and let out a small call from its mouth. It reared up at the sight of the man who attempted to charge directly at it. Unknown to the others was the true speed of such an animal, the deer charged with a ferocity that left Sadal agape as the deer swiped with its antlers. It lifted the man in the air briefly as he hit the ground, with pieces of flesh torn open from his chest. The man coughed and launched his spear. He missed as the agile deer maneuvered quickly past and turned to use its hind legs. It generated enough force to cave his chest in as he was knocked aside to the base of a tree. Splinters of wood ejected from the impact as the man recovered.

"We may need to reconsider our strategy..." Sadal said to herself as she saw the unfortunate soul get crushed before her very eyes.

With the giant deer now on the loose, it darted towards the western section of the woods. Sadal grabbed Jih and pursued as best as they could while keeping the image fresh in her mind. All she had to reference was just a cloud of dust that picked up from its feet. It wasn't enough for her to stall for time, it wasn't injured and she would need to figure out a way to get close, but it would either end up gored by the antlers or have no time to catch up.

"Sadal, this one is fast! How will we surprise it?" Jih questioned as he saw Narro and Trekkal resting by the stream to gather water.

"We have to keep it trapped in these woods. I haven't been able to get an idea of how large it all is. With antlers that big, it may get stuck and that could be our best chance. I just need to get close enough to toss one of my spears and wait it out." Sadal proposed.

Trekkal walked over with a bit of water pooling from her mouth as she attempted to swallow as quickly as possible. She wiped her mouth with her arm and looked up at the two of them.

"No way, have you seen the size of that thing? It can simply run through trees with force. Fighting it directly would be our best chance but the speed. Could you throw a shatterstick that well and that quickly? You are more delicate compared to us. One hit and it ends." Trekkal addressed Sadal's point. Sadal shrugged her shoulders on the matter, nothing would get done if they just sat around and continued talking. Narro walked over to address the others.

"I was the last one to have sight of it, when Trekkal and I were waiting back, I heard the sound of what I thought were Denmey in the distance. There may be caves around here for us to try and find another if all is lost. They also hunt these." Narro mentioned as Sadal frowned at her words.

"Why would we go find Denmey? That's another annoyance to consider which isn't worth our time right now." Sadal asked with folded arms.

"All we need is to find the antlers, remember? It may be likely that if we can steal the kill from one of these animals, we should be able to get what we need. Trust me Sadal. Not very honorable, but right now we need victory no matter the cost." Narro commented as Jih nodded in affirmation. Killing hyenas was second nature to their group, and the prospect of having actual fast hunters bring down their target was an interesting prospect if this gamble could be trusted. It was cleverness that kept them alive all this time after all. Jih decided to forgo water for now as he kept his eye on the deer's direction.

Jih left a deliberate trail for the others to follow and took apart a few branches as he made steady progress. Jih grumbled to himself and wondered if the effort to find this deer was enough to give what these people wanted. The fact that Jih was this close to the power rock meant that there was little that he wouldn't do to get further but his patience also ran incredibly thin when dealing with outsiders. What mattered to him the most were the lives of his friends, twice before that he felt he endangered them for his own aims, once to fight at The Gorge and the cannibals at base of the mountain. He hoped this Jarzill would be accommodating to the four of them once an audience was met. The other members of The Aligned spoke of him with such praise, he had to be an effective and powerful leader.

Sometime later, Jih was joined by the others as he held his fingers to his lips. In the outskirts of the forest there was the greater plains and the sight of depressions in the hills further from their vision that served as rock shelters and caves could be found there. The Aligned in this area contended with an assortment of animals to make their homes when materials for tents were not available. Hyenas were often their rival of choice, but other animals such as cave bears and cave lions also made their way in this land. Jih noticed that these hyenas that Narro claimed to hear were missing and instead they were in the presence of something greater.

"This is not Denmey land. Narro, you heard Kalpeu. Jih can smell urine from far away." Jih said matter-of-factly as Narro arrived out of breath. He got the rest of the group's attention and pointed to the obvious signs. He found it odd that cave lions would pass an opportunity to hunt for food with the forest this close. His face changed as he thought about the cave lions already having their scent.

Jih noted some differences between the two groups, most notably that cave lions had much smaller manes than the ones he was used to seeing in other areas of the world. Jih reasoned that the absence of these lions where they are may indicate that the deer was in their hunting range and decided to go after it. There wasn't much for the four to work from as they were now some distance from their intended target. Sadal advised that the group hug the forest in case they are unable to defeat them in combat, an escape to the forest would be a good line of defense. Narro looked over to notice a few spots of blood that were dried on the side of a tree and used that as the baseline to continue. Much to his surprise, the stifled sounds of conflict could be heard in the distance. The large deer the group hoped to find, contended with three cave lionesses that pursued, while one lone male stood in the distance and patiently watched. The giant elk was unable to use its speed to get away as the lionesses worked as a team to cut off the deer. It had no choice left but to fight. Narro saw the mighty deer lift its hooves to stomp one of the lionesses down while the remaining two jumped on its back. The animal hopped around in a panic, and shifted its body to loosen its grip, but the lionesses' claws dug right in.

The deer used its antlers to flip over the lioness on the ground, sufficiently goring it as its entrails fell to the soil, while the male lion went over to address the smell of the humans that were now closer to their domain. Trekkal held up her sling as the other three attempted to reach Narro. Trekkal stared the lion down and waited while Sadal wanted to move for the attack. The tension between them and the lion could be felt through the air. Both were occupied with the fate of the deer that showed no signs of slowing down just yet. The male lion noticed the difficulty of the kill and chose to intervene with its strength while leaving the others, the health of the pride was more important than these strange visitors. With a burst of speed, the male lion was able to lunge at the back of the deer and force it to collapse with three on its back. The lions were able to get the upper hand and slowly bring down the creature as it touched the ground with a resounding thud. Bits and pieces were taken apart of the deer as it was being stripped alive while Jih and the others observed. While Narro was concerned about retrieving the meat, Jih called him back as he led a short discussion with the others.

"We wait until Kalpeu eats, then, take what we need." Jih commented.

Jih remembered that no predator would want to fight on a full stomach unless they really needed to. With the meat of the deer now in their stomachs, the ravenous lions wouldn't be as contentious. Jih saw that some Thunderfeet imposed this strategy to capture scraps from larger animals that were far beyond the carrying capacity of predators. If the four could walk towards the carcass without fear in their eyes, the lions would observe with their stomachs full to not consider them food.

After a half hour of idling, the curious lions turned their attention to the four humans standing. They were aware of the impact humans could cause with their tools and so looked at them with suspicion as Jih was the first to move. Sadal slowly went behind him and withdrew her throwing spear but kept it close to her. Sudden movements would bring alarm, but having an effective display of force would hopefully show they were not to be trifled with. Narro's eyes dotted the ground for the presence of cubs that would trigger a response against them, but they were spared for now. Trekkal withdrew a knife while Jih, Sadal, and Narro kept their eyes on the lions. Trekkal worked to cut through the stringy meat of the deer's neck to decapitate it. Their trophy was incredibly difficult to hold, as it weighed almost sixty pounds, but between Narro and Trekkal's combined strength, they hauled it in their hands. The two walked backwards to keep their eye on the lions while Jih and Sadal guided them.

The surviving lionesses followed, with a visible trail of blood seeping from their mouths as the four slowly made their way away from the scene. Jih groaned as their next challenge was going to attempt to fit the massive antlers past some of the denser packed trees. He withdrew a hand-axe from his bag and chopped away splinters of wood falling at his feet. With the way inside now, Narro and Trekkal swapped positions with another taking control of where to go. Their persistence was able to keep them steady as they treaded through the forest. With the idea of victory at hand, the four closed the distance to find themselves some distance from when they first started the hunt, now with a much heavier prize in their hands. Trekkal guided the group to make their direction back to the village, citing the large snow-covered hill as their landmark to keep going.

The humble establishment they stayed at previously was a slight hub of activity with visitors from another band visible. These were different people than the ones Trekkal talked with before, but noticed they also held the symbols and coloration associated with Jarzill. She raised an eyebrow and wondered about how much reach one man and their ideas could truly go. The woman she met with before was engaged in discussion while another member of this village assisted in carrying over the antlers. Trekkal let out a small cough announcing her presence.

"So, it is true. The Agharudeu, you have slain it, and the antlers are large. We were hoping for something of this size. We have lost many and this ritual will bring us more members to restore our ranks." The woman proclaimed happily.

"Well-" Sadal said before getting cut off by Trekkal.

"Yes, our fine blades and rocks defeated such a creature. It was a noble display." Trekkal said as she hoped to stop Sadal's sense of sportsmanship from ruining their goodwill.

"Jih and friends have done part. Where is Jarzill?" Jih interceded while he received a quick pat from Sadal to keep quiet.

"Now that it has been mentioned, our visitors are from our sister village. They too have tasks that need to be done, but they were blessed by his arrival some time ago. Jarzill brought good news from the spirit that dwells within the meteor. If you wish to ask him this yourself, leave with this party. They are already aware of what you seek." The woman proclaimed.

Jih stewed in anger but understood that things worth having don't come easy. He turned around and noted the others that the group now found themselves with. He moved to their tent from the previous night and cleared it out of their belongings now that they would be on the move once more. He pointed to the others to gather their things and make the move as soon as everything was accounted for. The power rock would soon be in Jih's grasp.

The Trial: II

Jih's sleep on the cold ground was disturbed by Sadal rustling him awake. All around him, Jih could see the outline of bones that made up the walls of their hut for the night. Jih and the others hopped around with the generosity of others, but they were aware of the quest needed and were welcome to oblige. Jih saw Narro and Trekkal equipping themselves with spare furs that draped behind their backs like that of a cape. These were given to all four of them as a sign of trust and to ensure their greater survival out on the steppes.

"Jih, take these. It will be a cold one today." Trekkal said with some humor in her voice.

Jih could hardly keep his distaste, it was cold every day. Pockets of sparse grass dotted the landscape, but a cold harsh wind humbled many. Outside of their tent, ten of Jarzill's acolytes were armed and ready to participate in the great mammoth hunt. The man himself had two pockets of The Aligned that were allied to his cause to understand the secrets of the meteor. The first group numbered just around ten people and sought the antlers of the giant deer to provide spiritual balance to strengthen their numbers again. This group was more fortunate with their numbers at thirty. Jih and the three were to do yet another task for this group. For them, this was an important endeavor as one of their own was to give birth soon, and a new home would be needed to house the proud family. Jih dreaded this task the most as he remembered their demands to assist in their endeavors to claim a mammoth.

Jih took the extra furs with stride as he tied it in the same way that Narro and Trekkal did. Sadal was the first to exit as she looked at the strange brood who coated their faces in animal fat. Without having reliable clay up north, dousing the face in melted animal fat was a compromise to keeping warm as the wind wouldn't be able to cut as easily. Sadal found quickly that the trade-off for such a comfort was a hanging smell that lasted on the wearer that magnified with captured sweat.

"You bear the skin of the father that belonged to Jarzill. The Youngest does not venture into our territory." One of the women said to her as she looked over Sadal. Narro and Trekkal approached out next, while Jih was the last to hobble out.

"Her frame may be not like ours, but her throws are true. The Zaan will die tonight." Trekkal said in trusted defense of Sadal.

"We shall see if it is true. Jarzill is an important man with many goals." One of the men commented. Sadal wished to retaliate but the looks from both Narro and Trekkal had her keep her tongue silent. Jih observed the group as he waited to hear what the plan was.

Jih saw an older member of The Aligned, a few years his senior, address the group. His beard was grayed, and his hair drooped over his eyes slightly, but he could see the crowd with clarity. He pounded his chest with his fist and gave a mighty yell that invigorated the others.

"The Zaan come today before the frosts take hold to graze. We will fell a mighty one so that we may claim the bones for ourselves. Our target is simple, we will go after the strongest female. Killing her will demoralize the herd and bring great sorrow to the Zaan." The man opened.

Jih felt sick to his stomach, he was already having apprehensions about having to deal with one elephant, but an entire herd of them? The matriarch was no laughing matter when it came to the herd. Not only would she be a formidable opponent in her own right, but the other defenders of the herd would certainly come to her aid. The older man directed a few of the other warriors carrying long sticks. Timber was hard to find in this area, so it was often traded for or scavenged from dead logs when the opportunity struck.

"Firestarters. When we near our target, we will set the torches alight and begin our attack." The man commanded with a gruff nod received from the team.

Jih and the others headed out and chose to stay behind as they were to act as support. Out of the four of them, Narro was the only one with any real experience hunting elephants as he remembered his time with Fahlrit. The straight-tusked elephants were larger than woolly mammoths and he found that to be a possible endeavor, so a mammoth should be easier. Narro was unsure of how experienced these hunters were but trusted their experience in these bleak conditions. The four obeyed their instructions as given and absorbed the details around them. The landscape was dry and cold as the grass moved between their feet. Jih looked to see a herd of horses in the distance and rubbed his stomach. Their group calls sounded over the landscape as they ran with fervor across the hunting party.

Jih did his best to prepare himself to come to blows with the powerful mammoths that inhabited this land. He avoided elephants from a young age, mindful of their power and intelligence, no matter the type he came across. He was stuck in a loop of his own thoughts that broke as the group soon stopped in place. Narro peered out of their team to see the mammoths that they were going to attack. Jih remembered much about how Hyu had a keen eye regarding animal behavior and how she would describe various things to him on their travels. The elephants were arranged in a small circle and rubbed their trunks over the rotting corpse of one of their fallen in mourning.

"We will add another to their pile!" One of The Aligned women shouted and lifted her club in the air as she turned to Jih and the others to join them.

Sadal admired their resolve when it came to the hunt and she herself clapped happily to her words. Her expression of joy faded slightly as she saw Jih's reaction. Jih had many reasons to already feel apprehensive about this, but with the animals seen before them, he was unsure if this would be a wise hunt to make. Jih knew though this wasn't his place to make decisions. He grounded himself to stay calm and think about those back home who depended on him to find the power rock. The group convened some distance away from the mammoths, and Jih felt his entire body tense up as the imposing frame of the beasts came closer to view. The mammoth was no longer just some far off entity in the back of his mind, but a very real and visceral being he needed to face. Jih felt the supportive touch of Narro who nodded his head at Jih. Always thoughtful, Narro remembered most often about Jih's fear of elephants and would do his best to ensure everyone would be fine.

"We should get the calf as well, for their meat is the freshest!" One of the men insisted as the group agreed.

The leader of Jarzill's acolytes held his hand for the Firestarters to light their torches and advance slowly. Their plan was to overwhelm the mammoths into a panic by chanting and synchronizing their attack, while their remaining warriors along with Jih and the others were to go and target the matriarch. Sadal led the three forward as she urged Jih to catch up with the rest of them. Jih's entire core shook, but he powered through for the sake of his team. His teeth rattled and he felt sweat come on his forehead. Trekkal readied her sling and joined the others in the initial assault. Narro was happy to see Trekkal taking the lead on such a task, he felt his sister had truly grown since she and Sadal's battle back in the mountains.

"Sadal...This is bad idea." Jih said lowly under his breath as his eyes turned their gaze to the Firestarters that shouted and attracted the attention of the mourning herd.

These mammoths were ignorant of the destructive power that fire could hold, as with the group's signal, they set alight sections of the tightly packed grass of the steppes. To Jih's surprise, the harsh winds that filled the air didn't extinguish the fire. As the earth itself was incredibly dry, the fire spread quickly. The animals reared up in confusion to one another as retreated in different directions and shook the ground. Jih stood back and watched it all unfold. There was no mass death that he envisioned as a few of Jarzill's acolytes took their spears and clubs to begin their frontal assault on the matriarch. She was identified with a long scar that stretched from stomach to rib cage and a chipped tusk that remained sharp as ever. Trekkal flung rocks as well as she could with her sling and pelted the animal with brutal efficiency while the others attempted to have the elephant rear up and flip over to fall to the ground with her weight. Sadal ran forward with her throwing spears as well and hoped to assist some of them by targeting the elephant's massive feet. The mighty creature tried to calm down her frenzied horde as the grasses carried flame shortly by them, but all was lost.

"Jih! Keep your focus, we should go join the others. Sadal and Trekkal need our help!" Narro said as he held his hand out to Jih and dragged him forward in the process.

Jih closed his eyes as he felt Narro's pull on him, it was the only way he could find himself being remotely effective, but a harsh sound caused him to stop. In the chaos, a lone calf was on its own and a few of the warriors who wanted to attack the calf did so with much joy. It was an easy kill, as the elephant pleaded for its life, only to be pelted by an assortment of stones. Its skull was crushed by the resounding thud of a club from the men. Bits of brain matter littered the grass below. In any other instance, Jih would have expressed great joy at such a beast being returned to dust as all elephants should, but there was more to it than that. As Jih saw the dead calf, he turned his head to see the once frenzied elephants found common cause to unite.

It came to Jih quickly that a grieving mother was the cause of all this. There was already death in the air with one of their herd gone from this world, but a child had a life now extinguished, and they were the cause. The matriarch was embedded with three spears and was given a second wind as the other elephants converged towards the group. The odds were now against them. The matriarch used her trunk to grab a bashful member of The Aligned by the leg and dragged him across the ground without mercy. His furs were being torn apart into the ground as his body made an indent in the dirt. Jih was aware that The Aligned were a much more durable people than his own, but this was no match for what came next. Jih's mouth was agape as he practically saw the man ripped asunder as he was thrown high into the air and landed straight on the matriarch's tusk, only for his body to be torn in half as one half fell before the other.

The other elephants took this as a call to action as their dying matriarch realized that she wouldn't recover from this battle. Hyu always wondered if animals were capable of such thoughts and motivations for things as revenge, or the capacity to be petty like themselves, but now Jih would find that she was correct. From Jih's perspective, the matriarch wasn't going to leave this land without claiming the lives of as many as she could. Sadal's spear landed on the sole of the elephant's foot and caused an immense pain that only continued to fuel the bloodlust before them. One of the Firestarters attempted to wave off the mammoth, only to be knocked to the ground and trampled to death by another elephant who acted as support for their leader. The matriarch leaned on a juvenile male for support until she was able to get back up again for another resounding charge. Jih dropped his spear and punched the ground in agony as everything returned to him from long ago. He held no ties to these people and only cared about his friends. Jih watched as a woman who sought to recover the remains of her friend stepped forward and ran with a spear, unable to do anything else but brace for death. The elephant's massive body collided with the woman, throwing her a great length where she landed on the harsh ground like a ragdoll. She died before she touched the ground.

"Monster!" Jih shouted as he involuntarily teared up.

His vision blurred as the state of his being quickly shifted from the present before him to when he was small and powerless as a young child. It all felt so real, Jih saw the visage of Sundaland's trees in his view of the landscape. He remembered Chak's brutal death and the chaos it caused. Though the matriarch was much smaller than the straight tusked elephant he experienced in years past, its ferocity and intelligence was all the same. Jih shook in fear as he buried his head in the grass unable to control himself. Sadal changed course but was without a weapon as she realized the situation quickly unfolded to be too dangerous, even for her standards. Ronkalk always encouraged determination in the face of danger, but he was averse to running into suicidal endeavors as well. One thing that Sadal retained from The Broken Bone was not only to recognize her strength but also her limitations. She focused now on trying to find Narro and Trekkal to regroup and figure out what to do next. Her calls were interrupted by Trekkal's shriek as she attempted to make her way to save one of Jarzill's acolytes who found themselves frozen with fear.

"Sadal! I need help! This one is alive but wounded, help me drag them!" Narro shouted as he found one of their companions injured but still alive. Sadal was left with a choice as she was torn between which to help. She made the split decision to help Narro instead, in her limited assessment, she chose to prioritize someone physically wounded over one frozen by fear. As Sadal ran to catch up to Narro, she saw a furry lump in the dirt which on closer examination was Jih.

"Jih! We need you right now! Please! Trekkal is in danger, and I need you to help!" Sadal pleaded with him as she continued her run to Narro.

Jih wanted to pretend that he hadn't heard Sadal, but his conscience wouldn't allow such an action to happen. He wouldn't be able to forgive himself if his friends were injured on his behalf for his quest to get the power rock, even if they came originally of their own free will. He knew he had limited time to act and decided to run to Trekkal just as Sadal instructed. Jih wasn't going to clear his fear today, if anything, today's events justified everything he feared most, but Trekkal was the priority. One of the elephants in the fighting held an affinity towards launching rocks, a harmless enrichment item on its own, but was now tossed with resounding strength. Jih ran towards Trekkal as she was in the vicinity of the mammoth while it went to toss a medium sized rock in their direction.

Jih pushed Trekkal to the ground and placed his body over her as he closed his eyes to brace for impact. The rock was thrown a pitiful distance much to the relief of them both, but Jih was too paralyzed with fear to move at that point. Trekkal slowly left Jih's grasp and she and him were able to drag behind the survivor to safer ground. Sadal kept track of how much blood the matriarch was losing in the fighting that ensued. Their group would need to wait out the time given, but as she gave the elephant another glance, she was fading quicker than expected. The wounds present on her body beforehand were the work of all sorts of creatures and failed hunts as well. Narro hoisted the injured man up while Sadal strained to carry the back end while they regrouped. Narro turned his head to see that some of the warriors were out of breath but remained engaged in combat with the beasts.

For Narro, this was a pyrrhic victory at best. They already lost a few people to the elephants and were unsure of how to proceed from here. It was here, however, that the matriarch gave out as it landed with a sullen thud that humbled the combative mammoths. It was as if all at once, the herd decided to cut their losses with valued leadership now gone without cause. Rage filled the elephants as they let out a mighty cry at their misfortune, but revenge would come another day. The remaining mammoths herded their own away from the humans at their feet and swatted them away like flies with their trunk as they lumbered off into the distance.

Jih and the others were confused at the mammoths giving up after fighting so hard, but exhaustion was a universal feeling. The mammoths weren't entirely sure of just how many humans they needed to go through, as the fate of the entire herd wasn't worth it. In the distance, a few of the mammoths could be seen wiping their trunks on the defeated mother before they headed off from this cursed place. Jih knew that in the times to come, the mammoths would remember this day again and know how to quell their fears of fire, but that day would be experienced without his group being involved. The four stood in silence as the remaining companions that accompanied them tore apart the corpse and quickly claimed the pieces they saw fit. For their service as promised, the group considered this task complete and vowed to leave them with a portion of the meat as there was plenty to spare with both deceased matriarch and calf.

"Our bounty is fresh, and you fought with honor. Death happens to all, and it is with meat we may serve the call of the meteor once more. Bring this piece of ivory to our sister village to the east as proof of your battle here. Jarzill will be pleased. The road may take you one week if the weather is not fair, so I suggest you leave next dawn. As for your third trial, as we discussed, we are in contact with the main village. Find the Urain-Takom, slay it, bring the horn to Jarzill himself.[68] Once this is done, you will speak to him." The older man stated as he spoke to Narro and Trekkal. Trekkal waited as one of them chipped off a chunk of ivory to place it into her hands. As a gift, they were also given an additional supply of old mammoth furs taken off the dead. Trekkal was slightly disturbed but appreciated the extra layer of warmth for the times ahead.

"We will do that." Narro said, nodding his head in respect to the others. Now that their first duty was done, the time to rest fell on all their hands.

"Before we go, thank you Jih. You saved me, although the Zaan spared us the true wrath." Trekkal said as she gave Jih a tight hug. She rubbed his back while Jih gave a slow pat in return.

"Mmmm." Jih said lowly as he wanted to leave this behind him.

Without further delay, the four set out to find the next village as stated. Jarzill was a strange but powerful figure for those who wished to emulate his teachings. The four were curious about what power he truly had that existed on his own and how the meteor amplified these feelings.

---

[68] Emic word for wooly rhino.

The Trial: III

Jih reminded the group of their tasks to finally get an audience with the one known as Jarzill. They claimed the antlers of the giant deer and befell the mammoth with some of his allied warriors as witness to the triumph. At the far stretches of the North, massive glaciers made a giant wall of ice, impeding their progress any further in that direction. The four scoured along eastward, hoping to follow this barrier to find their target. The last task to prove themselves worthy was to claim the horn of a woolly rhino. Their purpose for it was kept vague, but Narro and Trekkal guessed it had to do with spiritual matters beyond their understanding. Jih was well aware of ivory and its uses among his people, a rhino horn was coveted by The Council as a good for trade among other things. At the beginning of their trial, Sadal felt deflated that none of these animals were the predators she yearned to do battle with, but these were still considered powerful opponents.

Jih and the others walked in relative silence for their target, as it was known that although rhinos had terrible eyesight, their sense of smell and hearing would wake them up quickly to their plans. Jih regretted not being much help during the mammoth hunt, as he only mustered up enough courage to quickly recover Trekkal from danger. He hoped to make it up to the rest of them with this hunt. A harsh wind picked up as they covered their eyes with the sun's reflection shining over the snow they walked in. Trekkal clapped loudly, giving a small smile to herself as the sound of her gloves carried through for some time while Sadal turned her head to frown at Trekkal. Not much was out there to accompany them, aside from a curious fox standing in the distance.

"Right...Sorry." Trekkal said, with a grin as she saw Sadal peering over some strange indents in the snow. She remembered they were told that the woolly rhino would rub its horn across the ground to graze much like the ones at home, and she decided to sniff it. Her nose was stiff as her breath materialized in the air.

"I can see some of these here. I'd say we're about an hour from finding one. It's been some time." Sadal said as she looked back to see the supportive nods of Narro and Jih who agreed.

Though Deeso was always the main tracker of the two, Sadal's skills improved considerably in the time since she left The Broken Bone behind her. In a way, it was this connection that was still able to keep them alive despite the ever-growing dire circumstances. Sunlight this far north waned quicker than usual, and their attempts to find a rhino have already been a few days. A few of the unaffiliated members of The Aligned taught the four how to survive, and the group were able to make do by constructing forts out of snow and huddling together for warmth. With no trees, mammoth bones and assorted animal furs comprised most of the dwellings here. Jih was filled with an unwavering will to find the rhino as this was just one step closer to reaching the power rock he set out to get so long ago. As the prelude to frostbite set in for the group, their calls were answered as noticeable tracks in the snow gave way towards a powerful animal in the vicinity. This was not the presence of mammoths who had large herds that could be seen in migration, but the humble rhino that stood by itself.

Narro silently pointed ahead and spotted a large furry animal in the distance. He was certain this was their target as he withdrew his club, now with noticeable frost placed on it. Narro felt his hand was practically glued onto the club as he manipulated his arm to get a good swing ready to practice. Sadal placed down her backpack and withdrew three of her throwing spears. One was still made of wood that she saved handy, but in the greater north, she now learned from Jarzill's flock to make spears from sharpened bone. Trekkal's supply of rocks were to be especially deadly now that they were additionally hardened by the cold. Jih took great care to retain his spears, wrapping the handle in mammoth fur so that the wood would remain hardy for combat and warm to the touch. As the four ventured forth, they carefully assessed the terrain and noticed that the rhino was at the edge of a frozen over lake. It used its massive weight to make small cracks in the ice and sip up the refreshing drink.

"Water has become land. We must be careful." Jih commented as he looked to Trekkal to toss a rock to test the ice's strength once they arrived closer.

While the other three descended from the snowy mound they walked on to near the rhino, Jih stopped as he looked closer at the animal's shape. Although Jih knew that this was their target, it hadn't occurred to him what he was actually looking at until just a moment ago. A small flash in his mind reminded him of his time back in Sundaland. A rhino was the last thing he hunted with his mother before her passing. He remembered her words and commands as he was with Kag and Hyu that day with the utmost clarity. This was a strange coincidence to Jih as reality struck back to the slightly dazed man. The facts spoke for themselves. Jih was in Hizo's position, though he now outlived her by four years. Now he would organize the plan for the hunt much as his mother did for the three of them back then. Jih nodded his head and trudged along, using his shoes to slide along the snow as he caught up to the others.

"Jih, what should we do? I saw you were taking longer on the hill so you must have a plan in mind." Narro asked as he leaned low to the ground.

"Follow Jih carefully. First, place snow on body." Jih said as he rubbed himself with the surrounding snow. Although this gave a few puzzled looks, Jih's orders were followed. Much like mud, Jih was hoping to mask their scent from the rhino that would be down wind. Their mammoth furs were exceptionally warm, but while the group exerted themselves to get through the snow and mounds of packed ice, they sweat in their clothing. Jih hoped by cooling them off, they wouldn't sweat as much and help mask their presence to the rhino.

"When we are close, do not speak. Use hand to talk. It hears better than us." Jih recommended while Trekkal fiddled with her glove to try and wave her hand.

Jih had no defense for the rhino's better hearing, but he hoped with the roaring wind returning, they would also be able to have an advantage. This rhino seemed much stronger than the one back home as he remembered being able to corner the animal using the base of trees. With no treeline in sight, he would need to construct a trap with the most barebone implements, and he figured the best part of that plan would be to use Narro and Trekkal in this way.

After some more walking, the four descended to find that the rhino was still at the frozen end of the lake sipping water from a small hole without a care in the world. Jih urged the others to wait as they assessed the ground. Jih lifted his hand and listened for the wind to sound before giving Trekkal the signal. Jih looked to Trekkal who gave a mighty swing and saw the rock that Trekkal leveled at the ground landed with a hearty thud. The ice was good and the four were able to pass without issue. The only problem that arose now was the rhino which was alerted to their presence. Droplets of still water descended from its snout as its breath dispersed through the air. The rhino faced their direction and although it could only make out a blurry outline of what was to come, anything that wasn't itself meant danger.

Sadal ventured first with a steady pace and sought to close the distance with the creature. The spears made of bone were far lighter than what she was used to and so she had a greater range to throw, but the effectiveness of these projectiles was not as reliable as traditional stone. She needed to attack the animal's vital areas with the utmost precision, or the kill wouldn't be sound. Sadal kicked a bit of snow in frustration as her bone spear landed some distance close to the rhino but failed to make the mark. She would be more careful with her second, but the rhino decided to test the four by going out further to the ice. Narro ran to support Sadal as he always did, and quickly realized he was now on solid ice. He was going to shout, but he remembered Jih's instructions to keep silent. He figured Trekkal and Jih would know this was to be the case shortly. Trekkal didn't anticipate having to hunt out on open ice, she struggled to keep her balance while she looked at Sadal who was trying to spread her weight out evenly.

Jih decided to use his spear as an anchor to restrict his sliding as he took slow steps. Much like the others, he nearly lost his balance but was able to slide along with a rhythmic motion as he neared the rhino. He lifted his hand up to call Trekkal to hurl another rock. The rhino turned and snorted as it ran in Sadal's direction. Jih moved his hand and guided Trekkal to launch a rock that blasted the rhino in the ear causing it to yelp in pain. It reared up and stomped as it followed the sound, now heading towards Trekkal's direction.

Thanks Jih... Trekkal thought as she attempted to slide out the way.

Jih called for Narro to do a risky move and try to slide over towards him as he hoped to use Narro's strength to bewilder the beast long enough for him to have an opening. Jih looked at Sadal once more and watched as she got up. She slid over as she went to help save Trekkal. Sadal took the second of her spears made from bone and used the momentum given by the ice to launch it straight into the ribs of the animal. The bone spear led a trail of red that dotted the ice as the rhino was put into a frenzy. While not exactly part of Jih's plan, he gave a nod of support to Sadal who smiled. All part of leadership was willing to be flexible and bend to the circumstances where they lay. The rhino huffed and thrashed to try to dislodge the bone spear from its hide. Jih's eyes expanded slightly as the rhino's movements made small cracks in the ice. The last thing he wanted to do was freeze in an attempt to swim back to shore.

Narro tossed his club to Jih who barely caught it with his glove. Jih gave him a confused look, but Narro illustrated that he wanted Jih to toss the club in the direction of the rhino as he had a better angle. Narro was hoping to throw off the animal's hearing by having it focus on another sound. Hunting by overwhelming the animal's senses was one of the practiced way the four could overpower foes larger than their own. Jih did as instructed, he was surprised at how heavy the stone was. He lobbed it together whereas expected it landed with a heavy thud. Jih ducked as he saw a rock from Trekkal soar above his head. From the rhino's perspective, it was being pelted with things all around it, but was unsure of what direction to head towards. The rhino's last trick was to lead it out into shakier ground where the ice could crack and potentially submerge its pursuers.

Jih took this challenge as he saw the other three express some hesitation. He knew he'd only have one shot to do this right, so he needed to be careful. The frenzied rhino sniffed the air and recognized Sadal's scent from the previous spear that still lay embedded in the ground. For the rhino, this was a personal endeavor. Jih moved his feet as quickly as he could to regain some traction and used his spear to propel himself further. He was positioned diagonally from the rhino and hoped to close the distance as it ran south in Sadal's direction. He held his spear out in a middling stance, ready to thrust it into the animal's eye. Much as he'd seen Hizo do before, he landed a solid blow, and embedded his spear directly into the eye. The hit was direct as a large amount of blood pooled out. Jih's collision with the animal caused him to lose grip of his spear and slide much further along the ice, but he looked to see his mark was made. He felt a slight friction burn on his arm as he attempted to get up.

"Jih! I'm coming! Stay where you are!" Sadal yelled. Now that the animal was on its last legs, she saw no reason to hide herself any longer.

Jih met the hand of Sadal who propped him up as the rhino bled out with the hit. As he saw Narro and Trekkal make their way back towards the two of them, Jih held an involuntary grin on his face. It dawned on him that the three before him in the snow and harsh winds weren't just his friends but in fact his very family. The four traversed the ice and made their way to the dying rhino which now was too weak to make any fuss. Sadal withdrew her dagger and slit the creature's throat to sip the blood, her face now with red streaks running down her cheeks. Sadal valued the rhino's use of terrain to try and challenge her combat ability, much like the snow leopard furs that made her old clothing. Narro hacked off the rhino's two horns with his club.

"Jih, take the small horn. This is a victory you earned for us all." Narro said happily as he ripped the bloodied appendage to place in Jih's hands. Jih lowered his head with a nod in thanks and felt the fur and ivory in his gloves. Sadal and Trekkal prepared the largest of the horns to return to Jarzill's followers. It was a massive horn but with enough creative storage space, Trekkal was able to hold it in her pack.

"This is quite heavy, you know. Good thing our backpacks are durable though!" Trekkal mentioned happily.

"With your muscles? It's an easy lift Trekkal." Sadal teased, as she pushed Trekkal forward a bit. Narro laughed as Trekkal attempted to catch her balance yet again. The four took what portions of meat they could for the trip and made their way in the village with the sun waning.

While the man ensured the four would need a week to cross the lands to find Jarzill's encampment, good fortune on them only made four days. Dusk was a gorgeous vista that remained bright with a fresh layer of snow. Standing torches displayed around the campsite melted portions of it and it was a lively place. With each of their long-awaited trials finally complete, Jih was shaking in anticipation of getting an audience with the man known as Jarzill. Someone who currently dedicated their entire life to studying the secrets of the power rock was certainly an interesting person to meet. The four carried the rhino's horn to the village and were greeted kindly by another Seer who waved their arrival. Jih and the others wondered how quickly all this was organized, but Jarzill had eyes and ears throughout the steppes.

As agreed, a representative from this village noted their immense efforts and rewarded them access to the base camp where Jarzill resided. He was made aware that someone would approach him, but he didn't know that there was in fact a group of four waiting for him. Their steps accompanied the guide as they walked in silence while the wind filled the void in their place. For much time there was very little in their surroundings, but small gray and brown dwellings were visible in the distance with smoke in the sky. The sound of small children playing with sticks filled their ears. Compared to everything they've seen thus far; it was a well-organized refuge isolated from the world. It was a proud establishment with fifty people strong that all listened to his words.

Jih, Sadal, Trekkal, and Narro stood in the center of the village that was devoted to Jarzill's teachings. Unlike most of the places they've been to, there was a deliberate effort in dress as all managed to emulate just a portion of his power by looking like Jarzill. The only differentiation they seemed to have was in their hair and face. Lacking ingredients for face paint in the far north, many voluntarily scarred themselves, with specific formations having meaning in their social structure. The four knew that Jarzill wore a mask made of wood and he had piercing brown eyes based on their accounts from neighboring areas. Sadal noted that much like Jih and herself, he also was said to have worn a necklace with a large cat claw, this being from the scimitar-toothed cat they now recognized and fought against. With many unwilling to answer their questions, the group looked for a solution. They were in a state of limbo, as they weren't perceived as a threat, but their appearance was cold much like the tundra that surrounded them.

"This man has seen power rock. Jih must talk." Jih said with heavy seriousness in his voice. As Jih and the others finally arrived at the cusp of their destination, the anticipation overpowered Jih immensely. Everything he sacrificed in the last year and a half would finally come to fruition and he could save his people. All that came to it now was just one conversation and a long trip back home.

As this was a village of The Aligned, much like the countless others they found in Europe, Narro and Trekkal knew it was common courtesy for others of their kind to enter an open tent. Narro and Trekkal advised Jih and Sadal to remain where they stood while they searched for the tent Jarzill resided in. Jih and Sadal watched as the two went separate ways and looked towards the ground, as they were outsiders once again. Trekkal peeked her head inside a few tents and saw many of the devout cupping small rocks that were to be used as an offering to the meteor. They additionally had pieces of bone and other small trinkets they would use to satisfy the spirits' hunger. Jarzill instilled to them that due to the meteor's long travel through the cosmos, it had a ravenous appetite and would need to be fed. Her luck ran low as she looked to see where Narro was heading. In his own stumbling through the snow, Narro entered an open tent. After the cold reception received by Jarzill's flock, he hoped to talk to the man in question and try to see his perspective. Jarzill adjusted the chords of his mask steadily before the newcomer addressed him.

"I heard your name mentioned before, are you the one known as Jarzill, yes? We have the horn you seek." Narro inquired as he saw the man fold his legs. A low campfire illuminated their surroundings and was a welcome visit as Narro felt his hands practically freezing. Jarzill gave no movement as Narro's shadow filled the tent in volume.

"Yes." Jarzill answered bluntly.

Jarzill's tone surprised Narro who wasn't used to receiving such treatment from his own kind. He noted the strange appearance of him, however, the mask that separated the two. He wanted to unveil it and see what lay behind, but there was a story behind the mask that he was afraid to learn. Narro was aware of the stakes and how important the meteor was for Jih, nothing would ruin his chances of getting its power.

"I am aware of why you are here. Your team worked well for my followers, but labor can only get you so far with me." Jarzill said with little enthusiasm in his voice. Narro picked this up and decided to recall events that happened quite some time ago.

"I came because hearing your name reminded me of someone I met some time ago. His name was Fahlrit, and I considered him a good friend. He told me you were his cousin. Is this correct?" Narro inquired of him. Jarzill's expression softened at the words, he hadn't spoken to Fahlrit since his long departure. It was hard to hide his surprise as he hadn't figured anyone would come across him.

"Was? How did he pass?" Jarzill asked, his folded arms going into a slump. Narro's eyes turned to the snowy ground where they sat. He wasn't sure how to exactly deliver the news, but he did his best.

"He died with honor after we hunted a Yaan together. Many of his hunting team were present and wished him well." Narro said, choosing his words as diplomatically as possible.

"I am aware that my cousin had...issues. One of these would one day best him in battle. To take a sacrifice such as this is an appreciated gesture. Perhaps I judged you too harshly as an outsider." Jarzill mentioned. Narro wasn't sure what else to say after that, but Jarzill spoke again and sensed a strange feeling of comfort in the man before him.

"Fahlrit was a good man. He lived a tragic life from an early beginning but did not let this stop him from achieving great things. We grew up together. My father is one of The Youngest, a wretched and pitiful soul. He accepted me like my own when nobody else would, we were only a dry season apart. He lost his One a long time ago, the day three of us fought the Mahaku that laid claim to our people. Fahlrit lost a good man and his leg. I lost my face, and I gained this claw. I wake up with strange pain over my body to this day and visions that torment my soul when I no longer hear the call of the rock. Was it worth it? Perhaps not." Jarzill poured out to him.

"Fahlrit gave me a piece of advice. He said not to kick when facing the Mahaku and I listened. I do live here, so I thank him for saving my life as he sees us from The Land of The Dead." Narro said, matter-of-factly.

A rare smile was obscured by the man's mask, but Narro could tell his words affected Jarzill a great deal as his position changed. Jarzill let out a stifled chuckle, it was clear that despite such hardships Fahlrit still retained his sharp tongue. Narro's kind nature showed through whenever it could, he hadn't expected to have gotten such a response from Jarzill. Narro decided to take this goodwill and extend it just a bit further. He was taking a real gamble, but now that he had established rapport with Jarzill, he felt the time was opportune.

"It is not by accident I have come here, Jarzill. I travel here on account of my friendship with a member of The First. He is more like an uncle to me than anything else. His people are dying, and we need just a small bit of the power the meteor has to reverse this fortune. I know they are not a popular subject in these lands, but you are an enlightened man." Narro explained in dismay to Jarzill.

Jarzill held his head in his fist in thought as he evaluated Narro's speech. He heard mention of The First and without a single deviation from Narro's cadence or expression. Jarzill asserted he was either telling the truth or was in front of the best liars that ever lived. Jarzill decided to table the issue of the matter surrounding Narro's tale and decided it would be best if they could be close by so he could see for himself.

"As you have listened to my tale, of the life I left behind, perhaps there is some good in outsiders after all. I will provide a tent for your party to stay for some time. Like my cousin Fahlrit, I have advice for you. I take it you plan to be a leader of your people someday. Notions of glory and splendor taint the visions of many. These quarters and Zaan furs mean nothing to me. Narro, power comes through sheer will and purpose with every step. I could tell a follower to fall before the blade and they would be they dead before they touch the ground. The meteor guides me and disavows all other spirits. This is the path one takes to enlightenment, lead for a strong spirit." Jarzill said to Narro. Narro wasn't sure what to make of these words as the mask obscured Jarzill's expressions. He nodded, shivering slightly as the cold was far more uncomfortable to him than the one he sat across from.

As Narro and Jarzill conversed, Leta humbly worked on threading furs in the next open tent and was curious about the new arrivals. While interned here, Leta hardly received any news of the outside world and felt woefully trapped with her imprisonment at the hands of Jarzill. She thought about her Seer and wondered if the path of death was appealing. The blade seemed a fitting end, but she was given a strong spirit to fight and resist. Submission is what Jarzill wanted out of all his captured subjects, and she wouldn't give this to him. She continued her duties but made an effort to learn more about these strange visitors as they weren't indoctrinated into the culture.

Jarzill wished to meet with Jih and confirm all he learned. Jarzill grew up hearing and revering The First as many of his kind did, but his travels up north exposed and complicated the legend. Jarzill also gained his own introspective of The First, independent of the influence of others. It was a negative outlook. Narro left the tent with Jarzill shortly behind him. The pair arrived to see the others as torches were lit to illuminate the village further. He studied their faces carefully and assessed their respective attributes. Jarzill watched as Narro mentioned to Jih all he discussed as Jih nodded in acknowledgment to his words. Jih stepped forward and looked at Jarzill with some suspicion. Jih's face was still obscured by his hood. One man's ability to claim such feats was something he marked with skepticism but was taken aback by his demeanor and mask. Jih extended his hand out to Jarzill and the two shook.

"I have heard from the one called Narro about you. Anyone else can tell me about why you have ventured here, but what does this path say for you?" Jarzill offered to let Jih speak.

Jih saw one last obstacle in his path, it wasn't another mammoth or a rhino, but just one man who seemed to hold unsurmountable power over others. Unlike Tur, he realized that Jarzill was one who built the community around him with his own hands rather than inheriting an already bloated structure. This wasn't someone who was an idle taskmaster, he was an ever-present force that demanded much but gave as well. He took a deep breath and chose his words carefully. Jih unveiled the hood and showed his full face to Jarzill.

"Jih has heard the calls of his people and must answer them. Home is not well, there is volcano that spits hot ash and kills everything. We are surrounded by those that seek to kill us. Our leadership falls to ground. What would one do when their home is under attack?" Jih proposed as he saw Jarzill made no reaction.

Sadal noted that Jih kept a cold expression as well, but his thoughts raced inside his mind. Jih sought to hit where it hurt the most. He saw that the others here have followed his example, extinction was a universal threat that could only be taken with the most severity. Jih hoped to appeal to Jarzill's sense of empathy that came with the burden of leadership. Jih knew that Jarzill needed to feed his flock, and while he didn't rely on cannibalism to do it, times were tough.

"Volcano has shown death for Jih and his people. The Council rule with fat stomachs while many starve. Jih finds power rock for those who could not go. It was not for Jih, but for everyone else." Jih mentioned. His hands sweat as he rubbed them against his fur lining.

"A volcanic spirit is strong with many demands, but Jih, I speak of another matter. Your ability is strong, and I respect it humbly. This Council you speak of. Why come here to me if there are problems that need your aid?" Jarzill asked, as Narro and Trekkal kept themselves quiet.

"Jih was exiled because The Council buried their mistakes. Jih will not return to Sunda until power rock is returned. This will bring balance to The Elders, for this is the way things are." Jih explained to Jarzill. Jih looked at the man before him and bit his tongue as there wasn't much to say left. It pained him to have to recall his fall from grace to an outsider, but his entire story was being evaluated now.

"Return? You speak as if you own the great gift from the sky. You hold no claim to this, it is not inherited to you. Your kind have claimed to have made everything; nature is not yours to claim. I can see it was for you after all. Your decision to go for the meteor is one of selfishness. Do not hold that expression, it is true. You see the meteor as a means to an end, rather than for what it truly is." Jarzill professed as Jih's expression was furious. Narro's face soured as he saw this intellectual discussion going south quickly. Jarzill was ill impressed with the man in front of him who lacked his fanaticism for such things.

"When I grew up, I heard the stories of The First, the infallible ancestors that gave us voice. I expected to see flowers bloom under your feet and Yaan rise from the ashes. All I see before me is a man. A man who broke the pact he agreed to and dragged these people for his ambitions. You live the life that I abandoned to the unenlightened of the south that barely make sacrifices. The First became too comfortable and lost their standing among the spirits. Now they send one of you in a vain hope to claim what is lost. You fail to understand what I have at stake." Jarzill proclaimed while he noticed Jih's expression darken.

"Jih does not care about rank or furs. People are dying and Jih must do something. Jih cares about Kag, Bani and Dran. They rely on Jih to deliver, and it will be done." Jih said sharply as he could feel his temper rising.

From Jih's perspective, he'd done everything he needed to get to where he was just moments away from victory. He couldn't understand why Jarzill had it out for him. His concern drew to Sadal, Narro, and Trekkal who could only stand idly by as they nervously listened to their discussion. For better, or for worse, they were here at this stage because of Jih's desire to find the meteor, but their own motivations were undoubtedly part of why they stuck together. Trekkal took great offense at Jarzill's insistence on his perspective on the group's relationship and shook her head in disagreement. Jarzill shook his head at Jih's answers to his questions. It was all focused on such material conditions and lacked emotional depth. Jarzill was an ideologue who sought to control the narrative regarding the meteor and its divinity.

"Jih and family have done all asked of us. We must go to power rock." Jih huffed.

"Plaguebringer, I answer you with the utmost honesty my spirit can muster. You have done what it took to meet with me. Given what Narro has done, I will allow you to observe but I will not allow you to destroy part of her soul. Your toolkit tells me you have much experience with stone, a useful utility but a futile endeavor. The meteor is beyond your ability to understand." Jarzill heeded with a smug arrogance. As Jih's expression seemed still to Jarzill, he interpreted it as him not understanding fully what was being asked of him. He spoke once more with a more targeted statement.

"You ask to take but a part of the meteor. Should I take your arm? These gestures are one and the same. Your selfishness has dragged the others behind you to peril and your cowardice has left those you consider important at the hands of these tyrants." Jarzill proclaimed.

Jih could barely contain his rage and he spit on the ground in Jarzill's direction in disgust. Jih considered himself by all metrics a patient man, but with very little in his way, there wasn't much he was keen on waiting for. Sadal and Trekkal shortly left to console the visibly angry Jih as he slowly walked off and gave the indication that the conversation was over. Narro attempted to salvage what goodwill they had left by talking to Jarzill once more.

"It has been a long day for us. I hope you can understand that this was not meant in good faith." Narro said, with a slight nervousness in his voice. He hadn't seen Jih this angry in a long time, if ever.

As Narro looked behind him, he saw that Jih studied the dimensions of the village they resided in. He could tell Jih was planning something as he left without much thought on the matter. Narro hoped that a solution would come between the two, but only time could tell. Jarzill let Narro go without any words as he stood where he left, recalling his conversation with Jih. Jarzill's devotion to the meteor outranked anything. He didn't like what he had to do, but Jih was but one man out of many who would endanger the spirit he worked so hard to protect.

"I don't agree with any of this. That self-righteous-" Sadal said lowly as she turned to see Narro.

"Jarzill left us a tent to use while we are in his village. We should figure out a plan in the next couple days. We are exhausted from the hunt and walk here you know." Narro proposed while the group got themselves situated. Jih continued to stew in anger as he felt Trekkal's comforting touch lay her head on his shoulder while she looked at Sadal and Narro.

"Jih will talk with wooden man once more." Jih noted to the three of them.

Sadal felt around the walls of their tent and noted the similar mammoth bone and fur structure as the previous villages they held refuge in. She noted the remarkable quality of the pelts here and was astonished that this is what they used to keep their homes steady instead of wearing as clothes on their bodies. The ground was mesmerizing as Sadal felt herself sink into the mammoth fur. Although Narro was about to correct Jih, he held his hand up. Jih was aware of Jarzill's name, as he continued.

"Like tree, his soul is hollow wood. Jih is master stoneworker and stone breaks wood." Jih said with a slightly ominous tone to his voice.

Jih would rightfully attempt to talk to Jarzill once more, but his goal is what mattered the most. He gave the rest of his friends a small grin to mask his true intentions as Narro and Trekkal returned it in kind. Sadal kept her thoughts to herself but waited as the group recalled their various exploits of the trials they endured. Jih's only course of action centered on the meteor and whatever means he would use to get there.

The Old And The New: I

Jih looked around and studied the tent that the four shared that they could keep as long as they were accommodating pilgrims of the meteor and the rules that Jarzill set in place. Their tent was well insulated, with sleeping bags provided by Jarzill himself, and a small fire lit inside. A tiny flap was opened to air out smoke periodically as they slept through the nights. Despite many nights of restlessness, Jih felt at ease. The group agreed to stay one week, which Jarzill agreed on, while they got themselves situated and mostly kept to themselves. By the fourth day or so, the others were getting acquainted with the inhabitants that made up the devoted members to the meteor and Jih continued to study the layout of their village and other details.

As access to the meteor was guarded, Jih made a mental note of the schedule of cultists that switched for the honor. Jih already spoke to Jarzill once more pleading for a fragment. His diplomatic approach faced a stone wall and Jih decided that he would need to take bolder action to get what he wanted. Jih waited until the cover of night to sneak away from his friends to find the power rock. He knew that this was a large risk, but he was too far now to give up. He kept a hand-axe placed inside a pocket in his heavy furs while his hands clutched a spear. He looked at Sadal, Narro, and Trekkal as they slept soundly. Jih's face felt true warmth as he had new additions to his family and that his aspirations would finally be realized. He adjusted himself, making sure that not a piece was out of place on his outfit as he carefully dressed himself. Jih placed his feet inside the shoes he left by his sleeping bag and made his exit. Sadal awoke for a small second of deliriousness as she saw an outline in the darkness and fell back to sleep. Luckily for Jih, the snow reflected enough light from the low visibility above that he didn't need to carry a torch. He stepped slowly, putting one foot after the other as he attempted to step forward. Immediately, the harsh winds blew, and a rush of immense cold went over him. Jih could only wonder how many more layers he could put on before he truly felt warm again.

Moments away from the meteor, Jih felt his very blood pulse with excitement. He looked around and willed himself to stay quiet, Jarzill ruled this village with a strange mixture of admiration and fear. Among his most devoted served as sentries to keep the camp safe at night. Sadal found this unnecessary, given their general isolation from anyone else, but Trekkal offered a darker conclusion, which was to keep people from leaving once they came in.

Just out of the boundary of their camp, Jih noted there was a sentry whose attention was aimed towards occupying himself by making faces in the snow. There were two sentries at night which guarded the vast openness where their place stood. Raids were incredibly rare, with most on the watch for bears or any other hostile animal wanting to make a quick snack. Jih made his move and waited quietly until it was all but confirmed he wouldn't bother to leave. He looked behind him and saw that the second of the sentries retreated into their tent to sleep. Jih knew he was past the point of no return on doing this but decided he would face the consequences alone. Jih inched by and immediately stuck his spear into the guard's neck with great force and aimed for the throat to keep the man silent as he fell the snow below. The small faces were now marred with a trail of blood that marked its way behind him. Jih grimaced at his actions. Jih took no pleasure in the death that followed, but this was the closest he could ever get now to achieving his dream. He took a deep breath and slowly dragged the body to a nearby tent before making his exit.

The walk to the meteor from the camp that was established was around thirty minutes, more than enough time for Jih to get away before people realized what transpired. As he walked, Jih used the back end of his spear to wipe excess snow over his tracks so that he couldn't be followed, either by the members of Jarzill's movement or that of his friends. If all was well, he could get the bits of the meteor he craved and return before anyone was the wiser. He remembered the directions to go directly north of the camp. It was so simple even a child could get there with ease. Jih remembered all that happened during his quest, rarely having a moment to himself to truly process everything that happened.

He thought of Sadal who slept soundly and heard her words. The jungles of Southern China were a distant memory by now but remained important all the same. The rush of their initial battle and subsequent friendship spoke volumes. Sadal was after all Jih's first traveling companion in all this.

"Jih! You outdid yourself this time. What a great hunt as the wind flows through my hair!" Sadal spoke to his mind.

Trekkal soon followed, her words more somber than usual, but still filled with her snarky personality. Jih remembered her words as well, obscured by her constant laughter at a joke she said at the time.

"You remind me of a Peymin I tried to catch the other day. It swam against the current for no reason that I could tell for such a long time. It was only after I realized from our travels together, that it is about the freedom to do such things. This I clearly took for granted hearing about your life, if I was twenty years older, the things I would have shown you!" Trekkal commented.

Narro was last, with his speech always keeping him and the others resolute. Jih looked behind him, with blood already on his hands, it was too late to go back now. He would have to rush and get the others to leave as soon as he was able to.

"Jih, I feel better knowing that you are here to help us. Working as a team has opened my eyes, well...eye, to many things. We have sacrificed much and now we will do what we set out to accomplish!" Narro's voice called to him.

The piercing winds of the tundra slowed Jih considerably and the looming glaciers miles high far in the distance dwarfed him on his walk. The feeling of Sundaland's warm shores gave Jih the shot of adrenaline he needed, and although it'd been some time, he thought of Bani, Dran, Kag, and lastly Hyu.

"Bani knows Jih will succeed." Her visage spoke to Jih. Simple and elegant, Bani always knew what to say. These were the last words he remembered her saying before his journey began. Kag stood next to her, with his familiar laugh and words inspiring Jih even further. The desire to tell him all that has transpired brought a resounding anxiousness that fell on him. The pressure to get away with what he was doing was immeasurable.

"Brother! Jih will return safe. Bring back gift for Kag?" Kag's words reinforced Jih as he now had a wealth of knowledge to give.

Dran said nothing but folded her arms and nodded at Jih to get the job done. Jih remembered the basics of his training and if it came down to it, he knew to not end in a tie like the two always managed to do. A tie in the art of spear combat was a pyrrhic victory where death could be delivered to both. Jih hoped that he wouldn't have to resort to any more violence to reach his aims, but with the life lost of the man behind him some time ago, the ends justify the means.

Jih's heart weighed with sadness as the last words he heard were that of Hyu's, these being the ones he imagined her speaking, as her actual last words were unknown to him. Her long flowing hair that ballooned in Sundaland's humidity vaguely resembled the fat clumps of snow that fell from the sky. Jih always found slight amusement in seeing his breath materialize in front of him. He internalized the breath that came from his body, part of his essence and soul. These were concepts he hadn't thought of much before his travels with Sadal, Narro, and Trekkal who discussed such matters from time to time.

"Hyu will never leave Jih. Let us venture together, our dream is almost complete." Hyu comforted him.

The site where the meteor landed wasn't a pristine landscape, underneath the layers of snow that inhabited it was blackened earth. Much of its size burnt away on impact but it could still impress. The meteor itself was smaller than Jih imagined. In the sky when he saw it with the others, it was a gargantuan entity of immense power, but here it was far smaller. It was wrapped in protective animal skins, mostly from mammoth but wolf as well. Jih stood by some distance, as the wind raged on, buffeting him with loose snow. Through the winds came the reason why Jih saw the meteor was coveted by so many including himself. He realized that the power the meteor held was not its size like that of an elephant or tiger, but what remained inside like that of a human. The meteor held substantial deposits of meteoric iron, a material completely alien to Jih and the others. Its very luster could steal one's soul if they weren't prepared to accept the power it held. While Jih's vision improved and he saw the meteor in his very eyes, nearly moved to tears at its existence, he quickly recovered as he noticed that another was present some distance away.

Jih saw but a glimpse of a wooden mask and immediately tensed up. Jih stewed in anger, and after being denied before, it would spell the end for both his mission and endanger his friends. He needed to approach this with much care. Jih wanted to avoid conflict by any means possible.

How is Jarzill here? Jih planned carefully. Jih thought.

Jih was unsure how to get out of this but decided to trust his instincts. The path that Jih took crunched beneath his snowshoes as he ventured forward. He lifted his legs and brushed what looked like debris off his shoes as he realized he was no longer stepping in just snow. He saw what appeared to be fragments of bones that were cut and drained of their marrow. He marveled at how many there seemed to be, for he felt the upper north was a barren wasteland.

Jarzill crowned himself as the meteor's steward, along with his followers that camped close to it. The bones of those who defied the will of Jarzill were arranged in rings, ritually spaced around the meteor. They were obscured by a layer of snow, but when the wind blew, the path was revealed. In the sky it appeared large but was now small. Jarzill fed the meteor with the hopes that it would regain its strength from the spiritual journey and give him another message. These remains were travelers who over the countless days have tried to dislodge the cult for personal grievances or were those who, much like Jih, thought they could get past the rules. The most unfortunate of these, however, arrived at the meteor for more sinister reasons. Jarzill commanded his followers to venture into the lower lands and subdue the strong and drag them home. He offered a choice of membership or death. The Aligned were a proud people and their refusal to submit before the prophet's call often sealed their fate.

With the expanse of the land behind him, Jarzill turned around and through the mask peered a figure out in the distance. He stood up now, to address this interloper who would dare go against his words. He gave a small laugh to himself as he felt this was inevitable. As he saw the man's gait approach closer, he recognized this one as Jih. Jarzill knew that Jih's stubbornness wouldn't allow him to heed the warning, and so he stood, hoping to explain to the man before him the extent of the mistake he was making. His breath emanated from his mask as he spoke. On the ground next to him was a spear of his own, a trophy that had seen wooden handles of various hues with multiple sections hafted onto it with birch bark tar. This makeshift construction started out as one spear, but Jarzill decided to keep each handle of the spear with the varying trees he gathered wood from in the far stretches of the south.

"These are the bones of the lesser who have defied my wishes. I will satisfy its thirst for blood." Jarzill mentioned. He said this to intimidate Jih, but his words were indeed true. His movement participated in human sacrifice, a fact that Sadal and Jih guessed but didn't have the heart to communicate to Narro and Trekkal.

Although he spoke without fanfare or any effort to project his voice, the silence and emptiness that filled the air was enough to carry his words far beyond Jih's range of hearing. A subtle echo carried over in the vast emptiness as nothing, but the harsh tundra awaited. Jih's expression soured as he remembered the words of the concerned people down south, he and some others talked to some time ago. Each one of these people lost someone they knew to Jarzill's zealotry, his desire to enrich himself under the veneer of his understanding of the greater mysteries was sickening to Jih. Jih was only reminded of Tur who could possibly equal the man in sheer callousness.

"I do not wish to bring death to you much like you did to one of my own and the sins of your forefathers onto mine. The dried blood on your hands speaks to that. Your face tells me everything about you Plaguebringer. The resilience of The First is one I understand more than anyone else. Your stubbornness, your inability to know when your time has passed, your pretentiousness. Your kind have given us much and we will remember you in the great stories to come. But I must ask you to turn away. You are not worthy. I am not one to repeat myself." Jarzill stated, watching as Jih went to close the distance from him.

"What is worthy to Jarzill? Jih and others have hunted Zaan. Jih has built your tents. Jih asks once more. Home is dying, the people of Jih need one piece." Jih said, holding up a single finger in his gloves as he spoke. Jih felt he was beyond begging, he only begged once in the past and vowed to never do so again. He knew that in doing so he would not only insult Hyu's memory but that of Hizo's as well.

"You are weak and hide behind wood. Show Jih your face. Jih may be called Plaguebringer, but Jih is also called Stone Breaker. What will it be?" Jih threatened.

"Your insults are meek, but your tale on further thought concerns me deeply. Though, I must ask, have you ever asked yourself that some things happen for a reason? Your world may be dying but we are stronger than ever. The way things look, you may take this sign from the spirits. I was put here to relay the meteor's message. What are you here for?" Jarzill taunted. Although Jarzill painted himself as an above the fray sort of person, Jih's comments got under his skin immensely.

All that mattered to Jih was the meteor and the means he would enact to get it. The blood on his spear already hardened with the cool air around him enveloping. Jih was tired and angry. The lives of his friends had been risked far too many times for his mission to become a failure. Jih exhausted all his options over his stay at the camp. He tried appealing as someone who wished to learn the power rock's secrets, and this wasn't enough. He tried to work past the bias against his people and that too wasn't enough. Jih felt a great and righteous anger swell over him that damned the consequences as they came. He had decided that only violence now could bring him to where he needed to go.

"Jih will kill for power rock. Back away." Jih warned Jarzill, grasping his spear tightly between his deerskin gloves. Tired of death that surrounded him, Jih's hands wavered in the cold, but his words hung true as his teeth chattered in the wind. Jih wore a small hood above his head as the wind blew harshly, leveling a small layer of snow between the two. Jarzill's appearance subtly faded into nothingness, only to show up again as the wind settled for just a moment.

"My death means nothing, for I am one man, known as Jarzill." Jarzill stated.

The two stood at a standstill where only the rising winds gave noise between the two men who stood apart, filled with emotions. Despite Jarzill seeing Jih as lesser, it was evident he respected his status as he clutched his own spear. Jarzill took this as a challenge for the two to fight for supremacy. He moved to give a speech, much like the one he did when Jih and the others had first arrived.

"Jih, I sense hesitation. It is not too late-" Jarzill said, getting interrupted. He gave a slight look of confusion but rushed to arm himself and brace himself in position. The footsteps of Jih grew closer and faster as he saw Jih rush in his direction. His eyes were filled with delirium and rage as he lunged with a spear. There would be no time for speeches now. Jarzill expected Jih to swing wildly, but it was clear he was in the presence of an expert. This would be a bout for the ages.

Jih let his emotions take the first strike. He never attacked first in spear combat, often figuring out his next moves based on his opponent's actions but Jarzill wasn't this forgiving. Where Jih chose to swipe, he was met with the clash of stone that cracked as the two collided. Jih needed to find an opening for Jarzill's ironclad defense. Jarzill was a renowned warrior prior to his encounter with the Mahaku of legend and was still incredibly deadly with a spear. Jarzill favored a mixed approach, much like his parentage, his fighting style varied extensively which caused Jih some trouble. Jarzill cemented himself on the ground, and swung high, hoping to kick Jih's spear out of his hand and leave him open for a second attack. Jih retreated backwards, himself weighed down by his furs and shoes. He remembered his fight with Dran when he fought in his Council ware that was also heavy and emulated her strategy for the attack. He timed his movements carefully and dodged Jarzill's assault. He plotted to tire the man out and punish the small deviations that came.

While Jarzill was an expert at the spear and decorated his own, he only saw it as a weapon. Jih and his people viewed the tool as part of their identity, he could produce great works, but there was more that could be exhibited from his ability. The two circled one another and made tracks in the snow that slowly lowered their bodies as they sank below. The two retreated to gain better footing, and then rushed towards each other. The rising winds once again interfered as snow resounded and obscured the other's vision. Jih could barely see in front of him as could Jarzill. The two stood still and waited to catch their breath.

Jih took advantage of the howling wind to obscure his position. He stepped slowly and timed his steps to the blowing wind. He stopped short when the snow settled but the mirage remained. As he circled Jarzill, he made a mental note to account for the distance between the two. With the storm, he emulated this in complete obscurity and stabbed blindly. He delivered a poke to Jarzill's back, confirmed by the man's grunt. It wasn't enough to do a killing blow, but it sent a message. The extreme cold made it more difficult for the wound to feel pain as his skin was already quite numb. Jih knew he needed to go for a decapitation or straight for the heart, nothing else would do.

Jih held his spear high towards his face, this was to defend himself, and separated his body from the point. Most of the opponents that Jih faced in the past used other weapons besides spears, where he held the advantage of range. Jarzill challenged this though by maneuvering his spear around Jih's and then slicing his arm as Jih attempted to bring his back up. Jih's planning ahead of time with his thick furs led him to only bleed slightly as he groaned to the pain he received. Jih jumped in the air slightly and moved his legs to switch position. His combat form was ambidextrous which allowed him to take any position he needed to counter Jarzill.

The two were locked in combat for some time where the clack of stone grew louder and louder as the two exerted more strength into their strikes. The most basic element of spear combat was the thrust, which Jih did considerably well. Jih sought to gain an advantage over his opponent. Thrusting in both long and short cases, allowed Jih to remain still while he used the length of his weapon to do the work for him. Unlike Sadal who cared for fighting for honor, Jih wasn't above any tactics to give him advantage now. Jih swung low with his spear towards Jarzill's legs, forcing him to jump out of the way as Jih took a bold risk to slam Jarzill harshly with his body. Jih knocked Jarzill over briefly as the man got up while he rotated his shoulder in recovery. Jih hadn't anticipated how much mass Jarzill had, but he had a plan for this as well. He noticed that Jarzill favored the slash, often attacking diagonally to try and cut off a counterattack. Jih was able to deliver a concise stab to the stomach with a quick thrust right as Jarzill was about to place the spear down to deflect from Jih.

Jih's fortune changed as Jarzill felt emboldened by his injuries. Jarzill chose to deliberately risk his position in battle and was able to use enough strength to shatter Jih's spear into an unusable husk with his own. Jarzill's spear disintegrated with the impact as the splinters of various colors fell to the snow below. Jih's eyes widened slightly as he was now unarmed and wasn't sure what to do. He retreated as fast as he could, making his way towards the meteor while he hoped to think of something. Jarzill was bleeding, but because the cold kept him in good shape, he had yet to feel the residual effects of this and pursued Jih with unrelenting speed. Jarzill's veneer of ethereal professionalism wore off as he sought to make an example out of Jih. He was filled with a passionate fury that made him want to hold Jih's head in his hands to his followers. The Plaguebringers were a dying race and he intended to do his part.

Clouds of snow piled behind the two men as they kicked up snow. The wind impeded them both, but Jarzill gained much more speed compared to Jih who was weighed down. As he turned behind him, he could see Jarzill's frame increase in size. A large fist torpedoed straight to Jih, and he took a hard punch to the forehead as he did so. Jih felt a portion of his vision fade as he got his grip on reality back. Jih was met with an overwhelming force of Jarzill that barreled towards him. Jih was powerless to fight this and opted to try and use Jarzill's weight against him as he grabbed onto his body. Jih propelled himself towards the snow, knowing that it would insulate the two as they rolled aggressively in the snow. Jih and his people in general didn't fare well in hand-to-hand combat. As their prowess was with the tools they made above all else, they had a severe deficit in this area. He placed his arms over his face, blocking Jarzill's barrage of punches. Jih returned with a jab or two, but quickly retreated into his former form. Jarzill had the frame and strength of The Aligned that gradually tore at Jih. He needed to find a way to get his situation changed and fast. Jih's gums filled with blood as he kept his mouth clamped tightly.

710

Jarzill saw that Jih's defense of his punches were quite strong, though he failed to match any of his own. Taking advantage of his position over Jih, Jarzill reached over and slowly separated Jih's tight arms with his hands and lunged his left hand into his throat, taking great pleasure in doing so. Jih could feel every individual finger and nail digging into his throat as he bled slightly. The worst part was the crushing. It came very slow to Jih at first, but suffocation hit him in waves. As Jih ran out of oxygen, the background that Jih witnessed faded into obscurity. The image gradually focused only on the immediate threat at hand, Jarzill and his wooden mask. Of all things, Jih thought about his exchange with Jarzill sometime earlier and remembered his quip about being also called a Stone Breaker. With what little strength he had left, he reached into his lower pocket and his fingers grasped a blessing comparable to his mother's love. A spare hand-axe he'd forgotten about some time ago.

Jih's right arm wavered as he was quickly losing strength to even lift his arms, but he persisted, nonetheless. He swung wildly as Jarzill lacked a crucial bit of peripheral vision from his mask. He felt the first hit by Jih was a complete surprise. It was struck with enough force that a portion of the wood cracked off and fell, exposing half of Jarzill's face to Jih. His flesh was sufficiently scarred, being practically flayed alive by the scimitar-toothed cat long ago. The subsequent healing from these injuries contorted a once proud face where only his piercing eyes remained.

Jih was disgusted at the sight before him and saw Jarzill's disfigured face as a keen reminder of the person that he truly was. Jih hacked some more, this time, reaching through the side of his head. Jih's gloves were splattered with an unsightly mixture of bone and brain matter as blood pooled out. Jarzill spasmed involuntarily as Jih's hand-axe made its way into his skull, his grip on Jih released immediately as he turned him over and worked to get himself up. Jih stumbled away as he hoped to catch his breath. Behind him, was Jarzill who left a trail of blood as he crawled, unrelenting in his desire to rip Jih apart. Jih sighed in pure exhaustion as he watched Jarzill crawl towards him. Jarzill's mouth sputtered out debris as he lost control of his body. Jarzill willed himself to move forward but he couldn't as he only grasped in fury. Jih sought to give no mercy to the zealot as he watched him collapse from blood loss. Jih walked over to the still body and saw that in one last attempt, Jarzill grabbed his ankle in an attempt to push him below. Jih withdrew his hand-axe from Jarzill's head and slammed it one more time, sufficiently putting him to rest. He hacked his head off and gripped it tightly by the dreadlocks. Jih looked into the eyes of Jarzill before dropping it and walking away. With the meteor just in sight, Jih's body betrayed him as his adrenaline held back the extensive trauma his body just endured. Jih tired slowly and the snow looked more and more inviting as he lost energy and collapsed to the ground. His body was still.

In the morning that followed, word spread quickly on the two bodies left behind in Jih's wake. The first guard was found behind the tent with horror on their faces. Jarzill's body would come as a surprise to everyone, including Sadal, Narro and Trekkal. Sadal woke up first, nudging the others awake as she could only hear people scattering around quite confused on what transpired. Her eyes quickly looked to see that Jih was missing. She gasped as she remembered seeing Narro and Trekkal got up slowly, but remained vigilant as they presumed, they were under attack from all the commotion.

"We must find our leader! Jarzill promised that we would be safe, but death comes within our homes." A man shouted in hopes to find answers to what happened.

The other cult members agreed, their promises of peace and security by Jarzill were certainly alluring ones but now the threat had come to their doorstep, miles away from those who were considered undesirable. Suspicion immediately came to Narro, Trekkal, and Sadal who were busy searching for Jih. The three looked for Jih in any tent and called out for his name but received no answer. Narro looked at Trekkal and Sadal as he reasoned Jih may have gone north to see the meteor and some sort of altercation occurred. He hoped he was wrong, but as the three made their way in the snow to test this theory, they were surely surprised. Narro and Trekkal covered their mouths in shock, while Sadal walked over and investigated the remains of Jarzill, now decapitated. She recognized the marks of the hand-axe, and saw the weapon left behind with dried blood and frost.

"This was Jih's work. As for where he could be, I have no idea." Sadal said with a solemn tone. Although the three were upset, Trekkal noticed that Jih's body was missing. The three had no love for Jarzill and so the commotion of the village was secondary to their needs.

"He may still live. Jarzill may be gone, but Jih is somewhere. I will find him if it is the last thing I do!" Trekkal said with the utmost severity.

The Old And The New: II

Jih's efforts at the meteor were controversial to put it lightly as he remained unconscious some distance away. Little did he know that someone would thank him kindly for this outburst. In the early morning, Leta was on her way from an expedition out to find lichen for a ritual. She often thought of trying to escape into the greater north, but the dangers of the wilderness were more dangerous to her than her internment. Her instinct to help others immediately kicked in as she saw the nonresponsive man before her. She slapped Jih with the back of her hand and he gave no reaction as she noticed blood that was lost. In her assessment of Jih, she found that the man before her was kept safe by the cold around them. She found that Jih was lighter than usual and as she looked at him, noticed that he was different. It was in her interest to revive Jih as she needed answers about why he appeared where he was. She carried him back to a small tent on the edge of a frozen lake distant from the main settlement where another healer waited with boiling water over an open fire.

Jih gradually felt his vitality return as warm water was forced down his throat. His eyes remained closed, but he coughed as the light around him returned. With some time, Jih's eyes opened as he stayed silent but was confused at his surroundings. The first thing in his vision was his previously injured body now covered with rags that felt wet to the touch. He saw two shapes come towards him that Jih recognized as members of The Aligned, but they lacked the markings that were typical of Jarzill's cult members. He saw the teen treating his wounds, and although his first reaction was to shout for Trekkal as the two looked similar, he slowly crawled back. While he was still in much pain from his injuries, he quickly realized the complete cataclysm of events caused by him. Jih's first thoughts were of his companions and felt great shame at his actions. He wasn't even close to the power rock as his injuries overtook him.

"Hold for a moment." Leta called out to Jih who turned his head. He watched as the other healer left to grab something unknown to him. The air was still as the two looked at one another. Jih wore guilt over his face, but his rescuer cared little about this.

"I found you in the snow outside, you know." She asked, as Jih kept his silence. He felt that saying more would put himself or his friends in further danger. His eyes darted towards a dagger that his healer had in her pocket. He noticed the blade was dull, but it would be more than enough to finish the job in his condition.

"You are in safe hands. I want to know what happened to you. Outsiders do not come here." Leta said as she placed her rags down. She folded her legs and plopped down on a patch of melting while looking into Jih's eyes. Jih felt slightly unnerved by such attention but felt somewhat assured by her words. Jih sniffed the air through his nose to prepare himself as he reiterated the previous night's events.

"Jih...went for power rock. Jarzill and Jih fought. The victor is here." Jih voiced.

Jih braced for what he felt to be his death as he openly admitted to murdering the leader of a powerful faction. The girl seemed confused more than anything else, but nodded as this was a perfect explanation for the wounds she saw on his body. Jih was astonished at her lack of reaction. The various people he encountered in this enclave were devout fanatics of his, even choosing to self-mutilate so that they could have a chance at his so-called gift.

"What happened to him? He should have sent someone by now." The girl replied, her voice low as she was waiting for more information.

"He is dead. Jih cut off head with hand-axe to be sure." Jih mentioned, as he saw the girl practically drop her mouth.

"I-Say that again. You just killed him? The man who fought Mahaku bare handed?" Leta said as she looked into Jih's eyes once more. Jih gave no further acknowledgment of his past actions, but the severity of his voice told her all she needed to know.

"I can go free. I have been held here for so long. I-I need a moment to think, but before I do that. You may be The Plaguebringer, but I owe you a great debt. We need to get you back to the village. There are belongings of yours I am sure you wish to get." Leta proclaimed as she gave her hand to lift Jih up.

While Jih set out on his walk with Leta, Sadal, Narro, and Trekkal were in the middle of a schism that brewed. As some of the members mourned the death of their leader, the opportunistic underbelly of such a system took root as pretenders immediately started to make orders and those who could see where the wind blew started to come forth. Jarzill encompassed his vision lasting through his lifetime and didn't have the foresight to name a successor just yet which made matters complicated. Try all they wish, for a copy is never as good as the original. Narro took advantage of the social unrest to have the other two join him further away as they made their way to find the meteor left undisturbed.

"This doesn't feel right without Jih. We should wait." Sadal said as she stopped her tracks while Narro and Trekkal soon followed.

Luckily for the three of them, waiting for Jih was not long. As promised, Leta who now had her freedom, supported Jih until he broke away at the sight of his friends in the distance. He hobbled over with some pride in his step as he fell to the snow but quickly got back up. Trekkal was the first to run over and give her warmth to Jih as she held him up with Narro and Sadal shortly behind. With them all reunited, Narro decided not to pry into the affairs with Jih and Jarzill before. This was the past and he was ready to leave this cursed place but not without something to show for it.

After walking for a bit, Jih and the others stumbled upon the location where their battle took place, indents in the snow evident and in the center was the meteor covered in animal skins that were pristine. With all the bloodshed, the meteor remained ever pure. The four approached it slowly and Jih unwrapped the skins. Jih was surprised at how small it was as were some of the others. The meteor at close glance was around the size of a large log from their perspective. It appeared much larger in the sky, but Jih knew well that there was much to be promised from a small package. He felt his clothing to find that he had nothing on him to obtain the fragment he sought, until he felt a tap on the shoulder from Narro.

"We figured this would be needed." Narro said as he passed Jih one of his hand-axes.

Jih gave a slightly embarrassed grin and waited as he absorbed his surroundings. Everything that Jih sacrificed up to this moment paled in comparison to what he witnessed. He took a long look at the rock and noticed that the material was completely different than what he'd seen before. As a Stone Breaker, Jih held an intricate knowledge of his environment but was unable to assess it as such. He placed his hand on it and felt the touch of meteoric iron. Far beyond the capabilities of his time, a find like this was remarkable and Jih could see the true power that this certainly held. Jih knew right away that carrying the entire meteor was not practical, but he slowly lifted his hand and slammed with his hand-axe, hoping to use gravity to hack off enough for himself and the others.

"Jih, now that we're here. What happens now?" Sadal asked with some worry in her voice. Jih held up his finger to Sadal and labored as he felt his hand-axe felt the full might of the meteor.

"Each will carry a piece of power rock for their own. It is what we earned." Jih directed, pointing to his backpack held by Narro. After a lengthy process that nearly ran Jih's hand-axe to have cracks in it, he was able to get the pieces he promised. He took the smallest piece for himself while he let the others decide which ones, they wanted to bring with them.

"Jih must return home now. The power rock is here and there is much work to do." Jih said as he looked at the others.

Sadal had nowhere to go as she left her entire life behind and made a new one with Narro. She nodded her head and agreed to help take Jih back home, it was the least she could do. Narro and Trekkal never saw Sundaland, and their eyes for adventure and respect for Jih gave no question for them as well. Jih gave a smile as he saw that his family were eager to help him return home. Jih entertained himself with the prospects of Kag learning about their adventures, but the problems of home crawled into Jih's mind and plagued his thoughts. Regardless of the circumstances at his feet, Jih knew it would be a long time until he returned home once again. He hoped that things truly would change for the better once he returned with the power rock. As long as Tur still ruled with a tight fist, there was little more that could be done.

Where Dreams Live And Die

Months after the death of Deeso, Zulag, and Cikya, Ronkalk stood alone in his tent. Ronkalk sent his partner out in his stead to gather the other bands to prepare for a remembrance of the fallen. His confidence in their return wavered significantly. Ronkalk's young child was poised in a rush to be the successor he desperately needed, but he still had several years before his son would be ready to undergo training and be a leader. For Ronkalk, the time for action was now as there was one more thing he needed to do. By now, The Broken Bone moved operations westward as the resources in their previous residence were used up. The land was purged and with it, a new batch of their kind could settle the land without fear. He sat down in meditation in his tent but was once again disturbed by the burden of leadership.

"Ronkalk...It's happened again. What do we do?" A man said, from the boundary of his tent where Ronkalk stood. The young man on the outside felt a cold touch to his shoulder as another voice came to him.

"It will be taken care of. Go and forget what you have seen. You require much rest." A strange voice said to the young man.

With a quick nod, he was off and the mysterious figure and Ronkalk were left alone. It was none other than the red priest that Ronkalk argued with before. In the low light of Ronkalk's tent, a fire baked on the ground. Ronkalk crushed a few berries in his left hand and mixed it with a red powder that the priests used for their markings. This solution was purple and applied on his face in a four-pronged direction with stripes on his face. Everything with Ronkalk was intentional. These four streaks represented the cardinal directions and the four bands under his leadership.

"It's you." Ronkalk said as he turned around to hear the red priest's words again.

"That it is." The red priest replied, still standing outside the tent. Although the red priest outranked Ronkalk and therefore could enter without permission, the two came to an agreement based on respect. Ronkalk let out a small grunt, signifying his approval for him to enter.

"The people grow restless on a solution. This Weypeu has caused trouble for even our most hardened warriors." The red priest mentioned.

"Warriors? I sent my best warriors out to die and I didn't know it." Ronkalk said to himself with a tinge of regret in his statement.

Ronkalk had been on hard times for a while, but the news of the tiger attack was the last straw. Since they arrived in the new region, tigers have been supplementing their diet with man as a food source. Unknown to The Broken Bone, a disease was spreading among the local deer making it more difficult to feed themselves. Ronkalk normally wore just a grass coverall on his body as he rejected the intricate fur designs worn by most of the leadership, but today would be different. At the edge of his bed of leaves was the folded pelt of a tiger that would be draped over him. Ronkalk often wore the pelts of the animal he was going to kill on a hunt as a reminder to the spirit which inhabited it that he was on top.

"I will go and bring the head of this Weypeu personally. There may be more around, but a leader must show by example. We have been embarrassed by such creatures. First with Sadal, and now with the others." Ronkalk explained as he looked back on the priest. He walked forth accompanied by the man as Ronkalk positioned himself to give a speech as he always did. Ronkalk roused the crowd who stopped working to heed his call as they saw the purple on his face and the tiger pelt on his back. The oldest among them saw that Ronkalk would take the hunt personally and bring balance to The Painted Hand that suffered at the hands of them.

"I will keep this brief. I am to venture into the deep jungle and lay waste to the Weypeu that have ravaged our people. This will no longer stand. We are warriors who hunt the best and biggest game! I will have a hunting party, who will-" Ronkalk said, stopping his speech as he saw a mass number of hands rise. The range was astounding, the youngest of them were practically fighting among themselves, and the old helped themselves up to sacrifice their lives in the field of battle for such an occasion. It moved Ronkalk emotionally to see such devotion to the ways of their people. He picked a group of seven, his hand faltering for just a moment on one person in his view. It was the Wanderer woman known as Bheyra.

"Bheyra, my last Wanderer. My primed Master Hunter. Are you sure this is a quest you wish to do?" Ronkalk asked as he saw the young woman's hand rise out of the crowd. Ronkalk saw a willing determination in her eyes but was unsure if he was willing to send her along with him. After some thought, Ronkalk nodded and allowed himself the company of the other seven to make an even group of eight. It took time no time at all for them to grab their arms and move in support of their leader.

Ronkalk had everyone lined up with their weapons of choice as they stood ready for orders. Ronkalk grabbed himself three sets of bolas for him to use from his pack in addition to one of Zulag's throwing knives left behind. Ronkalk generally fought with his hands but would use blunt instruments when the need suited him. While he was in good enough shape to run, he often preferred to wrangle his target so that he could have enough time to think of a plan afterwards. The other members of The Broken Bone stood as straight as they could with their eyes on Ronkalk as he spoke his next orders. The red priest followed Ronkalk and the others to serve as his personal protectors while he accompanied them on the journey.

"Your orders are this. Whatever beasts we find, kill them. If Forest Seekers stand in our way, kill them. If any of our kind try to intervene, kill them. This is a simple hunt. We search for the Weypeu with a harsh scar on its hind legs. We will head west, and I anticipate this will take about three days to travel. Let us move." Ronkalk ordered without further delay.

Three days' travel from The Broken Bone's current position was deep into Forest Seeker territory. Eshe returned from her campaign in the west some time ago and was searching to see how much of her influence remained where she started. By now, Eshe was well known among the various Forest Seeker bands with a contingent of warriors numbering around fifty at her disposal and representing over fifteen bands dispersed throughout the greater jungle who have sent a person or two in solidarity to her cause. She visited countless Forest Seeker bands selling her vision of a united front against the Thunderfeet and her efforts paid off.

Eshe was far from comfortable in her position, however. Some had grown accustomed to acting on their own accord without her direct presence, and some were beginning to question once again if the Thunderfeet were truly the menace she painted. Converted by the words of The Stone Breaker long ago, these early bands still remembered their roots. Eshe's return quelled this discussion as she knew that some people would question all she stood for, but her traveling band of hardened warriors showed what following her would do. Eshe sat quietly in thought as she chewed on a twig and watched the repair of the village that fell apart after the most recent migration. Akma stood some distance away as she dictated orders on Eshe's behalf and looked behind every once in a while with a smile. Eshe's peace for the moment was broken as she saw the familiar gait of some of her most trusted circle. Their faces were forlorn as they gave news worth hearing. One of the men stepped forward and lowered his head to Eshe before speaking.

"Eshe, our scouts have seen that we have an incursion of Thunderfeet in the area."

"What of them? Did we not establish an agreement with this band to not go past the river?" Eshe asked with a confused tone.

The duties of leadership matured Eshe and required her to make compromises where she could. While she opted for removal of the Thunderfeet when possible, she still had the issue of decentralization among her people to contend with. On occasion, Eshe would opt for containment of Thunderfeet settlement where established boundaries would keep ample supply for her people. Deviation of this was swiftly and brutally punished.

"No... They have left a trail of bodies where they come from. Negotiations may be impossible. We should attack." The man said as he waited for Eshe's orders. Eshe gave no delay on the matter, bloodthirsty Thunderfeet were a dangerous problem, and she saw the opportunity to raise her prestige further by the glory of battle.

Eshe and the other warriors equipped themselves and donned their signature Leaf Walkers and silently made their way to the scene in question without another word. Eshe clutched her blowgun closely as she once again walked the path of the forest floor with the village, they inhabited vanishing behind them. Eshe reflected on her long history, over two years she was now a hardened veteran, far from the inexperienced woman she was before. Eshe understood some of the Thunderfeet doctrine and incorporated it into her own strategies for raids. She and the other Forest Seekers would lay down a barrage of darts with their blowguns in hiding and once detected, run towards the enemy with blades in hand.

Ronkalk and the other members of The Broken Bone traveled with purpose as they took down many creatures that stood in their way, but the tiger still evaded them until a sign was given. The group of eight entered a clearing in the forest that was quite spacious. If the group was tired, this would be a suitable location for the hunt to continue another day. Ronkalk's hand rested on a tree as he turned to see strange indents in the wood. He deduced that these weren't human in nature and inquired further. He smelled the tree, hoping to see if there was any indication that the territory was marked. These claw marks were deep and Ronkalk asserted that they were within some distance of their target.

"Is everyone fine to press on, or must we stop and rest?" Ronkalk asked, as he waited to hear the call of everyone else.

While he waited for an answer, Ronkalk heard the faintest sound come by. His eyes widened as he alerted with hand signals to grab their attention. Ronkalk quickly made his way to the red priest and placed him down to the ground. Just as they anticipated, the Forest Seeker attack quickly was underway. The sound grew louder as the sounds of darts neared their location and hit nearby trees. There was a rapid succession of these darts that served as suppressing fire for the real threat to come by. At the rate they were going Ronkalk estimated a force of at least twenty were against them.

"How could they find us here?!" Ronkalk questioned as he stayed low to the ground, watching as the others did so to avoid the onslaught of darts in their location. One of their group lifted his head up prematurely, finding himself hit with a dart. Thinking nothing of it, he removed the piece only to find that a sudden sickness came over him. Ronkalk hadn't anticipated the darts being laced with venom, as The Broken Bone had no countermeasures for snakes.

"Stay down! Don't move until the order is given!" Ronkalk yelled again.

Their breathing was still as Ronkalk hoped playing dead would coax them out of their position to see if the marks were given. Their warrior that was hit writhed in agony as there was nothing that could be done for him. Ronkalk was angered as the man died in a dishonorable fashion, he couldn't even see the one who killed him. Ronkalk was cautious as he anticipated another round of darts to be used, but instead he saw the subtle movement of bushes. On a closer look, these weren't bushes at all, but long draping pelts that seemed to be covered with layers of leaves and debris to hide themselves in the foliage. He ordered his hunting party to get up and fight as he saw the advancing group in his direction.

Unusual in their delivery, the Forest Seekers ran towards the group with knives made from flint and wooden handles. A few of The Broken Bone carried long spears that they used to beat back the raving enemy. The clash of materials raged on as the sweat of Ronkalk's training was put to the test. Eshe decided to split her forces of ten into two groups of five that would surround their Thunderfeet opponents. Coming out of the brush, the Forest Seekers lunged in close towards their targets. Ronkalk was ill prioritized as due to his age he was looked at as the weakest. This was a big mistake. Ronkalk grabbed his bolas and rotated his arm with a mighty swing as he launched them in the direction of the Forest Seekers who mobbed together to keep things steady. Eshe prematurely removed her Leaf Walker so that it wouldn't interrupt her flow in battle. She was busy in combat with another of Ronkalk's group to not consider the appearance of the man herself until turning around to see his throw.

A sling? Really? Eshe thought as the bolas wrapped around her legs and she fell to the soil below.

With a look of surprise on her face, she realized that she was bound tightly together, and her legs prohibited her from walking. She quickly used her arms to reach down to the string that bound her tightly and cut with ferocious speed. Ronkalk, seeing he made his mark, ran towards Eshe with the utmost determination as the purple pigment on his face ran down while he sweated. Ronkalk gritted his teeth as he morphed his hand to a fist and rocketed it towards Eshe's face. As if the spirits themselves intervened, Eshe narrowly avoided the narrow punch of Ronkalk that felt as if it could shake the very earth itself. She quickly rolled herself on the ground, and used the momentum to break what was left of the tight strings. She got up and ran towards him. She swiped at him with the knife, only to be interrupted by Bheyra.

Eshe was remarkably quick with the knife, cutting her twice along her arms, as she was kicked to the ground by the crazed Thunderfoot before her. Eshe's hair was tugged as she felt the vengeful grab of her opponent. Bheyra laughed uncontrollably as she reveled in her own blood that fell on top of Eshe's face. It was a horrific cackle that unsettled Eshe, but she dared not falter in front of her subordinates. Eshe slid Bheyra off onto the ground and jumped on top of her and using her elbow to try and break the woman's teeth. She felt her own arm get scratched as she was bit on the arm but was able to stuff a rock in Bheyra's mouth as she bit once again and broke a tooth. The pain was incredible as Eshe kicked her harshly in the head, rendering her incapacitated for a brief period. She took her knife and moved to the next target.

Ronkalk had his hands busy as well with two Forest Seekers attempting to double team him in both directions. Ronkalk was an exceptional fighter on the ground, with his bolas not having much use up close. He grabbed the arm of the first Forest Seeker and contorted it heavily as the two collided heads in a headbutt. Ronkalk was dazed, that was certainly a maneuver for the young. The stunned Forest Seeker met an unfortunate end at Ronkalk's fists, caving the man's face with his nose contorting in on itself. His second attacker stuck his knife in Ronkalk's back, to which he screamed a great deal. Choosing to leave the knife in for the time being, he gripped the man by the arm and heaved with a mighty amount of strength to slam him on the ground as the man's entire body felt the shockwave. Ronkalk placed his foot on his neck as the man was too exhausted to do anything else. He slowly reached to his back and withdrew the knife as blood seeped down. His breathing was heavy as he concentrated on his next target.

The red priest, seemingly left alone due to his frame, slinked off into the distance and reached into his own bag, hoping to give his side the advantage that they would surely need. In his hands was a long wicking stick that could be lit as a torch with enough pressure as the fighting raged on. The red priest gathered in his studies of the Forest Seekers that much like the beasts they hunt after, the threat of fire would make them submit. The priest sparked a small flame that carried on the torch. He decided to step forward and end the hostilities as best as he could. As he stepped forward, the distant sound of a tiger's growl paused the fighting.

Eshe and the other Forest Seekers stopped as they looked to her for directions on what to do. She debated her options as she knew her forces would not be enough to take on such a creature on their own. She thought it would be better to let the tiger take care of those she opposed as it was a known man-eater. Although the Forest Seekers valued all the life of the forest, the tiger was a particular case as those with bad souls became these wretched creatures. Killing one in self-defense didn't violate their cause but many still sought to remain out of conflict with them when possible.

"It would seem we have an issue. Which one among you speaks for you?" Eshe said, breaking the silence now. A young man with blood caked on his face stepped forward.

"You dare address Ronkalk! Leader of The-" He said, getting cut off by the raise of Ronkalk's hand.

The young man bowed his head at his leader's gesture. Ronkalk rarely gave such bombastic displays of his rank and status, as he even spurned the furs allotted to him as his right. The group of Forest Seekers before him were not people he wished to impress; they were only a problem that stood in his way. Ronkalk anticipated being outnumbered as he brought a small group with him precisely to not attract attention, but as life would have it, this would not always be this way.

"I know who you are. The one known as Eshe. Now you know who I am. Ronkalk." Ronkalk said, as the other members of the Broken Bone waited quietly to hear his words.

"I am the one you wish to speak to. This is where we come to understand the circumstances we have here. There is a Weypeu in these forests. In my priest's hand is a lit torch. Consider this as my ultimatum. We will discuss terms as we are here, or I will burn this forest down with us in it. My demands are simple. Get out of our way and let us slay this beast." Ronkalk said, as he gestured to the priest, his arm poised to launch the torch to the forest floor.

The number of leaves and debris that would burn would be enough to consume most of the area here. Ronkalk knew an escape in these circumstances would be dire, so he hoped a bluff could work against their odds. Eshe felt in her heart that Ronkalk offered a strong bluff but given the brutality she witnessed from a man old enough to be her father kept her at bay. Sending her defenders to pointless battles and harming potential innocents of her own kind just to spite the Thunderfeet wasn't something she was willing to do so quickly these days. Perhaps some of Ozul's words she reflected on left some impact on her decision making. In the chaos of the fighting, it turned out that one of Eshe's men took a captive for their own. This was one of the women who happened to be knocked unconscious earlier in the fighting. Ronkalk was filled with fury as he saw this display. Eshe stood alone as the rest of The Forest Seekers retreated behind her. Eshe gave her subordinates a great deal of trust in the matters at hand, and she knew that their judgment would be the right call. She nodded her head at the man to speak to Ronkalk directly.

"You think you can just come here and start making demands? After we have slain two of your forces and hold one here?" The man said as he embedded the knife just a bit into her neck.

"Yes, actually. You are but a lone Teemba and I am an unhappy Yaan. You seem to forget that I have one of your own." Ronkalk said flatly, his foot on the neck of another one of Eshe's subordinates. He was too injured to move and could only gasp for air when Ronkalk allowed him to.

"The life of the one beneath my foot depends on the woman bloodied in your grasp. We shall wait for your decision." Ronkalk said, his eyes staring at the man gasping for air. The breathing stopped, as the Forest Seeker next to Eshe cut the woman's throat in cold blood. Eshe remained unmoved, but she was angered internally. Reasoning with Thunderfeet wasn't in her plans for today, but with the threat of the tiger growing nearer, her morality had more flexibility than anticipated.

At her core, Eshe was an idealist, but she molded into that practicality. Additional numbers could come well to serve. She wouldn't need to risk her own, but the man's brazen actions now endangered this possibility. Not bothering to look at what went below him, Ronkalk stared at Eshe as he slammed down on the Forest Seeker's neck without remorse. His windpipe was crushed instantly as he gasped for air one last time and died. Ronkalk gave a moment of silence to let the message stick. He decided to talk a bit more and, under the gaze of the red priest, attempted to understand the Forest Seeker perspective for the moment. The other members of The Broken Bone glared at the Forest Seekers while Eshe evaluated how to approach this situation.

"This creature is an eater of man. You say that we Thunderfeet, as you call us, do not care for the forest. Are we not doing those who live here a service? The Weypeu does not care for the target it seeks when it is hungry. It cares none of your spiritual connection. You impede my way and my hunt." Ronkalk stated, his eyes looking at Zulag's old knife.

"This is not for you to decide. The Weypeu has slain our own kind, yes, but it is acceptable to keep balance in the forest. With one life claimed, there is no stopping with any of you. You are a swarm that consume everything in their wake and leave nothing behind. This goes beyond the Weypeu." Eshe retorted as out of the corner of her eye, she saw the red priest moving to do something. A Forest Seeker withdrew their knife but waited as it was clear the man could pose no threat to them.

The red priest decided to step in the middle of the two's discussion that seemed to have no end as the two deconstructed the other's argument. Ronkalk gritted his teeth as he was bound by the code of his people to adhere to the wishes of the red priest. He already knew that he was going to offer something that he didn't wish to relent on.

"Ronkalk. I was not injured in the fighting that ensued. This would have been an easy kill. It's clear to me that if they can respect my role, we can come to an agreement that suits us all. My proposal is this. Eshe, let us claim the life of this Weypeu. The pelt will be yours to see as you do fit. As removed as you paint yourself to be, Forest Seekers still must trade for goods like the rest of us." The red priest mentioned.

Eshe and Ronkalk stood in mutual disinterest towards the priest's words. Despite how different they seemed to consider themselves, the two reflected one another far more than they thought possible. Incidentally, this is also how they came into agreement with the red priest as the motivator. He knew enough of the Forest Seeker philosophy with sustainability to propose a solution that would satisfy her people's needs, in addition to providing the righteous vindication for Ronkalk and the rest of The Broken Bone who felt unsafe with this creature. Eshe knew her forces wouldn't be strong enough to take on the animal on her own without significant losses. Ronkalk's skill within The Broken Bone was unmatched in hunting and under his leadership, the tiger would be killed.

The two begrudgingly agreed to call a truce with the danger of the tiger being a far more prevalent issue. Eshe and the Forest Seekers accompanied Ronkalk's hunting party to ensure that the kill would be delivered under fair terms and observed their strategies. For Eshe, this was an opportunity to see what they were up against in the battles to come. She watched with some surprise at the tenacity in which the fighters went up against the creature. For Ronkalk, this served two purposes. Not only did this motivate his hunting party and reinforce his status among the rest of The Broken Bone after the consequences of his decision making, but it sufficiently sent a message to the Forest Seekers that his band was not one to trifle with lightly. He anticipated that years after his own demise and the ascension of his son, the time to strike would be imminent for both parties. He needed to be ready. The previously unconscious and bloody Bheyra rose to join her comrades with a glare given to Eshe. Ronkalk and the rest of The Broken Bone that survived the endeavor slit the tiger's throat and sipped the blood as was customary. Ronkalk ignored the Forest Seeker presence before him and decided to address his tired and weary hunting party. The best reward wasn't the blood that came from the kill, or the honor itself, but from the speech that Ronkalk always did to rouse their spirits.

"We did a great thing for our people. A kill that would make my nephew proud. We take this blood for his name as my line. Zulag, son of my sister, Chindi." Ronkalk huffed.

Eshe gave a slightly surprised look as the name showed a small bit of familiarity to her, but she said nothing as she stood in silence, waiting for the pelt to come her way.

"I hope you return to me some day, for I mourn as it has been long without news. If you are truly gone, I have failed you and this will weigh on my shoulders. If you have made a life of your own with Deeso, I understand this as well." He said with a small laugh, humor which was rare from him, was one of the few ways he chose to cope. He'd lost almost everyone that he respected, whether through fate long ago, or his own actions that led to this resolution. He knew it was fruitless to dwell on it for too long.

Ronkalk delegated the task of skinning the tiger to one of his hunting party who skinned it with great effort as the two parties looked at one another in silence. Ronkalk would have words to give to the red priest along their long trek home. For now, the man with a mask whose face was unreadable held a small smile as this is what he hoped the spirits would reveal to him. Ronkalk presented the pelt as the initiator of the hunt where it was received by Eshe and the other Forest Seekers. The two locked eyes for some time until they mutually retreated to separate directions.

"Should we ambush them, Eshe? Their numbers are small, and we could-" One of the other Forest Seekers stated, stopping as she saw her leader's thoughts. Eshe weighed the decision. It was a practical one of course but she already lost people for today. She decided to save face on the matter.

"I have an injury that needs to be treated. Tomorrow though is a new day." Eshe proclaimed as she vanished with the others into the forest.

Ronkalk was also faced with this moral quandary as he and the rest of The Broken Bone walked back east to where their camps were situated. Opinions were mixed on the peaceful resolution to the Forest Seeker issue. There were some that called for blood and rightfully so, they proclaimed after the deaths of their fallen. To not retaliate back was a sign of weakness that should not stand.

"Ronkalk...We should take the pelt back. It's ours." One of the men said, hitting his chest in anger. Ronkalk shook his head, knowing fully well that the gaze of the red priest was upon him. He spoke loudly enough so that the troupe could hear his words as he walked to the rear. It was his instinct as he walked towards the back to ensure that even the weakest could have a fighting chance in case of attack.

"Do not embarrass me again with such foolishness. I am but one man and fate is nothing I choose to come up against. You can go if you wish, but our fight is with the beasts. It has always been this way." Ronkalk reprimanded them and kept them in line.

The Broken Bone and Eshe's forces were but two of the many bands that saw themselves as masters of their own destiny. On occasion, these would come to clash in the years to come, as the two found themselves at a crossroads. While a direct meeting between the two forces of nature that were Eshe and Ronkalk would never come to be again, each remained delightfully aware of the other's activities to some degree through a tight network of scouts.

Death of Tur

It was two years after the chaos that caused Tur's removal from The Council. Kag and Bani were spending time with Cren as they heard commotion outside of their tent. Bani kept the toddler in her hands while there was commotion going on outside. A few of the adults gathered around in the center of camp with looks of anguish. Bani kept her ears open to hear loud discussion over something. The crowd talked among themselves in dismay.

"Kag, Bani will put Cren to rest. Go and see what is happening. Bani will come soon." Bani said to Kag as he made his way over. Dran was already one step ahead, having heard the start of the commotion as she was maintaining the arena. The news brought a smile on her face. Tur was found dead in his hut in a puddle of urine. He died of a stroke, not that anyone could do anything about it.

The chaos unfolding in the wake of Kag, Dran, and Bani's efforts to unseat The Council brought much discourse within the ranks. Numbering about seventy strong now, The Elders held steady now that the priority of concern switched from pelts to actual food supplies. With the news of Tur's demise, it was easy to see for those who remained loyal to The Council and tradition to assume that foul play was involved. Those that were loyal to Tur glared at some of those who decided to align themselves with Kag and the others' philosophy. Aab was moved quickly as the leader of The Council, and while there was a general acceptance of her leadership, some of these critics were vocal that Kag and Dran specifically were forcing Aab to do things on their whim and not her own.

Despite everything thrown at them, Tur still had loyalists from the grave. The members of The Council who quit because of Tur's removal were also present and a schism seemed brewed. Kag saw this uneasy powder keg brewing as his eyes met Dran's. They needed to come up with a plan quickly before all their hard work would be put to waste. More adults crowded the center as the news of Tur's death spread quickly with others talking. While most deaths were reserved to the local family unit, or for an individual to grieve, the death of a member of The Council required all participants to attend. The question came as to who would succeed Tur, his demeanor was so cantankerous at times, nobody was able to retain his knowledge as an active understudy and a great fear set in. Kag of course realized that despite their good news, for Aab this was the worst day of her life. Aab was distraught to see her partner go in such a fashion despite how problematic his leadership was. It brought shame to her that she could not see Tur go when he did, but her obligation now was to lead The Elders with the others. Aab was escorted by a younger member of The Council who held her arm as she came to the scene. Kag decided to make a statement on the situation.

"Tur is dead. This is known. We will bury Tur and then discuss what to do." Kag said, attempting to bring order to the others.

"You could not wait, so he dies, his arms covering his face!" One of the other adults yelled at Kag with disgust spewing from his words. He mimicked the contorted nature of Tur's corpse and interpreted his spasms before death as him trying to defend himself from assault.

Kag blew air out of his nose in annoyance at the man's statement. He looked ahead but felt the supportive touch of Bani on his shoulder. She kept her head low but gathered what happened quickly. Bani saw Aab upset at the turn of events and she positioned herself closely to provide comfort and to get a better view of what was going on.

"Aab is leader and alive. Kag was put on The Council by Tur. Do you not remember? Tur died alone." Kag mentioned to him.

"We will proceed with burial. Grab your hand-axe, bring body of Tur to where he wanted. We will begin now." Kag said, slamming his fist into his hand to put finality on the statement, while his supporters rallied around him to get to work. Although Tur was immensely disliked at this point, there was still tradition that needed to be adhered to. Tur's loyalists also participated in the burial but said nothing to Kag or the others as they did so.

Aab felt the comforting presence of Bani as the rest of the adults fell in line. She looked back at her and Kag's home, remembering she would need to check on Creu again before getting back to her tasks.

"Will Aab be fine without Bani?" Bani questioned.

Aab shook her head no, which prompted Bani to stay longer while she watched the others work around. As Tur was a woodworker, the woodworking team mobilized to make an assortment of weapons that would be used to honor one of their own. With every able-bodied adult helping in the preparations for Tur, it was a quick turnaround. Four people carried his corpse from his home and walked backwards to shield the body from Aab's view. Kag went to delegate tasks as he organized the others. Kag or Dran wouldn't pick up a single stone or branch to honor Tur in death, but they had no qualms about making others do it. A small depression in the ground would be Tur's resting place some distance away from The Elders' camp into the deeper jungle. It was near a large amount of different colored woods and trees that bore fruit above. Kag and Dran were among the first present as they waited for people to gradually enter the space. Some of the woodworkers hacked away at some of the tight branches so that there would be more room for those to participate. Aab said nothing as she was last and mourned quietly away from the others. Kag took a deep breath and offered anyone to say a statement regarding Tur and his importance to The Elders.

Kag lifted his head as a few of the Tur loyalists spoke about what his leadership truly meant to them. Kag felt his eyes were going to melt as the sham of a funeral continued onward. His kindness only extended to the grieving Aab. Kag looked over Tur's body in the dirt. Kag, much like the rest of his friends, didn't understand how Tur could be so callous with his leadership. In years past, Kag grew to dislike Tur as much as anyone else, but he nor Hyu were given his wrath often, instead the origin points of their hate stemmed with his relationship to Jih and how Dran was treated by Tur. Kag always thought of Jih as he went by his routine and thought that he should have been here to witness Tur finally put to the ground. Seeing an opening, Dran decided to step forward and give a statement of her own. She was disgusted by the bold attempt at rehabilitating Tur's image even now as he was powerless to give them anything of value.

"None of you like Tur. You feared Tur. Dran protects all from weakness. Dran was strong so that you can be afraid." Dran said, lambasting the crowd before her that could only stand in silence or glare.

One of the men egged on by Tur's loyalists found Dran's comments to be so absurd, he moved his hand to a fist and moved to strike Dran. Another stepped forward to take the blow and now there was conflict between the two brewing sides as these comments devolved into a loud screaming match that Kag nor Dran could handle on their own. In the space given, the two factions argued among themselves, spouting insults about issues not related at all to Tur. The grieving widow of Aab stepped forward and yelled with a mighty call to stop their actions and focus on the matter at hand.

"Stop!" Her frail voice called out as it was paired with a resounding silence that filled up.

"How can you be this way? Is the word of Aab not enough?" Aab asked. The quarreling adults settled down as Kag and Dran looked in the old woman's direction from them. She gave a look of ire to the whole group, her partner's death was supposed to be in tradition, not a session for vented frustration that was meant for private ears or sycophants trying to obtain favor with her.

"The Neck-Shells told us we were weak. They were correct. Aab will make decision now. If you wish to leave, leave. The forest will take you." Aab opened, with her arm opening out to the group. To Kag's surprise, some chose to take Aab at her word, with them having put down what they owned and retreated.

Dran was in shock, she hadn't imagined anyone ever picking Tur of all things as the hill to die on, but for some people it was the first real decision they made in a long time. The silence that followed was incredibly awkward as Aab spoke to the rest of the group.

"This mocks our past. All of this." Aab said with a wave of her hand around at the proceedings. Aab voiced her complaints and ordered that if anyone had anything worth noting for Tur to stay, but she would not tolerate any pretenders. Kag nodded in respect to this notion and quietly made his exit with Dran not far behind him. The two would let the old widow grieve in peace.

Kag saw some of the other adults also leave the forest as they couldn't honor Tur in good faith, but still adhered to Aab's wishes. With nothing left to say, Kag decided to return to his tent so that he could spend time with Cren who was asleep. Bani returned much later, with an exasperated sigh as she was nice enough to stay with Aab the entire time. Kag rubbed noses with Bani as he could see the exhaustion on her face. Kag looked up at the roof of his home. While Tur was laid to rest and would be no more, Kag had a family of his own and a position where he was respected. This, more than anything else gave him a good night's rest.

Jih's Journey: II

Kag and Dran were out on a survey of the landscape as The Elders were preparing to make the move once again to their residence in Eastern Sundaland. Rather than do it all at once in the earlier days, fragments of the band dispersed in pieces to the location as this allowed for an easier transition. The seventy strong members that they had were now down to about thirty in this region. Under Aab's direction, the remaining members of The Council stayed behind while she pressed ahead. Aab decided to build operations ahead of time while the most essential teams operated as a skeleton crew to dismantle the previous pieces. As Bani refused to leave without Kag, she and the young Cren stayed with him in the process. Kag and Dran enjoyed the break from Aab, she proved to be a taskmaster much in the same way that Tur was, except that all her implements were for the benefit of their group. With limited numbers, The Council operated on a small capacity and Aab's micromanaging was what was needed for them to survive the next season. Kag looked to the volcano, which was for the moment dormant, but his concerns still loomed on things to come. His face turned to Dran who was busy assessing the area at hand. Dran's invitation into The Council was a diplomatic move by Aab to cleanse their sins of Tur's terrible leadership. Dran retained her dignity and refused to join The Council, but she ensured Kag alone, that her counsel would always be provided should he ask for it. Kag's eyes met the ground as he stopped in thought while Dran stormed ahead. He smelled the presence of animal dung and noticed that it was fresh. It was associated with a marked tree that had the smell of urine. Kag's face was concerned as he feared for the worse. The two were not far from the remains of their home.

"Weypeu tracks. Dran, come to Kag!" Kag yelled as Dran stopped her approach.

Dran turned around and raised an eyebrow at his call. Bigger threats like leopards and tigers usually stayed away from villages due to their size and amount of noise that would otherwise drive them off, but with a much smaller presence, the range of these animals increased as they left a void behind. The Hunting Team was off looking to recover some meat, and while they weren't hardened warriors, they exceled at combat against animals having intricate knowledge of their behaviors.

Kag knew he needed to take a proactive stance against this creature as Bani and Cren still remained. Kag and Dran observed the younger generation using fibers to tie their weapons to their backs around their stomach for easy access and allowed them to have free use of their hands at the same time. More than just a fashion statement, it came in handy as Kag was able to fasten his spear while on patrol. He held his out and took a stance while Dran followed in the same way, hoping to find the creature and kill it outright before it could do any harm to them.

While Kag and Dran rooted through the jungle in the search for their tiger, a lone boat drifted onto the coast of a wild yet familiar beach. The temperature of the surrounding waters was warm, and the ocean itself felt like a hot spring. Jih recognized the coast with some surprise on his face as two years had passed since he first left his home. Now returning with more than he imagined, Jih turned as he paddled to look at everyone else in tow. Sadal gripped the side of their canoe with utter fear as Narro served as her brace. The sun glistened on their skins in the heat of the sun. Trekkal looked at her face in the water while her eyes followed the movement of fish she'd never seen before.

Jih tried to remember all the names of them that he and the others came up with for specific ones that appealed to their interest as Trekkal let out a barrage of questions as they paddled. Shedding their great furs of the north for a lighter load, Jih and the others wore simpler outfits made from jackal fur carried over in their travels. In their backpacks were a few souvenirs from the lengths of their journey, and each one of them carried the most important piece, a fragment of the power rock. Jih spent months as the group returned from the far north attempting to work the power rock, but meteoric iron required many hands and many more hours to be used to any effectiveness. Jih exhausted what seemed like hundreds of stone tools and he could barely make a dent. He hoped that with the newfound respect given by his exploits, he could return to his fellow stoneworkers and do something worth noting.

Jih grounded the boat as he vaguely recognized where he first took his journey. Sadal was the first one to touch dry land as she let the sand go beneath her toes. She gave a large stretch as Narro and Trekkal soon followed. As the two landed, Sadal laughed as she saw their faces caked in sweat far more than her or Jih's. The plains that Narro and Trekkal belonged to were warm but were objectively less humid than what they were used to, even after hiking through earlier tracts of jungle at a higher altitude.

"How do you live like this? My own clothes stick to me!" Trekkal complained as she attempted to stretch out her animal skins to breathe.

Jih let out a small chuckle that soon resided as through the beach came a long and familiar walk. This was Neck-Shell territory through and through. Jih remained on guard, but he noted there was a distinct lack of people, particularly that of Bhet and his ilk. It was quite some time ago but Jih remembered the plan that he and Kag made before his departure. Was it truly done? Did Kag follow through and kill off the Neck-Shells as planned?

"We are home." Jih said with a solemn tone in his voice as he gathered the strength to go further.

In the excitement of the power rock in his grasp, everything that Jih avoided soon assaulted his mind. The death of Hyu, his exile, and what he internalized as abandonment of Kag and Bani. In the grand scheme of things, he hoped that this would be enough to bring balance to his home but also the respect of the others who've seen him as a pariah before his exile. At long last, Jih and the others returned to Sundaland. Jih now looked for any sign of his home. He hadn't bothered to keep track of the seasons and while he was aware that his band moved around, there were only three locations they frequented. For him, it would be a matter of finding where to go next. He led the others with a hand as he guided them through the familiar paths he knew since boyhood. Sadal watched with envy as Jih practically melted into the foliage surrounding them.

Jih turned and used his hand-axe to weave a path for them as he extended his hand. As Jih and the others embarked on what was former Neck-Shell territory, they were a fair distance away from The Elder's camp. Jih lifted his hand for the others to stay silent and to equip their weapons as he looked around for any threats. Narro and Trekkal were unsure of what to expect here and followed Jih's instructions to the letter. Sadal absorbed her surroundings and found that there was a strange presence she hadn't realized before. Jih stopped his movement as he came across the corpse of an animal that was not killed by tools but had a large claw mark on it. He took a deep breath as he turned to the others to realize that in the absence of the Neck-Shells living in this area, a tiger had taken refuge. Jih pointed up to the trees and saw that no such prey was hanging above. A leopard was by no means easy, but a tiger would be a difficult challenge.

"We walk into the lair of Weypeu. We must fight if we see it." Jih warned the others.

Jih and the others weaved through the dense foliage with caution in their step. Narro and Trekkal grew up fearing lions and the scimitar-toothed cat but Jih and Sadal feared the tiger above much else in the jungle. Sadal decided to split herself from the three for the moment as she headed directly ahead of them. Jih chuckled, even after having mastered the art of fighting as a team, Sadal couldn't override her programming to run headfirst into the dangerous predators. For Sadal, however, hearing about a tiger in the distance flooded her vision with red. She wanted revenge more than anything else for the fallen and the embarrassment she felt on the day that bound her to find Jih to begin with. Sadal saw the streak of orange through the treeline, and it was what she was searching for. She let out a large scream alerting all in the surrounding area that she was ready to fight. Sadal withdrew her first spear and readied to carefully throw as the sounds of Narro and Trekkal bumbling their way through the foliage soon followed. Trekkal found it hard to manipulate her sling in the thick underbrush as she usually could, but she attempted an underhand throw that required less movement to land its mark. No matter what, the four of them would come together. The tiger let out a roar as Narro ventured forth with his club, and carefully assessed where he should place his mark. After experiencing the horror of the scimitar-toothed cat, a tiger seemed almost trivial in comparison, but the two beasts were different. The scimitar-toothed cat had no need to know its surroundings, it only used brute force and sheer mechanical efficiency to kill its prey. Jih was the last to venture out as he saw Sadal engaged with the tiger as she lobbed a spear towards it. Jih ran forward and yelled as he jabbed his spear in the air to beat the tiger back. Narro quickly turned his head around to talk to Jih to which Jih harshly yelled at him.

"Narro! Face Weypeu, it attacks from behind!" Jih warned.

Narro heeded his instructions and boldly charged the tiger by sidestepping and keeping his gaze on it. Narro snatched its tail and hit its backside with his club. Sadal used her first spear and lobbed it with a powerful yell, piercing the tiger straight in the stomach. The spear fell apart from its thrashing, but blood poured out and now it was a race against time. By now, Sadal understood she needed to aim for the head or neck to finish it off, but she wanted this prey to suffer a little more. Jih assisted Sadal by rapidly poking the tiger with his spear in an attempt to get a good blow, while Trekkal supported the others as best as she could. The tiger's panic in fighting multiple opponents was known as it let out a large roar and swiped at Jih. He learned his lesson after his injury from facing the Mahaku and saw to keep his entrails inside. Jih's hope was to keep the tiger from lunging with its full strength as there'd be no way for any of them to take the full weight of the animal. In a burst of quick thinking, the injured tiger leaped towards the base of a tree and used it to encircle the others.

"All must stand back-to-back. Weapons out. Weypeu looks for weakness, we will not give it." Jih said as Sadal quickly linked backs with him, while Narro and Trekkal did the same.

Some distance away, Kag and Dran could hear the faint sounds of what seemed to be the tiger they were searching for. Tigers rarely had to defend their meals unless it was from a rival or a pack of hyenas so the two prepared for the worst. Dran ran ahead of Kag with mud kicking up as she looked to see Kag closely behind. The two weaved through the foliage as their surroundings dimmed around them. Their focus was so resolute that only the path to the tiger showed in their range of vision. Kag and Dran sunk themselves into the foliage and noticed a clearing in the distance. The growing signs of their tiger knew that the prey was near, and the hunt would finally begin.

Kag and Dran ran as fast as they could with their spears held at a middling stance, with their goal being to impale the tiger using momentum to assist them with greater power than they could exert on their own. Despite decades of experience, it was a great effort to face a tiger and keep your nerves. Every dangerous animal for Kag was now a potential threat that would deprive him of time spent with his son if he needed to heal or end his life entirely. The thought agonized Kag, but the duty to keep the land safe for his family came first.

While Jih remained steadfast in his effort to trace the tiger's movements with his eyes as it looked for an opening between the four of them, he was briefly distracted by the sound of footsteps. The tiger long heard these before anyone else and let out a warning snarl as its ears bent back. The sound of additional humans interfering in its plans enraged it dearly as it let out another roar this time, hoping to ward them off with its presence. Through the bushes, Kag and Dran emerged with their spears and charged the tiger. The impact from the blow knocked both over as they collided with the massive beast and Jih's formation broke, seeing an opportunity at last. Jih and the others relentlessly pounded the tiger with their weapons as it attempted to get up, but the assault was too great. The tiger's vision fell as it swiped wildly, hoping to claim one of them with it. Sadal's throwing spears were not particularly useful up close, but she saw that the tiger's neck was exposed, and with two hands, she jammed it inside as deeply as she could. The familiar cracks of neck vertebrae as she embedded the missile inside the tiger filled her with euphoria as blood dripped. After a few moments, the tiger was now slain. Though the pelt was in terrible condition, for Sadal it didn't matter, it was about revenge, and she'd gotten it. She knelt and cupped the blood that leaked from the wound she inflicted on the beast and drank. Jih walked over to Sadal and placed his hand on her shoulder in an affirmative nod while behind the two of them, Narro and Trekkal addressed their strange saviors.

Kag looked up to see the hand and a friendly grin from Narro. Kag hesitated but grabbed his hand, while Trekkal attempted to assist Dran, only for her to be shooed away as she stretched her body. As Narro and Trekkal looked over at Kag and Dran, their excitement for the day overpowered them significantly. Jih was their only frame of reference for what The First looked like, but now there were two more right in front of their eyes.

"Jih...Can you come here?" Trekkal asked for him.

Upon hearing his name, Kag and Dran's eyes widened in surprise. Amid the chaos, Dran and Kag hadn't noticed the arrangement of new people that accompanied the now deceased tiger. The two gave each other a look and were unsure of what to think. They knew about other people through their experience on Flores but saw nothing quite like this. How could they have understood her? More importantly, did she truly mention Jih's name? The Elders were unique in that names were never recycled as far as their oral histories could go. There would only be one Kag, one Dran, and one Jih. To share someone's name meant you would steal their accomplishments in life, and this was frowned upon in their society. For this strange woman to mention Jih, it was unmistakable. Going against everything he prepared himself for, Kag couldn't help himself but try just once.

"Brother?" Kag called out.

Jih's hand left Sadal's shoulder for the moment as he heard the familiar voice of Kag. He quickly turned around, as he was caked in blood to see him supported by Narro. Jih dropped his spear that fell to the ground as he slowly walked over to be sure it was Kag. With a grin he knew since boyhood, it was truly Kag. Jih said nothing more and gave Kag a silent embrace as Kag cried uncontrollably regarding Jih's return. Kag always remained optimistic about Jih being able to survive his ordeal, but he had to remain realistic as well. The realities of the road became more and more cruel to them as time went on, but Jih was adaptable, and he would overcome all else.

"It has been a long time, Kag." Jih said as he lifted his head up to notice that Dran accompanied him.

When Jih first left, he and Dran were not on great terms historically to begin with. Their relationship was guarded at best, but Jih had much time to reflect on things in his journey. Jih considered her a friend early on despite their arguments. He held no ill will towards Dran, the guilt on her face as her eyes met him was evident, she still felt terrible regarding all that happened. Kag's words gave her the motivation to keep going and be an effective force for The Elders, but this started to crumble as she saw Jih once more in the flesh. Sadal returned to the others to see what was happening as she gave Narro a look while he stepped back a moment to give them some space. Jih left Kag briefly and looked at Dran while Trekkal stood next to her. Jih walked forward and tightly hugged Dran who vibrated in embarrassment at such a gesture. It wasn't what she expected at all from Jih, but Kag's words were true. After a few seconds, Jih left the two of them and stood back.

"Kag and Dran. Jih has come home. These are fr-family of Jih. Come." Jih said as he waved over Narro, Trekkal, and Sadal to introduce themselves.

Narro and Trekkal introduced themselves happily as they shook in excitement. Kag and Dran, much like Jih originally, weren't aware of their status outside the world and Dran seemed impressed regarding this knowledge. Sadal introduced herself but was met with further confused looks from Kag and Dran. Jih laughed and assured his friends that they would understand her dialect in due time. The entire event was bewildering as a few of their eyes looked at the rotting corpse of the tiger attracting insects. The group of six agreed to walk together towards the shoreline and talk further out in the open.

Once they reached the beaches, Kag's face was bursting with questions. Dran had her own but would ask them in a more intimate setting. Jih and the others washed the blood and mud off their bodies with the ocean's water as they entered the water save for Sadal. Jih gave her a smug look as he was more than willing to dunk her in the water once more as Sadal begrudgingly stood at the shallow end and splashed herself.

"Brother...After all this time. Kag must ask..." Kag said with a gasp as he looked at Jih's clothing. He hadn't thought of Jih's attire at all, but it was especially strange as he walked over to see the various new pieces on his body. His eyes looked at the backpack present on Sadal and noticed that Jih had one of these as well.

"Jih has found power rock. Would you like to see it?" Jih said as both Kag and Dran turned their gaze and nodded in anticipation.

Jih placed his backpack on the sand and dipped his hand inside while Kag and Dran marveled at the various things Jih brought out. Aside from the basic implements, Jih kept a pair of rhino hide shoes from the north, he enjoyed the feeling on his feet that came with wearing them and did his best to keep them in good condition. He kept a single claw from a deceased scimitar-toothed cat to bring with him as well. Kag noticed that his spear design was also different from his own, Jih was a master stoneworker to begin with once he left The Elders but was blown away by the new sophistication. There was much to learn. After a few moments, Jih brought out the fist sized piece of meteoric iron to show Kag and Dran who covered their mouths in awe. The payoff was incredibly worth it. Jih gave a look of satisfaction to his friends as they nodded in respect. Jih looked to the ground though as the thought of returning home still unnerved him greatly. Kag saw this look on Jih's face and lifted an eyebrow as he wished to hear his friend's concern. Jih quickly pocketed the power rock once more and kept it safe.

"Jih is shunned by word of Tur. Can Jih return? Have things changed?" Jih said as he looked back at Narro, Trekkal and Sadal who were talking among themselves about the highlights of their travels.

"Tur?" Dran said with a laugh, as Kag shared her expression. Kag remembered that Jih was woefully uninformed about the past two years. Kag, Bani, and Dran were responsible for massive change in their community, but the biggest one came as a gift from nature itself.

"Tur is dead brother! There is no need to fear. Aab rules The Council now." Kag said as he happily shook Jih.

For the first time in a long time, Kag saw Jih have an absolute smile of joy on his face. His normally neutral face showed a straight row of teeth that turned to a smile. After years of torment by the man, Tur finally was laid to rest and Jih no longer had to squirm to try and meet his impossible expectations. A huge sigh of relief came upon him, as he knew that he would not be welcomed with open arms and a feast, but he was free to return, nonetheless. Kag waved for the others to join him and Dran on their walk back.

"The one known as Narro. Very strong! He can lift Kag with one hand!" Kag said as he looked over at Narro and gave a wave.

Narro, Trekkal, and Sadal were unsure of how they'd be received by the others of Jih's band, or if there were any other groups in the area to consider, but for now they would take it in stride. This was Jih's home and as his guests, they would abide by his customs as best as they could. Dran took an inquisitive look at all of them, especially Sadal as she noticed her strength in taking down the tiger previously.

"Dran trusts Jih on these strange ones. If their tongues can be understood, we may not be so different." Dran said with a huff.

As the group stood, Kag walked them to the direction of their village, but he stopped short as he realized Jih stood still where he was before. Dran walked over to collect the others while he and Kag shared brief words. Jih recognized the strip of beach where they were as due north, the grave of Hyu loomed over him as one last challenge to address. Jih took a deep breath as his gaze turned to the longer strip of land.

"Kag. Jih will go see her before we go to village." Jih said as Kag's face changed. Although he could hear Jih's sadness still in his voice, he was happy to see that Jih was willing to finally see Hyu's grave again. He avoided it from the time of the burial to his exile, and Kag was unsure if he would ever get the chance to once more. Kag gave a simple nod of understanding.

"The way has always been the same brother. Our village has not left." Kag said as he patted Jih's back. Jih took his backpack and hoisted it on his body while he walked ahead of the others to go due north. As Dran collected the others who asked her all sorts of questions, Sadal raised an eyebrow as she noticed Jih was walking off on his own.

Jih walked off quietly as he absorbed the sounds of the ocean. The waves hit the sand and the familiar smell of salt filled his nose. It hadn't set into Jih that he was truly home once again, and all the challenges that came with such an endeavor. He approached the arrangement of poison plants and first slid his backpack underneath while he crawled on the ground to avoid the plants from touching his skin. It all came rushing back. The first memories of when he was shown this place as a small child with Hyu were now nothing more than just that, memories. Jih felt his heartbeat as he felt slightly claustrophobic, but he calmed himself down. His eyes turned to face the mound that Hyu's grave. The original set of rocks placed over her grave were replaced with shinier new ones, but these too were now grown over with moss and dirt.

"Hyu. Jih has come and brought power rock. It is done, our dream has been finished." Jih said as he reached into his backpack to reveal the power rock.

He spoke more for some time as he told the mound about some of his adventures and how he couldn't have done this without her guidance. Although Jih wasn't exactly sure what to think regarding where people go after death, he found comfort in Narro and Trekkal's belief of the Land of The Dead and chose to adopt this to his own thinking. One day when Jih returned to the soil, he would find her there and recall his adventure with the utmost clarity. Jih sat with his eyes closed in focused meditation, a skill he picked up from his time with Eshe to realign himself in times of great stress. Jih attempted his best to remain aligned to the flow of wind that was on the outside. He stood like this for some time, but he felt an abrupt but soft touch on his skin. He wasn't sure what to think as he continued to breathe heavily and remained focused, but the grip was much tighter now. Jih opened his eyes and heard a soft whimper, but he was confused. Was he imagining things? Jih looked over his shoulder and saw a crying Sadal right behind him. Sadal had always known the struggles that Jih went through but now that she could actually see the reality, it overwhelmed her incredibly.

Soon after, Jih felt the touch of another, this time it was Narro. As Sadal was his One after all, Narro felt a special connection to Sadal, but his respect for Jih was paramount. Though Narro and Trekkal came from a supportive family who would one day see their return, Jih was just as important as their own flesh and blood, and when he felt pain, so did Narro. Hearing of Hyu was this far off entity that lacked real personhood until it all came into focus. He said nothing more as he took another side of Jih.

Trekkal also wasn't far behind, she hated to be excluded from anything, and despite Dran's insistence on not following, she chose to ignore it anyway. Trekkal stumbled through the foliage as she fell inside practically announcing her entrance to the others. She looked around at the serene atmosphere and Jih let out a small chuckle, knowing fully well that Trekkal arrived. By now, Hyu was much more than someone to just Jih but to the four of them throughout their travels, the core member of the group they never got to meet.

"Why are we all-Oh." Trekkal said to herself as her eyes met the large mound. She remembered bits and pieces of Jih's stories and as soon as it clicked for her, she felt incredibly embarrassed at her demeanor.

To complete the set, Kag and Dran eventually arrived but with a far cheerier mood. Bani was working with meat earlier and prepared skewers of tapir for the group to enjoy. Kag reiterated the news of Jih's return to her as she quickly cut some of the meat to give to the others while she had her hands busy with Cren. Kag held the meat and called the attention of the others.

"Let us eat. It is what Hyu would want." Kag said to the group as he gave Jih the biggest one for them to enjoy.

Jih and Kag shared the bulk of the exchanged stories regarding Hyu but even Dran commented at times to set the record straight, while Sadal, Narro and Trekkal listened intently as they ate together.

The group of six laughed together for some time and Jih felt the good times had finally returned. After giving Hyu a proper goodbye, they left to make their way back to the main village. Kag explained the situation to Jih as he nodded in understanding while Dran took the others around on a small tour showcasing the structures around them.

"Oh! Brother, Cren has been waiting for you." Kag explained with a nice grin as Jih raised an eyebrow in confusion. Kag noticed this and gave a small chuckle as he called for Bani. After Jih gave a warm smile to Bani, he realized that Cren was now their living son. Seeing that the boy was able to walk relatively on his own put it into perspective of just how long Jih was truly gone.

Jih looked at the small boy and took a knee to meet eyes with him. He opened his arms out for the young boy to approach. Much like the Forest Seeker named Ozul, Jih reserved his disdain for children as he patiently waited for Cren. Cren looked around as he slowly waddled to Kag who pointed to Jih who was waiting. Cren looked at the ground first and grasped a pebble, there were thousands of these that looked to be the same, but to Cren each one required the utmost amount of care. Kag gently lifted up Cren and placed him on the path to Jih. With a small pat on the butt, he was on his way. After a while, Cren finally made his way to Jih and sunk his head into him. Cren looked up to see Jih's rugged face while Kag happily smiled in the background.

"Cren!" The young boy said introducing himself.

"Jih. Jih is brother of Kag. Cren is son of Kag and Bani. Jih is uncle of Cren." Jih explained as he gently lifted Cren up to get a better look at him.

Bani came by and rejoiced at Jih's return while she kept her eye out regarding the new arrivals to their area. Bani mentioned in addition to Kag's words that the rest of their band hiked out to Eastern Sundaland while camp was deconstructed here. She offered to take them there with Kag, Cren, and Dran so that they would be able to show Aab that he succeeded in his quest. Jih agreed and knew that the others would be interested in the venture. As the day waned, Bani saw that it would be best for them to take this journey tomorrow. She held the hand of young Cren as she prompted Jih to follow her. Jih's house was one of the last structures they hadn't started to dismantle, Kag insisted on keeping it as long as he could. Jih waved for the curious Sadal, Narro and Trekkal to come.

"This is your house? How do we get in?" Sadal asked with some confusion.

Jih held up a finger and demonstrated how they crawled into their entrance only for the rest of the home to be bigger on the inside. It was pristine with the amount of love and care that Kag and Bani took into restoring what remained of his home after the Neck-Shell raid. Never actually having the ability to fit four people, it was a tight squeeze, but it was home. The four slept on comforting leaf beds in anticipation for the morning.

Dawn approached, and as promised, Bani was awake with Cren, Kag, and Dran in tow to make the trek to Eastern Sundaland. It would be a few days' travel as the party grew in size. Jih showed his friends the utility of the backpack and had the others place their spare meat inside for the trip ahead. Much of their time was spent asking all sorts of questions regarding the outside world. Sadal felt a bit out of place seeing as her dialect was hard to understand, but aside from Jih, Bani picked up her responses quickly and was able to reply.

The arrival to Eastern Sundaland was far from what Jih anticipated. He knew he would hardly receive a warm welcome as upon entering, Jih met the stares of onlookers who still carried resentment towards him. Kag took control of the situation and called for Aab. As she was now leader of The Council, she would be the one to make the call regarding Jih. Aab was busy delegating orders to construct new huts for the latter half of the band that would arrive in due time, but she stopped this as she heard news that gave her pause. Aab, unlike Tur, required no aid to walk, but members of The Elders felt compelled to support her as she did so. Aab's eyes widened as she saw that Jih returned but also arrived with strange foreigners in her wake. Aab gave no welcome to Jih, but she sympathized with his initial plight. Jih remembered that Aab abstained in the vote for exile. It wasn't one for innocence, as Sadal reminded him, but it wasn't complicit either.

"Jih returns with power rock." Jih said as Aab studied Jih and lifted her eye at his strange dress.

Jih placed his backpack down and a silence filled the group as all eyes converged on Jih. He withdrew the power rock and placed it at the feet of Aab who stepped back as she evaluated its power. Aab touched the rock with her hand, it was nothing she'd ever seen before. A nod from one of the other stoneworkers confirmed that the material was not known to them or any of the other bands they traded with. One wasn't sure if their tools could work the rock as well. Jih studied her expression as she assessed how this would influence her new beginning. Using her executive power as leader, she accepted the power rock and with this, Jih was able to return. Their wonderful moment lasted for some time, but the sound of Dran in a heavy argument with someone else took take root. A man pointed at Jih and hurled insults in his direction. Though he complied with Aab's demands, he voiced his distaste for Jih and the new arrivals.

"Jih comes and brings strange people to us. How do we know they bring peace?" One man voiced.

"You spit falsehoods into air. These are people who know our tongue." Dran spat back in irritation.

Jih felt embarrassed as he hadn't considered how his band would feel about the presence of Narro, Trekkal, and Sadal who could only stand awkwardly as he spoke louder. While some had a tolerance towards the others, years of propaganda from The Council spurned fear about the presence of outsiders. For much of their history, The Council quelled rumors about the existence of others with a strong persistence that culminated into abject hatred and even fear. Jih felt it was incredibly irrational but given the outcome, it was hard to think otherwise. Narro attempted to intervene, but a tug from Trekkal signified this wasn't their place. Their respect for The First was immense and they hung their heads as they discussed things. Aab, who was tired of the discourse, lifted her hand and offered Jih an ultimatum to make. She wanted this to be a smooth process, but she couldn't ignore the concerns of her band now that she was leader. She remembered that Jih's old position was held out of respect by the Stoneworking Team in the event that he would ever return, and he could serve with Kag as their equal. She offered this to him, and if he refused, he would have to leave with Sadal, Narro, and Trekkal. This was not out of distaste for him personally, and he wouldn't be shunned for his leave, but Aab had already dealt with one angry mob.

After so long of not having a home of his own but with the others, Jih was given an incredibly difficult task. He remained conflicted for a long time. If Jih were a younger man, he would have thought to reject Aab's offer and continue to travel with his friends as a vagabond, but much like Sadal, Jih abandoned his people and had a responsibility to meet. Jih looked back at his friends and was proud of his growth. In the time that passed, Jih cared little for his position with The Council, it was irrelevant in what gave him actual meaning, but people depended on him. His goal all along was to bring the power rock home to his people and to bring balance to the land. He could not do the latter half with his removal. Jih also locked eyes with the young Cren who already lost his aunt before he was born. Bani and Kag were great parents, but not everything could be done with them. Jih knew he needed to be a resource for Cren.

"Brother...You have seen much of world. Kag understands if here is no longer for you." Kag said, with a strong sense of empathy. Nothing would have caused greater pain to Kag more than to leave twice, but he knew that Aab twisted Jih's hand much like Tur did.

The world slowed down as Jih made his choice and slowly stepped to join the others in his band. He turned with hatred in his eyes towards the man that made an outburst. Jih knew that Sadal, Narro, and Trekkal couldn't stay forever, but he imagined that with their combined destiny far freer than his own, a different reality could one day be possible. Sadal was a Wanderer now who had no home of her own. Jih knew this and once offered her the chance to join him on his return home in secret, but her later union with Narro buried such discussion.

"Aab says this once. You have three days and then you will leave. Or we will make you." Aab said, as she pointed her finger to the other three while the rest of the band dispersed.

Jih walked over to his friends and gave them a hug. As agreed, Sadal, Narro and Trekkal would stay for three days and make their leave. While they tagged along with Jih, and kept their distance from the wary villagers, a question arose among them.

"Jih, do you have a home here made for you? Kag kept your old one." Narro asked as he looked around in some confusion.

"Jih has no home here." Jih said with his words hanging on.

Narro grabbed Jih by the arm and gave him a smile. Sadal raised an eyebrow as she could tell immediately what he was thinking.

"Well, I know how we will spend our time with you. Jih, we will build you a home." Trekkal said happily as she echoed Narro's tone.

Sadal rummaged around in her stuff to find the perfect tool to gather wood. Out of everything she held in her backpack, Deeso's axe remained as a memento to better times. Once caked with the blood of many, she decided to wear it down to its last nubs for something productive as they looked for a good source of wood. Jih used his crafted hand-axes along with a few members of the Stoneworking Team to assist in the process. The hours waned by and Jih laughed as the three of them attempted to build one of their homes from sight alone. On occasion, Kag or Dran would walk by and offer advice as they positioned the sticks and rocks into place. Jih remembered the first time he struggled to build his home after Hyu's death. In lieu of where Hyu's face was to grab or position a piece, he saw the faces of his friends all willing to help. At the end of the day, the proud structure was built and the four slept together on the dirt.

Sadal and the others made a point of spending the next day helping with various tasks that The Elders had to improve their image among the other members of Jih's band. The gesture was appreciated by some, but the terms of the deal still held. As the final day approached, Jih and the others returned home with a final hunt under their belt. A processed leopard pelt sometime later was given to Jih as a gift for his new home. With the short celebrations over, Aab was serious in her word as her and the remaining members of The Council appeared to see that the terms were met. Kag approached with a few warriors that were trained in the art of combat, not as a threat, but as an escort for the three out of their territory. He whispered in their ear another order out of the range of the rest of The Council. He urged them to go forward and return once contact was made with the outside. Aab was old, and eventually she too would die, Kag wished for The Elders to be ready for anything that would come, including outsiders who found their native territory.

Sadal, Narro, and Trekkal stood at the border of their village while Jih walked to see them off. He gave a look of confusion as he saw the three of them hold their backpacks out to him.

"Things to remember us by. We can make new ones on our way. Take my piece of the power rock and make something incredible. Think of me when you do this and kill something mighty." Sadal explained as she removed what she could bring with her and left a spare throwing spear behind. Narro and Trekkal followed suit and dropped their backpacks.

"Jih, please take these. You all will love pockets." Narro said as he attempted to keep a stoic face for the others. Trekkal said nothing as she dropped her backpack, she voiced many of her statements the night before.

Jih gave the three of them a long-lasting hug as it was soon time for them to leave. Kag nodded his head and waved over for the warriors to join them, he also gave them well wishes on their travels. Jih waited for some time as the three walked off and he turned his back to face the others. Jih kept a neutral expression as Aab and the others had gotten what she wanted. While Narro and Sadal were busy walking with the visage of the village behind them, Trekkal stopped in her tracks.

"Wait. I forgot something. I will be brief." She said with brevity that surprised both.

Trekkal looked back and trudged along back to the direction of the village, and this time her pace increased. Narro and Sadal looked at each other and decided to follow as Trekkal's pace was incredibly fast, quicker than she ran for almost anything. Trekkal was always one for the dramatic. Kag gave a look of interest as he saw Trekkal running in their direction. As tears filled her eyes, she jumped onto the previously busy Jih, and nearly knocked him to the ground as she dangled on his back. Jih, who managed to keep himself together beforehand, turned around to feel Trekkal on top of him. He cried as much as Sadal and Narro who returned to share a hug while the two attempted to rip her off him. After a brief struggle, Trekkal composed herself long enough for an actual coherent farewell. Dran watched with a still expression on her face.

"In another life Jih..." Trekkal said with a small grin on her face as Sadal and Narro's eyes were red with sadness. Jih wiped his own with his knuckles, the prospect of never seeing them again was truly a heavy toll.

"I hope to see you one day on the hunt, when you all change your minds, the land that is dry and hot awaits. The world is only as dangerous as you let it be." Sadal said as she placed her hand on Jih's shoulder before letting it fall. She moved back to the others and pushed Narro forward to say his piece. Narro's goodbye was the simplest and resonated with them all.

"You are loved by us Jih. Take care." Narro declared.

"Jih says the same. Sadal, Narro, Trekkal. Be well." Jih said as he watched the three of them walk into the distance before they morphed into amorphous figures in the distance. With that, Jih was now back in Sundaland proper with the weight of his travels on him. Jih returned to his new home to sleep the day off as he lit a fire in the center. Jih wondered if there was one day, he could see them again.

To his surprise, he heard a tug at the entrance of his home sometime later. The first to enter was young Cren, as Jih lifted his head up with the sound of Bani and Kag next. Dran's chewing on sugarcane could be heard as she entered Jih's new home. Narro, Trekkal, and Sadal built it to accommodate a larger group of people than two so there was plenty of room.

"Brother...Kag has question for Jih." Kag asked as Jih lifted his head up.

"Of course. Ask Jih anything, brother." Jih offered as he adjusted his position. He noticed the shared look on everyone's faces as Cren stumbled around and looked at the walls of Jih's home.

"What happened out there?" Bani said, stealing Kag's question with a sly grin. Dran nodded in agreement as she swallowed her food.

    "Tell us everything Jih! From the beginning." Kag said as he slapped the ground. He held his arm to rope Cren back to his grasp. Kag shook him slightly as Cren's head turned to face Jih.

    "This will take much time. Are you prepared?" Jih questioned, running his fingers through his beard. The group gave a collective nod that Jih saw as an opportunity to speak.

    "Come closer..." Jih said with a grin as he expanded his arms.

    Jih started the long process of telling the tale of his trials that he endured over the past two years. He spared no detail as he regaled the others and noted their reactions, Kag and Bani would tap the floor when they wanted to intercede with a question while Dran gave a slow and thoughtful nod as she envisioned what Jih spoke about. Although it was unclear to Jih about the fates of Sadal, Narro, and Trekkal, he knew that they would have what it took to survive wherever they chose to claim home. Jih still felt like an outsider from his time spent traveling the world, but in time, he became greater than he could ever have imagined. Surrounded by loved ones, Jih could begin again and build a new life.

References

In this section of Jih's Journey, here is where we separate fact from fiction. This section details all the resources I used for the writing of Jih's Journey and is based on some of the latest and greatest archaeological research at the time of publication. If you want to know more about the characters and the world as they existed in real life, please enjoy these resources!

Agam, A., & Barkai, R. (2018). Elephant and Mammoth Hunting during the Paleolithic: A

Review of the Relevant Archaeological, Ethnographic and Ethno-Historical Records.

Quaternary, *1*(1), 3. https://doi.org/10.3390/quat1010003

Anil, D., Chauhan, N., Ajithprasad, P., Devi, M., Mahesh, V., & Khan, Z. (2022). An Early

Presence of Modern Human or Convergent Evolution? A 247 ka Middle Palaeolithic

Assemblage from Andhra Pradesh, India. *Journal of Archaeological Science: Reports*,

45, 103565. https://doi.org/10.1016/j.jasrep.2022.103565

Anton, M., Galobart, A., & Turner, A. (2005). Co-existence of Scimitar-toothed cats, Lions

and Hominins in the European Pleistocene. Implications of the Post-cranial anatomy of

(Owen) for Comparative Palaeoecology. *Quaternary Science Reviews*, *24*(10–11), 1287–

1301. https://doi.org/10.1016/j.quascirev.2004.09.008

Bar-Yosef Mayer, D. E., Groman-Yaroslavski, I., Bar-Yosef, O., Hershkovitz, I., Kampen-

Hasday, A., Vandermeersch, B., Zaidner, Y., & Weinstein-Evron, M. (2020). On holes

and strings: Earliest Displays Of Human Adornment in the Middle Palaeolithic. *PLOS*

ONE, *15*(7), e0234924. https://doi.org/10.1371/journal.pone.0234924

Belfer-Cohen, A., & Hovers, E. (2010). Modernity, Enhanced Working Memory, and the

Middle to Upper Paleolithic Record in the Levant. *Current Anthropology*, *51*(S1), S167–

S175. https://doi.org/10.1086/649835

Blinkhorn, J. (2019). Examining the Origins of Hafting in South Asia. *Journal of Paleolithic Archaeology*, *2*(4), 466–481. https://doi.org/10.1007/s41982-019-00034-4

Blinkhorn, J., Achyuthan, H., & Petraglia, M. D. (2015). Ostrich Expansion into India during the Late Pleistocene: Implications for continental dispersal corridors. *Palaeogeography, Palaeoclimatology, Palaeoecology*, *417*, 80–90. https://doi.org/10.1016/j.palaeo.2014.10.026

Cantillo-Duarte, J. J., Weniger, G.-C., Cantalejo, P., Domínguez-Bella, S., Molina-Piernas, E., Otto, T., Rotgänger, M., Kehl, M., Espejo, M. M., Fernández-Sánchez, D., Tafelmaier, Y., Vijande-Vila, E., Becerra-Martín, S., Gómez-Sánchez, L., & Ramos-Muñoz, J. (2023). Molluscs as Personal Adornment in a Gravettian Context from Cueva de Ardales (Málaga, Spain). *Environmental Archaeology*, 1–22. https://doi.org/10.1080/14614103.2023.2218126

Costa, A. G. (2017). A new Late Pleistocene fauna from arid coastal India: Implications for Inundated Coastal Refugia and Human Dispersals. *Quaternary International*, *436*, 253–269. https://doi.org/10.1016/j.quaint.2015.07.002

d'Errico, F., & Banks, W. E. (2013). Identifying Mechanisms behind Middle Paleolithic and Middle Stone Age Cultural Trajectories. *Current Anthropology*, *54*(S8), S371–S387. https://doi.org/10.1086/673388

Dunham, W. (2021, September 17). Moroccan Cave Yields Oldest Clues About Advent of Human Clothing. *Reuters*. https://www.reuters.com/lifestyle/science/moroccan-cave-yields-oldest-clues-about-advent-human-clothing-2021-09-16/

Freidline, S. E., Westaway, K. E., Joannes-Boyau, R., Duringer, P., Ponche, J.-L., Morley, M. W., Hernandez, V. C., McAllister-Hayward, M. S., McColl, H., Zanolli, C., Gunz, P., Bergmann, I., Sichanthongtip, P., Sihanam, D., Boualaphane, S., Luangkhoth, T.,

Souksavatdy, V., Dosseto, A., Boesch, Q., ... Demeter, F. (2023). Early presence of Homo sapiens in Southeast Asia by 86–68 kyr at Tam Pà Ling, Northern Laos. *Nature Communications, 14*(1), 3193. https://doi.org/10.1038/s41467-023-38715-y

Gaudzinski-Windheuser, S., Kindler, L., MacDonald, K., & Roebroeks, W. (2023). Hunting and Processing of Straight-tusked Elephants 125.000 years ago: Implications for Neanderthal behavior. *Science Advances, 9*(5), eadd8186. https://doi.org/10.1126/sciadv.add8186

Ghasidian, E., Kafash, A., Kehl, M., Yousefi, M., & Heydari-Guran, S. (2023). Modelling Neanderthals' dispersal routes from Caucasus towards east. *PLOS ONE, 18*(2), e0281978. https://doi.org/10.1371/journal.pone.0281978

Gibbons, A. (2017). Neandertals Mated Early with Modern Humans. *Science, 357*(6346), 14–14. https://doi.org/10.1126/science.357.6346.14

Groman-Yaroslavski, I., Zaidner, Y., & Weinstein-Evron, M. (2021). Complexity and Sophistication of Early Middle Paleolithic Flint Tools Revealed Through Use-Wear Analysis of Tools from Misliya Cave, Mount Carmel, Israel. *Journal of Human Evolution, 154*, 102955. https://doi.org/10.1016/j.jhevol.2021.102955

Hagen, E. H., Blackwell, A. D., Lightner, A. D., & Sullivan, R. J. (2023). *Homo medicus*: The Transition to Meat Eating Increased Pathogen Pressure and The Use of Pharmacological Plants in *Homo*. *American Journal of Biological Anthropology*, ajpa.24718. https://doi.org/10.1002/ajpa.24718

Hallett, E. Y., Marean, C. W., Steele, T. E., Álvarez-Fernández, E., Jacobs, Z., Cerasoni, J. N., Aldeias, V., Scerri, E. M. L., Olszewski, D. I., El Hajraoui, M. A., & Dibble, H. L. (2021). A Worked Bone Assemblage from 120,000–90,000 year old deposits at Contrebandiers

Cave, Atlantic Coast, Morocco. *IScience*, *24*(9), 102988.
https://doi.org/10.1016/j.isci.2021.102988

Harvati, K., Röding, C., Bosman, A. M., Karakostis, F. A., Grün, R., Stringer, C., Karkanas, P.,
Thompson, N. C., Koutoulidis, V., Moulopoulos, L. A., Gorgoulis, V. G., & Kouloukoussa,
M. (2019). Apidima Cave Fossils Provide Earliest Evidence of Homo sapiens in Eurasia.
Nature, *571*(7766), 500–504. https://doi.org/10.1038/s41586-019-1376-z

Henry, A. G., Brooks, A. S., & Piperno, D. R. (2011). Microfossils in Calculus Demonstrate
Consumption of Plants and Cooked Foods in Neanderthal Diets (Shanidar III, Iraq; Spy
I and II, Belgium). *Proceedings of the National Academy of Sciences*, *108*(2), 486–491.
https://doi.org/10.1073/pnas.1016868108

Hershkovitz, I., Weber, G. W., Quam, R., Duval, M., Grün, R., Kinsley, L., Ayalon, A., Bar-
Matthews, M., Valladas, H., Mercier, N., Arsuaga, J. L., Martinón-Torres, M., Bermúdez
De Castro, J. M., Fornai, C., Martín-Francés, L., Sarig, R., May, H., Krenn, V. A., Slon,
V., … Weinstein-Evron, M. (2018). The Earliest Modern Humans Outside Africa.
Science, *359*(6374), 456–459. https://doi.org/10.1126/science.aap8369

Husson, L., Salles, T., Lebatard, A.-E., Zerathe, S., Braucher, R., Noerwidi, S., Aribowo, S.,
Mallard, C., Carcaillet, J., Natawidjaja, D. H., Bourlès, D., & team, A. (2022). *Javanese
Homo erectus on the move in SE Asia ca. 1.8 Ma* [Preprint]. In Review.
https://doi.org/10.21203/rs.3.rs-1818726/v1

Iurino, D. A., Mecozzi, B., Iannucci, A., Moscarella, A., Strani, F., Bona, F., Gaeta, M., &
Sardella, R. (2022). A Middle Pleistocene Wolf from Central Italy Provides Insights on
The First occurrence of Canis lupus in Europe. *Scientific Reports*, *12*(1), 2882.
https://doi.org/10.1038/s41598-022-06812-5

Jaubert, J., Verheyden, S., Genty, D., Soulier, M., Cheng, H., Blamart, D., Burlet, C., Camus, H., Delaby, S., Deldicque, D., Edwards, R. L., Ferrier, C., Lacrampe-Cuyaubère, F., Lévêque, F., Maksud, F., Mora, P., Muth, X., Régnier, É., Rouzaud, J.-N., & Santos, F. (2016). Early Neanderthal constructions deep in Bruniquel Cave in southwestern France. *Nature*, *534*(7605), 111–114. https://doi.org/10.1038/nature18291

Joordens, J. C. A., d'Errico, F., Wesselingh, F. P., Munro, S., de Vos, J., Wallinga, J., Ankjærgaard, C., Reimann, T., Wijbrans, J. R., Kuiper, K. F., Mücher, H. J., Coqueugniot, H., Prié, V., Joosten, I., van Os, B., Schulp, A. S., Panuel, M., van der Haas, V., Lustenhouwer, W., ... Roebroeks, W. (2015). Homo erectus at Trinil on Java Used Shells for Tool Production and Engraving. *Nature*, *518*(7538), Article 7538. https://doi.org/10.1038/nature13962

Kaifu, Y. (2017). Archaic Hominin Populations in Asia before the Arrival of Modern Humans: Their Phylogeny and Implications for the "Southern Denisovans." *Current Anthropology*, *58*(S17), S418–S433. https://doi.org/10.1086/694318

Koch, T. J., & Schmidt, P. (n.d.). OPEN A New Method For Birch Tar. *Scientific Reports*.

Kubat, J., Nava, A., Bondioli, L., Dean, C., Zanolli, C., Bourgon, N., Bacon, A.-M., Demeter, F., Peripoli, B., Mahoney, P., Albert, R., Kullmer, O., Schrenk, F., & Müller, W. (2021). *Dietary strategies of Pleistocene Pongo sp. And Homo erectus on Java (Indonesia)* [Preprint]. In Review. https://doi.org/10.21203/rs.3.rs-940427/v1

L. Hilgen, S., Pop, E., Adhityatama, S., A. Veldkamp, T., W.K. Berghuis, H., Sutisna, I., Yurnaldi, D., Dupont-Nivet, G., Reimann, T., Nowaczyk, N., F. Kuiper, K., Krijgsman, W., B. Vonhof, H., Ekowati, D. R., Alink, G., Ni Luh Gde Dyah Mega Hafsari, Drespriputra, O., Verpoorte, A., Bos, R., ... Joordens, J. C. A. (2023). Revised Age and Stratigraphy of The Classic Homo erectus-bearing succession at Trinil (Java, Indonesia).

Quaternary Science Reviews, 301, 107908.
https://doi.org/10.1016/j.quascirev.2022.107908

Li, Y., Li, H., Sumner, A., & Zhang, J. (2023). Lithic Technological Strategies of Late Pleistocene hominins in the Daoshui River Valley, Hunan Province, Central South China. *Frontiers in Earth Science, 11*.
https://www.frontiersin.org/articles/10.3389/feart.2023.1133499

Liu, W., Martinón-Torres, M., Cai, Y., Xing, S., Tong, H., Pei, S., Sier, M. J., Wu, X., Edwards, R. L., Cheng, H., Li, Y., Yang, X., de Castro, J. M. B., & Wu, X. (2015). The Earliest Unequivocally Modern Humans In Southern China. *Nature, 526*(7575), 696–699. https://doi.org/10.1038/nature15696

Livraghi, A., Rivals, F., Rendu, W., & Peresani, M. (2022). Neanderthals' Hunting Seasonality Inferred From Combined Cementochronology, Mesowear, and Microwear analysis: Case Studies from the Alpine foreland in Italy. *Archaeological and Anthropological Sciences, 14*(3), 51. https://doi.org/10.1007/s12520-022-01514-5

Maloney, T. R., Dilkes-Hall, I. E., Vlok, M., Oktaviana, A. A., Setiawan, P., Priyatno, A. A. D., Ririmasse, M., Geria, I. M., Effendy, M. A. R., Istiawan, B., Atmoko, F. T., Adhityatama, S., Moffat, I., Joannes-Boyau, R., Brumm, A., & Aubert, M. (2022). Surgical Amputation of A Limb 31,000 years ago in Borneo. *Nature, 609*(7927), 547–551.
https://doi.org/10.1038/s41586-022-05160-8

Mayoral, E., Duveau, J., Santos, A., Ramírez, A. R., Morales, J. A., Díaz-Delgado, R., Rivera-Silva, J., Gómez-Olivencia, A., & Díaz-Martínez, I. (2022). New dating of the Matalascañas Footprints Provides New Evidence of the Middle Pleistocene (MIS 9-8) Hominin Paleoecology in Southern Europe. *Scientific Reports, 12*(1), 17505.
https://doi.org/10.1038/s41598-022-22524-2

Milks, A., Parker, D., & Pope, M. (2019). External Ballistics of Pleistocene Hand-thrown

    Spears: Experimental Performance Data and Implications for Human Evolution.

    Scientific Reports, 9(1), 820. https://doi.org/10.1038/s41598-018-37904-w

Nabais, M., Dupont, C., & Zilhão, J. (2023). The Exploitation Of Crabs by Last Interglacial

    Iberian Neanderthals: The evidence from Gruta da Figueira Brava (Portugal). *Frontiers*

    in Environmental Archaeology, 2, 1097815.

    https://doi.org/10.3389/fearc.2023.1097815

Nabais, M., Portero, R., & Zilhão, J. (2023). Neanderthal Brown Crab Recipes: A Combined

    Approach Using Experimental, Archaeological and Ethnographic evidence. *Historical*

    Biology, 1–9. https://doi.org/10.1080/08912963.2023.2220005

Nishiaki, Y. A., Yoneda, M., Kanjou, Y., & Akazawa, T. (2017). Natufian in the North: The

    Late Epipaleolithic cultural entity at Dederiyeh Cave, Northwest Syria. *Paléorient*,

    43(2), 7–24. https://doi.org/10.3406/paleo.2017.5763

Nowell, A. (2021). *Growing Up in the Ice Age: Fossil and Archaeological Evidence of the*

    Lived Lives of Plio-Pleistocene Children. Oxbow Books.

    https://doi.org/10.2307/j.ctv13nb8xw

Pante, M., Torre, I. de la, d'Errico, F., Njau, J., & Blumenschine, R. (2020). Bone tools from

    Beds II–IV, Olduvai Gorge, Tanzania, and implications for the origins and evolution of

    bone technology. *Journal of Human Evolution*, 148, 102885.

    https://doi.org/10.1016/j.jhevol.2020.102885

Pleyer, M. (2023). The Role of Interactional and Cognitive Mechanisms In The Evolution of

    (Proto)language(s). *Lingua*, 282, 103458. https://doi.org/10.1016/j.lingua.2022.103458

Prévost, M., Groman-Yaroslavski, I., Crater Gershtein, K. M., Tejero, J.-M., & Zaidner, Y.

    (2022). Early Evidence For Symbolic Behavior in the Levantine Middle Paleolithic: A

120 ka old Engraved Aurochs Bone Shaft From The Open-air Site of Nesher Ramla, Israel. *Quaternary International, 624*, 80–93. https://doi.org/10.1016/j.quaint.2021.01.002

Roebroeks, W., MacDonald, K., Scherjon, F., Bakels, C., Kindler, L., Nikulina, A., Pop, E., & Gaudzinski-Windheuser, S. (2021). Landscape Modification by Last Interglacial Neanderthals. *Science Advances, 7*(51), eabj5567. https://doi.org/10.1126/sciadv.abj5567

Rots, V., & Plisson, H. (2014). Projectiles and the Abuse of The Use-Wear Method In A Search For Impact. *Journal of Archaeological Science, 48*, 154–165. https://doi.org/10.1016/j.jas.2013.10.027

Ruebens, K. (2013). Regional behaviour Among Late Neanderthal Groups In Western Europe: A Comparative Assessment of Late Middle Palaeolithic Bifacial Tool Variability. *Journal of Human Evolution, 65*(4), 341–362. https://doi.org/10.1016/j.jhevol.2013.06.009

Shea, J., Davis, Z., & Brown, K. (2001). Experimental Tests of Middle Palaeolithic Spear Points Using a Calibrated Crossbow. *Journal of Archaeological Science, 28*(8), 807–816. https://doi.org/10.1006/jasc.2000.0590

Suraprasit, K., Jaeger, J.-J., Chaimanee, Y., Chavasseau, O., Yamee, C., Tian, P., & Panha, S. (2016). The Middle Pleistocene Vertebrate Fauna from Khok Sung (Nakhon Ratchasima, Thailand): Biochronological and Paleobiogeographical implications. *ZooKeys, 613*, 1–157. https://doi.org/10.3897/zookeys.613.8309

Turk, M., Turk, I., Dimkaroski, L., Blackwell, B. A. B., Horusitzky, F. Z., Otte, M., Bastiani, G., & Korat, L. (2018). The Mousterian Musical Instrument From the Divje Babe I Cave

(Slovenia): Arguments on the Material Evidence for Neanderthal Musical Behaviour. *L'Anthropologie, 122*(4), 679–706. https://doi.org/10.1016/j.anthro.2018.10.001

Wragg Sykes, R. (2020). Kindred: 300,000 Years of Neanderthal Life and Afterlife. Bloomsbury Publishing USA.

Verheijen, I., Starkovich, B. M., Serangeli, J., van Kolfschoten, T., & Conard, N. J. (2022). Early Evidence For Bear Exploitation During MIS 9 From The Site of Schöningen 12 (Germany). *Journal of Human Evolution*, 103294. https://doi.org/10.1016/j.jhevol.2022.103294

Zhang, X., Witt, K. E., Bañuelos, M. M., Ko, A., Yuan, K., Xu, S., Nielsen, R., & Huerta-Sanchez, E. (2021). The History and Evolution of The Denisovan- *EPAS1* haplotype in Tibetans. *Proceedings of the National Academy of Sciences, 118*(22), e2020803118. https://doi.org/10.1073/pnas.2020803118

Zupancich, A., Lemorini, C., Gopher, A., & Barkai, R. (2016). On Quina and demi-Quina scraper handling: Preliminary Results From the Late Lower Paleolithic Site of Qesem Cave, Israel. *Quaternary International, 398*, 94–102. https://doi.org/10.1016/j.quaint.2015.10.101

Letter From The Author

Dear Reader,

Thank you for reading! This is my first production and I've put my heart and soul into this work for almost two years. My two illustrators, Andrew Loyd Smith and Ana Beatriz Moreira Lima have worked extensively to achieve my vision for this book, and I hope you can see it to the fullest. Andrew sacrificed much of his time getting everything together for the upcoming companion book, The Beasts of Jih's Journey, and Ana's been there since the first rough sketches of Jih and Sadal. I'd also like to extend thanks to my trailer artist Omar Jehangir for an amazing production. Jih's Journey came to me as something unexpected at first, a simple idea that snowballed into a grounded universe with all sorts of surprises. I wanted to set a novel in the past for a very long time, but I wondered what a good period would be. Being invested in archeology, I always had an interest in the very dawn of humanity, and after seeing a lot of media not really keeping up with all we've learned, I figured why not do it myself! As for you, I want to thank you for giving this a shot. It'd mean the world to us if you left a review!

Sincerely,

Xavier Giovanni McClean

Made in the USA
Middletown, DE
17 October 2023